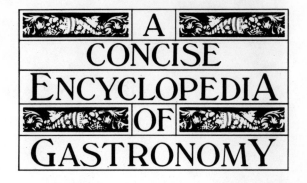

A CONCISE ENCYCLOPEDIA OF GASTRONOMY

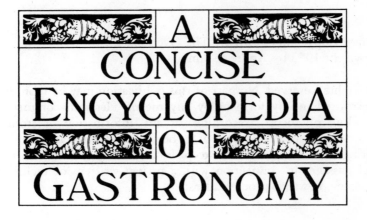

A CONCISE ENCYCLOPEDIA OF GASTRONOMY

BY ANDRE L. SIMON

PREFACE BY NIKA HAZELTON

COMPLETE AND UNABRIDGED
WITH DECORATIONS BY JOHN LEIGH—PEMBERTON

THE OVERLOOK PRESS

WOODSTOCK, NEW YORK

First Overlook edition published in 1981 by
The Overlook Press
Lewis Hollow Road
Woodstock, New York 12498

LIBRARY OF CONGRESS
CATALOGING IN PUBLICATION DATA

Simon, André Louis, 1877-1970.
  A concise encyclopedia of gastronomy.

  Originally published: 1st American ed. New
York: Harcourt, Brace, 1952. With new pref.
  Bibliography: pp. 785-791
  Includes index.
  1. Gastronomy. 2. Cookery — Dictionaries.
I. Title.
TX631.S53   1981   641'.03'21   81-47413
ISBN 0-87951-134-6   AACR2

PRINTED IN THE USA

CONTENTS

PREFACE TO THE AMERICAN EDITION

NIKA HAZELTON

FEW things in life are as rewarding as when, after many years, you find that a book has remained as wonderful as when you knew it in the first place. This happened with André Simon's *Concise Encyclopedia of Gastronomy,* for which I wrote an Introductory Note when it first came out in America. I felt as honored to do this then as I feel honored to do the same now because the book is the great culinary classic of our time, as delightful to cook from as to read.

As a cookbook, it offers an immense variety of recipes, plain and fancy, for about every food consumed by civilized man. As a reading book, it presents these recipes in a literate and informative manner that makes it hard to put down. Some of the information may have been superseded by new research, new sources, and other new information, but the book remains the cornerstone of our present knowledge of food, food habits, and nutrition. The recipes are as delicious as ever, as useful to the novice in the kitchen as to the expert well-traveled cook, to the home cook looking for a different way with a familiar vegetable as well as to the epicure wanting to be sure of the correct garniture for tournedos or seeking a true omelette Malmaison.

I have had the pleasure of knowing André Simon, without doubt the greatest food and wine man of our times and acknowledged as such—a professional chef and home cook to whom no trick of the trade was foreign, a wine merchant and sommelier, student and scholar, writer and founder of the prestigious International Wine and Food Society—and a man of immense charm and kindness, always ready to share his truly encyclopedic knowledge with others.

His magnificent library of ancient and modern works on gastronomy was recently auctioned off at Sotheby's in London. But he also roamed outside the books and manuscripts in his possession to become well acquainted with all books relevant to food and wine, the subjects of his extensive writings. His "List of Sources" (to be found on page 785) is a most valuable documentation. Many of the books may have to be found today in specialized bookstores or in the culinary collections of institutions such as the Library of Congress, the New York Public Library, and the British Museum. I strongly recommend seeking out at least a few of them; it is not difficult. It is from these sources, besides his own practical knowledge of food and wine, that André Simon compiled his *Concise Encyclopedia of Gastronomy,* creating an invaluable reference book, as well as a great international cookbook of the most diverse foods for anybody who cares for good food and its preparation.

Obviously, a number of André Simon's dishes presume certain culinary skills that come with practice, such as boning a chicken not yet cooked or turning out a flawless timbale. But home cooks are now familiar with skills and techniques that were unheard of for non-professionals when the book first appeared. Cooking has now become a national passion, as proven by the proliferation of cookbooks, food magazines, cooking schools, and cooking vacations; and by the star status of chefs—foreign and native—and the seemingly endless discussions of food, now the favorite topic of conversation at all occasions. A passionate interest in food creates a bond that immediately unites total strangers, perhaps because food is still one of the few subjects upon which it is possible to hold unorthodox opinions without getting into trouble with the established and not-established authorities.

The current interest in cooking has not only increased the skill of home cooks but has also brought within our reach a wealth of ingredients not as easily accessible and far more costly in André Simon's early days. Gourmet shops are now the norm everywhere, gourmet-food mail-order houses have sprung up like mushrooms after a rain, and shelves stacked with gourmet foods are part of today's supermarkets. In fact, ordinary supermarket shelves now regularly include foods once considered specialties, such as imported breads, cheeses, teas, jams, olive oils, and wine vinegars. However, the vast majority of dishes in this book could always be made with staples and ingredients readily found in our supermarkets. They are the everyday dishes of many lands, but they are the most civilized versions of these dishes, a pleasure to eat and no more difficult to make than the ordinary kind.

Another result of the current interest in native and foreign cooking is that people have been much more curious about the food they eat when they travel (and they travel more and farther) and are therefore much more familiar with foreign cooking terms. England, André Simon's permanent home, is well represented here. You will find a number of English cooking terms which become perfectly clear after reading the recipes carefully: to whisk in England is to beat in America, castor sugar is our granulated sugar, a tin of tomato paste is a can of tomato paste in our country, Demerara sugar is brown sugar, an aubergine is an eggplant, grill and grilling mean broil and broiling, and a pudding cloth can be made with several thicknesses of cheese cloth. But there is an important difference in the cooking habits of the two countries. American cooks measure their ingredients such as flour, butter, and milk, whereas British cooks weigh the solid ones. In the United States, few kitchens have scales but no kitchen is without a set of standard measuring cups and spoons. There is no simple, scientifically accurate way of converting ounces into cups because various foods—like flour, sugar, and so on—differ in weight and volume. The general conversion tables below are of necessity approximate and have been rounded off to the nearest convenient measure. But you can cook from them since, in any case, almost all cooking needs some adapting. Most cooks do this automatically, adding a little more liquid to dilute to a proper consistency or cooking down to thicken. Exact measurement matters little in dishes such as stews, roasts, and gravies, but it does affect baking which is (like all cooking) a chemical process based upon an exact relation between the various ingredients and should be followed accurately until you know the recipe very well. You may do a little experimenting along these lines or, better still, weigh your ingredients and then measure them. Again, thanks to our current passion for cooking, kitchen scales are now inexpensive and easy to find in the United States.

CONVERSION TABLES

Liquid Measures, United States of America

1 quart	=	2 pints	=	32 fl. oz.
1 pint	=	2 cups	=	16 fl. oz.
		1 cup	=	8 fl. oz.
		1 tablespoon	=	1/3 fl. oz.
		1 teaspoon	=	1/6 fl. oz.

Liquid Measures, Great Britain

1 quart	=	2 pints	=	40 fl. oz.
1 pint	=	4 gills	=	20 fl. oz.
1/2 pint	=	2 gills or 1 cup	=	10 fl. oz.
1/4 pint	=	8 tablespoons	=	5 fl. oz.
		1 tablespoon	=	just over 1/2 fl. oz.
		1 dessertspoon	=	1/3 fl. oz.
		1 teaspoon	=	1/6 fl. oz.

Approximate Equivalents

BRITISH	AMERICAN
1 quart	2 1/2 pints
1 pint	1 1/4 pint
1/2 pint	10 fl. oz. (1 1/4 cups)
1/4 pint (1 gill)	5 fl. oz.
1 tablespoon	1 1/2 tablespoons
1 dessertspoon	1 tablespoon
1 teaspoon	1/3 fl. oz.

AMERICAN	BRITISH
1 quart	1 1/2 pints + 3 tbsps. (32 fl. oz.)
1 pint	3/4 pint + 2 tbsps. (16 fl. oz.)
1 cup	1/2 pint − 2 tbsps. (8 fl. oz.)

OVEN TEMPERATURES

GAS NO. (REGULO)	FAHRENHEIT	ENGLISH DESCRIPTION OF OVEN HEAT
1/4	225°	Very cool
1/2	250°	Very cool
1	275°	Cool
2	300°	Cool
3	325°	Moderate
4	350°	Moderate
5	375°	Fairly hot
6	400°	Fairly hot
7	425°	Hot
8	450°	Very hot
8	475°	Extremely hot
9	500°	Extremely hot
9	525°	Extremely hot
9	550°	Extremely hot

ALL CONVERSION TABLES ARE APPROXIMATE. THEY HAVE BEEN ROUNDED OFF TO THE NEAREST CONVENIENT MEASURE.

Also, remember that a pound is a pound the world around (at least the Anglo-Saxon world), but a pint is not. The British Imperial pint is larger than ours; one British pint equals one and a quarter American pints and one British quart equals two and a half American pints. You must also remember that some of our American ingredients vary slightly from their English counterparts. The butterfat in English cream is different from that in American cream, English plain flour absorbs liquid somewhat differently from American all-purpose flour, and meat cuts are different which will affect their cooking times. But here again, a little experimentation and caution at the first try of a recipe will soon teach you how to achieve perfect results by letting your own experience guide you. There are occasional unavoidable discrepancies in the conversion tables; the cook should always follow one system or the other and not attempt combining the two.

Cooking from and reading the *Concise Encyclopedia of Gastronomy* have been a joy and comfort to me for many years, and to all the people to whom I gave the book when it was still in print. If nothing else, it is the best bedside reading. I am so happy to see it among us again and can find no better way to describe it than by taking the liberty of paraphrasing what Shakespeare said of Cleopatra: "Age cannot wither it nor custom stale its infinite variety."

FOREWORD

WHATEVER Plato really meant when he suggested that Gaster-the-Belly was the seat of the Soul, is a question that we are content to pass to Greek scholars and philosophers for their learned opinions. But every man, woman and child who reaches the age of reason should be made to grasp and hold throughout life the fact that Gaster-the-Belly is a most important part of our anatomy; one that has needs which must be satisfied, as well as fancies and moods which we must accept and understand.

It would be quite useless for us to have our house expertly wired for light and power, to buy the best electric cooker and radiators, to choose fine fittings and the right place for each one of them, if the generating station upon which we depend for power happens to work badly or not at all. So also will our brain and heart, our sight and hearing, our hands and feet fail us if and when Gaster-the-Belly fails them. This is not a matter of personal opinion or mere guesswork: it is a fact which nobody in his right senses would dare to challenge. Our dependence upon Gaster-the-Belly is universally acknowledged, in spite of which the number of Gastronomes is comparatively small, and Gastronomy, that is the proper understanding of our own inner regions, is much less honoured than Astronomy. This is probably mainly due to the widespread idea that so long as the fires are kept burning, all must be well, and that any food is fuel to the furnace that is Gaster-the-Belly. But Gaster-the-Belly is not at all like a coke oven: it is a temperamental furnace, one that may refuse one day what it accepted the day before, one that has likes and dislikes that must not be disregarded if we are to enjoy the best of health.

Gastronomy in England and in the United States of America has a very limited appeal; it certainly has none of the fascination which Nutrition has for a vast number of people. And yet Gastronomy is to Nutrition what health is to sickness. All who enjoy good health, which means, happily, the great majority of the population, could and should enjoy good food and good drink, the fuller and happier life which is the gift of Gastronomy for all normal people: that is to say people who are blessed with all their senses and a sufficient measure of common sense to make good use of them.

The sick and the unfit – diabetics, anæmics and others – whatever their trouble happens to be, had better apply to duly qualified dieticians who may help them return to the normality of good health. Nutrition and Dietetics is a science which belongs to the Lecture Room, the text-books, the laboratory and the surgery, not to the man and woman in the street, be they fat and anxious to get thin, or thin and anxious to get fat. The science of Nutrition and Dietetics is concerned with the chemistry of food, that is its composition, which can be ascertained scientifically and fairly accurately; and it is also concerned with its behaviour, that is its combustion or digestion and assimilation, which is much more a matter of approximation or experimentation, since so much depends upon the sometimes unpredictable behaviour of Gaster-the-Belly. Gluttons make a god of their belly, which is why gluttons can never be Gastronomes.

Gastronomes are not the slaves but the masters of Gaster-the-Belly, intelligent and kindly masters, who realize that a good servant is a friend in need and that he deserves to be well treated, listened to and at times humoured; no good service can possibly be expected from a starving servant any more than from a drunken one.

Gastronomes believe that all our senses were given to us to be used, not abused, and certainly not ignored. They do not make the mistake, for instance, of regarding their nose as an ornament placed more or less in the middle of their face, but as the chief organ of their sense of smell which enables them to detect, and enjoy and remember different smells and perfumes, just as the taste-buds of their palate can be trained to recognize and memorize different degrees of flavours and savours. Why children at school should be taught to distinguish various colours and tones, but never made aware that they are born with senses of smell and taste, is passing strange. Of course, like all other senses, smell and taste have an immediate utilitarian value: they warn us in time that something is burning, or to spit out a bad oyster or any tainted food. And, again like all other senses, smell and taste can be educated or trained and become a source of real artistic pleasure or sensual joy. The difference is that whilst the occasions to enjoy fine pictures or great music are very rare for the majority of people, Gastronomes are given not once, but twice or thrice, on every day of their lives, the chance to use critically their senses of taste and smell, and to train them to recognize that which is good, better and best. It does not mean that Gastronomes are hedonists, sensuous lovers of their ease: there may be such, but the true Gastronome is much more grateful than most good folks for Divine

Providence's wonderful gifts, simply because he has a far more highly developed sense of appreciation. Nobody expects the tank of one's car to be grateful for being refilled, and such is the ungracious attitude of many for whom food is just fuel: a Gastronome knows better.

Gastronomy teaches us how to serve and to be served by Gaster-the-Belly not only on festive or special occasions but every day. Since eat and drink we must, whether we like it or not, day after day, is it not better to make a hobby of our daily meals rather than let them become a duty or drudgery? This is exactly what Gastronomy proposes to do for us, showing us how to avoid monotony and how to achieve harmony between a variety of foods and drinks.

The variety of excellent foods available in all parts of the world is very great: far greater than most people, even most Gastronomes, imagine, as they will realize if they consult the far from complete list given in this Encyclopædia. But great as the diversity of raw materials may be, the methods of cooking or preparing most of them for the table are also almost beyond count, so that there is no possible excuse for monotony in our daily meals: lack of imagination and our incurable conservatism are alone to be blamed for this, and they are poor excuses.

Of course, the majority of the population must buy their food from the shops, the number of fisherfolk who eat the fish they catch is very small, and the number of farmers and gardeners who eat the vegetables they grow is not very large. Food shops cannot afford to stock foods for the few who like something better or at any rate 'different'; they will stock none but goods for which the demand is lively and profitable. Take greengrocers, for example. How many will bother to stock sorrel? Very few. Sorrel is really a weed, which can be grown anywhere, at all times and at very little cost; it is excellent in soups and sauces, and it is very good with tasteless white fish or with poached eggs and in a number of other ways. But it is too cheap; it does not pay to sell it, so one cannot buy it in shops. It is the same with unbleached sea-kale; the bleached and forced sea-kale is sold in the winter at high prices, but the unbleached sea-kale is never to be seen in our shops. Its sea-green curly shoots have not merely more colour but more flavour in them than the paler, earlier and much more costly ones which are on sale some three months earlier, but they are not worth any greengrocer's while to stock, simply because the public would not recognize it as sea-kale and would not buy it. It is the same with the blue 'coco' French beans which were first introduced by the late Edward Bunyard: they are absolutely stringless (probably the only kind of French Bean that is really stringless), they cook to a most beautifully vivid green, and they are tender, delicious and the best of French beans. The only thing against them is their colour before they are cooked; it is not at all an ugly colour, a rich purple, but it is not the colour which the public associate with French beans, and they will have none of them. But the greatest tragedy of all, in the list of missed opportunities among vegetables, is the utter disregard for Pokeweed, or *Phytolacca americana*. Every winter this American shrub is cut down and its roots are protected by straw or bracken from frost; in late April or early May, each plant will send a dozen or so little shoots, half of which are left to grow and bear seeds in time, whilst the other half may be cut when a few inches long, and all there is to do with them is to wash them and let them cook for about twenty minutes in hot water just off the boil, when they are ready to be served hot with Sauce Hollandaise, or left to get cold and served with a Sauce Vinaigrette. They are equally excellent hot and cold, as good as asparagus, and they demand no preparation whatever, no scraping, peeling or trimming. Yet nobody bothers to grow *Phytolacca americana*!

The same tale of missed opportunities could be told by fishermen: the sea is full of all manner of different kinds of fish which are good to eat, but there are a very few of them which the fishmongers will bother to buy because there are a few only that the public happen either to know or to trust.

Lobsters, for instance, are fashionable and extremely expensive as a result of being so highly prized, whilst their cousins, the crawfish, sometimes called 'spiny lobster' (*Palinurus*) is much cheaper although quite as good, if not actually better, in the opinion of many a Gastronome; but it does not happen to have any claws, so it finds its last home mostly in tins when it is sold as tinned 'lobster.' And because the Sole is quite rightly considered the best flat fish there is, a number of very inferior flat fish of the Plaice genus masquerade under the names of Lemon sole, Witch sole, Torbay sole. Credit must be given to the fishmongers, aided and abetted by the Board of Fisheries, for making the English eat fish that nobody would ever have bought some years ago, when meat was more plentiful. All that was needed was a little imagination to coin names that were more acceptable, such as *Flake*, the name given to different kinds of dog-fish, beheaded and skinned, of course; and *Rock Salmon*, the name that belongs to a member of the great Cod family but one that is now given to the repulsive looking, although quite good eating wolf-fish or cat-fish, which is never offered for sale, of course, with its great ugly head.

Two world-wars within twenty-five years have been responsible for a number of shortages and restrictions, and it is all the more important to make the best of all the resources within our reach and means; hence we shall find of practical value in this Encyclopædia of Gastronomy, a list and description not of *everything* that is fit for human consumption, but of a very large number of the more acceptable foodstuffs available in different parts of the world at different times of the year: it is true, unfortunately, that many of these are not to be found in the shops, but it is equally true that they *should* be there and *could* be there did the public demand them with sufficient perseverance. There is also a very important approach to the problems of 'enjoying' one's meals: besides the raw matèrials, the fish, flesh and fowl, the vegetables, cereals and fruits of fine quality and in great variety, there is the question of their proper preparation in as many different manners as possible to avoid monotony. This is where the cook comes in. But where is the cook? Or where is the money to pay for the services of a professional cook? There has never been such a shortage of professional cooks as there is at present, and owing to the ever rising cost of living there are fewer and fewer people every year who can afford to pay the high wages which professional cooks demand, whether they deserve them or not. On the other hand, there have never been so many or such good amateur cooks as there are now, and every year the number is growing of both men and women who find that it is quite a fascinating part-time hobby to do their own cooking. In all arts, as distinct from crafts, the amateur has as good a chance as the professional to become a master and to enjoy getting there by degrees. Whatever the trouble the artist may have to take to paint or sing or cook better to-day than yesterday, he is more than repaid by the results he achieves. For the amateur, cooking is both an art and a sport, and there is as much thrill in seeing one's first Cheese Soufflé rise in the oven like a chef's hat, as there is in bringing off a thirty yards putt or scoring a goal. And here again the cook, whether he or she, whether professional or amateur, will find in the *Encyclopædia of Gastronomy* a very great choice of recipes to be used as a guide how best to secure good results.

ACKNOWLEDGEMENTS

This Encyclopaedia of Gastronomy could not have been produced without the aid and labour of many hands, and it is both a duty and a privilege to avow assistance and to return thanks for many and valuable suggestions, emendations, corrections and contributions received from a great number of friends and well-wishers. Our greatest debt of gratitude is due to past and present members of the Advisory Council of the Wine and Food Society, to the late Mrs Jessop Hulton, the late Sir Stephen Gaselee and the late Sir Eric Maclagan; also to Sir Francis Colchester-Wemyss, Miss Elizabeth Craig, Sir Jack Drummond, Mr Vyvyan Holland, the Dowager Lady Swaythling and Mrs Doris Lytton Toye. Among other Members of the Wine and Food Society, great assistance was rendered by some gifted cooks, both amateurs and professional, chiefly the late Ernest Oldmeadow, Mrs M.D.Crittall, Mrs F.M.L.Douglas, Mrs W.H.Wynne Finch, and Lady Samuelson, among the first, and Mr William Heptinstall, of Fortingall fame, and Monsieur Eugène Herbodeau among the others.

We also wish to acknowledge with sincere gratitude the wholehearted help which was given to us by the specialists and technicians to whom we appealed from time to time, such as the late Sir Daniel Hall, the late Dr H.E. Durham, Sir E. John Russell, Director of the Rothamsted Experimental Station, Dr C. D. Darlington, of the John Innes Horticultural Institution, Professor H.A.D.Neville and Mr Waldie, of Reading University, Mr N.K. Gould, of the R.H.S. Gardens, Wisley, Mr H.T.Wilkin, of Messrs James Carter & Co., Raynes Park, and Mr W.T.Stearn, the Lindley Library Librarian at the R.H.S. Headquarters, in Vincent Square. Their help was invaluable when we were preparing the Sections of the Encyclopædia dealing with Vegetables, Fruit and Cereals. And so was the assistance which we received from Mr C.N.Hooper, then Clerk of the Fishmongers Company, when we were preparing the Fish Section; and from Dr Francis C. Fraser, of the British Museum (National History), Mr H.F.Goffe, Hon. Secretary of the Utility Poultry Society, Mr L.R.Brightwell, the London Zoo artist, Mr G.B. Stratton, Librarian and Dr S.A.Neave, Secretary of the London Zoological Society, when we were preparing the Sections dealing with Meat and also Birds and their Eggs. Thanks are also due to Nika Standen for assistance in preparing the American edition.

London　　　　　　　　　　　　　　　　　　　ANDRÉ L. SIMON

SECTION 1
SAUCES

SECTION I

Sauces: comprising the principal classical Sauce Recipes together with a classified index of Condiments, Garnishings, Dressings, Herbs, Flavourings, Seasonings and Stuffings, including Sweet Sauces for puddings and desserts

SAUCES

Epicurean cooks
Sharpen with cloyless sauce his appetite.
Shakespeare, ANTONY AND CLEOPATRA, Act II, Scene 1

INTRODUCTION

'SAUCE' is one of those French words that came over with the Normans and remains unchanged to this day. It still retains its original meaning of a relish to make our food more appetizing, but, whilst that is the only meaning of 'sauce' in France, the Elizabethans took 'sauce' out of the field of gastronomy, in England, and endowed it with a new meaning: a refreshingly impudent rejoinder was in a 'saucy' manner 'saucily' said; petulance became 'sauciness'; an impertinent fellow a 'saucebox'. And old-timers today still use 'sauce' in the jocular mood of 'None of your sauce,' which would be quite the wrong way to decline the horrid flour-paste-in-milk messes served to us as 'Cream Sauce' in many places that ought to know better.

In all mediæval household accounts of lordly feasts and homely meals, 'salt and sauce' are shown almost invariably as a single entry, a proof that sauce was then mostly, if not exclusively, a savoury relish served with fish and meat, to make them more palatable, or more acceptable, when they had suffered in transit or storage. Present-day rapid methods of transport and modern means of refrigeration have banished the need to sauce over unpleasant reminders of incipient mortification in highly perishable foodstuffs. Sauces are no longer the spicy pickles which they were originally. Their chief object to-day is to make our food look and taste better, to make it at the same time more appetizing and more nutritious.

A good appetite may be called the best of all sauces, and meat gravy as good a sauce as any roast requires. In both instances, however, the name 'Sauce' is used more figuratively than literally. Strictly speaking, sauces are liquid or semi-liquid foods devised to make other foods look, smell, and taste better, and hence be more easily digested and more beneficial. There are a few sauces which are quite simple, such as melted butter, an emollient, or mint sauce, a stimulant. But the majority of sauces are combinations of various elements affording to every cook a chance of displaying his or her own individuality, even when adhering to the main directions laid down in cookery books.

Most sauces have as a basis some nourishing substance, be it cream, butter, milk, olive oil or an 'essence', that is a concentrated form of meat or fish stock. Then there is the binding, mostly eggs, and, lastly, the flavouring agent or agents, one or more of the many varieties of herbs, spices, condiments and wines. Hence the possibility of countless combinations in sauces that will be different in colour, flavour, taste and consistency; sauces that will make us enjoy, digest and be duly grateful for boiled cod and baked beans.

Sauces, like all else, are continually changing in details whilst the foundations upon which they are built change but little if at all. There are five foundation sauces or basic sauces, called in French *Grandes Sauces* or *Sauces Mères*. Two of them have a record of two hundred years behind them; they are the *Béchamelle* and the *Mayonnaise*. They have lasted so long, not only because they are very good, but because they are so adaptable and provide a fine basis for a considerable number of other sauces. The other three, which also date back to the eighteenth century, are the *Velouté*, the *Brune* and the *Blonde*; Carême called these last two *Notre Espagnole* and *Notre Allemande*, to emphasize that both were French sauces and that their names were due to their dark and fair complexions.

These five sauces still provide the basis for the making of many modern sauces, but no longer of most of them. Modern sauces may be divided into two classes: the Carême and Escoffier classes. Among the faithful, in the great kitchens of the world, Escoffier is to Carême what the New Testament is to the Old.

Carême and his disciples produced sauces that were works of art: beautiful and delicious, but complicated. Their chief concern might have been – and probably was – to camouflage as much as possible the meat, game or fish served with some sauce. Many of the sauces which Carême used or introduced were strong and spicy sauces, such as the *vert-pré*, *Périgueux*, *matelote*, *bourguignotte* (now called *bourguignonne*), *chevreuil*, *aigre-doux*, *piquante*, *salmis*, *Robert*, *raifort*, etc. Of course, there were others, such as the *Sauce Suprême* and the

Sauce Hollandaise, for instance, as great favourites to-day as they were a hundred years ago. But, on the whole, Carême sauces killed more than they helped the flavour of the meat or game, fish or poultry with which they were served.

Escoffier took a different view: he was the apostle of simplicity; he wanted his sauces to help and not to hide the flavour of whatever dish they adorned. He introduced, and he had the greatest faith in, *fumets* and *essences*, that is, evaporated stock obtained by allowing the water, milk or wine in which meat, fish or vegetables happen to be cooked, to steam away slowly so as to leave behind a fragrant concentrate as a basis for whatever sauce will be served with them.

Grimod de la Reynière, a contemporary of Brillat-Savarin, the author of *L'Almanach des Gourmands*, allowed his enthusiasm once upon a time to run away with his discretion, when he exclaimed: 'I would eat my own father with such a sauce'. Escoffier would not have approved of such a sauce: he was not even too keen about the old French proverb: *C'est la sauce qui fait manger le poisson*. Fish that one cannot eat unless it be buried under a rich sauce had better be buried in the ground, but the fine flavour of a fresh Dover sole cooked in white wine is helped, not blurred, when served with a sauce made from the greatly 'reduced' wine in which the fish was cooked.

Espagnole and *Allemande*, the *roux brun* and *blond*, and all flour sauces, are less and less popular to-day; *fumets* and *essences*, which are of much more easy digestion, more delicate, lighter, and altogether better, are the greatest favourites, and they deserve to be.

Imagination and wit are gifts which are only too easily dulled by dull food and dull company, whether we be young or old. We cannot always choose the company, but we can, or should be able, to choose our sauces and banish dullness from our meals.

Far too long has England lain under the jibe that she has a hundred religions, but only one sauce. The reverse would be ever so much better for everybody, and as there are signs of a desire for greater religious unity, let us hope that the desire may also grow for more and better sauces. There is but one serious obstacle in the path of a 'sauce-conscious' England, and it is the sauce inferiority complex of the race. The belief is deep-rooted in Anglo-Saxon minds that the making of a French sauce is far too difficult a task to be attempted with any hope of success. But it is not the case. Most classical sauces, called French sauces, are well within the understanding and achievement of most of us. There are, of course, a number of complicated sauces, in the making of which strange ingredients, rarely available, are indispensable, and such sauces are better left alone or ordered at hotels and restaurants where they happen to be obtainable. But they are exceptions to the rule, and if they are mentioned in the following pages, it is merely as a matter of general interest. On the other hand, all the sauces for which detailed recipes have been given can normally be made in most households in England or the United States of America just as well as in France. The making of sauces is not confined to any nationality, and it offers a field which is positively unlimited to the cook who possesses imagination and taste.

Besides the names of the better-known sauces, there will be found in this Section the names of the *Garnitures* or garnishings which usually adorn the sauces themselves or dishes served with their own particular sauce; also various dressings and stuffings.

NOTES ON THE MAKING OF SAUCES

Some cooks prefer potato flour (*fécule*) to ordinary flour in the preparation of certain delicate sauces. When *fécule* is used, sauces need to simmer less, and, as a consequence, do not tend to become over-salted, as is sometimes the case when ordinary flour is used; further, the sauce looks more transparent and 'stands up' better when made with *fécule*. Once ready, a *fécule*-made sauce should not remain too long on the fire or it will become too clear in appearance.

To remove all fat from a sauce, greatly reduce cooking heat and throw a few drops of cold water into the pan. This at once causes the fat to rise to the surface, whence it may be easily removed with a spoon.

When egg yolks are added to a sauce they should be beaten with a teaspoonful of cold water, and then a little of the sauce stirred into the yolks. Remove pan from the fire and stir the mixture into the rest of the sauce by degrees. Stir until well blended. Return to the double-boiler. Stir constantly until thick, but do not allow to boil or the sauce will curdle.

Only the best butter must be used in the preparation of the perfect white sauce and eggs must, of course, be very fresh. If a very rich *blonde* sauce be needed for special occasions, use thin cream instead of milk.

HERBS, SPICES AND CONDIMENTS

A well-stocked kitchen cupboard should include sundry spices and condiments without which certain types of sauce cannot be made. Here is a recommended short list:

SPICES

Ground and stick cinnamon	Ground and whole nutmegs
White and black pepper, ground	Ground and whole cloves
Whole peppercorns	Root and ground ginger

SPICES (*continued*)

Dried and ground saffron	Paprika
Cayenne pepper	Curry powder

Ground and whole mace

HERBS, ETC.

Dried sage	Dried thyme
Dried chervil	Dried bayleaves
Dried mint	Dried basil

Dried marjoram, tarragon and parsley

SUNDRY SEASONINGS, ETC.

Garlic	Tarragon vinegar
Capers	Garlic vinegar
Chives	Shallots
Potato starch or flour (*fécule*)	French mustard
White wine vinegar	Celery salt
Red wine vinegar	Rock salt

OTHER HERBS, SPICES AND CONDIMENTS

POT-HERBS, SWEET-HERBS AND OTHERS

Alexanders	Comfrey	Pennyroyal
Anise	Costmary	Rosemary
Balm	Cowslip	Rue
Basil or Sweet Basil	Dittany	Safflower
Bergamot	Eschalot	Sage
Borage	Fenugreek	Samphire
Brooklime	Good King Henry	Sauce 'Alone'
Burnet	Horehound	Savory
Calamint	Hyssop	Scallion
Celery	Lemon Thyme	Spoonwort
Charlock	Lovage	Sweet Cicely
Cibol	Marigold	Tansy
Clary	Milfoil	Tarragon
Cochlearia	Mugwort	Thyme
Colewort	Parsley	Watercress

SPICES AND CONDIMENTS

Allspice	Chutney	Nasturtium
Aniseed	Coriander	Persicaria
Broom	Cumin	Pickles

OTHER SPICES AND CONDIMENTS *(cont.)*

Canella	Dill	Pignoli
Caraway Seeds	Elderflower	Pimentos
Cardamom	Fennel	Red Pepper
Cascarilla	Galangal	Saffron
Cassia	Horseradish	Turmeric
Cayenne or Red Pepper	Juniper	Vanilla
Chillies	Mace	

Definitions and Recipes

ACHILLÉE
Lat. *Achillea Patarnica*. A wild herb, the *Milfoil* or *Goose-tongue*, a little of which, chopped like chervil, improves any green salad or a *Sauce Verte*.

AFRICAINE
(*Garniture pour grosses pièces*). One of the elaborate *Haute Cuisine* garnishings, including *Cèpes*, cucumber, aubergines and tomatoes *sautés* in oil and *Pommes Château*.

AGRO DOLCE
The favourite 'bitter-sweet' sauce of Italy. It is made with a few lumps of sugar steeped in vinegar, and put in a pan until they run to caramel; white wine is then added and shallots; when reduced, some demi-glace is added, then stoned raisins and capers.

AGUAXIMA
A variety of Brazilian black pepper.

AIL
Lat. *Allium sativum*. Fr. for Garlic (q.v.). *Gousse d'Ail*, Fr. for a clove of garlic. *Aillade*, Fr. for a piece of crust rubbed with garlic.

AÏOLI
A Provençal olive-oil-cum-garlic cold sauce which may be described as a well-seasoned *Mayonnaise* (q.v.) with more or less pounded garlic. In Provence, the *Aïoli* is the name of the dish itself, whether it be cod or vegetables or snails, when served with such a sauce.

AIRELLES, Sauce
The French name of the English and American *Cranberry Sauce* (q.v.).

AJI, AGI
Guinea or Red Indian dwarf bird-pepper, a species of *capsicum* grown in Peru.

AJOLIO
The Spanish edition of the *Sauce Provençale*, i.e., oil and garlic.

ALBERT, Sauce
The French name for the English hot *Horseradish Sauce* (q.v.).

ALBONI
A brown sauce for venison with red currant jelly and grilled pignoli added.

ALBUFÉRA
A *Sauce Suprême* (q.v.) with *Beurre pimenté* (q.v.) added and flavoured with port wine. Served with game, roast pork and other rich meats.

ALECOST
Lat. *Chrysanthemum Balsamita*. Also known as *Costmary*. One of the old-fashioned English herbs; it has a faint flavour of mint and is useful in salads.

ALEXANDERS or **ALLISANDERS**
Lat. *Smyrnium Olusatrum*; Fr. *Persil de Macédoine* or *Macéron*. A plant now almost forgotten, which was formerly much used in England as pot-herb and in salads. It belongs to the cow parsley family and is somewhat of a cross between parsley and celery. The stems can be used blanched, and are in season in April.

ALGÉRIENNE
(*Garniture pour grosses pièces*.) French garnishing consisting of small tomatoes cooked in oil and *Croquettes* of sweet potatoes.

ALLEMANDE, Sauce
One of the classic French sauces, also known as *Sauce Blonde* and *Sauce Parisienne*. To make a *Sauce Allemande*, one requires:

    2 cupfuls of *Sauce Velouté* (q.v.)
    2 egg-yolks
    Fresh butter or thick cream
    A little nutmeg.

Reduce the *Velouté* upon a slow fire until it is but half the original quantity. Pour into a double-boiler, or, failing this, in a small saucepan which must be set in another larger pan containing hot water. Beat two egg-yolks and add to sauce, stirring gently during addition. Next, add cream or butter sufficient to enrich and improve the flavour of the sauce; also a light dusting of nutmeg, some essence of mushrooms, or lemon juice to taste. Cook in or over gently boiling water, stirring frequently until the sauce is thick and very creamy.

ALLSPICE
Lat. *Pimenta officinalis*. Fr. *Piment* or *Poivre de la Jamaïque*. The kitchen name for Jamaica pepper, one of the most aromatic of spices; it is the dried berry of *Pimenta officinalis*, the Allspice tree.

9

ALSACIENNE
(*Garniture pour rôtis, volaille et gibier.*) Fresh noodles *à l'alsacienne*, scollops of *foie gras sauté* in butter, slices of truffles with a little *Sauce Madère*. Sometimes denotes the presence of *Choucroûte* as part of the garnishings or as the background of the dish.

AMBASSADEUR
(*Garniture pour grosses pièces.*) An elaborate French *Haute Cuisine* garnishing consisting chiefly of *Pommes Duchesse*, artichoke bottoms filled with a *purée* of mushrooms, and grated horseradish.

AMÉRICAINE
The name of a sauce made of a *Velouté de poisson* and with added lobster meat and pounded shell; also the name of a *Garniture* including lobster tails and rounds of truffles.

Here is Marcel Boulestin's recipe (*The Finer Cooking or Dishes for Parties*, Cassell 1937, pp. 49-50):

'Cut in small dice one onion and one carrot, and cook them for a few minutes in a mixture of olive oil and butter, together with a bouquet.

'Meanwhile take a small raw lobster and cut the tail and claws in small pieces; put aside the thick liquid there is inside the body and scrape the "coral" out of the head.

'Add the pieces of lobster to the vegetables and cook 2 or 3 minutes, turning the pieces till the shell is red. Remove the excess of oil and butter, if any, and put in a liqueur-glassful of brandy. Set it alight and let it burn, shaking, till it dies out.

'Put in a glass of dry white wine, a little fumet of fish, a tablespoonful of tomato sauce, salt, pepper and paprika. Cook a few minutes more and remove the pieces of lobster.

'Pass the sauce through a strainer, pressing the pieces of vegetable well. Put it into a small saucepan, add a little fresh cream, and reduce a little more. See that it is highly spiced, add the inside and the coral mashed with a piece of butter and cook a few seconds on a slow fire. This acts as a binding.

'Pass once more through a strainer if you want it absolutely smooth, and serve in a sauce-boat.

'Some people add to it the flesh of the lobster cut in small cubes, but it is not necessary; it can be used for a pilaff.'

AMIRAL, Sauce
A butter sauce mostly used for boiled fish. To 1 breakfast-cupful of melted butter, add two well-pounded anchovies, four finely chopped chives and a number of chopped capers; also a very little thinly pared lemon-peel. Let the whole lot simmer over a gentle fire until the anchovies are well blended; then take out the lemon-peel, add the juice of one lemon, pepper and salt, and serve hot.

ANCHOVY SAUCE
An English sauce usually made by adding a little Anchovy Essence to a white sauce. It is the easiest way but not the best. The proper way is to make first a good, rich white sauce and add to it a couple of de-salted anchovies, pounded to a paste and rubbed through a fine sieve. The following are popular variants of the plain Anchovy Sauce:

Anchovy Butter Sauce
Beat up some *Beurre d'Anchois* (q.v.) the size of a small egg in 1 pint of good brown sauce; warm over a slow fire and add the juice of half a lemon, or more, according to taste.

Anchovy and Caper Sauce
Put ½ pint melted butter in a saucepan; dredge in a little flour to thicken; season with pepper and salt, a little dusting of nutmeg and some of the vinegar from the capers. Mix all well together and then add a boned anchovy, chopped finely, and a tablespoonful of chopped-up capers. Stir well in over a good fire; let the sauce simmer for 5 minutes, when it will be ready to serve.

Anchovy Cream Sauce
Melt some butter so as to have a pint of melted butter. When hot, add 3 oz. *Beurre d'Anchois* (q.v.); stir until dissolved, and then stir in quickly 2 tablespoonfuls of whipped cream, off the fire; do not let it boil.

Anchovy Essence
A preparation of pounded boned Anchovies, vinegar, pepper and spices sold under various brands and very useful as a flavouring agent.

ANCHUSA or ALKANET
Fr. *Orcanette*. A deciduous herbaceous plant the leaves of which are used in wine cups, like those of Borage, which they resemble.

ANDALOUSE, Sauce
A *Mayonnaise* (q.v.) with a *Purée de Tomates* added; also dice of sweet peppers.

ANDALOUSE
(*Garniture pour grosses pièces et volailles.*) Long peppers cut in two, braised, stuffed with rice *à la Grecque* and rounds of Egg-plant *sauté* in olive oil; served with tomatoes cooked in oil and dressed with chopped parsley.

ANGLAISE, À L'
Usually denotes a simple English method of cooking, such as plain boiling or steaming. *Garniture Anglaise*, for boiled beef, consists

of plain boiled carrots, turnips, cauliflower, runner beans and potatoes.

ANISEED

Lat. *Pimpinella anisum*; Fr. *Anis*. The fruit of anise—used to flavour sauces as well as creams, sweet puddings and cakes.

ANVERSOISE

(*Garniture pour grosses pièces*.) *Tartelettes* filled with *Jets de Houblon* (hop shoots) and plain boiled or *noisette* potatoes.

APPLE SAUCE

One of the classic English sauces, and one of the most popular sauces in the U.S.A. It is best when made with green, sharp apples, in the following manner:

Cook the peeled apples in a very small quantity of water, stirring often to prevent burning. When soft, pass through a sieve, add sugar—but not too much—and a very little cinnamon, if liked, or lemon if preferred. *To serve with cold pork.* Add to mashed apples about a tablespoonful of granulated gelatine, previously soaked in a little cold water. Heat mixture until gelatine is dissolved, flavour as directed, and pour into tiny Bar-le-Duc glasses, turning out, when set, on a glass plate to serve with meat.

APRICOT SAUCE

This is a sweet sauce usually made with apricot jam, a little flour and some 'cooking sherry,' stewed together for a little while and passed through a sieve. The correct way to make Apricot Sauce, however, is with fresh apricots, cut in halves, their stones broken and the kernel within peeled, pounded and put back with the rest of the fruit in a saucepan, on a gentle heat, with a little water to prevent sticking. When the fruit is quite soft, add a glass of Madeira to each dozen apricots used and some Demerara sugar. Stir well and reduce until the sauce is syrup in consistency and pass through a sieve into a sauce-boat.

ARLÉSIENNE

(*Garniture pour Tournedos ou Noisettes*.) Slices of *Aubergines* fried in oil; rings of onions and tomatoes cooked in oil.

ARMENONVILLE

(*Garniture pour grosses pièces*.) Pommes *Cocotte*, artichoke bottoms cut in quarters, tomatoes and French beans.

ASPIC

French for *Meat Jelly*. Meat gravy and calf's foot jelly flavoured with pot-herbs, one of these being the *espic* or *spikenard*, hence the name.

The more usual way to make a meat glaze for *Aspic* is as follows:

Onions and carrots
Meat trimmings
1 calf's foot
Small 'bouquet garni'
Salt and pepper
1 clove garlic
1 clove
Hot water

Cover the whole bottom surface of a heavy copper or iron saucepan with slices of onion; cover these in turn with trimmings of lean meat, preferably gelatinous things such as pieces of shank of veal, skin of fresh pork and scraps of beef, poultry or veal. Add one or two sliced carrots, a calf's foot cut into smallish pieces, the 'bouquet', clove, garlic, salt and pepper. Moisten with a ladleful of water and set on a good fire to *sweat*. When the juices begin to flow and the contents of the pan begin to colour and look like sticking to the bottom, reduce heat greatly and continue cooking very gently until the surface fat looks quite clear. Skim this fat off very carefully, then add hot water according to requirements. Do not touch contents of pan, beyond shaking gently now and then, that the browned onion may colour the glaze nicely, but do not allow contents to burn. Simmer gently over a low heat for 2 or 3 hours; then, again skim off any surface fat and strain the gravy through a very fine sieve lined with muslin. Set aside for use whenever wanted. It will keep well on ice.

To Clarify Glaze, for Aspic

This meat glaze may be used to make aspic jelly; if, when it is required for use, the weather happens to be particularly hot, add to the warmed glaze 1 tablespoonful of granulated gelatine and, if desired, a little lemon juice. To clarify, when the glaze is hot, add two lightly beaten white of eggs and their shells, broken up. Whisk the mixture briskly over a sharp fire until it reaches boiling point; then reduce heat, or draw to side of stove, and allow the mixture to simmer gently for about 10 minutes. Strain through a fine sieve and use as directed.

Quick Aspic Jelly

1 heaped tablespoon granulated
  gelatine
¼ cup cold stock
2 cups bouillon or diluted meat glaze
1 teaspoon lemon juice
Sherry (optional)

When there is neither meat glaze, bouillon, nor stock at hand, a tablespoonful of good meat essence or two or three meat cubes may be used, but the flavour will not be so delicate as if a well-made meat glaze is the basis of the jelly.

Soak the granulated gelatine in the cold stock – or water – until the latter is absorbed by the gelatine. Heat the stock, or whatever is used as a foundation, add the dissolved gelatine and remove pan from fire. Stir contents until the gelatine is entirely dissolved. Flavour as desired with lemon juice and dry sherry or white wine.

To Use Aspic Jelly

If to be used for decorating a mould containing sundry trifles such as pieces of breast of chicken, sweetbread, truffles, etc., pour half an inch of the aspic in the bottom of the selected mould. The aspic is ready to use when it is almost cold and just beginning to jell. Put the mould in a cool place so that the aspic may set. On the surface, place your decorations: tiny sprigs of chervil or parsley, truffles, thinly sliced and cut into fancy shapes, slices of stuffed olive or what-not. Cover this decoration with more semi-liquid aspic, pouring it gently on with a teaspoon, taking care not to disarrange the pattern. When this light layer is set, cover with more gelatine, allow this to set, then cover with whatever ingredients you are using. Continue filling the mould in this fashion, taking care none of the ingredients touch the sides of the mould. Be careful to use rather small pieces of whatever you are 'aspicing' or the jelly may split when turned out. Finish with a rather thick layer of jelly. If pieces of almost completely set aspic are placed on the layer of filling, then covered with a thin layer of the semi-liquid aspic, good and quicker results may be obtained. The use of ice for this job is important, but failing this, a cool room and lots of time and patience must do.

Tomato Aspic
(American)

For hot weather dishes, tomato aspic is very refreshing. It can also be used in conjunction with meat aspic in making up a jellied mould of vegetables or other ingredients, using one two-inch layer of tomato aspic and then the filling, covering this with a two-inch layer of tomato aspic. When turned out the result is charming. Aspic may also be coloured lightly with green colouring and made into a three-colour jellied dish.

    2 cups strained tomato juice
    ¼ cup boiling stock or water
    1 teaspoon lemon juice
    ¼ cup cold water
    1 teaspoon sugar
    1½ tablespoons granulated gelatine
    Salt and pepper

If a clear jelly is required, it must be clarified as indicated in the Aspic recipe. Leaf gelatine may, of course, be used in all recipes calling for granulated gelatine. Allow ½ oz. leaf gelatine for 1 tablespoonful of the granulated kind.

AURORE, Sauce

There are two sauces of that name, both pink, the one being a *Béchamel* with paprika, and the other a *Velouté* coloured lightly with a little tomato *purée*.

BADOISE

Garniture (a) *pour grosses pièces*: red cabbage, braised; lean bacon; mashed potatoes. (b) *pour tournedos et noisettes*: stoned cherries.

BANQUIÈRE

(*Garniture pour tournedos et noisettes*.) Boned and stuffed larks, braised, *quenelles* and truffles.

BASIL or SWEET BASIL

Lat. *Ocinum Basilicum*; Fr. *Basilic*; It. *Basilico*. A plant of the Labiate family and one of the pot-herbs; its leaves have a strong flavour of cloves. Always included in the making of *Turtle Soup*.

BÂTARDE, Sauce

A butter sauce with an egg yolk binding made as follows: Melt an oz. of butter in a pan and add to it an oz. of flour; mix well and add some salted hot water; whip up the lot smartly, then add the yolk of an egg which will have been beaten up in a spoonful of cold water beforehand. With the saucepan on the corner of the stove, away from the fire, and whilst beating all the while, add another 4 oz. of fresh butter, little by little. Season to taste and pass sauce through a fine sieve. A squeeze of lemon before serving is optional.

BATELIÈRE

(*Garniture pour Poisson*.) Mushrooms, small onions, fried eggs and *Écrevisses* are the outstanding component parts of this fish *Garniture*.

BAVAROISE, Sauce

A highly flavoured *Sauce Hollandaise* made as follows:

Beat the yolks of four eggs and put them into a saucepan in which about a cupful of wine vinegar has been boiled, whilst the eggs were being beaten, until reduced to about half the original quantity. Add, at the same time, about 1 oz. of fresh butter and grated horseradish according to taste. Beat the lot thoroughly and season with salt and a little grated nutmeg. Stir over a gentle heat until quite thick but do not let it come to the boil. Pass the sauce through a fine hair-sieve into another pan and then mix with it, little by little, some 3 oz. fresh butter. Beat the mixture over a slow fire until it becomes light and frothy, and then add 3 oz. of *Beurre d'Écrevisses*; serve at once.

BAVAROISE

(*Garniture pour Poisson.*) Crayfish tails.

BAYLEAVES

Lat. *Laurus nobilis*; Fr. *Feuilles de Laurier*. The dried leaves of the bay tree, used as a flavouring agent in some game pies and in court-bouillons. One or part of a bayleaf is always included in the *Bouquet Garni*.

BÉARNAISE

One of the most popular sauces for a fillet of beef, or most grilled red meats. It is not peculiar to Béarn, but was named by the chef of the Pavilion Henry IV, at St. Germain-en-Laye, near Paris, who first introduced this sauce, in 1835.

    1 or 2 shallots
    Spring fresh tarragon
    2 or 3 stalks chervil
    2 tablespoons wine
    4 egg yolks
    ½ lb. best fresh butter
    2 tablespoons cold water
    Salt and pepper

Chop shallots, tarragon leaves and chervil *very* finely. Place in a small saucepan, add white wine and allow the lot to simmer very gently until the wine has almost entirely evaporated; then add cold water. Strain and set aside. Place the egg yolks in the upper part of a double boiler, add the prepared herb and wine mixture and gently whisk with a wire whip, adding the butter one piece at a time, beating until absorbed before adding another piece. The beating must not be too fast; it must be steady and continuous over the *almost* boiling water until the sauce is as thick as Mayonnaise. Should the sauce curdle or *separate*, remove pan from fire, add a small teaspoonful of cold water and whip rather vigorously until sauce is thick and very smooth. Serve hot, either spread with a sprinkling of chopped chervil and tarragon on grilled meat or separately in a sauce-boat.

BÉATRIX

(*Garniture pour grosses pièces.*) *Morilles sautées* in butter; artichoke bottoms cut in quarters; new carrots and new potatoes *fondantes*.

BEAUHARNAIS

(*Garniture pour tournedos et noisettes.*) Stuffed mushrooms and artichoke bottoms cut in quarters.

BÉCHAMELLE, Sauce, or
BÉCHAMEL, Sauce à la

The name of one of the basic French sauces and one of the creamiest white sauces. It was named after, and believed to have been introduced by, Louis de Béchameil, or Béchamel, Marquis de Nointel, Lord Steward of the Household at the Court of Louis XIV.

The flour and water, sticky and lumpy horror so often served under this name is a libellous imitation, but it is not a *Béchamel*. To make a *Béchamel* in the old-fashioned and best manner, one should use butter and flour in equal quantities and the best and creamiest milk, as follows:

Melt the butter, but do not allow to sizzle, in a small saucepan over a rather low heat. When the butter is melted, add the flour, stirring well into the butter. Have some cold boiled milk. When the butter and flour mixture begins to bubble gently, add the cold milk, very little at a time, stirring and beating well until the whole amount of milk has been added and the sauce is thick and creamy. This is the Sauce Béchamelle. It may be used as a basis for other sauces by adding anything called for by the recipe chosen: mushrooms, chopped parsley, chopped hard-boiled egg, oysters, or whatnot. If to be served plain, and if a rich sauce be required, add the beaten yolk of an egg – after removing the pan from the fire – and a little lemon juice.

BELLE HÉLÈNE

(*Garnitures pour grosses pièces.*) Grilled mushrooms filled with tomatoes; green peas, new carrots and *Pommes croquettes.*

BERCY

A popular French sauce, of which there is a variant for fish and another for meat. The basis for both is white wine and shallots, a *velouté de poisson* being used for the first and *glace de viande* for the second.

BERGAMOT

Lat. *Monarda didyma*; Fr. *Bergamote.* An ornamental plant, the leaves of which, when dried, are used for flavouring. In some parts of the U.S.A. the Bergamot leaves are used to make what is known as *Oswego Tea.*

BERNY

(*Garniture pour gibier.*) *Croquettes* of potatoes *Berny* and *Tartelettes* filled with purée of chestnuts and lentils, capped with a slice of truffle.

BERRICHONNE

(*Garniture pour grosses pièces.*) Balls of braised cabbage; glazed button onions; whole chestnuts and slices of bacon.

BEURRE MANIÉ or BUTTER and FLOUR BINDING

When a sauce should be only very slightly thickened, it is customary to add what is known in *cuisine* as a 'beurre manié'. This is a piece of butter the size of a large walnut, rolled and indeed 'squashed' in flour; it is added to the sauce a few minutes before serving and given just sufficient time to simmer for the flour to be cooked.

BEURRE À L'ANGLAISE

French for *Melted Butter*.

BEURRE NOIR

A sharp sauce made of fresh butter, browned, but not burnt, and mixed with vinegar. It is used chiefly as a sauce for skate: *Raie au beurre noir*; brains: *Cervelle au beurre noir*, etc. Fried parsley is the usual garnishing of *Beurre noir* dishes.

BEURRE NOISETTE

Fresh butter melted in a small saucepan and cooked to a light hazel tint, and no more, when it must be moved away from the fire. It should be whipped off the fire the moment a light hazel tinge shows itself; it must be used at once as a sauce for fish more particularly and with or without a squeeze of lemon according to taste.

Not to be mistaken for *Beurre de Noisettes*, which is butter in which crushed grilled filberts have been mixed.

BEURRES COMPOSÉS

Preparations in which various more or less highly flavoured or coloured foods are mashed or worked into fresh butter and used as sauce or seasoning. They are known by the name of the principal ingredient responsible for the informing flavour imparted to the butter, the more usual *Beurres Composés* being the following: *Ail*, garlic; *Amande*, sweet almonds; *Anchois*, anchovies; *Bercy*, shallots; *Caviar*, caviare; *Chivry*, shallots, tarragon, chives and fresh garden burnet; *Colbert*, same as *Maître d'Hôtel*, with a little chopped tarragon added; *Crevettes*, shrimps; *Écrevisses*, fresh-water crayfish; *Estragon*, tarragon; *Hareng*, fresh herring; *Homard*, lobster; *Laitance*, fish roe; *Maître d'Hôtel*, butter mixed with chopped parsley, salt and pepper and a squeeze of lemon; *Meunière*, a *Beurre Noisette* with a squeeze of lemon; *Moutarde*, French mustard; *Paprika*, onions and paprika; *Raifort*, horseradish; *Ravigote*, same as *Chivry*; *de Tomatoes*, tomatoes; *de Truffes*, truffles.

BIGARRADE

An orange sauce made with the rind of the bitter or Seville orange (*Citrus Bigaradia*) as follows:

Cut off thin, regular, long pieces of the rind of two bitter oranges; cut them up into small pieces, matchlike, and boil them in plain water for five minutes; drain them and add them to about a pint or much reduced *Sauce Espagnole* (q.v.) and leave it on a gentle heat until the little pieces of rind are fairly soft. At time of serving, add the juice of an orange, a squeeze of lemon, and a little pepper and salt.

BLANQUETTE

A stew of veal, chicken or sweetbreads served with a white sauce which is usually made as follows: Put 2 oz. of butter in a saucepan, and when the butter is all but melted, sift in about two tablespoonfuls of flour; stir over the fire until well mixed, when you will add little by little some veal stock, mixing all the while, until the sauce is of the right consistency. Bind with egg yolks and add small onions and button mushrooms previously cooked; also a bouquet of herbs and pepper and salt to taste.

BLONDE, Sauce

This is an ordinary *Velouté* (q.v.) with a binding of egg yolks. For 1 quart of *Sauce Blonde*, here is Escoffier's recipe: Put in a pan a few spoonfuls of *cuisson de champignons* (stewed, chopped, fresh mushrooms); a pint of *fonds blanc* (white stock); five egg yolks; a little pepper; a mere dusting of grated nutmeg. Whip the lot thoroughly and then add a quart of *Velouté*. Bring to the boil and reduce by a quarter over a quick fire, stirring all the time. Then reduce further on a low heat and pass through a fine hair sieve.

BOHÉMIENNE

A *Mayonnaise* sauce with the addition of highly seasoned cream, and a little tarragon vinegar. As a *Garniture pour noisettes*, *Bohémienne* means pilau rice, tomatoes and fried rings of onions.

BOITELLE

(*Garniture pour poissons*.) Mushrooms.

BONNEFOY

Same as the *Sauce Bordelaise*, with some chopped tarragon added.

BORAGE

Lat. *Borago officinalis*; Fr. *Bourrache*. One of the four cardinal flowers of the Ancients, the use of which is now restricted to flavouring wine-cups.

BORDELAISE, Sauce

The generally accepted manner of making this sauce is as follows:

Streaky salt pork or mild bacon
2 or 3 carrots
2 onions
1 stalk thyme
1 small bay leaf
1 cup red wine
2 or 3 whole shallots
6 whole peppercorns
Dash cayenne pepper
1 clove garlic
1 tablespoon *Espagnole* sauce
A sufficiency of stock

Have a heavy iron pan or an earthenware casserole, not too large. Cover the bottom with thin slices of salt pork or bacon, cover these with diced carrots and onions, add thyme and bayleaf and place pan over a low heat to allow ingredients to *sweat* gently – that is, to bring out their juices slowly. When this is accomplished, add the wine, the whole shallots, peppercorns, a dash of cayenne, salt if needed, and the garlic, finely minced. Cook this very gently until the gravy produced is brown and sticky (technically this is now known as *réduit à glace*); then add the *Sauce Espagnole* and enough stock for your requirements. Boil up gently, skim to remove surface fat, and strain the sauce through a fine strainer. Return to pan and again reduce sauce by slow cooking; add a small piece of specially good butter when serving. Excellent with roast meat. If preferred, red Bordeaux may be used instead of white. In this case, add a little lemon juice and some chopped parsley when serving. This sauce must be rather highly seasoned.

The *Sauce Bordelaise* can be improved by adding at time of serving some poached beef marrow, cut into cubes, and a squeeze of lemon.

BOTTLED SAUCES

There are a number of liquid or semi-liquid condiments made industrially and sold commercially in bottles, under labels which are easily recognized. Among the most popular of these are the *A1 Sauce* and *Worcestershire Sauce*.

BOULANGÈRE

(*Garniture pour grosses pièces.*) Sliced or oval-shaped potatoes baked with onions in the same dish as the joint.

BOUQUET GARNI

This is just an assemblage of a sprig of thyme – fresh or dried may be used, but if the former it must be quite small as it is very pungent; a small dried bayleaf; stalks of parsley. These three herbs are tied together and used to flavour certain soups, stews, etc. The best way to deal with them and to have

them handy as required is to prepare a dozen or so 'bouquets', of varying sizes, in advance. In order that the 'bouquet' may easily be removed from the stew or what-not when done with, have a long piece of string left on, or, better still, place the herbs in a small piece of cheesecloth (butter-muslin), tying it tightly round the stalks and leaving a long piece with which to fish it out when desired. By this means no small pieces of thyme or parsley will be left in the dish. Kept in a tightly closed tin the 'bouquets' will keep for a very long time.

Sometimes other herbs, such as chives, chervil and so on are added.

It is often rather difficult to find even the simplest kind of herbs – with the exception of parsley – in the average greengrocer's shop. If a small garden is available, it is a good plan to plant the most customary herbs in it, or, failing a garden, chervil, chives and even tarragon may be grown on one's windowsill, in pots.

BOUQUETIÈRE

(*Garniture pour grosses pièces.*) Small potatoes *Château*, and as many fresh vegetables as possible arranged alternately round the meat: artichoke bottoms filled with small pieces of carrots and turnips; French beans; green peas; sprigs of cauliflowers with Hollandaise sauce.

BOURGEOISE

(*Garniture pour grosses pièces.*) Carrots cut to the size and shape of olives; browned onions; small pieces of bacon.

BOURGUIGNONNE, Sauce

A variant, somewhat more highly seasoned, of the *Sauce Bordelaise*, with red Burgundy in place of red Bordeaux wine.

BRABANÇONNE

(*Garnitures pour tournedos et noisettes.*) *Tartelettes* filled with a *purée* of brussels sprouts covered with a little *Sauce Mornay* (q.v.) *gratinée*, and thin potato *croquettes*.

BRAGANCE

(*Garniture pour tournedos et noisettes.*) Small tomatoes filled with Sauce *Béarnaise* and served with potato *croquettes*.

BRANDY SAUCE

There are many different methods of making this sauce, but the following is the method which we recommend:

Mix the yolks of three eggs with ¼ pint of cream, 1 dessertspoonful of Demerara sugar and 1 wineglassful of decent brandy. (It is a grave error to imagine that a wine or brandy used in cooking may be 'anything cheap'.) Beat well together and warm up in a saucepan for about 10 minutes in a double-boiler or *bainmarie*. Stir continuously to avoid curdling.

BREAD SAUCE
The most typically English of sauces and excellent with roast chicken or birds. There are three secrets to it: cook in a double boiler; beat with a fine whisk; and add a pat of fresh butter after removing from stove.

　½ pint milk
　1 small onion
　1 small clove
　1 blade mace
　2 oz. fresh, soft breadcrumbs
　½ oz. butter
　1 tablespoon cream
　Salt and pepper.

Crumble the bread very finely. Heat the milk slowly with the mace and the onion in which the clove has been stuck. Bring this to scalding point in the top portion of a double-boiler. Remove mace. Now sprinkle in the crumbs stirring and beating the while. Add salt and pepper to taste and half the butter. Cook, beating frequently for about 20 minutes; then add the cream and rest of the butter. Remove onion and clove and serve at once.

BRÉBAN
(*Garniture pour grosses pièces.*) *Purée* of broad-beans heaped upon artichoke bottoms; sprigs of cauliflower with *Sauce Hollandaise* (q.v.); Potatoes *persillées*.

BRETONNE, Sauce
Mostly used for fish and made as follows:
　Cook slowly in butter equal quantities of celery, leeks and onions, finely cut up in a *iulienne*; then add about the same quantity of fresh mushrooms as of the other three vegetables, also cut up in a *julienne*. Moisten with some fish *fumet*. Reduce almost completely. Add at the last moment, away from the fire, some white wine sauce or some Sauce Normande. Mix thoroughly, and if it is a great occasion add some finely chopped truffles before serving.
　There is also a *Sauce Bretonne* served with meat, which is usually an onion sauce with tomatoes or a tomato *purée*, but Carême's recipe for the *Sauce Bretonne* is without tomatoes; it is a *Sauce Espagnole* with onions.

BRETONNE
(*Garniture pour grosses pièces.*) White haricot beans and *Sauce Bretonne*.

BRILLAT-SAVARIN
(*Garniture pour gibier.*) Small *Tartelettes* filled with snipe or woodcock *mousse* or soufflé and a free display of truffles.

BRISTOL
(*Garniture pour grosses pièces.*) Small *croquettes* of rice in the shape of apricots; creamed *flageolets* and *pommes noisettes*.

BROOKLIME
Lat. *Veronica beccabunga*; Fr. *Cressonnière*. A bog-loving Veronica, known in Scotland as Water Purpie, and an excellent substitute for watercress.

BROOM
Lat. *Cytisus scoparius*; Fr. *Genêt*. The ordinary yellow Broom; its buds were universally used in England in olden times in the way that *Capers* are used now. They were preserved in vinegar.

BROWN SAUCE
Fr. *Sauce Brune*. See *Espagnole*.

BRUNE, Sauce
See *Espagnole*.

BRUXELLOISE, Sauce
The most popular sauce with asparagus in Belgium.
　Melt some first-class fresh butter gently over a low heat, add salt, pepper and lemon juice to taste. Finely chop or sieve one hard-boiled egg. Add to the melted butter and serve when heated through.

BURNET
Lat. *Poterium sanguisorba*; Fr. *Pimprenelle*. A valuable culinary herb used, chopped up, in salads and savoury omelettes.

BUTTER
The most delicate, delicious and digestible form of fat. It is, or should be, the cream of fresh milk, but it is most difficult to buy nowadays in its pure form.

BUTTERS
Savoury preparations, the basis of which is fresh butter.

Anchovy Butter
　6 de-salted anchovies
　Equal bulk of butter
Remove bones from fish and pound in a mortar or press through a sieve. Mix completely with the butter.

Montpellier Butter
　Assortment of herbs: chives, chervil, tarragon, etc.
　2 anchovy fillets
　1 pickled gherkin
　Dusting of nutmeg
　Olive oil
　2 or 3 hard-boiled egg yolks
　6 oz. butter
　Vinegar or lemon juice
　Green vegetable colouring
　Few capers

Place a handful of the mixed herbs in a little boiling water to blanch for a moment. Drain well and dry; then pound in a mortar with the other ingredients, all previously chopped. Flavour with nutmeg, lemon juice or vinegar and add enough oil, a drop at a time, to make a stiff creamy mixture. If nobody objects, the mortar may be rubbed with a little garlic before pounding the ingredients. Very good with any cold poultry or fish.

Crayfish or Shrimp Butter

If crayfish be used, boil and set aside tails and claws for other uses. Crush and pound the shells and heads in a mortar (if using shrimps, pound them whole). Add an equal amount of butter, pounding with the fish, then place mixture in a small pan with a little butter and simmer for 20 minutes. Place some cold water in a basin, cover with a fine muslin, then pour hot butter into this. Once cold, the prepared butter can easily be removed from surface of water, the shells remaining on muslin. Prawns may be also used, but their flavour is not so good as that of the plain brown shrimps.

The butter may, if wished, be lightly coloured by the addition of a little coralline pepper or suitable vegetable colouring. Season, if necessary, with salt and pepper, but if the fish was well seasoned, this is unnecessary.

Maître d'hôtel Butter

Fresh butter softened to a cream and seasoned with pepper, salt and lemon juice; finely chopped parsley is mixed with it.

CALAMINT

Lat. *Calamintha officinalis*; Fr. *Calamenthe*. A small plant with blue flowers; it has a hot scent similar to peppermint.

CAMBRIDGE SAUCE

The best English substitute for a *Mayonnaise*. It is a cold sauce, for cold dishes. It is made of oil and vinegar, the pounded yolks of, hard-boiled eggs, capers, anchovies, chervil tarragon and chives. A dusting of Cayenne pepper is optional.

CANCALAISE

(*Garniture pour poisson*.) Poached and bearded oysters; shelled shrimps; *Sauce Normande*.

CANELLA

Lat. *Canella alba*; Fr. *Cannelle blanche*. A West India tree from the inner rind of which a digestive, aromatic condiment is made.

CANNELLE

Fr. for *Cinnamon*.

CANNELLE DE CHINE

Fr. for *Cassia*.

CAPERS

Lat. *Capparis spinosa* and *capparis inermis*; Fr. *Câpres*; Ger. *Kapern*; It. *Capriole*; Sp. *Cabriolas*. The buds of a sort of hyssop which used to be grown in England in chalk pits and on walls; they are pickled in vinegar.

CAPER SAUCE

A white sauce served with boiled mutton. It is made of half milk and half liquor in which the meat was cooked. Allow 1 tablespoonful of coarsely chopped capers to 1 cup of sauce, together with a small dessertspoonful of the caper vinegar. Serve as soon as capers have been added, to avoid curdling of the sauce. Some cooks recommend the addition of a *soupçon* of tarragon vinegar and a tablespoonful of cream.

CAPSICUM

The family name of a number of green and red, round and long peppers or chillies. See *Cayenne*, *Chilli* and *Peppers*.

CARAMEL, Sauce

Put into a saucepan 6 oz. of sugar, the yellow rind of half a lemon, a little cinnamon and a pint of cold water; bring gradually to the boil and simmer for 10 minutes. In the meanwhile, put 4 tablespoonfuls of white sugar into another saucepan and a little water; place on the fire, stir constantly with a wooden spoon and in a few minutes the water will have evaporated and the sugar will begin to 'brown' or caramelize. Then is the time to add to the caramel the liquid prepared in the other saucepan, after passing it through a fine sieve. Add a glassful of Madeira wine or half a glassful of brandy. Stir well and serve hot with a pudding.

CARAWAY SEEDS

The seeds of the *Carum Carvi* (Fr. *Cumin des prés*), a plant widely distributed over Europe and parts of Asia. Used chiefly for flavouring in bakery and confectionery.

CARDAMOM

Lat. *Elettaria cardamomum*; Fr. *Cardamome*. The seeds of the *Cardamomum* plant, a native of the East Indies. Also known as *Grains of Paradise*. Used for flavouring confectionery and always in curry.

CARDINAL

The culinary equivalent of Scarlet, a colour usually obtained from the Coral of hen lobsters. The *Garniture* consists of pieces of lobster, rounds of truffle and *Sauce Cardinal*.

CARDINAL, Sauce
A *Béchamel* (q.v.) with fish *fumet* and a lobster *coulis*; or a *Béchamel* with fresh cream and some *Beurre de Homard* added; also a dusting of Cayenne pepper.

CASSIA
Lat. *Cassia cinnamomum*; Fr. *Cannelle de Chine*. The powder ground from the bark of *Cassia lignea*; a coarser and much cheaper sort of *cinnamon*.

CASTILLANE
(*Garniture pour tournedos et noisettes*.) Tomatoes cooked in oil placed on the meat, surrounded by small potato *croquettes* and fried onion rings.

CATALANE
(*Garniture pour tournedos et noisettes*.) Artichoke bottoms and grilled tomatoes.

CATCHUP
Also known as *Ketchup* (q.v.) or *Catsup*.

CAVOUR
(*Garniture pour grosses pièces*.) Semolina *croquettes*, timbale of *lazagnes* and *ravioli*.

CAYENNE or RED PEPPER
Lat. *Capsicum frutescens, var. longum* and *var. minimum*; Fr. *Poivre de Cayenne*. The powder of the dried pods and seeds of the capsicum, whether grown at Cayenne or elsewhere.

CELERY SAUCE
This is an American recipe for Celery Sauce.

    1 small bunch or head of celery
    1 tablespoon flour
    1 tablespoon butter
    2 cups stock or water
    6 tablespoons cream
    Salt and pepper

After well washing celery, cut into pieces, green tops and all. Place in a pan with the stock or water and cook until tender enough to rub through a sieve. Rub butter into flour, add the celery mixture and stir over a low heat until gently boiling. Simmer for a few moments then add the cream and season as desired. This is good with boiled mutton or with rabbit *fricassée*.

CHAMBORD
(*Garniture pour poissons*.) Large fish *quenelles*, mushrooms, soft roes, *écrevisses*; large rounds of truffles; *fleurons*.

CHANTILLY, Sauce
A *Mayonnaise* with a squeeze of lemon and some whipped cream added at the moment of serving. There is also a hot *Sauce Chantilly*, which is a *Béchamel* mixed with whipped cream. (In confectionery, *Chantilly* means fresh cream whipped and sweetened.)

CHARLOCK
Lat. *Brassica sinapis*. An uncultivated kind of Mustard, or Field Mustard, which can be used as a substitute for Mustard, although it is better not to encourage it, as it soon becomes a troublesome weed.

CHAROLAISE
(*Garniture pour grosses pièces*.) Cauliflower sprigs, *Villeroi* and *Croustades* filled with mashed turnips.

CHASSEUR, Sauce
A highly seasoned sauce with white wine as its foundation, mushrooms for flavour and shallots for pervasive bouquet.

CHATEAUBRIAND, Sauce
White wine, shallots and demi-glace sauce, greatly reduced, when fresh butter and chopped tarragon are added to it, a little Cayenne pepper and a squeeze of lemon just before serving. This sauce, which used to be invariably served with a grilled *Châteaubriand aux Pommes*, has now been superseded by the *Sauce Béarnaise*.

CHÂTELAINE
(*Garniture pour grosses pièces*.) Potatoes *Château* as well as celery, artichoke bottoms and tomatoes.

CHAUCHAT
(*Garniture pour poissons*.) Potatoes cut longways arranged as a border round the fish, with a *Sauce Mornay* (q.v.) over them and *gratinées*.

CHAUD-FROID, Sauce
    3 cups velouté sauce
    1 cup aspic jelly
    1 tablespoon thick cream
    2 egg yolks

The method of employing this sauce for covering pieces of chicken – or a whole cooked bird – will be found in the section 'Poultry and Game'. Having prepared a good smooth velouté, add the aspic and reduce over a low fire, beating and stirring well the while. When the sauce is sufficiently thick to coat the spoon (a wooden one should be used for stirring), remove the pan from the fire, add the cream and the beaten egg yolks. Taste the sauce to make sure the seasoning is right. Strain through a fine hair sieve and cool until almost jellified. Use according to recipes.

CHEESE SAUCE
    2 tablespoons butter
    3 tablespoons flour
    2 cups milk
    Salt and pepper
    1 cup grated cheese
    Few grains cayenne

Hard cheese is best, the hardest and best being Parmesan.

Melt the butter in a small saucepan, add the flour, stirring until mixture bubbles gently. Add the milk a little at a time and beating constantly until mixture is smooth and creamy. Remove pan from fire. Add salt and pepper, cheese, and a few grains of cayenne pepper, if you like. Very delicious with boiled cauliflower or poured over split baked potatoes. May be n ade a little thicker by adding more flour, and an egg yolk may be beaten into it with the cheese, should a richer sauce be desired.

CHERVIL
Lat. *Anthriscus cerefolium*; Fr. *Cerfeuil*; Ger. *Kerbel*; It. *Cerfoglio*; Sp. *Preifolio*. One of the most useful, fragrant, and universally grown garden or pot-herbs. Chervil looks rather like parsley except that the leaves are smaller and more curly.

Chervil Vinegar
Take a cupful of leaves, stripped from stalks, and let them be steeped in two cupfuls of white wine vinegar for a fortnight; strain off carefully without pressing the leaves into a clean jar; add another cupful of fresh leaves and let them macerate for another fortnight, when the *Chervil Vinegar* may be bottled for use. Cork tightly.

CHERVIL SAUCE
(The Hon. Mildred Gibbs' recipe.) Season some fresh cream with pepper and salt, add strips of chervil, finely cut, and serve with poultry or game instead of bread sauce.

CHESTNUT SAUCE
A popular American sauce.
- ½ pint chestnuts
- 2 cups white stock
- 1 tablespoon flour
- 2½ tablespoons butter
- ½ cup thick cream
- Pepper
- ¼ teaspoon salt

After removing outer and inner skins of chestnuts, boil them in the stock until soft enough to press through a fine sieve. Rub flour into butter and add to chestnut *purée*; place in a pan and bring gently to boiling point, stirring constantly. Add cream but do not boil mixture again. Season with salt and pepper. The sauce must be rather thick; it is mostly served with boiled poultry.

CHEVREUIL, Sauce
A Sauce *Poivrade* with some added red wine, a *mirepoix* of vegetables and some tit-bits of venison. The English version, or *Roebuck Sauce* (q.v.), is quite different.

CHEVREUSE
(*Garniture pour tournedos et noisettes.*) Artichoke bottoms filled with a mushroom *purée* crowned with a slice of truffle. Potatoes *noisette*.

CHILLI
Lat. *Capsicum frutescens, var. longeurm*; Fr. *Poivre de Guinée*. One of the hottest members of the Capsicum or Red Pepper family.

CHILLI SAUCE
Chop six green peppers and four large onions very finely; put them into a saucepan with two dozen peeled tomatoes, 8 tablespoonfuls of moist sugar and 3 of salt; also 3 breakfastcupfuls of wine-vinegar. Boil gently for an hour or so, then let the mixture cool, pour it into jars and it is ready to use. (Mrs William Hussey's recipe.) Chop two red chillies, chop a tablespoonful of capers, chop a little parsley; add salt, sugar, sherry and lemon juice. Particularly good with fried fish.

CHIPOLATA
(*Garniture pour grosses pièces.*) Braised button onions, *chipolata* sausages, mushrooms, whole chestnuts; small *lardons*.

CHIVES
Lat. *Allium schoenoprasum*; Fr. *Ciboulette*; Ger. *Schnittlauch*; It. *Cipollina*; Sp. *Cebollino*. The smallest and finest of the onion tribe. It is a native of England and is known in Spain as *cebollino de Inglaterra*. The leaves and tops of young plants are used as a pot-herb and chopped finely, for seasoning.

CHIVRY, Sauce
A sauce made of a *Velouté de Volaille* with chopped herbs: chervil, parsley, tarragon, burnet, chives; white wine and finished with a *Beurre Chivry*.

CHOCOLATE SAUCE
Put in a lined saucepan ¼ lb. chocolate, ½ pint milk, and a stick of vanilla; also some sugar if the sauce is to be particularly sweet. Stir over the fire until the chocolate is quite melted and the milk ready to boil, when the saucepan is moved from the fire and the yolks of four eggs, previously well beaten, are added and stirred in, over a gentle heat, being careful not to let the sauce come to boiling point again.

CHOISY
(*Garniture pour tournedos et noisettes.*) Braised lettuce and *Pommes Château*.

CHORON
(*Garniture pour tournedos et noisettes.*) Artichoke bottoms with green peas; *Pommes noisettes.*

CHORON, Sauce
A *Sauce Béarnaise* mixed with tomato *purée* to taste.

CHUTNEY
An Indian condiment in the preparation of which a variety of fruits are mixed with sugar, vinegar and spices.

CIBOL
Lat. *Allium fistulosum*; Fr. *Ciboule*, little onion. Vernacular: *Welsh Onion.* A hardy perennial of strong flavour, with no bulbs, its stalks only being used for flavouring. Sometimes, but wrongly, called *Scallion.*

CIDER SAUCE (American))
    3 tablespoons butter
    4 tablespoons flour
    2 cups ham liquor
    4 tablespoons cider
    Salt and pepper

Melt the butter, add the flour and moisten gradually with the ham liquor, stirring constantly. Simmer for a few moments, add cider and season to taste. Served in America with hot ham.

CINNAMON
Lat. *Cinnamomum zeylanicum*; Fr. *Cannelle*; Ger. *Zimmtbaum* or *Kaneel*; It. *Cannella*; Sp. *Canela*. Probably the oldest form of spice known in the West. It is a powder ground from the dry bark of a special species of laurel which grows best in Ceylon; also in the Madras and Bombay Presidencies and in Java. It is similar but finer and sweeter than the powder obtained from the *Cassia lignea*, a tree largely grown in China; hence the name of *Chinese Cinnamon* often given in Europe and the United States to *Cassia*. In medieval times, *Cinnamon* was known as *pulvis dulcis*, *poudre douce* or *sweet powder*.

CLAMART
(*Garniture pour grosses pièces.*) *Tartelettes* or artichoke bottoms filled with green peas *à la française* or green peas *en purée*. Small *Pommes rissolées.*

CLARY
Lat. *Salvia Sclarea*; Fr. *Saugé clarée*. A herb of the sage family which is very rarely used in cookery nowadays.

CLERMONT
(*Garniture pour tournedos et noisettes.*) Broken pieces of chestnut mixed with a *Sauce Soubise* poached in *Dariole* mould. Rings of fried onions as well.

CLOU DE GIROFLE
French for *Clove*.

CLOVES
Lat. *Eugenia aromatica* or *caryophyllata*; Fr. *Clous de Girofle*. The dried unexpanded flower bud of the clove-tree, a tree which belongs to the Myrtle family and grows best in the Moluccas.

COCHLEARIA, SCURVYGRASS or SPOONWORT
Lat. *Cochlearia officinalis*; Fr. *Cranson*. A wild plant, a native of English hedges, eaten as a salad.

COLD SLAW (English)
    6 yolks of eggs
    1 tablespoonful of butter
    1 teaspoonful of made mustard
    2 tablespoonfuls of fine sugar
    1 cup of white wine vinegar
    ½ teaspoonful of salt
    Juice of one lemon

Beat the yolks well. Cook in a double-boiler with vinegar, sugar, butter, salt and mustard, beating all the time. When nearly done, add the juice of the lemon. When thick remove from the fire. Let it get cold, then mix in one cup of whipped cream.

Put in a cool place. Serve on white hard shredded cabbage. (For American cole slaw, see p. 24).

COLEWORT
Lat. *Brassica campestris*; Fr. *Chou champêtre*. The wild cabbage used sometimes as a pickle and in sauces.

COMFREY
Lat. *Symphytum officinale*. An old favourite among pot-herbs, now hardly known in England.

COMMODORE
(*Garniture pour poissons.*) *Croquettes* of cray-fish tails or lobster; fish *quenelles*; mussels *à la Villeroy* and a crayfish *Coulis*.

CONDIMENTS
The name of a number of seasonings, mostly pickled or spicy.

CONTI
(*Garniture pour grosses pièces*). Lentils passed through a sieve and lean bacon cut in rectangles and cooked with the lentils.

CORIANDER
Lat. *Coriandrum Sativum*; Fr. *Coriandre*. An Eastern condiment introduced to Europe by the Romans.

CORNICHONS
French for *Gherkins*.

COSTMARY

Lat. *Tanacetum Balsamita*; Fr. *Baume de coq*; Ger. *Alecost* or *Rainfarn*. An old-fashioned pot-herb, rarely seen nowadays, similar to *Tansy*. It was introduced in England in the sixteenth century and was used extensively not only to flavour dishes, but to perfume linen and strew floors.

COULIS

Fish, meat or game gravy used as a sauce or with a sauce.

COWSLIP

Lat. *Primula veris*; Fr. *Coucou*. A wild spring flower which is sometimes eaten with fresh cream in England, or dipped in sugar to make crystallised cowslips. Chiefly used to make Cowslip wine, vinegar, mead or syrup.

CRANBERRY SAUCE

A favourite American sauce for game, turkey and chicken.

> 2 cups ripe cranberries (1 pint)
> 1 cup water
> 1 cup sugar

Wash the berries. Place them in an enamel saucepan, add the water and cover closely. Simmer on a gentle fire, watching occasionally while they cook. When each cranberry has burst open, remove lid altogether, and add sugar and simmer gently for 20 minutes uncovered, *without once stirring*.

CRAPAUDINE, Sauce

A *Sauce Piquante* to which have been added some chopped mushrooms and a little mustard diluted in tarragon vinegar.

CREAM

Fr. *Crème*; Ger. *Rahm*; It. and Sp. *Crema*. The fatter part of milk.

CREAM SAUCE

There are two Cream Sauces, one for fish, egg dishes, poultry and vegetables: it is made with two parts of reduced *Béchamel* to one of fresh cream mixed; off the fire, a little butter and a little more cream are added and the sauce is then passed through a fine sieve. The other Cream Sauce, for roast veal, is a *roux blanc* with cream added.

CREAM SAUCE FOR OYSTERS
(American.)

> 2½ tablespoons butter
> 3 shallots
> 3 medium-sized mushrooms
> 1½ teaspoons flour
> ½ cup thin cream
> 1 egg yolk
> Salt and cayenne
> ¼ teaspoon chopped parsley
> 1 tablespoon grated cheese

This is the sauce usually served with baked oysters. Melt half the quantity of butter in a pan, add the chopped shallots and finely chopped mushrooms, cooking all together gently for 15 minutes. Meantime, melt remainder of butter, add flour and, when mixture begins to bubble, moisten gradually with the cream. Stir until sauce is smooth and thick. Beat the egg yolk, add the sauce slowly to it, mixing well; then add the shallots and mushrooms and their butter. Season rather highly with cayenne and salt and sprinkle in some parsley. Cheese and paprika are sprinkled on top of oysters as directed in oyster recipe.

CRÈME, Sauce

French. A *Béchamel* with a good deal of fresh cream added at time of serving.

CRÉOLE, Sauce
(American.)

> 2 tablespoons chopped onions
> 2 tablespoons chopped mushrooms
> 2 tablespoons chopped green peppers
> 1 tablespoon chopped red pepper
> 1 tablespoon chopped parsley
> 2 tablespoons butter
> 2 cups sauce Espagnole
> Salt and pepper

This sauce is a great favourite with grilled steak, shrimps and eggs in the U.S.A. Chop all vegetables, simmer for 10 minutes gently in butter, then add the *Sauce Espagnole* (q.v.) and season rather highly. Simmer gently on side of fire for 1 hour, then serve.

CREVETTES, Sauce

A fish *velouté* with shrimps *coulis*.

CREVETTES À L'ANGLAISE, Sauce

See *Shrimp Sauce*.

CUCUMBER SAUCE
(American)

> 1 small firm cucumber
> ½ cup thick cream
> 2 tablespoons vinegar
> Salt and pepper

All ingredients must be pre-chilled thoroughly. Grate or dice the cucumber. Beat cream until thick but not stiff, add the vinegar gradually, beating constantly, season, and at the moment of serving fold in the cucumber. Delicious with salmon.

CUMBERLAND SAUCE
(Mrs Hyne's recipe.)

> 1 lemon
> 1 orange
> ½ gill Port wine
> ½ gill of water

2 tablespoonfuls red currant jelly
2 tablespoonfuls vinegar
½ teaspoonful made mustard
Cayenne, salt
Chopped glacé cherries

Peel the orange and lemon very thinly without taking off any of the white pith. Cut this peel into very fine shreds, cook in ½ gill of water for five minutes, strain, put back into the saucepan, add the Port wine, red currant jelly, mustard, Cayenne, salt, the juice of the orange and lemon, and the vinegar. Boil this for a few minutes. When cold add chopped glacé cherries.

CUMIN
Lat. *Cuminum cyminum*; Fr. *Cumin*. One of the hardy spices from the East which can be grown easily in England and Scotland.

CURRANT JELLY SAUCE
To about a breakfast cupful of *Brown Sauce* (q.v.) passed through a strainer, add a teacupful of red currant jelly, made warm, stirring until the jelly is well mixed and the sauce quite hot; it is then ready to serve.

CURRY POWDER
Medium Hot
1 lb. best powdered Turmeric, ¾ lb. powdered Coriander seed, 3 oz. powdered Ginger, 2 oz. powdered Black Pepper, 1½ oz. powdered Cayenne Pepper, 1½ oz. powdered Cadamom seed, ½ oz. powdered Caraway seed, 80 finely powdered Cloves.

The whole to be well mixed and put into a stoppered dry bottle or glass jar.

(Sir Ranald Martin's favourite recipe.)

Hot
4 lb. Coriander seed, 1½ lb. red Chillies, 2 lb. Turmeric, 1 lb. Caraway seeds, 1 lb. Fenugreek, 1 lb. Black Pepper.

All ingredients to be finely powdered and well mixed.

(Captain Wroughton's famous recipe.)

CURRY PASTE
(*For use on biscuits, fried bread or in sandwiches.*)
8 oz. Coriander seed (roasted), 1 oz. Cumin seed (roasted), 2 oz. dried Turmeric, 2 oz. dried Chillies, 2 oz. Black Peppercorns (roasted), 2 oz. Mustard seed, 1 oz. dry Ginger, 1 oz. chopped Garlic, 4 oz. Salt, 4 oz. Sugar, 4 oz. split Peas (roasted).

All these ingredients to be powdered very carefully, and when fine they must be mixed with some best white vinegar to the consistency of a thick jelly. Then warm some good, sweet oil, and when the oil bubbles put in the mixture and fry till it is all reduced to a good paste.

CURRY SAUCE
1 oz. dripping, 1 small onion, 1 carrot, 3 slices of apple, 1 gill of tomato sauce, 1 pint of stock, 1 teaspoonful of curry powder, 1 tablespoonful of flour.

Bring the dripping to the boil. When the dripping is boiling add the onion and carrot in fine slices and fry to a golden colour, but *not* brown. Then add the curry powder and flour, which must be first mixed to a smooth paste with a little water. Put in the sauce and sliced apple. Simmer for about half an hour. Skim, add a little more of the tomato sauce, and then pour the curry sauce over the hard-boiled eggs or slices of cooked fish and serve with an edging of well-boiled rice.

Vegetable Curry
This may be made either with fresh or previously-cooked vegetables in thin slices, or pieces.

If made with fresh vegetables, each vegetable should be separately boiled and the water well strained off before putting into the curry. Potatoes (finely sliced), beans, French beans, celery, cucumber, turnips, vegetable marrows in square blocks, small tufts of cauliflower, and tomatoes in judicious quantity; also green peas. Put the sliced vegetables with the tablespoonful of curry (which must be fried with butter and onions) into a saucepan. Add a breakfast-cupful of good stock and simmer until the stock is absorbed.

Toast Curry
Cut up an onion into very thin rings; chop two heads of garlic, two bay-leaves, and fry all these in 2 oz. of butter with twelve cloves until nicely browned. Then add 1 tablespoonful of curry powder and stir. Put in 1 large cupful of good tomato ketchup, a teaspoonful of tarragon vinegar, and the seeds of eight cardamoms; simmer gently for about 15 minutes until the mixture is thick. Spread generously on rounds of fried bread. Garnish with parsley and serve hot.

If left to get cold this mixture can be spread on biscuits. It can be put into a small glass dish for a picnic lunch, and is much liked on a grouse moor when the day is cool.

(These Curry recipes are from Mrs Jessop Hulton's *Curry Recipes*, published by the Wine and Food Society in 1938.)

CUSSY
(*Garniture pour tournedos, noisettes et volailles.*)
Large mushrooms grilled and stuffed with a *purée* of chestnuts, *rognons de coq*, and small whole truffles cooked in Madeira wine.

CUSTARD SAUCE
3 egg yolks
2 tablespoons thick cream
2 oz. butter
1 small teaspoon sugar
Salt and pepper
Small teaspoon tarragon vinegar

This sauce must be cooked in a double-boiler. Place the well-beaten egg yolks in upper part of saucepan, gradually add the cream, beating the while, then the butter, in small pieces. Stir until mixture thickens, then add sugar, salt and pepper as desired. Remove from hot water, add the tarragon vinegar or, failing this, lemon juice to flavour. Strain before serving. Some people are very fond of this sauce with salmon.

DARTOIS
(*Garniture pour grosses pièces.*) Pieces of carrots and turnips; braised celery; *pommes rissolées.*

DAUMONT
(*Garniture pour poissons.*) Large mushroom heads; Sauce *Nantua* (q.v.); fish *quenelles*; breadcrumbed and fried soft roes.

DAUPHINE
(*Garniture pour grosses pièces. — Pommes Dauphine* in straw potatoes nests.

DEMI-GLACE
A *Sauce Espagnole* (q.v.) reduced by simmering on a slow fire after some *Glace de Viande* or *Fonds de veau brun* has been added to it.

DEMI-GLACE TOMATÉE
A *Demi-glace* with tomatoes added.

DEVILLED SAUCE
Chopped shallots and vinegar; add *Demi-glace tomatée*. Add more or less of one of the patent bottled sauces to taste and a dusting of cayenne pepper at time of serving.

DIABLE, Sauce
Shallots, white wine and vinegar; simmer until greatly reduced; then add *Demi-glace*; pass through fine sieve and add *fines herbs* at time of serving.

DIABLE À L'ANGLAISE, Sauce
See *Devilled Sauce.*

DIANE, Sauce
A *Sauce Poivrade* flavoured with game essence and enriched with butter and cream.

DIEPPOISE
(*Garniture pour poissons.*) Shredded shrimps, bearded mussels and mushroom heads.

DILL
Lat. *Anethum graveolens*; Fr. *Aneth.* A condiment of the Fennel seeds type, with a strong smell and valuable digestive properties.

DIPLOMATE, Sauce
A *Sauce Normande* blended with lobster *coulis* and essence of mushrooms; garnish with dice of truffles and lobster meat.

DITTANY
Lat. *Cunila origanoides.* A small aromatic herb, fairly common in the U.S.A., where it is used like chervil (q.v.).

DORIA
(*Garniture pour Entrées et Poissons.*) Cucumber cut up to the size and shape of olives and stewed in their own steam and butter; *noisette* potatoes.

DRAWN-BUTTER SAUCE
Put 2 oz. of butter in a saucepan, and stir in 2 tablespoonfuls of flour; moisten with a quart of water, and season with pepper and salt to taste. Let it simmer at the side of the stove until it thickens, then add, little by little, ½ oz. of butter, beating continuously until it becomes quite white. Squeeze in the juice of a lemon; stir once more; strain through a fine hair-sieve and serve.

DRESSINGS, Salad
Fr. *Assaisonnements.* French dressings are the simplest, the American the most complicated, and the English much more like the French than the American.

The way of dressing a salad in thousands of French homes, from the humblest to the richest, has been for many years past, and still is, as follows: 2 tablespoonfuls of olive oil to 1 of wine vinegar; a teaspoonful of salt and 2 full turns of the pepper mill. Chopped herbs: chervil, chives, tarragon – burnet if you can get it. This is called a *Sauce Vinaigrette.*

There are different versions, of course, such as *Vinaigrette aux oeufs*, when hard boiled eggs are introduced, cut in quarters; *Vinaigrette au lard*, with *lardons*; *Vinaigrette à la crème* and *à la crème moutardée*, when plain cream or fresh cream whipped with some mustard is added.

In England, the same measures of oil and vinegar, salt and pepper are customary, plus a little mustard, and some people add a pinch of sifted sugar as well. Chopped herbs are not so easily obtainable in England, unfortunately, not because they are difficult to grow but because the demand is not large enough to make their cultivation a paying proposition. Olive oil is also often replaced by other oily patent preparations which *look* like olive oil, and malt vinegar is mostly used in place of wine vinegar.

Both in England and in France the practice is gaining ground of replacing vinegar in salad dressings with lemon juice.

It is not possible, however, to dismiss the question of American salad dressings in so few words, as will be seen from the following versions of American recipes:

Boiled Dressing

¼ tablespoon salt
1 teaspoon mustard
⅔ tablespoon sugar
Cayenne to taste
2 tablespoons flour
1 egg
¾ cup milk
2 tablespoons butter
¼ cup vinegar

Mix all the dry ingredients together, add the slightly beaten egg, the milk, the butter and the vinegar, the latter very slowly and beating well. Pour mixture into a double-boiler and cook, stirring all the time, over boiling water until the dressing begins to thicken. Cool after straining. This is a sort of cooked mayonnaise and will keep well on ice in bottles.

Chiffonade Dressing

2 hard boiled eggs
Vinaigrette
2 tablespoons minced parsley
2 tablespoons chopped red pepper
1 teaspoon minced shallot

The eggs, after shelling, must be finely chopped, as must all ingredients. Blend all well together and serve very cold.

Chicken Salad Dressing

½ cup vinegar
4 egg yolks
Cayenne to taste
Salt to taste
1 teaspoon salt
2 tablespoons French mustard
½ cup good rich chicken broth
½ cup thick cream
1 cup melted butter

Add the vinegar, slightly beaten egg yolks and seasonings to stock. Cook in double-boiler, stirring constantly, until the mixture begins to thicken; then strain, add cream and butter.

Cold-Slaw

(Sometimes called 'Cole' Slaw)
This is more in the nature of what is known in America as a 'relish'. It is made of finely shredded white cabbage, crisped in cold water, then drained, dried thoroughly, and mixed with either plain mayonnaise or boiled dressing.

Cream Dressing
(German-American)

½ cup thin cream
Salt and pepper
1 tablespoon mixed mustard
Vinegar to taste, or lemon juice
Onion juice (optional)

Beat cream with a rotary beater until stiff. Add salt, pepper, mustard (French is best for this; if English, use less), and the vinegar, beating very slowly and continuously. Onion juice may be added, if liked, with other ingredients. Chopped parsley and onion or chives are added when used for potato salad.

Russian Dressing

½ cup mayonnaise
1 tablespoon pimento
¼ cup chilli sauce
1 tablespoon green pepper
1 tablespoon finely chopped celery

The pimento and green pepper must be finely minced. Mix all ingredients and chill thoroughly before serving.

St Lawrence Dressing
(Canadian)

½ cup olive oil
8 green olives (chopped)
Juice ½ a lemon
Juice ½ an orange
¼ teaspoon paprika
¾ teaspoon salt
1 teaspoon grated onion
1 teaspoon Worcester sauce
1 teaspoon chopped parsley
¼ teaspoon mustard

Mix well all ingredients, chill and shake until thickened.

Thousand Island Dressing

Mix Russian dressing and mayonnaise, in equal parts. Add ¼ cup stiffly whipped cream and blend thoroughly before serving.

'Vivette' Dressing

1 saltspoon salt
Pepper to taste
1 teaspoon French mustard
1 teaspoon sugar
1 tablespoon wine vinegar
1 tablespoon chilli sauce
1 tablespoon thick cream
1 whipped egg white
Onion juice (optional)
2 tablespoons olive oil.

Mix together salt, pepper, mustard, sugar and vinegar, add chilli sauce, cream, onion juice and oil, beating well, then, when ready to serve, fold in the stiffly whipped egg white which must be very fresh and cold. Chill dressing well before serving.

DUBARRY
(*Garniture pour grosses pièces.*) Cauliflowers with *Sauce Mornay, Pommes Château.*

DUCHESSE
(*Garniture pour grosses pièces.*) *Pommes Duchesse* of various shapes and sizes.

DUXELLES
The name of a sauce made with white wine, chopped onions and shallots and *Duxelles*, a culinary preparation of shallots, parsley, onions and mushrooms, chopped and stewed together slowly until all the moisture has been evaporated, leaving a dry 'seasoning' in which the flavours of mushroom and shallots should predominate. Dry *Duxelles* is kept as a standby and used for seasoning sauces and soups.

EGG SAUCE
(Scotch.)
A light *Béchamel*, with the yolks of hard-boiled eggs passed through a sieve and the whites cut up in thin strips.

EGG AND PARSLEY SAUCE
(English.)

> 1 or 2 hard-boiled eggs
> 1 heaped tablespoon chopped parsley
> 1 or 2 drops onion juice (optional)
> White sauce as required

Peel the eggs and chop coarsely. Remove stems from clean but not wet parsley, mince or chop finely. Mix with the egg and add to the hot white sauce previously lightly flavoured with lemon juice.

Egg sauces are usually served with boiled fish.

ELDERBERRIES
Lat. *Sambucus nigra*; Fr. *Sureau*; Ger. *Holunder*; It. *Sambrico*; Sp. *Sauco.* The berries of the elder tree; they are used sometimes in the making of jellies, chutney or Ketchup.

ELDERFLOWER
The flower of the elder used for flavouring and sometimes also to make fritters.

ESCHALOT or SHALLOT
Lat. *Allium Ascalonicum*; Fr. *Echalote. Ciboule.* One of the most valuable of the culinary garden herbs.

ESPAGNOLE, Sauce, or
BROWN SAUCE
One of the three *Grandes Sauces – Velouté* and *Béchamel* being the other two – or basic sauces from which most others are made. Here is a classical recipe for making *Sauce Espagnole*:

> Trimmings of raw veal and ham or
> game
> 1 onion
> 1 whole clove
> 1 carrot
> 2 dessertspoons flour
> Hot stock or *bouillon*
> 1 small 'bouquet-garni'
> Salt and pepper

The meat trimmings must be lean, veal and ham for choice, but, if more convenient, scraps of rabbit, pork or game will do. Have a heavy iron pan and in this place the pieces of meat, an onion (cut up), a whole clove and a carrot cut into slices. The heat should be gentle and the pan closely covered. Cook slowly until a rich brown gravy is obtained; then sprinkle in a dessertspoonful of flour, stirring so as to work it into all ingredients until lightly browned. Moisten with some hot stock or *bouillon* and add salt, pepper and a *bouquet-garni.* Cook gently over very little heat or on the far edge of the stove for 4 hours. The sauce should be of the consistency of thick cream. When done, skim to remove surface fat, if any, and strain through a fine wire sieve. This sauce may be kept in a cool place for some time and may be used as a basis for other sauces. Mention will be made in other sections of this book of the various uses to which this sauce may be put.

ESSENCES
In culinary French *Essence* means the natural juices of whatever has been cooked after such juices have lost by evaporation a large proportion of their moisture and reached the degree of concentration when their flavour is greatest and their bulk least.

ESTOUFFADE
Another name for a *Fonds Brun.*

ESTRAGON
Fr. for *Tarragon*, one of the most fragrant of the garden pot-herbs.

EXCELSIOR
(*Garniture pour tournedos et noisettes.*) Braised lettuce and *pommes fondantes.*

FARCE
French for *forcemeat.*

FAVORITE
Garniture (a) *pour tournedos et noisettes*: sliced *foie gras*, truffles and asparagus points; (b) (*pour grosses pièces*): artichoke bottoms in quarters, celery and small *Pommes Anna* or *Château.*

FENNEL
Lat. *Foeniculum vulgare, var. dulce*; Fr. *Fenouil*; Ger. *Fenchel*; It. *Finocchio*; Sp. *Hinojo.* A

popular Italian esculent which may be compared to celery with a faint aniseed flavour. It is used either cold, as a *hors-d'oeuvre*, with an oil and vinegar dressing, or hot, as a vegetable. There is also a good fennel sauce, usually served with mackerel or mullet, which is an English Butter Sauce to which has been added blanched and chopped *fennel*.

FENUGREEK
Lat. *Trigonella Foenum-Graecum*; Fr. *Foin-grec*; also referred to as *Greek bay*, one of the pot-herbs greatly in favour in ancient times, and even in olden days, but practically out of cultivation in England nowadays. Still used in the making of curry.

FERMIÈRE
(*Garniture pour volailles et grosses pièces.*) A *Paysanne* of carrots and turnips, onions and celery or celeriac and potatoes.

FINANCIÈRE
(*Garniture pour volailles et Ris de Veau.*) *Quenelles, crêtes et rognons de coq*, truffles, mushroom heads, stoned olives.

FINANCIÈRE, Sauce
　　1 cup brown sauce
　　½ cup chicken broth
　　Truffle trimmings
　　4 or 5 mushrooms
　　½ glass Sauternes or Madeira
　　Seasonings as desired

Heat the brown sauce, add the chicken broth, the truffles and the chopped mushrooms. Cook over a good heat until liquid is greatly reduced, then add the wine, a little at a time, after reducing the heat. Strain and serve hot.

FINES HERBES
Parsley, tarragon and chives chopped up very fine; also a little chervil. They add just the right flavour to a green salad, to a plain omelette, a grilled steak, a white wine sauce (*Sauce aux Fines Herbes*), and many other dishes.

FLAMANDE
(*Garniture pour grosses pièces.*) Braised cabbage, carrots, turnips, bacon, cooked with the cabbage, *saucisson* and plain boiled potatoes.

FLEURISTE
(*Garniture pour tournedos et noisettes.*) Tomatoes scooped out and filled with a *Jardinière* of vegetables; *Pommes Château*.

FLORENTINE
(*Garniture pour poissons et ris de veau.*) Spinach.

FLORIAN
(*Garniture pour grosses pièces.*) Braised lettuce, browned button onions, carrots cut into olive shapes, *Pommes Fondantes*.

FONDS DE CUISINE
Basic preparations which are indispensable in large establishments as a standby for preparing sauces, gravies, soups, etc. The principal *Fonds de Cuisine* are: *Fonds Blanc*, veal broth, highly seasoned; *Fonds Blanc de Volaille*, veal broth with old hens or fowls added, highly seasoned; *Fonds Brun* or *Estouffade*, beef broth, highly seasoned; *Fonds de Gibier*, game broth, highly seasoned, and with white wine added during cooking.

FORCEMEAT
Fr. *Farce*. A preparation always somewhat rich and highly seasoned, used by itself or as part of the stuffing for fish, flesh and fowl; also for vegetables and patties. There are ever so many ways of making *Forcemeat*. The following are merely examples of how to set about making it.

　　¼ lb. ham
　　1 small onion
　　Salt and pepper
　　½ lb. cold chicken or veal
　　1 egg
　　1 teaspoon lemon peel
　　½ lb. breadcrumbs
　　1 teaspoon chopped parsley

Mince together the ham and chicken or veal, then pound in a mortar with other chopped ingredients. Bind the mixture with an egg, adding a little milk if necessary.

II
　　3 oz. lean bacon
　　¼ lb. suet
　　Peel of half a lemon
　　6 oz. breadcrumbs
　　Salt and pepper
　　1 teaspoon mixed herbs
　　1 teaspoon chopped parsley
　　1 or 2 small eggs
　　Flour
　　Bacon fat

Cut up the bacon finely, chop the suet, lemon peel, also finely. Add breadcrumbs to above ingredients, mixing well. Season and bind mixture with eggs, stock or milk. Divide it into small balls, roll in flour and fry brown in bacon fat.

FONTAINEBLEAU
(*Garniture pour tournedos et noisettes.*) *Bouchées* made of *Pommes Duchesse* filled with a *Jardinière* (q.v.).

FORESTIÈRE
(*Garniture pour grosses pièces.*) Either *Sautés Cèpes* or *Morilles*, according to season; dice of lean bacon and *noisette* potatoes.

FUMET
In culinary parlance *Fumet* is a concentrate of fish or vegetables stewed in wine or otherwise and gently reduced. It corresponds to *Essence*, which is a concentrated form of meat juices.

GALANGAL
Lat. *Alpinia officinarum*; Fr. *Galanga mineur*. A Chinese plant, the rhizome of which provides a mild form of ginger. Not to be confused with the English *Galingale*, Lat. *Cyperus longus*; Fr. *Souchet*.

GARLIC
Lat. *Allium Sativum*; Fr. *Ail*; Ger. *Knoblauch*; It. *Aglio*; Sp. *Ajo*. When used with care and discretion, this bulb is most useful. The small sections are known as 'cloves' of garlic (*Gousse d'ail*). It should be kept in a dark, dry place or hung up in a dry cellar.

Garlic Vinegar
Two ounces of peeled and bruised garlic must be allowed for 1 quart white wine vinegar. Place the garlic in the vinegar and set it in a cool spot for a month or so, then filter and bottle.

To flavour a salad, rub the interior of the salad-bowl with a cut clove of garlic or, if you can stand a little more, make a 'chapon', which is a small hard crust of bread well salted and rubbed over its entire surface with a cut clove of garlic. Leave this to soak awhile in the dressing before adding the salad, and remove before serving.

GARNISHES
Fr. *Garnitures*.

Breadcrumbs
Heat butter until lightly smoking, but not too coloured. Add rather coarse stale white breadcrumbs. Toss lightly till crisp and coloured. Sprinkle with salt and serve hot.

Croûtons
Take some rather stale and close-grained white bread, and cut it into quarter-inch slices; remove crusts and either cut slices into plain dice or stamp into fancy shapes with special cutters. Heat some butter until almost smoking but not brown, fry croûtons in this, tossing to colour on all sides. '*Croûtes*' are larger editions of the above, on which small birds and entrées are served.

Fleurons
Roll out scraps of puff pastry very thinly. Bake or fry and serve hot, as a garnish for soup or entrées.

Fried Parsley
Wash, pick off large stalks, dry very thoroughly and fry in boiling fat for a second or two or until crisp. Handle very carefully. Chiefly used as decoration for fish dishes, or eggs *au beurre noir*.

Suet Dumplings
4 oz. flour
Salt and pepper
2 oz. suet

Sieve flour, add a pinch each of salt and pepper. Chop the suet finely, add to flour and mix to a rather stiff dough with cold water. Shape into small balls with floured hands and poach in boiling water or stock for 10 minutes or until light.

GARNITURES
French for *Garnishes*, or odds and ends which not only decorate a dish when it is served, but add to its enjoyment, their colour and flavour being devised to combine and assist the colour and flavour of whatever fish, flesh or fowl is the chief part of the dish.

GASTRONOME
(*Garniture pour poissons, volailles et ris de veau.*) Glazed chestnuts, truffles, *rognons de coq* and *morilles*.

GÉNEVOISE, Sauce
This is a *Roux* which is moistened with some of the water used for cooking certain kinds of fish. This water may further be flavoured and greatly reduced – when it is technically known as a fish *coulis*, by cooking in it the bones, head and débris of the fish. When blended with the *roux* – a white *roux*, naturally – add a tablespoonful of butter, half a teaspoonful of finely chopped parsley, a few thin slices of mushrooms, which may or may not be *sautés* previously in a little butter, a few drops of lemon juice, a chopped shallot and, unless the fish dish contains wine already, a small wineglassful of dry white wine. Reduce by slow cooking for half an hour, or longer if convenient, strain and serve hot.

GHERKINS
Fr. *Cornichons*; Ger. *Pfeffergurken*. Pickled, small, prickly cucumbers.

GHERKIN SAUCE
Place over a gentle heat, in a lined suacepan, a breakfastcupful of wine-vinegar, and a sprig of thyme, a bay-leaf, a clove of garlic,

two finely chopped shallots, pepper and salt, and a little Cayenne pepper. Let all these boil gently in the vinegar for about half an hour. Then add a breakfastcupful of stock, thickened or not with some flour, according to taste. Place back on the fire and, when it boils, add some very finely chopped parsley and some peeled pickled gherkins, minced.

GIBLET SAUCE

Boil gently for three or four hours, in stock, or water should no stock be available, fowls' giblets, adding an onion, clove, a blade of mace and some peppercorns. When the giblets are quite tender, take them out, strain the liquor in which they were cooked into another saucepan, and chop up gizzards, livers and other parts into small pieces. Thicken the sauce, if so inclined, and serve with the chopped giblets in it.

GINGER

Lat. *Zingiber officinale*; Fr. *Gingembre*; Ger. *Ingwer*; It. *Zenzero*; Sp. *Gengibre*. The scraped and dried rhizome (root-stock and underground stem) of the *zingiber officinale*.

GINGER SNAP SAUCE
(American.)

    4 ginger snaps
    1 cup stock
    1 lemon
    ½ cup brown sugar
    ½ cup vinegar
    ¼ cup raisins
    ½ teaspoon onion juice

    Mix all ingredients together, cooking gently until smooth. In some States this sauce is greatly liked and usually served with meat, especially tongue, and sometimes with fish, in which case fish stock is used instead of meat stock.

GLACE DE VIANDE, DE VOLAILLE, DE GIBIER

Concentrated meat stock obtained by reducing a *Fonds Brun*, *Fonds Blanc de Volaille* or *Fonds de Gibier*.

GLOUCESTER SAUCE
(English.)

    A *Mayonnaise* flavoured to taste with Cayenne pepper, chopped chives, lemon juice and *Worcestershire Sauce*, and diluted with a little sour cream. Chiefly used for dressing meat salads.

GODARD

(*Garniture pour volailles, etc.*) Some small and some large *quenelles*, large mushroom heads, coxcombs, lamb's sweetbreads and truffles.

GODARD, Sauce

A rich wine sauce made as follows: Put ½ lb. of raw ham (cut up in smallish pieces) into a saucepan with a carrot and an onion, both sliced, and ¼ lb. of butter; fry the ham in the butter for 5 minutes or so and then add half a bottle of dry Champagne and simmer for half an hour. Then strain the liquor into a stewpan and add to it a quart of *Sauce Espagnole* (q.v.) and plenty of mushrooms previously cooked and chopped up. Boil gently the whole until it acquires a fairly thick, creamy consistency, then strain into a *bainmarie* pan or double-boiler and keep hot until wanted.

GODIVEAU

Veal forcemeat used in the preparation of some garnishes. It is made as follows: Chop as finely as possible 1 lb. of fillet of veal (knuckle of veal will do, but the *noix* is better), two veal kidneys and 1½ lb. of beef suet; add pepper and salt and finely chopped herbs and pound the whole in a mortar. Add four eggs and go on pounding in a mortar until the suet cannot be distinguished from the veal. Keep on ice until required.

GODIVEAU LYONNAIS

A fish forcemeat made in the same way as the Veal or classical *Godiveau*, but with boned pike instead of veal and beef suet. Pike, chopped veal kidneys, eggs and breadcrumbs are pounded in a mortar until they form one compact paste which is used for making *quenelles* and other garnishes.

GOLDEN SAUCE

An English sweet sauce made in many different ways in many different homes. The following is a favourite recipe for "not-too-strictly-teetotal families." Put 4 ozs. of butter into a basin, warm it before the fire, beat it by hand until creamy; then stand the basin in hot water and add 4 ozs. of brown sugar, stirring continuously until all the sugar is melted. Now stir in the beaten yolk of one fresh egg and go on stirring until the sauce is thick, when add a wineglassful not of 'cooking Brandy' but of genuine Cognac Brandy. Go on stirring over a slow fire until hot. Add a little dusting of grated nutmeg before serving.

GOOD KING HENRY

Lat. *Chenopodium Bonus Henricus*; Fr. *Bon Henri* or *Épinard Sauvage*. The best of the *Goosefoots* and formerly one of the favourite pot-herbs. It grows wild in many parts of England.

GOOSEBERRY SAUCE
(English.)

> ½ pint young green gooseberries
> 1 gill water
> 1 oz. butter
> 1 oz. sugar
> Salt and pepper
> Dusting nutmeg
> Fresh sorrel

Cook the gooseberries in the water until tender. Drain and rub through a sieve. Add to this pulp finely chopped well-boiled sorrel leaves to taste, butter, sugar, salt and pepper and a sprinkling of nutmeg. Re-heat and serve with boiled mackerel.

GRAINS OF PARADISE
See *Cardamom*.

GRAND-DUC
(*Garniture pour poissons et volailles.*) Truffles and asparagus points; also *Ecrevisses* for fish dishes.

GRAND VENEUR, Sauce
Sauce *Poivrade* with venison *essence*, and some hare blood, added to some of the marinade; also fresh cream at the last moment.

GRAVY
Fr. *Jus de viande* when the gravy is hot, and *Gelée de viande* when it is cold gravy. True gravy is merely meat extract, a rich and savoury liquid when hot and an equally rich and savoury jelly when cold. Unfortunately, gravy that is hot is usually coloured and flavoured hot water.

Gravy for Game

> Bones and trimmings of game
> Cold water to cover
> 1 small 'bouquet-garni'
> 1 small onion
> 1 teaspoon butter
> 3 or 4 peppercorns
> Salt

Break all the bones and tie in a piece of muslin. Cut up trimmings of game. Place these, with other ingredients, in a small pan, cover tightly and simmer for 2 to 3 hours. Strain and use, thickened or not, as required.

GREEN SAUCE
See *Sauce Verte*.

GRIBICHE, Sauce
The yolks of hard-boiled eggs are pounded to a paste which is worked up with olive oil in the same way as for a *Mayonnaise*. Vinegar is then added, and chopped gherkins, capers, parsley, chervil and tarragon. Finally a *iulienne* of the whites of hard-boiled eggs.

GROSEILLES, Sauce aux
Stewed green gooseberries mixed in equal parts with a *Sauce Bâtarde*. See also *Gooseberry Sauce*.

HARD SAUCE
In U.S.A., a *Hard Sauce* is made with one measure of fresh butter to two of castor sugar. The sugar is worked into the butter and the two are beaten together until their consistency is that of clotted cream. A squeeze of lemon is then added and this *Hard Sauce* is kept on ice until wanted, when little pats of it are cut off, shaped, and served.

Sometimes Brandy or Rum is added, drop by drop, whilst beating the sugar and butter, instead of lemon juice.

In England, a similar sauce is called *Brandy Butter* or *Rum Butter*.

HENRY IV
(*Garniture pour tournedos et noisettes.*) (1) Watercress and *Pommes Pont-neuf*. (2) Artichoke bottoms, *noisette* potatoes and a *Béarnaise* sauce.

HERBS
Various herbs used in cooking for their distinctive flavour. They are sometimes divided into *pot-herbs* and *sweet-herbs*, both sorts being included under the heading of Culinary Herbs, of which the most usual are the following: Basil, Bayleaves, Borage, Burnet, Celery, Chervil, Chives, Cibol, Eschalot, Garlic, Mint, Marjoram, Parsley, Rosemary, Savory, Sage, Thyme, Lemon Thyme and Tarragon.

Sage, mint, tarragon, chervil, parsley and thyme, if grown in one's garden, may be dried in the autumn in a dark, dry spot, the bunches being tied in paper to keep them from dust. When dry the leaves should be powdered and bottled for winter use.

HOLLANDAISE, Sauce
One of the most justly popular of sauces. It may be called a hot *Mayonnaise*, butter added very slowly in place of the dripping olive oil, to yolks of eggs upon a very gentle heat, stirring all the time. Cream may be added, but flour never.

The very finest butter obtainable must be used. Cut ¼ lb. butter in two equal halves; place one half in top of a double-boiler over hot water; when melted, add two or three well-beaten egg yolks. Stir gently until mixture thickens, adding remainder of butter in small pieces until all is used. Cream may be added and a little lemon juice or tarragon vinegar, as well as salt and pepper to taste. Take care surrounding water does not boil too fast or sauce may curdle.

In the United States, a quick imitation or *Mock Hollandaise Sauce* has been introduced which is made as follows:

> 2 egg yolks
> 1 tablespoon water
> 1 tablespoon lemon juice
> 1½ tablespoons butter
> 1 tablespoon flour
> Pepper and/or paprika
> 1 cup boiling water
> Salt

Mix and stir well together the egg yolks, tablespoonful of water, salt and the lemon juice. Place in a double-boiler. Melt the butter in a small pan, add flour as when making a white sauce and, when smooth, add the water and beat. Add this mixture to contents of the double-boiler, mixing thoroughly. Season with pepper alone or with pepper and a little paprika.

HONGROISE
(*Garniture pour grosses pièces*.) Sprigs of cauliflower with a *Sauce Mornay* (q.v.) and paprika. Plain boiled potatoes or *Pommes fondantes*.

HONGROISE, Sauce
A *Sauce Suprême* (q.v.) to which one adds chopped onions, separately cooked in white wine, and paprika.

HOREHOUND
Lat. *Marrubium Vulgare*; Fr. *Marrube blanc*; Ger. *Weisse Andorn*; It. *Marrabio bianco*. One of the commonest of the herbs growing wild in all parts of the British Isles; it can be used profitably for flavouring sauces and salads.

HORSERADISH
Lat. *Cochlearia Armoracia*; Fr. *Raifort* or *Radis noir*; Ger. *Meerretig*; It. *Rafano*; Sp. *Rabano*. A root with a somewhat peppery taste. It is sometimes used simply shaved as a condiment, but mostly as a savoury sauce, with cream.

HORSERADISH SAUCE
This sauce, which is not nearly as well-known as it deserves to be, is delicious with fresh-water fish. To a good smooth *Béchamel* sauce add a small teacupful of grated horseradish and half a cupful of thick cream. Season to taste and blend well, simmering only for a few moments after the horseradish and cream have been added.
(Mrs Hyne's recipe.)

> 2 tablespoonfuls of grated horse-radish
> ¼ teaspoonful of made mustard
> 1 gill of cream
> 1 tablespoonful of white wine vinegar
> 2 teaspoonfuls of castor sugar
> Salt and pepper

Mix the horseradish with the sugar, salt, pepper, mustard and vinegar. Whip the cream and stir it into the mixture by degrees.

Put in ice chest to get very cold. This sauce can also be frozen and cut in small cubes when set. It is delicious served with grilled salmon.

HORSERADISH FROZEN SAUCE
(American.)

> ¾ cup grated horseradish
> 1 cup thick cream
> 1 tablespoon pistachio nuts
> 1 teaspoon French mustard
> 2 tablespoons chili sauce
> 1 tablespoon lemon juice

The horseradish must be grated very finely. Whip the cream very thick, fold in all ingredients. The nuts must be finely chopped and salted. Season as desired, then pour into an oiled mould and set in an ice-pail surrounding with shaved ice, using four parts ice to one of freezing salt. Let the mould stand in this for 1½ hours, then serve with cold fish on a hot day. May be frozen in trays of ice-box if easier.

HORSERADISH AND MUSTARD SAUCE
(American.)

> 3 tablespoons butter
> 2 tablespoons flour
> 1 cup white stock
> 1 teaspoon mustard
> 1 teaspoon chopped onion
> Salt and pepper
> 2 tablespoons thick cream
> 1 teaspoon grated horseradish
> Lemon juice

Melt the butter, add flour, mixing well, then moisten with the stock, beating until mixture is quite smooth. Add salt and a little pepper, onion, mixed mustard (French and English) and grated horseradish. Cook together for 20 minutes gently, then strain and add lemon juice and cream, gradually. Usually served with Hamburger Steak (meat balls).

HUSSARDE
(*Garniture pour grosses pièces*.) Tomatoes hollowed and stuffed with *Soubise* and grated horseradish; *Duchesse* potatoes.

HYSSOP
Lat. *Hyssopus officinalis*; Fr. *Hysope*; Ger. *Echter Ysop*; Ital. *Isopo*; Sp. *Hinojo*. A sweet-scented plant, the flowers of which add to

the looks and charm of a green salad. (There is no better honey than hyssop honey.)

IMPERIALE
(*Garniture pour volailles.*) Foie gras, truffles, mushrooms and *quenelles.*

INDIENNE
(*Garniture.*) Rice.

INDIENNE, Sauce
A curry sauce made as follows: Brown in a saucepan a sliced onion and a little raw, lean ham; add 1 oz. of butter, a sprig of thyme and a dozen whole peppers. Dilute in some *velouté* a teaspoonful of curry powder and add to the rest. Let the whole boil gently for about 10 minutes, then strain into another saucepan. Add some fresh cream, the yolks of two eggs and lemon juice to taste.

ITALIENNE
(*Garniture pour grosses pièces.*) Artichoke bottoms and macaroni *croquettes.*

ITALIENNE, Sauce
There is a cold *Sauce Italienne* which is merely a *Sauce Mayonnaise* garnished with a *purée* of cooked calf's brains and chopped *fines herbes.* But the more usual *Sauce Italienne* is a hot sauce made as follows: Put a tablespoonful of fresh butter into a saucepan on a slow fire; add 2 tablespoonfuls of chopped parsley, one each of chopped mushrooms and chopped shallots; then a pint of white wine. Let it come up to the boil and let it boil until reduced to half the original quantity. Then add half a breakfastcupful of stock and twice as much *velouté,* and let the whole boil until it is fairly thick. Skim the sauce and serve it hot.

IVOIRE, Sauce
A white sauce made up of three parts *Sauce Suprême* (q.v.) and one part *Sauce Blonde* (q.v.)

JAPONAISE
(*Garniture.*) Tartlets filled with *Japanese Artichokes* par-boiled and tossed in butter; *croquette* potatoes.

JARDINIÈRE
(*Garniture.*) All manner of fresh vegetables, plainly boiled, arranged separately by kinds and alternate colours round a joint or piece of meat.

JARDINIÈRE, Sauce
Put in a saucepan, over a moderate fire, a tablespoonful of butter and a teaspoonful of sugar; add finely cut up carrots and turnips – say three of each if of moderate size – and about twenty peeled button onions. Fry gently 10 to 15 minutes; then add 2 cupfuls of broth and let the whole simmer gently until the vegetables are tender. Boil faster for a while to reduce bulk and skim off all fat. In a second saucepan, you will have made a *Sauce Espagnole* to which you will add some flowerlets of cauliflowers, some asparagus heads, green peas, French beans, as well as the vegetables cooked in the first saucepan. Let the whole boil gently together for 15 minutes; add pepper and salt to taste and serve hot.

JOINVILLE
(*Garniture pour poissons.*) *Salpicon* of cooked mushrooms, shrimps and truffles; *Sauce Joinville.*

JOINVILLE, Sauce
A *Sauce Normande* with a *coulis* of *écrevisses* and shrimps. A *julienne* of truffles is optional.

JUDIC
(*Garniture pour entrées.*) Stuffed braised lettuces; *Pommes Château.*

JULES VERNE
(*Garniture pour grosses pièces.*) Stuffed and braised potatoes and turnips; mushrooms *sauté* in butter.

JUNIPER
Lat. *Juniperus communis*; Fr. *Genévrier*; Ger. *Gemeiner Wachholder*; It. *Ginepro*; Sp. *Enebro.* The ripe berries of the juniper tree; they are very aromatic and contain a bitter principle called *juniperin.*

JUS
French for meat gravy.

JUS LIÉ
Short for a *Fonds de veau lié à l'arrowroot*, or veal gravy thickened with arrowroot.

KETCHUP: CATCHUP: CATSUP
Ketchup (Catchup, Catsup) from Chinese kôe-chiap or kê-tsiap, 'brine of pickled fish or shellfish'. A liquor extracted from mushrooms, tomatoes or (formerly) walnuts, used as a sauce or condiment.

LADIES' DELIGHT
The name of a home-made pickle, of which the following is one of the recipes: Put 8 oz. of apples, 8 of onions and 2 of chillis, all chopped into a pickle bottle. Pour over them a pint of white wine vinegar which has been boiled with a dessertspoonful of salt. In a few days it will be ready for use.

LAGUIPIÈRE, Sauce
A white wine sauce with fish essence and glaze.

LANGUEDOCIENNE
(*Garniture pour entrées.*) Stuffed aubergines, *émincé of cèpes* cooked in oil; tomatoes and parsley; *Pommes Château.*

LAURIER, Feuilles de
French for *Bay Leaves*. They are used in meat or game pies and in *marinades*, sauces and soups for the sake of their pungent flavour. Should be used very discreetly.

LAVALLIÈRE
(*Garniture pour volailles et ris de veau.*) Truffles served whole, lamb's sweetbreads larded with truffles; *écrevisses.*

LAVALLIÈRE, Sauce
A *Madeira Sauce*, flavoured with game essence, to which is added a *julienne* of tarragon and truffle. Thicken with some cream.

LEMON SAUCE
(American.)

> 2 eggs
> 1 teaspoon cornflour
> Juice of 2 lemons
> 1 cup fish stock
> 1 tablespoon butter
> ½ teaspoon sugar
> Salt and pepper

Beat eggs well. Mix the cornflour with the cold fish stock. Cook all ingredients together in a double-boiler, stirring until creamy. Serve hot with boiled fish. Sometimes almonds, cut into thin strips, are added to sauce at time of serving.

LEMON-BUTTER
(English.)
Put one measure of cornflour to two of castor sugar into a saucepan and the grated rind of one lemon; mix them thoroughly and, when mixed, stir in half a pint of boiling water with the juice of a lemon squeezed in it; also a small piece of butter; add gradually the beaten yolks of two eggs; stir, and be careful not to let it come to the boil.

LOBSTER SAUCE
Take the meat out of a freshly boiled hen lobster and cut it up into small pieces; mix the coral with them and put them in a saucepan with a lump of fresh butter and a fair allowance of thick cream. Stir over the fire until the sauce is steaming hot and serve.

LORETTE
(*Garniture pour entrées.*) Chicken *croquettes*, asparagus points and slices of truffles.

LORRAINE
(*Garniture pour grosses pièces.*) Braised red cabbage and *Pommes Fondantes.*

LOUISIANE
(*Garniture pour volailles.*) Sweet corn fritters; rice *darioles* on *sautées* sweet potatoes; rounds of fried bananas.

LOVAGE
Lat. *Levisticum officinale*; Fr. *Livèche*; Ger. *Echte Liebstäckel*; It. *Levistico*; Sp. *Ligustico*. A wild form of angelica of which the shoots are used for flavouring or candied. Scotch Lovage is a different sort of *Levisticum*, eaten raw as a salad, called *Shunis*, or cooked like celery.

LUCULLUS
(*Garniture pour volailles et ris de veau.*) Truffles cooked whole in Madeira wine, hollowed and refilled with *quenelles* of chicken forcemeat and chopped truffles.

LYONNAISE, Sauce
A white wine and onion sauce.

MACE
Lat. *Myristica fragrans*; Fr. *Macis*. The husk of nutmeg, used for flavouring, when ground finely.

MADELEINE
(*Garniture pour grosses pièces.*) Artichoke bottoms, *Soubise* and white haricot beans *en purée* in tartlets.

MADÈRE, Sauce
One of the best wine sauces. It is made like a *Sauce Piquante* (minus the pickles and vinegar) in which white wine takes the place of cold water. Add to the strained sauce ¼ lb. thinly-sliced fresh mushrooms and the gravy from whatever roast this sauce is to grace, after removing fat from surface. Finally, 5 minutes before serving, add a wineglassful of good Madeira wine and allow sauce to simmer gently. On festive occasions, sliced or chopped fresh truffles are also added.

MAITRE D'HÔTEL, Sauce
Cold, fresh butter, kneaded with finely-chopped parsley, pepper, salt and lemon juice. A pat of this butter is placed upon or under broiled meat or fish at the time of serving and melts on the dish.

MALTAISE, Sauce
A *Sauce Hollandaise* (q.v.) with some blood-orange juice and very thin little pieces of rind added.

MARAICHÈRE
(*Garniture pour grosses pièces.*) Salsify *sautés*. Brussels sprouts and *Pommes Château.*

MARÉCHALE
(*Garniture pour entrées.*) Truffles, and asparagus points.

MARGUERY, Sauce
A *Hollandaise* sauce flavoured with fish essence and *purée* of oysters.

MARIE-JEANNE
(*Garniture pour Noisettes et Tournedos.*) Tartlets filled with *purée* of mushrooms and capped with a slice of truffle.

MARIE-LOUISE
(*Garniture pour entrées.*) Artichoke bottoms filled with mushroom *purée* slightly covered with grated cheese and *gratiné*; a slice of truffle on top of each. Also green asparagus points served at the same time.

MARIE STUART
(*Garniture pour entrées.*) Tartlets filled with *purée* of turnips and rounds of marrowbone fat.

MARIGNY
(*Garniture pour entrées.*) Tartlets filled with green peas and French beans lozenge-wise; *Pommes Fondantes.*

MARIGOLD
Lat. *Calendula officinalis*; Fr. *Souci*; Ger. *Ringelblume*; It. *Fiorrancio*; Sp. *Flameniquillo*. One of the pot-herbs in olden times viewed with no great favour. Its presence on the table generally meant that the 'wittles were a bit flyblown'. It was used chiefly to hide the evil smell or taste of meat that was not fresh. Used in *Conger Soup*.

MARINADE
French for a 'Pickle' or a highly-seasoned liquid in which meat or fish is left to soak. In a French *Marinade* there is usually some wine; if not always vinegar as well as olive oil, lemon, pepper and salt, bay leaves, onions, shallots, thyme, parsley, cloves, garlic and any other herbs available.

MARINÉ
French for 'pickled' in a *marinade*.

MARINIÈRE
(*Garniture pour poissons.*) Bearded mussels and shredded shrimps.

MARINIÈRE, Sauce
This is a *Sauce Poulette* (q.v.) with a pinch of finely-chopped shallot and a little finely-minced parsley added.

MARJORAM
Fr. *Origan*. Sweet Marjoram, Fr. *Marjolaine*; Ger. *Majoran*; It. *Persa*; Sp. *Mejorana*. One of the pot-herbs possessing a most pungent smell; should be used discreetly.

MARMALADE SAUCE
A favourite among English sweet sauces. Put a breakfastcupful of orange marmalade in a saucepan with two wineglassfuls of white wine. Stir over a gentle fire until very hot. Strain and serve with steamed sponge pudding.

MARQUISE
(*Garniture pour noisettes et tournedos.*) *Salpicon* of *Amourettes*; asparagus points; *julienne* of truffles; *Sauce Suprême.*

MARSEILLAISE
(*Garniture pour tournedos et noisettes.*) Stuffed olives with anchovy fillets in hollowed tomatoes.

MASCOTTE
(*Garniture pour volailles.*) Quarters of artichoke bottoms *sautés* in butter; *Pommes en Cocotte*; truffles.

MASSÉNA
(*Garniture pour tournedos et noisettes.*) Artichoke bottoms with a *Sauce Périgueux* or *Béarnaise*. Slices of marrowbone fat or truffle upon the *tournedos* or *noisettes*.

MASSENET
(*Garniture pour tournedos et noisettes.*) Artichoke bottoms filled with marrowbone fat; French beans; *Pommes Anna*.

MATELOTE
(*Garniture pour poissons.*) Onions, mushrooms, *croûtons* and *écrevisses*.

MATELOTE, Sauce
A red wine court-bouillon in which fish has been cooked; it is first of all 'reduced' by simmering, and then a fish demi-glace is added. Pass through a sieve and add butter and a dusting of cayenne before serving.

MAYONNAISE
The most popular oil sauce. It is made from olive oil and the yolks of eggs. It is firm and golden, and it may be flavoured with a little vinegar or lemon juice, or coloured green by the addition of chopped *Ravigote* (q.v.).

    Best olive oil
    1 or 2 egg yolks
    Salt and pepper
    Chopped parsley, chervil, etc.
      (optional)
    Vinegar or lemon juice

The eggs used must be at least one day old, but they should not be more than three or four days old. Break carefully, removing every particle of white from yolk. In winter, one egg makes sufficient mayonnaise for two or three people; in summer, two yolks give

33

better results. All ingredients used, as well as the basin required, should be at same temperature. Use a wooden spoon or a whisk for mixing.

Place the egg yolk – or yolks – in a medium-sized basin. Add the olive oil a drop at a time, turning the mixture, that is, stirring, not beating it, all the time. As the mixture thickens, increase the flow of oil to a thin trickle until you have the desired amount of sauce. Add salt, pepper, chopped herbs and vinegar, or alternately, lemon juice to taste. The herbs are omitted in a plain mayonnaise and other ingredients may be added.

Note. Should the sauce become too heavy and thick, add a few drops of vinegar and continue turning to desired consistency. If the sauce does not coagulate, break another egg, start the operation all over again in another basin, adding the first mixture, drop by drop, as the second one thickens.

Mayonnaise
(Quick American method)
Ingredients as above. Use a rotary beater instead of a wooden spoon or even a wire whisk. Mustard may be added if wished.

Aspic Mayonnaise
(American)
½ cup thick mayonnaise
4 tablespoons cool aspic jelly
This dressing may be pressed through a 'star' tube and a bag to garnish salads or sundry cold dishes. Have the aspic jelly cool but not congealed. Add it, a drop at a time, to the mayonnaise, beating all the time. If desired, a little stiffly-whipped cream may also be added.

Red Mayonnaise
(American)
This looks well when served with lobster salad. Add the coral of the lobster and a little grated beetroot juice to thick mayonnaise.

Horseradish Mayonnaise
(American)
Add 3 spoonfuls of very finely grated horseradish to 2 cups of mayonnaise just when serving. Usually served with cold boiled fish, beef or salads.

East India Mayonnaise
1 teaspoonful good curry powder
1 clove garlic
Chop and rub the clove of garlic through a fine sieve and add, with the curry powder, to a thick mayonnaise. Serve with fish cakes or cold boiled salmon.

Tomato Mayonnaise
2 tomatoes
Yolks of 2 hard-boiled eggs
1 raw egg yolk
6 tablespoons olive oil
1 small clove garlic
Salt and pepper
Peel the tomatoes, cut them into halves and remove seeds. Chop fleshy part finely, then rub through a coarse sieve. Drain off all liquid. Rub bowl with garlic. Mash the hard-boiled egg yolks in basin, add the raw yolk and blend to a perfectly smooth paste, adding the oil, a drop at a time, and lemon juice. When the mixture is thick and smooth, add the tomato pulp and season to taste. A drop of tabasco sauce may be added to enhance flavour.

MAZARINE
(*Garniture pour entrées.*) Artichoke bottoms filled with a *Jardinière, croquettes* of rice, quenelles and mushrooms.

MÉDICIS
(*Garniture pour tournedos et noisettes.*) Artichoke bottoms filled with green peas, carrots and turnips or with carrots *Vichy* and green peas. *Pommes noisettes. Sauce Choron.*

MENTHE, Sauce
See 'Mint Sauce'.

MERCÉDÈS
(*Garniture pour grosses pièces.*) Grilled tomatoes; grilled mushrooms; braised lettuce; *Pommes Croquettes.*

MEXICAINE
(*Garniture pour grosses pièces.*) Grilled mushrooms; grilled long peppers; tomatoes and aubergines cut longways.

MIGNON
(*Garniture pour Volailles et Ris de veau.*) Artichoke bottoms filled with buttered green peas; round *quenelles* with truffles.

MILANAISE
(*Garniture pour escalopes.*) *Julienne* of tongue, mushrooms and truffles, and sometimes ham, added to spaghetti with a little tomato sauce, a dusting of grated cheese and a pat of butter.

MILK SAUCE
½ pint meat or fish stock
3 tablespoons flour
Salt and pepper
¼ pint milk
2 tablespoons butter
1 tablespoon chopped parsley
1 egg yolk
Few drops lemon juice

If to be used as an accompaniment to fish, use fish stock, if with boiled fowl, veal or calf's head, substitute liquor meat was cooked in. Melt butter in a small pan, stir in the flour and cook for 2 or 3 minutes, then add the liquor and milk gradually, stirring all the while, until the mixture boils. Reduce heat and season. Simmer for a few minutes, beating the while to prevent lumps, then add parsley. Remove pan from fire, add the lemon juice and the beaten egg yolk gradually. A little thick cream may be added to enrich sauce.

MINT

Fr. *Menthe*; Ger. *Munza*; It. *Menta*. There are very many varieties of mints, but only one that can be recommended for sauces, it is the *Mentha rotundifolia* of the botanists and the common mint of cottage gardens.

The use of fresh mint leaves with new potatoes or new peas is an entirely English culinary practice, and the Mint Sauce served with lamb, hot or cold, an English culinary monopoly.

MINT SAUCE
(English.)

> 1 dessertspoon finely-chopped
>   fresh mint
> ¼ pint wine-vinegar
> 2 dessertspoons sugar (about)

The mint should be young and freshly-picked. Strip from stalks and wash well; then dry in a cloth. Chop very finely, place in a basin with the sugar and vinegar and allow, if possible, to stand for 4 or 5 hours before serving. White wine-vinegar is best, and the amount of sugar used depends on individual taste. Some people also add a little warm water to dilute the vinegar.

Winter Mint Sauce
1 large bunch fresh mint
White wine-vinegar

Remove leaves from stalks, wash well, then allow to dry before chopping up finely. Place the chopped mint into a large bottle which must be filled with good wine-vinegar and tightly corked. The bottles should be sealed, like wine, to retain aroma of mint. When wanted, during the winter and mint-less days, pour out the quantity required, after shaking well, add a little more vinegar and sweeten to taste. Re-cork tightly.

(The Hon. Mildred Gibbs's Recipes.)
1 dessertspoonful of mint to 1 teaspoonful of vinegar, and 1 dessertspoonful of sugar and a little water to get the desired consistency. This is for cold lamb. For hot lamb it is preferable to heap finely-ground mint on thin slices of lemon, sprinkling a little sugar on the mint and moistening sufficiently with lemon juice to make it adhere.

MINT JELLY
This is preferred to mint sauce in Canada and the United States because, being solidified, it does not cool the hot meat or congeal the gravy. Here are two recipes.

I
> 3 or 4 sheets gelatine or 1 tablespoon
>   granulated gelatine
> 1 cupful vinegar
> Chopped mint
> Sugar to taste
> ¼ cup hot water

Some cooks use the sheet gelatine, others the new granulated gelatine – which is easier to handle. Dissolve the quantity specified in hot water, stirring until entirely melted. Add the vinegar, sugar to taste, and the finely-chopped mint. Sometimes the mint is, after being chopped, scalded in water which is drained off before being added to gelatine preparation. If wished, add a drop or two of green vegetable colouring. Set the mixture into small pots to cool, stirring as they jellify to prevent the mint from sinking to the bottom of the pots. Turn out into a small glass dish to serve. Will keep on ice for some time if you care to make double or triple quantities.

II
> 6 cooking apples
> Chopped mint
> Water
> Vinegar or lemon juice
> Sugar to taste

The apples should be rather under-ripe and of the tart kind. Cut into quarters, removing stems, but neither cores nor skins. Place them in a pan and add just enough water to cover. Cook gently until the apples are completely mashed up, then place them in a jelly-bag or a knotted cloth hung up and allow the juice to drip out all night, without pressing. Next day, measure and allow about 1 lb. sugar to every pint of apple juice. Boil up the juice, add the sugar, after warming it, and as soon as the sugar has melted, increase heat and boil mixture fast. The mint should be added before the boiling operation begins, also the white wine-vinegar or lemon juice. Continue fast-boiling until mixture 'jells' when tested in the usual way. Remember: *boil fast* to jell quickly – in 3 or 4 minutes it should be ready to set when tested.

MIRABEAU
(*Garniture pour Grillades.*) Anchovy fillets crossways, stoned olives and a *Beurre d'Anchois*.

MIREPOIX
Very small cubes of uncooked carrots, onion and ham lightly *sautés* in butter, with the addition of bay leaves and thyme; used for garnishings.

MIROTON, Sauce
2 onions, cut up finely
2 tablespoons butter
1 tablespoon flour
1 cup good stock
Pepper and nutmeg as wished
Salt to taste
1 teaspoon wine-vinegar
1 saltspoonful mustard

The onions, once peeled, must be finely minced. Brown to a nice even shade in the butter, stirring frequently. Add flour and moisten with stock or *bouillon*. Simmer gently for 20 minutes, then add pepper, a dusting of nutmeg, salt, vinegar and mustard. Simmer 20 minutes longer; then use, unstrained, as directed in recipe.

MOËLLE, Sauce
A *Sauce Bordelaise*, but with white wine instead of red, and some pieces of poached marrowbone fat added.

MONTMORENCY
(*Garniture pour noisettes et tournedos.*) (1) Artichoke bottoms filled with carrots the size of marbles. *Pommes noisette.* (2) Artichoke bottoms filled with asparagus tips and fancy *Macédoine.*

MONTPENSIER
(*Garniture pour noisettes, ris de veau, etc.*) Artichoke bottoms filled with asparagus tips. *Pommes noisette.*

MORNAY, Sauce
This is a 'cheesed' *Sauce Béchamelle* (q.v.) in a double-boiler. The desired quantity of grated parmesan cheese is stirred in the *Sauce*, and a little cayenne pepper may also be added before serving. If used with fish, add essence of fish.

MOSCOVITE, Sauce
A *Sauce Poivrade* with juniper berries. A glass of Malaga or Marsala added at time of serving.

MOUSQUETAIRE, Sauce
A *Mayonnaise* with chopped shallots and a garnish of chives, seasoned with cayenne pepper and flavoured with essence of veal.

MOUSSELINE or MOUSSEUSE, Sauce
This is a *Hollandaise* (q.v.) to which is added an equal amount of stiffly-whipped cream. Heat this mixture *very* carefully in a double-boiler, whipping gently all the while until hot through. Season to taste.

MOUTARDE
French for mustard.

MOZART
(*Garniture pour entrées.*) Artichoke bottoms filled with a *purée* of celery; *Pommes Copeaux.*

MUGWORT
Lat. *Artemisia vulgaris*; Fr. *Armoise.* An Eurasian perennial herb with aromatic leaves.

MUSHROOM SAUCE
Add fresh and thinly-sliced mushrooms to a *Béchamel* (q.v.). Cook gently in a double-boiler for about 30 minutes. Some cooks believe in the sliced mushrooms being lightly *sautés* before adding to the sauce, straining into it also the butter they have been cooked in.

MUSTARD
Lat. *Brassica alba* and *Brassica nigra*; Fr. *Moutarde*; Ger. *Senf*; It. *Mostarda*; Sp. *Mostaza.* Formerly known as *Senvy* in England, from *Sinapi*, the mustard seed which, being ground, yields mustard flour or powder.

MUSTARD SAUCE
This is just a white sauce to which, when thoroughly heated, one teaspoonful of French, and half a teaspoonful of English mustard are added. Delicious with grilled herrings.

NANTAISE
(*Garniture pour grosses pièces.*) Turnips, green peas and mashed potatoes.

NANTUA
(*Garniture pour poissons.*) *Écrevisses* tails, *Sauce Nantua* and truffles.

NANTUA, Sauce
White wine and *fumet de poisson*. *Mirepoix* of vegetables and *écrevisses*. Fresh tomatoes or tomato *purée*. *Velouté* of fish; pepper and salt and a dusting of cayenne.

NAPOLITAINE
(*Garniture pour escalopes.*) Spaghetti, tomato sauce and grated parmesan cheese.

NASTURTIUM
Lat. *Tropaeolus majus*; Fr. *Capucine*; Pickled Nasturtium, Fr. *Câpres de Capucine.*

NEMOURS
(*Garniture pour entrées.*) (1) Green peas, carrots and *Pommes Duchesse*. (2) Mushrooms *sautés* and olive-shaped potatoes.

NEMROD
(*Garniture pour gibier à poil.*) Mushrooms and chestnut *purée*. French beans. Rissoles of marrowbone fat. *Pommes Croquettes*.

NEWBURG, Sauce
(American.)

> 2 tablespoons butter
> ⅓ cup dry sherry
> 1 cup thick cream
> 1 teaspoon salt
> ½ teaspoon paprika
> 3 egg yolks

Melt the butter without cooking it, then add the sherry. Simmer for 2 or 3 minutes slowly, then add the cream, mixing well. Season with salt and paprika and pour mixture over the well-beaten egg yolks. Return to top of a double-boiler and cook the sauce, stirring often, until smooth and thick. Lobster coral may be added with advantage. A favourite sauce for lobster served hot.

NIÇOISE
(*Garniture pour poissons.*) Tomatoes, garlic, capers and lemon. *Beurre d'Anchois*.

NIVERNAISE
(*Garniture pour entrées.*) (1) Carrots and turnips, braised lettuce, onions, plain boiled potatoes. (2) Artichoke bottoms, stuffed with glazed button onions; small carrots and olive-shaped potatoes.

NORMANDE
(*Garniture pour poissons.*) Bearded oysters and mussels, mushrooms, *écrevisses*, fried smelts or fillets of sole *en goujons*; truffles.

NORMANDE, Sauce
Velouté with *fumet* of soles, *essence* of mushrooms and oyster or mussels liquor; egg yolks and cream.

The marinade used for the preparation of a *Sole Normande* (see Fish section), should be drained when the fish is done – the latter being kept hot between two plates the while. Strain this liquor and use to moisten a *roux blond*, adding, when the sauce is smooth, two egg yolks beaten in after removing the saucepan from the fire. When the sauce is creamy, add several small pieces of fresh butter, beating each in smoothly as for a *Béarnaise* sauce, but taking care the sauce does not boil. Season to taste with lemon juice.

NUTMEG
Lat. *Myristica fragrans*; Fr. *Muscade*; Ger. *Muskatennuss*; It. *Noce Morcada*; Sp. *Nuez Moscadas*. The nut of which the husk is called *Mace*; it is used ground for flavouring. The seeds of the *Myristica fragrans* or nutmeg tree.

ONION
Lat. *Allium Cepa*; Fr. *Oignon*; Ger. *Zwieffeln*; It. *Cipolla*; Sp. *Cebolla*.

ONION SAUCE
One of the classical English sauces. There are many different methods of making an onion sauce; here are two recipes:

(1) Boil some peeled onions in plain water until they are quite soft; cut them up, not too small, and mix them thoroughly with some white sauce. Add cream at the last moment. Serve hot.

(2) 1 cup rich milk
> 2 tablespoons butter
> Salt and pepper
> 2 tablespoons cream
> 3 tablespoons flour
> ½ lb. onions (2 medium ones)

Peel onions, place them in cold water, bringing same gently to boiling point. When this is reached, remove saucepan from fire, strain onions, afterwards returning them to pan with a sufficiency of salt and sufficient boiling water to cover them. Boil them until quite tender, then drain well and chop them coarsely. Make a white sauce with the butter, flour and milk, in the usual way and, when smooth, add the onions and season to taste. Simmer for a few minutes, then add cream and serve.

The three principal French sauces in which the onion is supreme are the *Soubise*, *Robert* and *Bretonne* sauces.

ORANGE SAUCE
(American.)

> 1½ tablespoons sugar
> 3 tablespoons currant jelly
> Grated rind one orange
> 1 tablespoon orange juice
> 1 tablespoon lemon juice
> Salt and cayenne

Place sugar, jelly and very finely-grated orange rind in a basin, beat well, then add remaining ingredients, blending thoroughly. The addition of a tablespoonful of good port is an improvement. Serve with cold roast duck or galantine of chicken or game.

ORIENTALE
(*Garniture pour grosses pièces.*) Half tomatoes or tartlet cases filled with rice *à la grecque* croquettes of sweet potatoes.

ORIENTALE, Sauce
A *Sauce Américaine* flavoured with curry powder and enriched with fresh cream.

ORLOFF
(*Garniture pour grosses pièces.*) Celery, *Pommes Château*.

OYSTER SAUCE

>   6 or more oysters
>   Dusting powdered mace
>   Strip lemon peel
>   1 tablespoon butter
>   1 teaspoon flour
>   Salt and pepper

Open oysters carefully, setting aside their liquor. Strain this through fine muslin. Place strained liquor in a pan, add a small pinch mace and a small strip of lemon peel. Simmer for 10 minutes gently, then add the butter, rubbed into the flour, stirring quickly to blend. Boil up, season to taste, add the bearded oysters, cooking gently until edges curl, then serve.

PAPRIKA

A condiment prepared from the fruit of the *Capsicum frutescens, var. tetragonum,* mostly grown for the purpose in Hungary; also in Spain.

Hungarian Paprika

The two districts of Hungary where the *Capsicum frutescens, var. tetragonum* is cultivated on a commercial scale for the making of paprika are those of Szeged and Kalocsa; in each district there are five distinct grades of paprika made: (1) Noble-sweet; (2) Semi-sweet; (3) Rose, or first quality; (4) Strong, or second quality; and (5) Commercial, or third quality.

The extraordinarily pungent quality of paprika is due to a substance known as *capsaicin,* a condensation product of vanillylamine and a decylic acid. Its red colouring is believed to be a hydroxy-derivative of carotene.

The better grades of paprika are relatively mild, and besides their gastronomic merit as a flavouring agent, they are valuable physiologically as a source of Vitamins A and C.

PAPRIKA SAUCE

A rich *Velouté* sauce, thickened with cream and flavoured with paprika.

PARISIENNE

(*Garniture pour entrées.*) Various vegetables, but always *Pommes Parisienne.*

PARISIENNE, Sauce

Another name for a *Sauce Blonde* (q.v.).

PARMENTIER

In culinary parlance *Parmentier* always means potatoes; it is the homage of French cooks to Parmentier, who introduced potatoes in France.

PARSLEY

Lat. *Carum crispum;* Fr. *Persil;* Ger. *Gartenpetersilie;* It. *Prezzemolo;* Sp. *Perejil.* The

ornament of many dishes. It is also used fried with fried fish and rissoles. If placed in a wire basket, dipped into the very hot fat of a frying-kettle and taken out 1 minute later, it should be crisp and ready to serve.

PAYSANNE

(*Garniture pour entrées.*) The same as *Fermière,* with *Pommes Cocotte* added.

PENNYROYAL

Lat. *Mentha Pulegium.* A European *Mint* with pungently aromatic leaves.

PEPPER

Lat. *Piper nigrum;* Fr. *Poivre;* Ger. *Pfefer;* It. *Pepe;* Sp. *Pimienta.* There are two main kinds of pepper: the black pepper, from the East, and the red pepper, from America. There is also a white pepper which is the dried seeds of the black pepper; it is milder than black pepper, or peppercorns, as black pepper is called before it is ground. Black pepper is better than white, and it should be ground as required in a small mill sold for that purpose; pepper contains oils which evaporate when left exposed to the air.

PEPPER DULSE

Lat. *Laurentia pinnatifida.* A pungent red seaweed gathered in the *Western Islands* of Scotland.

PERCE PIERRE or CHRISTE MARINE

A sort of marine fennel which grows near the sea and among the rocks; steeped in vinegar, it is used in the same manner as gherkins, as a condiment.

PÉRIGUEUX

The chief city of Périgord, the land of truffles, and the name given to one of the best sauces; it is a *demi-glace* with truffle essence and chopped truffles and flavoured with Madeira wine.

PÉRIGOURDINE, Sauce

Similar, but richer, than the *Sauce Périgueux,* some *foie gras* being added.

PERSICARIA

Fr. *Persicaire.* The *water-pepper* or *lake-weed,* formerly a favourite kitchen herb.

PERSIL

French for *Parsley.*

PÉRUVIENNE

(*Garniture pour grosses pièces.*) *Oxalis* and *Sauce Allemande.*

PICKLES

Condiments made of a large variety of vegetables such as gherkins, cucumbers, onions, cauliflower flowerlets, etc., and walnuts, which have been 'pricked', i.e. 'pickled', salted or otherwise treated with brine and then bottled by themselves or mixed together into a vinegary bath.

PIÉMONTAISE

(*Garniture pour entrées.*) Rizotto with shredded grey Italian truffles.

PIGNOLI

Fr. *Pignon de pin*; It. *Pinocchio*. The culinary name for pine-cone kernels, used in sauces and cakes in place of chopped almonds or nuts.

PIMENTO: PIMIENTO

Lat. *Capsicum frutescens, var. tetragonum*. Fr. *Piments* or *Poivrons*. The dried berries of the *Allspice* tree, the *Pimenta officinalis*, a most valuable flavouring agent.

PIMENTS

French for *Allspice* (q.v.)

PIMPRENELLE

One of the *herbes* most valuable in salads and savoury omelettes. It is usually and quite erroneously translated by *Pimpernel*, which is a poisonous flower; its English name is *Burnet*.

PIQUANTE, Sauce

    2 oz. butter
    4 oz. chopped onions
    1½ oz. flour
    Salt and pepper
    One or two vinegar pickles
    White wine

Gently melt the butter in a copper (or earthenware) saucepan until it begins to smoke slightly, then throw in the onions and stir, cooking them until they are a rather dark, even, golden colour. Now add the flour, stirring until the entire mixture is an even brown. Moisten with white wine, adding it little by little and stirring well all the time. The sauce should be of the consistency of a thick white sauce. Season to taste and allow to simmer over a low heat for 15 to 20 minutes. The sauce may be passed through a *chinois* (which is a conical metal sieve) or not, as preferred. Cut up one or two vinegar gherkins, add them to the sauce, with chopped parsley, chervil and tarragon, and simmer for 5 or 10 minutes longer. The gravy, from whatever meat is intended to be served with this sauce, should be added to it; failing this, add a little good meat essence. When adding the gravy, skim off fat first or the sauce will be too rich. Some cooks also add a little French mustard; this is entirely a matter of taste.

POIVRADE, Sauce

One of the most popular of the peppery French sauces.

    1 tablespoon butter
    1 carrot
    1 onion
    1 or 2 shallots
    1 clove
    1 laurel leaf
    Pinch dried thyme
    Pepper
    Good pinch flour
    1 small glass red wine
    1 tablespoon wine-vinegar

Put butter in a small pan, add cut-up carrot and onion, chopped shallot, clove, laurel leaf, thyme and salt. Cook, stirring frequently, until all is coloured, then add flour; stir, then moisten with mixed wine and vinegar. Simmer for half an hour. Add a good amount of freshly-ground pepper. Strain through a fine sieve and serve. A little meat glaze improves flavour, if available.

POIVRE

French for *Pepper*.

POIVRE MIGNONETTE

French for freshly, and not too finely, ground peppercorns.

POIVRONS

French for *Pimentos*.

PORT WINE SAUCE

    ½ cup meat gravy
    1 teaspoon red currant jelly
    1 glass good port wine
    Dash lemon juice

Use gravy from roast mutton or venison. Place all ingredients in a small saucepan, beating jelly to mix with gravy. Bring gently to boiling point and serve after straining.

PORTUGAISE

(*Garniture pour entrées.*) Small stuffed tomatoes and *Pommes Château*.

PORTUGAISE, Sauce

    5 or 6 ripe tomatoes
    1 clove garlic, minced
    1 tablespoon *Espagnole* sauce
    Salt and pepper
    1 teaspoon olive oil
    1 tablespoon tomato sauce

Peel tomatoes, cut up and place in a saucepan with the garlic, salt, pepper and oil. Cook gently until tender, then add the other prepared sauces (recipes for both of which will be found in this section) and heat. Serve without straining.

POULETTE, Sauce
A variant of the *Sauce Béchamel.*
> 2 tablespoons butter
> 2 tablespoons flour
> 2 cups bouillon or stock
> Salt and pepper
> 1 very small 'bouquet'
> 2 tablespoons thick cream
> Lemon juice to taste
> 1 or 2 egg yolks

Make in the same way as white or cream sauce, taking care the flour does not colour. Moisten with any good white stock or use the liquid of the meat to be served with this sauce. When the sauce is smooth and thick, remove from heat, beat in cream and egg yolks, add lemon juice and seasonings. An excellent sauce for mussels, as well as a ragout of veal.

PRINTANIÈRE
(*Garniture pour entrées.*) All manner of vegetables in season cut up in dice and arranged separately round the dish.

PRINCESSE
(*Garniture pour tournedos, etc.*) Artichoke bottoms filled with asparagus points. *Pommes Noisettes.*

PROVENÇALE
(*Garniture.*) Tomatoes, mushrooms, aubergines, garlic, etc.

PROVENÇALE, Sauce
> 3 tablespoons pure olive oil
> 3 shallots
> 1 small clove of garlic
> ¼ lb. mushrooms
> 1 dessertspoon flour
> Good stock or bouillon
> Salt and pepper
> 1 small glass white wine
> 1 small 'bouquet-garni'
> Lemon juice to taste

Chop together, rather finely, shallots and garlic and, after having heated some oil, lightly brown them, stirring frequently. Sprinkle with flour, moisten with meat stock or *bouillon*, season with salt and pepper; add white wine and *bouquet* and cover closely. Let it simmer gently for 15 minutes, then add the chopped mushrooms and let it simmer for 20 or 30 minutes more. Strain, add lemon juice and serve with, for instance, cold roast beef or veal.

> Sauce Provençale aux Œufs
> 2 cloves garlic
> 4 shallots
> 2 stalks fresh tarragon
> 1 or 2 stalks chervil

> 4 dessertspoons vinegar
> 4 egg yolks
> ½ pint olive oil
> Salt and pepper

Chop the herbs as for a *Béarnaise* sauce and set in the vinegar. Reduce by simmering gently until vinegar has almost entirely evaporated, then replace by same quantity of water; strain and cool. Place this liquid in upper part of a double-boiler, add egg yolks, salt and pepper, and beat as you would for a *Sauce Béarnaise*, adding the olive oil a little at a time, as when making *Mayonnaise*. Whip and beat until the sauce is thick. This sauce is excellent with grilled fish.

QUENELLES of Chicken, etc.
Add half a pound of raw, chopped chicken, veal or white fish to *Panade*, a pappy preparation of bread soaked in milk. Pound the chicken with it. Add a beaten egg and mix and pound again. Season and rub mixture through a hair sieve. Shape into small sausages and poach in boiling water or stock until they swell. Drain carefully and serve in soup, as a garnish – in which case they must be quite tiny – or in patties, cream or tomato sauce, as an *entrée*.

QUIN'S SAUCE
'Take a pint of walnut pickle, a pint of mushroom catsup; six whole and six bruised cloves of garlic; twelve large anchovies well bruised; 2 ozs. horseradish scraped; large teaspoon of cayenne pepper. Let them stand mixed together in a jar for a week, shaking it often.' (Kenneth Hare, in *Wine and Food*, No. 24, 1939, p. 358.)

RAIFORT, Sauce
See *Horseradish Sauce.*

RASPBERRY BUTTER
To one measure of fresh butter – say ¼ lb., allow two of sifted white sugar – say ½ lb. Put into a slightly warmed basin and work thoroughly together. Over this sweet butter pour enough raspberry juice to colour and flavour it, and it is ready to serve.

RASPBERRY SAUCE
Squeeze a pint of fruit juice out of fresh raspberries and boil in a small lined saucepan, having added as much castor sugar as may be desired, and a squeeze of lemon. Strain the juice and then work in it a tablespoonful of arrowroot in a basin. Return to the saucepan and bring to boiling point again, stirring all the while. Serve with vanilla ice cream, etc.

RAVIGOTE, Sauce
One of the most popular of French sauces. A *Ravigote* is the assemblage of onions and

such herbs as tarragon, chervil, chives and burnet, in a *velouté* with some white stock and vinegar. There are two versions of this sauce, the cold and the hot.

(Cold)

3 hard-boiled egg yolks
2 tablespoons or more olive oil
Salt and pepper
Chopped chives
Chopped French capers
Chopped parsley
2 raw egg yolks
French mustard
1 tablespoon wine vinegar
Chopped tarragon
Chopped shallots
Chopped onion

Crush and pound the hard-boiled egg yolks adding the raw yolks to them and blending to a smooth, thick paste. Now add the mustard and the oil, very little at a time and beating hard. Flavour with the chopped herbs, etc., and the vinegar, and season rather highly. More oil may be added if required and the amount of vinegar needed depends on individual taste. Serve ice-cold.

(Hot)

A cupful of *roux blond*
Salt and pepper
Beurre de ravigote
Vinegar
Tiny pinch grated nutmeg

(For *Beurre de Ravigote*.) Chopped parsley, chives, chervil, tarragon, shallots and garlic, to taste. Have a very little boiling water and drop all the above into this, just blanching for a moment or two. Drain and squeeze herbs to extract water completely. Pound the herbs in a mortar, press through a fine sieve and add this mixture to 2 or 3 table-spoonfuls of fresh butter, blending thoroughly and adding salt and pepper to taste.

Make the *roux* as directed for special recipe, using a little good chicken stock to bind flour mixture. Add a scant tablespoonful of wine vinegar, pepper and the nutmeg. Simmer this mixture gently for 5 minutes, then add a heaped tablespoonful of the prepared *Beurre de Ravigote*, beating the whole gently over a low heat until ready to serve. Do not allow to boil or the flavour of the butter will spoil.

REFORM, Sauce

A *Poivrade* (q.v.) with a *julienne* of whites of hard-boiled eggs, gherkins, mushrooms, truffles and tongue. (This sauce was introduced at the Reform Club, by Soyer, with *Cutlets*.)

RÉGENCE, Sauce

(For fish.) A *Sauce Normande* with white wine, mushrooms and truffles. (For fowls.) A *Sauce Suprême* with white wine, mushrooms and truffles.

RÉMOULADE

A salad dressing consisting of the yolks of hard-boiled eggs, oil and vinegar, salt and pepper. Mustard is sometimes added. When a *Ravigote* (q.v.) of chopped herbs is added it becomes a *Sauce Tartare*.

RICHE, Sauce

Another name for the *Sauce Diplomate* (q.v.)

RICHELIEU

(*Garniture pour grosses pièces*.) Stuffed tomatoes and mushrooms; artichoke bottoms stuffed with chicken *purée*; braised lettuce. *Pommes Château*.

ROBERT, Sauce

This is one of the oldest of French brown sauces, used with goose, pork and sometimes venison. It is a *roux* (q.v.) made with the addition of three large onions, very finely chopped, per tablespoonful of flour used to make *roux*. Moisten with *bouillon*, season well, simmer for half an hour, and add, when ready to serve, a suspicion of good wine-vinegar and French mustard as desired.

ROCAMBOLE

Lat. *Allium Scorodoprasum*. A variety of garlic grown chiefly in Denmark.

ROCHAMBEAU

(*Garniture pour grosses pièces*.) Carrots, lettuce and cauliflowers. *Pommes Anna*.

ROEBUCK SAUCE

The English *Sauce Chevreuil*. Chop ham and onions; brown them in butter; add a little vinegar and *bouquet garni*. Add sauce *demi-glace*. Finish with port wine and red currant jelly.

ROSEMARY

Lat. *Rosemarinus officinalis*; Fr. *Rosemarin*. One of the old English favourite pot-herbs used in stuffings and for flavouring sauces.

ROSSINI

(*Garniture pour tournedos et noisettes*.) *Escalopes* of *foie gras sauté* in butter; slices of truffle.

ROUX

A generic term for various flour bindings. A *roux* is sometimes brown, sometimes white or *blond*, according to the use that it is intended for. It is really but a *Béchamel* sauce (q.v.) in its essentials. One or more spoonfuls of butter are placed in a small saucepan and, when it is melted, the same amount of

4I

flour is added and stirred into the butter. If a 'thin' sauce is required, one spoonful of flour is used to two of butter. The mixture must colour gently to the desired shade, then the liquid indicated by the recipe is added, little by little, and the sauce seasoned as desired and allowed to mellow by the side of the stove. The dripping from a piece of roast meat is sometimes used instead of butter; this improves the flavour of the sauce if intended to be served with the roast.

RUE
Lat. *Ruta graveolens*; Fr. *Rue des jardins*. A hardy evergreen, with aggressively scented leaves which are supposed to possess beneficial medical properties.

RUM SAUCE
Beat to a smooth cream the yolks of two eggs, 2 tablespoonfuls of sifted sugar and a saltspoonful of grated nutmeg. Beat the whites of two eggs to a stiff froth. When the time has come to serve the sauce, mix with the egg whites 2 tablespoonfuls of sifted sugar, quickly and lightly; then mix with the yolks and, last of all, add a wineglassful – or more, according to disposition – of the best and oldest Jamaica Rum available.

SABAYON
     4 egg yolks
     1½ oz. sifted sugar
     2 gills Marsala wine
     Put into a saucepan the four yolks and the sugar; place the saucepan on a hot stove and beat the yolks and sugar smartly with a wire whisk for 2 minutes. Pour in the Marsala, or, failing this, some Madeira slowly, stirring all the time; then take the pan from the fire and strain the sauce through a fine sieve over the pudding with which it is to be served. It is also served with vanilla ice cream. This sauce must not boil.

SAFFLOWER
Lat. *Carthamus tinctorius*. A European thistle which has orange flowers that are used for colouring cakes and sweets.

SAFFRON
Lat. *Crocus sativus*; Fr. *Safran*. One of the fallen monarchs of the kitchen. Bacon wrote that 'The English are rendered sprightly by a liberal use of saffron in sweetmeats and broths'. It was used largely for its flavour and colour, but it was completely – or almost completely – ousted in England by the introduction of curry. It is, however, still a *sine quâ non* of the Cornish Saffron cake. It still holds it own in Cornwall and North Devon, and, of course, in Italy and Provence, the *Risotto Milanese* and *Bouillabaisse* being two of many saffron dishes.

SAGE
Lat. *Salvia officinalis*; Fr. *Sauge*; Ger. *Salbei*; It. and Sp. *Salvia*. The three chief sorts cultivated in England are the green, the purple and the narrow leaved. Sage is used mostly in forcemeat and sauces in England.

SAGE AND ONION Sauce
     2 tablespoons butter
     2 onions
     1½ cups brown stock
     1 teaspoon sage
     2 tablespoons soft breadcrumbs
     Salt and pepper
     Melt the butter in a pan, add the minced onions, cooking until a light brown. Add the stock, bring to boiling point, then add the finely-chopped sage leaves, the breadcrumbs – freshly made – and season to taste. Usually served with roast pork, when a tablespoonful or two of the meat gravy added to the sauce improves it.

SAINT-GERMAIN
(*Garniture*.) A *purée* of green peas.

SALT
Fr. *Sel*; Ger. *Salz*; It. *Sale*; Sp. *Sal*. Chloride of sodium, not only indispensable in cooking for the palatability which it imparts to food, but for the salinity which is indispensable to health and even to life.

SAMPHIRE
Lat. *Crithmum maritimum*; Fr. *St. Pierre* Ger. *Meerfenchel*. A common aromatic plant which grows wild at the seaside among rocks.

SARLADAISE
(*Garniture*.) Truffles.

SARRIETTE
French for *Summer Savory*.

SARSAPARILLA
Lat. *Smilax officinalis*. A Central and South American *Smilax* with cord-like roots which, when dried, are used in infusions and to flavour carbonated and sweetened so-called 'mineral' waters, reputed to be refreshing and tonic.

SAUCE ALONE
Lat. *Allium officinalis*. One of the old favourites among English pot-herbs. It is also known as *Garlick Mustard*.

SAVORY
The *Summer Savory* (*Satureia hortensis*) and *Winter Savory* (*Satureia montana*) are two of the most highly aromatic garden herbs; they are used, like chervil and chives, finely chopped, in salads and omelettes; also in

France, Holland, Germany and Scandinavia always with boiled broad beans.

SCALLION
Another name for *shallot*.

SERPOLET
French for *Wild Thyme*.

SÉVIGNÉ
(*Garniture pour entrées*.) Stuffed lettuce, grilled mushrooms and *Pommes Château*.

SHALLOT
Lat. *Allium Ascalonicum*; Fr. *Echalote*. A valuable member of the onion family, its bulb like that of garlic being divided into several bulbs called cloves, because cloven.

SHALLOT SAUCE
> 2 tablespoons finely-chopped shallots
> 5 tablespoons vinegar
> 2 cups *bouillon*
> *Bouquet-garni*
> *Beurre manié*
> Salt and pepper

Place the shallots with the vinegar in an enamel or earthenware saucepan over a good heat. Cook, stirring often, until the vinegar has almost entirely evaporated, then add the stock, salt and pepper and *bouquet*. Cook gently for 15 minutes over a low heat; when serving, remove *bouquet* but do not strain. Add the *beurre manié* a few minutes before serving.

SHRIMP SAUCE
> ½ pint brown, freshly-boiled shrimps
> 3 cups white sauce

Have a nice rich white sauce to which have been added a good amount of first-class fresh butter and a tablespoonful of thick cream. Peel the shrimps, setting the heads aside. Pound these with about six or more of the shrimps, to a paste, press through a small sieve and add to the sauce, stirring well in. When ready to serve, add rest of shrimps, simmering for a minute or two to heat thoroughly.

SMITANE, Sauce
Sour cream and onions. Brown lightly a finely-chopped onion; add a full glass of dry white wine; reduce on slow heat; add a pint of sour cream; let it boil for a few moments only, pass through a fine sieve and add the juice of one lemon.

SOISSONNAISE
(*Garniture*.) Large white haricot beans.

SORREL SAUCE
There are two versions of this old-fashioned English sauce, one without cream, usually served with roast goose, and the other, with cream, not necessarily for a gander.

1. Boil fast for about 6 or 7 minutes a quart of fresh green sorrel leaves in plenty of salted water. Drain them and drop them in cold water. When cold, drain them again and rub them through a sieve with a masher and put them in a saucepan with a fair lump of fresh butter, a little sifted sugar, the juice of a lemon and enough brown gravy made from the drippings of a goose to make the sauce of the right consistency. Serve very hot.

2. Wash two handfuls of fresh sorrel leaves and chop them up. Put 1 oz. of fresh butter into a saucepan with a tablespoonful of flour and stir over the fire until well mixed; then pour in half a pint of cream and a little stock; when it boils, add the sorrel and let it come to the boil again; add pepper and salt and a dusting of grated nutmeg and serve.

SOUBISE, Sauce
A *purée* of onions diluted with a *Béchamelle* sauce.

> 20 rather small onions
> 2 tablespoons butter
> Salt and pepper
> Dusting nutmeg
> 2 cups *Béchamelle* sauce
> Butter to taste

The *Béchamelle* should be gently reduced to almost half its original bulk by slow-cooking before using for this recipe. Peel the onions, lay in saucepan with the butter, salt, pepper and nutmeg. Cover closely and cook thus, gently, until tender. Press through a sieve. Add the *Béchamelle*, and see that it blends well, and add a little fresh butter at the time of serving.

SOY
The name of one of the most popular kinds of ketchup or bottled sauce in early Victorian times, judging from the number of silver *Soy* sauce labels still in existence. It is said, by Kettner and others, to owe its name to the fact that one of the chief ingredients used in its manufacture was the *Soy* bean (*Soya hispida*), from the Far East. *Soy* was black and rather sweet, especially the cheaper, spurious *Soy* sold in some shops, which was made, according to Cooley, by saturating molasses or common treacle with salt.

SPAGHETTI, Sauce
(Italo-American.)
> 2 large ripe tomatoes
> 1 slice lean ham
> 2 cloves garlic
> ¼ cup olive oil
> 2 bay leaves
> Salt and pepper

Peel the tomatoes after plunging first in boiling water, and then in cold. Remove cores and seeds and cut up finely, as well as some ham and garlic. Simmer together in olive oil, with bay leaves, salt and pepper, for 1 hour. Pour over spaghetti and sprinkle with Parmesan. The sauce must be rather highly seasoned and thick. An onion, or, better, a couple of shallots may also be added to ham and garlic.

SPANISH SAUCE
See *Espagnole*.

SPICES
Fr. *Epices*; Ger. *Gewurz*; It. *Spezie*; Sp. *Especia*. The usual spices obtainable in England are cayenne, cinnamon, ground or in sticks, chillies, cloves, coriander, curry, ginger, mace, caraway seeds, cardamom, mixed spice, nutmeg, paprika, peppers, white and black, whole or ground, saffron, and vanilla.

SPOONWORT
See *Cochlearia*.

STUFFINGS and GARNISHES
Goose Stuffing
1 large peeled onion
2 small leaves of sage
½ cup fresh breadcrumbs
Salt and pepper
Butter to blend stuffing

Chop the onion and sage leaves together, finely. Have the breadcrumbs of an even size – not too large – mix with onions and sage, season with salt and pepper, and blend to a thick mixture with butter.

Fried Apple Rings for Goose
Tart green cooking apples
Bacon fat

Do not peel the apples. Remove cores and cut into slices about half an inch thick. Heat some bacon fat – or butter if preferred – and gently fry the apple rings in this until brown on one side, then carefully turn and brown the other. Serve around goose, duck or pork, as a garnish when not serving apple sauce.

Apple Stuffing
(American)
¼ cup salt pork, diced finely
½ cup chopped celery
½ cup chopped onion
¼ cup chopped parsley
4 cooking apples, diced
Sugar (optional)
1 cup fine dry breadcrumbs
Salt and pepper
Cut the salt pork up very finely and brown

until crisp. Remove pieces of pork from pan. Cook the cut-up celery, onion and parsley in the fat for 3 minutes, then remove. Now place the apples in the same pan, sprinkling lightly with sugar if desired, and cook slowly until tender, after covering. When done, remove lid and continue cooking the apples until they are brown and glazed, then add to them the crumbs and other ingredients, including the bits of fried salt pork. Nice for duck, goose or with roast pork.

Chestnut Stuffing for Turkey
2 lb. chestnuts
1 cup good meat stock
2 tablespoons butter
Pinch sugar
Salt and pepper

Slit the chestnuts and bake or roast them for 20 minutes. Remove both skins and place them in a pan with the stock, using only just enough to cover them. Continue cooking the nuts until tender and almost dry, shaking to prevent burning. Rub through a fine sieve, add butter, salt, sugar and pepper. Some recipes also advise the addition of ½ cupful of fresh breadcrumbs and one beaten egg to bind mixture. The addition of a truffle or truffle peelings is a great improvement.

Hare or Rabbit Stuffing
3 oz. fat pork or bacon
Liver of the hare or rabbit
3 oz. veal suet
Herbs as liked
1 shallot
Salt and pepper
Dusting nutmeg
8 oz. fresh breadcrumbs
1 anchovy
1 egg

Chop the pork or bacon and fry until a light brown, then remove pieces of meat and fry liver in fat. Chop this when done. Mix pork or bacon pieces with chopped liver, chopped suet, herbs (mixed marjoram, thyme and parsley), add the minced shallot and season rather highly. Now add breadcrumbs and anchovy and pound all this thoroughly in a mortar. Beat up the egg and use to bind. If not sufficiently moist, add a little milk.

Fish Stuffing
2 oz. veal suet
2 oz. bacon
1 dessertspoon mixed herbs
Oysters (optional)
¼ lb. fresh breadcrumbs
4 tablespoons butter
Salt, pepper and suspicion of nutmeg
2 eggs

Chop the suet very finely and mix with the chopped bacon. Add the herbs and, if liked, a sprig of parsley, also chopped. If oysters are added, remove beards, and chop, if large. Mix all this with the breadcrumbs and just-melted butter. Season and bind with the beaten eggs. A light grating of lemon peel is a nice addition. If stuffing is too dry, add a little milk.

Sausage Stuffing for Chicken

½ lb. pork sausage-meat
4 oz. fresh breadcrumbs
2 tablespoons butter
1 teaspoon chopped parsley
Salt and pepper
1 egg or milk to bind

Mix sausage-meat and breadcrumbs, add the melted butter and seasonings, and lightly fry for a few minutes. Cool and blend with beaten egg.

Mushroom Stuffing

6 oz. fresh mushrooms
1 small rasher bacon
6 oz. fresh breadcrumbs
Salt, pepper, nutmeg
1 oz. butter
1 egg

Wash and dry mushrooms, using stalks if firm and white. Chop them rather finely. Cut up the rasher of bacon and fry lightly with the mushrooms, stirring all the time. Add this to the breadcrumbs and season well. Bind mixture with the butter and the beaten egg. Use for small game birds or pigeons.

Giblet Stuffing

Boiled and chopped giblets
½ cup butter or fat
1 small onion
Parsley
4 cups rather coarse fresh bread-crumbs
1 cup boiling water or giblet stock
1 egg

Boil the giblets in just sufficient water to cover, adding salt, a piece of onion and a small *bouquet-garni*, if wished, to flavour. Simmer until tender enough to chop finely. Soak crumbs in stock. Melt the butter or fat and use, with the beaten egg, to moisten all well-mixed and seasoned ingredients. Used for chicken or turkey.

Forcemeat Balls for Roast Poultry
(French)

½ lb. fresh breadcrumbs or large piece of breadcrumb
1 cup chicken stock
2 tablespoons butter

Trimmings of raw fowl (4 oz.)
2 or 3 egg yolks
Cream
Nutmeg
Salt and pepper

Soak the crumbs in the stock for an hour, then squeeze them dry. Melt the butter in a pan, add the bread and season. Stir this mixture, with a wooden spoon, over a moderate heat until it makes a smooth paste and a ball around the spoon, leaving the sides of the pan clean. Cool before using.

Add to the above, trimmings of fowl, and egg yolks. Blend all well together, season, add, if possible, some truffle trimmings, a touch of nutmeg, more butter, and, if wished, a touch of thick cream. Form into small balls, dip in flour, then boil for 2 minutes in salted boiling water.

SUPRÊME, Sauce
A *Velouté* to which some fresh cream is added just before serving.

SWEET Sauce
(English.)

4 oz. sifted sugar
4 egg yolks
2 gills sweet cream
1 orange

Stir the sugar and egg yolks in a saucepan with a wooden spoon until they are well mixed, then add the cream, little by little, beating all the time, and grate in the rind of an orange. Place the saucepan on a slow fire and stir contents for 4 or 5 minutes, being careful not to let them boil. Take the pan off, strain the sauce through a sieve and serve.

SWEET CICELY
Lat. *Myrrhis odorata.* An old English country name for *Chervil*.

SWEET WHIPPED Sauce
(Mrs Hyne's recipe.)

2 yolks of eggs
1 level tablespoonful of castor sugar
2 tablespoonfuls of cold water

Put eggs, sugar and water into a very clean saucepan and whisk all together over a fire (the saucepan standing in a *bain-marie* or one can use a double-boiler).

Whip it constantly until it begins to thicken, then add, little by little, one glass of sherry.

This sauce takes from 8 to 10 minutes and must be served at once.

SUCHET, Sauce
A white wine sauce with a *julienne* of potatoes, carrots and celery.

45

SWEET and SOUR SAUCE
(American.)

> 2 tablespoons butter
> 2 tablespoons flour
> 2 cups vegetable water or stock
> Salt and pepper
> 2 tablespoons vinegar
> 2 tablespoons sugar

Brown the butter nicely in a small pan, add flour and stir and brown well; then add remainder of ingredients. Cook, beating until smooth, and serve with boiled beef (*pot-au-feu* meat, for instance) or cooked vegetables served as a separate course. A dash of French mustard improves this sauce.

TABASCO
A small, very red and very hot Capsicum introduced from the State of Tabasco, in Mexico, in 1868, by E.McIlhenny, of New Iberia, Louisiana.

TARRAGON
Lat. *Artemisia Dracunculus*; Fr. *Estragon*; Ger. *Schlanger-Kraut*; It. *Targone*; Sp. *Estragon*. One of the most odoriferous of pot-herbs. Invaluable in salads, savoury omelettes and many sauces.

TARRAGON Vinegar
Place a handful of fresh tarragon leaves in a half-gallon earthenware jar filled with French white wine-vinegar. Close it tightly and let it stand for a fortnight in the sun (if you can), turning jar once a while. At the end of that time the vinegar may be filtered and bottled for winter use.

TARTARE, Sauce
A pungent French sauce, usually made like a *Mayonnaise*, with vinegar, mustard and a chopped *Ravigote* added in the following manner:

> Parsley, finely-chopped
> Tarragon, finely-chopped
> Salt and pepper
> French red wine-vinegar
> 2 or 3 shallots, minced
> Coarsely chopped gherkins (2 or 3)
> French Dijon mustard
> Dry white wine
> Good firm mayonnaise

Have all ingredients ready to add to the mayonnaise, together with about a teaspoonful of the mustard. Thin to required consistency with little dry white wine and vinegar.

TARTARE, Sauce
(Mrs Hyne's recipe.)
To one cup of *Mayonnaise* sauce add

> 1 dessertspoonful chopped gherkins
> 1 dessertspoonful of chopped capers
> 1 dessertspoonful of chopped parsley

Mix carefully together and season well.

THYME
Lat. *Thymus serpyllum*; Fr. *Serpolet*; Ger. *Thymian*; It. *Timo*; Sp. *Tomillo*. The wild *Thyme* grows freely in large clumps on moors and many other places; it bears purple flowers from May to October which have a pungent, pleasant scent. Dried *Thyme* is used in cookery as a flavouring agent. Garden *Thyme* is a favourite plant in rockeries and paved walks.

TOMATO SAUCE

> Water or stock
> 6 ripe tomatoes
> 1 onion
> 1 small *bouquet-garni*
> Salt and pepper

Fresh tomatoes, boiled to a pulp in stock, passed through a sieve, seasoned to taste and served hot, make the lightest, and some say the best *Tomato Sauce*; but, as a rule, *Tomato Sauce* is made thicker with flour and butter. The flour may be added to the same amount of butter as when making a white sauce; when the mixture begins to bubble, a sufficiency of water or, if convenient, white stock should be used to moisten and, when boiling, the tomatoes and seasonings should be added and cooked in the already thickened sauce. Another method consists in placing in a saucepan the amount of water – or stock – required, adding to this the cut-up tomatoes, the onion, *bouquet*, salt and pepper. All this is boiled together until the tomatoes are done, then the sauce is strained through a wire or hair sieve, all pulp being carefully extracted. This liquid is now placed in a pan, heated gently and, when boiling, the thickening should be slowly added, the sauce being stirred the while. A few moments should be given to cook the flour and thicken the sauce, which is now ready to serve, after a tablespoon of good butter has been added, but not cooked. To make the binding, mix the flour, by this latter method, with a little cold milk or cold water and strain into the boiling sauce. If made very thick, it may be used in many ways which will be indicated in other sections.

TRUFFLES
Lat. *Tuber aestivum* (English); *T. melanosporum* (French); and *T. magnatum* (Piedmont or Italian); Fr. *Truffes*; Ger. *Truffeln*; It. *Tartufi*. The most odoriferous of culinary tubers.

TYROLIENNE, Sauce
A *Mayonnaise* flavoured with tomato *purée*; served with fish.

VANILLA
Lat. *Vanilla fragrans* and *V. planifolia*; Fr. *Vanille*. The pod of an orchid plant: it is

greatly valued for its aromatic scent and it is used as a flavouring agent in puddings, sauces and ices.

VANILLA SAUCE

    1 pint milk
    1 pod vanilla
    3 eggs
    2 tablespoonfuls flour
    Sugar

Boil the pod of vanilla in the milk with as much sugar as you happen to care for, and then remove the saucepan from the fire. Beat the yolks of the three eggs with the flour and add to them the hot, vanilla-scented and sweet milk; stir over a slow fire until thick, but do not let the milk boil. Whip the white of the three eggs to a stiff froth with a tablespoonful of castor sugar; add this froth to the sauce and serve.

VELOUTÉ

    2 tablespoons of butter
    2 carrots
    2 medium-sized onions
    A slice or scraps of ham
    Scraps of white meat, raw and lean
    A *bouquet-garni*
    1 pint or more water
    Salt and pepper
    A few mushrooms
    1 or 2 cloves
    1 cup white sauce
    More cold water

The above ingredients are sufficient for a small houshold. If a large quantity of this basic sauce is needed to be kept on hand, a small fowl must be added.

Melt the butter in a heavy saucepan, add the sliced carrots and onions, then the pieces or slice of lean ham and the scraps of lean meat, also the *bouquet-garni*. A small boiling fowl is also helpful. All this must gently 'sweat' over a low fire, but the ingredients must *not* colour. To prevent this, add a pint of water as soon as colouring is likely to begin and continue gently cooking until the gravy is greatly reduced. If a fowl is in the pan, it must, at this juncture, be stuck all over with a fork to let the juices flow into the gravy. Now fill the pan with cold water, after adding the salt, pepper to taste, a few fresh, peeled mushrooms, if available, and the cloves. Cover closely and cook gently for 4 hours, after skimming carefully just as the contents of the pan start boiling. Strain, when done, through a fine sieve and pour stock into another saucepan. Bring contents to boiling point, then gently stir in the white sauce, stirring constantly until blended with the stock. This sauce may also be kept in the ice-box for some time, if required in sufficient quantities to warrant making a large amount. When the white sauce has been added, the mixture should gently simmer over a low heat, to improve the flavour, before cooling, to store.

VERTE, Sauce

1. Pound in a mortar parsley, chervil and tarragon leaves after mincing finely. Add a teaspoonful or two of cold water. Pass through a fine strainer, lined with muslin. Add to a seasoned mayonnaise. A drop of onion juice, or, better still, a little chopped chives, may also be added to the pounded mixture.

2. A *Mayonnaise* (q.v.) flavoured with a *purée* of chervil, spinach and tarragon. Blend with *Aspic* to taste.

VICTORIA SAUCE

This is a *Sauce Allemande* (q.v.) to which some good white wine has been added in the proportion of one measure of white wine to three of sauce; the two are thoroughly warmed up together with some chopped cooked mushrooms added, without being allowed to boil. In the meantime, some lobster coral is pounded with some fresh butter, and, when the two are thoroughly well mixed, they are added to the sauce and stirred until it is time to serve.

VINAIGRETTE
(Oil and Vinegar.)

    1 small saltspoon salt
    ½ saltspoon pepper
    1 saltspoon French or English prepared mustard
    1 tablespoon wine-vinegar
    2 tablespoons olive oil

This should be sufficient dressing for a green salad for two persons. In the United States other ingredients are sometimes added or, if a large quantity is made in advance (a bad practice), a small onion is placed in the bottle and left there to flavour the sauce.

Mix the mustard, salt and pepper thoroughly with the vinegar, then add oil and beat well.

VINAIGRETTE
(Mrs Hyne's recipe.)

Three parts of salad oil to one part of vinegar, salt, pepper, chopped capers, gherkins, parsley, tarragon, chervil and chives may be added if liked.

WHITE SAUCE

There are quite a number of different sorts of sauces known as 'White Sauce' because of their colour, some for meat and others for fish, some being made with milk, others with flour and others with both milk and flour.

Milk and Flour

Put ½ pint of milk into a double-boiler and stand it over the fire. Mix 4 tablespoonfuls of flour with ½ pint of milk, and stir it in with the milk on the fire when it comes to the boil. Remove from the fire and add a pint of cream, stirring all the time. Stir the sauce for 2 minutes, on a low heat, then cover it and let it cook for another 8 minutes. Beat the yolks of two eggs with one teacupful of cream, then mix them with the other ingredients and take them off the fire at once. Add some chopped parsley, pepper and salt and serve.

No Flour

Boil some sliced mushrooms in a pint of good white stock until it is reduced by a third; move the saucepan away from the fire and stir in the stock, the beaten yolks of four eggs and ½ pint of cream; season with pepper and salt, a dusting of grated nutmeg and a squeeze of lemon. Stir over the fire again until on the point of boiling, when it must be moved away at once and it is ready to serve.

Neither Milk nor Cream

Put a pint of the liquor in which fish was cooked into a saucepan, and boil until reduced to half; then stir into it a dessert-spoonful of flour that has been mixed with a little water, and stir over the fire until the flour be cooked. Beat two eggs in a little water, and mix them with the sauce, moving the saucepan at once to the side of the fire. Season to taste with pepper and salt, stir until the sauce be sufficiently thick and serve.

WORCESTERSHIRE SAUCE

Ordinarily, but wrongly, called *Worcester Sauce*. One of the most popular of all bottled sauces in England; garlic is its basis and its strength, but it does not assert itself unduly. Other ingredients are old and matured anchovies and West Indies tamarinds.

ZEGAKELIE

A small shrub the leaves of which possess a strong scent, somewhat similar to that of *Thyme*. It grows freely in Abyssinia, where it is used in the making of an aromatic sauce known as *Aoudze*; this sauce is always served with the Abyssinian national dish called *Brondo*.

ZINGARA, Sauce

A white wine sauce with some meat glaze, mushrooms, truffles, ham and tongue, all finely-chopped up, and a fair sprinkling of cayenne pepper.

SECTION 2
VEGETABLES

SECTION II

Vegetables: comprising an alphabetical list of Vegetables,
Herbs, Salads, Fungi and edible Weeds, and a
selection of American, English, French,
Scottish and Welsh Recipes for
their culinary preparation

VEGETABLES

All cooks agree in this opinion –
No savoury dish without an onion.

Kitchen Oracle.

INTRODUCTION

SCIENCE has placed beyond doubt the fact that our physical and mental fitness
depends to a great extent upon the presence in our daily diet of infinitesimal
quantities of various mineral salts and a whole alphabet of vitamins. We also
know now for certain that fresh vegetables are the richest – and incidentally
the cheapest – source of supply of most such precious minerals and vitamins.
We all know that vegetables are good for us. It does not mean that we all love
vegetables, any more than the average school boy loves soap because it is
good for him. It is true that vegetables, like many other good things and good
people, are often dull; but it is our fault, nearly always. There is neither sense
nor excuse for being content, as so many people are content, with the same
half-a-dozen 'usual' vegetables, mostly boiled to death in 'plenty of fast boiling
water.' There are ever so many different vegetables for us to enjoy at different
times of the year, and there are countless ways of preparing them for the
table, cooked and uncooked, as this book will show. Its publication has been
undertaken in order to make the less 'usual' vegetables better known than
they are at present, and to offer a large variety of recipes for all the more usual
vegetables.

There are four fundamental rules, practically without exceptions, to be
remembered whenever one buys or cooks vegetables:

51

1. The freshest vegetables are the best; young and small ones are better than large and old ones; wilted and bruised ones may cost less but are worthless;
2. Vegetables should be cooked in a minimum of water and of time; overcooked vegetables lose not only their flavour but their precious vitamins;
3. Salt should be added to the water in which vegetables are to be cooked, but not bicarbonate of soda;
4. The water in which vegetables have been cooked must not be thrown away but saved for soups or gravies.

VEGETABLE TIME TABLE

SINCE many Americans pressure-cook their vegetables, the following table may be useful. The time of cooking will of course vary with the age and freshness of the vegetables. The manufacturer's directions that accompany your pressure cooker should also be consulted.

	Boiled	*Pressure Cooker* *(at 15 pounds)*
Artichoke, French	25 to 40 min.	10 min.
Jerusalem	20 to 35 min.	2½ min.
Asparagus	15 to 35 min.	†2½ min.
Beans, Pod (string)	35 min. to 1 hr.	†2½ min.
Lima or other green beans	30 to 45 min.	†1 min.
Beets	30 to 45 min.	†5 to †10 min.
Broccoli	25 to 30 min.	†1½ min.
Brussels Sprouts	15 to 30 min.	†1½ min.
Cabbage, young, whole	25 to 30 min.	†1 min.
Carrot, young, whole	15 to 25 min.	4 min.
sliced	10 to 15 min.	†2 min.
Cauliflower	20 to 30 min.	not recommended
Celeriac	15 to 20 min.	2 min.
Celery	*20 to 35 min.	†2 min.
Corn, green	5 to 15 min.	not recommended
Cucumber	*12 min.	†5 min.
Eggplant	25 to 35 min.	not recommended
Greens, general rule	20 to 40 min.	not recommended
Kohlrabi	25 to 45 min.	†3½ min.
Leeks	20 min.	†6 min.
Okra	20 to 40 min.	†3 min.
Onion	30 to 60 min.	†8 min.

	Boiled	Pressure Cooker (at 15 pounds)
Parsnip	30 to 50 min.	10 min.
Peas, green	15 to 40 min.	†15 seconds
Potato	30 to 40 min.	8 min.
Sweet Potato	25 to 30 min.	8 min.
Radish	*15 to 30 min.	not recommended
Salsify	45 to 60 min.	10 min.
Spinach	15 to 25 min.	†1½ min.
Squash, Summer	15 to 20 min.	†2 min.
Tomato	*15 to 25 min.	not recommended
Turnip	30 to 60 min.	†5 min.

*Stewed

†Set cooker in cold water to lower pressure quickly

Definitions and Recipes

ACCOUB

Lat. *Gundelia Tournefortii*. A Thistle of which the roots, shoots and flower-buds are not merely edible but deserving of all gastronomes' attention. Its own home is Syria and it grows freely in the lands and islands of the Mediterranean. The roots may be eaten in any way suitable for *Salsify* (q.v.); they are very much the same as those of the *Golden Thistle* in size and appearance. The shoots, when six inches long, can be cooked like *Asparagus* (q.v.) and the buds are best parboiled in salted boiling water for a few minutes, then tossed in butter, seasoned and served like *New Potatoes*. Their taste is both pleasant and intriguing; it reminds one of both the Globe Artichoke and the Asparagus.

ADZUKI

Lat. *Phaseolus angularis*. A bushy Eastern *Bean* closely related to the *Rice Bean*; both are extensively grown for food in China and Japan; it is eaten as *French Beans* (q.v.) when freshly picked, but the dried seeds or beans are crushed and made into a kind of flour used for cakes and pastry.

AGAR-AGAR

Lat. *Eucheuma spinosa*; *Gelidium Japonicum*; *Gracilaria Lichenoides*; Fr. *Mousse du Japon*. A name given to a number of red Oriental seaweeds from which various gelatinous substances are obtained, known as *Ceylon Moss, Chinese Isinglass, Japanese Agar, Mousse du Japon*, etc. In Europe it is chiefly used in biological laboratories, but in the Far East it is used extensively for food; sold in thin strips of white and almost transparent leaves, it is rich in carbohydrates and makes good soups and also jellies. The Salanganes, or Chinese swallows, use *Agar-agar* in the building of their nests that *Bird's nests Soup* is made.

AGARICS

See *Mushrooms*.

AGRIMONY

Lat. *Agrimonia Eupatoria*. A common perennial weed growing, mostly in waste places, in many parts of the British Isles. It bears a spike of dainty little yellow flowers. Stems, leaves and, flowers are picked together to make *Agrimony Tea*, one of the oldest of the homely spring beverages believed to cool and cleanse the blood.

ALGA MAR

Lat. *Durvillea Antarctica*. An edible seaweed highly prized in Chile for food; it is exported from Chile to the U.S.A.

ALLELUIA

See *Wood Sorrel*.

AMAZOMBE

Lat. *Gynandropsis Pentaphylla*. It is a weed highly prized as a green vegetable of the *Spinach* (q.v.) type, by the natives of Bechuanaland, Natal, the Transvaal and Zululand. Its leaves are also dried for winter use.

AMERICAN CRESS. LAND CRESS. BELLE-ISLE CRESS

Lat. *Barbarea praecox*; Fr. *Cresson de terre*. A common weed which is quite easy to grow and worth cultivating as a winter salad. It is also known in the U.S.A. as *Bank Cress, Upland Cress* and *Hedge mustard*. It is prepared for the table like *Watercress* (q.v.).

ANGELICA

Lat. *Angelica Arcangelica*; Fr. *Angélique*. An Alpine plant which grows freely from Lapland to Spain. It is cultivated in France for making liqueurs and for flavouring as well as decorating sweets and confectionery. In England, it used to be bleached and eaten as a salad, but it is rarely seen now except in its candied form. In Norway and Lapland, they use the root as a substitute for bread.

ARRACACHA. ARRACACIA

Lat. *Arracacia Xanthorriza*. A South American perennial *Umbellifera*. Known in Spanish-America by the name of *Apio*. It is cultivated in Central and South America as well as in some of the West Indies for the sake of its farinaceous roots (*not* tubers); these are fried, boiled, baked and otherwise prepared in any of the many ways suitable for *Potatoes* (q.v.). The name is also given to the tuber of the *Oca* (q.v.).

ARROWHEAD

Lat. *Sagittaria Sagittifolia*; Fr. *Herbe à la flèche*. The name of some Chinese plants with leaves shaped like an arrow-head, and starchy roots. In the U.S.A. this plant is grown for, and used by, the Chinese.

ARTICHOKE

Lat. *Cynara Scolymus*; Fr. *Artichaut*. A Thistle, a native of Europe and Northern Africa, which has been cultivated for so many centuries that it has been improved beyond recognition. It thrives in every part of the temperate zone, all the world over, and nowhere better than in California. There are other vegetables called Artichokes, such as the *Jerusalem Artichoke* (q.v.) and the *Chinese Artichoke* (q.v.), but they have no *choke* and they owe their name to their flavour which is considered to approximate to that of the real *Artichoke*, the only one with a *choke*, which is also known as *Globe Artichoke*, *Crown Artichoke* or *French Artichoke*.

In Europe, *Artichokes* are in season from June to September; in the U.S.A. from November to May.

There are many different varieties of *Artichokes*; most of them are cultivated for their *bottom*, or *Fond*, the base of the scale of the flower and the flat receptacle out of which the *choke*, or flower-to-be, grows. There are, however, some varieties of small *Artichokes* such as the *Florence* and *Purple Venice Artichokes*, which may be boiled and eaten whole, when quite young. The smallest of all, really miniature *Artichokes*, are preserved in olive oil and packed in attractive little glass barrels, in Italy, and sold under the name of *Carciofini*. These *Carciofini* are greatly prized as hors-d'oeuvre.

Artichokes are comparatively rich in mineral salts, iron and iodine; wholesome and toothsome, but not helpful as regards the appreciation of fine wine. When quite young, small and tender, they are nutty and excellent, even if not suitable in cases of dyspepsia, and are eaten uncooked, as a hors-d'oeuvre, either *à la croque-au-sel*, that is with nought but a grain of salt; *poivrade* with a *Sauce Poivrade*; or *vinaigrette*, with a *Sauce Vinaigrette*.

Artichauts à la Barigoule
(Provençal recipe)

Tender artichokes
2 tablespoons olive oil
2 tender carrots
1 clove garlic
1 onion
Salt and pepper
1 glass dry white wine
A little hot water or stock

Only small and tender artichokes are suitable for the preparation of this dish. Place a tablespoonful of the oil in a saucepan — the type known as a '*Sauteuse*', which is a shallow broad-bottomed pan, is best. When the oil is hot, add the chopped onion and the carrots, cut into tiny dice. Lay the artichokes on this bed of vegetables, bases downwards. Sprinkle with salt and pepper and with the rest of the oil cover and cook gently, shaking the pan now and then to prevent burning. When the onion and carrots begin to brown, add the wine and continue cooking until reduced to half its original volume, then add the garlic, a few spoonfuls of either hot water or stock, cover closely and continue cooking until the artichokes are done. Serve as a separate course, straining the juice over all. Add a few drops of lemon juice just before serving.

Boiled Artichokes

Strip off the larger outside leaves; cut off the stalk, trim base neatly and rub with lemon to prevent it getting black. Snip off the end of each leaf with a pair of kitchen scissors to within a couple of inches of the base; remove the inner *choke* and tie a thread round the largest circumference of the artichoke. Plunge the *Artichokes*, head down, in fast boiling water, to which some vinegar or lemon juice has been added, as well as salt. Leave them to simmer for 15 or 20 minutes, according to size and age of the *Artichokes*, probe with a fork and when the bottom is tender, drain and dry the *Artichokes*.

Boiled artichokes may be served hot with a *Sauce Hollandaise*, a *Sauce Mousseline*, or any other unctuous sauce, or else simply with melted butter. Or they may be allowed to get quite cold and then be served with a *Sauce Vinaigrette*. They may also be stuffed and 'finished' in many ways.

Artichoke Bottoms (Fonds d'Artichauts)

The *Bottom* of the *Artichoke* is all goodness and it is the only part saved and served on ceremonious and other occasions when strict economy is not *de rigueur*. The *Artichoke* is first of all boiled, as indicated above, and then the leaves are carefully removed so that the bottom may be left unbroken. According to their size artichoke bottoms may be served either whole or in halves, either hot or cold, either as a vegetable course, 'finished' in many different ways, or as garnishings, with a 'filling' of peas, spinach, minced mushrooms or anything else in season or at hand.

Artichoke Bottoms

Fonds d'Artichauts Béchamel. Trim, blanch and drain the artichoke bottoms; toss in hot butter; season with pepper and salt and serve with a *Sauce Béchamel* poured over them.

Fonds d'Artichauts en fritot. Trim, blanch and drain the artichoke bottoms; cut them up and let them soak in a marinade of olive oil, lemon juice, pepper and salt and chopped chives until wanted; take them out then and dip them in a light batter; fry in deep fat and serve hot with fried parsley.

Fonds d'Artichauts farcis. Trim, blanch and drain the artichoke bottoms and finish cooking in butter with some stuffing, either mashed chestnuts (*Cévenole*); mushroom purée (duxelles); sausage meat and onion (*Lyonnaise*); spinach, Sauce Mornay and then browned (*Florentine*); olive oil and tomato fondue (*Niçoise*); risotto and Parmesan cheese (*Piémontaise*); onion purée (*Soubise*), etc.

Fonds d'Artichauts garnis. Artichoke bottoms are used very often as garnishings in the making of many elaborate dishes, whether hot or cold. When used whole, they serve as it were the part of a small saucer filled (i.e. *garni*) with some other vegetables or sauces, which give their name, on the menu, to the *Garniture*. Thus, when the artichoke bottoms are filled with hop shoots and cream, the name is *Anversoise*; if the name be *Argenteuil*, it means that the artichoke bottoms are filled with a purée of white asparagus; if *Bretonne*, a purée of white haricots; if *Conti*, a purée of lentils; if *Princesse*, a purée of green peas; etc.

Fonds d'Artichauts au Beurre. Blanch some artichoke bottoms in boiling, salted water from 10 to 15 minutes; drain them; toss them in hot butter; season with pepper and salt; add some finely chopped chives and serve with the butter from the pan poured over them.

Braised Artichokes

Artichauts Mireille. Take some tiny artichokes, remove coarse leaves and cook in a casserole with a glass of stock or water, a gill of salad oil, salt, peppercorns and twelve button onions. Then add two or three peeled tomatoes, cut in quarters, and cover. Let them cook fairly fast for half an hour and serve without dishing up.—A.G.

Cheesed Artichokes

Artichauts Milanaise. Blanch some large artichokes; drain and remove the choke; put the artichokes in a well-buttered dish and place in the centre of each one a pat of butter and a large spoonful of finely-grated Parmesan cheese. Cover the dish and put it over a gentle heat, leaving the artichokes to stew gently in their own steam until the leaves may be pulled off easily.

Artichoke Salad

Wash, trim and cut into quarters some small artichokes; scoop out the choke and rub with lemon juice; boil them in salted acidulated water for 10 minutes or so; drain, place in a buttered stewpan, season with pepper and salt, stew gently over a low heat and when tender remove and leave them to get quite cold. When wanted, dress them with a good sauce vinaigrette and some finely-chopped chervil and chives. Prawns, olives, filleted anchovies and ever so many other things may be added to the *Artichokes* to improve or vary the salad.

Stewed Artichokes

1. *Artichauts à la Provençale.* Take some small and tender artichokes; remove the first layer of outside leaves and cut off the tips of the remaining leaves. Put them into an earthenware pot and half cover them with warm olive oil. Season with pepper and salt; add a few onions and half a clove of garlic; cover the pot and stew on very gentle heat until leaves come off easily.

2. *Artichauts aux petits pois.* Prepare in the same way as the *Artichauts à la Provençale*, but do not use any garlic. When the artichokes have been stewing in their own steam for 10 to 15 minutes, add a pint or more fresh garden peas, also a lettuce and a bunch of parsley tied together, half a glass of water and some small pieces of bacon, ham or fat. Cover the pot again and go on stewing on a gentle heat until the leaves come off easily. Remove the lettuce and parsley 'bouquet' and serve in the pot.

ASPARAGUS

Lat. *Asparagius officinalis, var. altilis*; Fr. *Asperge*. A very widely-distributed plant which grows best in light, sandy soils, but adapts itself to almost any soil. It has been cultivated and highly valued for its excellent flavour and wholesome virtues from ancient times to the present day. There are a large number of different species of *Asparagus*, the most highly prized by gastronomes being the following:

Argenteuil, or *French Asparagus*, an improved variety of the Dutch asparagus, which produces very thick sticks with a pale purple tip.

Anglaise, or *English Asparagus*, which is thin and green and never grows to the size of the *Argenteuil*, but has more flavour and is greatly prized for asparagus salads and asparagus tips.

Belge or *Malines Asparagus*, a variety of the *Argenteuil*, large pale, fleshy and of a very good flavour.

Italienne or *Genoa Asparagus*, also known as *Asperge violette*, owing to its purplish colour; a free grower but not so good as the others in flavour.

Lauris, an improved variety of the *Green English Asparagus*, from the south of France; perhaps the finest all-round asparagus, for size, colour and flavour; equally delicious hot or cold.

Asparagus is rich in mineral salts and it stimulates the bladder, it also contains Vitamins A and B. Asparagus is probably the only vegetable that is acceptable not only hot or cold but even tepid. No less than 94 per cent of the weight of asparagus being water, it keeps the heat of the boiling water quite a long time.

The two most popular ways of serving asparagus are (1) plainly boiled, served hot with melted butter or a *Sauce Mousseline*, *Mousseuse* or *Hollandaise*; and (2) plainly boiled, served cold with a *Sauce Vinaigrette*, or with a *Sauce Mayonnaise à la Crème fouettée*.

Many people imagine that it is as easy to boil asparagus as it is to boil an egg, but, as a matter of fact, the proper cooking of asparagus is very difficult. One has only to be reminded that the point of the asparagus is tender whilst the stalk is not, to realise how difficult it must be to cook both at the same time. The Romans of old, who loved asparagus, always cooked it 'standing', and this is the only way to cook asparagus properly. The asparagus are prepared by cutting off the ends evenly and scraping from tip to stalk. They are then tied in a bundle. Water is brought to boiling point in an asparagus boiler, a narrow but very deep pan; salt is added to the water and the bundle of asparagus is then put in, standing, so that all the stalks are in the water and the points or tips are out of it; a lid, provided with one or two small holes for the steam to escape, is now put on the asparagus boiler which is left on the fire 15 minutes, for freshly picked asparagus, or 20 minutes for 'shop' asparagus. By that time, the *boiled* stalks will be tender and the *steamed* points will be cooked but not mushy, as they invariably are when the asparagus is boiled horizontally, and the whole of it treated alike. Failing a special asparagus boiler, a jar filled with boiling water and stood in a pan of boiling water will do, but then quite 30 minutes should be allowed for the cooking. Never put asparagus in cold water and bring the water to the boil: they will be tender enough in time, of course, but they will have no flavour whatever left and their taste will be no better than that of tinned asparagus. If you *must* cook asparagus in the bad old way, horizontally, put the bundle of asparagus in boiling salted water, boil them for 15 minutes and serve at once, after draining thoroughly; in that way there will be a good deal of the white stalks too hard to eat, but the green part will still hold together and retain its flavour.

The flavour of freshly-picked asparagus is so delicate that it is better to undercook rather than overcook this vegetable, and it is also advisable to eat it without any strongly-flavoured sauce. However, not all asparagus is freshly cut; it may come from a long distance and it may also remain in shops some time, in which case there are many sauces which it is justifiable to serve with asparagus. Moreover, there are traces of sulphur in all asparagus, not enough for the sense of smell to detect, but sufficient to spoil the enjoyment of red wine. Hence the different ways which have been devised of serving asparagus with grated cheese.

Cheesed Asparagus

Asperges Milanaise. Cook the asparagus, drain them thoroughly and dress them upon a long serving dish, in tiers; sprinkle the tips with grated Parmesan cheese and when ready to serve, pour some melted butter over the cheese and brown quickly under a hot grill.

Asperges Mornay. Cook and drain the asparagus; dress them in a long serving dish; cover the tips with some *Sauce Béchamel*; then sprinkle some grated cheese over them, and, at the time of serving, pour some melted butter over the cheese and brown quickly under a hot grill.

Pointes d'asperges

Besides hot, cold or tepid asparagus served as a vegetable course, the tips or points of the asparagus may be used in countless combinations, as hors-d'oeuvre, garnishings and fillings, in omelettes, with scrambled eggs, and practically with every form of egg, meat and poultry dish. Plain boiled asparagus points are best finished in butter or with cream, when hot; or with a light vinegary or lemon dressing, when cold, they are always welcome.

Asperges Polonaise

Cook and drain the asparagus, dress them in tiers in a long serving dish; sprinkle the tips with a mixture of finely-chopped yolks of hard-boiled eggs and parsley. At the time of serving, cover the tips with a mixture of *Beurre Noisette* and freshly-made breadcrumbs. (Grated cheese is sometimes mixed with the breadcrumbs, but not necessarily so.) Brown under a hot grill.

Asparagus Soups

Crème d'asperges. Cook for 5 minutes in salted water half a bundle of asparagus, two onions and two or three floury potatoes. Drain them well and put them in a saucepan with a piece of butter the size of a small egg, and two lumps of sugar; cover with a butter-paper and cook very slowly for a few minutes, being careful that these vegetables do not brown. Remove the paper, put in half water, half clear soup (preferably made with chicken or veal), allowing for reduction.

Bring to the boil and simmer for about half an hour. Meanwhile, make a little white *roux* in another saucepan.

Remove the vegetables, mash them through a sieve; add to the *purée* you obtain enough of the stock to make the soup fairly liquid. Pour it over the *roux*, bring to the boil and cook for 5 minutes more till it thickens. Finish by adding a yolk of egg diluted in a little cream, and a handful of asparagus previously cooked.—x.m.b. (3).

An Asparagus Soup made in a similar fashion but with tapioca instead of potatoes is known in culinary French as *Crème Montespan*.

Cream of Asparagus Soup. Boil the heads and stalks separately. When the stalks are soft, mash and rub them through a coarse sieve. Heat a pint of milk in a double-boiler. When scalding hot, thicken with two level tablespoonfuls of flour, and two of butter rubbed to a smooth paste. Add the water in which the asparagus was boiled and the pulp. Season with salt and pepper to taste and a very little sugar. Add half cup of rich, sweet cream, and then the heads. Let the soup get thoroughly hot and serve.—p.t.l.

Asparagus Soup. Asparagus Soup is well worth making with the heads that are not quite good enough for the table. For this you want thirty or forty heads and a quart of vegetable stock. The water which potatoes have been cooked in would be excellent. Cut off the tips of the asparagus and put them aside. Cut the stalks, which should have been well cleaned, into short pieces and simmer them for half an hour in the stock. Rub lightly through a sieve so that there can be no suspicion of stringiness in the soup; heat it up, and when it boils again add the asparagus tips and the seasoning required, and cook gently till the tips are tender, for about 10 minutes. Then stir in a gill of cream and serve with it *croutons* of fried bread and, if you wish, a garnish of a few very young peas.—a.h. (2).

Sprue or Wild Asparagus

The thin, green and hard stems of Wild Asparagus and of *Sprue*, the suckers of ill-kept asparagus beds are not to be despised, as their flavour is excellent and their cost trifling. They are quite good enough to use in the making of asparagus soups and with scrambled eggs or in any of the following ways:

Creamed. Wash, scrape and cut the sticks in pieces about an inch long, discarding all discoloured or woody ones. Boil gently until tender and serve with a white sauce to which the yolk of an egg should be added, either as an *Entrée* or on squares of buttered toast or within a border of rice.

Cold Asparagus

Asperges Vinaigrette. Boil the asparagus in the usual way, taking care not to overcook them. Drain upon a cloth and, when cold, set on ice. Serve with a very cold *Vinaigrette* Sauce.

Asperges à la gelée. Boil and drain the asparagus in the usual way and let them get quite cold. Cut up one or two hard-boiled eggs in even slices. Spread a little aspic jelly at the bottom of a mould, with a wooden spoon and let it get cold on ice or in a cool place. Place a layer of hard-boiled egg slices on the aspic and cover them with a layer of the same aspic jelly. Leave it alone until it is set. Then lay on it a layer of the asparagus tips and cover these with a layer of aspic jelly. Repeat alternate layers of egg and asparagus tips until mould is full and let the last layer of aspic jelly be thicker than the first. When this last layer is firmly set, and when time has come to serve the *Asperges à la gelée*, turn out upon a bed of young and fresh lettuce leaves. To turn out, wring a cloth out in very hot water and wrap it round the sides and bottom of the mould for a minute or two; it will help loosen the jelly which should then slip easily out of the mould.

Salade d'asperges. Green Asparagus are best for serving cold as a salad, with a dressing of oil and vinegar.

ASPARAGUS BEAN

Lat. *Vigna catjang*; Fr. *Volique asperge*. A South American Bean with pods from 1 to 2 ft. long and packed full of seeds of the kidney-bean sort, some reddish-brown and others yellow-brown. This bean cannot stand any frost; it cannot be grown in England except in some particularly sheltered places, but it flourishes in many of the southern parts of the U.S.A. A closely related species, known as the *Cuban Asparagus Bean*, is a vigorous, climbing plant producing pods some 3 ft. long. Another species, known as *Black-eyed Bean* or *Bird's Foot Bean* is grown extensively in Italy. It is cooked like *Haricot Beans* (q.v.).

ASPARAGUS BROCCOLI

See *Calabrese*.

ASPARAGUS BUSH

Lat. *Dracaena manii*. A West African plant, the young shoots of which are eaten cooked like *Asparagus* (q.v.). Natives of the Cameroons also eat the leaves, boiled, chopped up and mixed with rice.

ASPARAGUS LETTUCE

Lat. *Lactuca sativa, var. Angustana*. A peculiar form of *Cos Lettuce*, which never forms a head; its leaves are long and very narrow and of no value as a green salad. But its thick, swollen stem, when about 1 ft. high, may be boiled for about 25 minutes, drained, the outside fibrous cover removed and the inside pith is then eaten with melted butter or a *White Sauce*. It is also known as *Pamir Lettuce*.

ASPARAGUS PEA. WINGED PEA

Lat. *Psophocarpus Tetragonolobus*. An annual decorative plant, a native of Southern Europe, which has neither shoots, like *Asparagus*, nor seeds like *Peas*, but thin, green, rectangular pods; these are gathered when about 2 in. long; they are tender and tasty, but sometimes rather stringy; they should be simmered in a very little water during 10 minutes and no more. They are served with just a little butter, and pepper and salt to taste, either as a vegetable dish, by themselves, or else as an accompaniment to any meat or poultry or game course.

AYA
See *Chufa*.

BADDERLOCKS. MURLIN

Lat. *Alaria esculenta*. One of the edible sea-weeds gathered in the Faroe Islands and upon the northernmost coasts of the British Isles. It is also known as *Henware* and *Honeyware* in Scotland.

BALM. GARDEN BALM

Lat. *Melissa officinalis*. A hardy herbaceous perennial which grows wild nearly everywhere in the South of England and used to be cultivated extensively. It was one of the favourite 'strewing' herbs in olden days and was also used to flavour sour wine and to make a refreshing kind of 'tea'. Its leaves are sweet-scented with a faint and pleasing lemon flavour, and they may be chopped finely and added to green salad.

BALSAM APPLE. BALSAM PEAR

Lat. *Momordica balsamina*; *M. Charantia*. Two East Indian ornamental vines of the *Gourd* family which are widely naturalized in the West Indies. Their shoots are used in China and Japan as a green vegetable, but their fruits are not edible.

BAMBOO SHOOTS

Lat. *Bambusa arundinacea*. *Bambu* is a Malay name given to a large genus of woody or arborescent grasses which grow freely in most tropical and many sub-tropical countries in both hemispheres. The most important species is the *Bambusa arundinacea*, the hollow stems of which reach 5 and 6 in. in diameter; yet its shoots, when quite

young, are tender and tasty and they are used extensively for food. They are also canned and sold in England and the U.S.A. as a luxury food.

Bamboo shoots may be used in any way suitable for *Asparagus* (q.v.).

BAMIA

Lat. *Hibiscus esculentus*. The name under which *Okra* (q.v.) is known in the Near East and in France. It is chiefly popular in Turkey where it is eaten both in the summer when freshly picked in salads, uncooked, or fried in oil, and, in the winter, in the dried form: it looks then like haricot beans and may be cooked like *haricots*.

BANK CRESS
See *American Cress*.

BARBADOS YAM
See *Yams*.

BASELLE
See *Indian Spinach*.

BATATA
See *Sweet Potato*

BEANS

Originally the name of the large, smooth, kidney-shaped, edible seeds within the thick, furry uneatable long pods of the *Broad Bean*. In Europe where it has been cultivated from a very early date, it was the only vegetable known by the name of *Bean* until the sixteenth century. Since then, a number of other vegetables, mostly from South America and also from the East, are known as *Beans*. The following, selected as the more important gastronomically, are described briefly and will be found in their alphabetical order:

Adzuki Bean

Broad Bean (*Field* and *Horse Beans*).

Coco Bean.

French Bean (*Kidney Bean, Snap Bean, String Bean, Wax Bean, Wax-Pod Bean*).

Haricot Bean (*Boston Bean, Navy Bean*).

Kotenashi Bean (*Otenashi Bean*).

Lablab Bean (*Egyptian Bean*).

Lima Bean (*Burma, Madagascar Butter Bean, Rangoon Bean*).

Mung Bean.

Runner Bean (*Scarlet Runner*).

Sieva, Sibby or Civet Bean.

Soy or Soya Bean (*China Bean, Japanese Pea, White Gram*).

Sword Bean (*Jack Bean, Canavali Bean, Gotani* (S. Rhodesia) and *Sabre Bean*).

Tepari or Tepary Bean.

Velvet Bean.

BEAN SPROUTS

Bean Sprouts are greatly valued by the Chinese who serve them as a vegetable course or as one of the ingredients in Chop Suey. The best Beans for this purpose are the *Urd* (q.v.) and *Mung Bean*, but the *Soya Bean* is also largely used for the purpose; the Beans are soaked thoroughly in slightly warm water and germinated under a damp cloth for several days. *Bean Sprouts* are now obtainable, canned, in all parts of the U.S.A. and, fresh, in the vicinity of San Francisco.

BEET. BEETROOT

Lat. *Beta vulgaris*; Fr. *Betterave*. *Beet* is the more usual form in the U.S.A. and *Beetroot* the more generally accepted form in England. Both names refer to the cultivated form of a biennial plant producing, like the carrot, a thick, fleshy tap-root during the first year, and a branched, leafy, flowering stem in the following season. A very large number of varieties are cultivated, some for the sake of the sugar which is extracted from their roots (*sugar-beet*); others for cattle food (*mangel, mangold* or *mangold-wurzel*); others for their roots eaten as a vegetable (*Garden-beet*); and yet others for the sake of their leaves, stems and midribs or *Chards* (q.v.).

Boiled Beet Leaves

Take young leaves of garden beet, wash them, tie them together in bunches and put them into boiling, salted water; simmer till tender. Drain, chop and warm up again in open pan with a little butter or fat; season to taste and serve on buttered toast with or without a white sauce.

To boil Beetroot

Cut off all leaves and wash the roots, leaving all 'beards' or fibres and taking care not to cut or scratch the skin of the root; otherwise the red root will lose some of its juice during cooking and its colour will be spoilt. Put the washed roots in boiling salted water, cover the pan and simmer gently until tender. (Be sure that the water covers the roots completely.) Larger roots take longer. When cooked, take the roots out of the water, cut off 'tails' and rub off the outer skin and fibres.

To bake Beetroot

Wash beetroots carefully and if the skin has been scratched or cut anywhere, cover the damaged portion with a little flour-and-water paste. Arrange roots in a baking dish and bake in a moderate oven until tender.

Cold Beetroot
(Beetroot Salad)

Slice boiled or baked beetroot or cut up in small cubes, and serve as hors-d'oeuvre or salad, with a French dressing, some chopped parsley and, if liked, some chopped chives or onions. Sliced hard-boiled eggs may also be added, or/and some lettuce leaves, cold, boiled new potatoes, sliced, and practically any other vegetable.

Beetroot Soup

Bake three beetroots in water for 3 hours, then peel them and chop them up with a head of celery. Have a pint of water and the same measure of milk in a saucepan, and cook the beetroot and celery in this till they are soft enough to pass through a sieve. Having done this to them, add a spoonful of cream and a little butter, and serve.—A.H. (2).

Bortsch

This is the national Beetroot Soup of Poland and of some of the Western Provinces of Russia as well. There are many ways of making *Bortsch*, but two ingredients are quite indispensable, i.e. beetroot and sour cream. Here is one of many recipes for making *Bortsch*:

Make a rich *Pot-au-feu* with 2 lb. of beef, 1 lb. smoked bacon and a duck, and a faggot of dried herbs, a large onion with six cloves stuck in it, a spoonful of vinegar and a tumblerful of squeezed beetroot juice flavoured with some caraway seeds. Season with pepper and salt. Fry lightly in goose fat a *Julienne* of shredded or sliced beetroot, cabbage, white of leeks, celery roots and onions, and add it to the soup when the meat is nearly done. When quite done, take the meat out, cut it up, add some crisp Chipolata sausages and serve immediately after the soup. Before serving the soup itself, add as much sour cream as your taste tells you; heat again thoroughly; taste and season with more pepper and salt, if required, and a grating of nutmeg.

Beetroot Toast

Cut up a cooked beetroot in fairly thin slices and fry in hot dripping until well heated through. After removal from pan, drain the slices for a second, then season with pepper and salt to taste, add a little grated lemon rind to a teaspoonful of vinegar and pour over.

Arrange the slices of beetroot over rounds of hot buttered toast and serve immediately.—L.G.N.

Betterave à la Crème

Peel and slice some par-boiled beetroots. Finish cooking the slices in a good *Béchamel* sauce to which has been added a few muscatel grapes. Before serving add one or two tablespoonfuls of fresh cream and a dash of lemon juice.—D.B.

BELLE-ISLE CRESS
See *American Cress*.

BERGAMOT
Lat. *Monardadidyma*. An ornamental plant of American origin; its leaves have a strong scent of orange and are used both fresh and dried to flavour food and drinks. In the U.S.A., a kind of tea is made from the dried leaves of the *Bergamot*: it is called *Oswego Tea*.

BETONY
Lat. *Stachys Betonica* (U.K.); *Teucrium Canadense* (U.S.A.). Also called *Purple* or *Wood Betony*. A European weed which grows freely on roadside banks in many parts of England; it was grown in almost every cottage garden in olden times, and used to be as highly prized as *Vervain*. A wholesome hot drink is made in the same way as tea from its dried leaves and flowers. In the U.S.A. the name is given to a different plant altogether, the American *Germander*.

BLACK BRYONY
Lat. *Tamus communis*. A climbing plant which grows freely in many English hedges: it has bright, heart-shaped leaves and pretty red berries, but the only parts worth eating are its young shoots, in the spring: they must be soaked in salted water for an hour or two and then put in fast-boiling salted water and simmered until tender, when they can be served with a white sauce, a *Sauce Hollandaise*, or a *Sauce Vinaigrette*, in the same way as Asparagus (q.v.).

BLACK-EYED BEAN
See *Asparagus Bean*.

BLACK-EYED PEA
See *Cowpea*.

BLACK GRAM
See *Urd*.

BLACK JACK
Lat. *Bidens pilosa*; Afrikaans *Knapsekerel*. An annual herb from 2 to 3 ft. in height, which is a troublesome weed in many parts of the Union of South Africa, and is eaten by the natives as a green vegetable, in Zululand and Swaziland.

BLEWIT
See *Mushrooms*.

BONAVIS BEAN
See *Lablab Bean*.

BRACKEN. BRAKE
Lat. *Pteris aquilina*; Fr. *Fougère*. The young fronds of the common bracken are rich in potash and they are an important food in the Far East. Bracken fronds, shaped like a fiddlehead and known as *Fiddleheads*, are a popular food in Eastern Canada and are canned for export. They are eaten hot and cold, as a vegetable dish or a salad, cooked and served like *Asparagus* (q.v.).

Bracken roots are also edible; they have to be dug up deep so that they grow no more – which is all to the good. They are boiled till tender, left to cool and served with an oil and vinegar dressing, or any sauce likely to make them acceptable. In the Canary Islands, they grind to powder bracken roots, mix it with barley meal and use the mixture to make a coarse kind of bread called *gofio*.

BROAD BEAN
Lat. *Vicia faba* (*Faba vulgaris*); Fr. *Fève*. Broad Beans are flat and broader than other beans; they are at their best when quite small, but one cannot buy them in shops when they are very small; nor can one get them easily from one's own garden at that early stage unless one happens to be one's own gardener. When half grown, or less, broad beans may be cooked like *Runner Beans*: they taste much better than they look. As they grow, however, the pods soon become furry inside, leathery outside and quite unfit to eat, whilst the beans put on a parchment skin which gets thicker and thicker as the days pass by, until the broad beans are big enough to please both gardeners and greengrocers. This outer skin renders the broad beans coarse of taste and very indigestible: it should always be removed before serving. This is easily done by blanching the broad beans, that is throwing them in fast-boiling water for a couple of minutes, draining, drying and rubbing them in a coarse cloth, when the outside skin should come off and go to the pigs' bucket, whilst the inner broad bean can be stewed or simmered in a little milk and water, or prepared in any other suitable way, and served either hot or cold, as a vegetable dish, as garnishing, in soups, as a hors-d'oeuvre or in salads. Very small broad beans, freshly gathered, may be shelled and blanched, and served cold and uncooked with a *Sauce Vinaigrette*, as hors-d'oeuvre.

Boiled Broad Beans
Put very small broad beans in a saucepan. Cover them with hot water; add pinch brown sugar, salt and 1 oz. butter. Cook on slow fire, uncovered, until the beans are tender. Drain and serve with a little more butter and some chopped parsley.

If the beans come from the shop, not your own garden, blanch them in boiling salted water, then remove outer skin and cook them as if they were small and tender.

(A very good sauce to serve with boiled broad beans is made as follows: Four tablespoonfuls of melted butter, one of minced parsley, a few gratings of nutmeg, a dash of pepper and two tablespoons of lemon juice. Serve hot in a separate jug.—L.C.)

Broad Beans Purée

Shell, blanch and skin a pint of broad beans. Put the beans in hot water; add salt, an onion, some mixed herbs, and cook on slow fire until the beans are tender. Drain and press through a sieve; season with salt and pepper and work in some fresh butter; a little thick cream, if available, is better than butter.

Fèves à la Paysanne

1 quart small broad beans
3 artichoke bottoms
1 thick rasher bacon or ham
Salt and pepper
2 lettuces
1 onion
2 tablespoons butter or oil
Dash grated nutmeg

Cut the heart of the lettuces into fine strips; trim the artichoke bottoms and cut into four or six pieces, according to their size; chop the onion finely. Cut the bacon or ham into rather small dice and brown them lightly in the butter or oil, then add the onion, artichoke bottoms, lettuce and beans, cooking all together gently, shaking the pan occasionally. Season to taste, cover pan well, after adding a couple of tablespoonfuls of hot water. When the beans are tender, there will be but a little liquid left, just enough to pour over them before serving.

Broad Beans Croquettes

Shell the broad beans and plunge them in fast boiling water for a moment; drain and slip off the skins. Cook in simmering water in an uncovered pan until tender; drain and pass through a sieve. Season the broad bean *purée* with pepper and salt; when cool, shape it into *balls* or *croquettes*; dip each one in beaten egg and breadcrumbs and fry in deep fat; serve with tomato sauce.

Broad Bean Salad

Boil some very small and young broad beans; drain and let them get quite cold. Dress with oil and vinegar, pepper and salt, and some finely-chopped chives or chervil. May be served as hors-d'oeuvre or as a salad, by themselves or with some thin rounds of new carrots.

Broad Beans Soup

Boil 2 lb. of young broad beans in salted water; add a sprig of herb savory (*Sariette*) to the water; when tender, drain and rub through a sieve. Put the *purée* in a saucepan with 1½ pints of good meat stock; simmer and stir about 20 minutes. Taste and season if needed. Serve hot with little fried pieces of of bread and, if available, chicken or game-meat cup up in small cubes.

Broad Bean Milk Soup

Boil 1½ lb. of young broad beans in a quart of water, to which you have added some salt, an onion cut in halves, a sprig of fresh thyme or a *Bouquet garni*. When the beans are tender, drain, but keep the water in which they were cooked. Keep a dozen or two of the broad beans to garnish the soup, and rub the rest through a sieve. Replace the *purée* in a saucepan with the water in which they were cooked; bring to the boil and simmer for 15 minutes. Dilute in cold milk a spoonful of arrowroot and stir it in the soup. Bring to the boil again, then move away from the fire, add a little butter, the yolk of an egg and ¼ pint of cream. Garnish with the reserved beans and serve hot.

BROCCOLI

Lat. *Brassica oleracea, var. Botrytis*; Fr. *Chou Brocoli* or *Chou-fleur d'hiver*. A native of southern Europe introduced into France and England from Italy at the beginning of the eighteenth century.

Broccoli is the winter and early spring Cauliflower. From the English market point of view, the season begins with the *Roscoff Broccoli*, a Brittany variety which cannot stand the frost but is cultivated with success in Cornwall; its head is rather small but tender, and it is available at the time of the New Year. Then there are a number of English varieties of hardy broccoli, which carry on until Easter, and some of these have very big heads. Usually during the months of February and March, in England, a comparatively new type of Italian Broccoli, the *Calabrese* (q.v.), or *Green Sprouting Broccoli*, is available. It is one of the best vegetables to be obtained at that time of year. Two earlier varieties have now been introduced, the *Early Purple Sprouting Broccoli* and the *Early White Sprouting Broccoli*, which throw up sprout-like tiny cauliflowers at or near Christmas time. In the U.S.A., *Broccoli* are obtainable from November till June, Middle West and East Coast supplies becoming available when the Southern and Western States' season comes to an end.

To boil Broccoli

Select young heads, strip off any wilted stems, cut off stalk close to head and soak in cold, salted water to get rid of any insects. Remove and place in a large saucepanful of boiling water. If the heads be very small and tender it is best to cook them wrapped in muslin to prevent their breaking up. The lid of the saucepan should be off during the cooking. As soon as the broccoli is done, take it carefully out of the water, drain well and serve on slices of toast with melted butter. Broccoli, when cold, is very good served 'en vinaigrette', as a salad course, with a border of potato salad or hard-boiled eggs.

Broccoli 'alla Parmigiani'
Wash and clean the broccoli well and put them for one hour in salted cold water, then rinse again, and cook in boiling, salted water with a little butter. Put 10 tablespoonfuls of white sauce into a stewpan with a little chopped-up onion, and boil for a few minutes, then add a ¼ lb. of grated Parmesan cheese. When boiling, add the yolk of an egg and a very little cayenne pepper, mix quickly and pour a little on a dish; lay the broccoli on it, pour the rest of the sauce over them, sprinkle with breadcrumbs and grated cheese, and put it in the oven for half an hour, until of a nice brown colour, and serve. (If you have no white sauce, use melted butter, cooking it less or it will be greasy.)—J.R.

Broccoli may also be prepared as horsd'oeuvre, garnishings, salads, soups, and in every other manner suitable for cauliflower (q.v.).

BRUSSELS SPROUTS
Lat. *Brassica oleracea*, var. *Gemmifera*; Fr. *Chou de Bruxelles*. A variety of cabbage introduced from Belgium early in the nineteenth century; it has neither heart, like the common cabbage, nor head, like the cauliflower, and it is cultivated for its sprouts, which are produced in the axils of the leaves all along the stem; their small spoon-shaped leaves are very closely and compactly wrapped round one another to form what we call 'sprouts'. They come into use late in September and are one of the stand-by vegetables of the winter.

The tiny, tightly-closed sprouts so appreciated in France are seldom to be found in English or American shops, where they are usually much larger. Always choose the smallest and of as even size as possible: be sure they are green and very fresh, or they will taste and smell horrible. Before cooking remove outer leaves, cut end and make a cross cut on bottom of each stalk.

Boiled Brussels Sprouts
After soaking in cold, salted water, throw the sprouts into fast-boiling water. Cook fast, uncovered all the while. When tender, but only just, remove and drain off every drop of water. Serve with a good piece of butter, salt and pepper, or toss them in hot butter until lightly coloured. This latter method makes the sprouts no less digestible than if plain boiled and served as soon as drained.

Small 'left-over', boiled brussels sprouts can be very good if *sautés* in a little butter or good beef dripping.

Brussels Sprouts Bonne Femme
Blanch the prepared brussels sprouts in boiling salted water for 5 or 6 minutes. Drain, put them in a saucepan with 2 oz. of butter to each lb. of sprouts, the butter being divided into small pieces. Season with salt and pepper, cover and simmer in the oven for 15 minutes, turning occasionally with a spoon, being careful not to break the sprouts.—C.M. (1).

Brussels Sprouts Fritters
Boil some nice close sprouts for 5 minutes, then drain them in a colander. Plunge this into cold water and let them drain again very well. Heat them up in a little butter, and then soak them in a frying-batter. Plunge them in a frying-basket into deep hot oil, and give them 10 minutes, when they should be a nice golden brown. A tomato sauce would go well with them, if they are being served as a separate course.—A.H. (3).

Purée of Brussels Sprouts
Blanch the sprouts for 5 minutes in boiling water, drain thoroughly and cook in butter till tender. Rub through a sieve and add a third of their weight of potato *purée*. Mix well over a slow fire, remove the saucepan from the fire and add two or three lumps of butter.—C.M. (1).

Brussels Sprouts au gratin
After the brussels sprouts have been cooked, put them back into the pan with a good piece of butter, some pepper and a little grated nutmeg; then put into a fireproof dish, sprinkle with grated cheese, moisten perhaps with a little cream, and then brown quickly under the grill.—A.H. (3).

Brussels Sprouts Soup
1 lb. brussels sprouts
1 oz. butter
1 ham bone

Boil a ham bone in a quart of water for a full hour. Remove outer leaves from the sprouts and set aside the smallest ones; cook these in plenty of boiling salted water until *just* tender, and no more; drain them and keep them hot. Boil the remainder of the sprouts with the ham bone until they are quite soft; take them out, pass them through a sieve and return to the pan; season with salt and pepper and a dusting of cayenne; bring to the boil and pour into soup tureen in which you will have put the smaller brussels sprouts previously cooked; also 1 oz. butter. Stir and serve hot, with or without a little grated cheese, according to taste.

BUCHU. BUCKU
Lat. *Diosma Ericoides*. A South African plant which grows freely in the vicinity of Cape Town. Its leaves are very fragrant, and they are used to make an aromatic and diuretic hot drink, which is vastly improved in taste and virtue when a sufficiency of Brandy is added to it.

BUCKSHORN PLANTAIN
See *Hartshorn*.

BURMA BEAN
See *Sieva Bean*.

BURNET
There are two distinct species of *Burnets*:
1. Lat. *Pimpinella saxifraga*; Fr. *Pied de Bouc* or *Boucage*. *Burnet Saxifrage*, which grows in damp meadows and in chalky districts in many parts of Great Britain, and is one of the oldest of cordial herbs: its seeds used to be made into sugar plums, like caraway comfits;
2. Lat. *Poterium sanguisorba*; Fr. *Pimprenelle*. *Garden* or *Salad Burnet*, the young leaves of which taste and smell 'cool', like cucumber, which is the reason why they were used – and may still be used – in salads and wine cups.

CABBAGE
Lat. *Brassica oleracea, var. capitata*; Fr. *Chou cabus, Chou pommé*. A native of Western Asia and of Europe which may rightly claim to be one of man's oldest and best friends among the plants of the earth. It has been grown for the sake of its leaves for so many centuries and in so many lands that there are a considerable number of different varieties now in cultivation. These usually fall into two main classes, the smooth-leaved and curly-leaved or *Savoys* (q.v.). There are, besides, many other members of the large cabbage family, some of which are cultivated for their flower, like the *Cauliflower* (q.v.) and *Broccoli* (q.v.); or their stems, like the *Kohl-rabi* (q.v.); or their sprouts, like the *Brussels Sprouts* (q.v.); or their leaves, like the *Borecole* or *Kale* (q.v.), the Chinese Cabbage or *Pe-tsai* (q.v.), and others. There are early and late varieties of cabbage and there are green ones, white ones, and others purple red, but the green are in the majority. Cabbages may be eaten raw, cooked or pickled. They are more easily digested when suitably cooked, but they may lose in the cooking nearly the whole of their Vitamin C and the greater part of their mineral salts.

A considerable number of cabbage varieties is grown in the United States of America for all-year eating as well as for 'kraut'; they are generally named after the regions where they are grown.

The Cooking of Cabbage
To boil cabbage in plenty of fast boiling salted water, which is the way recommended in practically every cookery book, ancient and modern, and in some of the recipes – otherwise excellent – which are given hereafter, is, in our own opinion, wrong. It means the waste of the vitamins and salts which are the more precious parts of the cabbage; it also robs the cabbage of its flavour and renders it uninteresting, gastronomically and dietetically.

Before cooking cabbage, all tough and discoloured leaves should be removed; the cabbage is then cut in four, the hard core and all the tough stalk of the larger leaves are cut away, each quarter torn apart with the hands to make sure that there is no form of active animal left, and the cabbage should then be left to soak in some cold, salted water with a little vinegar added, for 20 or 30 minutes before it is put in a pan with a mere tumblerful of hot water and just a spoonful of butter or fat; put the lid on the pan and the pan on a gentle heat; the cabbage will soon sweat and provide the moisture necessary for its own steaming and cooking. This is a better way than steaming cabbage in a double-boiler or 'steamer' in which it loses its colour. There are people, however, who find it impossible or difficult to digest cabbage unless it has been boiled in fast boiling water, when there is but little of its original goodness left in it, and if such people will have cabbage, it must be boiled in plenty of water for them. But there can be no excuse for serving much or even any of the water in which cabbage has been boiled. *All* the water must be squeezed out before serving. This may be done with a wooden masher, pressing the cabbage in a colander; failing a wooden masher a small plate may be used by way of a tight lid pressed hard upon the cabbage.

Cabbage, and all green vegetables, should never be cooked in an iron saucepan, but in a tin-lined or enamelled pan.

One of the reasons why cabbage is so wholesome is that it contains, besides much nitrogenous matter, a certain amount of sulphur, which is responsible for the evil smell of cabbage, when cooking. Varieties have been hybridized which are guaranteed to be free from this smell; it merely means that such varieties have been deprived of their sulphur content and are, therefore, inferior dietetically. It is claimed that a piece of stale, crusty bread on top of cooking cabbage will save its smell pervading the house; it need not be left more than 20 minutes, by which time the cabbage will have cast all its sulphur.

Braised Cabbage

Blanch a cabbage in boiling salted water for 10 minutes. Drain and let it get cool. Separate the leaves and lay them on a cloth. Remove ribs of the larger leaves. Season with pepper and salt and put in a saucepan lined with strips of fat bacon, one sliced onion, one carrot cut in two or four, and a glassful of white wine or meat stock. Cover with bacon rashers, put on a close-fitting lid and cook in a moderate oven for 2½ hours.

Cabbage Croquettes

Remove outer coarse leaves of the cabbage; cut it in four, core it and wash it well in water and vinegar. Cook in a pan with a little butter and no water, with the lid on, until quite soft. Chop it up finely and return to the pan, this time leaving the lid off so that all moisture may evaporate. Then mix with a thick *Béchamel Sauce*, bind with the yolk of an egg and let it get cold. Shape into round or flat *Croquettes*. Brush over with flour, dip in yolk of egg, then breadcrumbs, and fry in deep fat. Drain and serve with a cream sauce.

Cabbage Hotpot

1 cabbage
2 onions
1 lb. potatoes
2 oz. butter
Seasoning

Boil cabbage and slice it. Peel, slice and parboil potatoes. Peel and chop onions and fry them till soft in butter. Grease a fireproof dish with a lid and arrange in it layers of cabbage, onions and potatoes, finishing with a layer of potatoes. Cover and cook in a moderate oven until the potatoes are done. Take off lid and finish cooking just to brown potatoes. Sufficient for six people.—L.G.N.

Cabbage Knabrus

Onions
Salt and pepper
Cabbage cut fine
2 tablespoons butter

Butter a large cooking-kettle well and fill with alternate layers of cabbage and sliced onions. Cover kettle and place over low

flame and steam until vegetables are tender. Season with salt and pepper and butter. (*Pennsylvania recipe*).—C.G.

Two Cabbage Pies

I

Steam a tender cabbage till it is nearly but not quite cooked. Drain it. Chop it up finely and then mix with it the beaten yolks of two eggs and a tablespoonful of butter (also well beaten) and 2 tablespoonfuls of cheese. Put the mixture into a buttered fireproof dish. Sprinkle with breadcrumbs, put a few small pats of butter on top, and bake in a good oven till the breadcrumbs are browned.

II

Steam a large tender cabbage. Drain it, but do not throw away the liquor, which should go into vegetable stock. Peel six large tomatoes and grate one large onion. Put in a buttered fireproof dish layers of the steamed cabbage leaves and sliced tomatoes (double the quantity of cabbage to tomatoes and grated onion), with a little butter in small pats between each three layers (too much butter spoils the dish and makes it greasy). Finish with a layer of tomatoes. Cover with browned breadcrumbs quite ½ in. thick, adding a few little pats of butter, and put in a quick oven for a few minutes till thoroughly hot all through.—E.S.R. (1) .

Cabbage Salad or Cole Slaw

Wash, trim, core and shred a small, crisp and fresh cabbage; soak in cold, salted water; drain and dry well. Serve with a French dressing to which mustard has been added.

Scalloped Cabbage

Cook cabbage in a covered pan with very little water, and with some butter or fat, until tender. Drain, chop or shred and reheat with cream or a white sauce. Put creamed cabbage in baking dish, sprinkle over with breadcrumbs, dot pats of butter and bake until nicely browned.

Cabbage Soup

Put a pound of pickled pork into a saucepan of cold water with a bouquet of parsley, thyme and bayleaf, bring it slowly to the boil and simmer it for an hour. While it is cooking, cut up a carrot and a small turnip in little pieces and shred finely a good solid savoy. Take the pork and the bouquet out of the water, and put in their place the vegetables, seasoning them with pepper and, if necessary, salt. Bring to the boil again and simmer for another hour and a half, when you must add a little chopped parsley, an onion (or if you prefer it, a clove of garlic) finely minced, and a little of the pork cut up in tiny dice. Cook for another half hour and your soup is ready, just as it is, the piece of pork waiting modestly for to-morrow's breakfast sideboard. (AMBROSE HEATH. *Autumn in the Kitchen*, in *Wine and Food*. Vol. III, p. 53).

The most popular form of cabbage soup in France is called *Garbure*; the Russian edition of it is known as *Stschi*.

Stuffed Cabbage
1 large white cabbage
Rice (uncooked)
3 tablespoons fresh breadcrumbs
1 small onion
Sausage-meat
Salt and pepper
Butter
Stock

Cut off end of stalk close to head of cabbage, remove wilted outer leaves. Wash in several lots of cold salted water, pulling leaves apart to inspect for grubs. Blanch the cabbage in boiling water, then drain thoroughly. Meanwhile mix together the chopped onion, and the breadcrumbs, previously soaked in a little milk or stock and squeezed dry. Season well. Use this stuffing between the leaves of the drained cabbage, pushing it well down. Wrap the stuffed cabbage in greased paper and tie neatly into shape. Put it in a baking-tin, pour stock around and bake for at least an hour, basting continuously. When done, unwrap and brown surface of cabbage after adding small bits of butter on top. The gravy may be slightly thickened, but it should be 'short'.

Red Cabbage
'Having bought a sound and fresh red cabbage, I tear off and throw away the soiled and untidy outside leaves, exposing a firm and purple orb. With a sharp long knife I cut this orb into two equal halves. These halves, when laid open, are a pretty sight, the white hearts and the purple crinklings of the close-set leaves contrasting bravely. It is safer to purify the halves in salted water in the ordinary way, although the close growth of the outside leaves usually protects the cabbage from vermin. The next stage is to cut out the tougher parts of the heart, where the stalk was growing into the cabbage. Then, with the same sharp knife, one cuts the cabbage into large thin slices. Two large Spanish onions are freed from their outside skins and are sliced up in the same way. Next, some cooking apples, of the same bulk as the onions, must be peeled and cored and cut up into thin pieces. Meanwhile, a stewpan or casserole should have been placed over a very gentle heat, with a lump of butter in it. Over the melted butter one gently piles up the slices of cabbage and

onion and apple, moistening the whole with a good spoonful of vinegar and a small tumberful of cheap red wine. If there is Claret or Burgundy in the house which has been opened a day too long, it can be used with the cabbage, and if it has begun to go slightly sour, the quantity of vinegar will be lessened. A little brown sugar, some pepper and a little salt are to be added. The lid is placed *tightly* on the vessel and the cooking goes on for 4 or 5 hours, as slowly as possible. Now and again the contents of the pan should be turned over with a wooden spoon so that the butter is equally distributed. When the dish is ready, the onions and apples and cabbage will be found blended together in such a way that the apple and onion will hardly be recognized, while the cabbage will taste mild and refined. I serve this dish with very thin slices from a hot ham or from a baked piece of bacon, or with sausages on a cold day. When one can get into touch with a butcher who makes beef sausages really well, they go finely with this dish of red cabbage, although they are much cheaper than good pork sausages. If the cabbage is not all eaten at one meal – and I ought to say that the recipe just given will yield several pounds in weight – it can be kept until the next day; as it is greatly improved by being warmed up once or twice. Indeed, I have warmed up red cabbage five days running and it got better every day. Some people dislike this dish of red cabbage at first, and a few dislike it to the end; but those who acquire a taste for it sometimes become slaves to it and eat it too often, thus running the risk of getting tired of a dish which is delightful as a change though unsuitable as daily fare.'—E.O.

Chou rouge à l'Alsacienne
Shred very finely a red cabbage, wash it and scald it. Melt in a deep pan some pork fat or goose fat and brown in it a finely-sliced onion. Then put in the shredded red cabbage, moisten with two glasses of red wine and cook slowly for about 3 hours.

Chou rouge Flamande
Cut the red cabbage in quarters, remove all the hard parts, wash them well in several waters and cut them like a fine *julienne*. Put in an earthenware saucepan a good piece of butter and begin to melt it, add salt, pepper and a tablespoonful of wine-vinegar, then your cabbage, stir well, put the lid on and cook very slowly for about an hour and a half. At this stage of the cooking, add a few eating apples cut in small pieces and a tablespoonful of castor sugar, and go on cooking slowly for another hour. Serve very hot in the saucepan.—X.M.B.(2).

Red Cabbage Poblano

2 small red cabbages
1 cup beef or chicken broth
1 cup red wine

Wash the cabbages, cut into quarters, and put them into a double-boiler to steam for about 20 minutes with the lid on. Add the broth and the wine and cook for another 40 minutes, very gently, until the cabbage is permeated with the flavours of the wine and broth. Season with salt and pepper and serve.—H.P.

CABBAGE, TURNIP-ROOTED
See *Swede*.

CABBAGE, PORTUGAL
See *Couve tronchuda*.

CAFTA
See *Khat*.

CALABRESE
Lat. *Brassica oleracea, var. Italica*. An improved variety of *Broccoli*, generally found in seedsmen's catalogues as *Asparagus Broccoli* or *Green Sprouting Broccoli*. It produces an abundance of small flowerlets, during the summer and autumn, but it usually suffers from the first frosts. Its little flower heads are green instead of white; the flavour is excellent and no gastronome's garden should be without it. All recipes suitable for *Cauliflower* (q.v.) are suitable for *Calabrese*.

CALALU
Lat. *Xanthosoma hastifolium* and *Xanthosoma sagittifolium*. A tropical American plant which is used, chiefly in the West Indies and South America, as a vegetable in the same way as *Okra* (q.v.). It is also known as *Malanga* and *Yauta*.

CALAMUS
See *Sweet Flag*.

CALLA LILY
Lat. *Zantedeschia aethiopica*. The *Calla* or *Arum Lily* grows freely in many parts of the Union of South Africa, where the natives eat the young leaves and small shoots plainly boiled, as a green vegetable.

CAMASS
See *Quamash*.

CANAVALI BEAN
See *Sword Bean*.

CANTALOUP
See *Melons*.

CAPSICUM
(See also *Peppers, Pimento*.)
The name of a large genus of tropical plants producing a variety of Peppers and Chilies. The fleshy Capsicums (*C. annuum*), known as Peppers or Piments, may be grouped into two categories, the hot ones and the sweet, the flesh of the latter being without fire, though the seeds in the fruit are intensely hot. *Paprika* (q.v.) is made from those seeds. The sweet Capsicum, also known as Green Pepper, sometimes turns red when ripe, is used in salads, uncooked, and in cookery, either stuffed like *Egg-plants* (q.v.) or in vegetable stews. The hot kinds of *Capsicum annuum*, or *Guinea Pepper*, are cut in thin strips and are used both for flavouring and decoration in many dishes, chiefly in Hungarian cooking, in Italy, Spain and Portugal. A dish of *Rizotto*, for instance, colourless and flavourless as it is, may be given both colour and flavour by strips of red Capsicum.

The slender, long, red Chilies (*C, frutescens*)are the chief source of Cayenne Pepper.

Capsicums Stuffed with Rice
Drop the capsicums into boiling water and cook for 10 minutes. Drain and, with a sharp knife, cut round the stalk and take it out together with the pips. Stuff the capsicums with a mixture of cooked rice, a little chopped fried onion, parsley, a little meat if you have it, salt and pepper. Place in a buttered fireproof dish, add a little tomato sauce or vegetable stock and finish cooking in the oven.—M.K.S.

Capsicum may be prepared for the table in any of the ways suitable for *Egg-plant* (q.v.).

CARDOON
Lat. *Cynara cardunculus*; Fr. *Cardon*. A species of European thistle which is a first cousin of the *Globe Artichoke*. It has been cultivated for a very long time in the South of Europe for the sake of both its roots and its stalks. Its main root is thick, fleshy and tender; its flavour is very pleasant and it provides an excellent hors-d'oeuvre or salad, plainly boiled (but *not* over-boiled) and served cold, dressed with oil and vinegar. Its stalks, or rather the ribs of its inner leaves are bleached and are a good substitute for *Celery*, as a winter vegetable. In England, *Cardoons* have never been grown to any large extent, and in the U.S.A. they are often known as *Chard*.

To cook Cardoon
The outer stems, which are tough before they are cooked, are tougher still after being cooked; they look fine but are useless and must be discarded. None but the inner leaves must be used. The outside 'prickles' of the inner leaves must be pared off and the

'strings' which run the length of the ribs must be carefully removed. This being done, the leaves are cut in lengths from 4 to 5 in. in length and blanched in boiling salted water for 10 to 15 minutes. It is advisable to add vinegar to the water so that the cardoon may remain white. Drain, make sure that no 'strings' remain, and finish off in any way recommended in various recipes for *Celery* (q.v.).

CARNAUBA
Lat. *Copernicia cerifera.* A Brazilian Palm, the *Wax Palm*, the root of which is starchy and edible.

CAROB. CAROUBE. ALGAR-ROBA. LOCUST BEAN
Lat. *Ceratonia siliqua.* A shrub which is probably a native of Asia but grows freely in most countries bordering the Mediterranean Sea. It bears long pods the pulp of which is rather sweet and flavourless. It is eaten either roast, fried, or mashed, in balls and cakes.

CAROSELLA
See *Fennel.*

CARRAGEEN. CARRAGHEEN. CARIGEEN. IRISH MOSS. PEARL-MOSS. SEA-MOSS
Lat. *Chondrus crispus.* A dark purple or green, branching, cartilagenous, translucent, edible, seaweed which is common on many coasts, of northern Europe and North America. When dried and bleached, it is known as *Irish Moss.* It is used as a vegetable gelatine, forming a somewhat spongy jelly, in the making of Moulds and Aspics. It has to be well washed in several waters, left to soak overnight in fresh water, then drained and dried over the stove and stored for future use.

Carragheen Mould
Soak half a cupful of dried carragheen in water for 10 minutes; drain it; simmer for 15 minutes in milk with a flavouring of dried Elderflowers (2 teaspoonfuls), laurel leaf or sweet spice, strain it into a basin or mould, sweeten with honey or sugar and allow it to set. The addition of a little cream is a great improvement.—J.H.

Irish Moss Mould
½ oz. moss
1 pint of milk
2 strips lemon peel
Sugar to taste

Wash and soak the moss in cold water and simmer the milk with the sugar and lemon peel for 10 minutes, strain the milk on to the moss and boil for half an hour, then strain into a mould. Turn out when cold. (A well-beaten egg may be stirred into the mixture before straining.) A fruit jelly is made by using water instead of milk and adding fruit juice to flavour. The moss may be bought at some chemists' shops.—M.K.S. (2).

CARROT
Lat. *Daucus carota, var. Sativa*; Fr. *Carotte.* A native of Europe of which there are many different varieties cultivated in practically every part of the globe. *Carrots* are grown for the sake of their roots, some of which are long and tapering; others shorter and with rounded ends; they are also of different colours, but the red carrots are by far the most popular. Carrots were first introduced in England as a vegetable by the Flemings during the reign of Queen Elizabeth, but they had been growing in the sandy soil of many English coasts for centuries before. Carrots are with us all the year round, but the best are the *New Carrots*, that is, the first of each season. During the winter, we have to depend upon storage carrots, which are not so good; they are larger and their core is often inclined to be woody, in which case it should be removed. Both with young and old carrots, the flavour and the precious vitamins and salts are in and close to the outer skin. This is why carrots should not be peeled nor even grated, except in the case of carrot salads. They should be scrubbed with a good, hard, vegetable brush and cooked with their skin. In the case of old carrots, the old skin, after cooking, looks unsightly and it is easy to slip it off, but even then it should not be thrown away but rubbed through a sieve and added to either soup, stew or sauce in which the carrots are going to be served.

Carrots have many uses as a vegetable, but all attempts at using them as fruit, in puddings, for instance, have proved failures and are not to be encouraged.

To cook Carrots
Whatever may be the way in which the carrots are going to be 'finished' and served, they should practically always be prepared in the following manner: wash them well; scrub them hard, but do not peel nor scrape. Do not boil them but steam them half an hour, if new, or an hour and a half if both old and large. If in a hurry, slice the carrots in rounds and cook them in very little water and in a tightly-covered pan until tender.

Brandade de Carottes
Tender carrots
Thick *Béchamel Sauce*
Butter
Dusting grated nutmeg

Grind new carrots finely in a mincing-machine. Place in a saucepan with just enough water to prevent burning and a good lump of butter, cooking gently and stirring frequently until tender and mashed. All liquid should have evaporated. Remove pan from fire and add an equal quantity of thick *Béchamel Sauce*. Blend well and season with a touch of nutmeg to taste.

Carrots buttered

Scrub and steam the carrots until tender. Drain and put in a stewpan in hot but not brown butter; shake over the fire for a few minutes; season with pepper and salt, a pinch of castor sugar and a squeeze of lemon juice. Dish up in a hot dish and sprinkle with finely-chopped parsley.

Carrots 'alla Casalinga'

Cut up some young carrots into small pieces, and put them into a saucepan of salted boiling water. Leave them to boil for several minutes, then drain and put them into a saucepan, with 4 oz. of butter, some salt, and a little pepper, on a hottish fire to bring out the flavour. Add a little flour, and a little broth (or water) and boil again, taking care the carrots do not fall to bits. Then make a sauce with the yolks of two eggs, the juice of half a lemon, and a little chopped parsley, and pour it over the boiling carrots. Take them off the fire at once to prevent the eggs from getting hard, put them on a dish, garnish with fried parsley and fried sippets of bread, and serve up hot. —J.R.

Carrots 'en Casserole'

1 thick slice bacon or streaky salt pork
1 or 2 onions
Salt and pepper
Young carrots
Butter
Chopped parsley

After scrubbing the carrots, cut them into thick 'matches', longways. Chop the onion. Cut the slice of bacon or pork into cubes. Brown these gently in a casserole, with a little butter. Now add the onion and carrots, seasoning with salt and pepper. Cover closely and cook gently until carrots are done, then remove lid and increase heat a little to somewhat crisp and brown contents of casserole. Sprinkle with chopped parsley and serve in casserole.

Creamed Carrots
(Carottes à la crème)

Wash and scrub the carrots and either leave them whole, if they be young and small, or cut them up if large and not so young. Put the carrots in a *sauteuse* (shallow pan) and cover them with water. Season with salt, castor sugar and butter. Put the pan upon a quick fire and as soon as the water boils reduce heat or move the pan away and simmer until practically the whole of the water has evaporated. Cover the carrots then with fresh cream which has been heated separately, stir well in and go on simmering until reduced to the desired consistency.

Carottes aux fines herbes

Wash, scrub and steam some young carrots. Drain them, slice them and toss them for a few minutes in a frying pan with some fresh butter; season with pepper and salt and plenty of finely-chopped parsley and chervil mixed.

Flan aux carottes

Line a flan tin with puff pastry, cover with mashed carrots (see *Carrot Purée*) and garnish with some *Carottes aux fines herbes* (q.v.) on top. Put in a brisk oven until the pastry is lightly browned. This *Flan* is usually served as a vegetable hors-d'oeuvre, but it can also be served as a sweet, in which case sugar must be liberally added to the mashed carrots.

Carottes au jus

The carrots are prepared in the same way as *creamed carrots* (q.v.), but instead of hot cream, to finish with, some good veal or other meat stock is added.

Fricassée of Carrots

Take a bunch of small, young carrots, scrape them and wash them. Melt a good bit of butter in a frying-pan, and when it is getting hot, add the carrots and cook them, shaking them and rolling them about now and then. When they are about three-quarters done, add a rasher of bacon cut in very small bits, and some chopped parsley. Finish cooking and sprinkle with salt before serving.— A.H. (3).

Fried Carrots

Wash, scrub and steam carrots. Drain, when tender, and slice in as thin slices as you can. Fry them in boiling olive oil and serve with salt and fried sprigs of parsley.

Glazed Carrots

1 lb. young carrots
2 tablespoons butter
2 lumps sugar
Good stock as required

Put into an earthenware casserole the carrots, enough stock to cover, the butter and sugar. Simmer gently, shaking once in a while and leaving pan uncovered. The liquid will evaporate and become glazed. Sprinkle with parsley and serve as a garnish or as a course.

Carrots au gratin

Cut six large carrots in quarters, and blanch them for half an hour; then drain them and finish cooking them in stock. Pass them through a sieve, keeping them warm the while, season the *purée* with salt and pepper, sprinkle in a good pinch of flour and one or two tablespoonfuls of the liquor in which they were cooked. Now add separately three yolks of eggs and six well-whisked whites, mix well together, and pour the mixture into a shallow fireproof dish, well buttered beforehand. Bake in a moderate oven for a quarter of an hour, and serve as quickly as possible.—A.H.(3).

Carrot Jelly

Wash, but do not peel nor scrape, the required number of red carrots (yellow carrots are rather too sweet). Boil these till quite tender, and then pass them through a colander, pressing hard with a wooden spoon; keep warm. Dissolve a leaf of gelatin in some boiling hot consommé. Put the carrots into a jelly mould, pour over them the consommé and gelatin and let it all get cold. Turn out when cold and you will have a delicious vegetable jelly to serve with a salad or with slices of cold sausage, sardines, or cold meat; it may also be eaten as an Aspic. This jelly can be poured into individual small moulds and served with watercress.—B.H.

Carrot Boats with Peas

Long but tender carrots
Butter
Cooked green peas
Salt and pepper

Wash and scrub the carrots; scoop out centre, leaving a shell an eighth of an inch thick all around and shaping into 'boats'. Boil gently in salted water until tender but take care not to break. Drain well and pour over the carrots a little oiled butter, salt and pepper. Fill boats with nice freshly-boiled tender green peas.

This makes a nice garnish. It may also be served ice-cold, as a salad with *Mayonnaise*.

Carrots and Peas

Wash and scrub some freshly-picked carrots. Cook in boiling salted water until tender, drain. Mix with freshly-cooked green peas, binding the sauce with a tablespoonful of thick cream; season to taste.

Carrot Pie

This is one way to make good use of old carrots. Wash them and steam them or simmer them in as little water as possible. When cooked, peel off the skins, cut in halves longways, and remove the core. Rub the cored carrots, and their skin also, through a wire sieve, and then grate a large onion – that is, if you have six to eight largish carrots. Beat some 6 to 8 oz. of fresh butter to a creamy consistency and mix thoroughly well with it the sieved carrots and onion. Season with pepper and salt. Fill a pie-dish with the mixture and bake in a hot oven for half an hour. Garnish the top with finely-chopped chervil and parsley.

Carottes à la Provençale

Steamed carrots, sliced and fried in olive oil, an onion (sliced) and a tomato (peeled and quartered) being fried at the same time, usually in a shallow fireproof dish with a plate over it, in a hot oven.

Carrot Pudding

Take one cup of grated raw carrots, one-half pound of fine dry breadcrumbs, one teaspoonful of nutmeg, two of cinnamon and one-fourth of salt. Over this pour one-fourth cup of sherry. Beat four eggs very light with one-half cup of sugar, add four large tablespoonfuls of butter. Bake in moderate oven in buttered baking-dish about 45 minutes. Serve hot with pudding sauce. (*Mrs E. Smith's recipe*, 1742. *Adapted Market Square Tavern Kitchen*, 1937.)—W.A.C.

Carrot Purée

Wash, steam and drain carrots when cooked. Rub off the skin. Cut them longways and remove core, if they are old carrots. Rub through a sieve and return to pan. Season with salt and pepper and as much butter as you can spare; also sugar to taste. Mix thoroughly well. Add a little fresh cream before serving.

Ragoût of Carrots

The carrots scraped and washed, cut them across in thin slices and cook them slowly in water flavoured with a little lemon juice, a bouquet, grated nutmeg, salt and pepper. When tender, remove the carrots, keep them hot and go on reducing the stock by at least half.

Prepare a white *roux* to which you add little by little the reduced stock. Bring to the boil, let it thicken and reduce again. Put in the carrots, cook for a few minutes more, and just before serving, add, off the fire, a little piece of butter. The sauce should be well spiced and the consistency of cream.—X.M.B. (3).

Carrot Salads

The simplest form of carrot salad is peeled and grated carrot served on lettuce leaves, with or without French dressing.

Grated raw carrots lend themselves to ever so many combinations, both salt and sweet, with blanched almonds put through a mincing machine for instance, garden peas, seedless raisins, sliced bananas and so on.

Carrot Sandwiches

Raw carrots, finely-grated, and, of course, the younger the better, provided they are ripe, make an excellent filling for bread-and-butter sandwiches.

Carrots Sautées

Young tender carrots
Butter
Chopped parsley
Pinch sugar
Salt and pepper
1 tablespoon thick cream

A dish fit for a king–but only for those who grow their own carrots. Pick them quite young, wash, scrub and dry well. Melt a couple of tablespoonfuls of butter in a casserole; when it is melted but not too hot, add the carrots whole, and season with sugar, salt and pepper as desired. Cover casserole and cook gently for 15 to 20 minutes, shaking the pan gently and taking care the cooking is very slow. When done, remove casserole from fire, add cream, shake pan, add chopped parsley and serve.

Carrot Soup

Wash and scrub five or six large carrots and simmer until tender in a little salted water. Peel off the skin, cut in two, longways, and remove the core. Rub the carrots through a sieve and reheat the water in which they were cooked; when it comes to the boil, put in ½ lb. rice and then the mashed carrots. Simmer gently until the rice is soft but not mushy. Season with pepper and salt and butter; add the beaten yolk of an egg and a little fresh cream if possible and serve hot.

Carrot Timbale

2 cups sliced carrots
1 egg
1 extra egg white
1 tablespoon butter
Salt and pepper
Boiling stock or water
1 hard-boiled egg

Slice the carrots thinly until you have two cupfuls. Melt the butter in a pan, add the carrot slices and cook for 10 minutes, stirring continuously; then add the stock or water – just enough to cover carrots. Cook until they are quite soft, then drain well and press through a sieve. Slightly beat one egg white and add to the other egg, also beaten, and the carrot *purée*. Season well. Butter some small timbale moulds and lay in the bottom of each a round of hard-boiled egg or cut same into quarters or fancy shapes. Fill each mould two-thirds full of the carrot mixture, set in a pan of hot water, cover with greased paper and bake for 45 minutes in a moderate oven. Turn out and serve with a *Sauce Poulette*.

Carottes Vichy

Carrots enjoy the reputation of being beneficial in all cases of liver complaints, and Vichy has long been the Mecca of all who suffer from liver complaints. Hence the association of Carrots and Vichy. Any dish described in culinary French 'A la Vichy' is sure to have a garnishing of carrots. There is also a dish called *Carottes à la Vichy*. It is, or should be, a dish of small, new and tender carrots, steamed or cooked slowly in very little water – not necessarily Vichy water – seasoned with a little salt, no sugar nor brandy nor any spices; tossed to finish with in a little hot butter and served with finely-chopped chervil and parsley sprinkled all over.

CATAWISSA
See *Welsh Onion*

CATMINT. CATNIP. CATNEP
Lat. *Nepeta cataria*; Fr. *Chataire*. One of the most useful edging herbaceous plants; its leaves are too strongly aromatic for use in food, but its very small young shoots are acceptable in small quantities in green salads and some stews.

CAULIFLOWER
Lat. *Brassica oleracea*; Fr. *Chou-fleur, var. Botrytis*. A variety of cabbage cultivated for its undeveloped flowers, and not for its leaves. It is believed to have originated in Cyprus and to have been introduced to Italy probably during the sixteenth century; it is described by Parkinson in his *Paradisus* as Cole Flowers and the best flavoured of the Brassica tribe; whereas Loudon, writing in 1822, calls it 'the most delicate and curious of the whole of the Brassica tribe', a proof that it was by no means a popular vegetable at the time.

In England, cauliflowers are sown early in the year, sometimes under glass; they come on from June onwards until the autumn frosts. In the U.S.A., they are obtainable from one part or another of the country practically all the year round.

Gastronomically speaking, the cauliflower may be described as a *Broccoli* (q.v.) with a larger and more compact head, but no better in flavour, if as good.

Only those who have a vegetable garden can tell how much better a cauliflower is which was gathered in the early hours of the day, with the morning dew on it, than one picked in the afternoon after the sun has dried it up. Grated raw cauliflower is quite good, as part of a vegetable salad, but it must be washed well since it is not protected by skin or rind that can be peeled or scraped.

To cook a Cauliflower

There are ever so many ways to cook a cauliflower so that it may be safe, digestible and flavoursome; it provides an excellent background for a number of sauces and it can be baked or fried in a number of different manners, but it should never be boiled. It should either be *steamed* or cooked in a parchment bag, so as to retain its shape, its snow-whiteness and its flavour. An average cauliflower requires about 30 minutes steaming, and a particularly large head 45 minutes. It should be firm, not mushy, and it needs no better sauce than a little melted butter to be enjoyed at its best. When it is boiled to a pappy state and has lost all flavour, it is usually served with either a rich, creamy sauce or else a highly-seasoned one, the cauliflower being introduced in the menu under the name of the sauce served on it or with it. Steamed cauliflowers are served either hot with different hot sauces, or cold with different salad dressings.

Baked Cauliflower

Trim, partly steam and drain a cauliflower; cut up its head in small pieces and fill with them a buttered baking-dish. Cover with a white sauce, which may or may not be thickened with grated cheese – or crushed nuts – or sieved boiled chestnuts – or anything else that you happen to fancy or possess. Then sprinkle a fair quantity of breadcrumbs; put on a few pats of butter and bake in a quick oven for 15 minutes.

Cauliflower 'alla Piemontese'

Boil a fine cauliflower in salted water, and when done pour the following sauce over it: Chop up one small onion, and one or two anchovies very fine, cook with some butter and stock, add a few drops of vinegar, and a teaspoonful of sweet herbs chopped up fine. Cook for a few minutes before serving.—J.R.

Creamed Cauliflower

Remove all outer leaves of the cauliflower and steam for 20 minutes or so. Drain and divide the sprigs, placing them in a buttered pudding basin and pour over them a thin cream sauce made separately. Leave the basin in a fairly hot oven for 20 minutes longer, after having seasoned the sauce to taste, and serve hot.

Cauliflower Fritters

1. *English way*: Wash, trim and parboil a cauliflower; drain it, tear it in strips; dip these in batter and fry in deep fat. Serve in a folded napkin with sprigs of parsley.

2. *French way (Beignets)*: Trim, steam and drain a cauliflower; cut it up in smallish sprigs and season with pepper and salt, a little vinegar and a sprinkling of finely-chopped parsley and chives mixed; let them stand for 15 or 20 minutes. Then dip them in batter and fry in deep fat. Serve with a *Sauce Béchamel* or a *Sauce Tomates*.

Chou-fleur au gratin

Trim, steam and drain a cauliflower, then put it in a fireproof dish and pour over it a thin white sauce thickened with a little grated Parmesan cheese or a *Sauce Mornay*. Sprinkle fairly thickly with breadcrumbs on top; add a few small pats of butter, brown in the oven and serve hot.

Mashed Cauliflower (Purée Dubarry)

Trim, steam and drain a cauliflower and rub it through a sieve. To every pound of cauliflower *purée* add ¼ lb. mashed potatoes. Mix thoroughly in the saucepan, over a slow fire, and add a little butter and a tablespoonful of fresh cream. Season with pepper and salt, stir and serve hot with little snippets of fried bread.

Chou-fleur Polonaise

Trim, steam and drain a cauliflower. Heat some butter in a pan and when nut-brown, put in the pan two hard-boiled eggs finely chopped; then a cupful of stale breadcrumbs. Mix well and pour the mixture over the cauliflower; serve at once.

Cauliflower Salad, Raw

Grate a raw cauliflower and mix with it either some grated radishes or some tomato pulp or any other vegetable you happen to fancy and possess. Serve upon lettuce leaves with a *Sauce Mayonnaise*, a *Sauce Verte*, or a *Sauce Tartare*.

Cauliflower Salad, Cooked

Trim, steam and drain a cauliflower. Detach the little sprigs without breaking them and arrange them in a bowl. Pour over them a *Sauce Vinaigrette* before they are cold and let them get quite cold before serving.

Cauliflower Soufflé

Trim, steam, drain and sieve a cauliflower. Mix with it two tablespoonfuls of grated Parmesan. Season with pepper and salt and a little onion juice. Make a paste with 1 oz. butter, 1 oz. flour, a pinch of salt and a gill of water to each 4 oz. of sieved cauliflower and cheese. Mix all together over a quick fire and then add the yolks of two eggs, one at a time, stirring well, then a whole egg, and then fold in the whipped whites of the two eggs. Fill a greased *soufflé* dish half-full of the mixture and bake for 10 minutes in a hot oven. Serve as soon as the *Soufflé* rises.

Cauliflower Soup

Boil a cauliflower in salted water for 20 minutes, then halve it. Pass one half through a coarse sieve, and keep the other warm. Chop up a small onion and fry it for a few minutes in 2 oz. of butter with a bayleaf. Take out the bayleaf and add an ounce of flour. Mix well and cook a little longer, then moisten with a quart of white stock, stirring well. Boil a pint of milk and mix it with the cauliflower *purée*. Add this to the stock, season with salt, pepper, a little celery salt, and, perhaps, a suspicion of nutmeg, and strain. Serve with *croûtons* and the flowerets from the other half, broken into convenient pieces. The addition of cream should not be despised. (AMBROSE HEATH. *Summer in the Kitchen*, in *Wine and Food*. Vol II, p. 35.)

CELERIAC. TURNIP-ROOTED CELERY

Lat. *Apium graveolens, var. rapaceum*; Fr. *Céleri rave*. A European variety of celery cultivated for its thick turnip-like stembase, and not its stalks, which are not fit to eat. It is easy to store during the winter months and supplies a valuable stand-by for hors-d'oeuvre, soups and *purées*. It was introduced in England during the eighteenth century.

To cook Celeriac

In spite of the fact that so much of the goodness of all vegetables is in and near their skin, celeriac must be peeled before it is cooked; its skin has such a parchment-like stringiness that it must be removed. Small roots are best; they may be cooked whole; large roots are sometimes hollow or woody; they had better be cut in halves or quarters. Celeriac should be boiled slowly in good vegetable stock whenever possible (if not, in salted water) until it is tender to the touch of a fork. It can then be served covered either with melted butter or a *Hollandaise* or a *Béchamel Sauce*. Celeriac may also be cooked in practically every way suitable for cooking *Beetroot* (q.v.).

Celeriac fritters

Cut into long 'matches', or dice some celeriac; boil them in salted water until tender; drain, dry in a cloth, dip in batter, fry crisp in hot fat and serve with fried parsley.

Purée de Céleri-Rave

One large celeriac, two dessertspoonfuls of butter, some consommé water, a pinch of sugar, seasoning. Cut the celeriac in dice and blanch in boiling salted water, then drain. Put in a casserole 1 dessertspoonful of butter, the celeriac, the sugar, seasoning, and barely cover with consommé or water. Let simmer gently until quite cooked and then pass through a sieve; return to the casserole and reduce to the required consistency. At the moment of serving add the second dessertspoonful of butter, stirring well.—D.B.

Celeriac Sautés

Wash and peel off outside skin, removing all discoloured parts. Cut into rather thick slices and cut these into rounds with a fancy cutter having a scalloped edge. (The trimmings make good soup.) Melt some fresh butter in a casserole, add the rounds of celeriac and cook gently, shaking pan frequently and carefully turning contents to brown evenly. No water is required for this dish. When a nice colour, serve, after seasoning well and sprinkling with chopped parsley.

Celeriac à la Crème

After washing and peeling, cut into thick slices and then into cubes. Boil until tender, drain well and cover with a rich cream sauce when serving.

Celeriac Vinaigrette

Dice, boil, drain and mix with a *Vinaigrette*, serving when cold, as a salad.

CELERY

Lat. *Apium graveolens, var. dulce*; Fr. *Céleri*. A native of Europe cultivated extensively for its leaf-stalks or ribs; these are bleached and may then be eaten cooked or uncooked. Celery is in season as soon as the first frosts are come and throughout the winter months right up to April.

Celery is really the cultivated variety of a common English weed called *Smallage*, which Italian gardeners improved beyond recognition during the seventeenth century.

How to cook Celery

Celery that has been boiled in salted boiling water, as so many cookery books direct, is utterly spoilt. Celery should *never* be boiled in plain water, salted or no. When it is not too large, celery is best uncooked. When it is rather large, it is best either braised or stewed, and stewed slowly either in veal or chicken stock, or else in vegetable stock, that is, water in which onions, carrots, Jerusalem artichokes, etc., have been boiled.

Baked Celery with Cheese

1 or 2 heads boiled celery
Salt and pepper
Butter
1½ cups white sauce
½ cup grated cheese
Brown breadcrumbs

The celery being cooked until tender and well-drained, cut into suitable lengths. Put a layer of this in a buttered baking-dish, cover with a layer of sauce and a sprinkling of seasoned crumbs and cheese. Repeat again and cover surface thickly with mixed cheese and crumbs. Dot with pieces of butter and bake for 10 minutes or until top is brown and crisp.

Braised Celery

Remove outer stalks; wash well; cut to desired lengths, place in baking-dish with just enough meat stock to cover; season with pepper and salt and a little butter rolled in flour; braise until quite tender and serve with what gravy is left in the baking-dish.

Céleri au Jus

Remove outer stalks from two or three fine heads of young celery. Braise the hearts until tender, drain well, then simmer in good stock or gravy until coloured and nicely impregnated with the seasoning. Tomato sauce may be used instead of gravy.

Celery Soup

Wash two heads of celery, cut them up in small pieces and toss these in hot butter for 5 minutes. Add a quart of good meat stock, bring to the boil, and then simmer gently until the celery is quite tender. Take it out and rub it through a sieve; return it to the saucepan. Mix 1½ oz. of flour in a pint of milk and add to the soup. Season with pepper and salt and bring to the boil; then simmer gently for another 10 minutes or so. The soup is now ready, but it can easily wait until the guests are ready for it. It must be served very hot, and fried sippets of bread served in the soup are an improvement.

Celery Soufflé

2 heads celery
3 eggs
½ cup grated cheese
Salt and pepper
1 cup milk
2 tablespoons butter
2 tablespoons flour
Dash lemon juice

Use hearts of celery. Boil in the milk, after cutting up, and simmer until celery is tender enough to press through a sieve after straining off the rest of the milk which must be set aside. Melt the butter, add flour and cook as if making white sauce, using the celery-milk and the egg yolks to moisten and bind mixture. Take great care it does not boil or, to make sure, cook in a double-boiler. Now add to this thick sauce the celery *purée*, the cheese, salt, pepper and the egg whites, beaten until very stiff. Do not beat mixture after these have been folded in. Pour mixture into a *soufflé* dish and bake in a fairly hot oven until risen well, then serve at once with very hot plates.

Note. A small onion and a tiny 'bouquet-garni' may be cooked with celery to add flavour to the milk.

CÈPE

Lat. *Boletus edulis*. The most popular member of the large *Boletus* family of mushrooms. It is found in large quantities in forests chiefly from the end of April until the autumn and it is dried, also bottled or canned, on a commercial scale.

Cèpes à la Bordelaise

Fresh or tinned cèpes
1 or 2 small cloves garlic
Salt and pepper
Shallots
Olive oil
Chopped parsley

Cèpes – large fleshy mushrooms found chiefly in France–are more readily available tinned than fresh in England and the States. Drain off liquid, cut off stalks and chop them finely with the shallots and garlic, using as much or as little of the latter two ingredients as liked. Pour a couple of tablespoons of pure olive oil in a frying-pan; when it is hot, use to fry the mushroom caps, cutting the very large ones into two or even three pieces. When they have been simmering gently for 10 minutes and have exuded their liquid, add the chopped stems and seasonings and continue cooking, turning the large cèpes to brown lightly. Add salt and pepper. When the oil is quite clear the mushrooms are ready to serve, with the addition of chopped parsley and a few drops of lemon juice.

Çèpes à la Crème

Cèpes
½ cup of rich cream
1 tablespoon flour
1 or 2 onions
Butter
Salt and pepper

Cut off the caps at end of stems and slice the latter rather thickly. Put a sufficiency of butter in a *sauteuse*, melt it, then add the chopped onions and cook until a light brown, stirring often, then add the cèpes, both caps and sliced stems. Season well and cover *sauteuse*, cooking to remove excess of water from mushrooms. As soon as they begin to boil remove lid and shake pan until all the liquid has evaporated, then add the cream into which the flour has been beaten. Boil up once, then serve. This method may be used for other kinds of mushrooms with success.

Grilled Cèpes

Blanch the cèpes for a few minutes in boiling water. Drain and sponge them dry. Dip in melted butter and grill under a hot grill; season with pepper and salt and some finely-chopped chives and parsley mixed.

CEYLON MOSS
See *Agar-Agar*.

CHARD. LEAF-CHARD. LEAF-BEET. SWISS CHARD. SEAKALE-BEET. SILVER BEET. WHITE LEAF-BEET
Lat. *Beta vulgaris, var. Cicla*; Fr. *Poirée*. These different names are given to a variety of Beets, cultivated for their *Chards*, or mid-ribs, instead of their roots. Chard is tender when young, and stringy when old; it has very little flavour of any sort at any time, but it is welcome at a time of the year when green vegetables are scarce. There are really two vegetables in one in chard, since the outer green of the leaves can be cooked just like *Spinach* (q.v.), whilst the white mid-ribs are cooked in any way suitable for *Sea-Kale* (q.v.). In large leaves, the mid-rib is some-times 3 and 4 in. wide, and it has to be cut up before being served. If one is to enjoy the faint asparagus-like flavour of the chard, which is seldom there because chard is usually cut up first and then boiled – it is important to remember that chard should be steamed and not boiled, and that it should not be cut up until after it has been cooked. Large chards require an hour's steaming; smaller ones, less time.

Chard is the name sometimes given in the U.S.A. to the *Cardoon*.

CHAYOTE
See *Chocho*.

CHERVIL (TURNIP-ROOTED)
Lat. *Chaerophyllum bulbosum*; Fr. *Cerfeuil bulbeux*. A native of Southern Europe which is cultivated for the sake of its bulbous roots which resemble, in shape and size, the *Early Horn* carrot; they are floury and rather sweet, with a distinctive aromatic flavour. They keep well and are mostly used in Italy and Southern France as a winter vègetable.

It is quite a different plant from the curly-leaf or salad chervil, a herb used for flavouring and garnishing.

Root chervil may be served plainly boiled and with a little fresh butter, like new potatoes; or with cream and chopped parsley, like new carrots; or mashed into a *purée* which, in culinary French, is known as *Purée Chevreuse*.

Chervil roots should be washed and scrubbed with a brush, but not peeled. Then they may be either boiled or steamed; if boiled they take about half an hour to be tender; if steamed, a little longer.

CHICKLING. CHICKLING VETCH
Lat. *Lathyrus sativus*; Fr. *Gesse cultivée*. It is also known as *Grass Pea* in the U.S.A. A European annual plant cultivated for its seeds: they are white in colour and irregular in shape. When unripe they are eaten like *Green Peas*; when ripe, they are dried and kept as a winter vegetable. They are used in the making of soups and in stews, like *Chick-pea* (q.v.), but they have no claim to the attention of gastronomes.

CHICK-PEA
Lat. *Cicer arietinum*; Fr. *Pois chiche*. A native plant of Western Asia and Southern Europe. It is extensively cultivated in all lands of the Mediterranean basin, in Turkey, India and the U.S.A. Its peas are used both 'fresh' and dried and mostly in soups and 'messes' or stews, such as the Spanish *olla podrida* and the Algerian natives' *Couscous*. Roasted *Chick-peas* are also used as a substitute for coffee. The best chick-pea is the white species grown in Spain.

In India the chick-pea is known as *Gram*, not to be mistaken for the *Green Gram*, which is the *Mung Bean* (q.v.).

CHICKWEED
Lat. *Stellaria media*; Fr. *Mouron blanc*. A troublesome and despised weed in times of plenty, but one that is quite acceptable as food for man, in times of scarcity; it can be cooked like *Spinach* (q.v.).

CHICORY. SUCCORY
Lat. *Cichorium Intybus*; Fr. *Endive Chicorée sauvage. Barbe de Capucin*. A European weed which has been used in its natural or wild form as well as when improved by cultivation, both as food and medicine, during many centuries. The roots of the wild chicory are long and thin, like over-grown radishes; they are lifted and planted in the autumn in moderately heated houses and in complete darkness; they produce long, thin, bitter leaves, silvery white at the base and pale yellow at the tip; they are used as a

salad, popular in France under the name of *Barbe de Capucin.* (q.v.). An improved variety which is popular in Switzerland under the name of *Salade des Alpes,* is known to seedsmen by the name of *Chicory de Trevise* or *Treviso.* Its tips are pale mauve and harmonize excellently with the deeper mauve of cooked beetroot.

The largest and best variety of cultivated chicory is known as *Chicory Witloof* or *Endive de Bruxelles*; its roots are like small parsnips and its tightly-packed silvery leaves are eaten either uncooked as a salad, or cooked in many different ways as a vegetable.

A closely related species, known as *Magdeburg Chicory,* is not suitable for forcing; it is grown chiefly for the sake of its roots, which are as large as those of the *Witloof,* and are used, roasted and ground, to adulterate coffee.

The salad known in England as chicory called Belgian endive in the U.S.A.

Braised Chicory
(Endives à la Flamande)

Remove outside wilted leaves and wash heads of chicory in salted water; arrange them in rows in a well-buttered shallow earthenware oven dish; season with pepper and salt and a squeeze of lemon; add a cup of stock or water, a few pats of butter on top of the chicory, cover with a greased paper and cook in a moderate oven till the chicory becomes soft; turn over and go on cooking slowly until the chicory is quite soft and almost transparent, and before it gets brown. It will take from 50 to 90 minutes to cook, according to size and degree of freshness of the chicory.

If you happen to be in a hurry, matters may be speeded up by plunging the chicory in boiling water for 5 minutes before braising. But chicory should never be boiled. When it is braised, however, in the classical manner, *à la Flamande,* it can be finished in many different ways, either *Au Jus* with plain meat gravy over it; or, *à la Béchamel, à la Crème, Mornay,* and so on; that is, served with a *Béchamel,* a *Cream,* a *Mornay* or any other sauce.

CHINA BEAN
See *Soya Bean.*

CHINA PEA
See *Cowpea.*

CHINESE AMARANTH
Lat. *Amaranthus gangeticus*; Fr. *Amaranthe de Chine.* The 'Spinach of the East,' a branching annual which is a native of China, and is grown in India and most warm parts of Asia, where it is one of the chief green-leaf vegetables. It can be prepared for the table in any way suitable for *Spinach* (q.v.).

CHINESE ARTICHOKE.
JAPANESE ARTICHOKE.
CHOROGI. KNOTROOT
Lat. *Stachys Sieboldii*; Fr. *Crosnes du Japon.* An Eastern perennial now being grown for the sake of its white, sweetish, underground rhizomes. These are not affected by frost and may be left in the ground all the winter, being lifted as and when required for immediate use. Once out of the ground, they rapidly shrivel and lose their flavour, a delicate flavour not unlike that of the *Globe Artichoke,* hence their name. They were first introduced into Europe by a Monsieur Pailleux of Crosnes (hence their French name) to whom rhizomes had been sent, in 1882, by Dr Bretschneider, the then doctor to the Russian Ambassador in Pekin.

The rhizomes of the Chinese Artichoke contain a substance known as inulin which looks like starch but behaves quite differently.

Boiled Chinese Artichokes
Wash and cut off stringy ends. Drop in boiling water for a moment only, take them out and rub the skins off in a rough cloth. Then put back into boiling salted water and simmer for 20 minutes, or until they are soft. Serve with melted butter or a cream sauce.

Fried Chinese Artichokes
Wash, cut off ends, parboil and rub off skins in a rough cloth. Then fry in butter, season to taste and serve; or dip in egg and breadcrumbs and fry in deep fat, and serve with fried parsley. *Some cooks do not rub off the skin of the Chinese Artichoke in order to avoid spoiling their attractive curly shape.*

CHINESE CABBAGES
See *Pak-Choi* and *Pe-Tsai.*

CHINESE MOSS
See *Agar-Agar.*

CHINESE MUSTARD
Lat. *Sinapis juncea* and *Sinapis rugosa.* An Asiatic Mustard, naturalized in many parts of the temperate zone; its leaves are as large as Spinach leaves and may be eaten uncooked like *Spinach* (q.v.). It is also sold under the name of *Tendergreen.*

CHINESE RADISH
See *Daikon.*

CHINESE TURBAN
See *Gourds.*

CHITO
See *Melons*.

CHOCHO. CHAYOTE
Lat. *Sechium edule*; Fr. *Chaiote*. The name of a
West Indian vine which was introduced in
Algeria in 1845, and is very popular in
Northern Africa. It is a fast-growing, climbing plant which may be either trained upon
stakes or allowed to run on the ground like a
gourd. Its fruit looks like a green pear with a
very thick and prickly skin. It must be
peeled, cut in two or four, and parboiled
after removing the seeds; it can then be
tossed in butter, boiled, fried, and, generally
speaking, prepared in any way that would be
suitable for the *Fonds* or bottoms of *Globe
Artichokes* (q.v.).

In South America and the West Indies,
where it is extensively cultivated, it is cooked
like *Pumpkin* (q.v.), made into soups,
mashed or made into tarts similar to the
New England *Pumpkin Pie*.

CHOROGI
See *Chinese Artichoke*.

CHOUCROÛTE
Choucroûte – Sauerkraut is made of white
cabbage which is shredded, a special kind of
wooden tub being filled with the shredded
cabbage, in layers, with a sprinkling of salt
and a few caraway seeds upon each layer,
until the tub is full to the top with closely-
pressed layers of cabbage. A little water is
added on top, then a cloth and then a wooden
lid with a heavy weight upon it to keep the
cabbage in its place. Every week, during the
next three weeks or longer, the lid and cloth
are lifted and the scum that has risen is
removed, a little salted water being added
in its place.

In England and in the U.S.A., however, it
is more usual to buy *choucroûte* or *sauerkraut*
ready for use, either freshly fermented from
the tub, in special *Delicatessen* shops, or in
tins, and all there is to it is to warm it up, if
out of a tin, or to cook it if out of a tub. The
Sauerkraut garnishings may be varied according to individual tastes and available supplies.

CHUFA. RUSH-NUT
Lat. *Cyperus esculentus*. A European sedge
with tangled roots intermixed with underground shoots, which become swollen and
form small, scaly tubers, brownish in colour;
their flesh is white, floury and rather sweet,
insipid when fresh; improving in flavour
with time, when properly dried; the tubers
keep well and are eaten during the winter
months both uncooked and roasted and
ground. They are also called *Tiger Nut*,
Earth Almond, *Aya* and *Zulu Nut*.

78

CLAYTONE
See *Winter Purslane*.

COCO BEAN
Lat. *Phaseolus vulgaris*; Fr. *Haricot vert*. The
Coco Bean is a variety of French Beans
which deserves special notice since it has
earned Sir Daniel Hall's verdict as 'the best
flavoured of the string beans class'. It has
small purple flowers and is very decorative
as a plant, being a climbing bean with beans
similar to those of French Beans but of a
deep purple colour. It should be grown as a
Runner Bean, although it does not grow
quite so tall and is a little later; it also has
better flavour and is more tender than any
other Runner Bean. In the cooking the
purple or 'blue' beans change to green. It is
listed in seedsmen's catalogues as 'Blue
Coco' or 'Indigo'. A dwarf variety of the
coco bean has also been introduced, usually
catalogued as 'Early White Coco'. When
picked young, coco beans are cooked just
the same as French beans; when picked after
the beans in the pods are fully formed, they
are shelled, like haricots and cooked as such.

COCO YAM
Lat. *Colocasia esculenta*. A tropical plant
grown chiefly for the sake of its tuberous
roots from which a starchy flour is obtained
which is called *Arum* or *Taro*. The roots of
the Coco Yam are usually peeled, steamed or
boiled and pounded to a paste, which is left
to ferment during two or three days, when
it is made into *Poi*, the staple food of the
natives of Hawaii. The leaves of the Coco
Yam, when small and quite young are also
eaten boiled and shredded, like spinach.
Also known as *Egyptian Ginger*.

COLE. COLEWORT
Lat. *Brassica campestris*; Fr. *Choux*. A general
name for all true members of the *Brassica
oleracea* genus or true cabbage family.

COLLARD. COLLARDS
Lat. *Brassica oleracea, var. Acephala*; Fr.
Choux verts. Any sort of cabbage the green
leaves of which do not form a compact
'head'. They are mostly large *Kales* (q.v.)
quite hardy and a useful standby, in many
English cottage gardens, during the winter
months. They can be cooked in any way
suitable for *cabbage* (q.v.).

COLTSFOOT
Lat. *Tussilago farfara*. A common English
weed, the leaves of which used to be
gathered, dried and used to make a medicinal
'tea'.

CORN
See *Maize*, p. 194.

CORN SALAD. LAMB'S LETTUCE

Lat. *Valerianella olitoria*; Fr. *Mâche or Doucette*. *Valeriana eriocarpa*, the Italian Corn Salad. A European weed which has been improved greatly by long years of cultivation and has become one of the most popular winter salads in France and Italy. The more extensively grown varieties are the French, or round-leaved corn salad, so-called in opposition to the Italian corn salad (Lat. *V. eriocarpa*), the leaves of which are lighter in colour, longer and somewhat toothed on the edges. Corn salad should be picked when the leaves are still quite small. It is one of the few green salads dressed without chopped herbs; it is usually served with thin slices of cooked, red beetroot; also with both cooked beetroot and thin sticks of uncooked celery: when dressed thus, its French culinary name is *Salade Lorette*.

COUVE TRONCHUDA. PORTUGAL CABBAGE

Lat. *Brassica oleracea, var. Tronchuda*; Fr. *Chou de Portugal*. *Couve Tronchuda* is the Portuguese name of a variety of cabbage which originated in Portugal and was introduced in England in 1821. It is also called *Braganza Cabbage* and *Sea-Kale Cabbage*. The white midribs are cooked in the same way as *Sea-Kale* (q.v.), and the head in any of the many ways suitable for *Cabbage* (q.v.). There is a very hardy variety known as *Curled Couve Tronchuda Cabbage* with smaller midribs, but leaves more undulated and curled. It stands frost better than almost any other kind of cabbage.

COW PARSNIP

Lat. *Heracleum sphondylium*. A common weed of many English meadows and hedges. Its leaves cooked like *Spinach* have an asparagus flavour, and make quite a pleasant change of green vegetables.

COWPEA

Lat. *Vigna sinensis*. A sprawling herb more closely related to the bean than to the pea. It grows wild in most tropical countries, and it is extensively cultivated in the Southern States of the U.S.A. for forage. The dried seeds, or beans, are also used for food. There are two sorts, the black and the white, and they are also called *White-eyed pea* or *Black-eyed pea*.

CRAMBE

See *Sea-Kale*.

CRESS. GARDEN CRESS

Lat. *Lepidium sativum*; Fr. *Cresson aliénois*. A native of Persia which can be grown quickly and easily almost anywhere. Its tiny leaves are used for garnishings and the fillings of sandwiches. Quite a different plant from *Watercress* (q.v.).

In England cress is usually grown and used with *Mustard* (q.v.), the latter being sown a week later than cress as it grows faster. Mustard and cress is served as a salad and used for making vegetable sandwiches. Cress is also served as a hors-d'oeuvre with either chopped olives, sardines, boiled beetroot, sliced hard-boiled egg, with an oil and vinegar or lemon juice dressing. But it is excellent by itself as a spread for sandwiches in the following way:

Cress Sandwiches

Wash the cress, dry it and chop it up roughly. Cream as much butter as you will require and work into it the chopped cress, as much as it will take; season with salt but no pepper. Spread on very thin slices of white or brown bread, and cut these in fancy shapes.

CRIN-CRIN. JEWS' MALLOW

Lat. *Corchorus olitorius* and *C. tridens*. Fr. *Corette*. A leafy vegetable which is extensively grown in many parts of the East, Far East and West Africa. It has also been introduced in France. Its leaves are eaten boiled and prepared in any way suitable for *Spinach* (q.v.). A slightly different species is grown for food in Angola.

CRINKLEROOT

Lat. *Dentaria diphylla*. An American toothwort with a knotted, pungent and succulent root-stock.

CUCUMBER

Lat. *Cucumis sativus*; Fr. *Concombre*. A creeping plant, a native of North-West India, introduced in England in 1573. It is cultivated both in hot houses and in the open for its fruit, which is mostly eaten uncooked or pickled; it is also cooked and eaten as a vegetable. There are many different sorts of cucumbers; the skin of some is white, of others yellow, but of most of them dark, shiny green and smooth. The *Chinese Cucumber* is light green and is marked longitudinally with white lines. There are small kinds of Cucumber known as *Gherkin* or *Pickling Cucumbers*, the most suitable for pickling being the small green *Paris Cornichon* in Europe, and the various *Pickling Cucumbers* in the U.S.A.

Cucumber is excellent for rubbing over the skin to keep it soft and white; hence cucumber soap is recommended to people of tender skin. There is practically no food value in cucumber and it is not easily digested by the majority of those who enjoy its flavour, but this is chiefly due to the fact

79

that uncooked cucumber is served, as a rule, peeled and cut in very thin slices indeed. Cucumber should be well washed and sliced thickly enough to ensure mastication. The rind of the cucumber is not merely rich in salts and flavour, like the rind or skin of other vegetables, but it contains minute – yet sufficient – quantities of a pepsin-like substance which helps digest the cellulose part of the pulp, with the assistance of the ptyalin brought forth by mastication. The value of cucumber lies chiefly in the subtle and *cooling* quality of its flavour. This can only be enjoyed when the cucumber is freshly picked and not cooked. Cucumber is served uncooked in a variety of ways, as hors-d'oeuvre, in salads and for the garnishing chiefly of cold dishes. Long strips of rind are also used in wine cups. Cucumbers, however, can also be used cooked in many different ways.

Boiled Cucumber

Wash a large cucumber and cut it crosswise in slices about 2 in. thick. Drop in boiling, salted water and simmer till tender. If you can spare the time, spare the cucumber the indignity of boiling and steam it till tender. It will be just as tasteless but not so watery and shapeless. Serve with a good white sauce, a Hollandaise or a cream sauce. The success of the dish depends upon the quality of the sauce.

Buttered Cucumbers

Pare and cut a good-sized cucumber into chunks of required size, removing seeds and stringy portions. Cook gently in salted, boiling water. Drain well, then *sauté* in butter and add half a teaspoonful of chopped parsley when serving. Once boiled, the cucumber may also be served in white sauce.

Fried Cucumber
I

Wash a large cucumber and cut it crosswise in slices about 1 in. thick. Steam for 15 minutes, then dry them and fry in butter till brown; season with pepper and salt and a speck of red pepper. Serve with fried parsley, or a tomato sauce.

II

Wipe, pare and cut lengthwise in $\frac{1}{3}$ in. squares. Dry between towels. Sprinkle with salt and pepper. Dip in crumbs, egg and crumbs again. Fry in deep fat (390 deg.) and drain.—w.h.w.f.

Cucumber Soup

Wash a couple of cucumbers and cut them crosswise in slices 1 in. thick. Toss them in sizzling butter 5 minutes and put them in a saucepan; do the same with two or three sliced onions; also cook in the same hot butter a handful of sorrel for a few moments and add to the pan. Fill pan with a quart of good stock, season with pepper and salt and simmer for an hour or so. At the time of serving, bind with egg yolk beaten with a glassful of fresh cream. Serve with *croûtons* of fried bread.

The best Cucumber Soup is the Russian *Rossolnick*, which is a *Velouté de Volaille* to which one adds some cucumber juice (*rossole*) and some pickled cucumbers (*agoursi*).

Squeezed Cucumber Sandwich

Cucumber, bread, butter, sour cream, chives, lettuce.

Sear with a fork one peeled hothouse cucumber and slice finely. Place in a porcelain bowl, sprinkle lightly with salt and add enough clear water to cover. Allow to marinate for 10 minutes, then drain and place cukes in a towel and squeeze. Spread thin slices of bread with creamed butter to which has been added a little sour cream. Cover lower slice with a layer of squeezed cucumber and sprinkle with finely-chopped chives. Press on upper slice and cut into any desired shape. Serve in napkin on bed of shredded lettuce.—a.s. (2).

Stuffed Cucumber

1 rather large cucumber
1 cup of stock or roast meat gravy
1 small 'Bouquet-garni'
Veal or sausage-meat stuffing
Salt and pepper
Fried croûtons

Peel the cucumber and cut into pieces about 2 in. long. Scoop out centres with care. Sprinkle with salt and leave it to disgorge water; then fill with any desired meat (or fish) stuffing. Set the pieces of cucumber in a saucepan with the stock or gravy and the 'bouquet' as well as the necessary salt and pepper. Cook very slowly until tender, then remove cucumber and allow gravy to reduce. To serve, place a piece of cucumber on a *croûton*, garnish the dish with tiny grilled tomatoes and parsley and hand the gravy separately. More stock or gravy may be added if desired.

CUSTARD MARROW

Lat. *Cucurbita pepo, var. Ovifera.* One of the most picturesque varieties of the *Squash* (q.v.) genus. It is sometimes called *Scollop Gourd.* Its fruit is flattened and broader than long, and it has regularly scalloped edges; its flesh is firm and rather floury, but not so sweet as that of the other members of the *Pumpkin* family. They are known according to their skin as Yellow,

Green, Orange, Striped and Warted Custard Marrows. They are also called *Elector's Caps*.

DAIKON

Lat. *Raphanus sativus, var. Longipinnatus*. The *Japanese Radish*, also called *Chinese Radish*. Its roots are long and hard; they are eaten both raw and cooked, like *Cucumber* (q.v.). *Daikon* keeps well and is an important article of food during the winter months in the East.

DANDELION

Lat. *Taraxacum officinale*; Fr. *Pissenlit*. A European weed which grows best in the poorest soils and is cultivated not only in Europe, but in Asia and North America for the sake of its bitter, toothed or pinnated leaves, which may be bleached, and are equally good uncooked as a salad or boiled like Spinach, as a green vegetable. The larger, outer leaves, however, should be removed as neither cooking nor dressing will make them acceptable. A brew made from *Dandelion* flowers used to be made in England and decorated with the name of *Dandelion Wine*.

DHAL

Lat. *Cajanus indicus*. Soak a teacupful of Egyptian lentils in cold water for 1 hour. Strain off the water and put the lentils into a stewpan with a small onion chopped very fine and 1 oz. of butter. Add a dessertspoonful of curry powder and 1 pint of good stock. Cover the saucepan and leave the mixture to boil for half an hour. Then add a little salt and continue cooking until the lentils are quite dissolved and are about the consistency of thick pea soup. Serve in a small well-warmed tureen with plain boiled rice in a separate dish.

The Dhal mixture may also be rolled with the boiled rice into rissoles and be dipped in egg and breadcrumbs and fried to a golden colour.—B.H.

DILLISK

See *Dulse*.

DOCKS

Lat. *Rumex Alpinus*, *R. Patientia* (*Herb Patience*); *R. Crispus* (*Curled Dock*). The *Mountain Rhubarb* or *Patience Dock*, and the *Curled Dock* are two valuable even if humble members of the large *Dock* family, which includes Sorrel and Rhubarb. All Docks contain a valuable alkaloid called *Rumicin*, as well as some chrysophanic acid, both of which have a beneficial effect upon the liver. They are best as pot-herbs, for flavouring, or added to spinach, sorrel or lettuce when cooked as vegetables.

DULSE

Lat. *Rhodymenia palmata*. Also known as *Dillisk* and *Dillesk*. A seaweed, reddish-brown in colour, which is gathered in some parts of Scotland, on the West Coast of Ireland and along the northern shores of the Mediterranean. Soyer introduced it to the *Grande Cuisine* as part of his *St. Patrick's Soup*.

DURRA

See *Dari Corn*.

EDDO

Lat. *Colocasia esculenta*. The root of the *Taro* and other related aroids which grow freely in many tropical lands. Also the leaves of an Egyptian variety, grown also in India, which are boiled and eaten like *Spinach* (q.v.).

EGGPLANT

Lat. *Solanum melongena*; Fr. *Aubergine*. A native of Asia introduced into England in 1597. There are many different sorts of Eggplant, some with egg-like fruit, others with cucumber-like or tomato-like fruit, and mostly deep purple in colour. There is also a white Eggplant, the fruit of which is like a hen's egg; it is used more as an ornament than in the kitchen.

Baked Eggplant

Do not skin the eggplants; steam them for half an hour; cut them lengthwise; scoop out the pulp as close to the skin as possible without breaking the skin. Mix the pulp with as much butter as you can spare and a finely-chopped hard-boiled egg. Fill the skins with this mixture, sprinkle over with breadcrumbs, then some small pats of butter, and bake in a fairly hot oven.

Aubergines Basquaise

Peel the aubergines, cut them in thin slices and put them in a dish with salt. After a couple of hours, when the water has oozed out, dry them, roll them in flour and fry them in hot oil till soft. Cook also in oil a few pimentos (sweet peppers), pips and skin removed; mix them with the aubergines and add a few tomatoes, also peeled. Cook slowly together about 20 minutes, see that it is well seasoned, and just before serving add chopped parsley. There should be about the same proportions of the three vegetables.—X.M.B. (1).

Broiled Eggplant

Do not peel the eggplants; cut them in thick slices; season with pepper and salt; dip in olive oil and broil for 5 minutes, each side. Serve with melted butter over them and some fried parsley.

Créole Eggplant

1 eggplant
6 spring onions
Bayleaf
Marjoram
Chopped parsley
1 tin tomato soup

Slice the eggplant in pieces ¾ in. thick, and cook, not too long, in a covered dish in a little water. Heat a little olive oil in a saucepan and cook slowly the cut-up onions with a little marjoram (chopped) and a bayleaf. When nearly cooked, add the chopped parsley, but this must be cooked only a little. Pour over this the tin of soup and simmer all together, stirring well. When hot, pour it over the eggplant and cook in a fairly slow oven for 10 minutes or so. A slight browning, almost scorching, at the edges, improves this type of dish. Serve garnished with grilled tomatoes.—H.P.

Fried Eggplant

Peel the eggplants, cut them up in thick slices; remove the seeds; dredge with flour and fry in olive oil or butter. Small eggplants may also be cut longways in 'fingers' and fried like *Pommes frites*.

Eggplant Fritters

Cut the eggplants in thin slices and let them stand, well salted for an hour or so. Drain and dry them, dip them in a good batter and fry in deep fat to a light golden brown.

Aubergines gratinées

Slice some aubergines as you would a cucumber and cook the thin slices in olive oil or butter till they are nearly black. Take them out of the pan and arrange them in thick rows in a shallow baking-dish. Cover them with equal quantities of cream and tomato *purée*; sprinkle some breadcrumbs on top and some pats of butter; bake in a moderate oven till browned.

Aubergines farcies Provençale

Carefully scoop out the flesh of four medium-sized eggplant fruits, cut the flesh into dice and fry until tender in butter with a few mushrooms, four or five skinned tomatoes, garlic and three onions. While this is cooking, par-boil the shells, being careful not to cook them too much, otherwise they will fall to pieces. When the flesh is cooked and seasoned, refill it into the shells, lay them in a baking-dish, sprinkle with breadcrumbs and dot with butter. Brown in the oven and serve very hot.—D.B.

Stuffed Eggplant

The eggplant is first of all cooked in butter or oil, steamed or boiled till tender. It is then cut in two, longways, the pulp is scooped out without the skin being cut. The pulp is then seasoned with pepper and salt and thoroughly well mixed with any and every kind of minced meat or sieved vegetables one may fancy or one happens to have ready for use. The mixture is then used for filling the half-skins, some breadcrumbs are sprinkled over, melted butter added and the stuffed eggplants are browned in a quick oven and served.

EGYPTIAN BEAN
See *Lablab Bean*.

EGYPTIAN GINGER
See *Coco Yam*.

ELDER
Lat. *Sambucus nigra*; Fr. *Sureau*. A widely distributed European tree which bears clusters of white flowers and of small black fruit, both the flowers and the fruit being used in the making of artificial wines, the flowers to impart a 'muscatel' flavour, much more aggressive than that of the best Muscat grapes; and the berries to give a deeper shade of colour to red wines. In England, in country districts, the buds, tops and early sprouts of the Elder used to be pickled, about mid-April; the flowers were picked in May and made into fritters or else dried and saved to make a kind of tea. Later on the berries were picked to make Elder Wine.

Elder Flower Fritters
Wash the heads of Elderflowers in salt and water; take out and dry carefully; then separate into nice-sized pieces; dip into a good batter and fry. Sprinkle with sugar before serving.—M.K.S. (2).

ELECAMPANE
Lat. *Inula Helenium*; Fr. *Aulnée*. An old-fashioned favourite of English Herb Gardens; it was cultivated chiefly for the sake of its rootstock from which candy, conserves and a sweet paste used to be made.

ELECTOR'S CAP
See *Gourds*.

ENDIVE
Lat. *Cichorium endiva*; Fr. *Chicorée frisée*. One of the finest of salads. It is a native of the East, and the date of its introduction into England is uncertain, but it is previous to 1548. There are many varieties of endive, all of them derived from *Cichorium pumilum*, the wild Mediterranean endive. In England, when not otherwise qualified, endive means one or other of the curled-leaved varieties, such as the *Anjou*; or small green curled summer endive, the *Meaux*, or small green

fine curled winter endive; the *Picpus*, or curled endive; the *Stag's Horn*, or *Rouen* endive; the *Louviers* or *Ruffec* moss-curled endive; the ever-white curled endive, etc. All broad-leaved varieties are called *Batavian Endive*.

A slate or tile placed in the centre of an endive, when almost fully grown, is all that is necessary to bleach its 'heart' or 'head', which is thereby rendered not only whiter or paler yellow, but more tender, hence more suitable for eating uncooked as a salad. Endive is also wholesome and of fine flavour cooked like *Spinach* (q.v.).

Endive also goes by the name of chicory, and is sometimes called *French Endive*. There is also a green salad known as *Green Endive*, which is neither endive nor chicory, but the *Prickly Lettuce*.

Braised Endives

1 lb. endives
Salt and pepper
Butter
Good gravy or meat glaze

If very young and tender, the endives need not be blanched in boiling water, but if they are rather large and somewhat open it is better to blanch them for 10 or 15 minutes. Drain well before braising. Lay the heads side by side in a large *sauteuse*, pour the gravy or meat glaze over them as well as a little oiled butter. Cover with a buttered paper; cover the pan and set in a moderate oven for 15 to 20 minutes. Serve the endives in their juice.

Endives à la Ménagère

This method is somewhat similar to the preceding, but simpler inasmuch as no oven-cooking is required. A large *sauteuse* – which is a shallow wide pan – is required as the endives should not touch one another while browning gently Put in the *sauteuse* two tablespoons of good butter, add the uncooked, well-washed endives, all dripping with water, but no other water is required. Season with salt and pepper, cover pan and cook very gently, turning each endive carefully to colour nicely on all sides. When ready to serve, the butter should be clear and the endives golden-brown. If accompanying veal, add, when serving, a couple of tablespoonfuls of the veal gravy to the endives, shaking them gently the while.

ERYNGO. ERYNGO CANDY

Lat. *Eryngium maritimum*. The candied root of the *Sea-Holly*, an English seaside weed with thistle-blue flowers and fleshy cylindrical roots. There is a similar *Eryngium* which grows wild on some of the northern coasts of the U.S.A., but its roots are fetid and unfit to eat.

EVENING PRIMROSE

Lat. *Oenothera Biennis*. A biennial plant, a native of Peru; its roots are tender and fleshy and may be eaten like *Parsnip* (q.v.).

EYEBRIGHT

Lat. *Euphrasia officinalis*. A European minute herb which is dried and used to make a kind of medicinal 'tea'.

FAN-KOT

See *Kudzu*.

FATHEN

See *Orache*.

FENNEL

Lat. *Foeniculum officinale*. A European weed which grows freely in the South of France and in Italy. Its only gastronomic merit is that it bears a multitude of little seeds which have a pungent smell and are used for flavouring. The cultivated or garden Fennel is grown for its fragrant seeds, which are used as a flavouring agent in confectionery and to make Fennel Sauce (*see p.* 25); for its bulbous roots which are eaten prepared in any way suitable for *Celeriac* (q.v.); and for its young shoots and small stems which are served like *Celery* (q.v.) either cold, with an oil and vinegar dressing, as hors-d'oeuvre or salads, or else cooked, as a vegetable. Fennel stems are available almost all the year round in Sicily, and are eaten, like celery, uncooked; they are very tender and in great demand in Naples, where a closely-related species of Fennel is grown, known locally as *Carosella*.

Boiled Fennel

Peel and slice the bulb and tender part of the stalk. Wash, drain, cook in boiling salted water until tender (from 25 to 45 minutes). Sprinkle with salt and pepper and either melted butter or hot olive oil and serve.— w.h.w.f.

There is quite a different kind of Fennel, the *Florence Fennel* (Lat. *Foeniculum vulgare, var. Dulce*), which is a native of Italy, where it is one of the staple vegetables, known as *Finocchio*. It is a thick-set, low-growing plant usually yielding two crops a year, the first early in the summer, and the other at the beginning of the winter. When the head or enlargement of the leaf-stalks at the base of the stem has attained about the size of a hen's egg, it is slightly earthed up, about half-way up, and cutting may begin a week or two later.

Finocchio should never be boiled in water but either steamed, or, better still, stewed in good meat stock. It can be prepared in practically every way that is suitable for *Celery* (q.v.). The more solid part of the finocchio base may also be served as hors-d'oeuvre, and in salads in the same way as *Celeriac* (q.v.).

FENNEL FLOWER
Lat. *Nigella sativa*; Fr. *Nigelle aromatique*. An erect-growing plant which is a native of the East and is grown in Europe for the sake of its seeds: they have a pleasant aromatic flavour and are used in confectionery. In Germany, the single-flowering variety is the kind chiefly grown; its seeds are known as *Schwartz-Kummel*.

FEVERFEW
Lat. *Chrysanthemum Parthenium*. A perennial European herb, once popular in England as a cure for headaches. Its leaves and flowers are dried and used to make a medicinal 'tea'.

FRENCH BEANS. KIDNEY BEANS. SNAP BEANS. STRING BEANS
Lat. *Phaseolus vulgaris*; Fr. *Haricot vert*. A native annual plant of South America. *French Beans* (U.K.) or *String Beans* (U.S.A.) are grown for their pods, gathered when the beans or seeds are still quite small or barely formed.

In the U.S.A., the name French Beans is sometimes given to String Beans. 'Frenched' beans are String Beans that have been shredded for quicker cooking. String Beans of a higher quality, not quite so copper-green in colour, are called *Haricots verts*.

There are early and late varieties of both the dwarf and the climbing kinds of French or String Beans, but climbing French Beans must not be mistaken for *Runner Beans* (q.v.). Most French Beans are green, but there are some varieties which are golden. The colour, however, is not quite so important as the mineral salts and vitamins content, to save which French Beans should not be *boiled*. They are best when smallest and stringless; all that is needed then is to 'top-and-tail' them, wash them, put them in a basin with a little butter and steam them, whole. When they are left to grow to what may be called a 'commercial' size as opposed to a gastronome's standard, it is usual to boil them, and regrettable; it is important to remove the string or filament binding the two shells together, and when they run to 'runner bean' size, it is also advisable to slice them thinly.

When French Beans or String Beans are left to grow long enough, the little beans inside become bigger and harder, whilst the green or golden pods themselves become tougher, fibrous and wholly indigestible. When they reach that stage, they cease to be French Beans, in England, and String Beans in U.S.A. They are shelled, like peas, the pods are thrown away and the seeds, known as Haricots, are eaten there and then, or else saved for winter use.

The name French Beans is supposed to have originated in England when their cultivation was introduced by French Huguenots during the reign of Queen Elizabeth. The American name String Beans is obviously due to the string which is by no means more stringy in American varieties than in Europe.

On both sides of the Atlantic, seedsmen have now introduced *stringless* varieties which can be relied upon to be stringless provided the beans are picked before they reach their full size.

Wax-pod Beans, in England, *Wax-beans* in U.S.A., refer to French Beans or String Beans with tender, golden yellow pods, which are stewed slowly, whole, when the beans inside the pods are nearly fully grown. In France they are known as *Mange-tout*. In England, they are sometimes called *Butter Beans*.

Plain Boiled French Beans
Have a rather large saucepan. Prepare beans by removing ends,– they should be young enough to have no 'strings'. When the water is boiling fast, add salt and a little soda if the water be 'hard'; plunge beans in and cover the pan until water is again boiling fast; then remove the lid and continue cooking until the beans are just tender enough to eat and have a slight 'bone' in them. Drain very thoroughly. Replace in saucepan, add a good piece of fresh butter and a sprinkling of salt and pepper. Some people also add a few drops of lemon juice to bring out the flavour of the beans. Serve at once, not allowing the butter to cook at all. Delicious as a separate vegetable course.

Haricots verts au beurre
Top and tail the smallest and freshest French Beans you can get; wash them, put them in a basin with a little butter and steam till tender. Toss them in an open pan with a little more butter for a minute or two and season with pepper and salt to taste. Serve hot *without* any chopped parsley.

Haricots verts panachés
Serve together, well mixed, half *Haricots verts au beurre* (q.v.), and half *Flageolets* (small, pale green haricot beans) cooked in the same way.

Haricots verts en salade

Allow some *Haricots verts au beurre* (q.v.) to get cold and dress them with oil and vinegar or lemon juice, finely-chopped chives and chervil; serve as hors-d'oeuvre or as a salad, either with or without other vegetables, such as new potatoes, garden peas, carrots, cauliflower flowerlets, etc.

Haricots verts Tourangelle

Top and tail the beans and slice them if necessary. Steam them, or stew them until nearly tender but not quite done, and finish cooking them with a rather thin *Sauce Béchamel*. Season with pepper and salt, finely-chopped chives (or a very little garlic) and some chopped parsley.

Wax-pod Beans, baked

Top and tail the beans but do not slice them. Put them in a thick earthenware pot with as much butter as you can spare, pepper and salt and two or three small onions. Cover the pot with a close-fitting lid and put it in a moderate oven where it can be left alone for an hour or so. Serve in the pot itself.

In the U.S.A. they sell a *Bean-pot*, which is made of crude, heavy crockery and has a lid to it, especially designed for the slow cooking of beans.

GLASSWORT

Lat. *Salicornia herbacea*. An inferior variety of *Samphire* (q.v.) which grows freely in salt marshes. It has cylindrical, jointed branches of a light, bright green, smooth, succulent and full of salty, bitterish juice. There are no leaves. Steeped in malt vinegar, the tender shoots are made into a pickle which is sometimes sold for *Samphire*, or under the name of *Marsh Samphire*.

GOA BEAN

Lat. *Pachyrhizus tuberosus*. A trailing plant which is sown in India towards the end of the dry season and trained over supports; it continues to fruit throughout the rainy season when other vegetables are scarce, and is used in any way that is suitable for *String Beans* or *French Beans* (q.v.).

GOAT'S BEARD

Lat. *Tragopogon pratensis*; Fr. *Salsifi sauvage*. The uncultivated or poor relation of the *Salsify*: it grows freely in some meadows; its roots are coarser than those of the *Salsify* (q.v.), but they may be prepared in the same manner.

GOBO

See *Great Bardock*.

GOLDEN GRAM

See *Mung Bean*.

GOLDEN THISTLE

Lat. *Scolymus hispanicus*. A native of Southern Europe; it is cultivated for its white fleshy tap-root, which is cooked in any of the ways suitable for *Salsify* (q.v.). It is also called the *Spanish Oyster Plant*.

GOMBO

Lat. *Hibiscus esculentus*. There are two different types of the same plant known as *Gombo*. One is a native of South America and is cultivated for the sake of its seed vessels which, when young, are tender and exceedingly mucilaginous; some are long and others round; the first are commonly known as *Okra* (q.v.), and the second as *Bamia* (q.v.). The plant itself as well as its pods are known as *Gumbo* in the Southern States of U.S.A., and as *Ochro* and *Okra* in the West Indies and in West Africa. In England, the pods are sometimes called *Ladies Fingers*.

The other is a native plant of West Africa, also known as *Wild Saur*, in Gambia. It is used as a potherb, and its leaves are also eaten like *Spinach* (q.v.). In India, where it is largely cultivated, its seeds are also eaten roasted.

GOOD KING HENRY.
GOOSEFOOT. MERCURY

Lat. *Chenopodium Bonus-Henricus*; Fr. *Epinard sauvage*. *Hondebossie* is the Afrikaans name of the various species of this weed, which is widely distributed in South Africa; it is called *Umbikicane* by the Zulus; it is an annual herb from 1 ft. to 3 ft. in height, with leaves covered with a white powdery substance; it appears with the pre-rain flora and is available at most times of the year. It is commonly used boiled, as a green vegetable, and is believed to be good against scurvy. In England the young shoots are earthed up and eaten, blanched, like *Asparagus* (q.v.) from April to June; later on its leaves are boiled like *Spinach* (q.v.).

GOOSE TONGUE

See *Sword Bean*.

GOTANI

See *Sword Bean*.

GOURDS

Calabash Gourd: *Lagenaria vulgaris*; Chinese Gourd: *Cucurbita Pepo, var. melo-pepo*; Crookneck Gourd, Dishcloth Gourd or Loofah: *Luffa cylindrica*; Gooseberry Gourd: *Cucumis anguria*; Malabar Gourd: *Cucurbita ficifolia*; Siamese Gourd: *Cucumis ficifolia*; Indian Gourd: *Luffa acutangular*; Snake or Serpent Gourd: *Trichosanthes anguina* and *T. dioica*; Towel Gourd: *Luffa aegyptiaca*; Wax or White Gourd: *Benincasa cerifera*; White-flowered Gourd: *Lagenaria leucantha*; Yellow-flowered Gourd: *Cucurbita Pepo, var. ovifera*.

The most picturesque and the least deserving of gastronomes' attention among the many members of the *Curcurbita* family. See *Pumpkin*, *Squashes* and *Vegetable Marrow*. The best gourds, gastronomically, are the *Turk's Cap* and *Turban*, the flesh of which is thick, floury, sweet and of a fine orange colour. There is also a small Chinese Turban Gourd, imported but lately from the Far East into England, which is a free bearer; its flesh is yellow, firm, floury and sweet. Gourds are mostly used for soups in the same way as *Pumpkin* (q.v.).

The fancy gourds called in French *Coloquintes* have no gastronomic value whatsoever; they are used as ornaments on account of their strange shapes and colourings.

The White Gourd is grown extensively in China and many parts of Asia; it is eaten in the same way as *Vegetable Marrow* (q.v.), and also in curries or made into a sweetmeat. Among the many other kinds of edible gourds esteemed in the East and Africa are the Calabash Gourd, the Towel Gourd, a small and highly-esteemed gourd, a native of India and Malaya; the Strainer Vine, called *Torai* in Hindustani, and *Djinji* in Malaya; the Snake Gourd, grown throughout India as a rainy season crop; the Dishcloth Gourd or Loofah, and a number of others.

GRASS PEA
See *Chickling Vetch*.

GREAT BURDOCK
Lat. *Arctium lappa, var. edulis*. The *Burdocks* of Europe are troublesome weeds, with edible but never-eaten roots. The *Great Burdock* is the aristocrat of the genus, and it has been cultivated so long in the East that it has become a vegetable of real gastronomic merit. In Japan, where it is known by the name of *Gobo*, its long, tapering roots are tender and tasty; some good judges have declared that they were better than the Salsify roots and they can be prepared for the table in any way suitable for *Salsify* (q.v.).

GREEN GRAM
See *Mung Bean*.

GROUND FURZE
See *Rest Harrow*.

GROUNDNUT
See *Peanut*.

GUINEA PEPPER
See *Peppers*.

GUINEA SORREL
See *Indian Sorrel*.

GUINEA YAM. KAAWI YAM
Lat. *Dioscorea aculeata*. A Polynesian Yam with prickly stems and sweet, starchy tubers.

HAI-TAI
The name of one of the most popular among the edible seaweeds of the Far East. It grows in separate strands fixed to the rocks on the bed of the ocean, among other seaweeds from which it has been carefully selected, separated and brought to the surface, where it is collected in boats. The best *Hai-tai* is collected by the women of the Japanese island of Quel-part, who, by long training, acquire the faculty of remaining under water quite a long time.

HAMBURG PARSLEY
See *Parsley* (turnip-rooted).

HARICOT BEAN. BUTTER BEAN. NAVY BEAN
Lat. *Phaseolus vulgaris*; Fr. *Haricot*. All *Haricot Beans* are highly nutritious and satisfying; they can also be delicious if and when properly prepared, and they possess over all vegetables the great advantage of being just as good, if not better, when kept waiting, an advantage in the case of people whose disposition or occupation makes it difficult for them to be punctual at mealtime. It is also well worth while to cook rather more than less haricot beans, since whatever quantity may be left over will be just as good, perhaps better, the next day, when warmed up, or served cold, with an oil and vinegar dressing, as hors-d'oeuvre or salad.

In Europe, haricots are the fully-grown or the partly ripe seeds of various kinds of dwarf and climbing beans. Some of these haricots are large and white (*White Rice, Comtesse de Chambord, Soissons*); others are smaller (*Flageolets*) and green (*Chevriers*), purple (*Chartres*) or brown (*Dutch*). In the Americas the same beans are cultivated as well as others, chief among them being the *Lima Bean* (q.v.). In India and China, in tropical and sub-tropical countries a large number of other beans are grown for their seeds or haricots and are described under their own names, such as *Adzuki, Kotenashi, Lablab, Mung, Sieva, Soya, Sword, Tepari* and *Velvet Beans* (q.v.).

Boston Baked Beans
'You soak in cold water a quart of navy beans overnight; drain and cover with more cold water, adding ¼ teaspoon of baking soda. Bring to the boil for 5 minutes. Drain and rinse with cold water – which firms up the beans. Then mix in the following: a

large-sized shredded onion, ¼ lb. of salt pork, scored, ⅛ cup of good molasses, ½ teaspoon mustard, 2 teaspoonfuls of salt. You lay the pork at the bottom of the casserole, pour over the beans, fill with cold water to cover, put on the lid and bake for *eight* hours in moderate oven. You may have to add more water after 4 hours. During the last hour and a half, lift up the pork from the bottom and let it cook on top. These are beans.'—F.G.F.

Boiled Haricot Beans

Wash the beans and put them in a deep pan; cover them with cold water and put the pan on a moderate heat so as to bring the water to the boil *very gradually*; when the water begins to boil, remove all surface scum and put in the pan two onions with cloves stuck in; two or three carrots cut in half or quartered according to size; a *bouquet garni* made up of a sprig of thyme, half a bayleaf, a clove of garlic and a stick or two of celery. Put the lid on the pot or pan and simmer gently till the beans are tender. Season with salt and pepper and finish cooking, or serve the beans in any way that you wish.

Creamed Haricots

Drain *Boiled Haricot Beans* (q.v.) when cooked and put them in another pan with a cream sauce poured over them; re-heat and serve.

Danish Beans

'Put ½ lb. of beans to soak in cold water for a day before using them; put them to cook with one onion and a pinch of herbs in well-flavoured stock with 2 oz. of bacon or ham; cook them for 3 hours. Remove the herbs and bacon; chop the onion fine and put it into a stew-pan with a gill of white wine, ¼ pint thick tomato sauce, four truffles chopped fine, or mushrooms. Add the beans, boil all together for 15 minutes, turn it out on a hot dish garnished with slices of hot smoked beef or tongue. Serve it very hot.'—P.A.

Haricots gratinés

Drain some *Boiled Haricot Beans* (q.v.) and put them into a fireproof dish, season with salt and pepper, moisten with a little meat stock or gravy, sprinkle with breadcrumbs, dot with pats of butter and brown in a quick oven.

Jugged Haricots

Wash some haricots, red or brown ones are best for this, put them into an earthenware pot, cover them with red wine, add a pair of pig's trotters, an onion or two, pepper and salt, and stew very slowly all day or all night on the back of the stove or in the oven.

Haricots Lyonnaise

Drain some *Boiled Haricot Beans* (q.v.) and mix well with some finely-chopped onions which have first been browned in butter. The proportion of beans to onions should be ¼ lb. onion to 2 lb. beans. Serve hot with a sprinkling of chopped parsley.

Haricot Mush

Drain some *Boiled Haricot Beans* (q.v.) and push them through a colander into a basin. Stir in a pint of milk to a pint of beans; season with pepper and salt and mix thoroughly, re-heat in a pan and serve hot from the pan or pot.

Purée Musard

Drain some *Flageolets* after cooking them as indicated (see *Boiled Haricot Beans*) and rub them through a sieve into a basin. Add 4 oz. butter to a lb. of beans, stir well in and thin with a little hot milk. Season with pepper and salt to taste. Re-heat and serve hot.

Purée Soissonnaise

The same as the *Purée Musard* (q.v.), but using instead of *Flageolets* the larger, white beans, known as *Butter Beans* in England, *Navy Beans* in the U.S.A., and *Soissons* in France.

Haricot Beans Salad

Drain *Boiled Haricot Beans* (q.v.) and let them get cold. Dress them with a *Vinaigrette Sauce*, with rather more vinegar than usual and some finely-chopped chives or onion.

Haricot Beans Soup

Drain ½ pint of *Boiled Haricot Beans* (q.v.), but save the water in which they were cooked. Slice an onion and shred a stick of celery; put them in a saucepan with some hot melted butter; then add the beans and stir together over the fire for a few minutes. Then add 2 pints of the water in which the beans were cooked, season with pepper and salt and bring to the boil. Strain, rub the beans through a sieve, put the *purée* back into the soup, stir well, re-heat and serve hot with some small *croûtons* of fried bread.

Butter Beans and Sorrel Soup (Purée Compiègne)

The same as *Haricot Beans Soup* (q.v.), but using only half the quantity of the water in which the beans were cooked and half milk. Also, before serving, a handful of Sorrel, shredded and cooked in butter is added to the soup.

Red Haricot Beans Soup (Purée Condé)

The same as *Purée Compiègne*, but with red haricot beans instead of white butter beans, and with red wine instead of milk.

87

Haricots aux Tomates

Cook the haricots as usual, but add, besides, half a dozen tomatoes, skin and pips removed, and cut in quarters, also one small piece of garlic, and let the whole thing simmer longer so that it is all well mixed, mellowed and rather over-cooked. This is a delicious accompaniment to grilled French sausages, which should be put in, already cooked, just for 2 minutes before serving.

HARTSHORN. BUCKSTHORN PLANTAIN

Lat. *Plantago coronopus*; Fr. *Corne de cef* or *Pied de corbeau*. A European weed which has been, and still is, cultivated for the sake of its green leaves, which make a pleasant green salad when young and tender. It is also called *Star of the Earth*. The wild species is widely distributed in sandy and stony places, more particularly near the sea.

HEARTSEASE

See *Violet*.

HEDGE MUSTARD

Lat. *Sisymbrium officinale*. A species of wild *Mustard* which is greatly appreciated and eaten as an anti-scurvy green vegetable by the natives in many parts of the Union of South Africa, chiefly the Eastern Cape, where it is known by the name of *Isiqwashumbe*.

HENWARE

See *Badderlocks*.

HERB PATIENCE. PATIENCE DOCK

Lat. *Rumex patientia*; Fr. *Oseille d'eau*. A European plant of the Sorrel genus; it is a free grower and used to be grown in most cottage gardens in England. It is prepared for the table like *Sorrel* (q.v.).

HERB YARROW

See *Yarrow*.

HONEYWARE

See *Badderlocks*.

HOP

Lat. *Humulus lupulus*; Fr. *Houblon*. Hops are not to be found in vegetable gardens, but whoever lives near a hop field should secure some of the tender shoots which, in the spring, sprout so freely that many are cut away in order to leave but two or three that will eventually be trained up the hop-pole. Hop shoots are used in the same ways as *Asparagus Points* (q.v.).

HORSE BEAN

See *Broad Bean*.

HYACINTH BEAN

See *Lablab Bean*.

ICELAND MOSS. LICHEN

Lat. *Cetraria icelandica*. A lichen with branched, flattened thallus, growing in mountainous and arctic regions and occasionally used medicinally or as food.

ICE-PLANT

Lat. *Mesembryanthemum crystallinum*; Fr. *Pourpier* or *Ficoïde glaciale*. The name of (*a*) a European plant (*Ficoïde*) with crisp, green leaves, eaten as a salad; and (*b*) the *New Zealand Spinach* (q.v.).

INDIAN CRESS

See *Nasturtium*.

INDIAN GRAM

See *Chickpea*.

INDIAN LETTUCE

Lat. *Montia perfoliata* and *Pyrola americana*. The name in U.S.A. of a round-leaved winter-green eaten like *Spinach* (q.v.).

INDIAN MUSTARD

See *Chinese Mustard*.

INDIAN POTATO

See *Yam*.

INDIAN RICE

In the British Isles, Indian-grown rice, chiefly Patna rice. In the U.S.A., another name for *Wild Rice* (q.v.).

INDIAN SORREL. ROSELLE

Lat. *Hibiscus sabdariffa*. Known in India as *Sour-Sour* and *Masha*. The leaves are used as a pot-herb for flavouring soups, stews, curries and salads. The fleshy calyces are made into preserves. In the West Indies, it is known as *Jamaica Sorrel*.

INDIAN SPINACH. BASELLE. MALABAR NIGHTSHADE

Lat. *Basella alba* and *B. rubra*. The names of two Asiatic plants, the white variety being a native of India, and the red a native of China. Both produce during the summer months an abundance of green leaves, which can be prepared in any way suitable for *Spinach* (q.v.).

INDIAN TREE LETTUCE

Lat. *Pisonia alba*. A coarse lettuce which occurs in the West Indies and is eaten boiled like *Spinach* (q.v.).

IRISH MOSS

See *Carrageen*.

IZIBO
Lat. *Nymphaea stellata.* A tuber which is eaten by the natives in Zululand and Natal. The seeds are also eaten in Senegal, fried in oil.

JACK BEAN
See *Sword Bean.*

JAMAICA SORREL
See *Indian Sorrel.*

JAPANESE ARTICHOKE
See *Chinese Artichoke.*

JAPANESE HORSERADISH
Lat. *Entrema wasabi.* A very pungent root much appreciated in Japan as a condiment, usually grated fine and served with uncooked fish.

JAPANESE PEA
See *Soya Bean.*

JAPANESE RADISH
See *Daikon.*

JERSEY CUDWEED
Lat. *Gnaphalium luteo-album.* A common European everlasting, which has been naturalized in South Africa where the natives eat it cooked like *Spinach* (q.v.).

JERUSALEM ARTICHOKE
Lat. *Helianthus tuberosus*; Fr. *Topinambour.* This very valuable vegetable was first observed as a cultivated plant by Champlain, in 1605, in Massachusetts. It was introduced in France in 1607 and was first of all called *Pomme de terre.* It was soon after given the rather ridiculous name of *Topinambour,* for no better reason than it was a curious looking root from overseas and that it had arrived only just before some curious-looking savages of the Topinambour tribe, who were brought to Paris and exhibited by one Claude Delaunay, Seigneur de Razilly, upon his return from a voyage of discovery to Brazil. From France the roots reached Holland and they were cultivated at Ter Neusen by Pastor Petrus Hondius who gave specimens to his friends abroad, including some in London, where the tubers first arrived under the name of *Artischokappeln van Ter Neusen,* which soon became anglicized to *Jerusalem Artichokes.* This is the explanation of the tuber's English name which was first suggested by Sir David Prain, and has been accepted by Professor Redeliffe N.Salaman. The name artichoke is easily accounted for since the flavour of the cooked Helianthus is not unlike that of the globe artichoke, but the 'Jerusalem' is more puzzling. As the name 'Jerusalem Artichoke' in England for this vegetable was used long before the name *Girasole* was applied to it in Italy, there can be no truth in 'Jerusalem' being an approximation of 'Girasole', which is the generally but wrongly accepted derivation of the name. More curious still is the name *Jerusalem Potato* given to this vegetable in some parts of the U.S.A., where Ter Neusen and Girasole have never been heard of.

Jerusalem artichokes are usually warty and unprepossessing-looking tubers; their taste is sweetish, their substance watery and their flavour not so fine, but quite as pleasing as that of the globe artichoke. They grow in the poorest as well as the richest soils, they are practically immune from most of the pests and diseases which attack other tubers, and they deserve a far greater measure of public favour than they have won up to the present in England and the United States.

There are different varieties of Jerusalem artichokes; the white variety is best for flavour; the reddish-skinned French variety is also very good and more pleasing to the eye, whilst the old fashion purple sort will always be popular, being a very free grower.

The Jerusalem artichoke tubers are rich in carbo-hydrates, particularly in inulin, which on hydrolysis yields *fructose* directly without intermediate products – apparently nine molecules of *fructose* being responsible for one of inulin. Hence some medical authorities have recommended Jerusalem artichokes to diabetic subjects who could not eat potatoes. Other authorities, however, absolutely disagree, and it seems probable that the suitability or otherwise of Jerusalem artichokes in cases of diabetes must entirely depend upon the personal idiosyncrasies and reactions of individual sufferers.

How to Cook Jerusalem Artichokes
To 'peel' or 'pare' the artichokes and 'boil in plenty of water', which is the advice given in ninety-nine cookery books in every hundred, is very bad advice indeed. Jerusalem artichokes should be well washed and scrubbed, but *not* peeled nor pared. They should be steamed or boiled in just enough water to cover them, and the water saved as the basis for artichoke soup, or any other vegetable soup ; it will set jelly-like, when cold, and it possesses the best of the flavour of the artichokes.

After they have been steamed or boiled in their skin until tender – which takes longer when steamed than boiled, and for big tubers than small ones – Artichokes should have their skin rubbed off before being 'finished' in butter or in the oven, or served with melted butter or any white sauce one cares to pour over them.

Baked Jerusalem Artichokes
Wash and scrub the artichokes and parboil them; rub off their skin and place in an oven-proof serving-dish with enough good meat stock to cover. Bake for about 40 minutes in a hot oven, covering the dish up to the last 15 minutes; season with pepper and salt and serve from the dish.

Béchamel Jerusalem Artichokes
Steam or boil the artichokes until tender, rub off skin and re-heat after pouring over them a good *Béchamel Sauce*.

Buttered Jerusalem Artichokes
Steam or boil Jerusalem artichokes until tender; rub off skin and serve whole, if small, or sliced if large, with hot melted butter and finely-chopped parsley over them.

Croquettes of Jerusalem Artichokes
Steam or boil Jerusalem artichokes until tender; rub off skin and cut up in small pieces; mix these with a *Béchamel Sauce*, bind with yolks of eggs to the right consistency; shape into *Croquettes*, brush with melted butter, coat with breadcrumbs and fry in deep fat. Serve with fried parsley.

Jerusalem Artichokes à la Daube
1 chopped onion
1 tablespoon lard
6 Jerusalem artichokes
3 garlic cloves
1 teaspoon salt
⅛ teaspoon pepper
¼ teaspoon nutmeg
1 pint white wine
Herb bouquet

Put onion into saucepan with lard and cook slowly until brown and tender. Add artichokes peeled and quartered, then the garlic, salt, pepper, nutmeg and herb bouquet. Keep covered and simmer 15 minutes very slowly, shaking the pan from time to time to keep the contents from catching on the bottom. In the meantime reduce wine to one cup by boiling in separate pan and add to artichokes. Add several tablespoonfuls of hot water if needed, and continue cooking slowly until artichokes are done.—C.R.B.B.

Fried Jerusalem Artichokes
Parboil some artichokes, rub off skin and dry well. Cut in very thin slices and drop in very hot deep fat, not too many at a time so that all may be equally caught by the boiling fat. When golden brown, take out and serve at once with a sprinkling of rock-salt and finely-chopped parsley over them.

Jerusalem Artichoke Fritters
2 bunches artichokes
Milk
Olive oil
Salt and pepper
Parmesan cheese, grated
Fritter batter
Vinegar

Pour boiling water over artichokes; rub the skins off. Cook them in milk about 25 minutes until nearly done. Cut into slices and whilst still warm marinate them for half an hour in olive oil, vinegar, salt and pepper. Drain, dry and sprinkle with grated parmesan cheese and dip in fritter batter. Fry until golden brown in deep hot fat.—A.W.R.

Jerusalem Artichokes au gratin
Steam or boil artichokes until tender; rub off skins; cut up in thick slices and mix these with a *Sauce Mornay*, filling a baking-dish and then sprinkling over a coating of bread-crumbs mixed with some grated cheese; dot with a few pats of butter and brown in a quick oven.

Jerusalem Artichoke Pie
Mash the cooked tubers or rub them through a fine sieve. Add a little lemon juice and some onion *purée*. Put alternate layers of this mixture and grated cheese in a pie-dish. Cover with breadcrumbs and cheese and a few small pats of butter and cook in a hot oven for 10 minutes.—E.S.R.

Jerusalem Artichokes Provençale
Steam or boil artichokes till tender; rub off skins and slice. Toss slices in butter in a frying-pan with some sliced tomatoes, a sliced clove of garlic, one chopped onion, one chopped stick of fennel, and season with pepper and salt. Mix all together and serve hot.

Purée de Topinambours
(Mashed Jerusalem Artichokes)
Steam or boil the artichokes until tender; rub off skins and mash or rub through a fine sieve; season with pepper and salt and warm up in a saucepan with a little melted butter and cream. This *purée* is improved when mixed with about one-third of another *purée* to two of artichokes, either a potato *purée* or mashed carrots; the latter is distinctly sweet-ish and appeals to children, whilst being most nutritious and wholesome.

Jerusalem Artichoke Salads
Steam or boil Jerusalem artichokes until tender; rub off skins and slice; let them get quite cold and serve the slices as hors-d'oeuvre salad, with a covering of *mayonnaise*.

The cold, steamed or boiled artichokes may be diced instead of being sliced and served with diced cold potatoes and lettuce with a French dressing.

Jerusalem Artichoke Soufflé

Prepare some *Mashed Jerusalem Artichokes* (q.v.), and make it lighter than usual by adding a little more cream, then add for every pint of *purée* the yolks of three eggs and the whites beaten to a stiff froth. Season with pepper and salt and fill, three-quarters full only, a *soufflé* dish. Put in a hot oven at first, and as soon as the *soufflé* begins to rise, lower the heat and cook for 20 or 25 minutes, until the *soufflé* is lightly browned.

Jerusalem Artichoke Soup

Wash and scrub well 2 lb. Jerusalem artichokes and boil them in salted water till tender. Take them out of the water, rub off skins, mash the artichokes and mix with the *purée* a *roux*, made with 1 oz. butter and a dessertspoonful of flour; then return to the water in which the artichokes were boiled; stir in a pint of milk and replace pan on the fire; bring to the boil, then reduce heat and let the soup simmer gently for 15 or 20 minutes, when it will be ready to serve, but may wait if necessary. Taste before serving and season to taste. Small pieces of stale bread fried in fat and added to the soup at the time of serving improve it.

JERUSALEM PEA
See *Mung Bean.*

JEW'S MALLOW
See *Crin-Crin.*

KAA HE-É
Lat. *Stevia rabaudina*. A native plant of Paraguay, where it is largely used as a sugar substitute; its leaves have an intensely sweet taste when chewed, raw: they retain their sweetness when dried, but lose it when cooked.

KAAWI YAM
See *Guinea Yam.*

KALE. KAIL. BORECOLE KALE. COLE. COLEWORT
Lat. *Brassica oleracea, var. acephala*; Fr. *Chou vert*. Any cabbage with sprouting, curled, finely dented leaves which do not form a solid head or heart. It is believed to be the original form of the great *Brassica oleracea*, or cabbage family. Its curly leaves are used in winter and the little shoots which sprout from the stem are welcome in late winter and early spring, at a time when green vegetables are scarce; they are usually sold under

the name of winter greens, Scotch kale, cottage kale, or curled kale, curlies. Borecole is the anglicized form of the Dutch *Boerenkool*, meaning peasant's cabbage. There are different varieties of kales, tall and dwarf, green and variegated, and the best of these, personally speaking, is the one sold by seedsmen under the name of Labrador. This and all curled kales are excellent cooked like *Cabbage* (q.v.), or merely thoroughly well washed and served as green salad, with or without lettuce or endive, and dressed like these.

An unusual and decorative kale is the *Cavolo Pavonazza*, or *Neapolitan Curled Borecole*: its stem swells a few inches from the ground, and it is eaten in any way suitable for *Kohl-Rabi* (q.v.).

KHAT. KAT. QAT. CAFTA
Lat. *Catha edulis*. A shrub of Arabia and Abyssinia, the leaves of which are used to make Arabian Tea, a stimulating – some say narcotic – drink of the Arabs. The leaves are also chewed by the Arabs and they are exported to India.

KIU-TS'AI. KUCHAY
Lat. *Allium tuberosum*. Two approximations of the Chinese name of a very fine species of garlic, one which the Chinese have introduced wherever they have settled. Besides the cloves, the leaves can be chopped up like chives, and the flowers have a faint garlic flavour and a honeyed sweetness which make them a welcome addition to any green salad.

KNOTROOT
See *Chinese Artichoke.*

KOHL-RABI. KNOL-KOHL
Lat. *Brassica oleracea, var. caulorapa*; Fr. *Chourave*. A hybrid of the cabbage family which must be grown quickly to be fit to eat. Its base stem is swollen and nutty in flavour and tender withal, unless its growth has been too slow when it is woody. It is quite a popular vegetable on the Continent, but it has never been grown to any extent in England, nor is it popular in the U.S.A.

The sprouting green leaves of kohl-rabi, when young, may be eaten prepared in any way suitable for the culinary preparation of *Spinach* (q.v.), but kohl-rabi is mostly grown for its base stem or overground root which must be picked young and may be prepared in any way suitable for *Turnip* (q.v.). The distinctive flavour of kohl-rabi is mostly in and nearest to the skin: hence this vegetable is best steamed before it is peeled or pared. The usual way, which consists in peeling the kohl-rabi and boiling it till tender, is not so good. For hors-d'oeuvre and salad, kohl-rabi is best when prepared in the same way as *Celeriac* (q.v.).

Kohl-rabi steamed till tender unpeeled, then allowed to get cold, peeled and cut in thin slices, dressed, with oil and vinegar or *mayonnaise* is excellent served with cold meat, as a salad.

KOTENASHI BEAN
Lat. *Phaseolus vulgaris*. Small, white *Haricot Bean* (q.v.), imported from Korea for canning. A smiliar haricot bean imported from Japan for the same purpose is known as *Otenashi*.

KUDZU
Lat. *Pueraria hirsuta*. An Eastern ornamental vine naturalized in the Southern States of the U.S.A. In China and Japan its starchy tuberous roots are valued as an article of food, and they are sold also in the Chinese markets of San Francisco and New York. *Kudzu* is its Japanese name; its Chinese name is *Fan-kot*.

LABLAB BEAN. EGYPTIAN BEAN
Lat. *Dolichos Lablab*; Fr. *Dolique d'Egype*. A native of India and a fast-climbing bean which supplies one of the staple foods of Egypt and the Near East. The beans are brown in colour, with a curious white keel along one of the edges; they are short, broad and thick. It is also called *Hyacinth Bean*, and *Tonka Bean*. Both the green pods and the ripe seeds are used as food; and even the leaves are sometimes dried and used as a vegetable.

LADIES' FINGERS
See *Okra*.

LAD'S LOVE
See *Southernwood*.

LADY'S SMOCK
See *Meadow Cress*.

LAMB'S LETTUCE
See *Corn Salad*.

LAND CRESS
See *American Cress*.

LAVER
Lat. *Porphyra laciniata*; *P. vulgaris*; *Ulva latissima* and *U. lactuca*. The name of two kinds of edible seaweeds common on most shores of the British Isles:
1. The *Red Laver*, also called *Slouk*, in Scotland, and *Stoke*, in Ireland. It is filmy, reddish-purple seaweed which is much in evidence on the rocky coasts of South Wales and Cornwall, and is 'in season' from June to March; its fronds are rich in iodine and

make a good pickle. It is produced commercially in Japan and is used under the name of *Asakusanori* for soup, as a vegetable, or raw, in salads, like cabbage.
2. The *Green Laver*, also known as the *Lettuce Laver*. Its fronds are bright green and crinkly, not unlike the curly lettuce; they are also in season from June to March.

How to prepare Laver
Wash and boil gently till quite tender, pour off the superfluous water, and beat a little salt into it. The resulting pulp may be kept in jars for a week and served in the following ways:
1. Add 3 oz. of butter or a little gravy or meat extract, lemon juice and pepper to 1 lb. of laver; heat in an aluminium saucepan (it is a tradition to avoid iron), stirring with a wooden spoon or silver fork; serve very hot with roast meat. Laver served in a silver chafing dish with a squeeze of Seville orange juice is a classical accompaniment to Welsh mutton.
2. Mix with vinegar or lemon juice a few drops of olive oil, pepper and salt; serve cold on toast. A delicious hors-d'oeuvre or savoury, suggesting a mixture of olives and oysters.
3. Mix with oatmeal and fry in the form of flat cakes for breakfast.—J.H.

LEEK
Lat. *Allium porrum*; Fr. *Poireau*. A native of Europe and one of the most useful of all vegetables. It is the most discreet member of the large onion family, but it is a mistake to imagine that because it has not the onion's assertiveness it lacks flavour. On the contrary, the leek has a very pleasant flavour of its own, and it is an asset to all vegetable soups and to most stews.

Baked Leeks
Trim some smallish, tender leeks and parboil them in boiling water for 10 minutes. Cut them up in 2 in. lengths, put them in a fireproof dish; cover with good meat stock, season with pepper and salt, and bake in a moderate oven for 20 minutes or so. Then cover with breadcrumbs and grated cheese; add a few pats of butter and brown in a quick oven.

Leeks Béchamel
Trim and boil leeks till tender; drain well and serve with a *Béchamel Sauce* over them.

Boiled Leeks
Trim some smallish, young and tender leeks, cut off roots and green part and remove outside leaves; they should not be more than 5 in. long. Boil them in as little water as possible – just enough to cover; put

some vinegar in the water to keep the leeks white. When still firm but sufficiently cooked, take leeks out of the water and drain well. Serve with melted or oiled butter, or any white sauce of your choice.

Braised Leeks

Trim and parboil some young and small leeks. Drain them and braise them on a gentle heat with a little stock and some butter; season to taste and serve with a meat glaze.

Leek Custard
(Flamiche Amiénoise)

Trim and boil some young leeks and drain them well; then shred them finely and mix them thoroughly with some fresh cream, enough to make it a soft, spongy mass; add the yolks of two eggs, well beaten and fill a Flan or light pastry with this mixture. Set under a hot grill until the custard has firmly set and serve at once.

Hachis de Poireaux

 5 or 6 large fresh leeks
 2 egg yolks
 1 teaspoon flour
 2 tablespoons butter
 2 tablespoons thick cream
 Salt and pepper
 Fried *croûtons*

Remove green upper part and outer skins of leeks. Wash well and blanch in boiling salted water. When tender, drain and squeeze well, removing every drop of water (which, by the way, will make good stock for a vegetable soup). Chop the leeks very finely. Place the butter in a pan, lightly brown the leeks in this, then sprinkle the flour over them and moisten with the cream. Simmer gently after seasoning to taste. Remove pan from fire and stir in the two well-beaten egg yolks. Serve in a dish garnished with parsley and fancy *croûtons*.

Leeks Mornay

Trim and boil some young leeks, drain them well and serve with a *Mornay Sauce*.

Leeks Normande

Trim and boil some young leeks, drain them well and serve with a *Sauce Normande*.

Leeks Paysanne

Dice some bacon and brown it in an earthenware pot in just enough butter to cook it. Trim and wash some young leeks and cut them up in ½ in. pieces; put these in the pot with the bacon; season with pepper and salt, and simmer for 30 or 40 minutes, according to age of the leeks, stirring occasionally.

Leek Pie

Trim some young leeks, wash them and cut them up in 1 in. pieces; half fill a pie-dish with these and add just enough milk to cover; season with pepper and salt, then add a covering of clotted cream and cover the dish with a good pastry cover; bake for about an hour in a moderate oven.

Leek Purée

Trim and boil the leeks till quite tender; then drain and sieve them and re-heat in a pan, adding first of all butter, seasoning with pepper and salt, and finishing with enough fresh cream thoroughly well worked into it to get the *Purée* of the right consistency.

Leek Salad

Trim some young leeks and boil them in just enough salted water; drain them well and let them get cold; serve with a *Vinaigrette Sauce*, as hors-d'oeuvre, or as part of a vegetable salad, with cold, diced potatoes and sliced tomatoes.

Leek Soups
I
Flemish

Wash a handful of picked sorrel and chop it up finely; also the same quantity of chervil; trim and wash half a dozen leeks and cut them up in ½ in. lengths; wash a couple of lettuce and shred finely. Put all these in a pan with just enough water to cover, and season with pepper and salt; add half a dozen medium-sized potatoes, peeled and quartered and a sprig of winter savoury. Simmer quite slowly for 4 hours and, before serving, crush the potatoes with a fork.

II
French

Trim and wash the leeks, leaving some of the green; slice them in ¼ in. rounds and cook in hot butter for about 15 minutes, but without browning. Then dredge with flour, stir and cook for another 10 minutes. Then add half the quantity of milk wanted, and simmer gently for 15 minutes, by which time the leeks should be quite tender. Strain and sieve the leeks and return the *Leek Purée* to the saucepan; add the rest of the milk, season with pepper and salt and cook for another 5 or 6 minutes; move pan from the fire and add fresh cream; serve with *croûtons* of fried bread.

III
Scottish

Put two quarts of chicken broth in a saucepan and bring to the boil; sprinkle in a tablespoonful of coarse oatmeal and add the white part of six leeks, washed, trimmed and shredded. Season with pepper and salt and simmer gently for as long as needed for the oatmeal to be quite soft and the leeks quite tender.

This is the most famous of Scottish soups, outside Scotland: it is known the world over as *Cock-a-leekie*.

IV
Welsh

Wash and trim three or four largish leeks. Cut each one longways and then crossways very finely. Peel four or five medium-sized potatoes, slice them and put in a saucepan with a pinch of salt and three pints of water. Melt some butter in a frying-pan and cook in it the shredded leeks and a finely-chopped onion; dredge with flour, moisten with some of the potato water and stir well for a few minutes; then put the leeks and onion into the saucepan and simmer gently until the potatoes are quite soft. Strain, sieve the vegetables and return to the saucepan. Reheat. Beat the two egg yolks and put them in the soup tureen; then pour the hot soup into the tureen and mix in ½ cup of fresh cream just before serving.

Leeks stewed

Prepare the leeks in the usual way and cut them into pieces about ¾ in. long. Place these in a saucepan with 1 oz. of margarine to every pound of leeks together with three tablespoonfuls of water. Sprinkle lightly with salt but be careful not to add too much. Put a grease-proof paper over the saucepan, jam on the lid very tightly and cook slowly over a gentle heat for about 35 minutes. Serve with the liquid.—D.H.

LENTILS

Lat. *Lens esculenta*; Fr. *Lentille*. A small branching plant, a native of Southern Europe, which is cultivated for its seeds. These are round and flat; dried, they keep for a very long time and provide an excellent stand-by vegetable for the winter months.

To cook Lentils

Soak in plain water overnight and cook very slowly with just enough water to cover at the beginning. As the water evaporates, replace with meat-stock or vegetable stock, if available, if not, with water. Season with pepper and salt and cook at the same time an onion or two. When the lentils are tender enough to be easily crushed with a fork, they can either be served as a vegetable, in their own cooking juice, with a good piece of butter added at the time of serving; or else they may be left alone to get quite cold and served with a dressing of oil and vinegar, either by way of hors-d'oeuvre or with cold meat, as a salad; or else they may be sieved and the *purée* re-heated with butter

and a little milk or cream, making a very nourishing dish and one that is much more easily digested by both the young and the old than mashed haricot beans.

Lentil Soup

Soak ½ lb. lentils overnight and simmer till soft in water or vegetable stock, if any, a piece of bacon or pork, a couple of small onions, half a clove of garlic, if you have no objection to garlic, and half a bayleaf. Only put just enough stock or water to cover and add more as it evaporates. Season with pepper and salt. When the lentils are tender, strain the soup into another pan, sieve the lentils and return the *purée* to the soup, reheat; warm up the soup tureen, put in it a number of small pieces of fried stale bread and then pour soup into tureen; add a large spoonful or two of fresh cream at the last moment and serve.

Lentils 'al Riso'

Leave 1 pint of lentils in cold water for 12 hours. Strain, put them into hot water, and boil them rapidly; then cook slowly for about an hour, drain well, put back into boiling water and cook until quite soft. Then take ½ pint of rice, and put it into an earthen pot of boiling water. When cooked, drain the rice through a sieve, and stand it near the fire for 10 or 15 minutes to dry. Place 2 oz. of butter in a frying-pan; when melted, add a small onion chopped up fine; when browned, put in the lentils and rice, and stir them over the fire for a quarter of an hour. Add a little salt and pepper, and serve up very hot.—J.R.

LETTUCE

The name of quite a number of different varieties of salads, the principal sorts being:

(a) *Cabbage Lettuce*. Lat. *Lactuca sativa, var. Capitata*; Fr. *Laitue*; (b) *Cos Lettuce*. Lat. *Lactuca sativa, var. Longifolia*; Fr. *Romaine*; (c) *Small* or *Cutting Lettuce*; this is a lettuce which never forms a head, but produces leaves almost continuously during the summer months; it is valuable where space is limited, as it does not run to seed, and it provides a green salad so long as its leaves are cut off regularly; (d) *Perennial Lettuce*. This is an uncultivated lettuce with leaves not unlike those of the *Dandelion*. It grows freely in light and chalky soils in many parts of France, and its young leaves are very much appreciated in the spring of the year for salads.

Best-known American lettuce varieties are the iceberg or crisphead, of medium green colour with white inner leaves; the New York with curly dark green leaves; the Simpson or New York State iceberg; the Boston, butterhead or bib lettuce with a loose head and tender leaves; the romaine or cos lettuce; the curly endive as well as various different kinds of garden-grown lettuces.

The first and foremost place for all kinds of lettuce is in the salad bowl. The lettuce should be washed very carefully in plenty of cold, salted water which is easy; then it should be thoroughly well dried, which is not so easy. The best way is to put the lettuce into a wire basket and either swing it or rotate it until all the water is forced out. Failing a wire basket, the wet lettuce can also be swung in a piece of thin muslin, but it must *not* be *pressed*, nor even patted, otherwise the salad will be lifeless and lose the crispness which is its chief gastronomical asset. Freshly picked, crisp, young cos lettuce is most acceptable with just a grain of salt, undressed, with bread and cheese. But, of course, any lettuce served as a salad, should be dressed; the usual dressing consists of two parts of olive oil to one of wine-vinegar or lemon juice, and two of salt to one of pepper, with variations according to individual tastes. That sort of dressing, however, is merely the beginning or under garments; a salad, to be properly dressed, should be given the added flavour of finely-chopped *Fines Herbes*, that is, tarragon, chervil and the green tops of chives or spring onions; there are other herbs which may be introduced by way of a change from time to time.

Lettuce may also be cooked, mostly braised, like *Chicory* (q.v.).

Baked Lettuce

Trim and wash the lettuces; drop them in boiling, salted water for 5 minutes and no more. Take them out; drain well and lay them in a well-buttered fireproof dish; press well down and add two or three small onions and one lump of sugar per lettuce; also one or two pats of butter on each lettuce; cover the dish and cook in a moderate oven for 40 or 45 minutes. Serve with their own juice as sauce, binding it with a little butter kneaded with flour. Season with pepper and salt to taste.

Braised Lettuce

Trim and wash some lettuces, then drain them and parboil in boiling, salted water for 5 minutes. Plunge them for a few seconds in cold water, then drain and press all the water out. Fold over the lettuces and tie them down with thread; put them in a baking-dish with some bacon rashers (one to two lettuces), and one sliced onion per lettuce. Just cover the lettuces with meat-stock and simmer in a slow oven for 1½ hours, turning them over once or twice.

When cooked, take them out of the dish, press most of the moisture out with the back of a wooden spoon, and arrange in the serving-dish which will then go back into the oven, there to keep the lettuces hot, whilst the sauce is being made from the liquor in which they were cooked.

Lettuce à la Crème

Wash three or four good-sized cabbage lettuces, trim them and blanch them for 8 or 10 minutes in fast-boiling water. Plunge them at once into cold water, drain them and dry them, and cut them in quarters or eight parts according to their size. Put 2 oz. of butter in a pan, add the lettuces with a seasoning of pepper, salt and a pinch of castor sugar. Simmer very gently indeed for 2 or 3 hours, stirring fairly often with a clean wooden spoon. When tender, stir in the yolks of two eggs beaten up with half a gill of cream or milk, and serve when hot. Do not allow it to boil after the eggs have been added. Serve garnished with *croûtons* of fried bread, or *fleurons* of puff paste.—A.H. (2).

Lettuce Fritters

Boil two lettuces in salted water, drain them and cut them up. Beat up four eggs, whites and yolks separately, then mix them; add the lettuce and fry it in spoonfuls of boiling oil. Serve hot. (Spanish recipe.)—P.A.

Mousse de Laitue

Have four good-sized lettuces (either the cabbage kind or the cos), clean them well and put them in boiling salted water. Boil them 1 minute and let them simmer 3 or 4 minutes more.

Boil also two floury potatoes, or one fairly large one – not more than a quarter of a pound.

Pound both the potatoes and the lettuces (well drained) and mix them well over the fire; add the yolks of three eggs, cook 1 minute more, see that it is well seasoned, and add, lastly, four whites of egg beaten to a stiff froth.

Fill a well-buttered Charlotte mould, stand it in boiling water and cook 15 minutes in a moderate oven. Or use an ordinary *soufflé* dish, cook in the ordinary way about 3 minutes less and serve in the dish.—X.M.B.

Lettuce Soup
(Crème Choisy)

    1 lb. of lettuce
    6 tablespoons of white stock or milk
    2 tablespoons of cream
    1½ pints of thin *Béchamel Sauce*
    Chervil butter and salt
    A little sugar

After having washed the lettuces, blanch in salted boiling water for 5 minutes. Drain and dip in cold water. Drain again thoroughly and chop the lettuce coarsely. Add to the hot *Béchamel* and simmer till the lettuce is quite tender. Rub through a sieve, replace the *purée* in a saucepan, add the white stock or milk, season with salt and a little sugar and, lastly, stir in the cream. Garnish with a little chervil. Serve with *croûtons* of fried bread.—C.M. (2).

LIMA BEAN

Lat. *Phaseolus lunatus, var. macrocarpus* (*P. limensis*). An annual, fast-climbing bean, a native of South America. It is extensively cultivated for the sake of its seeds or beans, which are short, flat, slightly kidney-shaped, one half nearly always larger than the other, and usually white and marked with wrinkles. The name is often given to another and closely-related bean, the *Sieva Bean*. Both the *Lima* and *Sieva Beans* are very floury and nutritious. Besides the more usual white *Lima Bean* and the green *Sieva Bean*, there are some variegated varieties known as *Mottled Lima Bean* and *Marbled Cape Kidney Bean*. All these beans may be prepared for the table in any way suitable for *Haricots* (q.v.).

In the U.S.A. different varieties of both the Lima bean and Sieva bean are grown very widely, and are available the greater part of the year. They are used extensively both fresh and dried. In the British Isles attempts to naturalize these beans have so far met with little success, owing to climatic conditions. In Brazil, Lima beans are to the population what potatoes are to the people of Ireland.

Three sorts of Lima beans imported by the United Kingdom are the *Burma Bean*, a white haricot bean, the trade name of which is new haricot; the *Rangoon Bean*, which is a red haricot bean; and the *Madagascar Butter Bean*, which is larger, white, and usually sold in tins under the name of Lima Beans.

LOCUST BEAN
See *Carob.*

LONG POTATO
See *Sweet Potato.*

LOOFAH. LUFFA
See *Gourds.*

MADAGASCAR BUTTER BEAN
See *Lima Bean.*

MALABAR NIGHTSHADE
See *Indian Spinach.*

MALANGA
See *Calalu.*

MALLOW
Lat. *Malva sylvestris*; Fr. *Mauve.* A common and pretty flowering European weed: its pale mauve flowers are picked and dried to make a kind of homely medicinal tea, and its leaves, when young, may be boiled and eaten in the same way as *Spinach* (q.v.).

MANGEL. MANGOLD.
MANGOLD WURZEL.
MANGEL WURZEL
Lat. *Beta vulgaris.* The 'field' variety of the common *Beet* or *Beetroot* grown on a large scale for cattle winter feed, but also in the vegetable garden for human consumption. They should be used when small, but any that may be allowed to get very large, woody and unfit to eat should not be thrown away; they should be hacked into pieces and dug in for manure. Small roots are prepared for the table in any way suitable for *Beet* or *Beetroot* (q.v.).

MARSH SAMPHIRE
See *Glasswort.*

MARTINOES
See *Unicorn Plant.*

MEADOW CRESS.
LADY'S SMOCK
Lat. *Cardamine pratensis*; Fr. *Cresson des prés.* European weed, which grows freely in moist meadows and on the banks of many streams in different parts of England. Its leaves have a peppery, biting taste and make quite a pleasant salad when picked very small; they are best, however, used in soups like *Sorrel* (q.v.).

MEADOWSWEET
Lat. *Spirea ulmaria*; Fr. *Reine des prés.* One of the most decorative of the wild flowers growing freely in all parts of the British Isles, more particularly in damp fields. A few leaves are a welcome addition in many vegetable soups, and its flowers are dried in many parts of the country to be used during the winter months in the making of a pleasant kind of medicinal 'tea', reputed to be a cure for colds. There is a closely-related species flourishing in the U.S.A., but little, if any, use is made of it.

MELILOT
Lat. *Melilotus officinalis*; Fr. *Tréfoil.* A perennial leguminous plant which grows wild in many parts of England, more particularly in the Eastern Counties. Its dried leaves and flowers are very aromatic, and they are used to flavour *marinades* and stews. In France, *Melilot* is used as stuffing for tame rabbits, and in Switzerland it is put in the green cheese known as *Schabzieger*: its Swiss name is *Ziegerkraut*, the curd herb. It is used also in the making of Gruyère cheese.

MELON

The fruit of a number of herbaceous plants with slender, flexible stems, furnished with tendrils by means of which they attach themselves to any suitable support, creeping along the ground or climbing, as opportunity offers.

Cucumis melo, Melon; *Cucumis melo*, var. *cantalupensis*, Cantaloup melon; *Cucumis melo*, var. *Chito*, Chito melon; *Cucumis melo*, var. *flexuosus*, Serpent melon; *Cucumis melo*, var. *inodorus*, Honeydew or Cassaba melon; *Cucumis melo*, var. *reticulatus*, Musk melon; *Citrullus vulgaris*, Water melon; *Citrullus vulgaris*, var. *Citroides*, Citron melon.

Melons are, like tomatoes, true fruit which it is customary to include among vegetables. But, unlike tomatoes, melons are mostly so sweet that their proper place is at the end of the meal, as dessert fruit. However, they are usually served at the beginning, as an hors-d'oeuvre, chilled, with sifted sugar and ground nutmeg: they are best with a little freshly-ground rock salt, and, being watery, cold and not of easy digestion, they should be followed immediately by a small glass of vodka, brandy or old Madeira.

There are many varieties of melons, the following being among the more popular:

Cantaloup or *Cantaloupe*. A variety of melon which owes its name to Cantalupo, in the province of Ancona, where it is believed to have been first grown in Europe, from seeds brought from Armenia. The rind is ribbed and warty and the flesh is either dark orange or pale green, very juicy, sweet, and of excellent flavour when fully ripe. One of the worst gastronomic heresies is to remove the seeds of the cantaloup and fill the cavity with Port wine: it ruins both the Port and the cantaloup.

The best *Cantaloup Melons* in the British Isles were imported from France; the cheapest from Holland. In the United States of America the name of *Canteloup* is usually given to *Nutmeg Melons* or *Musk Melons*. These are of many different varieties and of varying shape and size, with either white, green or red flesh, but they are all distinguished by their 'netted' or 'lace-patterned' rind, and they are invariably watery and sweet when ripe.

The *Cassaba Melon* is a musk melon introduced from Asia Minor and now extensively grown in California; one of its white-skinned varieties, rather small-fruited, is known as *Honeydew Melon*.

The *Winter Melon* is another variety of musk melon: its flesh is either green or white and it has practically no flavour whatever. One of the poorest members of the melon family, gastronomically, it is one of the most important, commercially, because it is a 'good traveller', and keeps well. It is also known as *Melone de oro* and *Melon de Portugal*.

Water Melons belong to a different genus. They are native of Africa and grow in none but warm countries. When ripe they are watery, refreshing and lacking in flavour, some being sweet and others bitter. They are often eaten, before they are ripe, as a vegetable, boiled, fried, stuffed and prepared in any way suitable for *Vegetable Marrow* (q.v.).

The *Citron Melon* is a variety of water melon with hard flesh, but valued for its rind which is used for preserves.

The *Serpent Melon* and the *Orange Melon*, or *Chito*, are also varieties almost exclusively used for preserves.

Small cubes or rounds scooped out from ripe melons are added to fruit cocktails and salads in the U.S.A.

MERCURY
See *Good King Henry*.

MILFOIL
See *Yarrow*.

MILKWEED
Lat. *Asclepias incarnata*, var. *pulchra*. The name given in the U.S.A. to a number of plants of the *Asclepias* and *Acerates* genera used in salads.

MUNG BEAN
Lat. *Phaseolus Mungo*, var. *radiatus*. The *Golden Gram* and *Green Gram* of India. The ripe seeds of the mung bean are boiled whole or split, like peas. They are also parched and ground into a floury meal.

MURLIN
See *Badderlocks*.

MUSHROOM
The name usually accepted as covering all edible fungi. The commonest and some of the best of these grow in open pastures, and where the grass is kept grazed short by cattle; they are the *Field Mushrooms*, usually referred to as just *Mushrooms*. (Lat. *Psalliota campestris*; Fr. *Champignon des prés*).

The same sort of mushroom is also cultivated in gardens, quarries, sheds, and cellars, in hot beds and nearly all the year round; it is picked and sold as *Mushrooms* at different stages of its growth, very small, as 'buttons' and up to its maximum opening up, to 5 in. in diameter. A larger and coarser variety grows in damp meadows and in moist and shady places; it is edible but inferior in quality. It is usually called *Horse Mushrooms*.

(Lat. *Psalliota arvensis*; Fr. *Pratelle* or *Boule de neige*).

Field and shop *Mushrooms* consist chiefly of a stem and a cap; the stem has a clothy ring round the middle and the cap is furnished underneath with numerous radiating pale pink coloured gills, free from the stem; as the mushroom grows older and after it is taken from the earth the gills turn dark brown to black.

Gastronomically, both the cap and stem of the field mushroom are of value, although not of the same value. The cap is best. When it is quite small, still in the 'button' stage, it only needs washing and scraping, then being dressed with lemon juice, a mere grain or two of salt, a little olive oil, and it is excellent, uncooked, as an hors-d'oeuvre and in salads. When the cap opens, it is better cooked. The cap is fleshy, firm and white within and light brown outside. The cuticle or silky skin of the cap easily peels off. The gills underneath the cap are white at the very beginning, then pale pink and of a deeper shade of pink in the fully-grown specimens, but never black as in the shops, except after they have been kept and exposed to the air for some time; at that stage they are not necessarily poisonous, but they are not worth buying. The mushroom caps are best stewed in cream in a pan with a closely-fitting lid to it; they are very good also grilled or tossed in butter. The stem of the field mushroom is always firm and slightly pithy up to the middle but never hollow. It is best cooked separately, and it is usually chopped up and used to flavour sauces or in garnishings or stuffings.

Besides the field mushroom, and its immediate relations, the cultivated or garden mushroom and the coarser horse-mushroom, there are a very considerable number of other fungi which grow in fields and woods from early spring to late autumn, a few of them being poisonous, but most of them being quite safe and valuable, not as food – since no fungus has any valuable nutritive value – but as condiments, that is on account of the delicate flavour which they impart to the food with which they are served.

One of the very best flavoured of all fungi is the *Fairy-ring Mushroom* (Lat. *Marasmius oreades*), which is very common in France, in Italy and in the U.S.A., but somewhat less common in England. Its cap is but 1 or 2 in. in diameter, wide bell-shaped, becoming flat as it opens but always retaining a small boss in the centre; in colour from deep cream to light buff; in texture, somewhat leathery; the gills broad and widely separated and lighter in colour than the outside of the

cap; the stem straw-thin, tough and without any ring or collar. It is found on lawns, in open pastures, but never in woods. Like other fungi, it has a habit of growing in rings, hence its name both in England and U.S.A. It has not only a better flavour than the field mushroom, but it retains it much longer when dried and kept for flavouring stews, sauces or soups during the winter months.

Among other common edible varieties of fungi we may mention the *Morel* (Lat. *Morchella esculenta*; Fr. *Morille*); the *Blewit* (Lat. *Tricholoma personatum*; Fr. *Russule*); the *Chanterelle* (Lat. *Cantharellus cibarius*; Fr. *Chanterelle*); the *Shaggy Cap* (Lat. *Coprinus comatus*; Fr. *Coprin chevelu*); the *Parasol* (Lat. *Lepiota procera*; Fr. *Lépiote Columelle*); the *Amethyst Agaric* (Lat. *Tricholoma nudum*; Fr. *Clavaire améthysta*); the *Funnel Agaric* (Lat. *Clitocybe maxima*); the *Honey Agaric* (Lat. *Armillaria mellea*); the *Giant Puffball* (Lat. *Lycoperdon giganteum*; Fr. *Vesse de loup*); the *Horn of Plenty* (Lat. *Craterellus cornucopioides*; Fr. *Corne d'abondance*); the *Scaly Agaric* (Lat. *Lepiota rhacodes*; Fr. *Lépiote raboteuse*); the *Sheathed Agaric* (Lat. *Amanitopsis fulva*; Fr. *Agaric porreau*); the *Warty Cap* (Lat. *Amanita rubescens*; Fr. *Amanita rougeâtre*); and the *Beefsteak Fungus* (Lat. *Fistulina hepatica*; Fr. *Fistuline hepatique*), which looks rather like a piece of liver jutting out from a tree trunk, usually oak; it is anything from 8 to 24 in. across, the upper surface, purplish red or liver-colour; underneath, pale buff to brownish-red and porous – no gills; the flesh is soft, like cooked beetroot, dark red, marbled, juicy; it has a faint vinous scent and is entirely different from any other fungus gathered in the British Isles or the U.S.A.

In France, where fungi are gathered and used in cookery to a much greater extent than in any other country, one of the most highly-prized variety of fungus is the *Boletus* or *Bolet*, which is known in culinary French by the name of *Cèpe* (q.v.).

How best to cook Mushrooms

Mushrooms should be skinned and placed *stalks uppermost* in a greased dish with a small dab of butter or margarine to each mushroom, and cooked till tender, always keeping the lid on the dish in which they are cooked and serving in the same dish; they are far more delicate in flavour and more tender than when either grilled or chopped up. The secret of all the most delicious mushroom dishes is to keep the cover on the dish when cooking and to serve the mushrooms in the dish in which they have been cooked.—B.H.

Baked Mushrooms
(English Style)

Remove the stems and peel the caps of bought mushrooms; if young, freshly-picked mushrooms, wash the outside of the caps, but do not peel them. Place in a baking-dish, the gills up; sprinkle pepper and salt and a very little pounded mace, if liked. Put a small pat of butter on each cap and bake for 20 or 25 minutes, according to size of caps. Serve in the dish in which they were cooked, with a light dusting of coralline pepper.

Baked Mushrooms
(French Style)

Clean the mushrooms, peeling or not, according to whether quite freshly-picked or not; if just gathered, they need only wiping or washing. Remove the stalks and cook the caps slowly in pork fat or olive oil for 2 or 3 minutes only; take them out and place them in a fireproof dish. In the meantime, chop finely the stalks and a little bacon fat and fry this in the pan from which you have just taken the partly-cooked caps. Put this mince over the mushrooms in the baking-dish, moisten with a glassful of wine; season with pepper and salt and the juice of a lemon; cook in slow oven for about half an hour and serve in the baking-dish.

Mushrooms Bourgeoise

Pick, wipe, trim and cut in half the required number of mushrooms. Put some slices of streaky bacon into a stewpan and cook them over a slow fire for 15 minutes; then add the mushrooms, some minced chives and a little finely-chopped parsley; season with pepper and salt; moisten with some dry white wine, dredge with a little flour, and stew very gently until the sauce is quite thick; the mushrooms and the sauce should then be served on squares of fried bread.

Broiled Mushrooms

Choose some fairly large, fully-opened mushrooms; clean them and peel them; then soak them in a *marinade* of olive oil or oiled butter for about half an hour. Brush the grill with the same oil or butter and put the mushrooms on the hot grill, stems and gills up; broil quickly, basting them with the oil or butter of the *marinade*. Serve very hot, with a dusting of salt and freshly-ground black pepper.

Buttered Mushrooms

Take a shallow earthenware fireproof dish, place therein one tablespoonful of butter. Let it melt. While the butter is melting, stick a head of garlic on the end of a fork and rub it gently round the dish. Peel and stalk enough mushrooms, arrange them symmetrically in the dish (you will serve the dish up to table) cut side up, put a pinch of pepper and salt in each mushroom, then a dot of butter to each, then a tiny sprinkle of paprika. Cook slowly, first of all covered to keep the steam in, then open to finish. It is advisable to baste occasionally. Serve with strips of hot buttered toast.—H.G.B.

Casserole Mushrooms

Pick, clean, peel and stem some fairly large and well-opened mushrooms. Put each cap upon a round piece of buttered bread, lining the bottom of a shallow casserole; season with pepper and salt and put a pat of butter on each mushroom; moisten with a cupful of fresh cream and put the casserole under a grill for 25 minutes, basting with the cream from time to time. Serve hot in the casserole.

Champignons sous Cloche

Choose mushrooms of the same size and not too large. Peel carefully, having washed them if necessary, and remove the stalks. Beat two tablespoonfuls of butter to a cream with half teaspoon of lemon juice and a little salt, and spread in a round glass baking-dish which has a lid. Cut a few rounds of bread ½ in. thick and about 2 in. in diameter, and put these in the dish and, over, put the mushrooms, piling up in the shape of a cone. Season with salt and pepper and a good squeeze of lemon juice; cover with five or six tablespoonfuls of cream, and cover with the glass lid. Bake in a moderate over for 25 to 30 minutes, adding more cream 10 minutes before serving, and just before serving flavour with one tablespoonful of sherry. Send to table with the lid on.—C.M. (1).

Creamed Mushrooms

Clean, trim and stem some small mushrooms and simmer them for 10 to 15 minutes in some rich *velouté*, or in a light cream sauce; season with pepper and salt. Have as many rasped French rolls as there are guests; scoop out of the rolls all the crumb, or as much as possible, and put the hollowed rolls in the oven until they are hot and crisp; fill them up then with the creamed mushrooms and pour in and over the rest of the *velouté* or cream sauce in which the mushrooms were cooked.

Devilled Mushrooms

Fresh mushrooms
Salt and pepper
2 hard-boiled eggs
Mustard
Butter
Lemon juice
2 raw eggs
Cayenne

Peel and wash mushrooms, *sauté* until tender in a sufficiency of butter; then cut into small pieces, seasoning rather highly with salt, pepper and cayenne. Add lemon juice and mustard to taste. Mash the yolks of the hard-boiled eggs, chop the whites finely. Blend to a rough paste with the yolks of raw eggs and heat gently in a small pan, taking care mixture does not boil. Pile on fried *croutes* or on hot buttered toast, decorating with hard-boiled eggs.

Champignons Flambés (for 4)

Sauté 1 lb. of mushroom caps in butter with plenty of salt in a chafing dish. Pour a cupful of sherry over them. Simmer until dryish. Then add a small amount of brandy and light it. When the flame has gone out, add cream to taste.—DALE WARREN.

Fried Mushrooms

Pick, clean, trim and peel some medium-sized mushrooms. Melt some butter in a frying-pan and fry the mushrooms in it for about 10 minutes; season with pepper and salt. Take the mushrooms out of the pan and keep them hot in the oven whilst you fry in the butter in the pan some small rounds of bread upon which to serve the mushrooms.

Mushrooms au gratin

Pick, clean, trim, peel and stem some mushrooms; place them, gills up, in a well-buttered baking-dish and sprinkle over them fresh white breadcrumbs, a little minced parsley and chives, and either a little Parmesan cheese or some finely-chopped ham; season with pepper and salt and pour over it all some liquefied butter, then bake for 15 or 20 minutes according to heat.

Gratin de Champignons

Have some mushrooms, wash them under the cold tap; if they are really fresh there is no need to peel them. Cook them for 5 or 6 minutes in butter with pepper and a little lemon juice, covered with a buttered paper. Remove them, add a glass of sherry to the butter and lemon in which they have been cooked and reduce by half. Add then a small quantity of thin *Béchamel*, same quantity of fresh cream, and bring to the boil. Let it boil and thicken. See that it is well seasoned. Put the mushrooms in a fireproof dish, cover them with the sauce, sprinkle all over with grated cheese and brown quickly. Serve in the same dish.—X.M.B. (1).

Grilled Mushrooms

Choose some rather large mushrooms, wash them and peel them; cut off the stalks to within ½ in. of caps. Let them stand for an hour in warm, melted butter, turning them over from time to time; season with salt and pepper. Then cook over or under a clear and

fierce heat, turning once only. Serve on buttered toast with a squeeze of lemon and a sprinkling of chopped parsley. Bacon fat may be used with advantage in place of butter.

Mushroom Omelette

Pick, wash, trim, peel some mushrooms and chop them up, caps and stems; toss them in hot butter till done, season to taste and fold them in an omelette just before serving.

Mushrooms sur le plat

Pick, wash, trim and peel some small mushrooms and put them in a fireproof soup plate or egg dish; put a pat of butter on each mushroom and just a little water in the plate; put a strip of any sort of ordinary paste round the edge of the plate or dish, then reverse another plate or dish, exactly of the same size, press the paste over it all round so that no steam can escape and bake in a moderate oven for 25 minutes. Then remove the top plate and the paste round the edges, wipe the rim of the under plate and serve the mushrooms straight from it.

Champignons à la Provençale

Clean and trim the mushrooms, which must be of large size, and cook them in olive oil and half a glass of white wine over a slow fire. Then arrange them in a shallow baking-dish, upside-down, and fill with a stuffing made of the finely chopped stalks, which have been fried in butter with some finely-chopped parsley, two anchovies and a little garlic. One may add a little bread that has been soaked in milk. The mushrooms all filled, sprinkle them with fine breadcrumbs and brown in the oven. Another good filling is made with the stalks, chopped and cooked in a little *Béchamel*, a pinch of nutmeg, lemon juice and cream.—D.B.

Mushroom Purée

Pick, wash and trim the mushrooms, but do not peel them; dry them carefully, then chop them finely, caps and stems alike. Cook them slowly in hot butter – they must not be *fried* but stewed in butter till soft; they are then seasoned with pepper and salt and a squeeze of lemon, mashed and re-heated with more or less *Béchamel Sauce*, according to taste, or some breadcrumbs soaked in gravy. The whole must be thoroughly well mixed together before use as a filling of puff paste *darioles*, scooped out tomatoes, egg-plant, baby vegetable marrow, and many other vegetables; or else served as a garnish with cutlets or many other meat, game or fish dishes.

Salade de Champignons

Pick, trim, wash, peel and stem some fairly large mushrooms. Dry them well and slice them in very thin slices. Cook these gently in hot butter – stew but do not fry – for a few minutes only, so that they are still firm, although not hard. Let them get quite cold and serve with a dressing of olive oil; lemon juice and freshly-ground black pepper.

Mushroom Soufflé

1 lb. mushrooms, peeled, stemmed
and coarsely chopped
1 cupful of mushroom stock made
from stems and peelings
4 tablespoons butter
Dash of white pepper
3 tablespoons flour
3 egg yolks
1½ teaspoons salt
3 egg whites beaten for a soufflé

Cook the mushrooms in one tablespoonful of the butter for 2 or 3 minutes, or just enough to draw out the mushroom flavour. Blend the remaining butter and flour in a saucepan as you would for a cream sauce. Pour in the mushroom stock gradually and cook and stir until thickened. Remove from the heat and beat in the egg yolks vigorously one at a time. Mix in the mushrooms and seasoning and set aside until cold. Fold in the whites. Turn into a 7 in. buttered baking-dish set in a pan containing an inch of hot water, and bake in a moderately hot oven (375 deg. F.) for 35 to 40 minutes, or until puffed and lightly browned. Serves four or five persons.—E.K.H.

Mushroom Soup

1 quart fresh mushrooms
2 oz. butter
2 oz. flour
¼ pint cream

Wash, but do not peel, the mushrooms; put them in water with a dash of vinegar in it, bring to the boil, and then simmer slowly until the mushrooms are soft enough to be rubbed through a sieve. This will give you a mushroom *purée* which you will set aside and keep warm. In the meantime, put the butter in a pan over a slow fire, and as it melts, sift the flour into the pan and work it with a wooden spoon into a smooth paste; then add gradually the required quantity of hot milk and water in equal proportions, stirring all the while over a good heat. Season with pepper and salt, and just a dusting of nutmeg; also the usual herbs (*bouquet garni*) in a muslin bag. When the soup comes to the boil, fish out the muslin bag of herbs and put into the pan the mushroom *purée*, stir well and when the soup comes to the

boil again, add the cream, stir well in and serve. Small square pieces of stale bread fried in fat added to the soup are an improvement.

Stewed Mushrooms

All kinds of mushrooms, large or small, may be stewed in a number of different ways, but always very gently and never for very long. Butter is the usual fat in which mushrooms are stewed, but bacon fat will do just as well, if not better. Mushrooms may also be stewed in meat-stock, in milk and cream, in red or white wine, always being seasoned with a little salt, pepper (the freshly-ground black pepper for choice), a squeeze of lemon juice, and, according to taste, coralline pepper, cayenne or paprika.

Mushroom Stuffing
(Duxelles)

Mince as finely as possible on a board the same weight of parsley and trimmed mushrooms; mince also a little less than half the weight of shallots and cook it all in hot butter on a brisk heat for 5 minutes; season to taste and stir with a wooden spoon. Sometimes breadcrumbs and a beaten egg are added to the mixture to give it greater consistency, and when this stuffing is used for filling boned pigeons, larks or quails, the bird's liver is also added to the *Duxelles*.

Mushroom Tarts

Fresh mushrooms
Butter
Sour cream
1 egg
Flour
Finely-chopped chicken
Short pastry crust
Milk

Having prepared the mushrooms for cooking, fry them gently in butter after rolling each lightly in flour. When done, chop them coarsely, add the chopped chicken – cold left-over will do, or ham or cold roast veal – and add sufficient sour cream to bind the mixture. Season rather highly. Roll out the pastry rather thinly and cut into rounds the size of a small teacup. Pile a spoonful of the chicken and mushroom mixture in the centre of one round of pastry, moisten edges and cover with another round of pastry, pressing edges well together. Brush surface of each tartlet with the beaten egg yolk mixed with a little milk. Bake in a sharp oven until brown and serve hot with tomato or any suitable sauce. If preferred, leave *sauté* mushrooms whole, pile meat mixture in centre and cut out the pastry rounds large enough to enclose the mushrooms, proceeding otherwise as indicated. NOTE. Add the butter and gravy from *sauté* mushrooms to the sauce accompanying this delicious light supper dish.

Mushrooms on Toast

Fry some rounds of bread about ¼ in. thick and a good quantity of peeled mushrooms. Place some thinly-cut and crisply-fried bacon on the rounds of bread. Pile up the mushrooms on them and serve very hot. A small piece of parsley butter, added to each portion, is a great improvement.—L.G.N.

MUSTARD, WHITE

Lat. *Brassica alba*; Fr. *Moutarde*. A European annual with small and tender green leaves, usually cut some six or eight days after the seeds have been sown, and used with or without *Cress* (q.v.) to make sandwiches, in salads or for garnishings.

MYRTLE

Lat. *Myrtus communis*; Fr. *Myrte*. An evergreen shrub which grows wild in many parts of Europe. Its aromatic leaves and seeds were much used in Roman cookery and have been used ever since as a substitute for bay leaves in *marinades* and stews. *Sweet Gale*, one of the *Myrtles*, also known as *Dutch Myrtle* and *Bog Myrtle*, and the badge of the Campbells, has been used from the earliest times to flavour beer.

NASTURTIUM. INDIAN CRESS

Lat. *Tropaeolus majus*; Fr. *Capucine*. Although the *Nasturtium* is grown mostly for its brilliant flowers, it is one of the *Cresses*, and its leaves are a welcome addition to the choice of green fillings of sandwiches, whilst its flowers in a green salad add a touch of colour as pleasing to the eye as unusual; the flowers are also quite good to eat. The green seeds of nasturtium, pickled, are also used as a substitute for capers.

The dwarf variety of nasturtium (Lat. *Tropaeolus minus*) is easier to grow as it does not require staking, and it flowers more freely.

To Pickle Nasturtium Berries

Take nasturtium berries gathered as soon as the blossom is off, and put them in cold spring water and salt; change the water for three days successively. Make a pickle of white wine-vinegar, mace, nutmeg, slice six shallots, six blades of garlic, some peppercorns, salt, and horseradish cut in pieces. Make your pickle very strong, drain your berries very dry and put them in bottles; mix your pickle well together, but you must not boil it; pour it over the berries and tie them down close.—C.F.L. (2).

Nasturtium Salad

Shred a lettuce finely; mingle with it a quantity of nasturtium leaves and two hard-boiled eggs cut in quarters. Place in a salad-bowl, dress with oil and vinegar, salt and pepper, and decorate with nasturtium flowers.

NASTURTIUM, TUBEROUS-ROOTED

Lat. *Tropaeolus tuberosus*; Fr. *Capucine tubéreuse*. A South American perennial plant with tuber-like roots as large as a hen's egg, yellow with red stripes and rather attractive in looks. These tuber-roots are not affected by frost, and are lifted as and when required during the winter months. Their taste is not pleasant on first acquaintance, but in Bolivia, where they are extensively cultivated in the high mountain districts, they are considered quite a delicacy. They can be boiled like *Parsnip* (q.v.).

NAVY BEAN

See *Haricot Bean*.

NEBUKA

See *Welsh Onion*.

NETTLES

Lat. *Urtica dioica*; Fr. *Ortie*. *Nettles*, commonly known as *Stinging Nettles*, are a troublesome weed, but they are very wholesome to eat and not at all unpleasant of taste; they may even be very welcome after a particularly severe winter when spinach and winter lettuce have been killed. The young tips are gathered (with gloves on), washed and boiled like spinach, either by themselves or together with some spinach, sorrel or lettuce, and they are 'finished' in any way suitable for spinach. The liquor in which young nettles have been cooked, like spinach, in their own steam, without any added water, may be drunk hot, with a little added milk: it has the reputation of being a wonderful blood cleanser.

Scotch Nettle Pudding

To one gallon of young nettle-tops, thoroughly washed, add two good-sized leeks or onions, two heads of broccoli or a small cabbage, and ¼ lb. rice. Clean the vegetables well, chop the broccoli and leeks and mix with the nettles. Place all together in a muslin bag alternately with the rice, and tie tightly. Boil in salted water long enough to cook the vegetables, the time varying according to the tenderness or otherwise of the greens. Serve with gravy or melted butter.—M.G.

NEW ZEALAND FERN

See *Tara*.

NEW ZEALAND SPINACH

Lat. *Tetragonia expansa*; Fr. *Tétragone*. A hardy but somewhat coarse spinach from Japan and Australasia; it is also called, in the London markets, *Patent Spinach*. It is prepared for the table in any way suitable for *Spinach* (q.v.).

NIGHTSHADE (Black-berried)

Lat. *Solanum nigrum*. A free-flowering European weed, now naturalized in many parts of the world. In Europe, most people look upon it with suspicion, and it is rightly regarded as poisonous, although in warm climates its green leaves are greatly prized as a green vegetable, which is prepared for the table just like *Spinach* (q.v.). Its black or purple berries sometimes called *Wonderberries*, are also eaten like the *Huckleberry* (q.v.). (*See* Section IV. FRUIT.)

NIPPLEWORT

Lat. *Lapsana communis*. A weed of the sow thistle and dandelion order which can be used uncooked in salads or cooked as a vegetable, preferably mixed with some more leafy and less bitter cultivated vegetable or salad, such as spinach or endive.

OCCA. OKA-PLANT. OXALIS

Lat. *Oxalis tuberosa*; Fr. *Oxalide crénelée*. This South American plant was introduced in England in or about 1829, from Lima, in Peru. It is extensively cultivated for food in Bolivia and Peru and grows quite well in England and Wales. It is a variety of *Wood Sorrel* which produces a number of small tubers – rather like a walnut in size but irregular in shape. Some of the tubers are yellow, others brown and others reddish in colour outside, according to the different species of *Occa*, but the flesh is white in all species, floury, but lacking in flavour. The occa is one of those very rare vegetables which are not best when freshest. They contain a certain acid which neutralizes their sweetness and deprives them of flavour. In South America occas, when picked, are dried in the sun for a few days and eaten like new potatoes, or else dried for some months and kept as dried figs as a reserve or winter food known as *Caui*. In Bolivia, occas are also treated by frost and the frozen tubers are then pounded to a flour.

In England, occas are mostly parboiled for 10 minutes or so in boiling salted water, drained, dried and tossed in sizzling butter, like new potatoes; or else boiled and served with a little melted butter or a white sauce.

In France, the occa has gained the recognition of the *Cuisine Classique* under the name of *Purée Péruvienne*, which is mashed occas, well seasoned and prepared with a little cream, just as one would make a good *Purée de Pommes de terre*. A. Paillieux (*Le Potager d'un Curieux*) recommends drying the occas in an oven, for lack of Peruvian sunshine, and eating them like *Pruneaux*, gently stewed with wine.

(*I am indebted to Mrs W.H.Wynne-Finch for our occas at Little Hedgecourt, where they have proved quite a success in spite of colder conditions than in Wales.*—ED.)

OKRA. OCHRA. OCRA

Lat. *Hibiscus esculentus*; Fr. *Gombo* or *Gombaut*. Also known in England as *Lady's Fingers*; and in the West Indies and South America as *Quimbombo*.

A mucilaginous and aromatic bean, a native of the West Indies, now grown extensively in the Southern States of America, in West Africa and in India. The young pods are used as vegetables and in soups; also in curries and as pickles. The roasted seeds have been used as a substitute for pearl barley.

Okra and Aubergine

Wash and slice a dozen okra pods; peel an *Aubergine* (Egg-plant) and cut it up in dice; peel and slice a medium-sized onion; peel, quarter and remove the pips of two large tomatoes and stew the lot together on a gentle heat without any added water but a spoonful of butter; season with pepper and salt and some finely-chopped parsley. Stir well together and when cooked – it should not take more than half an hour – serve hot straight from the pan, or use it as the filling of an open tart, as a separate vegetable course.

Okra Dobe

Fry until light brown three slices lean ham, one large onion and one tablespoonful butter. Add one pint of boiling water, one large can of tomatoes, 24 whole okras, pepper and salt. Cook slowly for about 45 minutes. Serve with rice. *Alabama recipe.*—C.G.

Fried Okra Rings

Select 1½ lb. of fresh okra and slice. Place in a mixture of two-thirds cup of milk and two beaten eggs; then dip in cornmeal to cover, seasoned to taste with salt and pepper. *Sauté* in butter until golden brown on all sides.—G.T.L.

French Fried Okra

Pour boiling water over the okra, then drain and cook and wipe dry. Dip in a batter made of three eggs beaten with two-thirds cup of milk, one cup of sifted flour, salt and pepper. Drop just a few pieces of the okra at a time in deep hot fat and fry to a golden brown. Drain on absorbent paper.—G.T.L.

Georgia Okra Fritters

Boil one quart of okra. Strain off water and mash. Season with salt and pepper: beat in two eggs, two teaspoonfuls baking powder and enough flour to make a stiff batter. Drop one tablespoonful at a time in deep hot fat and fry.—C.G.

Okra Salad

Wash, trim and slice a cupful of okra; put in a salad-bowl with a cupful of cold, cooked, sliced mushrooms, the small, inner leaves of a lettuce, and a handful of watercress greenest leaves. Dress with a lemon juice and olive oil dressing, with a little mustard added and the usual pepper and salt. Mix well and keep in ice box until wanted, so as to serve the salad quite cold.

Okra Soup or Gumbo

'*Gumbo*' is a soup with okra in it and usually pork flavouring. May be a vegetable, beef, chicken, oyster, shrimp or crab soup, and some recipes forget the okra, but this would be like 'Antony and Cleopatra' without Cleopatra.—C.B.

OLLUCO

Lat. *Ullucus tuberosus.* A South American perennial plant with a branching, creeping stem which roots wherever it touches the ground. It produces tubers on runners issuing from the base of the stem: these tubers are of an oblong-roundish shape, very smooth of texture, yellow of colour and their flesh is yellow, mucilaginous and starchy. They are gathered after the first frosts of the year and eaten like *Potatoes* (q.v.).

ONION

Lat. *Allium cepa*; Fr. *Oignon.* A native of Asia which has become the most indispensable flavouring agent in cooking all the world over. Onions are eaten raw, pickled, boiled, fried, mashed and in a great many different ways. There are numerous varieties of onions, differing both as to size and flavour. The smaller and more pungent onions are mostly used uncooked, in salads or with cheese. The smallest sort are those which are sown in autumn and winter in shallow boxes, in light soil, and at a temperature of 65 to 70 degrees, and grown very much like 'Mustard and Cress'. They are not allowed to reach the bulbous stage but are eaten in salads as small seedlings. The next size is that of the 'Spring Onion', which is not a special breed of onion, but any ordinary onion pulled out of the ground at the time when the beds of seedlings need thinning. Then come the 'Pickling Onions', the first to be picked after the plant has had

time to form a bulb or onion proper; onions are best for pickling when quite small and they are also used in cooking at that stage, either for garnishings or hors-d'oeuvre; they are known as *Button Onions*. Past that stage, onions are given every encouragement to grow as large as possible; they are usually harvested in September and keep well, if properly stored, for six months or more.

The U.S.A. grows many kinds of onions, strong and mild, *Bermudas* and *Spanish* being the best-known of the latter. *Shallots*, another member of the family, are very mild, tiny dry onions.

The *Potato Onion* or *Underground Onion* is a special sort of onion which is particularly early; it is usually harvested, in England, in July, hence its popularity with cottagers who have thus a chance of using the ground for some other crop to follow.

The *Tree Onion* or *Egyptian Onion* is also a peculiar kind of onion which produces small bulbs in place of flowers, as well as larger bulbs at the roots.

The *Welsh Onion*, or *Cibol*, and its Japanese relation the *Nebuka*, are somewhat different; they are perennials which produce small *Leeks* with tubular chive-like leaves. The *Welsh Onion* is of Siberian, not of Welsh origin.

Rocambole, or *Sand Leek*, is the European cousin of the *Welsh Onion*; it has been found in a wild state in Lancashire, Yorkshire, Perthshire, and Fife; also in Ireland and its name is the anglicized form of the Danish *Rockenbolle*, i.e. *Onion on rocks*. It has a distinctly, although discreet, garlic-like flavour.

How to cook Onions

Onions are not nutritious, but they are of the utmost value on account of the salts and vitamins which they possess, and these are mostly in or close to the skin. Hence the wisdom of boiling and baking onions without peeling them first; the outer skin can always be removed more easily after cooking, and by that time the best that was in the outer skins has passed into the onion proper. Of course, when onions are added to stews or soups, more as a flavouring agent than to be served as vegetables, they have to be peeled first. Onions must also perforce be peeled before they are sliced for frying; and, when frying onions, it is important to wait till the butter or whatever fat is being used is boiling hot; it is equally important not to leave the pan for a moment, and to stir the onions continually whilst they are frying.

Boiled Onions

'To prepare an ordinary dish of boiled onions, cut off the roots and tops of some Portuguese or Spanish specimens, remove the dark skin, and *blanch* them. Blanching is effected by putting the onions in a saucepan of cold water, and bringing the water to the boil. This water is thrown away, and the onions, after being rinsed, are laid in a panful of salted water which has just reached boiling-point. If they are very large, they ought to be cut in halves before blanching. They must be boiled in the second water for 2 hours, or a little less if they are small. By pricking them with a fork it is easy to know when they are tender. It is necessary to drain them well and sometimes even to put them back in the empty saucepan and let them dry by the side of the fire. They can be eaten with a lump of butter and plenty of pepper and salt, or with white or brown sauce, or with hot finely-minced meat.'—E.O.

Baked Spanish Onion
I

Place the onions in cold salted water with the skins on; bring to the boil and boil till tender. Drain, dry in a cloth and wrap each onion in a well-buttered paper. Place in a tin and cook in a slow oven for an hour or so; unwrap and serve with a pat of butter and a sprinkling of pepper and salt.

II

Peel the onions and parboil them 20 minutes in boiling salted water. Drain and place in a pie-dish. Sprinkle with pepper and salt and a dusting of flour; pour into the dish enough milk to cover the lower half of the onions and put a pat of butter on top of each onion. Bake until the onions be tender, basting frequently. Before serving, beat two tablespoonfuls of fresh cream with the milk from the dish; spoon it over the onions and serve.

Braised Onions

Pick out a dozen or 18 medium-sized onions as much alike as possible; trim and peel them and put them into about ½ in. of boiling stock in a pan. Cover the pan and cook on a low heat until the onions have absorbed practically the whole of the stock and become tender. If they are not, add a little more stock and cook a little longer. Season with pepper and salt and serve with veal cutlets or any other dish of your choice.

Fried Onions (Plain)

Peel and slice the onions; put a little fat in a pan on a quick fire, and, when hot, put the onions in the hot fat and shake the pan so that all the onions may have a coating of hot fat; cover the pan and reduce the heat greatly; cook slowly for 10 minutes or so; season with pepper and salt to taste, and go on cooking a little longer if need be, until the onions are brown but not burnt.

Fried Onions (Crisp)

Peel the onions and slice them rather thickly; divide the slices into rings with the sharp point of a knife. Mix pepper and salt with some flour; dip the rings of onion in the seasoned flour and drop into boiling deep fat or oil; fry the rings until brown and crisp; drain well and serve hot with grilled steak or fried pork chop.

Glazed Onions

Trim some small pickling or 'button' onions and toss them about in a very little hot butter for a few moments; then dust them freely with castor sugar and go on shaking gently in the pan over a slow heat; if the onions be quite small there is no need to add any water or stock; if they be a little large, it is better to add enough stock barely to cover them and let them simmer until the stock has all but disappeared. By that time, the onions will be cooked and the stock and sugar will have formed a glaze into which the onions are rolled so that all shall be glazed evenly. They are then ready to serve, not as a dish but as a garnish.

Onions au gratin

Trim and blanch some large onions and then simmer in milk till tender; sieve or mash them and season to taste; moisten with some of the milk in which they were cooked. Butter a pie-dish and sprinkle in it some fresh breadcrumbs and a little grated cheese; fill with the onion *purée*; cover with breadcrumbs and grated cheese; add pepper and salt, and dot about some pats of butter; brown in a quick oven and serve hot from the dish.

Onion hors-d'oeuvre

Choose some pickling, 'button' or 'silver' onions, all of the same size; peel them carefully and stew them on a slow heat in equal parts of olive oil and white wine-vinegar; season with pepper and salt, a dusting of castor sugar and a bayleaf; moisten with white stock, enough to cover the lower half of the onions. By the time all the stock has disappeared, probably 15 to 20 minutes, the onions will be sufficiently cooked. Take out the bayleaf, let the onions get quite cold in their own glaze and serve them as hors-d'oeuvre with or without a squeeze of lemon juice at the time of serving, according to taste.

Onion Omelette
I

Prepare a *Purée Soubise* (q.v.) and fold it in the Omelette.

II

Make an Omelette *Fines Herbes*, but instead of beating chopped tarragon and other herbs into the egg mixture, replace by finely-chopped spring onions and make the omelette in the ordinary way.

Pissaladiera

Bread dough
Small black-salted olives
1 clove
Filleted anchovies
Lots of onions
Olive oil
1 clove garlic
Salt and pepper
1 bayleaf

Cut the onions into thin strips. Heat a couple of tablespoonfuls of pure Nice olive oil in a frying-pan; when hot, but not sizzling, add the onions, clove, chopped garlic, salt and the bayleaf. Fry all this together very slowly and gently until a nice light, even brown. Line a flat tart-tin with bread dough. Spread thickly with the onions, having removed the bayleaf, pepper surface well and dot with the olives, and fillets of anchovy (the French ones, curled up in olive oil). Bake in a rather brisk oven for about 15 minutes. Serve very hot, cut in thin strips.

Note. If you feel uncertain about liking the flavour of olive oil, you can fry the onions in butter; if you do this, and omit the garlic, you will have a decent savoury tart, but it will *not* be 'Pissaladiera'.

Purée Soubise

Trim and parboil some large onions; drain, peel and simmer them till tender in a light *Béchamel Sauce*, seasoning with pepper and salt to taste. Rub through a sieve, return to pan, taste and season further if need be, leave uncovered on the stove until as much moisture has evaporated as will leave the *purée* of the right consistency or rather more stiff than desirable; then work in a little fresh cream and serve as a garnish with meat or as a filling for omelettes or pancakes.

Purée Bretonne

Trim and parboil some large onions; drain, peel and simmer them till tender in good stock, seasoning with pepper and salt to taste. When tender, rub through a sieve and return to pan, dredge with flour, stir well and cook gently until of the right consistency. Taste before use and season further if need be.

Onion Ragoût

This is very good with dishes of lamb and mutton. Put 2 lb. of small onions into a stew-pan with 2 oz. of butter and fry them a golden brown. Then add two tablespoonfuls of white wine, a few cloves, a small stick of cinnamon, and two bayleaves. Moisten

with ½ pint of good stock, and add ½ lb. of tomatoes rubbed through a fine sieve. Simmer all together for about an hour, or until the onions are tender, and serve hot.—A.H. (3).

Roast Onions

Trim, but do not peel, some large Spanish onions and roast in a moderate oven for at least 2 hours. Serve in their skins with a pat of fresh butter separately.

Onion Salad

Trim and parboil some medium-sized onions; drain and peel and slice them as finely as you can. Arrange in a dish with alternate layers of sliced tomatoes and pour over all a *Vinaigrette Sauce* (q.v.).

Onions Sautés

Trim and peel some small pickling or 'button' onions; blanch them for 15 minutes in boiling water; drain and dry well and toss them about in hot butter till done, but not browned. Season with pepper and salt to taste.

Onion Soufflé

A delicate dish, just the thing to serve with duck; cook in salted water and drain well, then chop and drain well, very well, 10 or more silver-skin onions, according to size. Force through a sieve; there should be one cup of *purée*, not at all watery. Add one tablespoonful butter and season with salt and pepper. Make a sauce of one tablespoonful each of butter and flour, one cup rich milk, ¼ cup soft, sifted breadcrumbs and one egg yolk. Add this sauce to the *purée* of onion and fold in the stiffly-beaten whites of three eggs. Pour into buttered baking dish, set into a pan of hot water, cover with buttered paper, and bake until firm to the touch. This will take about half an hour.—L.G.A.

Onion Soup

3 or 4 large onions
1 tablespoon butter
1 heaped tablespoon flour
1 quart good meat-stock

Peel the onions, cut them up, chop them up finely. Heat butter in a frying-pan; add the chopped onions; cook gently, stirring frequently until a nice, even and not too dark brown. Stir in the flour with the buttered onions. Moisten with a little good meat-stock and then slip the whole contents of the frying-pan into a saucepan in which there is about a quart of good meat-stock. Bring to the boil, then let the soup simmer for 20 minutes and it will be ready to serve. It may be strained before serving, but it is really better served as it is, with some pieces of toasted bread.—A.L.S.

Soupe à l'Oignon gratinée

Make an *Onion Soup* (q.v.) and pour it in as many individual soup bowls as there are guests; add two or three thin slices of French bread dried in the oven to each bowl, sprinkle with grated cheese, brown under a fierce grill and serve hot.

Soupe à l'Oignon Savoyarde

Take ½ lb. of onions and cut them in fine slices, cook them in butter slowly till they are quite soft and remove them at the precise moment when they are beginning to brown; then add three cups of boiling water and three cups of good stock, the classical *bouquet* (thyme, bayleaf, parsley) and one head of garlic. Season well, bring to the boil, let it reduce, remove the *bouquet*, put in a few finely-broken leaves or buds of thyme, the whole white of an egg and cook a little more till the white is cooked, and bind just before serving with the yolk diluted in a little milk and a drop of vinegar.—x.m.b. (2).

Stewed Onions

Trim, peel, and parboil some nice Spanish onions for 10 minutes in salted water; then dry them and halve them lengthwise. Put into a pan a slice of fat bacon, a *bouquet*, two or three cloves, some whole peppers and a lump of loaf sugar; cover well with good white or brown stock (according to what you want the onions for), bring this just to the boil, then let it simmer for about 2 hours. Now set the onions aside and keep them hot, meanwhile strain the liquor (if brown), remove all fat, and boil it up sharply till well reduced, then serve over and with the onions. If preferred the onion liquor may be, when reduced, added to any sauce to taste, which is then served with the onions, the name of the dish varying according to the sauce used. The first method is known as *au jus*.—s.b.p.

Stuffed Onions
I

Parboil as many onions as required and then throw them for 2 minutes into cold water. Bore a hole through the centre of each and fill with a well-flavoured forcemeat. Arrange the onions in a baking-dish and cover them with some slices of bacon, after having seasoned them with pepper, salt and a little sugar. Cook in a quick oven, remove the onions and reduce the sauce for 10 minutes. These may be served hot, or, if prepared with a little oil in place of the bacon, cold as an hors-d'oeuvre.—D.B.

II

Spanish onions
Salt and pepper
Butter

Fresh breadcrumbs
Brown breadcrumbs
Grated cheese (optional)

Peel the onions, scoop out part of the centre of each, at top, and parboil for 10 minutes, then drain well, turning upside down to remove all water. Chop the parts scooped out and lightly brown in butter. Mix with the fresh breadcrumbs, moisten with a little melted butter, season with salt and pepper. Use to fill centres of onions. Sprinkle tops with brown breadcrumbs and cheese, dot with bits of butter and bake in a covered pan, adding a little water or milk or stock and a little more salt and pepper. Cook until tender then remove lid, baste onions, increase heat and brown tops before serving. Chopped meat, chicken, ham or left-over meat, may be used instead of only breadcrumbs, but a few must be added to bind mixture in any case.

Tarte Bretonne aux Oignons

Peel five big ripe onions. Put them in cold water, add salt, and bring them to the boil. Take them out and let them drain. Next put a pound of good butter in a frying-pan, heat, and place the onions in it. Let them cook slowly. When they have become soft and golden, add half a pound of small rashers of bacon, fried. Let the whole cool together in an enamel dish tightly closed. Then add three fresh eggs and four spoonfuls of thick cream. Beat together. Place the whole in a cake-tin lined with shreds of green vegetables, sprinkled with melted butter, and cook until it browns. Serve very hot.—A.L. (1).

Tarte Alsacienne aux Oignons

Line a shallow tin with short crust. Cut up small a bunch of young spring onions, including the green part, brown them in some butter and a pinch of salt, and remove them from the fire. Stir in three eggs and three large spoonfuls of thick cream and when well mixed pour it into the pastry. Place on the mixture small pieces of lean smoked bacon (preferably unsalted). Cook it in a hot oven for half an hour. Ordinary onions can be used. (*Pampille's Recipe*.)—P.A.

Spring Onions Vinaigrette

One bunch spring onions; olive oil; vinegar; chopped chervil and tarragon.

Wash and trim the onions and tie in a bunch like asparagus. Cook till tender in boiling salted water. Serve with a *Vinaigrette Sauce*, made with oil, vinegar, and chopped herbs. This dish may be served hot or cold.—H.P.

ORACHE. ORACH

Lat. *Atriplex hortensis* and *A. hastata*; Fr. *Arroche*. A native plant of Tartary, now cultivated fairly extensively in France, but not to any great extent in the British Isles nor in the U.S.A. It has broad, arrow-shaped, slightly crimped, soft, pliable leaves, which, are cooked in the same way as *Spinach* (q.v.) and sometimes mixed with spinach in the cooking. It is also called *Garden Orache* and *Mexican Spinach*. The wild *Orache*, commonly known as *Mountain Orache*, is a troublesome but edible weed, called in some English country districts by the curious name of *Fat Hen*.

OTENASHI BEAN
See *Kotenashi Bean*.

OUDO
See *Udo*.

OXALIS
See *Occa*.

OYSTER PLANT
Lat. *Mertensia maritima*. A name which is sometimes given to the *Salsify* (q.v.), a vegetable without any trace of oyster flavour; it should belong to the *Mertensia maritima*, a native British plant, which grows wild on the sea-shore in certain parts of Scotland, Wales and Ireland. It belongs to the order *Boracinaceae*; its flowers are pale blue, rather like *Forget-me-nots*; its grey-green leaves are excellent eaten raw, like water-cress, and they have a distinctly oyster-like saltiness and flavour.

PAK-CHOI
Lat. *Brassica parachinensis*. A Chinese cabbage with dark green, shiny leaves and broad, white midribs, like *Chard* (q.v.).

PAMIR LETTUCE
See *Asparagus Lettuce*.

PARSLEY, PARSNIP-ROOTED
Lat. *Petroselinum crispum, var. radicosum*; Fr. *Persil à grosses racines*. A hardy variety of Parsley grown for the sake of its fleshy root which is eaten uncooked or cooked in the same way as *Carrot* (q.v.). Root-parsley is white and somewhat dry; its flavour is not unlike that of celeriac; it was considered a delicacy in England during the Victorian era, when it was known mostly under the name of *Hamburg Parsley*.

PARSNIP
Lat. *Peucedanum sativum*; Fr. *Panais*. A European long-rooted plant which has been cultivated for human food during many centuries past. Its long, fleshy, white roots are one of the best root foods available during the winter months, yet one of the least appreciated. This may be due to the lack of interest shown and trouble taken by cooks. First of all, parsnips should never be pulled from the ground before they have had the benefit of two or three good frosts; it makes all the difference to their flavour. Then, whether boiled or steamed – and steaming is much better even if it takes a little longer time – parsnips must always be cut in two, longways, and the core or spine being cut in two halves must, and can very easily, be removed with the point of a knife; this core may be quite soft after boiling, but it is quite tasteless and removing it gives a far better chance to the flavour of the parsnip to show its worth. The roots will keep well in the ground, if the ground does not happen to be wanted for some other crop; they may also be stored in a dry place.

Parsnips are mostly used to flavour soups and stews, but they are very good either plainly boiled and served with a white sauce, or mashed, or made into fritters, and in any other way which is suitable for the cooking of *Jerusalem Artichokes* (q.v.).

Cold, cooked parsnip, sliced and served with green lettuce and a *Mayonnaise* makes an excellent salad which is called the *Poor Man's Lobster Salad*: it is not fishy, yet has a lobster-like quality.

Creamed Parsnip Pie
Do not boil but steam the parsnips (previously well washed) in a bowl. The time taken depends on the size of the roots. A medium-sized root may take 40 minutes. When cooked, you will find a little liquor in the bowl which tastes very strongly of parsnips and honey combined. Do not throw this away but add to vegetable soup. Apart from its flavour it contains valuable salts. Skin the parsnips and then slit them open and take out the cores. Put all except the core (which is worthless) in a hot basin and beat it up with butter, allowing 1 oz. of butter to each medium-sized parsnip. Beat it to quite a froth, an impossible feat if the core were left in. Mix in a tablespoonful of finely-chopped parsley and a pinch of salt. Put the mixture in a pie-dish, strew breadcrumbs with little bits of butter on top, and heat in a hot oven.

This dish can be varied in many ways. For instance, the addition of grated cheese (preferably parmesan cheese) makes a good vegetarian supper dish. Or finely-shredded ham can be mixed in. Left-over mushrooms cut up small are a good addition. Just before serving the top can be garnished with powdered hard-boiled yolk of egg and paprika.—E.S.R.

PATENT SPINACH
See *New Zealand Spinach*.

PATIENCE DOCK
See *Herb Patience*.

PEA
The most popular of all summer vegetables in all but tropical and sub-tropical countries. It is cultivated mostly for its seeds, the peas, within its fruit, the pod, but there are certain varieties cultivated for their pods, which are cooked and eaten like French beans, before the seeds, or peas have had time to grow to their full size. Peas are also dried and kept for winter use, either whole or split.

(a) Garden Peas. Green Peas. Shelling Peas
Lat. *Pisum sativum*; Fr. *Pois*. There are a number of different varieties of *Garden Peas*, smooth and wrinkled, early and late, but all are eaten freshly-picked and freshly-shelled, whether forced under glass or grown in the open. The smaller and younger they are, the better they are if they are to be served as a separate vegetable course, hot, or as a salad, cold. When oldish, big and floury, they are better used for making soups or *purées* (mashed); they may also be added to stews.

Garden Peas English Style
Shell the peas, wash them and put them in plenty of salted boiling water; add a sprig or two of mint and a pinch of sugar; then cover the pan. When the water comes up to the boil again, take the pan away from the fire and go on simmering until the peas are tender. Drain at once, dish the peas in a warmed-up dish, season with salt and pepper and a piece of butter rammed in the middle of the peas and serve.

Garden Peas à la Française
Peel two or three small onions and toss them about in hot butter in a deep pan for a few moments; then put into the pan a head of washed cos lettuce, a lump of sugar, a spoonful of warm water and a quart of garden peas, shelled and washed. Cover the pan and cook gently, shaking the pan occasionally, for about 20 minutes, when the peas should be tender and ready to serve.

Garden peas cooked in the English or French way may be served hot, by themselves, as a separate course, or with any joint and *entrée*; or else used as garnishings and fillings for artichoke bottoms, puff paste tartlets, etc. They may also be 'finished' with cream or one or the other of many suitable sauces or mixed with other cooked vegetables. They may also be left to get cold and dressed with any salad dressing preferred and cooked and cold vegetables in salads.

Jugged Peas
1 lb. green peas
1 small teaspoon powdered sugar
1 tablespoon butter
Salt and pepper

Shell the peas and put them into a jar having a close-fitting lid or top, adding the butter, salt, sugar and a little freshly-ground black pepper. If wished, a few fresh mint leaves may go in as well. Shut bottle or jar securely and immerse, to the extent of half its depth, in a pan of hot water. Bring quickly to boiling point and cook, shaking the pot and turning upside down once or twice gently, for about half an hour.

Petits Pois au Lard
1 thick slice bacon or salt, lean pork
1 small *bouquet-garni*
Salt and pepper
Freshly-shelled peas
Butter
1 small lettuce

Cut the bacon or pork into dice and brown lightly in butter on all surfaces. Add the peas and just moisten with water. Add the heart of the lettuce and the *bouquet*, season with salt and pepper to taste. Cover saucepan and cook gently until the peas are tender. Remove *bouquet* and serve peas around lettuce.

Green Pea Soup
Boil two cups of large, elderly green peas in plenty of boiling water till tender, and no longer or they will get as hard as when they were put in. Press them through a sieve and save the water in which they were boiled. Peel and cut up an onion; brown it in a little hot butter and put in the same pan as the mashed peas and the water in which they were boiled. Add two or three small potatoes, peeled and sliced as finely as possible. Season with pepper and salt. Bring to the boil and then simmer for half an hour. Before serving stir in a little butter and the well-beaten yolk of an egg.

Pea-pods Soup
String the pea-pods and remove as much of the inner parchment as will come off easily. Wash and put in a saucepan with a peeled and sliced onion, two or three peeled and sliced potatoes and a quart of milk. Season with pepper and salt to taste and simmer until the potatoes are quite soft. Pass the whole through a fine sieve, return to the pan, re-heat and bind with the beaten yolk of an egg just before serving.

(b) Edible podded Peas. Sugar Peas. Pois Mangetout
Lat. *Pisum sativum, var. macrocarpum*; Fr. *Pois mangetout*. Sugar peas are a separate sort of

peas; their pods have no parchment lining, like the shelling peas, and when their seeds, that is to say the peas within the pods, are still very small, they are picked, 'tipped-and-tailed', and boiled like *French Beans* (q.v.), drained, buttered and eaten, pods and all.

(c) Split Peas. Pease

Dried peas are with us at all times of the year and of real value during the winter months, when no others are to be had. They are very good for soups and also soaked, boiled and mashed, for *purées*. There are two sorts of dried peas, the green and the yellow.

Irish Pease Pudding

1 quart dried peas
2 tablespoons butter
1 egg
Salt and pepper

Soak the peas over night. Boil until tender, drain and rub through a sieve. Beat the egg and add to the peas with the butter, salt and pepper. Beat the mixture well for about 10 minutes, then tie into a floured cloth (leaving room for the peas to swell), and simmer for 1 hour longer. Turn out and serve with salted butter.

N.B. A small *bouquet* and onion added to the peas when cooking greatly improve the flavour. With hot pickled pork, pease pudding is classical. Pickled pork and pease pudding was a favourite luncheon dish with King Edward VII.—B.H.

Split Pea Purée

Green or yellow split peas
4 or 6 oz. fat bacon
2 carrots
2 onions
1 or 2 cloves
1 *bouquet garni*

After soaking the peas overnight, put all the ingredients on to boil together. When done, remove the bacon, pass the other ingredients through a sieve after draining them well, and reserve the liquid, some of which will be used to moisten the *purée* to the desired consistency, and the remainder will be used for soup. Allow the *purée* to simmer gently by the side of the fire, after adding some of the liquid and a good tablespoonful of fresh butter. Serve hot with fried sausages, or with boiled Frankfort sausage.—B.H.

Split Pea Soup

1 pint split peas (soaked overnight)
2 quarts meat-stock or ham water
1 carrot
1 onion
1 stick of celery

Put the peas in meat-stock, or in water with a ham-bone and the cut vegetables. Bring to the boil and then simmer until the peas are soft enough to be rubbed through a fine sieve. Re-heat and add either a tablespoonful of butter at the time of serving, or, better still, two tablespoonfuls of thick cream, and serve hot. Small squares of fried stale bread added to this soup are an improvement.—B.H.

PEA BEAN

Lat. *Phaseolus vulgaris.* A variety of climbing *French Bean*, cultivated for its seeds or beans, which are round and resemble peas, hence the name. It is known in New York as the *Beautiful Bean*, and its bi-colour blooms are truly beautiful; its flavour reminds one of the *Mangetout Peas*, but it is finer. It is one of the least known and yet probably the finest of all beans gastronomically, provided, however, that it be eaten as soon as picked: it quickly gets tough after being picked. It is cooked in any way suitable for *French Beans* (q.v.).

PEANUT. EARTH-NUT. GROUND-NUT. ARACHIS

Lat. *Arachis hypogaea*; Fr. *Arachide* or *Cacaouette.* A Brazilian herb now extensively cultivated in many sub-tropical and even temperate countries for the sake of its oblong, oily, nutlike seed. This is chiefly used to make peanut butter and peanut oil, but it is also eaten roasted and cooked in various ways. *Peanut cake*, made of ground peanuts, is the staple food of millions of natives in Africa and the East. In Europe peanuts are used chiefly in vegetarian cooking, but their flavour is objectionable to many palates.

Peanut Brittle

1 quart sugar
1 pint water
1 quart peanuts

Dissolve the sugar in the water and boil in a covered saucepan only until the syrup is thick and has just taken on a light amber colour. In the meantime have the peanuts shelled and skinned. Sprinkle nuts generously over the bottom of a well-oiled platter or pan. Pour the caramelized syrup over the nuts. Do not scrape the pan. When cooled break the brittle into pieces. This makes 2¼ lb. candy.—P.D.P.

Peanut Sandwiches

Sandwiches of buttered brown bread spread with peanut butter mixed with clear honey are very good for children, and many grown-ups who are not cursed with a sensitive palate also like them.

PEPPERGRASS. PEPPERWORT

Lat. *Lepidium sativum*. The names of different species of *Cress* (q.v.).

PEPPERS

1. A condiment, the fruit of plants of the *Piper* genus, such as *Piper cubeba*, Cubeb Pepper, and more particularly *Piper Nigrum*, Black Pepper. Its dried berries yield black pepper, the ripe seeds with their original black outer skin left on; and white pepper, the same seeds after they are freed from their outer cover.

2. A condiment, the fruit of any species of *Capsicum* (q.v.), such as *Cayenne* (q.v.), or *Guinea Pepper* (q.v.), and *Paprika* (q.v.).

3. A vegetable, variously known as *Spanish Pepper, Long Pepper, Green* or *Sweet Pepper, Bonnet Pepper, Bell Pepper* or *Red Pepper*, according to shape and the colour of its skin when ripe.

Bell Pepper, *Capsicum frutescens, var. tetragonum*; Black Pepper, *Piper nigrum*; Cayenne Pepper, *Capsicum frutescens, var. minimum*; Cubeb Pepper, *Piper Cubeba*; Long Pepper, *Capsicum frutescens, var. longum* (*Piper longum*); Red Pepper, *Capsicum annuum* and *C. frutescens, var. tetragonum*; Sweet-Pepper, *Capsicum grossum*.

Fried Peppers

Peppers may be cut in strips, longways, or in rings to be fried. In either case, the seeds must be removed and as much as possible of the inner lining membrane. Then the peppers are either parboiled in salted boiling water, for 5 minutes, drained and tossed in butter another 5 minutes; or else dipped in egg and breadcrumbs, fried in deep fat and drained on absorbent paper.

Stuffed Peppers

Cut the peppers in half lengthwise and remove the seeds and some of the inner membrane. Parboil 3 or 4 minutes, drain, stuff and bake for 10 or 15 minutes in a hot oven. Stuffings suitable for stuffed tomatoes, eggplant or vegetable marrow can be used. Practically anything left over, whether meat, poultry, game, fish or vegetables, may be made into a tasty stuffing with a little imagination; mushrooms and cheese are always safe for the purpose.

PERPETUAL SPINACH

See *Spinach Beet*.

PE-TSAI. CHINESE CABBAGE

Lat. *Brassica pekinensis*. A Chinese cabbage which looks more like a cos lettuce than a cabbage. It may be eaten uncooked, as a salad, but it is best cooked in any way suitable for the common *Cabbage* (q.v.) and it has the advantage of being practically odourless whilst cooking. (*Pé* means white, and *Tsai* means vegetable).

PHILIPPINE SPINACH

Lat. *Talinum triangulare*. The name of two varieties of Eastern *Purslanes* which are cultivated for the sake of their green leaves which are prepared for the table in any way suitable for *Spinach* (q.v.).

PIGWEED

Lat *Amaranthus candatus, A spinosus*, and *A. Thunbergii*; Fr. *Pourcellaine* An annual herb from 3 to 5 ft. in height, with hard, shining, red, white or black seeds, which is cultivated in tropical Africa, India and Ceylon for the sake of its edible seeds, an important article of food among the hill tribes of India It is widely naturalized in South Africa, being called *Misbredie* in Afrikaans, and *Umbuya* by the Zulus

Among related species used as food, chiefly in the Union of South Africa and in Portuguese East Africa, mention may be made of *Amaranthus thunbergii* and *A. Spinosus*: their young leaves, shoots and young flower heads are boiled in water, with a little salt and are eaten, like green vegetables, with other foods, or are mixed with mealie meal and boiled until a thick paste is obtained. In summer, the young leaves are also dried for use when fresh vegetables are not obtainable.

There are a number of weeds also known as *Pigweed*, such as the *Goosefoot* (q.v.), and the *Purslanes* (q.v.).

PIMENTO. PIMIENTO

Lat. *Capsicum frutescens, var. tetragonum*; Fr. *Piment*. The Spanish Pepper. The seed, when ripe, is dried and is known as *Paprika* (q.v.), but the fruit itself is used as a vegetable. See *Pepper* (3).

Pimento Cream

One cup heavy cream, one egg white, two or more pimentos rubbed through sieve. Whip cream until thick, beat egg until stiff, combine mixtures, and lastly fold in the pimento.—P.D.P.

Pimento Soup

To beef *Consommé* or chicken broth add some parboiled and sieved pimentos and some cayenne papper; if the night be cold and the guests not wine-minded, add also some *Tabasco Sauce*.

PLANTAIN

Lat. *Plantago major*. Usually considered an objectionable weed in paths and lawns, this plant was highly prized by Chaucer and Shakespeare for its healing virtue, and its leaves were used to make a kind of 'tea', in

England, long before Bohea had ever been heard of. Its young leaves can also be used in green salads like *Corn Salad*. (Canaries are very fond of Plantain seeds.)

POKEBERRY. POAKBERRY

The red berry of the *Pokeweed* (q.v.). It has no gastronomic merit but may be used – and was formerly much used – as a vegetable colouring for pastries, jellies and creams.

POKEWEED. POAKE. POAKAN

Lat. *Phytolacca americana* and *P. Scinosa*. A native shrub of Northern America which was imported into Europe in the sixteenth century and cultivated for the sake of the red dye obtained from its tightly-packed bunches of red berries full of blood-red juice. (Its name, poake, means blood in idiomatic Indian). Its cultivation was abandoned in Europe when the cochineal was imported from Mexico and replaced poake red as a dye. The root is said to be poisonous, but its leafy shoots, in May or June, when some 6 to 8 in. long, are delicious. The leaves must be left on the shoots, which are tied in small bundles and boiled for 10 minutes in fast *un*salted water. The poake is then taken out, drained and served with melted butter or a *Sauce Mousseline*. The flavour of poake combines in a very happy manner both that of the asparagus and that of spinach. It is also very good served cold with oil and vinegar. Pokeweed may be forced in the same way as seakale and eaten like *Seakale* (q.v.).

The published American figure for the Vitamin C content of *Pokeweed* is 273 mgs. per 100 gs.

Another member of the pokeweed family, chiefly grown in Japan, is known as the *Yama Gobo*. Dried Gobo sliced diagonally may be bought occasionally from Japanese grocers in New York.

POMPION

See *Pumpkin*.

POPPY

Lat. *Papaver Rhoeas*; Fr. *Pavot*. The common field poppy; its very young leaves, if gathered before the poppy blooms, may be treated like *Nettles* (q.v.). They have a nutty flavour and are quite acceptable after a severe winter when green vegetables are rare.

POTATO

Lat. *Solanum tuberosum*; Fr. *Pomme de terre*. Potatoes are with us all the year round, new, not so new, or old. They are full of everything that is good for good people, that is normal people who do not suffer from diabetes or the craze for slimming. But, unlike good people, whose goodness is in the heart, most of the goodness in the potato is in its skin. This is why potatoes, except old and warty ones, should not be peeled before they are cooked. Potatoes are not only full of goodness, but again, unlike many people who are ever so good, potatoes are not boring. One could, and many do, eat potatoes every day without tiring of them as one would if one had to put up with a daily ration of turnips, Jerusalem artichokes, parsnips and other roots and tubers. The flavour of the potato is not aggressive, and yet it holds its own against all comers, be it steam or boiling water, sizzling butter, olive oil or any kind of fat. This is why there are more and more varied manners of cooking potatoes than all other vegetables, as one can easily ascertain by consulting any cookery book. There is only one thing that cookery books do not tell us, and that is how to boil potatoes. As a rule they do not bother even to mention whether the potatoes should be put in cold or boiling water, but most of them agree that 'approximately' 20 minutes' boiling will produce 'boiled potatoes.' It is sheer nonsense. Before one can begin to think about boiled potatoes, one must know what sort of potatoes one is dealing with; it is obvious that the waxy, firm sorts of potatoes cannot be treated successfully in the same way as the soft mealy, or floury sorts, and that old, warty potatoes are an entirely different proposition from the small new potatoes freshly dug up.

Boiled Potatoes

(*a*) Waxy, firm potatoes should be washed, scrubbed, *not peeled*, and put in a panful of cold, salted water; there must be enough water to cover the potatoes completely. Put the pan on a good fire, bring to the boil and boil for 15 or 20 minutes, according to size of tubers. Pour all the water away, leave the potatoes in the covered pan on a corner of stove or in a cool oven for another 20 minutes, or until wanted. Peel them then or not, according to taste.

(*b*) Floury or mealy, softer potatoes should be washed, scrubbed, *not peeled*, and put into a panful of fast-boiling salted water; there must be enough water to cover all the potatoes completely. Boil for 20 or 25 minutes, according to size, pour away the water and let the potatoes finish cooking in their own heat for another 20 minutes in the covered pan. Peel or not, according to taste.

(*c*) Old, warty potatoes, should you have no other, must be peeled and soaked in cold water for an hour, then put into boiling water and boiled fast for 30 minutes. They are then drained, and the best thing to do with them is to mash them, season, moisten with a little milk and serve as *purée*.

(*d*) New potatoes are best washed, rubbed, *not peeled*, and put in boiling salted water which is not allowed to boil again; simmer for 15 or 20 minutes, drain, toss in a little melted butter, season with a pinch of salt and serve without parsley, mint, or anything else.

Potatoes baked in their jacket
(Pommes de terre en robe de chambre)

Wash and scrub some fairly large potatoes and wipe them dry. Brush a little butter or bacon fat over the skins, prick them with the points of a fork and bake in a moderate oven for an hour, or longer, if the potatoes are large ones. Choose the red, pink or other floury, mealy or soft potatoes for baking. Unless the potatoes be quite old, the skin should be crisp and very good to eat. If you have to use old, thick-skinned potatoes, slit them longways with the sharp point of a knife, and press on either side to make the slit gape and the floury potato meal rise. Serve in a folded napkin with plenty of fresh butter separately.

Mashed Potatoes
Purée de Pommes de terre

Peel some boiled floury or soft potatoes and press through a sieve. Put the sieved potatoes back into a pan on the fire; season with pepper and salt; add a piece of butter and stir in; also enough hot milk to allow the potatoes to be whipped to the consistency of a thick cream.

Pommes Anna

Peel the potatoes and cut them into very thin rings, which you must soak in cold water for 10 minutes. Drain them and dry them in a cloth. Take a straight-sided fireproof dish (with a lid) just large enough to hold all the potato, and butter it well. Arrange the rings in this in layers, seasoning each with salt and pepper and dotting it here and there with butter (which you must not spare). When the dish is full, spread the top layer fairly thickly with butter, put on the lid and make it airtight with paste made with flour and water. Bake in a slack oven for three-quarters of an hour, when you must take out the potato cake and put it back in the dish upside down. Cover closely and cook for another three-quarters of an hour, then pour off all the butter, and turn out the lovely golden cake you will find. (AMBROSE HEATH. *Spring in the Kitchen*, in *Wine and Food*. Vol. I, p. 38.)

Pommes de terre à l'Auvergnate

Potatoes
4 oz. fat bacon or salt pork
2 or 3 onions
2 tablespoons good pure lard
Salt and pepper

Peel the potatoes and cut into thin slices. Cut the bacon or lard into smallish cubes. Slice the onions. Heat the lard in a *cocotte*, add alternate layers of sliced potatoes, cubes of bacon and sliced onions, seasoning as needed. Cover pot and cook gently for one hour. Serve in pot. If wished, the onions may be lightly browned before adding to pot as may also be the cubes of bacon, the fat from which will replace the lard.

Potato Balls

Sieve some boiled potatoes and allow a tablespoonful of butter per pound of mashed potatoes. Stir the butter little by little into the mashed potatoes over the fire, then move pan away from the heat and whisk in the beaten yolks of two eggs. Shape into balls, egg and breadcrumb these and fry them in deep fat to a golden brown; drain and serve hot.

Potato Cheese

6 cooked potatoes
2 oz. grated cheese
$\frac{1}{2}$ oz. margarine or dripping
$\frac{1}{4}$ to $\frac{1}{2}$ pint milk
Salt and pepper
Chopped parsley

The potatoes must be mashed very smoothly. Melt the dripping or margarine. Add this along with the milk, salt and pepper. Stir in the cheese, and re-heat in the saucepan. Garnish with chopped parsley. The same mixture can also be put in a greased pie-dish. Reserve some of the cheese. Sprinkle this over the top and brown under the grill or before an open fire.

Potato Colcannon

Rub the potatoes through a sieve and allow twice as much potato as of the other vegetables put together. The greater the variety of vegetables the better. Mash up the other vegetables as small as possible. Mix with a good tablespoonful of butter and fill a buttered fireproof dish with the mixture. Sprinkle the top with a layer of breadcrumbs and put a few pats of butter on top. Bake in a hot oven till the breadcrumbs are golden brown.—E.S.R. (1).

Potato Crisps

Very thinly sliced potatoes cooked in boiling fat, drained, salted and usually eaten cold.

Potato Croquettes

Freshly mashed potatoes
1 egg yolk
A few drops onion juice
Salt and pepper
1 whole egg
Brown breadcrumbs

Mix the potatoes and seasonings well together, binding to a thick smooth paste with the egg yolk. Form into whatever shape desired with the hands. Dip in breadcrumbs, then in the beaten egg and again in the crumbs. Fry until crisp and brown in boiling deep fat. Drain and serve very hot.

Note. Half a cupful of grated cheese may be added to mixture if desired.

Pommes de terre à la Dauphinoise

Good baking potatoes
½ cup grated Gruyère
Milk or thin cream
Salt and pepper
1 clove garlic
Butter

Cut the clove of garlic and use to rub over entire surface of an earthenware gratin dish. Butter this well with softened butter. Peel and cut potatoes into rather thick slices. Lay them in the dish, one overlapping the other and sprinkling with salt, pepper and half the grated cheese. Repeat operation, finishing with a layer of the rest of the cheese. Pour over all three tablespoonfuls of melted butter. Cook in moderately hot oven, seeing that the potatoes cook at first rather slowly, then faster to brown surface. This is the classical recipe, but some cooks add, when the potatoes are nearly done, a couple of beaten eggs with a little more milk or cream. The quantity of milk used depends on the quality and quantity of potatoes; in any case it should be no more than can be absorbed while cooking. Serve, of course, in gratin dish.

Fried Potatoes

Firm, sound, waxy potatoes
Good frying oil or fat

Scrub but do not peel the potatoes, cut them into sticks of even thickness and length, and place in ice-cold water for a few minutes, then drain and dry thoroughly in a clean cloth. Keep them covered while heating fat. As soon as this is of the right temperature – 375° F. if you have a frying thermometer – which will be when the fat is lightly smoking, put potatoes in. Fry only a few at a time until crisp and light brown. Keep hot on white kitchen paper while others are being fried, and take care to re-heat oil to right temperature before adding more potatoes. If too many are fried at one time they do not brown regularly and are inclined to stick together. If preferred, fry all together until soft but not brown. Drain well, re-heat oil and plunge the potatoes in all together, shaking and stirring to prevent sticking and to ensure even browning. The first frying should be in oil or fat at a temperature of 350° F., or when it is hot and still, but not yet smoking. Serve as soon as ready, or if there is some delay, re-plunge for a minute in very hot fat and then serve as soon as drained. Sprinkle with salt when serving.

Note. Do not have the potato chips cut too thick. They look unsightly and the interiors remain floury and sometimes, according to type of potato used, rather hard and underdone. If pieces are preferred larger, take care not to fry in fat which is too hot or surfaces will brown leaving insides hard.

Fried (mashed) Potatoes

Take six large cooked potatoes, mash them with the yolks of four eggs, and cream sufficient to make the mixture quite soft. Season with salt and pepper and a very little parmesan. Whip the whites of three eggs very stiff and add to the mixture: Put the frying basket into a pan of boiling fat or oil and then drop in small spoonfuls of the mixture. As these turn golden coloured, lift them out, and put on a piece of paper in a hot dish.— **F.C.W.**

Cottage Fried Potatoes

Dice cold boiled potatoes. Season with salt and pepper. Brown in well-greased heavy frying-pan; sprinkle some finely-chopped chives over them.

Gnocchis de Pomme de terre

2 lb. sound potatoes
2 eggs
1 slice boiled ham (optional)
2 tablespoons butter
2 tablespoons grated parmesan
Flour

The red floury Dutch potatoes are best for this job. Bake in their skins until tender, then split and remove pulp. Mix with this the chopped ham, half the parmesan and the butter. Beat the eggs and add to mixture, blending thoroughly; finally beat in sufficient sifted flour to make a thick paste which can be readily moulded. Flour the hands, cut or break off pieces of the potato paste, shape into long sausages and cut these into thick slices. Shape into tiny balls or 'corks'. Put some water on to boil, salt as desired and use to poach the gnocchis until they rise to the surface. Drain well and serve in a gratin dish, covering with thick fresh tomato or *Béchamel Sauce* and sprinkling surface with remainder of grated parmesan.

Potato Omelette
(Omelette Parmentier)

Peel some boiled potatoes and cut them up in small cubes; toss these in hot butter; season them with pepper and salt and some finely-chopped spring onion or chives. Make an omelette in the usual way and fold the potatoes into it at the time of serving. The potatoes may also be beaten with the egg mixture and the omelette made with it.

Pommes Persillées

Tiny new potatoes
Finely-chopped parsley
Butter or good pure lard
Salt

Select very young and quite tiny potatoes. Scrub and dry in a cloth. Put a couple of tablespoonfuls of butter or lard or good dripping in a metal *cocotte* or an earthenware casserole. Heat fat well. Add potatoes and cook for 10 to 15 minutes, shaking the pan frequently. When the potatoes begin to colour, reduce heat, cover pan and continue cooking until they are done through, then remove lid, increase heat and crisp up the potatoes nicely, shaking pan to prevent burning. Serve very hot with a sprinkling of salt and finely-chopped parsley. If there seems to be too much fat in pan when potatoes are done, pour some off so that they may crisp more easily and evenly. If small potatoes are not available, balls may be scooped from large, firm ones.

Potato Pie

Whip in plenty of *Sauce Mornay* with the required quantity of mashed potatoes; fill a baking-dish with the mixture, put a few pats of butter on top and bake in a hot oven until the top is golden brown, when the pie will be ready to serve.

There are, of course, ever so many different ways of using up left-over cold boiled potatoes into potato pies with other left-overs of all sorts.

Quenelles de Pommes de terre

5 or 6 potatoes
3 egg yolks
Dusting ground nutmeg
2 tablespoons melted butter
2 egg whites
Salt and pepper

Boil potatoes, mash and pass through a sieve after draining thoroughly. Mix with this the three well-beaten egg yolks, the nutmeg, salt, pepper and the melted butter, blending and beating well. Whip the egg whites quite firm and fold into potato mixture lightly. Shape into small sausages of desired size and thickness. Poach these in boiling bouillon or milk until they rise to surface of liquid, then skim out, drain and serve with a thick fresh *Tomato* or *Béchamel Sauce*.

Roast Potatoes
(Pommes de terre au four)

Peel some fairly large potatoes and cut them in two; if using smaller tubers, peel and leave them whole. Put them in the baking-dish round the joint which is to be roasted and let them roast in the fat of the meat till done.

Sautéed Potatoes
Pommes de terre sautées

Peel some boiled potatoes and slice them – ¼ in. thick slices are best. Melt a little butter or fat in a frying-pan and toss (*sauter*) the potatoes in the hot butter or fat, season with pepper and salt and a sprinkling of finely-chopped parsley, till all the butter or fat has gone into the potatoes and they are beginning to 'catch'. Serve at once, hot.

Savoury Potatoes

Add one tablespoonful of chopped watercress and one teaspoonful of chopped fresh mint-leaves to some mashed potatoes; then a few pats of butter and brown under quick grill.

Potato Salads

Potato salads should be made with yellow-fleshed, waxy potatoes. There are a few specially suitable varieties – such as *Vitelotte, Fir Apple* and *Kipfel* – which are firm and small in diameter, so that they are easy to cut into appropriate discs.

Hot Potato Salad

Wash six medium-sized potatoes and boil until tender. Cool, peel and cut into very thin slices. Cover the bottom of a baking-tin with these slices, seasoning with salt and pepper and sprinkling with a little finely-chopped chives and parsley mixed. Blend together two tablespoonfuls of wine-vinegar with four tablespoonfuls of good olive oil. Add the juice of one lemon. Bring this mixture to boiling point, then pour over the potatoes. Cover tin and allow to stand in the oven until contents are very hot.

Cold Potato Salad

Cold boiled potatoes
Pepper and salt
1 cup finely-chopped parsley, chives and celery
Vinaigrette Sauce

Slice the potatoes and cut into regular cubes, and mix with the chopped parsley, chives and celery; cover with sufficient *Vinaigrette* to marinate for half an hour before serving.

Pommes Soufflées

Choose some firm, waxy potatoes of medium size. Peel them and slice them roundways as thin as you can, and all of the same thickness. Do not wash them, just wipe them well in a clean cloth. To make sure of success, you should have two deep pans ready, each with some deep boiling fat at different temperatures. Plunge the potatoes into the first pan, in fat at a temperature of not more than 350°F., let them cook four or five minutes, shaking the pan or stirring the potatoes all the time; when they rise to the surface and begin to puff, skim them and transfer them at once to the second pan where the fat should be very hot and smoking, about 400°F. They will puff at once but should be left and stirred until they begin to brown. Then is the time to drain them and serve them at once, with a dusting of salt over them.

Potato Soup

There are different ways of making a potato soup, but the simplest – and best – is to simmer four or five medium-sized peeled potatoes, if making soup for six people, for quite a long time in a little water and a quart of milk, adding more milk if necessary to make as much soup as one requires. Season well with pepper and salt. Mash the potatoes, add a tablespoonful of butter and pour into the soup tureen over some little snippets of fried stale bread.

Stuffed Potatoes

Large potatoes baked in their skins and cut in two have their floury meal scooped out and returned after it has been mixed with any and every kind of minced meats, vegetables, truffles, etc. Or else the stuffing may replace the floury meal of the potato entirely.

French Potato Preparations

Allumettes. Fried potatoes cut as finely as matches.

Alsacienne. New potatoes tossed in butter with some button onions and small pieces of bacon; a sprinkling of fine herbs over them.

Anglaise. Steamed or plain boiled.

Anna. The potatoes are cut in regular, thin, round slices and arranged in a well-buttered dish closely together, tart-like, in a thick layer. Melted butter is then poured over them and they are baked in a hot oven.

Bataille. Fried potatoes cut in cubes.

Bénédictine. Fried potatoes cut turban-like by a special machine.

Berny. Fried croquettes of mashed potatoes and minced truffles mixed.

Biarritz. Mashed potatoes with some ham cut dice-like mixed with it, also some chopped-up green peppers and fine herbs.

Bohémienne. Baked potatoes with their meal scooped out and replaced by a stuffing of sausage meat baked in the potato.

Boulangère. Sliced fried onions and sliced potatoes mixed together and moistened with meat-stock and baked in oven.

Bretonne. Large dice of potatoes cooked in stock with chopped onions and garlic and some sliced tomatoes.

Byron. Little flat cakes made of the mealy part of baked potatoes mixed with cheese and some *Béchamel Sauce*, cooked in hot butter and browned in a hot oven.

Cendrillon. Whole potatoes baked in their jackets and shaped like *sabots* (wooden shoes); the mealy part is scooped out, mixed with grated cheese, returned and arranged dome-like in the potato skin and browned in a hot oven.

Chambéry. Boiled potatoes, peeled, sliced, arranged in a buttered dish in layers, each layer buttered and sprinkled with grated cheese, then browned in a hot oven.

Château. Peeled potatoes cut like large olives, parboiled and then cooked in a moderate oven in butter.

Chatouillard. They are *Pommes Soufflées* (q.v.), but cut ribbon-like with a special gimlet-like cutter.

Chips. Fried potatoes.

Cocotte. The same as *Pommes Château*, but of a much smaller size.

Copeaux. Potatoes very thinly sliced in the shape of shavings and fried in deep fat.

Crème. Parboiled in boiling water. Peeled, sliced and finished cooking in milk, with fresh cream added at the time of serving.

Dauphine. Mashed potatoes with butter and the yolk of an egg added; then about one-third of puff paste is mixed with it and the mixture is shaped somewhat like large corks, which are egg-and-breadcrumbed and fried in deep fat.

Dauphinoise. Peeled and sliced potatoes laid in a buttered dish and cooked in a moderate oven with milk to cover and some grated Gruyère cheese added.

Duchesse. Mashed potatoes with butter and yolks of eggs added; shaped, brushed over with beaten egg and lightly browned in hot oven.

Elizabeth. The same as *Pommes Dauphine*, but with a stuffing of creamed spinach.

Fondantes. The same as *Pommes Château*, but cooked with a little chicken broth and in a covered pan, so that they are softer.

Four, Au. Baked in their jackets.

Gratin, Au. Mashed potatoes to which butter, and the yolk of an egg have been added; also pepper and salt, a little cream and some grated cheese. The mixture is put into a buttered baking-dish, covered with breadcrumbs and grated cheese and browned in a hot oven.

Impériale. Potatoes baked in their jackets, then cut in two, their meal scooped out and returned after it has been mixed with butter, cream and minced truffles.

Lyonnaise. Sliced potatoes tossed in butter and then mixed with fried onions and sprinkled over with chopped parsley.

Macaire. Potatoes baked in their jackets, then cut in two, their meal scooped and returned after it has been mixed with butter and finely-chopped fine herbs.

Maître d'Hôtel. Same as *Pommes à la Crème*, but served with a thick sprinkling of finely-chopped parsley.

Mignonettes. Fried potatoes cut twice as large as *Pommes Allumettes*.

Mireille. The same as *Pommes Anna*, but with artichoke bottoms added; also some slices of truffle.

Mirette. Potatoes cut dice-like and cooked in butter, then mixed with a julienne of truffles (thin slices of truffles) and served in a timbale with some *Sauce Madère* over them, a sprinkling of grated cheese and browned in a quick oven at the last.

Monselet. Fairly thick rounds of potatoes cooked in hot butter and served crown-wise with the centre filled with shredded mushrooms tossed in butter and chopped truffles.

Noisettes. Potatoes cut like marbles or cobnuts, tossed in hot butter till cooked and served with finely-chopped fine herbs.

Paille. Potatoes cut longways and as thin as possible, like straws, then fried in deep fat and well drained; served with grilled meat.

Parmentier. The French culinary equivalent of potato.

Persillées. New potatoes simmered in stock, finished in butter and served with a sprinkling of chopped parsley.

Pont-Neuf. Fried potatoes cut rather thick and square.

Provençale. Same as *Pommes de terre sautées* with minced garlic added.

Rissolées. Same as *Pommes Château*, but cooked a little longer till dark brown.

Savoyarde. Same as *Pommes Dauphinoise*, but with stock in place of milk.

Vapeur. Steamed potatoes.

Voisin. Same as *Pommes Anna*, but with a little grated cheese and just a whiff of nutmeg upon each layer of potatoes.

There are other vegetables called *Potatoes*, such as the *Kaffir Potato* or *Umdondive*, a favourite tuber of the natives in Natal; the *Madagascar* or *Haussa Potato*, largely cultivated in many parts of tropical Africa, Java, Ceylon, Madagascar and Mauritius; the *Sweet Potato* (q.v.), and the *Yam* (q.v.).

POTATO ONION
Lat. *Allium cepa, var. solaninum*. See *Onion*.

PRIMROSE
Lat. *Primula veris*; Fr. *Primevère*. Primrose leaves, when young, may be eaten, boiled, like *Sorrel* (q.v.), and preferably with sorrel, as they are tasteless by themselves. A few primroses in a green salad look fresh and pleasant; they have no taste.

PUMPKIN
Lat. *Cucurbita maxima*; Fr. *Potiron*. Pumpkin is the name given in England to:

1. All members of the large *Cucurbita maxima* family known in the U.S.A. as *Squash*. Their flesh, sweetish of taste and orange of colour, is full of nourishment and vitamins; it keeps well and provides an excellent stand-by vegetable for the winter months, chiefly for soups but also as a vegetable, and;

2. The gourd-like fruit of a coarse prickly-haired pumpkin-vine, or field pumpkin, the *Pompion* – extensively cultivated in the U.S.A. as food for stock, as a vegetable and for making pumpkin pies.

To Cook Pumpkin
Slice, pare and cut into small pieces; add a little water only; cover and simmer until tender; pour into a colander to drain; when cool, rub through the strainer. You will then have a *purée* of mashed pumpkin, which is ready to be used for pumpkin soup or pumpkin pie; if served as mashed pumpkin, it only needs seasoning, buttering and re-heating.

Free State Pumpkin Fritters
(South African Recipe)
2 cups mashed cooked pumpkin (dry as possible)
4 tablespoons flour (or enough to thicken the pumpkin)
1 teaspoon baking powder
2 eggs
Pinch of salt

Mix the pumpkin, flour, baking-powder and salt. Add the well-beaten eggs. The mixture must be rather slack. Fry in butter or lard in a frying-pan. Sprinkle thickly with sugar mixed with a little ground cinnamon, and serve with cut lemon, as a dessert.

Pumpkin Pie
1½ cups boiled fresh or canned squash or pumpkin
1 cup sugar
1 cup milk
1 teaspoon ground ginger
½ teaspoon mace

1½ teaspoons nutmeg
4 eggs beaten
3 tablespoons brandy
½ teaspoon salt
1½ teaspoons cinnamon

Put squash in mixing bowl, add sugar, ginger, mace, cinnamon, nutmeg and salt. Mix in the milk. Whip in the beaten eggs and last the brandy. Bake in pie-crust in moderate oven one hour. This makes one deep pie.—C.R.B.B. (2).

To make one Squash or Pumpkin Pie
One cup of mash, one egg mixed unbeaten with the squash, a cup and a half of sugar, one milk cracker rolled fine, half a teaspoon-ful each of ginger, cinnamon and nutmeg, a pinch of salt and a dash of cayenne pepper. After these are well mixed, add half a cup of milk. Bake in either puff or plain paste.—H.L.D.

Pumpkin Soup
French Style
Put 1 lb. of cooked pumpkin in one quart boiled milk and a small onion or two, sliced and browned in butter. Season with pepper and salt and a little sugar. Simmer for half an hour or so. Mix the yolks of two eggs in a basin with a little cold milk at first, and then with some of the hot milk from the pan. Pour this egg and milk mixture in the soup tureen and pour the hot soup over it. Stir in a little cream and serve at once.

Pumpkin Soup
Italian Style
Cut two or three slices of white pumpkin into small dice. Put them into a saucepan with 4 oz. of butter and cook till they take a golden colour. Mince up one onion, some parsley, sweet basil, celery, thyme, and (for those who like it) one clove of garlic. Mix well, and add two cloves, one quart of water, and some butter, or pure olive oil, or both. Boil for one hour, serve very hot with *croûtons* (fried bread).—J.R.

PURSLANE
Lat. *Portulaca oleracea*, and *P. Sativa*; Fr. *Pourpier*. A troublesome weed of both hemi-spheres; its green leaves, when young, are quite acceptable in salads or in vegetable soups, in place of Sorrel. The *Garden Purslane* or *Rosemoss* is cultivated for its flowers in England, but its tuberous roots are excellent and an important article of food in South America. The Sea Purslane, also called Notch-weed, may be used as a vegetable, boiled like *Spinach* (q.v.), or pickled in vinegar and used as a condiment.

QUAMASH. CAMASS
Lat. *Camassia esculenta*. An American plant of which the bulbs are the staple food of the Indian tribes of the Western Coast.

QUATRE ÉPICES
A mixed bag of four spices which, formerly, was made up by each grocer according to his own formula. An average mixture consisted of 4 oz. white pepper; ½ oz. powdered cloves; 1 oz. ginger; and 1¼ oz. ground nutmeg.

QUIMBOBO
See *Okra*.

QUINOA
Lat. *Chenopodium quinoa*. A South American grass cultivated in the uplands of the Andes for the sake of its leaves which are eaten like spinach, but should be boiled in two waters so as to render them less acrid. In Peru, its seeds are also used in soups and in cakes, and also in the brewing of a kind of beer.

RADISH
Lat. *Raphanus sativus*; Fr. *Radis*. The pungent, snappy root of many varieties of radishes; round, oval, olive-shaped or long and taper-ing in shape; white, pink and scarlet in colour; mild, nutty and peppery in taste; large or small in size; early or late growing.

There are three main classes of radishes:

1. *Forcing or summer radishes*, all small in size, all meant to be grown quickly and eaten uncooked, some of them round in shape, others turnip-shaped, olive-shaped or tapering; some purple in colour, others scarlet, deep scarlet, salmon, white or white tipped;

2. *Main crop summer and autumn radishes*. Later and larger varieties, mostly parsnip or turnip-shaped, some grey, others yellow, white, scarlet or purple;

3. *Winter radishes*. Larger, firmer, more compact and later varieties which grow more slowly without sprouting or becoming hollow in the centre; some are black and long, like carrots, others are white, grey, purple or scarlet, and they may be prepared for the table in any way suitable for small *Turnips* (q.v.).

The *Wild radish* (Lat. *Raphanus raphanis-trum*), from which all cultivated varieties are derived, is common in English fields, and it may be used in place of and in the same way as *Horseradish* (q.v.).

The *Rat-tailed radish* (Lat. *Raphanus sativus*, *var. candatus*), is a native of Southern Asia. Its root is not edible, but its seed-vessels or pods are gathered before they are fully ripe and they are eaten freshly picked, uncooked, or pickled.

Amateur gardeners do not trouble to let their radishes run to seed for the sake of saving the seed, but it may happen that a few radishes are not pulled in time and do run to seed. If the little pods are picked when just formed, when the little seeds inside are still minute, these seed-pods can be added to any green salad; they are tender and their slightly peppery taste is quite pleasant, as well as likely to be quite new to most of one's friends.

Radishes, like grapefruit, can be and have been cooked, but they are not meant to be, and the practice is not to be encouraged.

RAMPION

Lat. *Campanula rapunculus*; Fr. *Raiponce*. A European weed which used to be cultivated in English gardens for the sake of its long, fleshy roots; these were cooked in the same way as *Salsify* (q.v.).

RAPE

Lat. *Brassica napus*. A European herb of the *Brassica* family: it grows prolifically in the Thames Valley and its leaves are gathered in the spring and eaten like *Spinach* (q.v.).

REDWARE

Lat. *Porphyra lacinata*. The name given in the Orkneys to an edible seaweed known in other parts of Scotland as *Tangle*; it is similar to *Laver* (q.v.).

REST HARROW. GROUND FURZE

Lat. *Ononis arvensis*; Fr. *Bugrane*. A vetch common on arable land. Its young shoots make tasty pickles; they may also be eaten green in salads.

RHUBARB

Lat. *Rheum rhaponticum*; Fr. *Rhubarbe*. A weed of Asiatic origin, cultivated for the sake of the fleshy stalks of its leaves, which are used cooked, for various sweets, and in the making of tarts, pies and preserves.

To Cook Rhubarb

'Cut into short lengths, *unpeeled*, covered with a small amount of water, stewed for 10 minutes or less and generously sweetened, the first rhubarb of the season is to the digestive tract of winter-logged inner man what a good hot bath with plenty of healing soap is to the outer after a bout with plough and harrow. Even the tongue and teeth have a scrubbed feeling after a dish of early rhubarb.'—D.L.

'Place a small quantity of brown sugar in a basin, put in the cut thubarb, cover with a saucer. Put the bowl into a steamer and cook over pan of boiling water until tender. The rhubarb remains whole, and no flavour is lost.'—B.L.L.

Rhubarb Chutney

2 lb. rhubarb
1 lb. sultanas
2 lb. sugar
2 lemons
1 oz. garlic
1 oz. salt
1 oz. ginger
1 pint of vinegar

Wash, strip and cut up the rhubarb very finely. Skin the lemons, cut the pulp finely, removing the pips. Cut and crush the garlic very fine. Bruise the ginger. Put the whole of your ingredients into the pan and boil till the mixture becomes very thick Pick out the ginger, and then cover the mixture in a jar. Keep one month before using.—B.H.

Compôte of Rhubarb

Make a syrup by cooking together equal parts of sugar and water. Trim and cut some rhubarb in 2-in. pieces and put them into the syrup; add a squeeze of lemon, and a piece of lemon rind; simmer till the rhubarb be tender but move away from the fire before it begins to come apart. Pour in a glass dish; remove the rind; let the *compôte* get quite cold and serve with cream.

Rhubarb Fool

Cook the rhubarb as you would for a *Compôte* (q.v.), then put through the sieve and stir in as much cream as you care to use. Chill and serve.

Rhubarb Fritters

Choose some small sticks of quite young and tender pink rhubarb. Cut into lengths 2 or 2½ in. long, dip in batter and fry in boiling lard. Serve with plenty of castor sugar over them.

Rhubarb Pie

Butter a pudding-dish and put in it a dozen stalks of young rhubarb, washed, scraped and cut in thin slices the length of the dish; cover the rhubarb with granulated sugar; dot about small pieces of lemon rind; then cover with white breadcrumbs; put small pieces of butter on the breadcrumbs and sprinkle castor sugar over it all. Bake 45 to 50 minutes in a moderate oven and serve hot with cream.

Rhubarb Snow

Prepare rhubarb as for *Compôte* (q.v.) beat stiffly two egg whites; fold half into the rhubarb and pile in a deep dish; put the other half of the beaten egg white on top and very lightly brown in the oven for a very few minutes.

ROCKET. ROCKET SALAD. TURKISH ROCKET

Lat. *Eruca sativa*; Fr. *Roquette*. One of the old-fashioned cottage garden herbs; its leaves have a pleasant, peppery taste when gathered young and are a welcome addition to green salads.

In the U.S.A. there is a green salad sold under the name of *Rocket Salad*, but it has nothing to do with the Garden Rocket; it is the *Winter Cress* (q.v.).

There is also quite a different plant called *Turkish Rocket*. It is a native of Western Asia and has been naturalized in France. It has the advantage of producing fresh green leaves earlier than any other type of salad; in the summer, its leaves are too coarse to be acceptable in salads, but they may then be treated like *Spinach* (q.v.).

ROSE

Lat. *Rosa canina*; Fr. *Eglantine*. The Rose, like so much else, is no longer what it was once upon a time, more particularly in England and in France, two countries so near geographically to one another and yet with so little in common, except the Rose, the National flower of both lands. The White Rose was the emblem of Lancaster and the Red Rose that of York, before the two warring families were united under the Tudor Rose. In those days the Rose was chiefly prized for its sweet scent, 'cabbage' roses and damask roses being mostly in request for the making of rose-water, whilst musk and Provence roses and sweet brier were in every cottage garden. Damask rose petals were added on top of the cherries in a cherry-pie, before putting on the crust; rose-water was used to flavour cakes; honey and the fresh juice of Provence roses were boiled together to make rose honey, besides the many vinegars, syrups, ointments and confections used for toilet and medicinal purposes and scented with roses.

Miss Rohde has published the most complete list we have of old-world recipes in which roses were and can still be used, not only rose leaves but rose 'hips'. (See *Rose Recipes*, by Eleanour Sinclair Rohde, London. Medici Society.)

ROSELLE

See *Indian Sorrel*.

RUE

Lat. *Ruta graveoles*. A decorative garden plant; its leaves are aromatic and can be used, finely-chopped, to make tasty sandwiches with brown bread and fresh butter.

RUNNER BEAN. SCARLET RUNNER

Lat. *Phaseolus multiflorus*; Fr. *Haricot d'Espagne*. This bean was introduced into Europe from Mexico in or about 1633. It is a fast-climbing, free-flowering and free-bearing bean, with pods which can be of a wonderful size to look at, when allowed to grow beyond the small and medium sizes when *Runners* should be picked. Although runners by name and habit, a variety called *Dwarf Gem* has been introduced which no longer runs. When they are small, runner beans are cooked whole, in the same way and ways as *French Beans* (q.v.). Fully-grown runner beans, large but not tough nor old, can and should still be cooked whole, even if cut up after cooking. In England, however, full-size runner beans are invariably spoilt, one may even say ruined, by being sliced, when they are not 'shredded', before being cooked. There exists a machine devised and sold to abet this sinful practice. When sliced or shredded before cooking, beans, runner or not, are bled in the boiling and lose most if not all their flavour and most of their vitamins.

RUSH-NUT

See *Chufa*.

RUSSIAN TURNIP

See *Swede*.

RUTABAGA

See *Swede*.

SABRE BEAN

See *Sword Bean*.

SAINT JOHN'S BREAD

See *Carob*.

SALADS

Salads, originally *Sallets*, were at first the uncooked, edible leaves of various herbs and plants, eaten with a dressing of *Sal* or *Salt*, but to-day the name is used for an enormous variety of cooked and uncooked herbs, vegetables, fruit, meat and fish with nothing in common except that all should be dressed in some way or other. Vegetable salads may be divided into the following classes:

1. Lettuce and other Green Salads;
2. Vegetables, uncooked;
3. Vegetables, cooked;

Lettuce, Chicory, Endive and Cress Salads

I

The lettuce and endive, of which there are a very large number of different varieties, are the most popular of all green salads during nine months of the year. During the worst winter months of the year, they give up the lead to the chicory and the dandelion, which are more suitable for bleaching. Both gastronomically and dietetically the lettuce and chicory grown out of doors, in the sunshine, are superior to bleached salads.

Allied to the more popular salads, lettuce, chicory and endive, we may mention the green foliage of spring turnips and salsify. Also the lamb's lettuce and the purslane. Another popular form of green salad is supplied by the cress family, which include the garden cress, winter cress and watercress.

All these green salads may be and are really best served by themselves, with a dressing of olive oil, wine-vinegar or lemon juice, in the proportion of three (oil) to one (vinegar); salt and pepper, and neither sugar nor mustard, but some finely-chopped mixed herbs, such as parsley, chervil, tarragon, chives, and, if liked, a mere suspicion of garlic. Radishes, tomatoes, cucumber and the like are very often added to green salads in England and the U.S.A., but their inclusion in the green salad bowl is sheer heresy: they are much better served separately, as hors-d'oeuvre, the radishes by themselves, the tomatoes in a more vinegary than oily dressing and the shaved cucumber with a dressing more oily than vinegary.

The average English middle-class household salad is an abomination, consisting of wet lettuce cut up small with a steel knife, uncored halves of tomatoes, stalky watercress and sliced hard-boiled eggs, with a covering of linseed oil salad 'Cream' from a grocer's bottle. In the U.S.A. salads are also mostly ruined by some bottled 'dressing,' in the manufacture of which pure olive oil is seldom used.

Salads of Uncooked Vegetables
II

There are quite a number of vegetables which are excellent in salads or hors-d'oeuvre, by themselves, with a simple dressing. Such are:

Artichokes, when very small and nutty, with a *Vinaigrette Sauce*;

Cabbage, green or white, cut julienne-wise with a *Sauce Moutarde*;

Cabbage, red, cut julienne-wise, with a *Vinaigrette Sauce* and some hard-boiled eggs cut in quarters;

Cabbage, Kohl-rabi, shaved fine, with a *Mayonnaise Sauce*;

Cucumber, in thin slices or shaved, with an oil or cream dressing;

Carrots, whole, if very small, or cut in thin slices, with a horseradish or a cream dressing according to taste;

Celery, cut fine, match-like, and dressed with a *Sauce Moutarde*;

Fennel, shredded and served with a *Vinaigrette Sauce*;

Tomato, sliced and served with a *Vinaigrette Sauce.*

Salads of Cooked Vegetables
III

Artichoke bottoms, cut dice-like, with a *Vinaigrette Sauce*;

Asparagus points, served whole with a *Vinaigrette Sauce*;

Aubergines (Egg-plant), sliced and served with a *Sauce Moutarde*;

Beans, all kinds, cooked, dressed, when hot, with a *Vinaigrette Sauce* and then allowed to get quite cold before serving;

Beetroot, cooked, sliced and served with a *Sauce Moutarde*;

Broccoli, detached cooked flowerlets, served with *Vinaigrette Sauce*;

Brussels Sprouts, cooked when very small and served whole with a *Vinaigrette*;

Cabbage, red, white or green, cut up julienne-wise and served with a *Vinaigrette Sauce*;

Cardoon, cooked, cut up dice-like and dressed with a *Mustard Sauce*;

Cauliflower, detached cooked flowerlets dressed with a *Vinaigrette Sauce*;

Celeriac, boiled, cut up julienne-wise and dressed with a *Mustard Sauce*;

Chinese Artichokes, cooked, served whole with a *Vinaigrette Sauce* and some quarters of hard-boiled eggs;

Jerusalem Artichokes, cooked, cut up dice-like and served with a *Mayonnaise*;

Lentils, cooked, dressed when hot with a *Vinaigrette* and served cold;

Leeks, boiled, well drained and served with *Vinaigrette*, quite cold;

Potatoes, cooked, sliced and dressed when cold with a *Vinaigrette* or *Mayonnaise*; *Vitelotte* and other waxy kinds are best for salads;

Peas, Garden Peas and *Sugar Peas,* cooked, dressed when hot with *Vinaigrette Sauce,* and served cold;

Salsify, cooked, sliced and served with *Mayonnaise.*

SALSIFY. SALSAFY.
VEGETABLE OYSTER

Lat. *Tragopogon porrifolius*; Fr. *Salsifi*. A European vegetable which is much more popular on the Continent than in England or the U.S.A. Its long, thin, white roots, when boiled and tender, probably did possess a flavour not unlike that of an oyster, hence its English name of *Oyster Plant* or *Vegetable Oyster*. If Salsify ever did possess such a flavour, it must have lost it, as Musk has lost its scent, but it is none the less one of the best winter vegetables. Whilst its roots are its chief gastronomical asset, its young leaves in the spring may be eaten in salads.

The Cooking of Salsify

Salsify is best scraped, parboiled, drained and finished cooking either in boiling fat or in sizzling butter.

As soon as salsify is scraped, each root should at once be dropped into a little vinegar and water to prevent it turning black, and it is also advisable to add a little vinegar to the salted water in which salsify is boiled or parboiled.

Salsify Fritters
(Beignets de Salsifis)

Scrape salsify and boil in acidulated salted water till tender; drain and dry them; cut them in 3-in. lengths; dip each length in batter and fry in deep boiling fat until crisp and brown. Drain on paper and serve at once, piled criss-cross, with fried parsley as garnish.

Salsifis gratinés

Scrape salsify and boil in acidulated, salted water till nearly tender; drain and dry them and cut them in 3-in. lengths; put the pieces in a baking-dish; pour a white sauce over them, then a liberal dusting of grated cheese mixed with white breadcrumbs and a few pats of butter; brown under a hot grill or in the oven.

Salsifis Poulette

Scrape and boil salsify till tender; drain and cut in smallish pieces. Pour a *Sauce Poulette* over the cut salsify, season with pepper and salt and a squeeze of lemon and serve hot.

Vegetable Oyster in the deep shell

The *Vegetable Oyster* idea may be carried out by dicing the boiled salsify, sprinkling with lemon juice and serving in scallop shell with an *Egg Sauce.*—D.H.

Salsifis Sautés

Scrape and boil salsify till tender; drain and dry and cut up in 3-in. lengths, splitting the thick upper parts. Toss the pieces in sizzling butter until nicely browned on all sides. Season with pepper and salt and a squeeze of lemon. Serve with fried parsley as a garnish.

Salsifis à la Vinaigrette

Boil, drain well, cool and serve with a good *Vinaigrette Sauce.*

SAND LEEK

See *Onion.*

SAVOY

Lat. *Brassica oleracea, var. bullata*; Fr. *Chou de Milan.* One of the oldest and most popular species of the *Brassica* or *Cabbage* family. It includes a large number of different kinds of cabbage with *crimped* leaves. They are at their best after the first frosts, and they have a more delicate flavour than the common cabbage. All recipes suitable for *Cabbage* (q.v.) are suitable for savoys.

Savoy Cabbage cooked in Milk

1 tender young Savoy cabbage
Milk
Salt and pepper
Butter

Wash the cabbage well and prepare as for boiling. Set it in a pan and cover with boiling water, and let it stand in this for 10 minutes, then drain, replace in fresh boiling, salted water and cook from 10 to 15 minutes, according to size of savoy. Drain very thoroughly. Replace in saucepan, covering with milk. Simmer until tender, then add butter, salt and pepper to taste, blending all well before serving. A very delicious dish, when properly cooked.

SCARLET RUNNER

See *Runner Bean.*

SCOLYMUS

See *Golden Thistle.*

SCORZONERA

Lat. *Scorzonera hispanica*; Fr. *Scorzonère.* This excellent vegetable is greatly underrated in the British Isles and the U.S.A. It is usually regarded as a poor relation of the *Salsify*, whereas it is its big and better brother. It is true that its roots are black and cylindrical instead of white and tapering, but they are of very good flavour. They can be prepared for the table in any of the ways recommended for *Salsify* (q.v.), and some of the roots should always be left in the ground for the sake of the shoots which they will produce early in the following spring; these shoots, which are more in the nature of chards than asparagus shoots, are both tender and tasty and very welcome at a time of the year when there is little variety in the kitchen garden.

A related variety, the *French Scorzonera* or *Picridie* (Lat. *Picridium vulgare*), is grown for the sake of its leaves more than for its roots, which are coarse, whilst the leaves are excellent as a green salad, and they may be cut three or four times from the same root during the same season; they look somewhat like the chicory known in France as *Barbe de Capucin*, but they have not got the bitter taste of the chicory.

SCURVYGRASS

Lat. *Cochlearia officinalis*; Fr. *Cranson.* A seaside weed which retains its typical saltiness even when it grows inland. In former times, it used to be gathered in many seaside places in England, and eaten fresh as a salad in the spring. It was also used to make a kind of medicinal 'tea', reputed to be valuable 'to clear the blood'.

SEA-GIRDLE
See *Redware*.

SEA-KALE. SEA-KAIL. SEA-COLE
Lat. *Crambe maritima*; Fr. *Cranson*. A native of most sea-coasts of Western Europe; it is cultivated for its leaf-stalks, which are usually bleached and forced so as to be on sale during the winter months. But sea-kale that is not forced and is cut in April and May is much better in flavour than any that is forced. It can also be used uncooked, in salads, or served with cheese, like celery.

To cook Sea-kale
Sea-kale is best steamed – not boiled – till tender; it will take about 50 minutes to cook, and it should then be served with a little melted butter or a very light white sauce, if the excellent flavour of the sea-kale is to be fully appreciated. Or else it may be simmered gently in vegetable stock till tender, and no longer. Whether steamed, boiled or stewed, sea-kale gets hard when over-cooked. Another way with sea-kale is to wash and trim it and tie it in a bundle; par-boil it in salted boiling water for a very short time and drain; then put the sea-kale in a fireproof dish, cover it with a *Sauce Mornay*, and bake in a hot oven till nicely browned.

Sea-kale Salad
The curly, crinkly, green tops of sea-kale, not of the forced but of the open-air variety, are usually boiled to a mush when cooked with the stems, being so much more tender. It is best to cut them off and serve them as a green salad, well washed, well dried, torn in small pieces if at all large, and dressed with oil and vinegar, finely-chopped chives and tarragon leaves, if available. They are tasty, nutty, and truly delicious.

SEAKALE-BEET
See *Chard Beet*.

SEA-MOSS
See *Carrageen*.

SEA-PURSLANE
See *Sea-Sandwort*.

SEA-OXEYE
Lat. *Borrichia arborescens*. A fleshy European weed which grows freely upon some beaches and in sandy ground near the sea. It is used, pickled in vinegar, as a condiment, like *Samphire*. (*See Section I. SAUCES.*)

SEA ROCKET
Lat. *Catrile maritima*. A seaside weed the leaves of which, when young, are used in salads.

SEA SANDWORT.
SEA PURSLANE
Lat. *Arenaria peploides*. A seaside weed of the Northern hemisphere coasts, pickled like *Samphire*. In Iceland they also use this sea-weed packed with salt and pressed down in the way *Sauerkraut* is prepared.

SHINLEAF
See *Indian Lettuce*.

SIEVA. SIBBY. CIVET BEAN
Lat. *Phasoleus lunatus*; Fr. *Haricot de Java*. A South American Bean related to the *Lima Bean* (q.v.), but a little smaller and often sold for Lima beans. It is prepared for the table in any way suitable for *Haricots* (q.v.).

SILVERWEED
Lat. *Potentilla anserina*. A common weed the roots of which contain some starch and are eaten like parsnips in the Hebrides; they have also been used in times of scarcity to make a kind of bread.

SKIRRET
Lat. *Sium sisarum*; Fr. *Chervis*. A native of China which produces a bunch of swollen roots not unlike Dahlia roots; they are tender, sweet and rather floury; being quite hardy they may be left in the ground during the winter months until wanted, and they are cooked in exactly the same ways as *Salsify* (q.v.).

The *Sweet Potato* (q.v.) used to be called, among other names, *Peruvian Skirret*.

SLAW. COLE SLAW
An American preparation of shredded cabbage which may be served *cold* or *hot*, and should rightly be called *Cold Cole Slaw* and *Hot Cole Slaw*.

Cold Slaw
Shred the centre part of the cabbage very fine, except the heart, and then soak in ice-water for an hour, drain dry, add a little oil and vinegar, chopped caraway seed, paprika and black pepper; salt last, so that the crystals are not dissolved. Serve on lettuce or romaine.—A.S.

Hot Slaw
Well wash a good white cabbage, using plenty of water for the purpose, shred it very fine (in America a special slicer is used), drain it thoroughly, place it in a pan, and for a quart of shredded cabbage pour in a good half pint of boiling water; dust it all with half a teaspoonful of salt, cover down the pan, and let it boil till nearly tender, which it should be in about half an hour; at the end of this time pour in a gill of milk and a tea-spoonful of butter, and let it cook till it is all

absorbed. Now turn it into a hot vegetable dish, and serve either with a *Béarnaise* or some other sauce.—S.B.P.

SLOUK
See *Laver*.

SNAKE BEAN
See *Sword Bean*.

SMALL SALAD
The name given in the U.S.A. to *Watercress* and *White Mustard* served together as a salad, or sandwich filling.

SNAKE CUCUMBER
Lat. *Cucumis melo, var. flexuosus*. An East Indian variety of Melon, long and slender when fully grown; its sole gastronomic use is that when quite small it is pickled in vinegar, like *Gherkins*.

SNAKE-ROOT
Lat. *Aristolochia serpentaria*. An Alpine grass the roots of which grow into one another, snake-like. The leaves, when young, are used in any way suitable for *Spinach* (q.v.).

SNAP BEANS
See *French Beans*.

SOJA BEAN
See *Soy Bean*.

SOLOMON'S SEAL
Lat. *Polygonatum officinale*. A decorative weed and favourite garden plant of the Lily family; young shoots may be eaten like *Asparagus* (q.v.).

SORREL
Lat. *Rumex acetosa*; Fr. *Oseille*. The leaves of all varieties of Sorrel contain more or less oxalate of potash; this is responsible for the peculiar acid taste, which some people greatly enjoy and others cannot abide. The Wood and Mountain Sorrel (Lat. *Oxyria digyra*) are the sharpest of all; the French Sorrel (Lat. *Rumex scutatus*) the mildest. The Indian Sorrel, commonly known in the East as *Masha* or *Sour-Sour*, is a potherb used to flavour soups and stews; also in salads and curries. The fleshy calyces are used for making jams and jellies; also for brewing a refreshing beverage called Sorrel Drink.

French Sorrel when young and small can be eaten uncooked in salads, but other sorts are better cooked; they are best served with flavourless meat, such as veal or sweetbreads; also with fish; a *purée* of sorrel, for instance, is excellent with *Shad* (q.v.; (*See* Section V. *FISH*.) Sorrel is also good for flavouring soups and stews, and to make a green, sharp sauce. (*See* Section I, *SAUCES*.)

Sorrel Purée
Trim 4 lb. freshly-picked sorrel, discarding the whole of the stalks; wash it well in several waters. Put it dripping wet in a saucepan without any other water, and leave it on a slow fire for half an hour, when it will have gone down a good deal in volume. Make a *roux blond* with some butter and half its weight of flour, and mix this with the sorrel. Then add a quart of good meat-stock, season with pepper and salt and a fair pinch of castor sugar; cover the pan and leave it in a moderate oven for 45 minutes. Put the sorrel through a sieve, then re-heat it and bind it with four or five yolks of eggs beaten in a little fresh cream and some butter.

Sorrel prepared thus makes a good background for poached eggs, roast veal or baked white fish; it can also be served as a vegetable course by itself with some fried *croûtons* of bread.

Sorrel Soup
Take four handfuls of freshly-picked sorrel and remove all the stalks and ribs; wash in several waters and put in a pan with a tablespoonful of butter; leave the pan on a moderate heat, stirring the sorrel, which will soon melt; add 1½ pints milk, little by little, season with pepper and salt, and bring to the boil. In the meantime fry some snippets of bread and beat a yolk or two of egg into a little cream. Warm the soup tureen, put the fried bread in it and the beaten egg and cream; pour the boiling soup on top and stir well, then serve.

SOUPS
Recipes for Vegetable Soups made chiefly with one kind of vegetable – carrots, cauliflowers, onions, potatoes, etc. – are given under the headings of all such vegetables. But there are many excellent vegetable soups made with a number of different vegetables; some of the best recipes for the making of such soups have been collected and are given here.

The Ideal Vegetable Soup
'To this day I do, and as long as I am able to handle pot and pan I shall continue to, make a vegetable soup as nearly like that my mother made as one hand can cut and contrive like another. Twice at least during the coldest months of the year I make it, and my mother made it even oftener – as often, in fact, as she could get a shank bone.

'For, say what you like, the ideal vegetable soup must be made with a shank bone – the shank of a beef critter. For a shank bone is the only bone of any consequence that has marrow in it, and it is the marrow that gives the peculiar richness, body and flavour, which a true vegetable soup should have.

'The bone must be cracked in order to get the value of the marrow. So, in case you should be inspired to try your hand at making a good, stout, sustaining soup for a winter's day, the kind that will warm you to the core and stick to your ribs until time for the next meal, go and buy a shank bone of a size according to your family, and ask the butcher to crack it.

'Wash and dry the bone and put it in a good-sized kettle of cold water. Enough water to cover the bone completely and some to spare.

'Set it where it will cook slowly. Of course, if you had a good old-fashioned wood stove you would put the soup kettle on the back griddle to simmer, but if you must struggle along with a gas or electric range and other folderols of an effete generation, turn the heat low and let it slowly cook.

'Now, prepare your vegetables, and, believe me, this is going to be a *vegetable* soup. Again you will proportion your vegetables to the size of your family, but this is what I do: I use a six-quart kettle and cover the bone with about four quarts of water. (It is a good-sized bone.) As this boils away I add *hot* water to keep the amount of stock about the same.

'Then I take onions, potatoes, carrots, celery, in reasonable porportions, but not stinting on the onions, and *one* parsnip; peel wash and chop them together to make about a quart of the mixture. I add about a cupful of shredded cabbage, and around an hour and a half before dinner time I put these all into the kettle together with a cup of washed barley. Then I add a sprig of parsley if I have it, and season it with salt and pepper to taste.

'Continue to boil slowly until the vegetables are done and the meat falls from the bone, adding water as necessary.

'I read the other day in some of the numerous admonitory columns regarding polite usages that a soup in which either meat or vegetables were left at serving was in bad taste and poor manners. It said you had to *eat* such a soup.

'Well, you do. You eat it with a spoon and you taste it, going down. You even have to chew it a little. First a cautious experiment of the tongue, exploring temperature and taste; hot, smooth, unctuous, with the rich flavour of marrow and the age-old wisdom of salt, it meets approval and is commended to all the outlying areas of sapidity and relish, and to that arbiter of savoury sense, the palate.

'Then our gustatory soul satisfied with

tentative essay, we meet substance – just enough resistance to halt the course of action and give the ravished senses time to speculate on varied savour. We meet:

'*Potato*: bland, amiable, and homely, an honest vegetable, giving honour where honour is due – in an honest soup. *Cabbage*, so revered by the Egyptians for its stimulating qualities as to warrant a temple built in its honour. *Parsnip*: the faint, sweet, fragrant flavour of which lends romance to the dish. *Onion*: humble kindred of the lily clan, rooted from oblivion by Alexander the Great and bestrewn by him, along with learning, to the civilized world, thus lending a touch of wisdom and sophistication to the whole. And *barley*. Barley lends a slight viscidity to the broth, a holding property superior to rice, and a rich quality to the dish, completing and fulfilling its nutritive mission to mankind. The *carrot* is an innovation of later date. In the culinary prime of my mother's day, carrots went, if anywhere, to the cattle – a gain to the latter, but a loss to us.

'This, then, was the soup that once warmed the hearts of a homely farmer and his humble family in Southern Michigan. And this is the soup that I still set before a more modern but none the less appreciative family who can – if they wish – listen to the Philharmonic concert as they eat.'—D.L.

Quickly-made Vegetable Soup

Dice some vegetables, such as two or three each of potatoes, leeks, carrots, one onion and one small turnip, and drop into boiling water. Simmer for 20 minutes. Mash them with a fork or rub them through a colander, and add 1 pint or so of boiling milk, a little choppped parsley and, just before serving 1 oz. of butter.—G.M.B.

Soupe Bonne Femme

First fry an onion, sliced, in a couple of ounces of butter, stopping short before it colours. When partly cooked, add lettuce and sorrel cut into thin strips and, say, $\frac{1}{2}$ oz. of flour, salt, and pepper; and cook for a few minutes. Then add a little stock, and continue cooking till very thick, when the balance of a quart of stock may be added, little by little, stirring all the time. Simmer for 20 minutes.

Meanwhile, beat two yolks of eggs in a basin with an ounce of butter, add a little of the stock very hot, and beat up till the egg, butter, and stock are thoroughly amalgamated. This is a liaison: pour this very slowly into the hot soup, stirring all the time, and finally pour the finished soup over some strips of very dry bread laid on the bottom of a tureen.—F.C.W.

Vegetable Broth

Lentils, barley, turnip, carrot, cabbage, leeks or onions, and any other vegetable available; salt and pepper; butter and water.

Wash lentils until quite clean; wash and scald barley; wash and prepare other vegetables and cut in small pieces. Put all in pot with two quarts cold water, bring to the boil and let them simmer for three hours. Season to taste, and just before serving add a tablespoonful of butter.

Chiffonade Soup

Stamp out the leaves of two good-sized lettuces with a round tin cutter about the size of a two-shilling piece, and put them into a stewpan with the heads of a few spring onions, half a dozen leaves of tarragon, a little chervil, two leaves of fresh mint and half a pint of young peas shelled. Moisten with clear *consommé*, season with a pinch of mignonette pepper and a small lump of sugar, and boil gently until the peas, etc., are done. Serve as it is.—A.H. (2).

La Potée Champenoise

This resembles the *soupe aux choux* in many respects, the main difference being that the *potée* is sometimes entirely meatless, whereas the *soupe* always includes salt pork and *saucisses*.

1 firm white cabbage heart
1 large cup dried haricot beans
2 or 3 carrots
1 lb. rather fat bacon (in one piece)
4 or 5 potatoes
1 cup dried green peas
1 or 2 turnips
1 or 2 onions

Soak the dried beans and peas overnight in cold water. The bacon is optional. Remove outer leaves from cabbage, cut into four, removing hard core, and soak for an hour in salted water. Drain, place in an earthenware *pot-au-feu* with all the other vegetables except the potatoes. Add salt and pepper to taste and about three pints of tepid water. Bring to the boiling point, add bacon, if used, cover closely and cook very gently for three hours. Add the potatoes about half an hour before serving. Pour the broth over thin slices of stale bread, serve the bacon, sliced, with the vegetables arranged nicely around.

Potage aux Herbes

Take 2 oz. of the white part of a leek cut in thin slices, and the same amount each of spinach and lettuce rather coarsely chopped. Stew these in an ounce of butter very gently for half an hour, keeping the pan covered and stirring its contents now and again with a wooden spoon. On no account should the leek be allowed to brown. When the vegetables are quite soft, add a quart of boiling water and a little salt, put on the lid and let the soup boil for 20 minutes. Now rub the whole through a coarse sieve, put it back into the pan and bring it to the boil. Add now, if you like, three or four spoonfuls of cooked rice, boil for a minute again, and finally bind with cream and beaten egg-yolk. Finish with a few small pieces of butter off the fire, correct the seasoning and serve as it is. (AMBROSE HEATH. *Spring in the Kitchen*, in *Wine and Food*. Vol. V, p. 45).

Potage Paysanne

Cook some potatoes, carrots and very small turnips, cut into slices, and a small heart of cabbage cut up, seasoned with salt and pepper, in enough water just to cover them. When cooked quite soft, and most of the water has evaporated, make up the original quantity of water with a good *consommé* and boil together for 20 minutes.—F.C.W.

Potage Printanier

This is a cream soup made with the vegetables of early summer. Cook in salted water one quart of fresh peas, the white of two small leeks (cut in small pieces) and two small lettuces.

When all these are cooked drain them well and keep the stock in a bowl; pound the vegetables in a mortar and add the stock little by little to this *purée*, stirring well, till you have a mixture the consistency of thick cream. Put it in a saucepan and add chicken stock till you have the required quantity. Bring to the boil and simmer it two or three minutes; finish by a liaison of two yolks of eggs diluted in two tablespoonfuls of cream. Serve with *croûtons*, or with a *julienne* of macaroni.—X.M.B. (1).

Vegetable Purée

Clean and slice six carrots, one large turnip, three Spanish onions, twelve large potatoes and a small head of celery. Put into a saucepan 2 oz. of good dripping or butter, fry the sliced carrots and onions for about 10 minutes, moving them about to prevent burning. Add the remaining vegetables and four quarts of water, boil together for an hour or until the carrots are tender. Now pass through a coarse wire sieve, return again to the saucepan, season the *purée* to taste, bring to the boil, and serve. If stock is preferred it may be used instead of water. (*Mrs W. Johnson Leigh, Penrith.*)—P.T.L.

Summer Soup

Chop up a small onion and a medium-sized carrot and turnip very small, and cut four or five lettuce leaves in thin strips. Melt ½ oz. of butter in a stewpan and in it 'melt' a handful of Sorrel for quarter of an hour. Now add a good quart of boiling water, then the carrot, onion and turnip, a pint of shelled peas and half a pint of French beans cut in pieces. Season with salt, bring to the boil, put on the lid and simmer gently for 1¼ hours. Ten minutes before serving let the soup boil more rapidly, add the strips of lettuce and shower in a level tablespoonful of very fine tapioca. Mix in another ½ oz. of butter and serve. (AMBROSE HEATH. *A Cook's Dozen*, in *Wine and Food*. Vol. XIV, p. 34.)

SOUR SOUR
See *Indian Sorrel*.

SOUTHERNWOOD. LAD'S LOVE
Lat. *Artemisia Alzotanum*; Fr. *Aurone*. A species of wormwood related to *Tarragon* and used in the same way, finely-chopped in salads. It can also be used as a vegetable and cooked like *Spinach* (q.v.).

SOW-THISTLE
Lat. *Sonchus oleraceus*. A troublesome weed, the leaves of which, bleached under a stone or tile, *in situ*, like dandelion, are very wholesome, even if somewhat bitter, in salads. Its roots are also edible but incorrigibly tough. The Ancients used the leaves of the *Sow-Thistle* as a vegetable, boiled like spinach; they considered it most beneficial for the health, but did not record their appreciation of its palatability. In Lapland, the young shoots of the *Mountain Sow-Thistle* (Lat. *Sonchus alpinus*) are considered a delicacy.

SOY BEAN. SOYA BEAN
Lat. *Glycine soja*; Fr. *Haricot de Java*. The most nutritious of all the beans; it is also the most easily digested, hence the least flatulent bean. It is a native of China and is grown very extensively not only in the East but in many parts of Africa, America and Australasia, and to a certain extent in Europe as well. There are a very large number of different varieties of Soya Beans, some early and others late, some yellow and others black or green, all equally good. They are eaten both fresh and dried in any way suitable for *Haricots* (q.v.). They are also called *Butter Beans* and *China Beans*.

SPEEDWELL
Lat. *Veronica officinalis*; Fr. *Véronique*. A handsome wild herb common in English fields. Its dried leaves were used formerly to make a kind of medicinal 'tea' which was believed to cure the gout.

SPIKED RAMPION
Lat. *Phyteuma spicatum*; Fr. *Clochette*. A modest member of the *Campanula* family. It is common in Switzerland and used in salads. It is still to be found wild in English fields, but no longer, as formerly, in cottagers' herb gardens.

SPINACH
Lat. *Spinacia oleracea, var. inermis* and *var. glabra*; Fr. *Epinard*. A native of the Far East introduced into Europe by the Dutch in 1568. The most universally cultivated species of *Spinach* are the common spinach or large prickly-leaf winter spinach; the round-leaf spinach, which is best for spring and summer use; and the *New Zealand Spinach*, which will grow in the poorest soils and the driest positions.

How to Cook Spinach
Spinach must be washed with great care in two or three lots of fresh water, the green part of the leaves being torn away from the mid-rib or stalk, which is useless. The wet, torn, or shredded leaves are then put in an earthenware pan – or any other if no earthenware pan is available – and the pan, with its lid on, is put on a slow heat. The spinach will provide all the necessary moisture to cook itself in a very short time. When spinach is cooked, it can be 'finished' either *en branches* or *en purée*. The first or *en branches* is best for flavour, and the other best for old and rather tough spinach. It also depends how the spinach is to be served, as a vegetable course or merely as a background or garnishing. If it is to be served as a vegetable course, it should merely be roughly chopped up, after being cooked, seasoned with pepper and salt and re-heated with as much butter as one can spare – there is practically no limit to the amount of butter that spinach will absorb. A little milk and flour may be blended in to soften any spinach inclined to be 'strong'. If the spinach is to be used to flavour a *soufflé*, to garnish some *Ravioli*, or to provide a bed upon which poached eggs are to rest, then it is best *en purée*, that is passed through a sieve after it has been cooked, and re-heated, seasoned with pepper and salt, butter and some rich milk or cream, but only very little, if any, flour. Spinach must always be served *dry*, which is easily done by leaving it in an open oven until all moisture has steamed itself away.

Spinach Balls
These are delicious for serving with roasts. Mix together three cups cooked, chopped spinach with two tablespoonfuls butter, two tablespoonfuls grated cheese, two tablespoonfuls grated onion, one cup fine dry

breadcrumbs, one egg, ⅛ teaspoonful Jamaica pepper, and a dash of paprika. Allow mixture to stand for about 10 minutes before shaping into balls and rolling them in breadcrumbs. Dip balls in beaten egg mixed with half cup cold water, then crumb them again and fry in deep fat. Serve on a flat dish garnished with tufts of fried parsley. (*Mabel Terry Lewis*.)—E.C. (2).

Spinach Croquettes

Prepare 3 lb. of Spinach. Steam for 20 minutes, then squeeze dry as possible and chop very fine. Fry one small chopped onion in butter until soft and mix well through the spinach. Add one cup of stiff cream sauce to which has been added one tablespoonful of crisp crumbled bacon (optional), mix well and heat. Add the yolks of two eggs and stir over fire constantly for two minutes. Spread out on a buttered plate and let get very cold. Form into Croquettes, roll in fine sifted breadcrumbs, then in a slightly beaten egg, and again roll in the crumbs. Fry in deep fat to a nice brown.—G.T.L.

Epinards à la Crème

Trim, wash and cook the required quantity of spinach; then either chop roughly or put it through a sieve, if preferred; put the chopped or sieved spinach in a fireproof dish with 2 oz. butter per lb. of spinach and stir well over a quick fire until all moisture has disappeared. Then add as much fresh cream as you can spare, season with pepper and salt, a little nutmeg and a pinch of castor sugar; stir well and simmer for 8 or 10 minutes. Serve hot.

Warmed up, with some cream added, spinach is quite good on the second day.

Epinards au gratin

Trim, wash and cook the required quantity of spinach and either put it through a sieve or not, as preferred. Well butter a fireproof dish, dust it with a mixture of fine breadcrumbs, grated parmesan cheese, pepper and salt; fill it with the spinach and cover this with the same mixture of breadcrumbs and cheese; add pepper and salt to taste and a dusting of coralline pepper; dot about some pats of butter and bake in a moderate oven for 15 minutes.

Epinards à l'Italienne

Trim, wash, cook and chop coarsely the required quantity of spinach. Stir into it 2 oz. butter per lb. of spinach, and, 5 minutes before serving, one heaped teaspoonful of raisins and one heaped tablespoonful of pine kernel nuts. Heat thoroughly and serve.

Epinards à la Mornay

Trim, wash, cook and chop coarsely or sieve the required quantity of spinach. Mix in first of all 2 oz. butter per lb. of spinach, and then about a quarter of the total amount of *Sauce Mornay*. Stir well and simmer for about 10 minutes.

Spinach Soufflés

Spinach *Soufflés* may be made with just spinach or else a mixture of spinach and chopped-up ham, truffles or anchovies, or any other tasty food available. The Spinach, in any case, had better be sieved after it is cooked; it is then put into a basin with the yolks of three eggs (supposing there is 1 lb. of spinach), a pinch of white pepper, a dusting of sifted sugar, two tablespoonfuls of stiffly-whipped cream, and the whites of four eggs whisked to a stiff froth; all this being well mixed together, pour the mixture into previously oiled, dried and papered *Soufflé* cases, put a small pat of butter on each, and bake from 12 to 15 minutes in a moderate oven. Serve straight from the oven.

Spinach Soup

2 lb. spinach
1 pint stock
½ pint milk
a little cream
1 oz. butter
½ oz. cornflour
seasoning

Prepare the spinach, cook with as little water as possible and rub through a sieve. Melt the butter in a stewpan and stir in the cornflour till smooth, be careful not to burn. Add the stock, stirring all the time, and then the spinach; add the milk and seasoning. Cook for 10 minutes, remove any scum and add a spoonful of cream. Serve very hot. Sufficient for four people.—L.G.N.

Spinach and Tongue Salad

Lettuce; spinach; tongue; capers; hard-boiled eggs; onions. Squeeze out boiled spinach and chop very fine. Season with a little finely-minced shallots or onions, nutmeg and salt. Julienne smoked ox-tongue very fine and mix with spinach. Press into a mould and allow to cool in ice-box for 2 or 3 hours. Turn out in nests of lettuce and garnish with chopped capers and quartered eggs. French dressing.—A.S.

Tarte Niçoise
I

Make a nice *purée* of spinach or of the green leaves of spinach-beet. Mix with this *purée* a small tin of sardines, skinned and broken up, a good handful of breadcrumbs, one egg beaten up, pepper and salt and the oil from the sardines. Put into a shallow fireproof dish; sprinkle a few breadcrumbs on top and cook in the oven for about quarter of an hour. It may be served hot or cold.—M.K.S.

II

Parboil about six large leaves of spinach-beet and chop into small pieces both the white ribs and the green leafy part. Make a batter with 2 oz. of flour, two eggs, some of water in which the beet was cooked, a little olive oil, pepper and salt. Add the beet to this together with some nice ripe olives. Line a shallow dish with pastry; fill with the mixture, cover and bake.—M.K.S. (2).

Spinach Tarts

Scald some spinach and drain it quite dry. Chop it, and stew it in some butter and cream, with a very little salt, some sugar, some bits of citron, and a very little orange flower water. Put it into very fine puff-paste, and let it be baked in a moderate oven.—W.A.H.

SPINACH BEET.
PERPETUAL SPINACH

Lat. *Beta maritima*; Fr. *Poirée*. Both are *Beets* cultivated for their leaves and midribs and not their roots.—See *Chards*.

SPROUTING BROCCOLI

See *Calabrese*.

SPRUE. SPRUE GRASS

Asparagus seedlings or thin sticks of wild asparagus.

SQUASHES

The fruit of a number of different varieties of *Cucurbita*, the cultivated forms of which may be divided into three principal sorts:

1. The *Winter Squashes*, which include the *Hubbard, Turban* and similar varieties (Lat. *Cucurbita moschata*).

2. The *Cushaw Squash*, from which the *Crooknecks* are derived (Lat. *Cucurbita pepo*, var. *melopepo*).

3. The *Summer Squashes*, better known in the British Isles under the name of *Pumpkin* (q.v.) (Lat. *Cucurbita maxima*).

Summer Squash

Boiled. Cut two or more small summer squashes in two and remove all seeds. Wash and pare, if nubbly, but if the skin be smooth and fresh, it is best not to peel the squash. Put in a heavy pan over a slow fire with just a little boiling water and stir until it begins to sweat. Cover the pan and let the squash cook in its own steam for 15 minutes or a little longer if necessary, until it is sufficiently tender to be mashed with a wooden spoon. After the squash has been mashed, add seasoning to taste and boil for 5 minutes. Add first some butter and then some fresh cream and let it be well stirred and hot; then serve.

Summer squash may also be boiled or steamed in cubes, not mashed, seasoned and buttered while cooking and served like *Carrots* (q.v.) with fried parsley or a cream sauce. Also cold, as a salad, with a *Mayonnaise*.

Fried. Wash and pare the squash; slice about ½ in. thick; remove all seeds; sprinkle with pepper and salt; dredge with flour and fry until nicely browned in half butter and half lard. Cook slowly with cover over frying-pan.

Baked. Three medium-sized yellow Summer Squashes; one teaspoonful salt; ⅛ teaspoonful of black pepper; ½ cupful of cream; ⅓ cupful of fine dried breadcrumbs; one tablespoonful of butter, melted.

Peel and cut the squashes in slices ½ in. thick. Remove the pith and seeds, leaving the slices in rings. Place in a colander, and steam, covered, over rapidly boiling water for 10 minutes. Arrange in a shallow oven-proof serving-dish, sprinkle with the seasoning and pour the cream over the top. Cover with the crumbs mixed with the melted butter. Bake in a hot oven (400°F.) for 25 minutes. Serves five to six persons.—E.K.H.

Winter Squash

Boiled. Cut a *Hubbard* or *Delicious Squash* in two, lengthwise; scrape out all seeds and stringy pieces. Cut up as many fairly large pieces as you will require and put them in a heavy kettle with 3 or 4 in. of boiling water. Cover tightly and simmer for 35 to 45 minutes, or until tender. Scoop out of the shell and use as desired for soups, *purées*, pies, garnishings, or fillings.

Steamed. Cut the winter squash in two and scrape out all seeds and stringy pieces. Peel and cut up in cubes the quantity required; put in a heavy kettle with just a little boiling water, cover and simmer gently in its own steam for 45 or 50 minutes, or until tender. Drain and use as desired after seasoning and putting it through a sieve.

Baked. Cut the winter squash in half, lengthwise, and scrape out all seeds and any stringy pieces; sprinkle with pepper and salt; dot about some pieces of butter and then sprinkle brown sugar over all the interior. Place the half to be baked in a baking-dish two-thirds filled with hot water. Cover and bake in a slow oven from 2½ to 3 hours.

STAR-OF-THE-EAST

See *Hartshorn*.

STOKE

See *Laver*.

STONECROPS

Lat. *Sedum album* and *S. album, var. reflexum.* The *White Stonecrop, Crooked yellow Stonecrop* and *Orpine Stonecrop* are ornamental rock-garden plants, but their leaves are, when young, tender and tasty, excellent in green salads. They may also be pickled.

SUCCOTASH

The name given in the U.S.A. to a combination of *Sweet Corn* and *Lima Beans*, each boiled separately and then combined in any proportion, but usually half and half. The two being well mixed are seasoned to taste, well buttered and re-heated. Cream added just before serving is an improvement.

STRING BEANS

See *French Beans.*

SUGAR BEET

Lat. *Beta vulgaris*; Fr. *Betterane à sucre.* The palest type of Beet or Beetroot and the sweetest. The more usual sorts are white both outside and in, but there are varieties with yellow and others with black skin. Although it is chiefly cultivated for the sugar-making industry *Sugar Beet* can be eaten, cooked, as a vegetable, like the *Garden Beet* or *Red Beet* or *Beetroot* (q.v.).

SUGAR CANE

Lat. *Saccharum officinarum*; Fr. *Canne à sucre.* A stout, tall, perennial grass extensively cultivated in tropical and warm regions for the sake of the sweet sap contained in its stalks or *Canes*. Cane juice is obtained by crushing, and, after it has been cleared of impurities and treated, the mother liquor – or molasses – is removed, leaving a crude, yellowish sugar, which is known in the U.K. as *Demerara Sugar* and in the U.S.A. as *Brown Sugar*: when refined, discoloured and re-crystallized it becomes *Cane Sugar*, *White Sugar* or *Lump Sugar*.

SUGAR MAPLE

Lat. *Acer saccharum.* A *Maple* of Eastern North America, the three to five-lobed leaf of which is the floral emblem of Canada, and the sweet sap of which is the chief source of *Maple Sugar.*

SUGAR PEA

See *Pea.*

SWEDE (SWEDISH TURNIP) RUTABAGA

Lat. *Brassica napobrassica.* A turnip-rooted cabbage mostly grown for cattle food in many northern continental European countries. It is a cabbage of the *Kohl-rabi* variety; its stem swells underground instead of above ground and forms a large root, like a huge turnip, the flesh of which is yellow in the *Rutabaga* and white in the *Chou-navet*. Swedes are grown in gardens as well as in large fields, but many good palates prefer the agricultural to the horticultural *Swede*, provided they are lifted before they have reached full size.

Swedes are also known as *Russian Turnips, Swedish Turnips, Rutabagas*, and *Turnip-rooted Cabbage.*

How to Cook Swedes

Cut into cubes and cooked till tender in salted, boiling water, swedes may be beaten smooth to a *purée*, like mashed potatoes and eaten with any hot roast; what may be left goes a long way towards a good thick soup of the *Garbure* kind. Swedes may also be cooked in any way suitable for *Turnips* (q.v.).

SWEET FLAG

Lat. *Acorus calamus.* A plant with flag-like leaves which grows in marshlands in many parts of the British Isles. Its roots possess carminative and tonic properties and a taste which is not unpleasant.

SWEET GALE

See *Myrtle.*

SWEET JAVRIL

Lat. *Osmorhiza claytoni.* An American perennial herb with aromatic roots.

SWEET POTATO. BATATA

Lat. *Ipomoca Batatas*; Fr. *Patate douce.* A native of South America cultivated for its tubers, like the potato but not nearly so hardy nor so universally popular. The flesh is very tender, sweet and somewhat perfumed.

In the tropics it is usually boiled, mashed or sliced, and served as a sweet, with milk, sugar and grated coconut and some sort of spice. It is also roasted in hot ashes, or cut in slices and fried in oil. In Brazil it is usually peeled, grated before being cooked and made into a pudding with milk and spices. In Siam and the East Indies, it is often preserved as a sweetmeat in a clear syrup.

SWEET TANGLE

Lat. *Laminaria saccharina.* One of the edible seaweeds of the British Isles. See *Laver.*

SWEET TEA

Lat. *Smilax leucophylla.* An Australian variety of *Smilax*, used in the making of a substitute for *Tea.*

SWORD BEAN. SABRE BEAN

Lat. *Canavalia ensiformis.* It is known as *Canavali, Jack Bean* and *Snakebean*, also *Gotani* in Southern Rhodesia. A bean which is extensively grown in many parts of the tropics. When picked quite small and young, it is cooked in the same way as *French Beans* (q.v.), which it resembles. When the seeds or beans are allowed to develop and mature, they are often roasted, ground and used as a substitute for coffee.

TACCA. TAKAK

Lat. *Tacca pirmitifida*. A small, tropical herb, known in India as *Pia*: it is cultivated for the sake of its starchy roots from which the *Madagascar Arrowroot* is made.

TANGLE

See *Laver*.

TANSY

Lat. *Tanacetum vulgare*; Fr. *Tanaisie*. A European weed common by road-sides and in rough places. Its bitter leaves are aromatic and were used to a large extent in England of old, traditionally at Easter.

Tansy Pudding

3 oz. white breadcrumbs
1 oz. sugar
½ oz. butter
2 eggs
½ pint milk
1 dessertspoonful of finely-chopped young Tansy leaves

Boil the milk and pour over the breadcrumbs; leave for half hour. Beat the eggs, add to them the sugar and tansy, mix with the breadcrumbs, add the butter and bake the mixture in a pie-dish in a moderate oven till set. Eat it cold with a little sugar and cream, if procurable.—(Miss Emma Crawshaw, of Kirton Lindsey, Lincs.)—J.H.

A Tansy

A *Tansy*, in olden days in England, was the name of a custard flavoured with tansy or other bitterish leaves, and baked in a buttered shallow pie-dish.

Blanch and pound ¼ lb. of Jordan Almonds; put them into a stewpan; add a gill of syrup of roses, the crumbs of a French roll, some grated nutmeg, half a glass of brandy, two tablespoonfuls of tansy juice, 3 oz. of fresh butter, and some slices of citron; pour over it 1½ pints of boiling cream or milk; sweeten and, when cold, mix it. Add the juice of a lemon, and eight eggs beaten. It may be either boiled or baked.—C.F.L. (2).

TANSY MUSTARD

Lat. *Descurainia pinnate*. An American cress-like herb with bitter leaves not unlike those of tansy in appearance.

TARA. TARA FERN

Lat. *Pteris tremula* and *Pteris vulgare*. A New Zealand fern or brake with swollen root-stocks which the Maoris eat boiled or baked and ground like *Yam* (q.v.).

TARO

See *Coco Yam*.

TEPARY BEAN

Lat. *Phaseolus acutifolius, var. latifolius*. A Mexican *Haricot Bean* (q.v.) grown in the South-Western States of U.S.A. on account of its high powers of resistance to drought and heat.

TERFEZ

Miss G.E.Simpson, in her book *The Heart o Lybia* (Witherby), refers to Terfez as a kind of truffle growing in the desert about 4 in. under the ground, and she relates how servants and slaves go out with the children to search for the little mounds that are thrust up by the growing tubers, digging them up with sticks. In some places these tubers are so plentiful, according to this author, that three or four camel-loads can be gathered and lived upon for quite a long while.

THRACIAN CRESS

Lat. *Barbarea longirostris*. A comparatively new kind of Cress in England, but one that is widely distributed in the Balkans. Like all cresses it is rich in vitamins and ranks very high among the 'protective foods', but it is also well deserving the attention of gastronomes, particularly those who have a garden; it combines the mustard-oil flavour of mustard (in the 'mustard-and-cress' seedlings) with that of raw cabbage, and it is a valuable addition to many green salads and to practically any vegetable salad, particularly potato salads, haricot salads and others.

TIGER-NUT

See *Chufa*.

TOMATO

Lat. *Lycopersicum esculentum*; Fr. *Tomate*. The fruit of a branching plant, a native of South America, introduced into Europe in 1596. There are many different varieties of Tomatoes; most of them bear bright red, round or oval fruit, but others have a golden yellow fruit. Tomatoes are eaten both cooked and uncooked and a considerable demand also exists now for Tomato Juice, either fresh or – and chiefly – in a preserved form in bottle, can or tin. The best tomatoes are the just-ripe freshly-picked ones, and they are best eaten uncooked. A cooked tomato is like a cooked oyster, ruined; its ruin, that is its loss of flavour and vitamins, is not in vain, since it helps whatever is being cooked with it.

To Peel Tomatoes

1. Hold them, if firm, on point of a fork, over a low gas flame until skin wrinkles and splits: then slip it off;

2. Drop them into boiling water for two minutes; remove; peel and cool them;

3. Rub entire surface of tomatoes over with the back of a knife to loosen skin from flesh. Slit and remove skin carefully.

Uncooked Tomatoes are served chiefly as hors-d'oeuvre, sandwiches and salads, by themselves or mixed with some other vegetable. *Tomato juice* is one of the popular forms of Cocktails in the U.S.A.

Tomato Juice Cocktail

1 cup tomato juice
1 tablespoon mild vinegar
1 teaspoon sugar
Dusting pepper
1 scant teaspoon grated onion
1 tablespoon lemon juice
½ teaspoon salt
Small piece bayleaf
¼ teaspoon Worcester sauce

Mix all ingredients and allow to stand in a cool place for half an hour, then strain through a fine sieve, or a piece of fine muslin, chill, and serve in small glasses with cheese straws.

Tomato Hors-d'oeuvre

Tomates à la Génoise. Sliced tomato dressed in the centre of a *ravier* (narrow, small side-dish), with pieces of red and yellow peppers on the edges and some slices of cold potatoes. Cover with a *Sauce Vinaigrette.*

Tomates à la Monégasque. Small round tomatoes, with the seeds and pulp scooped out and replaced by a stuffing made of shredded tunny fish, the mashed yolk of hard-boiled eggs, and finely-chopped parsley, onion, chervil and tarragon, the whole mixed in a *Sauce Mayonnaise.*

Tomates au naturel. Small, halved tomatoes or sliced larger ones, marinated in oil and vinegar, with pepper and salt and some finely-chopped chives, for some time; served in their marinade.

Tomates en Quartiers. Tomatoes cut in four quarters and served either *au naturel,* just with a *Vinaigrette Sauce,* or else with a filling of mashed cold fish, a *Macédoine* of vegetables or any other filling, mixed with some *Mayonnaise Sauce,* in place of the pulp and seeds which have been previously removed.

Tomato Sandwiches

1. On rounds of buttered bread, place thin slices of peeled tomatoes; season with pepper and salt and finely-chopped chives. Press another piece of buttered bread on top and cut in two, diagonally.

2. On a piece of buttered bread, place thin slices of peeled tomatoes; season with pepper and salt; sprinkle over a thick dusting of hard-boiled egg-yolk and some finely-chopped chervil or parsley. Press another piece of buttered bread on top and cut in two, diagonally.

3. Proceed as for No. 2, adding some very thin pieces of cold tongue on the tomatoes instead of the yolk of egg.

4. Proceed as for No. 3, but use small pieces of cold boiled bacon instead of tongue.

5. Proceed as for No. 3, but use small pieces of chopped fillets of anchovies instead of tongue.

6. Proceed as for No. 5, but use sardine paste instead of anchovies.

7. Proceed as for No. 1, but add finely-chopped watercress in place of chives.

(There are, of course, many more varieties of Tomato Sandwiches.)

Tomato Salads

Andalouse. Lettuce, tomato and celery.
Caprice. Tomato, celery, apples, asparagus tips, blanched almonds, lettuce.
Leopold. Lettuce, crabmeat, celery, tomato, shrimp, green pepper.
Lily. Lettuce, tomato, cucumber.
Mary Garden. Salmon, anchovies, green peppers, celery, olive, beet, lettuce and tomato.
Ponce de Léon. Lettuce, chicken, raw peas, kraut, beet, celery, cress and tomato.
Radisson. Cucumbers, asparagus tips, nuts, celery, chives, tomato and tomato *purée*; lettuce.
Robespierre. Tomato, pimolas, lobster, lettuce.
Sicilienne. Tomato, celery, artichokes, apples, hard-boiled eggs, chives, red and green peppers, lettuce.
Surprise. Tomato, apples, celery, hard-boiled eggs, lettuce.
Taylor. Tomato, Virginia ham, lettuce, celery, caviar, chervil, parsley, chives.
Trianon. Tomato, lettuce, celery, chives.
Tom Coryate. Lettuce, tomato, hard-boiled eggs, pineapple, Cheddar cheese, celery, green and red peppers, anchovies.—A.S.

Baked Tomatoes

I

Cut off the top of each tomato and scoop out some of the centre and bake in a moderate oven. In the meantime, fry in butter some breadcrumbs and chopped onion or chives, and press as much as you can of this seasoning into each baked tomato. Brown in a quick oven and serve hot.

II

Cut the required number of tomatoes (one per guest) in two; do not peel them. Put them in an earthen pan with some butter on each half, and season with pepper and salt. Bake for about one hour. In the meantime, prepare squares of buttered toast, place a half tomato on each piece of toast, pour the melted butter from the pan on each of them and serve hot.

Green Tomato Chutney

Peel and slice about 2 lb. of green tomatoes. Add 2 oz. mustard powder, 1 oz. ground cinnamon, 1 oz. ground cloves, 1½ lb. brown sugar, 3 pints brown vinegar and a pinch of cayenne. Boil all together until quite thick. Bottle securely, and keep a few weeks before using. Apples can be used instead of tomatoes if preferred.—B.H.

Devilled Tomatoes

3 large tomatoes
Salt and few grains cayenne
1 hard-boiled yolk of egg
1 teaspoon mustard
4 tablespoons butter
2 teaspoons powdered sugar
1 egg
2 tablespoons vinegar

Beat butter to a cream, add all dry ingredients, rubbing hard-boiled egg yolk to a paste. Blend with beaten egg and the vinegar. Cook in a double-boiler, stirring constantly until mixture is thick, then pour over the sliced tomatoes which have previously been lightly fried in butter.

Fried Tomatoes

Choose firm, medium-sized tomatoes; peel them, cut them in ½ in. slices; dip each slice in batter and fry in boiling olive oil or in deep fat.

Grilled Tomatoes

Brush over some smallish, firm tomatoes with softened butter or olive oil. Dust with pepper and salt and cook slowly under gas or electric grill. Large tomatoes may be cut in halves and grilled in the same way.

Tomatoes au Gratin

Peel some large and firm tomatoes; slice them and cover with the slices the bottom of a well-buttered pie-dish; sprinkle with grated cheese and breadcrumbs; season with pepper and salt; moisten with melted butter; then put in the dish another layer of tomato slices and treat them in the same manner, alternating layers of tomatoes and cheese-cum-breadcrumbs until the dish is filled. Finally moisten with butter and bake in a moderate oven for 50 minutes.

Tomato Eggs

6 large tomatoes
6 eggs
6 pieces of toast
Bacon for garnishing
Minced parsley

Cut off the tops of the tomatoes and scoop out the centres. Into each hollow break an egg. Bake in a moderate oven until the egg is set – about 15 minutes. Serve on toast garnished with crisp bacon and sprinkled with minced parsley.—H.P.

Tomato Fondue

2 medium-sized ripe tomatoes
½ teaspoon dried sweet basil
1 clove garlic
2 tablespoons butter
¼ glass dry white wine
2 cups grated Cheddar cheese
Paprika

Skin the tomatoes; remove the seeds, and chop the flesh very fine. Mix the basil with it. Rub the chafing dish with the clove of garlic, then melt the butter in it and when it is bubbling – it should not get brown – put in the tomato. Simmer for six to eight minutes, then season with paprika and add the wine. Do not add any salt because the cheese may be salted. Simmer the mixture until well blended, then add the grated cheese. Keep stirring, and when the cheese is melted and well blended, serve very hot on toast.—H.P.

Tomato Jelly

3 or 4 tomatoes or 1 cupful
    strained tinned tomatoes
1 tablespoon sliced onion
1 saltspoon sugar
1 tablespoon chopped carrot
Half a cupful of celery
Sprig of parsley
Salt and pepper
1 clove

Cut up vegetables and place all together in a pan with two cupfuls of water. Add seasonings and, if liked, a small *bouquet-garni*. When tomatoes are done, cool mixture somewhat and add granulated gelatine in the proportion of one tablespoonful of the latter to one cupful of the tomato liquid. Strain through a piece of muslin or a fine-mesh sieve (chinois). This jelly is useful for making small jelly rings, in the centres of which may be placed various small tasty tit-bits such as pieces of ice-cold foie gras, flaked crabmeat or tunny fish, mixed small vegetables in *Mayonnaise*, etc.

Omelette Portugaise
(Tomato Omelette)

Peel some large and very ripe tomatoes; cut them in two and remove the seeds; cut them up and put them in a saucepan with butter, pepper and salt, a shaving of garlic and a pinch of sifted sugar. Stir from time to time, and cook on a moderate heat until the tomato can easily be passed through a fine sieve. Return the Tomato *Purée* thus obtained to the pan and keep hot whilst making the omelette in the usual manner; then fold most of the Tomato *Purée* in the omeette and serve the rest of it round the omeette itself, by way of Tomato Sauce.

Tomato Pie

1½ lb. tomatoes
1 lb. onions
6 oz. rice
2 oz. grated cheese
4 oz. breadcrumbs
Pepper and salt to taste

Wash the rice and put it into a saucepan, covered with cold water, and boil quickly for 20 minutes. Grease a large pie-dish, strain the rice, and line sides and bottom of pie-dish with it, pressing it down with a spoon. Wipe tomatoes, place them in dish. Peel and grate the onions, and put them over the tomatoes, adding pepper and salt. Sprinkle the cheese over, and cover the top with the breadcrumbs. Bake for half an hour in a hot oven. Serve hot with good brown gravy. Sufficient for six or eight people.—L.G.N.

Tomato Pie (Green)

Line a pie-dish with short pastry, sprinkle it with dry flour, then put in a layer of green tomatoes sliced finely; sprinkle with flour again, then sprinkle thickly with sugar and a pinch of salt; dot several small pieces of butter over and add one tablespoonful of water. Cover with pastry and bake in a good oven for half an hour. This is like apple pie and is delicious served with cream or custard.—L.G.N.

Tomato Pie (Scotch)

Cut off the rind of the bacon and cover the bottom of a pie-dish with rashers. Sprinkle with a *little* oatmeal and a layer of tomatoes cut in slices. Repeat with alternate layers of bacon and tomatoes until the dish is three-parts full, always sprinkling the bacon with oatmeal. Beat up two eggs well and season. Pour them over the contents of the pie-dish and bake in a good oven for about half an hour. The eggs should be firm and the top nicely browned before serving. Sufficient for four people.—L.G.N.

Tomates Provençale

1 lb. firm even-sized tomatoes
1 or 2 cloves garlic
Salt and pepper
5 or 6 shallots
3 tablespoons olive oil
3 tablespoons breadcrumbs
Chopped parsley

Cut tomatoes into halves. Finely chop together the shallots and garlic. Crumble the stale white breadcrumbs finely and chop the parsley. Now put the oil in a large *sauteuse* so that the tomatoes may not touch one another. When oil is smoking, add shallots and garlic, then tomatoes, cooking gently after pricking with a fork to evaporate water they contain. When the oil is clear and the tomatoes have been cooked on both sides add the breadcrumbs, browning them in the oil. Serve the tomatoes sprinkling the browned crumbs and the parsley over them.

Note.—Once the liquid has been absorbed, the tomatoes should cook rather fast as they must be brown, slightly crisp and in no way watery or mushy.

La Ratatouille Provençale

1 or 2 small aubergines
Olive oil
5 or 6 ripe tomatoes
2 or 3 small green peppers
1 head celery
Salt and pepper

Cut all vegetables up. Place in a *sauteuse* with a couple of tablespoonfuls of pure olive oil. Add salt and pepper and cook gently, stirring once in a while, for about one hour. Serve either hot or cold.

Tomatoes 'Ripieni'

Choose 12 large and smooth tomatoes, cut off the stem end and take out the seeds. Put 4 oz. of grated bread, one quarter of an onion minced, a little salt, and 2 oz. of butter into a frying-pan; mix well and then fill the tomatoes with it. Put them in an earthen pan and cook for half hour over a hot fire; serve very hot.—J.R.

Tomatoes 'al Riso'

Take the pulp of six tomatoes and put it in a saucepan with 2 oz. of butter. Cook thoroughly, then strain through a sieve, add one large cupful of *consommé*, and cook till reduced one quarter.

Meanwhile cook some rice in *consommé*, when done add the tomatoes, stir, and serve hot.—J.R.

Tomato Soup (English)

1 lb. tomatoes
1 onion, 1 carrot and 1 turnip
1 or 1½ oz. sago
1 oz. butter
A sprig of parsley and a stalk of celery
4 cloves and 4 peppercorns
½ pint milk and 1 quart water

Prepare the vegetables, cut them up, add the water, and simmer 1½ hours. Strain, add butter and sago, and keep stirring till it boils. Let it boil for 15 minutes, then add the milk; heat, season to taste and serve.—M.C.B.

Tomato Soup (French)
(Velouté de Tomate)

Prepare a *Velouté à la Crème de Riz* (chicken broth with fresh cream, ground rice and a yolk of egg binding) and a *Purée de Tomate* (stewed ripe tomatoes passed through a fine sieve). Mix both together, half and half. Add some fresh butter and season to taste. Pearl barley, tapioca or any similar garnishing may be added at the last moment, if a thicker soup is preferred.

Crème Pompadour is a soup made with a *Purée* of Tomatoes, garnished with *Perles du Japon* and a *Julienne* of Lettuce.

Crème Portugaise is a soup made with a *Purée* of Tomatoes, garnished with rice.

Tomato Soup (U.S.A.)
(Tomato Chowder)

One No. 3 can of tomatoes, heated with three cupfuls of water; ¼ lb. salt pork; two small white onions, peeled and sliced; one teaspoonful of flour; ¼ cupful of uncooked rice, washed; two tablespoonfuls of sugar; three teaspoonfuls of salt. Pepper to taste.

Cut the pork in thin strips and place in a fairly hot small frying-pan. As soon as it begins to melt, add the onions, and fry until both pork and onions are lightly browned. Sprinkle in the flour and stir until blended. Turn into a heavy saucepan and add the remaining ingredients. Simmer, covered, for one hour, stirring occasionally. Add more seasoning, if needed. Serve in bowls or onion-soup casserole. Sprinkle a little cheese over the top. Serves six persons; halve the recipe for two or three, using a No. 1 can of tomatoes.—E.K.H.

Stuffed Tomatoes
(Tomates farcies)
I

These are prepared in the same way as *Baked Tomatoes* No. 1 (q.v.), but instead of buttered breadcrumbs being used as a filling, all sorts of other fillings are used, mixed with the pulp – freed from seeds – which has been scooped out of the tomatoes; cooked rice mixed with minced ham or tongue or any other kind of cooked meat, seasoned with finely-chopped shallots, parsley, chervil, pepper and salt, make a variety of excellent fillings for *Stuffed Tomatoes*. Mushrooms may be used instead of meat; truffles finely-chopped in place of or with rice. Broken-up cauliflower, asparagus tips, green peas and practically any and every left-over is suitable for use as stuffing for *Tomates Farcies*.

Stuffed Tomatoes
II

Rather large, even-sized tomatoes
Salt and pepper
Small pinch mixed herbs
Milk or stock
Sausage meat or other chopped meat
1 small onion
Fresh breadcrumbs
Brown breadcrumbs
Butter, ad lib.

After wiping tomatoes, remove stem and, with a pair of sharp scissors, cut out a small round piece from top of each. Scoop out seeds and pulp very carefully with a teaspoon, taking care not to break skin at edges. Sprinkle insides with salt and pepper and turn the tomatoes upside down so that the water may drain from them. Meanwhile prepare the stuffing, using breadcrumbs soaked in either stock or milk then squeezed dry, to bind mixture, and seasoning with finely-chopped onion and the herbs. Season rather highly and fry the stuffing lightly in a little butter before piling up inside the tomatoes, piling each high on top and covering with brown breadcrumbs, dotting all with bits of butter. The scooped out interiors, after being sieved, may be added to stuffing. Place them in a baking-tin, surround with good stock and bake until soft and brown, but take care not to overcook which would spoil their shape.

Note.—If flavour is liked, just a suspicion of either garlic or shallot or both may be added to stuffing. The stock should be all absorbed by tomatoes when ready to serve.

Alternative Stuffings

Interior flesh, mixed with breadcrumbs pre-soaked in milk or cream, seasoned with herbs, onion and salt and pepper. Blend with a little chopped garlic and melted butter.

Tomatoes are nice stuffed with boiled rice mixed with grated cheese. To serve cold, stuff with chopped raw celery, cooked peas and diced, cooked carrot, all mixed with *Mayonnaise.*

Stuff with any kind of creamed fish such as smoked haddock, cod, etc.

TONKA BEAN
Lat. *Dipteryx odorata*. The seed, or bean of a tropical South American tree. It contains a scented substance known as *Coumarin*,which is its chief asset as a flavouring agent; it is sometimes used as a substitute for *Vanilla*.

TOOTHWORT
See *Crinkleroot*.

TOPEPO
A tomato-like fruit which is said to be the hybrid of a *Tomato* and *Red Pepper*.

TRUFFLE
English Truffle: *Tuber aestivum*; French Truffle: *Tuber melanosporum*; Piedmont or White Truffle: *Tuber magnatum*. The best of the edible, subterranean members of the genus *Tuber*, found in the Périgord district of France. The English truffle, sometimes called *Bath Truffle*, or *Red Truffle*, is smaller and inferior in aroma. The *Italian Truffle*, or *Grey Truffle*, of Piedmont, has a distinctive peppery taste, whereas neither the French nor the English truffle has any taste at all. But the French truffle – and the English truffle in a very attenuated form – have a remarkable fragrance which pervades other foods coming in contact with them. New-laid eggs, for instance, left overnight on top of some fresh French truffles, will distinctly taste of truffle if cooked the next day. Whole truffles cooked in Champagne, or in any other way, are sheer extravagance. The only place of truffles in gastronomy is as a flavouring agent, and first of all in *Foie Gras*. This solid goose fat is improved beyond recognition when its complete lack of appeal to the olfactory sense is made good by the presence of some fresh truffles.

There is a flavourless subterranean fungus called an *Earthball*, which is sometimes found on the surface of the ground. It looks like a small round black potato and is black throughout; it is harmless and merely nasty; also without any market value; but it has been used fraudulently in *Foie Gras*, masquerading for truffle.

There is also a species of tubers related to the truffle, known as *Tuberales*, to which belong the *Terfez* (q.v.).

TURMERIC
Lat. *Cucurma longa*. An East Indian herb grown for its rootstocks which are boiled, sun-dried and used as a condiment, chiefly in curries. *Turmeric* is responsible for the yellowish colour of curry powder.

TURNIP
Lat. *Brassica rapa*; Fr. *Navet*. Although the 'tops' or sprouting leaves of the turnip are acceptable in the early spring, when there is a dearth of green vegetables, the turnip is chiefly cultivated for its root. There are many different varieties of turnips; they all belong to one or the other of the two main classes of turnips, the long-rooted and the flat-rooted, or round-rooted. The latter is superior to the first for flavour and sweetness.

Turnips possess a remarkable power of absorption which renders them most useful in stews and *ragouts*, specially with rich and highly-flavoured fare, such as duck and goose; whilst imparting their own sweet flavour, they become richer and succulent as they take to themselves the savour of their pot companions.

Like all root vegetables, turnips are best when quickly grown; slow growth results in a certain woodiness which no boiling can get over.

Boiled Turnips
Turnips should be steamed or boiled after being peeled. Young turnips ought not to require more than 30 minutes' boiling to be tender, or 45 minutes' steaming. Boiled turnips are best served mashed in a *Purée*, after being thoroughly well drained. They must be seasoned with pepper and salt, butter, a little thick cream well stirred in, and the whole re-heated before serving.

Turnip Soup
Wash and pare half a dozen medium-sized turnips. Cook them in gently boiling salted water till soft. Rub them through a sieve and re-heat the water in which they were cooked. When it comes to the boil again, put back the mashed turnips in it; season with pepper and salt and simmer for half hour or more. Add 1 oz. butter; stir in the well-beaten yolk of an egg and serve hot.

UDO. OUDO
Lat. *Aralia cordata*. A Japanese herb with shoots which are not merely edible but well worth the attention of gastronomes on account of their delicate aromatic taste; they need only be blanched, and they are eaten hot or cold,with a butter sauce or *Vinaigrette*, in the same way as *Asparagus* (q.v.).—L.C.

UNICORN PLANT
Lat. *Martynia proboscidea*. A trailing plant from Brazil; it produces an abundance of small ovoid fruit, with a curved or hooked point at the end. They are usually gathered before they reach their full size and pickled in vinegar like large capers.

URD BEAN
Lat. *Phaseolus Mungo*. A popular bean of the East, closely related to the *Mung Bean*, and known in India by the name of *Black Gram*.

The Bombay *Papad* is made of *Black Gram* or *Urd*. The beans are soaked in slightly warm water for two days and then crushed under a stone to a pulp and dried.

This bean is grown by the Chinese in the vicinity of San Francisco for *Bean Sprouts* (q.v.).

VALERIAN
(African)

Lat. *Fedia cornucopiae*; Fr. *Valériane d'Alger*. A North African herb which resembles *Corn Salad* (q.v.) and is used in the same manner.

VEGETABLE MARROW

Lat. *Cucurbita pepo*; Fr. *Courge* and *Courgette*. The most popular of all edible gourds in Great Britain, where Vegetable Marrows hold the place of Squash in the U.S.A. There are a very large number of different varieties of marrows, most of them belonging to one or other of the two main classes of (*a*) Trailing and (*b*) Cluster or Bush Marrows. When quite young, marrows are moist and tender; when fully grown, they are dry and tough. They must be picked before the first frosts and stored in a dry and frostproof place if they are to be kept at all. But they are ever so much better when picked small and eaten as soon as picked, baked, fried, or in pies and soups. The best use to make of vegetable marrows is to cook them very small and stuff them in any way suitable for *Stuffed Tomatoes* (q.v.). With the exception of the little African marrow and the *Cocozelle*, and maybe other small and finer species, marrows are a tasteless vegetable which has everything to gain and nothing to lose by the addition of highly-flavoured or spiced stuffings.

How to Cook Vegetable Marrow

Small and immature marrows should be peeled, as their skin when unripe is bitter and unwholesome; then they are cut in halves and the seeds removed; they may be cut up again in four or eight pieces, according to size, and the pieces are put in a steamer, or the top deck of a double saucepan with boiling water in the lower deck. They are steamed until tender and then seasoned and either served with a white sauce or mashed into a *Purée* or baked, or fried, or stuffed.

Fully ripe marrows, small or large, and usually 'store' winter marrows, should never be peeled, but steamed and peeled after, if they are to be mashed or used in soups; but not peeled at all if they are to be stuffed; their skin is hard; it is not eaten, but it provides a useful outside envelope, like that of the Egg-plant (*Aubergine*), as well as imparting a pleasant flavour to the pulp.— E.S.R.

Fried Vegetable Marrow

Take a medium-sized marrow; do not pare it but cut in slices. Dip these in egg and breadcrumbs and fry in butter. Season to taste and serve very hot. This recipe can be varied by cutting the marrow into short strips the size of a pea-pod and frying as above. In this case, however, it is necessary to pare off the skin.—E.S.R. (1).

Vegetable Marrow (Courgettes) Hors d'oeuvre

à la Benoiton. Slices of marrow fried in oil, then allowed to get cold and served as *canapés* for chopped hard-boiled eggs and tunny fish *mariné* with a *Mayonnaise*; chopped chives on top.

à la Caillou. Slices of marrow boiled in salt water, then marinated in oil and vinegar, and served with thin slices of tomatoes, a *julienne* of pimentoes and a *chiffonnade* of lettuce. Also hard-boiled eggs cut in quarters.

à la Grecque. Slices of marrow cooked for about 25 minutes in a *court-bouillon* of three parts of water to one of olive oil, lemon juice and a *bouquet garni* made up of celery, fennel, thyme and bayleaves; pepper, salt and coriander. Must be served quite cold and bathed in their own *court-bouillon*.

à la Turque. Same as *à la Grecque*, except for an addition of saffron.

Small Marrows au gratin

Peel tender young marrows, cut into thick rounds of equal thickness and boil for two or three minutes in salted water. Drain when a little tender but not soft. Brown the slices lightly in a little butter, taking care to have the rounds side by side in the pan. Turn and brown both sides. When done, season and place in a gratin dish. Cover with a good *Béchamel*, sprinkle with grated cheese, dot with butter and brown nicely. Serve in gratin dish.

Small Marrows with Marjoram

Take some long small marrows – a fair quantity as they shrink considerably in the cooking – and cut them in round slices, the size of a half-crown. Place a saucepan or a copper frying-pan on a good fire; half-fill the pan with olive oil, and when it starts boiling throw in the pieces of marrow, stirring them continually; when half-cooked, season with pepper and salt and when they begin to brown sprinkle with a generous pinch of marjoram, subsequently removing from the pan with a perforated slicer.— P.Ar.

Stuffed Courgettes

They can either be cut in half, lengthwise, or used whole. I prefer the last as more 'elegant' and because the little marrows show off better when served. In any case, they have to be emptied to make room for the stuffing. In order to empty them when used whole, employ a tin tube, inserting it through from one end to the other; should the hollow not seem sufficient, given the size of the marrow, widen with a small knife.—P.AT.

Marrow Jam

5½ lb. marrow
5½ lb. sugar
Salt
3 lemons
¼ lb. ginger

Cut up the marrow, place in a bowl and sprinkle with about half cupful of salt. Let it stand for 12 hours and then pour off the salty water. Mix the sugar with the marrow and again leave it for 12 hours. Add the juice of the lemons, the rind peeled very thin and chopped, and the ginger chopped, and boil all together until the marrow is transparent.—M.K.S. (2).

Vegetable Marrow and Cheese Pie

Cut a mature marrow in fairly thin slices and steam. Remove the seeds and put a layer of the slices in a buttered pie-dish that has been rubbed with onion. Then a layer of grated cheese, another layer of marrow, and on top grated cheese, some very fine breadcrumbs and tiny pats of butter. Put in a very hot oven to brown.—E.S.R. (1).

Vegetable Marrow Soup

Steam a sliced mature marrow. Remove the seeds and rub through a sieve. Mix the yolk of an egg with a little cream, and to this mixture add the sieved marrow and the liquor from it, stirring all the time. Stand the bowl in a *bain-marie* or a pan nearly filled with boiling water; heat, but never allow the *purée* to boil or it will curdle. Add seasoning to taste and milk to thin to right consistency.—E.S R. (1).

Stuffed Marrow Flowers

Pick the thin male flowers of the vegetable marrow, and whilst they are still fresh stuff them with a mixture of rice, chopped herbs, egg, and, perhaps, a little minced meat. Fold into neat little packets and fit them closely into a buttered fireproof dish. Add a little vegetable stock, dot with butter and cook in the oven for about 15 minutes.—M.K.S. (2).

Fritters of Marrow Flowers

Dip the fresh flowers in a well-flavoured frying batter and fry in deep fat, or in olive oil for preference.—M.K.S. (2).

VEGETABLE STEWS

There are many ways of preparing stews of various vegetables, with or without any meat, and the following is but a simple example of how to do it.

Vegetable Stew

Chopped parsley
Butter
1 small clove garlic
1 cup peas or French beans
1 large peeled tomato
Salt and pepper
1 or 2 stalks celery (optional)
2 or 3 sliced onions
2 or 3 shallots
8 or 10 young carrots
4 or 5 diced potatoes
Good pinch mixed herbs
2 or 3 small tender turnips
Flour

Mince the shallots and garlic very finely. Put a good piece of butter in an earthenware casserole or an iron cocotte. When hot, add shallots, onions and garlic and brown together lightly, then add peeled and cut up tomato. Season with salt, pepper and the herbs, and moisten with about two cups of hot water. Simmer for five minutes, then add all the other vegetables with the exception of the potatoes, which should not go into the casserole until the contents are nearly done. The peas or French beans should have previously been cooked for five minutes in salted boiling water. Simmer all gently until done, then add a tablespoonful of butter mixed thoroughly with the same amount of flour. This binds the sauce. Serve with hot toast or, better still, with hot American biscuits.

Note.—Tiny silver onions, left whole, are better than cut ones, and small new potatoes better than old diced ones. If available, a thick slice of ham, bacon or salt pork may be cut up small and browned with shallots and garlic, and rich meat-stock may be used instead of hot water. Dried beans, previously soaked and cooked, may be added and any other vegetables on hand: small pieces of cauliflower, broad beans, etc.

Fritto Misto of Vegetables

Cut up one or two young green pumpkins in thin slices about as long as a finger and half as wide, and lay them on a plate with a little salt. Mix 3 oz. of butter and three tablespoonfuls of flour in a saucepan and boil for two minutes, add half a tumbler of cream, half a tumbler of chicken broth, and boil it till it is a stiff *Béchamel*. Mix minced mushrooms or truffles with the *Béchamel* and roll into small balls, then dip into egg and grated bread and put aside till wanted. Take ten or twelve pumpkin flowers, some young artichokes properly prepared and cut into quarters (if not quite young and tender they must be boiled first), some cauliflower and bits of cardoon; dip them in egg and dust them with flour. Flour the slices of pumpkin and fry all together in pure olive oil. Use dripping or lard for frying if you have not got good oil, Season with a sprinkling of salt. Serve very hot.

VELVET BEAN

Lat. *Mucuna nivea*. One of the most esteemed vegetables of Burma and Bengal. It resembles, and is cooked like, *Haricot Beans* (q.v.).

VIOLET

Lat. *Viola odorata*. The wild Violet used for making syrups, conserves and pastes of violets; the leaves may be used for salads and in soups. On the Pacific Coast the wild Violet is known as *Heartsease*.

VIPER'S BUGLOSS

Lat. *Echium vulgare*. A European weed, naturalized in the U.S.A., where it is usually called *Blueweed*. It is used in place of *Borage*, which it resembles.

WASABI

See *Japanese Horseradish*.

WATERCRESS

Lat. *Nasturtium officinale*; Fr. *Cresson de fontaine*. An aquatic plant, a native of Europe, which grows freely in moist meadows and close to the banks of many streams. It is largely cultivated by market gardeners near all large cities and it is used for garnishing or decorating dishes as well as in salads. There is another European species of watercress, the meadow cress, which bears attractive clusters of pale mauve flowers in the early spring, but its leaves have no gastronomic merit whatever.

Watercress Soup
(Potage Santé)

One large bunch of fresh watercress is required; pick it over carefully, wash well, removing hard stalk. Peel and chop finely one onion. Peel and cut up roughly two or three potatoes. Chop watercress very finely and set aside. Boil potatoes in water and milk; add salt and pepper. Add onion and press through a sieve when potatoes are done. Re-heat, and when boiling, add chopped watercress. When it comes up to the boil again, pour in the soup tureen over one or two beaten yolks of egg; add a piece of butter and serve.—A L.S.

WATER LILY

Lat. *Nymphaea stellata*. A tropical water plant which is cultivated in India for the sake of its roots, its flowering stem and its seeds. The roots are eaten both uncooked and boiled; the stems, when young, are added to curries and its seeds are roasted and used in the making of cakes. There is another edible Water Lily which grows in tropical and South Africa; in Zululand, where it is called *Izibo*, the natives boil and eat the rootstocks. In Senegal, its seeds are made into balls, with flour, and fried in oil.

WATER PARSNIP

Lat. *Sium aquaticum*. A water weed with poisonous roots and edible leaves; the leaves resemble small celery leaves and are a welcome addition to green salads.

WAX GOURD

Lat. *Benincasa cerifera*. The fruit of a twining plant of tropical Asia. It is oblong, cylindrical in shape, from 14 in. to 16 in. in length, and 4 in. or 5 in. in diameter. The flesh is slightly floury and white; it keeps well and is a valuable store vegetable for the winter months in the East. It is also known as *White Gourd* and *Tallow Gourd*.

WELSH ONION. CIBOULE

Lat. *Allium fistulosum*. 'The so-called Welsh Onion, which has nothing to do with Wales, has a leek-like bulb, but with tubular leaves, and is known as *Allium fistulosum*. This is a useful vegetable, delicate in flavour, and perennial. One breaks off a leek or two as wanted, leaving the main plant undisturbed. This should be found in English gardens, as it is very hardy and easy to grow. One would like to think it was the Leek of Wales and Fluellen, but alas, chronology forbids. It is a Siberian plant, not known in England until 1629.' (Edward Bunyard, in *Wine and Food*. No. 6. 1935.)

There are related species which are known as *Nebuka* and *Catawissa*.

WHITE BASIL

Lat. *Basella alba*. An important food climbing plant with succulent stems and leaves. It is used extensively in many parts of India in the same way as *Spinach* (q.v.) is used in Europe. It is also an important potherb used in the making of curry and is particularly valuable as a rainy season plant, when other vegetables are scarce.

WHITE or BARBADOS YAM
A species of *Yam* (q.v.) widely cultivated in Australasia and Polynesia for its rootstocks which are eaten boiled and baked in different ways.

WILD RICE
Lat. *Zizania aquatica*. A tall, aquatic, North American, perennial grass bearing an abundance of hard seeds which are cooked like *Rice*.

WINTER CRESS
Lat. *Barbarea vulgaris*. A species of *Watercress* (q.v.) which grows freely in moist waste lands; it has smooth, shining, dark-green leaves, and an erect angular stem bearing yellow flowers. It is known in the U.S.A. as *Rocket Salad*.

WINTER PURSLANE
Lat. *Claytonia perfoliata*. A highly-prized vegetable in Central America and the West Indies. Its green leaves are eaten uncooked as a salad and cooked like spinach.

WOODRUFF
Lat. *Asperula odorata*. An old-fashioned English herb from the dried leaves of which a kind of medicinal 'tea' used to be made.

WOOD SORREL. ALLELUIA
Lat. *Oxalis acetosella* (U.K.) and *Oxalis montana* (U.S.A.). A common European weed the young leaves of which are excellent in green salads, being tender and tasty, slightly bitter but very pleasantly so. There is an American variety of Wood-Sorrel, a native of Mexico, with fleshy white roots which are insipid but edible, cooked like *Parsnips* (q.v.). Its leaves are prepared in any way suitable for the garden or common *Sorrel* (q.v.).

WORMWOOD
A strongly aromatic European annual herb used to flavour liqueurs, spirits and sweets.
' ... I did give them two quarts of wormwood wine.'—Pepys. Nov. 24th, 1660.
' ... to a little house behind the Lords' house to drink some wormwood ale.'—Pepys. March 21st, 1662.

YACON
Lat. *Polymnia edulis*. A Peruvian plant grown for the sake of its fleshy, edible tubers which are rich in inulin but are mawkish and tasteless.

YAMS
Barbados Yam; also Greater, Indian or Malay Yam or Winged-stalked Yam, *Dioscorea alata*; Common Yam, *Dioscorea sativa*, 'Cush-Cush' Yam of Trinidad or 'Yampi' of Jamaica, *Dioscorea trifida*; Indian Potato or Chinese Yam, *Dioscorea Batatas*; Malacca or Dark Purple Yam, *Dioscorea atropurpurea*; Otaheite Potato, Potato Yam or Climbing Air Potato, *Dioscorea bulbifera*; Upeh Chinese Yam, *Dioscorea Fargesii*; White 'Eight Months' Yam or Negro Yam, *Dioscorea rotundata*; Wild Yam, *Dioscorea villosa*; Yellow or 'Twelve Months' Guinea Yam, *Dioscorea cayenensis*; Guinea Yam or 'Kaawi', *Dioscorea aculeata*; Japanese Yam, *Dioscorea japonica*.

There are a considerable number of yams, the most universally grown being known by the name of *Sain*. Among other sorts, the *Winged-stalked Yam*, a native of India and the South Sea Islands, produces the largest tubers of all, up to 8 ft. in length and 80 lb. in weight; the *Dark Purple Yam*, also known as *Malacca Yam*, which is considered the third best yam in India, has dark purple stems and tubers.

A widely cultivated variety of yam both in West Africa and the West Indies is the *Yellow Yam*, also known as *Prickly-stemmed Yam* and *Guinea Yam* or *Afou*; it is distinctly inferior in quality to the Chinese and Indian yams.

YAM BEANS
Ajipa Bean, *Pachyrhizus Ahipa*; Goa Bean, Starch Bean or Yam Bean, *Pachyrhizus tuberosus*; Nigerian 'Giri-Gir', *Sphenostylis stenocarpa*; Short-podded Yam Bean, *Pachyrhizus erosus*.

Tropical climbing plants with turnip-like roots which are eaten finely-sliced, uncooked, in salads, or boiled and mashed. The pods are also edible, boiled as a vegetable.

YARROW. MILFOIL
Lat. *Achillea decolorans*. A European herb with strongly-scented leaves, which is widely naturalized in the U.S.A. Its leaves, finely chopped, are a welcome addition to salads in place of *Chervil*.

YAUTA
See *Calalu*.

ZAPALLITO
A South American *Gourd*, which can be grown in England in the open. Its round, glossy, mahogany-coloured fruits are cooked like marrows, their flesh being firm and of golden hue. They are best when no larger than a cricket ball.

ZEGAKELIE
A small shrub the leaves of which possess a strong scent, somewhat similar to that of *Thyme*. It grows freely in Abyssinia, where it is used in the making of an aromatic sauce known as *Aoudze*; this sauce is always served with the Abyssinian national dish called *Brondo*.

ZULU NUT
See *Chufa*.

SECTION 3

BREADS,
DESSERTS
AND
CEREALS

SECTION III

Breads, Desserts and Cereals: a list of Cereals, Grasses,
Plants and Trees, the seeds, roots, fruits or pith of
which are made into flour, meal or paste for human
consumption; together with the description of
various flours and meals and a number of
recipes, both old and new, for the making
of Bread, Biscuits, Cookies and Cakes,
Puddings, Pies, Pancakes and
Fritters, Macaroni, Noodles
and Rice, and many kinds
of Pastries

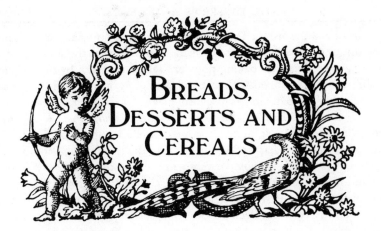

BREADS, DESSERTS AND CEREALS

She has given him a roll and a bun,
And a Shrewsbury cake. Of Pailin's own make.
THOMAS INGOLDSBY, *Bloudie Jacke of Shrewsberrie.*

INTRODUCTION

BREAD, Wine and Oil, that blessed trinity of the kindly fruits of the earth, have been, ever since Biblical times, the symbol of peace – and plenty, the reward promised by angels in heaven to men of goodwill upon earth.

In all times and among all nations bread has been regarded as the staff of life, the foundation upon which all kinds of widely differing diets have been built, according to age, climate and custom. Among free and civilized peoples the head of the family is known as the breadwinner. And for close upon two thousand years Christians of all denominations have had and still have one prayer in common – the Lord's Prayer: they all ask, as they were divinely ordered to do, that they may be given their daily bread, even before asking to be forgiven their trespasses, to be delivered from evil and not to be led into temptation.

Bread is made of the ground grain, the *flour* or *meal*, of wheat, barley, rye, oats and other cereals as well as of the seeds, fruits, roots or pith of many grasses, trees or plants, cultivated for the purpose in different parts of the world, according to the nature of the soil, climatic conditions and tradition.

Bread can be made in many different ways, and although there are many recipes given in the following pages for the making of different sorts of bread, no attempt has been made to reach anything approaching completeness, let alone finality.

Flour or *meal*, moistened with water or milk, or both; mixed with butter, margarine or some other form of fat; aerated or not, with the addition of some leavening agent, yeast or baking powder; lightened or not by the addition of well-beaten egg; seasoned with salt and flavoured or not with spices, sugar, fruit or other ingredients, is used to make *Biscuits, Buns, Cakes, Cookies, Crackers, Crumpets, Fritters, Macaroni, Muffins, Noodles, Pancakes, Paste* and *Pastry, Pies* and *Puddings, Scones, Shortbread* and all manner of 'Confections', the number of which has no limit other than the ingenuity of cooks. A very large but by no means exhaustive number of recipes of such 'Confections' will be found in this, the Third Section of our *Concise Encyclopædia of Gastronomy*. Many of the recipes are original ones and new, but many more, both ancient and modern, have been selected from some seventy-odd volumes of recipes, a list of which is given and supplies a valuable reference of cookery books well worth securing by all who are interested in the problems and pleasures of the table. A few recipes have been included which are merely of historical interest, and this does not apply only to the oldest of all, those from the seventeenth, eighteenth and early nineteenth centuries, some of which, such as the *Shrewsbury Cakes* recipe given among the *Tea Cakes*, are perfectly simple to follow to-day. It also applies to recipes given in quite modern books, such as the recipe for a *Black Cake*, requiring fifteen eggs, brandy and sherry, which nowadays, recalls an entirely different age from ours. Such recipes are but exceptions the *rôle* of which is to leaven the less exciting but more practical dough of everyday recipes.

American equivalents to some of the English terms used in the recipes that follow: 'Tins,' as in pie or cake tins, are always pans. Cornflour is cornstarch. Maize is cornmeal. A flan is a kind of open pie. A cake tray is a cake rack. Demerara sugar is brown sugar; castor sugar is plain granulated sugar; powdered sugar is extra fine granulated sugar; and icing sugar is confectioner's sugar. Biscuits are not the quick hot bread Americans call by that name, but plain or salt crackers as well as cookies. Treacle is an English syrup of the molasses kind, and you can always use molasses for it.

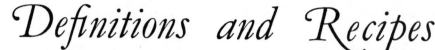

Definitions and Recipes

ABERNETHY BISCUITS

A 'digestive' biscuit which bears the name of a small Scottish town where they were first made.

1 oz. butter
1 lb. fine flour
½ oz. sugar
¾ oz. caraway seeds
2 eggs
A little milk

Rub the butter into the flour, then add the sugar and caraway seeds and mix with the eggs and milk. Knead well and roll out and shape into rounds. This quantity will make eight or ten biscuits. Prick them with a fork right through to the baking-sheet and bake slowly in a moderate oven.—M.K.S. (2).

ACHIRA

A species of *Canna* (q.v.); it has large root-stocks which yield a rich, starchy meal similar to *Arrowroot* (q.v.) and is used in the same way.

ADIRONDACK BREAD

Warm 2 oz. of butter, being careful not to let it oil in the least, or cream it with your hands or a wooden spoon, as you please; beat the yolks of five eggs till light, then whisk them into a pint of milk, adding in gradually from 5 oz. to 6 oz. of Indian corn meal and 4 oz. to 5 oz. of wheat flour, and beat it all together till smooth; now mix in the softened butter, working it well in, and finally mix in a full tablespoonful of sugar, a heaped teaspoonful of baking powder, and the whites of the eggs whisked to a stiff froth. Stir these all together as quickly and lightly as possible and pour the mixture into a well-buttered tin which should be both broad and shallow in shape, and bake 40 minutes in a moderately sharp oven (390° F.) and serve hot.—Q. (1).

AERATED BREAD

This is essentially a machine-made bread baked from dough made of flour, water and salt, without barm or yeast, but with carbon dioxide mechanically introduced. It is said to be of easier digestion than ordinary white bread, but it possesses a peculiar taste which one has to get accustomed to before liking it. This bread was introduced into England by a Dr. Dauglish, in 1856.

AERATED FLOUR

Another name for self-raising flour.

AFTERNOON TEA BISCUITS

3 cups sifted flour
3 teaspoons baking powder
⅔ cup milk
⅛ teaspoon salt
⅓ cup butter or shortening

Sift flour once, measure, add baking powder and salt, and sift and measure again. Put in shortening. Add milk gradually until soft dough is formed. Turn on floured board, knead slightly, roll ¾ in. thick, and cut with small floured biscuit cutter. Bake in hot oven 12 to 15 minutes.—L.R.

ALDERNEY CAKES

1 cup butter
1 cup milk
1 teaspoon nutmeg
1 cup brown sugar
1 teaspoon soda
2½ cups flour
1 cup broken nut meats

Cream the butter and sugar together. Mix and sift the dry ingredients and add alternately with the milk to the first mixture. Spread out in a well-greased, shallow pan and sprinkle with the nut meats. Bake in a quick oven (425° F.) for about 15 minutes and cut into squares while hot. This makes about two dozen squares.

These cakes may have a little more flour added and then be rolled out as any rolled cookies, but this makes them rather more troublesome to make, and the squares with nut meats on are very attractive.—B.S.R.

ALFALFA

An important leguminous forage plant, adapted to widely varying soil and climate conditions. It is grown as a cattle food in normal times, but it has proved valuable as food for man in times of scarcity.

ALICE'S CAKE

4 oz. butter
4 oz. castor sugar
2 eggs
1 dessertspoonful of boiling water
8 oz. flour
1 teaspoonful baking powder
Essence of lemon or any flavouring

Cream the butter, add the sugar and the beaten yolks of eggs (beat the yolks with a dessertspoonful of boiling water). Add the flour by degrees (after first mixing in it the baking powder). Well whisk the whites of the eggs and flavour the mixture. Beat well and bake in a moderate oven for one hour. —L.G.N.

ALLEGRETTI CAKE

Cream one-half cup of butter with one and fourth cups of sugar until very light. Sift two cups of pastry flour with three teaspoons of baking powder and a pinch of salt, and add to the butter and sugar alternately with two-thirds cup of milk. Beat hard, then fold in the whites of three eggs beaten stiff. Pour batter in a buttered and floured oblong pan and bake from 20 to 30 minutes. The cake should be about 1½ to 2 in. thick. Cover with fluffy white icing when cold. Over the icing spread three squares of bitter chocolates which have been melted. Cut in squares. —G.T.L.

ALLONYA

Lat. *Calathea Allonya*. The name of small, edible tubers grown for food in Trinidad, where they are known as *Topee Tamboo*. They are globose or egg-shaped, bound together by stalks: they contain little starch but a relatively large proportion of gummy matter; their flavour is nutty and rather pleasant.

ALMOND CAKES

> ½ lb. of flour
> ¼ lb. of butter
> ¼ lb. of ground almonds
> ½ a teaspoonful of baking powder
> 2 eggs
> ¼ lb. of castor sugar

Sieve flour, sugar and baking powder into a basin, add the almonds and rub in butter until free of lumps. Beat up the eggs, and use these for binding the mixture, making it very stiff. Roll out thinly, and shape into small rounds. Grease a tin, and bake in the oven until brown and crisp. Place two together with cream between and cover the tops with icing.

Cream for filling: Use 1 small jar of cream, 1½ dessertspoonfuls of sugar, 1 teaspoonful of vanilla flavouring.

Icing: Reduce 1 lb. of sugar to powder in a mortar or basin. Beat the white of an egg, add this to the sugar then add the juice of a lemon or orange or other flavouring desired. Mix thoroughly and spread on the cakes while they are hot.—L.G.N.

ALMOND DROPS

4½ lb. flour 1¼ lb. margarine ½ oz. baking powder, 4½ lb. sugar; when rubbed, make a bay, add 14 eggs and a little essence of almonds, roll in long, fine strips, cut off in ¼ in. pieces, stand on end ½ in. apart and bake in a cool oven.—L.G.M.

ALMOND FINGERS

Take 4 oz. of sweet almonds and 4 oz. of bitter, blanched and dried; mince them very finely (do not pound them). Have 4 oz. of castor sugar dissolved in a little water and fry the almonds in this in a pan. When they are crisp and well browned, drain them and pound them to a paste, which must be moistened with one beaten yolk. Weigh the mixture and to every 8 oz. add 12 oz. of flour, 8 oz. of butter and two extra yolks. Beat all well together, roll out, cut into fingers, glaze with egg and bake in a coolish oven upon a shallow buttered tin.—M.B. (2).

ALMOND FLOUR

Almond flour or meal is the residue left after almond oil has been extracted from the kernels. It is entirely free from starch and is used in making bread and biscuits for diabetics. Almond butter, made from almond kernels, is also a diabetic food.

ALMOND HORSESHOES

Take 4 oz. each of flour, rice, and ground almonds and mix them thoroughly. Cream 4 oz. of sugar, add two yolks and mix with the flour into a stiff paste. Roll out and cut into strips 6 in. long by 1½ in. wide. Form these into horseshoes and either stud them with blanched almonds or sprinkle with chopped almonds. Lay them on rice paper in a buttered tin and bake for about 20 minutes in a moderate oven.—M.B. (2).

ALMOND PASTE

Genuine Almond Paste is made from the blanched kernels of almonds and sugar; it is used in confectionery and chiefly in the making of *Macaroons* (q.v.). It is not unusual for so-called Almond Paste to be made from the crushed kernels of apricot, peach or plum.

ANDREW'S GINGERBREAD

Ingredients: 1¼ lb. of flour, ¼ lb. of sugar, 6 oz. of butter, 2 or 3 eggs, 1 tbsp. of ground ginger, 6 oz. of golden or other syrup.

Method: Beat the butter, sugar and golden syrup to a cream and beat in the eggs one at a time; add the flour, mixed with the ginger, till the mixture is thick enough to roll out. Roll into thin sheets, cut out with a plain round cutter, and bake on flat baking-tins. —B.E.C.

ANGEL CAKE

I

> 1 cup of cake flour
> 1¼ cups of powdered sugar
> 1 teaspoon of cream of tartar
> 1 teaspoon of vanilla extract
> ¼ teaspoon of almond extract
> 10 egg whites

In the first place it is necessary to bake an angel cake in angel-cake pan, the kind that has a centre tube and preferably one with a false or removable bottom. Do not butter it, but, of course, make sure the bottom is in securely. First light the oven, setting the regulator at 325° F. It must be a slow oven. Now sift about a cup of cake flour (bread flour won't do), then measure out carefully one level cup of it. Put the rest of the flour away. Then add to the flour quarter of a cup of powdered sugar and sift them together twice, then put it into the sifter ready to be sifted for the fourth time, into the cake. Measure out a level cup of powdered sugar, and have ready a level teaspoon of cream of tartar and some vanilla and almond extract. Now separate the whites from the yolks of 10 eggs. Put the yolks into a small bowl and pour a little cold water over them to keep them from drying out. Put them in the refrigerator for future use. Put the whites into a big bowl and add to them a pinch of salt, then, using a rotary beater, beat them until just foamy, and add the cream of tartar and continue beating, until just stiff enough to form and hold a peak when the beater is withdrawn. Be careful they are not what is known as dry. Now sprinkle over them a fourth of the cup of sugar and beat just long enough to blend. Repeat the process until all the sugar has been added; add a teaspoon of vanilla and a fourth of a teaspoon of almond extract and mix it in, then withdraw the rotary beater, and use instead a wire whisk, to fold the flour into the mixture (lightly), a fourth of a cup at a time. Don't beat it, just fold it. When all the flour has been added, pour it into the cake pan, letting it sheet in. Now take a knife and cut down into and through the mixture in several places to remove any air bubbles there might be in it. Place in the oven and bake slowly for 45 to 55 minutes, or until a delicate brown on top and firm to the touch. Do not open the oven for the first 25 minutes, and when you do look at it be careful not to slam the door shut nor to disturb it in any way. If the cake has not browned sufficiently, turn the light up a bit the last five minutes. When baked, remove from oven and invert the pan on a cake grill and leave it for one hour to cool before trying to remove it from the pan. Run a sharp knife around the edge and centre to loosen it, and the cake should fall out easily, especially if you give the false bottom a little poke. If the bottom falls out with the cake, run the knife between it and the cake before lifting it off. Either break the cake apart in pieces or use a gadget known as a cake-breaker. Never cut angel cake with a knife.

Note.—Left-over angel cake, lightly toasted for tea, is delicious, but the trouble is that there never seems to be any left.—J.P.

II

1 cup egg whites (8 or 10)
1¼ cups fine granulated sugar, sifted
1 teaspoon cream of tartar
1 cup cake flour
¼ teaspoon salt
½ teaspoon almond extract
1 teaspoon vanilla

Beat egg whites and salt with flat wire whisk until foamy, add cream of tartar, and beat until stiff but moist. Sift flour and sugar four or five times and fold carefully into beaten whites with flavouring, using whisk. Bake in unbuttered angel-cake tin 50 minutes in slow oven (300° F.), then turn off heat, and bake 10 minutes longer. Invert on cake cooler until cold.

Cocoa Angel Cake. Sift ¼ cup dry cocoa with flour and sugar.—B.C.S.C.B.

III

Take the whites of 10 eggs, 10 oz. of castor sugar and 6 oz. of fine flour. Whip the whites stiffly, take half and add the sugar gently, then dust in the flour. Add the rest of the whipped whites and bake in a quick oven in a tin with a hole in the centre. Ice with very thin white icing.—M.K.S. (2).

ARROWROOT

'A dry, powdery, and nutritive starch, used as a food; made from the pith of the roots of any of the plants of the type *Maranta*. It takes its name from the American Indian name for the plant *Araruta* (flour-root). The original is *Maranta arundinacea*, a native of South America but now grown largely in the West Indies, Bermuda and Port Natal, also in East Indies under the name of *Maranta indica*. Some East Indian so-called Arrowroot is made from *Curcuma augustifolia*, or narrow-leaved turmeric; really Curcuma starch. It is cultivated in much the same way as potatoes. The *Maranta* is a perennial herb, easily propagated by parting the roots. It grown from two to six feet high, with branching stems, broad pointed leaves and small white flowers.

'The fleshy roots, when a year old, are about a foot long, and as thick as one's finger. They are dug up, washed, peeled, grated or crushed between rollers, and strained through a sieve and the fibrous parts thrown out. The pulp is washed repeatedly, the milky top liquor left to settle, and the water afterwards poured off. The white starchy sediment is dried and reduced to a light white powder, and boxed or filled into barrels lined with paper fastened on with arrowroot paste, and exported.

'When good, arrowroot is a light opaque white powder, insipid and inodorous, and will keep many years in a dry place. When mixed with boiling water it swells up into a consistent jelly. Arrowroot is less apt to become sour during digestion than any other farinaceous food, hence its use for the sick and delicate.

'Arrowroot is imported into the United Kingdom from St. Vincent, Bermuda, Jamaica, etc.; the popular type being St. Vincent, whilst Bermuda is expensive and produced in small quantity.'—L.G.M.

ARROWROOT CAKE

> 4 oz. arrowroot
> 4 oz. butter
> 2 eggs
> ¼ pint milk
> 4 oz. flour
> 4 oz. castor sugar
> A little vanilla essence
> 1 small teaspoon baking powder

Sieve the arrowroot, flour and baking powder with a pinch of salt. Put the butter and sugar into a basin, and work together until a creamy consistency. Beat in the yolks of the eggs and stir in the flour as lightly as possible, adding the milk gradually. If necessary, a little more may be added. Then stir in the essence. Beat up the whites of eggs stiffly and fold in as lightly as possible. Put into a greased and paper-lined cake-tin, and bake in a moderately hot oven until golden brown and firm. The time required is about 1½ hours.—G.H. (4).

ARROWROOT WINE BISCUITS
(Old-fashioned)

> 1¾ lb. soft flour
> 4 oz. arrowroot
> 1 lb. fine butter
> 1 lb. fine castor sugar
> 3 eggs
> 2 yolks

Rub the butter into the flour and arrow-root until fine, make a bay, put in the sugar, eggs, and yolks, work together, and mix into a nice, smooth paste. Pin out into a sheet ¼ in. thick, cut out with a plain round cutter 1½ in. in diameter, set on plates ¼ in. apart, and stamp with a small wooden stamp that has the word 'Arrowroot' either in one or two lines. This can be bought for a trifle at the confectioner's tool shop. The pressure used to get a good impression will need to be considerable, but it must be even. Bake at once in an oven (450° F.) to a rich, bright colour.—A.A.B.

ASHLEY BREAD

> 1 cup rice flour
> 1½ teaspoons baking powder
> 1 cup milk

> ½ teaspoon salt
> 1 egg
> 1½ tablespoons melted butter

Mix and sift the dry ingredients. Beat the egg well and add the milk to it. Combine with the first mixture. Then stir in the melted butter and turn into a well-greased, shallow pan. Bake in a moderate oven (350° F.) for 45 minutes.

This is much like other spoon breads except that it has a characteristic rice flavour. Makes eight large pieces.—*Panchita Hayward Grimball, Wappaoolah Plantation, Cooper River.*—B.S.R.

BABAS AU RHUM

Make first a preparation with ½ oz. of fresh yeast, a tablespoonful of flour and a little milk. Work to a paste and leave it in a warm place. Also soak in warm rum a handful of stoned currants.

Mix in a bowl about a ¼ lb. of flour and three eggs, one by one, and make a smooth batter. Add the yeast preparation. Work it and beat it with the hand (in fact, almost whip it between the fingers) until it comes up easily and makes a kind of thin rubber band. Then add 2 oz. of butter well pounded to a soft ointment. All this takes almost 20 minutes. Leave it in a warm place.

Add the currants, a little sugar and a pinch of salt. Beat the batter back to the rubbery consistency and fill little Baba moulds (previously buttered) not more than half. Let the Babas rest at least a quarter of an hour, anyhow till the composition rises almost to the top of the mould. Then bake 12 to 14 minutes in a hot oven.

Turn out and keep till wanted. When cold, pour over them sugar syrup little by little to make them swell, and lastly the rum. Some people flavour them with Kirschwasser.—X.M.B. (1).

BAKING POWDER

This is the name given to a number of mixtures used as leavening agents for bread and pastry. They are made of ground rice, potato starch or some such farinaceous substance as a basis and they all contain a certain proportion of baking soda (carbonate) and one or other of three acid substances: (1) tartrate (Cream of tartar); (2) phosphate (Calcium phosphate); (3) alum (Aluminum Sulfate). When moistened, the carbonate and acid react and produce some carbonic acid gas (carbon dioxide) which 'raises' the dough. Baking powder must always be stored in a dry atmosphere.

BAKING POWDER BREAD

Sift well together four full pounds of flour, a heaped teaspoonful of salt, and three dessertspoonfuls of baking powder. When this is all thoroughly blended, work it to a nice dough gradually with about a quart of milk, milk and water, or water; shape it as quickly as possible into four loaves and bake from 1 to 1¼ hours, in a fairly heated oven. This must be put into the oven the moment it is shaped, and must be mixed as quickly as may be, on account of the baking powder.—Q. (1).

BANANA FLOUR
A flour, also known as *Plantain Meal*, made from unripe, starchy *Bananas*, sliced, dried and pounded.

BANBURY CAKES
> 1 lb. puff or rough puff pastry
> ½ teaspoon ground ginger
> Grated rind and juice of 1 lemon
> 2 oz. chopped candied peel
> 2 oz. cake crumbs
> 4 oz. butter
> 4 oz. sugar
> 4 oz. cleaned sultanas
> ¼ teaspoonful ground nutmeg
> 1 egg
> 4 oz. currants

Cream butter and sugar, beat in egg, add all the other ingredients and mix. Roll the pastry thinly and cut into 5 in. rounds, moisten edges with egg. Put a little of the mixture on to each piece of pastry, fold over, turn upside down, roll into oval cakes, and slash the top with a knife. Bake 20 minutes. —G.L.H.

BANNOCKS
The word Bannock is from the Gaelic *bonnach*, a cake or bannock; that is, a large, round girdle-scone or oatcake in the whole piece. A bannock is a thing of substance and may be made of oatmeal, wheatflour, barley or pease meal. Two famous varieties are the *Selkirk bannock*, a pleasant form of bun, and the *Pitcaithly bannock*, a kind of festive shortbread.—E.M.L.D.

Bannock
1 lb. flour, ½ lb. butter, 2 oz. sugar, 2 oz. almonds, blanched and sliced thinly, 2 oz. candied orange peel finely chopped. Mix the flour, sugar, almonds and orange peel together on a pastry board. Put the butter in the centre and knead until it is well blended. Roll out and form into round cakes, pinch the edges and prick the centre with a fork. Bake on a greased paper on a baking sheet for one hour in a moderate oven.—H.E.

Pioneer Bannock
Place two cupfuls of yellow corn-meal in a bowl with two teaspoonfuls of salt and two teaspoonfuls of sugar. Add four cupfuls of boiling milk, mix well and let cool. Then whip four yellows of eggs, mix into the mush, fold in the four beaten whites of eggs. Butter a flat earthenware dish about 10 by 7 and 1½ in. high, pour in mixture and bake in a very fast oven (400° F.) from 15 to 20 minutes.—E.E.A.

Selkirk Bannock
2 lb. bread dough, ½ lb. butter, ½ lb. lard, ½ lb. sugar, ½ lb. sultanas, ½ lb. currants, and ¼ lb. finely-chopped orange peel.

Work the lard and butter into the bread dough, add sugar, sultanas, currants and finely-chopped orange peel and knead well. Place the dough in a buttered tin and allow to stand in a warm place for about 30 minutes to rise, and bake in a moderate oven.— S.W.R.

'BANNOCK BROWN'
The registered trade name of a Pure Whole Wheat Bread (100 per cent extraction).
> 3½ lb. whole wheat meal
> 1 oz. yeast
> 1 oz. salt
> 1 oz. fat
> 2½ pints water

Mix and allow to stand in dough form for 45 minutes, knock back well and allow to stand for a further 15 minutes, tin off and prove for 45 minutes, or to suit bakery conditions.

The finished dough temperature should be between 72° and 75° F., not higher.

All the liquor should be added at the start.

Bake about 50 minutes, oven temperature 450° F. i.e. about 10 minutes longer in the oven than is usual for ordinary wholemeal bread.

It is necessary to warm the meal and dough receptacles, providing warm atmosphere to promote good yeast action.— J.W.

BAPS
Baps are the Scottish morning roll, at their best in Aberdeenshire. There are two sorts: the white, floury Bap and the buttery Bap, which, when well made and served hot, is deliciously light and flaky.—E.M.L.D.

Baps are made of good white flour, of which take 1 lb. and add to it a ¼ oz. of bicarbonate of soda, and ½ oz. of cream of tartar, well mixed and sieved finely. Work a hole in the centre and add 3 oz. of butter and a pinch of salt. Work it with the hand into a cream. Then add sufficient buttermilk or sour milk to make into dough. Roll it out and cut into scones and dust well with flour. Then bake in the oven for about a quarter of an hour. They should be white, and are good either hot or cold – Scotland generally eats them cold.—L.M. (2).

BARFORD PUDDING

Ingredients: Beef suet chopped, 1 lb.; raisins stoned, 1 lb.; flour, 4 oz.; castor sugar, 6 oz.; a little salt; half a nutmeg; five eggs.

Time to boil: 6 hours.

Method: 1. Mix all well together. 2. Boil in a cloth, which must be closely woven, wrung out in hot water, well floured, and tied very tight close to the pudding.—FL.W.

BARLEY

Lat. *Hordeum Sativum* (*H. vulgare*); Fr. *Orge.*
Barley, probably the most ancient of cultivated cereals, is grown over a wider climatic range than any other sort of grain. When the husk has been removed by machinery, *Barley* is used in the form of *Pot Barley*, *Scotch Barley* or *Hulled Barley* in soups, stews, haggis, etc. When steamed, rounded and polished in a mill, it becomes *Pearl Barley*, which is sometimes ground into a fine flour known as *Patent Barley*. Barley is also converted into malt used in brewing and distilling, and Barley offals are used in England in the same way as *Maize* is used in the U.S.A. for feeding domestic animals. See also *Barley-meal*.

Scots Barley Broth

Mutton or beef; barley; peas; carrots; onions or leeks; parsley or celery; greens and water.

Put one pound of neck of mutton or flank of beef into a pot with two quarts of cold water. Wash two tablespoonfuls of barley in cold water and add. Bring to the boil, then throw in a teaspoonful of salt to cause the scum to rise. Skim carefully. Add a small turnip and one or two young carrots cut into dice, two leeks or onions (leeks have a more delicate flavour) and half a young cabbage or a few greens roughly cut. Let the broth boil for a few minutes with the lid off after the vegetables are added, to let certain salts, which disagree with some people, escape in steam. Add salt and pepper to taste, put the lid on and let the broth simmer gently for three hours. Stir now and then. The meat should be removed when ready and re-heated at the last. A grated carrot may be added about 15 minutes before the broth is served. Add a tablespoonful of chopped parsley before serving.

A good marrow bone may be substituted for mutton or beef.—S.W.R.

Crème d'Orge

Put 6 oz. of well-washed pearl barley in a quart of fowl consommé with a stick of celery and a sprig or two of parsley, salt and pepper and cook slowly for 3½ hours. Strain off the consommé, pound the barley, and pass through a sieve. Add the consommé little by little, bring to the boil, and add a cup of cream just before serving.

With all the smooth thick soups are served *croûtons* of bread fried golden brown.—
F.C.W.

Barley Water

Take a small teacup of pearl barley, wash in cold water and place in a jug. Peel a lemon very thin and place the peel on the barley, add three or four lumps of sugar and pour on three pints of boiling water. Let it stand until cool and strain off carefully. It should be a light green colour.

BARLEY CAKES

Make some fine barley meal into a stiff dough with skim milk, roll out to the size of a pie plate ¾ in. thick and bake on a girdle or backstone if possible. Cut in pieces and eat with butter cold. (Welsh.)—L.M. (2).

BARLEY-MEAL

A whole-meal flour made from the ground *Barley*: it is darker in colour but lighter in weight than wheatmeal. It is still used for *porridge* and *gruel* (q.v.) in Scotland, and to a very large extent for breadmaking in many parts of Northern Continental Europe.

BARLEY-SUGAR

A brittle confection of sugar, boiled rapidly and drawn into long yellow strips, more or less transparent and generally flavoured with lemon. Originally it was an acid decoction of barley or barley-water and sugar.—L.G.M.

BARMBRACK. BARN BREAK

I

½ quartern of dough
6 oz. sugar
4 eggs
2 oz. caraway seeds
¼ lb. butter

Melt the butter and beat it into the dough with the sugar, then beat in the eggs one at a time, and lastly the caraway seeds. Make into a round loaf or put it in a large cake-tin and let it rise, then bake about 40 minutes —H.E.

II

1½ lb. flour
4 oz. butter
Sugar to taste
½ breakfastcupful of currants
1 dessertspoonful of caraway seeds
2 teaspoonfuls of bicarbonate of soda

Rub the butter into the flour, then the soda, sugar, currants and seeds. It must then be wetted with enough buttermilk to drop into shape and not be in a solid lump. Bake in a rather slow oven for two hours, with paper on the top of the loaf.—M.B. (2).

BARNSTAPLE FAIR GINGERBREAD

Ingredients: Treacle, 6 oz.; flour, 6 oz.; butter, 5 oz.; sugar, 6 oz.; ground ginger, 1 teaspoonful.

Method: 1. Warm the treacle. 2. Rub the butter into the flour. 3. Add the sugar and ginger. 4. Mix well. 5. Blend with the warm treacle. 6. Drop small pieces on a well-greased tin. 7. Bake at once in a very slow oven.—FL.W.

BATH BUNS

1 lb. flour
6 oz. butter
1 oz. yeast
1 gill (approx.) milk
1 to 2 oz. loaf sugar
2 eggs
5 oz. castor sugar
3 oz. sultanas
3 oz. peel

Rub the butter into the flour. Warm the milk, and cream the yeast with a little of it. Pour the milk and yeast into the middle of the flour. Add the beaten eggs. Beat very thoroughly, cover with a cloth, and put the dough to rise in a warm place until it doubles in size. This will take about 1½ hours. Add the castor sugar, sultanas and peel; beat well, and form into small, even-sized balls. Put on to greased tins and prove until they are double in size. Brush over with egg and milk, sprinkle with coarsely-crushed loaf sugar. Bake in a hot oven for 20 to 30 minutes.—G.H.(4).

Bath Buns (1807)

Rub 1 lb. of butter into 2 lb. of fine flour; mix in it 1 lb. of caraway comfits, beat well 12 eggs, leaving out six whites, with six spoonfuls of new yeast, and the same quantity of cream made warm; mix all together, and set it by the fire to rise; when made up, strew comfits over them.—A.A.

BATH OLIVERS

Many biscuits bear the name of the firm responsible for their manufacture, but England's very famous cracker, the *Bath Oliver*, is different: it bears the name of an eighteenth century doctor who was responsible for its excellence, but who never made or sold any biscuits. Dr William Oliver was born in 1695, in the Parish of Ludgran, near Penzance, and was christened in the Parish Church on 27th August 1695. He was admitted to Pembroke College, Cambridge, on 17th September 1714, took his degree of M.B. in 1720 and of MD. in 1725. He is believed to have practised at Plymouth to begin with, and he came to Bath with his cousin W.Borlase in 1734. It is said that Dr Oliver's coming to Bath was primarily due to his desire to test the virtues of the Bath Mineral waters and seek to cure his cousin, who was a sick man when he came, but soon after returned to Cornwall healed. Dr Oliver may also have been attracted to Bath by other reasons, since Bath was then the most fashionable Spa in England. In any case, he remained at Bath, where he died on 23rd March 1764, mourned by rich and poor, whose benefactor he had been for thirty years. Dr Oliver, when he made up his mind to remain at Bath, and that he would not require any longer the services of Atkins, his faithful coachman, decided to set him up in a little house, at No. 13 Green Street, as a baker. He gave Atkins 10 (some accounts say 12) sacks of the finest wheaten flour and One Hundred Pounds. He gave him also his own recipe for making a thin, palatable and easily digested biscuit, one that he had 'invented' himself, probably after a number of experimental trials, for the benefit of his dyspeptic patients. Atkins' Biscuits were known from the first as Dr Oliver's Biscuits and very soon became quite fashionable. When Atkins died, his shop and Dr Oliver's 'secret recipe' passed on to one Norris, by whom they were left to one Carter, passing on from Carter to Munday, from Munday to Ashman, and from Ashman to Fortt, whose heirs still manufacture 'Dr Oliver's Biscuits', with the Doctor's head stamped on every biscuit.

Besides Fortt's *Original Bath Olivers*, there are other biscuits which bear the name of *Bath Oliver* and possess some of the same characteristics: these are due to a well-leavened dough in the first instance; thorough kneading; rolling as thin as possible, i.e. 'paper thin'; the paste is then cut the size of an average tea-cup and pricked with a fork, taking care that the prongs of the fork go right through the paste, so that steam may escape freely and no blisters shall disfigure the biscuits; these are then set on flat baking-tins, dried in a warm cupboard or drawer for half an hour and then baked in a slack oven. Originally the biscuits were cut out by hand, placed one on the top of another, and then docked both sides and separated, this giving them a unique 'hand-made' appearance, but now this is done by an ingenious machine which preserves the 'hand-made' appearance.

BÂTONS À LA CANNELLE

Take ¼ lb. of flour, same quantity of butter, 2 oz. of sugar, one whole egg and a coffee-spoonful of ground cinnamon. Work the mixture well, roll it, cut out little sticks and bake quickly in a hot oven.—X.M.B. (1).

BATTER

The name of many semi-liquid, floury mixtures of flour, water or milk or both or some other liquid as well, salt, sometimes sugar and usually eggs, the whole being well beaten or 'battered' until of the right consistency for the purpose for which it is intended. Batters may be thin or thick, but even when thick they must be fluid enough to drop from a spoon; when thin they should pour out like a creamy milk.

A Batter to which yeast is added is known as *Sponge* (q.v.), and a Batter that is so stiff that it does not drop from a spoon and can be handled is known as *Dough* (q.v.).

BATTER BREAD

I

Take six spoonfuls of flour and three of corn meal, with a little salt – sift them, and make a thin batter with four eggs, and a sufficient quantity of rich milk; bake it in little tin moulds in a quick oven. (*Mrs Mary Randolph's Virginia Housewife*, 1831.)—H.B.

II

Add two well-beaten eggs to one and three-fourths cups of cooked rice or fine Hominy. Add two and one-half cups of sweet milk, then sift in one cup of meal, one teaspoon of salt and add one tablespoon of melted butter. Beat very thoroughly and bake in hot well-buttered baking-dish for forty minutes in a very hot oven. (*Old recipe, Richmond, Virginia. Prov'd Market Square Tavern Kitchen*, 1937.)—H.B.

BEATEN BISCUITS

Take one quart of flour, lard the size of a hen's egg, one teaspoonful of salt. Make into a moderately stiff dough with sweet milk. Beat for half an hour. Make out with the hand or cut with the biscuit cutter. Stick with a fork and bake in a hot oven, yet not sufficiently hot to blister the biscuit. (*From an old Williamsburg Cook Book.*)—H.B.

MARYLAND BEATEN BISCUITS

　　1 pint flour
　　⅓ cup lard
　　1 teaspoon salt

　　Milk and water in equal quantities
Mix and sift flour and salt; mix in lard with pastry mixer or finger tips. Moisten to stiff dough. Toss on slightly floured board and beat 30 minutes with rolling-pin or special utensil, continually folding over the dough. Roll ¼ in. thick, shape with round cutter 2 in. thick in diameter, prick with fork and place on buttered tin. Bake 20 minutes in hot oven (400° F.). Makes 12 to 18 biscuits.–B.C.S.C.B.

BEIGNET

This is a French word for which there is no English equivalent: it is usually described as a 'Puff paste fritter', but the name is misleading, as there are many *Beignets* which do not answer to such a description. There are as many different kinds of *Beignets* as there are *Fritters* (q.v.), but they should all possess the same family likeness of lightness. Among the classical *Beignets* one of the more popular is the *Beignet à la Dauphine*, named after Marie-Antoinette and sometimes called in English *Brioche Fritter*. It originated in Vienna where it is known as *Wiener Krapfen*: the same Fritter is known as *Berliner Pfannkuchen* in Germany.

Beignets de Confiture

Ask your druggist for some thin paper wafers, the kind that is used for prescriptions, cut them in round pieces about 2½ in. diameter, put in the middle of each a little jam, cover with another piece of rice-paper and wet it all round with water to make them stick.

When dry and well stuck dip them in batter and fry like any ordinary fritter. —X.M.B. (1).

Beignets Soufflés

Put in a saucepan ½ pint of milk, a pinch of salt, ½ oz. of sugar and about 6 oz. of butter. Bring to the boil, and when the butter has melted add, little by little, ½ lb. of flour. Stir all the time with a wooden spoon. Cook it, stirring, till, having become very thick, it does not stick to the saucepan.

Then add quickly, one by one, four eggs, and mix well again till the batter comes easily off the spoon. Let it rest a little and it is ready for use.

Take with a spoon little balls the size of a walnut and drop them quickly in deep fat. They revolve and puff, and in a few minutes they are cooked and pleasantly brown.

Drain well, sprinkle with sugar and serve with a jam sauce or Sauce Sabayon.

It is important that the fat should not be too hot when you drop in the fritters. It should not have attained the smoking point. When they are in increase the heat.—X.M.B. (1).

BELL FRITTERS

Put a piece of butter the size of an egg into a pint of water; let it boil a few minutes – thicken it very smoothly with a pint of flour; let it remain a short time on the fire, stir it all the time that it may not stick to the pan, pour it in a wooden bowl, add five or six eggs, breaking one and beating it in – then another, and so on till they are all in, and the dough quite light – put a pint of lard in a pan, let it boil, make the fritters small and fry them to a fine amber colour. (*Mrs Mary Randolph's Virginia Housewife*. 1831.)—H.B.

BELVOIR CASTLE BUNS (1869)

Ingredients: Flour, plain, 2 lb.; sugar, 6 oz.; butter, 5 oz.; currants, 6 oz.; milk, 1 pint; yeast, 1 oz.

Time: To rise, just 2 hours; then half an hour; and 10 minutes to bake.—FL.W.

BENNÉ
Lat. *Sesamum indicum*. An annual grass, a native of India, which is now cultivated in most warm countries. In the U.S.A. it is grown chiefly for the sake of its seeds which are used to make the *Oil of Sesame*. In Charleston cooking the seeds are also used for cake-making and in confectionery.

BISCOTINS. BISCOTTES
French names for particularly light biscuits given to infants; also for little balls of flour, or 'marbles', dried in the oven and added to clear soups.

BISCUITS. COOKIES. CRACKERS.
Fr. *Biscuits*; Ger. *Zwiebacken*; It. *Biscotti*; Sp. *Bizcochos*. This French name, which means literally twice cooked or baked, has passed unaltered into the English tongue. It covers a multitude of floury confections, mostly small. Some are sweet and others salt; some are neither sweet nor salt, just flour and water, whilst others are highly seasoned.

Whereas British usage lumps all these confections under the name of 'biscuits,' Americans distinguish them also as cookies and crackers, according to whether they are sweet, plain or salt. American biscuits, strictly speaking, are a quick bread leavened with baking powder.

Biscuits may also be divided into two other classes according to whether they are factory-made or home-made. All the standard makes of factory-made biscuits, such as Saltines, Fig Newtons, and others, are not included in this Section of the *Encyclopaedia* because they are not suitable for home baking: they are machine-made Biscuits and the recipes given in this volume are all for Biscuits that can be made at home without any special machine.

To Make Bisketts (1694)
Take a pound of fine powder shugar, put it into a stone morter and brake into it five eggs, leaving out 2 whites. Then beat them very well & put in 6 spoonfuls of Rose watter, & beat it very well againe till all ye lumps be broken, & then strike in by degrees a pound of fine flower, wanting 3 spoonfuls, & beat all together for half an hour, or not so much if your Ovon be hott. Let your Ovon be heating all ye while, if not before you go about them. When your Ovon is hott, put in 2 spoonfuls of caraway seeds or ye pell of a lemon greated & put a

spoonful into a plate, being buttered, and scrape over them a littil fine shugar when it goes in. As soon as they are a littil yellow, cut them out. If you lay them when warm it will be ye better.—A.B.

To Make Biscuits (1807)
Beat well eight eggs, the yokes and the whites separate, with three spoonfuls of rose water; when the yolks are beat enough, put to it, by degrees, one pound of loaf sugar, sifted, and beat them together; then put in the whites and one pound of fine flour; beat them till they go into the oven, and sift sugar over them.—A.A.

To Make Bath Biscuits (1807)
Take a pint of new milk, and set it on the fire, with four ounces of sweet lard, till it is melted; then pour it into a pint of cold water, and beat into it four tablespoonfuls of good yeast; strain it into four pounds of fine flour, and make it up into a stiff paste: cut them round with a tin, and prick them, and bake them in a moderate oven, on tins, keeping them turning till they are quite dry.—A.A.

BISCUIT DROPS (1843)
Beat well together in a pan one pound of sifted sugar, with eight eggs for twenty minutes; then add a quarter of an ounce of caraway seeds, and one pound and a quarter of flour; lay wafer paper on a baking plate, put the mixture into a biscuit funnel, and drop it out on the paper about the size of a half-crown; sift sugar over and bake them in a hot oven.—W.K.

BISHOP'S BREAD
    4 eggs, separated
    1 cup sugar
    1 teaspoon vanilla
    ¼ teaspoon salt
    2 teaspoons baking powder
    1 cup raisins
    1 cup flour
    1 cup almonds, blanched and
        chopped
    Powdered sugar

Beat yolks of eggs until light and lemon-coloured; then add sugar, and cream well. Add the vanilla. Sift the flour, baking powder and salt together and stir into the egg mixture. Add the raisins and nuts. Fold in the stiffly-beaten egg whites. Pour into an oblong buttered pan and bake in a moderate oven (350° F.) for 20 minutes. While cake is still hot, cut into squares and cover with powdered sugar.—C.G.

BLACK BREAD
Rub 5 lb. of brewer's grains to a paste, then work into this 4 oz. fresh yeast, 2½ lb. of

very coarse flour, and half a handful of salt. When well mixed, put it aside to rise, and when double its original size, make it up in loaves, and bake.—Q. (1).

HOME-MADE BLACK BREAD (SCHWARZES BROT)

50 per cent dark rye, 25 per cent white rye, 25 per cent wheat flour (2 lb. flour in all); 1 oz. yeast; ½ pint tepid water; 3 coffeespoons salt.

Put the flour in a bowl, make a hole in the centre. Dissolve the yeast in a fifth of the warm water and mix with 3 oz. of flour and leave to rise in a warm place. Add the yeast and salt to the flour and with the rest of the warm water knead into a stiff and smooth dough. Make into loaves and put on a greased and floured baking-tin and leave in a warm place to rise. Brush over with slightly salted water and leave again to rise. Repeat twice and bake slowly for one hour. When still hot, brush over again with salted water.—E.B.

BLACK BREAD PUDDING

Crumble finely ¼ lb. of dry dark bread and moisten it with a pint of red wine and two tablespoons of rum.

Beat ¼ lb. of powdered sugar with five egg yolks, add a pinch of cinnamon, 1 oz. of finely-chopped candied lemon peel, ditto candied orange peel, a ¼ lb. of grated almonds, and the moistened bread. Mix well and add to it the stiffly-beaten egg whites.

Grease a pudding form well with sweet butter and sprinkle with fine breadcrumbs. Fill into this form the pudding mixture, cover and cook in a water bath – Bain-Marie – for three-quarters of an hour; remove after that time from the bath and bake in a hot (400° F.) oven for 15 minutes with the cover removed.—W.R.

BLACK CAKE

      1½ lb. butter
      1½ lb. sugar
      ½ cup brandy
      15 eggs
      ¼ cup sherry
      1½ lb. flour
      2½ lb. seeded raisins
      1 lb. almonds, blanched and chopped
      ¼ lb. citron, chopped fine
      2 teaspoons cinnamon
      1 teaspoon cloves
      ½ teaspoon nutmeg
      2¼ lb. currants

Brown flour before using, cool, and sift with spices. Dredge fruit and almonds with half cup flour. Cream butter, gradually add sugar while beating continually. Whip into the mixture egg yolks beaten thick, whites beaten stiff. Beat in the brandy and sherry, add flour and then the fruits.

Put in buttered deep pans and bake four hours. If in one pan, bake five hours.—C.R.B.B. (2).

BLINI

Very small pancakes made of buckwheat flour and greatly used in Russia and Poland in place of puff pastry for *Canapés*, to serve caviare, smoked salmon and a number of other savoury foods, chiefly used for hors-d'oeuvre.

Russian Blenie

      3 oz. buckwheat or ordinary flour
      1 teaspoonful yeast
      ¾ pint of warm milk
      2 yolks of eggs
      Good pinch of salt
      ½ oz. melted butter
      2 teaspoonfuls of sugar
      ¼ gill of fresh cream
      2 whites of eggs
      6 drops of lemon juice

Mix yeast and warm milk together, gradually add to flour, then keep in warm place until it rises. Then mix the yolks of the two eggs with the sugar, melted butter and olive oil, and add a pinch of salt – mix these two mixtures together, put in a warm place for one hour until it rises for the second time. Afterwards whisk the whites of the eggs and the lemon juice, and gradually add it to the paste, and after that also add ¼ gill cream. Fry gently in butter in small portions at a time, dropping small quantities of butter on the *Blenie*: fry it until it becomes a golden colour and then turn it over, place on a very hot plate and serve it hot with Caviare Grivan, fresh sour cream and tablespoonful of melted butter or pressed caviare, or sliced smoked salmon.—A.Ma.

BOCKINGS

Take 4 oz. of buckwheat flour and mix it smooth with a breakfastcupful of milk just warm. Place this in a basin and set it before a fire. About an hour later stir in two well-whisked eggs and flour enough to make a fairly thick batter as for pancakes. Fry like pancakes and serve with lemon and powdered sugar.—M.B. (2).

BOODLE'S CLUB CAKE

1 lb. of flour, ½ lb. of butter or margarine, ¼ lb. of Demerara sugar, ½ lb. of raisins, 2 eggs, 2½ teaspoons of bicarbonate of soda, 1 gill of milk.

Beat butter and sugar together, then the eggs; chop raisins and mix with flour, stir in gradually; dissolve soda in the warm milk and beat all well together. Bake in a moderate oven for 2¾ hours. (Very good).—L.M. (2).

BOSTON BROWN BREAD

> 1 cup rye meal or white flour
> 1 cup corn meal
> 1 cup coarse entire wheat flour
> ¾ tablespoon soda
> 1 teaspoon salt
> ¾ cup molasses
> 2 cups sour milk *or*
> 1¾ cup sweet milk or water

Mix and sift dry ingredients, add molasses and milk, stir until well mixed, and fill well-greased mould not more than two-thirds full. Cover closely and place mould on trivet in kettle containing boiling water, allowing water to come half-way up around mould. Cover closely and steam 3½ hours, keeping water at boiling point. Add more boiling water as needed. In steamed pudding moulds steam 1½ to 2 hours. Take from water, remove cover, and set in slow oven (300° F.) 15 minutes to dry off. Remove from mould. Cut with string while hot, by drawing string round bread, crossing and pulling ends. Makes two loaves.

With orange peel. Add quarter of a cup finely-cut candied orange peel.

With raisins. Add one cup seedless raisins.

Boston Brown Bread may be steamed in a double-boiler. Grease top part and fill half full of batter. Set over lower part in which is enough boiling water to cover its base ½ in. Cover closely and steam three hours over low heat, keeping water at boiling point.—B.C.S.C.B.

BOUCHÉES

The French culinary name for *Patties*. Small, round, light pastries, with sufficient room within to be filled with fish, meat, game or any sort of tasty preparation. They can be served as *Hors-d'oeuvre chauds* or as trimmings with *entrées* or roasts. Some of the classical *Bouchées* are the following:

à l'Ancienne: breast of chicken, *en purée*, cream and truffles.

à la Banquière: Coxcombs, truffles, mushrooms, *velouté* of chicken, fresh cream and a little sherry.

Cambacères: Mussels, truffles, mushrooms, a *velouté maigre* with a *Brunoise* of vegetables.

Cardinal: *Salpicon* of crayfish, truffles, mushrooms and a *Sauce Nantua*.

Carême: *Purée de volaille à la crème*, foie gras and truffle.

Chavette: *Purée* of mushrooms and a *salpicon* of truffles and cream.

d'Aigrefeuille: A small scallop of sheep's brain fried in butter, and a *salpicon* of lamb's sweetbread and truffles.

Dino: A small mouthful of sole with a *Nantua Sauce* and truffles.

Grand-Duc: *Salpicon* of truffles and asparagus points, with cream.

La Varenne: *Salpicon* of calf's sweetbread, truffles and asparagus points.

Mazarin: *Salpicon* of shrimps and mushrooms, a piece of truffle and some soft roe cooked in butter and placed upon the truffle.

Montglas: *Salpicon* of foie gras, tongue, chicken, truffles and mushrooms.

Plumerey: *Salpicon* of game, truffles and mushrooms, with a slice of truffle on top and a piece of tongue upon the truffle.

Princesse: *Salpicon* of chicken, truffles and asparagus with a few asparagus points on top.

à la Reine: *Purée* of chicken with *velouté de volaille* with slices of truffles on top.

à la Royale: Truffles.

Saint-Hubert: Game.

Surcouf: Soles and truffles.

à la Tourangelle: *Quenelle* of pike and a *salpicon* of truffles and mushrooms.

BOWKNOTS

Two eggs, one-third of a cup of sugar, one tablespoonful of thick cream (sweet), one tablespoonful of melted butter, half a level teaspoonful of cream of tartar, quarter of a teaspoonful each of salt and mace, flour to make a stiff dough, one-eighth of a teaspoonful of soda. Beat the eggs without separating; add the sugar, cream and butter, then the flour sifted with the other ingredients, roll small pieces of the dough into shapes the size and shape of a pencil, tie in single knots, fry in deep fat and roll in powdered sugar.—M.K.S. (2).

BRAN

Bran is the ground husk of the grain; it is generally used as feed for horses and cattle, even as packing material. And yet Bran, and more particularly wheaten Bran, is rich in nitrogenous substances, phosphates and minerals, but man found Bran so difficult to digest that he gave it to his horse; it was only when motor-cars replaced horses that means were found to mill Bran in a manner that renders it digestible either in bread (wholemeal bread) or as bran flour.

BRAN BATTER BREAD

Recipe makes 2-lb. loaf.
Temperature: 425° F., then 380° F.
Time: 15 minutes, then 35 to 45 minutes.

> 1½ cups bran
> 1½ cups hot water
> 1 tablespoon shortening
> 1½ teaspoons salt
> ⅓ cup molasses
> 1 cake compressed yeast
> ½ cup lukewarm water
> 5 cups all-purpose flour

1. Mix wheat bran, water, shortening, salt and molasses. Let stand until cool.

2. Add yeast softened in lukewarm water.

3. Sift in about one-half the flour; beat well; add remaining flour to make soft dough.

4. Cover and let rise in a warm place until double in bulk (about 1¼ hours).

5. Beat and pour into greased bread-pan. Let rise again until it fills the pan (about 45 minutes).

6. Bake in a hot oven for 15 minutes; then reduce heat to moderate and finish baking.—M.E.A.

BRAN MOLASSES MUFFINS

Recipe makes 12 large Muffins.
Temperature: 400° F.
Time: About 25 minutes.

 2 cups all-purpose flour
 1½ teaspoons baking powder
 1 teaspoon soda
 1½ teaspoons salt
 2 cups bran
 1 egg
 ⅓ cup molasses or honey
 1¾ cups sour milk or butter-milk
 3 tablespoons melted shortening
 ⅓ cup chopped nutmeats, optional

1. Sift flour, baking powder, soda and salt together. Stir in wheat bran.

2. Mix beaten egg, molasses, milk and shortening; add to first mixture.

3. Stir together only enough to combine.

4. If nutmeats are used, stir into the dry mixture before adding liquid.

5. Fill greased muffin-pans two-thirds full and bake in moderate oven.—M.E.A.

BRAN MUFFINS

 1 cup flour
 1 teaspoon soda
 ½ teaspoon salt
 2 cups bran
 1 cup milk
 ½ cup molasses
 1 egg, well beaten (if desired)

Mix and sift flour, soda, and salt. Add other ingredients. Bake in buttered muffin-tins 30 to 40 minutes in moderately hot oven (375° F.). Makes 18 muffins.

Raisin Bran Muffins. Add three-quarters of a cup seeded raisins to bran.—B.C.S.C.B.

BRANDY-SNAPS

Thin, wafer-like, gingerbread biscuits, slightly flavoured with brandy and generally curled in baking. They may be made thus: 8 lb. of flour and 1 lb. of lard or butter is formed into a strong paste; 6 oz. of ground ginger, 6 lb. sugar and 2 lb. of treacle are then added, also a little salt and either a little brandy or a few drops of essence of lemon

to give flavour. The whole is afterwards well kneaded together on a well-floured board, rolled out very thin, and the snaps are then cut to shape with a tin paste-cutter and baked in a slow oven. When about half baked, and while pliable, the curled shape is given by rolling them round pieces of wood and then baking them till crisp.—L.G.M.

BRAZILIAN ARROWROOT

Another name of *Cassava* starch or *Tapioca* (q.v.).

BREAD

Bread is the name given to the oldest, commonest and cheapest form of human food: it is made of the flour or meal of one or more sorts of cereals, as well as the flour or meal which can be obtained from some grasses, seeds and rootstocks other than cereals.

The quality – that is the nutritive value, the taste and appearance of *Bread* – depends in the first place upon the nature and quality of the grain or grains from which the flour or meal is obtained. Then there is the milling, or 'extraction' of the flour, which comes second in point of timing but is of capital importance.

The grains of all cereals – and cereals are the chief source of flours for breadmaking – consist of four main parts: (1) the outer covering or husk; (2) the superficial layers of the grain itself – these are known as the bran layers; (3) the tiny embryo or germ from which the young plant springs on germination; and (4) the main mass of the grain known as the endosperm. The latter contains the starch and protein reserves upon which the young plant lives during its early days after germination. By contrast with the endosperm, a food reserve, the germ contains the building material of the plant itself. It is rich in protein, fatty constituents and certain vitamins as important to man as they are for the development of the growing plant.

The vitamins in cereal grains are not entirely concentrated in the germ, at least not in the case of wheat, which is the cereal of greatest importance in Great Britain and the U.S.A. There is quite a good proportion in a layer of protein – rich cells, known as the aleurone layer which underlies the innermost coat of bran. Modern research has shown the importance of trying to get as much as possible of the aleurone into the flour.

During centuries beyond count, *Bread* was made from flour obtained by the crushing of grain between two stones: such flour contained all but the coarsest part of the outer covering, the whole of the starch and the whole of the germ present in the grain. In colour it was any shade from light brown, in the case of wheaten flour, to black, in the case of rye flour. That was the bread which was deservedly known as the 'staff of life'.

Then came the roller mill from Hungary during the last quarter of the nineteenth century: it made it possible to crush the grain between revolving metal cylinders much more rapidly and economically. It also made it possible to separate fairly completely and easily the outer covering or bran, from the kernel or starch and the germ or vitamins storehouse. At the time, the vitamins were not yet understood and the chief merit(?) of the roller-mill was the possibility it gave to the millers of offering to the public a more attractive-looking loaf because of its snow-white crumb, at the same time, as having more and better 'offal,' i.e. left-overs in the shape of bran-cum-germ to sell as feed for cattle or poultry. Another fact that made the roller-mill popular with millers and bakers was that, by removing the germ, flour kept longer without showing rancidity. Actually stone-ground flour containing germ keeps well if it is milled dry and kept dry, but in milling 'roller' flour the grain has to be more moist. It is the relatively high moisture content of flours containing germ, made by the roller-mill, that results so often in an early onset of rancidity. Doctors and scientists warned the public that whilst the pure white flour was better than the brown for stiffening linen, being largely starch, it was a much poorer article as regards its food value. They were not listened to, and in the British Isles and the U.S.A., the public went on demanding white bread in preference to all others.

The discovery of the vital importance of vitamins, during the past twenty-five years, should have made the inclusion of the germ of the grain in the people's bread a moral as well as a legal obligation for the millers. However, most American bread manufacturers now enrich the soft white bread which is standard fare in the U.S.A., giving customers the benefit of added or replaced vitamins and minerals.

Whole grain bread is more wholesome, more toothsome and just as handsome as white bread, but all brown breads and all the so-called *wholemeal breads* are not necessarily *whole grain*: they may be brown because they contain bran, without any significant amount of germ. Such breads will not have the vitamin value of those containing germ.

There cannot be any question of scrapping the modern roller-mills and returning to the old and picturesque windmills; nor is there any need of going 'back'. On the contrary, there are indications that the modern roller-mill can be adapted to produce a flour acceptable by the mass of the public and at the same time almost as rich in nutriment as wholemeal. A new type of flour produced in Canada known as 'Canada approved' has these qualities and is proving very popular. The new National Wheatmeal now being milled in Great Britain is rapidly approaching the same character.

On the other hand, there are also new milling processes already in use which, it is claimed, enable for the first time flours containing the whole of the wheat berry to be produced in an assimilable form. In one process, the cells of the berry are exploded by intense air pressure, a process which reduces bran to a fine grist, liberates mineral salts, malt sugar and wheat oil, and produces a meal or flour from which bread is made that is pure, nutritive and digestible and contains the vitamins B1 and B2, and E, as well as valuable roughage.

Having secured the right flour for making *Bread*, one must make it into dough with water or milk or both, but water is the more usual liquid used for the purpose; also yeast and some salt. Whatever the kind of bread one may attempt to make, it is important to knead the dough regularly, steadily and thoroughly, so that the fermentation may be satisfactory and the bread free from holes and lumps. The flour must be dried before use, and the yeast must be fresh, or the bread will taste sour and bitter. All the ingredients should be slightly warmed before mixing. The oven should be raised to the right temperature before the bread is put in, i.e. 350° F., and it should then be gradually slackened or the crust may be too hard and dark.

In old-fashioned brick ovens, which were heated by wood being burnt in them before the bread was put in, the gradual cooling off process was, of course, automatic. Loaves, when taken from the oven, should be placed on a sieve or leant against something so that the air can circulate round them. If they are left lying flat the steam will condense into moisture and the bread become heavy.

There are exceptions to all rules, and there is *Bread* made without yeast:

Bread without Yeast

1 lb. of wholemeal flour, 1 level teaspoonful of bicarbonate of soda, 1 ditto of cream of tartar, 1 ditto of salt, 1 oz. of dripping or margarine, half teaspoon of sugar, ½ pint of milk.

Mix the cream of tartar with the milk. Take any lumps out of powders, mix ingredients stiff, and bake in quick oven for half an hour.—L.M. (2).

BREADCRUMBS

Fr. *Chapelure*. Well sifted and toasted crumbs of stale bread, white or brown, chiefly used for frying fish, meat balls and other foods.

BREAD SIPPETS

Bread 'Sippets' are small pieces of stale bread cut in the form of stars, the Maltese cross, triangles, diamonds and every imaginable shape; they are fried in hot dripping or lard and drained before the fire before being used as garnishings, as ornaments which one eats with pleasure.

BREAD PUDDING

Cut the bread into slices $\frac{1}{4}$ to $\frac{1}{2}$ in. thick. Square off by removing the harder crust. Pour a little milk into a large plate or flat dish, and place each slice into it until saturated, adding milk as required. Next, dip each slice into beaten-up egg, then into oatmeal, flour or baked breadcrumbs (which can be made of the crusts that have been removed), and fry in butter.

The bread can be served in this form, with jam or sugar added. Or, if there is an oven going, butter a dish and place the slices, when fried, one on top of the other, in the dish with a little jam or golden syrup between each. Whip up white of egg and put over the top. Bake until the white of egg has browned.—A.G.N.

BREAD AND BUTTER PUDDING

Cut thin slices of bread and butter without crust, of white and brown bread. Spread either sultanas, raisins or dates, or else jam or orange marmalade on each slice. Lay them in a buttered mould or basin and pour over a well-seasoned custard. Let it stand for half an hour, then steam it for an hour. This pudding is also delicious baked in the oven.

BREADSTUFFS

An American term for the various kinds of grain, meal or flour from which Bread is made.

BREAKFAST CEREALS

There are a large number of different kinds of partly or wholly cooked *Cereals* prepared, packaged and sold to provide an easily digested form of *Cereals* ready for consumption at a minimum of trouble and time, hence their great popularity in the U.S.A. and the British Isles. They are usually sold under the name of the firm responsible for their presentation, or some registered trade mark, as well as descriptive names. These *Breakfast Cereals* are usually ready to serve straight from their cartons or packets, or merely require some quick cooking. They are eaten with milk and sugar.

BREAKFAST SCHNECKEN

> 1 yeast cake
> 1 cup warm water
> 5 tablespoons sugar
> $\frac{1}{2}$ teaspoon salt
> 2 cups warm milk
> 2 eggs, well beaten
> $\frac{1}{4}$ cup melted butter
> Flour
> 4 tablespoons butter
> $1\frac{1}{2}$ teaspoons cinnamon

Dissolve the yeast cake in the warm water and add one tablespoon of the sugar, the salt and enough flour to stiffen to a sponge. Let rise for one hour, then add the milk, eggs, melted butter and enough sifted flour to make a soft sponge. Let rise again, then roll out dough on a floured board and cover with a mixture of the remaining sugar, butter and cinnamon. Roll like a jelly roll and cut in 2-in. pieces. Place on well-greased pans and let rise for a third time, then bake in a hot oven (400° F.) for twenty minutes. Delicious for breakfast or afternoon coffee. —C.G.

BREAK-OF-DAY FRITTERS

> 1 cup flour
> 2 tablespoons sweet wine
> 1 tablespoon brandy
> 1 tablespoon chopped, candied orange peel
> 1 tablespoon chopped, candied lemon peel
> 4 egg whites
> 1 tablespoon chopped citron

Mix flour to a rather thick batter with brandy and wine; if not sufficient liquid, add a little warm milk. Stir in the chopped fruit, mix well, and add the egg whites beaten to a stiff froth. Drop batter in lumps through a wide tin funnel into boiling fat and fry. Serve with powdered sugar strewn over.— C.R.B.B. (2).

BRIOCHE

A simple and most estimable cake made up of sifted flour, butter and eggs worked up to a paste which is particularly light owing to the quality and quantity of the yeast used to leaven the flour.

Brioche

$\frac{1}{2}$ lb. flour, $\frac{1}{4}$ lb. butter, 2 eggs, $\frac{1}{2}$ oz. yeast, teaspoonful of brandy, small tumbler of water, a little sugar and salt.

Mix the flour and yeast, crumbled; the eggs, sugar and salt; then add the butter, melted, and the water, making a thick batter. Beat with a wooden spoon until it becomes bubbly; add the brandy and leave to rise for 1½ hours. Bake in muffin pans in a sharp oven. The tins should be only half-filled with the batter. This recipe was given to me in Paris thirty years ago and is very successful.—M.K.S. (2).

BROAS. MADEIRA SMALL CAKES

1 lb. of flour, ¾ lb. of sugar, ¼ lb. of butter, 1 teaspoonful of powdered cinnamon, the peel of a lemon grated and two eggs. Put the butter into the flour, beat the eggs, mix well, roll out on a paste board and cut into rounds rather smaller than macaroons. If the mixture is not quite moist enough, add a little milk. Bake in a hot oven about twenty minutes.—M.B. (2).

BROOM CORN

An African Cereal of the *Sorghum* family, valuable both for its brush and its grain. It is grown in Illinois and other States of the Middle West where its relative, Dent Maize, is grown more extensively. It is also grown in California, in most countries bordering the Mediterranean Sea, and in the East.

BROSE

When not otherwise qualified, *Brose* means oatmeal and water, something between porridge and gruel. Boiling water is poured over the oatmeal, stirring hard all the time; salt is added to taste; also milk if possible and a lump of butter at the last moment. It is eaten with cream by the well-to-do farmers and without either cream or butter by the poorer people: it is then known as *Water Brose* or *Blind Brose*. *Brose and Butter* or *Aigar Brose (Oatmeal Brose)* might rightly be called the national dish of Scotland. The reddish pease meal is sometimes used in place of Oatmeal. *Milk Brose* is Brose made with boiling milk instead of boiling water.

Brose sometimes contains more than oatmeal, but it is then qualified in some manner indicating whether fish or flesh or cabbage has been added, as in the following instances:

Mussel Brose

Mussels, oatmeal, stock or milk-and-water. Wash the shells in several waters, scraping them well, then put them into a colander and run cold water on them until it runs away quite clear and free of sand, after which put them to steep for two hours. Drain them, put them on the fire in an iron stew-pan, closely covered, shake them occasionally until the shells open, and remove immediately from the fire. Strain the liquor into a basin, take the mussels out of the shells, and remove the beards and black parts. Put the

liquor with some fresh fish stock or some milk-and-water. Bring to the boil, add the mussels, and boil for ten minutes in all. Have some oatmeal toasting before the fire. Put a cupful of the boiling bree over it. Stir up quickly so as to form knots, return to the pan for a minute or two and serve very hot. Cockles may be served in the same way.— F.M.M. (2).

Kail Brose
(Old Cottage Recipe)

Ox head or cow heel, green kail, oatmeal, salt, water. Put half an ox head or cow heel into a goblet with three quarts of water. Boil till the fat floats on the top. Take a good stock of kail, wash it carefully and pick it down very small and put it into the broth. Now take a teacupful of toasted oatmeal, put it into a bowl with a little salt, dash upon it a teacupful of the fat broth and stir it up like oatmeal brose into knots. Put this into the pot for a moment or two before lifting off the fire. Stir well and serve.—F.M.M. (2).

BROWN BREAD

The name given to a large number of different kinds of bread, all of which have one common characteristic, that of being made wholly or partly with 'brown' flour, that is, flour of low extraction, whether fine or coarse. All breads other than white and black bread are 'brown', but they are also usually given some more distinctive names, under which they appear, in their alphabetical order, in this Section of the *Encyclopaedia*.

BROWN BREAD PUDDING

½ lb. of stale brown bread grated; ditto of currants; ditto of shredded suet; sugar and nutmeg; mix with four eggs, one tablespoonful of brandy and two of cream; boil in a cloth or basin that exactly holds it for three or four hours.—G.A.S.

BROWN SCONES

     3 oz. butter
     1¼ lb. wholemeal flour
     2 teaspoonfuls baking powder
     1 dessertspoonful flour

Make this into a rather stiff dough with sour milk or buttermilk; roll out, dent into shapes. Bake in a quick oven.—L.G.N.

BUCKWHEAT

Lat. *Fagopyrum esculentum*; Fr. *Sarrazin* or *Blé noir*. Botanically speaking, *Buckwheat* is not a true cereal, but from the gastronomical point of view it belongs to this class, since its seeds yield a flour from which bread is made as well as excellent pancakes and teacakes. Its original name was *Beechwheat*, which is the translation of the Latin name which it was given by botanists on account of its supposed resemblance to a beechnut. It is also known sometimes under the names of *Brank* or *Saracen Wheat*. (Its French name is *Sarrazin*.) A native of Siberia, where it is extensively cultivated for the making of bread. *Buckwheat* is largely grown in Holland, Brittany and in some of the poorest soils, sandy heaths and moorlands of other parts of France. In England it is grown on a small scale, chiefly as feed for pheasants. In some of the backwoods of America *Buckwheat* is grown extensively for the sake of its seeds which are ground and used as porridge or hasty pudding with maple honey; but in many parts of the U.S.A. hot buckwheat cakes are very highly valued as a breakfast delicacy.

BUCKWHEAT CAKES (1805)
One quart buckwheat flour, one pint of milk or new beer, 3 spoons molasses, 4 spoons yeast, stir well together, wet the bottom of the pan with butter or lard, and when the pan is hot, put in the cakes; when done, pour over butter and milk.—A.L. (2).

BUCKWHEAT CAKES
Mix a good teaspoonful of baking powder with 1 lb. of dried and sifted buckwheat flour; beat the yolks of two eggs with a little water till light (i.e. till the fork can be lifted without leaving any strings); then beat them into the flour, adding gradually enough water to produce a batter, which being lifted will fall in a kind of sheet from the spoon. Now stir in the whites of the eggs whipped to the stiffest possible froth with a pinch, and drop this batter by spoonfuls into a pan of very hot boiling fat (with a strong blue vapour rising from it). (They use butter in Brittany, olive oil in Provence, ghee in India, but dripping will do.) Cook over a good steady fire, then lift out, drain and serve very hot, spread with butter or honey.

BUCKWHEAT 'GALETTES'
To a quart of buckwheat flour, add 1½ tablespoonfuls of a yeast and a large pinch of salt; mix in a deep basin with enough water to make a smooth batter and leave it to rise in a warm (not hot) place until the next morning, when it should have risen. Shape into thin cakes and bake on a hot griddle, like griddle cakes. Serve hot with butter or honey.

BUN
A small cake, usually round and glazed, slightly sweet, with or without currants. In Scotland, however, the name is also given to a rich and spiced kind of cake; and in Ulster it is the name of a round loaf of ordinary bread.

To make Buns Marston way (1694)
Take two pounds and a half of flower well dryed, then rub in half a pound of butter; take a pint of good milk warmed, six or seven spoonfuls of Ale yest not bitter, five Eggs yoalks and whites: strain these through a sieve, then mix them well into your flower, and let it stand by the fire half an hour to rise. Then mix in half a pound of sugar, some Currons or Caraway seeds, which you like best, and a nuttmeg grated, then putt it in patti-pans or tins as you intend to bake it.—L.B.

To make Buns (1808)
Take two pounds of fine flour, a pint of ale yeast, with a little sack, and three eggs beaten; knead all these together with a little warm milk, nutmeg and salt. Lay it before the fire till it rise very light. Then knead into it a pound of fresh butter, and a pound of round caraway confitt, and bake them in a quick oven, on floured papers, in what shape you please.—L.E.

BURGOO
Seamen's name for oatmeal puddings. (In the U.S.A. the name is also given, in the Southern States, to a much-sauced stew.)

BUTTERMILK BISCUITS
Sift 1 cupful of flour, 1 teaspoonful of baking powder and ½ teaspoonful of salt into a bowl. Mix in lightly 6 tablesppoonfuls of soft butter and ¾ cupful of buttermilk to which has been added ½ teaspoonful of soda. Roll out dough lightly about ¾ of an inch thick and cut with biscuit-cutter. Place on lightly-greased pan and bake at 350° F. from 10 to 12 minutes.—E.E.A.

BUTTERMILK BUCKWHEAT CAKES
> 1 cupful of packaged
>   buckwheat flour
> ¼ teaspoonful of soda
> 1 tablespoonful of molasses
> 1½ cupfuls of buttermilk

Sift the flour and soda together twice. Stir in the buttermilk and then the molasses. Mix thoroughly but quickly so the soda will not lose its strength. Drop in tablespoonfuls on a hot well-greased griddle or skillet and brown on both sides. Serve with honey or syrup. Recipe makes about one dozen; double it for a larger amount.—E.K.H.

BUTTER ROLLS
> 3 eggs
> 2 yeast cakes
> 6 tablespoons butter
> 8 cups flour (approximately
> 4 tablespoons sugar
> 1 teaspoon salt
> 2 cups milk

Mash and mix together in a bowl the yeast. Add sugar, salt and eggs. Heat milk lukewarm. Add butter to the milk, then add to first mixture. Add seven cups of flour, mix well. Put remainder of flour on board. Knead until pastry blisters then set aside to rise for 1½ hours in a warm place. Roll out on floured board ¼ in. thick, brush with melted butter and cut with biscuit cutter. Fold each roll into pocket-book shape and let rise for another 1½ hours. Then bake in hot 450° F. oven about 15 minutes.—L.R.

CAKE

Cake is a name which covers a very large number of floury confections, sweetened and variously flavoured.

'*But cakes, it may be said, are childish things, and at the present day they run to hundredweights in the case of weddings; though before long wedding cakes will probably be discarded as evidence, or at least concomitants, of woman's already discarded slavery.*' (*Professor George Saintsbury's Introduction to* The Receipt Book of Ann Blencowe, A.D. 1694. London, 1925.)

CALAS-TOUS-CHAUDS

2 cups cooked rice
1 yeast cake
4 cups flour
2 eggs
4 tablespoons sugar
1½ teaspoons salt

Dissolve yeast in one-half cup lukewarm water. Stir into rice. Let rise overnight. Beat eggs until light, add salt and sugar, combine with rice mixture and stir in flour. Let rise for one hour. Drop by tablespoonfuls into deep medium hot fat and fry until browned. Drain and serve piping hot with cane syrup. Or, if preferred, sprinkle with powdered sugar and serve hot.—L.R.

CANARY PUDDING

2 oz. butter
2 oz. sugar
4 oz. flour
1 egg
½ teaspoonful baking powder
Rind of half a lemon

Cream together butter and sugar. Add egg and flour by degrees. Add baking powder, lemon rind and milk. Pour into greased mould. Steam one hour and serve with jam or lemon sauce or with golden syrup.—P.R.M.

CANAPÉS

Fr. for a settee or restful seat. In culinary French, it refers to small pieces of white or wholemeal crumb bread, sometimes of *brioche*, upon which sits a mouthful of fish, flesh or fowl; almost anything that is tasty and appetizing. Mostly used for *hors-d'oeuvre*, sometimes also as trimmings with *entrées*, and sometimes at the end of the meal, for *savouries*. *Canapés* may be round or square, star-like or any other shape, but they must be small. There is no limit to the number of *Canapés* any more than to human inventiveness. Here is a list of some popular *Canapés*, with an indication of their informing flavour:

à l'Arlequine: mixed; smoked salmon; tongue; ham; egg, etc.

à l'Américaine: lobster.

à la Beauharnais: truffles and chicken.

à la Bressane: truffles and chicken; coxcombs.

Coralie: chicken and tongue and horseradish.

Danoise: smoked salmon, herring and caviar.

à l'écarlate: tongue.

à l'Ecossaise: smoked salmon.

à la Grimaldi: chicken, tongue and truffles, red pimentoes.

à l'Indienne: shrimps, green pimentoes and curry.

Mireille: hard-boiled egg chopped with tarragon and fillets of anchovies.

Normande: shrimps, an oyster and Mayonnaise.

Printanière: yolk of egg and watercress.

CANNELLONI

A sort of Italian paste which might be described as a 'tubular' form of Ravioli.

Cannelloni ripieni alla toscana.

For the pastry: 6 oz. flour; 1 whole egg and 1 yolk and a pinch of salt. For the filling: Chopped, cooked meat; cooked chicken livers; truffles (optional); 1 egg; Parmesan cheese; gravy (*sugo*).

Work the flour and eggs to a stiff paste and roll out very thinly. Cut out into 3½ in. squares. Mix the finely-chopped meat, chicken livers and truffles with the egg and Parmesan cheese. Put the squares of pastry in a large saucepan of boiling water and cook for a few minutes, keeping them somewhat firm. Drain, and put them on a cloth. Put a little filling on each square and roll the pastry around it, so as to form a tube. Then toss the *cannelloni* in the *sugo* for a few minutes and sprinkle with parmesan cheese.—C.M. (4).

CANNA. QUEENSLAND ARROWROOT

The starch of the rootstock of a number of different varieties of *Canna* but more particularly of the *Canna edulis*, a native of the West Indies, which is known also as *Tous-*

les-mois, being available at all times of the year; it is used in the same way as *Arrowroot* (q.v.).

CAPE ANN PANNED JOHNNY CAKES

> 1 cupful of yellow corn meal
> 1 teaspoonful of salt
> 1¾ cupfuls of rapidly boiling water
> 2 tablespoonfuls of molasses
> 3 tablespoonfuls of bacon fat (or fat from 3 slices of salt pork)

Mix the corn meal and salt, cover, and keep warm until ready to use. Bring the water to a riotous boil and pour one-half cupful at a time over the meal, mixing as you pour. The water must be boiling each time that you measure it. Add the molasses and mix together thoroughly. Shape with wet hands into about seven little cakes, 2½ in. in diameter and ¾ in. thick. Have the fat in a skillet very hot, and brown the cakes on both sides, turning twice if necessary. Serve whole, or split, with plenty of maple syrup or honey. Very good for a late Sunday breakfast or a Sunday supper and easy to make in a boat or camp.—E.K.H.

CAPTAINS

Mix in a large basin 4 lb. flour, 2 oz. butter (broken up small), 2 whole eggs and a pint of water; rub and work these ingredients well together, slipping the hands down to the bottom of the pan, and throwing up the half-mixed dough till it is all well blended. Then knead it thoroughly, working it well and heavily. (The secret of bakers' 'Captains' lies in this kneading as they use either a 'break' or a biscuit machine, and thus knead the dough much more thoroughly than it is easy to do by hand, save in very small batches.) As soon as the dough is well mixed and smooth, cover it with a damp cloth and leave it for an hour or two; then roll it out quickly, as thin as possible (paper-thin is about right), cut out with a round plain cutter, prick the biscuits well with a fork, dust a baking sheet lightly with rice flour (do not butter it), arrange the biscuits on this and bake at once in a very hot oven. To ensure success with these biscuits, the dough must be worked in a warmish place and guarded from draughts till it gets into the oven. In baking, set the biscuits at first in the very hottest part of the oven, to blister and brown the surface, then shift them to a somewhat cooler part, but the oven must always be very hot and the work done very quickly. Like all plain, hard biscuits, *Captains* should always be well dried after baking, setting them for some hours in a dry, warm place or a slack oven. *Thick Captains* are made in precisely the same way,

only breaking the dough off in 2 oz. pieces, rolling these out a ¼ in. thick, in rounds (or rolling the dough in a sheet and stamping it out with a cutter), then pricking them well through.—Q. (1).

CARAWAY SEED BREAD

One cup of scalded milk; half cup of butter; half cup of sugar; half tablespoonful of salt; one yeast cake; one-third cup of lukewarm water; two tablespoonfuls caraway seeds; about four cups of rye flour or wheat flour, for kneading. Knead fully half an hour. When risen to double in bulk, shape into a long roll and bake. Serve either warm or cold.—M.K.S. (2).

CASSAVA

A West Indian name for a number of plants belonging to the genus *Manihot,* largely cultivated in all tropical lands for the sake of their fleshy rootstocks which yield valuable food. There are both bitter and sweet *Cassavas,* both sorts, but more particularly the bitter, containing some hydrocyanic acid, a poisonous substance which, however, loses its sting when the roots are exposed to light and air and dried. When dried and dressed, the *Cassava* roots are expected to produce about 40 per cent starch, 30 per cent syrup of glucose and 10 per cent tapioca, the rest being water. In Brazil *Mandioca* or *Manioca* or *Manioc* are the names given to *Cassava,* whilst in Peru and other parts of South America it is called *Yucca* or *Jucca.* Besides *Tapioca,* other foodstuffs are prepared from the *Cassava* or *Manioca* roots, such as *Farina, Brazilian Arrowroot, Cassareep, Onycou, Piwarree,* etc. *Bitter Cassava* is sometimes used to make *Casiri,* an intoxicating drink, whilst *Sweet Cassava* may be used as a vegetable.

CHARLOTTES

There are two different kinds of sweets known by the name of *Charlotte* in French Classical Cuisine, the one is always served cold and is known as *Charlotte Russe,* and the other is served hot and its prototype is the *Charlotte de Pommes* (See Part IV, FRUIT, under *Apple.*) Both have one feature in common: they consist of some sweet filling within a bread or biscuit framework. The earliest mention of a *Charlotte* is to be found in the works of Carême, who states that he was greatly complimented for the *Charlotte* he sent to some Minister's table in 1800 or 1802. He gives no indication why the name *Charlotte* was chosen, but the sweet is described as a cold pudding with a filling of sweet apple *purée.* It is therefore quite possible, even probable, that Carême, who was then just learning how to read and write, chose *Charlotte* as the nearest approximation to *Schaleth,* of which his dish was an improved edition. *Schaleth* is an old favourite among Jewish cookery recipes: it is a pudding made of mashed, sweetened apples (peeled and cored, of course), and some seedless or seeded raisins and sultanas previously soaked in wine; it is flavoured with various spices to taste and baked under a cover of hard wheat paste.

CHEESE BISCUITS

     3 oz. flour
     1½ oz. margarine
     4 oz. grated cheese
     1 yolk of egg
     A pinch of salt and of cayenne
       pepper

Rub the margarine into the flour. Add the cheese, pepper and salt. Mix the yolk of egg with a little cold water and add to the other ingredients. Mix all into a soft dough. Roll out and cut into neat, small rounds. Bake in a moderate oven till golden brown.—B.H.

CHEESECAKES

A very popular form of tartlets made differently in different parts of England. One of the old recipes for *Cheesecakes* is as follows:

Take ½ lb. of dry curd, 6 oz. of sugar, 6 yolks of eggs, 2 oz. butter, some nutmegs, salt and the zest of two lemons. Pound into a soft paste and distribute into tartlet-pans which have been lined with puff-paste; put citron-peel, currants or sultanas on the top of each and bake them in a moderate oven.

Lemon Cheesecakes

Cream ¼ lb. butter and 6 oz. of castor sugar, add two eggs, one at a time. Mix ½ lb. sieved flour with one teaspoon baking powder and add gradually to butter, etc. When these little cakes are cooked, set to cool and then cut in two, filling with the following lemon cream: ½ lb. loaf sugar, 2 oz. butter, juice of two or three lemons and some grated rind, two eggs. Put all except the eggs into the saucepan and melt gradually. When it is a little cool, stir in the beaten eggs and then stir over fire until the mixture thickens.–L.C.

CHEESE STRAWS BISCUITS

     1 lb. soft flour
     ½ lb. fine butter
     4 oz. parmesan cheese
     2 eggs
     ½ teaspoonful salt
     ¼ teaspoonful cayenne pepper
     Tablespoonful of milk

Rub the butter into the flour, make a bay, place in the cheese, eggs, milk, pepper and salt, work together a little and work all into a smooth paste, well rubbed down. Roll out into a sheet ⁹⁄₁₆ in. thick, and divide into

lengths ⅜ in. wide, and as long as the width of the baking-sheet. Now twist each length by turning one end towards and the other end away from you, and when twisted their entire length, set ½ in. apart across baking-sheets, pressing the two ends down to hold in position. When all are on, cut off the pressed ends with a scraper, and with the same tool divide the long strips into three rows of equal length. Work up the cuttings into the same lengths, and bake at once in an oven 450° F. to a rich golden colour. When cold tie into bundles of six with pieces of narrow bright red ribbon.—A.A.B.

CHELSEA BUNS

     ¾ lb. flour
     ¼ lb. butter
     ¼ lb. sugar
     ¼ oz. yeast
     1 lemon
     2 eggs
     ½ gill milk

Cream the yeast with a little sugar, and add it to warm milk. Rub half the butter into the flour and add half the sugar. Make a dough with this and beat in the eggs. Stand in a warm place to rise for about two hours; knead well and roll out on a floured board the same way as for a jam roll; spread the rest of the butter and sugar over. Fold in three and roll out again and then into a square. Roll up as for a jam roll, cut in thick slices all the same depth, and stand up on end to bake, each roll touching the other. Let them prove for about 20 minutes, then bake for the same time. The grated rind of a lemon is used for flavouring.—N.E.

CHESS CAKES

Cream one-half pound of butter and one-half pound of sugar well together. Beat the yolks of six eggs until light in colour and add to the butter and sugar. Put in a pinch of salt and stir in one-third of a cup of white wine. Bake in small pastry shells rolled thin in muffin-tins. Fill the shells about three-fourths full. Bake in moderately hot oven. Serve cold. Will keep for several days in a cool place. (*Traditional Virginia Recipe, Morgan family. Prov'd Market Square Tavern Kitchen*, 1937.)—H.B.

CHESTER CAKES

     6 oz. sieved flour
     6 oz. grated Cheshire cheese
     6 oz. butter
     Salt, cayenne, 2 tablespoons cream

Cream butter, then work in flour, and cheese, salt, cayenne and cream, with the hand on marble slab. Handle as lightly as possible. When blended, flour hands, make a ball, and allow to rest in cool place for about an hour.

Roll out about ¼ in. thick; stamp out in rounds the size of a two-shilling piece. Bake in good moderate oven till golden brown. Cool a little on sheet. Stick two together with a mixture of creamed butter and cheese. Reheat slightly and serve on hot dish.

Excellent without the filling, and they keep well in a tin.—D.L.T.

CHOCOLATE BISCUITS

> 1 oz. cocoa
> 4 oz. flour
> 2 oz. margarine
> ¼ teaspoonful of bicarbonate of soda
> 1½ tablespoonfuls of syrup
> 2 oz. sugar

Melt the margarine slightly. Mix it with the syrup. Then mix all the ingredients in the margarine and syrup. Beat thoroughly and roll out. Stamp out the biscuits and bake on a flat tin for 15 minutes.—B.H.

CHOCOLATE CAKE

I

¼ lb. of butter, ¼ lb. of castor sugar, ¼ lb. of flour, 2 oz. of chocolate powder, 2 well-beaten eggs, vanilla and a teaspoon baking powder. Mix flour, chocolate powder and baking powder together. Beat the butter and sugar together to a cream, add the eggs and then the dry ingredients. Bake in a flat tin in a quick oven.—L.M. (2).

II

> 8 oz. butter
> 7 oz. sugar
> 8 oz. flour
> ¼ teaspoonful baking powder
> 4 eggs
> 4 oz. chocolate
> 1 tablespoonful milk

Grease and line a tin 12 in. long by 8 in. wide. Dissolve the chocolate in a small saucepan in the milk. When thoroughly dissolved, remove from the fire and allow to become almost cold. Work the butter and sugar together until white and creamy, add the eggs one at a time with one tablespoonful of flour, and beat this in thoroughly before adding the next one. Add the dissolved chocolate and, lastly, the remainder of the sieved flour and a pinch of salt; mix well and pour into the prepared tin. Bake in a moderate oven of 350° F. for approximately 40 minutes. When cooked, turn on to a cake-tray to cool.—G.H.(4).

III

> 4 oz. butter
> 4 oz. castor sugar
> 2 oz. plain flour
> 1 oz. ground rice
> 1 teaspoonful baking powder
> Pinch of salt
> 4 oz. chocolate powder
> 2 eggs

Cream butter and sugar together, sieve the dry ingredients, add the eggs to this creamed butter, one at a time, beat well, stir in flour, baking powder and ground rice. The chocolate powder should be dissolved in a little milk over the fire; when cool add it to the mixture and pour all into tin; bake one hour and ice when cool.—L.G.N.

Chocolate Icing

Melt 2 oz. of chocolate in 2 tablespoonfuls of water, then add ½ lb. of icing sugar and water gradually until thin enough to spread. Keep it just warm.—L.G.N.

CHRISTMAS CAKE

I

¾ lb. fresh butter, 1 lb. flour, 1 lb. sugar, 1 lb. sultanas, 1 lb. raisins, ½ lb. ground almonds, ¼ lb. mixed and chopped peel, 6 eggs, a little nutmeg and mixed spice, grated rind and juice of a lemon, half a wine-glass of brandy.

Rub butter into flour and sugar, add fruit and other dry ingredients. Beat the eggs a little and add to the mixture with the brandy. Line the tin well with buttered paper and bake in a slow oven for at least eight hours.—M.K.S. (2).

II

(A Fruitless Christmas Cake)

> 14 oz. flour
> 2 oz. ground rice
> 2 oz. ground almonds
> 1 lb. butter
> 1 lb. eggs
> ½ gill sherry
> Almond flavoring
> 1 lb. sugar

Grease and line an 8 in. cake-tin. Sieve the flour, pinch of salt, rice, and ground almonds and mix thoroughly. Cream the butter and sugar. When pale in colour and of whipped cream consistency, beat in the eggs one at a time, adding some of the flour, etc., alternately with the eggs. When all the eggs have been added, stir in the sherry and a few drops of almond flavoring. Put into the tin and bake in a moderate oven of 350° F. for about 40 minutes, then at a temperature of 320° F. for about 1½ hours. Cool on a sieve.—G.H. (4).

CHRISTMAS PUDDING (EGGLESS)

½ lb. flour
6 oz. of raisins
6 oz. of currants
¼ lb. candied peel
¼ lb. chopped suet
¼ lb. brown sugar
¼ lb. mashed carrots
¼ lb. potatoes
1 tablespoon of treacle

Mix flour, currants, raisins, suet and sugar well together, stir in mashed carrots and potatoes, add treacle and lemon peel, but put no liquid into the mixture or it will be spoiled. Tie it loosely in a cloth, or put it into a basin (don't quite fill basin as it must swell). Boil for four hours. Serve with brandy sauce. Sufficient for eight or ten people.—L.G.N.

CHRISTMAS PUDDING ROYAL

1¼ lb. suet
1 lb. Demerara sugar
1 lb. raisins
1 lb. sultanas
4 oz. citron peel
4 oz. candied peel
1 teaspoonful mixed spice
½ teaspoon nutmeg
1 lb. breadcrumbs
½ lb. sifted flour
1 lb. eggs (weighed in their shells)
1 wineglass brandy
½ pint milk

Prepare all ingredients, well whip the eggs, add to milk and thoroughly mix. Let stand for 12 hours in a cool place, add brandy and put into well-greased basins, and boil 8 hours or longer. Sufficient for 20 or 28 people.—L.G.N.

CINNAMON STARS

8 egg whites
2 cups granulated sugar
6 teaspoons cinnamon
2 teaspoons grated lemon rind
2 cups powdered sugar
2 cups finely-crushed almonds

Use electric mixer if possible. Beat egg whites to a froth and gradually beat in mixture of granulated sugar and cinnamon, sifting about quarter of a cup at a time over top. Beat mixture until it becomes very stiff, about 15 minutes.

Remove half a cup of mixture and to the remaining mixture add the almonds and lemon rind. Knead in thoroughly the powdered sugar. Roll about ¼ in. thick and cut with star-shaped cutter. Brush tops with the half cup of reserved mixture. Bake in moderate oven (350° F.) for 20 minutes or until very lightly browned. Makes about two dozen stars depending upon size of cutter used.—A.W.R.

COACH WHEELS

Roll out your dough in a long narrow strip. Rub with soft butter, sprinkle with brown sugar and cinnamon. Roll up into a roll as round as your Buns are to be. Slice ¾ in. thick with a floured knife, and place almost touching in a well-buttered pan. Let them rise until light and bake in a moderate oven. (*Richmond Recipe. Prov'd Blair Kitchen*, 1938.) —H.B.

COCKTAIL BISCUITS

Cocktail Biscuits other than *Cheese* and *Cheese Straw Biscuits* (q.v.) are small in size but of any and every shape the cook fancies, and they must be rather highly flavoured. The more popular flavourings used in the making of savoury *Cocktail Biscuits* are *Tomato* (Tomato *purée*); *Onion* (Onion powder); *Celery* (Celery seeds); *Cayenne Pepper*; *Anchovy* and *Sprats*. In the case of fish, the bones must be carefully removed, and not too much of the shredded or pounded fish mixed with the biscuit paste before baking. Celery Seeds Biscuits are much better when sprinkled over with salt, but they must be eaten soon after being made. If kept for any length of time, the salt takes up the moisture from the air and the biscuits get mouldy.

COCONUT BISCUITS

Ingredients: 10 oz. of castor sugar, 2 whites of eggs, 6 oz. of desiccated coconut.

Method: Beat the whites of eggs to a stiff froth, add the other ingredients and form into pyramids; place the pyramids on paper, put the papers on tins, and bake the biscuits in rather a cool oven until they are just coloured a light brown.

Time: About a quarter of an hour. Sufficient for 15 to 20 biscuits.—B.E.C.

COCONUT CAKE

10 oz. flour
5 oz. butter
2 eggs
6 oz. castor sugar
1 orange
1 teaspoon baking powder
2 oz. coconut
Milk to mix

Sieve the flour with a pinch of salt and baking powder; mix thoroughly with the coconut and grated orange rind. In cold weather warm the butter and sugar and beat until light and creamy. Add the eggs and dry ingredients alternately to the creamed mixture, beating well between each addition. Stir in sufficient milk and a dessertspoonful of orange juice and beat well. Put the mixture into a tin 6 by 3½ in. lined with greased paper. Bake at 370° F. for 1¾ hours, or until cake is well risen, firm and golden brown in colour.—G.H. (4).

COCONUT CAKES

     ¼ lb. shortcrust pastry
     3 tablespoons desiccated coconut
     1 egg
     A little nutmeg
     1 egg yolk
     4 tablespoons milk
     1½ oz. castor sugar

Line some small patty-tins with shortcrust pastry. Prepare the coconut mixture by beating the eggs and milk thoroughly, and stirring in the rest of the ingredients. Put a little in each patty-pan and bake at a temperature of 380° F. for about 20 minutes. —G.H. (4).

COCONUT ROCK BUNS

     7 oz. flour
     4 oz. butter
     3 oz. desiccated coconut
     ½ an egg
     ½ teaspoon bicarbonate of soda
     4 oz. sugar
     ½ teaspoon cream of tartar

Beat the sugar and butter to a cream, add half the beaten egg. Then add the sieved flour, bicarbonate of soda, cream of tartar and coconut. Mix to a very stiff mixture, adding the remainder of the egg if the mixture will not bind. Place in rocky heaps on a greased baking-tray and bake in a hot oven of 425° F. for 15 to 20 minutes.—G.H. (4).

COFFEE BREAD

One cup of scalded milk, two cakes of compressed yeast, a quarter cup of water, enough flour to make a sponge, one-third cup of melted butter, quarter cup of sugar, half teaspoonful of salt, 2 eggs, well beaten, grating of lemon rind, flour. Soften the yeast in warm water and make a sponge with the yeast and flour. Then lightly add the other ingredients and flour to make a stiff batter; beat thoroughly. When light, spread it again on a buttered dripping-pan, cover and let rise. When ready for the oven, brush over with beaten egg and dust with sugar and cinnamon mixed. Bake in a hot oven. Alternatively the top may be covered with chopped nuts mixed with sugar, cinnamon, stale breadcrumbs and melted butter, and chopped stoned raisins may be added to the dough.—M.K.S. (2).

COFFEE CAKE

     2 cups brown sugar
     1 cup molasses
     ¾ cup butter
     1 teaspoon soda
     5 cups flour
     2 or 3 eggs, beaten
     1 cup cold coffee
     1 cup dried currants
     1 cup raisins
     1 teaspoon cinnamon
     1 teaspoon allspice

Blend dry ingredients, sifting twice, then add beaten eggs and butter blended, alternating with coffee and molasses and adding currants last. Bake in a moderate oven (250° F. to 300° F.) for 45 minutes.

The perfect breakfast cake in Michigan and, in fact, throughout the Middle West. —C.G.

COOKIES

Cookies are usually soft or stiff doughs. The softer mixtures are dropped from a spoon and baked. The stiffer doughs may be rolled, cut and baked; or formed into rolls, well chilled, then sliced and baked. Grease baking-pan or sheet with an unsalted fat.

Whatever the method of shaping a cooky it is important to use only as much flour in the dough and on the moulding board as is needed to make the dough easy to handle. To avoid using extra flour in the rolling and cutting, *all* cooky doughs are better for being well chilled before baking. A cold dough spreads or rises more than dough at room temperature. Make allowance for this when placing a cooky dough on the baking-sheet.

A cooky dough may be kept for some time in the refrigerator, well wrapped in waxed paper, and portions baked as needed.

Butter may be used if one prefers the flavour in a light-coloured or delicately-flavoured cooky.

Other shortenings: vegetable fats and oils, lard, chicken fat, clarified beef drippings, etc., may be used in darker cookies or those with definite flavours such as molasses, chocolate, spice and fruits.—M.E.A.

Coriander Cookies (1805)

1 lb. sugar boiled slowly in half pint water, scum well and cool, add 1 teaspoon pearlash, dissolved in milk, then 2½ lb. flour, rub in 4 oz. of butter, and 2 large spoons of finely-powdered coriander seed, wet with above; make rolls ½ in. thick and cut to the shape you please; bake 15 or 20 minutes in a slack oven – good three weeks.—A.L. (2).

Cookies (Scotch)

1½ lb. flour, 3 oz. butter, 3 gills milk, 1 oz. yeast, 2 eggs, 1 teaspoon salt, 6 oz. sugar

Sieve flour into warm basin. Melt butter, add milk and make lukewarm. Cream yeast with salt, pour over this milk and butter. Strain into flour. Add well-beaten egg and beat mixture till smooth and light. Allow to rise in warm place for two hours. Then mix in sugar. Form into small rounds, place on greased and floured tin. Set aside in warm place for 10 minutes, then bake in quick oven. When almost ready glaze with sugar dissolved in hot milk.—s.w.r.

Coolidge Cookies

1 egg, 1 cup sugar, ½ cup butter, 3½ cups flour, 2 teaspoons cream of tartar, 1 teaspoon soda, ½ cup milk, ½ teaspoon vanilla.

Filling: 1½ cups chopped raisins (seedless), ½ cup sugar, ½ cup water, 1 tablespoon flour. Cook until it thickens. Spread one spoonful between two pieces of cut cookie dough. Bake in a moderate oven.—p.d.p.

CORN

See *Maize*.

CORN BREAD

Corn Bread is especially acceptable on cold winter mornings and in camp. It is easier to make than regular bread and will absorb a lot of jam or maple syrup. Sometimes the corn meal is cooked first in a double-boiler for 10 minutes with sugar, salt, milk, and shortening, but usually, as everybody is in a hurry, the bread is made all at once.

Mix well one cup of corn meal with half a cupful of wheat flour, two teaspoonfuls baking powder (double acting, like Calumet), a teaspoonful each of salt and sugar; add enough milk or hot water to make a dough, and two beaten eggs and a tablespoonful of melted butter or vegetable oil and butter mixed. Bake in a hot oven in a greased pan – dough about 1½ in. thick. Should be done in 20 minutes.

Corn pone, ash bread, hoe cake, Johnny cake are all emergency corn 'breads' made with corn meal, salt, shortening and hot water to make a dough.

Spoon bread is a soft corn bread usually eaten from the pan in which it is baked. It may have boiled hominy or rice in it.—c.b.

CORN CAKE

One tablespoon of butter, 2 tablespoons of sugar, ½ teaspoon of salt, 1 cup of sifted flour, one ½ cup of yellow corn meal, 2 level teaspoons of baking powder, 1 egg, and, 1 cup of milk. Cream the butter and sugar, add the rest of the ingredients and bake in a flat square tin. Serve hot for breakfast or tea.—m.k.s. (2).

CORNETS

The French name of small conical pastries filled with cream; they used to be known in England by the name of *Cornucopias* (q.v.).

CORNFLOUR BREAD

To one quart of sifted (Indian) corn meal add one teacupful of cream, three eggs, a teacupful of bicarbonate of soda dissolved in water, buttermilk to make it quite soft; stir well and bake in a baking-kettle or oven.—m.k.s. (2).

CORNFLOUR NOG

     1 teaspoon cornflour
     1 cup new milk
     2 tablespoons of cream, if
       possible
     1 stiffly-beaten white of egg
     Flavouring

Gradually blend the milk into the cornflour. Turn into a saucepan and stir until boiling and cook for five minutes. Add flavouring and cream and sugar to taste, and just before serving stir in lightly the white of the egg. This mixture should be thin enough to drink and more new milk can be added if it is too thick.—l.g.n.

CORNFLOUR PUDDING

     ½ oz. cornflour
     ½ pint milk
     1 egg
     1 teaspoon sugar

Put most of the milk into a saucepan and allow it to heat. Mix the cornflour into a smooth paste with the remainder of the milk and add to it what is heating in the pan.

Stir constantly over the fire until the cornflour boils and thickens, and allow it to simmer at least five minutes.

Then remove from the fire and add the sugar and any flavouring desired. Next add the yolk of egg and mix it in.

Beat up the white of egg to a stiff froth and stir it lightly into the mixture.

Pour all into a greased pie-dish and wipe carefully round the edges of the dish. Bake the pudding in a moderate oven until it is nicely browned and well risen. Lift out, sprinkle lightly with sugar, and serve as quickly as possible. A little cream and some stewed fruit may be served with it.—g.h. (2).

CORNISH HEAVY CAKE

About ½ lb. of flour, 2 oz. of butter, 2 oz. of lard, 4 oz. chopped raisins, 4 oz. of currants or sultanas, ½ oz. of nutmeg, half a teaspoonful of mixed spice, 2 oz. of lemon peel, 3 oz. of castor sugar, 2 eggs, salt. Mix well together into a fairly stiff mixture, using milk to moisten if necessary. Roll out to 1½ in. thickness and bake on a flat greased tin for about half an hour.—m.b. (2).

167

CORNISH PASTIES

I

>   1 lb. of good, short pastry
>   ½ lb. of steak
>   ¼ lb. of kidney
>   ½ lb. of potatoes

Cut the steak, kidney and peeled potatoes into dice, season with pepper and salt. Roll pastry, cut into rounds about the size of a tea-saucer. Put a quarter of the diced mixture on the pastry rounds, fold over and crimp the edges, brush over with egg and bake in a fairly hot oven at first, and then reduce the heat a little and bake about one hour. Diced turnips and onions can be used as well as potatoes, if liked. The secret of this recipe is to use good, fresh meat; they are not good made with cooked meat. Sufficient for six people.—L.G.N.

II

Cornish pasties are also very good filled only with vegetables, such as leeks, with, if possible, a teaspoon of Devonshire cream (or top of the milk) added to each pasty. The leeks should be raw and cut up fairly finely and the cream added just before folding over the pasty. Bake for about 30 or 40 minutes (as there is no meat, less time is required than in the preceding recipe) and serve the finished pasty with a good, rich gravy. Of course, the pasties should be seasoned with pepper and salt.—L.C.

CORNISH SPLITS

>   3 lb. flour
>   ½ lb. butter
>   2 oz. lard
>   2 oz. yeast
>   A little milk, salt, sugar and about
>   half pint warm water

Put the yeast in a basin with a teaspoonful of sugar, the warm water and a teaspoonful of flour and leave to work in a warm place. Warm the milk, butter and lard together and warm the flour. Put flour in a basin, make a well in the middle and add liquid ingredients, make into a soft dough and leave to rise for 1½ hours in a warm place. When it is well risen, knead again and roll out ½ in. thick, then cut into pieces, which when rolled into balls are the size of a tangerine; flatten the top a little and bake in a medium oven for ¼ to ½ hour until each split is a golden brown. Serve cold, split open and fill with Cornish cream and jam.—M.K.S. (2).

CORN-MEAL BATTERCAKES
(for 4)

>   1 cup of white corn meal
>   ½ cup of flour
>   ½ teaspoon of salt
>   2 eggs

>   1½ cups of buttermilk
>   ½ cup of buttermilk
>   3 tablespoons of melted butter; melted or creamed butter; or cream and cinnamon mixed with powdered sugar
>   1 teaspoon of baking soda

Sift together one cup of white corn meal, half cup of flour, and half teaspoon of salt. Beat two eggs well, add to them 1½ cups of buttermilk and make a smooth batter by pouring into the dry ingredients. Now dissolve a scant level teaspoon of baking soda in another half cup of buttermilk and stir it into the batter. Then, last of all, stir in three tablespoons of melted butter. Cook on hot griddle, rubbed over with a piece of bacon rind. Be sure the griddle is not smoking hot, but very hot. Use a pancake turner to turn them over at the moment when the top surface is covered with little holes. Serve with melted or creamed butter, or try them with cream and a sprinkle of cinnamon mixed with powdered sugar.—J.P.

CORN-MEAL BREAD

A cup of sour milk is scalded, and a pinch of salt and enough corn meal to make a batter are added. The mixture is then left in a warm place overnight to sour. In the morning, a pint of warm milk and enough flour to make a batter are added, and this is then set in a warm place for about two hours, in which time it will have risen sufficiently. It should be baked in a slow oven for about 40 to 50 minutes.—L.M. (2).

CORN-MEAL DODGERS

Place a pint of milk in a saucepan with three saltspoonfuls of salt; set on the fire, and as soon as it comes to the boil, dredge in ½ lb. of Indian corn meal, briskly mixing while adding; let it boil for six minutes, stirring at the bottom occasionally. Add an ounce of butter, one egg yolk and a little grated nutmeg; mix well for one minute; put the mixture in a dish and let it cool. Divide the batter into 12 even parts, form into oval shapes and place on a buttered baking-sheet, lightly baste with melted butter and put into a slack oven for 20 minutes. Remove, split them open, put in a little good butter and serve.—M.B. (2).

CORN STICKS

>   1 cup corn meal
>   1¼ cups milk
>   ¾ cup flour
>   2 eggs
>   ¼ cup molasses
>   4 teaspoons baking powder
>   1 teaspoon salt
>   2 tablespoons cooking oil
>   2 tablespoons butter

Sift together flour, salt and baking powder. Pour scalded milk over corn meal and mix thoroughly. Let cool until lukewarm, then add molasses and well-beaten eggs. Lastly, add cooking oil and melted butter. Pour mixture into greased bread-stick pan and bake in hot oven for 20 minutes.—L.R.

CORNUCOPIAS À LA CRÈME (Cornets)

Have some tin moulds made in the shape of cornucopias. Line them with paste turning a bit over the moulds to form an edge. When baked fill them with a cream made like a rich custard, put them into the oven for a few minutes to dry, but take care they do not colour in the least.—G.A.S.

COULIBIAC

A Russian light or puff paste which may be made in many different manners. Here is the recipe for one kind of *Coulibiac*:

½ lb. flour, a tumblerful of warm milk and a pinch of yeast are worked with a spatula till it makes a smooth batter; it is then left in a warm place until it is risen well. Then add ½ lb. flour, ½ lb. melted butter, 7 eggs and a pinch of salt. Mix well and work it lightly on a floured board. Put it back in the basin to rest and ferment one hour in a warm place.

In the meantime you will prepare and cook whatever is intended to go into the *Coulibiac*, whether meat or fish with various garnishings such as mushrooms, olives, etc. These being ready, you will shape the batter as a ball, roll it, then flatten it on a floured board into a long shape, about 1 in. thick, 12 in. wide and 20 in. long. Place this on a well-floured cloth and build the *Coulibiac* in layers of meat, fish, sliced hard-boiled eggs, etc., in the middle of the batter. The ends and sides are then tucked up and in, as if making a brown paper parcel, the outside of which is painted with yolk of egg. Make two chimneys for the steam to escape and bake in a hot oven for 40 minutes.

COUNTRY GINGERBREAD

Rub 4 oz. of butter into 2 lb. of flour, add ¼ lb. brown sugar, 2 oz. ground ginger, ½ oz. ground caraway seeds, then mix to this 2 lb. of treacle and three well-whisked eggs and, last of all, ½ oz. of carbonate of soda dissolved in a small cup of warm water. Stir the whole briskly together, well grease a shallow tin and half fill it only, as the gingerbread should rise and be very light. Put it into a moderate oven and bake for an hour and a half; when cold, cut it up into thick squares.

The oven must be very steady, and it is well to line the tin with heavily-buttered greaseproof paper and to lay another sheet over the top, as all treacle cakes and puddings are liable to burn outside before they are cooked in the middle.—P.A.

CRACKERS

The American equivalent of the English *Biscuits* (q.v.), chiefly flour and water.

CRACKNELS

The English equivalent of the French *Craquelins*, little glazed *cornsticks* (q.v.).

To make Cracknels (1807)

Rub 2 oz. of butter into ½ lb. of fine flour, and put to it ½ lb. of loaf sugar, pounded and sifted, and ½ oz. of caraway seeds; mix it up with the yolks of three eggs, and as much cream as will make it into a paste; roll them very thin and bake them on tins, in a cool oven, 10 minutes.—A.A.

CREAM PANCAKES

Mix the yolks of two eggs with half pint of cream, 2 oz. of sugar, some beaten cinnamon, mace and nutmeg. Fry them as quickly as possible, and grate over them some lump sugar.—G.A.S.

CREAM WAFFLES

½ cup cooking oil
1½ cups milk
3 teaspoons baking powder
2 eggs
3 cups flour
4 tablespoons sugar
1 teaspoon salt

Mix and sift dry ingredients. Beat into the egg yolks first the oil and then the milk. Combine the two mixtures and beat until smooth. Fold in well-beaten egg whites. Pour three-quarters of a cup of batter on hot waffle iron. Bake three to four minutes.—L.R.

CRÊPES

The French name for *Pancakes* (q.v.), which were known in Chaucer's England and long after as *Cresp* and *Crisps*.

CRÊPES ANTONIN CARÊME

Faire les Crêpes selon l'usage.

Préparer d'autre part une Crème au Beurre comme suit:

Travailler dans un Bol avec une Spatule de bois un morceau de beurre très frais jusqu'à ce qu'il soit en Pommade; ajouter du sucre en poudre vanillé (soit pour 225 grammes de beurre, une cuillerée à soupe de Sucre) et un demi verre de Kirsch d'Alsace, ainsi que les larmes d'un quart de Citron.

Tartiner vos Crêpes avec cette pommade sans en mettre sur les bords; plier le Crêpe en quatre en avant soin de ramener auparavant les bords vers le centre.

Placer ces Crêpes sur un plat beurré, saupoudrer de Sucre vanillé et passer ce plat deux minutes dans un four vif ou sous la Salamandre.

Servir de suite, et arroser de Kirsch d'Alsace que vous flamberez.—F.L.

CRÊPES SUZETTE

There are practically as many different types of pancakes bearing this name as there are *Maîtres d'hôtel* to make them, as a rule, by the table of the expectant clients. The original *Crêpe Suzette* was introduced by Monsieur Joseph, in 1897, when in charge of the Restaurant Marivaux, in-Paris. There was a play at the Comédie Françaíse at the time in which a maid, called Suzette, had to bring in some pancakes, and these were supplied by the Restaurant Marivaux. Hence the choice of the name *Suzette*, which Joseph gave to his pancakes dipped into a sizzling mixture of butter, sugar and orange juice. The real and original *Crêpe Suzette* had no multicoloured liqueurs in it, but orange juice and naught else. Joseph came to London when Ritz left the Savoy; he replaced Ritz and introduced the *Crêpes Suzette* to London Society at the Savoy.

CRESCIONI

Boil a bunch of spinach, drain it well and put it to simmer with some pure olive oil, a taste of shallot, some chopped parsley and salt and pepper to taste; season with some raisins (stoned) and some currants, and a little sugar. Put the spinach into rounds of paste made of flour and eggs, about 2 in. in diameter, and fold the paste over the spinach (as you make a turnover). Fry in pure olive oil.—J.R.

CROISSANT

A fancy roll made with some *feuilletage* (q.v.) in the shape of a crescent. It originated in 1686, in Budapest, when the attacking Turks were defeated thanks to the Buda bakers who, during their night baking, detected the enemy's approach and gave the alarm in time. *Croissants* have been popular ever since in Hungary and in Austria, and in more recent times, in France and elsewhere as well.

CROMESQUIS

The French culinary name of the more elaborate forms of *Croquettes* (q.v.). They are usually made up of all sorts of *Salpicons* which are rolled in batter and then fried.

CROQUENBOUCHE

A French culinary term for any toothsome small, crisp pastry.

CROQUETTES

Crisp balls made up of all manner of *salpicons*

fried and served mostly as trimmings. The informing flavour of the most popular forms of *Croquettes* are the following:

Bignon: Crayfish.

Brantôme: Fois gras, truffles and chicken, in the shape of a cork, not of a ball.

Favart: Truffles, mushrooms and *palais de boeuf*, in the shape of a small egg, not of a ball.

Gorenflot: Soft roes, shrimps, mushrooms and truffles.

Judic: Celeriac, carrots, French beans, mushrooms, and a tomato sauce.

à la Monègasque: Macaroni, crayfish, mushrooms, truffles and a tomato sauce; in the shape of a small egg.

à la Nimoise: *Brandade de morue*: truffles and white wine sauce.

à la Reine: Chicken, truffles and mushrooms, in the shape of a cork.

à la Royale: Fois gras, truffles and mushrooms.

Sagan: Brains, artichoke bottoms, onions and curry sauce.

Sévigné: Chicken, *cèpes* and truffles, with a sauce *Soubise*.

à la Tyrolienne: Rice, sweet pimentoes, tomatoes, mushrooms, onions and paprika sauce.

CROQUIGNOLES

The French name of a certain kind of *Cracknel*, glazed, small hard biscuits of different shapes, some long like little sticks and others round like small buttons.

CROUSTADE

A French culinary term which refers to a large edition of a hot *Pâté* (q.v.).

CROÛTE, La or Une

French for a crust of bread.

CROUTES

The French culinary name for round or oval pieces of stale crumb fried in butter or any other fat, used as a foundation upon which all manner of fish, flesh and vegetables preparation are served either as hors-d'oeuvre, savouries, canapés or for garnishings.

Also the name of thin slices of stale crusty bread, toasted or not, which are added to some soups at the time of serving. The addition of these Croutes is optional except in the case of *Croûte au Pot* and *Petite Marmite*.

CROÛTONS

The French culinary name of dice of stale bread crumb fried in butter and added to some vegetable *purées*, chiefly spinach and peas, or to thick cream soups (*Veloutés*).

CROWDIE. CROWDY

'Oh that I had ne'er been married,
I wad never had nae care,
Now I've gotten wife and weans,
And they cry "Crowdie" ever mair.'

Burns

There are many kinds of Crowdie. The Lowland Crowdie is just milk and coarse oatmeal stirred together. The Highland Crowdie (Gaelic: 'Fuarag') is sometimes made of soured milk well whipped and mixed with toasted oatmeal. More often it is eaten as a very nourishing cheese, and here are the directions as made in Skye: Heat some sour milk slowly until it separates, but on no account must it boil. Strain off the whey. Season the cheese (or solid matter) with salt and a little pepper. To get out the moisture it should be pressed in a muslin bag. It should stand for a day or two.—M.D.

CRULLERS. CURLERS

Pastry which is cut in strips or 'curls' and fried in deep fat.

Crullers

Beat together three whole eggs, four table-spoonfuls of butter or lard (just heated enough to make it mix readily, but not oiled, or the mixture will be heavy); then work in enough flour to make a dough that will roll nicely, and roll it out in a sheet ¼ in. thick. Cut this into strips 3½ in. long by 2 in. broad; slit each piece twice, giving each a twist, and fry in plenty of smoking hot fat to a delicate brown. Drain well, and, if liked, dust with a little sugar.—Q. (1).

CRUMPETS

These are made in the same manner as muffins, with milk, flour, yeast and salt, and they share with muffins the honours of most middle-class tea-tables in England. They are usually bought from the baker, or from the itinerant street vendor in large towns, and toasted in front of a bright clear fire to a nice brown at tea-time, and spread with plenty of fresh butter.

Crumpets

One pint of warm milk, 1 lb. flour, ¼ pint brewers' yeast, 1 egg, 1 oz. butter and a little salt. Mix all ingredients together, beat well and leave to rise until bubbles are formed on top, then bake them in small polished iron rings on top of an iron baking-sheet. Crumpets may be cooked in an iron frying-pan with moderate heat underneath; turn when half done.—M.K.S. (2).

CRUSTS (Pastry)
Plain Short Crust

½ lb. flour
4 oz. butter
Salt
Water
Pinch baking powder or a few drops of lemon juice

Rub all butter into dry ingredients until like breadcrumbs. Add water and make into very stiff smooth paste. Yolk of egg may be added.—P.R.M.

Rich Short Pastry (For Tarts, Flans, etc.)

½ lb. flour
6 oz. butter or shortening
1 oz. castor sugar
Yolk of 1 egg
Water
Salt

Mix dry ingredients. Rub shortening in until like dry breadcrumbs. Mix to very stiff paste with egg and a very little water. Roll out and use.—P.R.M.

Suet Crust or Pastry

½ lb. flour
¼ teaspoon baking powder
Pinch of salt
Water to make a stiff paste
¼ lb. suet

Chop suet finely, or shred it if rendered suet is used. Add dry ingredients, mix well and make into stiff dough with water. Turn on to floured board, roll out and use. Wet the crust round the edges of basin to keep gravy from running out.—P.R.M.

CSIPETKE
(Hungarian Dumplings)

1 lb. flour
2 eggs
Water
2 spoonfuls of lard
Salt

Csipetke is a stiff paste made of flour, eggs and water. It is kneaded, then rolled out to the thickness of ⅛ in. and cut into strips of about the same thickness. Then little pieces the size of a bean are pinched off, rolled lightly between the fingers and either cooked in boiling water (they must boil a few seconds after rising to the surface of the water, when they are shaken and basted with lard to prevent them sticking together) or put into the gulyas (meat stew) to boil.—M.K.S. (2).

CUILLÈRE, BISCUIT A LA

2 lb. eggs (separated), less 4 yolks
1 lb. fine castor sugar
14 oz. cake flour

First of all prepare three or four baking sheets (according to size) by making them warm, covering well with clarified lard, and a coating of flour dusted on and well shaken off.

Now beat up the whites and sugar into a firm meringue (adding the sugar gradually), stir in the strained yolks lightly and then gently but thoroughly mix in the well-sifted flour. Scrape down the sides of the pan with the help of a spatula, tilt the pan to one side, and, using a dessert spoon, take up a spoonful and drop into oval form on to the prepared tins, beginning at the top end, and laying out in rows. Drop the biscuits as deftly as you can, all the same size, finishing each biscuit with a sharp little twist of the spoon that is quickly acquired with a little practice.

When all are ready, dredge lightly each biscuit with pulverized sugar and let them rest for 10 or 15 minutes, by which time the biscuits will have obtained a hold on the tins, and each tin can be turned upside down, just lightly to shake off any sugar that is not wanted. By this time also the sugar on the biscuits will be partially moistened, and when baked in oven at 400° F. the melted sugar will rise in the form of small pearls all over the biscuits.

When cold these biscuits will lift easily from the prepared tins.—A.A.B.

CURRANT LOAF

> 2 lb. of flour
> ¼ lb. of butter
> 5 oz. of sugar
> 5 oz. of currants
> 5 oz. of sultanas
> 3 oz. of candied peel
> 3 eggs
> ¾ pint of warm milk
> Pinch of salt
> 1 oz. of compressed yeast

Rub butter into flour, add fruit and sugar; beat eggs, milk and yeast; set aside for a little time, then knead and set aside to rise. Bake in good oven.—M.B. (2).

DAFFODIL CAKE

> 1 cup sifted cake flour
> 1 cup egg whites (about 8 eggs)
> 1 teaspoon cream of tartar
> ¼ teaspoon orange extract
> 1¼ cups sifted sugar
> ½ teaspoon salt
> ½ teaspoon vanilla
> 4 egg yolks beaten until thick and
>   lemon coloured

Sift the flour once, measure, add three-quarters of a cup of sugar, and sift four times. Beat egg whites and salt until foamy, add cream of tartar, and continue beating until stiff enough to hold up in peaks, but not dry. Beat in remaining sugar, two tablespoonfuls at a time. Sift flour over mixture in small amounts, folding it in carefully. Divide in two parts. To one, fold in vanilla. To the other, fold in beaten egg yolks and orange extract. Put in ungreased angel cake-pan by tablespoons, alternating mixtures. Bake in a slow oven (275° F.) 30 minutes. Then increase heat to 325° F. and bake 50 minutes longer. Remove from oven and invert pan one hour or until cold. *Mary G. Chandler.* —T.C.

DARI. DARRI. DURRA

Lat. *Sorghum durra*. The small, whitish, round seeds of *Sorghum* (q.v.), ground to make a meal or flour for human consumption in many parts of Africa, Arabia and India. In England the seeds are chiefly imported for cage birds, game and poultry food.

DARIOLE

A very old English word which is used in French culinary parlance and passes for a French word. It means a small cheesecake. In Chaucer's time it was called *Daryal*, or Maid Royal, and has survived as *Maid of Honour*, a form of pastry still popular at City banquets.

DARTOIS

Small pieces of light pastry paste, lightly baked, and used to serve little tit-bits of fish or flesh as hors-d'oeuvre or trimmings.

DATE BREAD

This is a variety of Cake Bread or Currant Loaf, made of a milk and flour dough with stoned dates worked into it, and baked in the usual way.

DEMEL TARTELETTEN

(Austrian)

Make some paste from 9 oz. flour, 6 oz. butter, 3 oz. sugar and 1 yolk of egg, little grated lemon rind. Follow same method as for Linzer paste. Let paste rest. Then roll out, cut in rounds about 2 in. across, and bake lightly. Should be about the thickness of Scots shortbread.

Stick two together with red currant jelly or jam, and glaze with chocolate icing, which must have a high gloss, and coat sides completely. Melt some sweet chocolate with a little bitter chocolate over very low heat in strong pan, or put pan in another pan containing water. When softened, add gradually enough stock syrup (see below) to make thick creamy consistency. Beat very well, and add at last moment tiny nut of butter. Chocolate icing should never be allowed to become hot or it goes dull.

Stock Syrup

Quarter of a pint water and ¼ lb. sugar boiled together. Can be bottled and kept; is useful for ices, syrups, etc.—D.L.T.

DERBYSHIRE PUDDING

Take a pint of milk and two tablespoonfuls of flour; mix by degrees, boil till thick, and set by till cold; then add 3 oz. of butter beaten to a cream, ¼ lb. of fine sugar, a little salt, the rind of a lemon grated, the yolks of five and whites of three eggs; mix thoroughly, put a paste round the dish and bake in a quick oven. This pudding is very good cold.—G.A.S.

DEVILLED BISCUITS

> Butter
> Cayenne pepper
> French mustard
> Anchovy paste
> Salt
> Salt flaky biscuits

Mix all ingredients – and be lavish with the butter. Spread thickly on the biscuits and grill them until sizzling. Strips of fried bread or of baked crisp pastry can be used instead of biscuits and grated cheese may be used instead of anchovy paste.—P.W.

DEVON CAKES

> ½ lb. clotted cream
> 1 lb. flour
> 1 egg
> ½ lb. sugar
> A little milk

Rub the cream into the flour, beat in the egg, add the sugar and mix into a smooth paste, adding a little milk if necessary to make it the consistency of dough. Roll out rather thin and cut into small shapes. Sprinkle each with granulated sugar and bake in a quick oven for about 10 minutes. —H.E.

DEVONSHIRE CHUDLEIGHS

They are made in the same manner as *Cornish Splits* (q.v.), but usually a little smaller.

DIABETIC BREAD

Mix together 4 oz. almond flour, two tablespoonfuls of gluten flour, two teaspoonfuls of baking powder, 10 oz. of butter previously creamed, and salt to taste; then work in two whole eggs, one by one, beating each in well, and pour the mixture into a shallow pan and bake for 20 minutes.—Q. (1).

DIET BREAD

Sift together 4 lb. granulated wheat meal, 2 oz. cream of tartar, and 1 oz. bicarbonate of potash; make a hollow in the centre of this meal with your knuckles (a 'bay', as it is technically called) and into this put 1 oz. fine salt, 2 oz. castor sugar, and just enough churned milk to dissolve the salt and sugar; when these are quite melted, work into it just enough churned milk to bring it all to a nice, smooth dough, then mould in buttered tins, and bake at once.—Q. (1).

DIGESTIVE BISCUITS

Rub 1 lb. of butter into 5 lb. of wheat meal; make a hollow in the centre and pour into this four lightly beaten up eggs, with 4 oz. sugar and ¼ oz. of carbonate of soda; mix this all to a little pool of batter in the centre of the flour, then gradually draw down the latter from the sides with a circular motion of your fingers, moistening the dough thus produced with about one quart of water, added by degrees, till you get it all to a nice workable consistency. Take up one-third of this dough and roll it out to the thickness of a penny; spread a clean cloth on the kitchen table, lift the dough on to the rolling-pin and roll it out again on the cloth, then cut it into oval or round cakes, prick these and place them in the oven. Finish off the rest of the dough in the same way.—Q. (1).

DIKA or ODIKA BREAD

This is made in the West African forests from the seeds (*oba*) of the Ibo tree (*Irvingia Carteri*). The plums are gathered, as they fall from the tree, into large heaps where they remain until the outside has putrified; then the stones are cracked and the kernels or almonds taken out and smoked for some days. Next they are put into a large mortar to be crushed and agglomerated into a homogeneous mass, weighing 10 lb. to 12 lb. This is exposed to the rays of the sun, which causes the fatty portion (like *Cacao butter*) to melt and separate. It is somewhat darker in colour than palm oil and about the same consistency. The flavour resembles that of cokernut oil and it is very suitable for confectionery purposes. *Dika* is generally moulded into cakes; it will keep good for six months, and the natives of the Cameroons eat it as a flavouring ingredient.—L.G.M.

DITALINI

A variety of Italian Paste in the form of thick pipes, cut diagonally, 2 in. to 4 in. long, and often artificially coloured yellow.

DOBOS CAKE
(Hungarian)

> 8 eggs
> 2 oz. sugar
> 2 oz. melted butter
> 4 oz. flour

Whip the whites of eggs very stiff with a little sugar and add gradually the other ingredients. Mix in last of all the flour. Spread the mixture thinly over three to four baking sheets and bake separately. Fill with the following cream:

Cream

4½ oz. butter, sugar to taste; three dessert-spoonfuls very strong black coffee; two dessertspoonfuls flour.

Cream the butter and add gradually the other ingredients, let the cream stand on ice for a few minutes. Ice the cake with caramel icing.—E.B.

DODGER BREAD

The Middle West name for *Corn Bread* (q.v.), known in the Southern States as *Ponebread*.

DOLLY MADISON CAKE

1 lb. of butter
1 lb. of sugar
1 lb. of flour
1 lb. of raisins
½ lb. of citron chopped fine
1 nutmeg (ground)
6 eggs
1 gill of brandy
1 gill of rosewater
½ teaspoon of soda dissolved in a
    little water

Mix in the usual way and bake in a moderate oven until you can run a straw through the cake without the dough sticking, or until the cake shrinks from the pan.

This recipe was given by a descendant of Dolly Madison.—G.T.L.

DOUGH

A soft mass of moistened flour or meal, the solid form of a *Batter* thick enough to roll or knead to make pastry, bread, biscuits or cakes.

DOUGH CAKE

Ingredients: Flour, 2 lb.; butter, ½ lb.; sugar, ½ lb.; currants, ½ lb.; warm milk, 1 pint; compressed yeast, 1 oz.

Time: To rise, over 1 hour; to bake, 1 to 1½ hours in hot oven which may be gradually slackened.

Method: 1. Rub butter into flour; 2. Add the dry ingredients and mix well; 3. Cream the yeast with a little of the sugar; 4. Mix it with the lukewarm milk; 5. Stir it into the flour, etc., and make it into a light dough; 6. Stand in a warm place to rise for more than 1 hour, then bake as above.—FL.W.

DOUGHNUTS

Cakes made of dough and lard and fried in deep fat. They are stodgy and more satisfy-ing than satisfactory, fare for the hungry schoolboy rather than for the discriminating gastronome. There are, however, some 'de luxe' *Doughnuts*, made with butter instead of lard, such as the following: they are not true to the original standard, but are all the better for it.

I

2 oz. butter
1 lb. flour
½ oz. yeast
2 eggs
1 oz. castor sugar
½ gill warm milk
Pinch of salt
Raspberry jam and frying fat

Mix flour, salt and castor sugar; mix well, divide into two lots and pass through sieve into two basins. Into one rub butter, in the other mix yeast and milk. Let it rise for half an hour, then mix both together and beat in the eggs. Now let the mixture stand in a warm place for an hour, to rise. Knead and divide into 24 pieces, shape each into a round ball, make a hole and insert a little jam into the centres; close up securely using a little egg to moisten the edges. Let them stand on a floured tin for 10 minutes to 'prove'. Cook them in deep boiling fat, only a few at a time, until they are a golden brown colour; dry on kitchen paper and roll in castor sugar.—H.E.

II

Doughnuts are made of dough fried in rings. The dough is made of butter, quarter of a cup, creamed with a cup of granulated sugar, three eggs, a teaspoonful of salt and two of baking powder, some 2½ cups of flour seasoned with powdered cinnamon and nut-meg, a large pinch of each (if one pinch be larger, make it the cinnamon), and enough milk to make a stiff dough. Roll it, cut with a doughnut cutter and fry in deep oil, not too many at a time. Dust with powdered sugar. The cut out centres may be fried 'as is' or rolled again. A doughnut by any other shape is called a 'cruller', usually long drawn out, doubled and twisted.—C.B.

DUKE OF CAMBRIDGE PUDDING

Line a dish or flan ring with paste, short or puff, and make the following mixture: Mix 3 oz. of butter, the same of castor sugar and the yolks of two eggs in a saucepan. Cut up 2 oz. of candied peel very finely and put it in a layer in the pastry case. Let the mixture in the saucepan come to the boil and pour it quickly over the peel, baking the tart till the top is nicely browned in a rather slack oven. Do not be afraid of boiling the mixture, as this results in a deliciously crinkled surface to the tart. There are two refinements of this dish: the first is to soak the cut-up peel for an hour or so in some liqueur, and the second is to use crystallized fruits instead of the peel. In every case it is really first-class.—w.f. (4).

DUMPLINGS

One of the most characteristically English contributions to cookery. Half a pound of beef fat finely chopped; ½ lb. of flour and ½ lb. of breadcrumbs form the basis; three eggs and a tumblerful of milk to moisten the whole; salt and pepper, of course. Mix well together, divide into balls the size of a turkey's egg, tie the balls in a cloth and boil for three-quarters of an hour. This is an old recipe which has many variants according to district and housewives. *Norfolk Dumplings*, for instance, are made of a batter (flour, eggs and milk) dropped in spoonfuls into boiling water and boiled for about 10 minutes. *Fruit Dumplings* are made of various fruits encased in batter, none being more justly popular than the *Apple Dumpling*. (See Section IV, *Fruit*.)

There is also a type of *Dumpling*, sometimes called *Hard Dumpling* or *Sussex Dumpling*, made simply with flour and water in the following manner:

Ingredients: 1 lb. of flour, ½ pint of water, ½ saltspoonful of salt.

Mode: Mix the flour and water together to a smooth paste, previously adding a small quantity of salt. Form this into small, round dumplings; drop them into boiling water, and boil from half to three-quarters of an hour. They may be served with roast or boiled meat; in the latter case they may be cooked with the meat, but should be dropped into the water when it is quite boiling.—b. (2).

DUNDEE CAKE

½ lb. each of flour, butter, sugar, currants, glacé cherries
¼ lb. ground rice
2 oz. mixed spice
3 eggs
2 tablespoons milk
2 tablespoons ground almonds
2 oz. whole almonds

Beat butter to a cream, add sugar, the yolks of egg, one at a time, adding some of the flour between yolks. Beat whites stiff and add them then to the ground rice. Beat well for 20 minutes, then add fruit, peel and ground almonds. Butter your cake tins and flour them before putting in mixture. Cover top of cakes with split almonds before baking. This mixture will make two cakes. —M.K.S.

EASTER BREAD
(Russian)

½ pint milk
1 lb. flour
6 oz. butter
6 oz. sugar
6 egg yolks
4½ oz. candied fruit
1 oz. yeast

Dissolve the yeast in the warm milk, mix with half the flour and let it rise. Beat up the yolks of eggs with sugar, and when the dough has risen mix the eggs with it and the butter, melted. Then add the rest of the flour and the chopped fruit. Beat the mixture well and leave to rise again. Form into a long loaf or twist and bake in fairly quick oven.—M.K.S. (2).

EASTER BUNS

Take 1 lb. of fine flour, some sugar, a little salt, a quarter of a pint of warm milk, 4 oz. of butter, 1 oz. of German yeast, one egg, and knead the whole up into a light dough. Let it remain in the basin in a warm place for one hour to rise, put the dough on the slab, make small buns, put in baking-tin to rise, bake in rather quick oven for 25 minutes, and in the top make a hole and fill it with marzipan. These may be served either hot or cold with powdered cinnamon. (*The Baroness Palmstierna*.)—L.M. (2).

EAST INDIA ARROWROOT

The starch obtained from the root-stocks of the *Curcuma*, a plant which is extensively grown in Southern India not merely for the sake of its starchy content but for *Turmeric* (q.v.).

ECCLES CAKES

Wash ¼ lb. of currants and mix them with one equal weight of moist sugar, a little nutmeg and a little rum. Rub 1 lb. of butter into 1 lb. of flour, roll out about ½ in. thick, cut into squares about 3 in. across, then put some of the currant mixture in the centre of each square. Wet the edges and join the four corners of the square in the centre. Turn over and roll lightly with the rolling-pin to make a round cake. Bake in a fairly hot oven. —M.K.S. (2).

ÉCLAIRS

Small, puff-paste buns, finger-like in shape and filled with either chocolate or coffee cream. Their name is believed to be due to the lightning speed of their consumption by children – and others – who have not reached the age of discretion.

2 oz. butter
¼ pint boiling water
Whipped cream .

Glacé icing
4 oz. flour
3 or 4 eggs
Sugar and flavouring

Use a saucepan to make the paste. Put in the butter and add the water gradually, stirring all the time. When the butter is melted, add the flour, dry and sieved, and stir vigorously. Cook until the mass is thick and smooth, and does not stick to the sides of the pan. Stir constantly to avoid burning. Then remove the saucepan from the fire and allow the paste to cool slightly. Add the unbeaten eggs one at a time, beating thoroughly until the mixture is smooth and pliable before adding the next one. The mixture should be of medium stiffness and the number of eggs depends somewhat upon their size; it is very important to have them absolutely fresh. Beat the mixture again when all the eggs are added. Put the paste into a pastry bag with a round tube of ¼ in. diameter. Force the paste through in strips 3½ in. to 4 in. long, and bake at 400° F. for 35 minutes. Allow to cool thoroughly, make slits in the side and insert the whipped cream and coat the top with chocolate (or coffee) glacé icing.—G.H. (4).

EIERKUCKAS

The name of rich Alsatian *Pancakes*, made with a cream batter and with either red currant or raspberry jelly folded in.

EINKORN

Lat. *Triticum monococcum*; Fr. *Petit épautre*. A chaffy wheat usually known by its German name (which means) one-grain'. It is a distinct type of wheat which is cultivated in poor soil in Spain, Switzerland and South Germany.

ELECTION CAKE (1805)

Thirty quarts flour, 10 lb. butter, 14 lb. sugar, 12 lb. raisins, 3 dozen eggs, 1 pint wine, 1 quart brandy, 4 oz. cinnamon, 4 oz. fine colander seed, 3 oz. ground allspice; wet the flour with milk to the consistency of bread overnight, adding one quart yeast; the next morning work the butter and sugar together for half an hour, which will render the cake much lighter and whiter; when it has risen light, work in every other ingredient except the raisins, which work in when putting into the oven.—A.L. (2).

ELECTION CAKE

(A Colonial Recipe)
1 cup chicken fat or clarified beef dripping
1 cup light brown sugar
1 pint milk
Flour
2 tablespoons finely-chopped citron
1½ yeast cakes

2 eggs
½ teaspoon salt
½ teaspoon each ground mace and nutmeg
1 cup seeded raisins
½ cup sherry
Few drops of rose extract
Grated rind of half a lemon
Pinch of soda

Begin making cake early in the afternoon. Cream fat and sugar, add milk, yeast dissolved in a few teaspoonfuls of tepid water, and flour enough to make a stiff batter. Beat mixture well, cover, and put in a warm place to rise. At night, when very light, add eggs well beaten, salt, mace and nutmeg, and additional flour to make the consistency of cake batter. Again cover and let stand overnight. In the morning, add raisins, sherry, rose extract, citron, and lemon rind. Beat the thick batter vigorously, add soda dissolved in a teaspoonful of hot water. Beat again and pour into a large pan lined with greased paper. Let stand until loaf doubles in size. Bake in moderate oven.—C.R.B.B. (2).

EMMER WHEAT

Lat. *Triticum dicoccum*. One of the most ancient types of wheat grown in Southern Europe; it is still grown in Switzerland and some of the adjoining parts of Southern Germany.

ENGLISH WHEAT

Fr. *Froment renflé*. A variety of wheat which, despite its name, is not grown in the British Isles. It is rarely seen outside the Mediterranean region and its flour is of low gluten content and makes but poor quality bread.

EUGENIES

Blanch 3 oz. of almonds and pound to a firm paste with 2 oz. of sugar and 1 tablespoonful of cold water. Add another ounce of sugar and 1 egg; mix with a wooden spoon; add 1 more yolk and mix well. Add 1½ oz. of flour, half a saltspoonful of salt, 1 tablespoonful of curaçoa. Mix well for 5 minutes and bake in buttered moulds for 15 minutes. Dredge a little vanilla sugar over them and serve hot.—M.B. (2).

FAIRY SPONGE CAKE

6 eggs
Salt
½ teaspoon cream of tartar
1¼ cups granulated sugar
1 teaspoon vanilla
1 cup flour

Beat whites of eggs until foamy. Add the pinch of salt and the cream of tartar, and beat very stiff. Add granulated sugar, sifted, and beat well. Beat yolks of eggs until light and add to mixture. Add vanilla. Fold in lightly the flour, after having been sifted four times. (Every stroke of the spoon after the flour has been added tends to toughen the cake.) Bake in a slow oven, in an ungreased pan, 45 to 50 minutes. Like Angel Cake, it must be put in a pan that has never been greased for baking, otherwise it will come away from the sides of the pan when taken from the oven and fall slightly. Turn cake in pan upside down, to allow to fall, then remove from pan.—P.D.P.

FARINA
A name which is used for a number of different articles of food, such as:
(a) A fine meal of flour of any kind of grain, starchy root, or nut;
(b) The purified middlings of hard wheat other than *Durum*;
(c) A purified starchy powder or meal made from potatoes;
(d) A patent breakfast food, prepared as follows: ½ lb. *Farina* cooked for 15 minutes in six cupfuls of water with half a teaspoonful of salt.

FARINA DOLCE
The name of an Italian 'sweet' flour made from dried and ground chestnuts.

FARINA DUMPLINGS
Recipe makes 18 small dumplings.

    1 cup milk
    1 teaspoon butter
    ⅓ cup farina
    2 eggs
    2 teaspoons salt
    Pepper

1. Scald milk in double-boiler; add butter.
2. Add farina slowly, stirring until thick and smooth. Cover and cook 15 minutes.
3. Cool; add well-beaten eggs. Mix well; add salt and a little pepper.
4. Form into small balls and drop into boiling salted water or soup stock about 15 minutes before serving.
5. Serve with meat stew or gravy. Buttered crumbs, or very small croûtons, may be sprinkled on the dumplings when served plain as a substitute for potatoes or rice.—M.E.A.

FARLS. FARLES
In Scotland in cottage and farmhouse the oatcake bannock was usually divided into four quarters before being placed on the girdle, and each quarter was called a farle (A.S. feorth-dael). At more elegant tea-tables the farles would be much smaller, being quarters of smaller bannocks, and trimmed into neat little three-cornered cakes. Some bakers call such cakes farles if thin and bannocks if thick.—E.M.L.D.

FASTNACHT KUCKA
    1½ quarts milk
    4 quarts flour
    2 cakes yeast
    ½ cup warm water
    1 cup butter
    4 eggs, beaten
    6 tablespoons molasses or honey

Scald milk, then cool to lukewarm; mix half of the flour with it, making a smooth batter, and add the yeast dissolved in the water. Beat together well and allow to stand overnight. Cream the butter and eggs together, add the honey or molasses and a little of the remaining flour. Beat well and combine with the batter. Reserve enough flour to dust a breadboard and add the remainder. Allow time for full rise and then roll and cut in form of doughnuts. Let rise again and fry in hot cooking oil or fat.—C.G.

FAT RASCALS
Take ½ lb. of flour, 3 oz. of butter or good margarine, 4 oz. of granulated sugar, 4 oz. of sultanas, about one saltspoonful of mixed spice, and one teaspoonful of baking powder. Mix thoroughly, moisten with a little milk and one beaten egg and bake in small patty-pans.—M.B. (2).

FECULA
The name often given to the starch obtained from potatoes, manioc, yams and legumes, as distinct from that which is obtained from cereals.

FEDELINI
The finest *Italian Paste* (q.v.), similar to but finer than *Vermicelli* (q.v.), and used in the same ways.

FEDERAL PANCAKE (1805)
Take one quart of boulted rye flour, one quart of boulted Indian meal, mix it well, and stir it with a little salt into three pints milk, to the proper consistency of pancakes; fry in lard and serve up warm.—A.L. (2).

FEUILLANTINE
Small 'puff-paste' tea-cake.

FEUILLETAGE
French for *Puff-paste* (q.v.).

FITZHERBERT'S, MRS, PUDDING
Take ¾ lb. of sharp apples, boiled, 3 oz. of clarified butter, 3 oz. of sugar, four eggs, well-beaten, a little nutmeg, lemon peel, orange flower water and grated bread. Mix well together and lay a thin puff-paste at the bottom of your dish.—W.F. (28).

FIVE HOUR BREAD

One pint of scalded milk or boiled water, 2 tablespoonfuls of butter, margarine or lard, 2 tablespoonfuls of sugar, 1 teaspoonful salt, 1 cake of compressed yeast, half a cupful of lukewarm milk, 6 to 8 cups of flour. Put the sugar, shortening and salt to the hot milk, and when lukewarm add the yeast which has been dissolved in the half cup of lukewarm milk, then add enough flour to make a dough and knead and leave to rise in a warm place. The dough will be ready in about three hours, then form into loaves. Leave to rise for one hour more and bake for the fifth hour.—M.B. (2).

FLAN

In France the name is reserved for any pastry filled with a custard, but in England and the U.S.A. it means any small pastry or tart with a filling of custard, fruit, cream or sweet rennet cheese.

FLAN PASTRY

Three oz. butter, 6 oz. flour (if unsalted butter is used, add a pinch of salt), yolk of one egg.

If for fruit or sweet dish add a teaspoonful of powdered sugar.

Rub the ingredients together, add the egg and roll out thinly. Line an oblong tin with the pastry and prick it well at the bottom. An oblong is easier to cut than a round dish.—L.M. (1).

FLOUR

In the kitchen, *Flour*, when not otherwise qualified, means commercial wheaten flour, i.e. the finely-ground meal of wheat, which consists essentially of the starch and gluten of the grain: the remaining of the wheat kernel being known as *Bran* and *Shorts*.

When the *Flour* has been milled in such a way as to include the whole or a proportion of the original *Bran* or *Shorts*, it is called *Wholemeal*, *whole-wheat*, *Pure whole-wheat*, or *entire-wheat* flour; or else it is given the registered name under which it is marketed, in the British Isles.

The meal obtained by grinding other cereals, vegetables or fruits is also called a flour, but it has to be qualified by the name of the grain or plant from which it is obtained, such as *Barley*, *Rye*, *Oats*, *Corn* (for *Maize*), *Buckwheat*, *Rice*, *Peas*, *Beans*, *Soya Beans*, *Potatoes*, *Cassava*, *Peanuts* or *Banana Flour*.

The different qualities of *Flour* vary according to the quality of the grain from which it is ground and to the manner of the milling. The important question is not so much to decide which is the best flour, but which is the most suitable for the purpose for which it is intended. What is known to bakers, in England, as the '*best pastry whites*', for instance, is the best flour for making fine pastry but not for making bread, and still less for making macaroni. All grades of flour have their uses and there is only one quality that they should all possess alike: they should all be pure, that is, free from dirt and adulterants.

In the U.S.A., the two principal kinds of flour sold to the public are known, the one as *All-Purpose*, *General-Purpose* or *Family Flour* (a blend of hard and soft wheats); and the other as *Cake Flour* or *Self-rising Cake Flour* (made from selected or 'soft' winter wheats).

FLUME FLANNEL CAKES

    1½ cups milk
    ¼ cup sugar
    ½ cup butter
    ½ teaspoon salt
    ½ yeast cake
    4 cups flour
    2 egg whites, beaten stiff

Scald milk and add sugar, butter, and salt. When lukewarm, add yeast cake and, when yeast is dissolved, flour. Mix thoroughly and add egg whites. Cover and let rise overnight, cut down, fill buttered, heavy muffin-pans half full. Let rise. Bake 20 minutes in hot oven (400° F.). Makes 24 to 30 cakes.—B.C.S.C.B.

FLUTE

The French name of the 'yard of bread', mostly crust, very popular in France.

FOCHABERS GINGERBREAD

Flour, butter, castor sugar, treacle, sultanas, currants, ground almonds, mixed peel, mixed spices, ground ginger, ground cinnamon, ground cloves, bicarbonate of soda, eggs, beer.

Beat 1 lb. butter and ½ lb. sugar to a cream. Warm 1 lb. of treacle slightly and add. Then break in four eggs one at a time, beating well. Mix together 2 lb. flour, ½ lb. sultanas, ½ lb. currants, 6 oz. ground almonds, 6 oz. finely-chopped candied peel, 1 oz. mixed spices, 1 oz. ground ginger, ½ oz. ground cinnamon, ¼ oz. ground cloves, and add these to the butter, etc. Dissolve two teaspoonfuls of bicarbonate of soda in a pint of beer and add. Mix thoroughly. Put into buttered cake-tins and bake in a slow oven for two hours. These quantities make 6 lb. of cake.—F.M.M. (1).

FOREST HALL CORN STICKS

    1 cup corn meal
    ¾ cup flour
    3 teaspoons baking powder

½ teaspoon salt
½ cup hot, boiled hominy
¼ cup butter
1 cup milk
1 egg, well-beaten

Sift together corn meal, flour, baking powder, and salt; then add hominy, mixed with butter, milk, and egg. Turn into buttered bread-stick pans and bake 20 minutes in moderate oven (350°F.).— B C.S.C.B.

FRANGIPANE
A sweet almond cream flavoured with some red jasmine extract or a similar essence, the scent of which is not unlike that of the Frangipane or red jasmine (*Plumeria rubra*).

Cream Frangipane
Mix 6 tablespoonfuls of sugar and 12 tablespoonfuls of flour with 3 yolks, 2 eggs and a pinch of salt, to which add 2 cupfuls of scalded milk and 1 teaspoonful of vanilla flavouring. Stir well until near boiling, remove from fire and add 3 tablespoonfuls of sweet butter and 2 tablespoonfuls of crushed stale macaroons. Stir until cold before using. —E.E.A.

FRENCH BREAD
Sift on to a table 2 lb. of the best quality flour, place half in a bowl sufficiently large to hold 6 or 7 quarts and carefully make a well in the middle of it. Place a ½ oz. cake of very fresh firm compressed yeast in a bowl, pour over it half a pint of lukewarm water and thoroughly dissolve with the hand for 2½ minutes. Pour into well, mix a little, gradually incorporate flour for 5 minutes and sharply knead well together for 6 minutes. Cover bowl with dry cloth, then lay vessel in a warm place (80 degrees) to rise during the night (or at least 3 hours) without touching it. The sponge will then have risen to proper size, fallen and risen again and be in a proper condition for dough. Place in a bowl half pint of lukewarm water or the same quantity of milk, ½ oz. of salt and dissolve for a minute, uncover bowl and pour water on sponge, thoroughly knead the whole together for 6 minutes, add little by little the remaining flour, briskly and constantly kneading. The kneading should continue for 30 minutes after flour has been added. Lift up dough with the hands and knock it as hard as you can against the bottom of the vessel, about 10 minutes; immediately cover vessel with dry cloth, put in warm place as before and allow to rise for 2½ hours. Remove cloth from vessel, transfer dough to lightly-floured board and cut into two even pieces. With the hands roll each piece into the shape of a ball, shift to corner of table and cover and let rest for 10 minutes, being careful to avoid draughts, then neatly roll out each piece with the hands to 4 in. and let rest for 2 minutes; then roll out again to 17 in. Have a board 18 in. square. Arrange over it a piece of dry cloth, the length of the board and 8 in. wide and flute cloth on both sides 2½ in. high and 3 in. wide. Carefully lay the loaf shape dough in sections on bed. Cover it with cloth on a lightly buttered piece of paper and place in temperature of 80° to rise for 1 hour. It should rise to double its size by that time. Shortly before time for baking bread, be careful to see oven is proper degree of heat. A simple way to determine whether the heat is right is to place a piece of white paper in oven, close door, and after 5 minutes open door and remove paper. If it is a dark brown colour the temperature is right; if it burns the oven must be cooled a little, and if it is only a light brown colour, it should be made hotter. Remove covering from loaf. Have a low-edged baking pan, large enough easily to hold loaf, placed alongside the board, then carefully turn over loaf into pan by means of the cloth without touching the dough with the hands. If loaf is not in exactly straight position in pan, use a piece of pasteboard to straighten it, then with sharp knife make several ½ in. deep diagonal incisions on top. Bake for about an hour and avoid opening the oven door for the first 20 minutes.—M.B. (2).

FRITTERS
To make Water Fritters (1778)
The batter must be very thick; take 5 or 6 spoonfuls of flour, a little salt, a quart of water, the yolks and whites of 8 eggs well beat, with a little brandy; strain them through a hair sieve and mix them with the other ingredients; the longer they are made before they are fried the better: just before they are fried, melt ½ lb. of butter and beat it well in. The best thing to fry them in is lard: do not turn them.—C.M.

Common Fritters
Three-quarter pint of ale, not bitter, 3 eggs, as much flour as will make it thicker than a batter pudding, a little nutmeg, and sugar; let this stand 6 or 8 minutes: drop them with a spoon into a pan of boiling lard, drain them, grate sugar over them; eat them with melted butter, wine, and sugar.—C.M.

Plain Fritters
Put a pint of boiling cream, or milk, to the crumbs of a small loaf grated; mix it very smoothly; when cold, add the yolks of five eggs, ¼ lb. of sifted sugar, some nutmeg grated; fry them in hog's lard; pour melted butter, wine, and sugar, into the dish. Currants may be added.—C.M.

Custard Fritters, a Pretty Dish

Beat the yolks of 8 eggs with 1 spoonful of flour, half a nutmeg, a little salt, and brandy; add a pint of cream; sweeten this and bake it in a small dish; when cold, cut it into quarters; dip them in batter made of half a pint of cream, a noggin of milk, 4 eggs, a little flour, a little ginger grated; fry them a light brown in good lard or dripping; serve them hot; grate sugar over them.—c.m.

Good Fritters (1808)

Mix ½ lb. of good cream very thick with flour, beat 6 eggs, leaving out 4 whites; add 6 spoonfuls of sack, and strain them into the cream; put in a little grated nutmeg, ginger, cinnamon and salt; then put in another half pint of cream and beat the batter near an hour; pare and slice your apples thin; dip every piece in the batter, and throw them into a pan with boiling lard.—l.e.

Plain Fritters

3 oz. of flour, 3 eggs, half pint of milk.

Mix the flour to a smooth batter with a small quantity of the milk; stir in the eggs, which should be well whisked, and then the remainder of the milk; beat the whole to a perfectly smooth batter, and should it be found not quite thin enough, add two or three more tablespoonfuls of milk. Have ready a frying-pan with plenty of boiling lard in it; drop in rather more than table-spoonful at a time of the batter, and fry the fritters a nice brown, turning them when sufficiently cooked on one side. Drain them well from the greasy moisture by placing them upon a piece of blotting-paper before the fire; dish them on a white doily, sprinkle over them sifted sugar, and send to table with them a cut lemon and plenty of pounded sugar. Time: from 6 to 8 minutes. Average cost: 4d.—b.·(2).

FRUIT CAKE

> 6 oz. flour
> 3 oz. margarine
> 2 oz. ground rice
> 3 oz. sugar
> 2 to 4 tablespoons milk
> 2 oz. currants
> 1 oz. desiccated coconut
> 2 eggs
> 1 teaspoon baking powder

Rub the margarine into the sieved flour, baking powder and ground rice. Add the coconut, sugar, and dried currants; mix into a paste with the beaten egg and milk until of the right consistency. Put in a lined greased tin and bake in a moderate oven (350° F.) until cooked (about 1 hour).—g.h. (4).

FURMENTY. FRUMENTY

From O.F. *Frumentèe* and L. *Frumentum*, corn or grain..

These are the names of a traditional 'harvest home' dish in mediaeval England. It was prepared by steeping new wheat in water and leaving it upon a slow fire for 24 or 36 hours when the kernel of the grain would be soft and all but malted. The grain was then dried, winnowed and washed, when it was ready to be boiled in milk, spiced, sweetened and served hot.

Furmenty is also the name given to a favourite custard pudding of the West of England, and there is also a nursery food of that name, which is made of hulled wheat, boiled in milk, with sugar, raisins and the yolk of an egg.

GALETTE

The French name for thin, round cakes, usually plain, made of different kinds of flour, wheat, barley, oats, buckwheat, etc., or pastry.

Galette

Work lightly ¾ lb. of butter into 1 lb. of flour, Indian meal, buckwheat, or rye flour; add a large spoonful of salt, and make it into a paste with a little water, or if you have them the yolks of two eggs beaten up with a little milk; roll this out into a round ¾ in. thick; score it into diamonds, brush it over with the yolk of an egg, and bake for half an hour in a quick oven. Eaten hot or cold. Often cooked on a girdle or frying-pan. —q. (1).

GAUFFRE

The 'de luxe' edition of the *Waffle* (q.v.).

Gauffres

Put into a warm basin ½ lb. of butter, and beat it with a wooden spoon till it becomes like thick cream; mix six yolks of eggs, one by one, beating them well, and add three tablespoonfuls of flour, with a little sugar rubbed on a lemon; take half a pint of double cream well beaten up; also whip the six whites of eggs very firm and mix all together very lightly. Make the Gauffre irons hot on both sides, pour in a little clarified butter for the first baking, bake the *Gauffres* quickly, serve them as hot as possible, and at the last moment throw over them a little powdered cinnamon, mixed with fine sugar.—g.a.s.

GENOA CAKE

> 8 oz. flour
> 6 oz. castor sugar
> 7 oz. butter or margarine
> 3 eggs
> 8 oz. sultanas
> 8 oz. currants
> 4 oz. candied peel

½ teaspoon baking powder
1½ oz. sweet almonds
Grated lemon rind

Grease and line a cake-tin. Sieve the flour, pinch of salt and baking powder together, add a little grated lemon rind and the prepared fruit and chopped candied peel. Cream the butter and sugar, add the eggs one at a time and beat hard. Fold in the dry ingredients, reserving a few of the almonds for the top of the cake. Put the mixture into a prepared tin, place the almonds on top, and bake in a moderate oven of 360° F. until golden brown or thoroughly cooked, approximately 1¾ to 2 hours.—G.H. (4).

GÉNOISE JEAN PAUL

Put 4 eggs and 4 oz. castor sugar in basin and whisk over hot water till mixture is light and creamy and holds its own weight (this can be ascertained by making figure of eight with whisk). Remove from heat and continue beating till cooler. Take out whisk and fold in gently with wooden spatula 3 oz. sieved flour and 1½ oz. ground almonds; flavour with vanilla. Lastly stir in 1½ oz. melted butter.

Note: The butter must be just melted and almost cool; any residue which falls to the bottom of pan must not be put in. The mixing of ingredients needs great care, otherwise the aeration whipped into eggs and sugar will disappear and the cake become heavy.

Pour into buttered, lined, and floured tin and cook in medium oven till knife comes out clean. Turn out and cool. Split and fill with reduced apricot *purée*, sprinkle with little rum. Glaze top with hot apricot syrup, sprinkle with granulated sugar, and powder with icing sugar.—D.L.T.

GENTLEMAN'S PUDDING

4 oz. butter
4 oz. flour
3 eggs
2 oz. castor sugar
3 tablespoons raspberry jam
½ teaspoon bicarbonate of soda

For the Sauce

2 egg yolks
1 tablespoon castor sugar
1 glass sherry
3 tablespoons raspberry jam

This is a simple but favourite sweet, the recipe for which can be used for a nursery pudding by omitting the sherry. To make it, cream the butter and sugar, stir in the flour and add the beaten eggs, then the jam and the bicarbonate of soda. Butter a basin and steam the mixture for 2 hours. The sauce is made by mixing 2 egg yolks with a table-spoonful of sugar and a glass of sherry and whipping these to a froth over hot water. Then mix in the raspberry jam and serve hot round the pudding. Cream may be served with the sweet.—H.P.

GEORGE WASHINGTON CAKE
(1780)

Rub two cups of butter and two cups of sugar to a light cream. Beat four egg yolks very light with one cup of sugar and stir together. Sift together four cups of flour, one teaspoonful of mace, two tablespoonfuls of baking powder, and add alternately with one cup of milk. Stir in one cup of raisins, one half cup of currants, and one-fourth cup of finely-cut citron. Fold in the well-beaten whites. Bake in square shallow pan in moderate oven about one hour; when cold, ice with white icing. (*Old Williamsburg Family Cook Book.*)—H.B.

GEORGE WASHINGTON PIE

Beat, till light and honey-coloured, the yolks of 6 eggs. Now sift 3 cups flour thrice with 2 teaspoonfuls cream of tartar; then sift this once with 2 cups castor sugar and beat lightly into the eggs. Lastly add the whites of 6 eggs beaten to a stiff froth, then 4 teaspoonfuls sweet milk in which has been dissolved 1 level teaspoonful of soda. Bake in buttered layer tins in a quick oven till firm and golden, then cool on a cake rack, and when perfectly cold put layers together with strawberry jam. Sift castor sugar lightly over. (*The Duncan Sisters.*)—E.C.

GINGER BISCUITS

Ingredients:

½ lb. of flour
¼ lb. of fresh butter
¼ lb. of castor sugar
½ oz. of ground ginger
1 egg and a little milk

Method: Rub the butter and ginger into the flour on the board, make a 'bay', or hole, break in the egg, and wet up into a nice, workable paste, using a little milk if necessary. Roll down in thin sheets, and cut out with a plain, round cutter; set on a greased baking-sheet, and bake in a cool oven.

Time: About 5 minutes to bake. Sufficient for two dozen biscuits.—B.E.C.

GINGERBREAD

A fancy kind of bread flavoured with ginger and usually sweetened with molasses. In olden times it used to be made in all sorts of fancy shapes and sometimes gilded.

Gingerbread

Beat 6 oz. of butter and 6 oz. of castor sugar to a cream, add 3 eggs, 8 oz. of treacle, 8 oz. of flour, well sifted, a teaspoonful of mixed spice, a teaspoonful of ground ginger, a pinch of baking powder and 4 oz. of shredded almonds. Pour into a greased and papered baking-tin and bake for three-quarters of an hour in a moderate oven.—M.K.S. (2).

Scots Gingerbread
(Traditional Recipe)

Flour, oatmeal, butter, green ginger, lemon peel, treacle, cream.

Beat 8 oz. of butter to a cream. Mix with it 12 oz. of flour, 4 oz. of oatmeal, and half a gill of cream. Stir in 12 oz. of treacle, 1 oz. of green ginger and 4 oz. of lemon peel cut into fine shreds. Work the whole into a light dough. Put in a well-greased tin and bake for 45 minutes.—F.M.M. (2).

Soft Gingerbread with Cream Cheese

Put in basin 1 cup black treacle, 3 oz. sugar, 2½ oz. butter; add 1 cup boiling water, stir till butter is melted. Sieve twice 2½ cups flour, 1 tablespoonful powdered ginger, half a tablespoonful cinnamon, good pinch salt and 1 teaspoonful bicarbonate soda. Beat into this the above liquid till very smooth. When well beaten, add quickly 2 beaten eggs. Pour into buttered and lined shallow tin and bake in slow oven 40 to 45 minutes. Let cool before removing from tin. Cover top with whipped cream cheese, made by stirring milk into 3 oz. fresh cream cheese till soft consistency, then beaten till light.—D.L.T.

White Gingerbread

1 lb. flour, 6 oz. sugar, ¼ lb. butter, 1 teaspoonful ginger, 1 to 2 eggs, 1 teaspoonful baking soda, 1½ teacupfuls milk. Mix well and let stand awhile, then bake in a moderate oven.—A.C.B.

GINGER CAKE

Take ¼ lb. treacle, ½ lb. butter, 6 oz. Demerara sugar, 1 lb. flour, 3 eggs, 1 teaspoonful carbonate of soda, 2 teaspoonfuls ginger, half a teaspoonful of spice and half a teaspoonful of salt. Melt butter, sugar and treacle. Sift together the dry ingredients, add the eggs (whipped) and lastly the flour, etc. Turn into a tin and bake in a moderate oven for 1 hour.—M.F.

GINGER NUTS

    6 oz. flour
    Salt
    2 oz. butter
    4 oz. brown sugar
    2 teaspoons ground ginger
    ½ teaspoon cinnamon
    ½ teaspoon mixed spice
    Golden syrup or honey to mix
      (approx. 1 tablespoon)

Sieve the flour, salt, spice, ground ginger, and cinnamon together. Cream the butter and sugar, stir in the dry ingredients alternately with the golden syrup (which may be warmed very slightly in order to make the mixing easier) to make a stiffish paste. Flour a pastry board lightly. Roll out the pastry and cut into small rounds with a pastry cutter. Place on a greased baking-tin and bake in a very moderate oven. These quantities make approximately 24 biscuits.—G.H. (4).

GINGER SNAPS

They are a second-rate kind of *Ginger Nuts*, thin, brittle, gingery in flavour and of lighter colour than *Ginger Nuts*.

GIRDLE or GRIDDLE CAKES

These cakes or scones are not baked in an oven but cooked on the top of the stove on a girdle or griddle, a thick, flat circular piece of iron with an arched handle. This should be heated, and greased or floured before the scone mixture is put on it.

A heavy iron frying-pan can be used in place of a girdle and is sometimes more convenient, when a batter is being used, as in buckwheat cakes.—M.K.S. (2).

Irish Girdle Cakes

    1 lb. flour
    1 teaspoon bicarbonate of soda
    Pinch of salt
    ½ pint buttermilk

Dissolve the bicarbonate of soda in milk, mix the salt with the flour and make it all into a stiff paste, roll this out and cut into rounds. Make a girdle hot, lightly grease the top and cook the cakes on this, turning them when they are half done.—H.E.

GIRDLE SCONES, SCOTS

    1 lb. flour
    ½ pint buttermilk
    2 teaspoons baking powder
    1 teaspoon salt

Mix dry ingredients together and pass through a sieve into a basin. Mix quickly with buttermilk. Turn out and knead lightly and roll out about ¼ in. thick. Cut into rounds with a tin cutter. Lightly grease a hot girdle with butter, lay the scones on and bake quickly. When well risen and a little browned underneath, turn and cook on the other side for a couple of minutes.—M.K.S. (2).

GLUTEN BREAD

Mix together a pint of cold milk and a pint of boiling water, pour this on to a teaspoonful of butter, and the same of salt, and let it stand till it is all lukewarm. Now add a well-beaten whole egg, a quarter of a compressed yeast cake, previously dissolved, and enough gluten to nake a soft batter. Cover the pan, stand it in a warm corner, and let it rise well; then knead in sufficient gluten to produce a soft dough, kneading this very thoroughly. Now shape it into four loaves, let it rise again, then bake for an hour. Remember gluten bread takes both less yeast and less time to rise than ordinary bread. It may be observed that a cake of compressed yeast is considered equal to half pint of liquid yeast. —Q. (1).

GNOCCHI

Italian Dumplings made of *Semolina* – but also of other kinds of flour – and cooked in fast boiling salted water, then drained, sprinkled with grated cheese, and served hot.

Golden Gnocchi

4 oz. semolina or golden maize, 1 oz. butter, lemon, thyme or parsley (1 teaspoonful in all), whites of 2 eggs, half a pint of milk, with salt and pepper to taste.

Cook the semolina or maize for half an hour with milk in a double saucepan. Add the butter, chopped herbs and seasoning. Cook 10 minutes longer. Add the whipped whites of eggs. When cool, form into shapes and egg and breadcrumb well in fine white crumbs. Fry in deep boiling oil. Drain well and sprinkle with grated cheese and serve with fried parsley.—L.M. (1).

Gnocchi Parisienne

Boil half a pint water with 2 oz. butter and little salt. Add 3 oz. flour away from fire, mix well. Return to fire and dry over flame till paste leaves sides of pan. Remove, add 2 eggs, one at a time, beating each in well. Add pepper, and 2 oz. grated cheese.

Allow mixture to cool a little, then shape with piping bag, using a pipe about ⅓ in. across. Let mixture drop into pan of boiling salted water, cutting lengths of 1 in. long with a knife, as the left hand presses up the paste.

Poach about 10 minutes, then drain Gnocchi well on sieve or muslin.

Prepare good half pint *Bechamel* (¾ oz. flour, ¾ oz. butter for 'roux', about half a pint boiling milk flavoured with bacon cuttings, parsley and bit of bayleaf), adding a spoon of cream if possible. Season well.

Put drained Gnocchi in buttered dish, pour over sauce. Sprinkle with 1 oz. grated cheese and dusting of paprika. Bake in hot oven till 'souffled' and brown.—D.L.T.

Gnocchi alla Piémontese

(Potato Dumplings à la Piémontese)
Ingredients: 1 lb. potatoes, 3 oz. flour, 1 whole egg 1 yolk, salt, pepper, 3 oz. or 4 tablespoons butter, 6 oz. grated Parmesan cheese.

Method: Boil or steam the potatoes and, while still hot, rub through a sieve, then mix in a bowl with the flour, the egg and yolk of egg and season with salt and pepper, roll into small balls the size of a walnut and flatten out in the shape of small cylinders and poach in boiling salted water for 20 minutes. Drain and serve with a little gravy or Espagnole Sauce and grated Parmesan cheese.

Gnocchi alla Romana

(Semolina Dumplings à la Romana)
Ingredients: ¼ lb. of semolina, 2 oz. butter, 2½ oz. grated Parmesan or Gruyère cheese, 2 eggs, milk and salt.

For the Sauce: 4 oz. of butter and 4 oz. grated cheese.

Cook the semolina in the boiling milk and when thick and smooth add 1 oz. butter and 1 oz. cheese. Remove from fire and add the eggs, mixing thoroughly. Then pour on a dish the mixture about ½ in. thick. Let the mixture stand till cold and then, with the fingers, roll into *Gnocchi* of the same shape and sizes as almonds. Put these in a baking-dish with the 4 oz. of melted butter and cheese and season with salt. Cook in a moderate oven for 30 to 35 minutes.—L.M. (1).

The paste may also be cut into rounds and arranged slightly over-lapping each other in a buttered dish, covered with melted butter and grated cheese and browned lightly in the oven.—M.K.S. (2).

GOFIO

The name given in the Canaries to Corn meal, i.e. ground maize, the staple food of the people of those islands. The peasants keep going for a long arduous day's work on a glass of milk into which some fine *Gofio* has been stirred, using it much as Highlanders in the old days used oatmeal and spring water. *Gofio* is also mixed to a consistency which is thick or not-so-thick, according to taste, and eaten as a quickly prepared snack in the form of paste. It is also used as a kind of breakfast cereals dish, like the Indian *Souji*, which is made of Semolina, or the Italian *Polenta* (q.v.).—E.M.L.D.

GOLDEN SYRUP PUDDING

6 oz. flour
3 oz. chopped suet
2 oz. sugar
1 gill of milk
Rind of 1 lemon (grated)
1 gill golden syrup
Small teaspoonful baking powder
1 egg

Pour the syrup into a well-buttered basin. Mix the dry ingredients well together, add egg well beaten and mixed in the milk. Pour on the syrup in the basin and steam for 2 hours. Sufficient for six people.—L.G.N.

GOLD CAKE

     1 cup granulated sugar
     ½ cup butter
     6 egg yolks
     1 white of egg
     2 teaspoons baking powder
     ½ cup milk
     1 teaspoon vanilla
     1½ cups flour

Cream sugar and butter together. Add egg yolks beaten light, add milk, add vanilla, add flour, after having been sifted four times. Add baking powder, add white of the one egg, having been whipped stiff. Put in three greased layer pans and bake 10 to 12 minutes.

Ice with chocolate, caramel or maple icing.—P.D.P.

GOLDEN CAKE. SAND CAKE

     4 oz butter
     4 oz castor sugar
     2 oz. ground rice
     2 oz. flour
     1 oz. potato flour
     2 eggs
     ½ teaspoon baking powder
     A pinch of salt

Sieve the flour, baking powder, salt, ground rice, and potato flour on to a piece of paper. Cream the butter and sugar, and add the yolks of the eggs, beating each one in separately. Beat the whites of eggs stiffly, and fold these into the creamed butter and sugar, alternately with the dry ingredients, adding a little milk if necessary. Put the mixture into a prepared tin and bake in a moderately hot oven of 375° F. for about 40 minutes.

N.B.—If potato flour is not available, 3 oz. plain flour should be used instead of 2 oz.—G.H. (4).

GRAHAM BREAD

Bread made wholly or partly with some Graham Flour.

GRAHAM FLOUR

Flour which has not been 'bolted', i.e. which has not been passed through a refining sieve after grinding. It is another name for wholemeal flour, and it was named after one Sylvester Graham, American champion of the wholemeal loaf.

GRANNY NICOLL'S CAKE

     1½ lb. flour
     1 lb. raisins
     1 lb. currants
     ½ lb. sugar
     ½ lb. butter
     1 teaspoon cinnamon
     2 tablespoons ground rice
     ½ teaspoon powdered nutmeg
     ½ pint buttermilk or sour milk
     2½ teaspoons bicarbonate of soda

Mix all together with buttermilk or sour milk in which the bicarbonate of soda has been dissolved. Bake about 1½ to 2 hours.—L.G.N.

GRANELLA BISCUITS

     1 lb. eggs
     14 oz. fine castor sugar
     12 oz. soft flour
     2 oz. cornflour
     Zest of 1 orange

Break the eggs into a small copper egg-bowl, put in the sugar and zest; warm these by stirring over a pan of hot water on the stove until they reach 100° F. Then remove and beat until cold and firm. Knock out the whisk, stir in the flour with a small spattle, and run out 3 in. long with a ½ in. tube on to baking plates, buttered and floured. Sprinkle all over with small Bath-bun sugar in pieces the size of granulated citrate of magnesia. Turn the plates over to shake off any sugar that may not adhere to the biscuits, and bake at once in an oven at 375° F. When nearly cold remove from plates by lifting with the finger nail.—A.A.B.

GRANTHAM WHITE GINGERBREAD

     1 lb. flour
     ½ lb. castor sugar
     ½ lb. butter
     1½ oz. ground ginger
     2 eggs
     1 dessertspoon baking powder

Cream the butter and sugar, beat in the yolks of eggs one at a time, sift in the flour, baking powder and ginger lightly, a little at a time. Lastly whip up the whites of eggs and fold them into the mixture. Bake on a buttered greased paper in a moderate oven and keep them quite pale in colour.—P.H.

GREAT CAKE (1694)

Take 5 or 6 pounds of currants, pick't, wash'd & dried, & plump'd if you please, & set them before the fire that they may be warme. Take 5 pound of flower, putt it into a pan. Take sixteen eggs, putt away half ye whites, & beat them very well, & strain them and a pint of ale yeeste, stirring together a pint of cream and a pound and half of butter, & putt them together that ye cream may warm ye yeeste and eggs; and with a warm liquor wett ye flower, and when it is mix'd cover it with a warm cloth, & sett it before ye fire, in a pan that you wett it in; & so let it stand, stirring it sometimes that it may be equally warm till ye oven be hott.

Take half an ounce of mace & two good nutmegs, & cinnamon or what spice you like best, & half a pound of sugar; & mix it all together, when ye oven is hott, with ye currants as they are warmed, putting it to ye dough, & when it is well mix'd have a large stronge paper, & butter it, & lett it be doubled with a paper hoope. Itt may be bak'd in an hour.—A.B.

GREEK BREAD

Sift and warm 6 lb. fine flour; then mix it with 3 oz. yeast, worked up with a little castor sugar, 3 oz. salt and a little water, adding gradually enough tepid milk and water to make it all into a not too stiff dough. Knead it well, cover with a cloth, and leave it for 3 hours in a warm place to rise, after which divide it into eight parts, set each in a buttered tin and bake in a very hot oven. When nearly done, turn them out of the moulds, and set them in the oven on tins to colour the crust nicely. This takes a very few minutes. Roll them up at once in flannel. —Q. (1).

GRISSINI. SALT STICKS

Take some light dough, such as is used for Vienna, French or Milk Bread; cut this into strips 8 in. to 10 in. long and rather thicker than a pencil; lay them on a buttered baking-sheet, dusting them well with salt, and bake till crisp. Some people use puff-paste, to which they have added a liberal dusting of salt, for these salt sticks; but abroad, where these *Grissini* are very popular, they are almost invariably made of light bread or rolled dough. Some cooks, having salted their dough before baking it, dust the little sticks with coralline or Nepaul pepper, when they are very useful with cheese. An egg worked into the Vienna dough is a great improvement to these little sticks, and, when shaped, brush them over with milk, and strew them liberally with coarse salt before baking.—Q. (1).

GROATS. GRITS

The seeds or kernels of oats deprived of their husk by machinery and either left whole or broken up. When crushed they are sometimes called *Embden Groats*, and when ground to a form of flour for making gruel or thickening broths they are called *prepared groats*.

GRUAU

The culinary name for decorticated grain, such as *Pearl Wheat, Barley* or *Groats*; *Gruau de Bretagne* is the coarsest and *Gruau de Paris* the finest, whilst *Semoule de Gruau* merely means *Semolina* (q.v.).

GRUEL

A thin form of *Porridge* which can be made with wheat, oats, barley or any other Cereal.

Barley Gruel

2 oz. of Scotch or Pearl Batley, half a pint of Port Wine, the rind of 1 lemon, 1 quart and half a pint of water, sugar to taste.

After well washing the barley, boil it in half a pint of water for quarter of an hour; then pour this water away; put to the barley the quart of fresh boiling water, and let it boil until the liquid is reduced to half; then strain it off. Add the wine, sugar, and lemon peel; simmer for 5 minutes and put it away in a clean jug. It can be warmed from time to time as required.

Time: To be boiled until reduced to half.

Sufficient with the wine to make 1½ pints of gruel.—B. (2).

A More Modern Recipe

Boil 3 oz. of Pearl Barley in a pint of water for 10 minutes; then strain the first water off and add two quarts of boiling water. When reduced to one-half it will be sufficiently boiled. Then strain, add sugar, lemon peel, or wine to taste, and simmer for a few minutes.—L.G.M.

Oatmeal Gruel
(Meg Dods' Recipe)

Fine oatmeal; water; salt; sugar; wine or honey, etc., to taste.

Take very finely ground oatmeal of the best quality. Infuse as much as you wish in cold water for an hour or two. Stir it up, let it settle, and pour it from the grits (or strain it), and boil slowly for a long time, stirring it up. Add a little salt and sugar, with any addition of wine, rum, fruit, jelly, honey, butter, etc., you choose. This gruel will be quite smooth, and when cold will form a jelly. With a toast it makes an excellent luncheon or supper dish for an invalid. It may be thinned at pleasure.—F.M.M. (2).

GUARDS PUDDING

Cream 4 oz. butter, add 4 oz. sugar and cream till white. Beat in 2 eggs, 2 oz. flour, 2 oz. fine breadcrumbs; add 1 egg first, then half flour and crumbs; beating carefully and lightly. Next, stir in 2 tablespoonfuls raspberry jam, sieved, and pinch carbonate soda.

Butter a soufflé dish, and place a buttered paper in bottom. Cover with buttered paper and steam 1½ hours. When cooked, remove top paper and let pudding stand for 7 to 8 minutes before turning out, or put in slow oven for 10 minutes, covered buttered paper, to dry the top. Then knock it free from sides and turn out on hot dish. Pour sauce around.

Sauce

Put several heaped tablespoonfuls raspberry jam in saucepan with little water and squeeze of lemon juice. Boil up and strain; thicken with small amount of arrowroot if not sufficiently consistent.—D.L.T.

HAMPSHIRE NUTS

¼ lb. flour
¼ lb. cornflour
¼ lb. castor sugar
1 egg
1 teaspoon baking powder
¼ lb. butter

Beat the butter and sugar to a cream, add the egg and beat, then add all ingredients. Mix into a paste, place teaspoonful on buttered tin and bake. When done, put two together with a little jam while hot.—L.G.N.

HANNAH MORE'S PUDDING

Shred ¼ lb. of beef suet very finely, mix with ¼ lb. of finely-grated breadcrumbs, ¼ lb. of stoned raisins, ¼ lb. of moist sugar and ¼ lb. of chopped apples weighed after they are pared and cored. A pinch of salt, a quarter of nutmeg, grated, 2 oz. of candied lemon, chopped small. When these ingredients are thoroughly mixed, stir into them 4 well-beaten eggs and 2 tablespoonfuls of brandy. Pour into a well-buttered mould and plunge into boiling water and boil for 3 hours.—W.F. (28).

'HARD TACK'

The sailor's name for Ship's Bread.

HIGH HOUSE TEA CAKES

2 tablespoons of butter
½ cupful of sugar
1 egg, beaten
1 teaspoon of lemon juice
2 cupfuls of sifted cake flour
3 teaspoons of baking powder
⅛ teaspoon of salt
1 cupful of milk

For the top:

1 tablespoon of butter
2 tablespoons of brown sugar
2 tablespoons of chopped pecans
Cake pan, 6½ by 10½, buttered and floured

Beat the butter and sugar together until creamy and light-coloured. Add the egg and lemon juice and beat until fluffy. Sift the flour, baking powder, and salt together. Add to the first mixture alternately with the milk. Turn into the pan. Mix the ingredients for the top together and spread over the batter. Bake in a hot oven (400° F.) for about 30 minutes, or until the edges leave the pan. Cut in small squares or oblong.—E.K.H.

HOE CAKES. JOHNNY CAKES

Scald 1 pint of Indian meal with enough boiling water to make a stiff batter (about 3 cups). Add 1 tablespoonful of salt. Drop on hot greased tin and bake in hot oven 30 minutes. (Some cooks prefer to spread their batter ½ in. thick in their dripping-pan and serve the cake up hot by cutting it in squares.) *Virginia recipe, c.* 1776.—H.B.

HOME-MADE BREAD

7 lb. flour
1 tablespoon salt
2 quarts warm water
1 gill of yeast or 2 oz. compressed yeast

Mix the flour and salt together in a basin and make a hollow or well in the middle. Mix the yeast with the warm water and pour it into the flour. If compressed yeast is used, cream it with a wooden spoon in a warm basin, then add the water to it gradually, before putting it in the flour. Have ready three pints of more warm water and stir in sufficient gradually to make the whole into a rather soft dough. The exact quantity of water cannot be given as some kinds of flour take more than others.

Knead dough well for about 20 minutes – when quite smooth sift a little flour over it and cover with a cloth. Leave to rise in a warm place for about 4 hours, then knead again for quarter of an hour. Cover and let it rise again for about 1 hour. Divide into four loaves and put these into greased and floured tins or make into cottage loaves or Coburgs. Leave these on the baking-tins to 'prove' for 15 minutes. Put the bread into a quick oven at first and bake for 2 hours if the loaves weigh 2 lb. each. When cooked turn the bread on to a sieve or lean it against a plate. If properly cooked bread should sound hollow when tapped.—M.K.S. (2).

Cottage Loaf

To shape a Cottage Loaf, take two pieces of dough one larger than the other, shape them into balls, put the smaller on top of the larger one, flour the forefinger and press it right through the centre of both.

Coburg Loaf

Shape the dough into an oval shape and make several deep cuts across the top.

HOMINY

Hulled, split and more or less coarsely ground and sifted *Maize*. The name is an approximation of *Auhuminea*, meaning *parched corn* in North America Indian dialect, or *Rockahoming*, of Algonquian origin. It is highly esteemed as a breakfast food and it makes good cakes and puddings. It is very cheap and not so heating as *Oats*.

HONEY CAKE (1805)

6 lb. flour, 2 lb. honey, 1 lb. sugar, 2 oz. cinnamon, 1 oz. ginger, a little orange peel, 2 teaspoons·pearl-ash, 6 eggs; dissolve the pearl-ash in milk, put the whole together, moisten with milk if necessary, bake 20 minutes.—A.L. (2).

HOT CROSS BUNS

(For Good Friday Morning)

1½ lb. flour
¼ lb. butter
1 oz. yeast
¾ pint warm milk
2 eggs
2 oz. sugar
¼ lb. currants
And a little spice

Let the butter dissolve in the milk, cream the yeast with a little of the sugar and pour the warm milk and butter on this. Then put the flour with the spice in a large basin, make a well in the centre and set the dough, which should rise in about 1½ hours. Then beat in the eggs, add the currants and let it rise again. Turn out on to a board. Knead, form into buns and lay them in rows on a baking sheet, leaving 2 in. space between each. These must now prove. When risen, mark them across and across with a bone paper knife and bake in a quick oven for 10 to 15 minutes. Brush over with milk and sugar whilst hot, to glaze them, as they come from the oven.—H.E.

HUNYADI CAKE

I

4½ oz. sugar
12 chestnuts
6 oz. chocolate
5 yolks
5 whites of eggs
Jam

Cook, skin and put the chestnuts through a sieve. Melt the chocolate. Mix the chestnuts, chocolate and yolks well together. Whip the whites of eggs and fold them carefully in. Bake the mixture in two round cake tins. Spread one cake with jam or whipped cream, cover with the second half and ice. —E.B.

II

4 oz. sugar
5 yolks
2 whole eggs
3 oz. chestnuts
Cinnamon
Peel of a quarter of a lemon
1 oz. breadcrumbs
6 oz. chocolate
5 whites of eggs

Beat the sugar, yolks and the whole eggs together until creamy. Add the grated chestnuts, lemon peel, crumbs, chocolate and the whipped whites of eggs. Bake in a moderate oven.—E.B.

INDEPENDENCE CAKE (1805)

20 lb. flour, 15 lb. sugar, 10 lb. butter, 4 dozen eggs, 1 quart wine, 1 quart brandy, 1 oz. nutmeg, cinnamon, cloves, mace, of each 3 oz.; 2 lb. citron; currants and raisins 5 lb. each, 1 quart yeast. When baked, frost with loaf sugar; dress with box and gold leaf.—A.L. (2).

INDIAN CHOCOLATE

The chocolate-coloured root of an Eastern *Geum*, ground and eaten in India by natives who believe that it has tonic properties.

INDIAN SLAPJACK (1805)

One quart milk, 1 pint of Indian meal, 4 eggs, 4 spoons of flour, little salt; beat together, bake on griddles, or fry in a dry pan which has been rubbed with suet, lard or butter.—A.L. (2).

IPURUMA

An edible fecula or sago-like flour obtained from the *Ita* palm, *Mauritia flexuosa*, in South America. It is obtained from the central part of the tree trunk and possesses an agreeable flavour.—L.G.M.

IRISH POTATO CAKES

Six good white boiled potatoes, salt, flour, and butter. Mash potatoes until they are of a creamy consistency, adding salt and then enough flour to make a dough stiff enough to roll. Roll out to ½ in. thickness, cut into rectangular pieces and bake on a griddle. Split and butter immediately and serve very hot.—H.E.

ISLE OF WIGHT DOUGHNUTS

Work smoothly together with the fingers 4 oz. of good lard, 4 lb. of flour, add ¼ lb. fine brown sugar, 2 tablespoonfuls of all-spice, 1 dram of pounded cinnamon, half as much of cloves, 2 large blades of mace beaten to a powder, 2 tablespoonfuls of fresh yeast which has been watered for one night, and should be solid, and as much new milk as will make the whole into a rather firm dough. Let this stand for 1 hour or 1½ hours near a fire, knead it well and make it into balls the size of a small apple, prod them with the thumb, put a few currants in the middle, enclose them well, and throw the doughnuts into a saucepan half-filled with boiling lard. When they are equally coloured, lift them out and dry them near a fire on a sieve. When they are made in large quantities, as they were on the island in certain seasons, they are drained upon very clean straw.

The lard should boil only just before they are dropped in, or the outsides will be scorched before the insides are done.—P.A.

ITALIAN PASTES

The generic name – *Pâtes d'Italie* or *Pâtes alimentaires* in culinary French – of a number of wheaten flour preparations which, until recent years, were made almost exclusively in the South of Italy and in Sicily. They must be made from the hard red or *Durum* wheat (see *Wheat*), or from Russian wheat (Taganrog or Black Sea wheat). The flour is well kneaded into a stiff dough which is forced through specially made perforated cylinders from which it emerges in various shapes and styles as thin sticks, tubes, pipes, ribbons, etc., being known eventually by different names such as Macaroni, Vermicelli, Spaghetti, Lasagnes, Crescioni, Ditalini, Fedelini, Ravioli, Reginette, Strichetti, Tagliarini, Tagliatelle, Tortellini, Zita, etc. A large manufacturer of *Italian Pastes* would have at least 200 different dies for making various shapes of paste.

In Bologna Macaroni is sometimes coloured yellow with egg, green with spinach or red with beetroot juice. In Genoa it is sometimes coloured with saffron.

The fresher one can get *Italian Pastes* the better, and if one keeps them they must be kept in a cool and dry place; otherwise they are liable to become musty in a damp place or to harbour weevils in a hot cupboard.

JAN IN DIE SAK
(John in the Bag)

    4 cups flour
    4 tablespoons butter (melted)
    4 eggs
    ½ teaspoon salt
    ¼ lb. raisins
    1 packet cream of tartar
    ½ packet bicarbonate of soda
    3 teaspoons mixed spice
    1 wineglass brandy, or wine
    3 tablespoons syrup or honey

    1 tablespoon apricot jam
    2 dry rusks, crumbled
    2 cups sugar

1. Mix all the dry ingredients, except carbonate of soda, together.
2. Add beaten eggs, butter, syrup, jam and brandy, then the soda dissolved in half a cup of warm water.
3. Add more water if necessary to make a stiff dough.
4. Add the raisins or dates, stoned and chopped.
5. Place in a floured bag or cloth and tie, allowing room for expansion.
6. Place in a pot of boiling water and boil for 3½ to 4 hours. Have a plate under the pudding and add a little salt to the water.
7. Serve with custard or wine sauce. (*South African recipe*).

JESSICA'S CAKE

    2 cups sugar
    1 cup butter
    4 cups flour
    6 egg yolks beaten until thick
    6 egg whites, beaten until stiff
    1 cup currants
    Few raspings of nutmeg
    4 tablespoons sherry or brandy

Cream butter and sugar until very light; add egg yolks and beat all together until light and creamy; grate nutmeg into brandy; dredge currants with a little of the flour and stir remainder into batter; then add currants with a little of the flour and stir remainder into batter; then add currants and fold in egg whites last.—C.R.B.B. (2).

JOB'S TEARS. COIX

Lat. *Coix lachryma*. An Asiatic grass cultivated in the more arid places of Spain and Portugal for the sake of its seeds which are ground and made into a coarse sort of bread. These seeds are very hard and of different colours and they are also made into homely necklaces, strung on fibre or silk.

JOHNNY CAKES. HOE CAKES

I

Scald 1 pint of milk and put to 2 pints of Indian meal and half a pint flour – bake before the fire. Or scald with milk two-thirds of the Indian meal, or wet two-thirds with boiling water, add salt, molasses and shortening; work up with cold water pretty stiff and bake.—A.L. (2).

II

1 cupful of yellow corn meal
¾ cupful of sifted all-purpose flour
1 teaspoon of baking powder
2 eggs
⅓ cupful of sugar
½ teaspoon of salt
1 cupful of milk
Pan 8½ in. by 11½ in. well buttered

Sift all the dry ingredients together. Melt the butter, add the milk, and drop in the eggs. Pour into a hole made in the centre of the dry ingredients and beat well together. Turn into the pan and bake in a hot oven (400° F.) for about 25 minutes, or until lightly browned.—E.K.H.

JUMBLES
(Old English *Jumbals*)

To make Jumbals (1807)

Rub 1 lb. of butter very fine into a pound of fine flour; mix in it a pound of loaf sugar finely sifted, and 2 oz. of caraway seeds, pounded; make it into a paste, with the whites of 4 eggs, and roll it out the thickness of your finger, and lay them on tins in the shape of the letter S, and bake them in a cool oven.—A.A.

Jumbles

5 oz. sugar
5 oz. butter
1 egg
10 oz. flour
1 teaspoon grated lemon rind
2 oz. ground almonds

Cream the sugar and butter together, add most of the beaten egg, stir in the flour, lemon rind, and almonds. Form the mixture into a roll and form into 'S' shapes. Place on a greased baking-sheet, and bake in a moderate oven for about 10 minutes.—G.H. (4).

KAFFIR BREAD

The farinaceous pith of some South African *Breadfruit* trees used as food by the Blacks.

KAFFIR CORN

Fr. *Mil d'Afrique*. One of the more important native African grasses (see *Sorghum*) extensively grown for bread-making as well as cattle food in most parts of Africa. It is also grown in the U.S.A. for poultry food chiefly.

Varieties of *Kaffir Corn* are known by a number of different names in different places, such as *Durrha*, *Milo Maize*, either white or brown, *Jerusalem Corn*, etc.

KENTISH HUFFKINS

1 lb. plain flour
1 oz. lard
1 teaspoon sugar

½ teaspoon salt
1 oz. yeast
About 2½ gills of warm milk and water

Sift flour and salt together into warm basin and rub in the lard. Cream the yeast in the sugar and add to the warm milk and water. Make up with the flour into a light dough. Mark the dough with a cross and leave to rise for 1 hour in a warm place, then knead well and divide into flat round cakes about ½ in. thick with a hole in the middle. Flour well, put on a warm tin and leave to prove in a warm place till well risen. Then bake in a hot oven for 10 to 20 minutes. Take out and wrap in warm blankets until cold; this keeps the outside soft.—M.K.S. (2).

KIPFEL
(Austrian Croissant)

Ingredients: 1 lb. of best flour, ¼ lb. butter, 1 yolk of egg, ½ oz. of salt, a little under 1 oz. of yeast, half a pint of milk.

Method: Cream the yeast in 5 oz. of warm milk. Put the flour into a bowl, add the creamed yeast and work into a dough, neither too stiff nor too soft. Let it rise for about half an hour, then add the rest of the milk and the salt, and knead until the dough no longer sticks to the hands. Now roll out on a board and spread with the butter. Fold the dough, shape into a ball and let it stand in a cool place for several hours or overnight. Roll out the dough, cut into 5 in. lengths, roll each piece into a cylindrical shape and let stand for 10 minutes. Flatten them slightly and form into crescents and let them rise for another hour – then brush them over with a yolk of egg and bake in a moderate oven.—M.K.S. (2).

KISS-ME-QUICK PUDDING

The weight of 2 eggs in brown sugar and butter; 2 teaspoons marmalade or jam; 6 oz. flour; 1 small teaspoon baking powder.

Method: Beat the sugar and butter to a cream; add the well-beaten eggs and beat to a cream. Add the jam, flour and baking powder. Steam in a basin for two hours. (*Miss Ruth Kennan, Maseru.*)—P.R.M.

KNEADING

Flour the hands and fold the fingers over the thumbs, making a fist. Then beat and pummel the dough, first one hand then the other, all over, turning it over and working it for not less than 20 minutes until it ceases to stick to the hands.

Flour a basin and put the dough into it, mark a cross on the top, cover with a cloth and let it stand in a warm place to rise for an hour or more. It should rise to nearly double its original size.

Dough may be set to rise overnight if covered and kept in a warm place.—M.K.S.(2).

KOEKSUSTERS

(Doughnuts with a coating of syrup)

1 cup milk
½ yeast cake
1 teaspoon salt
2 eggs
⅓ cup butter and lard mixed
Flour
1 cup light brown sugar
½ grated nutmeg

Bring milk to boiling point; when lukewarm add the yeast cake dissolved in a quarter of a cup lukewarm water, salt, and enough flour to make a soft batter, and let rise overnight. In the morning add melted shortening, sugar, eggs well-beaten, nutmeg, and enough flour to make a soft dough; let rise again, and if too soft to handle add more flour. Toss on floured board; then roll out, and cut each about 2 in. long. After being fried in deep fat, leave in a syrup made of three cups sugar, and two cups water, and flavoured with ground cinnamon, for a short while. (*South African Recipe.*)

KRINGLES

Beat well the yolks of eight and the whites of two eggs and mix with 4 oz. butter just warmed, and with this knead 1 lb. of flour and 4 oz. of sugar to a paste. Roll into thick or thin biscuits, prick them and bake on tin plates.—M.B. (2).

LADY BALTIMORE CAKE

1 cup butter
2 cups granulated sugar
3½ cups sifted flour
1 cup milk
3 teaspoons baking powder
1 teaspoon vanilla flavouring
½ teaspoon salt
1 teaspoon almond flavouring
Whites of 6 eggs

Cream the butter and sugar, then add the milk and the flour sifted with the baking powder, alternately. Fold in the beaten egg whites last of all, with flavouring. Bake in three layers in a moderately hot oven (375° F.) 25 to 30 minutes.

Filling: To one-half of the following frosting, when cool, add 1 cup of seeded raisins cut small, 1 cup of chopped nuts and 10 sliced maraschino cherries with half a teaspoonful of vanilla. Use the remainder of the icing plain for the top of the cake and decorate with cherries.

Melt one cup granulated sugar in half a cup of water with 1/16 teaspoon cream of tartar, stirring with wooden spoon till smooth. Cover and allow to boil without stirring for 4 minutes. Then cook to the hard-ball stage. (This takes 5 to 8 minutes after it boils, cooking to 254° F., or until a firm ball is formed in cold water.) Remove from fire whilst testing so that it will not overcook.

When done, remove from stove and when it stops bubbling pour slowly on to two stiffly-beaten egg whites (or one-sixth of a cup), beating it constantly. Continue beating it about 5 minutes till cool and thick.—C.G.

LADY CAKE

1 lb. sugar
¾ lb. sweet butter
1 lb. flour
2 oz. cornstarch
16 egg whites
Rose flavouring, lemon or almond extract
½ teaspoon baking powder

Cream butter and sugar together with 8 egg whites. Sift flour, cornstarch, and baking powder together and add to the creamed mixture. Beat the remaining 8 egg whites until very stiff and fold in gently. Stir in the flavouring mixing lightly. Pour into pans which have been greased and paper-lined. Bake in slow oven (300 to 325° F.) for 1¼ to 1½ hours depending upon size of pans. Makes two cakes.—A.W.R.

LANCASHIRE TEA CAKES

(One of Lancashire's many prides)

Make a dough with 1½ lb. of flour, ½ lb. each of currants and sugar, 2 oz. grated lemon peel, ¼ lb. lard, a teaspoonful of baking powder dissolved in milk, and 2 beaten eggs. Cook the cakes in an oven quick enough to raise them at once without browning them too much before they are cooked through.—P.A.

LANGUES DE CHAT

1 lb. fine butter
1 lb. fine castor sugar
12 whites of eggs
1¼ lb. soft flour
1 dessertspoon of vanilla sugar

Prepare the tins for baking by carefully waxing with melted white wax, or better still, good beeswax.

Beat up the butter and sugar and vanilla sugar as light as possible with a spattle, whisk the whites a little just to break them up thoroughly, and then beat into the mixture, using a ½ in. tube, and lay out on the waxed tins, 3 in. long. Bake in an oven 450° F., so that the centres of the biscuits remain only just tinted, and the edges which should run very thin should be richly coloured.—A.A.B.

LAPLAND BREAD

Put a pint of flour in a basin with a pint of cream or new milk, and mix it all well with the well-beaten yolks of 6 eggs, then at the last stir in quickly and lightly the stiffly-whipped whites of the eggs, pour the mixture in well-buttered tins dusted with flour, and bake in a moderate oven.—Q. (1).

LASAGNES, LAZAGNE

Long, thin, undulating, ribbon-like strips of Macaroni paste which are cooked like Macaroni (q.v.).

LAZY WILLIE CHOCOLATE CAKES

1 cup of sifted cake flour
1 cup of sugar
1 teaspoon of baking powder
⅛ teaspoon of salt
1 teaspoon of vanilla
2 tablespoons of butter
2 eggs, unbeaten
Milk
2 squares of chocolate (2 oz.), melted

Sift the dry ingredients together. Melt the butter in a measuring cup and cool. Add the eggs, fill up the cup with milk, and stir together thoroughly. Add gradually to the dry ingredients. Mix well. Stir in the melted chocolate and the vanilla. Fill small well-buttered cake-tins three-quarters full and bake in a moderately hot oven (375° F.) for 15 minutes. One-quarter cupful of chopped nuts may be added. Recipe makes about two dozen cakes.—E.K.H.

LEAVEN

Any substance used to provoke the fermentation of dough or to render it lighter, such as yeast, barm, baking powder, soda, etc.

LECRELET

A high-class, delicate and delicious pastry, sweetened with honey and flavoured with citron or orange, made nowhere so well as at Bâle, in Switzerland.

LEMON CAKE

5 oz. butter
5 oz. sugar
3 eggs
8 oz. flour
½ teaspoon baking powder
A little milk and a little grated lemon rind

Cream the butter and sugar together until they resemble whipped cream. Add the egg separately, with a little of the flour, and beat in very thoroughly. Lastly stir in the remaining flour, and the grated rind of half a lemon, pour into two greased and lined layer cake pans and bake at 350° F. for about half an hour. If liked, the cake can be split and spread with lemon curd.—G.H. (4).

LEMON CAKES

½ lb. butter
½ lb. ground rice
½ lb. castor sugar
1 lemon
4 eggs

Cream the butter and sugar. Add the well-beaten yolks of 4 eggs and the stiffly-whisked whites of two eggs. Sift in the ground rice and add the juice and finely-grated rind of lemon. Put in little tins and bake.—L.G.N.

LENA'S CORN BREAD

1 cup corn meal
1½ cups milk
1 cup flour
2 eggs
2 tablespoons sugar
4 teaspoons baking powder
1 teaspoon salt
2 tablespoons cooking oil
2 tablespoons melted butter

Sift together dry ingredients. Beat eggs and mix with milk. Add dry ingredients to eggs and milk mixture, then add the oil and melted butter and bake in a pan for 20 or 25 minutes in a moderate oven (350° F.).—L.R.

LIGHTNING CAKE

1 egg
½ cup sugar
1 cup flour
1 teaspoon baking powder
½ teaspoon vanilla
¼ teaspoon salt
¼ cup milk
3 tablespoons melted butter
¼ teaspoon lemon extract

Beat egg and add sugar while beating. Add flour sifted with baking powder and salt. Then add milk, melted butter, and flavouring. Bake 25 minutes in oil layer cake-pans in moderate oven (350° F.). Put together with any desired filling and frost as desired.—B.C.S.C.B.

LINZER TORTE (Austrian)
Linzer Paste

Sieve 8 oz. flour on to board; make a well, sprinkle on top 2 oz. ground almonds, 4 oz. sugar, grated rind of one lemon, half a level teaspoon powdered cloves, quarter of a teaspoon cinnamon. In centre of well place 6 oz. butter and one egg. With the fingers, cream the egg and butter together till like a pomade, and gradually work in flour and sugar and other ingredients till incorporated. Make into rough ball. Press paste away from you with the thumb end of the palm; do this in small sections, it blends the paste. Make into ball again and press away again. Form into ball once more, then put in piece of clean damp muslin and set in cold place till next day. To make successfully this 'pâte' requires as little handling as is possible; it is essential it should rest till next day.

Roll out paste and line a buttered flan ring; fill with raspberry jam liberally. Moisten edges of flan, and put a criss-cross lattice of paste on top. Brush over with beaten egg and bake in slow oven till pastry is well cooked and brown. Reduce some raspberry syrup and glaze top. Decorate with blanched split almonds. Better if kept for 2 to 3 days.—D.L.T.

LITTLE BUNS

Beat 6 oz. of butter to cream. Add the yolks of six eggs, 2 oz. of sugar, the grated peel of a lemon, an ounce of dried yeast mixed in a cup of warm milk, and 1 lb. of flour, with enough sour cream to mix the whole into a dough of light bread consistency. Put little lumps the size of a walnut in a buttered tin, and set them to rise. When they are light, put in the centre of each an almond, a raisin, or a dot of dried fruit, brush them over with egg and sugar mixed, or with egg and coarsely-pounded sugar, and bake them in a quick oven 10 or 20 minutes.—G.A.S.

LITTLE HOLLOW BISCUITS (1778)

Beat six eggs with one spoonful of rose or orange-flower water; add a full pound of loaf sugar sifted; mix these well; put flour to it which has been well dried till it is of a thickness to drop upon the sheets of white paper; drop them just as they are going to be baked, take them whilst hot off the paper; dry them in the oven on a sieve; keep them in boxes with paper between.—C.MA.

LITTLETON SPIDER CORN CAKE

1⅓ cups corn meal
¼ cup flour
1 cup sour milk
1 teaspoon soda (scant)
2 eggs, well-beaten
2 cups sweet milk
¼ cup sugar
½ teaspoon salt
1½ tablespoons butter

Mix and sift corn meal and flour. Add sour milk mixed with soda, eggs, one cup sweet milk, sugar, and salt. Melt butter in iron frying-pan and turn in mixture. Pour over remaining milk and bake 50 minutes in moderate oven (350° F.). Cut in pie-shaped pieces for serving.—B.C.S.C.B.

LITTLE WHITE CAKE

3 egg whites
⅔ cupful of sugar
¼ cupful of sifted cake flour
Grated rind of half a lemon
¼ cupful of butter, melted and cooled
2 teaspoonfuls of potato flour
7½ in. square cake-pan, buttered and floured

Beat the egg whites until stiff. Sift the dry ingredients together and add the lemon rind. Fold the egg whites into the flour until the two are blended. Add the cooled butter and mix lightly. Turn into the pan and bake in a moderately hot oven (325° F.) for 25 minutes, or until lightly browned and the edges leave the pan. Cool before removing. Frost or, if no frosting is desired, sprinkle with coarsely-chopped nuts before baking. —E.K.H.

LOOCHIES

Take 8 oz. flour, add half a teaspoonful of salt and rub in enough butter to make a pliable paste. Moisten it into a dough with a little water; pull it into small pieces, make these into balls about 1 in. in diameter and roll each as thin as paper. Fry them in deep fat in a frying-basket and let them dry on a sieve on the rack. Serve hot.—M.B. (2).

LOVE-AND-TANGLE

3 eggs, beaten
3 tablespoons sugar
3 tablespoons milk
Flour

Mix the eggs and sugar and add flour and milk to make it thick enough to roll. Roll in thin strips about 6 in. long and 3 in. wide, fold double by bringing one end up to the other. Beginning an inch or half inch from the folded end, cut several slits down the open end. Drop in hot fat and fry until light brown. Drain and sprinkle with powdered sugar.—C.G.

MACARONI

Macaroni is only one of the many pastes the names of which vary according to their thickness, shape, etc. Great care should be taken not to overcook these pastes. They should be put into a lot of salted boiling water and boiled for about 20 minutes according to size, the fine sorts and *nouilles* taking less time. Once boiled they can be served in a variety of ways, the simplest being to stir in a good lump of butter and hand some grated Parmesan cheese separately.

MACARONI À L'ITALIENNE

Plain boiled macaroni served with grated cheese.

MACARONI À LA MILANAISE
The same as *à l'Italienne*, but with tomato sauce added.

MACARONI AU GRATIN
The same as *à l'Italienne*, but heaped in a dish that will stand the fire; sprinkled with grated cheese and fine bread-raspings; bedewed with melted butter and put in oven till golden.

MACARONI, NEAPOLITAN
(*Pulcinella*)
Break tomatoes into pieces with the hand, and boil them with a few finely-chopped onions. Pass it all through a sieve. Boil about one quart of oil with 2 lb. of tomatoes till reduced to half, and combine the above with it. Cook the macaroni in salted water, pour over it the above sauce and sprinkle over it Parmesan cheese.—P.A.

MACARONI PUDDING
Take 1½ oz. of the best macaroni, and simmer it in a pint of milk with a little cinnamon till tender; put it into a dish with milk, 3 eggs (but only one white), some sugar, and a little nutmeg.—G.A.S.

MACARONI SOUP
Boil 4 oz. of the macaroni till three-fourths cooked. Have prepared strong gravy soup; take care that the macaroni does not get into lumps. Boil up. Serve rasped Parmesan in a glass dish or on a plate. Many strew it on the soup. This may be made a sort of white soup by thickening it with white sauce, and adding hot cream gradually when to be served, giving it first a boil up.—G.A.S.

MACARONI TIMBALE
One of the most elegant preparations of macaroni is the *Timbale de Macaroni*. Simmer ½ lb. macaroni in plenty of water, and a tablespoonful of salt, till it is tender, but take care not to have it too soft; though tender it should be firm, and the form entirely preserved, and no part beginning to melt (this caution will serve for the preparation of all macaroni). Strain the water from it – beat up 5 yolks and the whites of 2 eggs – take half a pint of the best cream, and the breast of a fowl and some thin slices of ham. Mince the breast of the fowl with ham – add them with from 2 to 3 tablespoonfuls of finely-grated Parmesan cheese, and season with pepper and salt. Mix all these with the macaroni, and put into a pudding-mould well-buttered, and then let it steam in a stew-pan of boiling water for about an hour, and serve quite hot, with rich gravy.—W.K.

MACARONI WITH TOMATOES
Put ¼ lb. macaroni in a large saucepan of boiling water and boil until tender, roughly 20 minutes, but it takes less time if freshly made. Drain well and mix with a tomato sauce made as follows: Heat two tablespoonfuls of olive oil and a little butter in a pan and add one onion roughly-chopped. Cook to a golden brown, then add about 1 lb. of tomatoes, also chopped, salt, pepper and a sprig of sweet basil or parsley. Bring to the boil and let simmer until the tomatoes are quite soft, rub through a sieve and reheat in the saucepan; then mix with your Macaroni together with about 2 oz. of butter and 4 oz. of grated Parmesan cheese.—M.K.S. (2).

MACARONI WHEAT
Lat. *Triticum durum*. A particularly 'hard' kind of *Wheat*, rich in gluten, grown on poor soils, particularly in Italy and Southern Russia. It is not suitable for bread-making but excellent for all kinds of *Italian Pastes* (q.v.).

MACAROONS
Almond Paste Biscuits.

I
8 oz. ground almonds
2 teaspoons orange flower water
1 lb. castor sugar
4 whites of eggs
2½ oz. ground rice

Whisk the whites of eggs stiffly, stir in the sugar, ground rice, and flavouring, then the ground almonds, and blend thoroughly until the mixture is light and creamy. Cover the baking-sheet with rice paper, place the mixture in small heaps on the paper, and bake in a moderate oven for 20 minutes or until golden brown.—G.H. (4).

II
Rub 1 lb. of almond paste with 2 cupfuls of sugar, 6 unbeaten whites of eggs and 2 tablespoonfuls of flour to a smooth paste. Fill into a pastry-bag, and squeeze ¾ in. wide drops on to Manila paper lying on baking-sheets. Bake in moderate oven (350° F.). When cold, wet bottom of paper so as to lift macaroons off easily.—E.E.A.

MADEIRA CAKE
8 oz. flour
Pinch of salt
½ teaspoon baking powder
5 oz. castor sugar
5 oz. butter or margarine
Little grated lemon rind
Few drops lemon essence
3 eggs
Milk to mix
Slice of citron

Prepare a cake tin. Sieve the flour, salt, and baking powder together and add a very little finely grated lemon rind. Put the sugar and butter into a basin and work together until they are of a creamy consistency. Beat in each egg separately, stir in the dry ingredients, and lastly add a little lemon essence and milk if required. Put into the prepared tin, place in an oven of 375° F. and bake for 1 to 1¼ hours. The slice of citron should be put on top of the cake as soon as it is set; if put on before the cake is put into the oven, it is inclined to sink.—G.H. (4).

MADEIRA GINGERBREAD

1 lb. flour, 1 lb. treacle, 1 lb. loaf sugar, ½ lb. butter or beef dripping, ¼ lb. citron, 2 eggs, 1 dessertspoonful ground cloves, one of ground ginger, 1 teaspoonful of bicarbonate of soda, the grated rind of 2 lemons, and 1 wineglassful of warm milk. Beat the eggs and sugar together, rub the butter into the flour, then add all the other ingredients, mixing well. The soda must be dissolved in the milk and added last. Place in a buttered tin and bake for nearly three hours.—M.B. (2).

MADELEINES

This is a little cake made of flour, butter, sugar and eggs, the same weight of each, as for the *Quatre-quarts* (q.v.), but in a small, grooved, deep, scallop shaped mould. It was called a *tôt-fait*, and was popular in Lorraine more than two hundred years ago. In or about the year 1730, the King of Poland, Stanislas Leczinski, a great gourmet and Louis XV's father in law, introduced *tôt-faits* to the Versailles Court, where they became fashionable. But it was only at the beginning of the nineteenth century that they were named *Madeleines* by one Avice, chief pastrycook to the Prince de Talleyrand, and they have been justly popular under that name ever since. The best *Madeleines* are those of Commercy, in Lorraine.

Here is an American recipe, not quite orthodox but none the worse for being a little lighter of texture than *Madeleines* made of *Quatre-quarts* dough:

Combine in a saucepan 10 oz. of powdered sugar with 8 whole eggs, place the saucepan into a large pot with boiling water – use the double-boiler, if you like – and beat this mixture till it thickens. Remove from the fire and add 7 oz. of fine, sifted cake flour, the juice of half a lemon and a pinch of grated ..mon rind – suit your taste – and 5 oz. of melted, lukewarm sweet butter. Mix all this carefully and thoroughly. Butter the muffin-tins well, sprinkle with fine breadcrumbs and fill the cavities with the dough to three-quarters their height. Bake in medium (300° F.) oven.—W.R.

MAGGIE'S BISCUITS

    4 tablespoons ground rice
    4 tablespoons flour
    1 egg
    4 tablespoons sugar
    3 tablespoons butter

Break the egg into the bowl on top of dry ingredients after the butter has been rubbed into it. Then roll out and make biscuits.—L.N.G.

MAHOGO

The name by which the *Cassava* (q.v.) is known in Zanzibar where it is cultivated to a considerable extent and supplies the staple food of the native population.

MAIDS OF HONOUR
I

Line some patty pans with good puff paste and fill with a mixture made as follows: half a pint of milk, 2 tablespoonfuls of breadcrumbs, 4 oz. butter, 2 oz. ground almonds, 1 oz. sugar, the grated rind of one lemon, 3 eggs. Boil the milk and crumbs and let them stand for 10 minutes, then add the butter, sugar and flavouring; beat in the eggs one at a time. Put a dessertspoonful of the mixture in the centre of the pastry and bake a golden brown.—H.E.

II

    ¼ lb. ground rice
    3 oz. moist sugar
    2 oz. butter
    2 eggs
    A little almond flavouring

Beat up butter and sugar and ground rice and flavouring and lastly, the eggs (well-beaten). When this is done, line some patty-pans with short paste, place in a little jam (raspberry, if possible), cover with the mixture and cross with two thin strips of pastry. Bake in a moderate oven till done.—L.G.N.

MAIZE. CORN

Fr. *Maïs*. The six main groups of this valuable cereal are:

1. *Pod Maize* (*Zea Mays tunicata*), probably the original plant from which the others have been raised; it is grown as a curiosity only;

2. *Pop Maize* (*Z. M. everta*), of which there are 25 named varieties, grown from Canada to Peru;

3. *Flint Maize* (*Z. M. indurata*), of which there are 69 named varieties grown as a field crop chiefly in Canada, the New England States, and the New York State;

4. *Dent Maize* (*Z. M. indentata*), of which there are 323 named varieties; it is the most extensively grown type of maize for grinding into meal or flour both for human consumption and fodder food;

5. *Soft Maize* (*Z. M. amylacea*), of which there are 27 named varieties, chiefly grown in South America;

6. *Sweet Maize* (*Z. M. Saccharata*), of which there are 63 named varieties both a garden vegetable and a field crop, and used in the kitchen freshly picked or canned as well as in the shape of flour or meal.

'Not only is maize in the collective sense the most important American cereal, but the acreage, as well as the money value of the crop, exceed those of any other crop – indeed, this statement doubtless applies to Dent maize alone, as it is this variety that is grown in the great corn-producing states of the Middle West. The national prestige of this giant grass is voiced in the saying "Corn is King."

'Only a small fraction of the enormous American crop is consumed by human beings, although in some states, notably in the South, maize ranks with wheat as a bread cereal. In most of the country, particularly the parts with the densest populations, maize in any form is a human food of secondary importance. By far the greater part of the crop is consumed by animals on the farm where it is produced, and a considerable part of what remains is consumed by animals in regions into which the corn or its products is shipped.'—A.L.W.
See *Corn*.

MAIZE MEAL PORRIDGE

    1 cup South African maize meal
    5 or 6 cups water, or water and milk
    1½ teaspoonfuls salt

Add the salt to the water (or water and milk). Bring to the boil, and gradually stir in the maize meal (dry, or mixed with a little cold water). Cook fast for 5 minutes, then slowly for about an hour, stirring occasionally in order to prevent burning. The porridge may be cooked for a longer period in a double-boiler, in which case stirring is not necessary.

N.B.—Left-over porridge (kaffir corn and oatmeal as well as maize meal) may be served with cooked, dried or stewed fruit and sugar, as a dessert, or used up in other ways.

MALT BREAD

    18 oz. white flour
    10 oz. wholemeal flour
    2 oz. malt
    ½ oz. yeast
    1 teaspoon salt
    2 tablespoons treacle
    ¾ pint water
    1 oz. butter

Mix the malt with quarter of a pint warm water, stir into the wholemeal flour, put into a double saucepan and surround by hot water at a temperature of about 140° F. (If poured from the kettle when it begins to 'sing', the temperature is approximately 140° F.). Put the lid on and leave for 6 hours, keeping the water at this temperature. Sieve the white flour and salt into a basin. Rub in the butter. Cream the yeast with a little water and stir the remainder of the water with which the treacle has been mixed into the flour. Leave for 1¼ hours to sponge. Add the cool malt mixture to the yeast dough and knead until well mixed. Put into greased tins and set to rise in a warm place for about half an hour. Bake at 400° F.—G.H. (4).

MANCHET. MANCHANT

An Old English name for a small loaf of fine wheaten flour baked specially for the lord of the house and persons of quality. In some parts of Cornwall they call a *Manchant* a loaf of bread shaped by hand and not baked in a tin.

MANIOC

Another name for *Cassava* (q.v.).

MANITOU BLACK CAKE

    3 oz. chocolate, melted
    1 egg yolk, well-beaten
    1 cup milk
    2 tablespoons butter
    1 cup sugar
    ½ cup milk
    1½ cups flour
    1 teaspoon vanilla
    2 teaspoons baking powder
    1 teaspoon soda

Mix the yolk of the egg with the milk and melted chocolate. Cook over the water until the mixture is thick and smooth. Remove from heat. Add the seven remaining ingredients in their order. Thoroughly beat in the flour before adding the baking powder and soda. Pour into a well-buttered pan, 12 by 9 by 1½ in. Bake in moderate oven (375° F.). Cover with boiled frosting. Cut in squares. Is a very rich cake, more like confection.—C.G.

MANNHEIM BREAD

Make a firm dough with 2 whole eggs, 6 oz. of fine flour, 2 oz. castor sugar, and ½ oz. powdered anise seed. When well mixed, divide the dough, rolling these pieces into long rolls 12 in. or so long and 2 in. or 3 in. across; lay these rolls on a buttered tin, score them down their length with a knife, brush them over with the yolk of an egg, and bake in a hot oven. They may be served whole or sliced and lightly dried in the oven, as rusks.—Q.

MARVELS

> 6 tablespoons sugar
> ¼ teaspoon nutmeg, mace or cinnamon
> 2 eggs, well-beaten
> 10 tablespoons flour

Add the sugar to the eggs and beat well. Sift the nutmeg or other spice with the flour and fold into the first mixture. A little more flour may be added if required, but we found that this was about the right amount to use for a batter which could be dropped into the hot fat.

Have ready a kettle of fat and drop the batter in by teaspoonfuls. When one side of the little cake is brown, turn it over to brown on the other side. Drain, roll in powdered sugar and serve. This will make about two dozen small cakes. (*Mary Leize Simons*).—B.S.R.

MARZIPAN. MARCHPANE

Fr. *Massepain*. It is very similar to the almond icing so much appreciated on wedding cakes. Take, for instance, ½ lb. of almonds, 20 bitter almonds, and ¼ lb. of sugar. Scald, peel and dry the almonds, pound them all in a mortar, and then press them through a sieve. To avoid too much stiffness in the paste, moisten occasionally during the pounding process with a little rose or orange flower water; crush and sift the sugar, which must be very finely-powdered, put it into a copper saucepan with the almonds, stand it over the fire, and stir steadily until the paste has attained the right consistency. Sprinkle some sugar on a pastry board and knead the almond paste; make it into a ball, wrap it in a sheet of clean paper, and keep it in a cool, dry place till wanted. It will remain good for some days, and need, therefore, not all be used at once; or it can be made beforehand. The rest of the process is quite simple. Roll it out on the board (if too stiff, moisten with some white of egg), work it to any desired thickness, cut the paste into fancy shapes, and dry (rather than bake them) in a moderate oven. They can also be covered with fruit, or merely be sprinkled with sugar.—Q. (1).

MASHLUM SCONES and MASLIN BREAD

Maslin Bread (sometimes spelt *Meslin*, signifying mixed grain) is made from a mixture of wheat and rye, sometimes sown and grown together, particularly in France, in the Alpes Maritimes, and in the North of England, where good wheat crops cannot

196

always be depended upon. After bad seasons *Maslin Bread* was largely used for local consumption. *Mashlum Scones* used to be commonly eaten by small farmers and agricultural labourers in Scotland in bygone Protection times. These scones were made of flour consisting of one part beans and two parts oats, ground and sifted by hand, and often even bran would be added. —L.G.M.

M'BELE MEAL

Ground *Sorghum* (q.v.) or *Kaffir Corn* (q.v.) meal: it is very popular as an article of daily diet in South Africa, in the form of *Porridge*, prepared in the same way as *Maize Meal Porridge* (q.v.), using a little more water and a little more salt. Europeans like *M'bele Meal*, as a rule, when they taste it in South Africa, but the brownish colour of the meal is not attractive: it is probably why so few people bought it when it was being offered for sale in some of the London Stores.

MEALIES

An African name for Maize or Indian Corn as grown in practically every part of the Union of South Africa, but chiefly in Natal and Cape Province.

MERINGUES

Whites of 2 eggs, 4 oz. of castor sugar, a pinch of salt. Whip whites very stiffly indeed, mix in sugar as lightly as possible. Take 2 dessertspoons, pile one with the mixture, and scoop out with the other on to a slightly oiled sheet of paper. Sieve over with castor sugar, and bake in a very cool oven till crisp and firm. Slip them off the paper with a knife, turn them upside down, and return to the oven till dry. Preferably Meringues should be baked on a board instead of a tin. It gets less hot, and therefore cooks them more slowly. Fill with whipped cream sweetened, with some strawberries coated with Melba sauce on the top.—L.M. (2).

MERINGUES CHANTILLY

Fill two Meringue Shells with *Crème Chantilly*, i.e. whipped cream sweetened and flavoured to taste.

MERINGUE SHELLS

Add to 6 well-beaten whites of eggs 1½ cupfuls of granulated sugar with vanilla or lemon flavouring. Fill mixture into pastrybag and form ovals about 2½ in. long on Manila paper atop a baking-sheet. Powder with sugar and bake for 35 to 40 minutes at 250° F. These will keep for some time in a dry, airy place.—E.E.A.

MESQUITE. ALGARROBA

The names of different varieties of spring shrubs of Mexico and some of the Southern

States of U.S.A.; their beanlike pods are rich in sugar and are used by the poorer natives pounded to a meal from which they make a kind of bread and some cakes. (See also Section II.)

MIGLIACCIO

An Italian delicacy made of a chestnut-flour paste about 1½ in. thick baked to a rich brown and with *Pignoli* sprinkled on top, or, failing *Pignoli*, chopped almonds and nuts.

MIGLIACCINI

Small edition of the *Migliaccio*; they are made in the same way but baked in small separate baking-tins.

MILDRED'S CAKE

Three eggs, 1 cup castor sugar, beat together for 15 minutes. Fold in lightly 1 cup of flour, to which has been added 1 teaspoonful cream of tartar, half a teaspoonful soda sifted five times. Melt and heat together 1 tablespoonful of butter, 4 tablespoonfuls milk; add to the above. Put into two layer cake pans and bake in a very hot oven about 450° F. 12 minutes.—P.D.P.

MILK BREAD

Two cups of scalded milk, 2 tablespoonfuls of shortening, 2 tablespoonfuls of sugar, 1 teaspoonful of salt, 3 yeast cakes, half a cup of lukewarm water, 6 or more cups of flour. Pour the milk over the shortening, sugar and salt in a bowl; when cooled to a luke-warm temperature add the yeast softened and mixed with the lukewarm water and stir in the flour. Knead well. Wash, dry and butter your bowl; put in the dough and set aside in warm place to rise; form into loaves and bake about one hour.—M.K.S. (2).

MILK ROLLS

½ pint of flour
1½ oz. butter
1 gill warm milk
½ oz. compressed yeast
1 oz. castor sugar
A pinch of salt
1 egg

Mix together the flour and salt in a basin, rub in the butter, beat the yeast and sugar to a cream, gradually stir in the warm milk. Put this into a hole in the centre of the flour and gradually work in all the flour. Make the mixture into a fairly stiff dough. Put into a floured basin, cover and leave for half an hour to rise. Then shape into rolls and brush over with beaten egg. Put them on a greased baking-tin and leave them in a warm place to 'prove' for about 10 minutes. Then bake in a fairly hot oven for about 15 minutes.

MILLE-FEUILLE
(Gâteau)

From some good puff-paste not too thinly rolled out cut some rounds, the first the size of a plate, the rest decreasing in size; place these separately on papered baking-tins and bake till lightly coloured and cooked. Now lift out the tins, lay white paper over the rounds, and a lightly-weighted iron baking-sheet on this and leave till quite cold, when you spread each round with any icing to taste, arranging each on top of the other till you have built them up into a kind of pyramid, put a glacé fruit on the apex, and serve when firm. If preferred, the rounds may be cut of equal size, and all but the top one spread with a sheet of bavaroise, jelly, Vienna icing, or any filling to taste; they are then built up as before, the whole cake being iced with any icing you please and garnished to taste with fruit, nuts and rosettes of pink and white Vienna icing.—Q. (1).

MILLET

Lat. *Panicum milliaceum*; Fr. *Millet commun*. 'True or common Millet has been culti-vated since prehistoric times in Asia, Northern Africa, and Southern Europe. It was grown by the ancient Egyptians, Lake Dwellers, East Indians, Greeks, and Romans. In China, Japan, India and parts of Europe it is still cultivated for human food. Under the Russian name "proso" it has been intro-duced into the United States.'—A.L.W.

The name *Millet* is also applied, with a qualifying prefix, to cereals and grasses which do not belong to the true *Millet* genus, such as *African Millet* or *Ragi* (q.v.), *Pearl Millet*, *Indian Millet* or *Great Millet*, which is not a Millet but the *Sorghum* (q.v.); the *Chena Millet*, which is extensively grown in the East; the *Little Millet* and the *Saniva Millet*, grown in Southern Europe and Northern Africa and also in the U.S.A. where, how-ever, it is not grown for its seeds but merely as forage. The *Italian* or *Foxtail Millet*, which belongs to a different order and bears larger seeds than the rest is grown not only in Italy but in Egypt and many parts of the Near East. It is used for both human and animal consumption, and it is the kind usually sold in shops under the name of *Golden Millet*, a name it owes to its yellow colour. The *Bulrush Millet* belongs to yet another class of forage grasses and its seeds are used in the East, ground, in the form of half-baked thin cakes.

MINCEPIES

¾ lb. flaky pastry
Mincemeat
Castor sugar
White of 1 egg

Enough for five or six persons.

Roll out the pastry and cut it into rounds. Line buttered muffin pans with the rounds, fill them up with mincemeat, moisten the edges with cold water, and cover with rounds of pastry. Cut the pies across in the centre, and bake in a quick oven. If the mince pies are to be glazed, brush them with beaten white of egg or water and dredge them with castor sugar when the pastry is half-cooked.

Note.—Mincepies can also be made without using muffin pans.

Mincemeat

1 lb. Valencia almonds
6 oz. mixed peel
Spices
¾ lb. Demerara sugar
1 lb. beef suet
2 lemons
1 gill brandy
1 lb. sultanas
1 lb. currants
¼ lb. crystallized fruit
1 lb. cooking apples
1 tangerine
1 gill rum

Utensils: Knife, chopping board, basin, gill measure, grater, teaspoon, lemon squeezer, wooden spoon, strainer.

Stone and chop the raisins and peel; clean the other dried fruit, and peel and chop the apples. Mix the fruit in a large basin with the finely-shredded suet, 2 oz. blanched and chopped almonds, the sugar, salt, half a teaspoon grated nutmeg, half a teaspoonful ground cloves, quarter of a teaspoonful ground mace, 1 teaspoonful each of ground cinnamon and ginger, the grated rinds of two lemons and of one tangerine. Add the strained juice of the lemons and the tangerine, the brandy and the rum. Pot and cover.—E.C. (1).

MOCHA CAKE

Make a round sponge cake, and cut a hole in the centre. Pour into the hole strong black coffee. Fill the centre of the cake with whipped cream, cover all the cake with whipped cream and sprinkle thickly with chopped nuts or almonds, browned. (*The Hon. Mrs Talbot-Rice*).—L.M. (1).

MOONSHINES

Mix and sift together into one beaten egg and one-half cup milk, one-third cup of sugar, one and a third cups of flour, two teaspoons of baking powder, one-fourth teaspoon of salt, one-half teaspoon of nutmeg, one teaspoon of melted butter. Drop into boiling fat, drain on brown paper. Split

and put currant jelly between. Roll in confectioner's sugar. (*Mrs Cole's Recipe, c.* 1837. *Adapted Market Square Tavern Kitchen.* 1937.) —H.B.

MOSS ROSE CAKE

2 cups sugar
4 eggs unbeaten
½ teaspoon almond flavouring
2 cups sifted cake flour
1 cup milk, scalded

Break eggs over sugar and beat 12 minutes. Heat milk to boiling point, add almond flavouring and let stand. Stir the flour into the egg and sugar mixture and then add the warm milk slowly. Beat until well mixed (about 3 minutes). Bake in a moderate oven (375° F.) in two layers about 25· minutes. Top with coconut-orange frosting.—C.G.

MOTHER'S CAKE

1 scant cup of butter
3 eggs
¼ teaspoon mace
3 cups pastry flour
½ teaspoon soda
1½ cups of sugar
1 teaspoon lemon flavouring
½ cup of milk
1 teaspoon cream of tartar
1 cup of currants

Cream butter, add sugar, and then egg yolks. Beat well together. Sift dry ingredients three times. Add alternately with milk. Fold in stiffly-beaten egg whites. Add flavouring and currants slightly floured. Bake an hour – oven 350° F. (*Mary G. Chandler.*)—T.C.

MOUNT VERNON POUND CAKE

Wash all the salt from a pound of butter, then put it dry between the folds of a clean cloth and set away in a cold place. Sift one pound of pastry flour and separate the yolks and whites of twelve eggs. Cream the butter and flour together very thoroughly and beat the yolks of the eggs to a thick, almost white, froth with one pound of granulated sugar. Add one teaspoonful of vanilla and a grating of mace. Gradually add the creamed butter and flour to the sugar and egg mixture and whip well, then fold in the stiffly-beaten whites of the eggs, pour into a well-greased and floured tube-pan, scatter a little grated lemon or orange rind over the top and bake in a moderate oven about one and a quarter hours. (*Old Recipe, Chase City, Virginia.*)—H.B.

MUFFINS (English)

I

To make Muffins (1807)

Take 4 lb. of fine flour, 2 spoonfuls of new yeast, 8 whites of eggs, a quart of milk, made warm, mix it well together, and let it rise for near an hour; then bake them. They must be made up with flour, so as not to stick to the hand.—A.A.

II

½ oz. compressed yeast
1¾ lb. flour
½ teaspoonful salt
1 pint water

Mix flour and salt in a basin and make a well in the centre. Cream the yeast with a wooden spoon and add lukewarm water. Stir yeast and water into the flour and beat well for about 20 minutes. Cover the basin and set to rise in a warm place for 1½ hours. Then beat the mixture up again and turn on to a thickly-floured board. Beat up the mixture again. Grease some hot muffin rings or large round cutters and place them on a greased girdle. Half fill them with the mixture and cook and brown on one side; remove the rings, turn the muffins and brown the other side. Split open, butter and serve hot.—M.K.S. (2).

III

1 pint of warm milk
2 lb. flour
¼ pint brewers' yeast
1 egg
1 oz. butter and a little salt

Mix all these ingredients together and beat up well with the hand. Set the mixture to rise. Make the muffins round, using a little extra flour to keep the dough from sticking. Let them remain a few minutes and then bake them on an iron or steel plate.—H.E.

MUSH

A sort of *Porridge* made by boiling some ground rice to a *Mush*: it has been called an American edition of the Italian *Polenta*.

MYSTERY BREAD

Sift together 2 cups of flour, 5 teaspoons of baking powder, half a teaspoon of salt, and 2 tablespoons of sugar. Mix with half a tablespoon of caraway seeds, half a cup of currants, and half a cup of seeded raisins. Beat 1 whole egg with 1 cup of milk and add to the mixture with 4 tablespoons of melted butter. Pour into a well-greased iron baking-pan or skillet and bake about half an hour in a moderate oven. Cut in wedge-shaped pieces and serve warm.—G.T.L.

NAPLES CAKES
(Zeppole)

Bring to the boil 2 glasses of water, half a glass of Marsala, half a pint of white wine and a little pepper. Sprinkle in ¾ lb. of flour and stir until the paste no longer sticks to the bottom of the pan. Put oil on the pastry board and turn the paste on to it, add 2 eggs and knead well and strongly. Roll it out, cut it into flat small cakes like biscuits, and fry in olive oil.—P.A.

NAPOLEON BISCUITS

4 oz. flour, 3 oz. of butter, 1 oz. castor sugar, 1 oz. ground almonds, 1 yolk of egg, jam.

Cream butter and sugar together, add the flour (sieved) and the ground almonds and the yolk of egg and a teaspoon of water with it. Leave the dough for one hour. Roll out very thinly and cut into small rounds with a cutter. Bake 10 minutes in a moderate oven. When cool put raspberry jam between two biscuits and place them together. This amount should make 15 double biscuits.—L.C.

NELL'S RICE CAKE

Ingredients: Ground rice, ½ lb.; fine white sugar, ½ lb.; eggs, 5.

Time: To bake in slow oven, about 30 to 40 minutes.

Method: 1. Mix the ground rice with the sugar. 2. Beat the eggs well. 3. Sift in the rice and sugar. 4. Beat all well together for 20 minutes. 5. Put into a lightly-buttered tin, dusted with rice flour and sugar mixed, and bake in slow oven.

N.B.—This makes an excellent sponge layer cake or a jam sandwich.—FL.W.

NEW ENGLAND BROWN BREAD

1 cup stale bread
2 cups cold water
½ cup molasses
1 teaspoon salt
1 cup rye meal *or* white flour
1 cup corn meal
1 cup coarse entire wheat flour
2 teaspoons soda

Soak bread in 1½ cups of the water overnight. Rub through colander, add molasses, dry ingredients mixed and sifted, and remaining water. Steam like *Boston Brown Bread*. Two loaves.—B.C.S.C.B.

NEW ENGLAND WEDDING CAKE

1 lb. sweet butter
1 lb. sugar
12 eggs
1 lb. flour

1 teaspoon cloves
1 teaspoon nutmeg
1 cup brandy
1 cup sherry
2 lb. seeded raisins, chopped
2 lb. currants
1 lb. citron shaved thin
1 teaspoon cinnamon

Cream butter and add sugar gradually. Beat egg yolk thick and add; whip in whites, beaten stiff. Dredge fruit with half a cup flour, sift remaining flour with spices, and stir into batter. Add wine and brandy. Stir in the dredged fruit, except the citron.

Line inside baking-pan with buttered paper. Lay in some of the citron, then a layer of the mixed batter, alternating until all citron and batter is used.

Bake in steady slow oven (275° F.) for 4 hours. Allow cake to cool gradually in oven.—C.R.B.B. (2).

NOODLES. NOUILLES. NUDELS

Fine ribbons of paste made of macaroni, or hard wheat flour and eggs. Noodles have been in great esteem in Northern China for centuries, and they were introduced to Italy from China by Marco Polo at the beginning of the fourteenth century; since then noodles have become popular in practically every part of Europe and America. Noodles can be made of any good flour available, but they are not true noodles if made without eggs.

To make Noodles

Make a paste with 1 lb. flour, 1 teaspoonful of salt, 3 whole eggs and 5 egg yolks, and as much water as may be necessary to moisten it. Roll this paste out twice upon a board and leave it to stand for 1 or 2 hours before cutting it up. Cut it up in long, fine strips. Plunge in boiling salted water and cook for 10 minutes. Drain in a colander and 'finish' in any way suitable for *Macaroni* (q.v.), or as follows:

Nouilles au beurre

Melt a sufficiency of fresh butter in a pan and pour over it the drained, freshly-boiled, noodles. Season with pepper and salt and toss the noodles about, turning them over occasionally with a fork so that they will all get a taste of the butter and be thoroughly hot when served.

Noodles sauté with Fresh Mushrooms

Slice thin 4 fresh mushrooms into 6 tablespoonfuls of butter, let smother for 3 minutes, then add ½ lb. of boiled noodles.

Season properly and toss about in pan until thoroughly heated.—E.E.A.

Thrifty Nouilles

Take ½ lb. of flour, salt, 1 egg and a tablespoonful of oil and mix with enough water to make a fairly stiff but elastic dough. Knead well and let it stand for about an hour or longer if convenient. Flour a pastry board and roll out your dough as thinly and as evenly as possible, sprinkle evenly with flour and roll it up like a 'Swissroll', then with a sharp knife cut the roll into slices. Unroll the slices and pile up the resulting ribbons lightly so that the air can get between them, or hang them over a towel rail to dry. I generally make my nouilles in the morning and they are dry enough by the evening, but I have kept them for two or three days.

They should be cooked in boiling salted water for about a quarter of an hour.

The same dough can be used for *Ravioli* or *Cannelone*.—M.K.S. (2).

NORTHUMBERLAND PUDDING

Make a thick batter by boiling and sweetening milk and flour. When cold and firm, mash it up, and add to it 4 oz. of melted butter, the same weight of currants, 2 oz. of candied lemon and orange peel, sliced, and a little brandy, if liked. Butter custard cups, and bake the puddings in them for 15 minutes. Turn them out on a dish, and pour wine sauce over them if to be eaten hot. If to make a cold, ornamental supper dish, omit the wine sauce.—G.A.S.

NUSSCREME TORTE
(Austrian)

Beat 4 yolks of egg with 1¼ oz. castor sugar till white.

Beat 5 whites of egg till stiff, then fold in 1¼ oz. sugar. Mix gently together, then add, very delicately, 1½ oz. sieved flour mixed with 3 oz. grated walnuts, little cinnamon, grated lemon rind. Next add little diluted caramel to colour; lastly, fold in 2 oz. melted butter, almost cool. Bake about 30 minutes in floured and buttered tins, not too deep, in very moderate oven. When cool, split or cut in half, and set one half on the other with following filling:

Cream 3 oz. butter; add 3 oz. icing sugar and beat till as whipped cream; flavour with coffee essence or strong coffee and add 3 oz. coarsely-chopped walnuts.

Cover top with icing sugar, mixed with lightly-whipped cream, flavoured with coffee. Put cake in oven for a minute or two to set icing. Decorate walnut halves.—D.L.T.

OATCAKES

They are chiefly Scots cakes and are made of two degrees of thickness, the one very thin, like the Passover Cake of the Jews, and the other about ¼ in. thick. They are known in the North of England as *Havercakes*.

Oatcakes

½ lb. oatmeal
2 oz. butter or lard
2 oz. sugar
A pinch of salt
1 teaspoonful baking powder

Put all ingredients in a basin and mix well, warm butter and add to the mixture. Knead into a pliable dough with warm water. Roll out thin on a baking-board, using plenty of dry oatmeal in the process. Let it remain to get firm a few minutes. Cut according to fancy. Bake in oven till very crisp.—A.C.B.

Oatcake

Mix 1 lb. of medium oatmeal with 4 teaspoonfuls of dripping, or lard, and a teaspoonful of salt, with just enough warm water to make a dough. Knead it till smooth; then dust a board with dry oatmeal, press the dough out on this with the knuckles into a round cake, roll it out quite thin, bake it on a hot girdle till firm (first cutting it across twice into triangles), then lift them off, rub them over lightly with dry meal, and toast till crisp before the fire. When ready they will curl up. Real Oatcake should be made of meal and water only, but this is a little too Spartan for most tastes, hence the fat.—Q. (1).

OATMEAL

The flour of meal of ground, hulled oats, and for a long time the staple food of the Scottish peasantry. There are many different grades and qualities of *Oatmeal*, the best being the Scots Oatmeal from East Lothian oats. Oatmeal is prepared in three grades or cuts: *pinhead*, *medium* and *fine*; or *rough*, *middle* and *small*.

Oatmeal needs much and very careful cooking in order to break the starch cells, and, of course, the larger and coarser the meal, the longer boiling it requires; but it is worth all the trouble.

OATMEAL BREAD

Take ½ lb. flour, ¼ lb. oatmeal, 1 teaspoonful salt, 1 teaspoonful baking soda, 1 teaspoonful cream of tartar, 1 breakfastcupful buttermilk. Soak the oatmeal in the buttermilk for two hours, then add the flour mixed with the other dry ingredients, knead lightly, form into a loaf and bake in a hot oven for 30 to 40 minutes.—A.C.B.

OATMEAL CAKES or BISCUITS

Mix together 6 oz. flour, and 6 oz. of medium or fine Oatmeal. Rub in 2 oz. of margarine, then rub in 2 oz. of grated cheese and a pinch of salt with 1 teaspoonful of bicarbonate of soda, mixed with a little water, to make a soft dough. Turn on to a floured plate and divide into two rolls (each ½ in.). Cut these into scone shape. Bake in a slightly greased tin in a moderately hot oven for 10 to 15 minutes. These scones or biscuits are excellent with cheese, or they can be split and served with butter or margarine.—B.H.

OATMEAL BROSE

Oatmeal, salt, butter and water.

Place two handfuls of oatmeal in a bowl. Add salt and a piece of butter. Pour over boiling water to cover oatmeal and stir it roughly, allowing knots to form. Serve hot with buttermilk or sweet milk. May be made with buttermilk or broth stock instead of using water.—S.W.R.

OATMEAL PANCAKES

I

2 heaped tablespoons of flour
2 heaped tablespoons of medium oatmeal
1 teaspoon of baking powder and a pinch of salt
1 egg and sufficient milk and water to mix

Lightly mix the dry ingredients. Break in the egg. Beat to a batter, gradually adding sufficient milk and water to make the mixture the consistency of thick cream. Allow to stand for half an hour. Take a frying-pan, grease with a lardy paper, and make very hot (as for omelettes). Drop the mixture on the hot pan with a tablespoon. Turn the pancakes as soon as little holes begin to form on top. They require only a few minutes cooking, and several can be cooked at once.

The resulting pancakes look very similar to thick drop scones, with a spongey light consistency. At our home they are served very hot with a little jam or syrup spread over, another pancake placed on top forming a delicious sandwich.

We find the pudding an advantage because (1) no sugar is used, (2) very little fat is needed for greasing the pan. (3) egg powder is equally effective if eggs are unobtainable, and (4) oatmeal is a valuable energy-producing food. Furthermore, this pudding need not be prepared until half an hour before the meal is due, a great benefit in these days when so many housewives are engaged in extra work of all kinds.—C.B.J.

II
A Way to use up Porridge

Beat up as many eggs as will be needed. To 8 dessertspoonfuls of porridge 2 eggs. Add the eggs to the porridge and sufficient milk to make a thin batter. Let it stand for a couple of hours; add if needed, a little more milk. At the last, mix in half a teaspoonful of powdered sugar and a tablespoonful of cold water.

These pancakes will make a good first course if filled with curry (chicken, lobster or minced meat), or they can be powdered thickly with grated cheese before rolling. —L.M. (1).

OATMEAL STUFFING

One cup finest oatmeal, 1 large onion, half a teaspoonful salt, half a teaspoonful pepper, 1 breakfast cup of dripping from roasted meat or from bacon.

Bring the dripping to the boil; add the oatmeal and finely-chopped onion, salt and pepper. Cook for 20 minutes. The mixture must be quite moist. (*Mrs Hemut Schroder.*) —L.M. (2).

OATS

Oats are the seeds of the cereal *Avena* which was already being cultivated in Central Europe in the days of Pliny. The best oats are known as the *Potato-oats*, a name due to the fact that they were first found in Cumberland, in 1788, growing among potatoes. The grain is white, fat and large, and it is mostly grown on land in a high state of cultivation. *Black Poland Oats* are also esteemed, and among other popular varieties the *Hopetoun Oat* is an early variety; the *Sandy Oat* is best for poor, wet land; the *White* and *Black Tartarians* and the *Siberian Oats* are coarser but excellent for horses.

Oats will grow in colder and wetter climates and on poorer soils than any of the other cereals; also in hotter climates than either wheat or rye.

The husks of *Oats* are particularly hard; yet they can be used and are prepared both in Scotland and Wales in the making of a sort of porridge called *Sowens* (q.v.). In the majority of cases, however, husks are removed and the oats are also sometimes flattened into what is known as *Rolled Oats*. Of all the cereals, oats are, when husked, the richest in fats and albuminoids.

Rolled or *Flaked Oats* are husked, softened by steam and rolled out flat to the size of a dime or a sixpence. They are then carefully dried by passing over steam-heated pipes along an endless woven-wire belt, and they are then carried to an 'aspirator' which cools them and rids them of any light bits and pieces.

ORANGE BISCUITS

¼ lb. castor sugar
¼ lb. shredded sweet almonds
3 oz. butter
3 oz. flour
Juice of two oranges
Grated rind of one orange

Drop this mixture in teaspoonfuls on a greased baking-tin. Leave plenty of room to spread and bake in a rather slow oven until done.

Orange Icing

Boil ½ lb. of good loaf sugar and a quarter of a pint of water for 15 minutes, then pour it gradually over a stiffly-whipped white of egg. Beat lightly, adding a little orange juice, and when thick pour it over the cakes. Sprinkle with chopped pistachio nuts. —L.G.N.

ORANGE BRAN COOKIES

Cream 1¼ cups of butter with 2 cups of light brown sugar. Add 2 eggs, well-beaten, and 1 cup of all Bran. Add the grated rind of 1 large orange, and 3 cups of flour sifted with 2 teaspoonfuls of baking powder. Form into a long roll, wrap in heavy waxed paper, place in refrigerator overnight. Slice thin and bake on light-buttered tins about 10 minutes in a hot (400 to 450° F.) oven.—J.P.

ORANGE CAKE
I

4 oz. flour
2 oz. lard
2 oz. margarine
1 grated orange
4 oz. sugar
½ teaspoon baking powder
2 eggs

For the filling:
3 oz. cake crumbs
1 oz. butter
1 grated orange
Juice of one orange
3 oz. sugar
1 yolk of egg

Cream the fat and sugar, add the grated orange peel and beaten eggs, then the sieved flour, gradually, adding baking powder with the last portion. Beat very thoroughly for 5 to 10 minutes, and place in two greased layer cake pans. Bake in a moderate oven of 370° F. for 15 minutes, then reduce heat to 350° F. until cooked (about 15 minutes). Turn out and allow to cool.

Put all the filling ingredients except the egg into a saucepan. Heat for 5 minutes, stirring all the time. Allow to cool slightly, add the egg and stir over a low heat. Spread on one layer and cover with other. Dredge liberally with icing sugar.—G.H.(4).

II

Take the weight of 2 eggs in fine sugar and flour. Beat the eggs and sugar together very thick and white. Mix the flour with the grated rinds of two oranges and 1 teaspoonful baking powder. Stir this lightly into the eggs and sugar. Well butter a tin and bake half an hour. Quick oven.

Ice with grated rind in the mixture and some juice. Put a layer of orange cream filling in it.—O.H.

ORANGE SHORTBREADS

Rub 6 oz. butter into 8 oz. flour; add 2 oz. sugar and grated rind of one orange. Work together into stiff dough. Turn on to floured board and knead thoroughly till smooth. Roll out thinly, cut in rounds 2½ in. in diameter. Prick well with fork. Bake in moderate oven till pale brown. Can be brushed with egg if liked and an almond, split, placed on each, or piece of candied orange peel.—D.T.L.

ORIENTALS

> 4 oz. castor sugar
> 4 oz. ground almonds
> 4 oz. butter
> 4 oz. flour
> 2 egg yolks well-beaten

Mix sugar and ground almonds, then rub butter into flour and add the sugar and ground almonds and egg yolks. Roll out as for pastry, cut into rounds. Bake and allow to cool, then put apricot jam between. Ice and decorate with cherries. Use the egg whites for icing. (*Mrs J.H.C.Midgley, Muizenberg.*) —P.R.M.

ORMSKIRK GINGERBREAD
(Biscuits)

Mix into 1 lb. flour, 8 oz. of castor sugar, 8 oz. mixed candied peel, 1 oz. ground ginger, half a teaspoonful of bicarbonate of soda. Rub into this mixture 8 oz. of butter. Warm 8 oz. of golden syrup, add to it half a teaspoonful of lemon essence and pour into the other ingredients. Work to a firm paste, roll it as thin as paper and bake in floured tins in a moderate oven.—M.B. (2).

OSTER FLADEN

> ¼ lb. flour
> 4 eggs
> 1 pint milk
> 2 oz. butter
> Sugar and flavouring to taste

Mix the flour with the eggs, warm the milk and melt the butter in it and mix with the flour and eggs; beat well until smooth. Pour into a large, shallow cake pan and bake until well risen to a nice brown. Can be served either hot or cold. (*Mrs H. Rhind. Masru.*)—P.R.M.

OTAHEITE ARROWROOT.
OTAHEITE SALEP

A perennial herbaceous plant with tuberous roots resembling new potatoes; when fresh, they are full of starch and used like *Arrowroot* (q.v.). It is also called *Tacca starch*, and *South Sea, Madagascar* or *Tahiti Arrowroot*. It is also known by the name of *Pia*.

OWENDAW CORN BREAD

Hominy gives this bread its distinctive flavour. Like all the spoon breads, it should be eaten very hot with much butter.

> 1 cup cooked hominy
> 2 eggs
> ½ cup corn meal
> 2 tablespoons butter
> 1 cup milk
> ½ teaspoon salt

While the hominy is hot, stir in the butter. Beat the eggs until light and add to the hominy, then add the milk and lastly the corn meal and salt. This makes a very thin batter. Pour it into a deep, buttered pan and bake in a moderately hot oven (375° F.) for about 30 minutes. This will serve six. When baked it has the appearance of a baked batter pudding, and when rich and well mixed it has almost the delicacy of baked custard. (*Southern Cook Book.*)—C.G.

PADDY. PADDEE

East Indian and Malay names for rough rice, i.e. before the husks have been removed.

PAILLETTES AU PARMESAN

Little sticks of *feuilletage* (flour and butter) flavoured with grated Parmesan cheese, cayenne pepper or paprika. Served with clear soups or *consommés*.

PAIN

Fr. for both *Bread* and *Loaf*. When not otherwise qualified, *un pain* means a loaf of bread. *Loaf sugar*, pain de sucre; *a wafer used as a seal*, pain à cacheter.

PAIN D'ÉPICES

Fr. for *Gingerbread* (q.v.).

PAIN PERDU

Soak small crustless slices of white bread, fruit loaf or brown bread in milk that has been boiled to half its bulk with sugar and flavouring to taste. When the bread has absorbed the milk and is half dry, sprinkle it with sultanas; fry the slices in butter till both sides are golden brown; dredge them with sugar and serve hot.—P.A.

Torriga
(A Spanish form of *Pain Perdu*)

Cut squares of bread about ½ in. in thickness, dip first into milk (do not soak too long), then into beaten-up egg. Drop them into boiling fat, fry a golden brown. Serve with golden syrup warmed.—P.A.

PANADA
Stale bread boiled with or without added flour, butter and salt, in stock or milk, wrung dry in a cloth when reduced to pulp, seasoned to taste and used to give consistency to various forcemeats; it is also used for soufflés and liaisons.

PANADE
The most homely of soups; it is made of stale crusts soaked in water (or milk), butter and an egg or two.

Panade is also the culinary name of a pappy preparation of bread and milk used in the preparation of *Quenelles*.

PANCAKES
The thinnest imaginable 'cake' made of batter cooked in an open pan and served plain or with any number of jams or liqueurs.

Célestine Pancakes
Into two tablespoonfuls of flour beat half a cupful of milk and one egg. Add a pinch of salt and a little ground nutmeg. If lumpy pass through a Chinese strainer. Add a little chopped parsley. Pour into hot buttered skillets and fry on both sides. When done cut into strips.—F.E.A.

Mrs Harvey's Pancakes (1694)
Take 3 pints of creame or good milk, putt in half a pound of butter, sett itt over ye fire till ye butter is melted; putt in a little mace & cinamon beat very fine, 9 eggs, and when it is almost cold putt them into ye creame. Stirr in about 3 spoonfulls of fine flower, fry them in a dry pan as thin as possible; as soon as that side next ye fire is browne, turn itt out upon ye wrong side of a pewter plate, and so throw them one upon another, ye brown side being still uppermost. Till you have fryed itt all you must strew a little sugar between every pan cake.—A.H.

Pancakes (1808)
Take a pint of thick cream, six spoonfuls of sack and half a pint of fine flour, six eggs but only three whites, one grated nutmeg, one quarter of a pound of melted butter, a very little salt, and some sugar; fry these thin in a dry pan.—L.E.

MRS MASON'S PANCAKES (1778)
Common Pancakes
Three eggs, a pound of flour and a pint of milk, or cream; put the milk to the flour by degrees; a little salt and grated ginger; fry them in lard; grate sugar over them.

Worcestershire Pancakes
The yolks of twelve eggs, four whites, beat them well; add one quart of cream, six spoonfuls of flour, two of brandy, one nutmeg, a quarter of a pound of melted butter; a little salt; for the first pancake rub the pan with a bit of cold butter; fry them without anything else in the pan: they must be very thin, clapt hot one upon another for about a dozen, and cut through when eaten.

If they are made with milk, double the quantity of butter.

To make Scots Pancakes
To a pint of cream, take the yolks of eight eggs, the whites of six, a quarter of a pound of butter, three spoonfuls of flour, a little white wine, sugar, and nutmeg; put the butter into the cream, and set it over the fire till it boils, then take it off; beat up the eggs well with the white wine, then mix it and beat it up well with the cream, and the other ingredients till it is a fine batter; put some butter into a small frying-pan; when it is melted put in a little batter, fry it till it is just brown next the pan; then turn it into a dish, with a little sugar strewed on it; put some more batter in the pan, fry it as before and then strew some more sugar over it.

Rice Pancakes
Take half a pound of rice, clean picked and washed, boil it till it is tender and all the water boiled away; put it into a tin cullender, cover it close and let stand all night; then break it very small; take fourteen eggs, beat, strain them, and put them to the rice with a quart of cream, a nutmeg grated, and a little salt; beat it all well together; then shake in as much flour as will hold them together, and stir in as much butter as will fry them.

Clary Pancakes
Four eggs, four spoonfuls of flour, a little salt; about a pint of milk; mix these exceedingly well; make some lard very hot; with a spoon drop in some batter very thin; lay in some clary-leaves washed and dried, then a little more batter; let them be a nice brown.

Paper Pancakes
Take six new-laid eggs, beat up the yolks, and half the whites; mix them by degrees into a pint of rich cream, three spoonfuls of white wine, one spoonful of orange-flower water, a little nutmeg and a spoonful of loaf sugar powdered; melt half a pound of butter and let it stand till it is near cold; mix by degrees three spoonfuls of flour in the batter, and then add the butter; set on the pan and fry them like other pancakes. They must be very thin.

New-England Pancakes

A pint of cream, five spoonfuls of flour, seven eggs (leave out three whites), a little salt; fry them thin in fresh butter; lay seven or eight in a dish; strew sugar and cinnamon between.—C.MA.

Pancakes Faletto

Make a batter of flour, milk and yolk of egg, and sugar and flavouring and melted butter, and cook a spoonful at a time in the pan. Make a sauce of Kirsch, butter, orange brandy, Cointreau and sugar, and serve the pancakes in the sauce.—P.A.

Hungry Man's Pancake

Take a breakfast cup of self-raising flour and a pinch of salt and rub into it about an ounce of lard or butter. Add a tablespoonful of sugar, a few currants, and mix with water, fairly thickly. Make into a round about an inch thick and fry on both sides in lard. Sprinkle with sugar and serve straight from the frying-pan. This makes enough for two people.—L.G.N.

Irish Pancakes

Take a pint of cream, eight yolks and four whites of eggs; beat the eggs with some grated nutmeg and sugar; then melt three ounces of butter in the cream, mix it with the rest, and add thereto about half a pint of flour smoothed fine. Rub the pan with some butter, and fry the cakes thin without turning. Serve several one on another.—G.A.S.

PARAGON CAKES

- 6 oz. flour
- 6 oz. castor sugar
- 3 oz. butter
- 4 oz. coconut flour
- 2 eggs
- 1 level teaspoon baking powder

Sieve the flour, coconut flour, and baking powder with a pinch of salt. Cream the butter and sugar until pale in colour. Then beat in each egg separately, and fold in the dry ingredients as lightly as possible, adding a little milk if necessary. Put into well-greased, small fancy cake-tins and bake at a temperature of 370° F. for 10 to 15 minutes, according to size.—G.H. (4).

PARKER HOUSE CHOCOLATE CREAM PIE

- 1½ lb. sugar
- 1 pint eggs
- 1 lb. 6 oz. flour
- ½ oz. vanilla
- 3 oz. lard
- 3 oz. butter
- 1 pint milk
- 1½ oz. baking powder
- ¼ oz. salt

Cream butter and sugar, add eggs gradually, add milk, blend, sift baking powder and flour mixed. Mix slowly with butter, sugar and eggs, add vanilla and salt. Bake in layer cake-tins. Makes 12 layers or 6 pies.

Filling:

- 1 quart milk
- 4 eggs
- 2 oz. butter
- ¼ oz. salt
- ½ lb. sugar
- 2 oz. corn starch
- ½ oz. vanilla

Scald milk, blend other ingredients together, add scalded milk slowly while beating. Cook 5 minutes and cool.

Icing:

- 2 lb. confectionery sugar
- ½ pint milk
- ¼ oz. vanilla
- 2 oz. butter
- 2 oz. cocoa

Mix sugar, cocoa and butter, add milk, beat and stir until well blended, add vanilla.—P.H.B.

PARKER HOUSE ROLLS

- 1 pint of milk
- 2 tablespoons of butter
- 2 tablespoons of sugar
- 1 teaspoon of salt
- ½ cake of yeast
- 1 quart of flour (measured after sifting)

Heat the milk to the boiling point and pour over the butter, salt and sugar. Cool to lukewarm, then add the yeast which has been dissolved in a little milk. Stir well. Add the sifted flour, beating until smooth. Make the batter about 9 a.m. Cut down with a knife about 1 p.m. Shake in a very little flour, let rise again. Roll out and cut about 2½ hours before serving. The mixture will be very soft, and hard to handle, but that makes the rolls light. If you should want the rolls for lunch, set the batter the night before.—G.T.L.

PARKIN

Oatmeal cakes which are popular in the North of England chiefly. They are mostly home-made and recipes vary from house to house. In Yorkshire, and more particularly in the country round about Leeds, the 5th November is the traditional day for *Parkins*, like Hot Cross Buns on Good Friday, or Pancakes on Shrove Tuesday.

I

- 1 lb. flour
- ¾ lb. medium oatmeal
- ¼ lb. butter
- 2 oz. sugar
- 1 lb. syrup or treacle
- 1 teacup milk

½ teaspoon bicarbonate of soda
1 teaspoon ginger
1 egg

Dissolve the soda in the milk, warm the treacle and butter and add to dry ingredients, also the beaten egg, adding milk last. Bake in a flat square tin for three-quarters of an hour. Turn out of tin when cold.—M.K.S. (2).

II

¼ lb. oatmeal
½ lb. flour
6 oz. syrup
¼ lb. lard
¼ lb. sugar
3 teaspoonfuls cinnamon
3 teaspoonfuls ginger
2 small packets mixed spice
1½ teaspoonfuls baking soda and
1 egg

Mix all the dry ingredients and rub lard into meal, flour, etc. Melt sugar and syrup together and pour over dry ingredients, and mix with egg beaten up. Take up in pieces and rub into balls with dry oatmeal, and bake till a nice brown.—S.W.R.

III

Rich Yorkshire Parkin

1 lb. medium oatmeal
½ lb. plain flour
1 teaspoon baking powder
1½ teaspoons ground ginger
2 oz. candied lemon peel
2 oz. ginger, crystallized
½ lb. butter
¼ lb. sugar
2 eggs
1 lb. syrup
½ lb. black treacle
Milk to mix

Sieve flour, baking powder and ground ginger; shred the peel and ginger. Put sugar, syrup, treacle and butter into a pan and melt gently. Add to the other ingredients with the well-beaten eggs and enough milk to make a soft mixture.

Allow to stand for 30 minutes and put in a well-greased and floured tin. Bake in cool oven till set. Should be about 2 in. or so in depth when finished, and have a glossy surface.

Parkin is a sort of first cousin to *Pain d'épices* and excellent if well made.—D.L.T.

PARLIES. PARLEYS

Parlies is the Scotch spelling and *Parleys* the English.

'*A species of Gingerbread supposed to have its name from being used by the members of the Scottish Parliament.*'—*Jamieson.*

Flour, sugar, ginger, butter, treacle.

With two pounds of the best dried flour mix thoroughly one pound of the best brown sugar and a quarter-pound of ground ginger. Melt a pound of fresh butter, add to it one of treacle, boil this and pour it on the flour. Work up the paste as hot as the paste will bear it and roll it out in very large cakes, a sixth of an inch thick, or less. Mark it in squares with a knife or a paper-cutter, and fire in a slow oven. Separate the squares when soft and they will soon be crisp.— (*Mrs Fletcher's Recipe, from Meg Dods's 'Manual.'*)—F.M.M. (2).

PASTE

Flour worked into a 'paste' with water, salt, butter or some other kind of fat, and sometimes with eggs or milk in proportions which differ and are responsible for different kinds of paste, such as: Pie-paste, puff-paste, tart-paste, dumpling-paste, brioche-paste short-paste, and *Pastry* (q.v.).

PASTRY

The utensils needed for making pastry are a board and a rolling-pin, flour dredger and knife – a slab of slate or marble is better than a board, as pastry must be kept as cool as possible. Make the pastry in a cool place and do most of the mixing with a knife, giving the final kneading only with the hands except in the case of short pastry. Mix the pastry with very cold water and always use very dry flour, dry it if necessary before the fire or in a cool oven after sieving it.

Flour the board and rolling-pin and lift the pastry occasionally to see that it is not sticking to the board. The pastry should be moist enough to handle easily without sticking to the hands. In baking, bottom heat is best for puff-pastry as this makes the pastry rise before the outside hardens. The oven should not be hotter on one side than the other for puff-pastry, or it will rise unevenly.

The temperature of the oven should be 300° F. when the puff-pastry is first put in; if the oven is not hot enough the butter will melt and run out before the starch grains in the flour have burst and absorbed the fat. The heat should be lowered gradually after the pastry has risen.—M.K.S. (2).

Biscuit Pastry
(Pâte Sucrée)

Sieve 8 oz. flour on to slab. Make a well. Strew round 3 oz. sugar and tablespoonful of ground almonds, sieved if necessary.

Place in centre 2 yolks with pinch of salt and 5½ oz. butter in pieces. Work butter and yolks together, then blend in other ingredients, using a little water if required to make into stiff paste. Do not overwork it, or it is 'burnt'. Form into ball, then press out once with palm of hand. Make into ball and put in clean cloth, and let it rest in cool place as long as possible. Roll out and use for *tartelettes*, sweet flans, etc.—D.L.T.

Chou Pastry

4 oz. flour, 2 eggs, 2 oz. butter, pinch of salt, half a pint of water.

Dry the flour and shake it through a sieve, with the salt, on to a piece of paper. Put the water and butter into a pan and bring to the boil. Draw the pan to the side of the fire and sift in the flour, stirring all the time. Return to the fire and stir very vigorously until mixture forms a ball in the centre of the pan, leaving the sides quite clean. Cool slightly, then beat in the eggs one by one, then beat very well.

The paste should be neither too soft nor too stiff. If too stiff, add another egg, or yolk of egg. If the pastry is too soft it spreads and loses its shape; if too stiff it does not rise well in the baking. This pastry is used for making éclairs, cream buns, etc.—M.K.S. (2).

Flaky Pastry

1 lb. flour, cold water, a pinch of salt, 11 oz. butter, or half butter and half lard, a squeeze of lemon juice.

In hot weather wash the butter in very cold water and then squeeze out all moisture in a cloth. Divide butter into three parts. Sieve flour and salt into a basin and rub in one-third of the butter. Make a well in the centre and add the lemon juice and gradually pour in enough cold water with the left hand, mixing in the flour from the sides with a knife. Work to a smooth but not too moist paste. Turn out on to a floured board and roll it into a long strip about ¼ in. thick. Flour the strip and put one-third of the butter in small pieces in even rows all over it, leaving a margin of about 1 in. from the edge of the pastry all round.

Flour the surface and fold the pastry exactly in three. Turn the fold to the left-hand side, press out the pastry gently with the rolling-pin, then roll lightly into a long narrow strip. Repeat this process with the remaining batter and the pastry is ready for use.—M.K.S. (2).

Hungarian Butter Pastry

1. Rub 2 oz. butter or margarine into 6 oz. flour, work in well one yolk of egg; then add little water with few drops of vinegar till soft dough is formed. Beat this in a basin with the hand till bubbles begin to form and paste leaves the sides of basin. This takes about 20 minutes.

2. Work 2 oz. flour into 6 oz. butter. Make into flat round. Roll out on floured board No. 1. Place No. 2 in middle as for puff pastry. Fold over top, then bottom end, next the left side, and fold right side under-neath. Put in cloth and rest in cold place for half hour. Roll paste out square; fold as before. Repeat twice. Rest paste each time. Use as for puff pastry; cuttings to be placed in centre of any left over paste and folded in. Roll out again as often as wanted. Keeps very well, and is a delicious crust.—D.L.T.

Indian Flaky Pastry

½ lb. flour, ¼ lb. butter, ¼ lb. lard, salt. Rub half the fats into flour sieved with salt, or cut in with knife; make into stiff dough with cold water. Make into ball, then roll out. Put rest of fats on the paste in alternate knobs, i.e., two of butter with one of lard in centre, then two of lard with one of butter in centre.

Fold over in three. Let rest 20 minutes. Roll out and give two half turns. Rest again 20 minutes. Give another two turns if to be used at once, or if needed next day give only one half turn. Excellent for flans, fruit tarts, etc.—D.L.T.

Light Paste, commonly called Puff Paste, is made by rubbing into sifted, fine flour, a little more than one-third its weight of the best fresh Aylesbury butter. Add a little water (fresh and clean), knead it; let it stand; roll it out; *thumb* it all over with butter; double it five fold; roll it out again.

For *Pies,* leave out the *thumbing.*

For *Tarts,* add a little powdered loaf sugar, a little cream of new milk, three or four eggs, and a little lemon sugar essence.

For *Raised Meat Pies,* use lard in lieu of butter, and more water.

For *Puddings* to be *boiled,* use *suet of beef* in lieu of butter; also a little milk, salt, and water. Knead all *well* together with your hands.—W.G.

Lining Paste
(*Pâte à Foncer*)

Sieve 3½ oz. flour on board. Make well in centre, put good pinch of salt in middle with 1 oz. butter, half a beaten egg. With very little cold water make into a paste as quickly as possible, using fingers only of one hand. The less this paste is handled the better; it speedily becomes tough. Form into ball, and put in cold place. When ready to use, roll out thinly. Cut with fluted cutter, then line tartlet cases or flan ring, etc. Bake 'blind' till golden, see below. Make more than needed at the moment; they keep well in a tin.

N.B.—'Blind' *means pricking paste well and filling with tissue paper and beans to stop crust rising.*—D.L.T.

PASTRY (1783)
Puff-paste
The best way

Rub ½ lb. of butter fine with a Gallon of Flour, and a little Salt. Make it up into a light Paste with cold water, just stiff enough to work it well up; then roll it out and stick small pieces of butter all over the paste, strewing a little flour upon it from a drudging Box or your hand; then roll it up together, and with a rolling Pin, roll it out again flatt and untill it is about half an Inch thick, and so do, nine or ten times, and untill you have rolled into your paste about a pound and a half of Butter. This is the Crust that is most usually found in good Pies of all kinds.

Beef Dripping Crust
A very excellent Crust
Boil a pound and a half of Beef Dripping in Water; then strain it and let it stand untill it is cold; when you must take off the hard fat, which scrape from all Impurities. Boil it, in Like manner, four or five times and then work it up well, into three pounds of Flour, as finely as possible, and make it up into a cold paste, with cold water. This makes as good a Crust, or better than any other Crust.—R.H.G.

PASTRY (1843)
Puff-paste
To a pound and a quarter of sifted flour rub gently in with the hand half a pound of fresh butter; mix up with half a pint of spring-water; knead it well and set it by for a quarter of an hour; then roll it out thin, lay on it in small pieces, three-quarters of a pound more of butter, throw on it a little flour, double it up in folds, and roll it out thin three times, and set it by for an hour *in a cold place.*

Paste for Meat or Savoury Pies
Sift two pounds of fine flour to one and a half of good salt butter, break it into small pieces, and wash it well in cold water; rub gently together the butter and flour, and mix it up with the yolks of three eggs, beat together with a spoon; and nearly a pint of spring-water, roll it out and double it in folds three times and it is ready.

Tart Paste for Family Pies
Rub in with the hand half a pound of butter into one pound and a quarter of flour, mix it up with half a pint of water, and knead it well.

Sweet, or Short and Crisp Tart Paste
To one pound and a quarter of fine flour add ten ounces of fresh butter, the yolks of two eggs beat, and three ounces of sifted loaf sugar, mix up together with half a pint of new milk, and knead it well.—W.K.

PASTRY (1854)
Very Good Light Paste
Flour 1 lb.; lard, 6 oz.; butter, 10 oz.; little salt.

Mix with a pound of sifted flour six ounces of fresh, pure lard, and make them into a smooth paste with cold water; press the buttermilk from 10 ounces of butter, and form it into a ball by twisting it in a clean cloth. Roll out the paste, put the ball of butter in the middle, close it like an apple dumpling, and roll it very lightly until it is less than an inch thick; fold the ends into the middle, dust a little flour over the board and paste-roller, and roll the paste thin a second time, then set it aside for three or four minutes in a very cool place; give it two more *turns*, and after it has again been left for a few minutes, roll it out twice more, folding it each time in three. This ought to render it fit for use. The sooner this paste is sent to the oven after being made, the lighter it will be: if allowed to remain long before it is baked, it will be tough and heavy.

English Puff-paste
Flour, 2 lb.; little salt; butter, 1 lb. 10 oz.

Break lightly into a couple of pounds of dried and sifted flour, eight ounces of butter; add a pinch of salt, and sufficient cold water to make the paste; work it as quickly and as lightly as possible, until it is smooth and pliable, then level it with the paste-roller until it is three-quarters of an inch thick, and place regularly upon it six ounces of butter in small bits; fold the paste like a blanket pudding, roll it out again, lay on it six ounces more of butter, repeat the rolling, dusting each time a little flour over the board and paste, add again six ounces of butter, and roll the paste out thin three or four times, folding the ends into the middle.

If very rich paste be required, equal portions of flour and butter must be used; and the latter may be divided into two instead of three parts, when it is to be rolled in.

Flead Crust
Flead is the provincial name for the leaf, or inside fat of a pig, which makes excellent crust when fresh, much finer, indeed, than after it is melted into lard. Clear it quite from skin, and slice it very thin into the flour, add sufficient salt to give flavour to the paste, and make the whole up smooth and firm with cold water; lay it on a clean dresser, and beat it forcibly with a rolling-pin until the flead is blended perfectly with the flour. It may then be made into cakes with a paste-cutter, or used for pies, round the edges of which a knife should be passed, as the crust rises better when *cut* than if merely rolled to the proper size. With the addition of a small quantity of butter, which may be either broken into the flour before the flead is mixed with it, or rolled into the paste after it is beaten, it will be found equal

to fine puff crust, with the advantage of being more easy of digestion.

Quite common crust: Flour, 1¾ lb.; flead, 8 oz.; salt, one small teaspoonful. *Good common crust*: Flour, 1 lb.; flead, 6 oz.; butter, 2 oz. *Rich crust*: Flead, ¾ lb.; butter, 2 oz.; flour, 1 lb. The crust is very good when made without any butter.—E.A.

PEARL BARLEY

The *Pearl Barley* of commerce is usually made by steaming Spring Barley to soften the skin, then drying it a little, and afterwards grinding it in a mill set wide, so as to round and polish the grains by a rasping or paring process, and so as to separate the whole of the husk except that portion left in the furrow of the seed.—L.G.M.

PEARL BISCUITS

1½ pints whites of eggs
2¼ lb. fine castor sugar
18 oz. cake flour
Tablespoonful of Maraschino

Beat up the whites into a firm meringue, adding the sugar gradually and beating well in; stir the sifted flour thoroughly, adding the Maraschino before the final mixing.

Cut strips of paper 4½ in. wide, and as long as the width of the baking-sheets.

Use a ¼ in. tube and small bag, and run out the biscuits 3 in. long and 1 in. apart. Dredge well with pulverized sugar, shake off all that does not adhere, and let stand for 15 minutes, partially to dissolve surface sugar. Then bake in an oven (375° F.), being careful that they take hardly any colour. Set in a warm room to dry for 24 hours, and then remove from paper with a thin palette knife. If good glazed paper has been used they will lift without using a knife at all. These biscuits are quite dry and very light. —A.A.B.

PEASE MEAL

This meal is used as a substitute for Barley meal to make *Bannocks* (q.v.) or in place of Oatmeal to make *Brose* (q.v.).

PEGGY'S CORN MUFFINS

2 tablespoonfuls of butter
3 tablespoonfuls of honey
¾ cupful of white corn meal
⅓ cupful of sifted rye (or all-purpose) flour
¼ teaspoonful of salt
3 tablespoonfuls of baking powder
1 egg beaten and mixed with
¾ cupful of milk

Heat the butter and honey until the butter is melted. Set aside to cool until ready to use. Sift the dry ingredients together. Gradually add the egg and milk, stirring lightly. Mix in the honey and butter. Pour into small, well-buttered muffin-pans and bake in a hot oven (400° F.) for about 20 minutes. Recipe makes two dozen muffins. —E.K.H.

PENNSYLVANIA CINNAMON BUNS

½ yeast cake
¼ cup warm water
1 cup scalded milk
Brown sugar
½ teaspoon salt butter
½ cup chopped raisins
2 tablespoons currants
2 tablespoons chopped citron
1 teaspoon cinnamon
3 cups flour

Dissolve yeast in warm water and add to milk which has been cooled to lukewarm. Add about 3 tablespoons sugar, the salt and flour, and knead thoroughly until it becomes a soft dough. Put the dough in a buttered bowl and butter the top of the dough. Cover bowl and put in a warm place. Let it stand until the dough triples in bulk. Roll to ¼ in. in thickness, brush with butter and spread with the raisins, currants, citron, cinnamon and brown sugar. Roll as a jelly roll and cut into ¾ in. slices, place in buttered pans, spread generously with brown sugar and bake in a hot oven (400° F.) for 20 minutes. —C.G.

PEPPERNUTS

(Pfeffernüsse)

Mix the following: A teaspoon of cinnamon, a saltspoon of powdered cloves, a saltspoon of powdered cardamons, a saltspoon of grated nutmeg and a pinch or two of freshly-ground pepper, a teaspoon of baking powder, 3 oz. of finely-minced citron peel, and the grated rind of half a lemon.

Mix thoroughly with 1 lb. of sifted flour, and 1 lb. of castor sugar. Beat up four eggs, well whipped, and add by degrees to the rest. Roll into small balls about the size of a golf ball, and place on a buttered baking-dish, not too close to each other as they swell in cooking.

Bake carefully in a slow oven. These will keep well if kept in a tin box, and are great favourites at tea-time.—L.M.(1).

PETITS FOURS

Sift into a bowl 11 oz. of flour, 1 oz. of cornflour, half teaspoon of baking powder and a pinch of salt.

Cream up ½ lb. of butter until very light, then fold in ½ lb. of castor sugar.

Add, singly, half pint of eggs and mix lightly. Stir in the flour, and add a few drops of vanilla flavouring.

Spread the mixture ¾ in. deep in a well-greased tin, and bake in a moderate oven until lightly coloured.

When cool, sandwich with butter cream and ground almonds, cut with fancy cutters or with a sharp knife, and ice the top with white or tinted icing.

Glacé fruits, nuts, and grated chocolate should be applied while the icing is soft.

Use either water or beaten white of egg for the icing, adding it gradually to fine icing sugar in a bowl and working it smooth with a knife to a useful consistency.—I.B.

PETITS SOUFFLÉS AU FROMAGE

This is a spécialité of the sunny town of Nice. The soufflés must be made quite small and served, as indeed should all savouries, *very* hot.

For 'Chou' Paste

¼ cup (4 oz.) butter
2 eggs
¼ pint (1 gill) water
2 oz. sifted flour

Other ingredients: A small quantity of puff or flaky pastry; grated cheese.

To make the 'chou' paste, put the water on to boil, add the butter and, when this is melted, add the flour, all at once, stirring fast the while and reducing the heat. Continue stirring until the mixture is thick enough to form a ball around the spoon and leave the sides of the pan clean. Remove latter from fire, add the eggs, one at a time, beating each one well in until the mixture is smooth, then add about half a cupful of grated cheese, salt and a few grains of cayenne pepper. The dough should be of the consistency of clotted cream.

Now line some patty-pans small ones, with thinly rolled-out pastry, either 'puff' or good flaky pie-crust. Trim off edges and cut a narrow strip to place on top of soufflé. Into each prepared patty-pan place a small spoonful of the 'chou' mixture. On top of each smooth ball of 'chou' paste place two thin, crossed strips of pastry. Set the pan in a moderately hot oven, having a good bottom heat. Bake for about 20 to 25 minutes, or until the soufflés are puffed up and nicely coloured. Serve hot, but they are also fairly good cold—as good as such things *can* be when cold!—P.W.

PETTICOAT TAILS

(Scottish)

'*An English traveller in Scotland and one very well acquainted with France states in his very pleasant book that our Club has fallen into a mistake in the name of these cakes, and that petticoat tails is a corruption of the French* Petites Gatelles. *It may be so: in Scottish culinary terms there are many corruptions, though we rather think the name petticoat tails has its origin in the shape of the cakes, which is exactly that of the bell-hoop petticoats of our ancient Court ladies.' Annals of the Cleikum Club.* —F.M.M. (2).

Rub 6 oz. butter into 1 lb. flour. Add 6 oz. sugar, and enough water to work into a smooth dough which divide in two. Roll into round cakes about size of a dinner-plate, cut small round cake from the centre of each with a cutter 4 in. in diameter. Then divide the outside of each into eight. Prickle on top with a fork, dust over with fine ground sugar, and bake in a moderate oven about 20 minutes. Cool on a cake rack. (*Ursula Millard.*)—E.C. (2).

PHILPY

½ cup rice, cooked
½ cup rice flour
6 tablespoons water
1 egg

Boil the washed rice until soft and tender. When cold rub the rice until it is smooth and add the rice flour and water which have been made into a smooth paste. Beat the egg until light and add to the rice mixture. Bake on a well-buttered, shallow tin plate in a quick oven (425° F.) for about 30 minutes.

If the Philpy is baked in a pie-pan, cut it into sections like those of a pie when serving. It must be very hot and split and buttered at once to be at its best. (*Carolina Housewife.*)—B.S.R.

PIA

Lat. *Tacca pinnitifida*. A perennial herb of East India and Australasia cultivated for its large, fleshy roots, especially in Madagascar. The roots yield a starchy, edible product known as *Otaheite* or *Madagascar* Arrowroot, which is used like *Arrowroot* (q.v.).

PIES

Meat, fish, fruit or vegetables served in the pie-dish in which they were cooked, *under a paste or crust*. A fruit pie is called *Tourte*, and a meat pie *Pâté*, in culinary French.

PIKELETS

To make Pikelets (1807)

Take 2 lb. of fine flour, 2 eggs, 3 spoonfuls of new yeast, and a little salt; beat the eggs, yeast and salt, well together; and add to them a pint and half of new milk, made just warm; put it to the flour by degrees, and keep it beating, which will make them very light and smooth; set it by the fire to rise, half an hour, and then bake them.—A.A.

Scots Pikelets

1 pint of warm milk
¼ pint of brewers' yeast
1 lb. flour
2 eggs
1 oz. butter

Mix all ingredients together and beat well and let it rise. Put about a dessertspoonful on a hot girdle and let it spread itself out quite thin. When lightly browned underneath, turn it with a palette knife and cook the other side. To be served hot and well buttered.—H.E.

Welsh Pikelets

½ lb. flour
2 oz. castor sugar
Pinch of salt
1 teaspoonful of bicarbonate of soda
¼ lb. buttermilk

Put flour and sugar into a basin and mix gradually into a thick batter with the buttermilk. Dissolve the bicarbonate of soda in half gill of boiling water and add to the mixture last. Take a tablespoonful of this batter and fry in a little hot lard the same as frying pancakes; turn when half-cooked. To be eaten hot and well buttered.—H.E.

PLAIN BISCUITS

Ingredients: 6 oz. of flour, 2 oz. of sugar, 1 oz. of butter, yolk of 1 egg, 2 tablespoonfuls of milk.

Method: Beat the egg with the milk, then mix with the other ingredients, and roll and cut out into very thin biscuits with a pastecutter. Bake for about six minutes in a quick oven.—B.E.C.

PLANTATION SPOON BREAD

1 cup of cooked hominy
½ heaping tablespoon of butter
2 eggs
1 cup of milk
½ cup of corn meal

Cook half a cup of hominy in a doubleboiler with half a cup of water and a pinch of salt. Take one cup of the hot cooked hominy and mix with the butter. Beat the eggs very light and stir into the hominy. Add the milk gradually, then the corn meal. The batter should be the consistency of a thick boiled custard. If thicker add a little more milk. Pour into a deep buttered baking-dish, place on lower rack of oven and bake from 35 to 40 minutes in a moderate oven.—G.T.L.

PLUMB BUNS (1807)

Rub ½ lb. of butter into 6 lb. of flour, sift into it ½ lb. of fine powder sugar, grate in a nutmeg and a little ginger, and caraway seeds to your liking; put in 3 lb. of currants, cleaned and dried; mix all together, with 3 pints of milk made warm, 2 eggs well beat, with 10 tablespoonfuls of yeast; run it through a sieve into the flour, and make it into a light paste; set it by the fire to rise, an hour; and when made up, rub them over with the white of an egg, and dust sugar over them. 20 minutes will bake them.—A.A.

PLUMB CAKES (1778)
A common Plumb Cake

Five pounds of currants, half a peck of flour; a quarter of an ounce of mace pounded, rather less of cloves, one pound of lump sugar sifted, twelve eggs, a pint of good ale-yeast, three pounds of butter melted in three pints of new milk, and a pint of brandy; mix all well together.

A good Plumb Cake

Three pounds of flour, three pounds of currants, three-quarters of a pound of almonds blanched and beat grossly, about half an ounce of them bitter, four ounces of sugar, seven yolks and six whites of eggs, one pint of cream, two pounds of butter, half a pound of good ale-yeast; mix the eggs and the yeast together, strain them; set the cream on the fire, melt the butter in it; stir in the almonds and half a pint of sack, part of which should be put to the almonds while beating; mix together the flour, sugar, and currants, what nutmegs, cloves and mace are liked; stir these to the cream; put in the yeast.

Another good Plumb Cake

Beat four pounds of butter to a cream; mix it with two pounds of loaf sugar, beaten and sifted very dry; add to that four pounds of flour, dried and sifted, a pint of brandy, and to each pound of flour eight eggs, the yolks and whites well beat separately; mix in the whites, then the yolks, three pounds of currants washed and dried, in three pints of new milk, half a pint of brandy; mix all well together.—C.Ma.

PLUMB CAKE (1808)

Mix one pound currants, one drachm nutmeg, mace and cinnamon each, a little salt, one pound of citron, orange peel candied, and almonds bleached, 6 pound of fruit (well dryed); beat 24 eggs and add with 1 quart new ale-yeast, half pint of wine, 3 half pints of cream and raisins.—L.E.

PLUM PUDDING

Take 2 lb. chopped suet, 2 lb. breadcrumbs, 1 lb. flour, 1½ lb. raisins washed and stoned, 2 lb. sultanas, 1 lb. chopped apples, 10 eggs, 1 lb. candied peel chopped small, 3oz. chopped almonds, the juice and extreme outside skin of a lemon chopped very small, a good sprinkling of nutmeg, ½ lb.

brown sugar, half a teaspoonful of salt, 2½ wine glasses of rum, 2 of sherry and 3 of stout. Soak the raisins and sultanas in the rum and sherry mixed. Sieve the flour and mix with the breadcrumbs, suet, salt, sugar, raisins, sultanas, lemons, almonds, apple and peel. Mix the egg with the rum, sherry, stout, and lemon-juice. Work till smooth, add the raisins and sultanas, and incorporate with the mixture, stirring for a long time.

Put the mixture into three or four pudding-basins well greased, tie up in floured cloth, and boil for six hours. The basins, tied in dry cloths, can be put aside for months. When required for use, the puddings are boiled again for three hours.

The best sauce. with plum pudding is brandy butter; creamed butter 4 oz., and sugar 1 oz. are thoroughly mixed in a basin, and then brandy or rum worked into it, as much as the mixture will absorb and remain stiff.—F.C.-W.

PLUNKETS

    4 eggs
    Weight of eggs in butter
    Weight of eggs in powdered sugar
    Weight of eggs in rice flour
    1 teaspoon vanilla, or juice and rind
      of 1 lemon

Cream butter and add sugar gradually beating all the while; add egg yolks and beat again. Beat egg whites until stiff and fold into the mixture; then gradually stir in the rice flour. Add flavouring and beat until fine and light; pour into greased small muffin- or patty-pans. Bake in moderate oven (350° F.) about 20 minutes. Dust tops with sugar. —A.W.R.

POLENTA
(Yellow Maize Flour)

Extensive use is made in Italy of this yellow maize flour which, when cooked, is not only served as a separate dish but also accompanies dishes of meat and fish. In certain parts of Italy *Polenta* is eaten instead of bread.

Ingredients: ½ lb. fine Italian maize flour; 2 or 3 tablespoonfuls butter; ¼ lb. grated Parmesan; a little over a pint of water, salt and pepper.

Method: Put the water in a saucepan, add a good pinch of salt, and when boiling stir in the flour with a wooden spoon. Stir till it thickens and simmer for 30 minutes, stirring constantly so that it is perfectly smooth. When done add the butter and grated cheese, season with salt and pepper, mixing thoroughly and serve very hot.—C.MY.

Polenta is sometimes made with chestnut flour instead of cornmeal; it is eaten both hot or cold. Cold *Polenta* cut up in strips and fried can be very good.

PONEBREAD

The name given in the Southern States of America to *Corn Bread* (q.v.).

POOR KNIGHTS OF WINDSOR

This is another and more appetizing name for the ordinary *Bread Pudding* (q.v.), but there is a 'not-so-poor knights' edition of this pudding: 'Cut a French roll in slices and soak them in sherry. Then dip them in beaten yolks of eggs and fry them. Make a sauce of butter, sherry and sugar to serve with them.'—A.H.

POP-OVERS

    1 cup flour
    ¼ teaspoon salt
    ½ teaspoon melted butter
    ⅞ cup milk
    2 eggs

Mix salt and flour; add milk gradually to make a smooth batter. Beat whole eggs until light and add to mixture. Add butter. Beat two minutes with egg-beater, turn into custard-cups or hissing-hot buttered iron gem pans. Bake 30 to 35 minutes, beginning with hot oven (500° F.) and decreasing gradually to moderate oven (350° F.) as Pop-overs start to brown. Make 8 to 12 Pop-overs.—B.C.S.C.B.

POPPY-SEED CAKE
(Makosteszta)

Ingredients: 1 lb. of ground poppy-seeds, half a pint of fresh cream, 6 tablespoonfuls of sugar, 1 strip of grated orange or lemon peel, 3 cups of flour, the yolks of 2 eggs, ¼ lb of butter, 1 teaspoonful of baking powder, 2 cups of milk.

Method: Make a dough with the flour, baking powder, the yolks of eggs, the milk, and a little sugar. Beat well and let stand for half an hour. Roll out to about ½ in. thick, cover with the poppy-seeds, which have been well mixed with the cream, sugar and grated peel, and bake in a moderate oven. —C.M.

PORRIDGE

The name given to pappy food made of any cereal or pulse steeped in hot water or milk, but, when not otherwise qualified, *Porridge* usually refers to *Oatmeal Porridge*.

Porridge
(The One and Only Method)

Oatmeal, salt, water. It is advisable to keep a goblet exclusively for porridge.

Allow for each person one breakfastcupful of water, a handful of oatmeal (about an ounce and a quarter), and a small saltspoon of salt. Use fresh spring water and be particular about the quality of the oatmeal. Midlothian oats are unsurpassed the world over

Bring the water to the boil, and as soon as it reaches boiling-point add the oatmeal, letting it fall in a steady rain from the left hand and stirring it briskly the while with the right, sunwise, or the right-hand turn for luck, and convenience. A porridge-stick called a spurtle, and in some parts a theevil, or, as in Shetland, a gruel-tree, is used for this purpose. Be careful to avoid lumps, unless the children clamour for them. When the porridge is boiling steadily, draw the mixture to the side and put on the lid. Let it cook for from 20 to 30 minutes according to the quality of the oatmeal, and do not add the salt, which has a tendency to harden the meal and prevent its swelling, until it has cooked for at least 10 minutes. On the other hand, never cook porridge without salt. Ladle straight into porringers or soup plates, and serve with small individual bowls of cream, or milk, or buttermilk. Each spoonful of porridge, which should be very hot, is dipped in the cream or milk, which should be quite cold, befor{ it is conveyed to the mouth.—F.M.M. (2).

Flour Porridge

Boil 1 pint of milk, reserving 2 tablespoonfuls to mix with 1 oz. of flour; stir this into the boiling milk, adding half a saltspoonful of salt; boil gently 10 minutes, and serve with sugar or treacle.—G.A.S.

Hominy Porridge

Wash the hominy clean, and boil with sufficient water to cover it. It should boil from 2 to 5 hours over a very slow fire. Eat it with butter and molasses or with sugar and milk. It is considered extremely wholesome food, especially for children and delicate persons.—G.A.S.

Sago Porridge

Take 4 tablespoonfuls of sago, 1 saltspoonful of salt and 1 quart of water. Soak the sago in cold water a few minutes, and boil it gently about an hour, adding the salt; pour into soup plates, and serve with molasses or sugar.—G.A.S.

Sago and Rice Porridge

This you make the same way as Sago Porridge, but using half the quantity of sago, with as much rice.—G.A.S.

Wheatmeal Porridge

To 1 quart of boiling water add a teaspoonful of salt; stir in gradually ¼ lb. of wheatmeal; boil 10 minutes and serve with milk or treacle.—G.A.S.

POTATO BREAD

Take the quantity of potatoes required and boil them in their skins. When done, peel them, bruise them with a rolling-pin to the consistency of paste. To this add as much flour as there is potato pulp and some yeast. Knead them well, putting as much lukewarm water as is necessary. When properly kneaded, form into loaves and place in the oven taking care that it is not so hot as for common bread or it will become hard on the outside before the inside is properly baked. The door of the oven should not be closed as soon as on ordinary occasions. This bread must be allowed longer to bake than any other.—M.B. (2).

POTATO FLAKES

The potatoes are washed and then cooked by low-pressure steam and dropped into the hoppers of the emasculators, where they are reduced to pulp. The actual drying takes place as the pulp is picked up by two smooth rollers or drums revolving in opposite directions at about five revolutions a minute. The heated drums drive the moisture from the thinly-spread pulp – they are set at about 0.039 sq. in. apart leaving a solid film of crisp potato, which is scraped off by knives set parallel to the axes of the drums. This film is broken into flakes or crisps and packed for sale.—L.G.M.

POTATO FLOUR MUFFINS

> 4 eggs
> ½ cup potato flour
> 1 tablespoon sugar
> Pinch of salt
> 1 teaspoon baking powder
> 2 tablespoons ice water

Beat whites of eggs very stiff and dry. Add salt and sugar to beaten yolks and fold into whites. Sift flour and baking powder twice and beat into egg mixture. Add ice water last. Bake in moderate oven 15 or 20 minutes.—T.C.

POTATO STARCH. FARINA

This is a meal or flour obtained by grinding potatoes and soaking the pulp in clean water: when the cellulose settles to the bottom, the starchy liquor is poured off into another vessel and allowed sufficient time for the starch to settle at the bottom; impurities are removed and eventually pure potato starch is scraped off. It is called *Fécule de pommes de terre* in culinary French, and not uncommonly, although quite erroneously, *English Arrowroot*.

POT BARLEY

Barley which has been hulled but not grounded and polished to the same extent as *Pearl Barley* (q.v.). It is used in soups and stews.

PROFITEROLES
Little balls of chou paste which may be filled with meat, vegetables or cheese fillings and are added to clear soups at the time of serving.

There is also a larger kind of *Profiteroles*, made of the same *Pâte* and filled with some cream or fruit syrup and served as a sweet, often with a coating of hot chocolate.

PUDDINGS (1783)
A Bread and Flour Pudding
One pound of fine Flour, a pound of white Bread, grated, the yolks of eight Eggs and the whites of four of them beat up, then strained, and then mixt with a Pint of good Cream, or for want thereof a pint of new milk, into which, when mixed, stir in the Bread and Flour, a pound of Raisins, stoned, a pound of Currants well washed and picked clean, half a pound of Sugar, and a little ground Ginger. Mix all well together and you may either boil or bake it; if the latter it will take three-quarters of an hour to bake.

A Bread Pudding
Cut or pare off the crust from a small loaf of Bread, and slice it thin into a quart of Milk where let it soak all night. Next Day take the Yolks of six Eggs, and the Whites of three of them, and beat them up, when strained, with a little rose-water and grated Nutmeg, and a little salt and sugar if you like that. Mix all well together and boil it half an hour.

A Spoonfull Pudding
The Yolks of five Eggs and the white of only one of them; to which add one large spoonfull of Flour and one pint of new Milk. Sweeten to your taste with fine Sugar. Boil it in a Bason covered with a cloth tied fast round it. Observe that your Bason be brim-full. Half an hour boils it.

A Spoonfull Pudding
Another Way
A Spoonfull of Flour, a Spoonfull of Cream or new Milk, an Egg, a little grated Nutmeg, ground Ginger and Salt. Mix all together and boil it in a little wooden Dish, or earthen Bason, for half an hour. Some add a few Currants.—R.H.G.

BAKED PUDDINGS (c. 1790)
Vermicelli Pudding
Take four ounces of vermicelli and boil it in a pint of new milk till it is soft, with a stick or two of cinnamon. Then put in half a pint of thick cream; a quarter of a pound of butter, the like quantity of sugar and the yolks of four eggs beaten fine. Bake it without paste in an earthen dish.

Sweetmeat Pudding
Cover your dish with a thin puff-paste, and then take candied orange and lemon peel, and citron, of each an ounce. Slice them thin, and lay them all over the bottom of the dish. Then beat up eight yolks of eggs, and two whites, and put to them half a pound of sugar, and half a pound of melted butter. Mix the whole well together, put it on the sweetmeats, and send it to a moderate heated oven. About an hour will do it.

Millet Pudding
Wash and pick clean half a pound of millet seed, put it into half a pound of sugar, a whole nutmeg grated, and three quarts of milk, and break in half a pound of fresh butter. Butter your dish, pour it in, and send it to the oven.

Oat Pudding
Take a pound of oats with the husks off, and lay them in new milk, eight ounces of raisins of the sun stoned, the same quantity of currants well picked and washed, a pound of suet shred fine, and six new-laid eggs well beat up. Season with nutmeg, beaten ginger, and salt and mix them all well together.

Transparent Pudding
Beat up eight eggs well in a pan, and put to them half a pound of butter and the same quantity of loaf sugar beat fine, with a little grated nutmeg. Set it on the fire, and keep stirring it till it is the thickness of buttered eggs. Then put it into a bason to cool, roll a rich puff-paste very thin, lay it round the edge of your dish and pour in the ingredients. Put it into a moderately heated oven, and about half an hour will do it.

Lady Sunderland Pudding
Beat up the yolks of eight eggs with the whites of three, add to them five spoonfuls of flour, with half a nutmeg, and put them into half a pint of cream. Butter the insides of some small basons, fill them half-full and bake them half an hour. When done, turn them out of the basons, and pour over them melted butter mixed with wine and sugar.

A Grateful Pudding
To a pound of flour add a pound of white bread grated. Take eight eggs but only half the whites; beat them up, and mix with them a pint of new milk. Then stir in the bread and flour, a pound of raisins stoned, a pound of currants, half a pound of sugar, and a little beaten ginger. Mix all well together, pour it into your dish, and send it to the oven. If you can get cream instead of milk, it will be a material improvement.
—W.A.H.

BOILED PUDDINGS (c. 1790)
Bread Pudding

Take the crumb of a penny loaf, cut it into very thin slices, put it into a quart of milk and set it over a chaffing-dish of coals 'till the bread has soaked up all the milk. Then put in a piece of butter, stir it round, and let it stand till it is cold; or you may boil your milk, and pour it over the bread, and cover it close, which will equally answer the same purpose. Then take the yolks of six eggs, the whites of three, and beat them up with a little rose-water and nutmeg, and a little salt and sugar. Mix it all well together and put it into your cloth, tie it loose to give it room to swell, and boil it an hour. When done, put it into your dish, pour melted butter over it, and serve it to table.

Batter Pudding

Take a quart of milk, beat up the yolks of six eggs, and the whites of three, and mix them with a quarter of a pint of milk. Then take six spoonfuls of flour, a teaspoonful of salt and one of ginger. Put to these the remainder of the milk, mix all well together, put it into your cloth, and boil it an hour and a quarter. Pour melted butter over it when you serve it up.

Hunting Pudding

Mix eight eggs beaten fine with a pint of good cream and a pound of flour. Beat them well together and put to them a pound of beef suet finely-chopped, a pound of currants well cleaned, half a pound of jar-raisins stoned and chopped small, two ounces of candied orange cut small, the same of candied citron, a quarter of a pound of powdered sugar, and a large nutmeg grated. Mix all together with half a gill of brandy, put it into a cloth and boil it four hours. Be sure to put it in when the water boils, and keep it boiling all the time. When done turn it into a dish and strew over it powdered sugar.

Plumb Pudding

Cut a pound of suet into small pieces, but not too fine, a pound of currants washed clean, a pound of raisins stoned, eight yolks of eggs and four whites, half a nutmeg grated, a teaspoonful of beaten ginger, a pound of flour and a pint of milk. Beat the eggs first, then put to them half the milk, and beat them together; and, by degrees, stir in the flour, then the suet, spice and fruit, and as much milk as will mix it well together, very thick. It will take four hours boiling. When done, turn it into your dish, and strew over it grated sugar.

Oatmeal Pudding

Take a pint of whole oatmeal, and steep it in a quart of boiled milk overnight. In the morning take half a pound of beef suet shred fine, and mix with the oatmeal and milk; then add to them some grated nutmeg and a little salt, with three eggs beat up, a quarter of a pound of currants, the same quantity of raisins, and as much sugar as will sweeten it. Stir the whole well together, tie it pretty close, and boil it two hours. When done, turn it into your dish, and pour over it melted butter.

A Spoonful Pudding

Take a spoonful of flour, a spoonful of cream, or milk, an egg, a little nutmeg, ginger, and salt. Mix all together and boil it in a little wooden dish half an hour. If you think proper you may add a few currants.—W.A.H.

PUFF-PASTE
(See also Pastry)

To make light puff-paste, attention is principally required in the rolling out; if it should be too light, it may be rolled out once or twice more than prescribed here, as it principally depends on the fold whether it rises evenly and high.

With a pound of good, stiff butter (free from water) take one pound of flour, wet it into a paste with a quarter of a pint of water, the juice of one lemon, and the yolk of one egg, beaten up with it (care must be taken not to make the paste too soft but hard enough to roll out the thickness of a crown piece, ¼ in.); lay the remainder of the butter in thin slices all over; fold it up, beginning at top and bottom, to the middle in five or six folds; roll it out as thin as at first, brushing up the flour before folding up; when rolled out and folded three times this way, try a piece in the oven; if so light that it falls over, roll it out once or twice more. The piece tried should not be thicker than a crown piece; if it rises properly, it has been folded evenly; if not the ends have not been laid straight.

This paste is used for all sorts of pies, patties, vol-au-vent, and light pastry generally.—G.A.S.

PUFF PASTRY
(See also Pastry).

Rough Puff Pastry

1 lb. flour
10-12 oz. fat
Salt and cold water to mix

Sieve flour and salt; add fat cut in pieces the size of walnut. Add water to bind to stiff paste, but do not break down fat. Use a knife to mix.

Turn on to floured board and press paste lightly together, without kneading.

Roll out in a strip, keeping ends and sides even; fold paste in three, sealing edges with pin. Give pastry a half turn, and roll out again in strip. Then repeat process, until it has had four rollings and four foldings. It is then ready for use, but less elastic if allowed to rest awhile.—D.L.T.

PUFF POPS

1 cup flour
1 egg, well-beaten
¼ teaspoon salt
1 cup milk

Sift the flour and salt together. Mix the egg and milk together and add to the dry ingredients. Beat for 2 minutes with a wheel egg-beater and put into very hot iron gem pans which have been liberally greased. Bake in a quick oven (425° F.) for about half an hour. This recipe makes twelve. (*Bossis*.)—B.S.R.

PULLED BREAD

Remove bread from oven before it is quite cooked, that is, reduce the ordinary time of baking by 10 to 15 minutes. Grate off a thin layer of the brown from the outside, then with the hands pull the loaf apart into pieces half the size of the hand and less than an inch thick; return to the oven or the warming oven in a dripping-pan and let cook or dry until slightly coloured. Serve it at once, or set aside and reheat before serving. —M.B. (2).

PUMPERNICKEL. SCHWARTZBROT

Black bread which is made of coarse, unbolted rye flour, mostly in Germany. It is sold in most German *Delicatessen* shops in London and is made by German bakers in New York and Chicago. It possesses a somewhat acid taste which is not unpleasant, especially when the *Pumpernickel* is freely coated with fresh butter.

PURDY'S PET COOKIES

½ cupful of butter (¼ lb.)
½ cupful of sugar
½ cupful of sifted flour
4 egg whites, unbeaten
1 teaspoonful of vanilla

Stir the butter hard with a wooden spoon until soft and creamy. Beat in the sugar gradually. Mix in the flour. Add the egg whites and *stir and stir* until the ingredients are thoroughly blended. Add the vanilla. Drop on an unbuttered cookie sheet in little mounds (about one-half teaspoonful) at least 4 in. apart to allow for spreading. Bake in a slow oven (300° F.) for about 10 minutes, or until lightly browned. While hot, remove and roll. Do not try to bake more than four or six at a time as they will harden before you can roll them. They can

be left flat, like jumbles, if you like. Keep in a cool place. Recipe makes about four dozen. —E.K.H.

QUATRE-QUARTS CAKE

Four eggs and their weight in flour, castor sugar and butter.

Separate the whites from the yolks and mix the latter with the sugar and a little lemon juice.

Beat your butter to a cream and add the yolks and sugar. When well mixed add the flour last of all. Stir all well with a wooden spoon.

Beat the whites of the eggs stiff, and mix lightly with the rest so that the white 'egg-snow' does not remain at the top.

Butter a cake-tin and half fill with the mixture so that it has room to rise. Put it in a medium oven (not too hot) for an hour. It should rise to double the amount.

Some chopped blanched almonds can be sprinkled into the mixture before putting into the oven.—L.M. (1).

QUEEN OF PUDDINGS

This pudding, one of the best known of all English puddings, needs careful preparation and good materials, otherwise it becomes a soggy and feeble ghost of what it should be.

Prepare some fine white breadcrumbs, about one breakfast cup full. Take 4 eggs and separate the yolks and whites of three of them.

With the yolks and the whole egg and 1 pint milk make a custard. Put a ¼ in. layer of raspberry jam in pie-dish; add the crumbs to the custard with little vanilla flavour, pour this on top, and allow to stand about half an hour. Then bake in moderate oven till set. Whip up the whites, adding 3 or 4 tablespoons castor sugar. Dispose this meringue on top of pudding, sprinkle with icing sugar and castor sugar and replace in oven till meringue is set and delicately browned.— D.L.T.

RAG CAKE

Cream 1 cupful of butter with 1 cupful of sugar; work in 4 yolks, blend and beat thoroughly; add 2 cupfuls of flour; 1 cupful of sour cream, 1 small teaspoonful bicarbonate of soda dissolved in the cream, 1 teaspoonful of cream of tartar mixed with the flour. Gradually add 4 whites whisked stiff. Mix well and put into a buttered tin. This cake can be iced at pleasure with a plain boiled icing.—M.B. (2).

RAGI

This cereal, which is also known as *African Milet, Kayur, Kurrakanor* or *Coracan*, is the staple crop of the State of Mysore; it is grown extensively in other parts of India and in Ceylon; it is made into cakes, bread, puddings and porridge, and it is one of the chief foods of the lower classes. It is extensively grown also in Central and South Africa: it is called by the Kaffirs *Luku*; in Tanganyika, *Uimbi*; in Mozambique *Upoko* or *Umngoza*. The bread made from *Ragi* or *African Millet* is said to be of excellent flavour.

Ragi enjoys the practically unique privilege of being almost immune from attacks by insects, so that it may be stored with safety.

RAIL SPLITTERS

(American)
Beat 1 egg, add 3 tablespoonfuls of sugar, 1 teaspoonful of salt, 1 cup of yellow cornmeal and 4 tablespoonfuls of cool melted shortening, and mix all thoroughly. Add 1 cup of fresh buttermilk and beat; then half a teaspoonful of soda, dissolved in 1 teaspoonful of cold water. Sift in 1 cup of flour, sifted with 4 teaspoonfuls of baking powder, and beat hard. Grease and heat to the sizzling point iron cornbread stick-pans and pour in batter immediately and bake in a hot oven about 15 minutes.—G.T.L.

RAISED MUFFINS

    1 cupful of milk
    ½ cupful of butter
    2½ tablespoonfuls of sugar
    1 teaspoonful of salt
    ⅓ yeast cake dissolved in
    ¼ cupful of warm water
    2 cupfuls of sifted all-purpose flour
    2 egg whites stiffly-beaten

Heat the milk with the butter, sugar, and salt, until the butter is melted. Set aside until lukewarm. Then mix in the dissolved yeast. Add the flour gradually, mixing thoroughly. Stir in the whites. Cover and let rise in a protected corner for six hours. This is not a stiff dough. Fill well-buttered muffin-tins three-quarters full with a spoon. Bake in a hot oven (400° F.) for 20 minutes. Recipe makes about two dozen small muffins. A good old-fashioned change from the modern quick muffin.—E.K.H.

RAISIN BREAD

    10 oz. wholemeal flour
    ¾ lb. flour
    3 teaspoons baking powder
    1½ teaspoons salt
    4 to 6 oz. sugar
    3 gills milk
    6 oz. seedless raisins
    1 egg

Mix together the wholemeal, flour baking powder, sugar, and salt. Add the raisins,

which have been cleaned with a little flour, and make a well in the centre of these dry ingredients. Pour in the milk and the egg slightly beaten, and form into a dough. Put it into greased bread-tins and bake in a moderate oven (375° F.) about three-quarters of an hour, or until done.—G.H. (4).

RAMEKINS. RAMAKINS

Fr. *Ramequins*. Small cheese-cakes which may be made with ordinary breadcrumbs but are much better when made with puff-paste.

Pastry Ramakins

To Serve with the Cheese Course
Any pieces of very good light puff-paste Cheshire, Parmesan or Stilton Cheese.

Mode: The remains or odd pieces of paste left from large tarts, etc., answer for making these little dishes. Gather up the pieces of paste; roll it out evenly and sprinkle it with grated cheese of a nice flavour. Fold the paste in three, roll it out again, and sprinkle more cheese over; fold the paste, roll it out and with a paste-cutter shape it in any way that may be desired. Bake the ramakins in a brisk oven from 10 to 15 minutes, dish them on a hot napkin, and serve quickly. The appearance of this dish may be very much improved by brushing the *Ramakins* over with yolk of egg before they are put in the oven. Where expense is not objected to, Parmesan is the best kind of cheese to use for making this dish.—B. (2).

RAVIOLI

Small paste envelopes, made of wheatmeal paste, and filled with a number of different stuffings, mostly minced meats or vegetables *purées*.

Ravioli Paste

Put 4 cupfuls of flour in a bowl. Make a depression in middle into which place 1 teaspoonful of salt, 3 whole eggs beaten with half a cupful of water. Gradually assimilate the flour until all is used, which will make a real stiff dough. Use as directed. —E.E.A.

Ravioli

1 lb. flour, 2 whole eggs and the yolk of one, 2 tablespoonfuls of olive oil, a little salt and enough water to form into a stiff dough. Knead the dough for about 20 minutes and then let it stand for about half an hour. Roll out very thinly on a floured board and then cut into squares 1½ in. across. Put a little stuffing on half of the squares and cover with another square, moistening the edges and pressing well together so that they will remain closed up. Boil in stock for 20 minutes, drain, put in a dish and pour over a good tomato sauce or a sauce made from some of the stock, improved with a little

meat glaze. Sprinkle with Parmesan cheese and heat in the oven.

Stuffings may be made of finely-minced chicken, veal, liver, etc., mixed with a little breadcrumb soaked in stock, a little Parmesan cheese and the yolk of an egg. *Ravioli* may also be filled with a *purée* of spinach and cheese.—M.K.S. (2).

Ravioli Alassio

Mince up meat very finely; boil spinach and pass it through a sieve; add salt and pepper, a very little nutmeg, an egg for every person and a little milk. Mix all well together.

Make a paste with flour and water. Cut out oblong pieces, put some mixture in each, fold it up, press the edges firmly together. Cook in a large saucepan in boiling water. Drain and pour over them some meat-juice. Sprinkle with Parmesan cheese.—P.A.

Ravioli alla Romana

Take 6 oz. of curd, 4 oz. of flour, 3 oz. of grated cheese, an egg, and 1 yolk and a little salt. Make a paste of it and turn it out on the pastry-board and make forms in the shape of a cylinder, cutting them in equal lengths. Boil them for 2 or 3 minutes in salted water. Sprinkle cheese over them or strong beef-tea.—P.A.

REGENT'S PUDDING

Grate 2 oz. of the white meat of a coconut. Mix with this 2 oz. of finely-grated breadcrumbs, 2 oz. of flour, 3 oz. of finely-shred beef suet, a tablespoonful of currants, a tablespoonful of chopped raisins and a little sugar. Mix these ingredients thoroughly and beat them up with 2 eggs and half a quarter of a pint of milk. Pour the mixture into a basin and put over it a piece of buttered writing paper. Plunge into boiling water and let it boil quickly until done enough. Turn it carefully and before sending to table pour over it a little custard sauce pleasantly flavoured with vanilla.—W.F. (28).

REGINETTE

Long, wavy, ribbon-like pieces of *Italian Paste* (q.v.) about ¼ in. wide and very thin. It is cooked and used like *Macaroni* (q.v.).

REVALENTA

An invalid food made up of prepared lentils and barley flour; it is sometimes sweetened and flavoured. It was introduced in 1845 under the name of *Revalenta Arabica* and a registered brand of it was very popular in France under the name of *Revalescière du Barry.*

RHEIMS BISCUITS

Put into bowl ½ lb. of finely-powdered and sifted sugar, and the yolks of 12 eggs and beat them together with a wooden spoon.

Whilst this is being done let another person whip the whites to a thick snow, then stir the two mixtures together very gently with the wooden spoon. Then sift in 6 oz. of fine flour, 2 oz. of powdered sugar and the grated peel of a lemon; mix all well but gently together so as to keep the whites frothy. Fill some buttered and sugared sponge finger-tins half full, and bake in a quick oven until the biscuits are a fine yellow colour. Turn them out of the tins while still hot. If properly made these biscuits will keep for some time. To be served with champagne or dessert.—M.B. (2).

RICE

Lat. *Oryza Sativa*; F. *Riz.* A cereal which is best and mostly used by way of a vegetable. Rice is poor in gluten and rice flour is poor altogether. It can be used in puddings and pastries, but it is advisable to mix some wheat flour with it.

There are many different varieties of rice and, generally speaking, a translucent rice of creamy tint has usually better cooking qualities than the chalky, dull white types of rice. By 'cooking qualities' we understand those factors which enable the grains of rice to retain their shape after being cooked.

In India, the best and most expensive rice is known as *Pillau*, of which there are different grades, but it is seldom that one may obtain the real *Pillau* outside India. The name, however, or its varieties, *Pillaw* and *Pillaff*, are commonly used in culinary French, for dishes prepared with rice, and with any kind of rice. In culinary French, the best sorts of rice among those obtainable in Europe and the U.S.A. are called, in order of merit, Patna, Carolina and Java. Italian rice is always known in culinary French as *Rizotto.*

Rice may be served as hors-d'oeuvre; in soups; as a vegetable by itself, or as an accompaniment to meat, fish and other vegetables; as a salad; as a sweet or savoury. Ground rice and rice flour also have many uses.

There are some uncultivated sorts of rice, true wild rice, but they are not sold in Europe. The so-called *Wild Rice*, which is sold in the U.S.A. on a large scale, and occasionally in England, does not belong to the genus *Oryza*; it is not a rice at all, but a perennial grass known to botanists by the name of *Zizania aquatica.*

THE COOKING OF RICE
The Western Way

Wash one cup of rice in several waters to get rid of all loose starch. Put two quarts of water in a pan; add three teaspoonfuls of salt; bring to the boil. Drop the rice slowly in the fast boiling water so that the water does not stop boiling. After 12 minutes take out a few grains and test for softness; so long as the grains cannot be crushed easily between two fingers let the rice boil. When the rice is soft enough to crush, but each grain still firm and whole, drain in a colander, cover the rice with a cloth and place it over some steaming water to fluff and dry out the grains.

The Eastern Way

Drop the rice you wish to cook in just enough boiling water for the grains to absorb the whole of the water by the time they are cooked, that is, just soft enough to eat but still firm and whole. This method, once the right quantity of water has been ascertained by trial and error, saves time and the vitamins – should there be any left in the milled rice, or the minerals which are surely wasted when the excess water is poured away and the boiled rice drained.

Rice Water

Water drained from boiled rice should be saved and used for sauces or soups; it may also be used for starching fine linen and lace. Rice starch is so easily digested and assimilated that rice water is often added to the milk given to infants.

Left-over Rice

The sooner rice is eaten after it is cooked, the better – as left-over rice spoils very quickly. In warm weather decomposition sets in cooked rice very soon. Left-over rice must be kept in a refrigerator until wanted. It may be added to boiling salted water for five minutes, then drained, allowed to fluff and dry out; or it may be re-heated in the oven, adding a little water to the pan, covering it and allowing the rice to get thoroughly hot.

Boiled Rice

Barkfare (Chinese Rice). Wash unpolished rice in three or four changes of water and allow to soak overnight. Place in boiling water and simmer for 20 minutes. Drain dry and serve in place of bread.—T.S.

Riz au gras. Wash the rice in several waters, blanch it in boiling, salted water. Drain it dry and boil in good chicken stock until nearly all the stock has been absorbed by the rice. Leave in the oven, with lid off the pan, for another 15 minutes. Taste and season, if necessary, before serving.

Japanese Rice. Take one cupful of rice. Wash well in a little water and *rub* rice thoroughly. After this rinse the rice *several times* in fresh water until the water is quite clear. This is an essential part of the recipe. The rice should be of a Japanese variety,

failing which Spanish is the next best. Take two cups of water to one cup of rice: put them in a saucepan; cover tightly with lid. When water boils, do not remove the lid, but leave the rice to steam undisturbed for about 20 minutes. When ready to serve, the water should have been completely absorbed and the rice should be a steaming, hot, snowy mass – rather sticky, but it smells and tastes more of *rice* than cooked in any other way.—D.L.S.

Rice Chowders
(Chinese)

Gai Jook (Rice chowder with chicken). Mince finely the breast of a chicken and wash some rice in several waters. Boil slowly for half-an-hour, adding a little ginger, some finely-chopped Chinese cabbage (*Pe-Tsai*, q.v.), and some spring onions. Simmer for 45 minutes.—T.S.

Ji Yuk Jook (Rice chowder with pork). Cut up some lean pork into very small pieces. Prepare some rice, add the minced pork and boil slowly for half-an-hour. Add a little ginger and a few drops of Chinese Sauce, and boil for a further half hour.—T.S.

Ngau Yuk Jook (Rice chowder with minced beef). The same as *Ji Yuk Jook*, replacing lean pork with lean beef.—T.S.

Cheesed Rice

Il risotto bianco (White rice). To every lb. of rice allow 1½ pints of stock, 3½ oz. butter, 3½ oz. Parmesan Cheese, and a small onion. Put half the butter in a pan and brown lightly the chopped onion. Add the rice and mix thoroughly. Then add the boiling stock and boil for about 13 minutes or longer, till the rice is soft and the stock absorbed. Season with salt and pepper. Then remove from the fire, stir in the remaining butter and the grated Parmesan Cheese.—C.M. (4).

Risotto à la Milanese. To 1 lb. of rice – preferably Italian rice – allow: 1 small onion, 4 oz. of butter, 2 oz. of beef marrow, 4 oz. of grated cheese, 3 tablespoons of white wine, 1½ pints of beef or chicken stock, ½ teaspoon of saffron, salt and pepper.

Chop the onion and cook to a light golden colour, but without browning, in 2 oz. of butter and the finely-chopped beef-marrow. Then add the rice and cook for 15 minutes, stirring almost continuously with a wooden spoon, so that it will not catch. Add the saffron, the white wine, the boiling stock gradually, mix all thoroughly and season with salt and pepper. Simmer for about 30 minutes, stirring frequently, and finally add the grated cheese and the rest of the butter. It is then ready to serve.—C.M. (4).

Risotto à la Parmigiana. This is done in the same manner as the *White Risotto* (q.v.), but small pieces of chicken livers are cooked with the onion. An abundance of Parmesan Cheese is used for this risotto – the *Parmesan stravecchio*, or 'Vintage' Parmesan.—C.M. (4).

Rice Cream
Take 4 oz. of rice, wash it well and boil it in plenty of salted water for 10 minutes. Pour away the water and add to the rice half a pint of milk. Stir over the fire until thoroughly cooked. Dissolve ¼ oz. of sheet gelatine in half a pint of milk, and add to the rice. (The gelatine and milk must not boil). Whip quarter of a pint of cream until stiff, flavour and sweeten to taste, and mix well with the rice. Have a mould ready, prepared with a little jelly, or a few dried cherries at the bottom; pour in the rice mixture, and set aside to cool. (*Mrs A G. Perkin, of Headingley.*)—P.T.L.

Fried Rice
(Chinese)
Chow Yurn Chow Fare. First boil the rice, then fry it with chopped onions, prawns, egg and any meat available, which must be cut up very small. Serve with Chinese Sauce.—T.S.

Pillau Rice
(India)
1 lb. of Patna rice well washed in cold water and set to soak in cold water for two hours or longer, then thoroughly drained; ½ lb. of butter or ghee, 1 large onion and 2 cloves of garlic, chopped; half a teaspoonful of saffron (steeped in half a teacupful of warm water); 12 cloves; 12 whole cardamoms; 2 sticks of cinnamon, each about 2 in. long, and half a teaspoonful of allspice (whole); 4 oz. of sultanas and 2 oz. of blanched almonds (lightly fried in butter).

Use a deep *sauté* pan with a close-fitting lid. Fry in the butter or ghee the onions (but do not brown), garlic and spices, then add the rice and, tossing it lightly, continue frying on a slow fire for 4 or 5 minutes longer. Add the steeped saffron and water, salt to taste and sufficient boiling water to cover the rice and stand an inch or two over it. Cover the pan closely, and cook on a very slow fire until the rice has absorbed all the water and is thoroughly cooked – each grain should be separate. Finally mix lightly into the rice the fried sultanas and almonds. —E.P.V.

Rice Pudding
Well wash the rice and soak in water overnight. Strain off the water, put the rice into a buttered pie-dish with a pinch of salt, a nut of butter, two tablespoonfuls of sugar and a pint of milk to a teacupful of rice. Bake in a slow oven for 1½ hours.

Dundee Rice Pudding
Boil sufficient rice in milk until cooked rather firm, sweeten and fill in therewith a fireproof glass – or nice-looking pie-dish – adding a spendthrift's spreading of juicy home-made marmalade and leaving a small valley in the centre for the following mixture to fill in:

Butter 2½ oz., melted butter, not allowed to oil, adding to it while warm 2½ oz. sugar and the yolks of five eggs, mixed well together and beaten until light. Pour this all over. Bake in a not very hot oven from half to three-quarters of an hour. It should be a pleasant *café au lait* brown on the top – like the ideal sponge cake – and there should be enough for six people. (*Lady Jekyll's recipe.*) —D.L.S.

French Rice Pudding
Riz pour entremets. Wash ¼ lb. Patna rice or Indo-China rice, blanch it in boiling water, drain it dry and rinse it in tepid water. Put the well-drained rice in a saucepan with 1½ pints boiled milk; this milk will have been boiled with a pinch of salt, a pat of butter, a pod of vanilla and sugar to taste. Put the pan on a quick fire to begin with, then put the lid on the pan and put the pan in a slow oven; leave it for half an hour and do not stir the rice. Take the pan out of the oven, stir into the rice with a fork six yolks of eggs, and add more sugar if necessary.

This rice may be served hot or cold by way of rice pudding, or improved by the addition of fresh cream, sugared fruit, etc., when it is called *Riz à l'Impératrice, Riz Montmorency*, etc.

Rice Salad
Col. Holden's Rice Salad. Rice, beets, tongue, asparagus, truffles, pimentoes, tomato, chervil, hard-boiled egg yolks, lettuce.

Mix equal quantities of whole steamed rice (each kernel to be separate and dry and not mashed together), diced red beetroot, smoked beef tongue and cubed asparagus, with a small amount of diced truffles and pimentoes. Season well and mix in a dressing made of oil and tarragona vinegar, proportion 3 oil to 1 vinegar.

Arrange the above in a crystal salad bowl lined with lettuce, and garnish sides with peeled and seasoned slices of red ripe tomatoes. Sprinkle chopped chervil and yolks of eggs over tomatoes. Should be made and seasoned at the last moment.—A.S. (1).

Rice Soup
Potage crème de riz. Wash, blanch and drain some rice, then cook it either in milk or chicken broth, adding pepper, salt and butter. When cooked, push through a fine

sieve, return to the pot in which it was cooked, re-heat and stir in some fresh cream before serving.

Stewed Rice

½ lb. rice, 1 cup lard, 1 cup tomatoes, 1 large onion, minced, 3 cloves garlic, 1 cup green peas, 1 cup diced potatoes, 1 teaspoon minced parsley, 4 cups water.

Soak rice in boiling water for 15 minutes, then wash in cold water in colander, draining well. Brown onion and garlic in lard, removing garlic when brown. Add rice, stirring constantly, and brown evenly. Pour off fat; add peas, potatoes, parsley and water, and cook slowly for 55 minutes. Put mixture into well-greased mould or pudding dish, packing firmly; set in hot oven in a pan of hot water till ready to serve.—C.G.

Rice Stew

(Chinese)

Subgum Chow Fan. Cut up in small pieces some chicken, ham, black mushrooms, prawns and Chinese cabbage. Place in a bowl and add a glass of white wine, in which an egg has been beaten. Throw in some prepared rice and stew for half an hour.—T.S.

Yellow Rice

(A South African Recipe)

2 cups rice
6 cups water (boiling)
¾ lb. yellow sugar
1 tablespoon butter
1 teaspoon turmeric
1 tablespoon salt
1 cup raisins
1 stick cinnamon

(1) Wash rice well.
(2) Put all the other ingredients into the boiling water.
(3) Gradually add the rice.
(4) Cover the saucepan and cook until the rice is tender and has absorbed all the moisture.

N.B.—Cook slowly towards the end.

Savoury or Yellow Rice

Using a deep *sauté* pan, with a close-fitting lid, lightly fry for about 5 minutes in ¼ lb. of ghee or butter, 2 tablespoonfuls of chopped onions, a small saltspoonful of finely-chopped garlic and 2 ordinary cloves. Add a teaspoonful of ground turmeric and a saltspoonful of ground cummin seed, cook for another minute or two and then add 1 lb. of well-washed, well-soaked and well-drained Patna rice and salt to taste. Stir and cook for another 5 minutes. Now add boiling water

sufficient to cover the rice and stand over it about an inch or two. Cover the pan closely and cook on a slow fire until the water is absorbed and the rice cooked.

Do not stir the rice into a pulp, but occasionally lift it lightly with a shallow spoon and toss it over and over until you are sure that every grain is cooked.—E.P.V.

Rice Biscuits

To every ½ lb. of rice-flour allow ¼ lb. of pounded lump sugar, ¼ lb. of butter, 2 eggs.

Beat the butter to a cream, stir in the rice-flour and pounded sugar, and moisten the whole with the eggs, which should be previously well beaten. Roll out the paste, shape it with a round paste-cutter into small cakes and bake them from 12 to 18 minutes in a very slow oven.—B. (2).

Rice Blancmange

¼ lb. of ground rice
3 oz. of sugar
1 oz. of fresh butter
1 quart of milk
Flavouring of lemon peel
Essence of almonds or vanilla or laurel leaves

Mix the rice to a smooth batter with about half a pint of the milk, and the remainder put into a saucepan, with the sugar, butter and whichever of the above flavourings may be preferred. Bring the milk to the boiling-point, quickly stir in the rice, and let it boil for about 10 minutes, or until it comes easily away from the saucepan, keeping it well stirred the whole time. Grease a mould with pure salad oil; pour in the rice and let it get perfectly set, when it should turn out quite easily; garnish it with jam, or pour round a compote of fruit, just before it is sent to table. This blancmange is better for being made the day before it is wanted, as it then has time to become firm. If laurel leaves are used for flavouring, steep three of them in the milk, and take them out before the rice is added: about eight drops of essence of almonds, or from 12 to 16 drops of essence of vanilla would be required to flavour the above proportion of milk.—B. (2).

Rice Bread

Boil 8 oz. of rice till tender, pulp it through a sieve, strain off any liquid, then blend it with 20 oz. of flour and 10 oz. of maize meal. Mix 1 teaspoonful of salt and 3 dessertspoonfuls of yeast in some of the rice water; make all into a smooth dough. Put it in a warm place, covered, to rise, and deal with it as wheaten bread, but it will take longer to bake.—M.B. (2).

Rice Buns

½ lb. flour
2 oz. of ground rice
1 egg
1 teaspoon baking powder
2 oz. butter
3 oz. sugar
Flavouring

Mix the flour, ground rice and the baking powder. Rub in the butter and then add sugar; then the flavouring, mix to a smooth paste with well-beaten egg. When thoroughly mixed, turn the mixture on to a lightly-floured board. Divide into about 20 pieces. Form these into a round ball, pressing them flat into some crystallized sugar. Bake until a pretty brown colour for about 10 minutes. —L.G.N.

Rice Cakes
(Kent, 1809)

A ¼ lb. of ground rice, the same of flour, 1 lb. of white sugar, sifted, a ¼ lb. of melted butter, 4 eggs, leaving out 2 whites. The rice, flour, and sugar to be mixed together, the eggs and butter to be added when the batter is nearly cold. If you choose currants, put a ¼ lb.—M.B. (1).

Rice Cheesecakes

Ingredients: Puff pastry about 6 oz.; butter 2 oz.; castor sugar 2 oz.; ground rice 2 oz.; egg 1; currants and cinnamon or other flavouring; sufficient for 12.

Time: To bake 15 minutes, in a quick oven.

Method: 1. Grease 12 patty-pans and line them with pastry. 2. Make the mixture to fill these as follows: Cream the butter and sugar, add the ground rice, well-beaten egg, cinnamon, and a few currants. Put a little of the mixture into each patty-pan.—FL.W.

RICE FLOUR

Rice flour is rice ground much finer than what is sold under the name of *Ground Rice*. Rice flour is used in cookery, for cakes, puddings and gruel for children, and also in the making of baking powders, custard and egg powders, face powders, etc.

RICE-FLOUR TODDLES

1 cup cooked hominy
1 egg
½ cup rice flour
1 teaspoon salt
½ cup milk (about)

Mix the rice flour and salt with the hominy and add the beaten egg which has been combined with the milk. Drop on a well-greased griddle and bake until each side is brown. This makes about 12 small cakes.

Wheat flour used in place of the rice flour, brings out the taste of the hominy more prominently. (*Miss C. Blanche Moodie*.)—B.S.R.

RICE-FLOUR WAFFLES

1 cup hominy
1 cup rice flour
¼ teaspoon salt
⅓ cup water
1 egg, well-beaten
1 cup wheat flour
1 cup milk
1 tablespoon butter, melted

Beat the cold hominy into the egg until it is smooth. Mix and sift the dry ingredients, mix to a batter with the milk and water. Then add the egg and hominy mixture and last the melted butter.

Bake in a hot waffle-iron for a trifle longer than usual – allow about 4 minutes. These waffles are not the crisp product with which we are familiar. They are crispish on the outside but moist within. The flavour is excellent, and while they may be served in almost any preferred manner, we found them particularly good liberally buttered and served with bacon. This recipe makes about 8 waffles. (*Mary Leize Simons*.)—B.S.R.

RIPON SPICE BREAD

3½ lb. flour
¼ lb. butter
¼ lb. lard
¼ lb. sugar
¼ lb. currants
¼ lb. raisins
¼ lb. peel
1 teaspoon mixed spice
2 oz. yeast
1 egg
A pinch of salt
Milk to mix

Prepare tins as for bread. Put the flour in a bowl, rub the butter and lard in, then add sugar, spice, salt, currants, raisins and shredded peel, and mix thoroughly in the dry state. Make a well in the middle. Cream the yeast in a teacupful of milk and warm water, add a sprinkle of sugar and set to rise. Break the egg into the well, add the yeast and with more warm milk make up. Knead lightly. Set to rise 15 minutes before baking in a slow oven.—P.H.

ROCK BISCUITS

6 eggs
1 lb. of sifted sugar
½ lb. of flour
A few currants

Break the eggs into a basin, beat them well until very light; add the pounded sugar, and when this is well mixed with the eggs, dredge in the flour gradually, and add the currants. Mix all well together, and put the dough, with a fork, on the tins, making it as rough as possible. Bake the cakes in a moderate oven from 20 to 30 minutes; when they are done, allow them to get cool, and store them away in a tin canister in a dry place.—B. (2).

ROCK CAKES

    12 oz. flour
    Pinch of salt
    1 teaspoon baking powder
    6 oz. butter or margarine
    1½ oz. finely-chopped peel
    6 oz. sugar
    3 oz. currants
    ¼ teaspoon grated nutmeg
    ¼ teaspoon mixed spice
    1 egg
    Little milk to mix

Grease a baking-sheet and dredge with flour. Sieve the flour, salt, baking powder, grated nutmeg and mixed spice into a basin. Rub in the fat with the tips of the fingers until it resembles fine breadcrumbs. Stir in the sugar, currants, and chopped peel and mix well. Make a well in the centre and stir in the beaten egg and just sufficient milk to make a stiff mixture. With the aid of two forks, place the mixture in rocky heaps on the baking-sheet and bake in a quick oven of 380 to 390° F. for 15 to 20 minutes, according to the size of the cakes.—G.H. (4).

ROLLS

Fr. *Petits pains*. Any kind of dough suitable for making bread, but a little only, and that little *rolled up* in any shape or form and baked till crisp.

French Rolls

Sift a teaspoonful of salt with a quart of flour, and work it all to a dough with 2 eggs, a tablespoonful of lard, 2 tablespoonfuls of yeast and enough milk to make it all a nice dough. Work this all well together, then leave it to rise in a warm corner till the morning, when you work it well again, divide into rolls and place them in proper French roll tins; let these rise again for a little then bake in a quick oven. Mind these do not burn on the top as they are apt to do, for then they must be rasped, which does not improve their appearance.—Q. (1).

'Gem' Rolls

Beat up an egg till light, then add to it half a teaspoonful of salt and a pint of milk, and mix this all gradually into a pint of flour. Bake in buttered 'gem' or small patty-pans. These should be made of Graham flour. —Q. (1).

Parker House Rolls

1 cupful of milk, 1 oz. of yeast, 3 tablespoonfuls of sugar, 2 eggs, quarter of a tablespoonful of salt, drop of lemon flavouring, 4½ cupfuls of flour and 6 tablespoonfuls of butter.

Dissolve yeast with milk, add sugar, salt, flavouring, flour and butter; work all into a smooth paste. Cover with buttered waxpaper and let rise in a warm place until double the original size. Interrupt the fermentation by working dough together again. Let rise anew by the same method as before and the dough is now ready to be moulded into rolls. Form 2 oz. balls and lay them in lightly-floured cloth. Let rise a trifle. With a ¾ in. thick rolling-pin press down in the middle of the dough ball and give a half-turn of the rolling-pin. Butter the inner side of one part of the roll and lap the other side over the other.

Place on slightly-buttered baking-sheets 1 in. apart and set in a warm place to rise; avoid draughts. Then bake in a moderate oven (350° F.). When done, brush over some melted butter. This will give about two dozen rolls.—E.E.A.

ROLY-POLY

    ½ lb. flour
    ¼ lb. suet
    A pinch of salt
    2 or 3 tablespoons jam
    A small teaspoon baking powder
    Cold water

Chop the suet finely, mix it with the flour, add the baking powder and salt, make a firm paste with cold water. Roll out on a floured board to a long strip, spread the jam to within an inch of the edge, wet the edge, roll up the strips, press the edges together, dip a pudding-cloth in boiling water, flour it well, put in the Roly-poly. Tie up the ends securely, place in a pan of boiling water, boil for two hours, take off cloth and serve hot. Sufficient for five to six people.

RUSKS

To make Rusks (1807)

Take 4 lb. of fine flour, a pint of new milk, with 4 oz. of butter melted in it; beat 4 eggs, with 4 spoonfuls of new yeast; mix it well together and let it stand 1 hour by the fire to rise; then make it up into small balls, and lay them on tins, and set them to rise for half an hour; then set them in a quick oven; and when they begin to look brown, take them out, and cut them through with a sharp knife, and set them in the oven again to crisp, with the door open.—A.A.

Italian Rusks

A stale Savoy or lemon cake may be converted into very good rusks in the following manner: Cut the cake into slices, divide each slice in two; put them on a baking-sheet, in a slow oven, and when they are of a nice brown and quite hard, they are done. They should be kept in a closed tin canister in a dry place to preserve their crispness.—B. (2).

RUSSELL BUNS

1¼ cups scalded milk
1 yeast cake dissolved in
¼ cup lukewarm water
3¾ cups flour
½ cup sugar
1 teaspoon cinnamon
1 teaspoon salt
2 eggs
1 tablespoon butter
1 tablespoon lard
½ cup currants

When milk is lukewarm, add dissolved yeast cake and three cups flour; cover and let rise until mixture is light. Add remaining flour with other ingredients, except currants; cover and again let rise until mixture doubles in bulk. Turn on floured cloth and knead in currants. Shape into biscuits, place in buttered pan close together, cover and let rise. Brush top with milk. Bake in moderately hot oven (375° F.) 25 minutes. Take from oven. Brush over with melted butter. Sprinkle with powdered sugar. Makes 24 to 30 buns.—B.C.S.C.B.

RUTLAND CAKES (1807)

Take 1 lb. of fine flour, and the same quantity of loaf sugar pounded and sifted; sift them together through a sieve; rub into it ¼ lb. of butter, and make it into a paste, with 4 eggs, leaving out 2 whites, which must be well beat, with 2 spoonfuls of rose-water; roll them very thin and bake them on tins of a light brown.—A.A.

RYE

Lat. *Secale cereale*; Fr. *Seigle*. Although not of the same genus, rye is closely related to wheat. It is more northern in its requirements than wheat, and until modern times was not found wild or cultivated outside of Central and Northern Europe. In Germany, Austria, Switzerland, and eastwards at the present time it ranks with wheat in importance as a bread cereal. It must also have been a common product in the British Isles for some centuries, from whence it was introduced into North America. As late as the latter-half of the nineteenth century rye was grown almost to the exclusion of wheat in New England, and ground locally for bread-making. The influx of Teutonic and Scandinavian emigrants into the United States has stimulated its culture in Middle Western and North Western States.'—A.L.W.

Rye flour is rich in nitrogenous matter, and *Rye Bread*, although darker in colour than wheaten bread, is very little inferior to it in nutritive qualities. In Sweden, *Rye Cakes* are to the peasantry what *Oat Cakes* are to the Scots. *Rye flour* is often used mixed with the flour of either wheat, oats or barley in the making of what is commonly called *Black Bread* (q.v.).

Rye is used in Holland to obtain the *mash* from which *Hollands* is distilled, whereas in the U.S.A. *Rye* is distilled into *Whisky*.

RYE BREAD

2⅓ lb. rye flour
2½ lb. wheat flour
1 oz. salt
1½ oz. yeast
1 quart warm water

Mix the two flours and salt together. Cream the yeast with the sugar, make a well in the flour and put in the yeast and mix to a dough with the warm water. Let it rise in a warm place for one hour, then knead well and leave to rise again for half an hour. Form into oval loaves, let them stand to prove again for about 10 minutes and bake in a medium oven.—M.K.S. (2).

Whole Rye Bread is known as *Pumpernickel* (q.v.).

SAFFRON BREAD
(Swedish)

2 lb. 14 oz. white flour
Bare pint of milk
1½ oz. yeast
1 teaspoon saffron
5 oz. butter
6 oz. sugar
1 egg
2 tablespoons ground almonds
6 pounded bitter almonds
3½ oz. raisins or
1½ oz. chopped candied peel

Covering: 1 egg, 2 tablespoons chopped almonds, 2 tablespoons granulated sugar.

Work part of the flour, tepid milk and yeast into a dough. Leave to rise to twice its size. Dry saffron in a very cool oven, pound finely with a little sugar, stir with a little milk and add to the dough. Cream sugar and butter and beat the egg. Work into the dough together with almonds and raisins, previously soaked in warm water and stoned. Add more flour if necessary and when well worked in, leave again to rise. Remove to floured pasteboard, knead well and divide into eight portions. Roll out, shape into strands and twist into a plait, which might be shaped into a wreath. Leave on greased tins to rise. Brush with lightly-beaten egg, sprinkle with finely-chopped almonds and sugar mixed. Bake in fairly hot oven.—I.N.

SAFFRON CAKE

1 lb. dough
Small pinch of saffron
2 oz. castor sugar
2 oz. currants
1 oz. candied peel
3 oz. butter
3 oz. lard

Make the dough in the ordinary way as for bread, but infuse the saffron in the warm water first to make it yellow. When the dough has risen, mix in the currants, sugar and candied peel. Melt together the butter and lard, which must not be made too hot or allowed to oil, pour on to the dough and beat in well. Then knead well; put into a cake-tin and leave to rise to the top of the tin before cooking in a moderate oven.—H.E.

SAFFRON WIGS (1807)

Rub a pound and a half of butter into six quarts of fine flour, add one ounce of caraway seeds; steep a quarter of an ounce of saffron in a quart of new milk; then beat eight eggs into a pint of very light barm; mix them with the milk, and make it up into a light paste, and set it by the fire to rise; then roll into it a pound and a half of loaf sugar, pounded and sifted; when made up, brush them over with milk and the yolk of an egg beat together.—A.A.

SAGO

A dry, brownish, granulated or powdered form of starch obtained in India, China, Borneo, Sumatra, Malaya, the Philippines, etc., from the mealy trunk-pith of various species of low palm trees. The ordinary sago palm grows to 20 to 30 ft. high, but only flowers once, and that when about 15 years old. When it is about to flower, the tree is felled, the hollow trunk, 18 to 22 in. in diameter, is split and sawn into pieces about 3 or 4 ft. long, soaked in water for a few days, after which all the soft white and spongy pith found inside is scraped out. This pith is then bruised in a mortar to a coarse powder like sawdust, kneaded and washed in long wooden troughs of cold running water and strained in a cloth until all the white fecula or starchy matter separates: it may either be caked right off for native use as bread, or dried and pounded up into *Sago Flour* or meal, which is passed through a sieve or cullender whilst moist and made into pill-shaped pellets and dried.

Sago is practically devoid of all flavour and consists almost exclusively of starch; it is easily digested and is used for young children or old people like *Arrowroot* (q.v.).

Sago Bread, as used by the natives of the Moluccas, is made simply by throwing caked lumps of *Sago Meal* into heated earthenware moulds, where it soon bakes in a hard mass.

German Sago is not *Sago* but *Potato flour*, made in Germany, and coloured yellowish with oxide of iron or burnt sugar.

SAGO PUDDING

Boil to a paste 2 oz. of *Sago* in 1½ pints of milk; when cold, add 1 oz. of butter melted in half a pint of cream, 6 yolks and 2 whole eggs, 1 lemon-peel, and half a nutmeg, grated; 2 dessertspoonfuls of orange-flower water, and ½ oz. of citron, cut; line a dish with paste, bake it half an hour.—G.A.S.

ST JOHN'S BREAD

A name given sometimes to the *Algarroba* (q.v.) or *Locust Beans*, and to a sort of bread made from their meal mixed with flour. The name is due to a tradition according to which the pods of the *Locust Beans* are identical with the 'locusts and wild honey' upon which St John the Baptist lived when in the wilderness.

ST MORITZ

Sieve 6 oz. flour on to table, make a well. Sprinkle flour with 1½ oz. ground almonds and 1½ oz. grated chocolate. Put 5 oz. butter and good ounce castor sugar in middle. Work the butter and sugar to a pomade, then work in other ingredients. Make into ball, then press away with floured hands to blend the paste. Roll out ½ in. thick. Put on buttered baking-sheet and bake in moderate oven 10 to 15 minutes, till firm and coloured but not too brown.

Cut down centre while hot; spread one half with melted chocolate and place other half on top. Cut into finger lengths. Dust with icing sugar when cold. This paste is very brittle.—D.L.T.

SALERATUS

The obsolete name for *Baking Powder* (q.v.).

SALLY LUNN

A tea cake originally made and sold by Sally Lunn at her tea-shop at Bath (England).

Sally Lunns

1 pint lukewarm milk
2 oz. castor sugar
1 oz. compressed yeast
A pinch of salt
1½ lb. flour
2 eggs
¼ lb. butter

Mix flour and salt in a basin. Beat the yeast to a cream with the sugar. Melt the butter in the milk and, when tepid, stir in the yeast. Strain this into the centre of the flour and add the beaten eggs. Mix in the flour from the sides carefully until a stiff dough is formed. Cover with a cloth and leave in a warm place to rise from 1 to 2 hours – then knead lightly until quite smooth and form into 5 or 6 cakes.

Put these on a greased and floured tin and leave to rise for 20 minutes. Then bake in a hot oven for about 15 minutes or until firm when pressed, or a nice brown. The *Sally Lunns* may be glazed by brushing with a little sugar, melted with a spoonful of milk, over the top.

When cooked, split open, butter generously and serve hot.—M.K.S. (2).

SAND TARTS

> 1 lb. castor sugar
> 1 lb. flour
> ¾ lb. butter
> 1 egg and yolk of 1 egg
> ¼ teaspoon soda

Mix thoroughly, roll very thin and cut out in rounds. A tumbler makes a good size. Brush with egg white, sprinkle with sugar, chopped almonds and cinnamon. Bake in a moderate oven very slowly.—P.D.P.

SANDWICH CAKE
(Inexpensive)

Cream 2 oz. butter or margarine; add ¼ lb. castor sugar and cream till white; add 1 egg, then 1 cup of sieved flour (4 oz.), 1 teaspoon of baking powder; add orange or lemon rind and a little vanilla; also a little milk to mix to dropping consistency. Bake in flat buttered pan or layer cake pans, 10 to 12 minutes in good oven.

Fill with lemon curd or any filling desired, and ice with white icing.—D.L.T.

SAVARIN PASTE

Quantities: 1 lb. flour, 12 oz. butter, ½ oz. of very fresh yeast, 8 eggs, about one-third pint milk, ¼ oz. of salt and 1 oz. sugar.

Procedure: Sift the flour into a basin (or a round wooden bowl, better suited to the work), hollow it out, add the yeast, dissolve the latter by means of tepid water, stirring slightly with the tip of the finger. Add the eggs, mix the whole, work the paste by hand for a few minutes, detach those portions of it which have adhered to the side of the utensil and add them to the whole. Distribute the softened butter in small quantities over the paste. Cover and place in a temperate room until the paste has grown to twice its original bulk. Then add salt, knead the paste that it may thoroughly absorb the butter and pat it briskly until it is sufficiently elastic to be taken up in one lump. At this stage add and work the paste again that the former may thoroughly mix with it. The sugar should only be added at the close of the operation, for, since it impairs the cohesiveness of the paste it would render the latter much more difficult were it added at the start.—A.E.

SCONES

Scones are griddle cakes or tea-cakes which originated in Scotland and used to differ from all other tea-cakes by their shape, being invariably cut in quadrants; the name is now given to all sorts of tea-cakes usually quadrant-shaped.

Barley Meal Scones

> ½ lb. barley meal
> 3 oz. white flour
> 1 oz. butter or lard
> 2 teaspoons baking powder
> ¼ pint milk
> Pinch of salt

Mix the flour and meal thoroughly, rub in the butter and add baking powder and salt. Mix with a knife to a soft dough with the milk. Work it lightly into a ball on a baking-board then pat it out to about ½ in. thick and bake on a girdle or in an oven.—A.C.B.

Drop Scones

> ½ lb. flour
> 1 teaspoon baking powder
> 2 tablespoons cream
> 1 egg
> ½ pint milk

Mix dry ingredients in a basin. Beat egg with the cream and some of the milk. Make a well in the centre of the flour and stir the mixture required, but keeping the batter fairly stiff. Drop the mixture in spoonfuls into a hot greased girdle or iron frying-pan. Brown on one side, turn, and brown on the other.

Irish Scones

> 6 tablespoons of plain flour
> 1 tablespoon Paisley flour
> 1 tablespoon lard
> A little salt

Mix with milk and roll out on a board. Cut with a sharp round cutter and bake in a quick oven. May be served hot or cold with butter.—M.B. (2).

Potato Scones (1)

> 10 oz. flour
> 8 oz. mashed potatoes
> ½ oz. margarine or butter
> 1 teaspoon baking soda
> 1 teaspoon salt
> 2 teaspoons cream of tartar
> ½ teacup milk
> ½ teacup water

Boil three or four potatoes and when ready, weigh ½ lb. and push through a sieve with a wooden spoon. Beat potatoes, margarine, salt together and leave till quite cold, then rub potatoes into flour, add baking soda and cream of tartar. Mix to a fairly stiff dough with milk and water. Roll out about ½ in. thick. Bake in an oven for quarter of an hour.—A.C.B.

Potato Scones (2)

1 lb. potatoes
½ lb. flour
1 oz. dripping
A pinch of salt
1 teaspoon of milk

Rub potatoes through sieve, add flour and salt, melt fat in milk and add to mixture. Roll out ½ in. thick and bake on greased girdle in moderate heat.—A.C.B.

Scotch Scones

1 lb. flour
1 oz. castor sugar
3 oz. sultanas
3 oz. butter
½ pint cold milk
2 teaspoons baking powder

Take a basin and sieve the dry ingredients into it, rub in the butter and add sultanas and sugar. Mix well; then add the milk. Turn on to a floured board and knead well. Form into two rounds and place them on a flat baking-sheet and cut each round across twice so as to form four scones in each round. Brush them over with egg and prick them with a fork. Bake in a quick oven from 15 to 20 minutes.—H.E.

SCOTS SEED CAKE

1 lb. flour
1 lb. fresh butter
1 lb. sugar
4 oz. bitter almonds
½ lb. orange peel
5 oz. citron peel
10 eggs
1 small grated nutmeg
1 small teaspoon caraway seeds
1 wineglass brandy

With the hand, cream butter and sugar. Beat eggs well and add gradually with flour. Then add all dry ingredients and lastly stir in brandy. Pour mixture into well-lined cake-tin. Sprinkle with caraway seeds and bake in moderate oven. Do not turn or move until nearly done as shaking will cause sweetmeats to sink to the bottom.—S.W.R.

SEED CAKE

4 eggs and their weight in butter, sugar and flour
½ teaspoon of baking powder
1 dessertspoon of cornflour
1 teaspoon of caraway seeds

Sieve together the flour, cornflour and baking powder and add the caraway seeds. Beat together the butter, sugar and eggs, add the flour mixture gradually. Beat thoroughly, put into a buttered tin and bake in a hot oven.—M.K.S. (2).

SEED CAKES

1 lb. of flour dried, 1 lb. of sugar sifted; wash 1 lb. of butter to a cream with rose-water; put the flour in by degrees; add 10 yolks and 4 whites of eggs, 1 oz. of caraway seeds; keep beating till the oven is ready; butter the pans well; grate over fine sugar; beat the cakes till just as they are set into the oven.

Small Plain Cakes for Tea (1807)

Rub ½ lb. of butter into 1½ lb. of flour; mix a few caraway seeds and ¼ lb. of loaf sugar, pounded and sifted together, and put to it; then make it into a light paste, with 4 eggs and 2 spoonfuls of new yeast, and cut them into any shape; when ready to set in the oven, rub them over with the white of an egg, and dust sugar over them.—A.A.

SEMOLINA

Fr. *Semoule*. The diminutive form of *Semola*, bran; *Semolina* should be the purified middlings of durum wheat, or of any other kind of hard or Macaroni wheat. It is chiefly valuable in the nursery, as pappy food for infants, being very nourishing and easy of digestion, but it is also used in the *Cuisine classique* in the form of *Gnocchi* (q.v.). The name *Semolina*, and even more the French culinary form *Semoule*, are used wrongly, but not infrequently, for fine forms of different flours.

SEMOLINA PUDDING

From a pint of new milk take sufficient to mix 2 oz. of *Semolina* into a smooth paste. Boil the rest, then stir in the *Semolina*, add a piece of butter and 3 tablespoonfuls of sugar, and stir over the fire for a few minutes.

Spread some jam at the bottom of a greased pie-dish. Stir the beaten yolk of an egg into the *Semolina*, then, lastly, very gently fold in the white of the egg whisked to a very stiff froth. Pour into the pie-dish. Bake in a slow oven for half an hour. Sufficient for four or five people.—L.G.N.

SEMOLINA CROQUETTES

Ingredients: 1 lb. of *Semolina*, 1 oz. of grated Parmesan cheese, 1 oz. of butter, 1 pint of milk, 3 yolks of eggs, 1 whole egg, breadcrumbs, frying fat, pepper and salt.

Method: Put the milk and butter into a stewpan, when boiling stir in the *Semolina*, and cook slowly for about 10 minutes. Now add the three yolks of eggs and the cheese, continue the cooking and stirring for a few minutes longer, then spread the preparation on a large dish. When cold, stamp out into rounds or other shapes, coat them with egg and breadcrumbs, and fry in hot fat until nicely browned. Drain well, dish in pyramidal form, and serve garnished with crisply-fried parsley.

Time: About two hours. Sufficient for five or six persons.—B.E.C.

SEMOULE, GATEAU DE

Put into half a pint of milk half a pod of vanilla, a little less than 3 oz. of sugar and a very small piece of butter. Bring to the boil, and when at the boiling-point throw in about 3 oz. of *Semolina* and cook it, stirring well. When it is ready, remove the vanilla pod (to be washed and put to dry for another time) and let the mixture cool.

When just tepid, stir in three yolks of egg, then three whites stiffly whipped, also very small dice of crystallized fruit which you have soaked for a couple of hours in rum, brandy or any liqueur you fancy (a small glass will be enough). Add also a few drops of the liqueur (and save the rest for another sweet).

Pour the mixture into a mould coated with caramel, and cook, standing in boiling water, in a fairly slow oven for about half an hour. —X.M.B. (1).

SHORTBREAD. SHORTCAKE

A cake or biscuit of Scotch origin, which is particularly rich in butter or 'shortening' and is usually sweetened. Shortcake used to be the more common name in England but it is practically never heard now. In the U.S.A., *Shortcake* is a name given indifferently to cookies and small tea-cakes, not necessarily of the *Shortbread* sort.

Austrian Shortbread

8 oz. fresh butter, 4 oz. sugar, 12 oz. flour.

Work butter and sugar to a cream, add flour. Roll out quite thin and cut out with a round cutter and in half of the biscuits make three holes with an apple corer. Bake in a slow oven to a golden colour, and when cool spread red currant jelly on bottom halves and put the halves with holes in them on top.—M.K.S. (2).

Ayrshire Shortbread

Mix together in a basin ¼ lb. of flour, 2 oz. castor sugar and a pinch of salt; rub in gently but thoroughly ¼ lb. of butter. Slightly beat up 1 egg and mix with it 1 tablespoonful of milk or cream.

Make a hole in the middle of the flour and pour in the egg and milk. Mix into the flour with a knife and then knead it well with the hand till the flour is well mixed; it must be a soft paste. Flour a board and roll out the paste ½ in. thick and cut into any shape desired. Ornament the edges and decorate the top with caraway seeds; place on a greased paper in a tin and bake.—A.C.B.

The Short Cakes made at ye Bathe (1694)
(Bath Shortbread)

Take a pound of flower and rube into it half a pound of butter, very fine; then put in half a pound of flo sugar & wet it with white wine to a paste; then rowl it very thick & cut it round with ye top of ye Drudger, & knotch it round with a squef & bake them upon tin.—A.B.

Christmas Shortbreads

Take 4 oz. butter, 8 oz. flour, 2 oz. castor sugar, 2 eggs, preserved cherries. Rub butter into flour and add sugar; mix into a paste with beaten eggs. Roll out on to a well-floured board, cut into rounds, triangles or squares, as desired; place a cherry on each piece and bake in slow oven till lightly browned.—L.G.N.

Edinburgh Shortbread

¾ lb. flour, ¼ lb. rice flour, ½ lb. butter, ¼ lb castor sugar.

Mix the flours and sugar together and knead the butter well in. Turn on to a board and continue kneading until quite smooth and free from cracks. Roll out and form into different shapes, crimping the edges and pricking the centre. Strips of candied peel or caraway comfits may be used as decorations if liked. Baked on a greased paper or a baking-sheet in a very steady oven from ¾ to 1 hour. Allow to cool before removing from tin. Dust over with castor sugar.—H.E.

Strawberry Shortcake

Make light dough; sift together 9 or 10 oz. flour, 1¼ oz. sugar, half a teaspoon salt, 3 teaspoons baking powder (level). Cut into it 2½ oz. butter; next, mix into it, stirring quickly, one-third to half a pint milk beaten with 1 egg. Form a light but not sticky dough. Turn on to floured board, and knead just enough to make into a smooth ball. Divide in two, then roll, or pat out ½ in. thick.

Place one-half in buttered pan, brush with melted butter; place other half on top, and brush also with butter. Bake in hot oven (450° F.) for about 15 minutes. Split with sharp knife and cover bottom half with warm berries, slightly crushed, and sweetened. Put other half on top, soft side up, cover with more fruit. Pile whipped cream on them and decorate with whole split berries.

Variations: Strawberries and raspberries, or raspberries alone. Cherries; pitted and simmered in syrup, and cooled. Peaches or apricots with dash of almond essence. —D.L.T.

SHREWSBURY BISCUITS
¼ lb. flour; ¼ lb. sugar; ¼ lb. butter; 1 beaten egg; half a teaspoonful baking powder.

Beat butter to a cream, add sugar, egg and baking powder; beat all well together and then add flour. Roll out ¼ in. thick; cut into round cakes; prick and bake in moderate oven; sprinkle sugar on top of each. (*Mrs Small*, of *Dirnanean*.)—F.C.B.

SHREWSBURY CAKES
These cakes have been among the most popular English Tea Cakes for many years past, and deservedly so as they are easy to make and very good. The old spelling was *Shrowsbury* or *Shrosbury* Cakes, which was the spelling, and still is among the old folks the pronunciation, of the County Town of Shrewsbury. They are made by mixing well together equal parts of dry flour, butter and sugar, then the white of one egg per ¼ lb. of the other ingredients. The mixture is then rolled out, cut into rounds and baked in a quick oven.—B.H.

SIENESE GINGERBREAD
(Panforte, a Tuscan Speciality)
Boil 4 lb. of honey with 12 oz. of blanched chopped almonds and walnuts, ½ lb. of chopped candied peel, a little pepper and cinnamon and 1 lb. of grated chocolate.

Mix well over the fire, add enough fine rye flour to make a firm paste. Form it into slabs about an inch thick. Put them in the oven for a few minutes to dry. With fine flour and more almonds a richer cake is made that is a great favourite in Tuscany; it is mixed wetter, baked in tins, and served with sugar over it.—P.A.

SILVER CAKE
    ¼ cup butter
    ¼ cup milk
    3 teaspoons baking powder
    Whites of six eggs
    1½ cups sugar
    2½ cups cake flour
    ¼ teaspoon cream of tartar
    ¼ teaspoon almond extract

Cream butter, add sugar gradually and cream together until creamy. Sift flour and baking powder together four times, and add alternately with milk. Add cream of tartar to egg whites and beat until stiff but not dry. Fold into mixture, add extract, and bake 45 minutes in a moderate oven (350° F.). Half the mixture will make two dozen small cup cakes. Frost as desired. (*Mary G. Chandler.*) —T.C.

SIMNEL CAKES or SIMNELS
(*These cakes are made for the fourth Sunday in Lent* or '*Mothering Sunday*').

For the cake mixture: 2 oz. each of butter, sugar and flour; ¼ lb. mixed peel, ½ lb. raisins, ½ lb. currants, ¼ lb. ground almonds, 4 eggs, a pinch of mixed spice and 1 wineglass of brandy or rum.

Cream the butter and sugar together, beat the eggs and mix with the flour; add fruit and spice last.

For the almond paste: ½ lb. ground almonds, ¼ lb. brown sugar, 1 egg, 1 oz. ground, bitter almonds; 1 tablespoonful brandy.

Mix well together. Butter a tin and line it with buttered paper, put in half the cake mixture, then a layer of almond paste and the rest of the cake mixture over it and bake for 1½ hours. When cooked cover with half of the remaining almond paste and form the rest into balls and put them round the edge. Brush with white of eggs and dust with castor sugar and put in a cool oven till paste is set. Decorate with angelica.—M.K.S. (2).

SINGING HINNIE
This is a kind of girdle cake very popular in the North Country, and it is made thus: Mix together flour and creamed butter (or thick cream) till it forms a thick stiff paste. Roll this out lightly twice till it is ¼ in. thick, shape it into round cakes, and bake on a girdle or hot plate, turning it as soon as one side is baked, to colour the other; split, butter well, and serve hot. Do not over-roll it or it will become a kind of puff-paste. —Q. (1).

SINGIN HINNY. NORTHUMBERLAND GIRDLE CAKE
    ¾ lb. flour
    2 oz. rice flour
    2 oz. sugar
    1 oz. lard
    3 oz. currants
    1 teaspoonful salt
    2 teaspoons baking powder
    1 gill liquid, half cream, half milk

Mix flour, ground rice, salt and baking powder. Rub in lard. Mix in currants, previously washed and dried. Then add the liquid and mix to a moderately soft dough. Roll out to a $\frac{1}{4}$ in. thickness. Prick all over with a fork and bake on a fairly hot griddle until nicely browned on each side It can be cut in halves or quarters for convenience in turning. To be served hot, split and buttered.—F.W.

SLAB CAKES

A 'shop' name for factory-made cakes supplied for stock and sold to the public by 'cuts' of the weight and price required.

SNICKERDOODLE

> $\frac{1}{2}$ cup butter and lard, mixed
> $\frac{1}{2}$ cup sugar
> 1 egg, beaten
> 1 cup water or milk
> $2\frac{1}{4}$ cups flour
> 2 teaspoons baking powder
> 1 cup raisins, dredged with flour
> Sugar
> Cinnamon
> Nuts

Combine all ingredients excepting the second listing of sugar, the cinnamon and nuts. Stir till mixed. This will be very stiff, but spread it out in a shallow bread-pan, sprinkle thickly over the top with the sugar, cinnamon and nuts. Bake about 20 minutes in a moderate oven (375° F.).—C.G.

SNOW CAKE

(A genuine Scottish Recipe)

> 1 lb. of arrowroot
> $\frac{1}{2}$ lb. of pounded white sugar
> $\frac{1}{4}$ lb. of butter
> The whites of 6 eggs
> Flavouring to taste of essence of almonds, vanilla or lemon

Beat the butter to a cream; stir in the sugar and arrowroot gradually, at the same time beating the mixture. Whisk the whites of the eggs to a stiff froth, add them to the other ingredients, and beat well for 20 minutes. Put in whichever of the above flavourings may be preferred; pour the cake into a buttered mould or tin, and bake it in a moderate oven for 1 to $1\frac{1}{2}$ hours.—B. (2).

SNOW PUDDING

Put 1 pint of water on to boil with a small cup of sugar, then stir in $2\frac{1}{2}$ tablespoonfuls cornflour mixed with juice of 2 lemons and 1 tablespoonful water. Boil a few minutes and then add whites of 4 eggs beaten to a stiff froth. Pour in a mould to set. With the yolks and 1 pint of milk make a custard and, when cold, pour round pudding. Sufficient for 6 or 7 people.—L.G.N.

SODA (or IRISH) BREAD

> 2 lb. flour
> 1 teaspoon of bicarbonate of soda
> $\frac{1}{2}$ pint sour milk or butter milk
> 1 teaspoon salt
> 1 teaspoon cream of tartar

Mix together the dry ingredients and put through a sieve into a basin. Make a well in the centre and stir in the milk, adding a little more should the mixture be too dry.

Mix well into a rather stiff dough. Divide into two and shape into rounds, prick the top with a fork and put in a greased, floured tin. Bake in a moderate oven for three-quarters of an hour.—M.K.S. (2).

SODA CAKE

> 8 oz. flour
> Pinch of salt
> $\frac{1}{2}$ teaspoon bicarbonate of soda
> $\frac{1}{2}$ teaspoon cream of tartar
> Little grated nutmeg
> 4 or 5 oz. butter or margarine
> 4 or 5 oz. sugar
> 6 oz. currants
> About $\frac{1}{4}$ pint sour milk to mix
> 1 egg

Well grease and flour a $6\frac{1}{2}$ to 7 in. cake-tin. Sieve the flour, salt, bicarbonate of soda, cream of tartar and nutmeg into a basin. Rub in the fat with the tips of the fingers until it resembles fine breadcrumbs, then add the currants and sugar and mix well. Stir in the beaten egg and sufficient milk to form a fairly soft mixture. Put into prepared tin and bake in a hot oven of 380° F. for the first 20 minutes or until the cake is golden brown, then lower the heat until a temperature of 340° F. is obtained, and bake for another 30 to 40 minutes.—G.H. (4).

SOFT BISCUITS

Baker's dough; butter; sugar. To every pound of baker's dough add 3 oz. of melted butter and a tablespoonful of sugar. Form into rounds shaped like flattened buns and about 3 or 4 in. in diameter. Bake in a good oven.—F.M.M.

The *Soft Biscuit* is made properly only in Aberdeen and the N.E. of Scotland. It looks like a round roll or flattish bun, and has a depression made in the centre. A good variety of nursery sops is made with a *Soft Biscuit* toasted for half a minute till it sizzles and gives off a pleasant baking aroma; it is then broken up into small pieces (not too small), hot milk is poured over it and plenty of sugar.—E.M.L.D.

SORGHUM

The family name of a number of different fodder grasses of the temperate zone and of the tropics, more particularly that of a cereal.

the flour of which is one of the staple foods of Asia and Africa under a variety of names, i.e. *Durra, Dura* or *Darri*, in India; *Kaffir Corn* or *African Millet*, in Africa; *Milo Maize, Egyptian Rice Corn*, and so on; it is often called simply *Millet*, but it is not a Millet, nor does it resemble corn or maize. In America it is used mostly as cattle food, but some good Griddle Cakes are also made with its flour.

A variety of *Sorghum* grown extensively in the East and in Africa, as well as in the U.S.A., at the end of the nineteenth century, was known as *Sugar Sorghum* (Fr. *Sorgho*). This variety is richer in sugar in the juice of the stalk than any of the others, and it is mostly grown for the sake of the sugar or syrup extracted from it.

SOUR MILK GRIDDLE CAKES

Dissolve 1½ teaspoonfuls of soda in sour milk. Add 1½ cups of flour, 1 tablespoonful of sugar and half a teaspoonful of salt which have been sifted together. Add 2 unbeaten eggs and beat well. Add 1 tablespoonful of melted butter. Drop on hot griddle. Brown on both sides. This recipe may be varied by using half corn meal and half flour, or half hominy grits and half flour. (*Virginia recipe, adapted and prov'd* 1937.)—H.B.

SOWENS. SOWANS

    Oatmeal Sids
    Water
    Salt

Put a quantity of sids (the inner husks of the oat grain) into a small wooden tub or jar and pour on to them twice their bulk of luke-warm water. Press sids down with spoon till all are wet. Leave for three or four days in a warm place until they are sour. When ready, strain off liquor, squeezing out all the goodness out of the sids, using a little more cold water in the process. Throw away the sids and let the liquor stand for a day or two till the starchy matter sinks to the bottom of the jar. The more solid part is sowans; the liquid is swats. When required for use, the clear liquid is poured off, and some of the sediment is put in a pan with as much water as will thin it. Add a little salt and boil it for 10 minutes or more, stirring briskly until it thickens. Pour into a bowl and serve with milk separately.—F.M.M. (2).

SOYA BEAN FLOUR

The flour or meal extracted from the *Soya Bean* is the richest as well as the cheapest source of vegetable protein known, and it contains also a fair proportion of fat; it is low in carbo-hydrates, compared to the flour of cereals, but, being practically free from all starch, it brings a welcome addition to the meagre choice of foods suitable for diabetics.

'Soya Beans are one of the few basic food materials which have survived the severe test of milleniums on a large scale natural experiment, involving today nearly one-half of the world's population, and are endorsed by modern science as well.

'In the Orient soybean curd (tofu) has been in daily use since times immemorial, and is called "the meat without the bones," as it serves as a food rich in protein.'— A.A.HORVATH, *Chief Chemist to the Agricultural Experiment Station of the University of Delaware, Newark, Delaware, U.S.A.*

A recent analysis of edible soya flour gives the following composition:

Moisture	7.65%
Protein	40.65%
Fat	20.38%
Carbohydrates	23.56%
Lecithin	3.08%
Ash	6.08%
Vitamins A, B, D, E, and K	

NO STARCH

One pound of this flour has a fuel value of 2,000 calories, and is equivalent in protein content to about 2 lb. of lean meat or 30 hens' eggs, or nine pints of cows' milk.— (KUPELWEISER.E, 'Veredelts Sojamehl,' *Das Oesterreichische Gesundheitswesen*, 1932, S.198.)

Besides the fifty odd centuries of Chinese consumption, we have the testimony of the German High Command as proof of the nutritive value of the *Soya Bean*: the canned meat and sausage of the last war have now been replaced, and replaced with advantage by '*Edelsoja*'.

'Edelsoja is a Soybean flour, with a high protein content of 40 to 45 per cent, and fat and carbohydrates. The flour is added to soups, bread, pastry, and macaroni. The soldier thus is supposed to get his balanced needs of protein, fat and mineral salts without the use of meat, milk or eggs. The savings in bulk tend to simplify the problems of packing and transporting. The German soldier can carry in his haversack a three-day ration of Soybeans, and reserves are not difficult to deliver. The High Command confidently feels that with a supply of Soybean rations, the Army can march anywhere without grave concern about its subsistence.'

It is only right to add that the writer of these lines, which appeared in the leading American Food Journal, *Food Industries*, in January 1941, went on to say:

'The German ration is not one that an American soldier would relish and perhaps does not satisfy the palate, but it apparently has what it takes to keep men well and strong.'

Since then, however, experiments have been made and improvements have been introduced which have resulted in making the best Soya Bean flour much more palatable than before when used by itself or mixed with cereals flour.

SPAGHETTI

One of the most popular forms of Italian Pastes; it is made from *durum* or other sorts of hard wheat, like macaroni, but solid, not tubular, in the form of long strings of paste, about twice as thick as *Vermicelli*.

The cooking of Spaghetti

'All paste should be boiled in a prodigal quantity of salted water in a pot big enough for the strands to swim actively about, unhampered by each other. About 15 minutes will bring spaghetti to the right firm tenderness, but it is safer to keep an eye on the pot rather than on the clock, since what is supposedly the same variety of paste may vary enough in thinness to make a difference in the cooking. The strands should be scraped from the bottom of the pot from time to time with a long fork to prevent sticking. At the end of 13 minutes or so they must be tested often, so that there will be no danger of over-cooking by so much as a minute. Just as soon as it has acquired the proper texture, the paste is taken from the fire and a couple of tablespoonfuls of cold water added to stop the cooking instantly. It is then drained in a colander, quickly but very thoroughly. If the dish is to be dressed in the kitchen, a part of the sauce is poured into a warm serving bowl of generous proportions, half of the paste is turned over it, and with salad spoon and fork the two are tossed about until each strand of spaghetti is well coated. The rest of the paste is then added, and covered with more sauce, the tossing and blending continue, and finally the remaining sauce is spooned over the savoury mound. This operation has taken place, of course, with the serving-bowl set in a pan of very hot water, the bowl itself has been well heated, the sauce is just off the fire, and with the last flourish of the mixing fork the dish is hurried to the table. If it is set in the oven to keep warm, even for a little while, the whole ritual will have been in vain, and the paste will turn up at table as a sorry, sticky mess.'

'If for one reason or another the time of serving the spaghetti course cannot be computed, the paste may be cooked beforehand to within a shade of complete doneness, then drained and rinsed by letting cold water run through it. In this way it may be kept for several hours, to be plunged (still in the colander) into boiling water for a final reheating.'

'Whether grated cheese is included in the dressing, or passed at table, is a matter to be decided by taste and by the quality of the cheese. The best Parmesan will stand up under the heat of the lengthy mixing, but many cheeses go stringy in the process, and it is, on the whole, safer to pass the cheese for individual mixing.'—S.H.

Spaghetti Reggio

Heat one tablespoonful of olive oil, and one chopped shallot, add boiled spaghetti and two tablespoonfuls of grated Parmesan cheese. Toss about until hot and serve. —E.E.A.

Tuscan Spaghetti

Mix cooked spaghetti with chopped chicken liver, chopped pimento, plenty of grated cheese, and a spoonful of tomato *purée*. Serve separately grated cheese and plenty of sauce made of grilled tomatoes, or tomato *purée*, poured over frying onion.—P.A.

SPANISH BREAD

    3 cups of flour
    2 cups of sugar
    1 cup of butter
    2 eggs
    1 teaspoon of ground cloves
    1 teaspoon of cinnamon
    $\frac{1}{2}$ lb. of blanched almonds

Sift the flour with the spices. Cream the butter and sugar. Add the ground nuts and mix all together with the slightly-beaten eggs. Form into a loaf and place in the refrigerator. It must be sliced while very cold into thin slices and baked in a slow oven. Be sure to keep the bread cold until put in the oven.—G.T.L.

SPATZLES

Into three soup-spoonfuls of flour, beat one egg and three soup-spoonfuls of milk. Add a pinch of salt, a pinch of pepper and a little ground nutmeg. Set a colander over boiling water and squeeze this mixture through; boil for a minute and pour into a sieve and serve as directed.—E.E.A.

SPELT

Lat. *Triticum spelta*; Fr. *Epeaute*. A chaffy wheat grown on poor ground in Spain, Switzerland and Southern Germany mostly for grits, coarse flour and feeds. It is believed to have been the chief cereal of ancient Egypt, Greece and Rome.

SPICE CAKES

8 oz. flour
Pinch of salt
½ teaspoon baking powder
3 to 4 oz. butter, margarine or
    lard
1 egg
4 oz. sugar
¼ teaspoon ground ginger
¼ teaspoon ground cinnamon
⅛ teaspoon grated nutmeg
Little milk to mix

Prepare patty-pans or fancy cake-tins by well greasing with melted lard or dripping. Sieve the flour, salt, baking powder, cinnamon, nutmeg and ground ginger into a basin. Rub in the fat with the tips of the fingers until it resembles fine breadcrumbs, then stir in the sugar and mix well. Make a well in the centre and stir in the beaten egg and just sufficient milk to make a soft mixture. Half fill the prepared tins with the mixture and bake in a quick oven of 380° F. for 15 to 20 minutes, according to the size of the cakes, or until they are golden brown and feel firm to the touch.—G.H.(4).

SPICED FRUIT CAKE

Boil for 3 minutes:
1 cupful of brown sugar
1 cupful of water
2 cupfuls of fruit (1 currants,
    1 sultanas)
3 oz. butter or margarine
¼ oz. mixed spice and nutmeg
    (grated)

When cool add:
1 teaspoon carbonate of soda dissolved in hot water
2 cupfuls of flour in which half teaspoon baking powder is sifted

Stir all well and bake for 1¼ hours.—L.C.

SPUNGE BISCUITS (1778)

Beat well the yolks of 6 eggs, and the white of 4, to a strong froth; mix them and beat them together; put to them 1 lb. of sifted sugar; have ready ¼ pint of water boiling hot, with one good spoonful of rose or orange-flower water in it; as the eggs and sugar are beat, add the water by degrees, then set it over the fire till scalding hot; take it off and beat it till almost cold (a silver or brass pan is the best); add ¾ lb. of flour, well dried and sifted, the peel of 1 lemon, pared very thin, and cut small; bake this in little long pans; a quick oven but not too hot, as they are apt to burn; sift sugar over before they are set in.—C.MA.

SPONGE CAKE

Ingredients: The weight of eight eggs in castor sugar and of five in flour. The grated rind and juice of one lemon. Butter two cake-tins and sift sugar all over the inside.

Method: Put your sugar into a basin and break in four whole eggs and the yolks of the other four. Beat up the remaining four whites in another basin very stiffly. Sift your flour and put it to warm on a piece of paper in the cool oven. Place your basin in another jar containing nearly boiling water, grate your lemon on to sugar and eggs and beat all together with a wire whisk for quarter of an hour, then add lemon juice, your stiffly-beaten whites, and lastly the flour, stirring it in as lightly as possible. Bake for 1 to 1½ hours in a moderate oven. This is a most excellent cake. Half quantities may be used. —M.K.S. (2).

Lemon Sponge

2 oz. of isinglass
1¾ pint of water
¾ lb. of pounded sugar
The juice of 5 lemons
The rind of 1 lemon
The whites of 3 eggs

Dissolve the isinglass in the water, strain it into a saucepan and add the sugar, lemon rind, and juice. Boil the whole from 10 to 15 minutes; strain it again and let it stand till it is cold and begins to stiffen. Beat the whites of the eggs, put them to it, and whisk the mixture till it is quite white; put it into a mould that has been previously wetted, and let it remain until perfectly set; then turn it out, and garnish it according to taste.—B. (2)

Royal Sponge Cake

1½ cups fine sugar
1 cup cake flour sifted six times
⅛ teaspoon cream of tartar
¼ teaspoon salt
6 eggs
½ cup water
½ teaspoon vanilla
1 teaspoon lemon juice

Boil sugar and water until it spins a thread. Pour over stiffly-beaten whites of eggs until cool. Stir in well-beaten yolks, vanilla and lemon. Fold in flour sifted with cream of tartar. Bake in a spring-side pan in moderate oven for 1 hour. (*Olive Evans*.) —T.C.

SPOON BREAD

3 cups milk
4 eggs
1 cup sifted corn meal
1 cup sifted flour
6 tablespoons sugar
1 teaspoon salt
½ cup butter
2 teaspoons baking powder

233

Separate egg yolks from whites. Beat, then add sugar, butter and salt. Cream until light. Sift dry ingredients, add alternately with milk to the first mixture. Fold in stiffly-beaten whites of eggs. Pour into well-greased Pyrex dish and bake in 350° F. oven for 50 minutes.—L.R.

SPRINGERLE

    4 eggs
    1 lb. of powdered sugar
    Grated rind of 1 lemon
    1 lb. of flour
    1 teaspoonful of baking powder
    ¼ teaspoonful of salt

Beat the yolks of the eggs until light coloured and thick, the whites until dry, then beat together, add the grated lemon rind and the sugar, sifted very gradually, beating all the time, lastly adding the flour with the baking-powder and salt. All of the flour may not be required. Knead and cover closely, leave for 2 or 3 hours, then roll—a small piece at a time— into a sheet ½ in. thick. Dust the sheet of dough lightly with flour, then press a wooden butter mould down very hard upon the dough so as to leave a good impression upon it. Cut out the little rounds and set aside on a board lightly floured to remain overnight. In the morning transfer to baking-tins buttered and sprinkled with aniseed and bake in a slow oven to a light straw colour.—M.B. (2).

STOUT CAKE

    1 lb. flour
    ½ lb. butter
    ½ lb. Demerara sugar
    1 lb. currants
    3 eggs
    1 teaspoon baking powder
    A little cinnamon and nutmeg
    ½ pint stout
    ¼ lb. peel
    Prepared fruit and bread

Rub butter finely into flour and add all dry ingredients. Mix with well-whisked eggs and stout and pour into a papered tin. Keep a few days before using.—L.G.N.

STRICHETTI

One of the 'fancy' *Italian Pastes* (q.v.), made of the gluten of hard wheat flour and eggs. It is used either in soups, like *Vermicelli* (q.v.) or with spinach or some other vegetable, like *Ravioli* (q.v.).

STRUDEL

    1 lb. flour
    1 egg
    Salt
    Lukewarm water and a cup of fried
      crumbs
    2 tablespoons fat

Mix one tablespoonful of fat with 1 lb. of flour, add salt and the eggs and water. Knead well, take the dough in your hand and beat it against the board, work it until it shows bubbles and comes cleanly off your hand and the board. Form it into one or two lumps and leave them a while on a floured board, covered with a warm napkin. Meanwhile, cover the kitchen table with a clean white cloth, sprinkled with flour. Put your dough in the middle of the cloth, pat and roll it out as much as possible and pull it with your hands. Put both your hands back upwards under the dough and pull carefully, doing this all the round so that the dough may spread uniformly over the whole cloth. It must be so thin as to be quite transparent, the thick edges, if any, should be cut off and put aside. Leave the dough to dry on the table. Afterwards heat one tablespoonful of fat, brown the crumbs in it and sprinkle them over the dough together with whatever stuffing you are using. Then take up one side of the cloth, and with a lifting movement roll up the *Strudel*. Have a flat tin ready greased and lift the *Strudel* on to it, forming it into a horseshoe shape as you do so, brush over with fat and bake in a hot oven, sprinkle with sugar when done.

This is a very popular sweet in Germany, Austria and Central Europe generally, and there are many different fillings, apple, nut, cherry, even cabbage and cheese. An Austrian cook I had used olive oil in mixing her dough and filled the *Strudel* with sliced apple, sultanas, spices, sugar, breadcrumbs and sprinkled it all with melted butter.—M.K.S. (2).

STUFFED MONKEY
(S. Africa)

    8 oz. flour
    6 oz. butter
    6 oz. brown sugar
    1 egg
    ½ teaspoon cinnamon
    Pinch of salt

For the Stuffing: 2 oz. citron peel, 4 oz. ground almonds, 1½ oz. butter, yolk of 1 egg; vanilla.

Sift flour, cinnamon and salt; rub in the butter; add the sugar; then mix to a soft dough with the beaten egg. Knead out the cracks, roll out and divide in two parts. Place the one half on a flat baking-sheet, cover with the filling or stuffing which should be well mixed, the butter being melted before it is added. Put the other half of the pastry over the filling; press the edges firmly together. Brush over with the white of one egg, and bake at 400° F. for 30 minutes until nicely browned. Cut into squares to serve.

The *Stuffed Monkey* may be made like sausage rolls if preferred. (*Mrs K.Whitaker, Maseru.*)—P.R.M.

SUFFOLK RUSKS

I

1 lb. flour
1 tablespoon brewers' yeast
3 eggs
2 oz. castor sugar
¼ pint milk
2 oz. butter

Melt the butter in the milk. Mix the flour and sugar in a basin, add the yeast and warm milk and butter, then beat in the eggs and form a smooth dough. Let this rise for 1½ hours, then knead and divide into 16 pieces. Roll these about 3 in. long and bake for 10 minutes. Take them from the oven, pull them in half lengthwise and put them back in the oven to get crisp. The sugar may be omitted.—M.K.S. (2).

II

½ lb. of flour, 1 egg and a little milk; 3 oz. of butter, salt and baking powder. Work all together as for pastry; cut into rounds with a cutter and bake. When nearly done take out and cut in half and bake again for a few minutes. To be eaten with butter or cheese.—M.B. (1).

SUMMER PUDDING

Prepare enough fruit to fill half a soufflé dish, i.e. *Black, White* or *Red Currants* and *Raspberries*, also *Strawberries*, mixed in any way you fancy (small, wild strawberries are best; if not available use garden strawberries cut in halves). Cook the fruit lightly with as much sugar as you like or can spare; do not allow it to boil. Grease a soufflé dish of the right size, line it with slices of stale bread nearly up to the rim, fill it up with the warm fruit off the fire, cover the fruit with more slices of stale bread; put a small plate on the top and a heavy weight on the plate. Let it get quite cold in a refrigerator, turn out on to a plate and serve cold with cream.—D.H.

SUNSHINE CAKE

7 egg whites
5 egg yolks
1½ cups sugar
1 pinch salt
⅓ teaspoon cream of tartar
1 cup flour
Flavouring

Sift sugar and flour five times, measure and set aside. Separate eggs, beat yolks to stiff froth, whip whites to a foam; add cream of tartar and whip stiff. Add sugar to whites, then beat; next add yolks and beat, then add flour and flavouring and fold lightly

through. Bake in moderate oven (300° F.) 40 to 50 minutes in a tube tin, ungreased but lightly floured.—C.G.

SWISS ROLLS

There are many different kinds of *Swiss Rolls* or *Sponge Rolls*, according to the cake mixture used in the making and the nature of the filling chosen; and there is the manner of the baking which is of the utmost importance.

Sponge mixture: The whites of 2 eggs; the yolks of 3 eggs; 5 oz. sugar; 4 oz. flour ¼ pint cold water.

Put the sugar into a clean saucepan with the cold water. Bring to the boil and boil hard for five minutes. Cool for five minutes, then pour the syrup on to the well-whisked yolks and whites of eggs. Continue whisking for 15 minutes or until the mixture thickens. Fold in the sifted flour as lightly as possible, blend thoroughly and pour into the prepared tin. Bake in a quick oven.—G.H. (4).

The baking: The temperature of the oven should be about 375° F. for the first 10 minutes, afterwards lowering the temperature to 350° F. Whenever possible, place the tin in the middle of the oven shelf and in the hottest part of the oven. When the cake is cooked, it should be golden brown in colour and firm to the touch.

The finishing touch. Have ready a clean tea-cloth wrung tightly out of water. Sprinkle liberally with castor sugar. Remove the cake by turning the tin upside down, thus allowing the upper surface to come in contact with the sugar. With a sharp knife trim off the edges as quickly as possible and spread with warm jam, taking care not to let it go too near the edge. If cold jam is used, it is likely to cause the cake to go 'heavy'. Roll up tightly with the aid of the cloth. Allow the sponge to remain a few minutes in the cloth and then place on a wire cake-tray.—G.H. (4).

TAGLIARINI

Tagliarini al fromaggio. Take 1 lb. of flour, 3 eggs, ½ tumbler of milk, and a pinch of salt; mix up into a paste and work it well. Lay it aside for half an hour, then roll it out very thin and let it dry before cutting it into long, thin strips (tagliarini). Boil these in boiling salted water over a very slow fire for 20 minutes and then drain well. Meanwhile, prepare 4 oz. of grated Parmesan cheese, 5 oz. of grated Gruyere, and 6 oz. of butter; put a layer of tagliarini into a baking-dish, and cover them with cheese and butter. Repeat the alternate layers of tagliarini, cheese and butter until the dish is full. Sprinkle the top with breadcrumbs and bits of butter, bake in the oven for quarter of an hour and serve in the baking-dish very hot.—J.R.

TAGLIATELLE

Tagliatelle with ham. Make a stiff paste with flour and eggs, roll it to the thickness of a florin, cut it into strips ½ in. or ¾ in. broad, and parboil with a very little salt. Meanwhile, cut up into small square pieces a thick slice of ham, mince some carrot and celery (about the same in quantity as the ham) and put them into a frying-pan, with two, or more, ounces of butter. When they begin to brown add some tomato juice, or tomato conserve and a cupful of broth (or water). Place the tagliatelle, well strained, on to a hot dish, season with grated Parmesan cheese, some bits of butter and the ham.—J.R.

TALMOUSES

The French culinary name of small individual soufflés, sweet or savoury, but usually flavoured with grated cheese.

TAPIOCA

A farinaceous substance derived from the *Manioc* or *Cassava* (q.v.) roots, chiefly in Brazil, but also extensively in Malaya and the Dutch East Indies. The crude juice extracted from the roots contains a large proportion of starchy matter which, when washed and dried is known as *Moussache* or *Brazilian Arrowroot.* This starch is roasted, dried and sifted into different grades and sizes of *Tapioca,* known in commerce as *Flake, Bullet, Medium* and *Pearl:* when ground to a powder it becomes *Tapioca Flour. Tapioca* is used like *Sago* (q.v.) in soups or for milk puddings.

TAPIOCA PUDDINGS

I

Boil 2 oz. of *Tapioca* tender in a pint of milk; beat up 5 yolks and 1 whole egg with ½ pint of cream; 2 oz. of butter, melted; 2 oz. of sugar; 1 lemon peel grated; bake half an hour in a dish lined with tart paste.—G.A.S.

II

Boil 4 tablespoonfuls of *Tapioca* in a pint of new milk; when thick, pour it on about 2 oz. of butter, stirring till cold; add 4 eggs, 2 whites, brandy and sugar to your taste. All to be well baked in a crust.—G.A.S.

Mrs Beeton's Tapioca Pudding

3 oz. *Tapioca,* 1 quart milk, 2 oz. butter, ¼ lb. sugar, 4 eggs, flavouring of vanilla, grated lemon-rind, or bitter almonds.

Wash the *Tapioca* and let it stew gently in the milk by the side of the fire for quarter of an hour, occasionally stirring it; then let it cool a little; mix with it the butter, sugar and

eggs, which should be well beaten, and flavour with either of the above ingredients, putting in about 12 drops of the essence of almonds or vanilla, whichever is preferred. Butter a pie-dish and line the edges with puff-paste; put in the pudding and bake it in a moderate oven for an hour. If the pudding is to be boiled, add a little more *Tapioca,* and boil it in a buttered basin 1½ hours.—B. (2).

TAPIOCA SOUP

Tapioca at the rate of 3 oz. per quart of stock put into cold *Bouillon,* whether meat or chicken broth, is brought to the boil and allowed to simmer for about an hour. It adds to the palatability of the *consommé* and even more to the nourishing value.

TARHONYA
(Hungarian Flour)

    2 lb. flour
    4 eggs
    Water

Put the flour in a bowl, make a hole in the middle and put in the eggs and enough water to make a very stiff paste. Work the ingredients with the hands until well mixed, then knead into a stiff paste and form into tiny balls with the palms of the hands. Spread them out on a tablecloth in the fresh air, sunshine if possible, to dry. Shake now and then to prevent them sticking to one another. *Tarhonya* can be made in greater quantities and kept in little sacks for the whole winter.—M.K.S. (2).

TART

Fr. *Tarte.* A flat piece of pastry with curled edge but no top crust and filled with fruit, jelly, custard, jam or any other sweet filling, but the name chiefly applies, in England, to a *fruit-filled* Tart.

TARTELETTES

Fr. for small pastry, *Tarts* or *Tartlets.*

TEA BISCUITS (1805)

2 lb. flour, 2 spoons yeast in a little warm milk, mix them together, adding ½ lb. melted butter with milk, to make it into a stiff paste; bake in a quick oven in any shape you please.—A.L. (2).

TEA CAKES (1778)
Little cakes for tea

Mix 1 lb. of dried flour, ½ lb. of fine sugar sifted, 1 oz. of caraway seeds, a little nutmeg and pounded mace; beat the yolks of two eggs with three spoonfuls of sack; put these to the rest, with ½ lb. of butter melted in a little thin cream, or new milk; work all together, roll it out thin, cut it into cakes with a tin or glass; bake them on tins; a little baking does in a slack oven.

Shrewsbury cakes

Beat ½ lb. of butter to a cream; add ½ lb. of dried flour, one egg, 6 oz. of sifted sugar, a few caraway seeds; mix these well; roll it out thin; cut it out with a glass or tin; prick them; bake them on tins in a slack oven.

Ratafia cakes

¼ lb. of bitter almonds, ¼ lb. of sweet almonds, ½ lb. of loaf sugar and the whites of three eggs; quarter of an hour will bake them.

Sugar cakes

Take 3 lb. of flour, dried well and sifted, 2 lb. of loaf sugar, beaten and sifted, the yolks of four eggs, a little mace, ¼ pint of rose-water (a little musk or ambergrease may be dissolved in the sugar, if agreeable); mix it all well together; make it up to roll out; sift some sugar over them, and bake them in a quick oven.

Portugal cakes

2 lb. of flour, the same of butter, sugar and currants, nine yolks of eggs, four whites; mix these with a little brandy; butter the pans; a pretty hot oven.

Heart cakes

Work 1 lb. of butter to a cream with the hand, put to it 12 yolks of eggs and six whites, well beaten, 1 lb. of sifted sugar, 1 lb. of flour dried, four spoonfuls of the best brandy, 1 lb. of currants washed and dried before the fire; as the pans are filled, put in 2 oz. of candied orange and citron; beat the cakes till they go into the oven; this quantity will fill three dozen of middling pans.

King cakes

1 lb. of flour, ¾ lb. of currants, the same of sifted sugar, one nutmeg, a little mace; rub the butter well into the flour; mix these together; add four eggs well beat; butter the pans; sift sugar on the cakes; a quick oven.

Queen cakes

Beat 1 lb. of butter to a cream, with some rose-water, 1 lb. of flour dried, 1 lb. of sugar sifted, 12 eggs; beat all well together; add a few currants washed and dried; butter small pans of a size for the purpose, grate sugar over them: they are soon baked. They may be done in a Dutch oven.

Marlborough cakes

Beat eight eggs very well, strain them, put them to 1 lb. of sugar sifted; beat these three-quarters of an hour, add ¾ lb. of flour dried, 2 oz. of caraway seeds; beat the cake well; bake in a quick oven.—C.MA.

TEFF

A valuable grass of Abyssinia with seeds as small as a pin's head from which a meal is ground; it is used for breadmaking in Abyssinia on a very large scale. The poorer among the natives make an inferior kind of bread from a *Millet* substitute known as *Yocusso* (q.v.).

TEN-MINUTE CAKE, MRS GARRETT'S

Take two teaspoonfuls of cream of tartar and mix it, by sifting, with one pint of dry flour, one even teaspoonful of soda, dissolved in a teacupful of milk; rub a piece of butter the size of an egg into the dry flour, then beat up one egg and a teacupful of sugar; mix all well together and bake without delay. Have your oven heated ready before you begin mixing, and you can make and bake the cake in 10 minutes. (*From Mrs Smith's Virginia Cookery Book*, 1885. *Prov'd Market Square Tavern Kitchen*, 1937.)—H.B.

THIRDED BREAD

    2 cups sugar
    Indian meal (about ½ cup)
    ½ cup milk
    ½ teaspoon salt
    1 teaspoon lard
    ⅓ cup molasses
    ½ yeast cake
    ¾ cup rye meal
    Flour

Boil the water and stir in the Indian meal, enough to make a thick batter, then stir in the milk and salt. Cool, add the lard, molasses, yeast and the rye meal, then mould as usual with flour. Yield: biscuits and a small loaf.—C.G.

TIMBALE

The French culinary name for an upstanding pie-crust filled with cooked meat, fish or fruit, as opposed to the *Tourte*, which is made of puff-paste and is wider but low.

TIPSY CAKE

One moulded sponge- or Savoy-cake; sufficient sweet wine or sherry to soak it, six tablespoonfuls of brandy, 2 oz. of sweet almonds, one pint of rich custard.

Procure a cake that is three or four days old, either sponge, Savoy or rice answering for the purpose of a Tipsy Cake. Cut the bottom of the cake level to make it stand firm in the dish; make a small hole in the centre, and pour in and over the cake sufficient sweet wine or sherry, mixed with the above proportion of brandy, to soak it nicely. When the cake is well soaked, blanch and cut the almonds into strips, stick them all over the cake, and pour round it a good custard. The cakes are sometimes crumbled and soaked and a whipped cream heaped over them the same as for trifles.—B. (2).

TOAST

Toast is stale bread browned either before red hot embers or in a dripping pan placed under a gas or an electric grill, or in any other available way. The bread may be cut very thin or fairly thick, and it may be 'toasted' swiftly or slowly, different kinds of toast being obtained accordingly.

Soft Toast is usually ¼ in. in thickness and 'toasted' quickly.

Crisp Toast is bread of the same or similar thickness but 'toasted' slowly. In any case one side of the bread is browned first and then the other.

Melba Toast, which we owe to Madame César Ritz, is stale bread cut in very thin slices, dried in a warming oven and 'toasted' or browned, in a slow oven or under not too hot a grill.

Pieces of toast must be placed standing in a rack and not piled up one on top of the other.

Toast may be cut in any shape and to any size; it can be served dry, in place of bread, or buttered, in place of bread-and-butter, and it can also be 'spread' with a number of different mixtures, such as butter and white or brown sugar, soft maple sugar, 'spiced' sugar, cinnamon, etc.

TOCUSSO

Lat. *Eleusine tocussa*. One of the poorer types of *Millet* grown in Abyssinia and also the name given to the inferior bread made thereof.

TOPS AND BOTTOMS

> 2 eggs
> 1 lb. flour
> 3 oz. of butter

Dissolve the butter in a sufficient quantity of warm milk to soften it; sift the flour into a pan; put the milk and butter into it together with enough yeast. Stir together, knead the dough on a paste-board, roll it out and cut it into whatever shapes you please. Put them on tins in a warm place for 20 minutes, then in rather cool oven. When cooked through, divide them and put them again in the oven until quite crisp.

TORTELLI

Take 7 oz. of curds (squeeze them through a cloth to extract all the water), 1½ oz. Parmesan cheese, one egg and one yolk of an egg, a little grated nutmeg and some allspice, a pinch of salt and a little chopped-up parsley. Mix well together and put a spoonful on to little rounds of paste (about 2½ in. in diameter). Fold the paste over the curds, as you would a turnover, and put them into boiling salted water. Take them out with a strainer,

season with butter and Parmesan cheese and serve hot. The quantities given ought to make about 24 *Tortelli*.—J.R.

TOURTE

The French culinary name of a puff-paste, round and low crust as opposed to the *Timbale*, which is narrower and higher.

TOUS-LES-MOIS

See *Canna*.

TRANSPARENT TARTS

Take 1 lb. of flour; then beat up an egg till it is quite thin, then melt ¾ lb. of clarified fresh butter to mix with the egg, and as soon as the mixture is cool, pour into the centre of the flour and form the paste. Roll it thin, make up the tarts, and on setting them in the oven wet them over with a little water and grate on them a small quantity of sugar. —G.A.S.

TREACLE SPONGE

> ½ lb. flour
> ¼ lb. suet
> ½ teaspoon carbonate of soda
> 1 teacup treacle
> 1 egg
> 1 oz. sugar

Mix together and pour into a greased mould. Steam 2 hours. Sufficient for four people.—L.G.N.

TSAMBA. TSAMPA

Barley parched and ground; the chief cereal food of the Thibetans.

TUILES D'ORANGES

Cream 1 oz. butter, add 1½ oz. castor sugar and cream together. Add 1½ oz. chopped blanched almonds, 1½ oz. chopped candied peel, dessertspoonful flour, dessertspoonful milk; colour lightly with carmine and place on buttered baking-sheet in coffeespoonfuls. Spread out flat with moistened fork. These should be given plenty of space— they spread in cooking. Cook in fairly hot oven 5 to 7 minutes. Remove from sheet with palette knife and press over rolling-pin to cool. These keep well in a tin.—D.L.T.

TUMBLES (1805)

Three pound flour, two pound sugar, one pound butter and 8 eggs, with a little caraway seeds; bake on tins; add a little milk if the eggs are not sufficient.—A.L. (2).

TURNOVER

A *Turnover* is a pasty doubled over with fruit or mincemeat inside. The most popular *Turnover* is the *Apple Turnover* and here is a recipe for making the pastry hereof. (The recipe for the filling will be found in Section IV. *FRUIT.*)

    8 oz. flour
    1 tablespoon butter
    1 heaped teaspoon baking powder
    2 tablespoons lard or mutton
        dripping
    Pinch of salt
    Water to mix

Add a pinch of salt to the flour in a mixing bowl and rub in the butter and lard. Mix the baking powder well into this and make a hole in the centre. Pour in a little cold water and stir round the hole with a wooden spoon until all the water has been absorbed into flour forming a sticky dough in the middle of the flour. Continue adding water in very small quantities and stirring the flour into it, till no dry flour is left round the sides. At the end the dough should be stiff enough to turn on to a floured pastry board and roll out without sticking to the rolling-pin, so be careful not to add too much water at a time. Remember that both mixing and rolling the pastry must be done as lightly as possible.

Divide the dough in two and roll it out thin. Put one half . at the bottom of a roasting-tin and spread it over nearly to the edges with the apple filling.—E.W.

TWELFTH-NIGHT CAKE
This should be made about three months before it is to be eaten.

Take 1 lb. of butter and 1 lb. of sugar and beat them to a cream; then add ⅛ oz. each of powdered cinnamon, powdered ginger, powdered coriander and ¼ oz. of powdered allspice. Beat separately the yolks and whites of nine eggs and add these to the butter, etc., with half a large wineglass full of brandy, then add very gradually 1 lb. of flour mixed with one teaspoonful of baking powder. Now put in 1 lb. of currants, 1 lb. of sultanas, 4 oz. each of sweet almonds, pounded, and of candied citron and lemon peel (this last should be chopped and put through a mincer). Let the whole mixture be thoroughly well beaten and then baked in a tin well lined with buttered paper in a slow oven for about 5 hours. Three months later you can cover the top of this cake with almond paste and white icing and decorate it as you please.—M.B. (2).

UPSIDE DOWN CAKES (American)

Pineapple Upside Down Cake
Melt ¼ lb. butter in pan, add 1½ cups brown sugar, and melt together; then spread on bottom of deep cake-tin. Arrange layer of tinned pineapple, cut in triangles, in the butter syrup. Beat three eggs with one cup castor sugar till very light, almost white in colour; add three tablespoonfuls hot water, beat again; add vanilla and lemon flavouring, and lastly one cup flour, sieved with one teaspoonful baking powder. Beat all well together and pour over mixtures in cake-tin. Bake in moderate oven for 40 minutes. Let cool a little in tin, turn on to sieve and let it drop by itself to allow caramel to drip into cake.

Garnish top with glacé cherries, and few blanched almonds, and glaze with apricot *purée*.

This can be served as an 'entremet' whilst still warm, with whipped cream, and fruit salad.—D.L.T.

Apricot Upside Down Cake
(or any fruit)
Sift together 1¼ cups cake flour, 1½ teaspoonfuls baking powder, good pinch salt, and half cup granulated sugar. Mix together well, one well-beaten egg, half cup milk, half teaspoonful vanilla; gradually add the flour and sugar mixture stirring till mixed. Stir in quarter cup melted butter or shortening then beat all together well till creamy in texture, about a minute or so. Have ready in cake-tin three tablespoonfuls butter and quarter cup of brown sugar melted; in this arrange 16 halves of apricots fresh or tinned. Pour over the cake batter. Bake in moderate oven about 50 minutes. Loosen cake from sides and turn out, letting cake-tin rest over cake for few minutes.

Note.—In all American measures a cup equals a good breakfast cup—D.L.T.

UXBRIDGE CAKES (1807)
Rub 1½ lb. of butter into 1 lb. of fine flour; mix into it 3 lb. of currants that have been cleaned and dried; grate a nutmeg and make it up into a light paste with some milk made warm, and new barm; mix it together and set it before the fire to rise, an hour; then make it up in small cakes.—A.A.

VERMICELLI
The little-appetizing name – meaning *little worms* – of the smallest among *Italian Pastes* (q.v.). It is used boiled in milk and sweetened as a nursery pudding, but it is chiefly used in classical cuisine in place of *Tapioca* in meat or chicken clear broths.

VIENNA BREAD
This is often made precisely like household bread, only using milk and water instead of plain water, and dissolving a little butter in the water. The great difference is that the very finest Hungarian flour being used instead of ordinary flour, more liquid is required than for household bread.

VIENNESE ROLLS

2 lb. best flour
Just over 1 oz. yeast
½ oz. salt
¾ pint of milk
Yolk of 1 egg
Water

Dissolve the yeast in half of the warmed milk and an equal quantity of water. Make a stiff dough with some of the flour and yeast mixture. Set to rise in a warm place for half hour. Work the remaining flour with the rest of the milk and water and add the dough that has risen. Knead thoroughly and let it rise for another hour. Divide the dough into 4 oz. pieces and shape into compact balls.

Let stand for another half hour. Shape into round rolls, brush over with yolk of egg and bake in a moderate oven.—M.K.S. (2).

VINEGAR CAKE

(Lunch cake in which vinegar is used instead of eggs)

¾ lb. of flour
6 oz. of butter or margarine
6 oz. of brown sugar
½ lb. of mixed fruits
½ pint of milk
2 tablespoons of vinegar
1 teaspoon of bicarbonate of soda

Rub the butter into the flour and add sugar, fruit and one small teaspoonful of mixed spice. Put the vinegar into the milk and add the soda. Beat to a froth and mix with the dry ingredients. Beat well and put into a prepared cake-tin and bake in a moderate oven for 1½ hours. A most excellent lunch cake.—L.M. (2).

VOL-AU-VENT

A much reduced and lighter edition of the *Tourte* (q.v.).

WAFERS

The thinnest and lightest of biscuits, usually sweetened. All biscuit-makers have their own registered brands of *Wafers* made according to their own recipes. Wafers are invariably offered in England with ice-cream.

Tunbridge Wells Wafers

6 oz. flour
1 teaspoon ground ginger
½ teaspoon baking powder
2 oz. treacle
2 oz. butter
2 oz. castor sugar or soft brown

Melt butter, sugar and treacle together in pan very slowly till quite blended. Must not be made very hot. Sieve flour with baking powder, add ginger; then mix all ingredients together to stiff paste. Divide into three portions. Roll out each portion as thinly as possible on floured board; cut in rounds with small cutter, and bake in very moderate oven till firm and coloured. Store in tin.

Note.—This paste is easier to handle if used while still warm.—D.L.T.

WAFFLES

About a quart of flour, scant teaspoonful of salt, tablespoonful of sugar, two tablespoonfuls of olive oil, two eggs and buttermilk.

Mix flour, salt, sugar and buttermilk until a thin batter is formed. Then beat in well two tablespoonfuls of olive oil and two eggs. Add soda and a little hot water. (*John Charles Thomas.*)—M.A.

To cook Waffles. On electric Waffle Iron. Put one teaspoonful water inside, put top down and turn on current. When it stops steaming, iron is at correct temperature for cooking Waffles. Electric waffle irons do not require greasing. Put one tablespoonful of waffle mixture in each compartment near centre of iron. Cover and mixture will spread to fill iron. Leave closed until no more steam escapes. Waffles should be well puffed and delicately brown. Lift from iron with fork.

On a non-electric iron. Heat on one side, turn and heat other side. Grease thoroughly the first time the iron is used. Grease each time before filling. Fill as above. If sufficiently heated, iron should be turned almost as soon as filled and covered.

To serve Waffles. Serve for breakfast with maple syrup. For a heartier dish, serve with small sausages, creamed chicken, mushrooms, bacon or fried chicken. As a dessert, serve with maple syrup or serve Chocolate or Ginger Waffles with whipped cream. —B.C.S.C.B.

WALNUT CAKE

Mix carefully six tablespoonfuls of sifted flour, 5 oz. butter creamed with a good tablespoonful of castor sugar, one tablespoonful of blanched and powdered almonds, two tablespoonfuls of blanched and powdered walnuts, the yolks of two eggs and a very little water. Bake in a flat, oblong or round cake-tin in a moderate oven till of a light golden-brown colour. Meanwhile heat together (*without letting it boil*) half gill each of cream and milk, the well-beaten yolks of three eggs, and three tablespoonfuls of castor sugar. When this is quite hot (but not boiling), lift off the pan and stir in the whisked whites of the eggs and four tablespoonfuls of blanched and chopped, or powdered, walnuts. Cover the cake evenly with this mixture, then put it in the oven till set. Serve dusted with sugar and chopped pistachios.—Q. (1).

WARM WRACK

    3 tablespoons of butter
    ½ cupful of brown sugar
    1½ cupfuls of sifted all-purpose flour
    2 teaspoons of baking powder
    ¼ teaspoon of salt
    Scant ⅓ cupful of milk and water,
      half and half
    ½ cupful of currants, soaked for 5
      minutes in scalding water and
      drained
    9-in. cake-tin, well buttered

Cream the butter and brown sugar together. Sift the flour, baking powder and salt together, and add to the first mixture alternately with the liquid. Stir in the currants. Spread evenly in the cake-dish and bake in a hot oven (425° F.) for about 15 minutes. Then spread generously with extra butter, sprinkle with extra brown sugar, and return to the oven until the butter is melted. Keep covered until ready to serve. Serve hot with afternoon tea or as a luncheon bread. Any left over is very good toasted for breakfast.—E.K.H.

WATER BISCUITS

Thin, round, white 'flour-and-water' Biscuits similar to, but rather thinner than, the average American *Cracker*.

Sieve ½ lb. plain flour, with ½ oz. Paisley flour and good pinch salt; rub in 1 oz. butter. Mix with milk to stiff dough. Roll out very thin, and bake in sheets; prick them lightly. Heat the tins before baking, then bake quickly. Serve with cheese, or in place of bread, in rough large pieces.—D.L.T.

WEDDING CAKE

    1 lb. butter
    1 lb. brown sugar
    12 eggs
    1 cup molasses
    1 lb. flour
    4 teaspoons cinnamon
    4 teaspoons allspice
    1½ teaspoons mace
    1 nutmeg, grated
    ¼ teaspoon soda
    3 lb. seeded raisins, cut in pieces
    2 lb. sultana raisins
    1½ lb. citron, thinly sliced and cut in
      strips
    1 lb. currants
    ½ preserved lemon rind
    ½ preserved orange rind
    1 cup grape juice or brandy
    4 squares chocolate, melted
    1 tablespoon hot water

Cream butter, add sugar gradually, and beat thoroughly. Beat egg-yolks until thick and lemon-coloured. Add to first mixture,

then add flour (reserving one-third cup, to dredge fruit), mixed and sifted with spices, fruit dredged with flour, lemon rind and orange rind finely chopped, grape juice or brandy, chocolate, and egg whites beaten until stiff. Just before putting into pans, add soda dissolved in hot water. Cover pans with buttered paper. If to be steamed, cover loosely with buttered paper, and tie paper firmly in place. Then steam 3 hours and bake 1½ hours in slow oven (300° F.). If desired, bake 4 hours in very slow oven (275° F.) without steaming. Rich fruit cake is always more satisfactory if part of the cooking is accomplished by steaming. Spread cake with almond paste, moisten with egg white. When firm, frost and decorate as desired.
—B.C.S.C.B..

WELLINGTONS

Rub together 8 oz. of fine flour with 8 oz. of butter, and 8 oz. of crushed sugar, one tablespoonful of sweet almonds, chopped, the grated rind of half a lemon and one egg well beaten. Form into small cakes and bake for about 15 minutes.—M.K.S. (2).

WHEAT

Lat. *Triticum vulgare*; Fr. *Blé*. Of the many different varieties of Wheat grown throughout the world that which is best is called, rather unfairly, *Common Wheat*, or *vulgare* in botanical Latin. A closely-related variety, which is known as *Club* or *Square Head Wheat*, is specially adapted to the Pacific Coast States of North America and to Chile; it is also grown in Turkestan and Abyssinia. There are a number of different sorts of spring and winter varieties, as well as softer, harder types of *Common Wheat*, which is the Wheat mostly grown to-day and the Wheat mostly used for the making of *Bread* (q.v.).

Durum Wheat, which is also called *Macaroni Wheat*, is grown very extensively in Spain and in Central as well as South America; also in Italy and other parts of the wheat-growing districts of the world. In Texas it is called *Nicaragua Wheat*, and in those parts of Canada where it is grown its local name is *Wild Goose*. The Bread made from *Durum Wheat* looks rather like *Rye Bread* and is of inferior quality. On the other hand, *Durum* is richer in gluten than *Common Wheat* and its flour is superior to *Common Wheat* flour for making Macaroni, Spaghetti, Ravioli and every kind of Noodle or Paste.

See also *Einkorn, Emmer, English Wheat* and *Spelt*.

WHITE FRUIT CAKE

    ⅔ cup butter
    ¼ teaspoon soda
    Whites of 6 eggs

⅔ cup candied cherries
½ cup thinly-sliced citron
1⅞ cups flour
½ teaspoon lemon juice
1½ cups powdered sugar
⅓ cup blanched and shredded
    almonds
1 teaspoon almond extract

Cream butter, gradually add flour mixed and sifted with soda and lemon juice. Beat whites of eggs stiff. Add sugar. Combine mixtures, add cherries, almonds, citron and extract. Bake in buttered deep cake-tin in moderate oven for 1 hour. (*Louise C. Martin.*) —T.C.

WHOLEMEAL BREAD

Take 2 lb. of wholemeal flour, 12 oz. of white flour, 2 large teaspoonfuls of sugar, the same amount of salt, ¾ oz. of yeast, 1 quart of warm water. Mix the yeast with the sugar; add the water and salt gradually, stir in the wholemeal flour, sprinkle a little white flour over the dough and put aside in a warm place to rise. When it has risen enough add the rest of the white flour, sufficient to make it into a firm dough when kneaded; make it into two loaves; put again to rise, then bake in a moderate oven for 1½ hours.—M.B. (2).

WHOLE WHEAT ROCK CAKES

2 oz. whole wheat meal, 2 oz. sugar, 2 oz. butter, 1 oz. raisins, 1 egg.

Cream sugar with butter, add yolk of egg, then meal, well mix above, then add well-beaten white of egg; bake 15 minutes. (*South African Recipe.*)

WIGS or WIGGS

A wigg was a wedge and these are wedge-shaped cakes.

Yorkshire Wigs (1769)

Take 2 lb. of flour, 1 lb. of butter, 1 pint of cream, 4 eggs (leaving out 2 whites), and 2 tablespoonfuls of yeast. Mix well and let it rise a little; then add ½ lb. of sugar and ½ lb. of caraway comfits. Make them up with these and bake them in a dripping pan. —M.B.(1).

Three Recipes for Wigs from the Complete Housewife (1737)

I

To make Wigs

Take 2 lb. of flour, ¼ lb. of butter and as much sugar; a nutmeg grated, a little cloves and mace and ¼ oz. of caraway seeds; cream and yeast as much as will make up into a pretty light paste; make them up and set them by the fire to rise till the oven be ready; they will quickly be baked.

II

To make the Light Wigs

Take 1½ lb. of flour and half pint of milk made warm, mix these together and cover it up and let it lie by the fire half hour; then take ½ lb. of sugar and ½ lb. of butter, then work these in the paste and make it into *Wigs* with as little flour as possible. Let the oven be pretty quick and they will rise very much.

III

To make very good Wigs

Take a quarter peck of the finest flour, rub into it ¾ lb. of fresh butter till it is like grated bread. Something more than ½ lb. of sugar, half a nutmeg and half a knob of ginger, grated; three eggs, yolks and whites beaten very well. Put to them half pint of thick ale-yeast and three to four spoonfuls of salt. Make a hole in your flour and put in your yeast and eggs and enough warm milk as will make a light paste. Let it stand before the fire to rise for half hour, then make into a dozen and a half *Wigs*. Wash them over with eggs just as they go into the oven and half hour will bake them.

WILLIAMSBURG BUNS

Scald one cup of milk, add half cup of melted butter, two teaspoonfuls of salt and half cup of sugar, cool to lukewarm. Add two yeast cakes which have been dissolved in one-fourth cup of warm water. Add three beaten eggs to liquids, then beat in well four and a half cups of flour. (One teaspoonful each of nutmeg and mace and a wineglass of sherry may be added.) Let the dough rise until double in bulk, turn it out and knead lightly. Fill muffin-pans two-thirds full and let rise until light (about 20 minutes). Brush with melted butter and bake in a moderately hot oven about 20 minutes. Makes about three dozen small Buns which are very nice for tea. (*Miss Bowdoin's recipe. c. 1801. Adapted Blair Kitchen*, 1938.)—H.B.

WILLIAMSBURG SALLY LUNN

Put one yeast cake in one cup of warm milk. Cream together half a cup of butter and one-third cup of sugar, add three beaten eggs and mix well. Sift in one quart of flour, alternately with the milk and yeast. Let rise in a warm place, then beat well. Pour into one well-buttered *Sally Lunn* mould or two smaller moulds. Let it rise again before baking in a moderate oven. (*Barlow family recipe, Williamsburg. Prov'd Market Square Tavern Kitchen*, 1937.)—H.B.

WILLIAMSBURG SPONGE CAKE
Beat three egg yolks until very light, slowly beat in one-third cup of sugar. Add one teaspoonful of lemon juice. Stir in lightly three well-beaten egg whites. Sift in one-third cup of flour and quarter teaspoonful of salt. Bake in small buttered muffin-tins, or in a small cake-pan in a very moderate oven about 25 minutes. (*Mrs Randolph's recipe. Adapted Blair Kitchen*, 1938.)—H.B.

WINE BISCUITS
     ½ lb. of flour
     ½ oz. of butter
     ½ pint of cream
     Pinch of salt

Mix the ingredients to a stiff dough; roll out to the thickness of ½ in.; cut with a 3 in. round cutter; roll out the thickness of a wafer cake; put in a hot oven to crisp. (*Mrs W. E. Crum.*)—F.C.B.

YARMOUTH BISCUITS
Take 6 oz. of currants, wash and dry them well; rub a little flour among them to make them white and put ½ lb. of powdered sugar with the currants on a clean board, add 12 oz. of sifted flour and ½ lb. of the best fresh butter you can get, break three eggs and mix all ingredients together to become a paste, so that you can roll it on the board ⅛ in. thick, then cut either rounds or what shape you choose and bake. Your oven must be rather hot.—M.B. (2).

YEAST or BARM
Yeast is a fungus which begins to grow at a certain temperature, blood heat, 98.4. This growth causes chemical changes to take place in the flour, which produce carbonic acid gas and aerate the dough, causing it to rise. Yeast requires warmth to start the growth, but should the heat be too great it will kill the germ. Use a warm basin when mixing the dough and dissolve the yeast in lukewarm water or milk.

Compressed yeast or baker's yeast is easiest to use; it must be fresh and sweet and smell good. Fresh yeast crumbles easily and creams easily when mixed with a little sugar or salt.

Yeast, brewers' barm, is a liquid form of yeast, it has a more bitter taste (1 oz. compressed yeast is equal to two tablespoonfuls of liquid yeast).

YORKSHIRE CHEESE-CAKE
Line flan-tin with good short crust; prick well and half bake. Let cool.

Filling: Sieve ½ lb. dry curds; then beat them with little cream, two egg yolks, sugar to sweeten, vanilla, grated lemon rind and juice of one lemon; fold in the whipped whites.

Fill case with this mixture and return to oven and bake till golden brown.—D.L.T.

YORKSHIRE PUDDING
A baked batter made of flour, milk and egg which is the traditional accompaniment of the roast sirloin of beef.

Mrs Beeton's Yorkshire Pudding
1½ pints of milk, 6 *large* tablespoonfuls of flour, 3 eggs, 1 saltspoonful of salt.

Put the flour into a basin with the salt, and stir gradually to this enough milk to make it into a stiff batter. When this is perfectly smooth, and all the lumps are well rubbed down, add the remainder of the milk and the eggs, which should be well beaten. Beat the mixture for a few minutes and pour it into a shallow tin, which has been previously well rubbed with beef dripping. Put the pudding into the oven, and bake it for an hour; then, for another half hour, place it under the meat, to catch a little of the gravy that flows from it. Cut the pudding into small, square pieces, put them on a hot dish and serve. If the meat is baked, the pudding may at once be placed under it, resting the former on a small three-cornered stand.—B. (2).

YORKSHIRE SPICE BREAD
     3½ lb. flour
     ¼ lb. butter
     ¼ lb. lard
     ½ lb. sugar
     ½ lb. currants
     ½ lb. raisins
     ¼ lb. peel
     1 teaspoon of mixed spice
     2 oz. yeast
     1 egg
     Pinch of salt
     Milk to mix

Put the flour in a bowl, rub in the butter and lard and then the sugar, spice, salt, currants, raisins and shredded peel and thoroughly mix all these dry ingredients. Cream the yeast in a teacupful of milk and warm water, add a little sugar and set to rise. Make a well in your dry mixture and break the egg into it; add the yeast and more warm milk to make into a dough. Knead lightly. Put the dough into bread-tins lined with greased paper, set to rise for 15 minutes, then bake in a slow oven.—M.K.S. (2).

YORKSHIRE TEA CAKES
Mix 1 lb. flour and 2 oz. currants with a pinch of salt. Rub in lightly 2 oz. lard and mix in 2 oz. castor sugar. Cream together 1 oz. yeast and one teaspoonful castor sugar.

Make half pint of milk warm and mix it with a well-beaten egg. Pour this and the creamed yeast in a hole in the centre of the flour. Leave it in a warm place to rise for 20 minutes. Now beat in all the flour round it and leave to rise in a warm place for an hour. Form into tea-cakes. Place them on a baking-tin, leave them for 20 minutes, and bake them in a moderate oven for about 20 minutes.—P.A.

ZEPHYRINAS

A breeze is probably created in the process, so quickly are these Zephyrinas made, being rolled paper-thin from an unleavened kneaded dough made of two cups of flour, one tablespoonful butter, salt to taste and enough water to combine. They are cut with a saucer, pricked with a fork, put in a moderately hot oven (375° F.) and baked instantaneously.—C.G.

ZITA, *pl.* ZITE

One of the fancy *Italian Pastes* (q.v.). It is made of the gluten of hard wheat and eggs, like *Macaroni*, in hollow, straight tubes of larger diameter than *Macaroni* (q.v.).

ZWIEBACK (Rusks)

1 lb. of flour, $\frac{1}{4}$ lb. sugar, $\frac{1}{4}$ lb. butter, half pint milk, two tablespoonfuls good yeast.

Warm the milk and stir the yeast into it. Put the flour in a pan and throw the sugar among it. Make a hollow in the middle and stir the yeast and milk into the hollow like a thin batter. Cut up the batter on the flour. Cover, and set it to rise. Then beat it until the dough no longer hangs to the hand or spoon. Let it rise again till it cracks on the top. Cut and mould from the dough long cakes an inch thick, 5 or 6 in. long and 2 in. broad. Set them on a buttered tin 2 in. apart, let them rise on this; then brush them over with milk and bake them. Next day, slice them open with a sharp knife, lay them on a tin with the crust under, and put them in a cool oven till they are crisp and baked yellow.—G.N.C.

SECTION 4
FRUIT

Fruit: comprising an alphabetical list of edible Fruits,

including Nuts, with Recipes for preparing them,

preserving them, and for cakes, pies, puddings,

fritters, dumplings and other desserts

wherein Fruits are used

FRUIT

'_No!_' _cried the staring Monarch with a grin;_
'_How, how the devil got the Apple in?_'
JOHN WOLCOT, _The Apple Dumplings and the King._

INTRODUCTION

FRUIT is the womb that holds, protects, feeds, matures and eventually delivers the seed responsible for the survival of the species and its propagation. Night and day the roots distil from the moist earth and the leaves distil from the moist air the food and the drink which tree, bush, herb or plant needs, not merely to live but also and chiefly to bring forth a living seed. Although this definition of _Fruit_ would, we trust, satisfy botanists, they would certainly use more scientific words. But this is not a scientific book; nor is it a literary one. Yet just as it is important not to disregard grammar even when one is not thinking of literature, so it is helpful to have some sort of general botanical background when one looks into the subject of _Fruit._

Gastronomes, and all who take an intelligent interest in what they eat and drink are entitled to the name, accord a very much more restricted meaning to the name _Fruit_ than the botanists do. The acorn, for instance, although a true fruit to the botanist is merely food for pigs to the gastronome. Peas and beans in their pods are also true fruits to the botanist, but the gastronome calls them vegetables; just as wheat, barley and oats are true fruits scientifically, but cereals in the vernacular.

Fruits, gastronomically speaking, are the fleshy and succulent seed-containers of fruit-bearing trees, shrubs, bushes, canes and other plants; and, in some cases, the name also applies to their edible seeds. Fruits are divided, botanically, into the following categories:

Pomes, known in British vernacular as *Pip* fruits; they are few in numbers but of greater importance in the British Isles and the U.S.A. than any other, since they include the *Apple* and the *Pear*.

Drupes, known in the vernacular as *Stone* fruits, bearing but one seed per fruit, and that enclosed within a hard stone; they include the almond, apricot, cherry, nectarine, peach and plum.

Brambles, the fruit of the *Rubus* family, of which there are over 3,000 different sorts; they are known to botanists as 'an agglomeration of drupelets', and to the rest of us merely as *Berries*; their prototype is the *Blackberry*.

Currants and *Gooseberries*, the fruits of the *Ribes* family, or *Groseilles*, which include the black, the red and the white currants as well as gooseberries and other berries.

Bush fruits, the fruits chiefly of the *Vaccinium* branch of the *Ericaceae* family, also known as *Berries*, such as the cranberry, blueberry, huckleberry and the like.

Citrus fruits, which are pulpy, juicy fruits with a leathery rind as outer cover and protection; of these the orange is the prototype.

Nuts, one-seeded fruits with a fibrous or woody shell protecting the kernel or edible seed – the meat – within; such are the hazels, chestnuts, pecans and all other nuts.

Freak fruits, which botanists do not recognize as true fruits at all, although everybody else does, the strawberry and the pineapple, for instance. It is somewhat of a shock to be told that the sweet and fragrant strawberry is a spurious fruit, but it appears that it is merely an enlarged receptacle terminating the flower stalk of the plant, the true fruits of which are the dry schenes borne on this enlarged receptacle. Happily, even such knowledge does not rob the strawberry of its charm, whilst it may be of some consolation to those who dare not eat strawberries for fear of urticaria.

In our opinion, not all, but most, fruits are best when eaten 'out of hand'; that is, when fully ripe and freshly picked. The only exception to that rule is in favour of the *Heath* berries: they must be cooked. Unfortunately, freshly picked, ripe fruit is not obtainable all the year round, and even when ripe and freshly picked there are varieties of fruit which are too acid or so lacking in flavour that they are best cooked and improved with sugar and some flavouring agent or agents. It is for such that a large number of recipes have been selected and are given in the following pages.

Of all fruits *Berries* are the most suitable for cooking, chiefly in tarts, puddings and pies, whilst *Citrus* fruits are the most unsatisfactory. Like caviare and like oysters, oranges and grapefruit are never improved by being served hot.

Science has made it possible to preserve fruits in wonderful condition for considerable periods, by heat or cold, vacuum or wax – the vapourised wax, which seals the pores of citrus fruit, has made it possible to allow the fruit to reach maturity before being picked, treated and shipped or stored. But long before any such scientific processes had been thought of and perfected, a very good way of keeping fruits ever at hand, at all seasons of the year, always acceptable and delicious, was and still is, to turn them into jam or jelly; also into other forms of preserves or conserves. All fruits lend themselves excellently to such treatment, not excepting *Citrus* fruits, which are used to make some of the most popular of all jams, in England usually called Marmalade.[1]

Home-made jam can and should be better than factory-made jam, since the first is made for love and the other for profit; also because the first is made with sugar and the other, as a rule, with sugar substitutes. But even love and sugar will not suffice to make really good jam: it is quite easy to make, provided one does not attempt to do anything else at the time. Jam must be boiled very quickly and watched all the time. Good jam is neither liquid – as it will be if under-boiled; nor solid, as it will be if over-boiled. It is difficult to give any sort of time-table that will ensure just the right consistency of the jam being made: so much depends upon the fruit and the heat used, but, as a matter of general rule, when a spoon is dipped into the boiling jam which sticks to it instead of dripping off it, the pan should be moved away from the fire, and its contents thoroughly well stirred before they are finally dealt with as jam or jelly. If jam is required, juice and fruit pulp are poured in clean glass or china pots or jars and left to cool off before covering. To make jelly instead of jam, none but the clear juice, which has been allowed to run of its own accord – not pressed – through a jelly bag, is bottled. Whole fruit may also be bottled in syrup or with various liqueurs, but as the processes for preserving most fruits are the same, they have not been repeated under each heading.

Botanists do not always agree among themselves as regards definitions and classifications, so that not only the general public, but gardeners and fruiterers, must be forgiven if they confuse the names of the fruits they grow or sell, and it is in the hope to dispel, as far as in us lay, such regrettable confusion that we have taken pains to ascertain from the most highly qualified quarters the correct botanical or Latin names of all the fruits hereinafter recorded, as the only safe means of identification. It has not been possible to give in all instances English·names corresponding to the botanical names of fruits either little known in the British Isles or the U.S.A., or known only by their original native names, which we have retained. As regards the corres-

---

[1]*Marmalade* is the English version of *Marmelo*, the Portuguese for *Quince*, and it meant originally Quince Jam, both in Portugal and in England; when and why it changed over from Quince to Orange has never been ascertained, as far as we know.

ponding French names of many fruits recorded, they are those of fruits the use of which in cookery and confectionery has been recognized by either the *Cuisine classique* or the *Cuisine bourgeoise*.

Definitions and Recipes

ACHOJCHA. ACHOJCHO
Lat. *Cyclanthera pedata*; *var. edulis*. A South American forest tree which bears edible fruits much prized by the Indians in some inland provinces of Argentina.

ADUWA or DESERT DATE
Lat. *Balanites aegyptiaca*. A date-like fruit of a small bushy tree which grows in Upper Egypt, Uganda, the Congo and Borneo. It has a bitter-sweet taste and aperient properties. It is used by the natives in the region of Fashoda to make their national dish, *Tuwon Aduwa*. The stone of *Aduwa* yields a medicinal oil known as *Zachum*. *Aduwa* is also called *Desert Date*.

AGUAY
Lat. *Chrysophyllum lucumifolium*. A South American shrub which bears edible berries chiefly used to make jams and preserves.

AKEE APPLE
Lat. *Blighia sapida*. A tropical fruit which is extensively grown in Jamaica, where 'Salt fish and *Akee*' is a very popular breakfast dish. The white arillus in which the seeds of the *Akee* are set have, when cooked, a very pleasant taste, but it must be gathered some time after it is well opened: if taken before, it is poisonous.

ALKEKENGI
See *Strawberry Tomato*.

ALLIGATOR APPLE
Lat. *Anona palustris*. The South American and West African *Custard Apple* and one of the least desirable of the *Annonas*.

ALLIGATOR PEAR
See *Avocado Pear*.

ALMOND
Lat. *Prunus amygdalus*, *var. amara*, Bitter Almond and *var. dulcis*, Sweet Almond (*Amygdalus communis*); Fr. *Amande*. The fruit of different varieties of Almond trees, which may be divided into two main classes according to whether they produce (*a*) sweet, and (*b*) bitter Almonds.

(*a*) *Sweet Almonds* are the more valuable, gastronomically and commercially; when freshly picked, they are eaten as dessert; when dried, whether salted or not, they are eaten with cocktails or with Port, before or after the meal, and they are also largely used in cookery and confectionery. There are five sorts of Sweet Almonds sold:

1. *Common*: it ripens at end of August; its shell is hard and woody. 1¼ to 1¾ in. long.
2. *Large*: it ripens in early October; 2½ in. long; sweet and of excellent flavour.
3. *Sultan*: it ripens early in September; the shell is tender but the fruit is small.
4. *Pistache*: it ripens at the end of August; its shell is tender and the shape is that of the Pistachio.
5. *Jordan*: it ripens at the end of August; tender shell, large fruit, sweet and of good flavour; often has double kernel. This is the kind mostly sold in shops.

(*b*) *Bitter Almonds*. These almonds are used mostly in confectionery and for flavouring; their bitterness is due to a benzaldehyde which develops, with minute quantities of prussic acid, when the almond is crushed and moistened. The skin which protects the almond should be removed; drop the almonds in boiling water for a minute or two, and then rub them in a rough cloth, when the thin skin will come off quite easily.

Almond Brittle is another name for *Almond Toffee* (q.v.).

Burnt Almonds are dried Sweet Almonds which are blanched, lightly grilled and coated with sugar. They are called *Pralines* in France.

Devilled Almonds are dried Sweet Almonds which are blanched and browned in a very little very hot butter; whilst being tossed in the pan they are freely dusted with salt and less freely with paprika.

Almond Crisps
½ cup butter
1 cup of light brown sugar
1 well-beaten egg
1 cup of all-purpose flour
¼ teaspoon of cream of tartar
½ cup of blanched and coarsely chopped almonds

Cream the butter and sugar until very light. Add the well-beaten egg. Sift the flour, cream of tartar, and a pinch of salt. Into this mix the nuts. Beat all together. Drop from the end of spoon on to a greased baking-pan and bake in a slow oven to a light brown.—G.T.L.

Almond Fritters
2 oz. ground almonds
½ oz. of cornflour
2 eggs
1 oz. castor sugar
A few drops of vanilla

Stir yolks of the eggs until creamy, then add the almonds and vanilla, cornflour, and the whites of the eggs stiffly mixed. Have a pan of hot frying fat, drop in the prepared mixture and fry and put on sieve to drain; sufficient for four people.—L.G.N.

Gâteau aux Amandes

Have ½ lb. pounded almonds; mix them with ½ lb. of soft sugar and the skin (no pith left) of a lemon grated or very finely chopped. Add about 3 oz. of potato flour, four eggs and one yolk and a pinch of salt. Having well mixed all these ingredients, add the remaining white of egg whipped to a stiff froth, mix well, fill a buttered mould with the mixture and bake in a slow oven almost half an hour.—X.M.B. (1).

Almond Ice Cream

Take 1 quart of cream custard as follows: Whisk four large or five small eggs, mix them into 1 quart of fresh cream, and add ¼ lb. castor sugar. Put these into a saucepan and place it over a moderate heat. Stir well until it thickens, but on no account let it boil or it will curdle and spoil. Strain through a fine hair sieve, and allow it to get quite cold.

Blanch ¾ lb. almonds, then grate them finely and add them to the cold cream custard just as it is finished making. Strain through a fine hair sieve and allow to get quite cold. When quite cold freeze and it is ready to serve.—E.C. (1).

Mandelkraenzen

½ cup butter
1 cup sugar
3 egg yolks, well beaten
4 cups flour
1 teaspoon baking powder
½ lemon rind, grated

Cream butter, add sugar, yolk and lemon; beat 10 minutes. Add flour sifted with baking powder. Quickly work the dough into long narrow roll. Cut off pieces, roll between hands and board, connect ends, forming circles. Dip in egg-whites and then into a mixture of sugar, cinnamon and finely-cut almonds. Bake in slow oven (250° F.) 10 to 15 minutes.—C.G.

Almond Milk

Blanch, peel and chop finely two or three dozen Sweet Almonds and put them in a jug with 1 or 1½ pints of water. Stir well until it looks like milk. Strain through a wet napkin, pound the almonds in a mortar and stir again in the same water. Strain and add sugar to taste; also a little orange juice. Serve very cold; a very good summer drink.

Almond Paste (Marzipan)

1. To 2½ lb. of freshly-ground almonds add 3½ lb. of cane icing sugar and the unbeaten whites of seven eggs. Work to a stiff dry paste and then add a wine-glass of old rum or the same quantity of new brandy and a dash of vanilla essence. Mix all together and work until the paste is of the right consistency.

2. Stir 1 lb. of freshly-ground almonds in 2 lb. of icing sugar, mix well into a paste; make a well in centre and put in it the yolks of four eggs, a little rosewater, vanilla essence and pineapple essence; knead and roll out on a pastry board.

Sirop d'orgeat

1 lb. of sweet almonds
6 oz. of bitter almonds
1½ quarts of water
3 lb. of crushed lump sugar

Blanch and skin the almonds and pound them to a smooth paste in a mortar with a little water. Add about ½ pint of water and mix well. Put the almonds and water in a saucepan, add the remaining quantity of water and the sugar, and simmer in a double saucepan till the sugar has melted. Remove from the fire, strain through a cloth into a terrine or large basin and, when cool, bottle it. Keep it in a cool place and use with plain water, barley water or soda water, iced, of course. It makes a most cooling and delicious summer drink. Do not make more at a time than you are likely to use quickly, as it does not keep well: it ferments of its own accord after a little while.

Gouffé recommends flavouring Orgeat with a little Fleur d'Oranger.

Tarte aux Amandes

Prepare the paste with a quarter of a pound of sifted flour, same quantity of butter, a little milk and one ounce of sugar. Mix well and lightly to a compact dough, roll and line a greased tart mould, about one inch high, with very thin paste.

Prepare the filling as follows: two eggs, 3 oz. sugar, 3 oz. pounded almonds, a small glass of milk; mix well. The mixture should be like thick cream.

Prick a few holes with a fork at the bottom of the tart, put in your mixture and bake in a fairly hot oven about 15 minutes. Two minutes before the end, sprinkle sugar all over. Serve hot, with cream, or cold.—X.M.B. (1).

Almond Toffee (English Style)

Blanch and skin some sweet almonds; cut them up longways and toss them in hot butter until nicely brown. Melt twice as much sugar as you have prepared almonds;

the melting must be done slowly and the sugar stirred all the time until it becomes a liquid golden syrup. Then is the time to stir in the almonds quickly, and to pour the toffee at once into an ungreased pan. Mark into squares before it gets hard.

Almond Toffee
(Spanish style. Turron de Jijona)

Blanch, skin and roast 1 lb. sweet almonds. Chop them up and pound them in a mortar with ½ lb. loaf sugar. Put into an iron saucepan and bring to the boil slowly, stirring all the while and adding ¼ lb. honey to the mixture little by little. When the mixture begins to brown, pour it into little wooden frames lined with rice paper.

AMATUNGULA

Lat. *Carissa grandiflora*. The refreshingly acid fruit of a South African tree: it varies in size from an olive to a damson and is known as *Natal Plum*.

AMERICAN CHERRY

Lat. *Prunus Virginiana*. The astringent fruit of an American bush-like tree chiefly used for hedges, like blackthorns in England. It makes good pies and is also used for sauces.

AMERICAN CRAB APPLE

Lat. *Malus coronaria*. A species of Crab Apple well worth growing for the sake of its beautiful pink blossom, but the little yellow apples which it produces are not worth eating.

AMERICAN DATE PLUM

See *Persimmon*.

ANGOSTURA

The bitter and aromatic bark of the *Galipea Cusparia* tree, a native of Venezuela.

ANNATTO-TREE

Lat. *Bixa Orellana*. A South American tree, known as *Urucú* in Argentina; it produces an edible but tasteless fruit, salmon-red in colour, used as a dye in confectionery; the seeds are used for flavouring.

ANNONA

Lat. *Anona Cherimolia*; *A. diversifolia*; *A. muricata*; *A. palustris*; *A. purpurea*; *A. reticulata*; *A. Squamosa*. This is a name given in tropical America and in India to a number of fleshy, edible fruits, of which the best are the following:

Cherimoya, from Ecuador and Peru; also cultivated in West Africa.

Soncoya, Central America, from Mexico to Panama; aromatic, mango-like.

Ilama, a variety of *Soncoya* and the most delicious of all.

Soursop or *West Indian Custard Apple*, fairly common in the West Indies; its flavour is somewhat like that of black currants.

Sweetsop or *Indian Custard Apple*, egg-shaped, its rind thick; its pulp luscious; commonly used in India to flavour rice puddings.

Bullock's Heart, an inferior variety which occurs chiefly in tropical America.

Alligator or *Monkey Apple*, also an inferior variety, which some even claim to be poisonous.

APPLE

Lat. *Pyrus malus*; Fr. *Pomme*. The fruit of any member of the genus *Malus*, of which there are many different species.

In Great Britain a distinction is made – and exists – between cooking apples and dessert apples. Cooking apples are usually large, green and acid, the acid being the cause of their flesh going to pulp when they are cooked. Dessert apples are usually smaller, darker of skin, sweet and fragrant; the best of them also possess a characteristic flavour, aromatic but difficult to define, and usually associated with a dull russeting of the skin.

In the U.S.A. the difference between cooking and dessert apples is by no means so well defined. As a rule, American apples possess a high colour and shining skin; they are sweet and very fragrant, but only one or two sorts possess the aromatic flavour so highly prized in English dessert apples. They are also much softer in texture than English apples and, when cooked, they do not 'pulp', but the pieces retain their shape.

Among the considerable number of varieties of English Apples only a few come to market: *Beauty of Bath* (August and September), *James Grieve* and *Worcester Pearmain* (September), *Ellison's Orange* (October), *Cox's Orange Pippin* and *Ribston Pippin* (October), *Blenheim Orange* (October and November), *Laxton's Superb* (December), are among the more popular dessert apples which can usually be obtained. Of cooking varieties, the best are *Victoria* (early), *Lord Derby* (October), *Bramley Seedling*, *Newton Wonder* and *Lane's Prince Albert*, which will keep until Easter.

Among American varieties the *Ben Davis*, *Winesap* and *Macintosh* are favourites. Other popular apples are *Northern Spy*, *Rome Beauty*, *Baldwin*, *Delicious* and *Golden Delicious*. The *Rhode Island Greening* is used for cooking and baking. Most American apples are grown in the State of Washington. New York State is the next largest producer, followed closely by Virginia.

Apple Amber

Skin and score 1 lb. of cooking apples; stew them in very little water and as much sugar as you happen to like. When the apples are cooked, rub them through a sieve and return to a pan in which you will have melted 1½ oz. butter. Add to the apple pulp the well-beaten yolks of two eggs; also the juice of one lemon. Mix well and heat thoroughly.

Line a tart tin with a light pastry and cover with the apple mixture. Bake in a moderate oven for half an hour. Beat the whites of two eggs stiffly with two tablespoons of sifted sugar; spread it over the top of the apple *purée* and bake until golden brown.

Apple, Baked

Both cooking and dessert apples may be baked, but not in exactly the same manner. Eating apples which are juicy and rather sweet should be baked in their skin and in a slow oven for a long time, two to three hours, according to size. Cooking and acid apples are best baked after they have been peeled and put into a hot oven (400° Fahr.) until soft. In either case the apples should be cored before being baked and placed in a baking-dish, the bottom of which is covered with boiling water. The centre of the apple, after the core has been removed, should be filled with sugar. Baked apples may be served either hot, straight from the oven, or quite cold and with a little fresh cream.

Apple Bonne Femme or Buttered Apple

A *Baked Apple* (q.v.) in which the cavity left by removing the core is filled not merely with sugar but with a mixture of butter and castor sugar.

Apple Butter

Pare and slice some sound apples; cook them in cider, with sugar, to a thick pulp; pour whilst boiling hot into hot, sterilized preserve jars; adjust rubbers and seal at once.—G.H. (1).

Apple Charlotte

A popular form of hot sweet, named after the heroine in Goethe's *Werther*. It is a combination of bread and butter and apples, prepared either with or without a mould. The Charlotte mould is a plain cylinder about 5 in. deep.

Peel and core 1½ lb. of cooking apples and cut them up in quarters. Stew them gently in ½ pint water and with 8 oz. sugar; also a strip of lemon rind. When the stewed apples are quite soft, add 2 oz. butter and mix in thoroughly.

Cut some stale white bread in thin slices; dip them in hot melted butter and line with them the bottom and sides of a deep pie-dish. Fill the dish with the stewed apples and cover with a layer of slices of stale bread,

dipped in melted butter. Sprinkle castor sugar over it all and bake in moderate oven until the top layer of bread is golden brown. Turn on to a warm dish and pour some diluted apricot jam over it before serving.

Charlotte Russe is the cold form of the *Charlotte*, finger biscuits being used instead of bread, apple marmalade instead of buttered apples and cream instead of butter.

Swedish Apple Charlotte

2½ lb. fresh apples
Bare teacup sugar
½ teacup water
½ stale brown loaf (about 1 pint breadcrumbs)
4½ oz. butter

Peel, core and cut into thin sections. Cook into pulp with sugar and very little water. Grate the loaf or pass through a mincer, and brown lightly in 3 oz. of the butter. Spread buttered and breadcrumbed tin with three layers of breadcrumbs and two of apples, the top layer of breadcrumbs. Dot on top with the rest of the butter. Bake for half an hour in moderate oven. Turn out and sprinkle with castor sugar. Serve hot or cold, with whipped cream or vanilla sauce. —I.N.

Apple Cobbler

Place a layer of chopped apples in the bottom of a round pudding-pan which has been well oiled. Sprinkle generously with sugar and a bit of grated nutmeg or cinnamon. Make a baking-powder biscuit dough, adding enough more liquid to make the mixture soft enough to drip from a spoon. Bake in moderate oven until the apples are soft and the crust brown – about 30 minutes. When done turn the pudding on to a plate upside down so that the apples are on top. Serve with cream and sugar or hard sauce.—P.D.P.

Apple Compôte
(Cosmopolitan Club, Lancaster County)

¼ peck cooking apples
1 lb. brown sugar
¼ lb. butter

Pare and core apples; cut into ¼ in. slices. Arrange apples in a flat baking-pan greased with part of the butter. Cover apples generously with sugar and dot with remaining butter. Cover dish tightly and bake in moderate oven (375°) about 30 minutes. Serve warm with heavy sweet or sour cream.—A.W.R.

Apple Condé

Pare and core some large apples and divide them in equal quarters. Poach the quarters of apple in a syrup made up of water and sugar and flavoured with some vanilla.

Dress the quarters of apple within a border of boiled and sweetened rice; decorate with some glacé cherries and pieces of green angelica and pour over it a syrup of apricots with a little kirsch added.—A.E.

Apple Dowdy

Apple Dowdy is not a dumpling, a pudding, or a pie – deep-dish or otherwise. It is just a dowdy – sort of common, homely, gingham-like, but it has character.

To make it, you peel and quarter firm tart apples, and you lay them in a deep earthen pudding-dish. (The dowdy would probably reconcile itself to a glass baking-dish if it had to.)

You will fill the dish with apples, and over this sprinkle light-brown sugar, the amount depending upon the tartness of the apples and the size of your dish. Add a slight scattering of nutmeg, a little less of cinnamon, a dash of salt.

Now, with generous judgment, cut some slivers of butter over the whole, say about a teaspoonful to each serving. Then add half a cup of warm, not hot, water.

Make a rich baking-powder crust. (One cupful of flour, two teaspoonfuls of baking powder, two tablespoonfuls of butter, ¼ teaspoonful of salt, and half a cup of milk.) Roll this out to ¾ in. in thickness, cut a dido in the centre – you know, a big S with eyelet holes slashed alongside – and lay the crust over the apples, pinching it to the edge.

So far so good, but the proof of the dowdy is in the baking. It must be baked in a *slow* oven (300-350°) at least three hours. When done, it will be delicately brown on top, a rich fruity red on the inside, and delicious withal.

Serve it as Aunt Hanner did, with thick cream slightly sweetened and flavoured with nutmeg.—D.L.

Apple Dumplings

Having pared your apples, take out the core with an apple-scraper, and fill the hole with quince or orange marmalade, or sugar, as may suit you best. Then take a piece of cold paste, and make a hole in it, as if you were going to make a pie. Lay in your apple and put another piece of paste in the same form, and close it up round the side of your apple, which is much better than gathering it in a lump at one end. Tie it in a cloth and boil it three-quarters of an hour. Serve them up with melted butter poured over them.— (*John Farley's London Art of Cookery.* 1787.)

French Apple Dumpling (Chausson aux Pommes)

A *Chausson* is a *Feuilletage* paste filled with apples stewed and sweetened; also, usually flavoured with vanilla or nutmeg. The paste is closed tightly all round and shaped like a *Chausson* (carpet slipper) and then baked in a moderately hot oven till golden brown.

Apples Flambées

Have some good eating apples, all the same size and rather small. Peel them carefully and cook them slowly, so that they do not break, in water and sugar.

When soft, remove and drain them, keeping them hot. Add a little more sugar to the water and boil it till it has reduced to a syrup.

Dispose your apples in a metal serving-dish, pour a little syrup over each; warm some rum in a small saucepan, set it alight and pour it all over the apples. Serve whilst still burning.—X.M.B. (1).

Apple Fool

Stew slowly the required number of apples in a syrup of water and sugar till tender. Rub the apples through a sieve and let them get quite cold. Before serving, add to the apples, and mix thoroughly with it, some sweetened whipped cream in the proportion of a pint of cream to 1 lb. of fruit.

Apple Fritters

Pare and core a couple of fair-size eating apples; slice them and sprinkle sifted sugar over them. Make a batter with two tablespoonfuls of flour, a little baking powder, a well-beaten egg and a little milk: the consistency of the batter should be that of thick cream. Dip the slices of apples in this batter and drop them in boiling fat. Take them out as soon as they are dark brown in colour, drain on crumpled paper, and serve with a sprinkling of castor sugar.

Apple Hedgehog

1 lb. apples
Cream or custard
¾ lb. sugar

This favourite nursery dish is often promoted to the dining-room. Peel and core the apples, add sufficient water to the sugar to moisten it (if lump sugar dip it in water), put apples and sugar into a saucepan, and boil till the mixture drops from a spoon. Put into a mould and when turned out stick strips of blanched almonds all over it and cover with cream or custard.—H.P.

Apple Pie

Take six acid cooking apples, say 1½ lb. in weight. Peel and core them; cut them into quarters and each quarter in two. Line a pie-dish with a thin coating of pie paste; fill it with the apples, add from 4 to 6 oz. of white or brown sugar, a dusting of grated nutmeg and a few small pieces of quince, or three or four cloves if no quince can be obtained; put pats of butter over the fruit and then put the dish in a fairly hot oven and leave it in, covered, 15 or 20 minutes. Take out of oven and let the dish get quite cold. Make ¾ lb. flaky or rough puff paste and fold in three; put the folded paste over the pie-dish and unfold without stretching; press edges all round the pie-dish and bake for 30 minutes in fairly hot oven. Serve hot with castor sugar or cold with thick cream.

Apple Pudding

Grease a bowl and line it with suet and flour paste (*Pudding Paste*); put in two apples, peeled, cored and sliced, a piece of quince or a couple of cloves; cover with sugar and add another layer of apple slices; sprinkle these also with sugar and put on top the remainder of the paste; trim edges, cover with grease-proof paper and steam for three hours.

Apple Pudding

Half a pound of apples boiled, and squeezed through a hair sieve; ½ lb. of butter – beaten to a cream and mixed with the apples before they are cold, six eggs well beaten, ½ lb. of fine sugar – the rind of two lemons or oranges boiled well, shifting the water several times – then beat all together – bake them on a crust; half an hour will bake it.— (*MSS. Cook Book, prior 1839, Morton Family of Charlotte County, Virginia.*)—W.A.C.

Apple Puffs

  1 lb. good cooking apples
  Sugar
  ½ lb. flaky or puff paste
  A small piece stick cinnamon

Pare and core the apples, then slice them. Put the slices into a saucepan with two table-spoonfuls of cold water, and the piece of cinnamon, and stew until the apples are quite pulpy. Remove the cinnamon, sweeten to taste, and put the pulp away to cool.

When the apple is cold, roll out the puff paste to ¼ in. thickness. Cut strips 4 in. wide, then cut these across to make 4 in. squares; brush the edges of the squares over with cold water; put a tablespoonful of the apple pulp on one half of a square, then fold the other half over, corner to corner, so as to form a triangle. Press the edges firmly together, brush the puffs over with beaten-up white of egg, and sift icing sugar thickly over the top. Wet a clean baking-sheet with cold water, lay the puffs on it and bake in a fairly quick oven for 15 minutes, opening the door as little as possible.—E.C. (1).

Apple Rings

Peel and core some large, acid, cooking apples and slice them up horizontally in ½ in. thick rounds or 'rings'. Melt a spoonful of butter in a frying-pan and add twice as much castor sugar; mix well and put in the apple rings, when the butter begins to smoke – before it gets brown. Cook the apple rings in the hot caramel mixture, first one side and then the other, until both sides are golden. Serve hot.

Apple Snow

Wash and dry three large cooking apples; prick them in a few places and bake them in a moderately hot oven until they are soft. Remove the skin and rub the pulp through a sieve. Beat the white of one egg to a froth, adding 3 oz. castor sugar, little by little; then add apple pulp and beat it all together until thoroughly well mixed, light and soft.

Apple Soufflé

Peel, core the apples. Cook till tender and strain. To three pints of apple sauce add two tablespoonfuls butter. Add sugar, nutmeg and rum to taste. Add yolks of three eggs well beaten – leave – add beaten whites. Turn in baking-dish – sprinkle with macaroon crumbs. Bake 30 minutes. (*Frances Fay Manning.*)—T.C.

Stewed Apples

Peel the apples, cut them into halves and then into quarters and remove the cores. Cut the quarters into two or three length-ways and put the apples into a saucepan with a very little water and sugar to taste. The quantity of sugar used will, of course, depend on how many apples you have. Also some apples require more sugar, some less, but 1½ tablespoonfuls to 1 lb. of apples is about the average. Bring them to the boil and then reduce the heat. Allow them to simmer very gently till quite done, and try to keep the pieces of apple as whole as possible. Cool them before serving and serve with cinnamon and sugar.

Fruit should not be cooked in an iron saucepan, for the metal and fruit acids act on one another and destroy the good colour.— E.W.

Apple Tart

Peel and core 1½ lb. acid cooking apples; slice them and put them in a pan with from 4 to 6 oz. sugar, according to taste, and three or four pats of fresh butter. Cover the pan and stew on low heat for 15 minutes; then remove from the fire and let the apples get cold.

Prepare ½ lb. rough puff pastry and line a pastry tin with it; fill with the cold and partly-stewed apple slices; brush over with sugar, glaze and bake for 20 minutes. Serve cold with fresh cream.

Apple Turnover

2 good-sized apples finely chopped
1 tablespoon currants
1 tablespoon Demerara sugar
½ teaspoon powdered cinnamon
1 teaspoon chopped mixed peel

Mix all together and spread over the pastry in the roasting tin. Damp the edges of pastry all round with cold water, roll out the other half of the pastry and place it over the filling. Press the upper and lower edges of pastry together all round, pressing downwards with your thumbs, prick over the whole with a fork to allow moisture to escape while the filling is cooking, and bake in a moderate oven for half an hour.—E.W.

This is the filling to put in the paste cover.—ED.

APRICOT

Lat. *Prunus Armeniaca*; Fr. *Abricot*. A native of North China, extensively cultivated in Armenia a long time ago and now grown in all temperate countries. The best apricots come from the Loire Valley and other parts of France, whilst the greatest quantities of dried apricots come from California, Australia and the Cape region of South Africa.

Apricot Compôte

12 large apricots
2 cups cold water
1 cup sugar
½ cup brandy

Peel, cut in halves and stone fruit. Boil sugar and water 10 minutes, removing any scum that rises. Put in fruit carefully and let it simmer, being careful that it does not burn. When liquid is all absorbed, remove from fire, add brandy, and set in cool place until wanted.—C.R.B.B. (2).

Apricots à la Condé

Unmould upon serving-dish a border of boiled, sweetened, cold rice, flavoured with vanilla. Set upon this border of rice either whole apricots or halves, peeled and cooked in a light syrup of sugar and water. Decorate with some *fruits confits* and pour over it an apricot sauce flavoured with Kirsch.

Apricot Croûtons
(Belgian)

Cut slices of bread about ½ in. thick into dice, without any crust, and fry them crisp and golden in butter. Pile them on a dish and cover them with hot apricots stewed to a *purée*. Pour over all a syrup, made of Madeira in the proportion of half a cupful to a cupful of sugar boiled together for at least 10 minutes. Serve hot.—P.A.

Apricot Dumplings
(Marillenknoedel)

2 cups milk
1 cup flour
3 tablespoons butter
Fresh apricots

Melt the butter in the milk over a low flame, and season with salt. When it simmers, stir in the flour and cook till it no longer sticks to the spoon. Spread this paste on a floured board and roll out very thin. Drop the ripe apricots into boiling water for a minute or two, then remove the skin, which should come off quite easily. Wrap each apricot separately in a square of paste, rolling them until they are smooth balls. Drop these dumplings into slightly salted boiling water and cook until they rise to the top. Drain them carefully in a sieve to avoid breaking. Serve with hot butter and sprinkle with castor sugar and powdered cinnamon.—H.P.

Apricot Ice Cream

Peel and stone the apricots or open a can of apricots and drain fruit well. Boil some sugar and water, remove scum as it rises and add fruit; simmer until mushy and then let it get quite cold. Freeze three cups of thin cream for each cup of apricot pulp; add pulp, a pinch of salt and more or less sugar according to taste; also a dash of lemon juice; then freeze the lot and keep in the ice-box until wanted.

Apricot Jam
(Fresh Apricots)

Pare, halve and stone some ripe apricots, and having weighed both apricots and sugar, place the fruit in layers covered with their weight of preserving sugar, pound for pounds, in a pan; bring to the boil and then simmer gently for an hour or so, without stirring. Skim as scum rises and add the blanched kernels from the broken stones of the apricots.

Apricot Jam
(Dried Apricots)

Wash 1 lb. dried apricots, cut them up and soak them overnight in a quart of water. Put in a pan, with 2 lb. of sugar, on slow fire and bring to the boil. Boil for about three-quarters of an hour, then add 1 oz. of finely-cut Sweet Almonds. When the fruit is soft and of the right consistency, ready to set, pot and seal the jam.

Apricot Pie

Put into a saucepan 1½ pints of milk with enough sugar to taste. Let it get hot whilst you mix two tablespoonfuls of cornflour with three tablespoonfuls of cold milk till smooth, then pour into the almost boiling milk and stir till it thickens. Pour into a small basin, adding the beaten yolks of two eggs and the well-frothed whites of the eggs. Put the contents of a tin of apricots into a pie-dish, pour the mixture over them and bake in a hot oven for 15 minutes. Whip two tablespoonfuls of cream till stiff, dot lightly over pie, return to oven and bake till nicely brown. Sufficient for six or eight people.—L.G.N.

Old English Apricot Pudding

Blanch firm, or even under-ripe apricots; peel them, cut them in half, crack the stones, put the kernels in hot water for 20 minutes and stew the apricots very slowly till tender in syrup sweetened according to their ripeness. In a buttered pie-dish, lay a layer of bread and butter. Sprinkle it with sugar and the merest hint of powdered cinnamon. On this place a layer of apricots, then some of the kernels. Moisten it with grenadine or fresh fruit-juice cooked in the apricot syrup, and repeat the layers till the dish is full, ending with bread buttered on both sides and sprinkled with breadcrumbs. Half an hour in a medium oven will be sufficient.—P.A.

Apricot Snowballs

Boil one cup of rice 15 minutes, or till tender. Wring small pudding-cloths (1 foot square) out of hot water, lay them over a small bowl. Spread the rice ⅓ in. thick over the cloth. Put an apricot in the centre, filling the cavity in each half apricot with rice. Draw the cloth around until the apricot is covered smoothly with the rice. Tie tightly and steam 10 minutes. Remove the cloth carefully, and turn the balls out on a platter, and serve with apricot sauce.—P.D.P.

APRICOT PLUM

Lat. *Prunus Simonii*. A Chinese species of plum which looks rather like an apricot or a small nectarine. It was first introduced in Europe in 1867, when Eugène Simon, a French Consul in the Far East, sent a specimen to Paris. It has been grown extensively in the U.S.A., chiefly in various hybridized forms, which are better than the original Apricot Plum in flavour.

ARACHICHU

Lat. *Rollinia emarginata*. A South American native tree which produces edible fruits.

ARBUTE

Lat. *Arbutus unedo*; Fr. *Arbouse*. The name of the scarlet granular berries, about ¾ in. across, of the Strawberry-tree, a native or Southern Europe and of the Killarney district of Ireland. The berries are much used in Spain and Italy in confectionery; also in France in the making of liqueurs.

AUSTRALIAN CHESTNUT

See *Black Bean*.

AVOCADO PEAR

Lat. *Persea americana* (*Persea gratissima*); Fr. *Avocat*. The fruit of a tree which is a native of tropical Africa, but is now extensively grown in the West Indies, in the U.S.A., and in many tropical and sub-tropical countries. There are a number of different varieties, the fruit of which varies from 6 oz. to 4 lb., but the shape is fairly constant and pear-like. The best weigh from ½ lb. to 1 lb. and have a shiny green skin.

The *Avocado Pear*, which is sometimes – and wrongly – called *Alligator Pear*, is very rich in oil and protein matter as well as vitamins, particularly Vitamin B. It is usually cut in two, the large kernel being easily removed, and the cushion of flesh between the kernel and the outside skin is scooped out with a spoon and eaten as it is; it is nutty in flavour, buttery in consistency and, when the Avocado happens to be of the right breed and just ripe, there is no need to add anything to it whatsoever. However, a perfect Avocado is very rarely to be bought in a shop in England, where, as a rule, some sort of dressing is helpful. Some people are content with a sprinkling of salt; others favour a little white pepper; others a squeeze of lime or lemon and some sugar; and yet others believe in a French salad dressing of oil and vinegar. The flesh of the Avocado so dressed makes a very good salad. It has become one of the most popular luxury foods in the U.S.A.

AZAROLE

Lat. *Crataegus azarolus*. The *Neapolitan Medlar*, the fruit of a species of hawthorn indigenous to all lands of the Mediterranean basin; it is also grown in the Paris region. In Algeria, Italy and Spain the *Azarole* berries are largely used to make jam; elsewhere they are chiefly used in confectionery and to make liqueurs.

BADIAN

Lat. *Illicium verum*. The carminative fruit of the Chinese Anise-tree.

BAEL or BENGAL QUINCE

Lat. *Aegle marmelos*. The fruit of an East Indian Citrus tree; it is mostly used in the dried form for preserves or as a flavouring agent.

BALIMBI. BILIMBI

See *Carambola*.

BANANA

Lat. *Musa sapientium var. paradisiaca* and *Musa Cavendishii*; Fr. *Banane*. The edible fruit of a large herbaceous plant, the Banana Tree, a native of tropical Africa, now introduced in most tropical and many subtropical lands. There are a number of different named varieties of Bananas, but the two that are mostly sold in England and the U.S.A. are the *Plantain* and *Dwarf* or *Canary Banana*.

'The banana is plentiful and cheap; it is enclosed in an almost sterile container; the fat and protein factors are almost negligible, carbohydrates being the chief food constituents. In addition to the easily assimilable carbohydrates, it forms a good source of lime and iron and offers abundant vitamins, except Vitamin D, and as an anti-scorbutic it ranks second only to the orange. Its calorific value is much higher than that of the common fruits, and its energy value is greater than that of the potato.' (*Von Meysenburg. The banana as a food for infants and children. In New Orleans M. & S. Journal.* 1927. v. 80.)

Although the best way to give bananas to infants may be in a mashed and sieved form, adults prefer the fruit in the natural state, by itself or with a little fresh cream. Besides its use as dessert, the Banana lends itself to many preparations and combinations.

Uncooked, bananas may be served as hors-d'oeuvre, cut up in thin slices and dressed with a vinaigrette or mayonnaise sauce. They are also used in various salads, both green salads with an oil and vinegar dressing and fruit salads with sweet fruit juice and various liqueurs. Ripe bananas are best uncooked. Unripe bananas are not fit to eat and over-ripe bananas are not safe to eat. Cooked bananas, ripe or not, lose most of their flavour and gain nothing in the cooking, but they supply a sweetish, pappy background in certain dishes. The *Cuisine Classique* has never encouraged the use of the banana in fine cooking, but there are a number of typically American dishes in which bananas are used, sometimes with meat or fowl, as in the *Chicken Stanley*, but mostly as sweets, pies, fritters, baked puddings, etc.

The Mexican and Central American *Platanao macho* or *Plantain Banana* is picked before it is ripe and when unfit to eat except cooked, like a vegetable. It is more starchy than the *Canary Banana*, and, being unripe, it is not sweet.

Baked Bananas with Lemon

3 small bananas peeled and scraped
3 tablespoonfuls of brown sugar
1 tablespoonful of butter
3 thin slices of lemon, halved

Place the bananas, whole, in a buttered oven-proof baking-dish. Cover with the sugar, patting down in place, and dot with the butter. Lay two half slices of lemon on each banana. Bake in a moderately hot oven (375° F.) for 15 minutes, basting only towards the end of the time. Serves three persons.—E.K.H.

Banana Dainty

4 very ripe bananas
2 cups whipped cream
½ tablespoonful orange or lemon juice

Skin and scrape the bananas; put through potato ricer or sieve and strain. Add sugar and orange juice; mix very lightly; then fold in the whipped cream. Serve in glasses and garnish with sections of orange. Serves six. —P.D.P.

Banana and Raspberry Cream

Cut up your bananas into rounds, put into a serving-dish and cover with a mixture of equal parts of thick cream and fresh raspberries crushed through a sieve, with sugar to taste.—M.K.S. (2).

Banana Creole

Slice your bananas lengthways into a buttered fireproof dish, sprinkle with brown sugar, pour over a good glassful of Rum and cook in the oven until the sugar is dissolved. —M.K.S. (2).

Creamed Bananas

3 large bananas
2 tablespoonfuls of powdered sugar
1 cupful of cream
¼ cupful of Sherry

Peel and force the bananas through a ricer or medium strainer. Mix in the sugar, add the cream, and beat with a wire whip for 10 minutes, or until thickened. Beat in the Sherry gradually. Turn into a serving-bowl and chill for 1½ hours. This may also be piled in scooped-out orange halves. Very good in place of ice-cream. Serves four to five persons.—E.K.H.

Banana Trifle

4 to 6 bananas
Apricot jam
½ gill Sherry
½ pint cream

Take off the skins of the bananas, cut them lengthways, spread with jam and lay them in a glass dish, pour over the Sherry and allow them to soak. Just before serving pour over the cream, which should be half whipped, garnish with some banana on the top.—P.D.P.

Amarillos al Sarten
(Stewed Ripe Plantains)

2 ripe plantains
¼ cup butter
1 stick cinnamon
1½ cups hot water
¼ cup sugar

Fry ripe plantains in butter until light brown. Add hot water, sugar and cinnamon. Cover and cook until bananas are soft. Number of servings, four. (*Puerto Rico Recipe*.)—C.G.

Renellos de Amarillo
(Stuffed ripe Plantains)

Filling: ½ lb. pork, 1 oz. ham, 1 oz. salt pork, 1 oz. onion, 2 oz. tomatoes, 1 oz. green pepper, ¼ cup water, 1 tablespoon fat, ½ tablespoon salt, 2 leaves coriander, 1 sprig parsley, ¼ cup olives, 2 tablespoons capers, 2 tablespoons raisins, ½ teaspoon annatto seeds; fat.

Boil three ripe plantains and mash them. Chop finely ham, salt pork, onion, tomato, pepper, and cook in one tablespoonful fat; add hot water and salt. Chop coriander and parsley very fine, cut olives, capers and raisins and add to pork Add half teaspoonful annatto seeds. Take about one-third cup of mashed ripe plantain, place on floured plate and spread flat into a circle. Put one tablespoonful filling into the centre, and bring edges together to shape into a ball. Fry in deep fat until brown. Drain on brown paper. Number of servings, nine. (*Puerto Rico Recipe*).—C.G.

BAOBAB

Lat. *Adansonia digitata*. A tropical tree, chiefly found in Africa, where it is also known under the name of *Monkey Bread Tree*. The mucilaginous pulp of the fruit has a pleasant if somewhat acid taste and is used chiefly to make a cooling drink. The leaves are powdered and used in soups and stews as a condiment.

BARBADOS CHERRY

Lat. *Malpighia glabra*. The acid berries of a West Indian tree; they resemble cherries in shape and size and must be cooked, in pies or tarts, to be acceptable.

BARBADOS GOOSEBERRY

Lat. *Pereskia esculenta*. The smooth, sweetish fruit of a West Indian Cactus; edible but not enjoyable. The name is also sometimes given to the *Tomato Strawberry* (q.v.).

BARBERRY, BERBERRY

Lat. *Berberis angulosa* (Himalayan Barberry); *B. aristata* (Nepal Barberry); *B. asiatica* (Asiatic Barberry); *B. buxifolia* (Magellan Barberry); *B. canadensis* (Allegheny Barberry); *B. Darwinni* (Darwin's Barberry); *B. vulgaris* (Common Barberry). The berry of the *Berberis*, a genus widely distributed in the temperate regions of the five continents. The common barberry, a native of temperate Europe and Asia, was introduced in North America at an early date, and it grows now in a wild state in a great many localities. Both in the British Isles and in the U.S.A. barberries are used for sauces, tarts and pies, and they are also preserved in sugar or syrup as comfits, but their use is not nearly so general now as it used to be. In Scandinavia, barberries are used to make cooling drinks and to flavour ices, sherbets and punches. In some parts of Normandy they use a seedless variety of barberry (*Epinevinette*) to make a delicious preserve.

Among Eastern varieties of the barberry, the following are deserving of mention: the *Himalayan Barberry*, which bears particularly large berries; the *Nepal Barberry*, with purple berries which are dried in the sun, in India, and used as dessert, like raisins; the *Asiatic Barberry*, which is said to make the finest raisins in India and is sometimes cultivated in English gardens; the *Magellan Barberry*, or *Calafate*, which bears large, black and well-flavoured berries in South America; and the *Darwin Barberry*, from Chile, grown a great deal in England as an ornamental shrub and bearing an abundance of edible little berries.

The *Blue Barberry* of the Pacific Coast is not a *Berberis* but a name given to the berries of several species of native American *Mahonias*; they are used in the making of refreshing drinks and as flavouring agents for ices and preserves.

Barberry Cheese

Prepare the ripe barberries carefully and put them into a brown earthenware jar, add 1 pint of water to 3 lb. of fruit and bake in a slow oven until quite soft. Pass through a hair sieve, and add an equal quantity of powdered sugar. Mix well together and put into a preserving pan, and bring to the boil and boil for about 15 minutes, or until it will set when tested.—L.G.N.

BEAR HURTLEBERRY

See *Huckleberry*.

BENGAL QUINCE

See *Bael*.

BERGAMOT

1. Lat. *Monarda di Syma*. An ornamental plant the leaves of which, when dried, are used for flavouring and to make *Oswego Tea*.

2. Lat. *Pyrus communis*. One of the oldest Pears known in England, where it was cultivated during the Middle Ages, and may have been introduced by the Romans. The original bergamot is not grown to any extent now. There are two other winter varieties of bergamot pears, *B. d'Esperen* and *B. d'Heimbourg*; also an early variety known as *Bergamotte de Pâques* or *Easter Beurré*. In English literature, up to the nineteenth century, bergamot invariably stands for the bergamot pear:

> 'Who, from his private garden, where
> He lived reserved and austere
> (As if his highest plot
> To plant the Bergamot)'
> *(Andrew Marvell on Cromwell)*

3. Lat. *Citrus bergamia*. Bergamot is also the name of a kind of orange, rather like a pear in shape, which is cultivated extensively in Calabria for the sake of an essential oil, the oil of bergamot, obtained from its rind. Bergamot rind is also used in confectionery and cookery as a flavouring agent.

BILBERRY, BLAEBERRY
Lat. *Vaccinium myrtillus*; Fr. *Airelles des bois*. An English berry, naturalized in the U.S.A. The name bilberry is given in the U.S.A. to a number of different berries mostly found in woods and copses on hillsides and used in the making of pies and tarts, jams and jellies, either by themselves or mixed with some other and more acid fruit. Bilberries are usually in season in late August and throughout September.

There are many local names given to bilberries in different parts of Great Britain, such as Whortleberries or Worts; Hurts, in Surrey; Whinberries, in the North of England; Blaeberries in Westmorland and in Scotland.

Bilberry Fritters
Make a good unsweetened fritter batter. Add enough bilberries to make it quite thick. Drop fritters into hot fat or butter (not deep) and cook as apple fritters. Drain and coat liberally with castor sugar and serve at once.

Bilberry Jam
Pick over 1 lb. of ripe bilberries carefully and warm them in a preserving-pan until the juice begins to run freely, then add 1 lb. of sugar, bring to the boil and go on cooking until the jam is of the right consistency.

BILIMBI. BALIMBI
See *Carambola*.

BLACK APPLE
See *Bush Apple*.

BLACK BEAN. AUSTRALIAN CHESTNUT
Lat. *Castanospermum australe*. The seeds – and also the wood – of a handsome Australian tree which bears large pods containing three or four chestnut-like seeds – sometimes called *Moreton Bay Chestnuts*; these are roasted and eaten like chestnuts (q.v.).

BLACK BEARBERRY
Lat. *Arctostaphylos alpinus*. A depressed Arctic-Alpine shrub, which bears edible, black berries.

BLACKBERRY
Lat. *Rubus Allegheniensis* (American Mountain Blackberry); *Rubus argutus* (American Wild Blackberry); *Rubus fructicosus* (European Wild Blackberry or Bramble); *Rubus laciniatus* (Oregon ever-bearing or evergreen Blackberry); *Rubus nigrobaccus* (American 'high-bush' cultivated Blackberry); *Rubus ursinus* (Pacific Blackberry). Fr. *Mûres de ronces*. Blackberries are the fruit of (*a*) the European thorny bramble, the growth of which is as difficult to check in woods and hedges, as it is to coax in gardens; and (*b*) of different varieties of hybridized native American brambles, cultivated on an important scale in the northern States of the U.S.A.

The wild blackberry has been gathered in the U.K. for many centuries past, but it has been cultivated on a commercial scale during the past few years only; in the U.S.A. the cultivated blackberry dates from the second half of the nineteenth century.

Blackberries deteriorate quicker than any other fruit after being picked; they should always be eaten on the same day as picked. Blackberries are not necessarily ripe when black; they must be soft, as well as black, and detached without bruising. Then, and then only, are blackberries sweet and juicy and probably the best of all bush berries.

Blackberries have long been used in English home cookery to a much greater extent than in the U.S.A. They are used with or without apples in the making of pies and puddings, jam and jellies. Many people, however, find the seeds in *Blackberry Jam* rather a nuisance, who have nothing but praise for *Bramble Jelly*, the old-fashioned name of an old English favourite, the *Blackberry Jelly*.

Blackberry and Apple Pie
Fill a pie-dish with a pint of washed blackberries and a pound of tart cooking apples, peeled, cored and cut up in small pieces. Place an egg-cup in the centre of the dish; cover the fruit with 3 or 4 oz. castor sugar. Cover the dish with pie paste, prick around edges and bake in a quick oven for 1½ hours.

Blackberry Dillie

Boil 1 lb. of blackberries slowly with a gill of water, then pass through a fine sieve. Boil for a few minutes 4 oz. of sugar in a gill of water and melt ¾ oz. of gelatine in a third of a gill of water. Mix the three liquids together and pour into a cold wetted mould. Sufficient for two or three people.—L.G.N.

Blackberry Pancakes

1 cup flour
2 tablespoons sugar
1 egg
1 cup blackberries
1 tablespoon butter
1 cup milk

Mix together the flour, blackberries, sugar, egg yolk, and milk to a smooth batter. Melt the butter and stir in, then add the stiffly-beaten egg white. Heat a little butter in a frying-pan and make small pancakes by covering the pan very thinly with the mixture. Brown on both sides. Serve hot accompanied by a sauce-boat full of ice-cream.—H.P.

Blackberry Batter Pudding

Cream one-third cup of butter with two heaping tablespoonfuls of sugar, add two well-beaten eggs, then alternately add one cup of milk and two cups of flour sifted with two level teaspoonfuls of baking powder and one-half teaspoonful of salt. Beat well. Place a layer of the batter in a round cake-pan which has been well buttered and lightly floured, cover with two cups of sugared blackberries, and over the berries pour the remaining batter. Bake in a moderate oven for 25 to 30 minutes. When done, spread over top creamed butter and a sprinkling of brown sugar. Run under flame a moment to melt the sugar. Serve with a hard sauce or heavy cream.—G.T.L.

Blackberry Mousse

Stew the blackberries and pass them through a sieve until you have at least a pint of *purée*. Sweeten it and mix with the whites of two eggs beaten to a stiff froth. Then mix in some whipped cream and serve cold.—P.G.

Blackberry Pudding

2 cups blackberries
2 eggs
2 tablespoons butter
¾ cup sugar
1 teaspoon baking powder
1 cup flour

Cream the butter, then add flour, sugar and beaten eggs. Then put in the blackberries. When all is well mixed, add the baking powder and a touch of bicarbonate of soda. Put in a pudding basin (or mould),

262

and steam for three-quarters of an hour. You can serve ice-cream with this hot pudding if you care to.—P.G. (1).

Bramble Jelly

Pick over some sound, ripe – but not over-ripe – blackberries and bake them slowly in a moderate oven until they are quite soft. Pour them then into a jelly bag, a little at a time, fruit and juice as it comes, but remove all solid parts of one lot before putting in another. When you have run all the juice in that way, add to it 1 lb. of sugar per pint of juice and boil gently until the jelly sets.

BLACK CURRANT

Lat. *Ribes nigrum*; Fr. *Cassis*. A European bush fruit which has been improved by cultivation during the last two hundred years or so. There is a native American species which is very similar but has never received much attention from horticulturists: it is found from Nova Scotia to Virginia and westwards to the Rocky Mountains; its wild fruits are edible but not greatly prized.

Black Currants have many more admirers in the British Isles than in the U.S.A. Some of the Black Currant Pies, Puddings, Tarts, Jams and Jellies are amongst the more popular English recipes. Black Currants also make very good ice-creams, and one of the best known French Liqueurs is made with Black Currants; it is known as *Cassis*.

The three varieties now generally grown in the United Kingdom are *Baldwin*, *Boskoop Giant* and *Goliath*; in France, the most popular variety is *Merveille de la Gironde*.

Black Currant Ices

1. Boil a pint of Black Currants with ½ lb. sugar as if making jam. When the fruit is quite soft, pass through a fine sieve, add a squeeze of lemon and beat in as much fresh cream as you can spare. Freeze and serve.

2. Wash a handful of young green Black Currant leaves and boil them for a few minutes in a syrup of sugar and water; cover the pan and let contents cool; strain when cold and put in a freezing machine; the result will be a cooling water ice with a delicate and very pleasant Black Currant flavour, not so good, of course, as the real fruit ice, but none the less acceptable.

Black Currant Jam

Boil 3 lb. of sugar in a pint of water until it throws up large bubbles and is quite clear. Then add 2 lb. *Black Currants* and boil 20 minutes or a little longer if necessary. Remove scum and fill pots.

Black Currant Jam Roll

Chop finely ¼ lb. of suet and mix it with ½ lb. flour and sufficient water to make a stiff dough, not forgetting a pinch of salt. Roll out and spread evenly with Black Currant Jam; roll up, pinching the ends together, tie in a cloth and boil for about an hour.

Black Currant Pie
A Black Currant Pie is made like any other fruit pie, fruit and sugar in a pie-dish baked with a paste over it until the paste be crisp and brown. Served with fresh cream, it is one of the best and most typically English fruit pies.

Black Currant Pudding
After removing any hard bottom crust, break into small pieces stale bread to fill three breakfast cups (about 1 lb.). Pour over as much cold milk as the bread will absorb and beat to a smooth mass, which should be fairly dry. Stir in a barely-filled teacup (4 oz.) each of chopped suet and sugar and two eggs. Spread one-third of this at the bottom of a greased pie-dish and add a good layer of Black Currants previously half-cooked with sugar to sweeten, draining off most of the juice. Cover with half of the remaining mixture, and another deep layer of fruit and spread what remains of the bread mixture on top. Bake in a moderate oven for 1½ hours. The juice drained off should be kept warm in readiness to serve with the pudding. Sufficient for six or eight people.—L.G.N.

To Preserve Black Currants
6 lb. of ripe Black Currants, 6 lb. of Demerara sugar, 12 cloves. Bruise the cloves, put them in a muslin bag and drop them into a 12 lb. stone jar. Fill up with alternate layers of Black Currants and sugar. Soak a piece of notepaper in brandy and place on top, then cover the jar, taking care to make it airtight and the currants will keep for any time.

Black Currant Tea
One of the old English household remedies for children with a cold, a hot drink made of Black Currant Jam diluted in boiling water. Adults prefer to cure or to ward off colds with a stronger edition of the same nature, either *Cassis*, a French liqueur made with Brandy and flavoured with Black Currants, or English cordials made with Gin and Black Currants.

BLACK GUAVA
Lat. *Guettarda argentea*. The black, edible fruit of a guava tree which grows in Jamaica and Guiana.

BLACK RASPBERRY
Lat. *Rubus occidentalis*. A species of raspberry bearing black fruit. It is a native of the Eastern States of America and is cultivated in New England for its fruit, which is commonly known as *Blackcap*.

BLACK SAPOTA
Lat. *Diospyros ebenastor*. A Mexican *Persimmon* (q.v.) with an almost seedless, dark-fleshed fruit of pleasant taste.

BLAEBERRY
See *Bilberry*.

BLUEBERRY
Lat. *Vaccinium canadensis* (Canadian Blueberry); *Vaccinium corymbosum* (High Blueberry); *Vaccinium pennsylvanicum* and *V. vacillans* (Low Blueberries); *Myoporum serratum* (Australian Blueberry). The berries of a number of *Vaccinium* bushes widely distributed in the U.S.A. and Canada. Here are the characteristics of the principal varieties:

High Blueberry. (Syn. *Swamp Blueberry*.) This species inhabits bogs and moist woods from Maine to Minnesota and southward. The fruit ripens from August to late September; it is blue-black with bloom when ripe, sweet and of pleasant flavour. It is grown in gardens as an ornamental shrub as well as for its berries.

Low Blueberry. (Syn. *Sweet Blueberry*.) This species is found covering great areas in dry heaths, pine barrens, and mountain lands from Newfoundland to Saskatchewan, and southward to Virginia and Illinois. Its fruit ripens in July and supplies most of the blueberries to be bought in markets. The berries are sweet and more agreeable than the *High Blueberries*, but they are soft and easily bruised.

Canadian Blueberry. (Syn. *Sour-top*.) This is a low blueberry found on dry plains, swamps and in woods from Labrador to Manitoba, southward to Illinois, and in the mountains to Virginia. The fruit ripens late; it is blue, small, acid and altogether inferior to the preceding two species.

The name blueberry is also given to the edible berries of an Australian tree known locally as *Native Myrtle*, *Native Juniper* or *Cockatoo Bush*. There is also in Australia a tree known as the *Blueberry Ash* which bears edible berries.

Blueberries are used in pies, puddings, jams, jellies, sauces and preserves.

Blueberry Pie
Line a deep pie-pan with pastry. Fill with blueberries and seasoning, using the following proportions:

    2½ cups blueberries
    ⅛ teaspoon salt
    ½ cup sugar
    2 tablespoons flour

Mix blueberries, flour, sugar and salt. Cover with pastry. Bake in a hot oven (425° F.) about 45 minutes or until crust is delicately browned. (*Maine recipe*.)—C.G.

BOG STRAWBERRY
See *Cowberry*.

BRAZIL CHERRY
See *Cape Gooseberry*.

BRAZIL NUT
Lat. *Bertholletia excelsa*; Fr. *Noix Péchurine*. The large, globular fruit of a South American tree; its hard, woody casing contains from 18 to 24 closely-packed oily, three-angled nuts, hard to crack but nutritious and much used in confectionery.

BREAD FRUIT
Lat. *Artocarpus incisa* (*Treculia africana*). A native fruit of the South Sea Islands now cultivated in all tropical countries, where it provides one of the most valuable foods of the natives. It is somewhat similar in shape and size to a green melon. It is usually treated as a vegetable, boiled and eaten like vegetable marrow, with a sauce, or stuffed with various preparations of meat. It may also be cut in slices and baked or fried in oil. The natives of Guam use it as bread, baking it in an oven; the Tahitians live on little else besides Bread Fruit, fish and bananas. Its starchy content is very high and it is comparable in food value to the potato. 'With meat and gravy, it is a vegetable superior to anything I know, either in temperate or tropical countries. With sugar, milk, butter or treacle it is a delicious pudding, having very slight and delicate but characteristic flavour, which, like that of good bread and potatoes, one never gets tired of.' (*A.R. Wallace*. Malay Archipelago.) Bread Fruit should be picked just before it is quite ripe; it should be eaten as soon as picked; it does not keep well, nor does it travel at all well.

BUCKBERRY
See *Hurtleberry*.

BUFFALO-BERRY. RABBIT-BERRY. NEBRASKA CURRANT
Lat. *Shepherdia argentea*. A North American bushy tree which grows wild in woodlands and waste lands chiefly in the Dakotas and Minnesota, where it is also used for hedges. It is cultivated in the colder parts of the Great Plains. The buffalo-berry is one of the hardiest of wild fruits, being found as far north as Manitoba and Saskatchewan. The berries are round or ovoid, the size of a large currant, red or yellow when ripe, acid but pleasantly flavoured. They are chiefly used for making sauces and are considered to provide the best sauce to eat with buffalo-meat, hence their name. They also make good jams and preserves.

BUFFALO-CURRANT
Lat. *Ribes odoratum*. This is a cultivated variety of the American currant, which grows wild from Missouri to Arkansas. The fruit has a distinctly aromatic quality of its own, which some people like very much and others dislike intensely. It is used chiefly in pies and preserves.

It is sometimes called *Missouri Currant*, a name which applies also to a closely related species, the *Golden Currant* (q.v.).

BULLACE
Lat. *Prunus insititia*. The name given to all the wild forms of the Damascus Plumtree; the fruit is not fit to eat as dessert but it is very good cooked or for making jam and jellies. It can be used in any way suitable for Damson (q.v.). Bullace should be left on the tree till the frosts come; in any case they ripen – when the summer is particularly hot – long after all other plums are ripe and picked.

BULLOCK'S HEART
Lat. *Anona reticulata*. The name given to a West Indian *Annona* (q.v.). It is a small tree which has been introduced in India, where it is now extensively cultivated, as also elsewhere in the tropics. The fruit is covered with soft prickles of a light-green colour; it has a peculiar but rather agreeable sour taste and a scent not unlike that of black currants. It is largely used to make a pleasant and refreshing beverage.

BURITI
See *Palmas*.

BUSH APPLE. BLACK APPLE
Lat. *Sideroxylon australe*. The large, plum-like fruit of an Australian tree (*Syderoxylon australe*); it is also known in Australia as *Native Plum*, *Wild Plum*, or *Rose Apple*.

CACAO
See *Chocolate Tree*.

CALABASH NUTMEG
Lat. *Morodora miristica*. The fruit of a tropical shrub; in size it resembles the average orange, and it contains many aromatic seeds which are used like nutmegs.

CALAFATE or MAGELLAN BARBERRY
Lat. *Berberis buxifolia*. The most highly valued *Barberry* (q.v.) of South America, bearing large, black and well-flavoured berries.

CAMAMBU
Lat. *Physalis viscosa*. The gooseberry-like fruit of a South American shrub.

CAPE GOOSEBERRY

Lat. *Physalis peruviana*. The edible, acid berry of different varieties of the bush *Physalis*, more particularly that of *P. peruviana*. It is a native of tropical America and it is now extensively grown in South Africa. It is also grown in Northern India, in the hills, where it is more usually known by the name of *Brazil Cherry*. It is also grown commercially in the South of France under the names of *Alkekenge*, *Coqueret* and *Physalis*. Cape Gooseberries can be eaten out of hand or boiled in a syrup, as a comfit, but they are best when made into jam, jelly or fruit cheese, in the same way as *Damson Cheese* (q.v.).

Cape Gooseberry Jam
1 lb. sugar to 1 lb. of fruit
Take off the hull and the stem from the gooseberries. Wash them well; weigh them and place them in preserving pan. Allow to simmer gently, break them up with a wooden spoon. Add the hot sugar, stir until sugar is dissolved. When boiling, cook quickly until it jellies – 20 minutes to half an hour. Do not cook past jellying point. Bottle while hot. When cold, put brandy paper on top and seal.—P.R.M.

CARAMBOLA

Lat. *Averrhoa carambola*. The acid fruit of a Malay and Indian tree. It is mostly used preserved in sugar as a sweetmeat and it is also known as the *Chinese* or the *Coromandel Gooseberry*.

CASHEW NUT

Lat. *Anacardium occidentale*. A South American tree now introduced in many tropical lands. The fleshy and juicy pedicle of its ripe fruit is eaten uncooked, as dessert fruit, and it also makes very good jam. Its astringent juice is fermented and made into an alcoholic beverage called *Cajuáda*.

CHAÑAR

Lat. *Gourliea decorticans*. A South American tree the fruit of which is eaten raw by the Indians; they also use it to prepare an alcoholic beverage known as *Aloja de chañar*.

CHECKERBERRY

See *Winterberry*.

CHERIMOYA

Lat. *Anona Cherimolia*. The custard-apple-like fruit of a small tree, a native of tropical America. 'Cherimoyas rank in delicacy of flavour and texture with the best fruits that grow and yet so little have they found their way into the markets of the world that I doubt whether one person out of 10,000 in the United States has ever seen one. The fruit grows best in an oceanic climate at altitudes of 1,000 ft. or so, but nevertheless I now grow hybrids of it and every year enjoy its fragrant and delicate flavour.'—D.F.

CHERRY

Lat. *Prunus avium*; *P. cerasus*; *P. pennsylvanica*; *P. serotina*; Fr. *Cerise*. Of the hundred and twenty odd different sorts of wild Cherries known to botanists, two are cultivated in all temperate regions of the world: the Sour Cherry and the Sweet Cherry.

Sour Cherries. There are over three hundred varieties of Sour Cherries cultivated for their fruit and they all belong to one or the other of the three following groups:

(*a*) *Amarelles*. They are pale red fruits with colourless juice. In spite of their name (*amarus*: bitter) they are the least acid of the Sour Cherries and the only ones suitable for eating out of hand as dessert fruit. The common representatives of this group are the *Montmorency* (often called in France *La Cerise Anglaise*), *Early Richmond*, and the various Cherries bearing the name Amarelle, such as *King Amarelle*, *Späte Amerelle*, etc.

(*b*) *Morellos*. The two main varieties of Morellos are the *Black Morello*, a dark coloured fruit with acid, coloured juice, and the *Red Morello*, a name given to a number of pale red, acid varieties of which the bitter Kentish Cherry is the prototype. Their French name is *Griottes*.

(*c*) *Damasca*. A Dalmatian Cherry from which the Maraschino liqueur is made. The fruit is much smaller than other Sour Cherries; it is dark red, almost black, and both the flesh and juice are deep red in colour and bitter of taste.

Sweet Cherries. There are about six hundred different varieties of Sweet Cherries, most of them belonging to one or the other of the three following groups:

(*a*) *Geans* or *Guignes*, of which the two main sorts are the *Black* with dark skin, sweet, tender and dark-coloured flesh; and the *Red*, with pale coloured skin, sweet, soft and translucent flesh. Typical Black Geans or Guignes are *Black Tartarian*, *Early Purple* and *Eagle*; typical Red Geans or Guignes are *Coe*, *Ida*, *Elton* and *Waterloo*.

(*b*) *Bigarreaus* or *Hearts*. These are distinguished by the firm, breaking flesh of the fruits. They are also distinguished by the colour of their skin as *Black Hearts*, of which *Windsor*, *Schmidt* and *Mezel* are popular varieties; and the *White Hearts*, of which *Yellow Spanish* and *Napoleon* are two out of a large number of varieties.

Duke Cherries. These are hybrids between the Sour and the Sweet Cherries; they are known in France as *Royale*. They originated in the Médoc and the parent variety was dubbed in England and the U.S.A. *May*

Duke; there are some sixty-five varieties of these Cherries and they are also subdivided into two categories according to their colouring. *Black Dukes* are dark of skin and flesh and their juice is deeply coloured. The *May Duke* is the prototype of this group. *Red Dukes* have pale red, translucent skin and flesh and their juice is colourless. *Reine Hortense* is the prototype of the group.

Morello Cherry Bounce

Gather and pick your cherries when perfectly ripe, put them into a tub and mash them with a rolling-pin, stones and all, and to every five pints of cherries put a quart of rum, let it stand a week; strain it through a flannel bag; to every gallon of bounce put three-fourths of a pound of brown sugar. Cheap rum answers equally as well as the best spirit for bounce.—w.a.c.

Cherry Brandy

Take 10 lb. of Morello cherries, pound them and their stones in a mortar, add 3 lb. of lump sugar and 1 oz. of bitter almonds, chopped. Put these into large stone jars, adding one gallon of Brandy. Cork and shake every day for the first month and then occasionally for three months. Strain through a jelly bag and bottle for use. It should be kept for a year before use.

Compôte of Cherries

Put some red cherries into a large shallow saucepan with just enough Claret to cover them. Flavour with sugar and a tiny pinch of cinnamon. Bring this slowly to the boil, and as soon as it boils take the pan off the fire, cover and let the cherries simmer very gently indeed (they should do no more than poach) for 10 minutes. Take the cherries out, reduce the syrup a little, and when it is cooling stir into it a tablespoonful of red currant jelly for each pound of cherries. It should be served very cold, and cream may be handed, though the flavour of the wine is better without it.—a.h. (1).

Flan de Cerises

Make a flaky paste and cover a round tartlet-dish. Make a French pastry cream, using half milk and half boiled cream. Fill the pastry with alternate layers of the cream and of cherries poached previously in a syrup of water and sugar. (*Sir Daniel Hall recommends a mixture of sweet cherries and of Morellos that have been soaking in brandy.*) Finally a top layer of cream; cook in a slow oven and serve either hot or cold.

Cherry Ice Cream

Two cups thin cream or one cup thin cream and one cup milk; one cup sugar; two cups chopped cherries, canned in syrup.

Add the sugar to the cherries, let stand for 15 or 20 minutes. Strain if desired, add the cream and freeze.—c.g.

Cherry Laurette

2 lb. large black cherries; 1 lb. jar red currant jelly; 2 tablespoons brandy; 1 lb. sugar; 2 lb. raspberries; half a lemon; 1 egg white.

This is a particularly delicious hot-weather sweet. First make some raspberry water-ice as follows: crush the raspberries in a pint of cold water and strain. Make a syrup with one pint water and 1 lb. sugar, cool, and add the raspberry juice and lemon juice. Freeze this mixture and when half frozen fold in the stiffly-beaten white of egg. While this is freezing, melt the currant jelly with the brandy, stone the cherries and add them to the malted jelly, then let cool. When ready to serve put a portion of raspberry ice on each plate and pour over some of the cherries.—h.p.

Cherry Pie

Boil the required quantity of cherries to fill the pie-dish. Put the cherries and the juice in which they were boiled in the pie-dish; add sugar to taste and cover with a lid of short crust, having first of all placed a band of paste upon the wetted edge of the dish, and having pressed it all round, put in a brisk oven to begin with, and then in a slow one for 40 or 50 minutes. Serve hot or cold with a sprinkling of castor sugar on top.

Cherry Tart

Line a flan-tin with a light 'Tart' crust; trim and crimp the edges. Bake the crust in a brisk oven until brown. Spread on the crust a rich cream filling and set in it enough cherries to cover the whole surface. The cherries must be stoned first and boiled in water and sugar; the syrup in which they are cooked is simmered, after the cherries are taken out, and long enough to become quite thick, when it is used to glaze the cherries.

CHESTNUT

Lat. *Castanea sativa* (European); *C. dentata* (American); and *C. crenata* (Japanese); Fr. *Châtaigne* and *Marron*. The nut of any variety of the *Castanea* tree, chiefly that of the Spanish or Sweet Chestnut tree, and that of the closely allied American species, now nearly extinct owing to the chestnut blight; also the nut of the Japanese Chestnut tree.

Chestnuts are used both in cookery, roasted, boiled or mashed, for stuffing and garnishing; and in confectionery, for cake filling, ices and sweet puddings; they are also greatly prized when steeped in a sweet syrup, from which they emerge as *Marrons glacés*.

Boiled Chestnuts

Split the skins at the pointed end and put the chestnuts into a saucepan; cover them over with cold water and bring to the boil. Take them out of the water and skin them. Put them back in a pan with just enough stock to cover, and simmer for 45 minutes or an hour.

Mashed Chestnuts

Split the skin at the pointed end and put in a hot oven in a dish with a little water for about eight minutes. Take them out and peel them whilst they are warm. Drop them into a panful of boiling water for a few moments and drain. Rub off the second skin and then simmer the chestnuts in some good vegetable stock. When soft, take them out and rub them through a sieve. Return the mashed chestnuts to the pan, stir in some fresh butter and season with either pepper and salt or sifted sugar, according to what you want to do with the *purée*. At the last moment, add a little warmed cream and stir well in.

Monte Bianco

One of the most popular of winter sweets in Italy. It is made of riced boiled chestnuts, with a little cream, Marsala or brandy added, and vanilla. It is then piled in a mound on a dish and covered with whipped cream.

Nesselrode Pudding

One of the best iced puddings; it was introduced by Mony, Chef to the famous Count Nesselrode. It is made of chestnuts, cream and eggs, as well as some currants and raisins.

Roast Chestnuts

Split the skin at the pointed end and roast in front of a bright coal fire (failing which in the oven) until the chestnuts gape open and are deeply coloured.

Soufflé de Marrons

Mash and pass through a sieve some boiled chestnuts, enough to fill a breakfast cup; add a little cream and sweeten to taste, bring to the boil and cook a few minutes to dry the mixture. Add four yolks of eggs and mix well, let it cool; add five whipped whites, fill the soufflé dish and cook like any soufflé, about 14 minutes in a moderate oven.—X.M.B. (1).

Chestnut Soup

1 lb. chestnuts
2 oz. butter
1 large Spanish onion
1 small head of celery
1 lb. potatoes
1 bouquet garni (mixed herbs)

Peel the chestnuts; scald them and skin them, then chop them up. Put three pints of water in a pan to boil, and when the water boils add the chestnuts, the butter, the potatoes peeled and sliced, the onion chopped, the head of celery and the *bouquet garni*. Season with pepper and salt. Bring to the boil again and then simmer gently for two hours or longer. Pass through a colander; return to pan; re-heat and stir in some thick cream before serving. Serve with some small square pieces of fried stale bread.

CHICKASAW PLUM

Lat. *Prunus angustifolia*. A native American *Plum* of the Southern States; sometimes known as *Mountain Cherry*. Its fruit is edible but small and of poor quality.

CHILEAN GUAVA

Lat. *Myrtus ugni*. The edible fruit of a Chilean shrub. It is mostly used in the making of jam and preserves.

CHILEAN NUT

Lat. *Gevuina avellana*. The nut which is in the coral-red fruit of a Chilean shrub. It is also called *Chile Hazel*, and is similar in taste to the *Hazel Nut* (q.v.).

CHINA ORANGE

The name given in Malaysia to a very large form of *Tangerine* (q.v.).

CHINESE DATE

See *Jujube*.

CHINESE DATE PLUM

See *Japanese Persimmon*.

CHINESE GOOSEBERRY

See *Carambola*.

CHINESE JUJUBE

Lat. *Zizyphus jujuba*. The name is given indiscriminately to a number of different species of the common *Jujube* (q.v.) grown and improved by Chinese horticulturists during the last 4,000 years for the sake of their fruits.

CHINESE NUT

See *Litchi*.

CHINESE OLIVE

See *Java Almond*.

CHINESE ORANGE

Not an *Orange* at all but a *Kumquat* (q.v.) differing from all other varieties by its globular shape which is that of an orange.

CHINESE PLUM or JAPANESE PLUM

Lat. *Prunus salicina.* A large, yellow or light red plum, very sweet and juicy, a native of China, where it is extensively grown, as well as in Japan.

CHOCOLATE

1. A solid or pliable substance obtained from the dried, partly fermented, roasted and ground seeds of the Chocolate tree (Lat. *Theobroma Cacao*), a native of South America, now extensively cultivated in the West Indies, Mexico and elsewhere. In the form of 'Bars' or 'Squares' or 'Croquettes', this plain or bitter chocolate is used to prepare the beverage of the same name, or it is eaten with or without bread, as a valuable food. It is also sweetened by the addition of sugar or sugar substitutes and there are also ways of mixing with it some dried forms of milk; it is then called milk chocolate.

2. A beverage made from grated or ground chocolate allowing an ounce of chocolate to half a pint of milk. When the milk is very hot, put in the chocolate gradually, stirring all the time, and until the milk reaches boiling point, when it must be taken away from the fire. Add sugar then to taste and go on stirring a little longer. Serve immediately or keep until wanted and re-heat to boiling point when required.

3. Small candy or sweet eaten as dessert or at any time out of hand, sometimes made entirely of chocolate but usually consisting of a core or centre of fruit, nut, nougat, fondant, or some such thing and a coating of chocolate.

Chocolate Cream Candy

1 tablespoon butter
2 cups sugar
⅔ cup milk
2 squares chocolate (2 oz.) or
2 oz. cocoa
1 teaspoon vanilla essence

Method: Melt butter, sugar, and milk by heating slowly. When it boils add the chocolate or cocoa. Boil 13 minutes. Remove from stove, add vanilla and beat till creamy. As soon as it begins to sugar round the edge, pour into buttered pan and mark in squares, when cool.

Chopped nuts may be stirred into this before pouring into the pan.—P.R.M.

Chocolate Ice Cream

Mix three cupfuls of cream with three oz. bitter chocolate and one cupful of sugar, three eggs and one tablespoonful of vanilla. Boil in a double-boiler and stir until the mixture thickens a little. Remove from heat and add two more cupfuls of cream. Stir until cold and freeze.—E.E.A.

Chocolate Mousse

The whites of three eggs beaten to a stiff froth, add castor sugar and two teaspoonfuls of powdered chocolate flavoured with vanilla. Mix it well in and serve in small pots. These are often served in France.—L.M. (2).

Chocolate Icing

4 oz. icing sugar
1 oz. grated chocolate
1 teaspoon good vanilla essence
¼ gill water (approx.)

Put the grated chocolate into a saucepan, add the water, allow the chocolate to melt and then let it boil for two minutes. Leave to cool. Rub the icing sugar through a hair sieve and add it to the tepid chocolate, together with the vanilla essence. Mix all together and allow the icing sugar to dissolve, but on no account allow it to get hot or it will become dull.—G.H. (3).

Chocolate Truffles

½ lb. of chocolate
¼ lb. fresh butter
3 tablespoons thick cream
2 oz. grated chocolate

Method: Melt ½ lb. of very good chocolate in a slow oven. Add the butter and cream. Mix into a paste and let it cool until it is the right consistency to make into balls. Grate some chocolate and roll balls in it, making them the size and shape of walnuts. Put each into a paper case. *Mrs Ashton, Maseru.*—P.R.M.

CHOKE BERRY

See *American Cherry.*

CITRANGE

Lat. *Poncirus trifoliata.* A citrus fruit, a cross between the sweet orange and the trifoliate orange.

CITRON

Lat. *Citrus medica.* The fruit of the Citron tree; its candied peel is used in confectionery and is called *Cédrat.*

CLEMENTINE

Lat. *Citrus nobilis; var. deliciosa.* A citrus fruit, a cross between the tangerine and the wild North African orange: it is practically seedless.

CLOUDBERRY

Lat. *Rubus chamaemorus.* A herbaceous little bramble of the boreal circle of the northern hemisphere. It is highly prized as an edible berry in Newfoundland, Labrador, Nova Scotia and North Quebec; also in parts of the U.S.A. close to the Canadian border; it also occurs on some moors of the Scottish

Highlands. It is found in greater plenty, however, further north, and it ripens its fruit occasionally in the arctic circle. The berries are golden-orange, tinged with deep red on the side of the sun; they have no taste and are unfit to eat until they are really ripe, when they acquire a honey-like sweetness and a flavour which is said to resemble that of some apples. They are used in pies and puddings and also for making a jam of fine quality. In some parts of Canada they are called *Baked-apple Berries*: they are also known in North Quebec and Hudson Bay as *Yellow Berries*.

COBNUT
See *Filbert*.

COCA
Lat. *Erythroxylum Coca*. A South American shrub: its leaves resemble tea leaves and they are chewed by natives, in Bolivia and Peru, as a stimulant.

COCKATOO BUSH
See *Blueberry*.

COCK'S CLAW. HONEY TREE. JAPANESE RAISIN TREE
Lat. *Hovenia dulcis*. A deciduous shrub or small tree of Eastern Asia which is also grown in some parts of South America. Its broad, fruit-bearing peduncles, or false fruit, reddish in colour and juicy, are edible.

COCK'S EGGS
See *Huero de Gallo*.

COCOA. CACAO
The pulverized form of Cacao or Cocoa Beans, the seeds of the Chocolate Tree (Lat. *Theobroma cacao*), a native of North America, now extensively cultivated in the West Indies, Mexico and elsewhere. The seeds are dried, partly fermented, freed from shell and germ and robbed of most of their fat, which is known as Cacao or Cocoa Butter, before they are ground to a powder.

The name cocoa also applies to the beverage made from cocoa powder as follows:

Put two teaspoonfuls of cocoa in a breakfast cup and pour over it sufficient cold milk to make it into a smooth paste, then fill the cup with boiling milk, boiling water or a blend of the two, stirring the cocoa paste all the while. Add sugar to taste. A cup of cocoa is a poor substitute for a cup of chocolate (q.v.) when made with water and unsweetened, but when it is made with rich milk in a saucepan, and boiled, instead of in the cup, it can be most acceptable.

COCONUT. COCOANUT
The fruit of the *Coconut Palm* (*Cocos nucifera*), the most important economic product of the Tropics. It consists of an outer fibrous husk and a nut or stone containing a thick edible jelly (endosperm), and in the fresh fruit, a clear, refreshing fluid called *Coconut Milk*. See *Palmae*.

COCO PLUM. COCOA PLUM
Lat. *Chrysobalanus icaco*. A West African fruit, naturalized in Central America, bearing a fruit which looks rather like a *Victoria Plum*; it is eaten uncooked, but is best used in the making of jams and preserves.

COCO YATAY
See *Yatay*.

COFFEE
See Section IX.

Coffee Icing
Cream ¼ lb. of sugar and ¼ lb. of butter and add a dessertspoonful of coffee essence by degrees.

Coffee Custard
For six glasses measure out four breakfast cupfuls of boiled milk, put it in a basin with one cupful of very strong, clear, and carefully strained coffee; add the yolks of five eggs, and one and half ounce of pounded sugar; mix thoroughly and strain. Skim off all froth, and cook the custard as already described in a saucepan plunged into a larger vessel filled with boiling water; when sufficiently thickened, pour the custard into the glasses, and set them in the ice-box.—WN.

COOCHIN-YORK
Lat. *Garcinia mangostana*. The name given in Australia to a popular variety of native *Mangosteen* (q.v.).

COQUITO
Lat. *Butia capitata*. One of the most valuable palm trees of Chile. The sap is used to make palm-honey, the Chilean version of the Canadian maple sugar; the seeds are eaten as sweetmeats whilst the fibre is made into cordage.

COQUITO DE SAN JUAN. IBAPOO
Lat. *Melicocca lepidopetala*. A pinnate-leaved palm tree of the Pacific coast of South America; its fruit is edible.

CORNEL CHERRY
Lat. *Cornus mas*. The olive-shaped, edible fruit of a small European tree or shrub; its red colour is attractive and the best part of an otherwise tasteless large berry.

COROMANDEL GOOSEBERRY
See *Carambola*.

COWBERRY

Lat. *Vaccinium vitisidaea*. A name given in the U.S.A. to a number of berries from pasture and wood low shrubs, belonging to the large family of *Cranberries* (q.v.), more particularly the *Mountain Cranberry*, *Foxberry*, *Partridgeberry* and *Bog Strawberry*.

CRAB APPLE

Lat. *Pyrus baccata*. 'The Crab-apple probably came originally from Siberia, northern China, and Manchuria, but has been cultivated for its fruit and flowers in China and Japan from time immemorial. The Chinese and Japanese have developed many forms differing in plant, fruit and flower, more particularly in the flowers, these being of many colours, various sizes, and in all degrees of doubling. The Siberian Crab-apple is the hardiest of the fruit trees, grows with great rapidity, thrives in many soils and bears year after year with increasing abundance.'—U.P.H.

Practically all the Crab-apples cultivated in the British Isles and in the U.S.A. are hybrids of *Pyrus malus* (the Apple), and *Pyrus baccata* (the Siberian Crab-apple), and they are chiefly grown for their blooms, although their fruit is also used for the making of jams, jellies and preserves.

Crab-apple Jelly

> 6 lb. apples
> 2 lemons
> 1 lb. sugar to each pint of juice

Wash and core the apples and cut into quarters; place in a preserving-pan with enough cold water to cover them. Boil for about three-quarters of an hour. Strain through a muslin bag Measure the juice and allow 1 lb of sugar to a pint. Boil them together for three-quarters of an hour, stirring well all the time, add the lemon juice strained, just before the jelly is done. Test occasionally and remove after it jellies easily on a cold spoon.—L.G.N.

CRANBERRIES

Lat. *Vaccinium oxycoccus, var. palustris* (U.K.); *Vaccinium macrocarpus* and *V. erythrocarpus* (U.S.A.); *Lissanthe sapida* (Australia); *Astroloba humifusum*, Tasmanian Cranberry; Fr. *Airelles*. The fruit of a small European shrub with wiry, creeping branches, which grows freely in swamps, marshlands, moors and wastes, where there is plenty of available water, in the British Isles, and in many parts of Central and Northern Europe. Its fruit is crimson, often spotted, about the size of currants and it ripens late in August or early in September, but even when ripe it is too acid to be eaten uncooked.

In America, however, there are many more varieties of the same genus; some grow wild from Newfoundland to the Carolinas and westwards to Wisconsin and Arkansas, and other sorts are to be found in plenty in the mountainous parts of the country from Virginia to Georgia. *Cranberries* are also cultivated on a commercial scale in the U.S.A., over a million bushels being marketed annually. They belong to three distinct categories: (*a*) the *Cherry Cranberry*, large, round and dark red; (*b*) the *Bugle Cranberry*, elongated and the skin of a lighter crimson; and (*c*) the *Bell Cranberry*, bell-shaped or turbinate, coral red and the favourite variety.

Cranberries are chiefly used in the making of tarts, pies, jams and preserves; also for sauces and garnishings. (See Part I. *SAUCES*.)

The Australian Cranberry is the fruit of the *Lissanthe sapida*; the Tasmanian Cranberry, the fruit of the *Astrolama humifusum*.

Cranberry Pudding

> ½ lb. of cranberries (2 cupfuls), washed and cut in halves
> ½ cupful of butter (¼ lb.)
> 1 cupful of sugar
> 2 eggs, beaten
> 3 cupfuls of freshly-grated bread-crumbs
> ¼ teaspoon of cinnamon
> ½ teaspoon of soda
> 2 tablespoons of finely-cut orange rind
> ¼ cupful of sultana raisins, scalded and chopped
> ¼ cupful of milk

1½-quart melon mould with cover, well buttered. Stir the butter hard with a wooden spoon until soft and creamy. Add the sugar and beat until light and fluffy. Add the eggs and beat thoroughly. Mix the breadcrumbs, cinnamon, and the soda and stir into the mixture. Add the orange rind, raisins and milk, and mix well. Mix in the cranberries. Turn into a mould, cover, and steam for three hours. Serve with hard sauce flavoured with brandy. Serves six persons.—E.K.H.

CROWBERRY. CRAKEBERRY

Lat. *Empetrum nigrum*. The berry of the *Empetrum nigrum*, a hardy bush which grows wild in the mountainous parts of Scotland, Russia and Scandinavia; its berries can be used like *Cranberries* (q.v.).

CURRANT

A small seedless *Raisin* (q.v.), grown chiefly in the Levant and originally obtained from Corinth, hence its French name *Raisin de Corinthe*.

CURRANTS

Lat. Red and White: *Ribes sativum, var. album* and *var. rubrum*; Fr. *Groseilles rouges et blanches* (*See also* Black Currants). The berries of the different sorts of *Ribes sativum*, or currant bushes; the three most important, gastronomically speaking, are the Red, the White and the Black. See *Black Currants* and *Red Currants*.

CUSTARD APPLE

Lat. *Anona cherimolia*. The name given to different varieties of tropical fruits, chiefly that of a West Indian *Annona*, the *Bullock's Heart* (q.v.), the *Sweetsop* (q.v.), and the North American *Papaw* (q.v.).

DAMASCENES

An inferior variety of *Damson* (q.v.), also called *Shropshire Damsons* or *Black Jack Damsons*: they are smaller and rounder than the ordinary *Damson*.

DAMSON

Lat. *Prunus domestica*; Fr. *Prune de Damas*. Damsons belong to a race of small rounded plums, deep blue in the skin with greenish flesh, ripening late, of which there are several varieties. They are regarded as derivatives of *Prunus institia*, or Damascus plum-tree, and are closely related to the *Sloes* of the hedgerows.

Although one enjoys uncooked *Damsons* after the age of reason and before the age of discretion, the fruit is much better when cooked. *Damsons* are used in any way suitable for *Plums* (q.v.), for tarts, puddings and pies, jams, jellies, pickles and preserves. Besides the usual *Damson Fool, Mould, Trifle, Whip*, etc., an excellent and wholly English way with *Damsons* is that known as *Damson Cheese*.

Damson Brandy

Steeped in brandy (or gin), *Damsons* are used to make cordials which some people prefer to *Cherry Brandy* and *Sloe Gin*.

Damson Cheese

Put 5 or 6 lb. of Damsons in a preserving-pan and add one quart of water. Boil until the fruit is tender and then rub through a sieve. Return the pulp to the pan, adding 1 lb. of sugar to each lb. of pulp. Bring to the boil, being careful to stir all the time. Test after a quarter of an hour and when the mixture sets, tie down in the usual way. A few sweet almonds or kernels from the damson stones are a great improvement.—L.G.N.

Damson Fool

Boil together for five minutes three dessert-spoonfuls of Demerara sugar and half a gill of water. Then add 1½ pints of damsons and cook the whole until the fruit is reduced to a pulp. Rub this through a sieve to remove the stones and skins, and then mix it with a pint of custard. Leave the mixture in a cool place to thicken, then pour it into small custard glasses and put a little whipped cream on the top of each. Sufficient for six or eight people.—L.G.N.

Damson Pickle

Boil one pint of vinegar with one stick of cinnamon, half teaspoonful of allspice and three blades of mace. Wipe, stalk, and prick 6 lb. of Damsons and pour the syrup over them. Allow to stand for 24 hours, then boil together with 3 lb. of sugar for three minutes. Bottle and seal. These are delicious.—L.G.N.

DANGLEBERRY

See *Tangleberry*.

DATE

Lat. *Phoenix dactylifera*; Fr. *Datte*. An oblong berry with a groved seed, the fruit of a palm tree cultivated on a very large scale in Northern Africa, also in Western Asia, and to a smaller extent in Southern California. In desert regions, like that of the Sahara, *Dates* are a food of the greatest value to the native population, and to their camels. The natural habitat of the Date Palm ranges from Persia through Arabia and Northern Africa to the Canaries, but it thrives also in Arizona and Southern California.

There are three chief varieties of dates: (*a*) the soft and juicy dates, the best and richest in saccharine, and the only ones to be exported to distant markets; (*b*) the dry and hard dates which keep well and are the Arabs' favourite; (*c*) the fibrous dates, low in sugar content, bad keepers, and inferior to the other two. The best dates to be exported were *Tafilats* and the *Tunisian*, which are packed 'on the stem'.

Date Cream Pudding

1 pint milk
2 oz. sugar
1½ tablespoons minute tapioca or sago
½ lb. dates, stoned
1 egg

Cook milk and tapioca together for 15 minutes, then add the beaten yolk of egg and sugar and dates. Cook another 15 minutes. Remove from fire and fold in stiffly-beaten white of egg. Serve hot or cold. Sufficient for four or six people.—L.G.N.

Date Gems

Beat ⅓ cup butter and 1 cup castor sugar to a cream; add 2 eggs well beaten, ⅓ cup milk, 1¾ cup flour, 2 teaspoons baking powder, ½ teaspoon ground ginger, ¼ teaspoon grated nutmeg, $\frac{1}{4}$ teaspoon powdered cloves, and 1 cupful chopped dates. Mix well and divide into buttered and floured gem pans, and bake in a moderate oven for 25 minutes. Cool on a cake-rack and when cold decorate each with icing sugar moistened with orange juice and a good squeeze of lemon, and top with a stoned date. (*Beryl Freeman's Recipe.*)—E.C. (2).

Date Moons

Put $\frac{1}{2}$ lb. dates, stoned, through the meat chopper, and add half cup walnuts and 2 oz. candied ginger coarsely cut. Knead and roll into sausages, using powdered sugar to prevent sticking. Serve cut in thin slices. (*Moyna Macgill's Recipe.*)—E.C. (2).

DESERT DATE
See *Aduwa*.

DEWBERRY
Lat. *Rubus caesius*; *R. hispidus*; *R. invisus*; *R. roribaccus*; *R. trivialis*; *R. ursinus*; *R. villosus*. The name given in the U.S.A. to any trailing *Blackberry* as opposed to the 'Bush' or upright *Blackberries*. There are different varieties of *Dewberries* which are cultivated as garden small fruit. The chief value of the *Dewberry* at the market gardener's point of view is that it ripens its fruit at least a week or two in advance of the *Blackberries*. It is used in cookery and confectionery in the same ways as *Blackberries* (q.v.).

DURIAN
Lat. *Durio zibethinus*. The oval or globose fruit of the *Durio zibethinus*, a Malayan tree which is extensively grown in the East and Far East. The flavour of the *Durian*, when at the right degree of ripeness and just picked, is delicious; so is its soft, cream-coloured pulp; but its smell, which is strong at all times, very soon becomes foul when the fruit is over-ripe or kept for any time after being picked. The seeds can also be roasted and eaten like chestnuts.

D. Fairchild calls the *Durian* 'the most remarkable fruit in the world'. The fruits weigh from 5 to 10 lb. and are about the size of small coconuts and completely covered with sharp prickles.

FIG
Lat. *Ficus carica*; Fr. *Figue*. The fruit of a number of different types of fig-trees. Figs may be divided into two main classes according to their shape, according to whether they are round, roundish or turbinate; or else long, pyriform or obovate. In each one of those two categories there are Figs with dark purple skin and others with green, or green tinged with brown. And in each case Figs may be further divided according to the colour of their pulp, which may be red or

from white to opaline. The natural home of the *Fig* is the Mediterranean basin from Syria to the Canaries, but Smyrna Figs, which are the best, and *Caprifigs*, which are wild Figs, have been introduced in California, together with the insect that is responsible for their fertilization, and they are now well established there as well as in the Gulf States. In England, Figs ripen out of doors in some sheltered positions, but they are mostly grown under glass. In France, Spain, Portugal and Italy they are grown extensively.

Wherever Figs ripen out of doors they are eaten when freshly picked as one of the most delicious of dessert fruits, but they are mostly used commercially in the dried form, when they travel and keep well.

Fig Mould
Chop up 1 lb. of dried Figs and put them in a saucepan with 6 oz. of sugar, $\frac{1}{2}$ pint water, $\frac{1}{4}$ pint white wine, some strips of lemon rind, and simmer gently till the Figs are quite puffed out and tender. Dissolve 1 oz. gelatine in a little warm water and add. Pour mixture into a mould and stand till set. Serve with whipped cream.

Fig Pudding
Chop finely $\frac{1}{2}$ lb. dried Figs and mix thoroughly with 6 oz. finely-chopped suet, $\frac{1}{4}$ lb. flour, $\frac{1}{4}$ lb. sugar, a pinch of salt and two well-beaten eggs. Moisten with about $\frac{1}{2}$ pint milk, and pack the mixture into a buttered basin. Steam for $3\frac{1}{2}$ hours.

Fig Sponge
$\frac{1}{2}$ lb. flour
$\frac{1}{4}$ lb. of suet finely chopped
1 teacupful of golden syrup
1 teacupful of milk
1 teaspoonful of bicarbonate of soda added last thing
$\frac{1}{2}$ lb. of chopped figs

Mix. Pour into a buttered mould and steam two hours. Sufficient for six or eight people.—L.G.N.

FILBERTS
Lat. *Corylus avellana pontica* and *C. a. grandis*; *Corylus maxima* and *C. tubulosa*; Fr. *Aveline* or *Noisette*. The name is a corruption of 'Nuts of St. Philibert', whose feast day happens to be August 22nd, when *Filberts* are usually ready to be picked. True *Filberts* are of excellent flavour but small and of less vigorous growth than Cobnuts and Hazels. There are two distinct varieties, known by the colour of their skin: (*a*) the *White Filbert* (*White Aveline* or *White-skinned Filbert*) or *Kentish Filbert*. The nuts are small, oblong, bluntly pointed, dark brown, often slightly grooved, and the skin of the kernel is white;

and (b) the Red Filbert (Red Aveline or Red-skinned Filbert), almost identical to the other but with a dark red skin of the kernel. There is a third but much less common variety known as the *Frizzled Filbert*, the husks of which are frizzled and cut at both ends.

In spite of some very slight botanical differences the Kentish Cobs are also classed among the *Filberts*, and the most extensively cultivated variety in England is known indifferently as *Kentish Cob* or *Lambert's Filbert*, the name being that of a Mr Lambert, of Goudhurst, Kent, who raised the nut in 1830. The nuts are large, long, rather flattened with well-defined suture, light brown in colour and of good flavour.

Another variety of nuts which is classed among the *Filberts* are those which belong to the *Bollwyller* group, a name derived from an old German variety. The nuts of this group are large, wider at the shoulder and tapering to a point.

Filberts grow in every part of the British Isles, but they are chiefly cultivated on a commercial scale in the County of Kent.

FOXBERRY
See *Cowberry*.

GOLDEN CURRANT or MISSOURI CURRANT
Lat. *Ribes aureum*. Both names are given to the same berry, in the U.S.A. It is the fruit of a native North American *Currant* which grows wild, and mostly on the banks of streams from Minnesota to Missouri and Arkansas, and westwards. This *Currant* is round or ovate, yellow as a rule, but sometimes black, and it is used cooked in tarts and pies, like *Blueberries* (q.v.). The *Golden Currant* has now been introduced by American horticulturists as one of the cultivated small fruit; the best known strain is that sold under the name of *Crandall*.

GOOSEBERRIES
Lat. *Ribes grosularia*; Fr. *Groseille à maquereaux*. R. *hirtellum* (American gooseberry). The *Gooseberry* is a native of Europe and North Africa, which was introduced in England in the sixteenth century. There is also a native American *Gooseberry* which bears small fruits, greenish, purple or black, very acid, but edible when cooked. European varieties have been imported in the U.S.A. on many occasions but without success as they are an easy prey to the Gooseberry Mildew. Hybrids, however, have been obtained from English and native American *Gooseberries* which bear large berries of good flavour and are quite hardy.

Gooseberries differ according to both shape and skin; as regards their shape they belong either to the round or roundish category, or else to the oblong, oval or obovate one. In each of those two categories there are varieties with smooth, downy or rough and hairy skin, and furthermore, such differences occur in four main classes of *Gooseberries* which are differentiated by the colour of the skin, when ripe: either red, yellow, green or white.

The *Grande Cuisine* all but ignores *Gooseberries*, but, in England, the selection, cultivation and cooking of *Gooseberries* have received a great measure of intelligent attention, and a boiled gooseberry pudding, made from young fruit no bigger than green peas, is one of the glories of English home cookery and an exquisite dish for all gourmets. *Gooseberries* are mostly picked young, in England, in the green state, for tarts, puddings and pies, or for bottling. Ripe *Gooseberries* provide a delightful dessert dish, but only when and if of the right dessert varieties; others, which are in the majority, are allowed to ripen only to be made into jam.

Gooseberry Amber
Put 2 oz. of butter in a saucepan, add 1 lb. of prepared gooseberries and a ¼ lb. of castor sugar. Cook all gently over the fire until the fruit is reduced to a soft, thick mass, then stir in 1 oz. of breadcrumbs, previously rubbed through a wire sieve, and beat in well the yolks of three eggs. Turn the whole in a buttered pie-dish. Bake the mixture in a moderate oven for about half an hour, then beat up the whites of the eggs to a very stiff froth, adding three level tablespoonfuls of castor sugar. Heap this mixture roughly all over the top, and sprinkle a little more castor sugar over all. Put the dish in a cool oven and bake until the mixture is pale brown and crisp. Serve at once. Sufficient for four or five people.—L.G.N.

Compôte of Green Gooseberries
For a quart of picked and washed green gooseberries, make a syrup as follows: Put 8 oz. of lump sugar into a pint of water and boil for 10 minutes. Then add a tablespoonful of apricot jam and a sherry glassful of Kirsch. Add the gooseberries which you have first blanched for two minutes in boiling water, and let them simmer gently until they are tender. Then drain them, put them into a dish and strain the syrup over them, reducing it a little more if thought necessary. This compôte should be very cold on serving.—A.H. (1).

Gooseberry Fool
Cook one quart of gooseberries in a light sugar syrup till tender. Rub through a sieve, and when quite cold add to it a pint of whipped cream. Taste and sweeten further if necessary and serve quite cold.

Gooseberry Meringue

Top, tail and wash 1 lb. gooseberries, melt 2 oz. butter in a saucepan, then add the fruit and ¼ lb. castor sugar. Let this mixture cook gently till the fruit has become a soft, thick mass, then stir in 1 oz. sifted cakecrumbs, and beat in the yolks of three eggs. Pour into a lightly buttered pie-dish and bake in a moderate oven for about 30 minutes. Now whip the whites of the three eggs to a stiff froth, add lightly three tablespoons castor sugar and a few drops of vanilla essence, and heap over pudding. Sprinkle lightly with castor sugar and put in a cool part of the oven till meringue turns crisp and pale brown. (*Marie Clavering's recipe.*)—E.C.(2).

Gooseberry Pudding, Boiled

Line a pudding basin with pudding paste and fill centre with very small green gooseberries, topped, tailed and washed, allowing a liberal sprinkling of brown sugar between each layer of fruit; cover with pastry lid and boil for 2 or 2½ hours.

Gooseberry Pudding, Baked

Top, tail and wash 1½ pints of green gooseberries; cook them in a light sugar syrup till tender; rub them through a sieve. Add to the *purée* ½ pint breadcrumbs, 1½ oz. butter, 2 oz. sugar and three well-beaten eggs. Line the edge of a pie-dish with short crust and pour in the mixture. Bake for about 40 minutes, sprinkle with sugar and serve hot.

GOUMI

Lat. *Eleagnus multiflora.* A Chinese berry closely related to the Buffalo-berry. It grows wild in China and Japan, where its berries are greatly valued for a number of culinary preparations, sauces, preserves, tarts and pies. The *Goumi* has been introduced in the U.S.A. and has proved hardy enough to thrive in the Eastern States, where it is chiefly cultivated as an ornamental plant. The berries ripen at midsummer and are produced in great profusion; they are most attractive in appearance, being orange coloured or reddish with tiny silvery specks. They are too acid to eat uncooked, but their flavour is quite pleasant, and they make excellent preserves.

GRANADILLA. GRENADILLA

Lat. *Passiflora coerulea*, Passion-fruit; *P. edulis* (Purple Granadilla of South Africa); *P. incarnata*, wild Passion-fruit; *P. lingularis* (Sweet Granadilla of Central America); *P. laurifolia* or *P. lutea* (Yellow Granadilla of Honolulu); *P. macrocarpa* (Giant Granadilla); *P. maliformis* (West Indies Granadilla); *P. quadrangularis* (Giant Granadilla of the U.S.A.). The names of a number of different species of Passion-flowers and their fruit; the following are the more extensively cultivated:

Passiflora quadrangularis, or *Giant Granadilla*, the American species, which is mostly used as dessert fruit, the moist, pippy pulp being scooped out with a teaspoon and mixed, or not, according to taste, with sherry or fresh cream and sugar.

Passiflora edulis, the South African species, also naturalized in Queensland. It is smaller but a more juicy variety and it is the best for making *Granadilla* ices.

Passiflora laurifolia, or *Water Melon* of Honolulu; it grows also in the West Indies, where it is usually known as *Pomme d'Or*.

Passiflora maliformis, the West Indian Passion-flower; its fruit is also known as *Sweet Cup* and *Sweet Calabash*.

Passiflora ligularis, a Central American species, cultivated mostly in Venezuela, where it is known as *Parchita*.

Passion-fruit Curd

Mix the pulp of six *Passion-fruits* and ½ lb. sugar and the juice of two lemons; beat slightly two eggs and put all ingredients in a double-boiler over a moderate fire. Stir occasionally, and when the mixture thickens cook 15 minutes longer, stirring frequently.

Passion-fruit Sorbet

In a wine-glass two-thirds Granadilla pulp mixed with one-third Sherry. Chill and serve.—F.C.-W.

GRAPE

Lat. *Vitis aestivalis*; *V. arizonica*; *V. Berlandieri*; *V. candicans*; *V. cordifolia*; *V. Labrusca*; *V. Munsoniana*; *V. riparia*; *V. rotundifolia*; *V. rupestris*; *V. vinifera*; *V. vulpina*. The fresh fruit of an immense number of different varieties of the *Vitis vinifera*, in Europe; also of the many varieties of indigenous species of vines, in the U.S.A.

In Great Britain grapes do not mature sufficiently regularly out-of-doors for vineyards to be planted for wine-making purposes, and grapes are grown exclusively for dessert, under glass, for size, flavour and appearance, but, in the first place, for continuity of supply. The most popular varieties grown are:

Early: Buckland Sweetwater; Foster's Seedling; Madresfield Court Muscat; Royal Muscadine, etc.

Mid-season: Black Hamburg; Muscat Hamburg; Prince of Wales, etc.

Late: Alicante; Appley Towers; Cannon Hall Muscat; Gros Colmar; Lady Downe's; Muscat of Alexandria.

In the U.S.A. wine-making grapes are grown exclusively in California; also in New York and some other States, both European and native American species being cultivated, the first for quality wines, and the second for the sake of larger quantities. Dessert or table Grapes are also grown on a large scale both out of doors and under glass.

Here is a list of the more popular Grapes in the U.S.A. which has been compiled from L.H.Bailey's 'Sketch of the evolution of our native fruits':

(a) Grapes grown on Vinifera, *i.e.*, European Stock

Actoni, greenish yellow, flesh sweet and firm.

Almeria, green, flesh hard and tasteless.

Bakator, pale red, juicy, sweet and good.

Black Hamburg, dark purple, firm, juicy, rich, good.

Black Malvoise, reddish black, early, sweet, juicy, no flavour.

Black Morocco, dull purple, firm and tasteless.

Chasselas, Golden, pale green to clear yellow; sweet, juicy, very good.

Chasselas, Rose, light red, sweet, juicy, very good.

Diamond, green with tinge of yellow, juicy, aromatic, very good.

Emperor, dull purple, firm, flavourless, late to ripen and keeps well.

Flame Tokay or *Tokay*, clear red, firm, crisp, sweet, good; the leading shipping grape of the Pacific coast.

Gros Colmar, black and very handsome, sweet, crisp, no flavour.

Lignan Blanc, yellowish green, very early, sweet, firm, good.

Malaga, yellowish green, firm, sweet, rich, good.

Mission, purple to black, firm, juicy, sweet, rich, delicious.

Moscatelo (Black Muscat), dark purple to black, sweet, rich, musky, juicy, very good.

Muscatel (White Frontignan), golden yellow, sweet, aromatic, very good.

Palomino, pale greenish yellow, sweet and vinous.

Rose of Peru, black, sweet, rich, very good.

Sultana, Sultanina, seedless and best for drying; also good dessert fruit.

Verdal, yellowish green, firm, good flavour, one of the latest to ripen, not juicy but keeps well.

(b) American Native Grapes and some of their Hybrids:

Agawam, red skin, foxy.

August Giant, purple skin, tough, but not foxy.

Barry, black skin, vinous, not foxy, good.

Brighton, light red, sweet, aromatic, good.

Campbell Early, dark purplish black, juicy, sweet, coarse, no flavour.

Canada, purplish black, juicy, vinous, sub-acid, pleasant flavour.

Catawba, dull purplish red, sweet and vinous, the standard red grape in the markets of the Eastern U.S.A.

Concord, black, tough and foxy; pure-bred and cross-bred *Concord* grapes represent 75 per cent of the grapes grown in the Eastern States.

Delaware, light red, sweet, vinous, aromatic, the best of the native American grapes.

Diana, light red, firm and vinous, an improved *Catawba*.

Downing, purplish black, juicy and vinous, very good.

Goethe, pale red, vinous and very good.

Hercules, black and very large, coarse and foxy.

Iona, red, sweet with a sub-acid taste, vinous, very good.

Isabella, black, sweet, coarse and slightly foxy.

Jessica, green, sweet, juicy, good.

Kensington, yellowish green, sweet, juicy, good.

Lady, light green, rich, sweet and slightly foxy.

Lindley, dark red, juicy, vinous, good.

Massasoit, dark brownish red; juicy, stringy, and foxy.

Merrimac, black, soft, juicy, good.

Mills, jet black, sweet, rich, juicy, good.

Niagara, pale yellowish green, juicy and foxy; the leading American green grape.

Noah, light green, juicy, vinous, coarse.

Triumph, golden yellow, vinous, juicy, very good.

Wyoming, amber-coloured, coarse and foxy.

Besides fresh grapes, which are crushed when ripe and as soon as they are picked to make unfermented grape-juice or fermented wine; or else, at a later stage, to be distilled into brandy, or fermented into wine-vinegar; and, besides the grapes which are eaten when ripe and as soon as possible after they are picked, as dessert fruit, or else are used for making jams and preserves, a large quantity of grapes are dried for future use, but they cease to be grapes then; they are called either *Currants* (q.v.), or *Raisins* (q.v.), and they are extensively used in either form in cookery and confectionery.

In the *Cuisine Classique*. grapes, usually *Muscat Grapes*, peeled and seeded, are used for garnishing and decorating certain dishes, such as *Sole Véronique* (q.v.).

GRAPE-FRUIT

Lat. *Citrus decumana*; Fr. *Pamplemousse*. A large, round or oblong citrus fruit, an improved variety of the *Shaddock* (q.v.), the original *Pamplemousse*, a name which now is made to serve for both shaddock and grape-fruit. There are a number of different varieties of grape-fruit, all of which, how-ever, belong to one or the other of two classes, the one having white pulp, and the other pink or red pulp; the coloured varieties are known as *Pomels* and are sweeter than the others.

Grape-fruit is most wholesome and re-freshing when ripe; it can be used for making cups and in fruit salads and generally speak-ing in any and every way suitable for oranges. It has also been tried cooked, but cooking deprives it of much of its goodness without adding anything to its digestibility or flavour: it is not to be encouraged.

Grape-fruit Jellies

 2 grape-fruit
 1 oz. isinglass
 Water to cover fruit
 1 tablespoon sherry

Remove rinds of fruit and cut each into two parts. Carefully remove the fleshy sections, avoiding white membrane and pips. Place fruit in a small pan with the isinglass and just nicely covering with cold water. Reduce fruit to a pulp by gentle cooking. Add sherry and press through a small sieve or a jelly bag, according to whether you prefer cloudy or clear jellies. Return liquid to pan with a scant pound of white sugar and boil rapidly. Pour while still liquid, but cool, into serving glasses and chill.

GREENGAGE

Lat. *Prunus domestica*; Fr. *Reine-Claude*. The popular name of all members of the *Gage* family. The *Gages* constitute a distinct class of *Plum* characterized by an almost spherical fruit, except for the seam, and a small stone, circular in outline. Of the old English *Gages*, the best is the *Cambridge Gage*; the French *Reine Claude* is a larger variety, named after the Queen of Francis I of France. Most of the gages are green, ripening to amber, but there are coloured varieties of the finest quality, as *Count Althann's Gage*, *Kirke's Blue* and the American *Jefferson*. *Coe's Golden Drop* does not possess the typical gage shape, in that it is attached to the stalk by a little pear-like neck, but if allowed to hang on the tree until the latter part of September or even October, it becomes a bag of sweet and fragrant juice.

Greengages are the sweetest and best of all dessert plums, but they are also used to make excellent jams and preserves, tarts and puddings.

GRUMICHANA

One of the earliest fruits to mature in Brazil in the early spring; it was introduced by D. Fairchild in South Florida where it now flourishes.

GUABIYU

Lat. *Eugenia pungens*. A South American fruit which the Indians have so far been alone in enjoying.

GUARANA

Lat. *Paullinia cupana*. The fruit, or rather the seeds, of a Brazilian climbing shrub, which, besides tannin, contain up to 4.5 per cent of caffein. The seeds are used to make a dry paste and also to flavour drinks; they are reputed to be good in cases of diarrhoea.

GUAVA

Lat. *Psidium guayava*; Fr. *Goyave*. An American tropical fruit which is grown in many tropi-cal and some sub-tropical countries for the sake of its apple-like fruit which is used to make a jelly as sweetly delicious in taste as it is wholesome. After the jelly has been made, the residue of the pulp is made into what is called *Guava Cheese*, still a palatable sweet, but, of course, not comparable to the jelly. In Brazil, a very good guava cheese is made which is known as *Goibada*.

In Puerto Rico and other West Indian Islands, as well as in some Central American countries, they call *Guava* the fruit of the *Inga vera*, a poor relation of the *Psidium* family, and the jelly, jam, and paste made from the *Inga* fruit are also poor; they ought not to be sold under the name of *Guava*, but they are.

GUINEA PLUM

Lat. *Parinarium excelsum*. The fruit of a large West African tree, *Parinarium excelsum*. It is not unlike a plum in size and colour, but a very poor substitute as regards its taste and lack of flavour.

HAZEL NUT

Lat. *Corylus avellana pontica* and *Corylus maxima*; Fr. *Noisette*. Although *Hazels* grow in England, they are not cultivated to nearly the same extent as *Filberts* (q.v.), and com-mercially speaking, the *Hazels* are the im-ported type of Cobnut, whereas the *Filberts* are the home-grown. In 1934, there were 90,406 cwt. of *Hazel Nuts* imported in the United Kingdom to the value of £233,334, mostly from Spain. The most important variety of *Hazels* is known as the Barcelona variety; it was introduced in the U.S.A. in 1885 and it is the most extensively grown variety there. The nuts are large, thick-shelled, round and broad shouldered with blunt point and of a rich chestnut-brown colour.

There is another group of *Hazels* which is distinguished by its thin shells and sweet flavour. The best specimen of the group is known as the *Cosford*; the nuts are oval, medium-sized, broad at shoulders, medium-brown in colour and very thin-shelled. It is one of the best English cob-nuts and is supposed to have originated at Ipswich in 1816. Very similar varieties, with the nuts a little larger, were imported from the Continent under the names of *Darviana* and *Italian Red*.

HICKORY NUT
The fruit of some of the American hardwood trees of the *Carya* genus, or hickories. It is used in the U.S.A. for confectionery.

HIPS
Lat. *Rosa canina*; Fr. *Eglantine*. The fresh fruit of the Dog-rose (*Rosa canina*), gathered when ripe and used to make jam, jellies, marmalade and preserves; also for sauces.

HOG PLUM
See *Spondias*.

HONEY TREE
See *Cock's Claw*.

HUCKLEBERRY
Lat. *Gaylussacia baccata* and *G. frondosa*. One of the North American wild edible berries chiefly used in the making of tarts, pies, preserves and syrups. They resemble the *Blueberries*, but their seeds are harder as well as larger, hence not nearly so good. The common Huckleberry ranges from Newfoundland to Manitoba and southward to Kentucky and Georgia. Some bushes bear blue fruits, covered with bloom; others white fruits, firmer than the other two, hence more suitable for sending to market, but not so pleasant of flavour as the berries of the *Tangleberry* (q.v.).

Another variety of Huckleberry, known as *Bear Huckleberry* or *Buckberry*, is found in woods from Kentucky to Georgia and North Carolina. The berries lack flavour but are acceptable for culinary purposes where they are gathered.

HUEVO DE GALLO
Lat. *Salpichroa rhomboides*. The fruit of a native South American tree; it is eaten raw, as plucked from the tree, by the Indians, and occasionally appears in the markets of San Juan and Tucuman (Argentina).

IBA
1. Lat. *Irvingia barteria*. The edible fruit of a West African inferior kind of Mango, which was introduced in Provence, in 1855. In Lagos and the Gaboon, natives eat the fruit itself, but they attach more importance to the kernel from which they make the so-called *Dika* or *Odika* bread, also known as *Gaboon Chocolate*. (See *Dika*).

2. Lat. *Cicca acida*. A tree of the Philippine Islands, cultivated for the sake of its roundish and greenish-white fruit.

IBAPOO
See *Coquito de San Juan*.

ICACO
See *Coco Plum*.

IGBA PURU
Lat. *Myrciaria islandica*. One of the best wild fruits of Argentina; it is produced by a native South American tree and it possesses a delicious flavour.

ILAMA
Lat. *Anona diversifolia*. The fruit of a variety of *Annona* (q.v.) very popular in Guatemala. It resembles in size and flavour the *Cherimoya* (q.v.) and 'it ranks with the best fruits that grow.'—D.F.

INDIAN CURRANT
Lat. *Ribes glutinosum*. The black, fragrant fruit of a *Ribes* which grows on the Pacific coast of North America; also the red berry of a different North American shrub, the *Symphoricarpos* or *orbiculatus*.

INDIAN FIG
Lat. *Opuntia ficus-indica*. A name given in England to an Indian star-anise, the Badian (q.v.), and in the U.S.A. to two varieties of prickly pears.

INGA
Lat. *Inga affinis*. The edible fruit of the *Jaboticaba*, a South American native tree which occurs chiefly in Argentina and Brazil. The purple fruits grow on both trunk and branches of the tree and they contain a white pulp which D.Fairchild describes as delicious.

JABOTICABA TREE
See *Igba purú*.

JACK-FRUIT
Lat. *Artocarpus integrifolia*. A variety of *Bread Fruit* which is a native of southern Asia but is now cultivated in most parts of the tropics. *Jack-Fruits* weigh up to 50 lb., and their pulp is eaten uncooked as well as cooked in various ways, chiefly in oil and with curry. It is also dried and preserved for winter use, whilst the seeds may be roasted like chestnuts, which they rather resemble in shape, size and taste.

The Ceylon variety of this fruit is smaller, whilst the *African Jack-Fruit* belongs to quite a different species, the only part of the fruit that is used for food being the seeds, which are ground to a meal; this meal is chiefly baked as bread or cakes, but it serves also to make a sort of almond milk.

JAMAICA BILBERRY
Lat. *Vaccinium meridionale.* The edible berry of a Jamaica mountain shrub.

JAMAICA CHERRY
Lat. *Ficus laerigata.* A West Indian Fig, globose and no bigger than a cherry.

JAMAICA COBNUT
Lat. *Omphalea triandra.* The sweet, edible seed of a West Indian tree, the *Omphalea triandra.*

JAMBERBERRY
See *Tomatillo.*

JAMBOLAN or JAVA PLUM
Lat. *Eugenia jambolana.* The plum-like fruit of a tree which occurs from the East Indies to Australia, and is common in most islands of the southern Pacific. The fruit itself does not appear to have any special gastronomical merit, but the seeds are strongly astringent and are used medicinally.

JAMBU
See *Rose Apple.*

JAPANESE MEDLAR
See *Loquat.*

JAPANESE PERSIMMON or KAKI
Lat. *Diospyros Kaki.* The commonest Asiatic variety of *Persimmon*; it is larger and has a better flavour than the American *Persimmon* (q.v.), and it has been introduced in Provence, where it is grown for the making of compôtes and jams.

JAPANESE PLUM
See *Chinese Plum.*

JAPANESE QUINCE
Lat. *Chaenomeles lagenaria.* A Japanese ornamental shrub with attractive clusters of red and reddish flowers. It bears globular or ovoid berries, yellowish-green in colour, stemless, very hard and not fit to eat as fruit. Yet they contain a rich, aromatic, lemon-like juice which can be used in the making of excellent jellies and preserves as well as to flavour ice-creams.

JAPANESE RAISIN TREE
See *Cock's Claw.*

JAVA ALMOND or CHINESE OLIVE
Lat. *Canarium luzonicum.* The drupaeceous fruit of an Asiatic tree which is cultivated in Manila, Malaya and the Dutch East Indies; the fruit is more valuable for the *elemi,* or fragrant resin made from it, than as food.

JUJUBE, T'SAO or CHINESE DATE
Lat. *Zizyphus jujuba.* These are different names for the same fruit, the date-like fruit of different varieties of tropical trees, natives of southern Asia, but now introduced in most parts of the tropics. *Jujube* is usually preserved in syrup or made into a jelly and sweetmeats greatly esteemed in China and most Eastern lands.

In California, the *Chinese Date* thrives; its fruit has long pointed seeds, a caramel-like texture with curious lines across, somewhat like scratches, and in taste it resembles dried dates: it is chiefly eaten candied. 'Ripe Jujubes, when eaten raw, are amusing rather than delicious and have a crisp, sprightly flavour different from other fruits.'—D.F.

JUNEBERRY
Lat. *Amelanchier Botryapium* (A. *oblongifolia*); *A. alnifolia*; *A. canadensis.* An American Berry of the *Amelanchier* genus, related to the shad-bush, service-berry, sugar-pear or grape-pear and some twenty-five other sorts of berries. The fruit is sweet and juicy, and it plays an important part in the diet of the North American Indians, who eat *Juneberries* both fresh and dried. They vary in size from that of a pea to that of a crab-apple; they vary in colour from dark red to a purplish-blue or black and all have more or less bloom. In the U.S.A. selected strains from wild Juneberry plants are offered by western nurserymen under the names of *Improved Dwarf Juneberry, Dwarf Mountain Juneberry, Western Huckleberry* and a few more.

KAFFIR ORANGE
Lat. *Strychnos spinosa.* This is not an orange at all, except in shape and size. It occurs chiefly in Portuguese East Africa; its rind is so hard that it is more like the shell of a nut, but it is filled with a brown, glistening pulp of the consistency of a very ripe banana and the flavour of which is aromatic and quite pleasing.

KAMACHILE. KAMANCHILE
Lat. *Pithecolobium dulce,* and *P. flexicaule.* A common and most valuable tree of tropical America, yielding good timber, a yellow dye, a mucilaginous gum and a fruit that is greatly prized.

KANGAROO APPLE
Lat. *Solanum aviculare.* The yellow, egg-shape fruit of an Australian grass; it is mealy in texture and sub-acid in flavour.

KUMQUAT

Lat. *Fortunella japonica (Citrus japonica)*. The small, bitter-sweet fruit of two Japanese shrubs: *Kumquat* and *Kumquat Nagami*. It grows in the open in Florida and California and it is grown in England under glass. It is used mostly in confectionery and for preserves. In the U.S.A. it is also served with ice-cream; in this case it is cut in halves, put in a pan with half cup of water, simmered gently until tender, when 1½ cups of sugar are added, and the fruit is cooked a little longer in its syrup, being stirred all the time.

LANGSAT. LANZONE

Lat. *Lansium domesticum*. An inferior kind of *Mangosteen* (q.v.) which occurs in Malaya and the Philippines. Also called *Boboa*.

LEMON

Lat. *Citrus limonia*; Fr. *Citron*. The fruit of the lemon-tree; its juice is rich in citric acid and its rind in oil of lemon. The juice is of the greatest use as a flavouring agent in cooking, and the rind also, but more so in confectionery. Many gastronomes and wine-connoisseurs use lemon juice in place of vinegar in salad dressings, even when oil-and-vinegar is recommended.

Lemon-water Ice

Put in a vessel half a pound of powdered sugar, with one quart of cold water, grate in the rind of a large lemon or of two small ones, squeezing in the juice of three good-sized ones, or of four if small, and with your spatula beat well together for five minutes. Have a syrup-weigher, place it in the centre of the preparation, and if it be twenty-one degrees it is correct, if not add a little more powdered sugar; remove the weigher, mix a little more, and then strain through a sieve into the freezer, putting on the cover and proceed to freeze precisely as for vanilla cream ice (q.v.) serving it in the same way. —G.A.S.

Lemon Ice Cream

Take from six lemons the rind, as thin as possible, and free from pith. Squeeze the juice of the lemons into a sugar-pan, with half a pound of sugar and half a pint of water. Place it over the fire and reduce it to a rather thick syrup. Have a pint and a half of milk upon the fire, into which, when boiling, throw the rind of the lemons; cover over, and let remain till half cold. In another stew-pan, have the yolks of twelve eggs (to which you have added an ounce of sugar) with which mix the milk by degrees, and stir over the fire until it adheres to the back of the spoon, when stir in the syrup and pass through a tammy. When cold, freeze, adding a pint of whipped cream when half-frozen. —G.A.S.

Lemon Sherbet

Mix two cupfuls of sugar with nine cupfuls of lukewarm water, squeeze in the juice of five medium-sized lemons and grate in the peel of one lemon, add two whites of eggs and whip all with an egg-beater for two minutes. Strain into an ice-cream freezer well surrounded with ice and rock salt. Turn crank for about 10 minutes until right consistency.

This recipe may be cut in half, but gives better satisfaction with above amounts.— E.E.A.

LICHEE

See *Litchi*.

LIME

Lat. *Citrus medica, var. acida (Citrus aurantifolia)*; Fr. *Limon*. The small, oblong, greenish-yellow fruit of the lime-tree which is cultivated in most sub-tropical countries, chiefly in the West Indies. Its juice and rind are used in cooking, confectionery and preserving in the same way as *Lemon* (q.v.). The fruit of the *Citrus medica* variety *limetta* is known as *Sweet Lime*.

LIMEBERRY. LIME MYRTLE

Lat. *Triphasia trifoliata* and *T. aurantifolia*. The berry of spiny Malayan shrubs; it is used in cookery and confectionery in the same way as the *Bilberry* (q.v.).

LITCHI or LYCHEE

Lat. *Nephelium litchi*. The fruit of a Chinese tree of the soapberry (*Sapindaceae*) family, the *Litchi chinensis*, cultivated in India, in the Philippine Islands and elsewhere, mostly in the East. It is oval, about 1 in. in diameter, not unlike a Gooseberry in shape and size, but its outer covering is hard and scaly, reddish and with occasionally some warty protuberances. The seed is small and hard; it is covered by a white, translucent, jelly-like, sweetish pulp, which is the only part of the fruit that is edible. The sooner *Litchi* is eaten after it is picked, the better. When *Litchis* are dried for export, their pulp turns black and becomes firm; it has little flavour left and is hardly worth eating. In that form it is called *Lichee Nuts* or *Litchi Nuts*.

LOGANBERRY

Lat. *Rubus loganobaccus*. The edible berry of an upright-growing *Dewberry* introduced in 1881, by Judge J.H.Logan, and now regarded as a hybrid between the American *Dewberry* and the true *Raspberry*. It is used as dessert fruit, for tarts and pies, jam and preserves, in the same ways as the *Blackberry* (q.v.).

LONGAN
Lat. *Euphoria longana*. A pulpy fruit related to the *Litchi* (q.v.) and produced by an East Indian tree.

LOQUAT or JAPANESE MEDLAR
Lat. *Eriobotrya japonica* and *Photinia japonica*. The plum-like diminutive fruit of an Eastern tree which has been introduced in countries bordering the Mediterranean as well as in California and Florida. It is of very little merit as fresh fruit but of value in the making of jams and preserves.

MACORA
Lat. *Eugenia javanica*. A variety of *Surinam Cherry* (q.v.) which occurs chiefly in the Dutch East Indies.

MAGELLAN BARBERRY
See *Calafate*.

MALAY APPLE
Lat. *Eugenia malaccensis*. A large, apple-like juicy fruit extensively grown in Malaya and the tropical parts of the southern Pacific; it is eaten raw as dessert fruit.

MAMMEE APPLE or MAMEY APPLE
Lat. *Otrocarpus africana* and *Mammea americana*. An inferior but edible fruit with brownish rind and yellow pulp which occurs both in the West Indies and on the West Coast of Africa.

MANDARINE
See *Tangerine*.

MANDUVIRA
Lat. *Geoffraea superba*. A South American fruit which the Indians toast to eat.

MANGO
Lat. *Mangifera indica*; Fr. *Mangue*. A native fruit of Malaya and the West Indies, of which there are a very considerable number of different varieties grown in many tropical parts of Africa, Asia, America and Australia. 'The choicest mango has no fibre in the pulp, and for flavour cannot be rivalled by any fruit in the world; but a bad mango tastes like tow soaked in oil of turpentine. Mangoes should not be eaten freshly plucked from the tree, but gathered when ripe and laid upon a shelf for a few days to mature. The green fruit is used in various ways, the stone being first taken out, and the mango cut into halves or slices: (1) put into curries; (2) made into a pickle with salt, oil and peppers (chillies); (3) made into preserves and jellies by being boiled and cooked in syrup; (4) boiled, strained, and with milk and sugar, made as 'mango fool'; (5) dried and made into *ambchur*; used for adding acidity to certain curries; (6) when very young cut into small pieces, mixed with a little salt, sliced chillies and milk, and made into a tasty salad. When ripe it is made into a curry cut into small pieces and made into a salad with vinegar and chillies, or the juice may be squeezed out, and allow to dry on plates, forming the thin cakes known as *Ambsath*, in India. Salted *Mangoes* are much eaten with fish curries.'—J.N.L.

MANGOSTEEN
Lat. *Garcinia mangostana*. A native fruit of Malaya now extensively grown in the moist and hot valleys of Ceylon, of India and the Dutch Indies; also in the West Indies. There is also a *Mangosteen* grown in Queensland named after the Cape York Peninsula *Coochin York*. The *Mangosteen* is a delicate fruit which must be picked when ripe and eaten as soon as possible after it is picked; its flavour is very pleasant and most refreshing, being sweet with an acid after-taste. In Java, they make quite a good *Mangosteen* vinegar.
'Resembling an apple of deep brownish-purple tints, *Mangosteens* have short stems and four thick, leaf-like bracts which form a rosette holding the purple fruit. The fruit has the consistency of a greengage plum, but a flavour which is indescribably delicious. Like many tropical fruits, there is a sprightliness of flavour, a suggestion of the Pineapple, the Apricot, the Orange.'—D.F.

MARMALADE
Originally quince jelly, from *Marmélo*, which is Portuguese for quince. Nowadays, *Marmalade*, when not otherwise qualified, means a preserve of bitter oranges and sugar.

Amber Marmalade
Slice thin one grape-fruit, one orange and one lemon, using everything but seeds and cores. Cover with three times volume of water and let stand overnight. Next day boil for 10 minutes and again let stand overnight. Then add pint for pint of sugar and boil very gently until it jellies, about 2 hours.—F.P.S.

MASTUERZO
Lat. *Coronopus didymus*. A South American tree of which the fruits are hardly fit to eat, but its leaves are aromatic and particularly rich in Vitamin C; they are eaten uncooked, in salads.

MEDLAR
Lat. *Mespilus germanica*; Fr. *Nèfle*. The fruit of the Medlar, or Mespil tree, a native of Europe, introduced into Louisiana by the Jesuits and thriving in most of the Southern States of the U.S.A. It is quite hardy and has been cultivated as far north as New Eng-

land, but its fruit has never been popular in America. In England medlars are picked when ripe and allowed to get soft before they are eaten, with the result that they look very unattractive when served – somewhat like a rotten crab-apple. Professor George Saintsbury professed to enjoy medlars and vintage port, but the taste for medlars is limited to comparatively few people in England. In Rome, medlars are eaten freshly picked, and they are a popular dessert fruit called *Nespoli*.

Medlar Jelly

Rub the medlars clean with a dry cloth. To 1 lb. of fruit add half a pint of water and let simmer until the pulp sinks to the bottom. Strain through a jelly bag and do not press the bag. Then add rather less than ¾ lb. of sugar to each pint of liquid and simmer until jelly begins to form slightly, as it stiffens in the keeping.

Medlar Jelly is practically undistinguishable from *Guava Jelly*.

MIRABELLE

The name of the smallest of cultivated species of *Plums*. The fruit is small, usually three-quarters of an inch in diameter, quite yellow or golden with red dots, round, cherry-like, the skin very thin and tender, the flesh soft, juicy and very sweet, with a pleasant flavour. The *Mirabelle* is sometimes called in England *Cloth of Gold*. It is extensively cultivated in Alsace and Lorraine, and to a lesser extent in other parts of France. It is very popular in Germany, but little known in England. In France it usually ripens towards mid-August. It is a pleasant dessert plum, but it is mostly used in fruit tarts and for making jams, jellies and preserves.

MIRACULOUS FRUIT

Lat. *Sideroxylon dulcificum*. The berry of a tropical African tree; it owes its name to the fact – or fancy – that without being particularly sweet itself it has the property of sweetening, or at any rate neutralizing the acidity of sour fruits or drinks.

MISTOL

Lat. *Zizyphus mistol*. A South American fruit which is sometimes eaten uncooked but is chiefly used to obtain from its fermented juice a strong *arrope* or spirit.

MOLLE DE BEBER

Lat. *Lithraea molleoides*. An Argentina fruit which is sometimes used in the Province of Cordoba with the *maté-tea*.

MONKEY PUZZLE NUT

Lat. *Araucaria araucana*, and *A. imbricata*. The nuts of two varieties of South American

Araucarias, the *Pino* and *Pehuen*, of Chile and Peru; they are large, very hard and oily.

MONSTERA

Lat. *Monstera deliciosa*. The cone-like fruit of a climbing plant, a native of Mexico. It is a delicious fruit with a most attractive and puzzling flavour that reminds one of both the fresh pineapple and the banana.

MOUNTAIN CHERRY
See *Chickasaw Plum*.

MOUNTAIN CRANBERRY
See *Cowberry*.

MULBERRY

Lat. *Morus nigra* (European); *M. celtidifolia* (Mexican); *M. alba* (Chinese); *M. rubra* (American). The berry or fruit of a number of different species of Mulberry trees, chiefly: (a) the *Black Mulberry Tree*, probably a native of Persia, but extensively cultivated in many parts of Europe for a very long time; (b) the *Red Mulberry Tree*, a native of the U.S.A., of which there are different sorts bearing berries either blue-purple, or long and red, or else reddish-black; (c) the *Mexican Mulberry Tree*, which reaches as far as Texas, New Mexico and Arizona; it is also an American native but its berries are smaller and inferior in flavour; (d) the *White Mulberry Tree*, a native of China, a tree grown chiefly for the sake of its leaves, upon which silk-worms feed; its berries are nearly white, sweet, small and flavourless.

Mulberries may be eaten raw, with sugar, or else cooked with or without other fruits, in pies, puddings and tarts in any way suitable for *Blackberries* (q.v.). *Mulberry Gin*, made like *Sloe* or *Damson Gin*, is far better than either.

MYRTLE, AUSTRALIAN
See *Blueberry*.

NAARTJE

Lat. *Citrus nobilis, var. deliciosa*. The South African native *Tangerine* (q.v.), and probably the best citrus fruit of the Union of South Africa. It is mostly eaten as fresh fruit, as dessert fruit or in fruit salads, but it is also delicious when preserved or crystallized (i.e. coated with sugar), and it also makes excellent jellies.

NASEBERRY
See *Sapodilla*.

NATAL PLUM
See *Amatungula*.

NEBRASKA CURRANT
See *Buffalo Berry*

NECTARINE

Lat. *Prunus persica, var. nucipersica*; Fr. *Brugnon*. A smooth-skinned variety of peach, smaller in size but firmer of flesh and richer in flavour than the *Peach* (q.v.). The colour of the flesh varies from white to yellow and also, but not so common, red.

The earliest ripening *Nectarines*, in England, are *Cardinal* and *John Rivers*, normally ready by mid-July; then comes *Lord Napier*, early in August; it is followed by *Dryden*, later on in August; then by *Pine Apple, Pitmaston Orange, Darwin* and *Milton*, early in September; *Spenser*, in mid-September, and *Victoria* late in September.

Nectarines may be used in cookery and confectionery, for jam and jellies, like *Peaches*, but they are really too good to be cooked and are best eaten as dessert fruit.

OGEECHEE LIME

Lat. *Nyssa ogeche*. The acid, olive-shaped drupe of a species of *Tupelo* (*Nyssa ogeche*) or Gum-tree of the Southern States of the U.S.A.

OLIVE

Lat. *Oliva europea*; Fr. *Olive*. The fruit of a tree which has been cultivated in the Near East, the South of Europe and North Africa for many centuries, chiefly for the sake of Olive Oil.

The olives of commerce are of two sorts, the *Green* and the *Black*. *Green Olives* are picked before being fully ripe, and they are treated in a different manner from the *Black Olives*, which are picked when fully ripe and are used more as relish, appetizer or hors-d'oeuvre. *Green Olives* are mostly used, stoned, for garnishing and flavouring, either whole or chopped up; they are also 'stuffed' with pounded anchovies, pimentoes, etc.

ORANGE

1. *Citrus sinensis*. The Malta, Portugal or common Orange, introduced into Europe from China and now cultivated on a commercial scale in many parts of the world. It is used as dessert fruit and for the sake of its juice, fresh and preserved orange juice being consumed in very large quantities in the U.S.A., and in a more limited measure in England and elsewhere. It is also excellent in fruit salads.

2. *Citrus Bigaradia*. The bitter or Seville orange, introduced into Europe from India. The bitter aromatic rind of this orange is closely dotted with concave oil cells and is much used in confectionery, for the making of preserves and marmalade. The flesh is juicy and acid. It is used in cookery and for the classic *Orange salad*, served with wild duck and other rich dark meats, also in the making of *Sauce Bigarade* (q.v.).

3. *Citrus aurantium*. The sweet orange, an improved variety of *Citrus sinensis*.

4. *Citrus bergamia*; Fr. *Orange bergamotte*. This orange has the most highly-scented rind of all orange rinds; it is used for preserves and in confectionery, but mostly in perfumery.

5. *Citrus nobilis*; Fr. *Mandarine*. The *Tangerine* (q.v.).

In all these main classes of *Oranges* there are different varieties. One of the most popular varieties of the *Sweet Orange* is that known as the *Navel Orange*, a seedless, or almost seedless, variety which originated in Brazil and is now extensively cultivated in California and elsewhere. There are also different vareities of the sweet orange with deep-red pulp known as *Blood Oranges*.

Orange Jelly

Proportions: To 4 lb. Seville oranges allow two lemons, 4½ pints cold water, and sugar as below.

Wash and dry the oranges and lemons, and grate off the rinds, being careful to take the outside yellow part only. Then peel all the white skin off the fruit, and do not use it in the jelly making. With a silver knife cut the inner part of the oranges and lemons into small pieces, and put all into a preserving-pan with the cold water. Bring to the boil and simmer for half an hour, stirring frequently. Then strain through muslin placed over a sieve, or through a jelly-bag, and leave to drip all night. Next day measure the liquid into a preserving-pan, and add the grated rind and 1 lb. of sugar to each pint of juice. Stir until boiling, and then boil until the jelly will set.—G.H. (3).

Orange Marmalade

Proportions: To 4 lb. oranges allow one lemon, 12 pints cold water, ½ pint boiling water and sugar as below.

First Day: Wash or wipe the oranges and lemon and cut them in halves. Then squeeze out the juice of the fruit on a lemon-squeezer, strain it into a basin and cover over. Put the pips and the jelly-like substance that adheres to them into another basin, pour the boiling water over it, cover, and leave to soak all night.

Second Day: Put the peel, with the water in which it is soaking, into a preserving-pan and boil it until tender. Boil the pips and their water for 10 minutes in a small saucepan, and then strain off the liquid into the preserving-pan. When the peel is sufficiently cooked, pour the contents of the preserving-pan back into the jar or basin, add the juice of the fruit, cover, and leave until next day.

Third Day: Measure the mixture with a quart or pint measure, put it back into the preserving-pan, and add 1 lb. of sugar to each pint. Bring to the boil slowly, stirring until the sugar is melted, and then boil until the marmalade will jelly. Pour into pots and cover when cold.—G.H. (3).

Marmalade d'Orange

Put six Seville oranges and three sweet ones in a saucepan with cold water. Boil till tender, remove them and let them cool. Cut the oranges, remove the pips and, in the case of sweet oranges, scrape off carefully all the pith. Cut all the fruit in small strips, but not too fine, and put back in the saucepan with 2 pints of juice from the first boiling and 4 lb. of sugar. Bring to the boil, simmer for two hours and put in pots. The above quantities will yield 8 lb. to 9 lb. of marmalade. Fruit preserves should be made in an untinned copper pan.—X.M.B. (1).

Marmalade, Juicy

This takes about 1½ oranges to a 1 lb. pot. Cut the oranges in quarters, squeeze out all the juice. Place all the white skin and pips in a jug of water, slice the rind fairly fine, add the juice and allow to each pound of fruit 3 pints of water. Strain the skin and pips and use the fluid as part of the water. Put it in an earthenware pan and let it stay till the next day. Then boil till the rinds are quite tender; then let it stand till the next day in the earthenware pan. To each pound add 1 lb. of loaf sugar and boil till the syrup jellies, about three-quarters of an hour. If the oranges are very juicy, decrease the water slightly.—L.M. (2).

Oxford Marmalade

One dozen Seville oranges put into a large pan of water and boiled gently two or three hours in *two* waters until quite tender. Drain, take out the pips only, slice the fruit very fine, well boil half an hour with 2 lb. of loaf sugar and ½ pint of fresh water to every pound of fruit. The first boiling may be done the day before if you like; and if you wish the marmalade to be bitter, do not change the water. Put 18 lb. of sugar to 10½ lb. of fruit. Five to six lb. of sugar, one dozen oranges, will make about 8 lb. jars of marmalade.—L.M. (2).

PACURI

Lat. *Rheedia brasiliensis, var. salicifolia.* A South American tree the fruit of which is edible.

PALMAE

The name of a very large family of ornamental trees and shrubs, many members of which are gastronomically and physiologically valuable, such as:

Areca catechu, the *Betel Palm,* which produces a nut-like drupe, known as *Areca Nut*

or *Betel Nut. Areca* nuts and *Betel* leaves are used in the making of a popular form of refreshing drink.

Arenga saccharifera, the *Arenga* or *Sugar Palm,* a native of India, Cochin-China, Japan and the Philippines. Ten-year-old *male* trees yield an average of 3 quarts of 'toddy' a day, during a couple of years. (Female trees bear the fruit but give no sap or 'toddy'.) From the 'toddy', sugar is extracted and *Arrack* may also eventually be distilled from it.

Nipa fructicans, the *Nipa,* or *Water Coco-nut Palm,* a low, stemless Palm growing in the soft marshes of the Indian Ocean, East Indian Archipelago, the Philippines, Queensland, and introduced into West Africa. Chiefly valuable for its saccharine juice or 'toddy'.

Phoenix dactylifera or *Date Palm.* See *Dates.*

Phoenix sylvestria, the wild *Date Sugar Palm,* which is grown for its sweet sap which is sometimes sold as a drink but chiefly made into sugar (*gur*).

Metroxylon sagu or *Sago Palm,* a low and thick-set Palm, a native of the East Indies, which flourishes in low, marshy situations. The pith or interior of the stem is made into *Sago* when the tree is about fifteen years old.

Eloeis guineensis, the Oil Palm, or *Guinea Palm,* one of the chief sources of *Palm Oil,* but the palm kernels are also used as food. It is widely distributed along the West Coast of Africa but also grows in East Africa. Palm Oil is to the African Native what butter is to the white man.

Cocos nucifera or *Coco-nut Palm.* This is the most extensively cultivated Palm tree in all tropical countries. There are three varieties cultivated in India and Ceylon: the *King,* which is very good; the *Dwarf,* much sought after in Ceylon for gardens; the *Brahmin,* with large nuts, principally esteemed for its milk. The oil is used as food and must be eaten soon after its extraction as it quickly decomposes. It is obtained in the usual way by expressing, or boiling and skimming. The kernel is often preserved in sugar and made into various sweetmeats. When young, the kernel is delicious food, being easily separated from the shell with a spoon, and when ripe is grated and added to puddings, etc. The young *Coco-nut* has a large cavity in the centre of the kernel containing the liquid commonly called 'milk', which is considered very refreshing and nourishing, and is used as a substitute for water. It is often substituted for cow's milk in the preparation of puddings. The white outer part of the kernel is, when dried, known as 'copra'. In India, *copra* is eaten with parched rice, or rasped and put into curries; or made into sweetmeats. The grated kernel produces a sweet milk, used instead of cow's milk in cookery. The other products of the Palm are sugar and vinegar.--J.N.L.

Borassus flabelliformis or *Palmyra Palm*, one of the most important sources of sugar, especially in Southern India, Burma and the East Indies. It is also grown extensively in Madagascar.

Borassus flabelliformis, var. aethiopicus, or *Deleb Palm*. A native of Africa; its ripe fruit is rich and has an apricot-like fragrance; the Arabs slice it and boil it with water to make a sweet syrup.

Caryota urens or *Toddy Palm* (in Bombay, known as the *Hill Palm*). A valuable Palm in life and in death. It is tapped for 'toddy' when from 15 to 25 years old and allowed no rest but tapped till exhausted. It is then cut down and the pith from the trunk is said to be equal to the best Sago. It is made into bread or boiled into thick gruel, forming in some places a great part of the diet of the people.

Raphia vinifera or *Wine Palm*, a West African Palm grown for the sake of the 'toddy' which it yields.

Hyphoene thebaica, Doun Palm or *Ginger-bread Tree*, an East African and Madagascar Palm grown for the sake of its 'toddy' or sap.

Copernicia cerifera or *Carnauba Palm*, a Brazilian and Bolivian Palm, yielding, 'toddy,' from which both sugar and vinegar are made.

Mauritia flexuosa, the *Ita Palm*, or *Tree of Life*, a native of tropical South America; its fruit yields different kinds of food according to the time when it is gathered; saccharine when fully matured; and farinaceous before it is mature.

Mauritia vinifera or *Wine Palm*, a Brazilian Palm from which 'toddy' is tapped.

Oenocarpus batawa or *Patava Palm*, a native of tropical America, the pulp and kernel of which yield equally good oils for food.

Astrocaryum tucuma or *Awarra Palm*, a tropical South American Palm which yields an oil which is excellent for frying fish; butter is also made from the kernel which is of fine quality.

Lecythis zabucajo or *Palmito*, a tropical American tree (*not* a Palm), which yields the *Sapucaia Nut*, a nut extensively used for food in the highlands of South America.

PAPAW or PAWPAW

Lat. *Asimina triloba*, and *A. grandiflora*. A member of the Custard-apple genus (*Annonacae*), widely distributed in the tropics and represented in many of the States of the U.S.A. by hardy varieties from New Jersey westwards through South-western New York, Southern Ontario, and Southern

Michigan to Kansas, and southward to Texas and Florida. It is rare in the East, but very common in the Mississippi Valley. A fully-grown Papaw is green with a heavy bloom. The flesh is greenish-white, being almost white in the centre, and it has at that stage an offensive smell and taste which make the fruit quite unfit to eat. But there is one variety of Papaw in which the skin becomes brownish-black as the fruit matures, the flesh becoming creamy yellow, custard-like, soft, succulent, sweet, and entirely free from all objectionable smell. It is then in great demand as a dessert fruit, but it has no culinary value. Its name is due to its fancied resemblance to the true and far better Pawpaw or *Papaya* (q.v.) of the tropics which is an entirely different fruit.

PAPAYA or PAWPAW

Lat. *Carica Papaya*. The fruit of an American tropical tree, *Carica Papaya*. It is large, oblong, angular, spherical or cylindrical and yellow, when ripe. Its flesh is pulpy; the rind is thick; its weight may be anything up to 20 lb. It is one of the most important food fruits of tropical and sub-tropical countries. It is grown extensively in Queensland; also in other parts of Australia and in South Africa. When ripe it is eaten like melon, either with sugar and a squeeze of lime juice or ginger; or else with pepper and salt. When it is still green, the fruit is peeled, boiled, cut up in small pieces and served with an oil and vinegar sauce. It is also preserved and pickled. The *Papaya* contains a fair quantity of an enzyme of the pepsin order, called Papain, which is an excellent digestive.

PARADISE NUT
See *Palmito*, under *Palmae*.

PARCHITA
See *Granadilla*.

PARTRIDGE BERRY
See *Cowberry*.

PASSION FRUIT
See *Granadilla*.

PEACH

Lat. *Prunus persica* (*Amygdalus persica*); Fr. *Pêche*. One of the most delicious and one of the most universally cultivated fruits we have. A native of China, there are now many varieties grown in Europe, America, Africa and Australia. U.P.Hedrick describes no less than 2,181 varieties in his work *Peaches of New York*, differing in size, shape, flavour, skin, colour and season. Gastronomically speaking, the two main categories of *Peaches* are the tender and juicy ones, the most delicious to eat when freshly picked, as dessert fruit, and the larger, firmer and darker ones, more suitable for canning but inferior in flavour. Peaches are grown in England mostly in greenhouses, but those which do ripen in the open, in sheltered positions, are far superior to the others as regards aroma and flavour. In the U.S.A. peaches are grown extensively in the open in many parts of the country, but nowhere to such an extent or to such perfection as in California.

Besides being in great demand as dessert fruit, *Peaches* are canned, bottled and frozen on a very considerable scale, and they are used, both fresh and preserved, in confectionery, to make jams, jellies and conserves, to flavour ice-creams and various liqueurs.

Peach Custard

Slice some canned peaches thinly and cover the bottom of small custard glasses with the thin slices. Make a milk and egg custard in the usual way, but mix into it the syrup from the can of peaches. Pour the custard mixture into the glasses over the peaches, put in oven to set and serve hot or cold.

Flaming Peaches

6 fresh peaches
½ cupful of water
1 cupful of cream (½ pint) slightly beaten
¼ cupful of sugar
¼ to ½ cupful of brandy

Place the peaches, unpeeled, in boiling water to cover, bring to the boil, and cook for four minutes. Remove and set aside until ready to use. Boil the half cupful of water with the sugar for five minutes in a small saucepan. Skin the peaches. Place two at a time – or three if the pan is large enough – in the boiling syrup and cook and baste for two minutes. Boil down the syrup to about one-half the original amount and pour over the peaches. Add the brandy and light. Pass the cream separately. When fresh peaches are out of season, use those that are canned whole. Heat in their own syrup and add the brandy. Serves six persons.—E.K.H.

Peach Ice Cream

Place one half pint of cream in a double-boiler, heat and add three-fourths cup granulated sugar and stir until the sugar is dissolved. Remove from fire and add one half pint of double cream and stir until cool. Freeze to a mush, then add one pint of mashed ripe peaches to which a little lemon juice and one tablespoonful of vanilla have been added. Continue freezing.—G.T.L.

Three of Escoffier's Peach-and-Ice-cream Recipes

Pêches Adrienne. Choose ripe peaches, one per guest. Drop them in boiling water and immediately after into iced water. Skin them, sprinkle sugar over them and keep in a cool place.

Prepare an ice-cream with some *Fraises des Bois* (wild strawberries) and some fresh cream; sweeten to taste and flavour with a little vanilla. Fill a crystal bowl with the ice-cream and press into the ice as many *Meringues* as there are guests. Place one peach in each *Meringue.* Pour over the peaches a very little *Mousse de Curaçao* and wrap up the lot in spun sugar.

Pêches Melba. Ripe peaches, skinned, served on a bed of vanilla ice-cream, and covered with fresh raspberry *Purée.*

Pêches Petit-Duc. The same as *Pêches Melba* with red currant jam replacing the raspberry *Purée.*

Peach Icebox Pudding

¼ lb. butter
1 cup of sugar
3 cups of sliced peaches
4 eggs
24 ladyfingers

Cream the sugar and butter until very light and frothy; add one egg at a time, beating well until all four eggs are used. Fold in the peaches, which have been lightly sugared and sprinkled with lemon juice. Line an oblong cake-pan with the split ladyfingers, both sides and bottom; over bottom place half of the mixture and finish with the ladyfingers. Place in refrigerator for 24 hours. Turn out on platter and garnish with sweetened whipped cream which has been flavoured with vanilla.—G.T.L.

Peach Island
(South African Recipe)

6 canned peach halves
2 egg yolks
2 egg whites
2 tablespoons sugar
⅛ teaspoon salt
1 cup hot milk
¼ teaspoon vanilla

Place the canned peach halves in serving dish. Beat the yolks with the sugar and salt. Slowly add the hot milk. Cook over water (e.g. in a double-boiler) until thick. Cool, add the vanilla and then fold in the stiffly-beaten egg whites. Pour this custard over the peaches and sprinkle with coconut.

Spiced Peaches

6 lb. peaches
3 lb. sugar
1 pint water
4 oz. stick cinnamon
2 oz. whole cloves
1 oz. ginger
1 pint vinegar

Clingstones make the best pickle, slightly under-ripe. Drop peeled peaches into a syrup made of water and half as much sugar. Boil five minutes. Cool quickly and allow to stand for two or three hours, then remove peaches. Add vinegar, rest of sugar and spices (in bag) to the syrup and boil for 10 to 15 minutes. Again add peaches and cook until tender and syrup is thick, about half an hour. Cook quickly and let stand a few hours or overnight. Remove spice bag. Pack; a piece of cinnamon and a clove or two without the bud or berry may be added. Pour re-heated syrup over peaches. Seal; store. (*Idaho Recipe.*)—C.G.

Peach Tart

Put peaches cut in halves or sliced in a baked tart shell and cover with a rich syrup in which should be mixed some finely-chopped fresh almonds. Serve with whipped cream sugared to taste.

Peach Whip
(South African Recipe)

Take soft loose-stone peaches and mash to a pulp, or take stewed peaches and press through a sieve. Take two egg whites and beat until stiff and dry; add two tablespoons sugar and again beat until stiff, then add two more tablespoonfuls of sugar and the peach pulp, which should measure a cupful. Beat thoroughly with an egg whisk until mixture is smooth and fluffy, then fill into long stemmed glasses and garnish with whipped cream and a glacé cherry on top. Serve with crisp cookies.

PEAR

Lat. *Pyrus communis*; Fr. *Poire*. Next to the *Apple* the *Pear* is cultivated more extensively than all other fruits in all parts of the world, except tropical and some sub-tropical lands. There are some 5,000 named varieties of European *Pears* and 1,000 American ones, practically every one of them descended from the same *Pyrus communis* or common pear. Another species, the *Chinese Sand Pear* (Lat. *Pyrus serotina*) furnishes about a score of named sorts with showy fruits which keep well but are scarcely edible uncooked and of very little gastronomical merit when cooked. A third species, the *Snow Pear* (Lat. *Pyrus nivalis*) is grown in Europe upon a much more restricted scale and solely for the making of Perry or Pear Cider.

In shape, pears are either *pyriform*, or pear-shaped, their proper shape, which varies, however, a good deal; or else elongated to what is known as the *Calabash* shape, sometimes shortened to what is known as the *Bergamot* shape, and yet sometimes round or oval. The colour of the skin also varies a good deal, from pale green to golden yellow and russet brown, plain, striped, flushed or dotted with red or russet. Many pears are exceedingly juicy and sweet and excellent as dessert fruit; other varieties are more suitable for cooking than for dessert, although there are no pears to compare with apples for acidity. Cooking pears are not particularly acid but lacking in flavour, and they are usually cooked in red wine or in some well-flavoured syrup.

Unless one has a garden, the right soil and the necessary knowledge to select and grow early and late varieties of dessert pears, one must be satisfied with the limited choice of pears which the growers find to be trustworthy 'croppers', such as the *Williams* (the *Bartlett* of U.S.A.), *Conference, Doyenne du Comice* (the best of Summer Pears), *Winter Nelis* and *Joséphine de Malines*. Best-known U.S. varieties are *Bartlett, Bose, Anjou, Comis, Nelis* and *Seckel.*

Baked Pears, au vin

Peel, core and quarter some pears and lay them in a baking-dish; sprinkle some castor sugar over them more or less according to taste; moisten with red or white wine, if available; failing wine, rum and water will do, and failing rum, water will have to do. Bake in a moderate oven until all or nearly all the liquid has disappeared and serve either hot or cold.

Baked Pears, au beurre

Peel and core some pears; cut them in halves and lay these in a pie-dish; fill the centre of each pear with a nut of fresh butter; sprinkle sugar freely over them and bake in a hot oven. Another way is to slice the pears finely and put a layer of thin slices at the bottom of the baking-dish; cover it with butter pats and castor sugar; then another layer of pear slices, more butter and sugar on top, and so on until the dish is full; then brown in a hot oven.

Poires Bourdaloue

Cook some pears in a syrup of sugar and water flavoured with vanilla; the pears may be whole, halved or quartered, according to size, but they must be peeled. Serve on a foundation of *Frangipane* and with a garnishing of apricot jam and macaroons.

Poires Bourguignonne

Peel, halve, and core the required number of pears; stew them gently till tender in a little water, much sugar and more red Burgundy. Serve in a glass dish and quite cold.

Poires Cardinal

Peel and poach some smallish pears in sugar and water; let them get cold in the syrup in which they were poached. When quite cold, serve them with a generous coating of sweetened strawberry *Purée*, flavoured with a little kirsch or maraschino.

Compôte of Pears

The same as *Poires Bourguignonne*, but replacing Burgundy wine by any other wine available, or water in place of wine if need be.

Poires Condé

Poach some small peeled pears in a syrup of sugar and water, flavoured with vanilla. (Should the pears be large, halve and core them.) Let the pears get cold in the syrup in which they were cooked. Serve them upon a border of rice cooked in milk, sweetened and flavoured with vanilla, and with a coating of apricot jam, livened up with a fair allowance of kirsch.

Poires Flambées

Poach some small peeled pears in a syrup of sugar and water, flavoured with vanilla. Drain and arrange in a fireproof dish; sprinkle castor sugar over the pears, then some brandy and set alight as you bring in the dish.

Poires Hélène

Poach some ripe pears, peeled, in a syrup of sugar and water, flavoured with vanilla; let them get cold in their syrup. Serve upon a foundation of vanilla ice-cream and with a hot chocolate sauce handed separately.

Pear Ice

Peel, core and pound ripe pears in a mortar with the same quantity of castor sugar, add the juice of one lemon to each pound of pears; rub through a sieve and freeze after adding water if you would rather have more ice and less flavour.

Poires Mary Garden

The same as *Poires Hélène* (q.v.), but instead of a hot chocolate sauce, serve a compôte of stoned cherries cooked with red currants and raspberries.

Poires Melba

The same as *Poires Hélène* (q.v.), but instead of a hot chocolate sauce, serve a *purée* of sweetened raspberries.

PECAN NUT

Lat. *Carya olivaeformis*. The smooth, oblong thin-shelled nut of a species of hickory of the South Central U.S.A. The kernel is much used in confectionery; it possesses quite a rich nutty flavour.

Georgia Pecan Brownies

2 egg whites
1 cup pecans, chopped
1 cup brown sugar
1 cup fine dry breadcrumbs
½ teaspoonful maple flavouring

Beat egg whites stiff, add sugar and flavouring. Stir well. Combine nuts and crumbs and fold in egg whites. Shape into small balls, place on buttered baking-tin, bake in slow oven until brown (325° F.).—c.g.

Hot Pecan Pudding

4 tablespoons ground pecan kernels
2 tablespoons granulated sugar
1 cup milk
2 tablespoons butter
2 or 3 tablespoons crumbled cake crumbs
2 eggs
Enough rich, flaky pie pastry to line a deep pudding dish

Cream the butter and sugar together. Beat in the eggs; then the cakecrumbs and pecans. Stir in the milk after it has been warmed a little in the top of the double-boiler.

Line the pudding-dish with the pastry, fill with the mixture and bake in a hot oven (400° F.) 20 minutes. Serve hot with grapefruit sauce.—c.g.

PEHUEN

See *Monkey Puzzle Nut*.

PEPERINA

Lat. *Minthostachys verticillata*. A South American bush tree, the fruit of which is hardly edible, but its leaves are dried and used to make a kind of tea and also to flavour sweetmeats and beverages.

PEPINO

Lat. *Solanum muricatum*. A plant which is a native of Peru; it is cultivated in Chile for the sake of its little yellow fruits, which are acid but refreshing and not unpleasant of taste.

PERSIMMON

Lat. *Diospyros virginiana* and *D. kaki*. The fruit of two distinct species of *Diospyros*, the Japanese and the American. The first, or *Kaki*, has been cultivated for centuries in China and Japan, and is sufficiently hardy to grow as far north as Pekin: its fruit is said to be delicious. The second, also known as *Virginian Date*, is usually found in woods, preferring dry lands, from Rhode Island, Southern New York, Iowa and Kansas southward to Florida and Texas. The American Persimmon is nevertheless chiefly considered as a cotton-belt fruit, as it grows more freely in the far south and its fruits are much less austere in the south. Fruits vary in size from that of a small cherry to that of a large plum; some are entirely seedless and they are the best for eating. The produce of some trees is sweet and luscious at maturity, whilst other trees in the same locality produce fruits so astringent to the end as to be unfit to eat. The persimmon ripens its fruit at midsummer in Florida, but not until late autumn in the north. Frost does not damage the fruit, and it is even considered as helping it to lose some of its asperity. The fruits vary in colour from yellow to orange and sometimes purplish red. The crop of late varieties, in the more northern States, often turns dark red, shrivelling and drying on the trees until the fruits resemble dry dates and are even credited with acquiring a taste not unlike that of dates.

Ripe persimmons can be eaten as a dessert fruit, more for curiosity than real gastronomic pleasure: the leathery skin is slit and peeled back petalwise without removing the stem, and the sweetish, sub-acid, mawkish pulp can then be sucked. Persimmons are also used for flavouring ices, jellies and for making preserves.

PERUVIAN MASTIC TREE

Lat. *Schinus Molle*. A South American tree which grows in the mountains of the Province of Cordoba (Argentina); its seeds are used as a condiment, like pepper, chiefly in the making of sausages.

PINDO

Lat. *Arecastrum Romanoffianum*. A South American tree which produces edible fruit.

PINEAPPLE

Lat. *Ananas sativus*; Fr. *Anana*. The *Pineapple* is neither a pine nor an apple; it is not even a fruit in the ordinary sense of the word, but a *sorosis*, i.e. a collective fruit formed by the union of originally separate flowers, with the bracts supporting them becoming fleshy and consolidated into one pulpy, succulent and perfumed mass, from milk-white in colour to deep yellow. The plant is a native of tropical America and is now cultivated extensively in many tropical parts, and with greater intensity at Hawaii than anywhere else. There are many varieties of pineapples, some large and decorative, and others small and usually of finer flavour.

In the Western Hemisphere, where pineapples are grown extensively, they can be divided into three main groups as follows:

(*a*) the *Queen* Group, of which 'Golden' is the type; the flesh is deep yellow and the eyes sloping from the sides;

(*b*) the *Cayenne* Group, of which 'Smooth Cayenne' is the type; flesh light yellow, eyes broad and flat;

(*c*) the *Spanish* Group, of which 'Abachi' and 'Porto Rico' are the types, the flesh white, the fruit mostly ovoid, tapering, the *Abachi* type narrow and the *Porto Rico* type broader.

A fully-ripe pineapple, neither cooked nor flavoured, is the finest dessert fruit grown in tropical and sub-tropical countries, and ever so much better than any of the made-up pineapple dishes. To serve a pineapple, the tufted top should be removed by a clean cut with a sharp knife; the uneven bottom of the pine should then be trimmed so that it can stand erect on a plate. Slide a long, saw-edged knife, such as a stainless steel bread knife, between the rind and the pulp, close to the pulp, from top to bottom and saw the pulp away from the rind all the way round. The whole of the inside can then be taken out, sliced, and the slices are put back into the unbroken rind. At dessert time, the erect pine may be passed round the table for all present to help themselves to one or more of the cut pineapple slices with the greatest ease.

Pineapples are canned or frozen, whole or in chunks or slices to an ever-growing extent, for export and for use at any time of the year either in fruit salads and in their own juice, or else in tarts, puddings, fritters and many other 'Sweet' forms. There is also, in the U.S.A., a considerable consumption of pineapple juice as fruit juice, and it is also used extensively to flavour ice-creams, jellies, preserves and liqueurs.

Pineapple Betty

2 cupfuls breadcrumbs
2 tablespoonfuls melted butter
2 tablespoonfuls sugar
1 tin pineapple slices
Grated orange rind
Orange juice

Mix the crumbs, melted butter and sugar, and put a layer in a buttered fireproof dish. Cover with a layer of pineapple cut in small pieces, and sprinkle over some pineapple and orange juice, and a little orange rind. Fill up the dish with alternate layers, finishing with a layer of crumbs. Bake in a moderately hot oven for three-quarters of an hour and serve with cream.—A.H. (1).

Pineapple Charlotte

A small tin preserved pineapple
4 oz. sugar (or less)
4 oz. raspberry jam
A few slices of freshly-buttered bread

Cut pineapple small and put it and sugar into a small pan to simmer until the fruit is tender. Line a plain oval mould with fingers of buttered bread and fill with alternate layers of pineapple and slices of bread buttered and spread with raspberry jam. Pour any pineapple syrup remaining over all.

Bake in a moderate oven about an hour. Turn out, sift more sugar over (optional), and serve. Sufficient for four people.—L.G.N.

Ananas à la Créole

Take a medium size pineapple and, with a silver knife and fork, scoop out the inside of the fruit and mash into a pulp. Skin three bananas and three oranges, slice the bananas into rings and mash the oranges, having removed pips and inner skin. Mix with the pineapple. Take a small fresh coconut and grate it finely and mix with the other fruit, together with sugar to taste and the juice of a lemon. Keep in the refrigerator for some time before serving.

Pineapple Custard

Grate a pineapple and cook a cup of its juice with a cup of sugar to a syrup. Let it cool. When cold, beat in the syrup four eggs, mix well and strain. Stir mixture in same quantity of milk and bake in a quick oven until firmly set. Let it cool and serve cold.

Pineapple Fritters

Cut the pineapple in thin pieces and coat these with sugar; dip them in breadcrumbs and then in a light batter and fry in deep fat; drain and sift sugar all over before serving; serve with a pineapple sauce.

Pineapple Ice

Mix in the pulp and juice of a pineapple, grated and pounded, a pint of melted sugar and a pint of water; pass through a hair sieve; add the juice of a lemon and a few small cubes of pineapple and put in the freezer till set hard.

Pineapple Ice Cream

Crush a pound of fresh pineapple and mix into 1½ pints of milk flavoured with vanilla and half a pint clarified sugar. Strain and freeze.

Pineapple Salad

Cut the top of a pineapple or melon and scoop out the flesh, chop it up and mix with some strawberries or raspberries (bananas or fresh figs can also be used); add sugar to taste and flavour with a liqueur. Put the fruit back into the pineapple and serve iced.

Pineapple or Grenadilla Sherbet

(A South African Recipe)

2 cups grated pineapple (fresh or canned), or 2 cups grenadilla pulp
¼ oz. gelatine
1 cup boiling water
1¼ cups cold water
2 cups of sugar
2 lemons

To the grated pineapple or grenadilla pulp, add the gelatine dissolved in the boiling water. After being softened in a little of the cold water, also add the cold water, the sugar and juice of the lemons. Freeze.

N.B. If canned fruit is used, the amount of sugar must be decreased slightly.

Pineapple Guava

Lat. *Feijoa selloviana*. A South American Guava, known in Argentina as *Guayobo*, which is used to make excellent jams, jellies and preserves.

PINO or MONKEY NUT TREE

Lat. *Araucaria angustifolia* (*A. braziliana*). A variety of *Araucaria*, the nuts of which are edible.

PIQUILLIN

Lat. *Condalia microphylla*. A South American fruit which is edible but is chiefly used to make a kind of syrup known as *arrobe*; also a fermented 'wine' which is distilled into a fiery brandy.

PISTACHIO

Lat. *Pistacia vera*. A small tree of Southern Europe and Asia Minor, which bears rather a large fruit with a stone containing one oblong greenish edible seed, the *Pistachio Nut*. It is used as a flavouring agent both in cookery and confectionery and has a distinctive yellow-green colour known as pistachio green.

In the U.S.A. the *Pistachio Nuts* are not easily obtainable, and pistachio has come to mean the pistachio green colour, not the nut. Pistachio ice-creams and pistachio pastes are ice-creams and pastes flavoured with almonds and vanilla and coloured with vegetable dyes as near the pistachio green as possible.

PLUM

Lat. *Prunus domestica*; Fr. *Prune*; American Plums: *Prunus angustifolia*, Chickasaw Plum; *P. angustifolia, var. watsonii*, Sand Plum; *hortulana*, American Plum; *P. maritima*, Beach Plum; *P. Munsoniana*, Munson Plum; *P. nigra*, Canadian Plum; *P. subcordata*, American Western Plum.

1. A drupe, i.e. a true stone fruit, of any tree of the genus *Prunus*, but chiefly of the Asiatic *Prunus domestica*, extensively cultivated in every European country; also of the American *Prunus americana* species.

2. The plum-like, edible fruit of a number of other trees, such as the *Spondias*, of Mexico and the West Indies; the *Diospyros* of Australia; the *Parinarium* of Africa; and the *Flacourtia* of India. This species has been introduced in Africa, and the fruit of the *Flacourtia ramontchi* is known in Northern

Rhodesia as *Batoko Plum*; the same fruit is called in Madagascar the *Madagascar Plum*.

3. Raisins, when used in certain cakes and puddings known as *Plum-cake* and *Plum-pudding*.

A distinct and very valuable species of American native plums is that known as the *Hortulanas*. 'The Hortulanas are particularly well-suited to the Mississippi Valley and Southern States, and fruit well as far north and east as New York. The product of Wayland, Kanawha, and Golden Beauty, best known of the score of plums belonging to this species, is especially suitable for preserves, spicing and jelly, being unsurpassed for these purposes by any other plums excepting damsons. They are quite too acid, and the flesh clings too tenaciously to the stone for dessert plums or even for ordinary culinary purposes.'—U.P.H.

Yet another variety of American Plums is the *Niagra* or *Canada Plums*, a distinct variety which grows farther north than any other, from Newfoundland to Michigan. They fruit early. There are about forty varieties under cultivation. The fruit is round-oblong, 1 in. in diameter, red, orange or yellowish in colour, with little or no bloom; the skin is thick and tough; the flesh yellow, firm and often acid or astringent. They are best cooked.

There are other varieties of native American Plums which bear edible fruit, such as the *Chickasaw Plum* or *Mountain Cherry*, a little red plum $\frac{3}{4}$ in. in diameter, found in the wild state from Southern Delaware to Florida; the *Sand Plum* of the plains of Southern Nebraska, Central and Western Kansas, and possibly Western Oklahoma; the *Munson Plums*, the most important group of native plums for the south; the *Beach Plums* of the sea beaches and sand dunes from New Brunswick to the Carolinas, and others.

Among the various species of plums which belong to the *Prunus* genus the best, from the gastronome's point of view, belong to the *Prunus domestica* family, of which both the Gages and the Quetches are members, the first being the finest plums to eat uncooked for dessert, and the second the best to dry into prunes. 'The *Domestica Plums* not only are the best known of the cultivated plums, having been cultivated longest and being most widely distributed, but also far surpass all other species, both in the quality of the product and in the characters which make a tree a desirable orchard plant.'—U.P.H.

Plums which are the most suitable for cooking belong to another branch of the *Prunus* genus, the *Prunus insititia*, or *Damson* (q.v.), whilst the native American plums

members of the *Prunus americana* family, owe their domestication to the fact that the *Domesticas* will not thrive in the Mississippi Valley, the prairie States, nor, for the most part, in the South. The fruit is reddish or yellowish, or a blending of the two, with the red varieties predominating. Wild or cultivated the fruits of the *American Plums* vary greatly in season, size, shape and flavour. The skin is thick, hard, acerb and astringent, but the flesh of some varieties is sometimes as sweet and luscious as the best Gage. Their greatest fault is their unreliability.

Other varieties of plums include the *Apricot Plum* (q.v.), the *Myrobalan Plum* (q.v.), also known as *Cherry Plum*, and the Japanese plums, of which there are many sorts, all of them bearing edible but inferior fruit and many of them being cultivated chiefly as ornamental trees.

Plum Caramel

Wash and stone some ripe blue plums; skin them, mash them and mix them with some finely-chopped, peeled, fresh almonds. Put in a glass dish and pour over them a good covering of tepid caramel. Let it get quite cold and serve with whipped cream.

Plum Compôte

Dissolve 2 oz. of granulated sugar per cup of water and boil until you get a light syrup. Wash, dry and stone some ripe plums, cut them in half and drop them into the syrup when boiling. Simmer gently until the plums be quite soft; take them out and go on boiling the syrup until it is reduced to the desired consistency; pour syrup over the plums, which must be all covered, and let it get cold. Serve with or without whipped cream, according to taste and circumstances.

Plum Flan

Wash, dry and stone some ripe plums; cut them in half. Line a flan tin or paste ring with a thin layer of short crust and cover with thin slices of plum, arranging them in neat rows, slightly overlapping each other. Moisten with a little light sugar and water syrup, sprinkle with granulated sugar and bake in a moderate oven for 30 to 35 minutes.

Plum and Apple Jelly

Take equal quantities of ripe plums, preferably red ones, and green cooking apples, cutting the latter into pieces, but including core and peel; just cover with water, boil till soft and then strain through a jelly-bag all night. Next day measure the juice, bring to the boil and boil briskly for five or ten minutes. Then add an equal quantity of warmed sugar, stir until dissolved and boil without stirring until a little will set on a saucer. Bottle and seal.—L.G.N.

POMEGRANATE

Lat. *Punica granatum*. An Eastern fruit introduced into Europe at a very early date. Its sweet juice is used for making a cooling drink and for flavouring ices.

POMELO

The pink-fleshed *Grape-fruit*, the sweetest variety and one which used to be served as dessert fruit in early Victorian England.

PRICKLY PEAR or TUNA

Lat. *Opuntia tuna* and *O. rufinesquei*. The fruit of tropical American cacti which grow only too freely in the districts of South-Western U.S.A. and many parts of Africa.

PRUNE

A dried plum, fully ripe and very sweet, such as are grown at Agen (France), in Portugal, etc. It may be eaten as dessert in its dried form, but it is usually stewed or sometimes stuffed first.

Prune Flory

Line a tart tin with puff pastry and cover the paste with prunes previously soaked in water for two or three hours and cooked in a light syrup till tender. Cover with a lid of puff pastry; press down and moisten edges; bake in a quick oven till lightly coloured.

Prune Fool

Stew gently in water a pound of prunes with more or less sugar added, according to taste. When the prunes are tender, stone them, put them back in the pan, add ½ pint warm milk and stir till it comes to the boil. Pass through a wire sieve and let it get quite cold. Stir in a little fresh cream before serving.

Prune Ice Cream

Stew a pound of prunes slowly till tender; take out the stones and pound the prunes into a *purée*, pass through a wire sieve, add sugar to taste, a squeeze of lemon and plenty of stiffly-whipped cream. Freeze.

Prune Mould

Remove the stones from 1 lb. of previously soaked prunes. Chop and put in a saucepan with 1½ pints of water, ½ lb. of sugar, and the juice and shredded rind of one lemon. Bring to the boil and simmer for 30 minutes. Then stir in 1 oz. of gelatine, previously melted in a little water, and turned into a mould rinsed out with cold water. Stand in a cool place till set.—c.m. (3).

Prune Mousse

Prunes should always be of first quality and soaked overnight. They should then be simmered in water, or in a little water to which you have added a glassful of red wine, a teaspoonful of lemon juice and a few pieces of lemon rind. Sweeten them when they are done, and if the water alone has been used, add a small glass of Port. When they are cold, put them through a sieve, and whip up some cream and stir it into the prune *purée*. Sweeten a little more if necessary, and then add the stiffly-beaten whites of two eggs. In summer it may be a good thing to include a little gelatine to make the *Mousse* as firm as you want it. See that it is served very cold.—a.h. (1).

Stewed Prunes

Soak prunes overnight. Put them in a pan with a glassful of water to two of red wine and sugar to taste. Stew gently for an hour or until quite tender. Pour into a glass dish and let them stand for a day or two before serving so that the wine may well soak in.

PULASSAN

Lat. *Nephelium mutabile*. A Javanese fruit, the size of an average plum; it has a deep pink, pebbly surface and a fairly thick skin. The single seed within the fruit comes out of the shell with its surrounding pulp and looks rather like a skinned grape, but it is not so juicy. Botanically it is related to the Chinese *Litchi* (q.v.), and gastronomically it is as good as the *Mangosteen* (q.v.).

QUANDONG, QUANDANG or QUANTONG

Lat. *Pusanus acuminatus*. An Australian drupaceous fruit which is usually referred to in parts of Australia, where it grows, as the *Native Peach*; it resembles the *Peach* in shape and size but in nothing else. Its stone holds a seed or nut which is locally known as *Quangdong Nut*, and is the best part of the fruit from the gastronome's point of view.

QUATRE MENDIANTS

A very old-fashioned French dessert plate of fruit at a time of the year when fresh fruit was a luxury, i.e. before California, Florida, South Africa and Australia sent fruit to Europe in large consignments. The *Quatre Mendiants* are dried figs, raisins, filberts and peeled almonds. The name is a reminder of the four chief orders of mendicant friars, the black friars (Dominicans, raisins); the white friars (Carmelites, peeled almonds); the grey friars (Franciscans, figs); and the Austin friars (Augustans, filberts).

QUINCE

Lat. *Pyrus cydonia* and *Cydonia oblonga* (*Cydonia vulgaris*); Fr. *Coing*. The *Quince*, the 'Golden Apple' of the Ancients, who looked upon it as the emblem of love and happiness, is the fruit of small trees or shrubs from 15 ft. to 20 ft. in height, native of the Mediterranean and Caucasus regions. It was introduced to

Rome from Greece before the Christian Era. Its cultivation spread throughout the West, and Chaucer speaks of it as growing in England in his day and being known by the name of *Coine*, from the French name of the fruit, *Coing*. It was the basis of *Cotignac*, a sweetmeat made in various parts of France, from mediaeval times to the present. *Cotignac* was offered to Joan of Arc when she entered Orleans, and Rebecca West wrote to the Editor that she was 'brought up on *cotignac*'.

Quince is either round or pear-shaped, with yellow, woolly skin and yellow flesh which turns pink in the cooking. The testa of its seeds abounds in a gum which possesses distinctive and valuable mucilaginous and demulcent properties; it is this gum which is responsible for the fact that *Quince* makes such good marmalades, jams and jellies. Its name in Portuguese – *Marmelo* – is the origin of the name *Marmalade*, which was at first applied to no other but *Quince Marmalade*. A little *Quince* improves practically every kind of jam or jelly, but it is best with apple jams and jellies, and in England there used to be small pieces of *Quince* invariably added to all Apple Pies. They make an excellent *Quince Cheese* in Spain, which is called *Membrillo*. The right sort is pink; golden *Membrillo* is insipid and is made of apple, not quince.

RAISINS

Grapes which have been sun-dried or dried by artificial means for storage use at any time in the making of puddings and pies, cakes and pasties of all kinds; jams, jellies, and preserves; also sauces and stuffings. Not all grapes are suitable for drying into *Raisins*: up to the latter part of the last century, *Raisins* were made almost exclusively from grapes grown in the vineyards of Malaga and those of Greece and districts bordering the Eastern Mediterranean. Grapes, which are dried into excellent *Raisins*, are now grown on a very large scale in California; also in the Cape Province of South Africa, in Australia and other lands.

RAMBUTAN

Lat. *Nephelium lappaceum*. A Javanese fruit related to the Chinese *Litchi* (q.v.) and very similar to the *Pulassan* (q.v.), but it is covered with soft, curled, tentacle-like hairs, which make it resemble somewhat a chestnut bur.—D.F.

RASPBERRY (O.E. Hind-berry)

Lat. *Rubus idaeus*; Fr. *Framboise*. Cultivated raspberries are red or yellow, and some varieties ripen their fruit in June and July, others in October and November. There are also some black raspberries, sometime called *Blackcap*; they belong to a closely-related species, *Rubus occidentalis*.

Raspberries are, with strawberries, the most popular of small dessert fruit and they are excellent either by themselves or with strawberries – chiefly the small wild strawberries (*Fraises des Bois*). They are served with a little sugar and cream, or else with Claret, Sauternes or Champagne.

'Spread the raspberries on a large dish and sprinkle with sugar: leave in a cool place overnight. By lunch-time, the next day, the raspberries will have melted and become merged in their own juice, but will have retained all the fragrance of the fresh fruit. You can doctor the dish with a little Claret or Cognac, but it does not need it. *Never stew raspberries*.'—D.H.

Raspberries make excellent jam, jellies and preserves, and they are used also in confectionery for ice-creams, tarts, pies and puddings, sauces, etc. They are equally valuable in the compounding of liqueurs and lastly for making vinegar.

Raspberry Bombe

Crush and strain through a cheese cloth two quarts of red raspberries. Make a syrup of one cup of sugar and one of water cooked together for five minutes after starting to boil. Add the syrup to the fruit juice and when cool add the juice of one lemon, then freeze hard. Line a two-quart mould about 2 in. deep, bottom and sides, with the raspberry ice and fill with one pint of stiffly-whipped cream which has been sweetened to taste and flavoured with vanilla. Cover with three sheets of wax paper and see that the lid is pressed down tight. Pack in salt and ice, using salt freely, for at least three hours. Unmould on platter and surround with red raspberries well powdered with sugar. Serve with a light cake.—G.T.L.

Raspberries and Chocolate

Whip 2½ cups of cream stiff with one cup grated chocolate and sifted sugar to taste; pick over one quart red raspberries, tail and fold them into the chocolate cream. Serve cold.

Raspberry Ice Cream

Simmer gently a pint of raspberries with a little sugar; rub through a sieve; thin with the juice of half a lemon and a tot of kirsch. Heat one pint of heavy cream and dissolve in it half a cup of sifted sugar. Let it cool. Then mix the cream and the raspberry *purée* and freeze stiff.

Raspberry Mousse

1½ cups of raspberry juice
Juice of half a lemon
20 marshmallows
1½ cups of cream

Strain and heat the juice. Cut up the marshmallows and dissolve in the juice. Cool, add the lemon juice and the cream which has been whipped stiff. Fill sherbet glasses with the *Mousse* and cool.—G.T.L.

Raspberry Pudding

Line a buttered pie-dish with pastry and put in half the raspberries you are going to use, also the same quantity of red currants, if the raspberries are red, or white currants with yellow raspberries. Then put a good coating of sugar over the fruit and the juice of half a lemon. Fill up the dish with the rest of the raspberries and currants mixed, with sugar on top and more lemon juice. Add a glassful of cold water. Roll out the pastry for the lid, moisten the edges and place on top. Join the 'lining' pastry and the 'lid', press round the edges; trim with a knife, cover with a well-floured cloth and boil for 2½ or 3 hours.

Raspberry Sponge

Dissolve five leaves of gelatine in ½ pint of milk (soak for one hour), mix with a ¼ pint of fresh raspberry juice, ½ pint of cream and sugar to taste. Whisk mixture in one direction until it stiffens and looks like a sponge; pour into a damp mould and turn out when set.—M.K:S. (2).

Raspberry Vinegar

Fill a jar with ripe raspberries, press them very lightly and add as much vinegar as the jar will take. After one month, strain the liquid. A teaspoonful in a glass of cold sugared water makes it a delicious beverage. —X.M.B. (1).

Raspberry Whip

Pick a quart of ripe red raspberries and mash them in a bowl with plenty of sifted sugar. Add the unbeaten whites of two eggs, mix well and then beat the lot stiffly to a froth. Chill and serve with whipped cream.

RED CURRANTS
WHITE CURRANTS

Lat. *Ribes sativus*; Fr. *Groseilles rouges* and *G. blanches*. Red and white currants are comparatively modern fruits; they have not been cultivated for more than four, or at most five hundred years, and they are hybrids of at least three different wild species. The *White Currants* are merely an albino strain of the *Red Currants*, and not a distinct variety, whilst the *Black Currants* (q.v.) are entirely different, being more closely related to the *Gooseberry* than to the *Red Currants*.

Red Currant Jelly

Proportions: To one pint of juice allow 1 lb. of sugar. This is the way our grandmothers made Red Currant Jelly and no other method is better. Pick and wash some red currants, drain them, but leave them rather

wet. Put them into a large jar or crock, stand this in a saucepan of water, and steam over the fire until all the juice is extracted from the fruit. Or the jar may be placed in a somewhat cool oven and left for several hours, or even overnight. Then pour the currants with their juice into a jelly bag, and let them drain until the juice has ceased to drip. Do not use pressure if you want the best quality of jelly. Measure the juice, and for each pint allow 1 lb. of sugar. Put both together into a preserving-pan, and boil five minutes, or until the jelly will set. A large quantity may require rather longer, but it is much better to boil only a little at a time. Pot in small glass jars. This should produce a perfect jelly with the full flavour of the fruit. A mixture of red and white currants will also make a very good jelly.—G.H. (3).

RIVER PEAR

Lat. *Grias cauliflora*. The fruit of a West Indian tree, which is not fit to eat as dessert fruit, but is used pickled like a gherkin; it is also called *Anchovy Pear*.

RIVERSIDE GRAPE

Lat. *Vitis vulpina*. The black, sour, small berry of an American wild grape, *Vitis vulpina*, often growing on river banks. It is not fit to eat as dessert fruit but makes good tarts or pies and preserves, with plenty of added sugar.

ROCK MEDLAR

Lat. *Amelanchier ovalis*. The small fruit of a European shad-bush and of a closely related American species. It is also known under the names of *Savoy Medlar*, *Sweet Pear* and *Grape Pear*.

ROSE APPLE

Lat. *Eugenia jambos*. The name of the large and edible berry of the *Eugenia jambos*, a tropical tree; the berry is aromatic and credited with possessing a rose-like fragrance. The name is also given sometimes to the *Brush Apple* (q.v.).

ROWAN

See *Sorb*.

FRUIT SALADS

In his *Edgewater Beach Hotel Salad Book*, Mr Arnold Shircliffe describes no less than 1,000 salads; of these 400 are *Fruit Salads*, and he does not claim to describe all the Fruit Salads which have been introduced in the past and may be invented in the future.

There are countless different ways of making a fruit salad, according to the variety of fruit available and individual tastes. The principle upon which a fruit salad should be made is that of contrasting flavours, so that there should be both bitter and sweet fruit in a fruit salad, whenever possible; the refreshing bitterness of citrus fruit – oranges, grape fruit, etc. – and the sweet fleshiness of peaches, ripe pears, etc. Dark fruit, such as black currants and damsons, are better left out of a fruit salad as they never look right, but a few cherries out of a bottle – that is stoned and sweet – always look well. The dressing of a fruit salad is provided by the juice of the fruit used, in the first place, and some sweet liqueur as well as some sharp lemon juice.

SALMONBERRY

Lat. *Rubus spectabilis*. An American wild raspberry or bramble found from California to Alaska and introduced in England. Its flowers are red and very attractive and its ripe berries are large, salmon-coloured, or wine red, conical and very pleasant as dessert fruit. They can also be stewed and used in any way suitable for *Raspberries* (q.v.).

SAND CHERRY

Lat. *Prunus besseyi*. The small, fairly sweet fruit of a small shrub, the *Prunus besseyi*, cultivated in the Western plains of the U.S.A.

SAND PLUM

Lat. *Prunus angustifolia, var. Watsonii*. A variety of *Plum* (q.v.) with thick-skinned fruit which is cultivated in the Southern States of the Western U.S.A.

SANTOL or SANTUL

Lat. *Sandoricum Koetjape*. The fruit of the Santal tree of Malaya; it may be described as an inferior or wild *Mangosteen* (q.v.).

SAPODILLA

Lat. *Achras sapota*. The fruit of an American tree, the *Achras sapota*. Its shape is that of a lemon, but it is grey-brown in colour, more like a medlar; it is very sweet when fully ripe or over-ripe. The pulp is reddish-yellow, somewhat like a reddish apricot. It is known in the U.S.A. by the name of *Naseberry*; in France it is called *Nèfle d'Amérique*; and in Java, where it is cultivated commercially and greatly prized, it is called *Sawo Manila.*

SAUCILLO

Lat. *Acanthosyris falcata*. A South American fruit which is gathered in Argentina chiefly, if not exclusively, for the distillation of a fiery fruit spirit known as Igba-jee.

SEA BUCKTHORN

Lat. *Hippophaë rhamnoides*. The orange red and edible berry of a maritime shrub with silvery leaves which occurs on some of the sea coasts both of Asia and Europe.

SERVICE BERRY

Lat. *Sorbus domestica*, and *Sorbus aucuparia*. The fruit, or berry, of any *Service* tree, such as the *Sorbus domestica*, in England a tree closely related to the Mountain Ash (*S. aucuparia*), but with larger flowers and larger berries; the Whitebeam, in Scotland, and any species of Shadbush (Bot. *Amelanchier*) in the U.S.A.

SHADDOCK

Lat. *Citrus maxima*. The largest but by no means the best citrus fruit. It was imported from the East Indies, in 1696, to Barbados by Captain Shaddock, whose name it bears. Its pulp is dry, coarse and of poor quality, but it has been improved beyond recognition and has now been superseded by the *Grape-fruit* (q.v.), a smaller fruit but one of far finer quality. The original native name of the *Shaddock* was *Pompelmous*, which has survived in *Pamplemousse*, which is the name used for *Grape-fruit* in culinary French.

SINGHARA NUT

See *Water Chestnut*.

SLOE

Lat. *Prunus spinosa* (U.K.) and *P. americana* (U.S.A.); Fr. *Prunelle*. In England the name is given to the fruit of the Blackthorn, and the best use that is made of it is to flavour one of the oldest and best of English liqueurs, *Sloe Gin*. In the U.S.A., the name is given to the fruits of various native *Plum* trees, and they are used chiefly to make conserves, jams and jellies, usually in combination with some other and less acid fruit, such as apples.

Sloe and Apple Jelly

3 lb. sloes
5 lb. apples
3¼ lb. sugar

Put Sloes in jar (a 7 lb. jam-jar). Fill up with water. Stand jar in a saucepan of cold water, half-way up jar, bring to the boil and cook till juice is fairly drawn and pour off one pint. (Fill up again with one pint boiling water and cook again, then pour off second straining 1½ pints and use it for Apple and Sloe Cake.) Meantime put apple parings and cores of 5 lb. apples in a preserving-pan, cover with water and cook till parings are quite soft, this should produce a good two pints of juice when strained. Put sloe juice (first straining one pint) and apple juice together, add 3¼ lb. sugar, bring to the boil, skim well and boil 45 minutes, or till it sets, and pot.—L.G.N.

Sloe and Apple Cake

3 lb. sloes
5 lb. apples
½ lb. sugar to 1 lb. pulp

Use the 5 lb. apples you have pared and cored for the Sloe and Apple Jelly, slice them and put them in a stew-pan with very little water and stew to a pulp, rub through a sieve. Add the 1½ pints sloe juice (second straining) from the 3 lb. sloes and mix well; then add half sugar to every pound of pulp and boil till it sets, about 30 to 45 minutes.

Fill into pots or tongue glasses. The Sloe and Apple Cake makes a delicious second course dish, turned out and served with custard or whipped cream. The sloes should not be gathered till after the middle of October.—L.G.N.

SOMBRA DE TORO
Lat. *Agonandra excelsa*. A South American tree which occurs chiefly in the hinterland of Argentina; Indians and the poorer people on the land eat its fruit.

SONCOYA
See *Annona*.

SORB or ROWAN
Lat. *Sorbus aucuparia*. The fruit of the Mountain Ash or Rowan; it is as large as a green pea and brilliant red, growing in highly decorative clusters. The Rowan is related to the Service Tree, and in the U.S.A. the *Service Berry* may be regarded as the same as the *Sorb* in England, and the *Rowan*, as it is called, in Scotland, where the berries are used chiefly in the making of jellies, either alone or with some other fruit.

Rowan and Apple Jelly

3 lb. rowans (stalked and washed)
7 lb. apples, cut in quarters and cored
7 pints cold water
7 lb. preserving sugar
Juice of 2 lemons

Boil the rowans, apples and water together, until quite soft. Strain through a jelly-bag. Boil the liquid for 20 minutes, and then add the sugar. Bring to the boil again, stirring all the time and add the lemon juice. Boil for about 10 minutes or until it sets when tested.—L.G.N.

Rowan Jelly

6 lb. rowan berries (stalked and washed)
3 pints water
Juice of 1 lemon
Sugar

Place the berries and water in a preserving-pan and boil gently until the berries are soft. Strain through a muslin bag. Measure the liquid and allow 1¼ lb. sugar to every pint of liquid. Add the lemon juice and boil for about half an hour or until it sets when tested.—L.G.N.

SOURSOP
Lat. *Anona muricata*. A small tropical American tree which produces a rather large, pear-shaped succulent fruit; it has short, fleshy spines and a somewhat fibrous and rather acid pulp; the best part of it is its flavour, which resembles that of *Black Currants*. It is fairly common in the West Indies and is known there as the *West Indian Custard Apple*.

SOUR SOUR
See *Indian Sorrel*.

SPONDIAS
Lat. *Spondias mangifera*. The edible fruit of an Indian tree resembling the common plum tree. It is called in India *Jungli Amba*, and in English by the less poetical name of *Hog Plum*. When ripe, it is eaten as a dessert fruit and also used for making jam or preserves; when unripe, it is used in curries or pickled.

STAR APPLE
Lat. *Chrysophyllum Cainito*. The apple-like fruit of a tropical American tree with silky, golden, oblong leaves. When the carpels of the fruit are cut across, they present a star-like appearance, hence the name. The Star-apple is related to the *Aguay* (q.v.) and is likewise used mostly to make jam and conserves.

STRAWBERRY
Lat. *Fragaria*; Fr. *Fraise*. Strictly speaking, the *Strawberry* is not a true fruit, but an enlarged pulpy receptacle, bearing numerous seed-like schenes. It belongs to the genus *Fragaria* which is widely distributed, indigenous species occurring in every continent. The strawberry grows more freely in temperate climates, but forms of the plant are found in the tropics and on the very borders of the arctic regions; hence the considerable number of different varieties of strawberries, both among cultivated and wild species. Probably no other fruit grows wild under such varied conditions and over such extended areas as the strawberry, and although the wild strawberry is much smaller than the cultivated sorts, its flavour and fragrance are usually greatly superior to the best strains of cultivated fruit. Strawberries have been divided into four main categories as follows:

(*a*) The *Scarlet* or *Virginian Strawberry*; fruit early, small, globular or oblong-conical, usually markedly necked; colour light scarlet, sometimes white; flesh usually pink, sprightly acidulous, aromatic.

(*b*) The *Pine* or *Common Garden Strawberry*; its berries are larger, conical or conic, firm; they are dark-red when ripe, more or less hairy and sometimes slightly necked; the flesh is white with a hollow core; the flavour is mild and a little musky.

(*c*) The *Alpine* or *Perpetual Strawberry*; the berries small, round and firm; sometimes round-conic and pointed; the flesh is white, delicate and sweetly aromatic. It is the *Fraise des Bois* or *Fraise des Quatre Saisons* of France and it grows wild in many parts of England.

(*d*) The *Hautbois Strawberry*, a species closely related to the *Alpine* but differing from it, its berries being rounder and larger, of a paler red and borne on longer, stouter stems which elevate them above the foliage; they also have a strong musky flavour entirely their own.

Strawberries may be served uncooked and cooked, hot and cold, but their flavour cannot be fully enjoyed except when they are eaten as soon as possible after being picked. Freshly-gathered garden strawberries, as the cultivated strawberries used to be called in England to distinguish them from the 'Alpine' or wild strawberries, if fully ripe, are best with just the point dipped into a little salt; it brings out both their sweetness and flavour. Another very good way with both the garden and Alpine strawberries, is to serve them in cups or deep plates, dredge them with sifted sugar and pour either Claret or Champagne over them; the wine not only helps the flavour of the fruit, but it acts as an antiseptic: Strawberries cannot be peeled; they should be rapidly washed under running water. The next best way to enjoy strawberries is to eat them mashed with sifted sugar and fresh cream. The enjoyment of freshly-gathered strawberries is not of very long duration, but preserved strawberries are with us all the year round in the form of jams, canned, tinned, bottled or frozen fruit; none of which have anything like the same flavour as fresh strawberries, but they are none the less very welcome in sweet omelettes, fruit tarts, fruit salads, ice-creams, jellies, meringues, charlottes and every kind of 'Sweet'.

Strawberry Shortcake

2 cups flour
4 teaspoons baking powder
½ teaspoon salt
1 teaspoon sugar
¾ cup milk
¼ cup butter

Mix the dry ingredients, sift twice, work in butter with finger-tips and add milk gradually. Put the mixture on to floured board and divide into two parts; roll out and put half into a round tin spread lightly with melted butter and place other half on top. Bake 12 minutes in a hot oven. When cooked, split cake with a fork and spread bottom half with strawberries slightly

crushed and sprinkled with sugar. Put the second half of cake on top and cover with strawberries, sugar and whipped cream. Cream may be put between the layers as well. This cake is also very good made with fresh figs, or raspberries.—M.K.S. (2).

Strawberry Jam with Lemon

Proportions: To 3 lb. strawberries allow the juice of 1 lemon and 2¼ lb. sugar.

The small or medium-sized red strawberries are the best for preserving. Pick the fruit and carefully reject any that is unsound. Put it into the preserving-pan, and bring it to the boil, stirring all the time. In the meantime have the sugar weighed out, crushed if necessary, and made very hot in the oven. Add it gradually to the fruit without letting it go off the boil. Pour in the strained lemon juice, and boil all together until the jam will stiffen.—G.H. (3).

Mousses aux Fraises

I

Have a pound of strawberries, mash them well and add sugar to taste, then ½ pint of whipped cream. Mix well, put in a soufflé dish and pack in ice for 2 hours.

II

Make a syrup with ½ lb. of sugar; it should be quite white, and at the temperature which you test in the following manner:

Dip your fingers in cold water, then quickly in the syrup. There will be a very small quantity of sugar left on the thumb and forefinger. Now dip your fingers in cold water; you should be able to roll a soft pellet of sugar.

Mash the same quantity of strawberries, reduce it well and add it to the syrup, and cook it so that it becomes thick and there is no juice left. Let it get cold, and add ¾ pint of well-whipped cream. Put this into a soufflé-dish and leave it in a refrigerator for about three hours. Raspberries can be treated in the same way.—X.M.B. (1).

STRAWBERRY BLITE

Lat. *Blitum capitatum*. An annual weedy herb of the north temperate zone, with succulent stems, small greenish flowers and little red, pulpy fruits.

STRAWBERRY-RASPBERRY

Lat. *Rubus illecebrosus*. This is not a hybrid but a bramble of the *Rubus* or Raspberry genus, introduced from Japan and grown for its berries as well as an ornamental climber. The berries are so tart, even when fully ripe, that they are not fit to eat uncooked, but when they are stewed with sugar they acquire a brilliant garnet-red colour, which is quite attractive, and a very pleasing flavour which is somewhat like strawberries and raspberries mixed.

STRAWBERRY-TOMATO or ALKEKENGI

Lat. *Physalis alkekengi* and *P. pubescens*. A small, yellow, diminutive tomato-like and edible fruit enclosed in the leafy calyx of several varieties of *Physalis*, the 'Chinese Lantern' flower of many English gardens

SUGAR APPLE
See *Annona*.

SUGAR CANE

Lat. *Saccharum officinarum*; Fr. *Canne à sucre*. A stout, tall, perennial grass extensively cultivated in tropical and warm regions for the sake of the sweet sap contained in its stalks or *Canes*. Cane juice is obtained by crushing, and, after it has been cleared of impurities and treated, the mother liquor – or molasses – is removed, leaving a crude, yellowish sugar, which is known in the U.K. as *Demerara Sugar* and in the U.S.A. as *Brown Sugar*: when refined, discoloured and re-crystallized it becomes *Cane Sugar*, *White Sugar* or *Lump Sugar*.

SUGAR MAPLE

Lat. *Acer saccharum*. A *Maple* of Eastern North America, whose three to five-lobed leaf is the floral emblem of Canada, and whose sweet sap is the chief source of *Maple Sugar*.

SULTANAS

Fr. *Sultanines*. The Turkish raisins, which used to be shipped almost exclusively from Smyrna, hence their name of *Smyrna Raisins*, in opposition to the Greek raisins, shipped from Corinth, and called *Currants*. They are now grown in and shipped from Greece, Crete, Persia, Afghanistan, as well as Turkey; also, in rapidly increasing quantities, from California, Australia and South Africa.

Sultanas are the fruit of a distinct type of vine which produces large, long, cylindrical bunches of small, round, firm, golden-yellow, seedless grapes. These are cured and not merely sun-dried, in order to bleach them and also to preserve them from the attacks of insect life.

'The best Sultanas are usually of a pale golden colour, with thin and delicate skins, almost transparent when new, and are very sweet, but without much flavour. Their chief characteristic is the absence of stones, seeds, or kernels, thus saving time in cooking, but they are also popular as a table fruit and for confectionery. New Smyrnas begin to arrive in England about the middle of September.'
—L.G.M.

California produces two distinct varieties of *Sultanas*, the *Sultana* proper and the *Thompson seedless*, which is grown on a vine originally produced by W.Thompson in 1878; it is a free-bearing vine but its fruit is not equal to that of the true sultana vine.

SURINAM CHERRY

Lat. *Eugenia uniflora*, and *Malpighia glabra*. The name is given to two different kinds of trees and to their fruit, i.e.(*a*) a Brazilian tree (*Eugenia uniflora*), often cultivated in Florida and California; its red, cherry-like fruit has a pleasant spicy quality responsible for the excellence of the jelly made from this fruit; (*b*) a tropical American tree (*Malpighia glabra*), which is rather uncommon; it bears an aromatic and edible fruit.

SWEET CALABASH
See *Passion Fruit*.

SWEET CUP
See *Granadilla*.

SWEETSOP or SWEET APPLE

Lat. *Anona squamosa*. The sweet, pulpy fruit of a tropical American tree, one of the large genus *Annona* (q.v.).

TAMARIND or INDIAN DATE

Lat. *Tamarindus indica*. An East Indian tree now cultivated in most parts of the tropics. Both its leaves and flowers are eaten in India, and the fruit or pod, of which the pulp is aromatic and acid, is used to make preserves and also a laxative or cooling drink. The seeds are also ground to a meal and baked into cakes.

TANGELO
See *Ugli*.

TANGERINE

Lat. *Citrus nobilus, var. deliciosa*; Fr. *Mandarine*. A small orange with loose rind and very sweet juice; chiefly from North Africa.

A recently introduced variety of Tangerine, from North Africa, with close rind like that of an Orange, practically seedless, and not quite so sweet, is called *Clementine*.

TANGLEBERRY

Lat. *Gaylussacia frondosa*. This variety of *Huckleberry* is found in the low copses on moist, peaty soils, from New Hampshire to Florida and westward to Ohio and Louisiana. It is most common along the seaboard. The berries are dark blue, with heavy bloom, when ripe; they are sweet and they possess a piquancy which is rather agreeable; it is responsible for the fact that the *Tangleberry* is considered the best of all the *Huckleberries* and *Blueberries*, whether eaten fresh or cooked. Its original name was *Dangleberry* on account of its extra long pedicels.

297

TASI

Lat. *Araujia sericofera, var. hortorum*. A South American fruit which is eaten toasted, chiefly by the Indians and the poorer rural population; it is credited with 'galactogenous' properties, i.e. it is recommended to nursing mothers.

THIMBLEBERRY

Lat. *Rubus parviflorus*. This is a wild American flowering raspberry found from Northern Michigan to the Pacific Coast and southward in the Rocky Mountains. The berries are light red in colour and of pleasing flavour. They can be used in any way suitable for *Raspberries* (q.v.).

TOMATILLO

Lat. *Physalis ixocarpa*. A name given in Spanish-America to a number of small globose fruits, red or yellow, resembling a small tomato, more particularly those of the *Physalis ixocarpa*, little berries more like gooseberries than tomatoes, from which a very good jam is made rather like the *Cape Gooseberry* jam; it is recommended with roast pork and goose in place of *Apple Sauce*.—D.D.

    Jamberberry is the name invented by Clarence Elliott for this fruit from which an amber jam is made with *Tomatillo*.

TOMATO-STRAWBERRY or BARBADOS GOOSEBERRY

Lat. *Physalis alkekengi* and *P. pubescens*. The yellowish fruit of a Mexican shrub, the *Alkekengi*, which is cultivated on a commercial scale in Italy and in the South of France. The fruit looks rather like a small tomato, and it is used chiefly in the making of jams and preserves. It is also known by a number of other names, such as the *Strawberry-tomato, Chinese Lantern, Winter Cherry* or *Ground Cherry*.

TREE TOMATO

Lat. *Cyphomandra betacea*. A South American tree-like shrub which bears an egg-shaped, reddish-brown, edible fruit, full of juice but lacking in flavour.

TUNA

Lat. *Opuntia tuna*. A South American tree, the fruit of which is eaten by the Indians in the Argentine.

UBAJAY or IGBÁ JAY

Lat. *Eugenia Myrcianthes*. A small South American fruit, rather pleasant of taste, which Indians and the poorer rural populations eat in the Argentine. It is closely related to the *Igbá Puru* (q.v.).

UBOCAYA

Lat. *Acrocomia totai*. 'A South American edible fruit.

UGLI

The name given in England to the citrus fruit called in the U.S.A. *Tangelo*. Its skin is loose, like that of the *Tangerine*, but it is much larger, irregular in shape and rather unprepossessing in appearance. It is eaten out of hand as a dessert fruit and also used in fruit salads and to flavour iced drinks in the summer.

URUCU

See *Annatto Tree*.

WALNUT

Lat. *Juglans regia*; Fr. *Noix*. The nut of any tree belonging to the genus *Juglans*, but more particularly that of the *Juglans regia*, which is known in the U.S.A. as *English Walnut*. Walnuts are eaten, like any other nut, either when fresh or dried. (In France the fresh or green walnuts are called *Cerneaux* and the dried walnuts *Noix*.) Fresh walnuts are oily and, where they grow in large quantities, as they do in some parts of France, they are crushed in order to obtain salad oil – *Huile de Noix* – which has a much stronger flavour than olive oil; many gourmets prefer it to olive oil.

    In England, where *Walnuts* rarely reach the state of edibility of dessert nuts, they are mostly pickled. Well-made *Pickled Walnuts* will keep for years and are highly esteemed with cold roast beef and even with cheese.

Walnut Bars

¼ cup butter
¼ cup lard
¼ cup boiling water
½ cup brown sugar
½ cup molasses
1 teaspoon soda
3 cups flour
½ tablespoon ginger
⅛ teaspoon grated nutmeg
⅛ teaspoon clove
1 teaspoon salt
Chopped walnut meat

    Pour water over butter and lard, add sugar, molasses mixed with soda, flour, salt and spices. Chill, roll, cut in strips 3½ in. by 1½ in. Sprinkle with nut meat and bake 10 minutes in moderately slow oven (325° F.). —B.C.S.C.B.

Caramel Walnuts

Mix together with a beaten egg to a very stiff dough 3 oz. icing sugar, 3 oz. ground almonds and 3 oz. castor sugar. Now lightly 'flour' your hands with icing sugar, take small pieces of the dough and roll them into balls in your hands. Press a walnut on each side and leave balls to firm for 24 hours. Then make a syrup of 1 gill water and 1 lb. loaf sugar, boiling till pale brown, then dip walnut balls in, stuck on a skewer, one at a time and as quickly as possible. Stand the caramel in a basin of boiling water while dipping, and then leave 'walnuts' to dry on an oiled plate (*Peggy Wynne's recipe*).—E.C. (2).

Sugared Walnuts

'Take green walnuts, in the proper state for pickling and boil them till tender; take them out and stick a piece of lemon peel to each nut; and to every fifth one a clove and a small piece of mace.

'To every pound of nuts, add 1 lb. of moist sugar with water enough to make a good syrup; put in the nuts and simmer them till the syrup is thick; let stand ten days; then clarify half the above quantity of sugar and boil as before, and when cold cover them close. By keeping, the syrup will shrink so that after a year or two it will be necessary to add a little more syrup.' (*Philips Companion to the Orchard*. New Edition. 1831. p. 219.)

Walnut Trifle

½ cupful of walnuts, coarsely chopped
1½ cupfuls of brown sugar
1 cupful of hot water
1 tablespoonful of gelatine
¼ cupful of cold water
2 teaspoonfuls of vanilla
2 egg whites, stiffly beaten
1 pint ring mould, wet with cold water

Boil the brown sugar and hot water together for three minutes. Sprinkle the gelatine in the cold water in a bowl and mix together. Add the hot syrup and stir until the gelatine is dissolved. Flavour and set aside until it is cool and begins to thicken. Add the walnuts and fold or lightly mix in the stiffly-beaten whites until blended. Set aside until thick enough to keep the nuts from sinking to the bottom, stirring occasionally. Turn into the mould and chill for five or six hours. Serve with whipped cream flavoured with sherry and pass cut-up fruit or berries separately. Serves five or six persons.—E.K.H.

(Walnuts are chiefly used in the making of cookies and cakes, for which recipes will be found in Part III of the *Concise Encyclopaedia of Gastronomy*.)

WAMPI

Lat. *Clausenia lansium*. A citrus fruit which D. Fairchild describes as 'the finest fruit in Thailand'. The fruit is about the size of a large marble. It is yellow, when ripe, and its flavour has been described by some people as resembling that of ripe grapes; by others that of the gooseberry. It is used to make a very good jam and also a pleasant, cooling drink.

WATER CHESTNUT

Lat. *Trapa natans* and *T. bicornis*. A fruit which is extensively grown in the East and in some parts of Africa; its seeds are very farinaceous and they are also rich in phosphorus; they are eaten uncooked, like nuts, or else roasted, boiled and mashed and generally speaking in any way suitable for *Chestnuts* (q.v.).

WHINBERRY

See *Bilberry*.

WHITE SAPOTA

Lat. *Casimiroa edulis*. A Mexican and Central America tree cultivated for its round, pulpy, edible fruit.

WHORTLEBERRY

See *Bilberry*.

WINEBERRY

Lat. *Rubus phoenicolasius*. The fruit of a bramble which is a native of the mountains of China and Japan and was introduced in the U.S.A. in 1889. It is a handsome, ornamental climber and worth growing as such. It bears small berries, bright orange-red when ripe, quite pretty to look at but insipid of taste. They are juicy and acceptable on a hot day with some very cold and sweet whipped cream.

WINTERBERRY. WINTERGREEN

Lat. *Gaultheria procubens*. The *Winterberry* is the red, spicy, berry-like fruit of the *Wintergreen*, a low, evergreen American herb, with white bell-shaped flowers; its berries are also called *Checkerberries*. They are mostly used in pies and puddings, also for sauces and stuffings and, generally speaking, in any way suitable for *Cranberries* (q.v.).

WORTS

See *Bilberry*.

YATAY

Lat. *Butia Yatay* (*Cocos Yatay*). A Central American palm tree, the shoots and fruit of which are edible.

SECTION 5
FISH

SECTION V

Fish: comprising an alphabetical list of edible Fishes and a selection of American, English and French Recipes for their culinary preparation

FISH

Je suis friant de poisson, et fais mes jours gras
des maigres: et mes festes des jours de jeusne.
MONTAIGNE, *Essais*, Lib. III.

INTRODUCTION

FROM the beginning of Time to this day the sea has been man's magic larder: without plough and without pay, there has always been – and there still is – in the sea a ready supply of all sorts of fish for man to catch and woman to cook. The same applies to all the waters of the earth: the sleepy or rushing waters of the humblest streams and noblest rivers, the icy cold waters of deep lakes in the mountains, and the shallow, brackish waters of lowlands and sea coasts – all are inhabited by fish, and mostly fish that is fit food for man.

In times of peace and plenty, fish does not receive the full measure of gastronomic recognition that it deserves. In wartime, however, when the importation of many foodstuffs is restricted, more attention is paid to fish, to its nutritive value and to its gastronomic merit.

Considering the importance of fish as food all the world over and in all times, it is somewhat strange that the names of fish known to everybody are, comparatively speaking, so few. The same name, such as *Bass*, for example, or *Dogfish*, is given to entirely different kinds of fish, and it is no exaggeration to say that there is much confusion as to the real meaning of many fish names. How many people, for instance, could tell what the difference is between the fish known as *Sole* in England and that which has the same name in the U.S.A.? Or how many people are quite sure whether there is a difference or none – and if there is, what it is – between a *Sole*, a *Dover Sole*, a *Lemon Sole*, a *Slip Sole*, and a *Torbay Sole*? And yet some fish or other is offered daily under those names in many famous hotels and restaurants. And how many people know the difference between *Crayfish* and *Crawfish*; *Lamprey* and *Lampern*? There is undoubtedly a great deal of confusion as regards the meaning of the different names of fish. Hence our first and our most difficult task has been to clarify the nomenclature of fish. It was, in our opinion, indispensable to remove all possible doubt as to the nature of the fish in question before attempting to give directions as to how it should be cooked.

The names of the edible fishes of the world, some 350 of them, are presented in the following pages alphabetically and they are gastronomically considered in concise form. The English name of every fish that has an English name is given first of all; then its scientific Latin name or names, when the same English name applies to different species. Its French name is then given and, in many instances, its German, Italian and Spanish names as well. A short gastronomic commentary follows, and then recipes for the most popular types of fish. These recipes have been largely supplied by Mrs Pauline Willsher and partly selected from the works of the most gifted American, English and French culinary writers, past and present, but no attempt has been made to offer more than a selection of fish recipes out of the considerable number to be found in all cookery books.

Recipes have not been given for any of the many Sauces mentioned as part of the Fish Recipes, since all such sauce recipes will be found in Section I of this Encyclopædia.

With a subject matter so extensive, omissions are inevitable and errors probable: pains have been taken to minimize both, but corrections and additions will be welcomed.

TO BUY FISH

There are many different kinds of fish in sea and rivers – flat-fish and shell-fish, small fish and large – and the best of them always is the freshest. Hence the best fish to buy is the freshest. There is no excuse for buying fish that is not fresh since it is so easy to tell fresh fish. Do not listen to the man or woman who has to sell the fish; look at the fish, it tells its own tale. The eyes must be bright and outstanding. The flesh must be firm (in some cases almost rigid), and the smell fresh and saline. Avoid all fish smelling, even slightly, of alkali or ammonia. Scales must adhere firmly to the skin and the gills must be a good red.

FROZEN FISH

More and more fish is brought to English and American markets every year which has been chilled or entirely frozen as soon as it leaves the sea. It is not so good as fresh fish caught close to the shore and sold the same day or the next, but it is cheaper and, in many cases, the only sort available. It is important to allow such fish to stand in cold water for several hours before cooking it, so that it may thaw gradually. It should then be thoroughly dried in a cloth and cooked immediately.

TO SCALE A FISH

Town dwellers are usually spoilt by having the fish they buy already scaled and cleaned for them. It is, however, useful to know how to prepare it for cooking in the event of catching it oneself or having it sent by some ardent disciple of Izaak Walton.

Lay the fish flat on a board. Take a small, blunt knife, or else use the back of a knife. Begin at the tail end, working towards the head. Hold the knife in a slanting position toward you, to prevent the scales from flying about, or use a proper scaler. Work, as it were, against the grain, taking care to remove *all* scales. Wash and dry fish after the operation.

Should the fish be slimy, pour boiling water over it, drain immediately, then scale.

TO CLEAN A FISH

Small fish are best cleaned by drawing entrails through the gills. If impracticable, slit abdomen and draw out entrails. Wash interior in cold, rather strongly salted water. If near the sea, use sea-water to wash out fish, but never use plain unsalted water. Also, avoid soaking sea fish in soft, unsalted water.

TO SKIN A FISH

Lay it flat on a board and cut the skin close to the fins on both sides of the back with a sharp knife. Remove the fins, and, if desired, also remove the head. Loosen the skin close to the flesh by inserting a finger under it, gently working the skin loose from the flesh then stripping it off towards the tail. Turn, and, if necessary, skin the other side. To remove the whole skin, bend the head backwards and, beginning at the base of the head, separate the flesh from the skin, as indicated, beginning the operation with a small, sharp knife and working towards the tail. With care, head and skin can be removed together. Most fish are easier to skin from head to tail.

TO BONE A FISH

Scale and clean the fish. Using a sharp knife, cut the skin through abdomen, remove entrails and cut close to the fins on both sides of back, pulling out the fins carefully. Starting at the back, separate the flesh gently from the bones with the help of a small knife, using the back of it to prevent cutting the flesh of the fish. Remove the backbone with the smaller bones attached to it in one piece, as far as possible. Pick out carefully any remaining bones, taking care not to break the skin. The flesh must be gently scraped from the bones, not cut.

Note.—Be careful to avoid pricking the fingers with the fishbones. Should this happen, wash in boiled hot water, then touch with iodine.

TO FILLET FISH

Using a sharp knife, cut through the thickness of the flesh on either side of the backbone. Slip the point of the knife under the incision, scraping the bones gently to avoid breaking or injuring the fleshy fillet. This done, turn the fillet towards the outer edge of the fish and either cut this or pull away from skin. This method is for flat fish such as soles, flounders, etc. For round fish, such as whiting, mackerel, etc., remove head, clean out the fish by slitting abdomen; scale if necessary. Cut the skin deftly along the backbone and work gently towards the slit. The fish will thus be split into two portions or fillets, leaving the backbone clean.

Note.—Retain backbone and head, which are useful in the preparation of fish stock or fumet for sauces, coulis, etc., to serve with the fish.

TO SALT FISH

Those who live in districts where fish is, sometimes, very abundant, may wish to salt what cannot be immediately consumed. To do this, remove entrails and heads and fillet as indicated. Prepare a brine, using one-fourth rock salt to three-fourths water, adding a little sugar, say a tablespoon to every quart of brine. Plunge the fillets in this brine and allow them to remain therein for thirty to fifty minutes, according to the size of the fillets. Damp a cloth in salted water. Place the fillets of fish in this and keep in a cool spot. Fish thus prepared will keep well for some time. When it is required for the table, wash it in several lots of fresh water before cooking it.

TO SMOKE FISH

The preservation of fish for household use by salting and smoking is not a difficult matter in places where suitable fuel for smoking can be obtained. Cabinet makers' sawdust or fragments of the different hardwoods produce the best results.Coniferous woods are less suitable, though they are sometimes used.

The essential parts of the apparatus needed are a fire bucket to hold a small smouldering fire, and in connection with it a barrel or box through which the smoke escapes, and in which the fish are hung in rows on sticks passed through their gills.

The fish should be cleaned, sprinkled with salt, and left with the salt on them for from six to twenty-four hours and then hung in the smoke for from six hours to some days, according to the time during which they are to be kept. It is not necessary to keep the fire burning continuously.

TO BOIL FISH

The first principle to remember is that fish should *never* actually boil: it should merely simmer, that is, the water should just be almost, but not quite, at boiling point, when the surface will 'shiver' or ripple gently. If boiled, fish loses a great deal of its savour and the flesh becomes stringy. Delicate fish should be cooked in a large piece of muslin to prevent it from falling to pieces. The use of a fish-boiler is a great advantage, as it contains a removable grid which enables the cook to take out the fish easily and without fear of breaking it. A home-made fish-boiler can be made by anyone who has a useful pair of hands. Cut a piece of fine wire netting to the size of the saucepan which you intend to use, fasten on either side a piece of wire, or of string, allowing sufficient length to project above the edge of the pan so that the netting may be pulled easily without disturbing the fish. Be sure the whole of the fish is covered by the liquid or the part standing out will not be cooked.

TO PREPARE A COURT-BOUILLON

Many cooks add to the water in which delicate fish is cooked different ingredients, which they cook at the same time as the fish. This method is wrong. The *court-bouillon* should always be prepared *before* the fish is placed in it.

All that one needs for a court-bouillon

Equal parts water and white wine	Small stalk celery
	Salt and pepper
1 or 2 cut-up onions	A 'bouquet-garni'
1 clove garlic	1 or 2 shallots
1 or 2 carrots	1 small clove

Put the water and wine on to boil; add about one tablespoon vinegar to every quart of water; add vegetables and seasonings. Let all this simmer gently for an hour before adding the fish. A fish *court-bouillon* may be used to make exquisite soup, in the Italian manner. Macaroni, spaghetti or vermicelli may be added and grated cheese served with it at the table. Every kind of fish may be cooked in this manner and the flavour of it will greatly be enhanced, whether eaten hot or cold. Whole peppercorns, bruised, should be used, not ground pepper. The bones and fish trimmings, head, etc., may be added to give more flavour.

Plain salted water may be used to cook fish, instead of a *court-bouillon*, or the fish may be steamed in a steamer. The flavour will be more 'natural' but also more fishy and less delicate. For invalids, fillets of fish may be placed in a soup plate, small pieces of butter and a little salt added; also a dusting of pepper, if the nurse sees no harm in it. The fish is covered with another soup plate and both are placed on top of a panful of boiling water. The fish must be gently turned and served, when done, with a little lemon juice.

TO GRILL FISH

Lightly oil the entire surface of the fish to prevent it from sticking to the grill. Be sure the fish has been well dried before attempting to grill. Turn the fish twice or four times, according to its size and thickness, while cooking, as both sides should cook evenly, that is, one side should not be done before the other has begun cooking. The use of wooden kitchen tongs is an advantage as they prevent the fish from breaking. It is advisable, where possible, to reserve a special grid for grilling fish as the smell clings despite careful washing. Begin fairly slowly and finish off a little quicker to brown skin evenly. One or two cuts across the fish enable the interior to cook more readily. The grid may be wiped over with an oily rag to advantage before the fish is placed on it.

TO BAKE A FISH

Oily types of fish, such as salmon, mackerel, etc., need the addition of *very little* fat when baking as the heat speedily causes their own fat to flow freely. On the other hand, dry fish such as whiting, pike, etc., must be given lots of butter if they are not to taste dry. The latter type of fish must be frequently basted while baking. Serve, whenever possible, the baked fish in the dish in which it was cooked as it contains its liquor. Sometimes baked fish is stuffed: it greatly improves the flavour of certain freshwater varieties.

TO FRY FISH

There are two methods of frying fish. Clean fish, wipe dry, sprinkle with salt and pepper, dip in flour, then in a beaten egg and then in white breadcrumbs. Fry in (A) deep fat, or (B) hot butter.

(A) DEEP FAT FRYING

The fish must be perfectly dried and well floured before immersing in the boiling fat; or egg-and-breadcrumbed; or else dipped in batter, as recipes indicate.

(B) SHALLOW OR BUTTER FRYING

To fry in butter, have sufficient to cover bottom of the pan nicely. Heat but do not colour. Place fish carefully in the butter, cook until brown, turn gently, drain and serve.

Note.—Frying by either method should be reserved for *small* fish or else fish slices or fillets only. Large fish are best boiled, steamed, baked or braised. Delicate fish, such as soles, trout, mullet, etc., are best grilled or pan-fried in butter. Good pure lard is suitable for frying flounders, whitings, and cod slices, while oil (the best olive oil) is preferable for frying eel and certain other types of fish. A mixture of olive oil and lard is suitable for nearly every type.

TO PICKLE FISH

2 cups French wine vinegar	5 bayleaves
2 cups water	1 teaspoon allspice
Salt to taste	4 or 5 onions
20 peppercorns	4 slices lemon

Boil the vinegar with the water, salt, peppercorns, broken up bayleaves and allspice, as well as the sliced onions for half an hour. Now add the slices of lemon and boil for five minutes longer. Simmer whatever fish you wish to pickle until it is soft enough to enable you to pull out a fin. Cook only a few fish or a few slices of fish at a time. As they are done, pack them in a stone jar with one or two thin slices of raw onion between each layer of fish. When all are done – and they should come to top of jar – cover with the hot liquid, without straining it. Put in a cool place and the fish will jelly and keep for several weeks. The quantities given above are sufficient for half a gallon of fish.

TO COOK FISH WHEN CAMPING

Build a fire of wood, allow it to blaze and then to die down completely. Wrap the fish, scaled and cleaned, headless or otherwise, in heavy wrapping paper, after sprinkling with salt and pepper. Place it in the hot embers and bake for half an hour, more or less, according to size. Rake the fish from the embers after turning it so that it be cooked on both sides; remove the paper, and as the skin sticks to the paper, it will be removed at the same time.

TO CAVEACH FISH,
AS PRACTISED IN THE WEST INDIES

'Boil as much Vinegar, covering it with Water to your Taste as you think will be sufficient for your Purpose, putting in black Pepper, mace, and Salt, and boiling all together gently. Slice as many Onions as you chuse, and fry well in the best of Olive Oyl (commonly called Sweet Oyl, and Sallad Oyl). Let your Fish, which must be of the large kind chiefly, and also of those Sorts which have firm, hard Flesh (In the West Indies they chiefly caveach Groupers, King Fish, Barrecooters and Hynds) be cut into Junks and fried in Oyl. When all is done put your Fish and fried Onions in a Jar or Stone Pot, laying first a Layer of Onions, then of Fried Fish, then fried Onions, then Fish again, and so on untill all is put in. Lastly pour in your prepared Vinegar, and as much cold Oyl as you chuse. Tie Down the Pot close.

Caveached Fish. In this Country, Bass and white, or silver Perch, seem to be as proper as any Sort of Fish to caveach. The Caveached Fish will keep good six months, even in the West Indies, as I have often experienced, keeping it in a dry, cool Place. It is an excellent Dish for Supper, and is allways ready to set upon Table.' (*Mrs Gardiner's Receipts from* 1763, p. 29. Boston, Mass.)

AVERAGE TIME FOR COOKING FISH (2 TO 3LB.)

Boiling	. .	About 10 minutes per lb.
Baking	. .	About 12 minutes per lb.
Frying	. .	10 to 20 minutes per slice or piece
Grilling	. .	15 to 25 minutes (according to size)

TO CARVE OR SERVE FISH

From Furnivall's *Early English Meals and Manners*, we learn that the right idioms used in the service of various fishes were as follows:

To *Tusk* barbels and breams; to *Fin* chevins or chubs; to *Tame* crabs; to *Transsene* eels; to *Side* haddocks; to *String* lampreys; to *Barb* lobsters; to *Splat* pikes; to *Sauce* a plaice or tench; to *Undertraunch* a porpoise; to *Chine* a salmon; to *Straunch* a sturgeon; to *Culpon* a trout.

Definitions and Recipes

ABALONE
Any gastropod mollusc of the genus *Haliotis*, with only one shell, used as a roof over the fish, which cling to rocks with a broad muscular foot. This is the only edible part of the Abalone. It is usually sliced, pounded and grilled or fried after being dipped in egg-and-breadcrumbs. Chiefly found on the Pacific coast of N. America.

ABOMA DE MAR
Lat. *Gobiomorus lateralis*. Spanish for sea snake. A *guavina* found on the Pacific coast of Central and South America.

ABOMA DE RIO
Lat. *Chonophorus banana*. Spanish for river snake. A large fresh-water *goby* found in rivers of the West Indies and East and West coasts of Central America.

ABURABOZU
Lat. *Erilepis zonifer*. The Japanese name of a large fish somewhat similar to the *Jewfish*, found in northern Pacific waters, from Japan to Alaska.

ACORN-BARNACLE. ACORN-FISH. ACORN-SHELL
Lat. *Balanus eburneus*; Fr. *Gland de mer* or *balane*. A small shell-fish of somewhat unprepossessing appearance but of very good flavour.

AGULHACREOLA
Lat. *Hemirhamphus brasiliensis*. A coarse fish of the South Atlantic, never seen but in the fish markets of Bahia and Rio de Janeiro.

ALBACORE
Lat. *Thynnus germo*. A species of tunny fish.

ALEC
An Old Latin word of Greek origin (salt fish), which used to refer to a herring or a pickle of small herrings.

'Alec, the Heringe, is a Fisshe of the See and very many be taken betweene Bretayn and Germania and also in Denmarke about a place named Schonen. And he is best from the beginnynge of August to december, and when he is fresh taken he is very delicious to be eten. And also whan he has ben salted he is specyall fod unto man.' (Lawrens Andrewe, in Furnivall's *Early English Meals and Manners*, p. 114.)

ALEVIN
The first stage of the *Salmon*.

ALEWIFE
Lat. *Pomolobus pseudoharengus*. A member of the Herring family very abundant off the Atlantic coasts of North America and of great gastronomic value.

ALLIS. ALLICE SHAD
Lat. *Alosa alosa*; Fr. *Alose*. The European *Shad* (q.v.).

AMBER FISH
Any of the many tropical and sub-tropical fishes, some of which are good food fishes, of the *Seriolidae* family.

ANCHOIS
Fr. for *Anchovy* (q.v.).

ANCHOVY
Lat. *Engraulis encrasicholus*; Fr. *Anchois*; Ger. *Anschove-sardellen*; Ital. *Acciughe*; Sp. *Anchoa*. A small, herring-like fish of the *Engraulidae* family, caught in large quantities in the Mediterranean and the English Channel. Dr. Badham says that it was to the ancient world what the herring is to the modern — compensating in some degree for its inferiority to the latter while fresh by surpassing when cured the very herring itself as a relish; and furnishing the materials for the finest fish sauce either on record or in use.

Anchovies were known to Shakespeare, even if Falstaff himself never tasted any. In *The First Part of King Henry IV* (Act II. Sc. 4), there appears a charge of 2s. 6d. in Falstaff's supper account for 'Anchovies and Sack after Supper'.

For some reason or other, Anchovies disagreed with T. Venner, who wrote in his *Via recta ad vitam longam* (Ed. 1628, p. 76): 'Anchova's, the famous meat of drunkards, and of them that desire to have their drinke, oblectate the pallat, doe nourish nothing at all, but a naughty cholericke blood ... and are therefor chiefly profitable for vintners'.

There is a variety of *Anchovy* in the West Indies (Lat. *Engraulis edentatus*) known as *Silverfish*, in Jamaica.

Anchovy Butter is made with from half an ounce to an ounce of butter for each anchovy.

Anchovy Essence, a flavouring made of pounded anchovies with capers, shallots, thyme, bayleaf, mace, red chillies and mushroom ketchup.

Anchovy Sauce, one of the best English sauces; it is made with anchovy essence or paste added to a white sauce.

Anchovy Toast, slices of bread fried in clarified butter, spread with anchovy butter and served with filleted anchovies.

The most popular French preparations of Anchovies, or *Anchois*, are the following:

Anchois saumurés. Whole fillets of boned anchovies, served with chopped yolk of hard-boiled eggs, chopped parsley, capers, with olive oil and a squeeze of lemon.

Anchois marinés à l'huile. Tinned anchovies in oil, like sardines

Anchois Chavette. Fillets of anchovies served on a *Chiffonnade* of lettuce with an oil and vinegar dressing, with beetroot and potatoes cut up dice-shape, the yolk of a hard-boiled egg and chopped parsley.

Anchois Gastéréa. Fillets of anchovies served on a *Julienne* of celeriac and truffles with a mayonnaise dressing. A row of very thin slices of tomatoes laid upon the anchovies and an alternate border of white and yolk of hard-boiled eggs.

Anchois Madrilène. Fillets of anchovies served upon a bed of tomato *fondue* (chopped tomatoes, onions, and a little garlic passed through a sieve and soaked in olive oil). Very thin slices of lemon laid upon the anchovies. Trimmings of cut-up sweet peppers.

Anchois de Norvège. Norwegian anchovies, also known as *Kilkis*.

ANGELFISH

Three kinds of fish bear this name, but the better known of the three is a *Squatina* (Fr. *Angelot*), also known in the U.S.A. as *Monkfish*, a raylike shark. It is found in the Atlantic, on both European and Northern American coasts, and its fins can be cooked in the same way as *Skate* (q.v.).

Another *Angelfish*, also called in the U.S.A. *Butterflyfish*, is the *Angelichthys ciliaris*, the yellow or blue *Angelfish*, and another is the *Pomocanthus arcuatus*, the black *Angelfish*, both being denizens of the warm waters of the West Indies and the Gulf of Florida.

ANGLER

Lat. *Lophius piscatorius*. A large and ugly member of the *Pediculati* family, found in the Atlantic seaboards of Europe and America. Sometimes called *Frogfish* and *Sea Devil*.

ANGUILLE

Fr. for *Fresh-water Eel* (q.v.).

ANGUILLE DE MER.
CONGRE

Fr. for *Conger Eel* (q.v.).

ARAPAIMA

A large-scale river fish belonging to the *Osteoglossidae* group; it is one of the largest fresh-water fishes, attaining 15 ft. in length and 500 lb. in weight. Its home is the Orinoco and other rivers of the northern part of South America.

ARCHER-FISH

Lat. *Toxotes jaculator*. A small tench-like fish of East Indian and Far Eastern waters.

ARCTIC FLOUNDER

Lat. *Liopsetta glacialis*. A small but highly prized food fish of the Behring Sea.

ATHERINE

Lat. *Atherina presbyter*. Commonly known as *Silverside* or *Sand-Smelt*. An excellent little fish which can be dressed in any way suitable for *Smelts* (q.v.).

AXOLOTL

Sp. *Ajolote*. Any of the several larval salamanders of the genus *Ambystoma*, found in the mountain lakes of Mexico and some of the western and southern States of U.S.A. Esteemed a delicacy by the natives of Mexico.

BAR

Lat. *Galeichthys marinus*; Fr. *Bar*. A white-flesh sea fish commonly known in England as *Dogfish* and in the U.S.A. as *Catfish*. The *Bar* enjoys, in France, a greater measure of popularity than either *Dogfish* in England or *Sea Catfish* in U.S.A. It lends itself to practically all the sauces and preparations suitable for *Salmon* (q.v.).

BARBEAU. BARBILLON

Fr. for *Barbel* (q.v.).

BARBEL

Lat. *Barbus barbus*; Fr. *Barbeau* or *Barbillon*; Ger. *Barbe*; Sp. *Barbo*. A fish of the *Carp* tribe found in several European rivers, where it rarely exceeds 16 lb. The *Nile Barbel*, however, is a much bigger fish, some weighing as much as 70 lb., but small or large, the *Barbel* is a poor fish, gastronomically speaking; its flesh is coarse and woolly.

Such, at any rate, is its reputation in England, but it has its admirers in France, and Escoffier gives the following recipes for *Barbeau* and *Barbillon*:

Barbeau au court-bouillon à la Ménagère
Cook the barbel in a white wine *court-bouillon*, flavoured with cut-up onions, twigs of parsley, a celery shoot, some thyme, bay-leaf, cloves of garlic, salt and peppercorns. Serve with a white sauce with capers and *Pommes de terre à l'Anglaise*.

The barbel cooked in a *court-bouillon* and served the next day, cold, with a *Vinaigrette* or *Mayonnaise*, is an excellent luncheon dish. A potato salad may be served at the same time.

Barbillon à la Meunière

Choose the smaller fish. Season with pepper and salt, dip in flour and cook in butter in an open pan. Dress in a dish; squeeze lemon over it, add small pats of fresh butter to the butter in which the fish was cooked; heat over a bright fire and as soon as the butter begins to sizzle, pour it over the fish.

Barbillon à la Bonne Femme

Choose a fairly large barbel – from 1½ to 2 lb. – and lay it in a baking dish generously buttered; season with pepper and salt; sprinkle some chopped parsley and shallots over it; cover it with finely-sliced mushrooms and some breadcrumbs. Moisten with a glass of white wine and the juice of half a lemon. Cook in a slow oven, basting it frequently with its own liquor.

BARBOTTE

Fr. for *Eelpout* (q.v.).

BARBUE

Fr. for *Brill* (q.v.).

BARRACOUTA

Lat. *Thyrsites atun*. A large sea-fish allied to the *Escolar* and common in Australian and New Zealand waters; it is also common at the Cape, and is called in South Africa *Snoek*.

BARRACUDA

Any of the voracious, pike-like, sea-fishes constituting the genus *Sphyraena*. The specimens caught on the Pacific coasts of the U.S.A. and on European coasts (*S. argentea*) are valued as food. The giant *Barracuda* of the Gulf of Florida and the West Indies is a serious menace to bathers, whilst in Cuba the *Barracuda* is considered poisonous.

BASS

Lat. *Morone labrax*. Originally *Barse*, the name given to a number of spiny-finned river and sea-fishes, from the *Perca fluviatilis*, the common river *Perch*, to the *Morone labrax*, the common European sea *Bass*, and including the following:

Black Bass

The name of three widely distributed and highly prized fresh-water game fishes of Eastern North America, viz:

1. *Huro floridana* or *Micropterus salmoides*: The large-mouthed black Bass, or *Bayou Bass*, which attains a weight of 20 lb.

2. *Micropterus dolomieu*: The small-mouthed black Bass, which never exceeds 5 lb. in weight.

3. *Micropterus pseudoplites*: The Kentucky black Bass, intermediate as to size and weight, and ranging from West Virginia to Kansas and Texas.

Black Sea Bass

Lat. *Centropristes striatus*. One of the more abundant and gastronomically important of the fishes caught along the eastern coasts of the U.S.A. They also call *Sea Bass*, in California, a gastronomically interesting seafish, the *Atractoscion nobilis*, allied to the *Weakfish*; also a *Jewfish* (q.v.), the *Stereolepis gigas*.

Calico Bass

Lat. *Pomoxis sparoides*. Also called *Strawberry Bass*. One of the best fishes of the rivers and lakes of the Mississippi Valley and parts of the eastern U.S.A. It owes its name to its variegated colours.

Rock Bass

Lat. *Ambloplites rupestris*. The poorest member of the large Bass family, gastronomically; its flesh is soft and often has a muddy taste; it is found in the Upper Mississippi Valley and Great Lakes region of the U.S.A.

White Bass

Lat. *Lepibema chrysops*. Similar in appearance to the *Rock Bass* and to be found in the same waters, but of far better flavour.

Sea Bass

Lat. *Morone labrax*; Fr. *Loup de Mer*. The European species and best of the tribe, gastronomically. It occurs from the Mediterranean to the British Isles, and is caught by sea anglers in the brackish waters of estuaries during the spawning season, from May to August.

Stone Bass

Lat. *Polyprion cernium* or *P. americanum*. A deep-water sea-perch of the Mediterranean and tropical Atlantic.

Striped Bass or Rockfish

Lat. *Roccus saxatilis*. A native of the Atlantic coasts of the U.S.A., but common now on the Pacific coast as well. It is olivaceous above and yellowish silvery on the sides and below; it is marked with numerous longitudinal black stripes. It frequently reaches 20 and occasionally 100 lb. in weight and is greatly esteemed as a game fish and as food.

All the recipes applicable to *Salmon* (q.v.) are also suitable for Bass.

BAUDROIE. LOTTE DE MER

Lat. *Lophius piscatoris*. A Mediterranean fish mostly used in the making of *Bouillabaisse*. Its English name is *Angler* or *Frogfish* and it is also called by the Marseilles fishermen *Crapaud de Mer*, *Diable* or *Marache*.

BÊCHE DE MER

A sea-slug of the *Echinodermata* genus found in the Pacific and particularly in the waters north and north-west of Australia – in the Timor Sea and inside the Great Barrier Reef. It is very highly esteemed by rich Chinese, who acquire nearly 100 per cent of the supplies. It makes a delicious soup resembling Turtle Soup. There is a similar but gastronomically inferior creature in the West Indies, Zanzibar and the east coast of Africa.

BELUGA
Lat. *Acipenser huso*. The Russian name of the *White Sturgeon* of the Black Sea, Caspian Sea and other waters. Its roe is highly prized as *Beluga caviar*.

BICHIR
Lat. *Polypterus bichir*. One of the largest and best fishes caught in the waters of the Upper Nile.

BIGORNEAUX
Fr. for *Periwinkles* (q.v.).

BIRT or BYRT
A small turbot (O.E.).

BISQUE
Fr. for a thick soup or *Purée* made from one or other kind of shell-fish, the name thereof follows immediately the name Bisque, thus: *Bisque de homard, d'écrevisses, de langouste, de crevettes, de crabes*.

The basis of all Bisques is a highly-seasoned white wine *court-bouillon* – Sherry for choice – in which the shell-fish is left to marinade overnight and then cooked with fresh tomatoes. When cooked, it is allowed to get almost cold, when the fish is removed and pounded in a mortar to a smooth cream; what will pass through a sieve is then put back in the bouillon and allowed to simmer very gently for quite a long time. When ready to serve, pour the bouillon into a soup tureen in which there are two or three lightly beaten egg yolks, stir, add a little fresh cream and a small glass of brandy or dry sherry, and serve.

BLACKFISH
The name given to a number of black or dark fishes, such as:

Centropristes striatus: the black sea bass.

Centrolophus niger: the black ruff.

Orthodon microlepidotus: a Californian cyprinoid fish.

Dallia pectoralis: a small but important food fish of Alaska and Siberia, remarkable for its ability to revive after having been frozen for a long time.

Gadopsis marmoratus: an Australian and Tasmanian fresh-water blenny-like fish.

Girella simplex: Australian bass-like food fish.

Girella tricuspidata: Australian bass-like food fish.

Leirus perciformis or *L. medusophagus*: also called *Barrel-fish, rudder-fish* and *log-fish*, a North Atlantic *Blackfish* often caught close to floating logs or barrels, which it seeks for the sake of the barnacles on them.

BLEAK
Lat. *Alburnus lucidus*; Fr. *Ablette*. A small river-fish of the Carp family, common in many European rivers. It is usually used for bait or dressed in the same way as *Sprat* (q.v.).

BLOATER
Fr. *Hareng Saur*. A *Bloater* is a herring that has been caught near enough to the shore to be brought into port and cured whilst still fresh – that is, without having had any salt put upon it in the hold of the drifter. A Yarmouth bloater is better than any other because the herrings which for some time past have been travelling the East Coast are in prime condition when they arrive opposite Yarmouth during October and November. A little later they cast their roe and are valueless. Unfortunately, bloaters do not keep so well as *Kippers*. To have them to perfection one must go to Yarmouth, and even there the epicure will eat them before he goes to bed rather than wait for breakfast.

Bloaters are good when grilled and served straight from the fire; they are best, however, when properly fried.

Bloater Paste
A popular relish made of baked, boned bloaters pounded with butter to a soft creamy paste.

BLONDE
Lat. *Raja brachyura*. A large and sluggish *Ray* – it grows to a length of 4 ft. – common near Plymouth.

BLUE COD
One of the best of the New Zealand sea-fish. It can be eaten fresh, but it is best lightly cured and smoked. Treated thus, smoked Blue Cod is like a Finnan Haddock gone to heaven. If cured sufficiently to enable a Blue Cod to travel – even to Australia – it loses some of its delicacy.

BLUEFISH
Lat. *Pomatomus saltatrix* and *Temnodon saltator*. A voracious fish esteemed in the Eastern States of the U.S.A. It varies from 3 to 15 lb. in weight. There are other fishes, mostly of the *sea bass*, *cunner* and *squeteague* types, which are also referred to as *Bluefish*, such as the *Apomotis cyanellus*, or *Green Sunfish*, a Sea Bass; the *Eriscyon parvipinnis*, or *Californian weakfish*; the *Scarus caerulus*, or

blue parrot fish; the *Girella cyanea*, of Australia; the *Girella nigricans*, or greenfish of California; the *Iridio radiata*, of Bermuda, and the *Scombresox saurus*, or *Saury*.

BOARFISH
Capros aper. A Mediterranean and North Atlantic fish allied to the *Red Mullet* (q.v.).

BOMBAY DUCK
Lat. *Harpodon negereus*. A small sea-fish of Eastern seas which is dried and used with curry dishes.

BONITO
Lat. *Pelamys thynnus*. A small species of *Tunny* (q.v.) found in the Mediterranean and the Atlantic, Pacific and Indian Oceans.

BOUILLABAISSE
The fishiest of fish soups, with saffron added. A perfect *bouillabaisse* cannot be made except on the shores of the Mediterranean, as some of the fishes used are not to be found elsewhere.

First Recipe
2 lb. mixed small fish (sea)
1 lobster or crawfish
3 or 4 cloves garlic
1 dried bayleaf
1 or 2 sprigs parsley
1 onion
1 small twig fennel
Good pinch saffron
Olive oil
1 peeled tomato
Salt and pepper
3 or 4 potatoes
Half glass white wine
Slices stale French bread

The fish may be almost any kind available, and a small crab or two improves things greatly. The traditional 'rascasse' is a Mediterranean fish unobtainable in England or America, but slices of cod, small whitings, a small mullet and so on will do. Clean and scale the fish. If either a small crawfish or lobster is being added, cook it separately, retaining a little of the water it was boiled in for adding to the *bouillabaisse* later.

Place the fish – if possible – in an earthenware *poëlon* with the garlic, bayleaf, parsley, onion (sliced), fennel and saffron. Add just sufficient good olive oil barely to cover bottom of pan. After peeling the tomato, cut it up finely and add to the rest, together with salt and pepper to taste. Cook for 10 minutes, stirring with a wooden spoon, then add three cups of hot water and *bouillon* from lobster, mixed, or water alone if no lobster is being added. Add the potatoes, sliced roundways, and cook fairly smartly for 20 to 30 minutes or until the largest fish

or pieces of fish are done, but take care they retain their shape. Add the wine five minutes before serving. Cut the stale French bread, or stale rolls, into rather thick slices and place in a tureen. Pour most of the fish liquid over them and serve with the fish, the remainder of the liquid and slices of potato, on a separate dish.

Second Recipe
Crawfish or lobster
Small crabs
Any small sea-fish
2 onions
1 tomato, chopped
½ glass olive oil
Salt and pepper
One small leek
Slices of stale French bread
Conger eel
Small whiting
Slices tail end of fresh cod
3 cloves garlic
1 small piece orange peel
Boiling water or fish stock
Saffron to taste
Herbs
Chopped parsley

This is, of the two, the better if a somewhat more complicated recipe. Remember that the cooking operation should, in all cases, be rapid and that the more different kinds of fish used, the better. If convenient – and this may be done at the seaside when one has been fishing – make a fish stock with the little fishes too small for any other purpose. Otherwise, the method of preparation is the same as indicated in the previous recipe. It is recommended that the soft types of fish be added when the firmer ones are already half-cooked so that they may all keep their shape nicely. Give the firm fish – conger eel, cod, etc. – 10 minutes' fast cooking before adding the whiting, etc. The herbs used as indicated in first recipe, with the addition of the small piece of orange peel and the small cut-up leek. The liquid must be strained on to the slices of bread and the chopped parsley sprinkled on top, but these refinements are not customary with the Provençal fishermen, who, it is said by the purists, prepare in their 'cabanons' by the sea, as soon as their boats touch land, the only real *bouillabaisse*.

BOUQUETS
Lat. *Leander serratus*. Also known as *crevettes roses*. Fr. for *Prawns* (q.v.).

BOURRIDE
A fishy soup of the Marseilles district; it is the same as the *Bouillabaisse*, except that there is no saffron, but garlic or *aïoli* instead.

315

BOWFIN
Lat. *Amia calva*. The mudfish of the Upper Mississippi Valley rivers and of the Great Lakes; of very little value gastronomically.

BRANCINO
A perch-like sea-fish, a native of the Adriatic and the best fish one is likely to eat in Venice. It is usually boiled in a *court-bouillon* and served either hot with a *Génoise* sauce, or cold with a *Mayonnaise*.

BRANDADE DE MORUE
A Provençal dish of pounded salt cod passed through a sieve and flavoured with garlic.

Genuine Provençal Recipe
Desalted cod, poached
Garlic (optional)
Milk
Pure Nice olive oil
Lemon juice
White pepper
Salt (if needed)
Chopped truffle (optional)

Two essential rules must be observed to make this creamy fish preparation as it is served in Provence. The mixture must be strongly and constantly stirred and the same moderate heat must be maintained throughout the operation. Pure olive oil is also an essential.

The cod must be soaked, but not too long; then cooked as directed. (See *Cod*.) Drain it well as soon as done; carefully remove all bones but *not* the skin, which assists coagulation of mixture. If wished, the fish may be pounded to an even pulp in a mortar, previously rubbed all over with garlic – if desired. In any case it must be reduced to a smooth paste, without any lumps. Heat about one cup of milk and the same amount of olive oil, having both warm, but only moderately so, and both at the same temperature. Add a spoonful of the warm oil to the pounded fish, working it well the while with a wooden spoon so that the mixture may become of a velvety smoothness. Now add a spoonful of the warm milk and continue using milk and oil alternately until the *brandade* is pure white and very smooth. Work over a very low heat or on the edge of the stove and do not have the oil and milk more than tepid. The stirring *must* be continuous and vigorous throughout the whole operation. Once made, season with lemon juice and pepper; some cooks add a pinch of nutmeg and a very little finely-grated lemon peel. The truffles may be mixed into the *brandade* or shredded and used to decorate its snowy surface. It may be eaten cold, but is nicer tepid. Fried croûtons or fleurons are sometimes also used as a garnish.

BREAM
Lat. *Abramis brama. Pagellus centrodontus. Chrysophrys aurata*; Fr. *Brème. Daurade*; Ger. *Brassen*; It. *Reina*; Sp. *Brema*. Yarrell refers to two kinds of *Bream*, the fresh-water bream or carp bream, which he calls *Abramis* or *Cyprinus Brama*, and the sea-bream, which he calls *Pagellus centrodontus*. Lawrens Andrewe (Furnivall's *Early English Meals and Manners*, p. 115) refers to the first as follows: 'Brenna is a breme, and it is a fisshe of the river and whan he seeth the pyke that will take hym, then he sinketh to the botom of the water and maketh it so trobelous that the pyke can nat se hym.' And Muffet (p. 148) refers to the second: 'Breams of the sea be a white and solid substance, good juice, most easie digestion, and good nourishment.'

The Carp-bream is of very little gastronomic value, whilst the sea-bream, which is common in most European waters, is a very delicate fish. It is at its best from June to December.

There is also the *Black Bream*, a name given to a number of different specimens of the *Sparus* family in Australia. The *Pomfret* (q.v.) belongs to the *Brama* genus and is an allied species.

In England, the sea-bream is usually served grilled or broiled.

Grilled Bream
Clean out and wash the fish, removing fins. Wipe dry in clean cloth; make one or two incisions on either side and marinade in olive. Wrap in greased paper and grill.

Bream Broil'd
Take a Bream, scale it, wash it, and scorch and cut it on the sides, then lay it on the Grid-Iron upon a little Straw that it may not stick to the Grid-Iron, keep it basted with Butter till it is ready; this done take fresh Butter and melt it in a Pan, add some Parsley minced very small, some Verjuice, Grapes, white Powder and a little Saffron beaten and steept in old Verjuice and Salt, boil it all together, and pour it over your Bream. (Giles Rose, 1682.)

Baked Bream à la Grand'mère
Choose a large bream.

Soak fine breadcrumbs in a little milk, then squeeze out all the moisture they have not absorbed. In a bowl work together the breadcrumbs with four tablespoons of melted butter seasoning, chopped parsley and a touch of nutmeg. Have ready a dozen small mushrooms which have been cooked in butter and a small sliced onion. Chop the mushrooms and onions; and add them to the breadcrumbs and butter, together with a well-beaten egg – white and yolk.

Sprinkle salt in the inside of your fish which should have been slit down from head to tail. Stuff it and tie it up. Put it on a fireproof dish which has been rubbed with butter. Pour over the fish a glass of white wine and sprinkle it with small dice of butter. Put the dish in the oven and baste it two or three times while it cooks. If the fish weighs about a pound it will be ready in 25 minutes. (La Cuisine au Coin du Feu. *Paul Bouillard*. (Albin Michel).)

The two more usual ways of serving a Bream, in France, are *à l'Angevine* and *à la Mode du Pêcheur*.

Brème à l'Angevine

Clean fish thoroughly and slit side half-way down. Soak a cupful of fresh breadcrumbs in half a cup of milk, adding a finely-chopped onion, butter and a coarsely-chopped egg. Mix to a paste, after squeezing out superfluous milk, and add salt and pepper. Add lemon juice according to taste. Use this to stuff bream, sewing up slit. Lay the prepared fish in a sheet of well-oiled white paper. Place in an oven dish and cook for three-quarters of an hour; then remove paper and serve with slices of lemon and fried parsley.

Brème à la Mode du Pêcheur

Clean fish thoroughly and scrape the scales. Make up a bed, in an oven dish, of *Duxelles* chopped shallots and breadcrumbs. Lay the *brème* upon it and cover it with the same preparation. Add white wine and cook in oven for 20 to 25 minutes, adding a little wine and pats of butter from time to time.

BREET
An obsolete name for *Turbot*.

BRÈME
Fr. for *Bream* (q.v.).

BRETT. TURBRET
A small *Turbot* (O.E.).

BRILL
Lat. *Scophthalmus rhombus*; also *Rhombus laevis*; Fr. *Barbue*; Sp. *Mero*. A European flatfish of real gastronomic merit, although generally regarded as inferior to *Turbot*, hence its price, usually slightly less than that of *Turbot*. Brill is in season all the year round, but at its best from April to August. There is in New Zealand a different sort of flatfish known as *Brill*; it is the *Caulopsetta scaphus*, and is of little gastronomic value.

For a whole brill, recipes are the same as for *Turbot* (q.v.); for fillets of brill they are the same as for fillets of *Sole* (q.v.).

Brill à la Dugléré
Have the brill filleted.

To 1½ lb. of fish, allow rather under 1 lb. of tomatoes. Plunge these into boiling water, remove and peel and chop them up.

Chop very finely sufficient onion to make a heaped tablespoonful.

Have ready also a tablespoon of tomato purée.

Butter a fireproof dish liberally. Put half of the mixed vegetables on it and the tomato purée. Then lay in the fillets, covering them with the rest of the chopped vegetables. Add also a small bouquet of herbs.

Over all pour a claret glassful of white wine, and one of fish stock.

Divide an ounce of very good butter into tiny pieces and sprinkle them over the fish.

Allow the liquid to boil up and then put the dish in a hot oven and bake from 15 to 20 minutes.

At the end of this time, take out the fillets very carefully, remove the skin, and set them on a hot dish placed over a pan of boiling water.

Take out the bouquet from the dish, and pour the tomatoes and liquid, etc., into a saucepan. Add a little *roux* and cook for five minutes, stirring all the time. If any more liquid has come away from the fish, add it to this sauce, and, at the last moment, stir in a piece of butter. Whip well together and season further if necessary, adding a little cayenne. Pour this sauce over the fish and serve at once.

Brill is very good cold with mayonnaise. (Mrs Lucas's *A Pretty Kettle of Fish*.)

BRIT. BRET. BURT
A small *turbot*, In England; a small *herring*, in U.S.A.

BUFFALO FISH
Lat. *Megastomatobus cyprinella*. One of the principal fresh-water fishes of the Mississippi Valley.

BULLHEAD
Lat. *Eleotris gobioides*, a fresh-water goby of New Zealand; also *Larimus fasciatus*, a seafish which enjoys a measure of gastronomic reputation in the Southern States of the U.S.A. Also various fishes with a large head.

BULTI
Lat. *Tilapia nilotica*. An esteemed food fish of the *Cichlidae* family, caught chiefly in the Nile.

BURBOT. LOTE
Lat. *Lota lota*; Fr. *Lotte*. A European freshwater fish Vid. *Lote*. An American *Burbot*, *Lota maculosa*, is found in northern waters in New England, the Great Lakes and further north.

CABRILLA
The name of a number of edible fishes of the genus *Seranus*, inhabiting the Mediterranean and the coasts of California and South America.

CALAMARY. PEN-FISH
Lat. *Loligo vulgaris*. A cephalopod or squid which is greatly valued in Spain and other lands bordering the Mediterranean, as a table delicacy. It is called *Chiriptia*, in San Sebastian; *Jibiones*, in Santander; *Chocos*, in Galicia, but it is best known under its Castilian name of *Calamares*, and its most popular culinary preparation is that which is called *Calamares en su tinto*, the fish being cut in pieces, fried, and served in a sauce made of the black liquid from the Calamary's pouch (it is used as a smoke screen by the fish when trying to avoid an enemy), and various aromatic herbs, as well as garlic.

CALIPASH. CALIPEE
Calipash is a corruption of *carapace*, the shell of the turtle, but it is used culinarily in reference to the green fat or gelatinous matter which adheres to the upper shell; *calipee* is the name given to the yellow fat or gelatine attached to the under shell.

CAMARONS
Lat. *Cambarus affinis*. The French name of the fresh-water crayfish of Mauritius.

CANDLE-FISH
Lat. *Thaleichthys pacificus*. One of the best fishes, gastronomically, of the Northern Pacific; somewhat like a *Smelt* but more oily.

CAPELIN or **CAPLIN**
Lat. *Mallotus villosus*; Fr. *Capelan, Caplan*. A small sea-fish of the *Smelt* family; it is very abundant on the coasts of Greenland, Iceland, Alaska and Newfoundland, where it is used as food and also as bait for cod fishing.

CARDINAL FISH
Lat. *Apogon imberbis*. A European sea-fish, also known as *King of the Mullets*: it is often red, but not always.

CARP
Lat. *Cyprinus carpio*; Fr. *Carpe*; Ger. *Karpfen*; It. *Carpióne*; Sp. *Carpa*. A soft-finned, fresh-water fish, indigenous to Asia and to be found in ponds and sluggish waters in every part of Europe. It is greatly valued as food on the Continent, but not in England (except by Jews), nor in the U.S.A. There exists a species of carp almost devoid of scales, commonly known as *Leather Carp*; another kind, with only a few very large scales, is known as the *Mirror Carp*. Carp may live to a very great age and may weigh 40 lb. or more.

Besides the carp proper, the carp family includes a number of other fresh-water – sometimes called 'mud' – fishes, such as the *Tench, Barbel, Gudgeon, Goldfish, Bream, Chub, Roach, Dace, Minnow* and *Bleak*. The best part of the carp is the roe ... and the sauce. A young carp is called, in French, *Carpeau*, and a very young one, *Carpillon*.

Carp sometimes have a muddy flavour, so it is advisable to soak them in running water in a box which has several holes in it, or, better still, to soak in two different lots of salted water and, finally, in a solution of weak vinegar and salted water – after scaling and cleaning, of course. If it is hard to remove the scales, dip the fish for a minute in boiling water and, when cutting off the head, be careful to remove the gall stone which lies at the back of the head or the fish will taste bitter.

To Roast a Carpe with a Pudding in his Belly
Take the Bones of a Pike and choppe them very small, then put in grated bread, two or three egges, Currans, Dates, Suger, Sinamon, and Ginger and Mace, Pepper and Salte and put in his bellye, and put him on a Broche and make sweete sauce with Barberyes or Lemmons minced and put into the sweete sauce and then put it on the Carpe when you serve it up. (*The Good Huswife's Jewell*, Thomas Dawson, 1596.)

'Your bait of falsehood takes the Carp of truth' (*Hamlet*. II. 1.)

And if the high swolne Medway faile thy dish,
Thou hast thy ponds, that pay you tribute fish,
Fat, aged carps, that runne into the net.
And pikes, now weary their owne kinde to eat.

(Ben Jonson's *Forrest*.)

A fresh Carpe, salted for the space of six houres, and then fried in oyle, and besprinkled with vinegar, in which spices have boyled, in all men's cinsure is thought to be the wholesomest kinde of fish. (Vaughan's *Directions of Health*, p. 38. London, 1626.)

Delicious Carp
Put a handful of prepared, washed and lightly-chopped sorrel into a saucepan together with a good sized piece of butter, a piece of crustless bread, chopped parsley, chives and shallots. Cook for 15 minutes, then add some good cream and simmer until well mixed. Take off the fire and add the chopped yolks of three hard-boiled eggs, three raw yolks, salt, and coarsely-ground pepper. Stuff a cleaned carp with the mixture, sewing the fish up so that nothing

escapes, and put it to marinade in oil, adding salt, pepper, whole chives, a clove of garlic, thyme, bayleaf and basilick. When ready, grill it, basting it with marinade and serve with this sauce.

Put chopped mushrooms and a little butter in a saucepan and simmer them for a quarter of an hour; then set them aside to cool. Then add a pinch of flour, capers, chopped anchovies, parsley, chives, shallots, a good lump of butter, stock, salt, and coarsely-ground pepper. Cook gently, and finish with a little lemon juice or a dash of good vinegar. (*Manuel de la Friandise*, 1796.)

Carp au Bleu in Aspic
(Czechoslovakia)

Put two pig's feet and half a pound of lean bacon rind into salted cold water. Bring the water to the boil and simmer until the contents are tender. Strain off the liquid and, when it is cold, remove all fat.

Clean the fish thoroughly, being careful to remove the scales. Cut it into portions or leave it whole. Set it in a pan and pour half a pint of boiling salted vinegar over it. This will have the effect of turning the skin slightly blue. Drain this vinegar from the fish and add it to the stock from the pig's feet. Add chopped vegetables of various kinds, pepper and herbs. Let all simmer for half an hour, then lay in the carp blue side downwards. When it is cooked, lift it out carefully and put it on a deep dish.

Strain all the liquid from the fish into another saucepan. Beat up the whites of two eggs and put them, with the broken shells, into it and stir constantly until it comes to the boil. Then let the pan stand in a half-open oven for 15 minutes. Strain through several folds of scalded muslin. (Do not press it through, let it drip.) Pour the liquid over the fish and set it in a cold place to become jellied. Garnish the dish with slices of lemon, tomato, and hard-boiled eggs. (Madame Ruzicka.)

Carpe à l'Alsacienne

Clean and scale a carp; insert fish stuffing in side slit and sew up. Poach in half white wine and half fish *fumet*. Serve with *Choucroûte*.

Carpe à l'Arlésienne

Clean and scale a carp, cut it up and place it in an earthenware jar with about two cups of warm water and the same quantity of red wine. Add salt and pepper, shallots and garlic, chopped mushrooms and chopped parsley. Simmer gently for 20 to 30 minutes according to size of the fish, then remove and keep hot. Let the sauce go on simmering until reduced to half its original quantity; strain over hot carp and serve.

Carpe au Bleu

Same as *Truite au bleu*. See *Trout*.

Carpe Chambord

The most elaborate way of serving a stuffed carp braised in red wine.

Carpe à la Juive

Clean, scrape and cut a carp into pieces. Cut up a large onion; brown in a little oil; add two tablespoons of flour; and moisten with water. Add salt and pepper, *bouquet garni* (q.v.), a clove of garlic and a little chopped parsley, and bring to boiling point. Then put in the pieces of carp and simmer gently for about 20 minutes: the sauce should only just cover the fish. When done, take out the pieces of carp and arrange them on a hot dish as nearly as possible to look like the original fish, and keep it hot whilst the sauce is reduced by simmering. Strain the sauce over the fish and let it cool. Serve very cold with horseradish sauce.

Carpe à la Juive au Persil. Same as above, but serve with much parsley.

Carpe à la Juive à l'Orientale. Same as above, but with saffron and chopped almonds added at the time of serving.

Carpe à la Juive aux Raisins. Same as above, but with sifted sugar and sultanas added at the time of serving.

Carpe à la russe

Clean, scrape and cut a carp into sections. Season some flour with salt and pepper and roll all the pieces of fish in it; then place them in a well-buttered oven dish. Add two glasses of dry white wine and heat on top of the stove until wine is almost boiling; then put the pan into a moderate oven. Have some choucroûte ready, as well as some small glazed onions and fresh mushrooms. When the fish is done, add a tablespoon of vinegar and some sour cream. Mix two tablespoons of grated cheese into the gravy, stir and blend well and strain over dished-up fish, re-assembling it into its original shape on a bed of choucroûte and garnishing with onions and mushroom heads and small pickles.

CARRELET

One of the French names for *Flounder* (q.v.).

CATFISH

There is a river fish of that name (Lat. *Pimelodus*), chiefly in the Mississippi and its tributaries, and there is also a sea-fish (Lat. *Galeichthys marinus*), common on the European and American coasts of the Atlantic, known as *Catfish* in the U.S.A., *Dogfish* in England, and *Bar* in France.

In England, the sea-wolf (Lat. *Anarrhicas lupus*) is usually known as *Catfish*.

CATLA
Lat. *Catla buchanani*. A carp-like food fish caught in Indian rivers; also in Burma and Siam.

CAVALLA
Lat. *Caranx hippos*; Sp. *Caballa*. An edible sea-fish of both the Eastern and Western coasts of Tropical America; it is sometimes found on the Atlantic side as far north as Cape Cod.

The *Green Cavalla* (Lat. *Caranx bartholomei*) is greatly prized in the West Indies.

CAVIAR
The prepared roe of one of the various members of the *Acipenserides* fish family, the *Beluga, Sturgeon, Ship, Sevruga* and *Sterliad*, which are caught in the estuaries of the rivers flowing into the Caspian Sea and also in the Danube estuary. The *Beluga* is the largest member of the *Sturgeon* family and the *Beluga* Caviar is the largest and best, but it does not keep. The Caviar from the *Sturgeon* proper is smaller and varies in colour from grey to black; it travels well and is the kind mostly exported in tins. The *Ship* Caviar is light in colour and samll; that from the *Sevruga* is smaller still. *Ketovaia* Caviar is the roe of the *Dog-Salmon* (Lat. *Onchorynchus Keta*), or *Keta*, caught in Siberia and in Canada; the grain is pink and large, but the flavour not so good as that of the real Caviar.

CEPHALOPODS CERO
Lat. *Sierra cavalla*. A large mackerel-like fish found mostly in the West Indies, where it is also known as the *Sawfish*.

CHANNEL CAT
Lat. *Ictalurus punctatus*. The most highly prized fish of the lower Mississippi Valley and Gulf States, U.S.A.

CHAR
Lat. *Salmo salvelinus*. A fresh-water fish found in Iceland, in some English lakes and Scotch lochs. Its name means *red* and its belly is red; it is obviously the *poisson rouge* recommended by St Evremond in one of his epistles. It is either identical or closely allied to the *Omble Chevalier* of the Swiss and Savoy lakes. In the U.S.A., the name *Char* is given to some species of *Trout*. All recipes applicable to *Trout* (q.v.) are suitable for *Char*, but *Potted Char* is a supreme delicacy.

Potted Char
(Sir Francis Colchester-Wemyss's Recipe) Clean and scale the fish and cook it slowly in white wine with a few slices of onion and carrot and pieces of parsley stalk. Allow to cool, skin it and remove the fillets. Be careful to take out all bones. Now arrange the fillets or pieces of fillet in an earthenware 'pot' and cover them with melted butter. Place the pot, with contents covered, in a moderate oven for 20 to 30 minutes and on withdrawing add more clarified butter if required. (Fillets must be covered with butter.) Will keep for some time in a cool place.

CHIRO
Lat. *Elops saurus*. A tarpon-like fish found in most tropical seas; of little merit gastronomically.

CHOPA BLANCA
Lat. *Kyphosus sectatrix*. A common rudder fish of the West Indies and Gulf of Florida. Also called *Bermuda Chub*.

CHOWDER
The American rendering of the Fr. *Chaudière*, the marmite in which soup is made. It is mostly used in connection with fish or clam soups.

Fish Chowder
2 lb. uncooked cod or fresh haddock
1 lb. potatoes, cut up into cubes or thick slices
1 onion, sliced
A 1½ in. cube of salt pork
About half a tablespoon salt
Pepper to taste
3 cups scalded milk
4 large dry biscuits
1 tablespoon butter

Have the fish skinned but the head and tail left on. Cut these later on and remove flesh from backbone. Divide this into 2 in. pieces and set aside. Place the head, tail and backbone – broken in pieces – in a good heavy saucepan, an earthenware one for choice – with two cupfuls of water and a little salt. Simmer gently for 15 minutes, then drain and set liquor aside. Cut the salt pork into tiny pieces and gently fry until fat is all out, in this cook the minced onion for five minutes and strain the fat into the stewpan. Add the potatoes in layers as indicated in clam chowder recipe, with two cups of water and boil for five minutes; then add the fish bone liquid and the pieces of fish, covering and simmering gently for 10 minutes longer. Now add the milk, seasoning, butter, and the coarsely crumbled biscuits (the nearest approach to the American 'crumbled' biscuits, in London, are the 'lunch' biscuits). (See *Clam Chowder*.)

CHUB
Lat. *Leucisus cephalus*; Fr. *Chabot*; Ger. *Kaulbarsch*; Sp. *Coto*. A common fresh-water fish of the carp family. A fully grown chub is 12 in. upwards and weighs from 4 lb. to 8 lb.

Should you have the misfortune to have caught a chub and nothing else, take Izaak Walton's advice:

'He is objected against, not only for being full of forked bones, dispersed through all his body, but that he eats waterish, and that the flesh of him is not firm, but short and tasteless. The French esteem him so mean, as to call him un Vilain: nevertheless he may be so dressed as to make him very good meat; as namely: if he be a large chub then dress him thus:

'First, scale him, and then wash him clean, and then take out his guts; and to that end make the hole as little, and near to his gills, as you may conveniently, and especially make clean his throat from the grass and weeds that are usually in it; for if that be not very clean, it will make him to taste very sour. Having so done, put some sweet herbs into his belly; and then tie him with two or three splinters to a spit, and roast him, basted often with vinegar, or rather verjuice and butter with good store of salt mixed with it.

'But take this rule with you, That a chub newly taken and newly dressed, is so much better than a chub of a day's keeping after he is dead, that I can compare him to nothing so fitly as to cherries newly gathered from a tree, and others that have been bruised and lain a day or two in water.' (Mrs Lucas's *A Pretty Kettle of Fish*.)

'A Chevyn or a Pollard: it is called in Latin *Capitus*, from its great head; by the Germans *Schwall*, or *Alet*; and *Myn* or *Mouen*; a *Schupfish*, from which we title it a chub fish.' (Randle Holme. Cap. XIV. par 27.)

CIRO

Lat. *Scomberomorus cavalla*. The name given in the West Indies to the larger specimens of *Kingfish* (q.v.).

CISCO

Lat. *Leucichthys artedi*. Canadian French *Ciscoette* or *Ciscovet*. One of the most highly prized whitefish or lake herring of Lake Superior and the other Great Lakes of Canada and the U.S.A.

CLAM

There are many different kinds of bivalves called *Clams*, but the two commonest sorts found on the Atlantic coast of North America are the *round* or *hard Clam* (*Venus mercenaria*) and the *long* or *soft Clam* (*Myra arenaria*).

Clam Chowder

1 pint clams
1 onion
2 sliced tomatoes
Butter
3 large potatoes
2 oz. rather fat salt pork
Salt and pepper
Crumbled crackers

This is what is known as 'Clam Chowder, New York Style'. The other way is known as 'New England Style'. *Clams* – real ones – are to be had in London, both fresh and tinned, but large cockles will do if needs must. Wash them well, set them in a saucepan with a cupful of cold water and place on the fire. As the water heats, the shells open. Remove fish and retain the liquid, straining through a very fine sieve lined with a double thickness of butter muslin.

If you have real clams, you will find that one part of them is hard and another soft. Chop finely the hard parts, setting aside the soft parts. Cut up the salt pork finely and fry slowly in a pan until the fat is melted, then add the chopped onion, fry it in the fat for five minutes and strain the fat into a heavy iron saucepan. Cut the peeled potatoes into, roughly, $\frac{3}{4}$ in. cubes and boil in salted water for five minutes. Drain them. Now – on the pork and onion fat – place a layer of these parboiled cubes of potato at the bottom of the iron pan. Add the chopped clams, the fried pork and onion, sprinkle with salt and pepper and dredge generously with flour. Add remaining potatoes, salt and pepper, dredge again with flour and add two and a half cups of boiling water. Cook for 10 minutes, add the peeled slices of tomato, the soft parts of the clams, and simmer gently until the tomato is dissolved into the chowder. Pour over some unsweetened dry biscuits, crumbled into separate soup plates or into a tureen, add a teaspoonful of good butter and the strained clam water, stirring well.

The 'New England Style' Chowder is made in the same way except for the omission of the slices of tomato and the addition of four cups of scalded milk in place of the water. Less milk or more water may be used as desired, but these chowders are really thick soups, more like a fish stew than soup.

Clam Chowder with Canned Clams

This recipe is simplified by the fact that the clams are already cooked.

Open can and strain off the liquor, which you reserve. Cut the clams into small pieces. Fry a small piece of salt pork (bacon is *not* a substitute) cut into dice, until brown. Add a layer of thinly sliced potatoes, a layer of sliced onions, a layer of chopped clams, and so on until your clams are used. Season each layer. Moisten with the clam liquor and water and simmer gently for 20 minutes.

Finally sprinkle with debris of 'cheese' crackers (i.e. any crackers not containing sugar, such as those usually eaten with cheese – any plain salted cracker will do) which have been soaked in a cupful of milk. Add remainder of milk and boil the whole again for a few minutes.

CLOVISSES. PRAIRES
Fr. for *Clam* (q.v.).

COALFISH
Lat. *Pollachius virens*; Fr. *Colin*. A first cousin of the *Cod* (q.v.) and closely related to the *Pollock* (q.v.). All recipes suitable for *Cod* apply to the *Coalfish*. It is called in Scotland *Saithe* (q.v.).

COCKLES
Lat. *Cardium edule*; Fr. *Coques* or *Palourdes*; Sp. *Bucardas*. Small bivalves which are very good with a *Sauce Poulette* or in fish sauces in place of oysters or mussels, when these are not available. Cockles also make good fish soups.

'Tis a cockle or a walnut-shell, a knack a toy a trick, a baby's cap.'
(*Taming of the Shrew.* Act IV. Sc. 3, l. 66).

COD. CODFISH
Lat. *Gadus callarias* or (Yarrell) *Morus vulgaris*; Fr. *Morue*, when salted; *Cabillaud*, when fresh. Ger. *Kabeljau*; It. *Merluzzo*; Sp. *Bacalao*, when salt, and *Merluza*, when fresh; Port. *Bacalho*.

A soft-finned fish, one of the most important food fishes of the world, from the cold waters of the North Atlantic. A closely allied species, the *Alaska Cod* (*Gadus macrocephalus*), inhabits the Northern Pacific. Cod is obtainable at all season, but it is at its best from October to January.

Fresh Cod from the Dogger Bank is usually boiled and served with a white sauce. It may also be baked with a forcemeat stuffing in its belly, fried or grilled.

Salt Cod, mostly from Newfoundland, must be soaked for twelve hours, heated very slowly, simmered but never boiled, for about an hour, and skimmed carefully from time to time. Usually served with egg sauce.

FRESH COD
Fresh cod, called in olden days, in England, *Greenfish* or *Haburdene*, and in French, *Cabillaud*, is usually boiled, steamed or poached; it may be served, according to Escoffier, with any of the sauces which are suitable for boiled, steamed or poached Turbot.

Cabillaud bouilli à l'Anglaise is just plain boiled fresh cod, whole or in thick cuts, served with plain boiled mealy potatoes.

Cabillaud Boulangère is fresh cod, either a small fish whole or else a large cut from a large fish, baked in the oven with sliced potatoes round it and plenty of butter used for the basting of both the fish and the potatoes. Chopped parsley is sprinkled over the fish before serving.

Cabillaud à la Flamande is usually the tail end of fresh cod poached in white wine, *fines herbes* and specially shallots. It is served with slices of lemon on it.

Cabillaud à la Provençale (for six people). Choose a piece of fresh cod of nearly 2 lb. in weight and cut it into three slabs about an inch thick. Divide each slab into two and remove the bones. Heat up in a flat saucepan three or four spoonfuls of olive oil with two spoonfuls of finely-chopped onion and two or three long peppers; season each piece of cod with pepper and salt; dip each one in flour and lay them all side by side in the saucepan, leave them but a very short time over a good fire, then turn them over and add four or five chopped tomatoes (peeled and pipped); parsley, a little garlic, a bayleaf and a glass of white wine. Put the lid on the pan and leave on the fire from 12 to 15 minutes. Plain boiled potatoes are served at the same time. (Escoffier's *Ma Cuisine*.)

Cabillaud à la Portugaise is prepared in the same manner as the *Cabillaud à la Provençale*, but it is served with rice instead of potatoes.

To Bake a Cod's Head
Make the Head very clean, and then lay it in the Pan you intend to bake it in, which must be buttered; put in a bundle of sweet herbs, an Onion stuck with Cloves, three or four blades of Mace, half a Spoonfull of black Pepper, a Nutmeg bruised, a Quart of Water, a little piece of Lemon peel, and a little piece of Horse-radish. Dust the Head well with Flour, grate a little Nutmeg over it, stick pieces of butter, and throw raspings of Bread all over that. Put it into your Oven, and when it is baked enough, take it carefully out of the Dish it was baked in, and lay it as carefully in another Dish and which you intend to send it to Table in. Set the Dish over boiling water, and cover it with a Dish Cover, to keep it hot. Pour all the Liquor out of the Dish it was baked in into a Saucepan, without Delay, and let it boil three or four minutes; then strain it, and put into it a Gill of red Wine, two Spoonsfull of Catchup, a pint of Shrimps, if to be had, half a Pint of Oysters or Mussells, Liquor and all, observing to strain such Liquor, a Spoonfull of Mushroom Pickle, a quarter of a pound of butter rolled in Flour, then stir all together untill it is thick and boils, when you must pour it into the Dish. Fry some toasted Bread, which hath been cut triangular very crisp. Stick pieces of this fried Bread about the Head and mouth and lay the rest about

the Head. Garnish with Lemon, horse-radish, and Parsley crisped in a Plate before the Fire. (*Mrs Gardiner's Receipts from* 1763, p. 37. Boston, Mass.)

Cod Custard

Take 1 lb. of nice flaky codfish and lay in a baking dish. Beat three eggs lightly and add three-quarters of a pint of milk and half a teaspoonful of celery salt. Pour over the fish and bake in a slow oven for three-quarters of an hour. (Mrs Turner's *Fifty Ways of Cooking Fish*).

Fried Cod Slices

One 1in thick slice of cod per person
1 small egg, beaten
Brown breadcrumbs
Butter
Salt and pepper
Lemon slices
Sprigs of parsley

Dry each slice of cod, after cutting off fins, in a cloth. Beat the egg, dip each slice of fish first in the beaten egg and then in the bread-crumbs, making sure that the entire surface is evenly coated. Allow to stand for a few minutes to harden the surface. Put about four or five tablespoons of butter in a pan and heat without browning. Add the slices of fish and cook gently, turning carefully when brown on one side. Sprinkle with salt and pepper and serve with slices of lemon and sprigs of parsley to garnish. Serve with *Tartare* sauce and mashed potatoes.

Cod en Cocotte

Slices of fresh cod
Thin slices of fat salt pork
1 sliced onion
Salt and pepper
Sliced cold boiled potatoes
Fish stock or hot water
Hot milk as needed

Cut the cod into thin slices. Lightly brown the slices of pork and the onion; drain off and keep the fat. Place the slices of crisp pork at the bottom of a *cocotte* or smallish casserole. Sprinkle them with the fried onions and lay the slices of cod on them. Sprinkle with salt and pepper and cover with slices of cooked potatoes. Fill in the dish with these alternate layers, then add sufficient fish stock or hot water to barely cover contents of casserole. Cook gently after adding the fat in which the pork and onions were fried. As the stock or water evaporates, replace with hot milk sufficiently to make a thick stew. Serve very hot.

Baked Codfish

1 small whole codfish
1 quart fish stock or water
1 small 'bouquet-garni'
Salt and pepper
2 tablespoons flour
Brown breadcrumbs
2 tablespoons butter
1 pint shrimps
Anchovy essence
Few sprigs parsley

Wash and dry the fish, place in a tin and add the stock – or water – the 'bouquet', salt and pepper. Dredge with the flour and coat with breadcrumbs. Dot with small pieces of butter. Bake in a moderate oven until done, basting frequently. Pick over the shrimps and blend them with some of the hot fish liquor and about a tablespoonful of anchovy essence, with, if wished, a little more butter mixed with flour (*beurre manié*) to bind the sauce. Place this in the dish, cook for about 10 minutes, again using liquor to baste the fish, and serve with slices of lemon, after removing the 'bouquet'. If desired, the codfish may be previously stuffed wth fish stuffing—A few mushroom heads, *sauté* in butter beforehand, may also be added to the sauce.

Old French Recipe for Preparing Cod

1 small whole cod or a thick slice
Slices of lemon
2 or 3 slices of onion
1 small 'bouquet-garni'
Salt and a few peppercorns
2 tablespoons butter
8 or 10 small firm potatoes
Hollandaise sauce

Place the cod, or thick slice of cod, in a pan in just sufficient cold water to cover it. Add three or four slices of lemon, slices of onion, 'bouquet', salt, six peppercorns or so, and the butter. Bring almost, but not quite, to boiling point; gently cooking, without boiling, until done. Drain carefully and keep fish hot. Cook the potatoes in the fish liquor, arrange them, when done, around fish and cover with a rich Hollandaise sauce.

Scalloped Cod
(American)

Butter
Cold steamed or boiled cod
Salt and pepper
Small raw oysters
Little onion juice
Lemon juice
Few grains cayenne pepper
Breadcrumbs

Butter an oven dish richly. Cover bottom with flaked cooked fish, sprinkle with salt and pepper, then cover with a layer of small oysters, previously 'bearded' and drained of their liquor. Each oyster, as drained, must be dipped in melted butter seasoned with a little of the mixed onion and lemon juice and dusted with the lightest of dustings of cayenne. Cover with 'cracker' or freshly made breadcrumbs, add three or four tablespoonfuls of the oyster liquor and repeat, finishing with a layer of crumbs. Bake for 20 minutes in a rather hot oven and serve with egg sauce, or, if preferred, a Hollandaise sauce.

Coquilles of Cod

Cold boiled or steamed cod
2 cups thick white sauce
Lemon juice
Salt and pepper
Fresh mushrooms
Mashed potatoes
Butter
Breadcrumbs

Pick over fish carefully, removing skin and bones. Flake with a fork. Mix with sauce, previously seasoned and flavoured with lemon juice. Place in scallop shells. The mushrooms must be sliced and *sautés* in butter. They may be mixed with fish and sauce, or else used to garnish the shells, within a border of mashed potatoes which should be 'piped' on, in rather large 'roses'. Dot some small pieces of butter over the fish; sprinkle some breadcrumbs and brown in a quick oven. If mushrooms be used as a garnish, add to the fish the butter in which they were cooked.

Cod Crimped

Cod ought to be crimped in thin slices, and you will then have the whole of your fish boiled quickly, equally, whilst in thick pieces the thin or tail part is overdone before the thick part is half boiled. Another advantage is, that you need not put your fish into the kettle until your guests have arrived. (*The Art of Dining*, Abraham Hayward, 1858.)

SALT COD

Salt Cod, or Ling, as it used to be called in England, has been a most important staple food of all European countries ever since the discovery of the Newfoundland fishing grounds, more particularly in Catholic countries where the Lenten Fast and the observance of other meatless days, such as Ember Days, called for immense quantities of fish that could be stored without danger of putrefaction and that could be sold to the masses at prices within their limited means. Salt cod has fulfilled both conditions for the last four hundred years. Like herrings, salt cod suffers from being too cheap to be fashionable, but it can be prepared in so many ways that it deserves the attention of all true gastronomes.

Salt cod must always be desalted before being prepared for the table: this means leaving the fish to soak in fresh running water overnight, whenever possible: if not, in fresh water which is changed as often as practicable, during 24 hours.

Desalted salt cod must *never* be boiled: it usually is, and it is usually tough and stringy as the result of boiling. The water in which cod is being 'boiled' must merely 'simmer'; it must be kept from actually boiling on very low gas heat or on the corner of the coal stove.

Allow a pound of desalted salt cod for three people.

Morue à l'Anglaise

Put the required number of square pieces of cod in a saucepan and cover them with cold water; put pan on fire, and as soon as the water comes to the boil remove the pan to a corner of the stove or lower the gas heat and leave the cod to poach in all-but boiling water for 15 to 20 minutes. Drain the pieces of cod, dress them upon a serving dish, garnish with parsley and serve with plain boiled potatoes and egg sauce.

Morue à la Béchamel

Cod poached in the same way as the *Morue à l'Anglaise*, but when it is cooked and drained, the skin and bones are carefully removed, the fish is flaked and the flakes are mixed with a *Béchamel* Sauce, then packed into a *Timbale*, with a little butter and a spoonful of fresh cream worked in at the same time. Usually served with plain boiled potatoes at the same time.

Morue à la Bénédictine

Poach, drain and flake the fish as for the *Morue à la Béchamel*; then pound the fish and mix with it half its own weight of *Purée de Pommes de Terre*, until it becomes one rather solid paste. Add to this paste, little by little, alternately, some olive oil and twice the same quantity of boiling hot milk, until the whole paste becomes unctuous. Fill a slightly oiled oven dish with this soft paste, sprinkle some breadcrumbs on top, add a little olive oil and leave in a hot oven for a short while, until it begins to brown.

Morue au Beurre Noir

Prepare in the same way as *Morue à l'Anglaise*, but serve with *Beurre Noir*, or *Beurre Noisette* poured over the poached fish.

Morue à la Lyonnaise

Poach some desalted cod, drain it, remove skin and bones, flake it and *sauté* it in butter, in a saucepan where you will have already begun to *sauter* some shredded onions. Season to taste with pepper and salt, and when ready to serve add a spoonful or two of wine vinegar. Dress in a *Timbale* or in a deep dish with sliced and *sautées* potatoes, in the proportion of 1 lb. of potatoes to 2 lb. of fish.

Salt Cod à la Princesse

When the cod fish has been cooked let it drain on a cloth.

Prepare a marinade made of 20 tablespoons of cold water, two of vinegar, a few peppercorns, chopped parsley and chives, a clove of garlic (which may be omitted), an onion cut in rounds and two cloves.

When the fish is thoroughly drained, divide it into pieces, being very careful to remove all the bones and skin, and place it in a deep dish, pouring the marinade over it. Leave it for two hours.

Take out the flakes at the end of this time, detaching the herbs, etc. Drain them again on a cloth.

Prepare a rather thick batter, made with flour, a pinch of salt, milk, the yolks of two eggs and a little grated Gruyère. When it is well mixed, dip the flakes of cod into it.

Then whip up the whites of eggs, but lightly only. Dip each piece of fish into them just before you throw them into very hot fat to fry. Let them colour on both sides.

When the fritters are ready, put them in a dish and serve them with egg sauce.

The Sauce. Melt 2 oz. of butter and add a tablespoonful of flour. Then add sufficient milk to make a rather thick sauce, season it, and add a little nutmeg. Let it boil for a few minutes and then add chopped hard-boiled eggs. (*Les Secrets de la Bonne Table.* B. Renaudet. Albin Michel.)

Kabiljo Pudding (Salt-dried Cod)

    1 lb. raw salted dried cod
    Or bare pint cooked finely-
        chopped fish
    2 teacups rice
    Bare pint water
    1¾ pints milk
    2 eggs
    3 tablespoons butter
    ½ teaspoon white pepper
    Salt
    1 to 2 teaspoons sugar
    Fireproof dish
    ½ tablespoon butter
    3 tablespoons sieved dried
        breadcrumbs

Soak fish overnight. Cook and, when cold again, bone and chop finely. Clean rice, put on in cold water and, when boiling, add milk. Simmer until almost soft, add butter and leave until cold. Season, add fish and beaten eggs. Pour into buttered and breadcrumbed pie-dish, sprinkle with bread-crumbs and bake in fairly hot oven for about an hour. Serve with melted butter.

Left-over pudding can be sliced and fried in butter. (I. Norberg's *Good Food from Sweden.*)

Codfish Balls
(American)

    2 cups of desalted cod
    2 cups raw cut-up potatoes
    2 tablespoons butter
    Pepper
    Frying fat

Tear the fish into pieces with two forks and soak overnight in cold water, renewing this twice or more should fish be very salt. Next day, shred the fish into small flakes or pieces and poach in water just off the boil with the same amount of cut-up raw potatoes in just sufficient water to cover. When potatoes are done, strain off any remaining water and place the dish in an open warm oven for a few minutes to dry out, shaking now and again. Chop or grind fish and potatoes, add butter and pepper to taste. Form into roughly-shaped balls and fry, without either flouring or coating of breadcrumbs, in boiling oil or fat. The balls will swell up and taste delicious with tomato or any other suitable sauce. To make them lighter and richer, add two or three slightly beaten egg yolks, folding in the stiffly-whipped whites last thing of all. A little onion juice and chopped parsley may also be added, if desired. Drop small pieces of this mixture into the boiling fat, where they will speedily puff up and brown. Drain and serve very hot.

Salt Cod Créole

    Desalted cod
    Water (lukewarm)
    Butter
    Cold boiled potatoes
    1 sweet pimento or red pepper
    Pepper
    Tomato sauce
    Fresh breadcrumbs

Cover the fish with the water, allow to stand until the former is soft and then drain well. Butter a baking-dish generously, place at the bottom of this a layer of the sliced cold potatoes and on this a layer of the shredded fish. Cut the pimento into strips and dot them over the fish. Season with pepper and repeat these layers until all ingredients are used up. Pour over the whole enough fresh tomato sauce to moisten, cover with the breadcrumbs, dot with small pats of butter and bake until the crumbs are brown. Serve in same dish.

Cod and Egg Ramekins

½ lb. desalted cod
1 lb. fresh breadcrumbs
2 beaten eggs
Pepper
Butter
Fresh eggs
Grated cheese

Poach cod and then shred finely, removing all pieces of skin and all bones. The breadcrumbs must be of even size, i.e. passed through a sieve, and mixed with the fish and beaten eggs. Take a little of this thick mixture, after adding pepper to taste, and use to line evenly well buttered oven ramekin dishes. Make a 'well' in centre and slip a fresh egg in this. Sprinkle surface of egg with grated cheese, dot with butter and bake until eggs are set but not hard.

Note.—Dried cod is not always very salt. After soaking as directed and cooking, it is advisable to taste mixture, as it may be found necessary at times to add a little salt.

Salt Cod Pudding

½ lb. desalted cooked cod
1 lb. hot mashed potatoes
2 beaten eggs
1 cup milk
2 tablespoons butter
Pepper

Shred poached cod finely, mix with the hot and seasoned mashed potatoes (from which all lumps have been beaten), add eggs, milk, butter and pepper. Blend well. Pour into a mould, well-buttered and, if wished, sprinkle evenly with brown breadcrumbs. Bake in a moderate oven, turn out, and serve with hot fresh tomato sauce.

Cassoulet of Salt Cod

Desalted and poached cod
Olive oil or butter
1 onion
1 shallot
2 slices salt pork or bacon
Pepper
Dried white beans (*Soissons*)
1 teaspoon tomato purée

Flake the cooked fish coarsely; it is then lightly *sauté* in olive oil or butter with minced onion, shallot and cut-up pork. When all is slightly brown, season and add the beans, also soaked overnight and boiled until soft, but not mushy. Mix all well and place in a deep earthenware pot or casserole. Lay one or two thin slices of salt pork on top, cover with hot water in which the tomato purée has been dissolved. There must be barely enough water to show under the surface of the ingredients in pot. Bake

gently until the beans are really soft and done, serving in the cooking pot.

Lenten Cod

Sundry diced vegetables, boiled
and drained
Thick cream sauce
Cooked desalted cod
1 beaten egg
Breadcrumbs
1 hard-boiled egg

Carrots, potatoes, turnips, small beans, small pieces of cooked cauliflower, small onions, all are acceptable. Cook in salted water (adding the diced potatoes last or they will be a shapeless mess). Drain well and add to rich, seasoned sauce. Cut the boiled fish into fillets, drain well, season and dip first in flour, then in beaten egg, lastly in fine brown or white breadcrumbs. Fry to a nice colour in deep oil or fat: when done and crisp, drain well and serve surrounded by the vegetable *macédoine*, decorating with slices of hard-boiled egg. After boiling the vegetables must be well drained, and they may be, if wished, *sauté* in a little butter before serving; a few fried mushrooms may also be used to garnish this excellent luncheon dish.

Salt Cod and Spinach
(Provençal)

Desalted and poached cod
2 lb. fresh spinach
3 tablespoons olive oil
1 onion
1 tablespoon flour
2 cups milk
Salt and pepper
Dusting of nutmeg
1 or 2 cloves garlic (optional)
Brown breadcrumbs

Poach fish, remove bones and skin and separate into flakes. Wash and cook the spinach as usual, squeeze out every drop of water and chop finely. Place the oil in a saucepan and heat; add the cut-up onion, brown it slightly, then add the spinach, stirring well with a wooden spoon. Add the flour, mixing well; then add the milk, which must have been heated. Season with salt, pepper and nutmeg to taste; simmer gently for 15 minutes, then add the garlic, if used, finely chopped. Take an oven dish and cover the bottom with a thick layer of prepared spinach, then cover this with a layer of fish and repeat the operation. Sprinkle surface, which should be a thin layer of spinach, with breadcrumbs, and either dot with small pieces of butter or – to be Provençal – with a few drops more of oil. Brown in oven.

CODLING

A small codfish.

'*Codd, first a Whiting, then a Codling, then a Codd.*' (Randle Holme, p. 324.)

COLIN

Fr. for *Hake* (q.v.) when cooked; before being cooked its name is *Merluche*.

CONGER-EEL. SEA-EEL

Lat. *Conger conger*, or *Muraena conger*; Fr. *Congre*. The true sea-serpent; mostly used for *Bouillabaisse* and other fish soups. A large – sometimes 8 ft. long – entirely scaleless, sea-eel.

'*... and he plays quoits well, and eats conger and fennel ...*' (*The Second Part of King Henry IV*. Act II. Sc. 4.)

The smaller conger-eels are best. They can be cooked by baking, boiling or frying, and are not sufficiently appreciated in England, although plentiful along the South Coast.

Conger à la Bretonne

Place two tablespoons of butter in an earthenware pan or casserole; when melted, add three tablespoons of flour and three or four chopped onions; stir until onions are light brown. Moisten with a sufficiency of cider, according to amount of fish. Season with salt and pepper. Add slices of eel and cover pan, cooking gently for nearly an hour. Remove fish and strain sauce over it, binding it, if necessary, with a little more flour blended with the same quantity of butter.

Conger à l'Italienne

Make a *court-bouillon* with water, white wine, shallots, garlic, herbs, clove, salt and peppercorns. Cook this for three-quarters of an hour, then strain. Place the conger in this liquid and half-cook it; then take it out from *court-bouillon*, remove skin and bones, cutting or separating the fish into fillets or rather large pieces. Make a sauce with equal parts of butter and flour, moistening with sufficient *court-bouillon* to make a thick creamy sauce. Cover the bottom of a gratin dish with a layer of this sauce, cover this in turn with pieces of fish and these again with an even coating of sauce. Sprinkle with grated cheese, dot with butter and bake until brown.

Note.—The remainder of the *court-bouillon* makes a delicious fish soup with added water, potatoes, carrots and leeks.

COQUILLES

French for Shells, usually fish shells filled with any and every sort of fish, meat, or vegetable preparations, the name of which follows that of *Coquille*.

COQUILLES ST. JACQUES

Fr. for *Scallops* (q.v.).

CORAL

Fr. *Corail*. A soft greenish matter, the ovaries of hen-lobsters, used in the making of most sauces served with lobster. It turns red in the cooking.

CORAMOUR

Lat. *Scomberomorus cavalla*. The name given in the West Indies to the young or small *Kingfish* (q.v.).

COULIBIAC

A Russian fish pie which is made in many different ways, but chiefly with eels and a variety of other fishes encased in puff-paste or fermented dough.

CRAB

Fr. *Crabe, Calappe, Poupart, Tourteau* and *Gourballe*; Ger. *Krebs*; Sp. *Cangrejo*. Any crustacean of the order *Decapoda*. Crabs are obtainable all the year round, but they are best from May to August. The best way to serve *Crabs* is in the form of *Dressed Crab*; all the meat, neatly removed from body and claws, is seasoned with oil and lemon or vinegar, and served in the shell.

Soft Shell Crabs are a delicacy which one must go to the United States to taste at its best.

Oyster Crabs. Tiny baby crabs found on the coast of New England in some oysters; they are excellent stewed in cream with a little Madeira added at the time of serving. They are stewed and eaten whole, shell and all.

Town-dwellers know crabs chiefly when all ready to eat, 'dressed' or otherwise, but, at the seaside, crabs which have just been caught can be made into a variety of delicious dishes at very little cost. The medium-sized crabs are sweetest, but the heaviest, when of the same size, are best.

'*A crabbe, breke hym a-sonder in a dysshe, make ye shelle cleane and put in the stuffe againe; tempre it with vynegre and pouder, then cover it with brede, and sende it to the kytchyn to hete; then set it to your soverayne, and breke the greate clawes, and laye them in a disshe.*' (Wynkyn de Worde's Boke of Kervynge. In Furnivall's *Early English Meals and Manners*, p. 167.)

'*The Crab is not easily digested; it is a meate best agreeing with those that are of a cholericke temperature, and that have hot stomacks.*' (Venner's *Via recta ad vitam longam.* Ed. 1628, p. 77.)

Note by Joseph Sinel, late of the Jersey Biological Laboratory.

'*When crabs are plunged into boiling water, they invariably throw off some of their limbs, hence fishmongers always place them in cold water, and either let them "drown", as they term it, or raise the temperature gradually.*

'The throwing off of limbs is not a mechanical result of the sudden heat, but is a natural procedure on the part of the crab when in pain or danger

'Many crustaceans – notably the little "Broad-claw Porcelain Crab" – throw off a claw or a leg or two when irritated, or even when danger threatens, so that the cast-off part may attract the attention of the aggressor while the creature itself escapes. (The same thing occurs with lizards, which throw off their tails when hard pressed by an enemy.) This throwing off of limbs on the part of crabs plunged into hot water is therefore evidence of pain. Plunged into boiling water, a large crab takes a considerable time to die, so that this method must inflict all the suffering which animals of this class can experience – an amount which we may, however, safely assume to be very much less than would be the case with a vertebrate.

'The most humane way of killing both crabs and lobsters is to place them in cold water and very gradually raise the temperature. The death which ensues is apparently totally unfraught with pain, and must be somewhat analogous to that of a person succumbing to a "heat wave", viz., loss of consciousness and a painless end.'

To Farse Crabs

'Take so many Crabs as you please, take the meat out of the Claws, and mix it with the meat of the body, the skin and strings thereof pick out, then take some Pine-apple, Pistaches, and Artichoke bottoms, minced with the body of an Eele half boyled, but not very small, and with the meat of the claws before you mix it, as also a handful of Oysters, put to it a little grated manchet, nutmeg, Cinamon, Ginger and Salt, with a Lemon cut in dice, with the yolks of two or three raw Eggs, and a quarter of a pound of Butter in small bits; make up this into a reasonable stiff force meat and force your shells. Make the rest into small balls, and put them into a deep tin dish, and bake them gently in an Oven; let your meat in your shells be a very tender meat; when they come out of the Oven, add to them some drawn Butter, and the juice of Oranges and Lemons, dish them with your forced balls round about them, stick them full of picked Sprigs of Paste about four inches long, and stick upon your Sprigs fried Oysters.' (William Rabisha, 1675.)

To Dress a Crab

Twist off the claws, both large and small, then remove the flaps and separate the upper from the lower shell or carapace. Remove the intestines and the stomach, which is a small bag placed near the head. Pick out carefully all pieces of meat from both body

and claws, chop it finely and mix with a little well-seasoned vinaigrette sauce. Wash and then dry the large shell and fill it with the prepared mixture. Decorate with some of the pieces of the small claws and chopped parsley. Take great care that no small pieces of shell are left in the crab meat.

Devilled Crab

1 good-sized crab
¼ pint thick cream sauce
1 teaspoon chili vinegar
1 teaspoon chopped gherkins
½ teaspoon made mustard
Salt and pepper
1 teaspoon chutney
½ teaspoon Worcester sauce
1 tablespoon brown breadcrumbs
Chopped parsley

Having removed all meat from shell and claws, heat the sauce. Add all the ingredients, including the crab, and stir over a low heat until hot through; then use to fill the shell. Sprinkle with breadcrumbs, lightly, and bake for 15 minutes. If wished, some flakes of the crab-meat may be set aside and used, after reheating in a little butter to garnish edge of shell all round, and a little chopped parsley may be used also to garnish. Use English mustard for this and, if liked, cayenne pepper.

Scalloped Crab
(Canadian)

1 or 2 cups crab-meat
2 oz. fine fresh breadcrumbs
4 tablespoons butter
Salt and touch cayenne
Lemon juice to taste
Chopped parsley

Prepare the shell or, if preferred, use small scallop shells or glass or china ramekins. Put a layer of crab-meat in shell, sprinkle with breadcrumbs and a little oiled butter, seasoning as desired. Repeat this until all ingredients are used up, finishing up with breadcrumbs. Dot with small pieces of butter and bake for 15 minutes. Sprinkle lightly with lemon juice and chopped parsley.

Partan Pie
(Scotch Farmhouse Recipe)

Pick the meat out of the claws and body of a *Partan* (boiled crab); clean the shell and claws and polish with a little salad oil. Chop the meat roughly, season with pepper and salt and mix with some mayonnaise sauce. Put mixture into the shell, decorate with claws and serve on a bed of lettuce leaves.

Crab Omelette
(French)

1 medium-sized boiled crab
Butter
4 eggs
Salt and cayenne

Remove crab-meat carefully, retaining soft interior of shell and beating this with the eggs, seasoned with salt and a dash of cayenne. Make omelette in the usual way and, when ready to serve, fold in centre the white meat of the crab heated in butter.

Crab Stew

1 boiled crab
2 tablespoons butter
2 tablespoons flour
1 cup bouillon
½ cup white wine
6 or 7 mushrooms
Butter for mushrooms
1 egg yolk
Salt and pepper

Having carefully removed all meat from body and claws of crab, chop coarsely. Melt the two tablespoons of butter, add the flour and stir until a nice light even brown (thus making a *roux blond*). Moisten with the mixed bouillon and wine, season rather highly and add the mushrooms, previously peeled, chopped coarsely and *sautés* in butter with a little salt and pepper. Add the crab and cook this mixture gently until rather thick. Bind with the egg yolk once the pan is off the fire and serve on toast or in ramekins.

Potted Crab

1 or 2 crabs
4 tablespoons butter
Salt and pepper
½ cup thick cream
2 or 3 egg yolks
Dash of cayenne
Clarified butter

Chop the picked-over crab-meat finely. Place in a pan with the butter and seasonings, cooking gently for 20 minutes, stirring frequently. Beat egg yolks with cream. Remove pan from fire, add egg mixture, mixing well. Place all this in a double-boiler and cook and stir until thick and creamy. It must have the consistency of a thick paste. Rub through a fine sieve, press into pots and cover with clarified butter. Keep on ice.

Crab Soup

1 large or 2 smaller crabs
3 cups chicken stock
⅔ cup stale breadcrumbs
1 slice of onion
2 tablespoons butter
2 tablespoons flour
1 cup cream
Salt and pepper
Parsley

Be sure the crabs are freshly boiled. Carefully remove all meat and chop finely; then add to it the stock, breadcrumbs, onion and parsley, simmering gently together for half an hour or so. Rub the soup through a fine sieve, re-heat and bind either with flour and milk, as indicated in previous recipes or, better still, with egg yolks beaten into the soup when off the fire. The soup may be lightly coloured with a little coraline pepper or red colouring – this will not affect the flavour but it pleases the eye.

CRAPPIE
Lat. *Pomoxis annularis*. One of the fresh-water fishes of the Mississippi Valley, related to the *Calico Bass* (q.v.).

CRAQUELOTS
The name given in France to herrings which are only half bloated; they are somewhere half-way between the fresh and the smoked herring and do not keep for any length of time. They are sometimes known as *Harengs bouffis*.

CRAWFISH
Lat. *Palinurus vulgaris*; Fr. *Langouste*; Ger. *Heuschrecken-Krebs*; Sp. *Langosta*. The spiny lobster, which is not nearly so generally appreciated in England as it deserves to be. The only explanation for this unpopularity of one of the very best shell-fish caught on the coasts of Devonshire and Cornwall more abundantly than anywhere else seems to be that the claw is reputed to be the best part of the *Lobster*, and the *Crawfish* has no claws; but the meat of the body is more tender and there is also more of it; its flavour, however, in the opinion of many good judges, is inferior to that of the *Lobster*. All recipes given for *Lobster* are applicable to the *Crawfish*.

Crawfish is caught in large quantities off the coasts of Chile and South Africa: it is extensively canned and shipped from Chile to the U.S.A. and from South Africa to England.

CRAYFISH
Fr. *Écrevisses*; Ger. *Fluss-Krebs*; Sp. *Cangrejo de rio*. The name of the small fresh-water lobster, of which there are two distinct varieties: the large and the small. The small is the one that is found in English rivers; its Latin name is *Astacus pallipes*, and its French name: *Écrevisses à pattes blanches*. The other sort, about twice as large, is called *Astacus fluviatilis*, in Latin, and *Écrevisses à pattes rouges* or *Écrevisses de la Meuse*, in culinary French. There is a third species, the

American fresh-water crayfish, or *Cambarus affinis* (Fr. *Camarons*), which is slightly different.

'*At Oxford, as I remember, on festivalls daies, they are wont to eate Crevices last, after flesh ... and this they name a feast royall.*' (*Cogan's Haven of Health*. Ed. 1612, p. 147.)

It is still the practice in France, on all ceremonious occasions, to serve the *Buisson d'Écrevisses* at the end of the meal, after the meat.

Écrevisses en Buisson
Boil for about 10 minutes in a highly-seasoned white wine *court-bouillon* and, when cold, serve gathered up in a heap or 'bush'.

Écrevisses à la Nage
Boil in a highly-seasoned white wine *court-bouillon* and serve hot 'swimming' in three parts of the *court-bouillon* in which they were cooked, and one part white wine. Care must be taken always to remove the central portion of the fan-shaped tail so as to draw out the black spinal cord, which has an unpleasantly bitter taste.

Crayfish Coulis
Boiled and pounded *crayfish* used as the foundation of either a *Bisque d'Écrevisses* or a *Sauce Nantua*.

Écrevisses Nantua
Boil the *Écrevisses* in white wine *court-bouillon*; let them cool in the *court-bouillon*; then remove the tails. Dry the shells and claws in a very slow oven; then pound them in a mortar to a fine powder. Mix this with twice the quantity of butter, place over a slow fire and, when the butter is melted, moisten with equal quantities of dry white wine and good white stock. Simmer gently for half an hour; then pass through a very fine sieve. Replace liquid in pan and continue simmering until greatly reduced; then add the thick cream (allowing about two or three tablespoons to two cups of prepared fish broth). Add the tails after reheating them in their *court-bouillon* and serve hot.

Rizotto of Crayfish
Make a *court-bouillon* in this wise:

Put into a saucepan a carrot, a large onion, two chopped shallots, a 'bouquet', two glasses of white wine and one of water, salt and a few grains of white pepper. Bring to the boil and simmer for a quarter of an hour. Clean and wash the *crayfish* and cook them in the *court-bouillon* for eight minutes. Take them out with a skimmer and put them into a basin.

Chop an onion and, when it begins to colour slightly in hot butter, sprinkle in about ¼ lb. of Carolina rice. Stir rice and

onion together for some two minutes, then pour over it the *court-bouillon* in which the *crayfish* have cooked, allowing three times as much *court-bouillon* as you have rice. Cook very slowly in a double-boiler, without touching the rice, for about 18 minutes.

Shell the *crayfish*. Put them into a saucepan in which you have heated some butter, and let them colour very slightly. Sprinkle them with a little flour. Stir quickly, so that each *crayfish* gets its share of flour. Add a little thick cream. Then very slowly, stirring all the time with a wooden spoon, bring the cream to boiling-point, but do not let it boil further.

Place the *crayfish* in the centre of a dish with the rice around it. Grated cheese may be served with the *rizotto*. (*La Cuisine au Coin du Feu*. Paul Bouillard. Albin Michel.)

Crayfish à la Mode de M. le Prieur
Take ten dozen fine *crayfish*, wash them in several waters, drain them and wipe them with a cloth.

Into a copper pan put two glasses of white wine, and as much white wine-vinegar, a glass of concentrated meat stock (*jus*) and half a glass of Champagne. Add 2 oz. fat bacon, two carrots and four onions cut in dice, ten shallots, two cloves of garlic; a bouquet of thyme, parsley, chervil and a quarter of a bayleaf; half the rind of a medium-sized orange, a big handful of uncrushed salt, a small handful of white pepper which has just been ground, two pinches of red pepper, or half a pinch of cayenne.

Cook together until the liquid is reduced by half. Put in the *crayfish*, stirring them often. After 10 or 12 minutes, if they are cooked, take them out and put them on a silver or porcelain dish, and, having passed the *court-bouillon* in which they cooked through a sieve, pour it over them.

At the appointed moment, the host raises the cover of the dish, a light vapour ascends towards heaven, vinous and acid aromas fill the room, the weariest heart takes courage, and appetite is born again. (*Brillat-Savarin*.)

CROAKER
The name given in the U.S.A. to various fishes supposed to produce grunting noises. Chief among them is the *Micropogon undulatus*, a small but gastronomically important fish of the Gulf coast and the North Atlantic, south of Cape Cod.

CROONER. PIPER
Lat. *Trigla lyra*. One of the *Gurnards* (q.v.).

CUNNER
In England, the name is given to the *Crenilabrus melops*, also known as the *Corkwing*

Brasse, and in the U.S.A. to the *Tautogolabrus adspersus*, both small denizens of the Atlantic of no mean gastronomical merit and both being credited with unusual cunning in nibbling bait.

CUSK. TUSK. TORSK
Lat. *Brosme brosme*. A large sea-fish closely allied to the *Cod*. It frequents the northern coasts of Europe and America. It is fairly well known in England In the U.S.A. *boiled Cusk* with *cream sauce* is deservedly popular.

CUTTLE-FISH. INK-FISH
Lat. *Sepia officinalis*. A cephalopod or squid of the Mediterranean and Adriatic. The bell-shaped body is cut into pieces 2 or 3 in. across, fried in oil and served with a sauce made from a *fumet* of the tentacles and the sepia dye saved for the purpose from the little sac carried by the fish; garlic is rarely absent from the sauce.

DAB
Lat. *Limanda limanda*; Fr. *Limande*; Ger. *Blieschen*; Sp. *Barbada*. The best member of the *Plaice family*, gastronomically. The *American Dab* is slightly different – it is called *Sand* or *Rusty Dab*. (Lat. *Limanda ferruginea*.) *Dabs* are cooked in the same ways as *Flounder*.

DACE
Lat. *Leuciscus leuciscus*; Fr. *Vandoise*; Ger. *Weissfisch*. One of the lesser fresh-water fishes. It is sometimes called *Dar* or *Dart*. The American *black-nosed* or *striped Dace* is a somewhat different fish. (Lat. *Rhinichthys atronasus*.) So is the *Horned Dace*, a common American cyprinoid fish (*Semotilus atromaculatus*).

DARWEN SALMON
Lat. *Acanthias vulgaris*. Not a Salmon, but a Dogfish, sold, without its head, and very cheap, in Lancashire: the name comes from Darwen, near Blackburn (Lancs).

DEMOISELLES DE CAEN. DEMOISELLES DE CHERBOURG
French culinary names for quite small lobsters.

DOGFISH
A name given to a number of different species of fish, such as (A) *Galeichthys marinus*, or *Bar* (q.v.); (B) *Squalus acanthias*, a destructive shark-like fish common in both th European and American waters of the North Atlantic, or *Spur Dogfish*; it is sold in England, without head and fins, under the name of *Flake*; (C) *Cynias canis*, or smooth *Dogfish*, so called because it has no dorsal fins like the *Squalus*; it is also a North Atlantic fish; (D) *Dallia pectoralis*, or *Blackfish* (q.v.); (E) *Lota maculosa*, or *Burbot* (q.v.); (F) *Amia calva*, or *Bowfin* (q.v.), and others.

DOLLARFISH
Lat. *Poronotus triacanthus*. A small marine fish of the *Stromateidae* genus common during the summer months on the Atlantic coast of North America. Sometimes called *Butterfish*.

DRUMFISH
The name given to a number of fishes of the family *Sciaenidae*. The common *Drumfish* (*Pogonias cromis*) of the North Atlantic, and the *Red Drumfish* (*Sciaenops ocellata*) of the South Atlantic are the best known, gastronomically. There is also a fresh-water *Drumfish* (*Aplodinatus grunniens*) in the Great Lakes and the Mississippi Valley which attains a weight of 50 lb. and more.

DUBLIN BAY PRAWNS
Lat. *Nephrops norvegicus*; Fr. *Langoustines*; Ital. *Scampi*. The largest and best of all *Prawns* (q.v.).

ÉCREVISSES
Fr. for fresh-water *Crayfish* (q.v.).

EEL
Lat. *Anguilla anguilla*; Fr. *Anguille*; Ger. *Aale*; Sp. *Anguila*. There are four kinds of eels: the *Snig*, the *Grig*, the *Broad-nosed* and the *Sharp-nosed*. The *Broad-nosed* are darkest, and the *Sharp-nosed* are the brightest and best. Large quantities of eels are imported from Holland, but the Thames eels are more silvery in appearance and sweeter of taste than the Dutch eels. Eels, in England, are at their best from August to May. They are mostly served collared, in pies, fried, grilled and jellied.

Smoked Eel is delicious and far superior, in the opinion of many gastronomes, to smoked Salmon.

The common eel of North America, although scarcely distinguishable from the *Anguilla anguilla* of Europe, is known as *Anguilla rostrata* or *chrysypa*.

Many rivers and lakes of New Zealand abound in eels of a most repulsive appearance. They are black, thick, with blunt heads, and of an average weight of 4 lb. to 7 lb., often reaching weights many times in excess of this average.

'*Cry to it, nuncle, as the Cockney did to the eels when she put them i' the paste alive; she rapp'd 'em o' the coxcombs with a stick, and cried: "Down, wantons, down!"*' (*King Lear*. Act II. Sc. 4.)

'*An eel, first a Fauser, then a Grigg or Snigg, then a Scaffling, then a little Eel; when it is large, then an Eel, and when very large, a Conger.*' (Randle Holme, p. 324.)

'Among all fishes that are pleasant in taste and not wholesome, the Yeele are most in use, which, as they be engendered of the very earth, dirt and mire, without generation or Spawne, so they be of a slimie substance, clammie and greatly stopping, whereby they are noysome to the voice.' (Cogan's *Haven of Health*. Ed. 1612, p. 143.)

Collared Eels

1 rather large eel
A little powdered mace
A little allspice
2 cloves
Salt and pepper
Salted water
2 tablespoons vinegar
Few leaves sage
Few sprigs parsley
Lemon slices to garnish

Cut the eel into chunks; bone it but do not remove skin. Rub the interior with the ground spices mixed with salt and pepper and roll up tightly, fastening with strong tape. The fish may, if preferred, be left whole. Cook in salted water to which vinegar has been added. Allow to cool and pickle in the water; the sage and parsley may be added when boiling, or the French method of preparing a *court-bouillon* may be adopted and the fish cooked in this and allowed to cool in it. Remove tape and serve with slices of lemon and parsley to garnish.

Jellied Eels

Cut up the required number of eels into chunks and let these marinate overnight in a white wine *court-bouillon*, with the usual vegetables, bayleaf and thyme. Boil gently for a long time the trimmings of mackerel, herrings, or any other oily fish with bones and if available, a cow's heel. You will thus get a fish jelly, and you will cook in it the chunks of eel, together with their wine marinade, for an hour or longer. Drain the pieces of eel; remove bone and skin. Pass through a sieve the liquor in which the eels were cooked, simmer a little longer to reduce it, and then pour over the eel in a deep dish or pot, after having carefully removed all surface fat. Let it get quite cold and serve.

Eel Pie

1 medium-sized eel
2 cups good stock
Salt and pepper
Pinch mixed herbs
1 onion
Lemon juice to taste
Good light piecrust

The eel should be cut into pieces, after skinning, and placed in a pan with the fins, head and tail portion. Add the stock, salt,

pepper, herbs and sliced onion. Cook gently until the fish is just done enough to enable one to remove centre bone. Strain liquid, skimming well. Place the pieces of eel in a pie-dish, season with lemon juice, add stock, cover with pastry and bake in a rather hot oven for about one hour. The stock may, if desired, be slightly thickened by the addition of a tablespoonful of flour mixed with half the stock, the remainder being added – warm – to the pie as soon as taken from the oven, pouring it in through a funnel under the central 'rose' decoration.

Eels Spatchcocked

Two pounds of eels will be required; the heads must be chopped off with a very sharp chopper to kill them. Skin and empty them, and divide into 3 in. lengths, bone these and sprinkle the inside with finely-chopped parsley mixed with sweet herbs and a little pepper and salt. Put in a tiny piece of butter and a squeeze of lemon juice. Close the pieces together and cover well with egg and breadcrumbs. Place in a frying basket and plunge into a saucepan of boiling fat and fry from 10 to 15 minutes until a nice golden brown. Drain on kitchen paper and serve very hot, garnished with fried parsley and cut lemon. (Mrs Turner's *Fifty Ways of Cooking Fish*.)

Pâté d'Anguilles

Cut the eel in rounds. Mix with it yolks of eggs, parsley, mushrooms, asparagus, soft roes, verjuice, or gooseberries if in season, and do not stint either butter, or salt, or pepper. Spread this on an undercrust and cover it with pastry. In order to hold it together, butter narrow bands of paper, and putting them round the pastry, bind them lightly on. Bake the *pâté* and, when it is cooked, mix the yolks of three eggs with a dash of verjuice and a little nutmeg; and when you are ready to serve, pour in your sauce into the *pâté* and mix it well. Open the *pâté* and serve with the crust cut in four. (*Le Cuisinier François*, Le Sieur de La Varenne, 1658.)

The most popular ways of preparing *Eels* in France, are the following:

Anguilles Beaucaire

The bones are removed. To the flesh of the eels is added a stuffing made of buttered whiting and minced mushrooms, the whole being braised in a terrine with chopped shallots, white Pouilly wine, a little brandy, butter, mushrooms and a few onions lightly browned beforehand.

Anguille Benoîton

Shredded fillets of eels, floured and fried, served with fried parsley and a red wine sauce.

Coulibiac

A *pâté*, the paste of which is made of *pâté à brioche*, or puff pastry, and the inside built up of poached eel, rice, hard-boiled eggs, chopped mushrooms and onions, cooked vesiga, in superimposed layers. Bake from 30 to 40 minutes.

Anguille Durand

Boned pieces of eel, with pike or whiting stuffing, poached in *mirepoix bordelaise*. Moisten with water and Pouilly wine. Brown in hot oven.

Anguille des Gourmets

Chunks of eel poached in Chablis and served with *fish velouté* (q.v.) and *crayfish coulis* (q.v.).

Matelote

Clean, skin and cut up eel and stew gently in red wine and water with salt and pepper, onion, garlic and bouquet. Brown small onions in butter and add to fish with a little more butter. When thoroughly hot, pour over thin slices of bread fried crisp in butter; remove bouquet before serving.

Matelote Mâconnaise

Same as above, with some *écrevisses* added.

Anguille Ménagère

Grilled chunks of eels; served with gherkins and a *Beurre Maître d'Hôtel*.

Anguille Meunière

Chunks of eels floured and cooked in butter, served with squeeze of lemon and chopped parsley.

Anguille Normande

Same as *Matelote Mâconnaise*, except that cider is used in place of wine and oysters replace *écrevisses*.

Anguille Orly

Fillets of eel dipped in breadcrumbs and fried; served with tomato sauce.

Anguille Pompadour

Rings of boned eels cooked in a white wine *court-bouillon*; left to get cold; strained; dipped in *Sauce Villeroy Soubisée*; rolled in breadcrumbs and fried. Served on a folded napkin with fried parsley and *croquettes à la Dauphine* with a *Sauce Béarnaise Tomatée* or *Sauce Choron*.

Anguille à la Poulette

Skin and cut up the eels; place the pieces in a saucepan and cover them with cold water; bring to the boil and then take them out and dry them. Melt a tablespoon of fresh butter in a saucepan and add to it a dessertspoonful of flour, stir well and cook the flour in the butter without allowing it to brown. Add the partly-cooked pieces of eel, moving them about so that they are all caught in the *roux*. Add a glass of dry white wine and three glasses of water; a dozen small onions; a *bouquet garni*; pepper and salt. Bring to the boil and then let it simmer for 25 or 30 minutes on gentle heat.

Dress the pieces of eel in a hollow dish with the small onions around and small mushrooms *sautés* in butter. Bind the sauce with three yolks of eggs beaten with a little fresh cream, pass it through a fine sieve, pour over the eel, add a dusting of finely-chopped parsley and serve with plain boiled potatoes. (*Escoffier Recipe*.)

Anguille à la Provençale

Cut up the eel as for the *Anguille Poulette*; let the pieces stand in boiling water for a few seconds; drain and cool them; dry them and season them with pepper and salt and then dip them in flour.

For 2 to 3 lb. of fish heat four or five large tablespoons of olive oil in an earthenware pot or pan; add four spoonfuls of chopped onions; as soon as the onions begin to brown, add the pieces of eel and mix well with the onions; add about half a bottle of white wine and, when it is reduced by half, add 1½ lb. of very ripe tomatoes, peeled and without any pips and cut up finely. Add also pepper and salt, a big pinch of chopped parsley and a little garlic. Cover the pan and let it all stew gently for 25 to 30 minutes. In the home, one may add at the same time as the tomatoes, some potatoes cut in quarters, to complete an excellent *ragoût de poisson* for luncheon. (*Escoffier Recipe*.)

Anguille à la Romaine

Sliced eel stewed gently in white wine with green peas and lettuce.

Anguille à la Rouennaise

Roll boned eel in rings; poach in red wine *mirepoix*. Serve with a *ragoût* of mushrooms, oysters and poached soft roes in the centre, and *Smelts Meunière* (q.v.) all round.

Anguille Sainte-Menehould

Sliced eel poached in white wine, drained, soaked in melted butter, rolled in a mixture of soft breadcrumbs and chopped (raw) mushrooms and then grilled and served with gherkins and diced anchovies.

Anguille à la Suffren

Sliced eel larded with fillets of anchovies, poached in white wine; this is reduced, then bound with a *purée* of tomatoes; a few pats of butter are added, and, to finish with, a little anchovy essence and a dusting of cayenne pepper. Served in *timbale*.

Anguille Tartare

Sliced eel poached in a white wine *court-bouillon* and either served cold with a *Sauce*

Tartare or else rolled in flour, beaten egg and breadcrumbs, fried and served with a *Sauce Tartare*.

Anguille Vénitienne

Slices of boned eel poached in white wine, mushrooms and soft roes as garnishings; *Sauce Vénitienne*.

Anguille a la Villeroy

Slices of boned eel poached in *court-bouillon*. When cold, covered with *Sauce Villeroy*, then rolled in breadcrumbs and fried. Served with tomato sauce.

EELPOUT

Lat. *Zoarces viviparus*; Fr. *Barbotte*; Ger. *Aalraupe*. Also called *Burbot, Bard, Greenbone, Guffer, Maroona Eel, Lote*, etc. A large-sized eel found in many European and American rivers, but not attractive as food.

EGLEFIN. AIGREFIN. EGREFIN

Fr. for fresh *Haddock* (q.v.).

ELVERS

Elvers are the young of the European eel, which, having been born in the primaeval depths of the Western Atlantic, reach English shores in the late spring, after a journey occupying two years. They ascend some rivers, notably the Severn, in incredible numbers and, during a month or so, are caught by fishermen in countless millions. They are complete little eels about 2 in. long, transparent, pale amber in colour and very thin.

There are two chief methods of cooking them:

1. Having well washed them under a tap spread them on a cloth and dry them. Dust them with flour and fry them in deep boiling fat after the manner of whitebait, and serve very hot with lemon.

If all goes well, each elver is separate and just crisp, and the dish is superb, almost beyond words. But it is very difficult. If there is too much flour, or if the elvers are not dry enough, they get into lumps of paste and are hopelessly revolting. If, on the other hand, there is not enough flour to dry them they cling together in a horrible gelatinous mass, which defies the frying medium. At their best, they are, compared to whitebait, what a *Cheval Blanc* of a great year is to pleasant *Ordinaire*.

2. Wash a quantity – say a quart – of elvers: season with salt and pepper, and put them into a basin. Tie up in a cloth, and boil for two hours or steam for three. This makes elver loaf, which, turned out of its basin, can be eaten either as it is, or, much better, cut into slices and fried.

EPERLANS

Fr. for *Smelts* (q.v.).

ÉQUILLES

Fr. for *Sand-eels*, a diminutive imitation of *Smelts*.

ESCABÈCHES

A Spanish and Provençal way of preparing small fish for hors-d'oeuvre, either fresh anchovies, sardines, whitings or mullets. The fish is first of all dipped in very hot olive oil, then piled in a hollow dish or earthenware pot. A marinade is then made of a little water, some vinegar, but chiefly olive oil; also a carrot, an onion and plenty of garlic, thyme, bayleaves, pimentoes, parsley, etc. When it has boiled for about 10 minutes, it is poured over the fish, which is left alone for 24 hours in a cool place. The fish is then ready to be served from its own dish with its marinade.

ESCARGOTS

Snails. They are neither fish or flesh, but being 'Abstinence' fare, i.e. permitted on 'meatless' days and not deserving of a section of their own, they have been included in this Fish Section. The edible snails are said to have been introduced into England by the Romans, who were fully alive to the gastronomic merit and medicinal value of the edible snail as food. But snails have never been accepted as an article of diet in England. The most popular *Escargots*, in France, are those served *à la Bourguignonne*. Other recipes, such as *Chablisienne* and *Dijonnaise*, are variants of *Bourguignone*. *Vigneronne* implies fried *Escargots*, Provençale, olive oil and garlic, and *Villebernier*, a red wine sauce.

ESCOLAR

Lat. *Ruvettus pretiosus*. A large, rough-scaled, mackerel-like, deep-sea fish of considerable gastronomic merit. It lives at depths of from 100 to 400 fathoms in the Mediterranean, middle Atlantic and Southern Seas.

ESPADON

Fr. for *Swordfish* (q.v.).

ESTURGEON

Fr. for *Sturgeon* (q.v.).

FALLFISH

Lat. *Leucosomus corporalis*. The name given in the Eastern States of America to the *Chub* (q.v.).

FERA

Lat. *Coregonus ferus*. One of the most delicate of the fishes caught in the Lake of Geneva and some of the other Swiss and Bavarian lakes. It is usually served *à l'Anglaise*,

Meunière, au Gratin, Mornay, and in other ways suitable for *Soles* (q.v.).

FIN

Fr. *Nageoire.* Any of the winglike or rudder-like membranes given to fish for propelling, balancing or guiding the body. In the *Skate* (q.v.) the very much developed pectoral fins are the best part of the fish, gastronomically; they are known as *Wings.* The best edible fin is that of the *Turtle.* Shark's fins can be used in the making of fish soups only.

FLAKE

The name under which *Dogfish* is sold in some parts of England.

FLOUNDER

Lat. *Platichthys flesus*; Fr. *Flet* or *Carrelet*; Ger. *Flunders*; Sp. *Lenguado.* The name of a flat sea-fish with a row of sharp little spines on its upper side, along the 'seam' or junction of its fins and body. In England, *Flounders* are at their best from February to September. In the U.S.A. the name *Flounder* is also given to two sorts of fresh-water fishes, the *Red-breasted Bream* and the *Sunfish* (*Eupomotis gibbosus*). In New Zealand, there is a common sea flat fish called a *Flounder.* See also *Witch Flounder.*

'The *fflounder is in taste, digestion and nourishment, like unto the Plaice, especially if he be young.*' (Venner's *Via recta ad vitam longam.* Ed. 1628, p. 70.)

Flounder Fillets in Tomato Sauce

Shred a small onion and one green pepper and cook in two tablespoonfuls of butter in a covered casserole till the onion is tender. Add six tomatoes cut in small pieces and a tablespoonful of minced parsley, blend two tablespoonfuls of flour with a little cream, or you can use a little more of the juice of the tomatoes only. When boiling add the fillets of flounder and cook for 10 minutes. (Mrs Turner's *Fifty Ways of Cooking Fish.*)

Flounder au Gratin

1 large flounder
Chopped parsley
Chopped chervil
1 or 2 chopped shallots
Onion or chives
Few mushrooms
Butter
½ cup water or fish stock
½ cup dry white wine
Brown breadcrumbs
Lemon juice
Salt and pepper

Remove head, cut off side fins and tail. Wipe fish well. Chop all herbs together, including onion, shallot, and (if available)

chives. Peel and chop mushrooms. Mix all these ingredients and set a third of the total amount aside. Butter an oven dish generously, cover bottom with two-thirds of the chopped herbs and mushrooms, add water with wine and season with salt and pepper. Sprinkle remaining third of chopped herbs, etc., on top of fish, covering with breadcrumbs and dotting with butter. Add a little lemon juice and cook from 20 to 30 minutes in a moderate oven, basting once in a while. Brown surface under a grill if necessary and serve in oven dish.

Marinaded Flounder

1 rather large flounder
Olive oil
1 sliced onion
1 chopped clove garlic
1 dried bayleaf
1 teaspoon chopped chives
Salt and pepper
1 teaspoon chopped parsley
Vinegar or lemon juice

Remove head, fins and tail. Wipe fish. Blend oil, sliced onion, garlic, herbs, salt, pepper and vinegar or lemon juice, using twice the amount of oil to either of these. Beat all this well and pour into a dish. Lay the flounder in the dish, turn frequently, keeping in a cool spot for a couple of hours. Drain, grill, basting with the strained marinading mixture. Serve with drawn butter.

Stuffed Turbans of Flounder
(American)

6 long fillets of flounder
½ cup chopped mushrooms
Few drops onion juice
3 tablespoons butter
4 tablespoons flour
½ cup cream
6 or 8 small oysters
Salt, pepper, cayenne
Few grains powdered mace

To prepare this rather more elaborate dish, metal rings, about 2½ or 3 in. in diameter and an inch high, are useful; failing these, large ramekins may be used. Have the fish filleted; trim to required size and coil the fillets inside the well-buttered rings or ramekins. If rings are used, place them when ready in a buttered tin; if ramekins, an ordinary baking tin will do. Cook the mushrooms and onion juice with the butter for a moment, add the flour, stirring well, then moisten gradually with the cream, mixing well. Simmer this mixture for a minute or two, then add the oysters, after removing beards and hard portions. Season well. Use this mixture to fill the centres of prepared rings or ramekin cases. Cover them with a sheet of well-buttered paper and bake for 20 minutes in a rather hot oven. Remove paper, then sprinkle with breadcrumbs, dot with butter and continue baking until surfaces are brown. Slip carefully out of rings, if used, or serve in ramekin cases. Hollandaise or rich cream sauce should be served with these. When lining rings or cases with the fillets of fish, care must be taken that the ends overlap or else the turbans will not retain their shape when being turned out. They may, however, be secured if necessary with a small splinter or a wooden toothpick.

Fried Filleted Flounder

Fillets of flounder may be fried in butter after being dipped first in beaten egg, then in white or brown breadcrumbs. They may also, if preferred, be fried in deep fat, after flouring well.

FLUKE

Another name for *Witch Flounder* (q.v.).

FOGAS

(Lat. *Lucioperca sandra*) is the name of a fish found in the Danube and Lake Balaton. The latter is whiter, has silver scales, and is more tender than its brother of the Danube. A fully-grown *Fogas* may weigh from 16 lb. to 20 lb. – under 2 lb. they are called *Fogas üllö* or *Sullö*. The export trade of this fish from Hungary is important enough to persuade the Hungarian Government to affix a leaden seal to genuine *Fogas* from Lake Balaton as a guarantee of authenticity. The frozen fish from Russia and the Caucasus cannot then be mistaken for it.

FRITURE

A French word which is used either for the fat – oil, butter, dripping, etc. – in which the fish, meat or anything else is to be fried; or also for the fried food out of the frying-pan. *Une friture*, for instance, is often – although incorrectly – used in reference to a dish of fried fish, usually whitebait or smelts.

FROG

Lat. *Rana esculenta*; Fr. *Grenouille*. One of many varieties of a leaping amphibian enjoying a certain gastronomical reputation in many parts of the world, but more particularly in France and the Southern States of America. Only the hind-legs are used – and only in the spring, chiefly during Lent. (Frogs are not *meat*.) They are either boiled and served with a *Sauce Poulette*, or else fried in butter. One of the more elaborate preparations of *Frogs' legs* in France is known as a *Chartreuse de Grenouilles*: the meat of the frogs' legs is served in a *Rizotto* with filleted

pike and *queues d'écrevisses*; grated cheese and browned before serving.

FROGFISH

Fr. *Baudroie* (q.v.). Also called *Angler* (q.v.).

FROSTFISH

The New Zealand name for the *Scabbard fish* (q.v.).

GAPER

Mya truncata. A bivalve living buried in sand or mud, in an upright position, at the mouths of rivers and estuaries, near low-water mark; they are dug up at low tide and are eaten boiled like *Cockles*. They are called *Cockle Brillion* at Belfast; *Brélin* or *Vrélin*, in Brittany; *Kunyu*, in Orkney; *Spoon-shell*, in Devonshire, etc.

GAR. GARFISH. GARPIKE

Lat. *Belone belone*; Fr. *Orphie*; Ger. *Hornhecht*. Names given to a number of pike-like, elongated, voracious fishes. The common European species (Lat. *Belone belone*) is a sea-fish of real gastronomic merit, but the fresh-water *Gar* (Lat. *Lepisosteus osseus*) of the U.S.A. is rank and tough; it can only be enjoyed pounded into *Quenelles*. There is a *Garfish* caught off the coasts of Australia which is considered one of the best of Australian sea-fish. It belongs to the *Hemiramphus* or *Halfbeaks* genus.

GIRELLE

Fr. for *Rainbow Wrasse*. See *Wrasse*.

GOBY

Lat. *Gobiidae*. The family name of a large number of sea-fishes and a few fresh-water spiny-finned fishes distinguished by their broad, depressed head and large mouth. Gastronomically, gobies do not rise above the *Bouillabaisse* (q.v.) standard.

GOUJONS

Fr. for *Gudgeons*.

GOURAMI

Lat. *Osphromenus goramy*. One of the most highly valued – gastronomically – of the fresh-water fishes of South Eastern Asia and the Malay Archipelago. The Dutch, in Batavia, rear the *gourami* in earthen vessels, feeding it exclusively on fresh-water plants. It has been introduced into South America, the West Indies and Mauritius.

GRAINING

Lat. *Leuciscus leuciscus*. Another name for the *Dace* (q.v.).

GRAVENCHE

One of the fishes peculiar to the lakes of Switzerland and Bavaria.

GRAYLING

Lat. *Thymallus thymallus*; Fr. *Ombre*. One of the best of the European fresh-water fishes. It is found in Great Bri ain, Scandinavia and Central Europe. In Northern America there are three slightly different kinds of *Graylings*, the *Arctic* or *Alaska Grayling* (*Thymallus signifer*), the *Montana Grayling* (*Thymallus montanus*); and the *Michigan Grayling* (*Thymallus tricolor*).

There is a Grayling in New Zealand (Maori name, *Upukororo*), which is the only indigenous representative of the *Salmonidae* in that country; strange to say it is identical, or nearly so, with a *Grayling* in the Falkland Islands. The New Zealand *Grayling*, being very easily trapped and netted, almost became extinct thirty or forty years ago; but a policy of strict preservation has, it is hoped, resulted in the survival of this very interesting fish.

The European *Grayling* spawns several months later than its cousins the Trout, so that instead of being in season from March to September it comes normally into condition in the latter month, and is, perhaps, at its best in November; but many small *Grayling* do not spawn during their first season of maturity, and these are in condition in the summer. The small *Grayling* up to ¾ lb. are best: in England, *Grayling* rarely weigh more than 4 lb.

Most methods of cooking *Trout* (q.v.) are suitable for *Grayling*, but the following is, perhaps, the best for a medium-sized fish.

Take a *Grayling* of, say, 4 oz. to 12 oz.; wash him well under a hot water tap; clean him and wipe him dry, inside and out. Dust him inside with salt and pepper.

Unless quite small, remove head and tail (this allows the use of a smaller pan and saves fat). In a suitable frying-pan, make some fat very hot (it should not be less than ½ in. deep). When the fat is sufficiently hot, put in the *Grayling*; after half a minute turn it over, and leave it till you estimate that the lower side is cooked; turn it over again and cook till a fork goes easily right through the thickest part. Serve immediately with melted butter or any of the butter sauces. If the cooking has been successful the entire skin will come away in one piece. Presented thus, a 10-oz. November *Grayling* has very few peers. (Sir Francis Colchester-Wemyss's Recipe.)

Grayling Cooked with Herbs

Clean, wash and dry the *Grayling*, cut off the fins, trim the tails, but leave the heads on. Mince very finely a bunch of sweet herbs. Put 4 oz. of butter into a fireproof dish and sprinkle some of the herbs over the bottom, put in the fish, either two large or four small *Grayling*, arranging them head to tail. Sprinkle over them the rest of the herbs and pour all over a gill of white wine. Bake in a moderate oven for 15 minutes. When cooked strain off the liquid. Blend ½ oz. of flour with a little stock or cold water and stir in the liquid you have strained from the fish, put it into a pan and stir until boiling. Season with salt and pepper and pour it over the fish, which is served very hot in the dish in which it was cooked. (Mrs Turner's *Fifty Ways of Cooking Fish*.)

GREENFISH

'The *Merlangus virens* of Cuvier or *Gadus virens* of Linnaeus.' (Yarrell. Vol. II p. 256.)

Greenfish which Halliwell calls Cod and Yarrell Green Cod is also referred to as Fresh Ling. It was the most popular Lenten fish in Elizabethan England.

'*Lings perhaps looks for great extolling being counted the Beefe of the sea and standing every fish day (as a cold supporter) at my Lord Maior's table; yet it is nothing but a long cod: whereof the greater sised is called* Organe Ling *and the other* Codling, *because it is no longer than a Cod, and yet hath the taste of Ling: whilst it is new it is called Green-Fish; when it is salted it is called* Ling.' (Muffet. pp. 154-5.)

There is also a *Bluefish* (q.v.) known in California as *Greenfish*.

GRENOUILLE

Fr. for *Frog* (q.v.).

GRIG

The name of a small fresh-water eel.

GRILSE

A young *Salmon* on its first leaving the sea to go up-stream.

GRONDIN. ROUGET-GRONDIN. TRIGLE

Fr. for *Gurnard* or *Gurnet* (q.v.).

GROUPER

Lat. *Epinephelus morio*. A bass-like sea-fish of some gastronomic merit found in Florida, West Indian and Central American waters.

GRUNT

The name given to a number of fishes of the *Haemulon* genus, mostly to be found off Florida and in West Indian waters. The best *Grunts*, gastronomically, are the *White Grunt* (*Haemulon plumieri*); the *Yellow Grunt* (*Haemulon sciurus*); the *Grey* or *Striped Grunt* (*Haemulon macrostomum*); and the *French*, or *Openmouthed Grunt* (*Haemulon flaveolineatum*).

GUDGEON

Lat. *Gobio gobio*; Fr. *Goujon*; Ger. *Gründling*; It. *Ghiozzo*. One of the best European fresh-water fishes. The *Gudgeon* belongs to the Carp family. It is usually fried and served like fried *Smelts* with fried parsley.

'*But fish not with this melancholy bait*
For this fool gudgeon, this opinion.'
(*Merchant of Venice*. Act I. Sc. 1. 1. 102.)

GURNARD. GURNET

Lat. *Trigla hirundo*; Fr. *Grondin*; Ger. *Seehahn*; Sp. *Trigla*. A very ugly and not a very good fish, which received a much larger measure of attention from cooks in the past than it does now. It is called *Tubfish* in Lancashire; also *Yellow Gurnard*. Sticklebacks and flying fish are *Gurnards* or *Gurnets*, two names for the same fish. The red *Gurnets* (Lat. *Trigla cuculus*), or *Sea-Cuckoo*, are best and they are in season from July to April. *Gurnets* are not expensive to buy, but they are not particularly economical, as the head weighs a good deal and a fish from 10 oz. to 12 oz. is required for each person.

Other British (waters) members of the same family are the *Streaked Gurnard* (T. *lineata*); the *Grey Gurnard* (T. *gurnardus*); the *Piper* (T. *lyra*), or *Sea-hen*; and the *long-finned Gurnard* (T. *obscura*).

'*If I be not ashamed of my soldiers, I am a soused gurnet.*' (*The First Part of Henry IV*. Act IV. Sc. 2.)

Gurnets Broiled

Draw, clean and scrape the gurnets and dry well. Cut off the heads and fins. Dip in flour and brush over with plenty of melted dripping. The bars of the grid-iron must be heated and well greased before using Make two or three cuts in the skin on each side and put them on the grid-iron over a clear fire, or under a gas griller, and cook slowly; turn them carefully several times and be sure they keep nice and greasy, as gurnets are rather dry fish. Serve very hot and hand melted butter in a tureen. (Mrs Turner's *Fifty Ways of Cooking Fish*.)

GWYNIAD

A white fish or fresh-water herring found in Bala Lake, North Wales.

HADDOCK

Lat. *Gadus aeglefinus*; Fr. *Aigrefin* or *Eglefin*; Ger. *Schellfisch*; Sp. *Merluza*. A fish which inhabits the Northern Atlantic from Iceland to France. It is at its best in Scotland, England and Ireland from September to February. There is no Haddock comparable to the *Finnan Haddock*, or Smoked Haddock – Findon (The place is Findon, corrupted into Finnan) is a fishing hamlet some six miles from Aberdeen – skinned, rubbed with butter, broiled and served with pats of cold fresh butter. Famous also, through the *Waverley Novels*, the *Rizzared Haddock* is rubbed inside and out with salt and left overnight before hanging in the open air, preferably in the wind, but always out of the sun. Afterwards, for breakfast, its head is cut off and the *Rizzared Haddock* is rubbed with butter, dredged with a little flour and broiled. In England, the *Haddock* is usually boiled in milk and water and served with plain English butter sauce. The *Norway Haddock* (Lat. *Sebastes norvegicus*), known as *Rodfisk*, in Denmark, is a red haddock, abundant from Trondjhem southwards and greatly prized gastronomically in all northern European countries.

Haddock (fresh)

This may be cooked according to any recipe for flounder, small fresh cod or any similar white fish. It may be stuffed and baked, filleted and fried (in deep or shallow fat), made into fish cakes, quenelles or soufflés or plain boiled and served with parsley sauce and boiled potatoes.

Haddock Fillets Fried
(Epicurean Sauce)

Choose two small haddocks weighing about 1 lb. each – this gives you four nice fillets. Sprinkle each fillet with salt, pepper, and lemon juice. Mince a few chives and a sprig of parsley and lemon thyme very finely and mix with half cupful of breadcrumbs. Beat up an egg and brush the fillets over with the egg and dip each one in the seasoned breadcrumbs. Place in the frying basket and fry in boiling fat to a nice golden-brown; drain well and serve on a hot dish.

For the sauce, beat half cupful of good cream till it is very stiff, then slowly stir in three tablespoonfuls of mayonnaise sauce, a teaspoonful of mustard, a tablespoonful of grated horseradish root, a good pinch of salt and a dash of cayenne pepper. (Mrs Turner's *Fifty Ways of Cooking Fish*.)

Haddock is chiefly served in one of the three following ways in France:

Beurre Fondu. Poached in salted water, served on a serviette, with bouquet of parsley at each end and plain boiled potatoes. Melted butter as a sauce served at the same time.

Fines Herbes. Baked in white wine in hot oven, with chopped mushrooms, onions and parsley, and served in baking dish.

Flamande. Poached in white wine.

To Smoke Haddock
(Scotch Farmhouse Recipe)

Clean the haddocks thoroughly; split them and take off the heads. Put salt on them and let them lie for two hours, but if required to keep for more than a week, let them lie overnight. Hang them in the open air for two or three hours to dry; smoke them in a chimney over peat or hardwood sawdust or fir cones.

To make a suitable chimney, use an old cask open at both ends. Place rods of wood across top of cask; tie the haddocks by the tails in pairs and hang them on the stick to smoke. Be sure to keep the heat as even as possible, as changes in temperature spoil the fish. When done the fish should be of a fine, yellow colour, which they should acquire in twelve hours at the most. Haddocks may also be smoked without splitting

To Cook Smoked Haddock

The best way to cook a smoked haddock is to broil or grill it over a quick, clear fire: rub it with butter and serve piping hot.

Stappit or Crappit Heids
(Scots Farmhouse Recipe)

The heads and livers of fresh haddocks. Oatmeal, pepper and salt and milk.

Take the heads of the haddocks and clean thoroughly. Chop the liver, which must be perfectly fresh; mix them with an equal quantity of raw oatmeal; add seasoning and bind with milk; stuff the heads with this mixture and place on end in bottom of buttered pan; pour water gently over them and boil for half an hour.

Baked Stuffed Haddock

This is the modern version of 'crappit heids'. Wash thoroughly a good-sized boiling haddock and remove the fins. Scrape from head to tail and dry. Now fill the aperture where it was cleaned with stuffing. This may be of oatmeal mixed with finely-chopped onion and plenty of suet, or of breadcrumb made as follows:

2 oz. crumbs, 1 oz. butter, a pinch of dried herbs, chopped parsley, salt and pepper, all mixed with the yolk of an egg.

Sew up the fish, lay on a baking-sheet greased with dripping, and cover the haddock with melted dripping. Baste well. The time needed to cook it will depend on the size of the haddock. Put some nice bits of parsley or tomato on it before serving, according to the sauce which is to be handed with it.

HAIMORA

Macrodon trahira. One of the best food fishes of tropical American waters; also a good game fish.

HAKE

Lat. *Gadus merluccius*; Fr. *Merluche*; Ger. *Kabeljau*; Sp. *Merluza*. A cousin of the Cod, whose chief claim to the attention of cooks is that its backbone is more easily detachable than that of any other fish. It is the safest fish for the nursery, because the most free from bones. Hake is in season all the year round, but at its best from June to January. The Silver Hake (*Merluccius bilinearis*), which is common on the Northern New England coast, is superior to the European kind, gastronomically. There is a third type of Hake (*Merluccius productus*) which is abundant on the Pacific coast from Puget Sound to Southern California.

HALIBUT

Lat. *Hippoglossus hippoglossus*; Fr. *Flétan*; Ger. *Heilbutt*; Sp. *Mero*. The largest species of flatfish to be found in the cold waters of the North Atlantic. It is one of the most useful food fishes; it is usually cheaper than Turbot – and not so good – but a welcome change from Cod. *Halibut* is obtainable all the year round, but it is at its best from August to April. Being so large, *Halibut* sometimes weighs as much as 200 lb. – it is retailed in small slices or squares, as desired. When freshly caught it is a delicate fish, but when kept on ice, as is too often the case, or when caught in Icelandic waters and frozen, it is somewhat insipid and must be accompanied by a good sauce. The best *Halibut* is the very young fish, one that weighs 3 lb. or less: it is called *Chicken Halibut* and is at its best from March to October.

Halibut Baked with Lobster Sauce

A piece of halibut weighing about 2 lb. will be required. Cut stripes in the top, large enough to insert a narrow strip of fat salt pork in each gash or stripe. Place in a baking pan, sprinkle with salt and pepper and dredge with flour. Pour in enough water to cover the bottom of the pan and 4 oz. of butter and add a slice of onion, a sprig of parsley, two slices of carrot cut in pieces, and a bayleaf. Bake for one hour, basting with the liquor in the pan.

For the sauce, remove flesh from a lobster weighing about 1 lb., and keep the tender claw meat. Chop the body meat and cover with three cups of cold water and add the body shells, cook until this is reduced to two cups, strain and add to it gradually 4 oz. of butter and 4 oz. of flour, which must have previously been cooked together. Add half teaspoonful of salt, a pinch of cayenne, dessertspoonful of lemon juice, and finally add the claw meat cut into neat dice. (Mrs Turner's *Fifty Ways of Cooking Fish.*)

Chicken Halibut with Cheese Sauce

Choose a chicken halibut weighing just about 2 lb., and this will give you four nice fillets. Season with salt, brush over with

339

lemon juice and roll them up neatly. Steam for 15 minutes and place on silver serving-dish, garnish with small shrimps and pour over the sauce. Serve very hot.

For the sauce, cook the skin and bones of the fish with three slices of carrot, one slice of onion, sprig of parsley, bayleaf, a few peppercorns, in two cupfuls of cold water for 30 minutes and then strain – there should then be one cupful. Melt two tablespoonfuls of butter, add three tablespoonfuls of flour and the fish stock and stir in half a small cup of cream. Bring to boiling-point and add the yolks of two eggs. Season with salt and pepper, a pinch of cayenne and a large tablespoonful of grated cheese. (Mrs Turner's *Fifty Ways of Cooking Fish*.)

Halibut Fillets or Collops

Court-bouillon
About 1½ to 2 lb. halibut
2 tablespoons butter
2 tablespoons flour
1 blade or pinch mace
Salt and pepper
Butter or dripping to fry collops
1 teaspoon lemon juice

Prepare the *court-bouillon* and, when ready, add the piece of halibut and very gently simmer for about 10 minutes. Remove fish, take off skin, remove bones and divide the fish into fillets or, as sometimes called, 'collops', of desired size. Retain some of the *court-bouillon* after straining. Melt the two tablespoons of butter in a saucepan, add the flour, mix well and moisten with the *court-bouillon*, using about two cupfuls of it. Add the mace, salt, pepper and Worcester sauce according to taste. Heat some more butter or some good dripping in a frying-pan, fry the fillets of fish in this, seasoning lightly with salt and pepper. When light brown on all sides, remove from pan and add to pre-pared sauce, simmering until properly cooked. Season with lemon juice and serve with sauce strained over the collops.

Baked Halibut
(Canadian)

1 or 2 lb. halibut
Boiling water
Salt and pepper
Milk
Small pieces butter
Fresh, hot, tomato sauce

Dip the dark side of the fish into boiling water, then remove that skin entirely. Sprinkle both sides of the fish with salt and pepper, then place it in a casserole and add enough milk to come half-way up the piece of fish. Add a few small bits of butter and cover. Bake gently, basting frequently, for

about an hour. Serve with tomato or egg sauce and potatoes.

HAMLET
Lat. *Epinephelus striatus*. A large *Grouper* (q.v.), common from Key West to Brazil and of more than passing gastronomic merit. The name is also given, in the West Indies, to one of the most valued sea-fishes, the *Gymnothorax moringa*, a yellow and black thickly-spotted tropical eel.

HARENG
Fr. for a *fresh herring*.

HARENG FUMÉ
Fr. for *Kipper* (q.v.).

HARENG SALÉ
Fr. for *Bloater* (q.v.).

HARENG SAUR
Fr. for *Red Herring*.

HERRING
Lat. *Clupea harengus*; Fr. *Hareng*; Ger. *Häringe*; It. *Aringe*; Sp. *Arengues*. One of the most nutritious and one of the cheapest of all the fishes out of the sea. *Fresh Herrings* are best broiled; *Salt Herrings* are best pickled; *Bloaters* and *Kippers* are best grilled. Herrings travel in schools of millions of individuals in the more temperate waters of the North Atlantic. They are in season all the year round, but at their best from June to December. A closely allied species, the *California Herring* (*Clupea pallasii*), is caught in the North Pacific Ocean. The *Thread Herring* (*Opisthonema oglinum*) is another species of herring to be found in the West Indies and off the East Coast of the U.S.A. Another gastronomically valuable species of herring, known in the U.S.A. as *Walleyed Herring*, is called, in England, *Alewife* (q.v.).

The herring fisheries of England and Scotland depend upon the presence of shoals of herrings off different parts of the coasts at different times of the year. In May and June there is great fishing off the Shetlands. Later on, beginning with July, the fishing is carried on from the Shetlands to the Orkneys and at Aberdeen, Peterhead, Fraserburgh and Wick. These fisheries, which last several weeks, are for fish almost ready to spawn. The English drift-net fishery for herring is practically confined to the East Coast, and it follows the Scottish fishery. The East Coast fishery commences at North Shields, in May, and it goes on at an increased rate during June, July and August, when Grimsby, Hull and Scarborough begin fishing. In September, the landings begin at Yarmouth and Lowestoft, reaching their maximum in November and December.

Were the herring a rare fish, it would be considered one of the greatest delicacies of the table. Its flavour is excellent; its food value very high and its cost very low: it supplies very nearly as much body-building material as the same weight of fresh salmon, but at a tithe of the cost. The fact that herrings are inexpensive is the only excuse for their being unfashionable among the well-to-do classes, but it is impossible to find an excuse why they should not be more popular than they are among the masses.

Many people do not like herrings because of their many small, fine bones. If care be taken, nearly all these may be removed with the central bone, but, to do this, the fish must be neatly split, with the fish knife, both sides being separated. Slip the knife under the backbone and gently lever it out, taking care that as many as possible of the small bones come away with it. Naturally, this method applies equally to kippers and bloaters, which are one and the same fish differently treated. The splitting operation may be done before the fish is cooked: it will make it much easier, hence more agreeable to eat.

Grilled Herrings

Clean, scale, remove heads, sprinkle with pepper and salt after wiping fish with a damp cloth. Rub over with olive oil and score both sides. Heat grill before placing the herrings under a sharp flame, cooking one side brown before the other. Serve with mustard sauce.

Savoury Herrings

1 fresh herring per guest
Butter
Chopped parsley
1 chopped shallot
Salt and pepper
1 egg, beaten
Flour
Frying fat
Parsley
Quarters of lemon

Take a thin, sharp knife and split each herring right along the centre of the back, taking care not to split the skin on the other side of the fish. Remove head and entrails (leaving roes in) as well as the tail and the backbone. Mix the butter, parsley, shallot, salt and pepper well together without melting it too much. Spread this paste on one side of the open herring, close the other over it, dip in beaten egg and then in flour; fry in deep boiling oil or fat. Drain well and serve with parsley and lemon slices.

Fried Herrings
(Scots Style)

This was King Edward VII's favourite dish of herring.

Scale herring and remove head. Open down back and take out backbone with as many of smaller bones as possible. Throw away entrails, leaving roe, if any. Season with salt and pepper and cover with oatmeal (medium ground). Press a little to make this adhere. Fry the herring in butter, bacon fat or dripping both sides and dish up with parsley and cut lemon. A pat of butter placed on the fish at the last moment is an improvement.

Herrings à la Bordelaise

1 herring per guest
Olive oil
Parsley
Shallot
1 clove garlic
Salt and pepper
1 tomato
Hot boiled potatoes

Clean and prepare herring. Grill on both sides, then remove when nearly done and place in an oven dish with the oil, chopped parsley, garlic, shallot, salt, pepper, and peeled and cut-up tomato. If available, add also a little chopped chives. Set the dish again under the grill, finish cooking fish, basting with the oil and herbs. Serve, when brown, with potatoes around the same dish. Lemon juice may be squeezed on when serving.

Herrings Cooked in Claret

Choose four large fresh herrings and have them cleaned and the heads and tails cut off, but they must not be washed. Cut three or four stripes across both sides and rub all over with mustard mixed into a paste with Tarragon vinegar. Put the fish in a flat fire-proof dish, sprinkle with finely-chopped parsley and 1 oz. of butter on each fish. Pour over a large glass of Claret and bake in the oven for 10 minutes. Turn the herrings over, baste all over with the liquor and sprinkle with a handful of fine breadcrumbs. Bake again for 10 minutes and serve very hot. (Mrs Turner's *Fifty Ways of Cooking Fish*.)

Herrings à la Meunière

Clean, scale and trim the required number of herrings; score on both sides; flour them and cook them in butter; season with pepper and salt and a squeeze of lemon; add chopped herbs and serve with the butter in which they were cooked and a slice of lemon on each fish.

Fresh Herring Stew

Clean, scale and trim as many herrings as may be required. Brown them for an instant in butter, then cover with an equal quantity of red wine and hot water, adding small onions and a clove of garlic, as well as salt and pepper. Cook gently, without boiling, for about half an hour. Mix a little more butter with an equal amount of flour, add to pan, simmer for a few minutes and serve fish hot, with baked potatoes.

Marinaded Herrings

Fresh herrings
Salt and pepper
Finely-chopped onion
1 bayleaf (if liked)
Best red wine vinegar
Water

Clean, wipe and split the fish, remove backbone and season well with salt and pepper. Cover with the chopped onion and broken-up bayleaf, if used. Roll each half up very neatly and tightly and place them in an earthenware jar, pouring over them equal quantities of the vinegar and water to cover. Tie over top of jar with paper and bake in a slow oven for at least one hour. Allow to cool, then add a little more cold vinegar.

Bismarck Herrings

Fillets of herring marinaded in white wine and vinegar with onions and carrots, salt and peppercorns.

Potted Herrings

6 fresh herrings
Salt and pepper
Small pinch powdered mace
Flour
Butter
Chopped parsley

Prepare fish, removing heads, entrails and backbones with as many of the small ones as possible. Set the herrings in an oven pan with barely enough water to cover them, adding seasonings and lightly dredging with flour. Cook gently until tender enough to rub through a sieve. Add to the paste butter as desired, taste to see if seasoning is sufficient, mix in parsley and mace and press into pots, covering with clarified butter. Keep in a cool place for a week or two, no more. Nice on toast.

Yorkshire Herring Pie

Wash and bone four fresh herrings, cut them into fillets and let them lie in a little salted water. Peel three or four potatoes and cut into thin slices, as for chips. Take a pie-dish and butter and grease well. Build the potatoes round the dish as for a *Charlotte*. Take two sour apples; peel and chop fine.

Place a layer of the herring fillets in the dish: season and cover with apple: so repeat until the dish is full. Put slices of potatoes on the top, and cover down. Bake in moderate oven for three-quarters of an hour. When done, turn out or not, as you like. (Sir Stephen Gaselee's Recipe.)

Baked and Stuffed Herrings

1 fresh herring per guest
Fresh breadcrumbs
Butter
Chopped parsley
Salt and pepper
Lemon juice

Prepare fish, separate into two parts, removing roes and backbone. Curl roes to serve as garnish. Mix together the breadcrumbs, butter softened – but not melted – parsley, salt, pepper and lemon juice to a thick paste. Spread this on the herrings, roll each separately or lay one half on another, place in a baking tin, cover with buttered paper and bake for 10 to 15 minutes. Some made mustard may be added to filling, or mustard sauce may be handed separately. Decorate with roes, *sautés* in butter.

Herring Pancakes

Pancake batter
Freshly cooked spinach
Flesh of boiled herrings
Thick white sauce
Butter
Parmesan cheese, grated

Prepare the batter, if possible, overnight. Pick over, wash and boil the spinach but do not chop, merely squeeze out all water and keep hot. Flake the boiled herrings, carefully removing all bones, season well and mix with the thick sauce. As each very small pancake is fried, place a spoonful of the fish mixture inside and roll up tightly, placing them as done on the hot spinach. When all are ready, sprinkle surface of entire dish with grated Parmesan cheese and brown quickly under a grill, serving at once.

Fried Filleted Herrings

Fresh herrings
Beaten egg
Breadcrumbs
Salt and pepper
Frying fat
Parsley
Lemon
Piquante sauce

Split fish open as directed, removing bone and roes. Each herring will give four small fillets. Egg and breadcrumb them in the usual way, seasoning with salt and pepper, fry crisp in fat and serve with lemon and parsley after draining well. Serve with *Piquante* sauce.

Herrings à la Lorraine

Fresh herrings
Flour
Butter
Salt and pepper
Cream
Lemon juice
Breadcrumbs

Clean the herrings. Flour and brown them lightly in butter (and to this, by the way, some people add a small finely-chopped shallot or onion), then season with salt and pepper; add lemon juice and cream as wished – about two tablespoons of the latter for four or five herrings would be correct. Sprinkle lightly with fine brown breadcrumbs while fish is still in pan – turning it to sprinkle each side. Simmer for an instant, then serve hot.

Herring au Gratin

Three or four herrings, three tablespoons breadcrumbs, one shallot, grated lemon rind, one teaspoonful chopped parsley, pepper and salt, tomato purée.

Split the herring open and remove the backbone and as many of the small bones as possible. Score the skin across two or three times and divide each fish into two lengthwise. Chop the shallot very finely and mix it with the breadcrumbs, parsley, pepper, salt and a little grated lemon rind. Well grease a flat fireproof dish with butter and sprinkle over the bottom half the breadcrumb mixture. Lay the fish on this and cover with the rest of the mixture. Pour round one or two tablespoonfuls of tomato purée, or fresh tomatoes, pulped and passed through a sieve, put a few pieces of butter on the breadcrumbs, and bake in a good oven from 15 to 20 minutes. The fish must be thoroughly cooked and the breadcrumb nicely browned. (From *Cookery for every Household*, by Florence Jack.)

American Pickled Herrings

3 soft roe herrings
½ cup cream
½ teaspoon sugar
1 large sliced onion
¾ cup vinegar
4 slices of lemon
6 peppercorns

The herrings, after cleaning, are soaked in cold water for 24 hours. Then remove skin and bones as well as the roes. Rub these latter through a sieve with the cream and sugar. Lay the sliced onion, vinegar and lemon on the fish, place in a pan, add the peppercorns and the sauce. Allow to stand on ice for another 24 hours before serving with potato salad.

Herrings, in France, are mostly grilled and served with either a *Sauce Ravigote* (their culinary name is then *Harengs à la Diable*); or with a *Beurre Maître d'Hôtel*. They are also stuffed and baked (*Calaisienne, Nantaise* or *Paramé*, according to the stuffing); and they are also used to a considerable extent in different guises as hors-d'oeuvre:

à la Livonienne. Fillets of smoked herring cut up in small dice and served with both potatoes and apples, plain boiled and also cut up dice-like, dressed with oil and vinegar, chervil and parsley, tarragon and chives and a little fennel, all chopped, served on small fish dish, made up to look like a herring, with the head added at one end and the tail of the fish at the other.

à la Potocka. Fillets of smoked herring, soaked in milk, then cut up in thin strips and laid crosswise on a salad of *reinettes* apples; dressed with alternate dice of cucumber and beetroot and thin slices of peeled lemon; moistened with oil and vinegar.

à la Suédoise. Thin scallops of smoked herrings, soaked in milk, then dressed on a long and narrow dish, alternating with round pieces of celeriac and with a border of the chopped white and yolk of hard-boiled eggs in alternate order. A little *Sauce Vinaigrette* over it all and a pinch of shavings of horseradish at each end of the dish.

à la Hongroise. Fresh herrings cooked in white wine and served cold with onions, olive oil and plenty of paprika.

à la Dieppoise. Fresh herrings poached in a marinade of one-third white wine and two-thirds vinegar, with pieces of carrots, celery, onion, pepper and salt, thyme, bayleaves and parsley. Allow to cool in marinade.

au vin blanc. Same as *à la Dieppoise*, except that there is no vinegar in the marinade.

à l'Espagnole. Fresh herrings cooked in olive oil, with tomatoes, onions, and paprika; sweet pimentoes and garlic. Let it get quite cold in its own juice and serve with slices of peeled lemon.

HILSA. HILSAH

Lat. *Clupea ilisha*. A valuable food fish of India, allied to the *Shad* (q.v.). It is sometimes called *Indian Salmon*.

HOGFISH

Lat. *Scorpaena scrofa*; Fr. *Rascasse* (q.v.). Also a large West Indian and Florida fish (*Lachnolaimus maximus*) of some gastronomic merit.

HORSE MACKEREL
Lat. *Trachurus trachurus* and *Caranx trachurus*. Not a *Mackerel* and not a good food fish. It is mostly seen near the European coasts of the North Atlantic. The young fish are tinned by the Portuguese and sold as *Sardines* of a very inferior kind.

INK-FISH
See *Cuttle-fish*.

ISABELITA
The Spanish name of *Angelfish* (q.v.).

JEWFISH
Any of the large *Groupers* (q.v.) but more particularly the *Promicrops itaiara* or *Jewfish* of the West Indies and the West Coast of Mexico. More highly valued by anglers for the sport it gives them than by epicures.

JOHN DORY. DOREE
Lat. *Zeus faber*; Fr. *Poisson de Saint-Pierre*; Ger. *Sonnenfisch*; Sp. *Dorado*. A European sea-fish of no mean gastronomic merit. A similar species exists in Australia; it is known as *Zeus australis*.

Fillets of Dory in batter
Clean the fish and take it off the bone, dividing it into good sized pieces. Prepare a thin frying batter, coat the fish with it and fry until a golden brown and quite crisp. Serve with Tartare sauce. (*Lady Maclagan's recipe.*)

John Dory Cooked with Tomatoes
Put three tomatoes in boiling water for a minute. Take them out and peel them. Cut them in half and press out the seeds. Chop a medium-sized onion finely and cook it for two or three minutes in butter, without allowing it to colour. Add to it the chopped tomatoes, a coffeespoonful of powdered sugar, and seasoning. Pour this into a fireproof dish, adding a little water or white wine.

On this mixture lay the filleted fish. Bake in the oven, turning the fish over once. When it is done, take it out and place it where it will keep hot. Put tomatoes, liquid and onion through a sieve and add this *purée* to a good white sauce. Season well and serve with the fish.

John Dory is excellent used as a salad. (Mrs Lucas's *A Pretty Kettle of Fish*.)

John Dory à la Provençale
Clean and thoroughly dry a small fish. Cut off the head, fins, etc., then sprinkle it with salt and pepper and dredge it lightly with flour.

Heat clarified butter in a frying-pan and when it is very hot lay the fish in it. Cook it on both sides, allowing about 10 minutes to each. Take it out and set it where it will keep hot.

To the butter in the pan add a tablespoonful of very finely chopped onion and a dessertspoonful of flour. Stir well together until you have a smooth, thick mass, then dilute it with three tablespoonfuls of white wine and a little fish stock. Add seasoning, a chopped tomato, and a teaspoonful of finely-chopped herbs. Cook the sauce for about 10 minutes, put it through a sieve and pour it over the fish. (Mrs Lucas's *A Pretty Kettle of Fish*.)

KEDGEREE
For four people: Boil 5 oz. unpolished rice in five pints of salted water for 15 minutes, then strain water through a sieve and dry rice for a minute or two in the oven. Mix with the rice an equal or greater quantity of boiled, boned and flaked fish, according to what you happen to have. Best results are obtained when one-third salt fish (haddock, as a rule) is used to two-thirds of fresh white fish (cod, halibut or hake). Add one sliced or crumbled hard-boiled egg and a dessertspoonful of fresh cream or butter per person and mix the lot thoroughly well whilst the dish is standing in very hot water so that the contents shall remain hot. Season with pepper and salt and a little grated chives. In the summer time, the kedgeree can be made in the usual way but left in the ice-box and served cold.

KILKIS
Norwegian anchovies.

KINGFISH
The name given to different species of fish in different parts of the world; in U.S.A. to the *Menticirrhus saxatilis* and other members of the *Menticirrhus* family; in the West Indies to a species of mackerel which is much esteemed gastronomically, the *Scomberomorus cavalla*; in Australia to the *Seriola grandis*; in Tasmania to the *Thyrsites micropus*; in New Zealand and in India to the *Polynemus indica*.

KIPPER
A *split*, salted and smoked fish; mostly *Herrings* (q.v.).

KLIP. CLIPFISH
The name by which is known a certain kind of Smoked Cod from Norway.

KNOBBARDS. KNOBBERDS. KNOBS
Little sea-shells similar to whelks.

In *Henry V* (Act III. Sc. 6) Fluellen describes Bardolph's face as: '*full of bubukles, whelks and knobs and flames of fire.*'

LAKE HERRING
See *Cisco.*

LAMPERN
Lat. *Lampetra fluviatilis.* The fresh-water *Lamprey* (q.v.).

Lamperns and Lampreys are almost pre-historic creatures: they are eel-like, they have a cartilaginous skeleton, but no limbs, no ribs, no backbone, and no jaws. The Lamprey averages about 30 in. in length, and lives in the sea. The Lampern is much smaller and inhabits the lower parts of certain rivers. They both live by attaching themselves to fish, and sucking nourishment from them. Lampreys are esteemed by fishermen as the best bait for cod and turbot, and are best left alone by cooks.

Lamperns are by many regarded as a great delicacy. They come into season in October or November, and can be cooked in any method suitable for *Eels* (q.v.). It is usually agreed that they should be served with a sauce made with their blood and that they are especially estimable in a pie with veal stock and mushrooms.

LAMPREY
Lat. *Petromyzon marinus*; Fr. *Lamproie*; Ger. *Lampreten*; It. *Lampede*; Sp. *Lampreas.*

'*A Lamprey, first a Lampron Grigg, then a Lampret, then a Lamprell, then a Lamprey.*' (Randle Holme, p. 324.)

'*Lampreys or Lampurnes be partly of the nature of Yeeles, yet somewhat wholsomer, and lesse jepardous, for that they bee not so clammie and so grosse as Yeeles. ... After Yeeles and Lamprayes, we should drinke good strong wine, as saith Arnold (Arnaud de Villeneuve) and generally with all kindes of fish, wine is very wholsome, for as the French man saith: "Poisson sans vin est poison".*' (Cogan's *Haven of Health.* 1612, p. 143.)

Both Lampreys and Lamperns have the reputation as being dangerous as food, which is no doubt because they each have two filaments in the back which are poisonous and which must be removed before cooking.

LAMPROIE
Fr. for *Lamprey* (q.v.).

LANGOUSTE
Lat. *Palinurus locusta*; Fr. for *Spiny Lobster* or *Crawfish* (q.v.). All recipes applicable to *Lobster* are suitable for *Langouste.*

LANGOUSTINES
(*Nephrops norvegicus*).
Fr. for *Dublin Bay Prawns* (q.v.).

LAVARET
One of the best fishes from the deep waters of the Savoy Lakes.

LEMON SOLE (English)
Lat. *Microstomus kitt*; Fr. *Limande.* A small European flat fish resembling a *Sole* in shape, but its flesh has not the same fine flavour. It is at its best from December till March. All methods of cooking a *Sole* are suitable for its poor relation, the *Lemon Sole.*

LIMANDE
Fr. for *Lemon Sole* and *Dabs* (q.v.).

LIMPETS
Lat. *Acmaea testudinalis.* Unattractive rock-fish of real gastronomic merit; in many dishes in which cooked oysters appear they could easily and advantageously be replaced by limpets.

LING
Lat. *Molva molva.* The largest member of the *Cod* family, it is usually salted and dried. The name is also given to the *Burbot* (q.v.) of Lake Ontario, and to the *Genypterus blacodes*, in New Zealand.

'*I have no mind to Isbel, since I was at Court; our old ling and our Isbels o' the country are nothing like your old ling and your Isbels o' the Court.*' (*All's Well that Ends Well.* Act III. Sc. 2.)

All methods of cooking suitable for *Cod* are applicable to *Ling.*

LOACH
Lat. *Nemachilus barbatulus*, the *Stone Loach*, and Lat. *Misgurnus fossilis*, the *Spined Loach* (Fr. *Loche*), are two of the minor fresh-water fishes. Cooked as *Smelt* (q.v.).

LOBSTER
Fr. *Homard*; Ger. *Hummer*; It. *Gamberi marini*; Sp. *Langosta.* The male and female lobsters are known as Cock and Hen.

Lat. *Homarus gammarus*, the common European lobster, and *Homarus americanus*, the common North American lobster, are never found in the Southern hemisphere like the spiny lobster or common sea craw-fish (*Langouste*) and the South African Cape lobster, which is also a crawfish.

In England, supplies of lobsters are short from December to March; they improve in April and are abundant throughout the summer.

Mr Joseph Sinel, late of the Jersey Marine Biological Laboratory, at the request of the S.P.C.A., made some experiments to ascertain which was the more humane way of boiling crabs and lobsters, whether by immersion in boiling water or by putting them in cold water and bringing the water to boiling-point. With the lobster placed in cold water and the boiler put on the fire, there was no evidence of discomfort, nor any attempt made by the lobster to emerge from the water, until the temperature reached 70°, when the lobster gradually collapsed and fell on its side. At 80° all movement ceased; the lobster was dead. With the lobster plunged alive into boiling water, there were violent attempts made to emerge, and life was manifest for 58 seconds; slight movement, probably reflex, up to 70 seconds. Reddening of the shell occurred before death. It is claimed that in the case of lobsters put in cold water, the temperature of which is raised gradually, the warmth penetrates them slowly and destroys the sensitive nervous system gradually and painlessly.

Grilled Lobster

Kill the lobster by inserting the point of a knife at the junction of tail and body, and split it in two, longways; brush the shell over with a thin coating of salad oil. Grill over a very red fire – or under gas flame – flesh side to the heat. When done, sprinkle with salt, cayenne and butter, melted but uncooked. Serve very hot, in shell. If inconvenient to grill (or 'broil'), split and place the two halves in a frying-pan, season well with salt, cayenne and butter, and cook until done in a very hot oven, basting occasionally with the butter and its own liquor.

To Boil a Lobster

Prepare a *court-bouillon*, put in it a live lobster; put on the fire and cover pan. Cook for 20 to 30 minutes, after it has come to the boil, reducing heat a trifle after first 10 minutes. Let the lobster cool in the *court-bouillon* and do not use an iron pan; if you do, the flesh of the lobster will be dark and unsightly.

Whenever possible, buy live lobsters and boil them at home. The medium-sized ones are preferable and they should be chosen by weight, the heaviest being the best. The flesh of the male lobster is better for boiling as it is firmer than that of the female or 'hen' lobster, the latter, however, contains eggs or 'coral', which is useful for sauces and decoration. The hen lobster may be recognized by its broader tail. When lobster is to be served in the shell, rub it over with a little oiled butter or salad oil before serving.

Some recipes indicate the cutting in two of live lobsters. Those who dislike this operation may run a skewer into the spinal cord, which is situated at the joint between the tail shells and the body; it means instantaneous death for the lobster, which may then be split and used as directed.

To Dress a Cooked Lobster

Separate tail from body, remove large claws, cracking each through the centre and at the joint. Split the tail down the middle with a sharp knife, remove the dark thread (spinal cord) and serve the body set upright on a dish, that is, the head portion upright, arranging the halves of the tail on either side, alternating with the claws and sprigs of parsley. The small feelers and legs must be removed when preparing to cut the lobster in two. The tail portions may be served in or out of the shell, as preferred, but are usually left in it.

Lobster and Sherry

There is a remarkable affinity between lobster and sherry, and it is always safe to marinade cooked lobster for some little time in pale sherry before 'finishing' and serving.

Homard à l'Américaine

Maître Escoffier was convinced that this dish originated in Le Restaurant Français in Nice, where, in 1860, the 'Langouste de la Méditerranée' was prepared with tomatoes and white wine. Maître Escoffier used to say that the title 'Homard à l'Américaine' was eventually given to this dish by a Provençal chef who, tempted by American dollars, went to the United States and there introduced the method of preparing lobster used at Le Restaurant Français. Since langouste in America is rather scarce, he used lobster and called the dish 'Le Homard à l'Américaine'. In 1860, 'Homard à l'Américaine' was served at Noël et Peters Restaurant, and from that moment it became famous. The 'Classic Recipe' is essentially Provençal. Here it is:

'Take a hen lobster. Cut it in even pieces. Carefully keep the coral and the water of the lobster. (1) Cook these pieces of lobster in hot olive oil of good quality. (2) Add salt, pepper, pimentoes and quarters of nice ripe tomatoes, and one tablespoonful of chopped onions. (3) Add one pint of dry white wine. Let the whole cook for 20 minutes. (4) Take the pieces of lobster out of the saucepan. Put the saucepan back on a fierce fire and reduce the stock by half. Now knead 4 oz. of fresh butter with the coral and the lobster water. Thicken the sauce with this butter, adding a little light meat glaze, some lemon juice, some chopped parsley and some chopped tarragon. Pour the whole of the sauce over the lobster, which has been kept hot in a suitable dish.' (Escoffier.)

Homard à l'Américaine
(Another Recipe)

1 live lobster
2 tablespoons butter
1 sliced onion
1 sliced carrot
1 'bouquet-garni'
1 small stalk celery
1 small glass good brandy

2 teaspoons meat glaze
1 tablespoon fresh tomato purée
1 glass white wine
Salt and red pepper
Additional butter
Chopped parsley

This is a French family recipe. Cut the lobster up into four or five pieces, setting aside the coral and the greenish liver. Place the butter in an earthenware saucepan, heat thoroughly, then add the pieces of lobster (flesh side downwards), and *sauté* over a quick fire, shaking the pan well during the operation. Now add the onion, carrot, 'bouquet' and celery; *sauté* all this well together for a few minutes; then pour the cognac over the whole, setting it alight and allowing it to burn itself out. Next add the meat glaze, the purée of tomato and the white wine, which has been reduced to half a glassful by quick boiling. Season rather highly. Keep mixture hot. In another oven dish place a tablespoonful of butter, set this on top of the stove and, when very hot, add the coral and the green mixture, blending all this well for a moment or two. Remove and pound this mixture in a mortar with more butter – a couple more tablespoonfuls. When ready to serve, arrange the pieces of lobster on a hot dish and keep hot. Mix the sauce in the first pan with the pounded mixture and pour this over the lobster, sprinkling the whole with finely-chopped parsley.

Homard à l'Américaine
(Third Recipe)

1 large live lobster
1 onion
Olive oil
Butter
White wine
Cognac brandy
1 fresh tomato
Salt and cayenne

Cut up the lobster as in preceding recipe. Chop onion and brown very lightly in a mixture of olive oil and butter; the latter must be very hot but must not brown. Add the pieces of lobster and cook fast for about five minutes. Add enough white wine and cognac (two-thirds wine to one-third cognac) to come one-quarter way up the side of the pan (which must be only just large enough for the purpose) and cook fast for three minutes; then add the peeled and cut-up tomato, continuing cooking for 15 to 20 minutes *fast*. Remove pieces of lobster and keep hot while the sauce is reduced (by quick cooking) a little; then add a good piece of fresh butter, season to taste and serve immediately.

Homard à l'Armoricaine
The name said to have been introduced after the first World War to replace *Américaine*.

Lobster Beaugency

1 boiled lobster
Butter
1 small glass dry sherry
2 tablespoons cream sauce
½ pint cream
2 egg yolks
Additional butter and cream

Select a medium-sized lobster and boil as directed. When cold, split in two and dice flesh. Heat about a couple of tablespoons of butter and lightly fry the pieces of lobster in this for a few minutes; add sherry, then add gradually the cream sauce – well seasoned – and half-pint of cream. Simmer gently for 10 minutes, then remove pan from heat. Beat the egg yolks with a little more cream and a tablespoonful of melted butter, mix this slowly with the lobster and use mixture to fill shells to the brim. Bake in a hot oven until bubbling and brown slightly.

Lobster Chowder

One 2 lb. lobster
3 tablespoons butter
Salt and pepper
4 cups milk
1 slice of onion
1 cup cold water
Paprika or cayenne
¼ cup crumbled biscuits

This is a great delicacy, if a somewhat extravagant one. Remove all meat from lobster and cut it into small dice, carefully setting aside the green portion (coral) of the fish. Beat the butter to a cream, add the coral and the crumbled biscuits. Scald the onion with the milk and pour slowly on to the mixture, stirring well. Place the carapace and other parts of the lobster (claw, shells, legs, etc.) in a pan and barely cover them with cold water. Bring slowly to boiling-point, seasoning as necessary, and strain; then add to previous mixture, with pieces of lobster. Serve very hot after dusting with either paprika or cayenne. A few drops of lemon juice improve greatly the flavour of this soup, which is a dish in itself.

Lobster Chow Min
(Chinese-American)

1 lb. boiled lobster meat
1 small tin bamboo shoots
1 tablespoonful butter
1 small onion
2 stalks celery
½ lb. fresh mushrooms

1 teaspoon Worcester sauce
1 egg
Salt and cayenne
½ lb. crispy noodles

For 'Crispy Noodles'

8 oz. flour
Pinch of salt
¼ teaspoon grated nutmeg
2 egg yolks

Tinned lobster is frequently used for this dish in the States, although freshly-boiled lobster is very much better. There must be 1 lb. of the flesh when removed from shell. The bamboo shoots are, really, optional, but should be used if obtainable. Tinned ones may be purchased in England in some of the big stores. Heat the butter, add half the lobster meat, *sauté* for a few minutes, then add the finely-chopped onion and celery and the mushrooms, cut into fine strips, also the bamboo shoots, if any are being used. Mix all this together, add the Worcester sauce and cook, covered, for about 10 minutes.

To Make the 'Noodles'

Make a stiff paste with the flour, salt, nutmeg, and egg yolks. Roll this dough out very thinly and cut into strips as thin as spaghetti. Let these dry for a while then throw into boiling oil or frying fat, frying a delicate brown. Drain on crumpled-up blotting paper (or brown absorbent paper). Then place three parts of these 'noodles' in a hot deep bowl, covering with the prepared lobster mixture. Fry the other half of the lobster in a little more butter for a few minutes and arrange it on top of the first lot. Beat up the egg and pour it in a little hot butter in a small frying-pan, just large enough to make a very thin sheet or layer of fried egg. Turn this out on top of the lobster, covering it, and sprinkle the remainder of the hot crisp 'noodles' on top or arrange around, in a border.

Lobster Cutlets

Flesh from a boiled lobster
Cream sauce
Salt and paprika
Brown, fine breadcrumbs
1 raw egg

Cut the lobster flesh up finely, mix with the sauce, which must be quite thick, season to taste and spread mixture in a pan to cool. Cut out or roll into any desired shape, dip in crumbs, then in the beaten egg and again in crumbs. Allow to stand a little while to harden surface, then fry in deep oil or fat until brown and crisp, and serve with any sauce you like.

Le Homard gratiné à la Dunkerquoise

Choose living and lively lobsters; split them in two, longways; take coral out and plunge in hot butter for a moment. Then soak them in cognac and set them alight. Put them to rest in a saucepan and cool them with a good, dry, white wine; put in also a tomato or two, a *bouquet garni*, chopped onions and some carrots cut up *brunoise* fashion.

When cooked, the lobsters should be taken out of the saucepan, but the rest is left to simmer on and reduce itself. In the meantime, the claws are broken up and the meat within is placed in the shells with the bodies.

The *cuisson*, that is the gravy and vegetables still in the saucepan, are now passed through a sieve, and a *duxelle* of mushrooms is mixed with it; salt and pepper to taste; a little cream; and as a last binding the coral is added, which has been worked into some very fresh butter.

A few shelled shrimps are added at the last moment to the sauce, which is poured gently over the half lobsters in their shells. Brown for a few moments under a quick grill and serve. (*Ecu de France* Recipe.)

Homard au Gratin à la Normande

Lobster
Court-Bouillon
2 cups rich Béchamel sauce
¼ cup grated Gruyère
2 tablespoons thick cream
Butter

Boil the fish until tender, allowing it to cool in the *court-bouillon*. Drain well when cold, split in two and remove all flesh from claws. Cut this and the tail portions into rather large dice, using a stainless steel knife. Mix with the hot sauce, add the grated Gruyère and the cream, and place this mixture in the tail shells. Sprinkle with a little more Gruyère, dot with small pieces of butter and cook in a sharp oven until surface is nicely browned, serving immediately it is ready. When removing flesh from shell, care must be taken not to detach the head from the tail. Should this be unavoidable, place the head in position, fill the shell and serve, but the shape will not be as good as if the head is left attached to the body.

Homard à la Newburg

1 boiled lobster
2 tablespoons butter
Few drops onion juice
1 small fresh truffle
Salt and cayenne pepper
1 small glass sherry
1 or 2 egg yolks
½ cup thick cream

After boiling the lobster in a well-flavoured white wine *court-bouillon*, in which it should cool, drain it, remove flesh from shell and claws and cut it into 1 in. pieces. Melt the butter in a saucepan without allowing it to frizzle, add the onion juice, the truffle cut up into small pieces, salt and cayenne to taste. Cook this together for a few minutes very gently, then add the sherry and simmer for a minute or two longer. Beat the egg yolks with the cream, add the pieces of lobster and pour this mixture into the pan, gently 'shuffling' contents over a low heat until the mixture is nicely thickened, but taking great care it does not boil. Serve hot. May be served on rounds of hot, buttered toast or otherwise. The addition of a few drops of lemon juice when serving is considered an improvement by many connoisseurs. If unskilled in this type of cookery, the use of a double-boiler is advisable, but care must be taken to heat the second mixture just sufficiently to thicken it or the pieces of lobster will break and look messy.

Note.—Lobsters should not be boiled in an iron saucepan, as it gives a darkish tinge to the flesh. White wine *court-bouillon* is best for cooking this delicate fish.

Lobster Filling for Patties

Diced boiled lobster
Thick Béchamel sauce
1 or more egg yolks
Thick cream
Mushroom caps
Butter
Sherry
Lemon juice to taste

Hen lobsters are again indicated for this recipe. Dice the flesh, add to the sauce, heating well in a double-boiler. Beat the egg yolks with the cream. Fry the mushroom caps, or sliced mushrooms, in butter, add them and the butter in which they were cooked, to the lobster mixture, season rather highly and flavour with dry sherry and lemon juice when ready to serve. The coral should be added to mixture when ready to use for filling small patty shells or a vol-au-vent case. Be careful not to mash up the pieces of lobster. If the sauce be all ready, it only needs heating thoroughly before adding flavourings and serving.

Lobster Salad

1 cold boiled lobster
Vinaigrette sauce
Lettuce
Mayonnaise
Sliced hard-boiled eggs
A few capers

This method of preparing an apparently simple dish will be found to make a great deal of difference. Remove flesh from a nice hen lobster, cooled in its own *court-bouillon* Cut the tail portion into round slices; leave flesh of large claws either whole or cut into two pieces, longways. Marinade all this in a well-seasoned vinaigrette sauce for several hours. Prepare the hearts of one or two lettuces, wash and crisp on ice, if possible. When ready to serve, lay the lettuce leaves in a salad bowl or on a flat crystal dish and season lightly with salt, pepper and vinegar, *no oil*. On this, lay the drained pieces of lobster and cover the whole thing with ice-cold, well-seasoned mayonnaise. Garnish with the slices of egg, sprinkle with a few capers and serve as soon as ready or the lettuce will wilt. If desired, cress, fancy slices of cooked beetroot, etc., may be added as a garnish, but the essentials are: crispness of salad and flavour of marinaded lobster.—The coral—if any—may be added, sieved.

Cold Lobster Soufflé

Whipped cream
A little aspic jelly
Mayonnaise sauce
1 boiled hen lobster

This is a delightful summer supper dish. Add some stiffly-whipped cream and a little aspic to some well-flavoured mayonnaise, the proportions being, roughly, two tablespoons whipped cream and the same quantity of aspic to one cupful of mayonnaise. Beat this mixture to a froth over ice, after adding the diced lobster. Pour the mixture quickly into small soufflé cases or cups and sprinkle the tops with a little of the coral and chopped aspic jelly. If larger soufflés are desired, place a band of kitchen paper inside each soufflé case, allowing it to stand about one inch above the top of each case or cup. When serving the dish, which must be kept very cold in summer, remove this paper band carefully. Garnish with parsley. If ice be unobtainable or the weather very hot, prepare the soufflés beforehand and allow to set in as cool a spot as possible. A little more aspic may be added also to ensure better results, but mixture must not be a solid jelly, naturally.

Lobster Stew
(American)

This is a New England fisherman's recipe. Kill a lobster when ready to prepare the stew. Split in two, dot with pieces of butter, sprinkle with salt and pepper and place in a tin in a rather quick oven. When the flesh is tender and juices begin to flow, remove flesh from body and claws and cut this up rather finely, taking care to keep the 'gravy' in the tin. Put this in an enamel saucepan, add the lobster and about a cupful of cream. Allow this mixture to boil up once, then add a tablespoonful of butter, a dash of red pepper and serve immediately on toasted biscuits. Be sure the lobster does not cook too long or the flesh will become tough.

Stuffed Lobster

Boiled and cooled lobster
Good Béchamel sauce
Fresh mushrooms
Chopped herbs
Brown breadcrumbs
Dusting cayenne pepper
Cognac brandy
Butter

Cook lobster in *court-bouillon* and let it cool. Split in two very carefully without separating the head from the body, if possible. Cut the flesh into round slices. Mix the green portion of interior—the liver—and the coral, if any, with the sauce, chopped mushrooms, chopped herbs (chervil, parsley and chives), a sprinkling of brown breadcrumbs, salt and pepper, adding a touch of cayenne, if liked. Use this mixture to fill the half shells and brown in a hot oven for a few minutes; then cover each surface with the pieces of lobster, one round overlapping the other. Sprinkle with a little Cognac brandy, spread with a layer of nicely seasoned Béchamel, dot with butter, heat well through in a quick oven and serve at once.

Homard Thermidor

2 small boiled lobsters
2 tablespoons butter
½ teaspoon finely-minced onion
Dash cayenne pepper
¼ glass dry white wine
¼ lb. fresh mushrooms
1 tablespoon tomato purée
1 cup white sauce
Grated Parmesan cheese

Pick all the meat out of the shells and claws of lobsters, dicing the tail portions, claws and coral—if any. Heat the butter and add the onion to it, as well as the lobster, cayenne to taste and the white wine. Simmer mixture gently for five minutes, stirring constantly, then add the finely-chopped peeled and washed mushrooms, the tomato purée and salt, if needed. Cook for five minutes more; then place this mixture into the lobster shells, cover with a sufficiency of thick white sauce, sprinkle with the Parmesan and bake in a sharp oven till mixture is well heated. Remove and brown surfaces for a minute or two under a grill. Serve very hot. Tinned tomato purée may be used, but it has neither the colour nor the flavour of a purée made from fresh tomatoes.

LOCHE

Fr. for *Loach* (q.v.). One of the freshwater fishes caught in France for *friture*.

LOTE. BURBOT

Lat. *Lota lota*; Fr. *Lotte*. The whiting of fresh waters, mostly caught in the lakes of Savoy and more rarely in English lakes. It varies, in size, from 1 to 3 ft.; its flesh is very white and rather tasteless; its liver is unusually large and is considered a great delicacy, but its roe is quite uneatable. Its liver is cooked and served in the same way as carp's soft roe. They also serve, in Geneva, an excellent *Omelette au foie de Lotte*. The three recipes given by Escoffier as the most suitable for the *Lotte* are the following:

Lotte à la Dugléré

Lift the fillets of the fish and cut them scallop-wise; season with pepper and salt, dip in flour and lay them side by side in a well-buttered pan (*sauteuse*). For a pound of fish, add one heaped-up tablespoon of finely-chopped onion, three or four tomatoes, peeled, seeded and cut up; a pinch of bruised parsley, pepper and salt and a glass of white wine. Cook over a quick fire and dress the fish upon the service dish. Add a little more fresh butter to the liquor in the pan and a squeeze of lemon before pouring it over the fish.

Lotte à la Provençale

Cut up the fish, scallop-wise, as for the *Dugléré*; season with pepper and salt; dip in flour and lay the pieces side by side in a shallow pan (*sauteuse*). Add, for 1 lb. of fish, two tablespoons of finely chopped onion, four or five tomatoes, peeled, seeded and cut up; some parsley; a pinch of saffron and a little garlic. Pour over it all four to five spoonfuls of olive oil, a glass of white wine and a glass of water. Cover the pan and leave it upon a quick fire from 15 to 18 minutes. Dress the fish upon slices of toasted bread and pour the sauce over. When the *Lotte à la Provençale* is served with a *riz Pilaw*, the toasted bread is left out.

Lotte à la Meunière

Cut up the fish scallop-wise. Season with pepper and salt; dip in flour and cook in butter in an open pan. Dress upon a dish and pour over it sizzling hot butter (the butter in which the fish was cooked and some more fresh butter added to it and heated before serving).

LOTTE

Fr. for *Lote* (q.v.).

LOUP DE MER

One of the French names for *Sea-bass* vid. *Bass*.

MACKEREL

Lat. *Scomber scombrus*; Fr. *Macquereau*; Ger. *Makrelen*; Ital. *Sgombri*; Sp. *Escombro*. One of the best, even if one of the cheapest of all the fishes out of the sea. It is excellent both hot and cold; hot, in ever so many ways, none better, however, than plain broiled and served with a *Maître d'Hôtel Sauce*; cold, soused. The one drawback of the mackerel is that it will spoil more quickly than almost any other fish, a fact which gained for it the privilege of being the only fish, once upon a time, allowed to be hawked in the streets on Sundays, in England. Mackerel are available all the year round, but they are in their prime in April, May and June, when they are caught in large numbers along the south coast of England. In July, August and September, mackerel are best left alone. At all times, but chiefly during the hot weather mackerel should be eaten as soon as possible after being caught. When very fresh they are quite stiff, opalescent, with bright protruding eyes and bright red gills. Beware of the limp mackerel, which is indigestible always, and may be poisonous.

The *Spanish Mackerel*, Lat. *Scomberomorus maculatus*, and other members of the genus *Scomberomorus*, are closely allied to the common *Mackerel*. They appear off the coasts of America during the warmer months, from Cape Ann to Brazil. They often weigh from 6 lb. to 10 lb. each. An allied but unspotted species, the *Monterey Spanish Mackerel* (*S. concolor*), occurs off the coast of California.

'*You may buy land now as cheap as stinking mackerel.*' (*The First Part of King Henry IV*. Act II. Sc. 4.)

Caveach or Pickled Mackerel

Take six large mackerel and cut them into round pieces. Then take an ounce of beaten pepper, three large nutmegs, a little mace, and a handful of salt. Mix your salt and beaten spice together, then make two or three holes in each piece, and with your finger thrust the seasoning into the holes. Rub the pieces all over with the seasoning, fry them brown in oil, and let them stand till they be cold. Then put them into vinegar and cover them with oil. They are delicious eating, and if they be well covered, they will keep a long time. (*The London Art of Cookery*, John Farley, 1787.)

Grilled Mackerel

2 rather small mackerel
Salt and cayenne
Maître d'hôtel butter
Slices of lemon and parsley

Cut off heads and fins. Make one or two rather deep cuts on either side of the fish.

Pre-heat a fish grill, grease it well and broil the fish either over a hot, clear fire or under a gas griller, turning once to brown second side of fish. Season with salt and a dusting of cayenne and serve as soon as ready, putting the prepared butter on the fish and garnishing the hot dish with quarters of lemon and sprigs of parsley. If available, a little finely-minced fresh tarragon may be added to the butter.

Mackerel Fines Herbes

Grill fresh mackerel as indicated; when done, split open the fish, remove backbone and sprinkle the surface with a mixture of chopped shallot, parsley and tarragon. Dot with small bits of butter and season with salt and pepper. Place in an oven dish, add a little water and a dash of wine vinegar and cook for a few minutes in a hot oven, serving in the dish and its own juice.

Mackerel à la Nantaise

1 large mackerel
Olive oil
1 onion
Salt and pepper
Vinegar court-bouillon
White sauce
Chopped chives
Chopped capers
Lemon juice
Butter

Cut the fish open, longways, after cleaning and removing both head and tail. Place in a dish and marinade for an hour or so in olive oil, chopped onion, salt and pepper. Drain and wipe, then cook until done – simmering but never boiling – in the prepared *court-bouillon*. Drain and serve with the white sauce to which the chopped chives and capers have been added as well as lemon juice and fresh butter to taste.

Small Mackerel Meunière

Small mackerel
Flour
Frying oil or fat
Butter
Lemon juice
Chopped fines herbes

Clean and prepare fish but do not remove heads. Roll in flour, then fry in deep oil or fat until crisp and brown. Sprinkle with salt and pepper and keep hot. Melt a sufficiency of butter in a tiny saucepan, add to this the juice of a lemon, chopped herbs (parsley, chives, chervil and tarragon), and pour this hot mixture over the fish when serving.

Filleted Mackerel
Fillets of rather large mackerel
Butter, melted
Salt and pepper
White wine
Lemon juice
Slices of lemon

Fillet the fish, after cleaning, removing skin. This may, of course, be done by the fishmonger, but select the fish whole, then have them filleted.

Place the fillets in an oven dish, sprinkle with a little melted but unbrowned butter and season with salt and pepper. Melt more butter in a small saucepan, add to this equal amounts of white wine and lemon juice. Bake the fish and, as it cooks, baste it with the wine and lemon mixture. Garnish with slices of lemon.

Cotriade de Maquereau à la Concarneau
Water
Salt and pepper
Thyme, bayleaf, onions, garlic
Several floury potatoes
Fresh mackerel
Butter

This is a very special Brittany dish well worth the attention of gourmets; a shallow saucepan, known as a *sauteuse*, is best for the preparation of this dish. Cover the bottom to the depth of 1 in. with water, and salt, pepper, a bayleaf, a branch of thyme, one or two small cut-up onions, and a small clove of garlic. Simmer these ingredients gently for 15 or 20 minutes, then add a few floury potatoes, cut into thick slices. When they are almost done, add the fish cut into chunks, and a good piece of butter. Cover the saucepan and continue the gentle cooking for another quarter of an hour. The fish and potatoes (which may be left whole if small) should be more steamed than boiled and the sauce must be very 'short', i.e. reduced. Remove herbs before serving. This dish can also be cooked in an earthenware or glass casserole, in which it should be served when ready.

Soused Mackerel
Remove heads from two or three medium-sized mackerel. Clean and split open. Lay them in an earthenware baking dish. Add a good sprinkling of salt and pepper (a few whole peppercorns are best), as well as a little dried thyme and a broken-up bayleaf. Cut an onion into thin rings and finely chop some parsley. Sprinkle these over the fish, adding as well, if desired, a few thin slices of carrot. Barely cover with a mixture of water and wine-vinegar or, better still, white wine and a squeeze of lemon. Bake in a rather slow oven until the vegetables are done,

basting frequently. Allow to cool in the liquor, removing peppercorns, herbs and slices of carrot when serving. They should be served cold, but some people say they taste better when served hot. A little olive oil is sometimes added to the marinade.

Mackerel au Gratin
2 medium-sized mackerel
2 shallots
1 onion
Chopped parsley
White breadcrumbs
White wine
Salt and pepper
Butter

Clean fish, removing heads and tails but not splitting. Wipe well after washing in salted water. Place in an earthenware or china baking dish which has been well buttered. Sprinkle generously with the mixed chopped shallots, onions, parsley and the breadcrumbs, and moisten with a sufficiency of white wine, which should come at least one-third up the fish. Season and dot with small pieces of butter. Bake for about 25 minutes in a moderate oven and serve in baking dish.

Mackerel à l'Italienne
1 large or two medium fish
White wine court-bouillon
2 small onions
2 tablespoons olive oil
1 small clove garlic
Salt and pepper
2 large fresh mushrooms
White wine
1 bayleaf
Chopped parsley

Half-cook the cleaned fish in the *court-bouillon*. Brown the chopped onions, mushrooms, garlic and parsley in olive oil, then moisten with wine and season as wished. Add the mackerel, well drained and not too much done, and the bayleaf. Simmer very gently until the fish is sufficiently cooked; then serve, covering with its own strained liquor.

Mackerel Baked in Milk
(American)
Split one or two very fresh mackerel, clean and remove head and tail. Put in a buttered baking dish, sprinkle with salt and pepper, dot over with bits of butter and add about two-thirds cup of milk. Bake for 25 minutes in a hot oven, basting frequently.

Boiled Mackerel with Gooseberry Sauce
Make several incisions in the back of the fish, and cook them very gently for 15 minutes in simmering water. Remove and drain them.

The Sauce: Take about ½ lb. of gooseberries and cook them in plenty of boiling water, but not long enough to let them burst. Pour off the water and pass the fruit through a sieve. Sweeten very slightly.

Or: Make a *purée* of gooseberries and add it to a white sauce together with a little chopped fennel. (Before the fennel is chopped it should be plunged for two minutes into boiling water and then be well dried.) (Mrs Lucas's *A Pretty Kettle of Fish*.)

Fried or Grilled Mackerel

Having cleaned your mackerel, split them down the back, and season them with pepper and salt, some mint, parsley and fennel, chopped very fine. Flour them, and fry them of a fine light brown, and put them on a dish and strainer. Let your sauce be fennel and butter, and garnish them with parsley.

If you choose to broil your mackerel whole, wash them clean, cut off their heads, and pull out their roes at the neck end. Boil their roes in a little water; then bruise them with a spoon, beat up the yolk of egg, a little nutmeg, a little lemon peel cut fine, a little salt and pepper, and a few crumbs of bread. Mix these well together, and fill the fish with them. Flour them well, and broil them nicely. Butter, ketchup and walnut pickle, will make a proper sauce. (*Ibid.*)

MAHASEER. MAHSIR. MAHSUR

Lat. *Barbus mosal*. A much appreciated fish of Indian mountain streams

MAIGRE

Lat. *Sciaena aquila*. A large European sea-fish of some gastronomic repute.

MANGO-FISH

Lat. *Polynemus paradiseus*. One of the edible fresh-water fishes of India.

MAQUEREAU

Fr. for *Mackerel* (q.v.).

MARLING

Old-English name of the *Whiting*.

MATELOTE

A fish stew, usually rather rich, made with red wine, sometimes with white wine or cider, and eel, herrings, bream and other types of fish. Here is the classical *Matelote* recipe:

> 2 large onions
> 2 tablespoons butter
> Flour
> 1 bottle red wine
> ½ lb. fresh mushrooms
> ¼ lb. small onions
> Sundry spices

About 2 lb. skinned and cut-up eel or other fish
Pepper

Cut up the large onions and, as soon as the butter begins to smoke slightly, put them in to fry. When golden brown, add the flour to onions, stirring well, then moisten with the red wine (Burgundy for choice). Add the small onions and the sliced mushrooms as well as such spices as are customary: one clove, dusting of nutmeg, pinch of ginger, pepper (not too much) and a small pinch of cinnamon. Cover closely and cook this sauce gently for nearly an hour, then add the pieces of eel and cook for a quarter of an hour. Decorate the dish with small fried *croûtons* and, on special occasions, add, before serving, a small glassful of brandy which has been previously set alight. Add this just one minute before serving.

MEGRIM

A common flat-fish of the *Flounder* (q.v.) family. It is called *Lantern flounder* in the U.S.A.

MELWEL

Fr. *Merluche*. Old-English name for *Hake*.

MERLUCHE. MERLUS. SAUMON BLANC

Fr. names for *Hake* (q.v.).

MEURETTE

A variant of the *Matelote* (q.v.). There are two sorts of *Meurettes*: the *Rose*, which is made up of a variety of fishes, *flambés* in *Eau de vie de Marc* and cooked in red wine; the *Blanche*, or *Normande*, is also made with a variety of fishes, but *flambés* in *Eau de vie de Cidre* and cooked in cider, whilst the *Matelote Meunière* is also *blanche*, but the fish is *flambé* with brandy and cooked in white wine.

MILT

The scientific name for *Soft Roe*. Fr. *Laitance*.

MINNOW

Lat. *Phoxinus phoxinus*; Fr. *Véron*. Very small cyprinoid fish common in many European gravelly streams.

MONKFISH

Lat. *Squatina squatina*; Fr. *Angelot*. The U.S.A. name for the fish known in England as *Angelfish* (q.v.), *Mongrel Skate* or *Shark-Ray*.

MOONFISH

See *Opah*.

MORUE

Fr. for *Salt Cod* (q.v.). See also *Bouillabaisse* and *Brandade*.

MOSTÈLE. MOUTELO. MUTELE. MOTELLE

Names given in the South of France to the *Lote* (q.v.), a fish caught in the Rhône estuary and used in the making of *Bouillabaisse* (q.v.).

MOULES

Fr. for *Mussels* (q.v.).

MULLETS

(a) *Red Mullet*. (1) Lat. *Mullus surmuletus*; Fr. *Mulle Rouget, Rouget, Rouge d'Yport*; Ger. *Meerbarbe*; Sp. *Barbo de mar*. The common *Red Mullet* of the English Channel and the Mediterranean Sea.

(b) *Grey* or *Gray Mullet*, or *Striped Mullet*. Lat. *Mugil chelo*; Fr. *Mulet, Muge* or *Meuil*; Sp. *Mugil* or *Mujol*; Ger. *Meeräsche*. This is a coarser fish found on both the European and North American coasts of the Atlantic as well as on the Northern Pacific coasts of America.

The *Red Mullet*, which is probably the best fish there is in the Mediterranean Sea, is very red, shortish and firm to the touch. *Red Mullets* are at their best between April and October. Clean very carefully, drawing out the gills, which will remove the intestines at the same time. Scrape lightly and be sure to retain the liver, which is considered a great delicacy. This must be left inside the fish. Some cooks claim that *Red Mullets* are best cooked without being cleaned. This fish may be either grilled, fried or baked, but never steamed nor boiled.

Baked Red Mullet

2 mullets
Breadcrumbs
Salt and pepper
Chopped parsley
Lemon juice
Butter

Score the fish on both sides, put them in a well-buttered earthenware baking dish and sprinkle with breadcrumbs, salt, pepper, and a little of the parsley. Strain lemon juice as required on fish, dot with small pieces of butter and bake in a moderately hot oven for about 15 to 20 minutes, basting now and again; if preferred, use a little white wine instead of lemon juice, but the fish is so delicate in itself that this is unnecessary.

Red Mullet Meunière

Roll small red mullet lightly in flour, after scraping and cleaning as indicated. *Sauté* in hot butter, cooking not too fast for about 15 minutes. Place on a hot dish, sprinkle with a little chopped parsley and a few drops of lemon juice. Add a tablespoonful of fresh butter to that used for cooking the fish, brown lightly, then strain over the mullets.

Marinaded and Grilled Mullet

Mix together oil, vinegar, pepper, salt, lemon juice and thin slices of onion. Put the cleaned fish in this, allowing it to marinade for at least one hour, turning now and then. Drain, grill and baste while cooking with the marinade. When brown, serve with the strained marinade, re-heated, to which a little finely-chopped tarragon and a suspicion of mustard have been added.

Rouget en Papillote

Cut off fins and tail; remove gills; wipe the fish dry and rub it over with melted butter. Mix some finely-chopped fennel with fresh breadcrumbs and a little salt; put some of this mixture in the fish and sprinkle the rest over it, then wrap it up in buttered paper and cook it for 20 minutes under a moderate grill.

Red Mullet with Mushrooms

An earthenware or glass casserole or small cocotte should be used for this delicious dish. Butter the pan, add the cleaned and scaled fish with about a tablespoonful of butter, salt, pepper, and a little chopped parsley. Cook gently, turning the fish carefully once during the operation, and keeping the pan covered. This recipe, being French, the small yellow mushrooms, known as *Mousserons*, are suggested. Failing these, small fresh mushrooms will do. Simmer them, after peeling, in just enough white wine to cover, add the herbs (parsley, chervil, a small bit of tarragon and some chives), as well as a reasonable amount of butter. When the mushrooms are done, add to the cooked fish and continue gently simmering together until the sauce is well blended and reduced. Serve in casserole.

Red Mullet Niçoise

Cook the fish in hot oil in a frying-pan, turning them very gently once. Take them out and lay them in a fireproof dish, sprinkle them with salt and small pieces of butter.

Have ready a number of tomatoes which have been skinned, sliced, lightly cooked in butter and seasoned. Lay these with a few very thin slices of lemon and thin strips of anchovy on the fish and place them in a quick oven for 10 minutes. Baste twice. (Mrs Lucas's *A Pretty Kettle of Fish*.)

Red Mullet in a Marinade
(Cold)

Red Mullet can be prepared in the same way as soused mackerel (q.v.), or in the French way, as follows:

Chop a shallot and a carrot and brown them lightly in good salad oil. Add half a pint of white wine-vinegar and a gill of water, a little parsley, a sprig of thyme, a bayleaf, a pinch of cayenne, a teaspoonful of white peppercorns, a clove, and a little nutmeg. Let the mixture come to the boil; simmer gently for half an hour.

Put the red mullet in a fireproof dish and, covering them with the marinade, let them simmer for about 10 minutes in the oven. These will keep for some days if they remain in the strained marinade. (Mrs Lucas's *A Pretty Kettle of Fish*.)

MUSSELS

Lat. *Myrtilus edulis*; Fr. *Moules*; Ger. *Muscheln*; Sp. *Mariscos*.

The name is given to all bivalve molluscs of the genus *Myrtilus*, found upon the seashore both in Europe and U.S.A.

Clean shells well, scraping with an old knife to remove corrugations and mud. Wash in several waters. Place in a frying-pan or saucepan, over a rather slow fire, covering the pan; shake continuously while cooking. When the shells open the mussels are done.

'Mussels were never in credit, but amongst the poorer sort, till lately, the lily-white mussel was found out about Romerswall, as we sail betwixt Flushing and Bergen-up-Zon, where indeed in the heat of the summer they are so commonly and much eaten without any offence to the head, liver or stomach: yea, myself, whom once twenty mussels had almost poisoned, at Cambridge, did fill myself with these mussels of the Low Country, being never a whit distempered with my bold adventure.' (Muffet, p. 59.)

Mussels to Stew

Wash them very clean from Sand, in two or three waters; then put them into a Stewpan, which cover close and let them stew untill all the Shells are opened; then take them out and pick them out of their Shells. When they are all picked, and the little Crabs which may have been in any of them, are thrown away, put them into a Sauce-pan, and to every quart of Mussels put half a pint of the liquor that came from them in stewing, which you must strain through an hair Sieve; add a blade of Mace and a piece of butter, as big as a Wallnut, rolled in Flour. Let them stew, and when done sufficiently, toast some Slices of Bread cut triangular, brown, and lay them round the Dish, pour in the Mussels, and send them hot to Table. (*Mrs. Gardiner's Receipts from* 1763, p. 43. Boston, Mass.)

Mussels to Stew, another Way

Clean and stew your mussels as in the preceding Receipt, only putting in a Pint of the Strained Liquor, and a quarter of a pound of Butter rolled in a very little Flour, to every Quart of Mussels. When they are stewed suffi-

ciently, have some Crumbs of Bread ready, and cover the bottom of your Dish thick therewith; grate half a Nutmeg over them, and pour the Mussels and Sauce all over the Crumbs. (*Mrs Gardiner's Receipts from* 1763 p. 43. Boston, Mass.)

Moules Marinière

Vinegar court-bouillon
Fresh mussels
Butter

Some cooks prefer a white wine *court-bouillon* but, in either case, it should simmer gently, with its herbs and vegetables, for about half an hour. Strain, add the well-cleaned mussels and cover the pan closely. Shake pan until shells open, removing them on the half shell one by one as they open and keeping covered to prevent them from drying up. When all are ready pour the *court-bouillon* (which will also contain the sea-water and juice of the mussels) over the fish in the shells and sprinkle with a little chopped parsley and shallot.

Stewed Mussels

1 pint fresh mussels
2 tablespoons butter
2 tablespoons flour
½ pint liquid from fish
Chopped parsley
Few drops lemon juice
Hot, buttered toast

Clean mussels and open them, removing completely from shells but retaining and straining their liquid. Heat the butter, add the flour, blending thoroughly, then moisten gradually with the strained liquid. Season well with salt—if necessary—and add the chopped parsley, and a few drops of lemon juice. Serve very hot on freshly toasted slices of buttered bread.

MUTTONFISH

Lat. *Haliotis naevosa*. An ear shell or abalone of Australia; called *Paua* in New Zealand. The edible contents of the shell are said to resemble mutton in taste.

Also the name of a *Mojarra* (*Diapterus olisthostomus*) of the Gulf of Florida and West Indies.

NAMAYCUSH

Lat. *Cristivomer namaycush*. A large *Char* of the North American lakes from New Brunswick to Alaska; it weighs normally 20 lb., but occasionally much more.

NATIVES

The popular name in England of English Oysters, spawned and bred in Kentish or Essex beds.

NIGGER-FISH
Lat. *Cephalopholis fulvus*. A *Grouper* (q.v.) of the West Indies and Southern Florida, ranging in colour from bright yellow through vivid scarlet to dark brown, and more or less spotted with blue or black.

NONATS
The 'fry' or young of a small Mediterranean *Goby*. They are usually served hot, fried like whitebait, and also cold in salad with oil and vinegar or mayonnaise sauce.

NYMPHES
French culinary name of *Frogs* (q.v.).

OMBLE CHEVALIER
Lat. *Salmo umbla*. A *Char* (q.v.). The best fish of the Swiss and Savoy lakes; it never leaves the lakes for the running waters of rivers.

OMBRE
Lat. *Thymallus thymallus*. A *Grayling*. One of the most sought after fishes from the rivers of France; it is never to be found in any of the lakes and it is at its best in October and November.

OPAH. GREAT OPAH
Lat. *Lampris luna*. A deep-sea fish caught from Newfoundland to Madeira. It is also known as *Sunfish*, *Kingfish*, *Jerusalem Haddock* and *Moonfish*.

OQUASSA
Lat. *Salvelinus oquassa*. A small *Char* found in the Rangeley Lakes of Maine, U.S.A. In the lakes of Arctic America it is represented by a related form: *S. oquassa naresi*.

ORANGE ROCKFISH
Lat. *Rosicola pinniger*. A common market fish of California. It grows to 2 ft. in length and is found from Puget Sound to Southern California.

ORMEAUX. OREILLE DE MER
Fr. for *Ormers* (q.v.).

ORMERS. ORMER-SNELLS
Lat. *Haliotis tuberculata*. Commonly called *Sea-ears* or *Ear-shells* on account of the ear-like shape of the shell.

A shell-fish which abounds on the rocks off the islands of Jersey and Guernsey; it has a considerable gastronomical reputation locally, and is dressed as *Scallops* or pickled.

OURSINS
Fr. for *Sea-urchins* (q.v.).

OYSTERS
Lat. *Ostrea edulis*; Fr. *Huîtres*; Ger. *Austern*; Ital. *Ostrice*; Sp. *Ostras*. Any marine bivalve mollusc of the genus *Ostrea* or family *Ostreidae*. The *Native*, whether *Colchester*,

Whitstable, or from any other Essex or Kentish bed, should always be eaten uncooked and unspoilt by its beard being removed or palate-paralysing vinegars and sauces added to it. A squeeze of lemon is said to be permissible, but it is the thin end of the wedge of heresy. Portuguese oysters, Blue Points, or the large American oysters are the only ones that should be used for cooking.

Oysters must be very fresh, plump and firm, and the shells must be tightly closed. The best way to open an oyster is to insert the oyster knife at the hinge, snap the ligament which attaches the fish to the top, or flat shell and serve the oyster in the deep shell, in its own liquor.

American oysters are sometimes very large indeed and may be cut in pieces when cooking. French oysters have a peculiar savour and are usually small; the best are the *Marennes*, both *Blanches* and *Vertes*, and the *Belons*. *Colchesters* and *Whitstables* are the best *Natives*.

When cooking oysters, do no more than allow the edges to curl or they will become tough.

'*Why, then the world's mine oyster.*' (*The Merry Wives of Windsor*. Act II. Sc. 2.)

Although oysters remain so true to type that shells discovered in ruins of the ancient city of Rome are recognizable as belonging to fish from the Essex rivers, their cultivation is nevertheless subject to great changes. Despite modern scientific investigation, there is as yet no certain knowledge of the method by which the oyster reproduces itself, nor of the causes of the epidemics which have almost emptied the beds of Brittany, Holland and England in turn during the past fifty years. The fisheries thus decimated have been restocked from those which suffered least, and there is in consequence a tendency on the part of those trading in oysters to confuse together all oysters of the European type (*Ostrea edulis*) under the general name of *Natives*, as opposed to the American type (*Ostrea virginica*). Strictly speaking, however, the word 'native' is restricted to those oysters spatted and reared between the North Foreland and Orford Ness. It may more reasonably be applied to any oyster which is fattened in the waters in which it was bred; and in that sense it offers a valuable distinction from the *relaid* oyster, i.e. the oyster which, for purposes of the market, is transferred from the original breeding ground to another, so that it may grow and acquire the flavour of the food in the waters in which it finds a new home.

The following are among the more popular European oysters:

Portuguese (Ostrea angulata). Though these are geographically a European oyster, they resemble the American type. As the name implies, they derive originally from Portuguese beds, but the main source of supply is now the Bay of Arcachon, wherein they became acclimatized through the shipwreck of a boat carrying a cargo of them. The Portuguese is much the hardiest of all oysters, and is able to endure long exposure to the sun at low tide without suffering either in health or flavour.

Brittany. The Brittany oyster, excellent in its own native waters, is also the one most suitable for relaying, and it meets that fate in very large quantities. During recent years the beds of Holland, Whitstable, the Helford river in Cornwall, the Yealm in Devon and the Roach in Essex, have been largely restocked from Brittany. The Brittany is a neutral oyster, very ready to assume the local flavour of its adopted ground, and consistently excellent wherever it is laid. It can often be identified by a small trace of lime on the outer side of the shell, at the hinge, owing to the fact that it is laid on tiles, placed in the water for the purpose. The tiles are previously covered with a solution of lime to prevent the oysters becoming so firmly attached that they will be difficult of removal when developed.

Marennes Vertes. These oysters have enjoyed a high reputation on account of their distinctive colour for more than two hundred years. They are cultivated in *claires*, or pits connected together by trenches wherein the tide circulates, and in which a fine green weed is encouraged. Each oyster is given about a square foot of ground, and in due time the beard through which the oyster filters his food collects the spores of the weed and becomes green. The greenness is not due to decay or copper, but to chlorophyl, the colouring matter of vegetables, derived from the weed, together with iodine and other valuable properties. The *Marennes Vertes* are, therefore, usually preferred to the *Marennes Blanches* in France, where the reason for the greenness of these oysters is better understood than in England.

Dutch Natives. The Dutchman is as excellent a cultivator of oysters as of bulbs, and in the past very large quantities of oysters have been shipped from Holland to England. Unfortunately, the Dutch beds were badly hit by the post-war oyster epidemic, and in consequence they have been largely restocked from Brittany. Recent falls of spat have, however, been very good, and there is a probability of increased supplies in the future.

Royal Whitstables. The Kentish beds, like those of Essex, won Roman favour, though the principal supply was then from Richborough, which no longer yields oysters. Shortly before the 1914 war the English spat was so free that Brittany beds were relaid from our own; but since 1921 the reverse course has been necessary. Most Whitstable oysters to-day are therefore relaid Brittanys or Belons. The oysters known as *Royal Whitstables* are, however, genuine natives, taken from a breeding ground the boundaries of which were settled by law about 1900, the property of the Whitstable Oyster Company, which alone has the right to call its Oysters *Royal Whitstables*. This Company (strictly, The Company of Free Fishers and Dredgers of Whitstable) has existed from time immemorial; it obtained an Act of Incorporation in 1793, but the Act did no more than confirm the traditional constitution, by which a foreman and jury are elected annually at a Water Court or Court of Dredging for the management of the Fishery for the ensuing year. The freedom of the Company is an hereditary right enjoyed by eldest sons of freemen dredgers. For the time being the supply of Whitstable natives is very small, but there is hope for better abundance in the future. The Whitstable oyster has a particularly pearly shell, a sweet, almost nutty, flavour, and – distinguishing mark of the real English native – a very small beard.

Colchester Pyefleets. Among the many varieties of the oyster, those of Essex in general and the Colne fishery in particular are probably the most famous. There is good ground for supposing that they were exported to Rome during the Occupation, for a great number of shells have been found among the ruins of the ancient city bearing the distinctive characteristics of the Colne oyster. Richard I, in confirmation of previous rights, gave the borough of Colchester by Charter the sole right to the fishery from the North Bridge to the West Ness. The Corporation has ever since successfully defended its claim, and among the treasures of its insignia is a beautifully modelled silver oyster (1804), setting the standard size below which it is illegal to sell Colne oysters. The Colne fishery is about 4½ square miles in extent; the Pyefleet creek is admittedly one of the best fattening grounds in the kingdom, and the rest of the fishery is admirably productive as a spatting ground. Other Essex estuaries share, in a lesser degree, the fame of the Colne, notably the Blackwater, the Roach, and the Crouch. During recent years, and particularly since the American slipper limpet reached England, the re-laying of oysters from other parts has been extensively practised in the Blackwater and the Crouch, with excellent results.

All oysters sold on the London market must satisfy stringent tests imposed by the Fishmongers' Company, and there is, therefore, no ground whatever for regarding the oyster as in any way dangerous to health. On the contrary, they are exceptionally rich in vitamins, iodine, and organic phosphorus; and as they are both nutritive and easily digestible they are a healthy food for all save the small minority who are allergic to oysters.

AMERICAN OYSTERS
(*Ostrea Virginica*)

Gulf of Mexico
It is not generally realized that fine oysters come from the west coast of Florida, where the trade speaks of oysters as 'plants'.

Crystal Rivers. From the mouth of the Crystal River come oysters, fairly small in size, but sharp and distinct in their mineral flavour.

Apalachicolas. In Florida's north-west corner is Apalachicola Bay, where oysters, highly favoured in the local markets, are grown. Of salty flavour, they often possess a readily detected copper taste.

North Carolina
The Atlantic shores of North Carolina provide many inlets and bays where the North Carolina oyster thrives and grows to a medium size. The higher copper content of the waters is believed to be the cause of the slightly metallic flavour.

Chesapeake Bays
Two states, Virginia and Maryland, share the Chesapeake Bay, which has been recognized as one of the world's largest oyster-producing areas.

These oysters are medium or small in size and have a mild salt flavour frequently inducing the metallic aftertaste.

Choptanks. These oysters, prized for their flavour, but not their appearance, are grown at the mouth of the Choptank River, which empties into the Chesapeake Bay.

Chincoteagues. Little known beyond the Chesapeake region, these oysters have a high salt and high metallic flavour, and in size often border on the mammoth. They are grown in Chincoteague Bay.

Delaware Bay
The Delaware Bay oyster beds have a reputation and an oyster of their own. Few oysters have as attractive an appearance as these fat white Delaware Bays. But a strong copperish flavour requires a cultivated appetite.

Long Island
Long Island waters rival the Chesapeake region in importance in the industry, employing thousands of men and cultivating hundreds of acres of land under water. Here oyster-growing has been recognized as a type of farming, and the crop, harvested after five years of growth, goes not only to cities along the coast, but into export trade.

Great South Bay. Along the Atlantic coast of Long Island lies Fire Island, forming the Great South Bay and shoal water highly suited to growing two of America's famous oysters, *Bluepoints* and *Fire Island Salts.*

Bluepoints are one of the most popular varieties on the half-shell. The meat is creamy and the interior of the shell pearly. Transplanted many times before growing, these oysters are required by law to grow at least their last three months in Great South Bay.

Fire Island Salts are much like the *Bluepoints,* but larger and in greater demand for oyster fries.

Gardiners Bay. At the far tip of Long Island is Gardiners Bay with its oyster beds 30 ft. or more down on the hard, clean sandy bottom.

Gardiners Bays and *Gardiners Island Salts* are the most famous products of these beds. These oysters have large rugged shells and a high salt flavour, and the salts are exported to South America and Europe.

Peconic Bay. Separated from Gardiners Bay by Shelter Island is Peconic Bay with oyster beds 60 ft. under water.

Seapure is the name of another type coming from the deepest waters of the bay. The meats are firm and very salty and the shells are heavy.

Oyster Bays. Grown in Oyster Bay along the north shore of Long Island, are the *Oyster Bays.* Heavy-shelled, they have a sweet-flavoured and darker meat. Hardier qualities ensure perfect condition during long distance shipping.

Virginia
Tidal waters of Virginia have offered the world many famous kinds of oysters, which include *Lynnhavens* and *Chincoteagues.*

Rappahannocks. These oysters are slightly smaller and usually prove more satisfactory on the half-shell.

Robbins Islands are a thin-shelled type, possessing a salty flavour, a light-coloured meat and a fine appearance when open. The shell often is dotted with a red coral substance.

Rhode Island

Inlets and bays have formed many a natural oyster bed in Rhode Island, where the industry has flourished since pre-revolutionary times. More important in Rhode Island's industry now are seed oysters, bought by other growers to restock their beds.

Narragansett Bays. Largest of all the State's bays is Narragansett. There the brackish waters produce fairly large and oval oysters. The meats, sweeter than usual, are creamy white. Slightly saltier are the Sea-to-Home brand, a Narragansett type.

Silver Leafs. Rocky bottoms are the beds from which this type is dredged. These oysters are remarkable in their similarity to the symmetrical scallop. A salty tang characterizes their taste.

Nayatt Points. The plumpness of this sweet-flavoured variety is attributed to the crystal-clear water into which the sunlight penetrates to a great depth and develops the diatomic marine growths on which oysters feed.

An Oyster Pye

Take about a quart of oysters and take off ye black fins and wash 'em clean and blanch 'em and Drayn the Liquor from them; then take a quarter of a pound of fresh butter and a minced anchovie and two spoonfulls of Grated bread, and a spoonful of minced Parsly, and a little pepper, and a little grated Nuttmeg, no Salt (for ye anchovie is salt enough). Squese these into a lump, then line your Patepan with good cold crust, but not flacky, and put one half of your mix's Butter and anchovie, etc., at the bottom; then lay your oysters, two or three thick at most; then put to 'em ye other half of ye mixed Butter and anchovie etc., and pick some grayns of Lemon on ye top (and some youlks of hard egg if you like 'em). Put in 2 or 3 spoonfulls of ye oyster liquor and close it with ye Crust which should be a good deal higher than ye oyster to keep in the Liquor. Bake it, and when it comes out of the oven cut up the Lid, and have ready a little oyster Lyquor and Lemon juce stew'd together, and pour it in and cut ye lidd in Peices and lay round it. (Anne Blencowe's *Receipt Book*, 1694.)

Oysters in Scallop Shells

Take a saucepan and put a piece of butter in it, with chopped parsley and chives, truffles too, if you have them. Stir over the fire for a few moments, then add the oysters. Season with ground pepper, fresh herbs, and spice, then pour into the shells (silver ones if you have them). Sprinkle with breadcrumbs and little pieces of butter. Let them colour in the oven, and when they have taken on a fine shade, place them on a dish, and serve them with lemon. (*Cuisine Moderne*, Vincent La Chapelle, 1733.)

'Angels on Horseback'

Select rather large oysters. Simmer them in their strained liquor until edges curl, then drain and wrap each one in a thin slice of bacon, skewering tidily or fastening with thread. Grill until bacon is crisp and serve on toast, or *croûtons*.

AMERICAN OYSTER RECIPES

Fried Oysters

12 large oysters
Fine brown breadcrumbs
Salt and pepper
Frying oil or fat
1 egg

Carefully remove any specks of shell as well as beards of oysters. Dry in a cloth, then roll in the breadcrumbs, seasoned with salt and pepper. Let them stand for a quarter of an hour, then dip in the beaten egg and again roll in crumbs. Allow to stand for another quarter of an hour, in a cool spot, then fry for one minute in deep fat at a temperature of 400° F., or, if no thermometer is available, when the fat is smoking. Drain on special paper; serve on a hot dish; garnish with some parsley and slices of lemon.

Broiled Oysters

12 or more large oysters
Salt and pepper
¼ cup oiled butter
Fine cracker crumbs

Clean oysters, drain off all liquor and dry them in a cloth. Dip each one in the melted butter, then in the seasoned crumbs. Place in a broiling pan fitted with a fine-mesh grid and broil (i.e. 'grill') over a clear, red fire or under the flame of a gas broiler until the juices flow. Turn once during the cooking operation. Serve with *Maître d'Hôtel* butter. In lieu of biscuit crumbs, fine white breadcrumbs must do.

Oyster Fricassée

18 medium-sized oysters
2 tablespoons butter
Salt, pepper, cayenne
Thick cream

Place the butter, salt, pepper and as much cayenne as is required in a chafing-dish or a small saucepan over a rather low heat. When the butter is melted but not sizzling, add the cleaned, bearded and drained oysters. Cover, shake pan occasionally and cook gently until the oysters look plump and edges curl up. Remove and keep them hot. Add sufficient cream to the pan in which they cooked to make about a cupful of liquid in *all*. Pour, when hot, over oysters, serving, if wished, on hot buttered toast. A few drops of lemon juice improve the flavour of this dish.

Escalloped Oysters
½ cup stale breadcrumbs
1 cup biscuit crumbs
½ cup oiled butter
24 medium-sized oysters
Salt and pepper
2 tablespoons oyster liquor
2 tablespoons cream
Few drops lemon juice

Mix the bread and biscuit crumbs and stir in the melted butter. Put a thin layer of this mixture in the bottom of a shallow baking dish, cover with drained and cleaned oysters, sprinkle with salt and pepper and add half each of the oyster liquor and cream. Repeat the operation, covering the top with remaining crumbs. Sprinkle with lemon juice, sparingly, and dot with butter, if wished, but the cream is usually sufficient to make a rich dish. Bake for 25 to 30 minutes in a rather hot oven.

Note.—Never allow more than two layers of oysters or the centre one will not be sufficiently cooked. Some American housewives spread on top of the dish one or two chopped hard-boiled eggs, mixed with the breadcrumbs.

Oysters, Manhattan Style
Allow three oysters for each serving. Open them when ready to use, keeping them, naturally, in the deep shells and removing beards and any pieces of shell. Beat about a couple of tablespoons of butter to a cream, adding to it, while beating, salt, a touch of paprika and a little very finely-chopped parsley. Divide this mixture into as many pieces as you have oysters. Place a piece of the prepared butter on each oyster and cover this with a thin piece of bacon. Put the prepared oysters in a baking tin and cook for 12 minutes in a hot oven to crisp bacon.

Oyster Stew
Oysters
Hot water
Salt and pepper
Butter
Boiling milk
Biscuit crumbs

Open the oysters when required. Drain off liquor, straining and mixing with sufficient hot water to cover the oysters set in a small pan. Season to taste and heat until the oysters begin to curl or 'ruffle' around the edges, then add a sufficiency of butter and,

when this has melted, at once add enough boiling milk for requirements, removing the saucepan from the fire. Special small 'oyster crackers' may be served, dry, with the stew, or some people prefer it to be thickened by the addition of crushed biscuit crumbs, or even a little flour, but the latter is not the choice of real gourmets.

Roast 'Saddle Rocks' in the Shell
3 large oysters per serving
Oiled butter
Salt and pepper

This is a very special American delicacy, the oysters used being the large 'Saddle Rocks.' Be sure they are tightly closed. Wash shells well in salt water, scrubbing thoroughly. Wipe with a clean cloth and place them, deep part of shells down, on live coals (charcoal is very suitable). As they open, carefully remove the shallow upper shell, taking especial care not to spill a drop of the liquor. Place at once on a very hot dish, each guest seasoning his own, as liked, with butter, salt and pepper. If the use of live coals is impracticable, a very hot oven may be substituted, the oysters being set in a tin or even in the plates on which they are to be served, but it is essential that both the top and bottom heat be equally good. This is another of those dishes which require the guest to wait for them rather than have them wait for him.

Pan Oysters
Cut stale bread into thin slices, removing crusts. Cut each slice to fit a small patty-pan, toast, butter them and set them in the buttered pans. Moisten each with some of the oyster liquor and fill up the small pans with raw oysters. Season with salt and pepper and dot each one with butter. Put all the pans into a hot oven, covering as tightly as possible with a large tin or lid having a weight on top. Cook for seven or eight minutes or until edges ruffle, then remove cover, sprinkle with a few drops of lemon juice and serve at once in the pans. Small china or even cardboard ramekin cases do nicely for this.

Oyster Fritters
12 or more large oysters
Salt and pepper
2 eggs
⅔ cup flour (about)
½ pint milk
Frying fat

Open the oysters, clean and drain, reserving the strained liquor. Set this on to boil gently; add oysters, cooking as directed after seasoning liquor with salt and pepper. Break the eggs in a basin, mix in the flour, then the milk, gradually. If batter is too thin to coat a spoon, add a little more flour, beating out all lumps. Dip the oysters in this batter and fry in deep boiling fat at 375° F. until brown and crisp. Serve at once with lemon and fried parsley.

OTHER RECIPES
Oysters with Grilled Steak
Fried oysters served with a thick grilled *entrecôte* and a good Hollandaise sauce are to be highly recommended.

Huîtres Délicieuses
2 tablespoons vinegar
1 teaspoon chopped chives
1 small pinch grated nutmeg
Salt and a dash of cayenne
½ teaspoon lemon juice
18 medium-sized oysters
2 hard-boiled eggs
1 cup cream
1 teaspoon chopped parsley
Rounds of hot buttered toast

Mix together the vinegar, chives (or a drop or two of onion juice must do in the absence of chives), the nutmeg, salt, and a few grains of cayenne pepper. Add the lemon juice, blending well with other ingredients. Open the oysters, trim, clean and drain. Put them in the above mixture and prepare the sauce. Mash the yolks of the eggs, season with salt and pepper or a dash more of cayenne, then blend with the cream and parsley. Put this in a small saucepan, bring gently to boiling point, drop in the oysters, cook slowly for four minutes, then serve on rounds of freshly-made and well-buttered toast.

Oyster Loaf
Take a good-sized tin loaf, remove top and set aside. Scrape out all crumb. Stew two or three dozen small oysters in their own liquor to which is added a blade of mace and a strip of lemon rind. When the oysters are done, remove and keep hot. Continue cooking strained liquor until reduced to half its original quantity, then add a tablespoonful of flour blended with twice that amount of cream, then salt and pepper. Beat well. Butter inside of loaf generously, put the oyster stew inside – that is, the sauce to which the oysters have been added – replace top and bake the loaf for about 10 minutes in a hot oven. It is advisable to brush the exterior well over with melted butter. The beards and hard parts of oysters must, of course, be removed before putting into sauce. Serve very hot with lemon.

Oyster Loaves
Make a round hole at the tops of some little round loaves, and scrape out all the crumb.

Put some oysters into a tossing-pan, with the oyster liquor, and the crumbs that were taken out of the loaves, and a large piece of butter. Stew them together for five or six minutes; then put in a spoonful of good cream, and fill your loaves. Then lay the bit of crust carefully on the top again, and put them in the oven to crisp. (*The London Art of Cookery*, John Farley, 1787.)

PACOU
Lat. *Gobius martinicus*. A *Goby* of the Caribbean Sea, highly prized when split, salted and cured.

PAK-FAN-EU
A small, nearly transparent, fresh-water fish, greatly esteemed in Southern China; also known as the *White Rice Fish*.

PALOLO
Lat. *Nereis*. A small marine worm esteemed a great luxury in some of the Pacific islands. At a certain time of the year vast shoals of it appear on the surface of the sea near Samoa, Tonga, Fiji, and other islands. They are tied up in bread-fruit leaves and baked.

PALOURDES
Fr. for *Cockles* (q.v.).

PAMPANITO
Lat. *Trachinotus rhodopus*. Spanish-American name of a small *Pompano* (q.v.) found from Panama to the Gulf of California.

PAMPANO
See *Pompano*.

PARGO CRIOLLO
Lat. *Lutianus analis*. The *Mutton-snapper* of Cuba and a fish in season at all times of the year, in the West Indies.

PARR
A young *Salmon* in the stage when it has dark transverse bands, called *parr marks*. It is illegal to fish *Parr*.

PARROT-FISH
Any fish of the family *Scaridae*; they are more remarkable for their bright colouring than valuable as an article of diet.

PEJERREY
Lat. *Basilichthys bonariensis*. The *Pezrey* or the king of fishes, caught off the coasts of the Argentine, Uruguay and Brazil; also in the Pacific, off Chile.

PERCH
Lat. *Perca fluviatilis*; Fr. *Perche*; Ger. *Barsch*; It. *Bertiche*; Sp. *Perca*. A perch from running waters is one of the most delicate of all fresh-water fishes. The American species are

the *Yellow Perch* (*P. flavescens*), and the *White Perch* (*Morone americana*). The *Giant Perch* of Germany, the *Zander*, abounds in the Elbe and is one of the gastronomical glories of Dresden. The best ways of cooking a *Perch* are the same as for the *Grayling* (q.v.).

The *Mountain Perch* (Lat. *Lates niloticus*) belongs to the *Serranidae* family and, when not too large, is one of the best fish from the Nile.

The Perch is a very good and very bold biting fish ... He is of great esteem in Italy, saith Aldrovandus: and especially the least are there esteemed a dainty dish. Gesner prefers the Perch and Pike above the Trout, or any fresh-water fish ... and he says the River Perch is so wholesome that physicians allow him to be eaten by wounded men, or by men in fevers, or by women in child-bed. (Izaak Walton.)

PERIWINKLES
Lat. *Littorina littorea*; Fr. *Bigorneaux, Bigourneaux*. A small, round, black shell inside which there is a small sea-snail or fish. Also certain American species of *Thais* and Australian *Turbo undulatus*. *Periwinkles* are abundant along the shores of England and Scotland. They are in season all the year round. They require about 20 minutes' boiling in salt water.

PICKEREL
A young or small *Pike* (q.v.). In U.S.A. the name often refers to a particular kind of *Pike* (*Esox niger*), which grows to 2 ft. in length and enjoys great repute among epicures.

PIDDOCK
Pholas Dactylus. A bivalve mollusc or *Clam*, which bores wood, clay, or soft rock, into which it lodges itself.

PIKE
Lat. *Esox lucius*; Fr. *Brochet*; Ger. *Hecht*; It. *Luccio*; Sp. *Lucio*. The Pike, also known as *Jack* or *Luce*, is 'the king and tyrant of other fishes, because hee not onely devoureth fishes of other kindes, but also of his owne kinde'. (Cogan's *Haven of Health*. Ed. 1612, p. 141.)

The pike has a bad reputation also among cooks, because it is dry, rather coarse and very bony. The pike runs to 30 lb. and more, but those of from 3 lb. to 7 lb. are best for the table.

Before it is cooked, and before it is even cleaned, a pike should be hung by the jaw and as much salt as possible should be forced down its throat; it should then be left hanging during eight to twelve hours. If so treated, the flesh of the pike will be more tender and many of the smallest bones will disappear during cooking.

Here is a recipe vouched for from personal experience by the Rev A.R.Batchelor Wylam:

'If a Pike of from 4 lb. to 8 lb. be cleaned as soon as caught, not washed, but wiped dry, cut into ¾ in. steaks (fins, head and tail removed), and salted each side overnight, and in the morning the salt wiped off, fry in shallow fat: the scales will come away with the skin and most of the bones with the backbone, and "as pheasant is to chicken, so is pike to cod".'

Brochet grillé
A small pike, well seasoned, bread-crumbed and grilled before not too hot a fire; usually served with a horseradish sauce.

Izaak Walton's Recipe
This dish of meat is too good for any but anglers, or very honest men.

First, open your Pike at the gills, and if need be, cut also a little slit towards the belly. Out of these, take his guts; and keep his liver, which you are to shred very small, with thyme, sweet marjoram, and a little winter savoury; to these put some pickled oysters, and some anchovies, two or three; both these last whole, for the anchovies will melt, and the oysters should not; to these you must add also a pound of sweet butter, which you are to mix with the herbs that are shred, and let them all be well salted. If the Pike be more than a yard long, then you may put into these herbs more than a pound, or if he be less, then less butter will suffice. These, being thus mixt, with a blade or two of mace, must be put into the Pike's belly; and then his belly so sewed up as to keep all the butter in his belly if it be possible; if not, then as much of it as you possibly can. But take not off the scales. Then you are to thrust the spit through his mouth, out at his tail. And then take four or five or six split stocks, or very thin laths, and a convenient quantity of tape or filleting; these laths are to be tied round about the Pike's body, from his head to his tail, and the tape tied somewhat thick, to prevent his breaking or falling off from the spit. Let him be roasted very leisurely; and often basted with claret wine, and anchovies, and butter mixed together; and also with what moisture falls from him into the pan. When you have roasted him sufficiently, you are to hold under him, when you unwind or cut the tape that ties him, such a dish as you purpose to eat him out of; and let him fall into it with the sauce that is roasted in his belly; and by this means the Pike will be kept unbroken and complete. Then, to the sauce which was within and also that sauce in the pan, you are to add a fit quantity of the best butter, and to squeeze the juice of three or four oranges. Lastly, you may either put into the Pike, with the oysters, two cloves of garlic; and take it whole out, when the Pike is cut off the spit; or, to give the sauce a *haut-goût*, let the dish into which you let the Pike fall be rubbed with it. The using or not using of this garlic is left to your discretion.

Brochet à la Hongroise

Cut the meat of a Pike into pieces about three inches square, salt them and place them in an oblong pan with bacon cut into dice, sliced green paprika and tomatoes. Put the pan in a moderate oven.

Fry some chopped onion, add a tablespoonful of red paprika, and, a minute after, enough cold water to cover all. Simmer gently for a minute or two. Add a teaspoonful of sour cream into which a teaspoonful of flour has been stirred. Add also about half a pound of cooked, sliced potatoes.

Ten minutes before the fish is ready, pour the mixture over it. Cover it and let it finish baking in a moderate oven. (Madame de Szasz.)

Quenelles de Brochet au Montrachet

Crush in mortar 2 lb. of pike and mix in one pint of cream; season well, and make into balls with the help of spoons. Add Montrachet wine to stock and cook, but do not boil. Take fish out, reduce the wine stock, add cream, reduce again, then add ¼ lb. butter. Garnish with mushrooms.

Brochets are served with quite a number of sauces and under the name of whatever the sauce happens to be. The following ways of serving a *Brochet* are also popular:

Benoîton. Fried fillets; red wine sauce.

Bleu, au. Same as *Truite au bleu*.

Bordelaise. Slices poached in red wine with a *Mirepoix*.

Martinière. *Brocheton* marinaded in white wine, olive oil, and *Aromates*. Take out of marinade; dry and grill over a gentle heat, adding olive oil during the process. Serve with a *Sauce Mayonnaise* with chopped walnuts added.

Orly. Breadcrumbed fillets, fried and served with tomato sauce.

Pain. Poached in buttered mould. Remove from mould; decorate with mushrooms and truffles; serve with *Sauce Bâtard*.

PILCHARDS

Lat. *Sardina pilchardus*; Fr. *Royans*. Pilchards are fine, fat sardines, too large to be tinned and excellent when plain broiled. They have also been called *Gypsy Herring*. They are very abundant upon the coasts of Devonshire and Cornwall. The best season is between July and Christmas. The fact that Pilchards are the fattest of herrings makes it very difficult

to enjoy them except near the coasts where they are caught; they are very bad travellers. A related species, *Sardinella jagax*, visits the coasts of Australia in large schools.

PILOT FISH

Lat. *Seriola zonata*. A transversely banded amberfish, common in parts of the Atlantic. Also the local name, in the Eastern States of the U.S.A., given to the *Menominee Whitefish*.

PIRARUCU

One of the best edible fishes of the Amazon; when fully grown it attains a weight of about 250 lb.

PLAICE

Lat. *Pleuronectes platessa*; Fr. *Carrelet* and *Plie*; Ger. *Schollen*; Ital. *Passeri*; Sp. *Platijas*. The least interesting – gastronomically – flatfish there is; it is best as fried fillets. It grows to 8 lb., 10 lb., and more. The best Plaice are caught between Hastings and Folkestone, and are usually known as Dover Plaice. Plaice is in season from May until Christmas; when in condition, the underside should be quite white and the upper side dark with bright orange spots; the body should be thick and firm and the eyes and spots bright. In U.S.A. the name is given to the Summer Flounder (*Paralichthys dentatus*) and other similar flat fishes. Most of the sauces and preparations suitable for Soles are applicable to Plaice.

PLIE

Fr. for *Plaice* (q.v.).

POLLACK. POLLOCK

Lat. *Gadus pollachius*. A valuable substitute for *Cod*, which it resembles, found off Newfoundland and upon the European coasts of the Atlantic. A darker species (*G. virens*, syn. *carbonarius*), also known as *Coalfish*, occurs on both the European and American coasts of the Atlantic. *Pollack* is sometimes called *Green Cod*.

POMFRET

The name of two very different kinds of fish: (*a*) the *Brama raii*, a sooty-black, spiny-finned food fish of the Northern Atlantic and Northern Pacific; and (*b*) the *Stromateus argenteus*, and allied members of the *Stromateidae* genus of the Indian Ocean. *Pomfret* is one of the best fishes one gets in India, more particularly in Bombay. It is a flat fish, which swims sideways, and is excellent either hot or cold, fried, grilled, boiled, steamed or smoked like *Salmon* (q.v.).

POMPANO

Lat. *Trachinotus carolinus*. One of the best fish of the Southern Atlantic and Gulf coasts of Northern America. It reaches a length of 18 in. and is covered with small scales with blue, silvery and golden lustre.

Pompano au vin blanc

Place into a large, not too deep pan a rack, to be able to steam the *Pompano* without having it touched by the broth. Fill the pan with white wine – Riesling – up to the height of the rack, add one whole onion, salt, pepper – whole, black – and a few sprigs of dill. Stuff the cavity of the pompano, where it has been drawn, with fresh dill, place upon the rack, cover the pan tightly and let the fish steam for about 40 minutes. Forty minutes is just right if the pompano weighs about a pound, which is the ideal weight. After the steaming is finished, remove the fish from the pan, throw the dill away, skin the fish and serve either whole or filleted. The only accompaniment for this is the following sauce: Mix two tablespoons of freshly – and I mean very freshly – ground horseradish with three soupspoons of un-sweetened whipped cream. That's all. (*Of Cabbages and Kings*, by William Rhode. Stacpole Sons, New York.)

PORGY

Lat. *Pagrus pagrus*. A food fish, commonly called *Red Porgy*, of the Mediterranean as well as of the European and American coasts of the Atlantic: the compressed, ob-long body is crimson, with blue spots.

PORKFISH

Lat. *Anisotremus virginicus*. A *Grunt* (q.v.), black, yellow-striped, occurring in the West Indies and vicinity.

POUTING

Lat. *Gadus luscus*. Sometimes known as *Bile* or *Whiting Pout*. A species of *Cod* (q.v.) with copper-coloured body which is found in the North Atlantic. It is good when quite fresh, but it decomposes very quickly

POWAN

A white fish or fresh-water herring found in Lochs Lomond and Eck and nowhere else; it is one of the best food fishes of Scotland, and closely resembles the Irish *Pullan* (q.v.).

PRAWNS

Lat. *Leander serratus*; Fr. *Crevettes roses* or *Bouquets*; Ger. *Flohkrebs*; Sp. *Langostin*. Prawns are in season all the year round, but at their best from February to October. They are sold by the pint, in England, and a pint is reckoned to be sufficient for four people.

The black filament in the back of prawns should be removed before eating; it is poisonous for people who suffer from an anti-shell-fish intestinal complex.

Prawns are largely used for garnish, but they are also excellent plain boiled and by themselves as hors-d'oeuvre or folded into a lightly cooked *omelette*, or as *buttered prawns*, i.e. cooked in gravy and butter – simmering gently for six or seven minutes, turned into a glass jar and allowed to set. *Curried prawns* can be excellent if prepared by a talented Indian cook.

Mousse of Prawns

Shell some prawns. Pound them, mix with butter, a little velouté mixed with fish stock pepper, and salt; and if available some coral of lobster, and melted gelatine, about a wine-glassful to thirty or forty prawns. Put through a fine sieve, heat over a slow fire, and when hot add the white of an egg beaten stiff. Finally, add a little whipped cream. Beat the whole with a fork, and mix thoroughly. Turn into a low mould, and leave to become cold. (Sir Francis Colchester-Wemyss' *The Pleasures of the Table*.)

Prawns Curried

Cook half a sliced onion in two tablespoon-fuls of butter till brown, add two tablespoon-fuls of flour mixed with half teaspoonful of curry powder (or more to taste), a little salt and pepper, and gradually pour on a cupful of rich milk or cream. Put a handful of sultanas with each pint of prawns, which have been carefully peeled. Heat the prawns and sultanas well through in this sauce and serve with a border of steamed rice. (Mrs Turner's *Fifty Ways of Cooking Fish*.)

PULLAN. POLLAN

A white fish or fresh-water herring netted in large numbers in spring and summer in Loughs Neagh and Erne, in Ireland: it also occurs in Loughs Derg and Ree. It is closely allied to the *Powan* and *Vendace*.

QUAHOG

Lat. *Venus mercenaria*; Fr. *Praires* or *Clovisses*. The American round *Clam*.

QUERIMAN

Lat. *Mugil curema* and *M. brasiliensis*. Any of several small West Indian *Mullets* (q.v.).

QUINNAT SALMON

Lat. *Oncorhynchus tschawytscha*. The most im-portant species of salmon of the Pacific from Monterey Bay to Bering Strait. It has now been acclimatized in New Zealand. It is not a salmon and it is, gastronomically, very inferior to the Atlantic salmon (*Salmo salar*). It averages 22 lb. in weight, but much larger specimens are not unusual. The whole fish, however, is rarely seen by the public, whose acquaintance with it is out of tins or cans.

RABBIT-FISH
Lat. *Promethichthys prometheus*. A sea-fish related to the *Escolar* (q.v.).

RASCASSE
Scorpaena scrofa. The Mediterranean *Hogfish*, chiefly used in *Bouillabaisse*.

RAZOR-SHELL
Solen Siliqua. The largest of the *Razor* bivalves. It is the *Aulo* of the Romans. It is widely distributed and is eaten either raw, boiled or fried.

REDFIN
Lat. *Luxilus cornutus*. A small *Shiner* (q.v.) widely distributed in Eastern and Central U.S.A. Also the *Lythrurus umbratilis* of the Mississippi Valley.

RED SNAPPER
Lat. *Lutianus campechinus*. A large *Snapper* (q.v.) and the most valuable of the genus, gastronomically. It is caught from Long Island to Brazil, mostly in the Gulf of Mexico and off the coast of Florida.

Creoled Red Snapper
Either slice in 1 in. slices or bake a whole large *Red Snapper*. Fry one large chopped onion and one minced green pepper in two tablespoons of butter. When soft, add one large tablespoon of flour, stirring until flour is absorbed; add a large can of tomatoes, a sprinkling of allspice, three sprigs of parsley, one crushed bayleaf, and one sprig of thyme. Simmer for 30 minutes. Run through a colander. Dredge fish with salt, pepper, and flour and place in a baking-dish with two tablespoons of bacon drippings and brown in a hot oven. Pour over sauce, reduce heat, and bake for at least one hour, basting frequently. During the cooking, if sauce becomes too thick add one cup of claret wine or water. Serve with slices of lemon. (*The Complete Menu Book*, by Gladys T.Lang. Houghton Mifflin Company. Boston, Mass.)

ROACH
Lat. *Rutilus rutilus*. (Yarrell: *Cyprinus rutilis*.) Fr. *Gardons*; Ger. *Rotaugen*. A silvery river fish of the *Carp* family common in English, French and other European rivers. It should be cooked like the *Grayling* (q.v.). There is also a river fish called *Roach* in the U.S.A., but it is a different kind altogether, the *Leiostomus xanthurus*, a *Spot* (q.v.).

ROBALO
Lat. *Centropomus undecimalis*. Also called *Snook*. A pike-like sea-fish of the West Indies and tropical American waters, of real gastronomic merit. The small *Robalo* is called *Robalito*.

ROCKFISH
Any of the many fishes which live among rocks or on rocky bottoms, but more particularly the *Red Rockfish (Sebastopyr ruberrimus)*, and the *Black Rockfish (Sebastodes mystinus)*, which are valuable market fishes of the towns of the Pacific coasts of North America and Asia; also the *Striped Bass*, the *Log Perch* and several *Groupers* of Bermuda and Florida waters.

ROCK HIND
Lat.*Epinephelus adscenscionis*. A brown spotted *Grouper* (q.v.) of the West Indies and southern coasts of the U.S.A. Also a *Grouper* (q.v.) found only in the waters to the east of Puerto Rico, the *Mycteroperca bowersi*. Also a variety of the *Niggerfish* (q.v.), common in the West Indies, the *Cephalopholis fulvus ruber*.

ROCK SALMON
Lat. *Pollachius virens*, in England, or *Coalfish* (q.v.); and *Zonichthys falcata*, and *Amberfish* (q.v.), in the Southern States of U.S.A.

ROCK WHITING
Any of several Australian marine fishes of the genus *Odax*, of no mean gastronomic merit.

ROES
Fr. *Laitance* (soft roe), and *Oeufs de poisson* (hard roe); Ger. *Rogen*. Hard roe is eaten fresh or dried. The best of all hard roes is the *Caviar*, the hard roe of different members of the *Acipenserides* family, the *Beluga, Sturgeon, Sevruga, Ship* and *Sterlind*, fishes caught in the estuaries of the rivers flowing into the Caspian and Black Seas. The roe of the *Grey Mullet* is known as *Botargo* and the cod's hard roe dried is a popular delicacy. Soft roe is a favourite relish as a savoury or as a garnishing of many fish dishes.

Devilled Soft Herring Roes
Butter
Made mustard
Salt and pepper
Soft herring roes
Hot toast
Chopped parsley

Place, say, two tablespoons of butter in a small pan by the side of the stove, add half teaspoonful of mustard, then salt and pepper. When the butter is liquid, but not cooked, add the roes and allow them gently to simmer until the butter be absorbed by them. Serve on hot buttered toast, sprinkling with parsley.

Fried Hard Herring Roes
Roll each roe, after sprinkling with salt and pepper, in flour. Next roll them lightly in breadcrumbs and fry in deep boiling fat

until crisp and brown. Drain well and serve with fried parsley, slices of lemon and hot tomato sauce.

Note —Cover pan when frying the roes as some of the tiny eggs explode while cooking and make the fat splutter dangerously.

Fritters of Hard Herring Roes

Simmer the roes in salted water for 10 minutes. Dry well in a cloth, then dip in frying batter and fry in deep fat. Serve with fried parsley and quarters of lemon. Soft roes may also be prepared in the same way.

Hard Herring Roes Vinaigrette

Boil as indicated above, dry well and then dip in ice-cold water to render them firm. Drain when ready to serve and hand separately a good vinaigrette sauce with chopped parsley, chives and chervil. Soft roes may also be prepared in the same manner.

Coquilles of Hard Herring Roes

Cook as directed, in salted boiling water. Dry, press the roes to a paste with a fork, add a sufficiency of melted butter (oiled butter) and the yolks of two hard-boiled eggs. Season well, then add an equal quantity of very fine fresh breadcrumbs. Place this mixture into scallop shells, brown in a hot oven and serve hot, sprinkling when eating with just a little lemon juice and maybe a dusting of cayenne pepper.

Hard Herring Roes Croquettes

Boil the roes, drain well and separate into small pieces. Mix some fine fresh breadcrumbs with a little softened butter and a dash of thick cream. Season rather highly, adding a little chopped parsley. Shape into small sausages, dip first in beaten egg then in fine brown breadcrumbs and fry in deep boiling oil or fat.

Soft Herring Roes in Sauce Poulette

    Soft roes
    Lemon juice
    Sauce Poulette
    Salt and pepper
    Parsley

Boil the soft roes in salted water for 10 minutes. Drain well. Make the *Sauce Poulette* as you would a white sauce, adding cream instead of milk with a little of the water the roes were boiled in. Remove from fire, then beat in a raw egg yolk. Season to taste and flavour with lemon juice. Place the roes in a dish, on toast or not, cover with the sauce and garnish with fresh parsley.

Soft Herring Roes à la Provençale

Cook the roes as indicated, simmering for 10 minutes. Drain. Make a good rich white

sauce to which s added the chopped yolks of two or three hard-boiled eggs, as well as one pounded and sieved anchovy. Place the hot roes on thin slices of fried or toasted bread and cover with the sauce when serving.

ROHU

Lat. *Labeo rohita*. One of the best of the fresh-water edible fishes of India and Burma.

ROLL-MOPS

Soused bloater fillets.

ROSEFISH

Lat. *Sebastes marinus*. A large fish, also known as *Norway Haddock*, which is found on both the European and American coasts of the North Atlantic; when fully grown it is usually bright rose-red or orange-red; of real gastronomic value.

ROUGET

Fr. for *Red Mullet* (q.v.). The two best *Rougets* are the *Rouget barbet* or *Surmulet* (*Mullus surmuletus*), chiefly from the Mediterranean; and the *Mulle Rouget* or *Rouge d'Yport* (*Mullus barbatus*), from the English Channel.

ROYANS

Fr. for *Fresh Sardines* grilled.

RUDD

Lat. *Scardinius erythrophthalmus*. A first cousin of the *Roach* (q.v.) and living in the same waters.

RUFFE. POPE

Lat. *Acerina vulgaris* or *A. cernua*. A freshwater species of perch which occurs in the Midlands and South of England, in Scandinavia and in Siberia. It is prepared like *Pike* (q.v.).

RUNNER

The name given in the U.S.A. to two distinct types of fish: (1) an amber-fish (Lat. *Elagatis bipinnulatus*), widely distributed in warm seas; and (2) a jurel (Lat. *Paratractus*, or *Caranx crysos*), common from Cape Cod southwards, known as Blue Runner.

SAILOR'S CHOICE

The name given in U.S.A. to different fishes which are supposed to possess real gastronomic merit, such as the *Lagodon rhomboides*, a small porgy fish found from south of Cape Cod along the Atlantic coast; the *Orthopristis chrysopterus*, or pigfish; the *Haemulon parra*, a Grunt (q.v.), found from Florida to Brazil, and *Diplodus holbrooki*, a pinfish.

SAITHE
A Scotch name for *Coalfish* (q.v.).

SALMON
Lat. *Salmo salar*; Fr. *Saumon*; Ger. *Salm*; Ital. *Salmone*; Sp. *Salmon*. The true salmon, or Atlantic salmon, a fish living in the sea and ascending at the spawning season the many European and North American rivers. The salmon is the most popular fish among all who love sport as well as good food. Gastronomes consider the *Salmon* caught in Norwegian waters as the finest of all; *Scotch Salmon* comes next. *Canadian Salmon* is at its best when smoked.

The best time for English and Scotch salmon is from February to August, but salmon fishing on the River Tay and its tributaries opens on January 15th for rod fishing, and on February 4th for nets; the fish that is caught during the first fortnight or so is of a delicacy and excellence never to be attained again during the rest of the fishing season. Salmon caught in European rivers weigh from 10 lb. to 25 lb., but some rare specimens have been caught that weighed as much as 75 lb.

The name *Salmon* is also given to other members of the *Salmonidae* family, such as some of the large trouts, and to other fish which do not belong to the *Salmonidae* genus, such as the *Quinnat Salmon* (q.v.).

'*There is a river in Macedon; and there is also moreover a river at Monmouth; it is called Wye at Monmouth; but it is out of my brains what is the name of the other river; but 'tis all one; 'tis alike as my fingers is to my fingers, and there is Salmon in both.*' (*King Henry V.* Act IV. Sc. 7.)

When at its best, salmon is said to be the king of fish. It must be very stiff, shiny and red in the gills, with scales bright and silvery. Medium-sized salmon are better than the very large ones and good judges prefer hen fish, i.e. those which have small heads and thick 'necks'. Scale carefully. Scrape away the blood when cleaning out but wash the fish as little as possible.

Salmon may be boiled, poached, grilled, stewed, baked, fried and prepared in ever so many different ways. It is excellent both hot and cold; also smoked, potted and pickled.

How to Bake a Joll of Fresh Salmon
Take Ginger and Salt, and season it, and certaine Currans, and cast them about and under it, and let the paste be fine, and take a little Butter and lay about it in the paste, and set it in the oven two houres, and serve it. (*The Good Huswife's Jewell*, Thomas Dawson, 1696.)

How to Seethe Fresh Salmon
Take a little water, and as much Beere and Salte, and put thereto Parsley, Time, and Rosemarie, and let these boyle togeathere. Then put in your Salmon, and make your broth sharpe with some Vinegar. (*17th-century recipe.*)

To Pickle Salmon the Newcastle Way, according to a Receipt procured from England, as is said by the infamous Governour Sir Francis Bernard
Scale your Salmon, split it down the back, and take out the back bone; then, with a Cloth, wipe off all the Blood, and then cut it into Junks of about four or five Inches thick. Put on your Pot of Water, making it sharp with Salt, and when it boils put in your Junks of Salmon, and let them boil for twenty-three Minutes. Then take it off the Fire and let it cool. Make a Pickle with two ounces of Allspice, two ounces of black Pepper and one Gallon of Vinegar, which boil, and into which, when cold, put an handfull of Salt. Place the Salmon in a Keg, and, when the Salt is dissolved, pour the Pickle upon the Salmon. After it has stood one night in this manner, strain off the Oyl that may have arisen on the Top, to prevent its acquiring a strong taste, then head up the Keg. (*Mrs Gardiner's Receipts from* 1763. Boston, Mass.)

To Boil Salmon
Scale the fish, clean and cook it in plain salted water to retain its own delicate flavour; this, of course, for Scotch or English salmon. Canadian salmon, having been chilled to travel, of necessity has less flavour in England and may be cooked in a prepared *court-bouillon*. Allow 10 minutes per pound and 10 minutes over for cooking, and never let the water boil, just simmer, or, as the French say, 'shiver'.

Grilled Salmon
Select a middle cut no more than an inch thick per serving. Dust lightly with salt and a speck of cayenne. Grease a gridiron with a piece of fresh veal suet, after heating well. The fish may be wrapped in oiled or buttered paper to grill or may come into direct contact with the heat, but, should 'chilled' salmon be used, cook by steaming; it will be dry and unappetizing if grilled. Serve with *Tartare*, *Ravigote* or *Mayonnaise Sauce* when done.

Smoked Salmon
The salmon are prepared for smoking by being split, and the head, tail and backbone removed. They are then placed in layers and salted for six or eight hours. The salt is then removed and the fish washed, placed over gas jets or in smoke ovens and cooked slowly for two hours. The fish is then

smoked and after this operation it is ready for eating without further cooking. Another method occasionally used is to split the salmon like a kipper with head and bones left on the fish and salted and smoked only, without cooking.

Potted Salmon

This is an old recipe and makes a delicious filling for sandwiches. Butter the entire interior of an earthenware crock, having a well-fitting lid. Place in it slices of fresh salmon together with a few peppercorns, salt, a pinch of mace and allspice to taste, quantities depending, naturally, on the amount of fish being potted. Add a little good fish stock, about one inch in depth, to prevent burning. Put on lid, covering with paper and a weight. Cook for an hour or more in a moderate oven, then let it cool in the crock. Remove fish when cold, drain on a sieve, add, if necessary, more salt and pepper, remove skin and all bones and pound flesh in a mortar with a little clarified butter. Press through a fine sieve and put into pots, covering with a thin layer of clarified butter. If desired, the flavour may be greatly enhanced by the addition of a little raw or blanched lobster spawn or a little essence of shrimps.

Old Recipe for Souchet of Salmon

Thin slices of raw salmon
1 cup stock
1 cup cold water
1 raw onion
1 small parsnip
1 small white turnip
Salt and pepper
1 or 2 small sprigs parsley

Place the slices of salmon in a large *sauteuse*, side by side. Add the stock and water which, when combined, should come about half-way up the slices of fish. Add the sliced onion, parsnip, parsley, and turnip, salt and pepper. Cover and cook gently, turning the slices from time to time, for about 30 minutes. Use the liquor in which the salmon was cooked for the sauce.

Salmon Tindish
(Canadian)
1 small whole salmon
1 tablespoon salt
1 cup fine breadcrumbs
1 teaspoon chopped parsley
Salt and pepper
Milk
Butter
Slices of lemon
1 or 2 hard-boiled eggs

Scrape and wash and clean the fish; dry it well. Rub in the salt and put the salmon in a

baking tin, scoring it across four or five times on each side with a sharp knife. Mix together the breadcrumbs (fresh), the parsley, salt and pepper, and moisten with milk. Plaster this over the fish and put one or two lumps of butter in each of the gashes. Cover the bottom of the tin with more milk and bake in a rather hot oven, basting frequently with the milk, adding more as required. When done, lift the fish carefully out of the tin on to a hot dish. Garnish with slices of lemon and slices of hard-boiled egg, straining the liquor over the whole. Allow about 10 to 15 minutes per pound for cooking.

Salmon Jelly
(Canadian)
1 cup cooked and shredded salmon
Allspice
Nutmeg
Salt and pepper
Aspic jelly
Lettuce leaves

Season the shredded fish with small quantities of the spices, salt and pepper. Soften, by gentle heating, some good aspic jelly, add the fish and use this mixture to fill small fancy moulds two-thirds up. Cool until set, then fill the moulds to brims with aspic jelly only. Set on ice, then turn out on lettuce leaves, decorating with slices of tomato, hard-boiled egg, or anything fancied.

Salmon Loaf
(American)
1 cup cooked and flaked salmon
1 cup hot milk
1 tablespoon butter
1 cup fresh crumbs
2 eggs
Salt and pepper

Mix all ingredients, beating eggs well and using to moisten. Press into a buttered tin and bake for 30 minutes in a moderate oven, serving hot with any preferred sauce or cold with sliced cucumber or a salad. If wished, a cupful of grated cheese may be added, but this is inadvisable when the salmon is fresh, not chilled.

Salmon Fricassée
(Canadian)
1 lb. fresh salmon
Salt and pepper
Smallest pinch mace
1 teaspoon mustard
3 or 4 tomatoes
¼ cup water
1 clove
1 shallot
¼ cup vinegar
Chopped parsley
Triangles of dry toast

Cut the salmon into 1 in. square pieces, removing bones. Put these pieces in a saucepan with all the other ingredients, first mixing the mustard to a paste with the vinegar. Boil up once, then add the peeled and cut-up tomatoes. Simmer gently for 35 minutes, then serve very hot in a border of hot mashed potatoes, garnishing with tiny triangles of toasted or fried bread. Canadians also serve this dish ice-cold in summer, substituting a border of sprigs of watercress and small lettuce leaves for the potato and bread sippets.

SEVEN 'ESCOFFIER' RECIPES

Coquilles de Saumon
Coquilles are usually made from boiled salmon. Carefully remove all bones; mix with a *Sauce Béchamel*; fill in the *coquilles*; sprinkle some grated cheese on top; pour some melted butter over it and brown under grill. Chopped slices of truffles, mushrooms and even hard-boiled eggs may be mixed with the salmon and *Béchamel*. (This is an excellent·way of disposing of left-over salmon.)

Côtelettes de Saumon
Prepare a paste made up of mushrooms (one-fourth) and boiled salmon (three-fourths); also some truffles; cover the lot with a *Béchamel* greatly reduced and with a binding of yolks of eggs. Spread the mixture upon a marble slab; let it cool and cut it up in slices, which can be shaped cutletwise; dip in beaten egg and breadcrumbs and fry just in time for serving. Dress upon a napkin with some fried parsley.

Côtelettes de Saumon Pojarski
Cut up roughly some salmon with a knife and mix with it thoroughly half its own weight of fresh butter and breadcrumbs soaked in cream in equal parts. Chop the whole together until it makes a fine, well-mixed paste; season with pepper and salt. Spread upon a floured board, divide in equal parts and shape cutletwise. Cook in clarified butter at the last moment, browning both sides alternately and dress crown-like upon a serving dish.

Garnishings: *Queues d'écrevisses*; shrimps; oysters; truffles; mushrooms; *cèpes*; rice with curry or paprika is suitable with these cutlets. Garnishings are served with either a *Sauce Béchamel à la crème* or a *Sauce Normande*.

Darne de Saumon Chambord
Poach a *darne* (middle cut) of salmon on slow fire in an open pan, in some good red wine, which must just cover the fish; season with salt, peppercorns, and add an onion and a carrot cut up; some twigs of parsley; a bayleaf; some sprigs of thyme. When sufficiently cooked, dress the fish on an oval serving dish and surround it with the following garnishings: *Quenelles* of fish stuffing; mushroom heads; carps' soft roes, seasoned, floured and *sautées* in butter; truffles cut up in quarters; *écrevisses* and *croutons* fried in butter. The sauce to serve with it is a *Génevoise*.

Darne de Saumon Daumont
This is the same as the *Darne Chambord*, except that white wine is used instead of red and a *Sauce Normande* instead of a *Sauce Génevoise*.

Darne de Saumon Régence
This is practically the same as the *Darne Daumont* with some *petits pâtés aux huîtres* added to the garnishings.

Darne de Saumon Royale
This is practically the same as the *Darne Daumont*, without the *écrevisses* and soft roes and served with *Pommes de terre à l'anglaise*.

(The above seven recipes are from Escoffier's *Ma Cuisine*.)

Salmon Cutlets
Cut about 1½ lb. of the middle cut of a large salmon into four cutlets, place in a fairly deep dish and cover with a cupful of good olive oil, add a tablespoonful of chopped parsley and one of chopped chives. Let the cutlets lie in the oil for two hours and turn several times. Broil them over a slow but clear fire about half an hour or a little longer, according to the thickness of the cutlets. Serve with horseradish sauce.

For the sauce, four tablespoonfuls of grated horseradish root, one and a half tablespoonfuls of vinegar, half teaspoonful of salt, a dash of cayenne pepper. Beat half cupful of good cream very stiffly and add the other four ingredients after mixing them together. (Mrs Turner's *Fifty Ways of Cooking Fish*.)

Salmon Fillets with Cucumber (Cold)
Take four slices of fillets of salmon from near the tail end; they should weigh just over 1 lb. Remove the skin, season with pepper and salt and a squeeze of lemon juice on each slice, put in a stewpan with enough fish stock or water to cover them, and allow them to cook for quarter of an hour. When done, place on serving dish and allow to get very cold. Cut half a cucumber into thin strips in Julienne style, after it has been cooked in boiling water till tender. Mix in with the cucumber a little warm clear butter, a sprinkling of chopped tarragon and chervil and squeeze over it a few drops of lemon juice. This is placed round the salmon fillets like a wreath and then the whole dish is run

over with aspic jelly, or, if preferred, chopped aspic can be put on the top. (Mrs Turner's *Fifty Ways of Cooking Fish*.)

Pickled Salmon
(Gravlax)

Gravlax is a Swedish 'Gentleman's relish' and much appreciated by Scandinavian gourmets. It may, or it may not, appeal to the British palate, but no harm in trying it. Here is the recipe:

> About 4 lb. salmon
> 1 oz. kitchen salt
> Pinch of saltpetre
> 2 teaspoons sugar
> ½ teaspoon coarsely pounded white peppercorns
> Small bunch fennel

92. Cut from a 7-8 pounder salmon a piece in the middle, weighing about 4 lb. Clean and scrape well, carefully removing the bone, and divide into two equal pieces. Wipe with cloth wrung out in cold water. Sprinkle with a mixture of sugar and finely-pounded salt and saltpetre, rubbing it in lightly. Pepper and a few sprigs of fennel might be added, but are not necessary. Put the two pieces together, with the thick part of one against the thin part of the other. Press lightly between two boards overnight.

Cut in fairly thick slices and arrange on a dish. Garnish with the skin, either grilled or fried, and sprigs of fennel. Serve with oil and vinegar, sugar, French mustard, salt and pepper.

The salmon could also be cut in thin slices and grilled. (I.Norberg's *Good Food from Sweden*.)

BLUE-BLACK or RED SALMON
Lat. *Oncorhynchus nerka*. A species of salmon living upon the northern Pacific coast, similar to the *Quinnat Salmon* (q.v.). There is a spiny finned fish called King Salmon in Australia and New Zealand, but it has nothing in common with the real Salmon and is but poor fare: its Latin name is *Arripis trutta*.

DOG-SALMON
Lat. *Oncorhynchus keta*. A species of salmon abundant in the streams of the Pacific Coast from the Sacramento northward; also found on the Asiatic side of the Pacific.

ROCK SALMON
Lat. *Pollachius virens*. It is not salmon at all: it is the name given by courtesy to the *Coalfish* (q.v.) or *Black Pollack*, known in Ireland as *Glassin*; it is also the name given to the *Amberfish* in the U.S.A.

SALMON TROUT
Lat. *Salmo trutta*; Fr. *Truite saumonée*. The European sea-trout, which is in season from March to August only; also the Dolly Varden trout of Alaska; and the young *Arripis trutti*, in Australia. For recipes see *Trout*.

SARDINE
Lat. *Sardinia pilchardus*; Fr. *Sardines*; Ger. *Sardellen*; It. *Sardelle*; Sp. *Sardinas*. The young of the *Pilchard* (q.v.). It is never found except off the coasts of Europe. In U.S.A. they catch small fishes which are called *Sardines*, such as the young of herrings, anchovies and others, but they are not the true *Sardinia pilchardus*.

Fresh sardines just grilled are delicious. Sardines in tins vary in goodness according to the quality of the olive oil used and the time allowed for the sardines to mature in oil.

SAUREL
Lat. *Trachurus trachurus* and *T. symmetricus*. Closely allied species of elongated sea-fishes, the first inhabiting the European and Northern American wastes of the Atlantic is known as the *Horse Mackerel*; the second is never caught but on the northern coasts of the Pacific.

SAURY
Scombresox saurus. A species of *Bluefish* (q.v.).

SCABBARD FISH
Any large compressed, silver-coloured fish of the genus *Lepidopus*, especially the widely distributed *Lepidopus caudatus*. It is not valued as a fish food in Europe nor in America, but in New Zealand, where it is also called *Frostfish*, it is considered of real gastronomic merit.

SCAD
Another name for *Horse Mackerel* (q.v.).

SCALLOPS. SCOLLOPS
Lat. *Pecten maximus*; Fr. *Coquilles St. Jacques*, *Pétoncle* or *Pélerine*. Any of the numerous sea bivalve molluscs of the family *Pectinidae* characterized by having the shell radially ribbed and the edge undulated. *Scallops* or *Scollops* are in season from October to March and at their best in January and February, when the roe, commonly called the foot, is full and of a bright orange colour.

Select those with shells firmly closed and pick out the heaviest ones available. To open, place on top of the stove, when the shells will soon open by themselves. Remove black part and gristly fibre, leaving intact the red 'coral', which is a great delicacy. American scallops are of two kinds, the smaller inwater *Bay Scallop* and the large offshore *Sea Scallop*. Be sure to keep the shells which, after a good scrubbing and boiling, may be used again and again for heating left-overs of fish, etc.

To Broyl Scollops
'First boyle the Scollops and then take them out of the shells, wash them, then slice them and season them with nutmeg, ginger and cinnamon, and put them into the bottom of your Shells again, with a little butter, white wine and vinegar, and grated bread, let them be broyled on both sides; if they are sharp, they must have sugar added to them, for this fish is luscious and sweet naturally. There is, therefore, another proper way to broyl them, with Oyster liquor and gravy, with dissolved Anchovies, minced onyons and tyme, with the juice of a lemon in it.'

One of the dishes served at the table of Elizabeth, commonly called 'Joan Cromwel', the wife of the late Usurper.

Baked Scallops
Open shells as indicated, removing beards and black parts. Take scallops completely out of shell to clean, scrub shell and line bottom with a layer of fresh breadcrumbs mixed with a little chopped parsley, shallot, salt and pepper. Place scallop on top of this and cover with another good sprinkling of the breadcrumbs, etc. Moisten well with melted butter and lemon juice. Bake in a moderately hot oven for about 20 to 30 minutes according to size of fish. Serve in shells. If wished, a few peeled and coarsely-chopped mushrooms, previously *sautés* in a little butter, then mixed with breadcrumbs, shallot, etc., may be added. In all cases, the coral, whole or diced, is used as decoration.

Scallops with Shrimps
Open scallops and clean as indicated. Cut the white portions into cubes after boiling for a few minutes in salted water. Toss chopped mushrooms in butter, add pieces of boiled scallop and the tail portions of large brown shrimps. Season well, sprinkle with breadcrumbs, dot with butter and bake as above. A little grated cheese may be sprinkled on top, with breadcrumbs.

Fried Scallops and Bacon
Open and clean scallops. Separate coral from white portion. Wash and dry in a cloth. Dip first in beaten egg then again in breadcrumbs. Fry crisp and brown in deep fat at 375° F., or when fat is smoking. Serve with crisp rashers of fried bacon and tartare sauce, the latter being as cold as the scallops are hot.

The most popular French recipes for *Coquilles St. Jacques* are:

Au Gratin. Braised in white wine; mushrooms; *Sauce Gratin;* breadcrumbs; and *gratiné* in oven or under *Salamandre.*

Mornay. Same as above, but with *Sauce Mornay.*

Nantaise. Same as *au Gratin,* but with poached and bearded oysters and mussels added.

Ostendaise. Shrimps, oysters, truffles, and *Sauce Nantua.*

Parisienne. Pommes Duchesse and chopped truffles.

SCAMPI
Italian giant *Prawns* closely allied to the *Dublin Bay Prawn* (q.v.).

SCHELLY. SKELLY
The schelly, which is found only in Ullswater, Haweswater, and the Red Tarn (near Helvellyn), is one of the white fishes of the genus *coregonus.* As *C. stigmaicus* it has been considered a distinct species, but modern opinion tends to regard it as a subspecies of the powan, of Loch Lomond, *C clupeoides.* Another subspecies is *C. pennantii,* the gwyniad of Lake Bala; and the pollan, found in Ireland, is, though a distinct species, also closely related. Similar forms occur in the lakes of Scandinavia and Central Europe. All these fish are among the poorest members of the salmon and trout family, gastronomically speaking; the flesh being dry and insipid.

SCUP
Lat. *Stenotomus versicolor.* Also called *Porgy.* A common 'pan fish' found along the northern coasts of the Atlantic. An allied species which inhabits southern Atlantic waters is known as *Stenotomus chrysops;* syn. *Aculeatus.*

SEA-BEEF
The name given in the Western Isles of Scotland to the flesh of young whales.

SEA-CUCKOO
Sailors' name for the *Red Gurnard* (q.v.).

SEA-DEVIL
Sailors' name for the *Angler* (q.v.).

SEA-EAGLE
Sailors' name for a large *Ray* (q.v.), called *Manta* by the Spaniards.

SEA-EEL
See *Conger Eel.*

SEA-EGGS
See *Sea-urchin.*

SEA-HEN
Sailors' name for the *Crooner* (q.v.).

SEA-OWL
Sailors' name for the *Lumpfish* (q.v.).

SEA-ROBIN
An American name for several species of *Gurnards*.

SEA-SLUG
Any naked marine gastropod of the *Holothuria* family, of the *Echinodermata* genus.

SEA-SWINE
See *Porpoise*.

SEA-URCHIN
Lat. *Echinus esculentus*; Fr. *Oursins*. Any edible specimen of *Echinus*.

SEAWIFE
Lat. *Labrus vetula*. A *wrasse* (q.v.) found on the European coasts of the Atlantic.

SEIRFISH
Lat. *Cybium commersonii*. A fish from 1½ to 2½ ft. long, found in the Indian Sea and also off the coasts of Zanzibar. It is known as *Chambam* in the Malay Straits.

SHAD
Lat. *Alosa sapidissima*; Fr. *Alose*; Ger. *Alsen*. Any of several herring-like fishes of the genus *Alosa*, including the *Twaite Shad* (Lat. *Alosa finta*) and *Allis* or *Allice Shad* (Lat. *Alosa alosa*), but differing from the true herring in having a much deeper body. It is one of the finest white-flesh fish caught in the rivers which flow into the Atlantic, in Europe and, to a far greater extent, along the Atlantic coasts of the U.S.A. Introduced on the Pacific coast, it is now abundant there. The *Shad* migrates from the sea to the rivers, like Salmon, and it is caught during the winter months only.

Baked Shad
Clean and bone a *Shad* weighing from 4 lb. to 5 lb. Season with salt and pepper and spread with creamed butter. Butter a Pyrex platter and heat thoroughly, then place on the platter and bake in a moderate oven about 25 minutes. Around edge of platter pipe well-beaten and seasoned mashed potatoes and fill in space between potatoes and fish with cucumber boats filled with creamed peas. Run under flame to brown potatoes slightly and to heat all thoroughly. Serve a savoury sauce from a gravy boat. (*The Complete Menu Book*. By Gladys T. Lang. Houghton Mifflin Company, Boston, Mass. 1939).

Fried Shad Roe
Boil the *Shad's* roe for 20 minutes in salted water with a little vinegar in it. Drain and plunge in cold water. Drain again, season with pepper and salt, dip in flour and fry in very hot deep fat until nicely brown, but not dark. Serve with crisp, fried bacon.

The more popular ways of serving *Alose* in France are as follows:

Bercy. Baked and served with a *Sauce Bercy*.

Farcie. Stuffed with a fish stuffing and cooked in oiled paper bag in oven from 30 to 40 minutes. Served with *Sauce Bercy*.

Gratin. Baked in oven from 30 to 40 minutes, with *Duxelles*, breadcrumbs, a glass of white wine, and plenty of fresh butter.

Grillée. Marinaded in oil, lemon juice, parsley, thyme and bayleaves overnight. Grilled and served with *Beurre d'Anchois*, *Maître d'Hôtel*, or *Béarnaise Sauces*.

Hollandaise. Cooked in salt water and vinegar, and served with plain boiled potatoes and a *Sauce Hollandaise*.

Oseille. Breadcrumbed, grilled and profusely basted with fresh butter during the grilling. Lemon juice, before serving, and serve with a *Purée d Oseille* (mashed Sorrel).

SHEEPSHEAD
Lat. *Diplodus probatocephalus*. A greatly valued food fish, found off the Atlantic coasts of the U.S.A. Its body is thick and chumpy, its flesh white and flaky, and it weighs from 8 lb. to 10 lb. In Maine, they call *Sheepshead Fish* the *Dollar Fish* (q.v.).

SHILBAYA
Lat. *Schilbe mystus*. A small fish, which is one of the best of the Nile.

SHINER
Any of the small, silvery fresh-water fishes of the *Cyprinidae* family of the Mississippi Valley and Great Lakes region.

SHRIMPS
Lat. *Crangon vulgaris*; Fr. *Crevettes grises*; Ger. *Krabben*; Ital. *Squille*; Sp. *Camarones*. Largely used for garnish in fish dishes – *Normande*, *Dieppoise* and others. Excellent as *Buttered Shrimps* and *Shrimp salad*.

Potted Shrimps
Melt a ¼ lb. of butter in a saucepan, and into it put a pounded blade of mace, as much cayenne pepper as you fancy, a little grated nutmeg and a pint of shelled shrimps. Heat them through gently and thoroughly, until they are impregnated with the buttery spices, but on no account let them boil, or they may toughen. When they are ready, pour them, butter and all, into small pots and seal them down with clarified butter.

Care should be taken to select fresh shrimps of good quality.

The method here recommended can also be applied to prawns, lobster and crawfish. (Ambrose Heath in *Wine and Food* No. 4, Winter No. 1934.)

Shrimps au Gratin

Heat three-quarters of a pint of white sauce and add a tablespoonful of Yorkshire relish or Worcestershire sauce, half a teaspoonful of finely chopped onion, a pinch of cayenne pepper, a pinch of celery salt, and half a pint of picked shrimps, but take out the four biggest to use later. Stir well over the fire for a few minutes and then turn into four buttered ramekins or a small soufflé dish. Sprinkle with buttered crumbs and bake for 15 minutes in a hot oven. Decorate with one whole shrimp in centre of each ramekin, or all four in the centre of the soufflé dish, and make a border of finely-chopped parsley. To make buttered crumbs, melt 1 oz. of butter in a pan and stir in the crumbs until coated with fat. (Mrs Turner's *Fifty Ways of Cooking Fish*.)

SILLOCKS

The fry of the *Saithe* or *Coalfish*, a fish of the Cod family. Clean the fish, wash in salt water and hang them up in bunches outside. Leave them until they become quite hard. They are eaten, in Scotland, uncooked and are very popular with the school-bairns of Ultima Thule, as a relish with their midday 'piece' of oat-cake or bere bannock.

SILVERFISH

The name given in Jamaica to the *Anchovy* of the West Indies (*Engraulis edentatus*).

SILVERSIDES

The name given in the U.S.A. to fishes of the *Atherinidae* family, related to the *Grey Mullet* (q.v.), having a silvery stripe along each side of the body; also to the *Silver Salmon* and to some small cyprinoid freshwater minnows.

SKATE

Lat. *Raja laevis* and *Raja batis*; Fr. *Raie*; Ger. *Meer-Rochen*. There are quite a number of different sorts of *Skates*. Skate is a coarse fish and it gains by being eaten not as fresh as possible. In cold weather, it is better to give skate a couple of days in which to get tender. Skate is best from October to April. The most popular way to serve skate is *au beurre noir*. The two most abundant of the many large *Rays* of the genus *Raja* are, in European waters, the *Raja batis*, and in American waters of the Atlantic, the *Raja laevis*. The allied species of the Pacific is the R. *binoculata*; also the *Thornback* (q.v.). There is also a small species of skate upon the Eastern coasts of the U.S.A., the R. *erinacea*.

In England, this fish is always sold cut into pieces or 'crimped'. In France, where it is often quite small, it is sold on the markets whole or cut into pieces of different size. In the States, it is undervalued because there is little knowledge of its nutritive value or its many culinary uses.

When buying, select a thick piece, as near the middle of the fish as possible. Steep in cold water, to which rock salt has been added, for an hour or so. If desired it may be boned, by removing the skin on both sides and cutting the flesh from bone with a very sharp knife. This will give long fillets which should be cut in two, making individual portions.

'Having cut the meat clean from the bone, fins, etc., make it very clean. Then cut it into thin pieces, about an inch broad, and two inches long, and lay them in your stew-pan. To one pound of the flesh put a quarter of a pint of water, a little beaten mace, and grated nutmeg, a small bundle of sweet herbs and a little salt. Cover it and let it boil fifteen minutes. Take out the sweet herbs, put in a quarter of a pint of good cream, a piece of butter, the size of a walnut, rolled in flour, and a glass of white wine. Keep shaking the pan all the time one way, till it be thick and smooth; then dish it up, and garnish with lemon. (The London Art of Cookery, John Farley, 1787.)

This fish used to be esteemed, when eaten cold with mustard and vinegar, quite a grand regale by those sober citizens of Edinburgh who repaired on holidays to the fishing hamlets round the city. It is thought to eat like lobster – by persons of lively imagination.' (From Meg Dods' *Cook and Housewife's Manual*, 1838.)

'Skate needs to mortify to be tender, and the transport from sea to Paris adds to its quality. As a matter of fact it is the only fish that can be kept for two or three days, even in thundery weather.' (Alexandre Dumas.)

Raie au Beurre Noir

Court-Bouillon
1 lb. skate
Butter
Wine vinegar
Chopped parsley and capers
Salt and pepper

Prepare the *court-bouillon* in advance, as previously suggested. Gently cook the fish in this, allowing about 15 minutes per lb. When done, remove carefully and keep hot. Brown some butter until almost, but not quite, black. Remove pan from fire and pour in a tablespoonful of good wine vinegar, taking care of the spluttering. Pour this over the fish, sprinkle with the parsley and whole or chopped capers.

Skate with Cream Sauce

Cook in *court-bouillon*, drain well and serve with boiled potatoes and a rich cream sauce to which chopped parsley, chives and a hard-boiled egg have been added, as well as lemon juice to taste.

Fried Skate

Cook gently in *court-bouillon* until done but not too soft. For this purpose, it is advisable to bone and fillet the skate. Roll and tie each half fillet around a small piece of the liver, dip in breadcrumbs, beaten egg and again in breadcrumbs, or dip in frying batter, if preferred; then fry as usual.

Skate Liver

Whenever possible, secure part of the liver, which is a delicacy. Boil with fish, then pound with butter, lemon juice, salt, pepper, and a tiny pinch of mixed spice. Serve this with the boiled skate.

SLIP SOLE

The name of small *Soles* (q.v.) weighing about 6 oz. each.

SMELT

Lat. *Osmerus eperlanus*. In Scots, *Sperling* or *Sparling*; Fr. *Éperlan*; Ger. *Stinte*; Sp. *Esperlán*. Smelts are in season from September to April. Best fried and served very hot with fried parsley. Smelts live along the coasts and ascend the rivers to spawn, or are land-locked in lakes.

This is a very delicate small fish which requires careful cleaning. Pull out gills, which will also remove entrails. Wipe and dry gently but do not wash.

How to Stew Smelts

Put your smelts into a deep dish with white wine and water, a little Rosemary and Tyme, a piece of fresh Butter, and some large Mace, and salt, let them stew half an hour, then take a handful of parsley and boil it, then beat it with the back of a knife, then take the yolks of three or four eggs, and beat them with some of your fish broth, then dish up your fish upon sippets, pour on your sauce, scrape on sugar, and serve it. (*A True Gentlewoman's Delight*, Elizabeth Grey, 1682.)

Fried Smelts

Any recipe for frying fish may be used except that they should be rolled in flour, not breadcrumbs, first, then in egg, and finally in breadcrumbs. Serve with a good shrimp sauce.

Smelts in Savory Jelly

Having gutted and washed your smelts, season them with mace and salt, and lay them in a pot with butter over them. Tie them down with paper and bake them half an hour. Take them out, and when they be a little cool, lay them separately on a board to drain. When they be quite cold, lay them in a deep plate in what form you please, pour cold jelly over them, and they will look like live fish. (*The London Art of Cookery*, John Farley, 1787.)

Baked Stuffed Smelts

6 smelts
3 or 4 mushrooms
5 or 6 oysters
½ teaspoon chopped parsley
A small onion
Salt and pepper
1 tablespoon thick cream
Lemon juice
Buttered crumbs
1 tablespoon butter

Clean and wipe fish dry. Peel and *sauté* the mushrooms. Parboil, then drain and chop oysters. Mix together finely chopped parsley, onion, salt, pepper, chopped mushrooms, oyster and cream. Use this mixture to stuff smelts. Lay them in an oven dish, sprinkle with salt and pepper and brush over with lemon juice. Cover with a buttered paper and bake for five minutes in a hot oven, then remove paper and sprinkle with buttered breadcrumbs and continue baking until these are brown and fish is done. Serve with a good Béarnaise Sauce.

Skewered Smelts

Clean smelts, remove heads and tails. Cut each fish into ½ in. slices, crossways. Cut thin rashers of bacon into pieces of equal size. Skewer fish and bacon alternately, brush over with either olive oil or oiled butter, salt and pepper. Roll in crumbs and grill, turning frequently or, if preferred, fry in deep fat.

The more popular ways of serving *Éperlans* in France are as follows:

A l'Anglaise. Slit the back. Remove main bone. Roll in breadcrumbs. Cook in clarified butter, serving with *Maître d'Hôtel* in the slit.

Buisson. Fried; served with lemon and parsley.

Brochette. Floured and fried and served with skewer through the heads; garnished with lemon and fried parsley.

Colbert. Same as *A l'Anglaise*, but a *Sauce Colbert* in place of *Maître d'Hôtel*.

Gratin. Same as *Merlans au Gratin*.

Grillés. Split the back; remove bone; dip in melted butter and flour. Grill. Serve with lemon and parsley and any fish sauce to taste.

Meunière. Same as *Mullet Meunière*.

Orly. Fried whole and served with a tomato sauce.

Plat. Same as *Sole sur le Plat* (q.v.).

Richelieu. Same as *A l'Anglaise*, but some slices of truffles added to the *Maître d'Hôtel*.

Pickled Smelts

When smelts be in great plenty, take a quarter of a peck of them, and wash, clean and gut them. Take half an ounce of pepper, the same quantity of nutmegs, a quarter of an ounce of mace, half an ounce of saltpetre, and a quarter of a pound of common salt. Beat all very fine, and then lay your smelts in rows in a jar. Between every layer of smelts strew the seasoning, with four or five bay-leaves. Then boil red wine, and pour over them in sufficient quantity to cover them. Cover them with a plate, and when cold, stop them down close. Many people prefer them to anchovies. (Mrs Lucas's *A Pretty Kettle of Fish.*)

SMOLT

A salmon about two years old when it first descends to the sea; i.e. between the *Parr* (q.v.) and *Grilse* (q.v.) stages. There was a time when smolts were caught freely, and in the whole range of fish cuisine there was nothing more delicious than a dish of smolts fried in butter. This delicacy is, however, a thing of the past, as taking, or possessing, smolts is illegal in the British Isles. Smolts vary in size from 4 in. to a maximum of 8 in.

SNAILS

Lat. *Helix pomatia*; Fr. *Escargots*; Ger. *Schnecken*; Ital. *Lumache*; Sp. *Limazas*. See *Escargots*.

SNAPPER

The name given in England to different members of the *Mesoprion* genus, some of them being highly valued in the West Indies. The name is given in the U.S.A. to many different members of the *Lutianidae* genus of carnivorous marine fishes. Also the name of an important food fish of the Australian and New Zealand coasts, the *Pagrosomus auratus.*

SNOEK. SNOOK

Another name of the *Barracouta* (q.v.).

SOLE

Lat. *Solea solea*; Fr. *Sole*; Ger. *Seezungen*; Sp. *Lenguado*. The European flatfish, the most universally praised by gastronomes. The *Sole* keeps relatively well and is on that account the best sea-fish away from the sea. What are called *Soles* in America are flat-fishes belonging to the genera *Achirus* and *Symphurus*, on the East Coast, and the *Eopsetta jordani* and *Psettichthys malanostictus* on the Pacific (American) coasts.

The *Dover Sole* is a name given by fish retailers and in restaurants to the real *Sole* to distinguish it from the inferior flatfishes, to which they give, quite erroneously, the name of sole, such as the *Lemon Sole* (q.v.), the *Torbay Sole* (q.v.), the *Witch* (q.v.) and the *Megrim* (q.v.).

The fish must look shiny and be firm to the touch. Select those without roes as their flavour is more delicate.

Fried Sole

Remove, or have removed, the dark skin. Clean, wash in salted water and wipe dry. Sprinkle with salt, pepper and lemon juice, then dredge evenly with flour. Brush over or dip into beaten egg, then dip in finely sieved white breadcrumbs. Fry in deep boiling pure oil or clarified fat. Drain well and serve with lemons and fried parsley.

To Fry Soals

Flea them and drudge them with Flour, and get a Pan almost full of clarified Butter, or good Dripping of Beef, when it is boiling hot, put in the Soals and fry them a good Brown on both Sides; drain them very well from the Fat, put crisped Parsley and slices of Orange over them. (*A New and Easy Method of Cookery*. Elizabeth Cleland, 1759.)

Grilled Sole

Trim the fish and wipe well with damp clean cloth. Rub the entire surface over with salt and a little freshly ground pepper and brush all over, on both sides, with liquified butter. Grill over a clear charcoal fire, if possible; if not, under a gas-griller after pre-heating and buttering the grid. Turn carefully to brown both sides. Serve with lemon and parsley, after dusting again with a little salt and pepper when serving.

Filet de Sole Bercy

On the bottom of a flat fire-proof dish, of such size that the fillets just cover it, sprinkle chopped shallot. Lay the fillets on this and pour over them white wine and fish stock, just not enough to submerge them. Season with salt and pepper and chopped parsley, and put several small lumps of butter on each fillet. Cover with a piece of paper and cook in a hot oven. When half cooked, remove the paper and baste with the sauce in the dish. Just before serving, pour on a little melted butter and a squeeze of lemon juice and finish under the grill or a salamander. (Sir Francis Colchester-Wemyss' *The Pleasures of the Table.*)

Sole Bonne Femme

Cook together in butter some minced mushrooms, a chopped shallot, and some parsley, salt, pepper and lemon juice. Cook a sole

375

slowly in white wine and an equal quantity of velouté made with fish stock in a small braising pan or a casserole. When cooked, remove the fish and keep hot, reduce the sauce somewhat, add some butter and the yolk of an egg or two; mix in the mushrooms, etc. Arrange the sauce over the fish and put under the grill or into a hot oven for three or four minutes before serving. (Sir Francis Colchester-Wemyss' *The Pleasures of the Table*.)

Fillets of Sole Carmen Sylva

1 firm cucumber
1 glassful white wine
1 lb. firm red tomatoes
Salt and cayenne
2 tablespoons butter
1 tablespoon flour
Fillets of sole
½ cup thick cream

Peel the cucumber and cut into slices. Put the wine in a pan, add the cucumber and the peeled and cut up tomatoes, seasoning to taste with salt and cayenne. Cook until the cucumber and tomatoes are done enough to press through a sieve. Heat the butter, add the flour and moisten the mixture, stirring all the while, with the cucumber and tomato purée. Poach the fillets of sole in this sauce and, just before serving, add the cream, boiling up just once, then serving.

Soles au Chablis

For four persons take four soles weighing about 7 oz. each; wash and trim them, and break the backbone of each in the middle so that they will lie flat. Butter a large fireproof dish, and put into it four thin rounds of onion. On these lay the soles, placing them so that they will not touch each other. Add half a glass of Chablis or dry white Burgundy, the liquid from a handful of mussels (which have been opened in a little hot white wine) and enough water just to cover the fish. Cover with greased paper and cook for about 15 minutes in the oven.

The Sauce. Strain off the liquid from the soles and placing them where they will keep hot, reduce it to half its original volume. Thicken with a little flour and butter. Take the sauce off the fire after it has cooked for eight minutes and add the yolks of two eggs diluted with a few drops of water. Beat well till thoroughly mixed. Put the sauce back on to a strong flame and let it come just to the boil, stirring all the time. Add the juice of half a lemon, and 3 oz. of butter, a little at a time. Stir vigorously, without letting the mixture come to the boil, until it has thickened.

Put the soles in a fireproof dish, cover them with sauce. Set the dish in another

containing hot water and brown in a very hot oven. Serve at once. (Ch. Bergerand, Hôtel de l'Etoile, Chablis.)

Fillets of Sole Cooked in Cider

Put a teaspoonful of very finely chopped shallot in a fireproof dish with a wineglass of cider, adding pepper and salt. Then lay in the fillets of sole. Cover and cook in the oven for about 15 minutes. Pour off the liquid into a small saucepan. (Keep the fish hot over boiling water.) Thicken with roux. Cook gently for eight minutes, stirring all the time. After having carefully seasoned the sauce add a little more butter in small pieces, whip it in and serve with or over the fish. Cider is used often in Normandy instead of white wine and is more delicate than vinegar.

The fish may be finished in the oven after it is covered with the sauce. Sprinkle with very fine breadcrumbs and tiny pieces of butter and brown. (Mrs Lucas's *A Pretty Kettle of Fish*.)

Sole Colbert

Cut off the head and remove the black skin. Detach fillets from the bone with the point of a sharp knife and break up the bone in two or three places so that it may be removed more easily when the sole has been cooked. Dip the sole in milk, then in a very little flour. Shake it well. Then dip it in egg and breadcrumbs and fry in very hot fat from 10 to 12 minutes.

Lay it on a cloth just inside the oven so that any excess of fat will drain off. Remove the whole of the backbone and put *Maître d'Hôtel* butter in the opening. Serve at once

Sole aux Crevettes

1 large sole
1 glass white wine
½ lb. large brown shrimps
Flour
Butter
Thick white sauce
Breadcrumbs
Lemon juice to taste
Salt and pepper

Remove skin and head of sole; cook it gently in the wine with the heads and shells of the shrimps which have previously been pounded thoroughly. When this mixture has simmered for about 20 minutes, strain through fine sieve and use to moisten the flour and butter to make a white sauce instead of milk. Place the whole in a buttered dish, cover with sauce, sprinkle with shrimp tails, breadcrumbs, salt, pepper and lemon juice, and bake for 25 to 30 minutes, according to size of sole. Serve in dish.

Note.—Be sparing with the breadcrumbs and generous with butter.

Fillets of Sole Florentine

Cook fillets of sole in butter; season with pepper and salt and a squeeze of lemon.

Line a fireproof dish with leaf spinach boiled, drained and tossed in butter. Place the fillets of sole on it, cover with a white or Mornay sauce and brown in the oven.

Fillets of Sole au Gratin
(A Danish way)

Take two soles, weighing about a pound each. Have them filleted and skinned on both sides. If the fillets are rather large, divide them. Roll them up and tie them securely.

With their bones make a fish stock and in this cook the fillets.

Wash a good pound of spinach thoroughly. If the leaves are large tear them into small pieces, but do not chop them. Cook it, drain it, and press out all moisture. Line the bottom of a fireproof dish with it, and over it pour a little seasoned melted butter. Then, having untied the little rolled fillets, arrange them on the spinach.

Make a white sauce of milk, roux, a little of the fish stock and grated cheese. Finish this sauce with a gill of thick cream. Cover the fish with it, sprinkle with grated cheese and bake for from 15 to 20 minutes in a quick oven. (Madame Lennard Grut.)

Sole Meunière

Heat some butter in a frying-pan; season the fish with salt and pepper—black for choice —and dust with flour. When the butter is just boiling, put the fish into it, turn it after 20 or 30 seconds, and once more when the original top side is sufficiently cooked.

When both sides are cooked (when a skewer goes right through fairly easily) put the sole on a hot dish, squeeze some lemon juice over it, dust with a little pepper and salt, and finally pour some hot melted butter over it immediately before serving. (Sir Francis Colchester-Wemyss' *The Pleasures of the Table.*)

Sole Mornay

Cook some fillets of sole in a covered pan with a little fish stock and butter; when cooked, remove the fillets and keep hot; add to the stock a little *Béchamel* sauce made with a small quantity of Parmesan, or equal parts of Parmesan and grated Cheshire or scraped Gruyère, and season. Cook together for three or four minutes, then pour about a quarter of the sauce into a very hot dish of such a size that the fillets nearly cover its bottom, and lay in the fillets $\frac{1}{2}$ in. apart to facilitate helping.

Cover with the rest of the sauce. Dust a little Parmesan over the surface and brown

under the grill or in a very hot oven. (Sir Francis Colchester-Wemyss' *The Pleasure of the Table.*)

Sole Normande

1 large sole
1 pint fresh mussels
12 oysters
$\frac{1}{2}$ pint shrimps
White wine
Salt and pepper
Butter
$\frac{1}{2}$ lb. mushrooms
Flour
$\frac{1}{2}$ cup thick cream
1 shallot

Have the sole filleted. Open the mussels over the fire and set liquor aside, removing mussels. Open the oysters, carefully straining their liquor and setting that, too, aside. Peel some fine shrimps, setting aside the shells and heads. Place about one cupful of white wine with the same amount of water in a small saucepan. Add to this the head and bones of the sole, the heads and shells of the shrimps, the liquor from mussels and oysters, salt, pepper, the shallot and the butter in which the sliced mushrooms have been gently cooked. Cook all this slowly for half an hour, then strain through muslin. Re-heat and use to poach the fillets of sole until done – which will take about 10 to 12 minutes' gentle cooking. Remove fillets and lay them in a buttered baking dish, longways. Mix a couple of ounces of flour with the same amount of heated butter, as when making an ordinary white sauce, moisten with the strained extract of fish and cook for five minutes gently, then add cream and see that the seasoning is as it should be. Pour this over the fillets of sole, decorating with mushrooms, shrimps, mussels and oysters, nicely arranged to form a border. Pass under the flame of a gas griller or in a Dutch oven to colour surface slightly, and serve in cooking dish. This is the Sole *par excellence.*

Sole Plougrescant

Potatoes
Salt and pepper
1 large filleted sole
White wine
Water
Fines herbes
Breadcrumbs
Butter

Firm potatoes must be used so that they may be sliced *very* thin indeed. Butter a shallow earthenware dish generously. On the bottom put a layer of thinly-sliced raw potatoes. Sprinkle with salt and pepper. Lay the fillets of sole on this and cover them with another layer of sliced potatoes. Mix half a glassful of white wine with a glassful of warm water. Pour over the dish, season. Add chopped parsley, chives and chervil, sprinkle with breadcrumbs, dot with butter and bake for about half an hour in a rather hot oven.

Filets de Sole Orly

1 large sole, filleted
2½ oz. flour
2 eggs
Breadcrumbs
Salt and pepper
Quarters of lemon

Roll up each fillet neatly and secure with a wooden toothpick or, if preferred, a little thread. Roll each fillet thus prepared first in flour, then in beaten eggs, then in fine brown breadcrumbs. Fry in deep boiling oil or fat. Sprinkle when brown with salt and pepper and serve garnished with quarters of lemon and sprigs of fried parsley. Ice-cold mayonnaise or sauce piquante may be served with this dish, but the correct accompaniment to any *Orly* dish is a *Sauce Tomates*.

Sole St Germain

Fillets of Dover sole
Fine brown breadcrumbs
Melted butter
Salt and pepper

Flatten each fillet evenly. Dip first in melted butter, then in breadcrumbs. Grill on both sides, seasoning with salt and pepper, and serve very hot with a *Béarnaise* sauce.

Sole à la Villette

Cut several fillets of sole into small pieces, dip them in milk, drain them well, season them and dip them in flour. Brown these in a wide pan in very hot butter.

Have ready the required quantity of parboiled new potatoes, diced and *sauté* in butter with blanched and diced artichoke bottoms. Season well. Serve round the fish. (Mrs Lucas's *A Pretty Kettle of Fish*.)

Sole Voisin

1 large sole, filleted
White wine
Fresh tomato sauce
Salt and pepper

Have the fish filleted, retaining head and all bones. Stew these gently for 20 minutes with salt and pepper. Strain. Make a 'short', i.e. much reduced tomato sauce. Lay the fillets of sole longways in a baking dish, cover with the well-seasoned sauce and serve after baking for about 25 minutes. Add plenty of butter and a touch of cream to the sauce.

Other Sole Recipes

Alexandra. Poached fillets of sole in white wine and fish *fumet* with mushrooms and seasonings; dressed with a sliced truffle upon each fillet and served with a Sauce *Nantua*.

Alice. A whole sole lightly poached and finished cooking at table in chafing dish with half a glass of champagne, a sprinkling of chopped onion, a few uncooked oysters and some dry biscuit crumbs.

Ambassade. Poached fillets of sole served with some lobster-butter, slices of lobster, rounds of truffle and small *croissants* of puff paste.

Ambassadrice. A poached sole served whole with a *Sauce Normande* to which poached oysters and minced mushrooms have been added.

Américaine. Poached fillets of sole served with scollops of lobster 'à l'américaine' on each fillet of sole and the 'américaine' sauce of the lobster over them.

Amiral. Whole sole poached and garnished with oysters, mussels, truffles and small mushrooms; served with a *Sauce Nantua*.

Ancienne. Whole sole poached, garnished with small onions and mushrooms and served with a fish *Velouté*.

Anglaise, à l'. Fillets of sole, breadcrumbed and cooked in butter in the oven. Served with lemon and chopped parsley.

Argenteuil. Whole sole or fillets with asparagus points as garnishings and served with a white wine sauce.

Arlésienne. A whole sole cooked in a fish *fumet* with chopped onions, tomatoes and parsley and a clove of garlic crushed. Served with a garnishing of thick dice of vegetable marrow on each side and fried rings of onion at each end of the dish.

Bagration, Aspic de Filets de Sole. Poached fillets of sole folded over, allowed to get quite cold and dressed over scollops of cold lobster around a stand of *Salade Russe*; they are garnished with slices of truffles and surrounded with some *Aspic* jelly.

Beurre Noir. A sole floured and cooked in butter; dressed upon an open dish, some *Beurre Noir* poured over it, also a little vinegar and a spoonful of capers.

Bordelaise. A sole poached in red wine with some chopped shallots. Served with a *Sauce Bordelaise*.

Bosniaque. A sole poached in a fish *fumet* and served with a white wine sauce with paprika added to it; also a *Julienne* of carrots, truffles and mushrooms.

Bourguignonne. A sole poached in red Burgundy with chopped shallots and mushrooms; served with small onions and mushrooms and its own liquor as sauce.

Caprice. Fillets of sole dipped in bread-crumbs and egg, then grilled; served with slices of banana cooked in butter and a tomato sauce.

Cardinal. A sole poached in white wine and served with a *Sauce Béchamel* to which a *Beurre de Langouste* has been added.

Carême. Fillets of sole poached, stuffed, folded in two and dressed crownwise; garnished with poached herring soft roes, slices of truffle and small mushrooms; the whole covered with a white wine sauce before serving.

Chambord. Fillets of sole poached in red wine, garnished with small onions, fish *quenelles*, small mushrooms and slices of truffle; served with a *Sauce Chambord* over it.

Chauchat. A poached sole dressed and garnished with round slices of boiled pota-toes, the whole being covered with a white wine sauce with chopped *Fines Herbes* and browned in a hot oven.

Coquelin. A sole cooked in a baking dish with a fish *fumet*, some chopped shallots, mushrooms and *Fines Herbes* and white wine. Served with a *Velouté*.

Dieppoise. Fillets of sole poached and garnished with mussels and shrimps, all being covered with a white wine sauce.

Doria. Fillets of sole floured and tossed in hot butter; served with cucumber cut up like olives and steamed; also some *Beurre Noisette* and a squeeze of lemon.

Dugléré. The sole is usually cut in three pieces and cooked in some fish *fumet* and white wine, butter, shallots, *Fines Herbes* and quarters of fresh tomatoes. Served with the liquor in which it was cooked with some fish *Velouté* added to it; also a sprinkling of chopped parsley.

Goujons, En. Fillets of sole cut up in strips, floured and fried. Served on a white napkin with fried parsley in the centre and a sauce (named and served separately).

Grand Duc. Poached fillets of sole, folded in two, dressed crownwise with slices of truffle between each fillet, covered with a *Sauce Mornay*, browned under the grill or in a hot oven, and served with asparagus points in the centre of the crown.

Grecque. Fillets of sole floured and fried in olive oil; dressed upon a foundation of rice Pilaff and with a tomato sauce, with red pimentoes added to it, all round in the dish.

Hongroise. A poached sole covered with a fish *Velouté* to which some tomato *Purée* and a dusting of paprika have been added; before serving, a little butter is added on top and the dish is left a few minutes in a hot oven.

Marguery. Fillets of sole poached and garnished with shelled shrimps and mussels, the whole being covered with a white wine sauce with *Fines Herbes*.

Marie-Louise. Poached fillets of sole, folded in two, dressed upon a foundation of mashed potatoes and covered with a white wine sauce; served with a sprinkling of finely-chopped truffles.

Minute. Fillets of sole floured, cooked in butter and served with the butter in which they were cooked.

Mirabeau. Fillets of sole cooked in *Beurre d'Anchois* and dressed with fillets of anchovies and leaves of tarragon.

Murat. Fillets of sole shredded, floured and cooked in butter with some artichoke bottoms, potatoes and truffles cut up Julienne-wise; served with a squeeze of lemon and *Beurre Noisette*.

Plat, Au. A sole cooked in the oven, in a baking dish, with some butter, fish *fumet*, mushroom purée and a squeeze of lemon, and served with the liquor in which it was cooked.

Provençale. A poached sole garnished with tomatoes and mushrooms, some shallots, garlic and parsley finely chopped and cooked in olive oil, and served with a sprinkling of capers and chopped parsley.

Véronique. Stuffed fillets of sole, rolled and poached, garnished with one muscat grape upon each fillet and muscat grapes round the dish.

Walewska. Poached fillets of sole dressed longways upon a silver dish, with scollops of lobster and rounds of truffles between each fillet, a *Sauce Mornay* over it all and quickly browned in a hot oven just before serving.

SPARLING
The Scottish name for *Smelts* (q.v.).

SPET
Lat. *Sphyraena sphyraena.* A small *Barracuda* (q.v.) of southern European waters. Also called *Sennet.*

SPOT
Lat. *Leiostomus xanthurus.* The American name of a small food fish of the Atlantic (American) coasts; also of the *Red Drum* (*Sciaenops ocellata*); also of the *Pinfish* (*Diplodus holbrooki*).

SPRAT
Lat. *Clupea sprattus*; Fr. *Sprats*; Ger. *Sprotten*; Sp. *Clupeo.* Sprats are in season from October to March, when they cost a few pence per lb., and a lb. is sufficient for four people.

The best way with *Sprats* is plainly grilled and served with a mustard sauce. Smoked *Sprats* also are delicious.

Sprats Fried in Batter
Dry the sprats thoroughly in a clean cloth. For the batter, melt 1 oz. of butter in a

tablespoonful of boiling. water and add ¼ pint of cold water. Put 4 oz. of flour in a small basin and stir in the water, a little at a time, making a very smooth paste. Beat the white of an egg to a stiff white froth, stir it into the flour and the batter is ready. Have your frying basket ready in a saucepan of boiling fat; dip the sprats carefully into the batter, and drop them into the fat, fry to a delicate golden-brown. Drain thoroughly and serve very hot with fried parsley and cut lemon, and hand thin slices of brown bread and butter. (Mrs Turner's *Fifty Ways of Cooking Fish*.)

SQUIDS

See *Calamary* and *Cuttle-fish*.

STERLET

Lat. *Acipenser ruthenus*; Russian *Sterlyad*. A small sturgeon found in the Caspian Sea and the rivers flowing thereinto. The finest caviar is from its roe. It is an excellent fish as prepared in Budapest.

STURGEON

Lat. *Acipenser sturio*; Fr. *Esturgeon*; Ger. *Stor*; It. *Storione*; Sp. *Esturion*. A shark-like 'royal' fish chiefly represented on the tables of all civilized lands by its prepared hard roe: *Caviar* (q.v.). The sturgeon is very widely distributed among the waters of the Northern Hemisphere and is caught at the spawning season in the estuaries of many rivers in Europe, Asia and America, but nowhere in such quantities as in the Caspian Sea and the Black Sea. The flesh of the sturgeon is white but hard, and it requires a good chef to make it acceptable gastronomically. It is advisable, and customary, to hang sturgeon for two or three days and then steep it in a strongly flavoured white wine marinade for twenty-four hours. It can then be treated in the same way as *Escalopes de veau, sautées* in butter or grilled.

Sturgeon is in season from August to March.

SUCKER

A name given to several species of fresh-water fishes closely related to the *Carp* (q.v.), but differing from it by having thick, soft lips. Except for two Asiatic species, they are confined to North America, where the commonest sorts are known as *Buffalo Fish* (q.v.) and *White Sucker* (*Catostomus commersoni*).

SUNFISH

The name is given to (1) a remarkably ugly marine fish found swimming lazily near the sun-baked surface of tropical and semi-tropical seas; its flesh is edible but tough; and (2) a number of American perch-like

fresh-water fishes, usually with brilliant colourings. The common fresh-water *Sunfish* (*Eupomotis gibbosus*) is but from 6 to 8 in long; it abounds in most clear streams and ponds of the northern U.S.A.

SWORDFISH

Lat. *Xiphias gladius*; Fr. *Espadon*. A large and widely distributed oceanic fish; it is valued as a food fish; it can weigh up to 600 lb.

Baked Swordfish

Choose a thick piece of swordfish weighing about 3 lb. Lay strips of salt pork in a baking pan and over them some onions cut up in thin slices; then the fish over the onions. Season with pepper and salt and cover with a paste made of equal parts of butter and flour. Sprinkle with biscuit crumbs on top with thin slices of salt pork. Cover with a buttered paper and bake in a moderate oven for about an hour. Discard paper, baste and cook about ten minutes longer, so as to brown the crumbs. Serve with *Hollandaise* sauce.

TARPON

Lat. *Tarpon atlanticus*. A noted game fish common on the coast of Florida, but of no gastronomic value.

TAUTOG

Lat. *Tautaga onitis*. A marine food fish of the *Labridae* family found on the American coasts of the North Atlantic. Also known as *Blackfish*.

TENCH

Lat. *Tinca tinca*; Fr. *Tanche*; Ger. *Schleie*; It. *Tinca*; Sp. *Tenca*. One of the small members of the large cyprinoid or carp family, inhabiting English and Continental rivers; unknown in the U.S.A. Of real gastronomic value either *au bleu* or grilled.

TERRAPIN

Lat. *Malaclemys centrata*; Fr. *Terrapine*. Any of the edible North American turtles living in fresh or brackish water, but the best of all is the *Diamondback Terrapin*, which lives in salt marshes along the Atlantic and Gulf coasts of North America. There are five sorts of *Diamondbacks*, those of Florida, of North Carolina, of Alabama and Louisiana, and of the West Coast of Florida, including Texas. Not so highly prized, gastronomically, are the *Red-bellied Terrapins* (*Pseudemys rubriventris*) of the tributaries of Chesapeake Bay; and the *Yellow-bellied Terrapin* (*Pseudemys scripta*) and allied species of some Southern States of the U.S.A. There is the same affinity between *Terrapin* and madeira as exists between Lobster and sherry.

Diamondback Terrapin

Throw *Terrapin* in water and let them be cleansed from all dirt – about an hour. Plunge into boiling water for 10 minutes, remove and take off toe-nails, rubbing off the skin from shell, head, neck and legs.

Put into fresh boiling water and cook until tender (the legs). When done, set off to cool and open the shell. Detach the meat from shell, being careful to remove the stomach and gall bladder, which are thrown away, also the lower intestines. Cut up all other parts into small pieces, allowing ½ lb. of butter to a *Terrapin*. Season with salt, cayenne pepper and ½ gill of sherry to each *Terrapin*. Only use water the *Terrapin* is last cooked in for essence. (*Maryland Recipe*, in Crosby Gaige's *New York World's Fair Cook Book*, p. 220.)

Terrapin Stew

Three large *Terrapin*; 3 pints water; salt; 1 onion; ½ lb. butter; 6 tablespoons flour; juice and rind of one lemon; half grated nutmeg; 2 cups cream; 1 cup sherry; 1 tablespoon Worcestershire; red pepper; 6 hard-cooked hen eggs.

Cut off heads of *Terrapin*, dip in boiling water for a short time and carefully pull off outer skin from feet, and all that will come off the back. With a sharp hatchet, cut open the *Terrapin* and take out the eggs, and put aside in cold water. Throw away entrails and gall bags, saving the livers, which are very much liked. Leave all the legs on the back and put on to boil. Put them into the water with salt and onion and let simmer and steam (not boil) about 45 minutes. When tender, take meat from back and remove bones. Cook meat a little more if not tender enough.

Cut up meat, across the grain to prevent stringing, and set stock aside for a few hours to jell. Rub yolks of hen eggs and butter and flour together. Put on jelly or stock to cook, and as soon as it boils add this egg mixture, also lemon and nutmeg. Then put in the *Terrapin* eggs and meat, and last of all cream, wine, Worcestershire and salt and pepper to taste, being careful not to let curdle or burn. Add chopped whites of hen eggs. Always have enough hot milk to thin out if it is too thick. (*Georgia Recipe*, in Crosby Gaige's *New York World's Fair Cook Book*, p. 71.)

THORNBACK

Lat. *Raja clavata*; Fr. *Raie*. A European *Ray* having spines on its back. All recipes suitable for *Skate* (q.v.) are also suitable for *Thornback*.

TILEFISH

Lat. *Lopholatilus chamaeleonticeps*. A large, coarse, but edible fish, caught off the East Coast of the U.S.A. in deep waters.

TOHEROA

Lat. *Amphidesma ventricosum*. A marine bivalve which lives in the 'Ninety-mile' beach in north-west New Zealand. It means, in Maori, long-tongued, and, cooked as a *Bisque* (q.v.), makes one of the most superb of all thick soups. Toheroa has been successfully canned for export.

TOMCOD

Lat. *Microgadus tomcod*. A small fish resembling the Cod, found off the Atlantic coast of the U.S.A. An allied species of the Pacific coast is called *Microgadus proximus*.

TOMTATE

Lat. *Bathystoma rimator*. A Florida and West Indian *Grunt* (q.v.).

TOPKNOT

A somewhat rare edible North Atlantic fish, of which three species are known, i.e. the *Common Topknot* (*Zeugopterus punctatus*); *Block's Topknot* (*Z. unimaculatus*); and the *Norwegian Topknot* (*Z. norwegicus*).

TOPSI-MUTCHI

The name given in Bengal to the *Mangofish* (q.v.).

TORBAY SOLE

Another name for *Lemon Sole* (q.v.).

TOTUAVA

Lat. *Eriscion macdonaldi*. A very large *Weakfish* (q.v.), reaching 150 lb. and over, found in the Gulf of California and highly prized as food fish.

TRIGGERFISH

Lat. *Balistes capriscus*, syn. *carolinensis*. A brightly-coloured small fish of the Mediterranean, fit for *Bouillabaisse*; it belongs to the genus *Balistes*, many members of which are poisonous.

TRIPLETAIL

Lat. *Lobotes surinamensis*. A large, coarse, but edible fish inhabiting the warm waters of the West Indies, but occurring also on the Atlantic coast from Brazil as far north as Cape Cod.

TROUT

Lat. *Salmo fario*; Fr. *Truite*; Ger. *Forellen*; It. *Trote*; Sp. *Trucha*. Broadly speaking, the name 'Trout' includes all those *Salmonidae* which live entirely in fresh water except *Grayling* and *Char*; and it is applied also to several of the migratory *Salmonidae*, including, in Europe, the Salmon Trout – *Salmo trutta* – (in Devonshire, *Salmon Peal*, in

Wales, *Sewin*). And in America, the Rainbow Trout (*Salmo irideus*) and others.

The common European Trout is *Salmo fario*, and others, whether or not they have special names, e.g. *Levenensis* or *Ferox* or *Great Lake Trout*, are merely varieties of *Fario*.

Sea Trout are found in all the countries, from Spain northwards, facing the Atlantic. Like salmon also, they are pink-fleshed and their life history is the same as that of salmon – they are begotten and hatched and spend their first two years in a fresh-water river, whence they go into the sea, and after an interval of a year or more, during which time they vastly increase in size, they return to their parental river to carry on the cycle of reproduction.

Rainbow Trout and similar fish, such as *Steel-heads*, may, quite unscientifically, be classed as half-way between fresh-water trout and sea trout, inasmuch as some of them go to the sea, some treat a large body of fresh water as the sea, running to it as two-year-olds, returning to the rivers to spawn and then going back to the lake to regain condition, while still others spend their whole lives in their parent river just like the *Brown Trout*.

In the Southern Hemisphere, there are no indigenous *Salmonidae* (except a rather rare *Grayling* (q.v.) in New Zealand and – *mirabile dictu* – in the small river in the Falkland Islands), but *Salmo fario* and *irideus* have been introduced and have prospered amazingly, especially in Tasmania and New Zealand, and later in Chile, where their average size is far larger than in their native waters. The American Brook Trout, so called, *Salvelinus fontinalis*, is really a *Char*, and so is the Dolly Varden Trout – *Salmo malma spectabilis*, and several similar varieties common in American rivers running into the Pacific.

For gastronomical purposes, trout may be divided into two classes – non-migratory and migratory – trout and sea trout – *truite* and *truite-saumonée*: *Char* may be included with the former.

As a rule, *Sea Trout* and the large *Trouts* should be treated and dealt with as salmon.

The smaller river or lake trouts are excellent smoked, fried, grilled, boiled and otherwise prepared in many different ways.

Fried Trout

For really small fish – say four to the pound and less – there is only one satisfactory method – having cleaned and wiped them, and dusted a trifle of pepper and salt inside them, fry them in a frying-pan, in any good fat (butter is the best) till crisp.

Larger sizes must be split open and fried, the backbone having been removed, they may be dipped in oatmeal, Scots fashion, and fried in a little butter or dripping. In either case serve hot, with either plain melted butter or a *Maître d'Hôtel Sauce*.

'*Here comes the trout that must be caught with tickling.*' (*Twelfth Night*. Act II. Sc 5.)

Grilled Trout

Suitable for fish up to 4 lb. to 5 lb. Clean the fish: open it out flat, remove the backbone, wipe it dry, and dust with pepper (not salt, which has a tendency to splutter in the eyes of the cook). Fix the fish in a folding gridiron and grill flesh to the fire, till about half cooked. Turn the grill over, baste with butter, and finish cooking skin side down, sprinkling some salt at the last moment.

With *Rainbow Trout* the butter is not necessary, as Providence has provided them with sufficient oil. The best fire for this method of cooking is a good wood fire which has ceased to blaze.

If it is necessary to grill the fish under an electric grill, the order must be reversed – finishing with the flesh to the fire: the important point is that the skin must be underneath during the second part of the cooking

River Trout

The Trout is a fish highly valued, both in this and foreign nations. It may be justly said, as the old poet said of wine, and we English say of venison, to be a generous fish: a fish that is so like the buck, that he also has his seasons; for it is observed that he comes in and goes out of season with the stag and buck. Gesner says, his name is of a German offspring: and says he is a fish that feeds clean and purely, in the swiftest streams, and on the hardest gravel: and that he may justly contend with all fresh-water fish, as the Mullet may with all sea fish, for precedency and daintiness of taste: and that being in right season, the most dainty palates have allowed precedency to him. (Izaak Walton.)

To Boil a Trout

The best way of cooking a trout is to boil it in white wine with two or three spoonfuls of good meat stock and salt. When this mixture boils throw in the trout well stuck with cloves and cinnamon and let it cook over as fierce a fire as may be. When it is half-cooked throw in some white bread crusts, as much to thicken the liquid as to prevent the fish from smelling of the pan. A little later add good herbs, such as thyme, marjoram, rosemary, summer savory, parsley and sweet spices. Finally pour butter which has been melted in a pan with a little vinegar over the fish. Boil up for a moment or two and serve all together. (*Le Thrésor de Santé*, 1607.)

Trout with Wine

Clean some fine trout. Put inside each a piece of butter which has been worked with fresh green herbs, salt and pepper. Place them in a fish-kettle and pour over them white wine – sufficient to cover the fish a thumb's breadth over – season with pepper, salt, nutmeg, two onions and two crusts of bread with two cloves stuck in each. Cook them over so fierce a flame that it will set fire to the wine. When they are cooked and the sauce reduced, add a piece of butter and stir it well in. When ready, and you are satisfied as to the seasoning, take out the fish, arrange them on a dish, and pour the sauce over them. (*Dons de Comus*, 1739.)

Hell Fire Trout

Clean and prepare a large trout. Work together butter, finely-chopped parsley, chives, a speck of garlic, mushrooms, two shallots, and basil, adding salt and coarsely ground pepper. Put the mixture inside the trout. The fish must then be placed in a pan just long enough to hold it, together with a carrot, a leek, and an onion stuck with three cloves. Pour over it a mixture of white and red wines (two-thirds white and one-third red). This should rise two thumbs deep above the trout. Cook over a very fierce flame. When the liquid is boiling fiercely, set light to it with a piece of burning paper, and cook until the wine is almost the consistency of a sauce. Take out the vegetables, add a good piece of butter to the wine, season and serve the fish very hot. (*Manuel de Friandise*, 1796.)

Truite Meunière

See recipe given for *Mullet Meunière*.

Truite au Bleu

Clean the trout but do not attempt to scale it. Place it in a dish with a little vinegar, coating on all sides, which 'blues' it. The *court-bouillon* – a vinegar one is usually used – being ready and nicely perfumed with herbs, etc., must be boiling when you put the trout in it. Let liquid just come to boiling point once after the trout has been put in and then draw saucepan to side of fire and cover closely. Allow to stand, covered, for five minutes, then remove fish carefully, draining well, and serve with parsley and either *Hollandaise* or *Ravigote* sauce.

Filets de Truite Vauclusienne

Rather large trout, filleted
White wine
Crayfish, boiled
Fresh mushrooms
1 chopped truffle
Thick Béchamel sauce
Egg yolks
Lemon juice
Salt and cayenne

1 beaten egg
Brown, fine breadcrumbs
Deep fat for frying
Butter

This is a somewhat sophisticated, entirely delicious recipe. Boil the fillets of trout in white wine, or, rather, poach them in it. When done, remove, drain and cut into rather large triangular pieces. Shell the boiled crayfish, keeping claws aside, after cracking neatly. Cut the tail portion of these miniature lobsters into small dice, mix with chopped mushrooms, the truffle and sufficient thick *Béchamel* to bind the mixture to a thick paste. The *Béchamel* should have been thickened by the addition of one or more egg yolks and flavoured with lemon juice, salt and cayenne to taste. Spread the mixture on each triangle of fish, coating evenly and pressing flat with a palette knife. Dip each piece of fish thus prepared first into beaten egg, then in breadcrumbs, allow surface to harden, then fry a golden brown in deep fat. Serve piled on one another, the corners of each triangle being ornamented with one of the tiny crayfish claws, stuck into it at right angles. An accompanying sauce may be made with the fish stock to which is added crayfish butter at the last moment.

Salmon Trout in Jelly

Clean and prepare a salmon trout the size you require, and put it in a fish-kettle with some cold water and a little salt. Bring it to the boil and keep it boiling from 15 to 20 minutes. Be sure your fish does not break. When cooked take it out very carefully and drain it well, then let it get quite cold. Lay the fish on a silver dish with some small peeled tomatoes, slices or cubes of cucumber, to which one or two gherkins are added cut into small pieces. Cover with jelly and decorate the top with thin strips of the peel from the cucumber.

For the Aspic Jelly, take 1 lb. of lean beef and cut it into dice, cover with a quart of cold water, and as soon as it boils take off the scum on the top. When it has simmered gently for half an hour, add four onions, a carrot, turnip, a bunch of herbs, and a few peppercorns. When it has boiled again for one hour, strain carefully. Let it stand till cold and remove all the fat, boil it up and add about $\frac{1}{2}$ oz. of gelatine previously soaked in cold water. When the jelly cools stir in the whites and shells of two well-beaten eggs. Let it boil briskly for two minutes, then stand for 10 minutes by the side of the fire, strain through a jelly bag and it will be quite clear. Finally add a little salt and some tarragon vinegar. (Mrs Turner's *Fifty Ways of Cooking Fish*.)

Trout Stewed in Port

Clean the trout and wash them and dry in a clean cloth. Melt 2 oz. of butter in a stewpan and dredge in one tablespoonful of flour, stir over the fire for three or four minutes until thick but smooth. Add three-quarters of a pint of good stock and a wineglassful of port, a little at a time, letting each lot boil before the next lot is added. Put in the trout and some finely-chopped parsley, and pepper and salt. Simmer for 40 minutes. Dish up on a very hot dish, straining part of the sauce over and serve the rest in a sauce-boat. (Mrs Turner's *Fifty Ways of Cooking Fish*.)

TRUITE

Fr. for *Trout* (q.v.).

TRUITE SAUMONÉE

Fr. for *Salmon Trout* (q.v.).

TUNNY (Tuna)

Lat. *Thunnus thynnus*; Fr. *Thon*; Ger. *Thunfisch*. The largest and most useful member of the *Thunnidae* or *Mackerel* family. Fresh tunny is somewhat coarse, but it lends itself admirably to tinning in oil. It is found in all warm seas, but chiefly in the Mediterranean. It grows to a length of 10 ft. and weighs 1,000 lb. On the northern Atlantic coast of America a closely allied species (*T. secundo-dorsalis*) is called *Horse Mackerel*. On the Pacific coast, another species (*T. saliens*) is chiefly valued as a game fish. The *Little Tunny* (*Gymnosarda alleterata*) of the Mediterranean and the *Long-finned Tunny* or *Albacore* (q.v.) are smaller species.

Fresh tunny fish being almost unobtainable in England, it will suffice to say that it may, after being cut up into 'steaks', be grilled or boiled in the usual way, serving with a *Maître d'Hôtel* sauce. When tinned in olive oil, it is useful for the preparation of hors-d'oeuvre and savouries.

TURBOT

Lat. *Scoputhalmus maximus*; Fr. *Turbot*, or *Turbotin*; Ger. *Steinbuthe*; Ital. *Rombo*; Sp. *Rodaballo*. A large European flatfish of considerable gastronomic value. It often weighs from 40 lb. to 50 lb. The same name is also given to some Flounders such as the *Hypsopsetta guttulata*, in California, and the *Ammotretis gunther*, in New Zealand. In the West Indies, the so-called *Turbot* caught locally are altogether different fishes from the real *Turbot*. Turbot is 'in season' all the year round, but 'in its prime' from March to August.

The best Turbot is caught on the Dogger Bank; then come the Holland, Norway and Devonshire Turbots; Scotch Turbot is not so good.

The flesh should be firm and white. It is retailed – being a very large fish – as required. It may be boiled, either in plain salted water or in a *court-bouillon*, baked or fried, and is usually served with shrimp, lobster or anchovy sauce. When boiling, drain well and do not remove fins. Small or 'chicken' turbot may be cooked *à la Meunière*.

Turbot Bonne Femme

In a saucepan put a level dessertspoonful of chopped shallot with a tablespoonful of melted butter. Cook gently for a few minutes, then add 3 oz. of sliced mushrooms. Simmer again for a minute or two, then add one wineglassful of white wine and two of water.

Butter a fireproof dish generously. Lay in it slices or fillets of turbot. Pour over them the contents of the saucepan, and sprinkle the fish with small pieces of butter.

Cover the dish with a piece of greased paper and set it in a moderate oven. Cook for about 30 minutes, basting several times, being careful to put back the paper after doing so.

Carefully pour off all the liquid from the fish into a saucepan. Keep the turbot hot by standing it over a large pan containing boiling water.

Thicken the liquid with a little roux and, standing it in a bain-marie, let it cook for at least five minutes. Season it, and just before you pour it back over the fish, whip in several small pieces of butter and a tablespoonful or two of cream. (Mrs Lucas's *A Pretty Kettle of Fish*.)

Turbot Cooked in Cream

Butter a baking tin and place the turbot in it and squeeze over it the juice of half a lemon, a pinch of salt and pepper, and cover it with about half a pint of cream. Place the baking tin inside another larger tin of boiling water and let it bake slowly for about a quarter of an hour, basting occasionally, then for about 10 minutes longer basting constantly, and if it gets at all dry add a little more lemon juice and cream. When nicely cooked take it out very carefully and serve on a hot dish with the cream liquor poured over it and garnish with slices of lemon. If you have a large enough fireproof sole dish, it can be served in the dish in which it was cooked. (Mrs Turner's *Fifty Ways of Cooking Fish*.)

TURBOTIN

Fr. for *Chicken Turbot*.

TURTLE

Fr. *Tortue*. The edible, herbivorous members of the order *Chelonia*, which are widely distributed in many parts of the world except the colder regions. Neither fish nor flesh, but excellent in the shape of *Turtle Soup*, a very rich and most nourishing *Consommé* which is served either thick or clear, with a squeeze of lemon and a glass of old Madeira. The only true *Turtle Soup* is made from live turtles killed for the purpose. The turtles which die on their way to England and are kept in cold storage are known in the trade as 'angels' and are no good at all for soup or anything else. The turtle fins, and again from live turtles only, can be very good grilled and served with a *sauce Madère*.

SOFT-SHELL TURTLE
Lat. *Amyda ferox*. Any of the many aquatic turtles of the family *Trionychidae*. They live in parts of Africa, Asia and North Mississippi Valley, the Great Lakes and many Southern Rivers.

GREEN TURTLE
Lat. *Chelonia mydas*. Large sea turtle.

UKU
Lat. *Aprion virescens*. A fish of the *Herring* family much esteemed at Hawaii.

ULUA
Lat. *Carangus sem*. A large food fish of the Southern Seas greatly esteemed by natives and Europeans.

UMBRA
Lat. *Umbrina cirrhosa*; Fr. *Ombre*. One of the rarer market fishes of the Mediterranean.

VENDACE
A 'white-fish' or fresh-water herring found only in the Castle Loch and Mill Loch at Lochmaben in Dumfriesshire, and in Derwentwater and Bassenthwaite in the Lake District.

WALLEYED or YELLOW PIKE
Lat. *Stizostedion vitreum*. An American fresh-water fish of the *Perch* type.

WALLEYED POLLACK
Lat. *Theragra fucensis*. A large sooty-black *Pollack* (q.v.) of the Pacific coast from Monterey northwards.

WATERZOOTJE
A Dutch name for a stew of small fish or larger fishes cut up in small pieces. The *zootje* is always eaten with thin slices of brown bread and butter.

WEAKFISH
Lat. *Cynoscion regalis*. A very acceptable fish, gastronomically speaking, which is found in large numbers along the American coasts of the Atlantic from Cape Cod to Florida. It is represented in the Gulf of Mexico by a closely related species (*C. arenarius*), called also *Sand Trout*. The *Weakfish* is also called *Squeteague*, *Gray Trout*, *Sea Trout*, and it is cooked in any manner suitable for *Trout* (q.v.).

WEEVER
Trachinus draco; Fr. *Vive*. This is the **Greater Weever**, the only member of the *Trachinus* family of any gastronomic value. Mostly found in the Mediterranean, but it occurs as far north as Scandinavia.

WHELK
Lat. *Buccinum undatum*. A marine gastropod mollusc popular as an article of food in Europe. The *Red Whelk* (*Fusus antiquus*) is gathered in large quantities on the Cheshire coast and sold chiefly in Liverpool.

WHITEBAIT
Fr. *Blanchailles*. The 'fry' or young of the common Herring (*Clupes harengus*) and Sprat (*C. sprattus*).

These tiny fishlets are at their best from March to August.

Whitebait, Plain
Wash and drain well, drying in a cloth; then lightly toss in flour and fry in deep fat, cooking only a few at a time and shaking the frying basket gently as they fry. Drain well, dip a second time in the re-heated and very hot (400° F.) fat to crisp, then sprinkle with salt and serve at once. Brown bread and butter and lemon should be served with this.

Whitebait Devilled
Wash the whitebait well in iced or very cold water and dry them in a cloth. Take a sheet of paper and put a cupful of flour on it, sprinkle the whitebait in the flour; they must be fingered as little as possible and not allowed to touch each other. Shake the fish about in the flour till they are completely covered. When the saucepan of fat (clarified dripping is the best) is smoking hot, put in the frying basket and drop in the whitebait for one minute, but only fry a few at a time. Lift the basket out of the fat and, after shaking the fish, sprinkle over it a little ground black pepper and fry again for a few seconds. The whitebait should be quite crisp when placed on kitchen paper to draw off the grease. Sprinkle a little red cayenne pepper upon the fish before serving, and hand thin slices of brown bread and butter and a lemon cut in quarters. (Mrs Turner's *Fifty Ways of Cooking Fish*.)

WHITEFISH
Lat. *Coregonus clupeiformus*. The largest and, gastronomically, the most important of the many members of the *Coregonidae* family of the Great Lakes and other Lakes of Northern America.

Planked Whitefish

Clean and bone a Whitefish weighing about 4 lb. Season with salt and pepper and rub the entire fish with creamed butter. Butter an oak plank, which should be 1 in. thick, and heat in oven for five minutes. Place fish on buttered plank and, to keep the plank from burning, cover space around fish with salt. Bake in a moderate oven for 30 minutes. When done, brush off salt. Pipe mashed potatoes with a pastry tube around border and fill in space between fish and potatoes with baked tomatoes filled with creamed mushrooms, and small mounds of cooked string beans. Place plank in a hot oven just long enough to brown the potatoes lightly. Remove from oven, garnish with parsley and lemon slices, and serve from plank. If you have no plank, heat a flat Pyrex dish and prepare in the same way. (*The Complete Menu Book.* By Gladys T. Lang. Houghton Mifflin Company, Boston, Mass. 1939.)

THE ROCKY MOUNTAIN WHITEFISH

Lat. *Prosopium williamsoni.* Ranging from Colorado to Vancouver Island, and the *Menominee Whitefish* (*Prosopium quadrilaterale*) are other important species.

WHITE PERCH

Lat. *Morone americana.* A small anadromous food fish of the coast and coastal streams of the Eastern U.S.A. It is closely related to the *Yellow Bass* (q.v.).

WHITING

Lat. *Gadus merlangus*; Fr. *Merlan*; Ger. *Weiszlingen*; It. *Naselli*; Sp. *Merlán.* It is one of the commonest European sea-fishes and one that is gastronomically important; its flesh is tasteless, but it is also very light and easily digested. Whitings are procurable all the year round, but are at their best from November to March. It is often served with its tail between its teeth, called in culinary French *Merlan en colère*. The American *Whiting* (*Merluccius bilinearis*) is a different fish, and the name is given in different parts of the U.S.A. to a number of other species, such as the *Sand* and *Carolina Whiting* (*Merluccius Americanus*), found from Chesapeake Bay to Texas; the *Northern Whiting* (*M. sexatilis*), found from Cape Ann to Southern Florida; the *California Whiting* (*M. undulatus*), found off the southern coasts of California; the *Silver Whiting* (*Umbrula* syn. *Mentiarrhus littoralis*) of the South Atlantic and Gulf Coasts.

When fresh, the eyes are very clear, the fish fairly rigid and wettish, and the colour a lovely silver.

Whiting au Gratin

1 or 2 medium-sized whiting
Butter
Half a glass white wine
Salt and pepper
Brown breadcrumbs
Lemon juice

Remove heads and split fish open on their entire length, then remove backbones. Place the whiting in a well-buttered baking dish. Add the wine, salt, pepper and breadcrumbs. Dot with pieces of butter. Bake in a moderate oven for about half an hour, basting with the liquor in dish. When done and nicely browned, serve in dish after sprinkling with the juice of a lemon.

Merlans à la Provençale

Rather small whiting
Flour
Good olive oil
1 shallot
Half a clove garlic
Fines herbes
Salt and pepper
Lemon juice

Clean fish, scrape and wipe. Roll in flour and place in a frying-pan containing a sufficiency of olive oil, shaking gently and turning carefully to colour on both sides evenly. When done, keep hot. Add to oil in pan the finely minced shallot and garlic as well as the chopped herbs (parsley, chives and chervil, with, if possible, a small sprig of tarragon). Add to this a little water (or a couple of tablespoonfuls of good bouillon) and the juice of a lemon. Blend well, cooking for a few seconds, then pour over fish and serve.

Merlan à la Pourvillaise

Take the fillets of four medium-sized whitings.

Put them in a frying-pan in which you have melted, without allowing it to boil, clarified butter. Season them with salt and pepper and sprinkle with lemon juice. Let them cook over strong heat, turning them once. Then take them out of the pan carefully and drain them on a white cloth.

Chop 4 or 5 oz. of peeled mushrooms very finely. Cook them for 10 minutes in milk with salt, pepper and a clove of garlic. (If garlic is disliked, substitute shallot.) Pass the liquid through two thicknesses of fine muslin, and add to it a dessertspoonful of butter, a wineglassful of stock and half a liquor glass of eau de vie (Brandy – but not the best). Cook the mixture gently over the fire, and just before you are ready to serve, add to it the yolks of two eggs. Stand the saucepan in a bain-marie, and beat the sauce until it thickens, but do not allow it to boil.

Put the fillets on a hot dish and cover them with the sauce, which should have the consistency of a purée.

This recipe was given by Madame Paumelle, who kept a small pension near Pourville. (*Les Secrets de la Bonne Table*, Benjamin Renaudet. Albin Michel).)

Whiting Cooked in the Italian Way

Place the whiting, when cleaned, on a fireproof baking dish with a large piece of butter, some parsley and two shallots cut up very fine. Bake in a moderate oven and after 10 minutes pour over them a glass of good stock and one of white wine, to which has been added a little essence of anchovy and a squeeze of lemon. Should the whiting get at all dry in baking, add more butter and baste with the white wine liquor. Serve very hot. (Mrs Turner's *Fifty Ways of Cooking Fish*.)

Fried Whiting, Tomato Sauce

Clean, scrape and wipe fish dry. Roll in flour and fry in oil with a *soupçon* of garlic or rub interior of frying-pan with that useful bulb. When brown, serve covered with thick tomato sauce made from fresh tomatoes. Or, when the fish are fried, put them in a baking dish and cover with the sauce, baking gently for 20 minutes and serving in dish they were cooked in.

There are many other ways of serving *Whitings*, such as the following:

Merlans à l'Anglaise

Split back from head to tail and remove backbone. Season the fillets and flour them lightly; dip in beaten egg first, then in very fine breadcrumbs and cook in clarified butter. Dress on a hot serving dish and put some *Maître d'Hôtel* butter over them. (Escoffier's *Ma Cuisine*.)

Merlans Bercy

Split four very fresh whitings of medium size; clean them and open them along the backbone so that they may cook better; lay them side by side in a butter baking dish with a teaspoon per whiting of finely-chopped shallots; and half a glass of white wine and the same quantity of water; pepper and salt and the juice of one lemon. Distribute a few lumps of butter over it all and cook in a moderate oven, frequently basting the fish with the liquor from the dish. When there is none left the whitings should be cooked. Before serving, sprinkle chopped parsley over the fish. (Escoffier's *Ma Cuisine*.)

Merlans Boitelle

The same as *Merlans Bercy* with mushrooms added.

Merlans Bonne Femme

The same as *Merlans Boitelle* with plain boiled potatoes served at the same time.

Merlans Colbert

Split back and remove backbone; season with salt; dip in milk, then flour, then beaten egg, then breadcrumbs, and fry in deep fat just in time to serve when cooked. Dress upon a long serving dish and put in a *Maître d'Hôtel* butter in slit of that back. (Escoffier's *Ma Cuisine*.)

Merlans en colère

Fried whiting with its tail through the eye sockets. Usually served with a *Sauce Tomates*.

Merlans Diable

Same as *Merlans à l'Anglaise* with a dusting of red pepper.

Merlans Dieppoise

Split four whitings along the backbone and cook them in the oven with just half a glass of white wine, some mushrooms and mussels. Make a long serving dish very hot and dress the whitings upon it, garnishing with mussels and small mushrooms freshly cooked, pouring over it all a white wine sauce with the *fonds de cuisson* passed through a fine sieve and greatly reduced. (Escoffier's *Ma Cuisine*.)

Merlans à l'Italienne

Split back and remove bone. Make a marinade with olive oil, white wine, a little wine vinegar, pepper and salt and a *bouquet garni*. Lay the whiting, boneless and open flat, in the marinade and leave it for an hour or two. Then drain and dry the fish; flour it and fry it in deep fat.

Merlans à la Juive

Fillets of whiting dipped in a light batter and fried in olive oil. Usually served with a *Sauce Tartare*.

Merlans sur le Plat

Split four whitings of medium size. Remove the backbones and cut off their heads, which you will chop up and put in a saucepan with a chopped onion, some parsley, half a bay-leaf and a few peppercorns. Add some water and boil the whole for 12 to 15 minutes. Pass through a sieve and keep this *court-bouillon* by you, but do not let it get cool.

Flour the whitings and lay them, flat open, in a well buttered serving dish; season with pepper and salt; add a few spoonfuls of white wine, the juice of a lemon and the *court-bouillon* already prepared. Bake in an oven, basting frequently, until the cooking liquor is reduced to a syrupy consistency; pour it over the fish and serve at once. (Escoffier's *Ma Cuisine*.)

Merlan Richelieu

The same as *Merlan à l'Anglaise*, with the addition of a row of sliced truffles over the *Maître d'Hôtel* butter.

Merlan Tyrolienne

The same as *Merlan en colère*, but served with a *Sauce Tyrolienne*.

Merlans Verdi

Poached fillets of whiting served with chopped up truffles and a *Sauce Choron*.

WITCH FLOUNDER

Also known as *Pole Flounder* and *Fluke* (Lat. *Glyptocephalus cynoglossus*). A large deep-water flounder of the North Atlantic.

WOLF-FISH

Lat. *Anarrhicas lupus*. A deep-water fish found in the Arctic and Northern waters. It grows to 6 ft. and more. They are caught when coming inshore to breed and, with head and skin removed, are sometimes sold as *Rock Salmon*.

WRASSE

The name of a number of edible marine fishes of the *Labridae* family, chiefly the *Rainbow Wrasse* (*Labrus vulgaris*), the Fr. *Girelle* used in the making of *Bouillabaisse*. Also the *Ballan* or *Ballan Wrasse* (Lat. *L. bergylta*), the *Red Wrasse* (*L. ossiphagus*), the *Green Wrasse* (*L. viridis*), and the *Black Wrasse* (*L. merula*), found on the European coasts of the Atlantic.

YELLOW TAIL

Lat. *Lutianus chrysurus*. A *Snapper* (q.v.) of the Caribbean Sea.

ZARTHE

Abramis vimba. A species of *Bream* (q.v.) found in most European rivers except the Rhine.

MADE-UP FISH DISHES
(Left-Overs)

Fish Pudding

Any cold boiled fish (about 1 lb.)
5 oz. bread (crust and crumb)
1 glass of the court-bouillon
Half a glass white wine
2 egg yolks
1 oz. butter (2 tablespoons)
2 egg whites
Butter for mould

Pick over the fish, carefully removing skin and any bones. Flake with a fork. Soak the bread in the mixed *court-bouillon* and wine. When very soft, pound and sieve, then add the egg yolks, fish and the two tablespoonfuls of butter, blending well. Season rather highly with salt and pepper and, finally, lightly fold in the stiffly-whipped egg whites. Pour this mixture into a well buttered basin or mould, cover with a greased paper, add a lid, securing it in place with a weight. Stand this in half a saucepanful of boiling water and cook (bain-marie) for half an hour, renewing boiling water when necessary. Turn out and serve hot with a rich *Béchamel Sauce* or, if cold, with mayonnaise.

Fish and Potato Salad

Cold boiled fish
Parsley
Cold boiled potatoes
Chives
1 small minced shallot
Tarragon
Oil and vinegar
Salt and pepper
A few chopped capers
Mayonnaise
Slices of hard-boiled egg
Lettuce

Pick over fish, separating into small flakes. Mix in a large salad bowl with all the other ingredients, except the eggs. There should be twice the amount of potatoes to the quantity of fish. Blend and stir well, seasoning as liked. Prepare two or three hours before serving, keeping very cold. Serve in a wreath of small heart of lettuce leaves, decorating with the slices of egg and anything else you may desire.

In the States and Canada this is sometimes served as a light luncheon course in hot weather on deep hollow lettuce leaves, as individual portions. Sometimes diced beetroot and a few cooked peas are added, and slices of lemon as a garnish.

French Fish Cakes

Remains of cold boiled fish
1 large onion
Butter
Pinch grated nutmeg
2 egg yolks
Water or court-bouillon
Salt and pepper
Flour
Frying fat

Mince the onion finely. Pick over and flake fish. Fry the onion a light brown, slowly, in sufficient butter. Mix this with the fish, nutmeg, beaten egg yolks and sufficient water or the flavoured *court-bouillon* in which the fish was cooked – and it is a good plan to keep some aside – to make a thick paste. Shape as wished, roll in flour and fry brown in deep fat or oil, serving, as soon as ready, with tomato sauce.

Timbale of Fish and Rice
Cleaned rice
Oil or butter
1 small onion
Salt and pepper
Remains of cold boiled fish
Grated cheese
White sauce
Butter, for mould

Brown about a cupful of cleaned rice in either oil or butter; when evenly coloured, moisten gradually with the *court-bouillon* and allow to cook until done, shaking during the cooking process but not stirring. Add the minced onion, salt and pepper about 10 minutes before it has finished cooking. Butter a round soufflé mould. Put a layer of the rice on the bottom of mould, on this a layer of picked-over cold fish, sprinklivg it with grated cheese. Add remainder of rice, almost filling mould with it and completing with some rich white sauce. Add a good sprinkling of cheese on this and bake in a moderately hot oven for 20 to 30 minutes. Serve unmoulded and hot with *Béchamel*, tomato or any hot sauce of your choice.

Curried Fish
1 lb. raw or cooked fish
2 tablespoons butter
1 small onion
1 dessertspoon good curry powder
2 tablespoons flour
1 gill milk
1 cup fish stock
A small tart apple
Salt
¼ lb. rice

If cooked left-over fish is used, simply flake and heat through in sauce. If raw fish, such as salmon, cod, halibut, or any other kind is preferred, it must be cut up, boned and skinned. Melt the butter, add the finely-minced onion, cooking gently without browning for a few minutes, then add the curry powder and the flour, stirring over a low heat together for five minutes without colouring the flour. Moisten gradually with the combined milk and stock, beating gently until smooth, then add pieces of fish and chopped up apple, seasoning with salt. Simmer very gently until fish is done, then serve with boiled rice and chutney.

Fish Soufflé
4 level tablespoons butter
4 heaped tablespoons flour
1 large cup milk
Salt and pepper
1 cup cooked, flaked fish
3 eggs

Melt the butter, add the flour, stirring well, then the milk, working to a smooth sauce. Season as wished with salt and pepper, then pound the fish to a paste and add it to the sauce with the well-beaten yolks of the eggs. Whip the egg whites very stiffly and fold into fish mixture. Put into a buttered soufflé mould with band of buttered paper round, set in a pan of hot water and cook in a moderate oven, without opening the door during cooking process, for 25 minutes. Serve with some nice sauce.

Sea Pie
(American)
Flake fish, removing all skin and bones. Mix with white sauce and season nicely. Add stiffly-whipped egg whites, folding them lightly in but not beating or stirring mixture. Have some freshly-made well-whipped mashed potatoes ready. Place the prepared fish in a buttered mould or tin and cover with the potatoes, which must be lightly piled on in 'rocks'. Sprinkle sparingly with breadcrumbs, dot with butter and bake for 20 minutes, or until brown on top and 'souffléd', serving hot.

LA TERRINE DE FRUITS DE MER
à la façon du Chef
Mettre à mariner dans un bon verre de Chablis et un verre de Cognac:

    Filet de sole
    Filet de truite
    Filet de hareng
    Filet d'anchois
    Escalope de homard
    Quelques truffes

Préparer d'autre part une bonne mousseline de turbot bien relevée en échalottes hachées, persil, cerfeuil, estragon et thym, quelques grains de poivre, le tout bien assaisonné.

Montez la terrine selon la méthode utilisée pour les terrines de gibier, en ayant soin d'intercaler les divers poissons avec une couche de mousseline, de façon que les truffes se trouvent dans le coeur de la terrine.

Faire cuire au bain-marie au four pendant 40 minutes. Laisser refroidir et servir.

Une bonne sauce Tartare n'est pas à dédaigner pour servir avec. (*M. Doumenc. A l'Ecu de France.*)

FISH SOUPS
I
Cut up 1½ lb. of different kinds of white fish in 2 in. lengths and chop an onion finely; cook in butter without browning during 20 minutes; then add two pints of *Velouté* (q.v.), stir well and simmer for 30 minutes longer. Pass through a sieve; replace soup in the saucepan and warm it up; season with pep

per and salt to taste; add the beaten yolk of an egg before serving.

II

Chop up two onions and brown them in butter; add ½ lb. sliced tomatoes and a handful of finely-chopped mixed herbs; cook for 15 minutes or so and add three pints of fish stock (failing which water will have to do). Season with pepper and salt. Bring to the boil and simmer for 20 minutes or half an hour. Then add 1½ lb. of white fish cut up in pieces or steaks and simmer until they are tender. Then add a wineglassful of dry white wine and simmer a little longer. Put a piece of toasted bread in each soup plate, a piece of fish upon the toast and then the soup over both.

III

Cut up 1½ lb. of whiting, bones and all, into small pieces and put them in a saucepan; add one carrot and one onion, sliced; cover with cold water and bring to the boil. Skin and season with pepper and salt; simmer for one hour, then strain into another saucepan, bring to the boil again and add 1 oz. butter worked to a paste with 1 oz. flour and stir well. Remove the saucepan from the fire and add two yolks of egg beaten into half gill of fresh cream; warm up on a very gentle heat, and at the time of serving add a little lemon juice and some chopped parsley.

IV

1 lb. haddock or cod
½ lb. of potatoes
1 onion
½ pint of milk
1 quart of water
2 oz. of dripping or butter
Seasoning

Cut the fish up into neat pieces. Peel and slice the potatoes and onion. Melt the fat in a saucepan and then put in the vegetables and toss over the fire for a few minutes; then add the fish and water and cook slowly until tender. Rub the fish through a sieve, return to the saucepan, add the milk and seasoning. Boil up again and serve. A little chopped parsley is an improvement. Sufficient for six or eight people. (Lucie G. Nicoll. *The English Cookery Book*. Faber.)

V

Fry two chopped onions in butter till they are golden, then add two dessertspoonfuls of flour mixed with a teaspoonful of curry powder, and put in the cod's head. Cover with water, add three tomatoes cut in slices, a bayleaf, two or three sprigs of parsley with plenty of stalks and a pinch of thyme, and simmer gently for two or three hours. Strain finely, season with salt and pepper and serve with fried croûtons or with vermicelli which has been cooked with the soup for 10 minutes or so before it is ready. (Ambrose Heath. *Good Soups*. Faber.)

VI

Boil 6 oz. of eel, cleaned and cut in small pieces, in three pints of water. When tender, remove the pieces of eel, add 2 oz. of capers and a few sprigs of parsley to the stock and bring to the boil. Simmer for 15 minutes, thicken with 1½ oz. of butter worked with an equal quantity of flour; stir and simmer for another 10 minutes. Just before serving, add the pieces of cooked eel. (Countess Morphy. *Soups. Kitchen Library No. 1*. Herbert Joseph.)

VII

2 lb. halibut or cod
4 large onions and 6 small **ones**
4 carrots
4 potatoes
1 tin tomato paste
1 teaspoon saffron
Chopped parsley
1 quart water

Chop the four large onions and cook in butter in a large pot until golden. Pour the boiling water over them, add the tomato paste, and cook for 5 minutes. Then put in the fish, in one piece, the small onions whole and the carrots cut up, and let this cook slowly for two or three hours. Half an hour before serving, add the cut up potatoes, the saffron and the chopped parsley. (Vogue's *Cookery Book*. Condé Nast Publications Ltd.)

SECTION 6
MEAT

SECTION VI

Meat: comprising an alphabetical list of all edible Meat,

drawn from both wild and domestic animals,

and a selection of American, English

and French Recipes for its

culinary preparation

MEAT

Oh! *the roast beef of England,*
And old England's roast beef.

HENRY FIELDING, The Grub Street Opera.

INTRODUCTION

MEAT, in its wider sense, means food, any food. In its more restricted sense, Meat means butcher's meat, beef and veal, mutton and lamb, also pork. In this Section of our *Concise Encyclopædia of Gastronomy*, Meat means any and every part of mammals which are or have been considered fit food for man.

Whether man's diet was wholly vegetarian or not before the Flood is a question for Biblical students: we are unable to throw any light upon it. Since the Flood, however, and this is surely as far back as we can reasonably be expected to search for evidence, the business of shepherds and goatherds has been to ward off danger from their charges, not that they might reach an honourable old age, but to keep the wolf from the door. Frederick W. Hackwood gives it as his considered opinion that 'the dish which was presented by Abraham to the angels on the plains of Mamre is identical with that which to this day is presented by the Arabs of Morocco to their more distinguished guests – a shoulder of veal well roasted, and covered with butter and milk.' (*Good Cheer: The Romance of Food and Feasting.* T.Fisher Unwin, 1911, p. 41.)

Although man kills man in these enlightened times upon a scale quite undreamt of by our uncivilized ancestors, we do not kill to eat our enemies, which is to the cannibals plain logic. Nor is there any record that the English

393

were at any time of their history so sentimental as to emulate those Eastern tribes where dead relatives were eaten by the surviving members of the family, thus to be endowed with a fuller life. Be that as it may, the eating of human flesh has not been considered in this Section of our Encyclopædia: it is outside the pale of Gastronomy.

We are aware of the fact that not only individuals but whole tribes and even nations live and love, work and rest, are strong of body and alert of mind in spite of a wholly meatless diet. Vegetarians would say 'because' instead of 'in spite of,' but we cannot agree. We maintain that since man was given teeth capable to tear, champ and cut, he was intended to use them just as any of the other animals – carnivorous all, which also enjoy the same or similar teeth. And Byron was not far wrong when he wrote:

> 'But man is a carnivorous production
> And must have meals at least once a day;
> He cannot live, like woodcock, upon suction,
> But, like the shark and tiger, must have prey.'

Of course, there is this difference between man and either shark or tiger: the flesh that man eats is cooked and dressed by him or for him. This is a great improvement; flesh is both more appetizing and more digestible when suitably cooked, seasoned and carved: thus the innkeeper in Massinger's play:

> 'There's no want of meat, Sir,
> Portly and curious viands are prepared
> To please all kinds of appetite.'

One should bear in mind the fact that meat has a grain, just like wood, and that it is important to carve meat according to its grain, and never to tear it away from it. Sharp knives also are of great value to avoid the tearing of meat and to ensure its full enjoyment.

American cooks should not be discouraged if some of the recipes that follow call for unfamiliar cuts of meat. Consult with your butcher, who can always suggest a proper substitute, if he cannot give you the American cut that corresponds to that called for by the recipe.

Definitions and Recipes

ADDAX
Lat. *Addax nasomaculatus.* A large antelope, with light-coloured coat and twisted horns, found in Northern Africa, Arabia and Syria. It is believed by some to be the *Pygarg*, which the Hebrews were allowed to eat as a beast that 'parteth the hoof and cleaveth the cleft into two claws, and cheweth the cud'. —(*Deut.* chap. xiv, v. 6.)

AGOUTI
Lat. *Dasyprocta aguti.* A rodent, as large as an average rabbit, found in Central and South America and in some of the West Indian Islands. The best part of it is its grizzled fur, but it is also eaten and, as a rule, cooked and served whole in the same way as *Sucking Pig* (q.v.). Some writers refer to it under the name of *Hare of Brazil.*

AITCH-BONE. EDGE-BONE
The bone of the rump, or the cut of beef lying over it. It is called also the 'poor man's sirloin'. It may be boiled, braised or roasted.

'This is a very nice joint for a small family, but not so economical as is generally supposed; it should be pickled carefully, and cooked in the same way as the round; one weighing 10 lb. will take two hours and a half; it should be trimmed on the top, and served with some of the liquor under it. It is very good when fresh and braised like ribs.'—Al.s.

ALDERMAN'S WALK
The name given in the City of London to the longest and best cut of meat sliced off a haunch of mutton or venison.

AMOURETTES
French culinary name of the marrow from calf's and sheep's bones; it is usually poached, seasoned and used among the garnishings of some meat dishes.

ANDOUILLE
A large, cooked, pork sausage usually served as hors-d'oeuvre, like *Saucisson.* It is made in many parts of France but nowhere better than at Vire, in Normandy.

ANDOUILLETTE
A smaller edition of the *Andouille.*

ANTELOPE
The name given to a large number of different ruminant mammals of the Old World, and chiefly Africa. They have been divided into four categories known as the *True*, the *Bush*, the *Capriform* and the *Bovine* Antelopes. They vary in size from the *Eland*, as large as an ox, to others barely 1 ft. high and without any food value. Particulars of each edible variety will be found under its own name.

'It is the fashion in this country (India) rather to despise antelope venison, as being lean and dry, and this, I think, for two reasons. In the first place, the old bucks being exceedingly shy and difficult to stalk, the majority of the animals killed are does and young bucks, the flesh of which is decidedly inferior to that of an old one. And, in the second place, I met with few people who when they had got the buck, knew how to cook him. My own experience is that the haunch of an old buck, when properly cooked, never lacks customers; and I have seen a party of old gentlemen, who knew right well what good living meant, dine off it without touching anything else. If roasted alone it certainly is rather dry, although delicate and well flavoured. But just take the fat from the inside of a loin of good mutton, envelop the haunch in this, and roast them together, and if you do not find it "an excellent good dish of meat" – as Old Isaak Walton would call it – never ask me for another recipe. It must be an *old* buck, mind you; for the flesh of a doe, or young buck, is very deficient in flavour'. —c.w.c.

AOUDAD
Lat. *Ammotragus lervia.* A North African wild goat which is probably the animal referred to in the Bible as *Chamois*, one of those which the Hebrews were allowed to eat.—(*Deut.* chap. xiv, v. 5.)

ARGALI
Lat. *Ovis ammon.* An Asiatic large-horned wild sheep which is probably the *Aoudad* and similar to the American *Bighorn.* It inhabits the mountains of North-West China.

ARIEL. SOEMMERING'S GAZELLE
Lat. *Gazella soemmering.* The *Antelopei* of Arabia.

ARMADILLO
Lat. *Tolypeutes tricinctus.* A South American mammal with body and head encased in an

armour of small bony plates. Its flesh is said to be very good, and it is prepared in the same way as that of the *Hedgehog* (q.v.).

ASADO

One of the most popular dishes of the Argentine.

'The "asado", or roast, must be cooked in the open. True, it is served in the restaurants of Buenos Aires, but in such a form it is urban and insipid. It is made by taking a section of the ribs of a sheep or an ox, and skewering it on a long metal spike, like that of an iron hurdle. Then a wood fire is lit on the ground, and when this has passed its early and smokier stages, the spike is driven into the ground at an angle, so that the meat hangs over the embers. Thus it is slowly roasted, the fire being fed carefully to keep a certain heat.

'The "criollo", the true Argentine, pours a strong garlic sauce over the meat at intervals, and when the "asado" is eaten, the flavour of garlic is indiscernible, leaving only a pleasant savouriness in the meat. He eats the resulting roast with his fingers, having hacked the piece of his choice from that appetizing carcass. And if there is anyone who thinks that less primitive ways of cooking meat can compare with this one for fulness of flavour and tenderness, let him try it. An "asado" would serve in England as a much-needed variation from the usual fare provided at picnics. It is both simple and exciting.'—RUPERT CROFT-COOKE in *Wine and Food*, XXII, p. 140.

ASS

Lat. *Equus asinus*. In times of emergency the *Ass* has provided most acceptable meat for the hungry, its flesh being both wholesome and nutritious. Labouchère, who was in Paris during the siege of 1870, said that the donkey meat which he ate then was like mutton in colour, firm and savoury. 'I can most solemnly assert,' he added, 'that I never wish to taste a better dinner than a joint of donkey, or a *ragoût* of cat, *experto crede*.' In China *Wild Asses* used to provide sport in times of peace and food for the troops in times of war.

ASSIETTE ANGLAISE

The name given in French restaurants to different kinds of cold meat served on the same plate: usually some very underdone roast beef, a wafer of York Ham and a fairly thick slice of Ox Tongue.

AUROCHS

Lat. *Bison bonasus*. The European *Bison* (q.v.), now all but extinct.

AXIS DEER

Lat. *Axis axis*. A South Indian *Deer*, distinguished by the white spots of its coat. See *Venison*.

BABIRUSA. BABIROUSSA

Lat. *Babirussa babyrussa*. A large hog-like beast inhabiting the wooded marshlands of the Malay Archipelago – its name is from the Malay *babi*, Hog, and *rusa*, Deer. It can be domesticated like the pig and may be prepared and served in any way suitable for the *Wild Boar* (q.v.).

BACON

Originally the French name for pig, and its meaning in England in former times was pork: Thus, in *Henry IV* (Act II, Sc. 1), 'I have a *gammon of bacon* and two razes of ginger to be delivered as far as Charing Cross' Shakespeare meant 'a leg of pork'. To-day, however, bacon means exclusively the back and sides of a pig after they have been cured, dry cured or tank cured, and smoked. The quality of bacon varies in the first place according to the breed, age and feeding of the animal responsible for it and the manner and degree of the curing; in the second place, according to the 'cut' or the part of the carcass. In England the practice is to cut a 'Wiltshire side' into ten different 'cuts' i.e., 1. Fore Hock; 2. Collar; 3. Prime Streak; 4. Thin Streak; 5. Flank; 6. Back Thick End; 7. Back and Loin; 8. Corner of Gammon; 9. Middle of Gammon; 10. Gammon Hock.

Other cuts of bacon are mostly used for boiling. Incidentally, a teacupful of vinegar and six or more cloves added to the water in which bacon is boiled improves its flavour. Boiled bacon whether hot or cold is a very popular dish for luncheon. Hot boiled bacon is excellent with roast turkey or veal, somewhat dry and tasteless meats by themselves and greatly benefited by a boiled bacon backing. Cold boiled bacon, a little mustard, some small onions and a crunchy cos lettuce make a meal fit not merely for a king but for the most fastidious gastronome.

In the U.S.A. bacon proper comes from the breast and flank sections of the side of pork. After the spareribs are removed, it is trimmed to make a rectangular bacon strip. Due to the different American ways of cutting meats, many cuts of English 'bacon' correspond in the U.S.A. to hams, salt pork, picnic shoulders, etc.

Breakfast Bacon

Bacon alone. Grilling or toasting in the old-fashioned Dutch oven is the best way of cooking breakfast bacon. It is not properly cooked until the fat has entirely lost its transparency – though this returns when it is taken out of the pan. The rind is most easily removed with a pair of kitchen scissors; but even this trouble can be avoided by placing the rashers so that they overlap like slates on a roof, with all the rinds exposed to the flame (above – for a gas or electric grill; underneath – in a frying-pan). In this way the rinds can be made crisp and edible, like the crackling on pork, while the leaner edges are shielded from the flame by the rashers next to them. In any case, this is the best way to arrange bacon, since it allows the lean to be kept soft and well-basted while the fat is cooked thoroughly. —G.M.B.

Fried Bacon and Eggs (*No.* 1). Use a large frying-pan. Remove rinds and trim the required number of bacon rashers. Fry rinds and scraps first, to get the pan greasy, then gather them up at the handle end of the pan. When the pan is very hot, put a piece of bacon in it at the very end furthest from the handle; as soon as done, turn it over and move it up, making room for another piece in its place; as soon as ready, this second piece should be turned and moved to the place of the first piece, which is edged up nearer the handle end of the pan; and so on, piece after piece, all starting at the 'bottom' end of the pan and moving up until all the rashers are gathered at the handle end of the pan upon the little pile of cooked rinds and scraps, where they will keep warm but not go on cooking. Something is wedged under the handle end of the pan to keep it up and there will be a nice lot of bacon fat at the lower end, in which to fry the eggs. This is the best way when cooking on a hot place but not on an open fire.—M.D.Cr.

Bacon and Eggs (*No.* 2). To each new-laid egg allow two rashers of bacon, half slice of bread and a little parsley. 1. Remove the rind and rust from the bacon; 2. Place the rind in the frying-pan and make it hot; 3. Put the bacon in the frying-pan; 4. Fry fairly quickly on either side, turning with a fork. When cooked, the fat of the bacon should be quite transparent; 5. Lift out the bacon and keep it hot; 6. Break the eggs one by one into a cup; 7. Turn each into the bacon fat, which should be just at smoking-point; 8. Cook slowly, basting the egg well with the fat; 9. When the egg is set, remove it carefully from the frying-pan, using a fish-slice, and place it on the hot bacon. If necessary add a little dripping or margarine to the pan; make it smoking hot and fry the bread, cut in fingers, until golden brown on either side; 10. Arrange the bread on the

dish and garnish with a little parsley.— C.M.D.R.

Bacon and Eggs (*No.* 3). This is a new way to cook bacon and eggs and is most appetizing. Cut some nice pieces of bacon in 3-in. lengths, cut off the rind, place in baking dish, and pour three tablespoons of fresh milk over and bake in moderate oven. When done a golden brown, take out and turn. When cooked sufficiently turn out on serving dish. While bacon is cooking, poach the eggs, and serve on bacon.—L.G.N.

Bacon and Tomatoes. Place baking-pan in oven. When hot place in it thin strips of bacon. When bacon begins to curl turn over. Do not leave bacon in more than five minutes for both sides. As bacon continues to cook after it is taken off, take it out of the pan while the fat is still transparent. Cut raw tomatoes in thick slices, using firm tomatoes that are not quite ripe. Sprinkle each slice with salt and pepper, dip in flour and cook until brown in frying-pan in which is one tablespoon hot butter.—A.W.M.

Bacon and Cymlings. (*Cymlings* are small Squashes.—Ed.). Fry some slices of fat bacon in a pan. Remove the bacon and keep hot. Fry in the drippings some cymlings that have been boiled tender and cut in slices. While frying, mash fine with a large spoon and add pepper and salt. Fry brown and serve with the bacon. (Old recipe. Toana, Virginia.)—A.W.C.

Bacon for Luncheon

Boiled Bacon. As bacon is frequently excessively salt, let it be soaked in warm water for an hour or two previous to dressing it; then pare off the rusty parts, and scrape the underside and rind as clean as possible. Put it into a saucepan of cold water, let it come gradually to the boil, and as fast as the scum rises to the surface of the water, remove it. Let it simmer very gently until it is *thoroughly* done; then take it up, strip off the skin, and sprinkle over the bacon a few bread raspings, and garnish with tufts of cauliflower or brussels sprouts. When served alone, young and tender broad beans or green peas are the usual accompaniments. *Time*: 1 lb. of bacon three-quarters of an hour; 2 lb. 1½ hours. *Sufficient*: 2 lb. when served with poultry or veal, sufficient for 10 people.—B. (2).

Liver and Bacon. Fry bacon as for *Bacon and Tomatoes* (q.v.). Cut liver in serving pieces, sprinkle each piece with pepper and salt and dredge with flour. Put pieces of liver in hot bacon fat, as soon as the rashers of bacon have been taken from the pan; brown on both sides, five minutes if slices be thin or eight if fairly thick. Place slices of liver on a hot serving dish, the rashers of bacon on them and the fat and gravy from the pan over it all. Serve hot with grilled tomatoes or *Pommes paille*. (See *Potatoes* in Section II, *VEGETABLES*.)

Cold Bacon Pie. (Eighteenth-century recipe.) Steep a few thin slices of bacon in water to take out the salt, lay your bacon in the dish, beat eight eggs with a pint of thick cream, put in it a little pepper and salt, and pour it on the bacon, lay over it a good cold paste, bake it in a moderate oven a day before you want it.—M.B. (1).

Bacon Rolls or Curls

Thin and short pieces of lean bacon are rolled loosely and kept rolled by a metal skewer or a little cocktail stick; they are then quickly grilled, fried or baked and may be served with cocktails or as a garnish with scrambled eggs, roast fowl or veal.

Bacon Stuffing

½ cup chopped, fried bacon
1 tablespoon minced onion
1 tablespoon bacon fat
2 cups breadcrumbs
½ teaspoon minced parsley
¼ cup stock

Mix all ingredients together and use for stuffing rabbit to be roasted —E.C.

BADGER

Lat. *Meles meles*. 'Still fairly common in England, but it is not generally known to be edible A fat autumn badger provides, however, two hams which, if cured in the proper way at any bacon-curing factory, furnish a real and unusual delicacy. They should be smoke-dried as well as salted.'

Until at least quite recently a Badger Feast has taken place for many years in the bar of an inn at Ilchester, Somerset. The badger is roasted whole in front of an open fire, while the guests, each with his slice of meat on a slice of bread, sit around drinking their ale from old-fashioned horn cups. (*Bath Chronicle*.)

L.R.Brightwell says that a big boar weighs up to 30 lb. and that the flesh is rather rich and 'porky'.

BALORINE

A favourite Russian hash of minced meat with finely-chopped spring onions and boiled beetroot and a sprinkling of caraway seeds; it is usually served with a border of either spinach or sorrel.

BARBECUE

'Whatever the actual definition for barbecued meat is, in the cow-country West it means meat cooked in a pit. Not meat cooked over a fire-pit, but meat cooked by hot rocks and coals, buried beneath 3 ft. of earth. It means seasoning the meat (a piece weighing not less than 25 lb.) with salt, pepper, sage, garlic salt, and clove garlic, wrapping the meat in cheesecloth, then putting this bundle into burlap sacking, sewing it up and burying it in the coals. That is the tradition of the plains. But barbecue plants are now in many patios and gardens, and barbecued meat has come to mean meat cooked over a live coal fire on a grate.'—M.A.

'Dig a hole 3 or 4 ft. deep and as large as you think you will need for the animal you wish to cook. For a polite party of to-day, I should say a pit about 3 ft. square. Line it well with rocks of good size and start a rip-roaring good wood fire in it. Let it burn for an hour or two and remove the coals very carefully. The rocks should be sizzling and crackling hot by this time. There should be some extra stones in the fire, too.

'Pour a good quart or two of warm water over the hot stones. Put a thick layer of grape leaves or corn husks or seaweed on the stones; next place your prepared, cleaned meat, whether it be a whole pig or a quarter of beef or three turkeys or whatever you may desire. Then more leaves. Then fish or meat of another type or vegetables, as you may desire. Then more leaves or husks or seaweed, then hot rocks, then a tarpaulin to cover all, then sand or earth to keep the steam in.

'Your cooking time will depend on the amount you have in the pit, but about three to three-and-a-half hours is usually enough to cook almost anything!'—J.B.

Barbecued Beef

3 lb. tender young beef
1 onion, grated
1 garlic clove, grated
1 teaspoon chili powder
2 cups white wine
Dash of cayenne
Salt
A little bacon grease

The beef should be boned sirloin or the inside of the round. For two hours before cooking, it is marinated in the white wine with which the onion and spices have been mixed. While marinating, turn occasionally. Then take it out, dry and rub with salt and fat, preferably bacon grease. If possible, grill over hot coals; if not, place under gas grill, not too hot, and turn often. Heat the sauce in which the beef was marinated, reduce one-third and pour over the meat when done.—c.r.b.b. (2).

Barbecued Steak Ventura
This begins the previous night, by cutting two cloves of garlic and placing them in a bottle with one half cupful of olive oil. Select tender steak (1 lb. per person will not be too much). This should be cut an inch thick by the butcher, who should also gash it about every 4 in. around the edge to prevent it from curling during cooking. While a good barbecue plant is best, a hole in the ground and a grate will produce delicious and juicy results. Build a good hot fire, and while waiting for the blaze to burn itself out, marinate your steak in the garlic-saturated olive oil, using a shallow pan, and first removing the garlic from the oil. When your fire has achieved red-hot and glowing embers, place your steak on the grate to cook. Turn with a clean cloth, a fork will puncture the seared surface and allow juices to escape from the steak. A brush dipped in water and flicked on the burning steak will advantageously put out occasional bursts of flame. Season with salt and pepper only after the steak is two-thirds done. Cook to desired rareness or medium rare, and serve sizzling. It will stir atavistic memories of the days when our ancestors lived in, and enjoyed the caves.—m.a.

Barbecued Spareribs
Select a strip of fresh pork spareribs. Have butcher trim ends and crack ribs through the middle. Lay ribs out flat in baking pan, cover with greased paper and start to cook in hot oven (450° F.) for 15 minutes. Reduce heat to moderate and continue roasting allowing 25 minutes to the pound. When ribs are half cooked, remove paper, baste with drippings in pan and dredge lightly with flour. Baste every 10 minutes thereafter until cooked. Serve with sauce Diable. —w.m.c.

BARON OF BEEF
The noblest joint of beef consisting of both Sirloins cooked and carved whilst left uncut at the backbone. The Baron of Beef is usually roasted upon a spit and it has been for many years one of the outstanding features of the banquets served at the Guildhall in the City of London.

BAT
A name covering all flying mammals constituting the order *Chiroptera*. In the Bible, *Bats* are named among the unclean birds which the Hebrews were not allowed to eat (*Deut.* chap. xiv, v. 18), an indirect admission that *Bats* were eaten by some people. In modern times a writer in the *Spectator* (30th

June, 1894) said: 'There are those who have tried the Bat and found it taste like a housemouse, only mousier.'

In India, the large *Fruit Bat* (*Pteropus giganteus*) is taboo to the Hindus, but it is eaten by the 'untouchables' ... and by the Europeans. L.R.Brightwell tried it once, *en casserole*, and found it 'delicious, very like chicken'. As Fruit Bats live exclusively on fruit, there is no reason why their flesh should not be excellent.

BATALIA PYE
Once upon a time this was a very popular meat pie in England: it was made of various tidbits such as cockscombs, gizzards, sweetbreads, etc. Its name is derived from *Béatilles* (q.v.).

To make a Batalia Pie
Take 4 game pigeons and truss them to bake, and take 4 ox palats well boyled and blanched, and cut it in little peeces, take 6 lamb-stones and as many good sweet breads of veal cut in halfs and parboyled, and 20 Cockscombs boyld and blanched, and the bottoms of 4 Artichokes and a pint of oysters parboyld and bearded, and the marrow of 3 bones, so season all with mace, nuttmeg and salt, so put your meet in a coffin of fine paste proportionable to your quantity of meat, put a little water in the Pye before it be set in the oven, let it stand in the oven an hour and a half then take it out, pour out the butter at the top of the pye and put in a leer of gravy, butter and lemons, and serve it up. (From *The Compleat Cook*, 1655).

BATH CHAP
The lower half of a *Pig's Cheek*, cured somewhat like *Bacon* and eaten cold, like *Ham*. When not too fat, a boiled *Bath Chap* served cold is very good indeed and superior to cold pickled pork.

BEAR
Fr. *Ours*. Any member of the family *Ursidae*, chiefly the European *Brown Bear* (*Ursus arctos*), the American *Black Bear* (*U. americanus*), and the white *Polar Bear* (*U. maritimus*). Bear is edible, and *Bear Paws* are considered a delicacy.

'Bear steak should be treated like beef, but should be marinated for two days. Treat it precisely like stewed beef (*à la mode*), but with the marinade it has lain in. Thicken the sauce with starch or arrowroot, add paprika pepper, and serve on a bed of sweet corn and butter.

'Bear Paws are a celebrated delicacy and are, I believe, cooked best in the ashes in a wood fire by the man who shot the bear. No one else ever gets a chance at this dish.'— m.h.p.

The flesh of the *Grizzly Bear* (*U. horribilis*) is also edible but coarser. 'We tried to eat the grizzly's flesh, but it was not good, being coarse and not well flavoured; and besides we could not get over the feeling that it had belonged to a carrion feeder. The flesh of the little black bear, on the other hand, was excellent; it tasted like that of a young pig. Doubtless if a young grizzly, which had fed merely upon fruits, berries and acorns, was killed, its flesh would prove good eating; but even then, it would probably not be equal to a black bear.'—TH.R. (1) (p. 316).

Nansen and his companions enjoyed the flesh of the Polar Bear: 'Meanwhile we have lain here – Longing Camp, as we call it – and let the time slip by. We have eaten bear-meat morning, noon and night, and, so far from being tired of it, have made the discovery that the breast of the cubs is quite a delicacy. It is remarkable that this exclusive meat and fat diet has not caused us the slightest discomfort in any way, and we have no craving for farinaceous food, although we might, perhaps, regard a large cake as the acme of happiness'.—F.N.

L.R.Brightwell states that all types of bear flesh are excellent, distinctly beefy in quality but requiring slow cooking. He praises particularly the smoked hams which could be purchased occasionally in pre-war times in England.

BÉATILLES

'*Béatilles* are all kinds of ingredients, that may be fancied, for to put together into a pie, or otherwise, viz. Cock's combes, stones, or kidnies, sweetbreads of veal, mushrums, bottoms of hartichocks, etc.'

'Take wings, livers and combs, all being well blanched in water, seeth the combes by themselves; and when they are sod peele them, and then soake all together, with good broth well seasoned; and when you are almost ready to serve, fry the combes and beatilles with good lard, a little parsley, spinach, and chibols minced, put them again to stove in their broth, untill you be ready to serve; you may mince with it some yolkes of egges; serve.'—*La Va.*

BEEF

Beef is the flesh of the *Ox* (*Bos taurus*), a bovine quadruped domesticated (and usually castrated as well), reared for food, when a year old or over, and fattened for the market before it is slaughtered. It may also be the flesh of a cow or of a bull used for breeding or for work on the farm as a beast of burden, in which case it never can hope to be *Prime Beef*.

Prime beef is firm to the touch, the lean is of a brilliant red colour, pleasing to the (butcher's) eye, and the fat is nearly white: the lean should be 'peppered' with small flecks of white fat. The quality of Prime Beef depends upon the breed of the ox, its age, its mode of feeding and fattening, and the manner of its slaughtering. The quality of any individual joint or piece of beef depends upon the 'cut', or the part of the carcass from which such joint or piece was cut.

Since American beef is 'cut' differently from English beef, American readers should consult their butcher in case of doubt in any of these recipes.

All the main joints and best pieces of beef are known by their Norman-French name *Beef*, but all tidbits which were presumably left by the Norman lords to their Anglo-Saxon menials have retained their original Anglo-Saxon Ox prefix: here is a list of them with their corresponding names in culinary French:

Ox brains, *Cervelle de boeuf*
Ox cheek, *Joue de boeuf*
Ox head, *Tête de boeuf*
Ox heart, *Coeur de boeuf*
Ox kidney, *Rognon de boeuf*
Ox liver, *Foie de boeuf*
Ox marrow, *Moëlle de boeuf*
Ox muzzle, *Museau de boeuf*
Ox palate, *palais de boeuf*
Ox pith, *Amourettes*
Ox tail, *Queue de boeuf*
Ox tongue, *Langue de boeuf*

In culinary French, *Boeuf* means meat from either ox, heifer, bull or cow. The more usual 'cuts' and *abats* of *Boeuf* are the following:

Aloyau de boeuf, Sirloin
Bifteck, Steak
Cervelle de boeuf, Ox brains
Coeur de boeuf, Ox heart
Côte de boeuf, Rib of beef
Culotte de boeuf, Rump of beef
Entrecôte, Rump Steak
Filet de boeuf, Fillet of beef or 'undercut'
Gras-double de boeuf, Belly
Hampe de boeuf, Shaft or handle
Langue de boeuf, Ox tongue
Museau de boeuf, Ox muzzle
Palais de boeuf, Ox palate
Palerone de boeuf, Shoulder blade
Pièce de boeuf or *Pointe de Culotte*
Poitrine de boeuf, Brisket
Queue de boeuf, Oxtail
Rognon de boeuf, Ox kidney
Tripes de boeuf, Tripe
Trumeau, Leg of beef

Boiled Beef (Fresh Beef)

Select a nice piece of fresh beef for boiling – round, aitchbone or thick flank will do nicely for this purpose. Cover meat with boiling water, add a few sprigs of parsley, a few celery tops, one small bayleaf and about 10 peppercorns. Simmer gently and allow 30 minutes for each pound of meat. Boiled beef must be cooked until it is very tender and the quality of beef has a lot to do with the time allowed for cooking. A 5 lb. piece of beef should be tender after 2½ hours of gentle simmering. About 45 minutes before meat is cooked add six medium-sized carrots, which have been washed and scraped, and a few small white turnips. When meat is cooked place it on a large platter and garnish with carrots at one end of the platter and turnips at the other end. Sprinkle a little finely-chopped parsley on the carrots and a few grains of paprika over the turnips. Serve with horseradish sauce separately.—w.m.c.

Boiled Beef (Salt Beef)
Salt beef (about 4 or 5 lb.)
5 or 6 carrots
8 or 10 peppercorns
2 or 3 turnips
2 large onions
A 'bouquet-garni'

Select a nice compact piece of salted brisket, aitchbone or silverside. Skewer or tie it up neatly. If very salt, put into sufficient *cold* water to cover completely, if it does not appear to be over-salted, place in sufficient *tepid* water to cover. Heat the water very gradually, carefully removing scum as it rises. When no more appears, add the vegetables and seasonings, cutting the carrots lengthwise into two or three pieces, the turnips into thick slices and leaving the onions whole. Cook gently, barely letting the water simmer, allowing 25 minutes per pound and 20 minutes over. When done, serve with or without dumplings, and a thick tomato sauce. The broth in which the beef is cooked makes good soup stock. If too salt, add more water.—p.w.

Cold boiled beef or pot-au-feu meat
Salt boiled beef may be used up according to recipe given for corn-beef hash or in any of the following ways, though it is less tasty than *pot-au-feu* beef because it was not cooked with the same seasonings.
Note.—It is advisable to strain any left-over bouillon or to retain enough of the water salt beef was boiled in, and to keep the left-over meat in this until required as it will otherwise become dry and look unappetizing.—p.w.

A very pretty way to eat Cold Boiled Beef (1728)
Slice it as thin as 'tis possible. Slice also an onion, or a shallot, and squeeze on it the juice of a lemon or two, then beat it between two plates, as you do cucumbers; when 'tis very well beaten and tastes sharp of the lemon, put it into a deep *china* dish, pick out the onion, and pour on oil, shake in also some shred parsly, and garnish with sliced lemon; 'tis very savoury and delicious.—m.k.

Made-up Dishes with left-over Boiled Beef (bouilli)
Boulettes de Bouilli
Finely-minced *bouilli*
Onion juice as desired
Breadcrumbs
Thick white sauce
Salt and pepper
1 or 2 raw eggs
Frying fat

The meat should be passed twice through the food-chopper or mincer, then pounded in a mortar. Season according to taste and mix with the sauce to a thick, smooth paste. Cool this mixture, then shape into balls, dip in beaten egg, then in breadcrumbs, repeating the operation twice if mixture is at all 'slack'. Fry in deep fat until brown and crisp and serve with tomato, mushroom or horseradish sauce, very hot.—p.w.

Boeuf gratiné
Mince a few onions and cook them in butter; cut some cold boiled beef in thin slices, cook them for a few minutes, add a tablespoonful of stock, a little tomato sauce, salt, pepper and parsley finely chopped. Put in a fireproof dish, sprinkle with breadcrumbs, add a few small pieces of butter and cook in the oven till well brown.—x.m.b. (2).

Bouilli au Gratin
Cold *bouilli*
Breadcrumbs
1 onion
Chopped parsley
Tomato purée
Butter
Fresh mushrooms
1 shallot
Bouillon
Meat glaze or extract

Cut the cold beef into even slices. Melt a sufficiency of butter in an oven-dish, when melted, sprinkle bottom of dish thickly with brown breadcrumbs. Add slices of beef, cover them with sliced mushrooms, the chopped and mixed onion and shallot and parsley, as desired. Moisten with bouillon, tomatoe purée, and meat glaze, sprinkle surface with more breadcrumbs and brown in oven for 15 minutes.
Note.—When serving the 'bouilli' *au naturel*, it is customary to surround it with

the vegetables from the *pot-au-feu* and to serve with it coarse rock salt, pickled gherkins and French mustard.—P.W.

Boiled Beef Hash with Eggs

4 eggs
1 onion
Brown gravy or sauce
White wine
Boiled beef
Butter
Tomato sauce
Salt and pepper

Chop onion finely and lightly brown in butter. When melted and blended to a blond purée – the cooking *must* be slow – add the finely-chopped beef, mixing well. Moisten with white wine, add salt and pepper and enough gravy or brown sauce to make a moist hash. Cook, the pan being covered, in a moderate oven, for half an hour, then turn into a hot dish, serving poached eggs on top, and surrounding hash with hot tomato sauce.—P.W.

Boeuf Bouilli en Salade

Cold pot-au-feu beef
A little chopped onion and parsley
Sliced boiled potato
1 or 2 hard-boiled eggs
Lettuce and other garnishes

Shred the meat with a fork or cut into small dice. Stand for an hour or more in vinaigrette sauce. Slice some waxy potatoes thinly, after boiling them, and season while still warm with a well-seasoned vinaigrette, adding the chopped parsley and onion and a coarsely-chopped or sliced hard-boiled egg. Add the meat, mix well together and serve in a mound, decorating the salad dish with small lettuce leaves, a few slices of tomato and some capers. Serve as a hors-d'oeuvre or entrée.—P.W.

Boeuf à la Bordelaise

2 lb. sirloin of beef
Salt and pepper
1 or 2 bay leaves
1 onion
2 tablespoons extra butter
1 tablespoon vinegar
Olive oil
Parsley
2 shallots
Butter
2 tablespoons flour
1 or 2 chopped gherkins

A thick slice of sirloin or, if preferred, any other tender piece of beef will do. Marinate this for at least 12 hours in oil to which minced shallots, onions, salt, pepper, bay-leaves and parsley have been added, turning the meat now and then during marinating.

When ready, drain and roast meat in the usual way, starting with a hot oven after adding butter, salt and pepper in small quantities. When done, serve with a sauce Bordelaise made as follows: keep meat hot, remove fat from gravy; melt the two tablespoons of butter, add flour, stirring until blended, moisten with the strained *marinade*, add the gravy from roast, the vinegar and one or two coarsely-chopped pickled gherkins.—P.W.

Boeuf à la Bourguignonne

2 lb. tender cut lean beef
2 oz. fat salt pork
Salt and pepper
Cognac (optional)
3 or 4 onions
2 tablespoons flour
Half bottle Red Burgundy
'Bouquet-garni'

Cut the beef into 2-in. cubes. Place the cut-up salt pork in a heavy iron stewing-pan or 'cocotte' and cook until all fat has run out; then remove small pieces left in pan and brown the cubes of beef in the pork fat, together with the sliced onions. When all is browned, sprinkle in the flour, stir for a moment, then moisten with the wine. Add salt, pepper, bouquet and, if to your taste, a small pinch of mixed spice. Cover closely and cook *very* gently for three hours or until beef is tender. Just before serving add a small glass of cognac, previously *flambé* (set alight), and simmer with meat for a minute before dishing up, after removing *bouquet*. There are many variants to this dish, some chefs adding button mushrooms, others omitting the cognac, etc.—P.W.

Braised Beef

4 or 5lb. fresh brisket of beef
1 or 2 small turnips
1 stalk celery
3 tablespoons butter
1 or 2 leeks
2 or 3 carrots
A 'bouquet-garni'
Salt and pepper
3 tablespoons flour
12 or 15 small onions

Prepare the carrots and turnips as a garnish by either dicing or 'turning' them with a French vegetable cutter. Peel the tiny onions and set aside with above. Shred the rest of the vegetables as well as remnants of carrots and turnips and use as a 'bed' on the bottom of a heavy iron stewpan. Lay the piece of meat on this, add 'bouquet', salt, pepper (or peppercorns) and sufficient water, or, better, good stock barely to cover the meat. If wished, thin slices of fat salt pork or bacon may be laid on meat. Cover pot closely and cook *very* gently indeed for about four hours; then add the prepared onions, etc., and continue cooking until they are done. Heat the butter in a small pan, add the flour, stirring and cooking until the mixture is a brown roux, then moisten with stock from stewpan and strain into the large pan, cooking until gravy is thickened. Serve with vegetables arranged in groups around sliced meat. This is the English method of braising beef.—P.W.

Beef braised in the French way is called Boeuf à la mode (q.v.).

Collared Beef

Ingredients: 7 lb. of the thin end of the flank of beef, 2 oz. coarse sugar, 6 oz. of salt, 1 oz. saltpetre, 1 large handful of parsley minced, 1 dessertspoonful of minced sage, a bunch of savoury herbs, half teaspoon of pounded allspice; salt and pepper to taste.

Mode: Choose fine tender beef, but not too fat; lay it in a dish; rub in the sugar, salt and saltpetre; and let it remain in the pickle a week or ten days, turning and rubbing it every day. Then bone it, remove all the gristle and the coarse skin of the inside part, and sprinkle it thickly with parsley, herbs, spice, and seasoning in the above proportion, taking care that the herbs are finely minced, and the spice well pounded. Roll the meat up in a cloth tightly; bind it firmly with broad tape, and boil it gently for six hours. Immediately on taking it out of the pot, put it under a good weight, without undoing it, and let it remain until cold. —B. (2).

Boeuf Créole

The characteristic of this dish is that no water or liquid is added to it.

Put 2 or 3 lb. rump of beef in an earthenware casserole, on a few slices of fat bacon. Season with salt, pepper and chilli pepper, finely chopped, and cover the meat with 2 lb. of sliced onions and the same of tomatoes. Cover and simmer for 3½ to 4 hours. —C.M. (5).

Daube of Beef

There are many ways of preparing *Boeuf en daube*. Originally the name applied to beef cooked in a closed earthenware pot buried in hot cinders, with hot charcoal added on top, and left alone to stew gently for a very long time. Now it means a stew of beef which has been cooked slowly and for a longer time than is usual for other stews.

Boeuf en Daube Provençale. The ideal dish for a cold meal, without exception. Get 3 lb. of good beefsteak – rump would do, but fillet is better – cut it into thin slices and beat them well. Have 1 lb. of pork, half fat and half lean, minced finely, and prepare some thin rashers of streaky bacon. Put the first slice of beef on a board, season it with salt, pepper, a little very finely-chopped onion, or onion salt, a pinch or so of mixed herbs, preferably fresh ones. On this place a layer of the minced pork, and on this enough rashers of bacon to cover it. Now put on another slice of beef, and repeat the process until you have ended up with the last. Tie the piece up well with string, and brown it quickly in a mixture of half butter, half olive oil.

Now, put it into a stewpan very little larger than itself, and with it put an onion cut in half, a couple of carrots cut in slices, a calf's foot split in two, a clove of garlic, a bouquet of parsley, thyme and bayleaf, salt, pepper, a grating of nutmeg, a claret-glassful of dry white wine, the same of water and a tablespoonful of tomato purée.

Put a sheet of greaseproof paper right on top of the meat, then the lid, and cook very slowly for about three hours. When done, take out the beef and put it in a long deep dish.

Strain the sauce into a basin, and when it is cold remove the fat from the surface. Warm it slightly again, and pour it over the beef which will be served invitingly submerged in this admirable jelly.—AMBROSE HEATH in *Wine and Food*, XIV, p. 37.

Daube à la Montigny-en-Vexin

(A cold dish perfected by none other than Jean-Jacques Rousseau)

Needed are: 3 lb. of tender beef, a good slice of ham and a calf's or pig's foot. Chop up the ham with a large onion and a large carrot, very fine. Cover the bottom of your casserole with this, and place on it the beef and the calf's foot. Sprinkle with a mixture of one-third dry white wine and two-thirds water, so that the beef bathes well therein. Cook slowly in a covered earthenware casserole for six hours, turning the meat at the end of three hours, taste for seasoning and add salt if needed. Continue cooking until done. Allow it to cool, skim the fat from top of gravy, and put in a cool place, after removing the calf's foot. Serve the meat the following day in its own jelly. —CL.K.

'Filet' of Beef

In culinary French *Le Filet* is the undercut, the most tender and best part of the beef, but *Un Filet* is merely a rather long and flattish piece of flesh, usually butcher's meat, but not necessarily so: there are *filets* of poultry, game and fish. This is the sense in which the English equivalent *Fillet* is used.

In Classical Cookery *Filets de Boeuf* are fairly large loin steaks, served whole and carved at the table. As a rule such *Filets* are larded or barded before being cooked. When a large *Filet* is cut in small, individual steaks before being cooked, their names in culinary French are *Filets Mignons or Tournedos* (q.v.).

Filet de Boeuf

Filet de Boeuf garni. The meat is barded with pork fat, after having been freed from every vestige of muscle, skin or fat. It is then broiled, grilled or fried, on a spit, or in the oven or in an open pan, allowing 10 minutes if one likes 'rare' or blue meat; 15 minutes to have it rosy or 20 minutes for juiceless meat. These are average times when there is a brisk fire and the fillet is not very thick. When the meat is cooked to your satisfaction, serve it with a *garniture* of your choice, the name of which will be added to *garni* and indicate the nature of the said *garniture*, such as:

Anversoise, hop shoots.

Andalouse, egg-plant and tomatoes.

Bouquetière, a number of fresh vegetables.

Bruxelloise, Brussels sprouts.

Châtelaine, chestnut *purée* and *Pommes noisettes.*

Clamart, green peas.

Dauphine, with *Pommes Dauphine.*

Du Barry, artichoke bottoms with cauliflower filling and a *Sauce Mornay gratinée.*

Duchesse, with mashed potatoes made up into little castles and browned (*Pommes Duchesse*).

Favorite, asparagus tips and truffles.

Forestière, mushrooms.

Frascati, mushrooms asparagus tips and truffles.

Hussarde, grilled mushrooms, cucumber slices, stuffed onions, braised celery, spinach and potatoes.

Italienne, stuffed tomatoes, quarters of artichoke bottoms and grilled mushrooms.

Jardinière, artichoke bottoms filled with asparagus points, green peas and other fresh vegetables.

à la Moderne, braised lettuce with truffles and braised cabbage stuffed with minced ham and mushrooms.

Niçoise, tomatoes.

Nivernaise, carrots.

Provençale, tomatoes and mushrooms.

Richelieu, stuffed tomatoes, mushrooms and lettuce as well as *Pommes Château.*

Sarde, tomatoes, stuffed cucumber and *croquettes* of rice seasoned with saffron.

Talleyrand, macaroni, minced ham, truffles and foie gras.

Filet de Boeuf Bressanne

Soak a fillet of beef (larded) in a marinade of white wine, olive oil and spices for 48 hours. Roast it in a very hot oven 20 minutes to the pound. Take it out, take off fat and add a little of the marinade to the gravy. Let it reduce. Add the juice of a lemon and strain it on a garniture of diced truffles, pistachios, tiny mushrooms and small olives, which have been previously blanched. Pour sauce over the fillet, let it simmer for a few minutes and before serving sprinkle meat with chopped parsley. (*Mary Pickford, Hollywood, Cal.*).—S.D.L.M.

Fillet of Beef Hollandaise

Trim and cut the short fillet into slices about $\frac{1}{2}$ in. thick. Season these well with salt, and then lay in a pan with six tablespoonfuls of butter, just warm enough to be oily. Squeeze the juice of half a lemon over them. Let them stand one hour; then dip lightly in flour, place in the double-broiler, and cook for six minutes over a very bright fire. Have a mound of mashed potatoes in the centre of a hot dish, and rest the slices against this. Pour a Hollandaise sauce around. Garnish with parsley.—OR.C.B.

Filet de Boeuf Madère

Middle piece of a fillet of beef
Butter
Larding bacon
Salt and pepper

Roasting spits being no longer in everyday use – more's the pity! – the centre portion of a fine fillet of beef must perforce be oven-baked. Trim, shape and tie up neatly after larding the meat in regular rows as described in 'Boeuf à la mode' recipe. Be sure the oven is *very* hot before putting in the meat so that the surface is quickly browned. For underdone meat, which is best, allow 15 to 20 minutes per lb. Baste well while cooking and, when done, use the gravy as a foundation for the *Sauce Madère*. Mushrooms and thin slices of truffle are the classical accompaniment and garnish of this sauce, which should be handed round, *not* poured over the roast fillet.—P.W.

Fillets of Beef

They should be cut out of the tenderloin in small pieces about $\frac{3}{4}$ in. thick, one fillet per guest. They are best grilled under a gas or electric grill or over a charcoal fire; 10 minutes suffice for fillets tender and blue; quarter of an hour for fillets 'in the pink', and 20 minutes for people who like meat to be well done.

The next best way with fillets of beef is to pan-broil them in the same way as pan-broiled steaks. Before being put into the pan, the fillets are rubbed with pepper and salt and dredged with flour. When one side is sufficiently cooked, turn over and cook the other side, but avoid pricking the meat with the point of a fork or knife.

Filets Mignons à l'américaine
Individual fillets of beef
Bananas
Brown breadcrumbs
Hot mashed potatoes
1 egg
Maître d'Hôtel butter

Prepare the pieces of fillet as directed in previous recipe and pan-fry quickly on both sides in hot butter. Dish up, one overlapping the other on a bed of hot freshly-mashed and fluffy potatoes. Cut the bananas, using as few or as many as may be desired, into quarters, dip in the beaten egg then in breadcrumbs and fry in the fat in which the meat was cooked. Use as a garnish, placing a small pat of Maître d'Hôtel butter on top of each fillet when serving.—P.W.

Filets de Boeuf à la Mode du Pays de Vaux
Small fillet steaks
Hard-boiled eggs
Lemon juice
Salt and pepper
Fines herbes, chopped
Butter

Grill the fillets in the usual manner, season when done, on both sides. Chop the eggs, mix with the fines herbes (chives, chervil, parsley and a tiny sprig of tarragon, if liked – and available). Moisten with lemon juice. Spread this mixture in a dish, add the fillets, place on each a nice piece of butter and, as soon as the butter has melted in a slow oven, serve very hot.—P.W.

Kimmel Beef
Place a piece of round of beef in a deep baking pan, with a pint of water, 2 oz. of caraway seeds tied in a piece of muslin, salt, pepper, and a few cloves and allspice, cover the pan down tight with the lid, and tie brown paper over it. Put it in a moderate oven for three or four hours. This is a good relish for luncheon.—B.J.C.

Boeuf à la Mode
3 or 4 lb. lean beef
1 or 2 strips fresh pork skin
Butter
1 clove garlic
2 or 3 shallots
1 small 'bouquet-garni'
6 or 8 carrots
1 calf's foot, split
1 slice fat salt pork
White wine
1 small glass cognac
Small button onions
Salt and pepper

First Method.—Melt two or three tablespoons of butter in a heavy iron stewpan,

and, when hissing-hot, put in the beef, browning it quickly on all sides but taking care not to pierce it with a fork in so doing. Then remove beef, and at the bottom of the pan place the strips of pork fat – that is, the skin, cut off with about quarter of an inch of fat adhering to it. (This is known as a 'couenne' in cuisines.) Place the beef back into the pan. Have the calf's foot split longwise and again across. Add this and all the other ingredients, except the carrots, leaving the garlic, shallots and onions whole. Cover very closely and cook as slowly as possible for about five or six hours, without once removing the lid except to add the sliced carrots a couple of hours before serving.

Second method.—Cut the slice of salt fat pork into strips and use it for larding the beef: to do this a special larding needle is required and special larding pork, or bacon, may be procured in most large shops for this purpose; if unobtainable, salt fat pork will do. The strips of prepared bacon or pork, which must be cut to the size of the larding needle, are known as 'lardons'. Put a strip of prepared fat into the needle, pierce the beef with the point of the needle unti it emerges from the opposite side of the joint, then gently draw the needle out, the strip of fat remaining in the meat, leaving the ends projecting at either side. The operation takes a little practice but imparts to otherwise dry meat a flavour and suavity which greatly improve it.

Once the meat is ready, lay it on the strips of pork skin, surround with the pieces of calf's foot and all the other ingredients, except the carrots. These are also added at the same time by many chefs but it is wrong. Cover closely and cook as indicated in first method.—P.W.

Beef Olives
Thin slices of tender steak
Stale breadcrumbs
Chopped onion
Butter
Chopped ham
Chopped parsley
Salt and pepper
Flour to thicken gravy

Remove all fat, flatten each slice of steak well, cutting to even-sized squares or oblongs. Add all chopped ingredients, blending thoroughly and use to stuff pieces of steak, seasoning well. Roll each one up, tie securely and brown in butter on all sides, then reduce heat and continue cooking until meat is tender. Serve with the gravy, thickened slightly, if preferred.—P.W.

Potted Beef
Ingredients: 2 lb. of lean beef, 1 tablespoonful

of water, ¼ lb. of butter, a seasoning to taste of salt, cayenne, pounded mace, and black pepper.

Mode: Procure a nice piece of lean beef, as free as possible from gristle, skin, etc., and put it into a jar (if at hand, one with a lid) with one tablespoonful of water. Cover it *closely*, and put the jar into a saucepan of boiling water, letting the water come to within 2 in. of the top of the jar. Boil gently for 3½ hours, then take the beef, chop it very small with a chopping-knife, and pound it thoroughly in a mortar. Mix with it by degrees all, or a portion, of the gravy that will have run from it, and a little clarified butter; add the seasoning, put it in small pots for use, and cover with a little butter just warmed and poured over.—B. (2).

Pressed Beef

Ingredients: 10 or 11 lb. of the flank, 2 lb. of salt, ½ lb. of moist sugar, ¼ oz. saltpetre, 1 teaspoonful mace broken in small pieces, 1 bayleaf powdered, 10 peppers, 10 cloves with the bloom picked off and crushed, 1 tablespoonful vinegar.

Method: Take about 10 or 11 lb. of the thin flank and rub well into every part 2 lb. of salt and ½ lb. of moist sugar, mixed with the saltpetre dissolved. Repeat the rubbing with pickle every day for a week, and then roll it round, and bind it with a wide piece of tape. Have a stew-pan of scalding water ready, put in the beef, and when it simmers allow five hours for 10 lb. of beef.

With boiling beef, boil a piece of bacon to give it a better colour. When sufficiently done, drain off the water in which it was boiled, and pour cold spring water over it for six or eight minutes; drain it on a sieve reversed and then place it on a board with a weight on it to press the meat well. Remove the tapes, trim it neatly, and serve when required.—C.N.

Ribs of Beef

Ribs may be either roasted whole, or they may be boned, rolled and either roasted or braised. In weight, they vary according to the size of the ox, from 2½ or 3 lb. to 14 lb. The best are the *Foreribs*, those next to the *Sirloin*: the *Middle Ribs* and *Chuck Ribs*, sometimes called *Wing Ribs*, are both uneconomical and ungainly as joints owing to the larger proportion of bone to meat.

Braised Ribs of Beef

Take four ribs, not too fat not too thick, remove the chine bone neatly, and 4 in. of the tips of the rib-bones, run with a larding needle several pieces of fat bacon through the thick part, trim over the flap and tie it well round, put into the braising-pan; put a ¼ lb. of butter, one teaspoonful of pepper,

and six teaspoonfuls of salt, into the pan, cover it over, and place it on a slow fire for 30 minutes, stirring it now and then, then add two quarts of water; at the expiration of one hour and a half, add eighty small button onions and sixty small young carrots, or pieces of large ones cut in the shape, which place around the meat; a bouquet of ten sprigs of parsley, three bayleaves and four sprigs of thyme tied together; half an hour after, add sixty round pieces of turnips; then place some live coals on the lid, and let it stew gently for one hour and a half longer, being altogether about four hours. Take out the meat, remove the string, and trim it. Skim off the fat from the liquor in the pan, remove the bouquet, etc., add a few pieces of butter, in which have been mixed a tablespoonful of flour and a teaspoonful of sugar, two of browning, stir gently with a wooden spoon, and, when just on the boil, dress round the meat and serve. In case it has reduced too much, add water. The vegetables and meat are excellent cold.—AL.S.

Ribs of Beef Bones

Ingredients: Rib of beef bones, 1 onion chopped fine, a few slices of carrot and turnip, quarter of a pint of gravy.

Mode: The bones for this dish should have left on them a slight covering of meat; saw them into pieces 3 in. long; season them with pepper and salt, and put them into a stewpan with the remaining ingredients. Stew gently, until the vegetables are tender, and serve on a flat dish within the walls of mashed potatoes.—B. (2).

Spare Rib

Wash and dry your spare rib, and season it with salt, cayenne pepper and powdered sage. Put it in a pan, and set it in a moderate oven. Instead of roasting, you may broil it on the gridiron.—H.W.

Roast Beef

Sprinkle a joint of beef with plenty of salt and a little pepper, then place it in a baking dish or pan, fat side up and without any water. Make sure that the oven is very hot and then put in the joint. Leave it in some 20 minutes, when the meat should be seared and browned. Then reduce heat and leave the joint to cook, basting it occasionally. Allow 16 minutes per lb. for underdone beef, 22 minutes for medium and 30 minutes for overdone beef, which some people prefer.

For roasting.—Sirloin and middle ribs are best. If the chump end of the sirloin be selected, the fillet may be detached and used separately.

Pan-roast Beef

Heat a frying-pan or a griddle on a hot fire. When it is nearly red-hot, throw your meat on it, but have in your hand a fork to prevent it from sticking to the pan and burning. 2½ minutes on each side will be enough if the meat is not more than 1½ in. thick.

Take it off the fire. Salt and pepper it, put a piece of butter the size of a walnut on top and let the butter melt under the gas. If there is a small burnt crust, take it off; you will find that the meat has been very thickly 'sealed', that it has a faint smell of wood, and that it bleeds abundantly under the knife.—CLARISSE.

American Pot Roast

2½ lb. rump of beef
2 tablespoons beef dripping
Hot water or stock
1 onion
Salt and pepper
2 tomatoes
Small pinch ground ginger

This is an old 'Yankee' recipe. Heat the dripping; gently brown the chopped onion in it; add the piece of beef and brown it well on all surfaces, seasoning with salt and pepper. When well browned, add about a cupful of hot water or stock and two peeled and cut-up fresh tomatoes. A very tiny pinch of ground ginger is also here added; then the pot is closely covered and the meat very gently cooked for about three hours. A stalk of celery and a couple of carrots may also be added, as well as a dried bayleaf. In all cases, a heavy thick-bottomed iron pot must be used as slow simmering is essential. —P.W.

To Reheat Roast Beef

If centre slices of a roast of beef are left over and are to be reheated they should be put on a hot dish and covered, when ready to serve, with gravy, reheated to boiling-point. Or they may be put between two soup plates, covered with gravy and a little dripping, and reheated over boiling water just long enough to make sure that the meat is hot right through, no more. Any spicy sauce, such as tomato, Mexican or piquante sauce may be used, instead of gravy.—P.W.

Round of Beef

The round is often divided in two, the inner side being called the *topside* or 'tender round', the outer one being known as the *silverside*. The whole round is usually roasted; or else spiced, stewed, and pressed, and then served as 'spiced beef'. When divided, the topside, from its freedom from bone and superfluous fat, forms a most economical roast, though the meat is perhaps hardly so fine as that of the sirloin.—Q. (2).

Round of Beef

This magnificent joint is, in general, too large for small families, but occasionally it may be used; the following is therefore the best method of cooking it: having folded the fat round it, and fastened it with skewers, tie round it, not too tight, some wide tape and a thin cloth, place it in a large stockpot with plenty of cold water, set it on a good fire, and, when beginning to boil, draw it to the corner, where let it simmer until done; five hours will be enough for a large one of 30 to 35 lb.; when done, remove the cloth and tape, and dish it up, previously cutting a slice 2 in. thick from the top, pouring a pint of the hot liquor over it when serving. —AL.S.

Half-round of Beef

This joint is now commonly known as the *silverside* (q.v.).

Rump of Beef

The *Rump* is the portion from which the finest steaks are cut for broiling; when cut in a single piece with the two sirloins, saddle fashion, it forms what is called the *Baron of Beef* (q.v.).

Beef Rump en Matelote

Cut a rump of beef in pieces; parboil, and then boil them in some common stock, without any seasoning; when half done, stir in some butter with a spoonful of flour till brown, and moisten it with the liquor of your rump; then put your rump in with a dozen large parboiled onions, a glass of white wine, a bunch of parsley, a laurel leaf, a bunch of sweet herbs, and pepper and salt. Let them stew till the rump and onions are done; skim well, and put an anchovy cut small, and some cut capers into the sauce. Put the rump in the middle of the dish with the onions round it. A beef rump will require four hours.—D.M.

Stewed Rump of Beef

Cut it away from the bone, cut about 20 long pieces of fat bacon, which run through the flesh in a slanting direction; then chop up the bone, place it at the bottom of a large stewpan, with six cloves, three onions, one carrot, one turnip and a head of celery; then lay in the rump (previously tying it up with string), which just cover with water, add a tablespoonful of salt, and two burnt onions (if at hand), place upon the fire, and, when boiling, stand it at the corner; let it simmer nearly four hours, keeping it skimmed; when done, pass part of the stock it was cooked in (keeping the beef hot in the remainder) through a hair sieve into a basin; in another stewpan have ready a ¼ lb. of butter, melt it over the fire, add 6 oz. of flour, mix well together, stirring over the fire until becoming a little brownish; take off, and when nearly cold, add two quarts of the stock, stir it over the fire until it boils then have four carrots, four turnips (cut into small pieces with cutters), and 40 button onions peeled; put them into the sauce, when again boiling; draw it to the corner, where let it simmer until tender, keeping it skimmed; add a little powdered sugar and a bunch of parsley; if it should become too thick, add a little more of the stock; dress the beef upon a dish, sauce round, and serve. Brown sauce may be used, and the gravy will make excellent soup.—AL.S.

Rumpsteak à la Hussarde

2 lb. lean rumpsteak
2 tablespoons chopped onion
¼ lb. mushrooms
1 pint consommé or good stock
A little milk
3 oz. stale breadcrumbs
3 oz. calf's liver
2 egg yolks
6 tablespoons butter
Salt and pepper

Select a thick, square piece of meat. Chop the liver finely. Soak the breadcrumbs in a little milk and squeeze dry. Mix with the liver, the onions, salt and pepper. Mix all this thoroughly and brown in a couple of tablespoons of butter. Allow stuffing to cool, then mix with the egg yolks and set aside.

Taking a very sharp knife, cut the piece of steak into slices, without, however, separating them entirely. There should be four or five 'pages' of them, in between which some of the stuffing must be spread, not allowing it to come nearer than ½ in. of the edges. When ready, tie up securely but not too tightly or the stuffing will be pressed out. Brown this prepared square of meat in the rest of the butter, on all sides; salt again and when nicely coloured moisten gradually with the consommé or stock. Add the mushroom caps and any of the left-over stuffing. Cover closely and allow dish to simmer. very gently for about four hours. Serve with mashed potatoes.—P.W.

Boeuf à la Russe

1 lb. tender cut of raw beef
1 raw egg
2 tablespoons uncooked rice
Lemon juice to taste
Flour
1 small cabbage
Thin fresh tomato sauce
1 pinch mixed herbs
Sugar to taste
Salt and pepper

Chop the meat finely, mix with salt, pepper, herbs and rice; shape into small sausages. Parboil the cabbage, detach leaves and remove hard stalks. Wrap each little meat sausage in a cabbage leaf. Tie into neat shapes and place them in a deep pan, covering with tomato sauce made from fresh tomatoes. Cook slowly for one hour then strain in the flour, blended with cold water or stock. Season to taste with lemon juice and sugar.—P.W.

Shin of Beef

One of the so-called inferior cuts of beef usually reserved for making soups or gravy, although it deserves better and may be made into a very palatable stew.

Stewed Shin of Beef

Ingredients: A shin of beef, 1 head of celery, 1 onion, a faggot of savoury herbs, half teaspoon allspice, half teaspoon whole black pepper, 4 carrots, 12 button onions, 2 turnips, thickening of butter and flour, 3 tablespoons mushroom ketchup, 2 tablespoons port wine; pepper and salt to taste.

Mode: Have the bone sawn into four or five pieces, cover with hot water, bring it to the boil, and remove any scum that may rise to the surface. Put in the celery, herbs, onion, spice, and seasoning, and simmer very gently until the meat is tender. Peel the vegetables, cut them into any shape fancy may dictate, and boil them with the onions until tender; lift out the beef, put it on a dish, which keep hot, and thicken with butter and flour as much of the liquor as will be wanted for gravy; keep stirring till it boils, then strain and skim. Put the gravy back in the stewpan, add the seasoning, port wine, and ketchup, give one boil, and pour it over the beef; garnish with the boiled carrots, turnips and onions.—B. (2).

Silverside

The outer part of the *Round*, also known as *Half-round*. The *silverside* is usually salted and boiled, though if stewed with fresh vegetables, spice, etc., it makes a most excellent joint.

Roast Sirloin

In weight a *sirloin* may vary from 5 lb. or 6 lb. to 14 lb. It may be roasted whole with the undercut, or it may be boned, rolled and roasted, after the fillet or undercut has been removed.

Sirloin of Beef

Sirloin of beef should never be less than three of the short ribs, and will weigh more or less according to the size of the ox from which it is taken; that from a small, well-fed, Scotch heifer I consider the best, and will weigh about 12 lb.; it takes about 2½ hours to roast, depending much on the fire. Having spitted or hung the joint, cover it with buttered paper, and place it about 18 in. from the fire; about an hour after it has been down, remove the paper, and place the joint nearer the fire, and put half a pint of water, with a little salt, in the dripping-pan; about a quarter of an hour before removing from the fire, dredge it with flour and salt from the dredging-box; when taken from the fire, empty the contents of the dripping-pan into a basin, from which remove the fat; pour the gravy in the dish, and then place the joint on it; serve some scraped horseradish separate. A Yorkshire pudding is very excellent when cooked under this joint.—AL.S.

Stuffed Skirt

Ingredients: 1 skirt, 1 teacupful oatmeal, 4 tablespoons melted dripping, 2 onions, pepper and salt.

(N.B.—Do not let the butcher cut the skirt in pieces.)

Method: Wipe it thoroughly and tear the tough skin that you will find on one side of it. Do not remove the skin altogether, but just so that it forms a pocket. Mix the oatmeal thoroughly with the chopped onions, pepper and salt, and the dripping. Add a little water if the mixture is not moist enough. Fill the space between the skirt and the skin with this mixture, then sew up and roll in seasoned flour. Brown thoroughly and stew for about 2½ to 3 hours.

(N.B.—This makes a delicious and nourishing dish for a cold day, and the kiddies will just love the rich gravy that it gives.)—C.N.

Smothered Beef

3 lb. rump or clod
Flour mixed with salt and pepper
3 large onions sliced
3 tablespoons oil or dripping
2 tablespoons mild prepared mustard
1 teaspoon celery seeds
1 cup strained tomatoes, or
½ can tomato soup

Dredge the meat with flour and brown it in a heavy pan. Brown the onions in the oil; add the mustard, celery seeds and tomatoes. Pour this sauce over the meat and simmer three hours or more.—B.C.B.

Steak

A piece of beef cut from the fillet, rump or any other lean and meaty part. The best steak is the thickest steak from the fillet. The best way to treat the best steak is to grill it and serve it with its own blood gravy. If served in one large piece, it is called a porterhouse steak (Fr. *Châteaubriand*); if cut in small round, individual pieces, they are called *fillets* (Fr. *filets mignons* or *tournedos*). When cut from the rump, the steak is called a *rumpsteak* (Fr. *rumsteck* or *rumsteck château*).

Grilled Steak

Choose a steak about 2 in. thick and cut from the sirloin or the rump. Trim off excess of fat. Grill under an electric grill, in the broiler of a gas stove or over live charcoal. Sear quickly on one side, then turn. Reduce heat and cook both sides alternately to the desired degree: A steak 2 in. thick will be 'blue' after 12 minutes, 'red' after 15 minutes, 'pink' after 20 minutes and 'black' after 30 minutes.

Pan-broiled Steak

Cook in hissing-hot frying-pan rubbed over with fat. Pour off all fat so that steak cannot 'fry'. After searing a thick steak in this way, slip a rack under the meat in the pan and finish cooking in a hot oven.

Steak Eros

¼ lb. fillet steak
¼ lb. butter
Salt
1 teaspoon Worcester Sauce
Parsley (chopped)
Pepper

Beat steak and flatten it out to a very thin shape, salt and pepper to taste. Cook butter in a pan till brown. Add sauce. Cook steak in this, then sprinkle with parsley. (*Mrs Vincent Astor*, N.Y.C.).—S.D.L.M.

Hamburg Steaks

Mince 2 lb. lean, raw rump of beef, lay it on a plate, add a good sized onion, finely-chopped and fried in butter for three minutes. Add one teaspoon salt, half ditto white pepper, one saltspoon grated nutmeg, one tablespoon chopped parsley and one whole raw egg. Mix all well together, then divide the meat into six equal parts. Roll them in flour and make them into flattened cakes. Heat ¾ oz. butter in a frying-pan; slide in the steaks and fry for six minutes on each side; they should be brown outside and pink, or even red, inside. Remove, drain and serve on a hot dish with their own gravy poured over and the fried onions around them. —A.F.

American Planked Steak

This is the most decorative manner of serving a steak. Special boards, called 'planks', grooved and with a well at one end to catch the gravy, are used for the purpose.

The plank must be previously seasoned. Brush over several times with butter and set in a coolish oven, wipe clean with a cloth. When this operation has been done several times it is ready to use.

A thick sirloin or porter-house steak must be selected, of a good thickness and well hung. Grill, in the usual way, for seven minutes, turning once to brown both sides and taking care to have a good direct heat whether it be gas, an electric grill, charcoal or coal. Brush the steak-plank over with melted butter. All around the edge and close to it must be piped a border of mashed potatoes using a large 'rose' nozzle for the purpose. Put the half cooked steak on the plank, after seasoning with salt and pepper, and set it in a *hot* oven, baking until steak is done – when small pools of blood will form on its surface – and potatoes are coloured nicely. Spread steak with butter, sprinkle with finely-chopped parsley and garnish with any of the following combinations:

Cauliflower flowerlets and green peas; fried mushrooms; small grilled tomatoes and sprigs of watercress; button onions, browned and glazed; small balls of carrots, etc.

All vegetables must, of course, be previously cooked and ready to serve when steak emerges from oven. They must be arranged in small groups, due attention being paid to colour, etc. It is possible to buy planks in silver or metal holders but failing such niceties, the plank may be served on a dish of the same size and shape and even, at a pinch, a thick oval wooden chopping board will do as it will not show when decorated.—P.W.

Plank Steak à la Parker

36 oz. sirloin steak
4 egg yolks
3 stuffed sweet peppers
Julienne carrots
Mushroom caps
1 qt. riced potatoes
3 stuffed tomatoes
Green beans, green peas
Cauliflower buds
Fresh asparagus in season

Sauté or broil steak on a fast fire about three minutes on each side. Place steak on plank, butter and put into medium oven for 10 minutes, remove. Add egg yolks to riced fresh-cooked potatoes, season with salt, pepper and butter. Whip lightly. Place potatoes through a pastry bag around edge of plank, then place stuffed peppers and tomatoes on potatoes, return to oven for about eight minutes. Remove from oven and arrange precooked vegetables around steak artistically, butter all and serve immediately. Serves three.—P.H.B.

Stuffed Steak, Canadian

1 slice of round steak
Salt and pepper
¼ lb. chopped boiled tongue
Chopped parsley
Butter
Chopped onions
Mushroom sauce

The slice of steak must be not less than ½ in. thick and neatly shaped, trimmings being used for stock or gravy. Cut the slice of steak into halves, crosswise. On the lower half sprinkle salt, pepper, chopped parsley and a few small bits of butter. Put the chopped tongue in the centre and cover the whole thing with the other half of the steak, fastening them securely together by deep stitches, using thin string and a trussing or big darning needle for the job. Cover the top with a thick layer of finely-chopped onions, bits of butter, salt and pepper. Put the steak in a tin, add a cup of either water or stock to it and small cut-up pieces of the beef fat or suet. Bake in a hot oven for three-quarters of an hour, basting three or four times. When done, remove string and serve with a rich mushroom sauce.—P.W.

Vienna Steaks

Mince finely 1 lb. lean raw steak, an onion and a teaspoon each of parsley and sweet herbs, season with pepper, salt, and a spoonful each of mushroom and tomato ketchup and make into small flattish rolls. Melt 2 oz. dripping in a pan and when very hot put in the rolls with a slice of fat bacon on each and bake for half an hour, basting well. Drain thoroughly and serve with braised onions and a good hot brown gravy.

Boeuf Strogonoff

Here is a pleasant, simple, and rather imposing dish for luncheon. All the provision needed is a supply of cream going sour in the kitchen, unless you make an imitation by adding lemon juice; but naturally sour is best. Cut some slices from a fillet of beef, beat them very flat and cut them again into short, thin strips. Slice some onions and mushrooms, and cook them slowly in butter and when they are done, fry the beef very quickly in butter in a separate pan, and then mix it with the vegetables, adding some thick sour cream. Strain the sauce or not, as you like (personally, I like the 'bits' in it), and if you want to heighten the flavour, mix in a little French mustard just before you add the cream. It must be served very hot, and I think a potato purée should accompany it.— AMBROSE HEATH in *Wine and Food*, iv, p.23.

BEEF TEA

A time-honoured pick-me-up for invalids and others. It is in effect a concentrated meat broth or *Consommé double*, but with this difference that it is made with boiling water and some more or less solid form of beef extract, as tea is made with boiling water and the dried tea leaves. It used to be known in England as 'Portable soup' and it is better known now under the names of the various well-advertised brands of meat extract which are sold to make beef tea, such as Brand's, Liebig's, Bovril, Lemco, Oxo, etc. How any of these commercial products are obtained is the business of the firms responsible for their marketing, but here is the method which was recommended by Alexis Soyer for the making of *Real Essence of Beef*:

'Take 1 lb. of solid beef from the rump, a steak would be the best, cut it into thin slices, which lay upon a thin trencher, and scrape quite fine, with a large and sharp knife (as quickly as possible, or the juice of the meat would partially soak into the wood, your meat thus losing much of its strengthening quality); when like sausage meat put it into a stewpan or saucepan, and stir over the fire five or six minutes until thoroughly warmed through, then add a pint of water, cover the pan as tightly as possible, and let it remain close to the fire or in a warm oven for 20 minutes, then pass it through a sieve pressing the meat with a spoon to extract all the essence.

If wanted stronger, put only half instead of one pint of water; seasoning may be introduced, that is a little salt, sugar and cloves, but no vegetables.—AL.S.

BELLY
Generally speaking the name applies to the edible part of any mammal's stomach, but, in practice, the ox's belly is made into *tripe* (q.v.), in the British Isles, and is used for making what is called in France *Gras-double* (q.v.). It is only the *Pork Belly* which retains the name.

BELLY OF PORK
'I have bought it from our butcher when possible, before pork was rationed, and I have cured it as one does bacon, that is about 4 lb. at a time, rubbed it over with Demarara sugar first, and then with coarse kitchen salt, and left it for about five or six days, turning and rubbing with the liquid every day. Then I wash it and put it in the pan with three or four bayleaves, a tablespoonful of sugar and about 12 to 14 peppercorns. I boil it in wine for about six hours and then press it between two plates. When it is cold it is really delicious. One can eat skin and all. Then from the stock I get enough lovely fat to make 1 lb. of flour into scones. The rest of the liquid goes into the stockpot and is a solid jelly. This pork is most useful with turkey, or chicken or pheasant.'—N.M.

BHARAL
Lat. *Pseudois nahoor*. A wild sheep, with down-curved horns, found in the Himalayas and Tibet.

BIFTECK
The French phonetic rendering of *Beefsteak*: it is used in culinary French both for steaks and for minced beef shaped and served to look like steaks; such are the following:

Bifteck à l'américaine
About 1 lb. of fillet of beef finely-minced and shaped into four small round 'steaks'; make a little nest in the centre of each one of these, with a spoon or the base of an eggcup; in the hollow thus made pour the yolk of an egg; sprinkle over all some finely-chopped chervil and spring onion. (Raw meat and raw egg are good for some people but not all good people like them.—Ed.).

Bifteck à l'andalouse
Make four small round 'steaks' out of 1 lb. fillet of beef finely-minced and mixed with just a little chopped onion cooked in butter. Dip in flour and fry quickly in very hot olive oil. Serve each 'steak' on a half tomato fried also in olive oil. Make a sauce with the oil in which the meat was cooked and a glass of sherry, allowing both to reduce on a gentle heat. Serve with boiled rice.

Bifteck à la russe
See *Bitokes*.

BILTONG
A peculiarly South African form of dried meat which is eaten uncooked.

Well-made biltong is one of those foods with the power of retaining their nutriment and flavour for many years. In fact, the old ladies of the veldt claim that biltong aged ten years or more has definite medicinal properties, especially if it has been made from beef. It is the custom in some households to nourish the sick with biltong finely-grated. At this age the meat is so hard that it is cut with difficulty, and even a man with a very powerful pair of jaws would have trouble in masticating it. But when it is reduced to powder form, the meat still yields its valuable essences. On the few occasions that biltong of such age has been offered up for sale doctors have attended the bidding, and usually the price per lb. has been run up to a surprisingly high figure. Biltong is favoured by many people in South African towns, but the men who know real biltong declare that the stuff they buy so readily is not real biltong. Good biltong is not made in the sun, for that reduces the meat to a shrunken mass and draws out most of its nutriment. This is really dried meat, for it has none of the appetizing qualities of the true product. Yet very high prices are often charged for it.

If cured properly, biltong never comes in direct contact with the sun. The farmers who know the real art of preparing it, hang the meat in strips from the rafters of large and airy rooms, through which a continual draught of air plays. And there it remains until it is properly cured, for the process must not be hurried. The eagerness of certain farmers to get their beef or game biltong on to the market, is actually ruining their trade, for by hanging it up in the sun so that it may be dried in the shortest time possible they are producing a very inferior product.

The average quality of the meat sold in South Africa is poor, yet it is claimed that poor though this meat may be, the skilled biltong-maker could produce from it a form of food to satisfy the most exacting.

In a number of countries, something similar to biltong is produced, but this is really sun-dried meat, which cannot be eaten raw, as biltong is eaten. This sun-dried meat must be roasted for a few minutes before use: to roast properly prepared biltong would be to spoil it.—W.L.SPEIGHT in *Wine and Food*, vi, p. 34 *et seq.*

BIGHORN

Lat. *Ovis canadensis*. The wild sheep of the Rocky Mountains, closely resembling the Asiatic *Argali*.

Mountain mutton is in the fall the most delicious eating furnished by any game animal. Nothing else compares with it for juiciness, tenderness and flavour; but at all other times of the year it is tough, stringy and worthless.—TH.R. (1), p. 240.

BINDENFLEISCH.
BUNDNERFLEISCH

A Swiss hors-d'oeuvre; beef at its driest, cut up in very thin wafers and dressed with oil and vinegar.

BISON

Lat. *Bison bonasus* and *B. bison*. The first is the European Bison, known as Aurochs, and the second the American Bison, more commonly known as Buffalo. The *Buffalo* formerly roamed in large herds over most of the temperate part of North America; it is now almost extinct, except for herds in Yellowstone and other parks. It is a large, shaggy-maned, ox-like quadruped with short horns and heavy forequarters.

On February 7th 1871, Morton C.Fisher, of New York, gave an 'American Dinner' at the Langham Hotel, in London, with especially imported American delicacies, including some *Tournedos de Buffalo*, of which Frank Buckland, one of the guests, wrote:

'The buffalo was exceedingly tender, more so than any rumpsteak I ever tasted. Buffalo tongue and hump are also very good.'—F.B.

BITKIS

Minced fillet of beef made up into small *palets* or discs, with or without bread and milk added, then dusted with breadcrumbs and cooked in butter; served with a little buttery sauce and *sautées* potatoes.

BITOKES

(Russian Meat Balls or Cakes)

Bitokes à la russe
1 lb. fillet or sirloin of beef
Salt and pepper
Butter
Flour
Fried onions

If the meat be very juicy and tender, chop or grind finely. If tougher, scrape to a pulp, discarding the fibre. In the latter case, allow 1½ lb. beef, as there is wastage, though the portions scraped off may be used for soup.

Mix with the chopped or scraped beef a sufficiency of salt and pepper and work in two tablespoons of butter thoroughly with the hands. Shape into flat round cakes about 2 in. thick. Flour each one nicely and cook in hot butter until brown on both sides, but the centre portion should be underdone. Serve with a topping of hot freshly-fried onions. If preferred, grill the *bitokes* instead of frying them.—P.W.

BLACK BUCK

Lat. *Antilopa cervicapra*. The common, medium-sized Antelope of India; it has spirally-twisted horns. See *Venison*.

L.R.Brightwell declares that the flesh of the *Indian Black Buck* is better flavoured than that of any other antelope, and he adds that, in peacetime, the animal was occasionally fattened at the London Zoo, for the privileged few.

BLACK PUDDING.
BLOOD PUDDING

Fr. *Boudin* or *Boudinnoir*; Ger. *Blutwurtz*; It. *Sanguinaccioni*; Sp. *Morcilla*; A large sausage made of pig's blood and suet. It is usually fried and served very hot with mashed potatoes.

BLANQUETTE DE VEAU

Cut veal in cubes and pour boiling salted water over it and let it soak for 20 minutes. Drain it and put in a pan; cover with water. Add small white onions, salt, pepper, a carrot sliced in quarters, bayleaf, a sprig of parsley. Bring to a boil and simmer slowly. When meat is done, make a white sauce with the stock. Let it cook for 20 minutes. Bind it with two yolks of eggs mixed with half cup cream. Pour over meat and onions and add mushrooms cooked separately. (*From Mrs Carroll Carstairs, N.Y.C.*)—S.D.L.M.

BLANQUETTE D'AGNEAU BOURGEOISE

    2 lb. breast of lamb
    1 large carrot
    4 oz. lean ham
    1½ oz. flour
    2 egg yolks
    Squeeze lemon juice
    1 large onion stuck with clove
    Parsley
    2 oz. butter
    2 cups mutton broth
    Milk or cream
    Salt and pepper

Cut the meat into neat pieces, trimming off excess fat. Put it into cold, slightly salted water for half an hour to whiten meat. Drain and put the meat into a stewing-pan, covering with fresh cold water. Bring gently to boiling-point, skim as required, then add the onion stuck with a clove, the carrot cut into pieces, and a sprig or two of parsley. Simmer very gently until the bones can easily be removed, then keep meat hot. Strain the stock, or broth, from meat. Cut the ham into small dice and cook it gently in the butter but do not allow to colour. Sprinkle on the flour, stirring well, then gradually moisten with the broth and beat vigorously to obtain a smooth mixture. Simmer to cook flour, beating the while, then strain and remove pieces of ham. Add the pieces of meat, heat well through, remove pan from fire and add the egg yolks, previously beaten up with a little thick cream or milk. Season with lemon juice to taste, and, if liked, a few grains of cayenne pepper. Serve very hot with mashed potatoes.—P.W.

BLOND DE VEAU
A double veal broth, valuable for mixing with soups and sauces on account of its smooth gelatinous texture.

BOAR
Fr. *Sanglier*. Young Boar, *Marcassin*. Boar's Head, *Hure de sanglier*. The uncastrated male of the swine, whether wild or tame, but in culinary parlance it always means *Wild Boar* (q.v.).

BOBOTIE
(South African Curry)
    2 lb. cooked lamb or mutton finely minced
    1 thick slice bread
    2 medium onions, sliced
    1 apple, sliced

    2 eggs
    2 tablespoons curry powder
    1 dessertspoon castor sugar
    1 oz. butter
    8 almonds, finely chopped
    Handful of raisins or sultanas
    ½ pint milk
    Salt to taste

Soak the bread in the milk, beat lumps out with a fork, and drain off any surplus milk.

Fry onions and apple in butter, add curry powder, sugar, salt, almonds, raisins, and one well-beaten egg; then the meat. Mix well, stirring over the fire for a few minutes, then put into a well-buttered pie-dish. Beat the second egg, add the rest of milk (strained off the bread, which should not be less than a quarter of a pint). Add salt and pepper to taste, and pour over the mixture; then bake gently until the custard is set.

The same mixture, put into an open shortcrust flan and served cold, makes an excellent picnic dish.—Miss E.Randall Haybittel in *Wine and Food*, XXI, p. 50.

BONES
Bones are, of course, invaluable in the preparation of stock and soup, but cooked bones, when denuded of most of the meat, have long been a supper favourite. Some, among whom are the immortal 'Gubbins' and the present writer, like the bones grossly overgrilled, so that the charred fragments of meat left on are reduced almost to a cinder and impart a delicious savour of the grid, but most epicures prefer a less drastic treatment, as for example the subjoined from the Café Royal:

Os Diablé
'Take one or two ribs of beef which have been cooked the day before and put them on to the grill. Then cover them with mustard and grill them again for a few minutes.'

Or the following, propounded by Soyer as long ago as 1857 for his 'Bill of Fare for London Suppers', which, instead of the elaborate messes most present-day Savoyards might expect, contained for the most part merely the plainest of fare cooked in the simplest fashion.

Devilled Bone
'The remains of the rib of a sirloin of beef or bladebone of a shoulder of mutton should be slightly cut all round with a knife and well rubbed with cayenne, salt and a teaspoon of chilli vinegar, or catsup or relish, and broiled gently until hot through and brown. Serve very hot.'

BOONTJIE BREDEE

The favourite 'Bean Stew' of the Cape Province.

3 lb. ribs of mutton; three onions; two tablespoons dripping or fat; six potatoes and lots of green beans. Cut the mutton into small pieces; flour each piece thoroughly and season with pepper and salt; skin the onions, chop them up finely and fry them to a golden brown in dripping or fat; then add the meat and the green beans cut in small pieces; add a little water, also the potatoes, peeled and halved. Stew gently for at least three or four hours.

Tomatoes, a green chilli, a small cauliflower and other vegetables may also be added; also peeled, cored and sliced quince, previously parboiled in water and sugar, if the fruit be acid and hard.

BOUDIN. BOUDIN NOIR

Fr. for *Black Pudding* (q.v.).

BOUDIN BLANC

A fat sausage made with white meat and seasoned with onions: the best are made with chicken and pork; the worst with veal and breadcrumbs.

BOUILLON

Fr. for *Broth*. The basic liquid of all *Consommés gras*. It is obtained by boiling (*bouillir*) in water, beef and/or veal, and/or a fowl, together with a variety of vegetables. *Bouillon, Bouillon Restaurant, Pot-au-feu*, all have beef as a basis. When there is no beef in the *Bouillon* and it has been made by boiling a chicken or some fish, it is called *Bouillon de Poulet* or *Bouillon de Poisson*.

Gilt-edged Bouillon

3 lb. beef (without bone or fat)
2 quarts cold water
1 piece red pepper pod
1 teaspoonful salt
1 leek
1 carrot (pieced)
1 bunch parsley
Cayenne
Shell of 1 egg (crushed)
4 cloves
1 cup canned tomatoes
1 small bayleaf
6 allspice
1 garlic
1 tablespoonful celery seed
1 onion
1 sprig thyme
2 tablespoonfuls sherry
1 egg white

Put above ingredients in soup kettle, cover and boil. When boiling smoothly, set aside where it will simmer steadily. After cooking 2½ hours add carrot, onion, thyme, parsley. Replace cover, leaving top one-third open. Boil for 2½ hours. If not strong enough boil longer. Strain all the broth off through a hair-sieve into a bowl. It should measure a full quart. Let it stand until next morning and then remove all grease. When clear, add sherry, salt and cayenne. To clarify *bouillon*, pour into clean kettle, add unbeaten egg white and crushed shell; stir these into cold soup until well mixed. Set it upon fire and cook for 10 minutes. Let settle and pour through jelly-bag. Do not squeeze bag, but allow to drip. (*Mrs Thomas Blagden, Lawrence, L.I.*)—S.L.L.M.

BOULETTES

(Little Meat Balls)

Soak a slice of bread in water, squeeze it well and put through the mincer with the remains of any cold joint and a tiny onion. Add seasoning, a beaten egg, and form into balls or flat cakes. Coat with raspings and fry quickly in hot butter. When cold, wrap each boulette in a crisp lettuce leaf.

BRAINS

The 'grey matter' contained in the skull of man and other vertebrates. The average weights of different sorts of brains are: ox brains, 22 oz., calf's brains, 11 oz., sheep's brains, 5 oz., pig's brains, 7½ oz. The best brains are the sheep's brains, and the worst, in the Editor's opinion, are pig's brains. In culinary language, when brains are not otherwise qualified, sheep's brains are implied, at least in England.

Brains au Beurre Noir

Poach in boiling salted water, drain and cut into two or three pieces of equal size. Flour each piece and toss gently in butter until brown on both sides, seasoning with salt and pepper. When done, add more butter to pan, cook it until nut-brown, remove it from fire and add a tablespoonful of vinegar or lemon juice. Pour this browned and savoury butter over brains and sprinkle with chopped parsley.

Brains in Fritters

Dip each piece of pre-cooked brain in frying batter and fry crisp in deep boiling fat. Drain well and serve at once, with fried parsley and tomato sauce.

Calf's Brains

One set of brains; one cupful white sauce; one yolk of egg; two rounds of toast; lemon; seasoning. The brains must be very fresh. Wash them in cold salted water, removing the loose skin and any clot of blood. Then let them lie in fresh cold water for an hour at least. When thoroughly cleansed, put the brains into a small lined saucepan with cold water to cover them, a pinch of salt, and a good squeeze of lemon juice. Add a small bunch of herbs (parsley, thyme and bayleaf) and simmer slowly for a quarter of an hour. Then strain and keep the brains hot. Make a good white sauce and add to it the yolk of an egg and a good squeeze of lemon juice. Place the brains on two rounds of toast, strain the sauce over, and garnish with lemon, a few potato balls and cooked green peas.—G.H. (1).

Cervelles de veau au Beurre Noir

Soak four calves' brains in cold water for one hour. Parboil them for five minutes, drain, skin and clean. Place them again in boiling water to which you have added half cup vinegar, salt, an onion, and a *bouquet-garni* (without the cloves). Then boil slowly for about half an hour, drain, and place them on a platter. Pour over the brains a good quantity of *Beurre noir*. Prepare this by melting butter in a saucepan until dark brown. Then let it cook a little, add a few drops of vinegar and re-heat. Sprinkle with chopped parsley and serve.—CL.K.

Fried Ox Brains

1 ox brain
2 tablespoons butter
Salt and pepper
1 clove garlic
1 or 2 cloves
Chopped chives or an onion
Parsley for frying
1 tablespoon flour
1 tablespoon vinegar
1 or 2 shallots
2 stalks parsley
Additional flour
Frying fat

Put in a saucepan the butter, blended previously with the flour, the vinegar, cut-up garlic and shallots, the cloves, the chives or chopped onion and the parsley. Season with salt and pepper and slightly heat the mixture to melt butter but do not cook. Keep the pan on a low heat or on edge of stove. Wash brains in cold salted water, drain when white, cut in rather thick slices and set in above mixture to marinate for a couple of hours, turning now and then. Drain well and dip each slice of brains in flour, then fry in boiling fat until brown. Serve at once, after draining, and garnish with sprigs of fried parsley.—P.W.

Brain Pie

Ingredients: 1 brain, ¼ lb. chopped ham, ½ lb. sliced tomatoes, 1 egg, teacup cream or milk, breadcrumbs, pepper and salt.

Method: Soak brain in cold water. Clean and remove fibre. Drop in boiling, salted

water, and simmer for 15 minutes. Lift out, remove skin and chop up. Fill a pie-dish with layers of brain, ham and tomatoes. Mix beaten egg, cream, pepper, salt and pour over the contents of dish. Sprinkle thickly with brown breadcrumbs and bake for 30 minutes.—C.N.

Pig's Brains

'Pig's brains, which, in my opinion, are the best, are blanched in a 'court-bouillon' highly scented with onion, bayleaf and thyme, and are then prepared with black butter and a dash of well evaporated vinegar in a frying-pan.—CLARISSE.

BRAWN

A boned confection of boar's meat or pig's head, always eaten cold in the shape of a *Galantine* (q.v.).

Brawn figures on most 'meat' days, in the accounts of the Lords of the Star Chamber, from 1534 to 1590, either as 'collars' or 'rounds' of brawn, or simply as *in brawn* ... so much. The money spent on *Brawn* varied from 3*s*. 4*d*. to 13*s*. 4*d*. per day.

According to Wynkyn de Worde's *Boke of Kervynge*, Brawn used to be served at the very beginning of the meal; 'Fyrste sette ye forthe mustarde and brawne' (Furnivall's *Early English Meals and Manners*, 1868, p. 156). This is confirmed by John Russell, in his *Boke of Nurture*: 'Furst set for the mustard and brawne of boore ye wild swyne.' (*Idem*, p. 48).

Presskopf (Brawn)

Boil a pig's head, tongue and heart soft. They must be covered close, simmering gently in just enough water to keep them stewing. When tender, take up the meat and cut it into small pieces. Boil down the liquor to a creamy thickness; add to it salt, pepper, grated lemon-peel, a little powdered cloves or mace, a quarter of a pint of white wine, and the same of vinegar. Stir the meat into the sauce, and give it a simmer together. Put it into any kind of form. Turn it out the next day.—G.N.C.

BRISKET

The meat covering the breast-bone of any mammal, but usually the breast of beef.

Brisket braised

In a thin layer of hot fat in the boiling pot, cook two onions, three carrots and a turnip of medium size, and cut into large pieces. When nicely browned, drain away the fat, add a bunch of mixed herbs, and barely cover with boiling water. Lay the meat on top, and, should the lid not fit closely, place beneath it a double fold of greased paper. Cook gently by the side of the fire or in the oven for at least five hours, keeping the vegetables almost covered with water. Have ready one or two tablespoonfuls of flour cooked to a fawn colour in enough butter to moisten it (use a small saucepan). Strain in the liquid after dishing the meat, and stir and boil till smooth, adding as much diluted meat extract as may be necessary to thin it. Season to taste and add a little vinegar or chopped gherkin. The bones may be removed before cooking and brown with the vegetables. Carrots and turnips should be served as a vegetable; cut in finger shapes and half-cook the carrot before adding the turnip.—L.G.N.

BROTH, Meat
Fr. *Bouillon*; Ger. *Fleischbruhe*; It. *Brodo*; Sp. *Brodio*. The water in which meat, as well as vegetables, as a rule, have been boiled. It is the basis of all clear meat soups: it is to soup what the material is to the dress.

Mutton Broth
> 1 lb. best end neck of mutton
> Cold water to cover
> 1 onion
> 1 carrot
> 1 turnip
> 1 stalk celery
> 1 leek
> 1 teaspoon pearl barley
> Salt and pepper
> Chopped parsley

Trim off some of the fat but do not remove bones. Place meat in water in an earthenware or iron pot and bring to boiling point. Be sure and remove scum as it rises and then add the vegetables, evenly sliced, with the barley. Simmer for three hours, after seasoning according to taste with salt and pepper. Then remove meat; cut into small pieces, replace these in soup and serve very hot.

Sheep's Head Broth
Split and clean the head, removing the eyes, and keep the brains out to make a savoury.

Skin the trotters carefully and wash with the head in lukewarm water. Leave all in cold water for two hours, with the neck and other odd scraps if available.

Put on the fire two gallons of cold water and add ¾ lb. of Scots barley. When it comes to the boil, put in the head, trotters, and neck of mutton, with carrots and turnips cut small. Boil for three hours, remove the meat and skim carefully, but if preferred scraps of the sheep's head can be left in. Half an hour before serving, put in some chopped onions. Serve very hot.—B.C.

SCOTCH BROTH
The Scottish edition of the French 'Pot-au-feu', with mutton instead of beef as its meat foundation.

BUBBLE AND SQUEAK
A 150-year-old English dish, traditionally employed for disposing of the remains of cold salt beef, though in the earliest named recipe that I have actually seen, Mrs Rundell prescribes for its use the plain roast variety. Soyer's method is as follows: Boil a few greens or a well washed savoy in plain water until tender, drain it quite dry in a sieve, chop it rather fine with a knife and season well with pepper and salt. Cut some rather underdone salt beef into slices not thicker than a five-shilling piece, and some slices of fat; put 2 oz. butter in a *sauté* pan and when it is melted lay in the meat, and, over a quick fire, fry both sides to a yellowish brown colour, when take them out on a dish and keep hot; place the vegetables in the same pan and keep turning them until quite hot, when dress them on a dish with the beef on top and serve.

The name is derived from the behaviour of the vegetables when introduced to the hot fat in the pan.

BUCK
The male of the fallow deer and the roe deer, as distinct from the male of the red deer, called *Stag*. It is also much used in its English form or in its Dutch spelling *Bok* added to the name of various deer and antelopes, such as *Roebuck* and *Springbok*. When so used, the name applies equally to male and female of the species. (See *Venison*.)

Braised Buck
Braise in veal stock, to which port wine, carrots, onions, and herbs are added. 'Best neck' cutlets are excellent done in this way. Red currant or cranberry jelly should be added to the sauce, which should above all things have a smooth demi-glaze texture.—M.H.P.

BUFFALO
(a) Lat. *Bison bison*. The American *Bison* (q.v.).

(b) Lat. *Syncerus caffer*. The Cape *Buffalo*, reputed to be the most dangerous beast of the African jungle.

(c) Lat. *Bubalus bubalis*. The Indian *Water Buffalo*, or *Carabao*, now domesticated and used as a draught animal.

The flesh of all buffaloes is edible, but not to be compared with beef in point of quality. As a matter of fact, the American species is now too rare to be killed for food, and the Indian Buffalo too useful on the farm to be killed before it is past working: it is also past eating by then. The African Buffalo is the only one which is still slaughtered for the market; it can be prepared in any way suitable for *Beef* (q.v.), all except its *hump*, a flabby growth between the two shoulder blades, which is coarse and stringy but can be prepared for the table in the same way as the hump of the *Camel* (q.v.).

BUFFLE

French for *Buffalo* (q.v.), and the name used by the English translators of the Bible for the Hebrew *Jemur*. Some authorities believe that *Jemur* means *Fallow-deer* and others *Wild Ox* or *Buffalo*.

BULLY BEEF

The English name of the American *Corned Beef*, that is pressed beef cured in a way that makes it suitable for long keeping in a tin or can. 'Corned' is an old English word meaning 'cured', and the cuts of beef commonly corned are the fancy brisket and the rattle-ran.† The red colour of Bully Beef is due to a liberal use of saltpetre in the curing, but in New England the custom is to use little saltpetre and New England corned beef is of a grey-brown colour which is quite distinctive.

Bully beef may be eaten straight from the tin, sliced, as cold meat, with pickles and a salad; or it can be stewed and made the basis of a *ragoût*, with any vegetables available; or it may be mixed in with sliced onions and fried in an open pan, which is the nearest approach – and a very good one – to the *Miroton* (q.v.) which soldiers on the march used to prepare for themselves.

Corning Beef

To 4 gallons water, 6 lb. salt, 2 oz. saltpetre, 1½ lb. brown sugar. Salt beef and let lay in a cool place four or five days. Then pack in a close barrel and pour the above mixture upon it. The drying pieces are ready for use in three weeks – the other in a month. (*Mrs Sarah D. Avirett Thomas, Allegany County.*) —F.P.S.

BUSHBUCK. BOSCHBOK

Lat. *Tragelaphus sylvaticus*. A small South African harnessed Antelope, with spirally twisted horns. Also any of several related species.

'This antelope is found everywhere in the belt of bush running all along the coast-line of the Cape Colony and Natal, and which in some places extends to a considerable distance inland.'—F.C.S.

'They are good eating; the flesh appears to me to have a distinct aromatic flavour, probably caused from its fragrant vegetable diet.'—F.V.K.

†*The* Rattleran *is described in* Webster's *as the upper back section of the plate piece of beef, especially a strip above the navel and brisket.*

BUSHPIG. BOSCHVARK

Lat. *Potomochoerus koïropotamus*. A South African wild hog which is mainly vegetarian and very destructive near cultivated lands; they move in troops of eight or ten as a rule, but sometimes 15 or 20, and they can do a great deal of damage in a little time. 'Their flesh is very coarse, yet generally eaten, but they never become very fat.'—F.V.K.

CALF

The young – under one year – of any bovine animal, but more particularly of the domestic cow is called *Calf*. Saxon *Calf*, in the cottage, became Norman *Veal*, in the mansion, said Wamba, the jester, to Gurth, the swineherd, in *Ivanhoe*: hence the roast, braised, boiled Veal; the *fricassées*, *ragoûts*, loins, and cutlets of Veal. But the offals evidently did not reach the lord's table, and they have always been known by their Saxon names; hence calf's or calves' brains (see *Brains*), chitterlings, ears, feet, head, heart, kidneys (see *Kidneys*), liver (see *Liver*), lungs, pluck, sweetbread (see *Sweetbread*) and tongue.

Calf's Ears à la Tortue

Procure four white calf's ears (cut with a broad base), scald them in boiling water for five minutes, after which plunge them in cold water, and let them be wiped dry; then hold them on the point of a skewer over the flame of a charcoal fire, to singe off any remaining hairs; wipe them clean, rub them over with lemon-juice, and braise them in some *blanc* (broth) for about 1½ or 2 hours. When the ears are done, drain them on a wet napkin, and with the back of the blade of a small knife scrape off all the soft skin; trim them neatly, and with the point of a knife cut the white gristle of each into slits – taking particular care not to draw the knife through – so that when the thin part of the ears is turned down, the strips may form themselves into loops or curls. When the ears are ready to dish up, fill each with a decorated *quenelle* or a round truffle, garnish with a *ragoût à la Tortue*, and serve.—A.F.

(The *Ragoût à la Tortue* is a rich stew with a *Sauce Madère* as its basis, tomatoes, truffles, olives, mushrooms, cocks' combs and such tasty trimmings stewed in it.—ED.)

Calf's or Calves' Feet

The feet should be split into halves, longways, carefully cleaned, singed and scalded; they are then boiled in salted water or, preferably, stock, until the flesh comes easily away from the bones. The flesh is then drained and it may be served in a number of ways, either dipped in breadcrumbs and egg or in batter and fried, or served as an *Entrée*, with any number of different sauces such as vinaigrette, ravigote, piquante, poulette, etc.

Pieds de Veau à la Ménagère

Boil two or three split feet as indicated, carefully boning them when done. Melt some butter in a pan, brown the feet in this, with a cut-up onion, add a small *bouquet*, a little tomato *purée*, salt and pepper. Brown all this nicely together, dredge with flour, stir and moisten with a mixture of white wine and *bouillon* or stock. Simmer for 20 minutes and serve with some mashed potatoes.—P.W.

Calf's Foot Broth

Ingredients: 1 calf's foot, 3 pints of water, 1 small lump of sugar, nutmeg to taste, the yolk of 1 egg, a piece of butter the size of a nut.

Mode: Stew the foot in the water, with the lemon-peel, *very gently*, until the liquid is reduced to half, removing any scum, should it rise to the surface. Set it by in a basin until quite cold, then take off every particle of fat. Warm up about half pint of the broth, adding the butter, sugar, and a very small quantity of grated nutmeg; take it off the fire for a minute or two, then add the beaten yolk of the egg; keep stirring over the fire until the mixture thickens, but do not allow it to boil again after the egg is added, or it will curdle and the broth will be spoiled.—B.

Calf's Foot Jelly

Jelly stock, made from calf's feet, requires to be made the day previous to being used. Take two calf's feet, cut them up, and boil in three quarts of water; as soon as it boils, remove it to the corner of the fire, and simmer for five hours, keeping it skimmed, pass through a hair-sieve into a basin, and let it remain until quite hard, then remove the oil and fat, and wipe the top dry. Place in a stewpan one gill of water, one of sherry, ½ lb. of lump sugar, the juice of four lemons, the rinds of two, and the whites and shells of five eggs, whisk until the sugar is melted, then add the jelly, place it on the fire, and whisk until boiling, pass it through a jelly-bag, pouring back again what comes through first, until quite clear; it is then ready to be poured into moulds or glasses.—AL.S.

Calf's Head

Fr. *Tête de veau*. A light and very popular *Entrée* served either plain boiled with a white sauce or with a *Vinaigrette*: or else *à la Financière* or *en Tortue*. *Calf's head soup* is known as *Mock Turtle* (q.v.).

Tête de Veau Vinaigrette

Half or a whole calf's head
1 large onion
2 carrots
Juice 2 lemons
Peppercorns
1 tablespoon flour
2 whole cloves
1 'bouquet-garni'
Salt

Have the head boned and cleaned by butcher. Mix the flour into sufficient boiling water to cover the head, add the vegetables, bouquet, cloves, salt, peppercorns and lemon juice and allow to boil for 10 or 15 minutes to flavour water before adding the head. The addition of the flour keeps the head white and is known as a 'blanchaille'. Cook gently in the court-bouillon until quite tender. Drain well. Serve hot with a well-seasoned vinaigrette sauce.—P.W.

Tête de Veau en Tortue

1 boiled (or half) calf's head
Few blades fresh basil
Strip red pepper
1 tablespoon tomato purée
2 sheep's kidneys
Stoned olives
Few button mushroom caps
Croûtons
1 cup bouillon
1 glass dry sherry
Salt and pepper
2 cups brown *roux*
1 tablespoon beef essence
1 truffle
Chopped pickled gherkins
Butter
1 or 2 hard-boiled eggs

The sauce of this otherwise inexpensive meat dish is in the nature of a court dress for a village maiden, and, at that, still other ingredients were called for in this old French recipe such as cocks' combs and crayfish!

Cook the head as described in preceding recipe. Now for the sauce. Place the sherry and bouillon in a saucepan with the basil. Cook fast to reduce to half original quantity, adding salt, pepper and strip of red pepper. Thicken by addition of the *roux* (see Section *SAUCES*) and the tomato *purée*, add beef extract, cut-up kidneys, cut-up truffle, stoned green olives, chopped gherkins and mushroom caps. Simmer all together for 15 to 20 minutes then add the head, cut into neat pieces, and simmer 10 minutes longer with more *bouillon* if required. Garnish dish with croûtons – rounds of hard-boiled egg, fried in butter, and ... crayfish!—P.W.

Calf's Heart

One calf's heart; three tablespoons breadcrumbs; one dessertspoon chopped ham; one tablespoon melted butter; chopped parsley; grated lemon rind; seasoning; egg or milk; tomato sauce. Wash the heart thoroughly and remove the large veins and arteries. Soak it for half an hour or longer in cold water to which a little salt has been added. Then blanch it, i.e., put it into a saucepan with cold water to cover, bring to the boil, throw the water away, and rinse the heart. It should now be clean and ready for stuffing. Mix all the dry ingredients in a basin, season them carefully, and bind together with the melted butter and a little egg or milk. Put this stuffing into the heart and sew it up, or tie a piece of greased paper over the top. Then roll in flour to make it thoroughly dry. Melt a small quantity of dripping in a stewpan, put in the heart and brown all over. Pour in a cupful of water or stock and stew slowly until the heart is tender, from 1½ to 2 hours. When ready, lift it on to a hot dish and remove the string or paper. To make a sauce prepare one cupful of tomato *purée* by rubbing some fresh or tinned tomatoes through a sieve. Mix this with a tablespoonful of flour and add to liquid left in the saucepan. Stir until boiling, season to taste, and when thoroughly cooked strain over the heart. Garnish with lemon and roast or *sauté* potatoes.—G.H. (1).

London's clever Soho Restaurateurs have discovered that the texture of suitably cooked calf's heart is very similar to that of wild duck, and the breast of wild duck served in Soho with a spicy brown sauce and sliced orange has often been in reality thin slivers of calf's heart.

Love in Disguise

After well cleaning, stuff a calf's heart, cover it an inch thick with good forcemeat, then roll it in vermicelli, put it into a dish, with a little water, and send it to the oven. When done, serve it with its own gravy in the dish. This forms a pretty side dish.—D.M.

Calf's Pluck

Roast a calf's heart stuffed with suet, sweet herbs, and parsley, crumbs of bread, pepper, salt, nutmeg, and a little lemon-peel all mixed together with the yolk of an egg. Boil the lights with part of the liver; when done, chop them small, and put them into a saucepan, with butter rolled in flour, some pepper and salt, and lemon juice. Fry the other part of the liver with some thin slices of bacon. Lay the mince at the bottom of the dish, the heart in the middle, and the fried liver and bacon round, with crisp parsley. Serve with plain melted butter.—D.M.

Calf's Tongue (Fresh)

This may be braised, as indicated in recipe for preparing ox tongue, or boiled, as calf's head, and served with any good sauce: ravigote, tomato, etc. It is nice, after being boiled in a well seasoned *court-bouillon*, served with pease pudding.

Calf's Tongue (Pickled)
(Marble Veal)

1 calf's pickled tongue
¼ teaspoon mace
Parsley
1 lb. fresh butter
4 lb. lean veal
Salt and pepper
Clarified butter

This dish is handy to have ready if the family is large and the weather hot. Boil either a dried or a pickled tongue until very tender. Remove skin and cut into as thin slices as possible. Pound these in a mortar with the butter and the mace until mixture is like a paste. Stew the veal in enough water barely to cover, adding salt and pepper, until very tender, then cut up and pound it in the same way. Have a large earthenware pot – called a 'crock' in some parts – and put a good layer of the veal in this, covering it with lumps of the tongue paste. Cover this with remainder of veal, nearly filling pot, press down hard and pour clarified butter over all. When serving, turn out of pot very carefully, cut into crossways slices and garnish with parsley. Any of the meat that is not used should be kept in a cool place, in the original pot.—P.W.

CAMEL

(*a*) *Camelus bactrianus*, the Asiatic *Camel* with two humps.

(*b*) *Camelus dromedarius*, the Arabian *Camel* or *Dromedary*, with only one hump.

The Camel is the chief beast of burden in Western Asia and Northern Africa, and much too valuable as such to be slaughtered for food, but in olden times, when there were probably many more camels than there are now, the *Camel* was greatly valued for the table. Aristotles places the flesh of the *Camel* above all other delicate viands, and it was highly valued by the Persians and Egyptians, but not by the Romans: the Jews were forbidden to eat it.

'The flesh of the young dromedary is as good as that of veal, and the Arabs make of it their common food. They preserve it in vases, which they cover with fat. They make butter and cheese with the milk of the female.' (Desmarest).

The best part of the Camel, according to Western Desert epicures, is the Hump. It is marinated in a pickle of olive oil, lemon juice, pepper and salt and various spices for as long as the weather will permit, a couple of days at most, and it is then roasted on a spit or baked in the oven, and served with a gravy made from its own fat and the marinade simmered down.

In the *Larousse Gastronomique* there are various recipes given for camel dishes, including *Couscous au chameau, filet de chameau rôti, pieds de chameau à la vinaigrette, pilaf de chameau, ragoût de chameau à la tomate, tranches de chameau aux poivrons* and *ventre de chameau à la marocaine.*

CAMELOPARD
The medieval name of the Giraffe – long-legged and long-necked like the camel and the skin spotted like that of the leopard. The Hebrews were allowed to eat its flesh, being a 'beast that parteth the hoof and cleaveth the cleft into two claws, and cheweth the cud.' (*Deut.* chap. xiv, v. 6).

CAPE HARE
Lat. *Lepus capensis*. Gastronomically speaking just as good as the European species.' —M.S.A., p. 98.

CARBONADES
Originally French for a grill 'over the coals', but now chiefly used for braised beef in the Belgian manner, either *Carbonades de boeuf à la flamande* or *au lambic.*

CARBONADO
This is one of the national dishes of the Argentine.

'The "carbonado" is an excellent and most practical dish – and, as eaten in Buenos Aires, an unforgettable one. Its recipe is as follows: Fry four onions in four teaspoonfuls of butter, and just before they brown put in a peeled and peppered tomato. When these are fried, add about 1 lb. or 1½ lb. of minced beef and let this brown lightly. Add salt, pepper and a little stock; cover, and allow to cook over a very slow fire for the best part of an hour. Then add fruit. In Argentina, where peaches are cheap, these are chiefly used as well as pears, but apples, or plums, are as good – about nine in all.

'At the same time, add some potatoes cut in small pieces, and cover again till the fruit is cooked. At the last minute drop in a handful of raisins. The result is unexpected and delicious.'—RUPERT CROFT-COOKE. 'Some Argentine Dishes', in *Wine and Food*, XXII, p. 140.

CARIBOU
Lat. *Rangifer tarandus*. The name of a North American and Greenland *Reindeer* (q.v.), the main source of food supply for the Eskimos of Alaska.—V.S.

'As an article of food, its (*Woodland Caribou*) flesh is not highly prized. Indeed, it is deemed inferior to any other venison, although, when in good condition, it is both palatable and nourishing.'

CAT
Lat. *Felis domesticus*. A carnivorous quadruped mostly hand-fed and never (knowingly) eaten in the British Isles. But its flesh has been described by Englishmen who have tasted it as very good. Labouchère, who ate cats during the siege of Paris in 1870, wrote that a cat was 'something between a rabbit and a squirrel with a flavour of its own. It is delicious. Don't drown your kittens, eat 'em.'

CERVELAS
Fr. for *Saveloys* (q.v.).

CHAIR À SAUCISSES
Fr. for sausage meat or *Forcemeat* (q.v.).

CHARCUTERIE
The name serves both for the wares sold by the pork-butcher, in France, and the shop in which they are sold. Among the many varieties of pig-meat preparations sold under the name of *Charcuterie*, the more usual are: Andouilles, Andouillettes, Boudin, Boudin blanc, Cervelas, Chair à saucisses, Confit de porc, Fromage de tête, Mortadelle, Pâté de foie, Rillettes, Rillons, Saucisses and Saucissons.

CHATEAUBRIAND
A steak of superlative quality: it is cut in the fillet; it is particularly thick; it is broiled or grilled and served with *Pommes Château* and a *Sauce Béarnaise*. Its name is due to Montmireil, who was chef to Chateaubriand when he introduced it. His own method – too wasteful for our times – was to place a thick steak from the fillet between two other steaks of exactly the same size; the two covering pieces of steak were burnt black in the grilling, whilst the *Chateaubriand* in between them was evenly pink throughout.

CHIPOLATA. CIPOLLATA
The name given to small (*little fingers*) sausages, which should be plentifully seasoned with chives, their name being derived from the Italian for *Chives*.

CHILE CON CARNE
1 lb. beef, diced in ½ in. cubes
½ lb. red peppers, or 2 tablespoons chile powder
4 slices onion, minced
Salt
2 tablespoons lard
¼ cup flour
Pinch of wild marjoram
3 cloves garlic

Fry garlic in lard until brown, then remove. Sprinkle flour over meat, then put meat in hot lard and brown. Make thin paste of chile powder or red peppers. (If red peppers are used, have seeds, veins, stems and skins removed by soaking in hot water.) Pour this and other ingredients over meat. Cover with hot water. Simmer until meat is very tender and sauce thickened.—c.g.

CHORISOS
The most popular Spanish sausages, usually highly seasoned with pimentoes, and sometimes with garlic as well.

CHUCK
One of the cheapest cuts of beef: usually used for making soups or stock; sometimes for stews and pies.

CHURRASCO
An almost universal dish in Argentina, especially in small restaurants which specialize in the cookery of the country. It is a thick beefsteak which is placed, already salted, on an almost red-hot flat-iron, and fired till it is about to burn, then turned over and cooked again. It is served without the addition of more salt, so that it retains the appetizing flavour which its contact with fire has given to it.—RUPERT CROFT-COOKE in *Wine and Food*, XXII, p. 140.

CITY CHICKEN LEGS
Two square smallish pieces of ham and two pieces of the same size and thickness of veal, in alternating order upon a skewer; dipped in biscuit crumbs and beaten egg, and fried brown in a frying-pan before being baked in a hot oven for an hour.

CIVET
A name which has nothing to do with the wholly inedible Civet Cat; it comes from the old French name *Civette*, now *Ciboulette*, or *Chive*, a savoury herb which used to be the informing flavour of this dish. In modern culinary parlance, a *Civet* is a *ragoût* or *fricassée* of game, sometimes also of poultry, cooked in wine and with the blood of the freshly-killed animal also used in the cooking thereof.

COLLOPS
Pieces of cut-up meat, now mostly beef, but formerly veal and mutton as well, and even chicken.

Beef Collops
2 cups of diced cold roast beef
3 tablespoons flour
Salt and pepper
Chopped parsley
3 tablespoons butter
Additional butter

Onion juice
2 cups fresh breadcrumbs
1½ cup stock

Cut meat up into small dice, after removing fat and gristle. Melt the butter, blend in the flour and moisten with the hot stock, stirring all the time and beating until smooth and thick. Add the onion juice and parsley. Put half the quantity of the breadcrumbs into a well-buttered baking-dish. Cover with the pieces of meat, pour the hot sauce over this and cover with rest of crumbs. Dot with butter and bake for 20 minutes.—p.w.

Minced Collops for Invalids
Minced collops of raw meat are sometimes recommended for invalids. Beef of the best quality should be obtained and minced finely, raw. It is then thoroughly heated in a little good stock in a casserole or double saucepan, seasoned and served on sippets of toast within a border of boiled rice or macaroni.

Scotch Collops
Best stewing steak put through the mincer, cooked with onion to flavour, seasoned to taste, and served with sippets of toast on the mince and sliced hard-boiled egg round the dish.—E.M.L.D.

Veal Collops
Cut long, thin collops, beat them well, and lay on them a bit of thin bacon of the same size, and spread forcemeat on that, seasoned high and also a little garlic and cayenne. Roll them up tight, about the size of two fingers, but not more than 2 or 3 in. long; put a very thin skewer to fasten each firmly; rub them over; fry them of a fine brown, and pour a rich brown gravy over.—M.E.R. (1814).

CONSOMMÉ
When unqualified, *Consommé* means, in culinary French, a clear soup made by simmering meat and vegetables together for a long time, after which it is strained and served either hot or cold. It is the strained liquor from the *Pot-au-feu* (q.v.). It varies in richness of flavour according to the proportion of meat to water that is used: when much meat is put in the pot or much time allowed for the water to steam itself away, the more highly concentrated form of stock which is obtained thereby is known as *Consommé Double* or *Consommé Riche*. When a *Consommé* is made with chicken, game, fish or vegetables, in place of beef, it is called *Consommé de volaille, de gibier, de poisson* or *de légumes*, accordingly. When the *Consommé* is merely the basis of a clear soup, with various garnishings added, its name is immediately followed by some culinary name indicating the nature of such garnishings. There are a

great many such names and new ones may be added to the already long list of them by any cook, but the few which are indicated here merely serve to illustrate the variety of Meat *Consommés*.

A l'Ancienne. A beef *Consommé* garnished with hollowed crusts of bread filled with the vegetables which have cooked with the meat; they are mashed to a *purée* first of all, and the crusts filled with this *purée* are browned under the grill before being served in the *Consommé*.

Andalouse (Consommé à l'). A clear *Consommé* with tomato *fumet*, garnished with dice of *royale* and tomatoes, a *julienne* of ham, rice and eggs *filés*.

Anversoise (Consommé à l'). A beef *Consommé* garnished with hop shoots and thickened with some tapioca.

Aurore. *Consommé* with a tomato *fumet* and a light tapioca binding. Garnished with a *julienne* of chicken white meat.

Beatrice. A beef *Consommé* with semolina, tomato *purée* and *royale*.

Belle-Gabrielle. A beef *Consommé* with a tapioca binding, garnished with rectangles of *mousse de volaille* and crayfish tails.

Bergère. A beef *Consommé* with a tapioca binding, garnished with asparagus points, shredded *mousserons*, tarragon and chervil.

Berny. A beef *Consommé* with a tapioca binding, garnished with a potato *purée* made up of potato *Dauphine*, marble-like in size, chopped grilled almonds, chopped up truffles and sprigs of chervil.

Boieldieu. A beef *Consommé* with a tapioca binding and garnished with three kinds of *quenelles*: foie gras, chicken and truffles.

Bouchère. A *Petite Marmite* garnished with squares of cabbage cooked in *Consommé*, and pieces of marrowbone fat served at the same time.

Bourbon. A beef *Consommé* with a tapioca binding, garnished with chicken stuffing, *perles du Japon* and sprigs of chervil.

Bourdaloue. A beef *Consommé* garnished with four kinds of *royale*: ordinary (white); tomatoes (red); asparagus points (green); carrot *purée* (pink).

Brieux. A beef *Consommé* with a tapioca binding, garnished with *royale* cut in the shape of small stars, dice of truffles and *perles du Japon*.

Britannia. A beef *Consommé* with a tapioca binding, garnished with crayfish *royale* and a *julienne* of truffles.

Carmen. A beef *Consommé* with *fumet* of sweet peppers and tomatoes; garnished with tomatoes, a *julienne* of pimentoes, rice and sprigs of chervil.

Catalane. A beef *Consommé* garnished with dice of egg-plant, sweet peppers and tomatoes, also rice; served with grated cheese.

Charolaise. A *Petite Marmite* garnished with small pieces of ox-tail, small onions, carrots and cabbage cut up small.

Chartreuse. Beef *Consommé* with a tapioca binding, garnished with pieces of tomatoes and ravioli filled with foie gras, spinach and chopped truffles.

Chasseur. A game *Consommé* with port wine added, garnished with a *julienne* of mushrooms and sprigs of chervil; served with *profiteroles* filled with game *purée*.

Colbert. A beef *Consommé* garnished with all sorts of fresh vegetables, cut up small, and poached eggs.

Cultivateur. A *Consommé* with some pork in it and a *brunoise* of carrots, turnips, leeks and onions; also potatoes.

Diane. A game *Consommé* garnished with game stuffing, and dice of truffles; a glass of Madeira wine is added at time of serving.

Douglas. A beef *Consommé* garnished with rounds of sweetbread, artichoke bottoms and asparagus points.

Dubarry. A beef *Consommé* with a light binding of tapioca garnished with rounds of *royale*, sprigs of cauliflowers, and chervil.

Ecossaise. Mutton broth with pearl barley and a *brunoise* of vegetables.

Favorite. A tapioca *Consommé* with small round potatoes, a *julienne* of artichoke bottoms and mushrooms; also sprigs of parsley.

Flamande. A meat *Consommé* with *royale* of sprouts *purée*, green peas and sprigs of parsley.

Germaine. A meat *Consommé* garnished with *quenelles* of chicken and *royale* of green peas.

Germinal. A meat *Consommé* with tarragon *fumet*, garnished with green peas, beans, and a *julienne* of carrots.

Grimaldi. Meat *Consommé* with tomato *fumet*, garnished with dice of *royale* and a *julienne* of celery.

Hongroise. A meat *Consommé* with tomato *fumet* and some paprika, garnished with quenelles of calf's liver and *rondelles* of chicken stuffing seasoned with paprika.

Indienne. Meat *Consommé* with curry powder and garnished with dice of *royale* made with coco-nut milk. Rice *à l'Indienne* is served separately with this *Consommé*.

Italienne. Meat *Consommé* garnished with dice of *royale* made with tomato *purée*, dice of *royale* made with spinach *purée* and some spaghetti. Grated cheese is served separately.

Léopold. Meat *Consommé* with semolina, garnished with a *chiffonnade* of lettuce and sorrel.

Macdonald. Meat *Consommé* with *royale* of sheep's brains, dice of cucumber and small ravioli.

Madrilène. Cold *Consommé* with *fumet* of celery and tomatoes, highly seasoned.

Médicis. Beef broth with a light tapioca binding; garnished with a sorrel *chiffonade* and dice of *royale*, some made of carrots, some of mashed green peas.

Mégère. Beef broth garnished with potatoes, *chiffonade* of lettuce and large vermicelli.

Mercédès. Beef broth, with some sherry added at time of serving, garnished with crowns of red peppers and stars of coxcombs.

Metternich. Meat broth with *fumet* of pheasant, garnished with dice of *royale* made of artichoke *purée* and with a *julienne* of pheasant.

Mirette.✦ Meat broth garnished with *quenelles* of chicken, a *chiffonade* of lettuce and some chervil. Cheese straws are served with this soup.

Parisienne. A meat broth with leeks and a *julienne* of potatoes and leeks.

St Hubert. Game broth (hare or venison) with added white wine; garnished with *julienne* of game and *royale* made of game *purée* and mashed lentils, cut in the shape of crosses.

CONY. CONEY

The old English name for *Rabbit* (q.v.). It is still used in the Statutes and Heraldry, but no longer in Gastronomy.

COWBOY STEW

(West Texas Recipe)

      5 lb. tenderloin of beef
      5 lb. sweetbread
      4 sets brains
      3 lb. calf liver
      3 calf kidneys
      1 calf heart
      1 lb. tallow
      1 large onion
      2 whole small hot green peppers
        (or dry hot chilis)

Cut steak, liver, heart, and kidney in cubes about ¾ in. in size. Cut tallow in small pieces using the tallow for braising all of the above separately until a little brown. Salt and pepper. After taking membrane from sweetbreads, cut in small pieces, and put all of this in large vessel, large enough to cook all the stew. Cover all the ingredients with water and cook slowly three or four hours. Then put in the brains, the whole onion and hot pepper and allow to cook one and a half hours more. Then take out the onion as it is for seasoning only.

Do not put any flour or thickening of any kind, as the juices from the meat should make a good, thick gravy. If you have to add any water on account of it cooking down too much, be sure your water is boiling hot and be careful not to add too much. (Serves about 30 people.)—M. BRAINARD.

COW-HEEL

A major edition of the *Calf's-foot* (q.v.), so rich in gelatinous substance that, when used for making soup, it may impart a glue-like quality to the broth unless adequately watered.

Cow-heel, Boiled

Ingredients: 1 cow-heel, 1 oz. butter, 1 oz. flour, 1 dessertspoon finely chopped parsley, salt and pepper.

Method: Wash the heel, put it into a saucepan, cover with cold water and cook gently for about two or three hours. Fry the flour and butter together, but do not let them brown, strain on to them three-quarters of a pint of the liquor in which the cow-heel is cooking, stir until boiling, simmer for a few minutes, then add the parsley and salt and pepper to taste. When sufficiently cooked, remove the bones, arrange the pieces of meat on a hot dish, and pour the sauce over. Time: about three hours. Sufficient for four persons.—B.E.C.

Cow-heel à la Hendy

From the butcher get a good, hefty cow-heel, well-dressed, and a pound of shin of beef, or hough; split the cow-heel lengthwise and cut it up into sizeable pieces, cut up your shin and put the whole lot into a stew-pan with a few peppercorns, a blade of mace and a spot of parsley, pepper and salt to taste; cover with water, or beef stock, and simmer for four hours; add a small glass of sherry, if you like it; thicken your gravy, garnish with sippets of toast and parsley when you serve it up.—H.G.B.

COYPU. NUTRIA

Lat. *Myocastor coypus.* A South American aquatic rodent which is easy to rear and is extensively farmed for its pelt; it has webbed hind feet and is a cousin of the *Musk Rat*. Its flesh is not only edible but, according to L.R.Brightwell, speaking from personal experience, it is most palatable and nutritious: it should be treated like hare and its flesh is very much like that of the hare, but it also has a slightly 'beefy' quality. *Coypu* weigh up to 15 lb.

CRACKLING

The scored skin or rind of a joint of pork after it has been roasted or baked crisp, on spit or in the oven.

CRÉPINETTES

Small and flattish sausages cooked in a piece of caul (Fr. *crépine*) or oiled paper, but not encased in a gut or skin. *Crépinettes* may be made of all sorts of forcemeat, not necessarily but usually pork, and highly seasoned; the best sorts also have some chopped truffle mixed with the forcemeat and are served with a slice of truffle over each *crépinette*. *Crépinettes* are usually buttered and grilled and served with a creamy *Purée de Pommes de terre*; they may also be fried or baked.

CROQUE-MONSIEUR

Rounds of thin, stale bread
Very thin slices of ham
Savoury prepared mustard
Softened butter
Grated Gruyère cheese
Frying-fat

Cut the rounds of bread thin, spread with butter mixed with a little French savoury mustard. Sprinkle rather thickly with the grated cheese and lay on this a round of thinly-cut ham the size of the round of bread. Cover the whole with another well-buttered round of bread, press firmly together and drop in frying-fat at the 'smoking' stage of heat (or 375° if you use – as you should – a frying-thermometer). If desired, each round may be dipped in a good batter and fried like tiny fritters. Serve very hot with crisp fried parsley.—P.W.

CROQUETTES

Croquettes of Pork-meat
(*Varkenscroquettes*: Dutch East Indies)
¼ cup onions, minced
1 tablespoon butter
¾ cup mushrooms, minced
2 cups (1 lb.) cooked pork, minced
½ cup flour
1¼ cups bouillon or stock
½ teaspoon salt, or more
¼ teaspoon pepper
½ teaspoon nutmeg
½ teaspoon turmeric
¼ tablespoon vinegar or lemon juice
2 eggs, beaten
1 cup breadcrumbs
Deep fat for frying

Sauté onions in butter. Add mushrooms and brown slightly. Add meat. Set aside. Brown the flour and mix with melted butter. Add stock slowly to the mixture to keep from lumping. Next add salt, pepper, nutmeg, turmeric, and vinegar or lemon juice. Stir constantly. Allow to thicken. Mix with meat and mushrooms, pour into flat dish and allow to cool. When cold, shape with spoons into rolls 2½ in. long and 1 in. thick. Carefully roll in beaten eggs, then in dry breadcrumbs. Coat well and, if necessary, repeat process; however, do not coat too thickly. Drop into deep fat (375°-380°F.) and allow to brown to light golden colour. Drain on paper to remove fat. Serve very hot. Serves four to six persons.—P.V.M.

Croquettes of Cooked Meat
Ingredients: 1½ lb. meat, 3 eggs, 5 oz. butter, dried thyme, 9 oz. flour, mint, marjoram, sage, parsley, breadcrumbs, lemon juice.

Method: Mince finely the meat and prepare the paste. Take ½ lb. flour and mix with a teaspoonful of salt in a bowl, add ¼ lb. butter or dripping and rub lightly between the fingers till it becomes like breadcrumbs, mix in with a spoon the yolk of an egg and a few drops of lemon juice and add sufficient water to form the paste. Turn it out upon the board and work it inwards, then roll it out thin once and cut into rounds. Take 1 oz. flour, 1 oz. butter, a tablespoonful cream, some thyme, mint, marjoram, sage and parsley dried and rubbed down to a fine powder and put on the fire in a saucepan. When it has boiled for about three minutes, add pepper and salt and two eggs beaten. Mix in bowl with minced meat. Take the rounds of paste and lay a little of the minced meat in the centre. Moisten the edge of half the round with water and fold over. Pinch round the edges. Brush with egg and roll in breadcrumbs, put in frying-basket and fry in boiling dripping for about one minute.–C.N.

Croquettes
(French fashion)

Take some *bouilli* or the remains of almost any cooked meat or fowl, remove skin and bones and chop the meat, but not too fine.

For 250 grammes (9 oz.) of chopped-up meat put in a casserole an egg of butter, a tablespoon of flour and melt it on the fire; when the butter is melted and well mixed with the flour, dilute with half a glass of water, then add the meat prepared as above, a little finely chopped parsley if liked and some chopped mushrooms if you have any. Simmer for a quarter of an hour without covering, so as to let the sauce evaporate; it is necessary that none remain. Let it get cold. Add two egg yolks and if you like, a spoonful of cream. Make little heaps which you mould into shape of corks or little balls; flour them and dip in yolk and white of egg, beaten as for omelettes and mixed with a small spoonful of water and one of oil, then roll them in finely crumbled breadcrumbs. Fry in deep fat and serve with fried parsley. —L.B.C.

Lamb Croquettes
Fry a tablespoonful of onion in butter then remove and add quarter cup flour to butter in pan, stir, moisten with one cup stock, cook for a few minutes, then add a cupful of cold minced meat and two-thirds of a cupful of chopped boiled potatoes. Cook gently until mixture is practically dry; then cool, shape, egg and breadcrumb in usual way and fry. Serve with any desired sauce such as tomato, mushroom, etc., very hot, when ready.

CROÛTE-AU-POT

Having removed excess of fat from the '*Pot-au-feu*' (q.v.), either by straining or by removing congealed fat from cold soup left over from the previous day, heat to boiling point and add a few scraps of cooked beef, some cubes of cooked vegetables and pour the whole in an earthenware marmite, having placed in it a toasted square of bread per person. Grated cheese is usually handed round at the same time.

CURRIES

Curried Beef

2 lb. lean beefsteak
3 or 4 tablespoons butter
1 scanty tablespoon flour
1 small tart apple
Lemon juice to taste
2 cups good stock
1 minced onion
1 dessertspoon curry powder
Tiny pinch sugar
Boiled rice

Cut the meat into cubes or squares and fry quickly in the butter until lightly browned. Remove meat and add the onion, chopped apple, curry powder and flour to butter in pan, cooking gently for about 10 minutes, stirring the while. Moisten with the stock, add sugar and salt to taste. Replace pieces of meat, cover pan and cook gently until quite tender, then dish up in a border of dry boiled rice, after adding lemon juice as desired to curry sauce. Cold roast beef may be used, the slices being heated in the sauce made as directed above.—P.W.

Bindaloo Curry

Slice and brown six onions with ¼ lb. butter, then in this same fry two tablespoons of curry powder; cut a pound of rump steak in small pieces and brown them slightly, then add them to the butter, onions and curry powder, and drop by drop stir in three-quarters of a small teacup of pure vinegar, with a good pinch of salt, and simmer very slowly for two hours. Serve with carefully boiled rice in a separate dish.—B.H.

Brown Bengal Curry

4 oz. onions to be fried in 4 oz. butter until nicely browned. To this add 1½ lb. fresh rump steak which has been par-boiled for 20 minutes in good strong stock; cut the meat in small pieces and add stock and all to the butter and onions, add three-quarters of a pint more stock with two tablespoons of curry powder, a small teaspoon salt and a tablespoon cream or milk. A tablespoon mango sauce, or a slice of coconut is a great improvement. Stir constantly with a wooden spoon till all the stock is absorbed, and when the butter separates from the stock the curry is finished.

Serve steaming hot with the rice plentifully piled up in a separate dish. All dishes and plates must be hot.—B.H.

Dry Minced Curry

Ingredients: 1 lb. minced steak, ½ lb. minced onion, two bananas cut up, two apples, one sweet and one sour, chopped fine. Mix together, and add one heaped tablespoon curry powder, salt to taste. Mix well and fry in a tablespoon butter till a nice brown. Then put in a saucepan, add one cup stock or water; simmer gently for two hours. Serve with rice and lemon slices, and instead of handing chutney, pour some chutney liquid over the rice.—D.T.

Hooseinee Curry

Take a tablespoon of curry powder and two small onions: pound these fine with a little water and when thoroughly mixed into a paste, put into a saucepan with 2 oz. of butter. In about three or four minutes add a tablespoon of milk. Keep on stirring this mixture for about 10 minutes, adding, if necessary, a tablespoon of water to prevent it burning. Have ready some slices of cold mutton or beef, cut into pieces about an inch square. Put these pieces of meat on skewers and between each piece of meat lay a thin slice of green ginger and of onion alternately. Put these skewers of meat into the spices and butter and then stir them about in it for a few minutes. Then add a breakfastcup of good gravy from stock. Put the lid on the saucepan and let it boil until the gravy is entirely reduced and the curry is dry. When the butter separates from the gravy and looks like oil, you may know that the curry is completed. If the curry is made with *uncooked* meat it must be done on a slow fire; allow one hour to every pound of raw meat.—B.H.

Indian Curry

Fry two sliced onions and a chopped clove of garlic in ¼ lb. clarified butter till golden brown. Add half tablespoon curry powder and a pinch of salt. Stir well, then add a tomato skinned and cut in quarters. Simmer five minutes, then add ½ lb. raw mutton (shoulder is best) cut in ½ in. cubes; cover pan and let the curry simmer slowly for 30-40 minutes. Stir occasionally, and add four more skinned and sliced tomatoes before removing pan from stove.—(HESTER VALENTINE in *Daily Express*.)

A good Wet Curry

Take ¼ lb. good butter, shred three large onions in it and fry till a light brown colour. Put this in a stewpan.

425

Mix a large tablespoon of curry powder in a pint of new milk or cream; take 1½ lb. lean veal or mutton, cut into small pieces and pour over it half the mixture of milk and curry powder, let it soak for a time and then fry it until half done; then put it, with the remainder of the mixture, into the stewpan with the shredded onions, and simmer gently for at least four hours, stirring it occasionally. More milk can be added if required, as the meat must be well covered while cooking.

A good Dry Curry

Fry plenty of onions, cut in thin slices, in butter (with salt) or bacon fat (without salt) till brown; take them out and put into the hot butter the curry powder (Vencatachellum is best), a few stoned and chopped raisins, 12 for four people, and a very little desiccated coconut. Bring these ingredients to the boil, stirring all the time, then add the meat, cut into pieces an inch square, which have previously been lightly fried, also the onions; let all simmer for one and a half hours, stir continuously and never allow it to boil after the meat is added, or it will become hard.

This curry should be a dark brown and served on a separate dish from the rice.

Potted Curry
(for Camps and Picnics)

Cut 2 lb. of veal in small pieces with large onion sliced fine. Put in a stewpan with some fresh butter – a copper stewpan is best. Shake in two tablespoons of curry powder and one of flour. Toss all together, add one tablespoon of grated carrot, one apple, finely chopped, the juice of half a lemon, a good pinch of salt, a teaspoon of powdered white sugar and a pint of good broth. Stew gently for about three hours; then set aside in a bowl to get cool. When cold put into a small pie dish. Can be eaten in slices or like potted meat on toast.—B.H.

Cold Curry

An excellent breakfast or luncheon dish. Useful for camp or picnic hampers.

Take a large knuckle of veal, or one large fowl.

Cut the meat in slices and fry with some apples, onions also cut finely, and a teaspoonful of chutney. No thickening is required. Add a tablespoon of curry powder and allow to simmer in meat stock for four or five hours. Pour into a wet mould and turn out when cold.—B.H.

CUSHION

That part of the leg of a cow or ewe that is closest to and partly covered by the udder.

CUTLET

Fr. *Côtelette*. The name originally applied to one of the smaller ribs of lamb, mutton or veal, cut off and cooked with its bone attached, either grilled, fried or stewed. The name has now been extended, in culinary parlance, to other preparations shaped to look like a cutlet, chiefly minced chicken mixed with some rather thick sauce, buttered, breadcrumbed, fried, and served with an imitation bone of macaroni, often ornamented with a paper frill, to make it look more like the real cutlet.

DAMAN. SYRIAN HYRASE

Lat. *Procavia syriaca*. A small herbivorous mammal of Palestine and Syria. The cony or rabbit of the Old Testament.

DASSIE. DASSY

The African species of the *Daman*, a cony or rabbit. 'Their flesh though dry is edible and somewhat like that of a young rabbit in flavour.'—M.S.A.

DEER

The name of many different members of the family *Cervidae*, ruminant quadrupeds differing from others by having branching horns, called antlers, which they lose at moulting time and replace soon after. From the gastronome's point of view, the best deer is the *Roe Deer* (Fr. *Chevreuil*), followed, in order of merit, by the *Fallow Deer* (Fr. *Daim*), the *Red Deer* (Fr. *Cerf*), the *Moose Deer* (Fr. *Elan*), and the *Reindeer* (Fr. *Renne*). In the kitchen, these and all other kinds of deer are prepared for the table under the name of *Venison* (q.v.).

'Young deer are worthless for the table, though in the sub-tropics I have eaten savoury dishes of fawn which were most excellently tender. So much depends on condition, sex, age, and the recent feeding of deer, that it is difficult to lay down any particular canon of excellence. The haunch of a hart of grease may be equalled or even surpassed by that of a yeld hind, or the cutlets of an undistinguished young stag may be far better than the civet of a monarch of the forest.'—M.H.P.

Deer's Liver

Cut into thin slices and lay in cold water for 10 minutes. Put butter in pan and fry the liver a light brown. A cupful of stock with a very little flour and cooked in the saucepan after the liver is taken out will make gravy if required.

Note—An old stag's liver is apt to taste rank after the middle of September, while male calf's liver is prone to have flukes, so is best avoided. For these reasons, a hind's liver is preferable, after mid-September.—B.C.

Highland Relish

Boil the liver of a hind, roe deer or fallow deer for 1½ hours. To every 1 lb. of boiled liver take 1 lb. of bacon fat, deer or mutton fat.

Boil together for one more hour.

Mince both together very fine.

Press the mixture through a sieve.

Add pepper and salt.

Press into a potted meat dish and, if not required at once, pour melted butter over the top and keep in a cool place.

Note—If spread upon toast or bread and butter, it makes a good mock *pâté de foie gras* sandwich.—B.C.

Deer Pudding

Put the pudding in salt and water immediately it comes in. Wash the pudding in warm water. This is necessary in order not to tear the fat. Turn the pudding inside out, i.e. the fat to the inside. (This is best done by running the handle of a wooden spoon inside the pudding, tying it to one end, and pulling it back through the pudding.) Tie up one end and fill with coarse oatmeal and a very little chopped onion. Add pepper and salt. To do the filling, push the oatmeal in with a porridge stick or the handle of a wooden spoon. Do not stuff too tightly, otherwise the pudding will burst. No suet should be added or the fat from any other animal, but if there is not enough fat in the pudding, some deer fat from the inside of the beast can be added to the oatmeal as it is pushed in. Tie up the other end. Then tie the two ends together loosely to make a circular pudding. If a little play on the string is not left, the pudding may burst. Now put the pudding into boiling water until the oatmeal is cooked, i.e. about 20 minutes, but to commence with, keep pricking the pudding for a few minutes, with a long needle. Then take out of the boiling water and fry in butter and brown.

If the pudding is sloshy or sodden like porridge, it is wrong. The oatmeal should be fairly crisp after frying.

Serve whole very hot and not cut up.

Note 1. If several puddings come in together, it will save trouble to stuff them all at the same time, par-boil them and hang them up until required.

Note 2. The stuffing of the pudding is made easier if the meat is pushed into it through a short length of ¾ in. piping.—B.C.

Deer's Head Broth

Deer's head broth is prepared much in the same way as sheep's head broth. Half a hind's head is just about a convenient size for cooking, and any odd scraps of deer's meat or bones can be added to help the soup.

See that the head is properly skinned before cooking, and all hair removed.

Remove brains and tongue to make separate dishes.—B.C.

DEVILLED MEAT
A Nice Devil (Admiral Ross's)

Ingredients: 4 tablespoons cold gravy; 1 of chutney; 1 of ketchup; 1 of vinegar; 2 tablespoons made mustard; 2 saltspoons salt; 2 tablespoons butter.

Method: Mix all the ingredients as smooth as possible in a soup plate, put with it the meat or whatever you wish to devil. Stew gently until warmed. Remove meat and grill for three minutes. Pour over gravy and serve on hot dish and you will have a delicious devil.—(*Mrs Noltenius*) K.C.B.

DJUVEE

(Jugoslavian)

¼ lb. chopped onions; ½ lb. any meat (usually pork and veal mixed) or fish; 1 lb. tomatoes; 1 cup rice; olive oil; butter or lard for frying; 1 large cup stock or water.

Fry the onions, and when soft add parsley, seasoning and rice. Cook until the rice is clear, stirring well. In a fireproof dish arrange layers of the rice mixture and thinly sliced tomatoes, with slices of the meat or fish interspersed, making the last layer of tomatoes. Pour in the stock or water. Cover the dish and cook slowly in the oven for about two hours till all the mixture is absorbed, shaking it gently from time to time so that the rice does not stick, and serve in the same dish.

DOG

Lat. *Canis familiaris*. Although no Member of the Wine and Food Society could possibly entertain for a moment the horrible thought of eating dog, it is on record that the great Hippocrates recommended dog's flesh as being of light digestion and excellent taste. The Greeks of old were very partial to it, but in ancient Rome the patricians left dogs to the poorer people to eat. In China, dogs, especially Chows, have long been specially fattened for food, and are a highly-esteemed article of diet in some parts of the country. Whether Labouchère really meant it or merely wished to shock his friends, he wrote that when he was in Paris, during the siege of 1870, he enjoyed various breeds of dogs, and he placed them in the following order: 'Spaniel, like lamb; Poodle far the best; Bulldog coarse and tasteless.

DOLPHIN

Lat. *Delphinus delphis*. The common *Dolphin* of the Mediterranean and North Atlantic about 7 ft. in length.

'The flesh of the Common Dolphin used in former times to be eaten in England.' —F.C.F.

DORMERS

Sausage-like shapes with rice added to the mince.

Allow a cup of cooked meat to a cup of cooked rice, two tablespoons chopped suet, a yolk of egg, a teaspoon of chopped parsley, quarter of a teaspoon powdered herbs, egg and breadcrumbs, a little flour, dripping and gravy sauce.

Well cook the rice and dry; mix it with the meat, which is finely-chopped, add the parsley, suet and herbs; season and bind together with the egg and gravy. Make into sausage shaped pieces, using a little dry flour; roll in egg and breadcrumbs, fry thoroughly, drain and serve with a good sauce.

DRIPPING

Good and fresh dripping answers very well for basting everything except game and poultry, and, when well clarified, serves for frying nearly as well as lard; it should be kept in a cool place, and will remain good some time. To clarify it, put the dripping into a basin, pour over it boiling water, and keep stirring the whole to wash away the impurities. Let it stand to cool, when the water and dirty sediment will settle at the bottom of the basin. Remove the dripping, and put it away in jars or basins for use.—B.

Good beef dripping, spread upon some rather thick freshly made toast, then put under the grill until it melts into the toast, a little salt on it – and a large mug of mulled ale with it – will keep cold and wet out, and keep peace and good will within.

DUGONG

Lat. *Dugong australis*. An aquatic herbivorous mammal, allied to the *Manatee*, but with a tail like the whale's. The male has tusklike upper incisors. It is widely distributed from the East Coast of Africa to the Philippines and Formosa; also along the East Coast of Australia to the Solomons.

'On account of the palatability of the flesh the animal is much hunted wherever found, hence it is in danger of extinction.' —M.S.A., p. 529.

DUIKER. DUYKER. DUIKERBOK

Lat. *Cephalophus grimmi*. A small and very timid South African Antelope which plunges through the bush at the approach of man: hence its name of *ducker* or *diver*. It is rarely seen for sale in the markets: thus, during the 1904 season, there were but 174 Duiker sold on Kimberley Market, when 1,415 Steinbok

and 4,025 Springbok were sold.—B.HO. See *Venison*.

EASTER MEAT BALLS
(Swedish)

Pass through mincer 10 oz. veal, one small onion, pepper, salt, one egg and one tablespoon potato flour; mix well with milk and work it till smooth; make into little balls and fry ready to serve with brown sauce.

ELAND

Lat. *Taurotragus oryx*. A large African antelope which is found in South and East Africa, where it is greatly valued for its flesh. In Western and Equatorial Africa, there is a related species (*T. derbianus*), which is also known as *Giant Eland*. See *Venison*.

'The flesh of the Eland is always reported to be the best game meat in South Africa, that of the red males being loaded with fat.' —M.S.A., p. 252.

'Towards the end of the dry season, when the old grass is nearly all burnt off and the new has not yet sprouted, Elands will in some parts of the country (in the Mashona country, for instance) live entirely upon the leaves of bushes, and their flesh then becomes utterly tasteless. Their flesh has been very much over-estimated, in my opinion, and is not to be compared for flavour to that of the buffalo, giraffe, hippopotamus, or white rhinoceros, supposing, of course, that the animals are all fat and in good condition.' —F.C.S.

L.R.Brightwell describes the flesh of the *Eland* as the 'most beefy of the antelopes'.

ELEPHANT

Lat. *Elephas maximus* and *E. africanus*. There are two main families of elephants, the Asiatic and the African. In Asia, the elephant is too valuable a beast of burden, as well as too tough, to be killed for food, but the more carnivorous natives of Africa have killed elephants for food ever since the days of Ptolemy Philadelphus. Here is a record of how a traveller and a gastronome, Le Vaillant, tasted elephant in Africa: 'They cut off the four feet of the animal, and made in the earth a hole about 3 ft. square. This was filled with live charcoal, and, covering the hole with very dry wood, a large fire was kept up during parts of the night. When they thought that the hole was hot enough, it was emptied: a Hottentot then placed within it the four feet of the animal, covered them with hot ashes, and then with charcoal and small wood, and this fire was left burning until the morning ... My servants presented me at breakfast with an elephant's foot. It had considerably swelled in the cooking; I could hardly recognize the shape, but it appeared so good, exhaled so inviting an odour, that I hastened to taste it. It was a dish for a king. Although I had often heard the bear's foot praised, I could not have conceived how so heavy, so material an animal as the elephant could furnish a dish so fine and delicate ... And I devoured without bread my elephant's foot, while my Hottentots, seated around me regaled themselves with other parts, which they found equally delicious.' (Le Vaillant. Voyages. Vol. II. Quoted in Soyer's *Pantropheon*, 1853.)

'The flesh of the elephant appears to be coarse, except certain tit-bits as the heart, the thick part of the trunk, and the fat meat in the hollow just under the eye, all of which were considered as special delicacies by the old-time hunters of South Africa.'—M.S.A., p. 824.

'I am not fond of elephant meat; in fact it is tough, strong and distasteful to me, but I had to subsist on it occasionally. I had not made any biltong of elephant meat as I might have done, I had grown to dislike it so.'—C.H.S.

'That evening, for the first time, I tasted elephant's heart, roasted on a forked stick over the ashes, which I thought then, and still consider, to be one of the greatest delicacies that an African hunter is likely to enjoy. The meat from the thick part of the trunk and from the cavity above the eye is also very well tasted, but needs much stewing to make it tender; the foot I consider tasteless and insipid.'—F.C.S.

L.R.Brightwell says that he enjoyed elephant's foot and that it makes a delicious 'porky' brawn.

ELK
Lat. *Alces alces*. The largest existing member of the Deer family in Europe. Its American variety is called *Moose*. Elk is also the name sometimes given to the American *Wapiti* (*Cervus canadensis*).

'The flesh is fine flavoured, but differs from all other venison. It is more nutritious than any other meat of which I have knowledge. A hungry labouring man is satisfied with about half the amount which would be required of beef. This nutritious quality of the elk is first alluded to by Lewis and Clark, and is fully confirmed by my observations'.

Elk with Sour Cream Sauce
Lard the underneath of the joint with fat ham or bacon. Fry in butter till coloured and moisten with a pint of sour cream, pepper, two cloves, bayleaf, and half pint of white wine. Braise slowly for three hours, basting frequently with the sauce. Skim off the fat from the sauce, squeeze in the juice of half a lemon and a little coarse pepper

from the pepper-mill. They do this in New Brunswick still.—M.H.P.

'Elk tongues are most delicious eating, being juicy, tender and well flavoured; they are excellent to take out as a lunch on a long hunting trip.'—TH.R., p. 282.

'For a steady diet no meat tastes better or is more nourishing than elk venison.'—TH.R. (1), p. 175.

ENTRECÔTE
The French name for a steak from the *contre-filet*, known in the U.S.A. as Sirloin Steak.

Entrecôte Bercy
Individual tender steaks
Butter
¼ lb. beef marrow
Salt and pepper
1 or 2 shallots
1 cup white wine
1 tablespoon meat glaze
Lemon juice as desired
Chopped parsley

Heat a sufficiency of butter in a *sauté* pan, add the small steaks, browning quickly, but leaving interior underdone. Keep hot. To the butter in pan add the chopped shallots; when lightly browned, add the wine, salt and pepper, and simmer until greatly reduced. Skim off excess fat, then add the meat glaze and the marrow, cut into tiny pieces. Cook this mixture gently for five minutes, then add lemon juice to taste, a piece of fresh butter and a good pinch of finely-chopped parsley. Pour this over the steaks, and serve very hot.—P.W.

Other classical modes of serving

Entrecôtes:
Béarnaise: Grilled steak served with *Pommes Château*, watercress and *Sauce Béarnaise*.

Bonne Femme: Steak cooked in butter in an open pan with some small onions and diced potatoes.

Bordelaise: Grilled steak with a garnish of poached marrowbone fat and served with a *Sauce Bordelaise*.

Bourguignonne: Fried steak finished cooking in red wine, which is used to make the accompanying gravy.

Forestière: Steak fried in butter and served with fried mushrooms.

Lyonnaise: Steak fried in butter and served with shredded fried onions.

Maître d'hôtel: Grilled steak served with a *Maître d'hôtel* butter.

Minute: The thinnest possible piece of steak fried in very hot butter.

Mirabeau: Grilled steak garnished with anchovy fillets, chopped tarragon, stoned olives and a *Beurre d'Anchois*.

Niçoise: Steak fried in olive oil, garnished with tomato *purée*, new potatoes tossed in butter, and black olives.

Vert-pré: Grilled steak served with straw potatoes, tufts of watercress and *Maître d'hôtel* butter.

ESCALOPE

A French word derived from the English *Collop*, used to designate a cut, slice or scoop of meat without any bone in it. Thus a slice of *foie gras* scooped out with a silver spoon is known as an *Escalope de Foie Gras*, but the name is mostly used in connection with narrow strips of veal, either cut from the cushion or fillet, which are the best, or from the loin. These strips of meat, or *Escalopes*, may be broiled, braised, stewed or *sautés*. They may also be prepared for the table in any way suitable for *Noisettes*, *Côtelettes* or *Tournedos*, but here are some of the more popular ways of serving *Escalopes de Veau*:

A l'anglaise: Flattened out, trimmed dipped in egg-and-breadcrumbs and cooked in hot butter; served with *Beurre Noisette*.

Casimir: Seasoned with salt and paprika, cooked in hot butter and served on cooked artichoke bottoms, garnished with a *julienne* of carrots and truffles.

A la jardinière: Prepared and cooked as *à l'anglaise*, but served with a *jardinière* of mixed fresh vegetables.

A la viennoise: Flatten out the escalopes, season them, dip them in egg-and-breadcrumbs, cook them in hot butter, serve them with a *Beurre d'Anchois*, some small fillets of anchovies and stoned olives.

FAGGOTS

The old English name of a substantial farm-house dish which is both nutritious and flavoursome.

Faggots or **Poor Man's Goose**
¾ lb. pig's liver
4 oz. fat salt pork
Mixed herbs to taste
Dash ground nutmeg
Pig's caul
1 small onion
Salt and pepper
1 egg
Fresh breadcrumbs
Good gravy

Chop the liver up finely with the onion and the salt pork. Place in a pan with the seasonings, cover and cook, very gently, for about half an hour, but do not allow meat to colour. When done, drain off the fat, add the beaten egg, the breadcrumbs and the nut-meg, using just enough breadcrumbs to bind mixture to a stiff paste. Shape into squares, rolls or oblongs, enclosing each in a piece of the pig's caul. Set them side by side in a baking dish, add a cupful of good gravy or rich stock and bake until nicely browned. Baked potatoes make a nice accompaniment to this dish.—P.W.

FLANK

The side, below the ribs, of a beef carcass; the best part is retailed under the name of *thick flank* and that from the hindquarters as *mid-flank*.

FLITCH

Fr. *Flèche de lard*. The flitch of bacon is the side with the leg cut off and the bone taken out. It has become the recognized reward for marital felicity, through the Dunmow Flitch ceremony, which takes place on Whit Monday, at Dunmow, in Essex, when a couple who can swear that for a year and a day they have neither quarrelled nor re-pented of their marriage may claim a Flitch of Dunmow bacon.

FORCEMEAT

Fr. *Farce*. Forcemeat is a generic name which covers a large number of pappy prepara-tions, made out of fish, flesh or fowl with the aid of pestle and mortar. The two most popular forms of forcemeat, in English cooking, are the *Veal Stuffing*, or fat force-meat, made usually of ox-kidney fat and breadcrumbs and used for stuffing veal, turkey and fish; and the *Sage and Onion Stuff-ing* for ducks, geese, pork, etc. There is also, in the winter time, the *chestnut forcemeat* used for stuffing turkeys. In French classical cooking, the two most extensively used forms of forcemeat are the *Quenelles* and the *Godiveau*.

FRICADELLES. FRICANDELLES
Fried balls of minced meat or *Rissoles*.

Frikkadels (South African Rissoles)
2 lb. minced mutton (raw rather than cooked)
A little chopped onion
1 or 2 slices white bread, soaked in milk
1–2 tablespoons tomato sauce
1 egg (beaten)
¼ nutmeg (grated)
Salt, pepper

Mix the ingredients well, shape into balls, egg and crumb and fry in hot fat.

FRICANDEAU
Fr. for a *Fricassée* of Veal (q.v.).

FRICASSÉE
Any kind of meat cut up in rather small pieces and cooked as stews and *ragoûts* of poultry or butcher's meat.

Fricasse of Veal

Take some veal, and cut into thinne slices, flowre them a very little, and passe them in the panne, and season them with salt, with an onion stuck with cloves, then soak them with a little broth, and the sauce being thickened, serve. (*La Va.*)

N.B.—To 'pass in the panne' means to fry, just a little, the equivalent of 'to parboil', but in a frying-pan.—ED.

FROMAGE DE PORC

Fr. for *Brawn* (q.v.).

Fromage de Porc

Thin slices of fresh pork fat (*couennes*)
1 pig's foot (fat)
3 cloves garlic
3 shallots
1 or 2 sprigs parsley
2 cups white wine
2 lb. pig's head
Salt
2 onions
Peppercorns
1 pinch or stem thyme
1 bayleaf
Pinch mixed spice

Take a heavy iron or earthenware casserole, of the deep sort. Line bottom with the slices of pork fat. On this lay the pig's head (select the cheek portion which is the meatiest), the foot, cut into four pieces, salt and sufficient water completely to cover the meat. Into a piece of fine muslin (with a long piece of string which can hang outside the pot for the easy removal of the bag when required), put the garlic, sliced onions, cut-up shallots, parsley, thyme, bayleaf, eight or ten peppercorns, and a pinch of mixed spice. Tie all up securely. Cook gently by the side of the fire or over a mere pinprick of gas (once the pot has boiled up) for seven to eight hours. Remove meat, taking out all pieces of bone, skin, etc. Replace the broth, after removing muslin bag, and strain into pan, add the meat, cut into rather large dice, and the white wine. Simmer for another hour, quite slowly, when the mass should be rather thick. Pour into a round, deep basin, and while it is cooling stir once or twice to prevent pieces of meat from sinking to bottom. When quite cold, chill and cut into slices to serve as a supper dish, with a salad.—P.W.

GALANTINE

A French word borrowed from England, where *Galyntynes* were among the most popular dishes throughout the Middle Ages. The name referred to a variety of dishes, differing from others by the addition of the powdered roots of *Galingale*, a wild flower of the snowdrop family, sometimes called *rush-nut*, known to botanists as *Sweet Cyperus* and in France as *Souchet*.

The present-day *Galantine* was introduced by one Prévost, Chef to the Marquis de Brancas, previous to 1789, and Master Cook on his own account in Paris during Napoleon's reign.

Galantine differs from *Brawn* in one respect only: *Brawn* is a blend of cooked meat and its jelly, i.e. the liquor in which it is cooked; *Galantine* is the same type of cooked meat but it is cased in or covered over with its jelly.

Beef Galantine

1 lb. lean beef
6 oz. breadcrumbs (stale)
1 small chopped onion
½ lb. bacon
2 eggs
½ cup good stock
Salt and pepper

Cut the bacon up finely with the beef or grind in mincing machine with the onion. Add the fine breadcrumbs, salt and pepper and mix well together. Beat the eggs, add them to the stock and use to moisten meat mixture. Shape into a short and rather thick roll, tie up in a buttered pudding-cloth, like a roly-poly pudding, and boil gently in water or, better, stock, for 2 to 2½ hours. Remove, shape when cool enough to handle, lay a thin board and a weight on top to press into a nice shape and, before serving, brush all over with meat glaze. Serve cold.—P.W.

Galantine of Sheep's Head

('Ingelegte Kop en poetjes', an old Cape Dutch recipe)

Take a well-cleaned sheep's head and feet, put them into a deep saucepan; cover them with cold water; add a few bay leaves, one dessertspoon coriander seeds, one tablespoon allspice, four cloves, tied up in a piece of muslin; boil for some hours till the bones can be taken out, skin the tongue and lay it in a mould; fill up with the rest of the meat and pour over it the sauce, which is made by boiling up a pint of the broth with a small cupful of vinegar, one small onion sliced, one teaspoon turmeric and a little salt; leave it in the mould till next day and turn out.—(*Cape Times.*)

Galantine of Veal

One small entire breast of veal
A grating of lemon peel
Salt and pepper
A few pistachio nuts
Pinch mixed herbs
About 1½ lb. good sausage meat
1 hard-boiled egg
1 small truffle
Rashers of bacon

This is a delicious hot weather or picnic dish. Remove all bones from breast of veal and lay it out flat on a board. Be sure the sausage-meat is well seasoned and good (home-made is best). Spread half of it in a flat even cake on half the veal. Sprinkle with the herbs, lay slices of the egg on top with more salt and pepper, alternating with the nuts and chopped truffle. Fry the bacon slowly until crisp; cool rashers and lay them on top of all; sprinkle very sparsely with grated lemon rind. Cover all this with the second half of the sausage-meat and roll the veal up tightly, wrapping next in a pudding cloth, as a roly-poly pudding, securing ends of cloth with string, as usual. Cook meat from three to four hours in a *court-bouillon* prepared beforehand. When done, allow to cool in the *court-bouillon*. When nearly cold, take out galantine, remove cloth and tie it up again neatly into a nicely shaped roll, flattening between two boards on which a weight is set.

Before serving, brush all over with glaze and garnish with sprigs of parsley and cubes, diamonds and other fancy pieces of aspic jelly.—P.W.

GALIMAFRÉE
Buy a small shoulder of mutton weighing not more than about 3½ lb. Separate the skin from the flesh and cut off the meat from the bone entirely – or ask the butcher to do this for you. 'When these surgical operations are finished, you will mince the meat finely, you will mix with it a little chopped bacon, some chopped lemon peel and some fine herbs, and you will cook the mixture, moistened with a little stock in a pan, keeping it well stirred. Of course you will take care that it is not in the least sloppy. When, with taste and smell and sight, you perceive that it is cooked, you will build it into what I may call the empty shell of your shoulder of mutton, the bone forming a support. You will very carefully bring back the skin to its original position and will tie it in place with a string. Flour it all over and bake it in the oven just long enough for the floured skin to take a good colour, so that the whole appears to be an ordinary roasted or baked joint. This last stage of the process will be quite short, as the meat has been separately cooked. It would appear that this sort of Galimafrée was served with a sauce like Ravigote.'—E.O.

GAMMON
The lower part of a 'flitch' or side of bacon. The *Gammon* is cured and prepared in the same manner as *Ham* (q.v.).

GAZELLE
Lat. *Gazella dorcas*. One of the most graceful

Antelopes of North Africa; it has soft brown eyes and dry, rather tasteless flesh.

Gazelle Steaks
Cut some steaks about ½ in. thick and pound them hard with a thick stick. Soak in Italian red wine; and add an onion cut thin and a handful of bruised wild sage leaves. Allow the steaks to marinade in this for about 18 hours. Next day beat up an egg and make a paste with ordinary oatmeal. Thickly coat the steaks with the paste and place in a frying-pan in which there is a very hot mixture of bacon fat and margarine. Fry over an open wood fire.

This takes some time, but it is essential that they should be very well cooked and the oatmeal cover done to a rich brown. When cooked, put on a plate beside the fire to drain. Serve with hot diced beetroot (tinned) and new potatoes (also tinned).

This seems a long job, but gives the flesh a piquancy that is lacking when the meat is roasted or cooked plain. If there is no wine, i.e. if no wine has been captured lately, the *marinade* can be made from vinegar with a little whisky or gin added. (*Evening Standard*, to which it was communicated by an officer of the Eighth Army in 1942.)

GEMSBOK
Lat. *Oryx gazella*. The largest and most handsomely marked species of the *Oryx* Antelopes.

'The Gemsbuck is almost entirely confined to the arid deserts of South-West Africa. In the Kalahari Desert, to the west of Griqualand West, it is fairly plentiful.' —F.C.S.

An allied but much more unusual species (*Hippotragus leucophaeus*) is known as the *Bastard Gemsbok* by the Orange Free State Dutch, as the *Bastard Eland* by the Transvaal Dutch, and as the *Roan Antelope* by the English.—F.C.S.

GIGOT
Fr. for a leg of mutton or lamb. In Scotland *Gigot*, pronounced *Jig'ot*, also means a leg of mutton.

GIGUE
Fr. for a leg of roebuck or venison.

GIRAFFE
Lat. *Giraffa camelopardalis*. The *Giraffe* is not very often killed now; it has become too rare, but it is quite fit to eat; trustworthy people who have partaken of giraffe meat have stated that it was not unlike rather coarse beef, and that the best way to eat it was to treat it like *Venison* (q.v.).

'Giraffe are splendid eating, and in good condition and fat are a luxury that no one can properly appreciate till he has lived for a time on nothing but the dry meat of the smaller antelopes.'—F.R.C.S.

GITE À LA NOIX
Fr. for *Fillet of Veal*.

GLAZE
A preparation of gelatine dissolved in stock – about 3 oz. of gelatine per quart of stock – mixed with caramel, burnt onions or other colouring substance, and brushed over a tongue, a ham or other cooked meat with a soft brush or feather: the meat to be glazed must be perfectly cold and wiped dry before applying the glaze. *Glaze* can also be made by boiling a shin of beef and a knuckle of veal in about six quarts of water, well seasoned, and simmering till there is but a quart of liquid left.

GOAT
The name of various members of the genus *Capra*, ruminant, hollow-horned mammals, closely allied to the sheep, but more particularly to the domestic goat (*C. hircus*). The He-goat (Fr. *Bouc*) is not fit to eat, but its hide is of use, and if of the Cashmere breed, its hair or wool is valuable. The She-goat or Nanny-goat (Fr. *Chèvre*) supplies an abundance of milk, which is excellent for the young; cheese is also made from it, which many grown-ups like very much and others dislike intensely.

Goats can subsist on the coarsest and scantiest of food; they are very destructive and poor converters, but they are fast breeders and their young, the *Kid* (q.v.), is well worth eating.

GODIVEAU
Fr. for *Veal Stuffing*.

GOULASH
Usually known as *Hungarian Goulash*. A Hungarian stew or *ragoût* of beef or veal seasoned with paprika.

American-Hungarian Goulash
2 lb. rump of beef
1 carrot
2 saltspoons paprika
Salt and very little pepper
2 gills hot stock
1 gill tomato sauce
1 teaspoon chopped parsley
Butter
2 onions
1 heaping tablespoon flour
1 gill red wine
Bouquet-garni
1 clove minced garlic

This dish is better re-heated, as indeed are all dishes containing wine. Cut the meat into 2 in. cubes and brown them in butter, adding the sliced carrot, the chopped onions and the paprika after the browning operation. Cook for a few minutes, then dredge with the flour and moisten with the stock and wine. Add the *bouquet-garni*, the tomato sauce, salt and a little pepper. Cook gently for an hour then add the minced garlic and the parsley and simmer until meat is tender. —P.W.

GRAS-DOUBLE
French culinary name for that part of the *Belly* of beef which is kept apart, in France, and not used as in England for *Tripe* (q.v.).

GRAVY
Fr. *Jus*. Gravy was originally the name given to the juices oozing from roasting meat, but it has been extended to cover all concentrates of the stock in which fish, flesh or fowl is cooked. The main difference between gravy and a sauce is that the first is made in the same pan in which meat or fish has been cooked, and almost if not entirely from the juices extracted during cooking, whereas a sauce, although some of the same ingredients may be incorporated in it, is made in a separate pan and with the admixture of other ingredients, seasonings and flavourings. Nobody, however, who has watched a sirloin of beef being roasted, can have any illusion about the hot, brown liquid served with it under the name of 'its own gravy'. What runs off the joint during roasting is mostly fat, whilst 'its own gravy' is mostly hot water, either coloured with caramel, or made up with a commercial preparation known as *Gravy Salt* or *Browning*. The best gravy is made with beef or veal, or both, usually with a knuckle of veal added, the whole being simmered long enough to produce a rich glaze or gravy concentrate, which may be thinned by adding hot water, and flavoured by adding onions, bayleaf and various vegetables and spices during cooking, but neither thickened with flour nor bound with egg yolks, which would make the gravy into a sauce.

GRAVY SALT. BROWNING
'A fluid preparation used to colour gravies, beef tea, soups, etc. A good one is made of following proportions – say 1 lb. of caramel (burnt sugar), ¼ lb. common salt and half pint of mushroom ketchup flavoured with spices. Some use strong beer, wine, or water, instead of the ketchup.'—L.G.M.

GRENADIN
Another name for a *Fricandeau* or *Fricassée* of butcher's meat.

Grenadins aux Olives
1 in. thick slices of beef fillet
Oil marinade
Larding bacon
Butter
Stoned olives

Prepare the marinade, using for the mixture thyme, parsley, minced onion, a spot of lemon juice or vinegar, salt, pepper and a crumbled bayleaf; blend well with olive oil. Prepare the grenadins, giving them a somewhat oval shape, trimming off fat and larding with the bacon, as directed in recipe for *Boeuf à la mode* (q.v.). Heat butter in a *sauté-pan*, cook the grenadins in this, after draining off the marinade in which they should have remained from five to six hours. Arrange, when done, on a hot dish and garnish with the olives. Add the gravy from the pan in which the meat was cooked. The grenadins must be nicely browned, quickly cooked and, when brown, placed for a few moments in a very hot oven slightly to glaze their surface. For a change, garnish with tiny stuffed and baked tomatoes or *sauté* mushroom caps.—P.W.

GRISKIN
The name of the spine, chine or backbone that is cut away when preparing sides of bacon; the name is also sometimes given to a poor, thin piece of loin of pork.

GROUND-HOG. ANT-BEAR. AARDVARK
Lat. *Orycterpous afer.* A South African anteater with a long snout with which it burrows into ant-heaps, and a long slimy tongue with which it catches scared ants, upon which it feeds almost exclusively. 'The flesh, which is often loaded with fat, is very much appreciated and is often salted or smoked.'—M.S.A., p. 223.

GROUND-PIG or CANE RAT
Lat. *Thryonomys awindernianus.* A large African burrowing rodent known to the Boers as *Riet-muis (reed-mouse).*

'Common throughout along the banks of streams and in the kloofs. Much amusement can be obtained by hunting them with dogs. The flesh is white and of good flavour, being particularly tasty if boiled and eaten cold.' —F.V.K.

GUINEA-PIG
Lat. *Cavia porcellus.* The domesticated form of the *Cony* or *Cavy* of South America, which the early Spanish explorers named *Canejo, Rabbit,* the name by which it is still known in Peru and Bolivia, where the *Rabbit* is called *Canejo de Castilla.* To-day it is chiefly used for bacteriological experiments in

Europe, and not regarded as fit for the table, but we have the word of Lady Dorothy Nevill, no mean Victorian hostess, that it is quite fit to eat. 'There's a dainty dish for you,' she wrote of the Guinea-pig, 'but it was always a job to make your cook do it. They want baking the same as the gipsies serve the hedgehog.'—E.L.B.

More recently, C.Cumberland, F.Z.S., has given a whole chapter of his book on the Guinea-Pig to various recipes for its culinary preparation: 'Cavies are excellent as *entrées* in various stews – with mushrooms cut up and stewed brown, in a white stew with button mushrooms, with brown onions, with green peas, *à la Soubise,* and especially in curry. A practical cook will have no difficulty in varying the preparations, and I will undertake to say that it will be found difficult to make them other than 'very good meate.' ... I do not wish it to be supposed that I recommend cavy as a cheap food, but rather for its delicious flavour and *recherché* quality. ... I consider the smooth-haired white cavy as best adapted for the table, on account of the whiteness of its skin. Cavy sows of about eight months old, when well fattened, are the most tender and best flavoured. I have made experiments with cavy hogs, and find them excellent eating. Boars do not fatten so well, and are best killed small, say when about four months old. Cavies should be prepared for cooking by scalding, and should not be skinned. All the wild varieties, as well as the Kerrodons, are eaten in their native countries. I have both eaten and hunted the Pàca or spotted cavy, in Brazil, and found it first rate, either for sport or food.'—C.CUM.

HAGGIS
A popular Scots dish, named by Burns *Great chieftain o' the puddin' race.* It is made of the heart, lungs, and liver of the sheep, hashed or finely-minced (about a quarter of the liver being grated), with suet, onions, oatmeal, salt and pepper. The whole is usually sewn up in either the large stomach bag, or a smaller one called the 'king's hood', of the sheep, well cleansed.—L.G.M.

Burns's poem '*To a Haggis*' begins thus:
"Fair fa' your honest sonsie face,
  Great chieftain o' the puddin' race!
Aboon them a' ye tak' your place
  Painch, tripe, or thairm;
Weel are ye wordy of a grace
  As lang's my arm."

As a rule one does not attempt to make a haggis; one just buys a haggis and does not inquire too closely as to how it was made. A bought haggis must be simmered in all-but-boiling water long enough to be thoroughly hot and steaming when a slit is made in the paunch for a large tablespoon (previously dipped in boiling water) to be inserted and the haggis scooped out. It is usually served wrapped up in a stiffly starched napkin to cover the none too appetizing bare looks of the sheep's stomach. Neat whisky is the orthodox liquid accompaniment of the haggis, and it should be drunk from a Quaich, a kind of shallow wooden drinking cup with two lugs or handles.

Edward Spencer (Nathaniel Gubbins of the *Pink 'Un*) tells in 'Cakes and Ale' how haggis was introduced into Scotland by the Romans, who made it by filling a pig's boiled stomach with fry and brains, raw eggs and pulped pineapples, seasoned with a disgusting decoction called *liquamen*, based on putrefied intestines of fish mixed with spices and wine; but the Scots, who hated any form of pig, adapted it for use with the 'innards' of the sheep, and this being so, it is rather surprising that old English classical authors, such as Mesdames Glasse and Mason, modify their Scotch Haggis or Hagas by the use of calf. Here, however, is the official recipe taught in the schools of Edinburgh at the present day, which appears to embody most of the principles necessary for success with the age-old Scottish favourite.

Haggis

A sheep's bag and pluck (liver, lights and heart); ½ lb. minced suet; ½ lb. oatmeal; ½ teaspoon powdered herbs; ½ ditto pepper; 1 ditto salt; 4 medium sized onions.

Wash the bag in cold water, scrape and clean it well, let it lie all night in cold water with a little salt; wash the pluck, put it into a pot of boiling water with a teaspoon of salt, boil for two hours with the windpipe hanging out; when cold cut off the windpipe, grate half the liver, the other half of which is not used, mince the heart, lights, suet and onions, add the oatmeal (which should first be toasted to a golden colour), the pepper and salt and herbs and one pint of the water the pluck was boiled in. Mix well, fill the bag rather more than half full of the mixture, sew it up. Place the haggis in a pot of boiling water, and boil for three hours, pricking it occasionally to keep it from bursting. Serve very hot with mashed potatoes and turnips and of course a *quaich* if desired.

It has been recently stated that this creature 'can be used whole and uncut, to boil with a thick vegetable and water stew, making a nutritious soup. It can then be cut open, and eaten either as a vegetable or as the meat course. What is left is cut in slices and fried instead of bacon for breakfast, and the remains put in pastry cases make useful savouries. The case which holds it is tripe, so every bit (but the string) is edible.'—D.T.

HAM

Fr. *Jambon*; Ger. *Schinken*; Sp. *Jamon*; It. *Prosciutti*; Port. *Presunto*; Dutch, *Hammen*. A Ham consists of the hind leg of the pig, separated from the carcass at about the second joint of the vertebrae, in the case of the 'long-cut' hams, and taking in part of the flank fat.—L.G.M.

ENGLISH HAMS

York Ham. It owes its universal popularity to the firmness of its body – firm and yet tender; to the mildness of its flavour – mild but far from insipid; and to the attractiveness of its pink meat – attractive but not artificial-looking. The York Ham has no monopoly of those three excellent qualities, of course, but it possesses them in a more consistent degree than, perhaps, any other cure of ham. They are due to the cure, not to the bracing air of York – to what is known among porkers as *Dry salt cure*.

Bradenham Ham. This is the registered name under which the finest Wiltshire Hams are marketed by the Bradenham Ham Company, of Chippenham, Wilts. The Bradenham hams are cured according to a special recipe dating back to 1781. It is a sweet and mild cure, and after pickling, the hams have to be hung many months to mature and develop their delicate and characteristic flavour. Each ham is branded with the registered trade mark of the word 'Bradenham' and a Horse Rampant; they can always be easily identified by their coal black outside, a feature due to the method of their curing.

Wiltshire Ham. What is commonly called a Wiltshire Ham is technically speaking a *Gammon*, that is the leg of the pig cured on the side, before it is cut off from the carcass. Gammons are 'mild' and do not keep so long as hams, but they are preferred by those who object to strong-tasting food.

Suffolk Ham. The special feature of this ham is its 'sweet' cure and full maturity. It is full-flavoured, and yet delicately mild, with just the right degree of sweetness that comes from maturity.

Epicam Ham. This is another registered name under which are sold the hams cured by the Epicure Ham Co. Ltd., of Pershore, in Worcestershire. All the hams bearing this name are guaranteed to come from specially fed Worcestershire pigs to ensure a right proportion of fat and lean, and they are cured according to a very old and famous family recipe.

Home cured hams. There are a great many farmers who still cure their own hams by their own fireside, so to speak, and as they all have a recipe of their own, and views of their own as well, there is still a great deal of individuality and degrees of flavour to be expected in English-cured hams to be bought in England. Here is a typical farm-house recipe.

Method: Rub each ham with 1 oz. saltpetre and same of brown sugar. The following day boil in a bottle or two of beer, 1 lb. bay salt, same of common salt; ½ lb. brown sugar, a small pit of salt prunella (for curing bone) and ½ oz. pepper. Let it cool, then pour all over the ham, and rub each day for a month. —C.N.

AMERICAN HAMS

There are many types of American hams, according to the breed of hog raised, to the methods of feeding and of curing. The best hams are generally considered to be the Virginian hams and the Kentucky hams.

Virginian Hams. The true Virginian hams come from the breed known as 'razor-backs'; they are fed on peanuts and peaches, and cured according to age-long and greatly treasured recipes, smoked over fires of apple and hickory wood, and aged in suitable smoke houses until the right flavour has been achieved.

A popular brand of Virginian hams is known as Smithfield hams; they are not named after the London Meat Market of that name, but after the little town of Smith-field in Virginia. The pigs are of 'razor-back' ancestry and are allowed to roam wild in the woods for the first nine months of their existence, feeding on acorns, beechnuts and hickory nuts. Then they are turned into the peanut fields and lastly fed on corn before being slaughtered. They are then dry-salted, spiced with black pepper and heavily smoked with hickory, apple and oak, and are aged for never less than a year. They are excellent.

But there are hams sold as Virginia hams which are the produce of western soft pork merely cured in Virginia; they are poor.

Kentucky Hams. These hams are from the finest Hampshire hogs and not from 'razor-backs'. When weaned, the piglets are turned out to roam where they fatten on acorns, beans and clover, until the time for slaughter-ing approaches, when they are penned and fed on grain. They are dry salted for about 30 days, smoked over hickory and apple wood for another 30 days, and then matured for another 10 or 12 months. They weigh from 10 to 15 lb.

'Quick-cure' Hams. Many American hams are scientifically and economically cured by various chemical hypodermical injections. They have their quick-cooking advantages, though slow-cured hams taste best.

IRISH HAMS

Irish hams are produced in Northern Ireland, where their production is closely connected with the making of Irish roll bacon. In the Irish Free State ham production is less im-portant, being merely a side-line in factories producing Wiltshire-cut sides. Belfast is well known for its hams, which are dry-salt cured, and well trimmed and squared at the butt. Boneless Irish hams are usually cut deep into the side, pickle-cured, and boned before they are smoked. As a general rule, Irish hams are long-cut and dry-salt cured and are smoked (often peat-smoked) by the curers; they are normally graded as 10-12 lb., 13-14 lb., and 15-16 lb.—L.G.M.

BAYONNE HAMS

The *Jambon de Bayonne* is mostly eaten raw, in very thin slices, as a *hors d'oeuvre*. It does not come from Bayonne, but is cured in a peculiar manner at Orthez, a village near Bayonne.

DANISH HAMS

Danish hams are a subsidiary product of some of the bacon factories and are shipped green. Average weight about 12-14 lb.— L.G.M.

PRAGUE HAMS

Prague hams (*Pragerschinkers*) are first salted in large vats and left in a mild brine for several months; they are smoked with beech wood and matured in cool cellars until marketed.—L.G.M.

Hot Boiled Ham

A hot boiled ham should be sliced as thinly as possible and the only orthodox sauce to serve with it is a tablespoonful of dry Cham-pagne per slice of ham: *Sherry Sauce* and *Madeira Sauce* are heresies, although many otherwise orthodox gastronomes approve of them.

To Boil Hams and Bath Chaps

Hams, being so very thick through, may be deceptive, and to make sure that the meat is sound to the core, run a long, sharp narrow knife into it, close to the bone. If, when withdrawn, the point of the knife has an agreeable smell and comes out quite clean, the ham is sweet, but not otherwise. A ham which is very dry-looking through long hanging should be soaked in cold water for 24 hours, changing the water occasionally. An ordinary ham needs only about eight hours' soaking. Wash well, trim off rusty parts from underside, put into a pot deep enough to allow it to be completely im-mersed in cold water. Bring the pot grad-ually to boiling point, skimming constantly as required, and simmer very gently, allow-ing 25 minutes per lb. for a medium-sized ham, 30 minutes per lb. for a very large one. The water must NOT boil: if it does, the lean will be tough and stringy. When done, remove ham, strip its skin off, and replace it in cooking water to cool. Sprinkle, when quite cold, with brown breadcrumbs or glaze surface, as desired. Bath chaps are cooked in the same way, but they, being much smaller, require only about 20 minutes per lb. and the addition of a small piece of orange rind to water greatly improves their flavour. Keep stock for making pea soup.

Cold Boiled Ham 'En Cornets'

This is an elegant manner of serving ham as a light luncheon dish. Prepare (1) a *macédoine* of fresh vegetables (see Section II, *VEGE-TABLES*) and (2) some good *mayonnaise* (see Section I, *SAUCES*). Mix both lightly together. Cut some thin slices of boiled ham and roll them into a point, like the old-fashioned grocer's bags. The best way to do this is first to make the 'cornets' out of strong white paper of the desired size. In these roll the slices of ham, fastening neatly inside with a wooden toothpick. Now fill each 'horn of abundance' with the mayonnaise and vegetables and carefully slip from the paper by undoing it deftly. Place each 'cornet' on a lettuce leaf to serve.—P.W.

Casserole of Ham and Peas

1 thick slice mild gammon
Freshly-boiled rice
10 or 12 small onions
Tender green peas
Mustard

Grill the gammon on both sides, after spreading lightly on one side with prepared French aromatic mustard – *fines herbes* or tarragon. When nearly done, remove and place in a casserole with a little of the fat from pan and the small onions. Continue cooking until all is lightly coloured, then cover, reduce heat and simmer until ham is tender. Cook the rice and peas separately, having the former dry and fluffy and the latter a good green and well drained. When ready to serve, remove ham and onions to a hot dish, add cooked peas for a minute or two to gravy and fat in casserole. Serve ham, surrounded by small onions, then by a ring of green peas and this, in turn, by a larger ring of snowy white rice. Or, if preferred, add peas and rice to ham in casserole and serve in this, which tastes equally good but does not look so attractive.—P.W.

Ham Croquettes

1 cup thick, rich white sauce
2 egg yolks
1 or 2 raw eggs
Frying fat
1 cup minced ham
Salt and cayenne
Breadcrumbs

Make the white sauce in the usual way, keeping it thick: (see Section I, *SAUCES*). Season rather highly as regards either plain or cayenne pepper. Add finely-minced ham and well-beaten egg yolks. Mix all well together and allow to cool. Shape as desired, dip each croquette first in beaten egg then in fine breadcrumbs. Fry until crisp and brown in boiling oil or fat, drain well and serve with any desired hot sauce.—P.W.

Mousse of Ham

½ lb. cooked ham
1½ gills of good stock
¼ oz. gelatine
A tiny pinch of cayenne
½ pint of cream
A little aspic jelly

Put the ham three times through the mincer, then pound in a mortar, keeping a little back. Season with pepper and cayenne. Melt the gelatine in the remainder of stock, and strain it into the ham mixture. When smooth, add the cream (whipped) and whip together until light and frothy. Place the *purée* in a soufflé dish, and smooth top as evenly as possible without pressing down too heavily. Just as it is setting, pour some *cold* liquid aspic gently on to the mousse. Serve very cold with a sauce of Champagne, with tangerine skins cut into matches.–CH.J.

Potted Ham

1 lb. lean ham
⅛ teaspoon ground mace
Salt, pepper, cayenne
¼ lb. fat ham
⅛ teaspoon nutmeg
Few drops onion juice

Pass ham through mincer, using finest knife, then pound in a mortar, add seasoning, and press through a fine sieve. Place in a pie-dish and bake in a moderate oven for three-quarters of an hour and if to be used fairly soon, press into small glass jars and cover with clarified butter.—P.W.

Scalloped Ham
(Canadian)

4 hard-boiled eggs
2 cups rich white sauce
¾ cup buttered biscuit crumbs
¼ cup chopped ham

Butter an earthenware, metal or oven-glass baking-dish well. Put a good layer of the crumbs, mixed with a sufficiency of melted butter, on the bottom of dish, cover this with two of the eggs, finely chopped, then half the chopped ham and cover this with half the sauce and repeat operation, finishing off with a sprinkling of crumbs. Bake in a moderately hot oven until crumbs are brown. Breadcrumbs may replace biscuit crumbs. They must be well mixed with the melted butter and, if liked, a little cayenne may be added.—P.W.

French Ham Soufflé

2 tablespoons butter
2 cups milk or thin cream
1 cup finely minced lean ham
2 tablespoons flour
½ cup grated Gruyère cheese
4 eggs
Few grains cayenne

Melt the butter without allowing it to sizzle, add the flour, stirring continuously; when blended, add the milk or cream, a little at a time. If the ham is very mild, add a little salt and allow mixture to simmer gently for a few minutes. It should be quite thick and smooth. Cool somewhat, then add cheese, finely-minced or pounded ham, cayenne to taste and the egg yolks, well beaten. Now beat egg whites very stiffly and fold into the mixture. Turn into a buttered soufflé mould and either cook *bainmarie*, i.e. in a large saucepan half-full of boiling water, covering mould with a paper; or bake in a moderate oven for 25 to 30 minutes, serving as soon as ready. If baked, it will be more *Soufflé* than if steamed, which makes it more of a light custard.—P.W.

Ham Suprême
(American)

2 centre cut slices lean ham
1 tin of sweet corn
¼ cup minced green pepper
Hot potato croquettes
3 firm tomatoes
¼ cup minced onion
Salt and pepper
Parsley

Cut the ham into ½ in. slices, then into rounds slightly larger than the sliced tomatoes. Heat the corn, draining off any excess of liquid, season and add a little butter. Put the corn into a pan such as is used under a grill. Set the rack on top and grill the slices of ham gently, turning once. When done, put a slice of uncooked tomato on top of each piece of ham, and on each of these a tablespoonful of mixed green pepper and onion, well seasoned. Continue cooking under grill until slices of tomato are hot through then serve on a hot dish with hot corn in centre and rounds of ham and tomato around, alternating with freshly fried potato croquettes (*see* Section II, *VEGETABLES*). Garnish with parsley. —P.W.

Ham and Egg Timbales

Finely chop some rather fat but mild ham, and then pound it to a paste. Blend with a little mustard, pepper or paprika and enough thick cream to form a smooth paste. Have some small ramekin or timbale moulds. Butter them, then line with the ham mixture, pressing it down on bottom and along sides to an eighth of an inch thickness. Break a fresh egg in centre. Set the timbales in a panful of hot water in a moderate oven. When eggs are set, turn them carefully out on *croûtes*, serving hot tomato sauce separately.—P.W.

HARE

Lat. *Lepus europaeus*; Fr. *Lièvre*; Ger. *Hase*; It. *Lepre*; Sp. *Liebre* A rodent quadruped with long ears and longer hind legs, a short tail and a dented lip or 'hare lip'; this last characteristic is but faintly marked in young animals, which makes it easy to tell a young hare from an old 'un.

Incidentally, let it be recorded, in fairness to Mrs Glasse, that there never was any mention in her *Art of Cookery* of 'first catch your hare'. This was laid at her door by some unscrupulous, facetious or merely ignorant reviewer, who turned 'case' to 'catch'. To case a hare meant to Shakespeare, to Mrs Glasse and to her readers 'to strip off its skin'. (See Johnson's Dictionary.)

The two most usual methods of cooking a hare are roast and jugged, besides two hare soups, the one using the animal's blood and the other without. But there are also a large number of more complicated recipes for serving hare with various sauces and garnishings, all of them somewhat rich. Practically all these different recipes have the same beginning, that is a well-seasoned *marinade* for the hare to spend at least a night and sometimes 48 hours soaking before it is cooked. This practice is fully justified whenever one has to deal with an elderly hare, but it is not to be recommended for cooking a young and tender hare. Young or old, a hare must always be well cooked, rather too much than too little. So long as the meat of the hare is red or reddish it is not fit to serve; many say that it is not even safe to eat.

Hare Brawn

Ingredients: 1 hare, 1 rabbit, 1 lb. fat ham or bacon, shallot, thyme.

Method: Stew all well together in good stock until tender, then put it all in a sieve to take the liquor from it, and take out all the bones. Reduce the liquor to a glaze. Mince the meat fine. Add the glaze to it with white pepper, salt and cayenne. Press it in a brawn mould and turn out when cold.–C.N.

Le Civet de Lièvre de Diane de Châteaumorand

Choose a pot into which you can settle your hare comfortably. You will then pour over it a glassful of wine, vinegar, half as much olive oil, pepper and salt, a bouquet of thyme, and an onion cut in strips. Keep the liver and the blood of the hare.

You must leave the hare in this dressing or *marinade* at least 12 hours before cooking it, and the more often you can turn it over and about so as to get it thoroughly soaked, the better it is for the hare. Chop together an onion and a little bacon fat; put this into a black pan with the hare that you will have cut up in pieces; also three or four pats of fresh butter.

After about 20 minutes' cooking, the hare will look greyish and will be sweating freely. Then is the time to give it a dusting of flour, and let it cook on a slow fire, tossing it about frequently.

By this time the hare will be partly cooked but still firm, and you should now add to the pot a large ladleful of good meat broth and the same quantity of red wine of good quality; also a little more pepper and salt, and then let the hare stew gently for another 35 minutes or so.

Take out of the *marinade* the thyme and onion and use the liquid to make a paste with the liver of the hare and the blood which you will have saved. This you will add to the hare only five minutes before it is ready to serve; bring to the boil and serve the hare with the rich sauce in which it was cooked. Taste before serving and if need be, add a little vinegar at the last moment. A little olive oil as a parting gift as the hare leaves the kitchen is also to be commended.

The *Civet* – what may be left of it – is all the better for being warmed up the next day. —Eugéne Herbododeau.

Braised Hare en 'Casserole'

Skin, draw, and bone a good hare, lard it or stuff with chopped fat bacon and seasoning, roll into a ball, dust with flour, and tie in shape.

Put 2 oz. of butter in a casserole, heat up, and brown the breast nicely. Take it out and put a layer of fat bacon at the bottom of the pan, then replace the hare and add round it the bones, etc., which you have broken in a mortar, a calf's foot cut in chunks, carrots and onions cut in rings, add a selection of spices and seasonings as in a braise. Add a glass of white wine, a squeeze of lemon, and enough good rich meat stock, and above all a dessertspoonful of brown sugar. Put a disc of buttered paper to fit between the lid and the pot, or lute it down with paste. Let it cook on the side of the stove, simmering slowly for four hours at least. (It does well in a hay box or fuelless cooker.) Strain before serving. This dish can be eaten hot or cold, which is the reason for the calf's foot.

If hot, subtract a good cupful of the gravy and reduce to half, adding red-currant jelly and wine to make a sauce. If cold, strain it all out into a big pudding basin or game-pie dish, when the gravy will set as a jelly and the excess fat can easily be removed.–M.H.P.

Hare (Flanders Style)

Cut up a hare into joints; fry in butter in a saucepan. Thicken with flour, fill up to half way, level with half and half stock and white wine, pepper, salt, spices, etc. Then add half a cupful of stoneless dried raisins and a similar amount of stoned, dried prunes. Roast chestnuts can also be added. Finish with a glass of red wine and the blood poured in a moment or two before serving.

A variety of other flavours, notably pears and even anchovies, are sometimes added to continental forms of jugged hare. In the same way the blood of the hare is sometimes made into omelette, particularly when the hare is an old stager, needing long hanging or marinading; and the blood will not keep until he is ready.—M.H.P.

Haricot Hare

This has nothing whatever to do with haricot beans, but is a *ragoût*. Make a stiff brown sauce with flour fried in butter, add stock, and onions, and let it cook. Chop the hare, and colour it in butter in a saucepan. Fry separately a dish of rounds of turnip in dripping, then add to the hare and pour over the whole the sauce you have made. Allow it all to cook very slowly for an hour or two, and add either a glass of red wine or a dash of lemon before serving.—M.H.P.

Jugged Hare

A young hare is, of course, best. Hang it for a week in a cool and well-ventilated place. Cut up the hare in nice serving pieces, and brown these in a little very hot butter or margarine. When they are nicely coloured, place the pieces of hare in a casserole or saucepan. In the fat used for colouring the hare, you then fry two or three sliced onions and one or two small carrots (sliced or diced). Put these in the casserole on top of the hare. Season with pepper and salt to taste. Cover the hare and vegetables with good meat stock, or, failing this, with hot water. Add a small faggot of dried herbs (*bouquet garni*) and, if you can buy, borrow or steal ½ lb. of fat ham or bacon, put that also into the pan. Then put on a closely-fitting lid and simmer *very gently* for not less than 1½ hours, preferably 2 hours and even 2½ hours if the hare be large or not so young. If necessary, add more stock or hot water during cooking.

When the hare is cooked and tender, move the pan away from the fire and add little by little the blood of the hare, if you have saved it for the purpose, stirring all the time gently. Warm thoroughly, but do not let it boil as it would curdle.

The Jugged Hare is now ready to serve, and this is the time when the 'finishing touch' can make all the difference.

Most cooks at this stage add a little butter blended with a good deal of flour and so thicken the sauce.

I do not like flour thickening at all. My own recipe is to heat a tumblerful of ordinary claret or any left-over red wine with a tablespoonful of red currant jelly in it. Stir and bring to the boil, when you will have a thick sweetish liquid which can be stirred into the Jugged Hare with advantage.

Hare Omelette

The blood is beaten up with the yolks of six eggs and two spoonfuls of cream and a teaspoon each of chopped parsley, shallots, and any other suitable *fines herbes*. A walnut-sized piece of butter is melted in a frying-pan and the mixture just poured in and stirred with a spoon till it thickens and begins to stick to the pan. Put a hot buttered plate on top of the frying-pan, and turn the whole upside down on to the plate and serve without folding it in two.—M.H.P.

Lièvre en Danube à la Provençale

1 young hare
Good pinch mixed spices
1 large onion
1 bayleaf
1 slice streaky salt pork
2 cups hot bouillon or water
Salt and pepper
2 cloves garlic
1 sprig dried thyme
Half a bottle white wine
1 or 2 smallish onions

Cut the hare into suitable pieces. Place these in an earthenware *terrine* or deep round pot, add salt, pepper, spices, large onion cut into pieces, thyme, bayleaf and garlic minced finely. Cover the whole with the wine. Cover with a lid, set in a cool plate for 12 hours, turning the pieces of meat once in a while to mix with the seasonings.

Next day, fry the cut-up pork gently in a heavy iron pan, removing pieces of meat left from this operation. Add the other onions, finely cut up, and, if wished, a few more dice of salt pork or bacon. Brown all this gently, then add the drained pieces of hare, browning them until the liquid in the pan has almost entirely evaporated. Now add to this the *marinade*, with its seasonings. (It is advisable to tie the thyme and bayleaf together for easier removal later.) Add the hot *bouillon* or water, cover pan closely and

cook gently until the hare is very tender. Serve 'as is', covering with the sauce.

This dish, by the way, is excellent cold. If wished, the hare may be entirely boned and left whole, to be sliced neatly when cold. Good aspic jelly as a garnish is an advantage.—P.W.

Roast Hare

1 hare
Thin rashers of bacon
¾ pint good stock
½ teaspoonful chopped shallot
Forcemeat (optional)
Pinch dried thyme
Butter
1 glass port wine
Flour
1 small chopped onion
½ teaspoon chopped parsley
Salt and pepper
Milk for basting

A young hare should be selected for this excellent dish and it may or may not be stuffed with forcemeat, as preferred. It should be hung for a week, weather permitting, before cooking. Truss as indicated in recipe for roasting a rabbit and brush all over with melted butter. Cover the back with the rashers of bacon, tied or skewered on. Place in a baking tin with about two cupfuls of milk, sprinkle with salt and pepper. Roast for 1½ to 2 hours, basting frequently with the milk. A little additional butter will enrich the milk. The liver should have been set aside, and the gall-bladder most carefully removed. While the hare is cooking, boil the liver gently for five minutes then drain and chop finely. Melt a couple of tablespoons of butter in a small saucepan, add the chopped liver, the parsley, the shallot, the onion and the thyme. Fry all this gently, seasoning well, for about 10 minutes, then, if possible, pound the mixture in a mortar or rub through a hair sieve. Take the butter that drained from this mixture, reheat it, add a good tablespoonful of flour and cook together until it is a light brown (*roux blond*), then add either stock or some of the milk used in basting the hare, stirring until the little saucelet boils. Add the liver mixture, simmer 10 minutes longer, then add the port wine. When the hare is nearly done, remove rashers of bacon, to brown the back, dredging it lightly with flour and basting frequently while it finishes browning. Remove strings, serve with the liver sauce and red currant jelly, handed separately.—P.W.

Hare Soup (English Style)

Cut down a hare into joints, and put it into a soup-pot, or large stewpan, with about 1 lb. of lean ham, in thick slices, three moderate-sized mild onions, three blades of mace, a faggot of thyme, sweet marjoram, and parsley, and about three quarts of good beef stock. Let it stew very gently for full two hours from the time of its first beginning to boil, and more if the hare be old. Strain the soup and pound together very fine the slices of ham and all the flesh of the back, legs and shoulders of the hare, and put this meat into a stewpan with the liquor in which it was boiled, the crumbs of two French rolls, and half a pint of port wine. Set it on the stove to simmer 20 minutes; then rub it through a sieve, place it again on the stove till very hot, but do not let it boil; season it with salt and cayenne and send it to table directly.—E.A.

Hare Soup (Scots style)
Bawd Bree

1 hare, fresh killed
Onion, carrot, turnip
Sweet herbs and peppercorns
Oatmeal and water
Port wine

Skin hare and clean thoroughly, holding it over large basin to catch all the blood, which contains much of the flavour. Joint the hare and put into pot with water, carrot, onion, turnip, peppercorns, herbs, salt and pepper, and simmer for three hours. Strain soup. Cut the meat into small pieces and return to pot with stock; add a handful of oatmeal. Strain the blood and gradually add to the soup, stirring all the time, and bring to the boil. Then add a glass of port wine and serve. A boiled potato should be served separately for each person.—S.W.R.

Baked Stuffed Hare

A stuffed hare takes about 20 minutes to half an hour longer to cook than an unstuffed one, and is cooked precisely like a roast but in the oven.

The stuffing is usually breadcrumbs, onion, suet, parsley and mixed herbs, but a trace of cinnamon, a very little chopped lemon rind and a clove or two improve the usual mixture out of all recognition.

An excellent French stuffing is as follows:

Crumble stale breadcrumbs, not crust, into a cup of cream. Add two onions stuck with cloves, and let it simmer for a few minutes to take flavour. Chop the hare liver finely, and add it to this *panade*, or base; then pound the whole with an equal quantity of butter, the yolks of two raw eggs, pepper, salt, and a sage-leaf or so. Stuff the hare with this and sew it up. Tie the forepaws back through the hindpaws, and cross these to the front so that the beast is in the natural attitude of running. Cover the whole with strips of fat bacon, and wrap in buttered paper. Cook for an hour and a quarter, then remove the paper and larding, sprinkle with pepper and salt, and brown nicely. Stir two spoonfuls of gooseberry or red currant jelly into a glass of port or Madeira and serve as a sauce.—M.H.P.

Lièvre en Terrine

1 hare
1 lb. lean fresh pork
Parsley
Small pinch dried thyme
Pinch powdered cloves
Thin slices fat salt pork
1 glass cognac
1 lb. leg of veal
2 oz. beef suet
1 small bayleaf
1 clove garlic
Salt and freshly ground pepper
1 thick slice streaky salt pork

The hare must be freshly killed, not 'hung'. Bone carefully. Cut up finely, with the veal and pork. Chop together the suet, parsley, thyme, bayleaf, garlic, cut the slice of salt pork into pieces the size of the pieces of hare, veal and pork. A suitable 'terrine' – which is a china or earthenware pot, oval or round in shape and having a well-fitting lid – must be available. Line this with the thin slices of fat salt pork. Mix all the other ingredients together, seasoning well with salt and pepper, add the nutmeg and pour the cognac over all. There must be enough to fill the terrine to the top, leaving just sufficient space for a covering of additional slices of fat salt pork (*bardes de lard*). Place cover on securely and fasten it down with a mixture of flour and water to seal contents in completely. Set in a medium oven and cook for four hours. Cool before opening. Rabbit – wild or tame – may be used instead of hare.—P.W.

HARTEBEEST

Lat. *Alcelaphus caama*. A large African antelope, light brown in colour with a yellow patch on the buttocks and black markings on the face. The horns, ringed and divergent, are bent back at the tips.

The range of this antelope is very similar to that of the Gemsbuck. It is still found in Griqualand West, in some parts being fairly plentiful. The *Bastard Hartebeest* (*A. lunatus*) is found throughout Central South Africa. —F.C.S.

HEDGEHOG

Lat. *Erinaceus europaeus*. A small European insectivorous quadruped with innumerable spines and a pig-like snout. The name is also given to other animals armed with spines, such as the Australian Porcupine ant-eater; *Hedgehogs* are not sold in shops for food.

they are among the farmer's best friends and should not be killed for food, but in the autumn, when they are at their fattest and best, hedgehogs are often run over, whilst on their leisurely way to their winter quarters, and killed by passing cars. They are well worth picking up and cooking, being as tender as young pork and of excellent flavour. Gipsies are always on the look out for hedgehogs to kill and eat: they either broil them on a hazel spit or bake them in clay.

Hotchi or Roast Hedgehog
In the typical gipsy fashion a hole is dug in the ground, lined with stones, and a fire is made here; then, when there is a bed of red hot ashes the animal is placed on them, encased in clay, skin and spikes left on. When it is cooked the clay is broken and the spiny covering comes away with the clay. The flesh is said by some to taste like roast chicken and by others like sucking pig.

HIPPOPOTAMUS
Lat. *Hippopotamus amphibius*. Next to the elephant, the bulkiest quadruped on earth; it is confined to Africa and is mostly aquatic in its habits. It is not killed for food, but, when killed, it has been eaten and declared fairly good eating by Puleston and other travellers. Sclater, in *Mammals of South Africa* (p. 272) says that all authors are agreed that the flesh of the hippopotamus is excellent eating, closely resembling succulent pork or veal.

HORSE
Lat. *Equus caballus*. A large quadruped which has been domesticated since prehistoric times. Horseflesh has never been popular in the British Isles, but it has long been in demand on the Continent. The fillet of a three-year-old thoroughbred is a costly luxury, but it is very good meat indeed: one has no chance of tasting it unless the horse happens to break its neck at exercise or otherwise injures itself so badly that it has to be destroyed. The majority of horseflesh sold by horse butchers is sound and wholesome meat, but too muscular to be enjoyable: it usually comes from horses too old for work as well as too old to roast: it is best boiled, stewed or in pies. Any of the recipes suitable for beef may be applied to horseflesh.

On February 29th, 1868, a horseflesh dinner was served at the Langham Hotel, in London, and Frank Buckland who was invited to it, said that he 'gave it a fair trial, tasting every dish from soup to jelly', but he did not approve of any of it.—FR.B.

HOT-POT. HOTCH-POTCH. HODGE-PODGE
A stew of meat – usually mutton – and vegetables, chiefly favoured in the North of England, where it takes the place of – and resembles – *Irish Stew*.

Lancashire Hot-pot
I
1 lb. neck of mutton
1 lb. loin chops
1 lb. Spanish onions
2 lb. potatoes

Put the meat, with bones and trimmings and the onions, in a stew pan and cover with cold water; bring quickly to the boil and then simmer until the gravy has been reduced by half. Grease a fireproof dish and cover bottom with a thick layer of sliced potatoes; arrange the meat over them and cover them with the rest of the sliced potatoes. Pour into the dish the meat gravy in which the mutton was cooked; brush the upper layer of potatoes with dripping and bake in moderate oven for two hours with lid on.

II
2 lb. neck of mutton
2 lb. potatoes
3 onions
½ lb. fresh mushrooms
3 sheeps' kidneys
12 oysters
2 oz. butter

Remove all excess of fat and cut the meat into cutlets. Peel the potatoes and cut them up in thick slices. Peel the onions and cut in thin slices. Wash but do not peel the mushrooms and cut them in two. Skin and halve the kidneys, removing core. Put all ingredients in a deep pan in alternate layers, with a layer of potatoes on top and seasoning each layer with pepper and salt. Melt the butter and pour it over; also two breakfast cups of meat stock. Cover closely and cook very gently in the oven or on top of stove for 2½ hours. Serve in cooking pot.

To make a Hotch-pot
Take a piece of brisket-beef; a piece of mutton; a knuckle of veal; a good colander of pot-herbs; half-minced carrots, onions and cabbage a little broken. Boil all these together until they be very thick.—*Sir Kenelm Digby's Closet Opened*, 1665.

IGUANA
Lat. *Iguana tuberculata*. A giant lizard, usually from 3 to 4 ft. long, but some reaching 5 ft. and more, found in Central and South America, also in some of the West Indies.

'A clean feeder, the creature lives in the tree tops of the steaming jungles below or at sea level, and subsists on the green leaves round it. ... Now it may be the Iguana is no pleasant object to look at. Its small eyes, pail-shaped snout and shark-like jaws, lined with a saw's teeth of steel, are, I know, repellent to many. Even the reptile's best friends, indeed, will be obliged to admit it presents at first sight a somewhat case-hardened exterior, and that its saurian countenance bears an unpleasing expression, both sarcastic and ferocious. But it is good, *very good*, to eat; and its cost does not amount to more than the equivalent of a shilling: two facts which must both tell in its favour. The ways of cooking it are many, but the best seemed to me to be roast saddle, cooked with herbs, and served in a circle of its own eggs with a rich brown sauce, flavoured with Madeira or port. The saddle is white and tender as the best capon, and the eggs, too, are a suitable, and even delicious, concomitant, once the consumer has grown accustomed to the idea of them.'—(OSBERT SITWELL, in *Wine and Food*, XXXIV, p. 61.)

IMPALA. ROOIBOK. ROODE-BOK

Lat. *Aepyceros melampus*. A large African antelope of a brownish-bay colour, white below, with a black crescent-like stripe on the haunch. The male has slender, annulated, lyrate horns. 'The ewes become very fat in the spring, and are excellent eating.'—F.V.K.

'They are nowhere more plentiful than along the Chobe, and may often be seen in herds of from twenty to a hundred together.' —F.C.S.

IRISH STEW

An excellent stew with a neck of mutton as its foundation, potatoes as its inevitable ornament, onions and other vegetables at will.

Irish Stew

Trim off all excess of fat from loin or neck of mutton and cut up in pieces suitable for serving. Put meat at the bottom of a good-sized earthenware pot or iron 'cocotte', just enough to cover; on the meat, place a layer of thick slices of potatoes and on these a layer of onions cut in rounds; salt and pepper. Then another layer of meat, another of potatoes and another of onions; more salt and pepper; and yet a third time, should you have a large family to feed. Add cold water, not quite enough to cover the whole. Put on a closely-fitting lid and put the pot or pan on a brisk fire for ten minutes. Remove scum as it rises and reduce heat to a minimum; let the lot stew very slowly until the meat is quite tender and the gravy has practically disappeared. Serve hot straight from the cooking pot.

JELLY

A soft, usually semi-transparent article of food obtained by boiling bones and tissues rich in gelatinous matter, such as calf's foot or cow-heel, removing the scum that rises and leaving the rest to cool. It is used for garnishing and decorating various dishes, also for glazing hams and tongues and other meats.

There are also Jellies made from fruit and sugar and from certain seaweeds and mosses. (*See* Sections II and IV, *VEGETABLES* and *FRUIT*.)

Meat Jelly

Take 1 lb. of gravy beef and 1 lb. of knuckle of veal; cut the meat very small and put into a stewpan; well cover with water and a pinch of salt. Simmer gently for about six hours. Strain into a basin and leave till next day; then remove all fat; put into a stewpan leaving the settlement at the bottom of the basin. Reduce the jelly till you have enough to fill a 1 lb. jam pot; leave till set and it is ready for use.—(The Lady Carrington in *Cookery Chronicle*, 1932.)

KANGAROO

The name is given to all herbivorous, leaping, marsupial mammals of the family *Macropodidae*, but practically the only one ever represented in the kitchen is the large *Kangaroo* (*Macropus giganteus*). Its long, thick tail which is used as a support by the animal, when it is standing on its hind legs or walking, is used in the making of soup, exactly in the same way as ox-tail is used in the making of ox-tail soup.

L.R.Brightwell, who has eaten a number of kangaroos from the London Zoo, where casualties were occasionally the result of free fights among the inmates, says that the flesh is very much like that of the hare, both before and after cooking.

KEBOBS

A dish of oriental origin, usually made by alternating highly seasoned pieces of various meats on small skewers and serving them broiled, on the skewers, with a sharp sauce; but quite the best recipe I know for them is English, and from its ingredients would not easily be feasible in most eastern lands:

Place three or four thin curls of cooked veal and of bacon, about $3\frac{1}{2}$ in. long, on a skewer alternately; in each curl of veal put a little bit of fat bacon, and in both veal and bacon put a morsel, sweet or savoury, of anything you like; chutney, walnut or other pickle, mushroom, onion, apple, stoned raisin or preserved cherry. Broil on a grid-iron over a quick fire and serve on the skewers very hot on buttered toast.

KID

Fr. *Chevreau, Cabri*. A kid some three or four months old is a great delicacy in mountainous countries and grassless lands of southern Europe and northern Africa, where lambs are few or else poorly fed. A kid some three or four weeks old, before it leaves its mother for the bark of trees is a great delicacy anywhere.

Loin of Kidd with Ragoûst

When it is well stuck, spit it, and when it is halfe rosted, bast it with pepper, vinegar, and a little broath; thicken the sauce with some chippings of bread, or chippings searced, then serve.—*La Va.*

Roast Kid

Take the joint and plunge it into a bowl of boiling water for about 10 minutes and then wipe dry before putting it in the baking tin. Make one or two incisions in the skin and slip under a leaf of mint or a tooth of onion. In Italy a few leaves of rosemary are sprinkled over the meat while cooking, as it helps to make it tender. It wants well basting, and a good plan is to have a tin of hot water at the bottom of the oven, so that the steam from it keeps the meat tender. Serve mint sauce or fruit chutney with it and plenty of green vegetables.—(*Woman*).

Kid en Casserole (an Irish dish)

Take a little haunch and hang till tender. Cover well with flour, then put into a big iron pot, with as many vegetables of different kinds as you can get, 4 oz. butter, pepper, salt, and a glass of white wine. Cook very slowly and very thoroughly. Cook at the same time in an earthenware dish plenty of potàtoes cut in pieces, *sautées* in butter and well seasoned. Serve the kid in a large dish deep enough to hold most of the gravy, and the vegetables together with it or separately.

KIDNEYS

Fr. *Rognons*; Ger. *Nieren*; It. *Arnioni*; Sp. *Riñons*. The kidneys of cattle, sheep and pigs, although dubbed 'offal', are excellent food. They are rich in protein, poor in carbohydrates and supply fat in varying proportions.

Beef Kidney	13.7%	Protein, 1.9% fat	
Veal ,,	16.9%	,,	6.4% ,,
Mutton ,,	16.5%	,,	3.2% ,,
Pork ,,	15.5%	,,	4.8% ,,

In England, *Kidneys*, when not otherwise qualified, means *Sheep's Kidneys*.

Kidneys cannot be too fresh; they quickly lose both their flavour and goodness. Buy kidneys whenever possible 'in the fat', when it is so much easier to tell the fresh from the stale.

Beef Kidney

Cut the kidney in thin regular slices and soak them in water and vinegar for an hour. Clean and dry them; then dredge a little flour over them. Put into a pan some butter; add salt and pepper. Put pan on a quick fire and when the butter begins to sizzle put the kidney in; reduce heat at once and stir until the pieces of kidney are nicely browned. Serve with a rich gravy and some fried parsley.

Kidney Curry

1 lb. of beef kidney and six (sheep's) kidneys. Stew these very slowly until quite tender in a little good stock or water. Cut the beef kidney into small square pieces and the sheep's kidneys into halves. Fry the butter and onions together as in all other curries, and then the curry powder; add these to the kidneys and simmer together for a little while. It is better to serve this curry with some of its own gravy, and not as dry as the others.—B.H.

Beef Kidney à la Parisienne

1 very fresh beef kidney
Salt and pepper
1 clove garlic
1 teaspoonful vinegar
Butter
Chopped parsley
Chopped chives or onion
1 pinch flour
1 cup stock

Remove skin and centre core from kidney, cutting into thin fillets or smallish pieces. Heat the butter until melted and fry the pieces of kidney in it with the finely-chopped garlic, chives (or onion), salt and pepper. When lightly coloured, add the vinegar (or lemon juice, if preferred) and a scanty cupful of stock, mixed with the pinch of flour. Heat but do not cook again, and serve at once, or the kidneys will become hard.—P.W.

Ragoût of Ox Kidney

1 lb. ox kidney and a small basket of button mushrooms. Cut kidney into slices ½ in. thick and lay on bottom of a stewpan with a slight sprinkling of pepper; add one pint water and simmer gently for two hours; then add mushrooms, salt and a little more pepper; when all has simmered gently for one hour longer pour it into a dish and let it stand all night. Next morning carefully skim off all fat and replace rest in stewpan; while heating, make two rounds of rather thick toast, place them side by side on a dish and pour the kidneys over them.

Lamb Kidneys

Lamb kidneys
Butter
Pepper
Salt
Orange juice
Thin cream
Hot toast

Split kidneys; soak in ice water. Grill kidneys in hot sweet butter. Squeeze orange juice over kidneys. Slightly pepper and salt. Last thing stir in thin cream. Serve on hot toast. Pour over sauce from pan. (*From Mrs S.K.de Forest, N.Y.C.*)—s.d.l.m.

Rognons à la Bérichonne

Sheep's kidneys
Fried croûtons
Salt pork
Tiny 'button' onions
Butter
Red wine
Fresh mushrooms
Salt and pepper

Skin and cut kidneys in halves. *Sauté* them in butter and place each half on a hot *croûton* of same size. Pour half a glass of red wine into the pan the kidneys were cooked in, stirring well; season and cook rapidly until reduced to half original volume, then add a 'nut' of butter and, if available, a spoonful of good meat extract or glaze. Cover kidneys with this gravy and serve them around a small *ragoût* composed of fried cubes of salt pork, *sauté* mushroom caps and glazed onions.—p.w.

Rognons Bretonne

4 large onions
1 cup stock
Chopped parsley
Butter
Sheep's kidneys
Lemon juice
Fried *croûtons*

Slice the onions and fry them in butter until an even brown. Add stock and reduce, by slow cooking, to a glaze. Slice the kidneys thinly, fry quickly in butter, add glaze, season with lemon juice, salt, pepper and parsley to taste. Re-heat and serve in a border of tiny crisp *croûtons* and any desired vegetable such as tiny glazed onions, green peas, mushrooms, etc.—p.w.

Brochettes of Kidneys

Lamb or sheep's kidneys
Mushrooms
Thick rashers mild bacon
Butter
Salt and pepper

Skin, core and cut up kidneys into chunky pieces. Cut the bacon into pieces of similar size and thickness. Peel and wash mushrooms, cut them also into similar sized pieces and lightly *sauté* them in butter, seasoning with salt and pepper. Retain the butter they are cooked in for other uses. Allow mushrooms to cool and do not cook too much. Now thread on special skewers first a piece of kidney, next a piece of bacon and thirdly a piece of mushroom, continuing until skewer is full. Cook under the grill, lightly dusting with salt and pepper. Serve very hot, on skewers, either on toast or *croûtons*.

Another Method

Prepare kidneys and bacon as directed, but use no mushrooms. When brochettes are ready, dip in fine breadcrumbs and either fry in deep boiling fat or *sauté* in butter until crisp and brown.—p.w.

Rognons au Madère

Sheep's kidneys
Butter
Dry sherry
Fresh mushrooms
Flour
Drop or two lemon juice
Chopped parsley

This makes an excellent *entrée*. Skin kidneys and cut each into halves, then each half in two or three pieces, according to size. Heat some butter in a *sauteuse* (shallow copper pan), add the pieces of kidney and the peeled and cut-up mushrooms, cooking rather fast, stirring frequently, until water has evaporated from mushrooms, and butter runs clear. Sprinkle with salt and pepper and then with flour. Moisten with a sufficiency of sherry, flavour with a drop or two of lemon juice, sprinkle with chopped parsley and serve at once. To be tender, the whole job must be quickly done and the sauce must be very 'short'. White wine or even champagne may be used instead of sherry, and mushrooms may be omitted and chopped shallots substituted. The above recipe is Lyonnaise and much more delicate than when shallot is used to flavour.—p.w.

Stewed Kidneys

Skin sheeps' kidneys, cut them in two, fry them in butter for two or three minutes, then put them with some good stock into a pan and stew very gently. Cut up for every six kidneys two medium-sized Spanish onions and four small apples; fry them in butter for 10 minutes, then add them to the kidneys and stew the whole lot very gently for five or six hours. If the gravy is not thick enough, thicken with a little cornflour.

The great point is to let the kidneys stew slowly for a very long time. (*Old Warwickshire Recipe, from a late Mayor of Warwick.*)

The Earl of Howth's Devilled Kidneys
1 oz. butter
1 tablespoon dry mustard
1 dessertspoon Worcestershire sauce

Split kidneys and shake a little seasoning inside; cook in stewpan with butter and pour the sauce around.

Pig's Kidneys
These are less delicate but also less expensive than sheep's kidneys. Skin, skewer, brush over with melted butter, sprinkle lightly with salt, pepper and sage, then grill, cooking cut side first and turning over when that side is done. Serve *à la Maître d'Hôtel*, with chip or straw potatoes.—P.W.

Veal Kidneys
5 veal kidneys
1 lb. mushrooms chopped very fine
1 tablespoon onion, chopped very fine
1 tablespoon fat (butter or bacon grease)
2 tablespoons white wine
Salt and pepper

Parboil kidneys a few minutes. Remove skin. Soak in cold water half an hour. Slice and season with salt and pepper. Cook mushrooms in a little water three-quarters of an hour. Cook onions in melted fat for three or four minutes. Add kidneys to onions and cook five minutes. Add mushrooms and cook all together five minutes. Add wine and serve. (*From Mrs Edwin White, St. Paul, Minn.*)—S.D.L.M.

Rognons de veau Clémentine
Cut open two good, light-coloured veal kidneys, remove the hard core, but leave some of the fat. Salt and pepper them and cook in butter in a covered earthen casserole in a slow oven, basting frequently. After 20 minutes (or when the kidneys are three-quarters cooked) place around them 18 mushroom caps and six small onions previously *sautéed* in butter to a pale gold colour. Let all this simmer five minutes in the fat of the kidneys, then baste the whole with three or four tablespoons of port wine and cover tightly. When the port is half reduced, blend in a teaspoon of prepared mustard (French type). Just five minutes more in the oven and your dish is ready to serve.—CL.K.

Veal Kidney à la Liégeoise
The best of kidneys is the calf's kidney, and the best way of cooking it is this:

Cook the kidney in a casserole with butter.

It should be whole, and a little of the fat surrounding it should be left. Just before serving throw in a wineglassful of burnt gin and a few crushed juniper berries.

These berries can be bought dried, but if you find or beg or even steal some fresh ripe ones great reward will be yours. (AMBROSE HEATH, in *Wine and Food*, II, p. 39.)

Vol-au-vent Surprise
2 lb. potatoes
1 oz. butter
½ lb. mushrooms
Salt and pepper
2 egg yolks
3 kidneys

For Kidneys
Salt and pepper
Dusting of flour
1 egg yolk
1 oz. butter
1 pint good rich stock
Breadcrumbs
Butter

To prepare potatoes, boil them until tender, drain well and dry out thoroughly on side of fire. Mash, adding salt and pepper and egg yolks, well beaten, with the butter. Cool a little, then turn this mixture out on to a floured pastry-board. Mould with the hands into a round 'raised' pie or *vol-au-vent*, keeping back enough of the mixture to make a cover. Brush over with beaten egg and bake in a hot oven until golden brown. Peel the mushrooms and the kidneys and cut both up, then place together for a few moments in boiling water (or, better still, *sauté* gently in butter until tender). If boiled, drain well, add salt and pepper, the butter, flour and stock. Simmer slowly for half an hour (if the mushrooms and kidneys have been *sauté* the method is the same, simmer after they are lightly browned). When done, add the beaten yolk of egg after removing the pan from the fire, stir well and use to fill the prepared *vol-au-vent*. Pop on the potato 'cover', brush this also lightly over with beaten egg and brown under the grill or in a sharp oven. If wished, some cooked peas or coarsely-chopped hard-boiled eggs may also be added to filling.—P.W.

KLIPBOK. KLIPSPRINGER
Lat. *Oreotragus oreotragus*. This little antelope is found from the Cape to the Zambesi, wherever there are stony hills.—F.C.S.

'The flesh ranks before that of all the smaller antelopes as an article of diet.'—F.V.K.

KROMESKIES
Cut some very thin slices of bacon, about 1½ in. broad and 2 in. long. Lay them flat and place a little well-seasoned minced meat on each. Roll up the bacon tightly, taking care that the mince does not escape, and put aside in a cool place. To serve, dip each into batter, fry a golden brown and garnish with fried parsley.

KUDO. KOODOO

Lat. *Strepsiceros strepsiceros*: syn. *S. kudu*. A large African antelope, grey-brown in colour, with vertical white stripes on the side. A similar but smaller antelope, mostly found in Somaliland, is known as the *Lesser Kudu* (*S. imberbis*).

'The flesh is generally reported to be good, and most sportsmen mention the marrow bones as being particularly delicious.'—M.S.A., p. 246.

'The flesh is quite equal to that of other antelopes.'—F.V.K.

LAMB

A *Lamb* is a young ovine animal that has not acquired its first pair of permanent teeth: when it has acquired those teeth, it becomes a *Hogget* – either a *wether hogget*, if a male and castrated, or a *ewe hogget*, if a female – until it reaches the period for clipping. In culinary language, however, there are two sorts of lambs, the *Baby Lamb* or *Agneau de Lait*, also known as *Agneau de Pauillac* and the *Lamb* proper, or *Agneau*. The first is milk-fed, i.e. fatted off its mother without weaning. The meat is very white and tender, without flavour, but none the less a great and costly gastronomic delicacy. The second, in Great Britain, is either lamb or hogget, that is a sheep not yet twelve months old, after which it becomes mutton. In olden times, however, mutton was the meat of wether or ewe when three, four or five years old; it was darker in colour, better in flavour, with plenty of white fat and very much finer meat than that of the 'old lambs' or yearling sheep of the present day. In the U.S.A., mutton is not mentioned at all in polite culinary society: one never gets anything but lamb.

Breed, age and feeding are the three main factors responsible for the degree of quality of both lamb and mutton, but when none of these important factors is known – and such is the case when one enters a butcher's shop – one has to be guided by the appearance of the meat, and here is the advice given by the Ministry of Agriculture in its Report on the marketing of sheep, mutton and lamb in England and Wales (Economic series, No. 29, p. 102):

'To sum up it may be said that in a lamb or young mutton carcass of high quality, the bone should be fairly soft, the flesh light in colour, fine in grain, firm, well developed and full of sap, the fat of a correct colour and well distributed, and the conformation good. The ratio of muscle to gristle and bone should be relatively high.'

The best joints of both lamb and mutton are the saddle and the shoulder, but they are also the least economical as they carry a greater proportion of bone to meat than other joints; next come the loin, the leg, and then the neck, which is divided in two parts, the 'best end', which is definitely best, and the 'scrag end', which is always much cheaper and about the same price as the 'breast'. From the loin, chops and cutlets are cut off, which are the best 'small cuts'; there are also the innards and the odds and ends, from head to tail.

Lamb Chop, *Côte d'agneau*
Lamb Cutlet, *Côtelette d'agneau*
Breast of Lamb, *Poitrine d'agneau*
Lamb Kidney, *Rognon d'agneau*
Leg of Lamb, *Gigot d'agneau*
Loin of Lamb, *Longe d'agneau*
Lamb's Liver, *Foie d'agneau*
Neck of Lamb, *Collet d'agneau*
Saddle of Lamb, *Selle d'agneau*
Shoulder of Lamb, *Epaule d'agneau*
Lamb's Sweetbread, *Ris d'agneau*
Lamb's Tail, *Queue d'agneau*
Lamb's Tongue, *Langue d'agneau*

Carré d'agneau rôti

The *Carré* is really the breast, the part between the neck and the saddle, and it is often grilled or baked in the oven; if small it can also be pan-fried, but on the whole it is best roast, if well basted all the time: 12 minutes per pound should be sufficient time for roasting.

The principal recipes of the *Cuisine Classique* for *Carrés d'agneau* are the following:

Beauharnais: Breadcrumbed and grilled and served with *Pommes noisettes* and *Fonds d'artichauts* filled with *Sauce Beauharnais*.

Bonne Femme: Cooked in a moderate oven, in a cocotte, with plenty of butter, a dozen small onions and a dozen *lardons*.

Bordelaise: Baked in a cocotte with half butter and half olive oil, with some *Cèpes*, chopped parsley and garlic.

Clamart: Pan-fried and finished cooking with green peas *à la française*.

Maraichère: Cocotte cooked in oven with butter and served with cooked salsifies, brussels sprouts and small potatoes.

Nouilles: Cocotte cooked, some freshly made noodles being added to the *cocotte* before the meat is quite done; finish cooking, with the noodles, in moderate oven, adding some meat gravy.

Languedocienne: Baked in open dish with butter or goose fat, some small onions, some ham cut up in small pieces and chopped garlic; garnish with some small *Cèpes* cooked in olive oil.

La Varenne: Boned and flattened; seasoned and dipped in egg and breadcrumbs and then cooked in butter; served with creamed mushrooms.

447

Monselet: Grilled, breadcrumbed and browned in sizzling butter; serve on a bed of *Pommes Anna*.

Niçoise: Baked in a moderate oven and garnished with small vegetable marrows cooked in olive oil, cut in small pieces; a large tomato, peeled, and quartered, and some small potatoes, the whole being rather highly seasoned.

Lamb Chops

Cut a neck of lamb neatly into chops, and rub them over with egg yolk. then strew over them some breadcrumbs, mixed with a little clove, mace, pepper and salt. Fry to a nice brown and place the chops regularly round a dish, leaving an opening in the middle, to be filled with stewed·spinach, cucumber, or sorrel.

Obs. Spinach and sorrel are two of the most wholesome vegetables served up at table, and should never be allowed to retire without being abundantly noticed.—C.F.M.

Stuffed Lamb Chops

Thick lamb loin chops
Salt and pepper
1 or 2 chicken's livers
1 or 2 fresh mushrooms

The chops must not be less than 1½ to 2 in. thick, one bone, or even two if lamb is small, having been removed. Split the lean part of the meat in half, cutting to bone. Peel off skin. Chop the livers and peeled mushrooms and *sauté* in butter, seasoning well, until done but not browned. Use to stuff incision in chops, sew up with large needle and coarse thread, sprinkle with salt, pepper and place on a greased griller, under a hot flame or over a clear charcoal fire. Brown on both sides, remove thread and serve very hot. If preferred, once the chops have been stuffed, egg and breadcrumb them, then bake in a hot oven after placing a little butter on top of each chop. Turn once to brown other side.—P.W.

Côtelettes Bruxelloises

Best loin cutlets
1 small chopped truffle
Sausage-meat
Salt and pepper

Select thick chops, trim into cutlets, removing all bone and fat. Flatten each one nicely. Coat, using the hands, with well-seasoned, freshly made sausage-meat, pressing well down, adding the chopped truffle. If available, cover all with the thin lamb's membrane, known in France as the 'toilette'; if unavailable, sprinkle with fine breadcrumbs and let surface harden before grilling. The chop should be underdone and the sausage-meat covering well browned and crisp.–P.W.

Côtelettes d'Agneau Café Américain

Small lamb cutlets
Fried croûtons
Balls of potato
Salt and pepper
Butter
Asparagus tips
Port wine
Thick cream

Allow two tiny cutlets per serving. *Sauté* them in butter, in an earthenware casserole, keep hot and add a soupçon of good port and a spoonful of cream to fat and gravy left in pan, after seasoning to taste. Serve cutlets on hot fried *croûtons*, garnish with buttered asparagus tips and tiny balls of boiled potatoes.

Fresh mushrooms, *sauté* separately in butter, may be also used as a garnish, their 'gravy' being strained into sauce.—P.W.

Cheesed Lamb Cutlets

Small trimmed lamb cutlets
Breadcrumbs
Frying fat
Beaten egg
Grated Parmesan cheese
Hot tomato sauce
Salt and pepper

Dip each cutlet in beaten egg, then in a seasoned mixture of breadcrumbs and grated cheese, pressing down firmly. Allow to harden, then fry in deep fat until brown and crisp. Serve very hot, as soon as ready, with a well-seasoned fresh tomato sauce.—P.W.

Côtelettes Edouard VII

Take very tender and rather large lamb chops. Dip each one, after neatly trimming, first in fine breadcrumbs, then in beaten egg, then again in breadcrumbs, pressing down evenly. Grill over a very hot flame so that the mark of the gridiron may show across each surface. Serve chops very hot with iced mayonnaise and potatoes baked in their skins. The latter must be served on a separate plate without any butter as the mayonnaise suffices to enrich dish.—P.W.

Côtelettes Estivales

Tender lamb chops
Beaten egg
Flour
Salt and pepper
Chopped mixed *fines herbes*
Butter
Milk

This is, as its name indicates, a nice summer dish. Trim chops, dip each one first in beaten egg, then in a mixture of finely chopped parsley, thyme, chervil and chives, pressing herbs well in. Heat some butter in a frying-pan, fry chops, or, rather, *sauté* them in this, quickly. Prepare a green sauce by finely chopping together a small quantity of parsley, thyme, mint, and one tiny sage leaf. Melt a tablespoonful of butter in a small pan, stir into this a dessertspoonful of flour and a cup of milk, beating well. Season with salt and pepper and cook over a low heat for five minutes, beating the while. When ready to serve, add the herbs and hand sauce separately.—p.w.

Côtelettes Jardinière
Olive oil
Carrots and onions
1 egg yolk
Salt and pepper
Mixed fresh vegetables
Tablespoon thick cream
Grilled chops

Marinate the chops for a couple of hours in a little oil, mixed with salt, pepper, a cut-up onion and a grated carrot. Put the trimmings of the chops, but not too much fat, in a pan with water, salt, pepper and any fresh vegetables handy: peas, French beans, small broad beans, carrots, small onions, etc. Cook them until tender, when the water will have all but disappeared; then remove pan from fire, beat together the egg yolk and the cream, stir into vegetable stew and serve this in centre of a hot dish, surrounding with the freshly grilled chops.—p.w.

Côtelettes à la Millionnaire
Mutton or lamb cutlets
Salt and pepper

Two out of every three of the cutlets must be cut rather thin and the third a good deal thicker. Season each one and tie or firmly skewer three together, the thickest in the centre. Cook under a hot flame, or over a clear fire, turning very frequently so that the gravy from the outer two may penetrate the third. Serve middle cutlets only.—p.w.

Côtelettes d'Agneau à la Provençale
Tender lamb cutlets
1 tablespoon butter
Salt and pepper
1 dessertspoon flour
3 egg yolks
1 beaten egg
3 onions
2 or 3 tablespoons *bouillon*
Additional butter
½ cup milk
1 small clove garlic, grated
Breadcrumbs

Sauté the cutlets in butter, using a good heat to brown surface quickly but without cooking interior too much. Slice onions and blanch them in salted, boiling water. Drain thoroughly. Place them in a small pan with the *bouillon*, season well and cook gently, covered, until they are soft enough to rub through a sieve. In another pan, melt a tablespoonful more butter, add the flour and moisten with the boiling milk, beating mixture well. Add the onion *purée*, simmer for a few moments, withdraw pan from fire and stir in the beaten egg yolks carefully. Cook for a moment over a low heat, stirring constantly, until thick. Add as much or as little as you may wish of the grated garlic. Work mixture well with a palette-knife until almost cold and quite thick. Take up a small piece of mixture and place on top of each cutlet, shaping like the cutlet itself. Brush this over with beaten egg and sprinkle with breadcrumbs. Set cutlets in a very hot oven to finish cooking rapidly and serve at once with any desired sauce or, more piquantly, with iced mayonnaise or *aioli*. (*See* Section I, *SAUCES*.)—p.w.

Lamb Cutlets
Lamb cutlets are cut single or double, and they are best just grilled, that is if one is to enjoy the delicate flavour of the cutlets of a Southdown or other well-born and well-fed lamb. There are, however, many different ways recognized by the *Cuisine Classique* to prepare lamb cutlets for the table. Here are some of them:

à l'anglaise: Dipped in egg-and-bread-crumbs and either grilled or pan-fried in butter; served with boiled potatoes.

à l'anversoise: Pan-fried in butter and served with creamed hop shoots.

Barman: Grilled and served with grilled tomatoes, mushrooms and bacon.

Brossard: Dipped in egg-and-breadcrumbs mixed with finely-chopped truffles, pan-fried and served with creamed mushrooms.

en chaufroid: Braised, allowed to cool and dressed with a *Sauce Chaudfroid*, garnished with cold tongue, truffles and the whites of hard-boiled eggs.

Conti: Dipped in vegetable *Mirepoix* and then pan-fried in butter; served with mashed lentils.

Dubarry: Grilled or pan-fried and served with flowerlets of cauliflowers, boiled or steamed and dressed with a *Sauce Mornay gratinée*.

à la maréchale. Dipped in egg-and-bread-crumbs, pan-fried and served with a large slice of truffle with each cutlet and some asparagus tips.

à la minute. Beaten flat, seasoned and cooked very quickly in sizzling butter; served with the hot butter from the pan poured over them and a squeeze of lemon.

Montrouge: Dipped in egg-and-bread-crumbs, pan-fried in butter and served with a *purée* of mushrooms.

449

à la parisienne: Dipped in egg-and-bread-crumbs, grilled or fried *à l'anglaise*, and served with creamed mushrooms and asparagus tips. (The breadcrumbs should be mixed with plenty of finely-chopped truffle).

à la portugaise: Pan-fried in butter and served with small grilled stuffed tomatoes, a *purée* of tomatoes and a little garlic.

princesse: Dipped in egg-and-breadcrumbs, pan-fried and served with asparagus points and pieces of truffles; also a brown sauce flavoured with mushrooms.

Rossini: Pan-fried in butter and served with a slice of truffle and a thicker slice of *foie gras* with each cutlet.

à la rouennaise: Pan-fried in butter and some small onions and shallots cooked at the same time and served with the cutlets on fried pieces of bread cut in the shape of hearts.

à la turque: Pan-fried in butter and served with *riz pilaf* and a tomato sauce.

Epigrammes d'Agneau

1 thick, meaty breast of young lamb
1 or 2 carrots
1 leek
1 sprig fresh mint (optional)
2 egg yolks
Fresh breadcrumbs
1 onion
1 *bouquet*
Salt and peppercorns
2 oz. melted butter
Additional butter
Squeeze lemon juice
Additional mint

This makes a novel and excellent luncheon dish which is economical as well as being delicious. Place the breast of lamb in a deep pot, cover with cold water, bring gently to boiling-point, skim carefully, then add salt and a few peppercorns as well as the vegetables and herbs. Cook very gently for about two to three hours or until bones may easily be removed. When this is done, lay the meat flat on a dish, cover with another and lay a board with a weight on top to press flat. When cold, cut into rather thin squares or strips. Beat the eggs, mix with the melted butter, dip each piece of meat in this mixture, then cover carefully with the fine, fresh breadcrumbs. Grill under a moderate flame, on both sides, seasoning with salt and pepper. Skim all fat from broth, boil fast until reduced to the amount desired as gravy or sauce; add to this, when ready to serve, a pinch of freshly-chopped mint, a squeeze of lemon juice and a couple of table-spoonfuls of butter, blended with the sauce when it has been removed from the fire.

Hand this with the grilled meat. If preferred, serve with a *Béarnaise* sauce.—P.W.

Roast Forequarter of Lamb, Rector

Purchase a forequarter of lamb and have the butcher trim it and remove bone for stuffing. The stuffing to be made as follows: six cups of soft breadcrumbs, one-third cup of melted shortening, one teaspoon of salt, half teaspoon pepper, half teaspoon of sage, half teaspoon of thyme, one tablespoon of chopped parsley and one cup of chopped mushrooms. Mix thoroughly by tossing lightly with a wooden spoon. Stuff the lamb and place in a very hot oven for 20 minutes – then reduce heat to moderate (325° to 350°) and continue roasting, allowing 20 minutes for each pound. Baste occasionally and season with pepper and salt just before removing from the oven. Place lamb on a hot platter and pour off all but two tablespoons of the drippings from the pan in which the lamb was roasted. Mix two tablespoons of flour in the pan with the drippings and when flour and drippings are thoroughly mixed, add gradually one cup of water and half cup of strained tomato juice. Stir over low flame until the boiling-point is reached, scraping and stirring all particles of meat essence well into the sauce. Remove from fire and season with salt and pepper, one tablespoon of lemon juice and a dash of Worcestershire sauce. Strain and serve with the lamb.—W.M.C.

Lamb's Head and Mince

The head should be scalded, scraped, and well washed. Don't have it singed, in the Scottish fashion, as lamb's wool is not nice to eat. Then put it, with the liver, into a stew-pan, with a Spanish onion stuck with cloves, a bunch of parsley, a little thyme, a carrot, a turnip, a bayleaf, some crushed peppercorns, a tablespoon of salt, and half a gallon of cold water. Let it boil up, skim, and then simmer for an hour. Divide the head, take out the tongue and brain, and dry the rest of the head in a cloth. Mince the liver and tongue, season with salt and pepper, and simmer in the original gravy (thickened) for half an hour. Brush the two head-halves with yolk of egg, grate breadcrumbs over, and bake in oven. The brain and sweetbread to be chopped and made into cakes, fried, and then placed in the dish around the head-halves.—E.S.

Lamb's Heads à la Ravigote

Remove the jaws, the muzzle and the eyes of two lambs' heads. Keep them in boiling water for seven or eight minutes and rinse them in fresh water in order to clean them thoroughly.

Put them next into a saucepan with *bouillon*, a large bunch of very aromatic herbs, salt, pepper, two onions, and the half of a peeled lemon, and let them cook on a slow fire.

When finished, lay the tongues and brains in a dish and serve with a *Sauce Ravigote*.

When preparing a sheep's or calf's head, or a rabbit or hare, I advise you always to remove the jaws and eyes, as these have a deplorable effect on a table. The sight of them can make the soundest persons feel sick; and how really horrible is the sinister gaze of those hollow sockets, and those mangled, moist, sad eyes !—Clarisse.

Leg of Lamb

Roast leg of lamb, allowing 10 minutes per pound, well basted and served with its own gravy and a little watercress, is the simplest and best of all methods of cooking this excellent joint. There are, of course, many other ways, and here are some of the more usual ones:

à l'anglaise: Coat a leg of lamb with butter and dredge it with flour, then tie it up in a cloth and put it in a panful of boiling salted water, with a couple of carrots, two or three onions, one of them with cloves stuck in, and a *bouquet-garni*. Simmer in the all-but-boiling water at the rate of 15 minutes per pound weight of the leg. Untie the leg, drain and serve with a caper sauce and various boiled vegetables in season.

à la bordelaise. Braise a leg of baby lamb in a *cocotte*, in olive oil and butter, half and half, for 20 minutes or so; then add to the pan 1 lb. potatoes cut up olive-wise and ½ lb. *Cèpes* already tossed in olive oil. Put the pan in a moderate oven and continue cooking until the meat is well done; add chopped parsley and garlic towards the end of cooking, and serve with the rich gravy from the *cocotte*.

à la périgourdine: Brown a leg of baby lamb in hot butter and bake it in hot oven for 10 minutes; then let it get cold. Cover it entirely with a blanket of sausage meat mixed with pounded *foie gras* and minced truffles and wrap it up in a *crépine de porc*, and then in two layers of paste; bake in a moderate oven for 1½ hours, being careful to allow a funnel in the paste for the steam to escape. Serve with a *Sauce Périgueux*.

persillé. Leg of lamb roasted on a spit or baked in the oven, and covered, when nearly done, with well-mixed fresh breadcrumbs and finely-chopped parsley and then browned in sizzling butter before serving with no other garnishings than a little watercress and some slices of lemon. In the South of France the *Persillade* is made of fresh breadcrumbs, minced parsley and finely-chopped garlic.

Roast Loin of Mutton or Lamb

Ask the butcher to crack the bones so that carving may be easier. Rub with salt and pepper and a little flour. Put a few rashers of fat bacon on top and place on a rack in open pan, ribs down. Roast in hot oven for the first 20 minutes or so, then reduce heat and finish cooking in the same way as if you were roasting a leg of mutton or lamb.

Noisettes d'Agneau

Small pieces of lean meat of lamb, cut round-wise, and taken from the forequarter or fillet: they are tender and delicate morsels, really at their best when plainly grilled or pan-fried, although they lend themselves to a very large variety of different preparations, of which the following are a few selected from the *Larousse Gastronomique*:

Armenonville: Pan-fried in butter, served with creamed morels, *Pommes Anna*, cox-combs and other trimmings.

Béatrix: Pan-fried in butter, served with small morels cooked in butter, dressed on fried pieces of bread, with small pieces of cooked artichoke bottoms, small carrots and new potatoes.

Beauharnais: Pan-fried in butter and dressed on fried pieces of bread; served with very small whole artichoke bottoms filled with a *Sauce Beauharnais* (*Sauce Béarnaise* with a *purée* of tarragon).

Chasseur: Pan-fried in half olive oil and half butter and served with a *purée* of mushrooms seasoned with minced shallots, also a *Sauce Chasseur*.

à l'italienne: Pan-fried in olive oil, dressed on fried bread, and served with a slice of lean ham cooked in oil with each *Noisette*.

Montpensier: Pan-fried in butter and served with pieces of truffle and asparagus tips.

Rivoli: Pan-fried in butter and served with *Pommes Anna* and truffles.

Lambs' Purtenances with Ragoust

Take the feet, the ears and the tongue, passe them in the panne with butter or lard, a chibol, or some parsley, then soak them with good broth, when they are almost enough, put in it some minced capers, sampire minced, broken sparagus, the juice of mushrums or truffles, and season all well ; serve neatly with a sauce well thicknd with what thickning you will, and a garnishing of leaves and flowers, and above all, let your purtenances be very white.'—*La Va*.

Crown Roast

This is an American speciality and a very pretty dish it is. In American cities this joint is ordered beforehand from a good butcher who delivers it all ready to roast, but it is, as a joint, practically unknown in England.

It is composed of an entire loin of small mutton or large lamb. The upper portions of the bones are trimmed and scraped, as when made into cutlets, and each chop is cut through to the skin, care being taken that this is not injured when cutting. The joint is now folded inside out and fastened together (either sewn or tied) thus making a 'crown'. On top of each bone place a cube of bread and a cube of salt pork, alternately. Stand the joint upright in a baking-tin, spread, as usual, with butter or dripping, sprinkle with salt and pepper and add a cupful of water to tin. Bake in a hot oven for 10 to 15 minutes to brown all surfaces quickly, then reduce heat and continue cooking, allowing about 20 minutes per lb. of meat. Baste frequently. Mash some good floury potatoes, season and whip to a smooth foam. When the meat is done, remove pieces of bread and pork and all string. Fill the centre of the crown with the piled up mashed potato, garnish outside with groups of freshly-cooked green peas and tiny young carrots, boiled before being *sauté* in butter. Hand gravy. Some cooks place a small cutlet frill on each bone-end when serving.—P.W.

Saddle of Lamb
(See *Saddle of Mutton*)

Salmis d'Agneau
Thin slices cold roast lamb
½ tablespoon chopped onion
Sippets of toast or croûtons
1 or 2 mushrooms
2 tablespoons butter
Salt and pepper
1 cup stock or gravy
Few stoned olives
Chopped parsley

Brown the onion in the butter lightly. Add the lamb, heat through, season with salt and pepper and cover with the stock or, if possible, lamb gravy. Serve up, slices overlapping one another, surrounding with pieces of toast or *croûtons*, the stoned olives and mushroom caps, previously *sauté* in butter.—P.W.

Shoulder of Lamb
The baby lamb shoulders are best grilled or pan-fried, and the shoulders of fully grown lambs may be prepared in any way suitable for shoulder of mutton. In the *Cuisine Classique* it is usual to bone the shoulders of lamb and mutton and prepare them in a number of different ways (see *Mutton*). Here are, however, two recipes for boned shoulder of lamb, the first being an English one and the second French:

Shoulder of Lamb with Turnips
Bone a shoulder of lamb and brown it on all sides in butter. Remove it while you brown a tablespoonful of flour in the same butter, and then moisten it with three good cupfuls of stock, adding salt, pepper (black), a *bouquet* of parsley, thyme and bayleaf, and a pinch or two of mixed spice. Replace the shoulder, put on the lid and cook slowly in the oven for three hours. As the end of the cooking nears, fry some pieces of young turnip in butter till they are soft and golden, and put them in with the meat just half an hour before it will be ready. Serve with the turnips round it, and the sauce strained over.
—AMBROSE HEATH, in *Wine and Food*, II, p. 38.

Epaule d'Agneau Meunière
1 shoulder of lamb
Butter
Salt and pepper
'Bouquet-garni'
4 oz. lean salt pork
Bouillon
1 clove garlic
New firm potatoes

Have the shoulder boned and rolled, the interior having been seasoned with salt and pepper. Cut the pork into dice and fry gently in a cocotte until fat has run out. Take out pieces of pork and brown the shoulder, on all sides, in the pork fat. Now put the shoulder in a second heavy iron pan, add a couple of cups of *bouillon*, salt, pepper, the garlic, the *bouquet* and the pieces of browned salt pork. Scrape or peel the potatoes and *sauté* them, whole, in the fat still in the first pan. Ten minutes before serving, add them to the meat so that they may be flavoured by the gravy without absorbing it. Remove string from meat, serve on a very hot dish, surround with the crisp, brown potatoes, skim fat from gravy, strain it and pour it over the meat.—P.W.

Epaule d'Agneau
Bone and season a shoulder of lamb. Stuff it with 200 grammes (about 7 oz.) of butter mixed with mushrooms, cooked and chopped, and chopped parsley. Roll the shoulder and fasten with string. Stew this in butter. Cut it in slices, and between the pieces place a slice of ox tongue.—D.A.

Lamb Stew
(*Ragoût d'Agneau*)
2 lb. best end neck of lamb
1 small and 1 large onion
1 tablespoon butter
1 dessertspoonful mushroom catsup
2 cups bouillon or stock
Turnips and carrots
1 tablespoon flour

1 glass dry sherry
3 ripe tomatoes
Salt and pepper

Cut up the meat, trimming off excess fat. Fry in the heated butter until brown. Remove meat, sprinkle flour in and brown all carefully. Add the *bouillon* or stock and stir until mixture boils, then add the meat, or put all into a casserole if the browning operation was done in another pan, add the onions and the peeled and cut up tomatoes, the sliced or diced carrots and turnips, salt and pepper. Cover closely and simmer for about two hours, or until the meat is nice and tender, either in the oven or on top of the fire.

As a garnish, more carrots and turnips, cut into balls with a special French vegetable cutter, boiled and *sauté* in butter, may be grouped around meat. In order to give the dish a better appearance, the gravy should be strained off first vegetables, which have become mushy, the others replacing them when serving, as described. The catsup and the sherry must be stirred into the stew last of all, when ready to serve.—P.W.

American Lamb Stew

2 lb. lean part shoulder of lamb
1½ cups tomato purée or pulp
1 scanty cup sour cream
2 onions
2 tablespoons butter
1 tablespoon parsley
Salt and paprika

Trim meat and cut up neatly. Heat the butter, add the chopped or sliced onions and the meat, previously rubbed all over its surface with salt mixed with a little paprika. Brown meat and onions together, then add the tomato *purée* or pulp and the chopped parsley. Cook gently for two hours, adding, if necessary, a little water or *bouillon* as required. When ready to serve, add the cream which *should* be sour, blending well with the gravy. This is a very excellent dish and veal may be prepared in the same way, either breast or chops.—P.W.

Lamb's Tail Pie

Obtain the tails as soon as possible after docking; they are only in season just after lambing time and must be docked from living (not dead) lambs, when a month or two old; when stewed they are gelatinous and very delicious; if cut from killed lambs they are shrivelled and useless.

Put the tails in boiling water and after a short time dip them in cooler water and pull off the wool by hand; the tender flesh will at first come away with the wool, but after a little experience the tail will be easily stripped of wool without a tear in the flesh. The tail is not wasted even if a little flesh does come away with the wool, which, dried and cleaned, is one of the finest things for wearing as boot socks, or for kneeling mats, cushions, etc.

1. After scalding off the wool and preparing the tails, cut them up into small pieces and make into pie, with pepper and salt and a *little* water and a good crust; a layer of chopped mint can be added, or mint sauce can be served; or

2. First trim the tails and divide each into two parts. Put some slices of bacon into a stewpan and over these place an inch layer of sliced carrots, turnips and onions; on top of all lay the tails.

Put the stewpan over a low gas for 10 minutes and then add one pint of stock flavoured with herbs and spices to taste, and let simmer for 2½ hours.

When the tails have simmered long enough, drain them from the liquor, dip them in flour and arrange them in a pie dish. Strain the broth from the vegetables; add a little browning to colour it and put it in the pie. Cover with a good crust; brush over with beaten egg and bake till the pastry is well done.

Fried Lambs' Tails

Cut the large parts from the tails and fry them; the smaller pieces of tail can be put in a stew jar and will make splendid stock for gravy or soup.

Lambs' Tongues
(American)

3 or 4 lambs' tongues
2 tablespoons butter
1 teaspoon Worcestershire sauce
½ cup vinegar
1 'bouquet-garni'
1 onion
1 teaspoon mushroom catsup
Salt and sugar to taste
Chopped parsley

Boil the tongues in salted water with *bouquet-garni* until they are quite tender. This will take about an hour and a half. Drain, skin and split them in half, longways. Heat the butter, add the sliced or chopped onion, the sauce, the catsup, and the flour, beating well until smooth, over a low heat. Now add the vinegar and season as wished with salt and a touch of sugar, adding a cupful of the water the tongues were boiled in. Add the pieces of tongue and simmer gently in the sauce for 15 to 20 minutes, stirring to prevent burning. Sprinkle with parsley and serve hot.—P.W.

Braised Lambs' Tongues

4 or 5 lambs' tongues
Butter
Larding bacon
Poivrade sauce (hot)

It is advisable to soak the tongues in cold salted water before cooking to whiten and remove blood. Blanch them, after this operation, for half an hour in hot salted water, then again put into cold water for a few moments. Drain again, lard as directed in recipe for *Boeuf à la Mode*, heat butter in a heavy iron cocotte and braise the tongues gently in this for four or five hours or until very tender. Remove skins and continue cooking in the glaze for half an hour, then serve with a hot *Poivrade* sauce.—P.W.

Lamb Tournedos

Have tender young lamb chops cut 2 in. thick. Remove fat and all bone and skewer the meat into circular pieces. Coil around each a thin rasher of bacon, tying or skewering it on so that it overlaps the meat about an inch. Sprinkle with salt and pepper, grill and serve with meat gravy.—P.W.

LAPEREAU

Fr. for a young Rabbit, up to six months old. (See *Rabbit*).

LAPIN

Fr. for Buck rabbit. Coney. *Lapine*, is a doe; *lapin de choux*, hutch rabbit; *lapin de garenne*, wild rabbit. (See *Rabbit*.)

LARD

Fr. *Saindoux*. Pork fat: a soft, white, odourless fat used for frying and making pastry.

LARD FUMÉ

Fr. for *Bacon* (q.v.).

LARDON

Fr. for a thin strip of fat bacon, mostly used for 'larding'.

LEG

In culinary language, a leg of beef is called *trumeau*, a leg of lamb or mutton, a *gigot* and a leg of pork, a *jambon*. (A fowl's leg is a *cuisse*, and a game-bird's leg a *patte*.)

LIGHTS

The name given to the *Lungs* of the animals we eat. They are known in French as *Mou* and in the vernacular as *Cat's meat*.

'I will say little about these, for fear of upsetting the Cat (whose perquisite these strangely marbled entrails usually are), except to note that I see the French, who here can rightly be called more frugal than we are, serve them *en Civet*. The adventurous may try this if they like. Cut the lights in cubes, season them and fry them in butter

with a *mirepoix*; that is, equal parts of onion and carrot and less celery, all cut in little dice, with a tiny piece of thyme and a small bit of bayleaf. Sprinkle with flour, and moisten with half red wine, half brown stock. Add a *bouquet-garni* and a touch of garlic. When cooked, strain the sauce, and garnish with *lardons* of bacon, slices of raw mushrooms, and glazed onions. Finish cooking these and serve in a timbale.'—AMBROSE HEATH in *Wine and Food*, XXII, p. 263.

LION

Lat. *Felis leo*. A man-eating mammal not usually eaten by man but apparently fit to eat. 'The Caffres eat lions; but Bruce, the celebrated traveller, was listened to with incredulous ears when he related that he had dined on the flesh of a lion in the North of Africa.'—I.O.E.

There is also on record an *Estouffade de Lion à la Méridionale* and a *Coeur de Lion à la Castellane*, served in Paris, at the Restaurant Magny, in January, 1875. The lion was shot by Constant Chéret, a well-known French sportsman, near Philippeville, Algeria; and sent to the editor of *La Chasse Illustrée*, Paris, who asked Magny to prepare it for himself and his staff. 'When Mr Lion was placed upon the table there was a religious silence, which, however, only lasted for a few seconds, for at the first mouthful a murmur of approbation ran round the table, and the guests with one accord drank to the health of Mr Chéret and Mr Magny, coupling in their admiration the valiant lion-slayer and the clever *artiste* who had proved himself able to prepare such a delicious dish out of the flesh of this ferocious game, which is more frequently in the habit of eating others than of being eaten itself.'—F.B.

LIVER

The most important – both as regards its volume and excellence – of the innards of all mammals, but more particularly of the calf. Lamb's liver is rarely served as such, but is included in various garnishings; sheep's liver is of poor texture, but may be prepared for the table like calf's liver; ox's liver is coarse and a second rate substitute for calf's liver; pig's liver is used mostly in the making of stuffing and sausage meat. Fresh calf's liver is by far the best and it lends itself to a great number of culinary preparations of which the following are but a small selection:

Liver of Veal Fryed

'Cut it into very thin slices, then passe them in the panne with lard or butter, well seasoned with peper, beaten cloves, and mace, onion, minced very small, and one drop of broth, vinegar or verjuice of grapes;

and for to thicken the sauce, put therein some chippings of bread well searced; you may serve it without soaking, least it should harden, with capers, sampire, mushrums, and garnished about the dish with what you like.—*La Va.*

Liver and Bacon

1 lb. calf's liver
1 tablespoon flour
¼ lb. streaky bacon
2 tablespoons dripping or bacon fat

Wipe the liver, removing all tubing and core. Cut into ½ in. slices. Spread flour and season it with pepper and salt. Dip each slice of liver in the flour. Fry the bacon lightly and keep hot. Fry the liver in the bacon fat on a gentle heat for 15 to 20 minutes according to taste. Remove liver to a hot dish; place rashers of fried bacon around; pour strained and seasoned gravy over liver.

Calf's Liver and Bacon

Liver and bacon is good, though somewhat dull fare, a more savoury variant being the following. Fry the slices of liver quickly in butter, so that each side is only just browned, and lay them in a fireproof dish on a bed of chopped onion, chopped streaky bacon rashers and chopped parsley. Pour over them the butter in which they were fried, cover the dish with some buttered paper, and bake in the oven for a quarter of an hour. Served with mashed potatoes, this is a first-class simple luncheon dish. Here are one or two other simple ways: *à la Bercy*, sliced and grilled, and served with *Sauce Bercy*; *à l'Espagnole*, sliced and grilled, and served garnished with grilled tomatoes, fried parsley and onion rings fried in oil; *frit*, cut in thin strips, egg-and-breadcrumbed and fried, and served with fried parsley; *à la Lyonnaise*, sliced and fried, and arranged round a heap of minced onions fried in butter, the frying-pan being 'unglazed' with a few drops of vinegar, and this poured over the dish; *à la Provençale*, sliced, fried in olive oil, and with a *Sauce Provençale* handed separately. (AMBROSE HEATH, in *Wine and Food*, Vol. XXIII.)

Liver and Bacon Pie

½ lb. liver
½ lb. fat bacon
½ lb. onions
2 lb. potatoes
2 teaspoons packet sage
Salt and pepper
Stock from bones, or water

Slice the potatoes and onions, cut the liver and bacon into small pieces; put a layer of potatoes at the bottom of pie dish, then a layer of onions. Sprinkle with sage, pepper and salt, then repeat layers until the dish is full, finishing with potatoes on top. Pour some stock or water into the dish, and bake for 1½ hours. Sufficient for six people.–L.G.N.

Liver Dumpling

Method: Mix in a basin: two tablespoons oatmeal, two tablespoons breadcrumbs, one tablespoon flour, and a small onion chopped fine. Take ½ lb. of liver (previously boiled and grated), add this with one tablespoon of suet well chopped to other ingredients. Season with pepper and salt; add some stock of the liver, and turn in to a greased bowl; cover with greased paper and boil for four hours. Serve with mashed potatoes.—C.N.

Calf's Liver
(*à la Française*)

Slices of calf's liver
Salt and pepper
Lemon juice
Flour
Butter
White wine
Chopped parsley

The liver must be cut into ¼ in. slices, after wiping and trimming. Dip lightly in flour – or not – some cooks preferring to thicken the gravy with a small *roux* when the liver is done. Cook in butter over a good heat until the blood oozes out in clear drops. Keep liver hot. Add a small quantity of wine to pan, thicken with *roux*, if wished; if not, stir sediment in pan to thicken and colour gravy. Add another small piece of butter, a teaspoonful of lemon juice and chopped parsley. Pour gravy over liver and serve hot.—P.W.

Foie de Veau Brochette

Cut the liver into 2 in. squares and about 1 in. thick. Season on all sides with salt and pepper. Thread on a skewer alternately with pieces of rather fat ham or bacon of the same size, but thinner. Roll the prepared brochettes in a little oil and grill on all sides until crisp and brown. If preferred, dip in beaten egg and in breadcrumbs and fry in butter. Mashed potatoes should accompany this dish; *sauté* mushrooms or small grilled tomatoes are also often served with it.—P.W.

Calf's Liver Moissonnière

Ingredients: Calf's liver, onions, one glass of red wine, butter, one bay leaf, a bouquet of mixed herbs, salt and pepper.

Method: Slice the onions, and fry them in hot butter. When they are beginning to brown, add the liver, cut up in small dice, the herbs and bay leaf, and season with salt and pepper. And lastly, a few minutes before serving, add one glass of red wine.—C.M.(6).

Calves' Liver à l'Italienne

Cut the liver into thin fillets; chop up finely some spring onions, some mushrooms, half a clove of garlic and two shallots, and powder half a bay leaf, a pinch of thyme and a little basil.

Take a small saucepan, put at the bottom a layer of the fillets of liver, season with salt and pepper, olive oil and a little of all your herbs and aromatic plants. Continue in this way until you have used up all your fillets, seasoning each layer as you have done the first one. Cook on a slow fire for an hour, then take the liver out of the saucepan with a skimmer, skim the sauce and add to it a small piece of butter worked with flour; over all sprinkle a few drops of vinegar and bind the sauce on the fire by stirring it with a spoon. Then dip the liver into the sauce again for a minute and dish up. Do not forget to offer mustard with this dish. —CLARISSE.

Roast Calf's Liver Nivernaise

4 lb. liver
2 oz. butter
2 onions
2 bay leaves
1 sprig thyme
1 glass dry white wine
1 cup breadcrumbs
2 hard-boiled eggs
1 raw egg
2 spoonfuls chopped parsley
1 clove garlic
1 spoonful chopped shallots

The liver is cut open on one side, the knife cutting round in the thickness so as to form a sort of pocket, then stuffed with the mixture described hereunder.

Closed and sewn or tied up with string if a piece of flare not available to wrap it up in. It is next placed in baking dish with butter, salt, pepper, thyme, bay leaves and a few small onions, and then put into a warm oven, basting frequently. The liver should not be cooked too much. The sauce in the baking dish should be *déglacée* with dry white wine and strained before serving.

The stuffing: This is made of breadcrumbs soaked in milk, chopped hard-boiled eggs, chopped parsley, a little shallot and fine chopped or grated garlic, salt and pepper, with raw egg for binding.—H.S.

Liver Pie

Ingredients: Equal quantities of liver and bacon, a little spice, a little good stock, a little aspic jelly.

Method: Cut up and fry equal quantities of liver and bacon. Put through mincer three times. Add a little spice and a little good stock. Put into a mould and let it get cold.

To improve, take off the fat when cold and add aspic jelly for decoration.—C.N.

Liver and Oatmeal Pudding

½ lb. cooked liver
¼ lb. suet
2 onions
1 teacupful of oatmeal
1 gill of stock
1 oz. dripping

Melt the dripping in a saucepan, add the onions, fry without burning, and fry the oatmeal until it is a golden brown; mix with the liver and suet and season. Add the stock and mix well, adding more stock if the mixture appears to be too dry. Press into a greased basin, cover with greased paper and steam from one to two hours. Serve with thick brown gravy. Sufficient for four people.—L.G.N.

Quenelles of Liver

Chop finely ¾ lb. calf's liver, put in basin with ¼ lb. chopped beef marrow, one handful baked breadcrumbs, one tablespoon flour, salt and pepper, two shallots, finely chopped and fried in butter, and two whole eggs; mix well.

Have ready a saucepan with boiling water away from the fire, on a corner of the stove; take the mixture in a soup spoon, and with another spoon drop it into the saucepan in balls. Cook for 10 minutes; drain quenelles and strain them, place on a dish and keep very hot; clarify 3 oz. butter in a small pan, fry yellow with a pinch of baked breadcrumbs, throw over and serve very hot.

Lamb's Liver

Foie d'Agneau Provençale: Lamb's liver every time for me! And this is as good a way of serving it as any. Cut the liver in slices and season these and flour them lightly. Fry them in olive oil, and dish them sprinkled with finely chopped parsley. Serve separately some *Provençale Sauce*, which is made as follows: Peel half a dozen ripe tomatoes, remove the core and pips and press out the water. Chop up the red flesh that remains and put it into a saucepan in which you have ready smoking four tablespoons of olive oil. Season with pepper and salt, add half a clove of garlic crushed, a pinch of sugar and a teaspoon of chopped parsley. Cook gently with the lid on for 20 minutes only, and your sauce is ready. (*Wine and Food*, XIV, p. 36.)

Pig's Liver with Cauliflower

½ lb. liver
1 very small cauliflower
A few mushrooms
2 oz. ham or bacon
1 tablespoon green peas

Small teaspoon salt
Large teaspoon soya bean sauce (or ½ a teaspoon of some savoury extract dissolved in boiling water)
A little stock
2 oz. lard for frying

Slice the ham finely and break up the flower of the cauliflower (only the flower to be used). Heat the lard, add the ham, cauliflower, peas and savoury sauce and fry them for a minute or two. Next add the mushrooms, chopped, the liver cut in small, thin slices, and the stock. Cook very quickly for three or four minutes, stirring all the time.

In this and other Chinese dishes the vegetables are more lightly cooked than we are accustomed to eat them. Your prejudice may at first make you consider them underdone, but once you have tasted them cooked in this way, you will probably find you like their crispness and fresh flavour.—M.F.C.S.C.

Liver Pâté

Put a pig's liver in a saucepan with four small onions, half teaspoon sugar and enough water to cover. Boil until it is quite tender, then drain and cool. Run through the mincing machine twice, then put in a bowl with ½ lb. butter, salt and pepper, kneading until it is a smooth paste. Put it into a stone jar in which it can be served, press down well, and pour melted butter over it. Keep in a cool place until required. (*Morning Post.*)

LLAMA

Lat. *Lama glama*. A South American domesticated ruminant the flesh of which is described by L.R.Brightwell as 'very like mutton, with a suggestion of venison'.

MANATEE

The name of different varieties of aquatic herbivorous mammals allied to the *Dugong*. The American *Manatee* (*Trichechus manatus*) is hunted for its meat, bones and hide in the Caribbean Sea, and from the Gulf of Mexico to Florida. It is about 10 ft. long, nearly black in colour, thick-skinned and almost naked. Another variety, the South American *Manatee* (*T. munguii*) inhabits the Amazon and Orinoco regions and is in great demand, for both flesh and hide. 'Its fat is as sweet as butter and can be used to advantage in all kinds of pastry, *fricasseés* and soups.' Dr A. Horner, in *Land and Water*, 1875, p. 551.

There is also a West African species (*T. senegalensis*) found along some of the coasts of West Africa.

MANIS. PANGOLIN

Lat. *Manis temminckii*. A South African ant-eater mammal called by the Boers *Ijzermagauw*; it is found chiefly in the Kalhamba-Libombo hunting veldt. 'The flesh is eaten by the Basuto and Tonga natives.'—F.V.K.

MARROW BONES

Fr. *Os à moëlle*. (See also *Bones*.) Marrow bones were served to the Lords of the Star Chamber on nearly every 'meat' day from 1519, when they cost 12*d.*, 16*d.* and 18*d.*, to 1639, when their cost had risen to 3*s.* 6*d.*

Boiled Marrow-Bones

Have the bones neatly sawed into convenient sizes and cover the ends with a small piece of common crust, made with flour and water. Over this tie a floured cloth, and place them upright in a saucepan of boiling water, taking care there is sufficient to cover the bones. Boil them for two hours, remove the cloth and paste, and serve them upright on a napkin with dry toast. Many persons clear the marrow from the bones after they are cooked, spread it over a slice of toast and add a seasoning of pepper; when served in this manner it must be very expeditiously sent to table, as it soon gets cold.—B. (2).

MEAT

Fr. *Viande*. The flesh of animals used as food; also, in a more extended sense, *food* in general.

Broken meat, *graillon*
Brown meat, *viande noire*
Forcemeat, *farce*
Minced meat, *Hachis*
Roast meat, *Viande rôtie*
Stewed meat, *Ragoût*
Butcher's meat, *Viande de boucherie*
White meat, *viande blanche* (*volaille* or *veau*)
To abstain from meat, *faire maigre*
Meatless days, *jours maigres*
Meat-balls, *Boulettes*
Meaty, *charnu*

MEAT CAKE

1 lb. cooked meat; 4 oz. breadcrumbs; two hard boiled eggs; one chopped onion; chopped parsley; some gravy; one egg; salt and pepper; half pint brown or tomato sauce.

Well grease a pie dish, cut the hard boiled eggs into slices and decorate the dish. Mince the meat, add breadcrumbs, onion, parsley, salt and pepper; mix with some gravy and well beaten egg. Put the mixture into the pie dish, press it well in and bake for 20 minutes. Turn out on a hot dish and pour tomato or brown sauce round it. (*Lady Playfair.*)—R.R.E.

Veal, Ham and Egg Cake

Ingredients: Short crust paste, salt, 4 oz. sliced veal, pepper, 2 oz. lean ham, chopped parsley and herbs, two eggs, water.

Method: Line a greased sandwich tin with rich short crust paste. Spread in the bottom of it 4 oz. sliced veal. Season with salt, pepper, chopped parsley and herbs. Sprinkle over it a little chopped pickle. Spread over 2 oz. lean ham, and over the ham spread two sliced boiled eggs. Pour into this half a teacupful of stock or water. Cover it with short crust and decorate with a few leaves; brush over with switched egg. Put two small holes in it with point of knife. Bake in a moderate oven 30-45 minutes.—C.N.

MEAT LOAF

Meat Loaf Bourgeoise

1 lb. ground beef
½ lb. ground pork
½ lb. ground veal
4 slices bread (soaked in warm
    water and drained)
1 onion finely chopped
1 tablespoon salt
¼ teaspoon pepper
Few grains cayenne
2 eggs
¾ cup chili sauce
1 tablespoon butter
1 cup stock or water

Mix thoroughly meat, bread, onion, seasonings and beaten eggs. Form mixture into 2 in. loaf and place in greased baking pan. Cover the surface with chili sauce, dot with butter and pour stock or water in pan. Bake in moderate oven 50 minutes.—W.M.C.

MILLE-FANTI

(Soupe Niçoise)
1½ pints good beef *bouillon* or stock
2 eggs
Fine freshly made breadcrumbs
1½ oz. grated cheese

About 1½ pints of *bouillon* or stock to 1½ oz. of breadcrumbs and same amount of mixed grated Parmesan or Gruyère cheese. The breadcrumbs must be freshly made and very fine. Mix with the grated cheese and the well-beaten eggs and pour this mixture through a colander into the boiling *bouillon* (boiling for 10 minutes), stirring fast the while. Serve at once. A small pinch of grated nutmeg may also be added.—P.W.

MINCE

Cut 1½ lb. lean meat into very small dice, which put on a plate; in a stewpan put a good teaspoon of finely chopped onions, with a piece of butter the size of a walnut; stir over the fire till the onions become lightly browned, when stir in half tablespoon flour, with which mix by degrees half pint broth to which you have added a few drops of browning and a teaspoon of vinegar; let it boil for five minutes, stirring it the whole time; then throw in the meat, season rather highly with pepper and salt, and when hot pour it into a deep dish and

serve with sippets of toast round, or a poached egg on top of it. (After Soyer.)

Mince au Gratin

Cut all skin, gristle and discoloured bits from the remains of cold meat, and either chop it or put it through the mincer. Mix together three tablespoons breadcrumbs and the same of grated cheese. Grease a rather deep casserole and put in some of the crumbs and cheese; then a layer of meat, and a little seasoning, and moisten with gravy or stock. Repeat the layers until the casserole is almost full, having the top layer one of crumbs and cheese. Put some small bits of butter on top and bake in a good oven until nicely browned.

MINESTRONE

The Italian version of the French *potée*. A thick soup with a *consommé* as its basis, pork, onions, potatoes, cabbage and all sorts of fresh vegetables, besides either spaghetti or rice and grated cheese added at the time of serving. A meal in itself.

MIROTON

Cold boiled beef (*bouilli*)
2 tablespoons butter
1 tablespoon vinegar
1 teaspoon chopped parsley
Light brown breadcrumbs
3 or 4 onions
1 tablespoon flour
2 cups stock
1 tablespoon tomato *purée*
Additional butter

Cut the onions up finely and cook gently in the butter until very soft and a light, even brown, then sprinkle the flour over them and stir well for a minute or two. Now moisten with the vinegar first then with the stock. Add the tomato *purée*, the chopped parsley, and season rather highly with salt and pepper. Turn this preparation into an earthenware baking-dish, using only half for the bottom part and covering the slices of cold boiled beef, laid on the sauce, with the other half. Sprinkle lightly with breadcrumbs, dot with tiny pieces of butter and brown in oven, serving in baking-dish.–P.W.

Variations to Miroton

A la Parmentier. Prepare the onion *purée* as indicated above. Mash some potatoes nicely, beating in a couple of egg yolks with salt and pepper. Pipe or lay a border of the potatoes around edge of dish, laying the slices of meat in between the two layers of onion, as described in preceding recipe.

A la Méridionale. Additions to first Miroton recipe:
2 or 3 aubergines (egg-plant)
2 or 3 peeled tomatoes
Olive oil
1 clove garlic

Prepare the beef and onion *purée* as indicated. Cut the aubergines into long slices, after peeling, and brown them in oil, seasoning to taste with salt and pepper. Peel the tomatoes, remove seeds and chop them coarsely. Cook for 10 minutes in oil, adding the grated or minced garlic, salt and pepper. Put a layer of aubergines in a baking-dish, cover this with a layer of slices of beef, this, in turn, with the tomatoes, and top off with the Miroton sauce made as indicated in first recipe. Finish off, as described, in oven.

MIXED GRILL
A testing dish for the cook, owing to the need to allow the correct frying time to each of the various kinds and sizes of meat which compose it, so that each is done to a turn at the instant of serving. An assortment usual in England is one for each person of a grilled cutlet, sausage, kidney and tomato, served plain but accompanied by choice of bottled sauces, and this may be varied by the addition of mushrooms, curls of bacon, or brains or especially sweetbreads – in fact, almost any delicacy suitable to the purpose which may be to hand at time of cooking.

Mixed Grill en Casserole
Have some little oval brown fireproof dishes just large enough to hold a cutlet comfortably.

Put in each a lamb cutlet, a rasher of bacon and two or three not-too-large mushrooms all carefully grilled. A Chipolata sausage can be added if liked.

This way of serving keeps the grill very hot and is incidentally economical because only the exact quantity for each person is used.—W.H.T.

Huntsman's Grill
For each person allow one cutlet or small fillet steak, a slice of streaky pork, some sweetbreads, sheep's heart and liver, a few asparagus tips and peas.

Stew the sheep's heart and liver till tender and cut in slices about ½ in. thick. Boil the sweetbreads; let both get cold. Dust all the pieces of meat in seasoned flour and fry. Place a poached egg on each portion and serve with a good gravy flavoured with tomato sauce.

Fritto Misto alla Romana
1 teaspoon salt
4 eggs (beaten)
⅛ teaspoon cayenne pepper
1⅓ cup milk
2 cups flour
3 tablespoons melted butter
Fat or oil for frying

Sift salt and cayenne pepper with flour. Combine eggs and milk and blend thoroughly with flour. Add melted butter and mix well. The batter can be used for vegetables, meat or fish, which are sliced, dipped into it and fried in deep fat. This batter is sufficient to fry an assorted serving for six people. A combination of various foods, cut in pieces, is used on one platter. These foods consist of meats and vegetables, such as calf's liver, calf's brain, lamb's kidney, cooked artichoke heart, peeled, scalded eggplant, and partially cooked string beans.
—P.V.M.

Friture Mixte
Brains and calf's liver are required for this homely and excellent dish. Break an egg in a deep dish with a pinch of salt. Beat it with a fork for a minute. Cut the brains into small pieces about the size of a walnut, roll them in the egg, and then in the crumbs. Cut the liver into pieces about the size of the palm of the hand. Roll them in flour. Place a lump of butter in a frying-pan on a quick fire and when steaming hot fry the brains and liver on both sides. When brown they are cooked. Serve on a hot dish surrounded with slices of lemon.—F.K.

MOCK DUCK
(American)
American butchers are accustomed to being asked for a 'forequarter of lamb dressed as a duck' – which order would surprise our hewers of meat! To prepare the joint oneself, order a forequarter of very small, young and tender lamb. Bone it and roll tightly, after salting and peppering interior, as near as possible in the shape of a duck, lifting both ends by means of a skewer and securing them upright with string. Cover these parts with buttered paper, tied on. Roast in the usual way, the only thing different about this joint being its shape. Some cooks go in for fancy decorations such as a couple of 'tail feathers', eyes and a 'bill' made of two pieces of macaroni.—P.W.

MOCK TURTLE SOUP
2 lb. lean shin of beef
Half a calf's head
1 onion
1 carrot
1 turnip
1 *bouquet garni*
2 or 3 cloves
1 blade or pinch mace
1 tablespoon butter
1 tablespoon flour
1 small glass sherry
Salt and pepper

Using a sharp knife, remove all meat from shin of beef. Procure the lower half of a calf's head, soak in salted cold water for an hour after having it boned. Tie the bones in a piece of muslin. Place the calf's head, rolled and tied up, and the beef, as well as the bones, in about two to three quarts of cold water, adding about two tablespoons of rock salt. Bring gently to boiling point, skim well, then add half the onion (a large one or two smaller may be used, half being retained for later use), the carrot, the turnip, the *bouquet-garni*, the mace – fresh or dried – the cloves and a few peppercorns. Cover closely and allow to simmer gently for four hours; then strain and set to cool. When cold, remove every speck of fat from surface.

Melt the butter in a frying-pan, add the other onion, sliced, and fry brown; add the flour, browning it also, then moisten with some of the stock and add to the rest of soup, which has, of course, been re-heated to boiling point. When the soup slightly thickens, withdraw the pan from fire, add sherry, season to taste (some cooks add a little mushroom catsup and others brown colouring) and garnish with the diced meat from calf's head and small pieces of the lean beef. Egg balls are handed separately, if desired.—P.W.

MONKEY

The name of a large number of different members of the *Cebidae* family of mammals inhabiting mostly the tropical forests of Africa, South America and South Asia. Monkeys are not killed for food but we have the late Colonel Theodore Roosevelt's recorded testimony that it is quite good to eat. 'In the afternoon, from the boat, Cherrie shot a large dark grey monkey, with a prehensile tail. It was very good eating'. —TH.R.(2).

This verdict was endorsed by Percy Selous who wrote: 'Whilst waiting I tried roast monkey and found it not at all bad.'—P.S.

In South Africa, the Grivet Monkey (*Cercopithecus griseo-viridis*) and the *Vervet Monkey* (*C. lalandii*), both called by the Boers *Apje* (*Ape*), are common in kloofs and bushlands of different parts of the country. 'They become inordinately fat, in which condition they are highly prized as an article of diet by the natives.'—F.V.K.

MOOSE

Lat. *Alces americana*. The 'big brother' of the European *Elk*. It inhabits the forests of Canada and the northern United States. A variety which is found in Alaska (*A. gigas*) is the largest member of the great *Deer* family.

'All agree that the flesh of the moose possesses one excellence over all other venison, in this, that the external fat, which is connected with the muscle, is soft and retains its fluidity at a low temperature, while the internal fat is very hard, like the fat of all other deer. It is coarse grained, no doubt, but for all that it is sweet and juicy, although not in the best of order. When from an old animal it is tough, but still it is always nourishing, and for that reason it is always esteemed where food is a desideratum. Richardson says: "The flesh of the Moose is more relished by the Indians and residents in the fur country than that of any other animal, and principally, I believe, on account of its soft fat." The flesh of the young, fat Moose is always highly prized, even by epicures whether in the camp or in the dining-room. This, like all the other deer, is in the finest condition at the commencement of the rutting season, when the flesh of even the old males is considered rich and delicious.'—J.D.C.

'The flesh of the moose is very good; though some deem it coarse. Old hunters, who always like rich, greasy food, rank a moose's nose with a beaver's tail, as the chief of backwood delicacies; personally I never liked either.'—TH.R. (1), p. 214.

MOUFLON. MOUFFLON

Lat. *Ovis musimon*. A wild sheep, with large curved horns, found chiefly in Sardinia and Corsica; also in North Africa. It is stringy, dry and strong when adult, but fit to eat when quite young and prepared for the table in the same way as *Kid* (q.v.).

John Gibbons, who ate Moufflon at Colomb-Bechar when entertained by the officers of the French Foreign Legion, does not recommend it. 'I remember being told', he wrote, 'that what I was eating was moufflon. I raise my hat to it, as one of the very few animals that has ever been able to give me indigestion. *Vive le moufflon*, and as far as I am concerned, it can.'—*Wine and Food*, No. 34.

MUSK DEER

Lat. *Moschus moschiferus*. A small ungulate Deer which occurs at rather high altitudes in Central Asia.

MUSK OX

Lat. *Ovibos moschatus*. A quadruped larger than a sheep but smaller than an ox, which occurs in Greenland and Arctic America.

MUSKRAT. MUSK RAT

Lat. *Ondatra zibethicus*. An aquatic rodent only too abundant in many parts of the U.S.A. and Canada, It is about the size of a small cat, with dark, glossy brown fur and webbed hind-feet. Muskrats live in holes in banks or in dome-shaped houses made of rushes and mud. They are sometimes killed and used for food under the name of *Marsh Rabbit*.

Marsh Rabbit
(Muskrat)

Let them soak in salted water one day and night, put them on and parboil for about 15 minutes. Change the water and cut up. Add onion, red pepper and salt to taste and a small quantity of fat meat. Add just enough water to keep them from burning, and a little thickening to make gravy, and cook until very tender. — *Mrs E.W.Humphreys, Wicomico County.* F.P.S.

The Province of Quebec sends cooked, boned muskrat packed in its own broth, to be sold in American gourmet stores at surprisingly reasonable prices for such a specialty. It is solid meat.

Did you ever dress muskrats? They are a fine network of bones. It's a pleasure for once to dip the dark-red, gamy flesh without first applying fork and knife in a boning technique.

MUTTON
See also *Lamb* and *Sheep*

The flesh of a sheep from one to five years old. The best mutton is the flesh of a well-bred, well-fed sheep three or four years old, and kept in an airy, cool place from two to three weeks after the sheep has been slaughtered. As in the case of *Beef* and *Pork*, the Norman name *Mutton* is used for the best parts of joints of the sheep, whilst the innards and less *recherchés* parts have kept their Saxon name, *Sheep*. Thus:

Mutton-chop, *Côte de mouton*
Mutton Cutlet, *Côtelette de mouton*
Breast of mutton, *Poitrine de mouton*
Haunch of mutton, *Quartier de mouton*
Leg of mutton, *Gigot de mouton*
Mutton ham, *Gigot de mouton fumé*
Loin of mutton, *Longe de mouton*
Neck of mutton, *Collet de mouton*
Saddle of mutton, *Selle de mouton*
Shoulder of mutton, *Epaule de mouton*
  But:
Sheep's Brains, *Cervelle de mouton*
Sheep's Head, *Tête de mouton*
Sheep's Heart, *Coeur de mouton*
Sheep's Kidneys, *Rognons de mouton*
Sheep's Tail, *Queue de mouton*
Sheep's Tongue, *Langue de mouton*
Sheep's Trotters, *Pieds de mouton*

Mutton Chops Paysanne
This is a homely but delicious winter dish. Allow two or three potatoes for each serving; slice them rather thickly, then arrange them in layers in a buttered earthenware or oven-glass dish which can be sent to table. Sprinkle a little salt and pepper between each layer and add enough stock or water to prevent burning. Put the dish in a very hot oven in order to brown top layer of potatoes quickly. Trim some nice tender chops, remove bones and skewer meat into rounds. Put the chops thus prepared on top of the brown potatoes, add salt and pepper and a little more liquid, if needed, and reduce heat of oven. Cook gently, turning chops to brown on both sides, and serve in dish as soon as both potatoes and chops are done. If liked, a clove of garlic may be cut and rubbed all over inner surface of baking-dish.—P.W.

Côtelettes à la Soubise
  8 or 10 mild onions
  Butter
  Bouillon
  Flour
  Meat extract
  Boiling water
  Thick cream
  Dijon mustard
  Salt and pepper
  Mutton chops

Peel the onions and cut them into quarters. Plunge them in boiling, salted water and cook gently until tender. Drain well and chop finely. Place in a pan with a little water and a good lump of butter. Cook gently, stirring to prevent burning, until very soft, then press through a sieve, after pounding to a pulp. Replace this *purée* on the fire, add enough thick cream to moisten mixture, mixed with a spoonful of good meat glaze or extract, and a small amount of good *bouillon*. Season with mustard and, finally, add another lump of butter, previously blended with flour. Cook this mixture gently until thick, then turn out on a hot dish and place freshly grilled chops on top.—P.W.

Escalopes de Mouton aux Champignons
  Slices of cold roast mutton
  1½ cups fresh tomato sauce
  Fresh mushrooms
  Cayenne pepper and salt
  Hot fried croûtons

Slice the meat carefully, not too thinly. Boil the peeled mushrooms until tender in salted water to which a squeeze of lemon juice has been added. Cut the mushrooms into thin slices. Have some freshly-made hot tomato sauce. Season rather highly with cayenne and salt. Add the slices of meat and the mushrooms, just heating both nicely through, but not boiling. Serve with *croûtons* as a garnish, cut into fancy shape.—P.W.

Hachis de Mouton
  Cold roast mutton
  1 onion
  Salt and pepper

1 tablespoon tomato *purée*
2 tablespoons butter
1 glass white wine
2 cups good *bouillon*
Poached eggs
Hot tomato sauce

Carefully remove all skin and gristle from meat, as well as fat. Chop coarsely or cut into tiny dice. Melt the butter, add the chopped onion and fry until a nice brown, then moisten with the wine. Season to taste, add *bouillon*, or stock, and tomato *purée*. Put the meat into this mixture, cover and simmer for three-quarters of an hour, adding a little more *bouillon*, if necessary, to prevent burning and to make a slack mixture. Serve up on a hot dish and surround with poached or fried eggs, covering the meat with thick hot tomato sauce.—P.W.

Haricot of Mutton

Cut up either the thin end of a loin of mutton or the best end of a neck, take off all fat, put the meat into a stewpan with a little butter; place it on a quick fire until it is of a golden brown, strain all the fat into a frying-pan into which you have put some slices of carrots and turnips; when the vegetables are brown add them to the mutton and a *bouquet-garni*, a little parsley, two onions, one pricked lightly with cloves, pepper, salt, and a little good stock; let it simmer for half an hour, take off all grease; if the gravy is too liquid, take out meat, etc., and reduce the gravy by boiling it up quickly before adding it to the haricot.—ST.J.C.B.

Braised Haunch

Trim a small haunch vigorously and put it in a casserole or braising-pan with two onions sliced, three sliced carrots, two cups of chopped celery, thyme, parsley, peppercorns, bayleaves, three cloves and a blade of mace. Add half a bottle of good claret and as much stock. Close the casserole tight with buttered paper between lid and joint, and bring it to the boil; then allow to cook in a moderate oven for three hours, basting with the juice from time to time.

When done, change the joint over to a buttered baking-pan and add a portion of the juice of the braise. Brush the surface of the joint with glaze to colour, strain the remainder of the sauce, and add a glass of port and a saltspoon of cayenne pepper. Thicken before reducing, and pour over the joint before serving.—M.H.P.

Roast Haunch of Mutton

This is baked in the same manner as the saddle with the exception of the care necessary in evenly cooking the loin and the leg. To avoid the former being overdone and the latter half-raw, cover the loin with several thicknesses of well-buttered paper and take care that the leg portion is placed to receive the hottest rays of heat from the fire.

To carve, cut the joint lengthways to the bone into thin slices. Be sure all plates, etc., are *very* hot when dishing up.

Roast Leg of Mutton

Roast in hot oven at first, then reduce heat, basting occasionally and allowing 20 minutes per lb. – in England, where underdone mutton is not appreciated. In France, the meat is preferred slightly underdone or 'pink' inside. Serve with onion sauce or red currant jelly and good rich gravy. Large dried 'Soissons' or small, green 'Flageolet' beans are delicious with roast mutton.

Boiled Leg of Mutton

Have a pan large enough to cover the leg completely with water, which must be boiling when it is put in. Add salt as required and boil fast for five minutes, then reduce heat and just allow the water to simmer gently until the meat is tender. Allow 20 minutes per pound and 20 minutes over and be sure to remove all scum as it rises. Keep the pan covered while the cooking is being done and use the stock for soup, adding to it any and every kind of diced vegetables available and some pearl barley.

Serve the boiled leg of mutton with mashed carrots and small round turnips; also potatoes, if liked; hand caper sauce separately.

Gigot Mariné
(Old French Recipe)
3- or 4 lb. leg of mutton
¼ lb. onions
Pinch mixed spice
6 tablespoons pig's blood
1 quart claret
2 oz. salt pork
Bouquet
Small glass cognac
Salt and pepper

To prepare Marinade: Add to the wine spices (as many and as varied as possible), salt, pepper and the *bouquet*. Slice the onions and add these as well. Bone – or have boned – the leg of mutton and leave it in this marinade for three whole days, turning occasionally and keeping in a cool place.

When ready to cook, dice finely the salt pork in an iron *cocotte* and brown the mutton in the fat on all surfaces. This operation will take some time, as it colours slowly after its immersion in the marinade. When nicely browned, add the rounds of onion and moisten with the strained marinade. Cover and cook gently for three hours, adding more wine as needed. When the meat is done, remove from fire and reduce the combined gravy and marinade, by fast boiling, to half its original volume. Strain, then add the pig's blood. (It may be omitted, but is used to thicken and at the same time flavour the dish.) Boil for five minutes, then add the cognac, previously *flambé*. Serve the sauce separately and garnish dish with plain, steamed or boiled floury potatoes.—P.W.

Mock Venison
To a large leg of lamb take 1½ lb. of pork fat. Cut the fat into long thin strips (¼ in. square). With a thin sharp knife pierce holes all over the leg and insert the strips of pork into the holes. Try to get the holes right through the leg.

Sprinkle with salt and pepper, and allow to soak for a day and night in half a bottle of vinegar, turning it over every now and then.

Roast in oven. Serve with apple or quince jelly.

Mutton Olives
Ingredients: Cold mutton; 2 tablespoons of veal forcemeat; ¾ pint of brown sauce; red currant jelly.

Method: (1) Cut the mutton into moderately thin slices, trim off skin and fat, and spread with well-seasoned forcemeat. Roll up and tie with stout thread (thus making 'olives'). If any forcemeat is left over, shape it into small balls, egg-and-crumb, and fry or bake in the oven.

(2) Place the olives in a deep pie-dish, pour the sauce over, cover with greased paper, and cook in a moderate oven for about half an hour.

(3) Remove the thread, dish the olives with the sauce strained over them, garnish with the forcemeat balls, and serve with red currant jelly.—H. & G.

Palettes à la Framingham
Cut slices from a cold leg of roasted lamb or mutton, cutting around the bone first with a small knife so as to have the slices whole and shaped like an artist's palette. Decorate all around the edge of each slice with small rounds of tomato, green pepper, spots of yellow and green mayonnaise, small heaps of chopped hard-boiled egg whites and yolks and rounds of truffle, all the above to represent blobs of paint. Set a piece of crisp celery upright slantways in centre to represent mahl-stick. Serve on individual plates, surrounding each slice with a wreath of small lettuce leaves and sprigs of watercress.—P.W.

Saddle of Mutton
The saddle of lamb or of mutton is the *back* of the animal with the vertebrae *not* disjointed, as they are in the loin. Spread with softened butter or good dripping, sprinkle generously with salt and add a little pepper.

Add a cupful of water to the baking tin and set the joint in a *hot* oven to close pores and seal gravy in. After 10 to 12 minutes reduce heat and continue cooking, basting frequently and allowing about 15 minutes per pound. Make gravy as described in recipe for roast beef and serve on very hot dish. Carve carefully thin slivers from neck to tail ends; also thin slices of the crisp fat from the sides; a piece of kidney, cooked in the pan for the last 15 minutes, should be served with each helping. Red currant jelly is always served in England with a *Saddle of Mutton*; either red currant jelly or mint sauce with a saddle of lamb.

Shoulder of Mutton
One of the joints far better understood in England than in France, where it is usually boned and rolled. A roast shoulder or better still a grilled one supplies some of the most delicious cuts of mutton, but one must know where to go for them. The meat from the bend of the joint is easier to carve, but not comparable to that upon the upper surface of the bladebone, against the ridge, and then that which nestles under the blade.

Roast Shoulder of Mutton
The usual way, in England, is to roast a shoulder in the same way as a leg, that is with its bone. But, for a change as well as for the sake of the carver, one may ask the butcher to bone the shoulder and deliver it neatly rolled and tied up. There are many ways of roasting, braising or stewing a boned shoulder, and here is a good recipe for a

Braised Shoulder of Mutton
Brown the joint all over in hot butter; remove it whilst you brown a tablespoon of flour in the same butter, and then moisten it with three good cupfuls of stock, adding salt, pepper (black), a *bouquet* of parsley, thyme and bayleaf, and a pinch or two of mixed spice. Replace the shoulder, put on the lid and cook slowly in the oven for three hours. As the end of the cooking nears, fry some pieces of young turnips in butter till they are soft and golden, and put them in with the meat just half an hour before it will be ready. Serve with the turnips round it and the sauce strained over. (AMBROSE HEATH, in *Wine and Food*, II, p. 38.)

Épaule de Mouton aux Navets
1 boned and rolled shoulder of
    mutton
1 clove
Bouillon or hot water
2 lb. young turnips
Pinch ginger
Salt and pepper
Butter

Sprinkle meat with salt, pepper and a touch of ground ginger. Brown the meat in a couple of tablespoons of butter and sparsely cover with *bouillon*, stock or plain water. Cook gently, allowing 15 minutes per pound. When nearly done, add the turnips, the clove and, if needed, more seasoning. Cover, cook for a quarter of an hour longer per pound of meat and serve very hot, after skimming off excess fat. The addition of a clove of garlic is considered a great improvement by many.—P.W.

Stuffed Shoulder of Mutton

1 boned shoulder of mutton
6 oz. bacon or salt pork
3 small onions
1 *bouquet*
3 oz. uncooked ham
2 carrots
Salt and pepper
1 small glass cognac
Butter

Chop together the ham, bacon (or pork), one onion and, if liked, a very small clove of garlic. Season with salt and pepper. Spread the shoulder flat and sprinkle with salt and pepper. Spread with the stuffing to within a couple of inches of the edge, all round. Roll up shoulder and sew it neatly into shape to prevent stuffing from coming out. Brown the meat in butter on all sides, adding the other onions, whole. When nicely coloured, add the sliced carrots – or a few whole baby ones – and the *bouquet*, with salt, pepper, the cognac and a cupful of water. Cover closely and cook gently for nearly two hours, or until meat is tender. Serve with gravy, after skimming off fat.—P.W.

Stewed Mutton

2 lb. leg of mutton with skin
1 tablespoon cooking sherry
1 dessertspoon soya bean sauce
  (can be omitted)
1 oz. dried orange peel
1 piece ginger or 1 clove garlic
1 teaspoon salt

Cut meat into neat shapes of fairly large size and simmer in two pints water on very low heat with the lid on. Add sherry, ginger or garlic and orange peel when it has been brought to the boil. Stir a few times during the process of cooking. Season with soya bean sauce or salt before serving.—ch.c.

Dutch Stew

Ingredients: 1 lb. neck of mutton, two onions, one small firm cabbage, half tablespoon dripping, six potatoes, pepper and salt.

Method: Put the dripping into a pot and let it get hot, then slice the onions and fry them gently in it. Wash the mutton well, and put it in the pot with the clean water that hangs about it. Put the lid instantly and closely on the pot, and let it stew slowly for three-quarters of an hour. Take a nice firm cabbage, wash it, remove the withered leaves and cut it into eight pieces lengthways; place the cabbage in water, peel six potatoes and cut them in slices ½ in. thick and place them also in the water. When the meat has stewed for three-quarters of an hour, lift the cabbage dripping with water, and the potatoes and pack both round the meat; sprinkle with salt and pepper, replace the lid closely and stew quickly for three-quarters of an hour. It must be cooked slowly, else it will burn. The whole is cooked by steam, and it is a most delicious as well as a profitable dish.—C.N.

Sweet Pepper Stew
(Hungarian)

Mutton, flour, paprika, potatoes, bacon, stock, wine, caraway seeds, onions, pepper and salt.

Cut up and fry an onion in butter, and add the mutton cut into small pieces, some pieces of bacon, and potatoes peeled and cut in slices. Fry all a pale brown. Put the potatoes, meat and onions in a casserole and cook slowly. Season it with paprika, salt and pepper, and add a quarter of a pint of red wine and a quarter of a pint of water or stock, and a few caraway seeds put into a muslin bag.—C.F.L. (1).

Navarin Printanier

This delicious dish is well within the range of all, but it is a test of a good cook, because it requires very great care and attention. Perhaps, therefore, I may be forgiven if I set down rather minute instructions for its preparation. In the usual way, we should make this with cutlets from the neck of mutton, well trimmed and as lean as possible. The quantities given are for about eight people. First, melt an oz. of fat in a pan, and season the meat with salt, pepper and a pinch of sugar. When the fat is smoking put in the meat and fry it until browned on each side. Then pour away three-quarters of the fat, sprinkle in a tablespoonful of flour and draw the pan to the side of the fire, leaving it there and moving the pieces now and again until the flour is lightly browned. Now add about a quart of water or stock, just enough to cover the meat, bring it to the boil stirring all the time and scraping the caramelized juices from the bottom of the pan. As soon as it has boiled, add a pinch of salt, a shaking of pepper, two tablespoonfuls of tomato *purée*, a *bouquet* of parsley, thyme and bayleaf and, if you like it, a clove of garlic crushed with the flat of a knife. Cover and cook slowly in the oven, if possible, for a good hour.

This ends the first part of the cooking.

While it is going on, you must prepare the garnish. Peel and brown in a little fat about a dozen button onions. Peel a couple of pounds of new potatoes about the size of a pigeon's egg. Peel and cut in halves or quarters, according to their size, enough carrots to leave three ounces, and cut the same amount of turnips into pieces the size of a large clove of garlic. In the same fat in which you have browned the onions lightly brown also the pieces of turnip, sprinkling them with a little sugar. Cut a couple of ounces of French beans into lozenges about an inch long, and have ready a cupful of shelled peas.

The meat having had its hour of cooking, take out the *bouquet garni* and fork out the pieces of meat, putting them into a warm basin. Tilt the stewpan and (this is most important of all) remove with a metal spoon as much grease as you can. Pass the remainder of the sauce through a fine strainer on to the pieces of meat, rinse the stewpan quickly, put back the meat and sauce and bring to the boil again. Cover the pan, and let the meat resume its cooking slowly and evenly, as before. Add the carrots and turnips and, after 20 minutes, the onions, peas, beans and potatoes, burying them well in the sauce. Put on the lid again, this time with a round of paper under it, and cook as before for three-quarters of an hour. Then, take the pan from the fire, let it stand for a minute or two, and remove with a metal spoon every trace of grease. Serve the *navarin* in its casserole (if it is of earthenware) or arranged on a very hot dish. The plates should be as hot as possible. An adventurous friend of mine also added asparagus tips, with a good deal of success.

Vegetables in spring and early summer provide such a succession of delights that it is difficult to single out any one for comment. But it may be worth while noting here, for lovers of seakale, that some years ago when this really delicious vegetable was served (plainly, with melted butter as an accompaniment to saddle of lamb) at one of the Vintners' Banquets, some pickled walnuts were handed with it, making a rare combination of flavour that well rewarded the bolder diners who tried it.—*Wine and Food*, V, p. 17.

Navarin aux Pommes or Ragoût de Mouton

    2 lb. mutton
    2 oz. dripping or butter
    2 oz. flour
    2 pints *bouillon* or water
    2 cloves garlic
    ½ lb. onions
    Salt and pepper
    Potatoes as desired
    Bouquet-garni

Select 'best end' of neck of mutton or, better still, the meaty part of shoulder. Trim off excess fat. Melt the dripping or butter in a heavy iron pot and, when sizzling hot, add the meat, cut into neat pieces. Brown them well on all surfaces then add the sliced onions and continue the browning operation until the mass is a golden colour. Stir almost continuously. Now sprinkle in the flour, stir again, to coat all pieces of meat with it. Moisten with the cold *bouillon* or water, using barely enough to cover the meat. Cover closely after seasoning with salt and pepper and adding the garlic and *bouquet*. Cook gently for an hour, then add the potatoes in whatever quantity desired. If possible, whole new potatoes are better than sliced ones as they keep their shape. Cook until the potatoes are done. Be sure the meat is tender before serving, skim off all fat and serve very hot.—P.W.

NEAT

Old English name for an Ox, retained in *Neat's Tongue* – for *Oxtongue*, and *Neat's Foot*, the foot of an ox.

'A netes tongue well dressed is best to be eaten, and if it be pricked with cloves it is the better, because thereby the moysture is diminished.'—Cogan. *The Haven of Health*. 1589. p. 125.

'Silence is only commendable in a neat's tongue dried and in a maid not vendible.'— *Merchant of Venice*. Act I, Sc. 1, 112.

'You starvelling, you elf-skin, you dried neat's tongue !'—*Henry IV*. Act II, Sc. 4, 271.

To make a Neat's Tongue pie

Let two small neat's tongues or one great one be tenderly boiled, then peel them and slice them very thin, season them with pepper and salt, and nutmeg; then having your paste ready into your baking-pan, lay some butter in the bottom, then lay in your tongues, and one pound of raisins of the sun, with a very little sugar, then lay in more butter, so close it and bake it, then cut it up and put in the yolks of three eggs, a little claret wine and butter, stir it well together, and lay on the cover, and serve it; you may add a little sugar if you please.— Hannah Wolley, *The Queen-like Closet*, 1672.

NILGAI

Lat. *Boselaphus tragocamelus*. One of the large Antelopes of India.

NUTRIA
See *Coypu*.

OKAPI
Lat. *Okapia johnstoni*. A curious-looking mammal, somewhat like a short-necked giraffe; it was discovered in 1900 in the tropical forests of the Belgian Congo. Puleston, in *African Drums*, says that its flesh is good, tasting like venison but looking more like veal.

OLIO
A festive form of Spanish *Pot-au-feu*, beef, mutton, veal, ham, pigeons and partridges, with spices and all manner of vegetables, but chiefly *Garbanzos* – split peas, are boiled together till tender; the resulting stock is served as soup with toasted bread and the rest as a 'mixed stew.' (*See* Charlotte Mason's *The Lady's Assistant*. Dublin, 1778, p. 282.)

OLLA PODRIDA
The national stew of Andalucia made with beef, pork, a hen, *Garbanzos*, *Chorizos* and all kinds of available vegetables stewed in an earthenware pot (the *Olla*).

OPOSSUM
Lat. *Didelphis virginiana*. An American marsupial, chiefly nocturnal and practically omnivorous. It is found in the western U.S.A. to the Great Lakes and Texas.

'Possum and sweet 'Taters
(Tennessee)
After cleaning the 'possum nicely, lay it on ice overnight, then wash and drain dry and rub with pepper, salt and sage. Lay in a baking pan, cover with thin slices of bacon, set in a slow oven, bake and baste one hour, and remove bacon. Around the 'possum lay six medium sized sweet potatoes that have been boiled until half done. Bake until brown, basting occasionally with the drippings. Serve with corn bread and thick cold buttermilk.—M.A.

ORIBI. ORIBIKI
Lat. *Ourebia ourebi*. A small African Antelope; the coat is a light tawny above and white below; the horns are straight, annulated and about 5 in. long.
   'North of the Zambesi they are reported by the natives to be very common on Shesbek Flat; and on the open downs of the Manica plateau I found them very numerous.'—F.C.S.

OSMAZOME
The name given by Thénard to that part of the aqueous extract of meat which is soluble in alcohol and contains those constituents of the flesh which determine its taste and smell. Soyer stated that this was known in different cookery books under the names of *Fumet*, *Essence*, etc., and regarded it as the purest essence of meat, but according to Dr Thomson, it is very doubtful if Osmazome is anything but fibrin, slightly altered by solution in water.

OXCHEEK
Bone and wash the cheek clean; then tie it up like a rump of beef, put it in a braising pan with some good stock (or water); when it boils, skim it; add two bay leaves, a little garlic, some onions, champignons, celery, carrots, half a small cabbage, turnips, a bundle of sweet herbs, whole black pepper, a little allspice and mace. Let the cheek stew till nearly done, then cut off the strings, put the cheek in a clean stewpan, strain the liquor through a sieve, skim off the fat very clean, season with lemon juice, cayenne pepper and salt, add a little colour, clear it with eggs, strain it through a tamis cloth to the cheek and stew it till tender.—J.M.

Ochsenmaul
An oxcheek and palate must be well washed in lukewarm water, then laid for some time in cold water. Set them on the fire in cold water, and simmer till tender; but first take up the cheek as soon as the water is scalding hot, and pare away any black and white skin from the palate. When the meat is cooked quite tender, take it up. Cut it in slices, brown some flour in butter and make a nice thick sauce, using any approved seasoning of spice, herbs, etc. Stir in one or two yolks of eggs. Add lemon juice, pour the sauce over the meat, and garnish with slices of lemon.—G.N.C.

Oxcheek Soup
Ingredients: An oxcheek, 2 oz. butter, 3 or 4 slices of lean ham or bacon, 1 parsnip, 3 carrots, 2 onions, 3 heads of celery, 3 blades of mace, 4 cloves, a faggot of savoury herbs, 1 bayleaf, a teaspoonful of salt, half that of pepper, browning, the crust of a French roll, 5 quarts of water.
   Mode: Lay the ham in the bottom of the stewpan, with the butter; break the bones of the cheek, wash it clean and put it in the ham. Cut the vegetables small, add them to the other ingredients, and set the whole over a slow fire for three-quarters of an hour. Now put·in the water and simmer gently till it is reduced to four quarts; take out the fleshy part of the cheek, and strain the soup into a clean stewpan; thicken with flour, put in a head of sliced celery, and simmer till the celery is tender. If not a good colour, use a little browning. Cut the meat into small square pieces, pour the soup over and serve with the crust of a French roll in the tureen. A glass of sherry much improves this soup.—B. (2).

OX-HEART
Ox-heart en Daube
One ox-heart
Salt and pepper
Chopped parsley
2 onions
1 *bouquet-garni*
1 tablespoon vinegar
2 or 3 cloves garlic
Larding pork
Mixed spices
Chopped garlic
2 or 3 carrots
1 small glass red wine
Salt fat pork
Small piece orange rind

Have the heart cleaned. Cut into rather large square pieces and lard each piece, first rolling each *lardon* in salt, pepper, chopped and mixed parsley and garlic and a tiny pinch of mixed spice. Prepare a *marinade* by placing in an earthenware pan the cut-up onions, carrots, the *bouquet*, salt, pepper, a pinch of mixed spice, the vinegar and the wine. Turn the pieces of heart in this, allowing them to marinate for five or six hours. At the end of that time, fry the cut-up fat salt pork, remove pieces of lean, and brown slightly the drained pieces of heart in the fat with a sliced onion. Add the cloves of garlic, the orange peel and the liquid in which the meat was marinated. Simmer until this has reduced greatly, then moisten with hot water or stock, using about a cupful of either. Season if needed, cover closely and cook gently until heart is tender. Skim off fat and serve with the strained gravy.—P.W.

OX-PALATE
To fricassée Ox-Palates
Boil and peel your palates, and cut them in small fillets; put them in a stew-pan with a little butter, a slice of ham, mushrooms, a nosegay (a faggot of parsley, onions, shallots, etc.), two cloves, a little tarragon, a glass of white wine, and broth; simmer them till they are quite tender; add salt, pepper and a little chopped parsley. When ready to serve, add a liaison made of three yolks of eggs, cream, and some bits of good butter; and add the squeeze of a lemon when ready.—M.CO.

OXTAIL
The tail of the ox is mostly used for making one of the best English soups but it is also excellent as an *entrée*.

Oxtail
(American Style)
2 rather small oxtails
1 tablespoon chopped onion
Salt and pepper
2 cups stewed tomatoes
2 slices of lemon
2 tablespoons butter
1 tablespoon chopped green
  pepper
Flour
½ teaspoon ginger
Water or stock

Heat the butter, add the chopped onion and green pepper and fry gently for a few minutes. Wash the oxtails, previously cut into suitable pieces, and cover with boiling water. Stand for a few moments then throw this water away and drain and dry the pieces of tail. Roll each one in flour, seasoned with salt and pepper, and brown in the butter with onions and green pepper. When coloured nicely, add as much water or stock as desired – about two cups is sufficient as the tomatoes and the other ingredients supply liquid. Tinned tomatoes will do if fresh are not available. Cover pot closely and stew gently until the meat falls away from the bones.—P.W.

Le Hochepot de Queue de Boeuf
Soak an oxtail, cut in joints, in cold water for several hours, wipe with a clean cloth, and brown in butter with four onions and three carrots coarsely chopped. When the meat is brown, add two crushed cloves of garlic. Cover for two minutes, then add half cup of brandy. Light this and let it burn for a moment, then add half bottle of dry white wine, and enough *bouillon* so that the meat bathes in the liquid. Add salt, pepper, a *bouquet-garni*, and cook slowly for three hours with the cover on. *Sauté* in butter ½ lb. mushrooms, a good handful of diced fat bacon and about one dozen small onions. Add the meat to this and pour over all the liquid which has been strained and from which the fat has been removed. Cover and cook for one hour more in a slow oven. The meat should be soft and the sauce unctuous without recourse to thickening with flour.—CL.K.

Stewed Oxtail
One oxtail; one small stick celery; one small turnip; parsley, thyme; one onion; one carrot; one tablespoon dripping for frying; pepper and salt; a little flour and browning.

Cut up the oxtail into small pieces, dip in flour, and fry till brown. Put into stewpan, adding all vegetables cut up in medium-sized pieces, and tying together the parsley and thyme. Cover with water and allow to simmer till tender. Put aside to cool and skim off all fat. Bring to boil again. Thicken with a little flour to which a little browning has been added and season to taste. *It is always better to start cooking this dish a day before it is wanted.*—(*Farmhouse Fare.*)

Oxtail Soup

1 oxtail
1 onion
1 small turnip
1 stalk celery
1 carrot
8 cups rich stock
Salt and pepper

Have the tail cut into 1 in. pieces at thin end and the large root pieces sawn into four portions of equal size. Clean and dice the vegetables. Soak the pieces of tail in boiling water for a few minutes, then drain, dry, and fry them in butter, with the cut-up vegetables. Season rather highly, cover after putting the oxtail and vegetable in the stock, in a saucepan; simmer for four hours, skimming frequently. Cool after straining, remove fat and serve. Small pieces of the oxtail meat should be served in soup.

A small *bouquet-garni* is thought an improvement by many; and a small glassful of very dry sherry is liked by some, this must be added when ready to serve.—P.W.

OX TONGUE
Baked Ox Tongue

Trim tongue neatly, wash in salted water then boil in more salted water, gently, until tender. Remove the skin. Put the tongue in a heavy iron pan with such vegetables as you may prefer: carrots, onions, turnips, celery and so on. Season with salt and pepper and add a couple of cupfuls of the water the tongue boiled in with small pieces of butter. Bake in a moderate oven, covering meat closely and basting now and then. It should take about two hours to bake, if a good size. Slice and serve with vegetables and gravy. —P.W.

Boiled Ox Tongue Tomato Sauce

1 large ox tongue
4 leeks
4 carrots
4 parsnips
2 large onions
2 cloves garlic
Large sprig thyme
2 bay leaves
2 sprigs parsley

The tongue (must be fresh) is soaked in water with a little vinegar for at least five hours, then put in a boiler with water, leeks, carrots, parsnips or turnips, onions, parsley thyme, bayleaves, garlic, salt and peppercorns, brought to the boil and allowed to boil slowly for at least 2½ hours. It must be skinned before being sliced and served.

The Tomato Sauce.—This is made with fresh tomatoes and onions boiled with a little water until melting point is reached, then sieved and mixed with a very light

béchamel (white sauce), salt, pepper and fresh butter. Garnish with parsley.—H.S.

Braised Ox Tongue

1 ox tongue
Onions
2 peeled tomatoes
Bouillon
Salt and pepper
2 cloves garlic
Pieces of fresh pork skin
Carrots
1 glass white wine
Hot water
Bouquet-garni

Select a nice plump tongue with smooth skin. Soak in cold water for about 12 hours, changing the water once or twice if the tongue is already salted and dried. If freshly pickled, soak for three or four hours only. Wash well, trim off root, removing hard nerve. Take a heavy iron stewing-pot. Place on the bottom the pork skin (*couennes*), covering them with thick slices of onion and carrot. Lay the tongue on this, cover pot and place on fire. Cook until the vegetables begin to brown, turning tongue now and then; add tomatoes, cut into pieces, and the wine. Cook gently until the latter has reduced to half its original bulk then, as the vegetables begin to glaze, moisten with hot water mixed with an equal amount of stock or *bouillon*, having sufficient liquid to come half-way up the tongue. Add *bouquet*, garlic and pepper (salt also, if needed); cover closely and simmer for three to four hours, or until tongue is very tender. Skim off fat, remove garlic and *bouquet* and slice tongue, serving with gravy or any preferred sauce, such as tomato sauce or *Sauce Madère*.—P.W.

PAMPAS HARE or PATAGONIAN CAVY

Lat. *Dolichotis magellanica*. A South American Guinea-pig which is easily bred in captivity and grows to be the size of a hare; its flesh resembles that of the hare, according to L.R.Brightwell, and should be cooked like hare.

PANDORAS
Spanish Pandoras

About 1 lb. of any cold, cooked meat, equal quantities of fat and lean; one egg yolk; one teaspoon cream or Ideal milk; bread fingers and frying batter; pepper, salt and shallots.

Mince or finely chop the meat, add pepper and salt and the finely-chopped shallots and mix to a paste with the egg yolk and cream. Spread on narrow fingers of bread, dip in frying batter and fry in deep fat till a nice golden brown.

PASTY

Cooked meat enclosed in a crust of pastry and baked.

For the filling, if using meat, always use fresh steak or good cuts of mutton, potatoes cut small, pepper and salt, and more or less onion according to taste.

The Cornish Pasty

The Cornish Pasty is, and has been from time immemorial, the staple dish of the county; the method does not vary but the name of the pasty varies according to the nature of the filling. When the pasties are being made, each member of the family has his or hers marked at one corner with identifying initials, so that each person's tastes may be catered for. The true Cornish way to eat a pasty is to hold it in the hand, and begin to bite it from the opposite end to the initial, so that, should any of it be uneaten, it may be consumed later by its rightful owner. And woe betide anyone who takes another person's 'corner'!—E.M.

Pasty rolled out like a plate,
Piled with 'turmut, tates, and mate',
Doubled up, and baked like fate,
That's a Cornish Pasty.
(*Breage.*)

PAUPIETTES

Small, thin pieces of any meat used as a wrapper for various meat garnishings rolled up sausage-wise.

Paupiettes de Veau

Thin veal steaks
Thin slices fresh pork fat
1 egg
Boiled ham
Salt and pepper
Breadcrumbs

Cut the veal steaks into pieces about two fingers wide and three fingers long. Flatten out the pieces of meat and lay on each a roll of finely-chopped ham. Roll each one up and wrap in a piece of pork fat (*bardes*), tying them up securely, then cover each with a piece of kitchen paper. Bake in a hot oven or grill under a low flame, turning often, until gravy begins to ooze out, then remove paper and pork fat, roll each *paupiette* first in beaten egg, then in breadcrumbs, and continue cooking until a golden brown, seasoning with salt and pepper. Serve with any sauce of your choice.

Paupiettes, colloquially known as 'birds without heads', may be cooked also without either *bardes* or paper. Brown them in butter, cover and cook gently until done, uncovering 10 minutes or so before serving. They are nice cold. for picnics.—P.W.

Paupiettes de porc

Very thin slices of leg of pork
1 slice fat ham
Pinch mixed herbs
½ cup fresh breadcrumbs
2 egg yolks
2 onions
½ lb. pig's liver
Pinch ground nutmeg
1 minced shallot
Butter
Salt and pepper
Cooking apples (small)
Hot, freshly-boiled rice

Have the slices of lean pork cut very thin. Trim into oblongs of desired size. Chop together the liver and the ham, add the nutmeg, herbs, shallot, about a tablespoon of softened butter, salt, pepper and breadcrumbs. Mix all well together and lightly fry in a little more butter. Cool mixture, then bind with beaten egg yolks. Divide this mixture into as many heaps as you have pieces of pork. Flatten each piece of meat, spread with the stuffing and roll up, like cigarettes, tying or sewing neatly. Heat some butter in a heavy iron pan; when hot, brown the *paupiettes* in it on all sides. Add the onions and the peeled and cored apples. Cook over a low heat until meat, onions and apples are nicely browned. If necessary, add just a very little hot stock or water now and then to detach from sides and bottom of pan the brown sediment which makes deliciously-flavoured gravy. Serve in a border of hot, well-dried boiled or steamed rice.—P.W.

PEMMICAN. PEMICAN

The phonetic approximation of the name given by the North American Indians to a preserve of meat which used to be made chiefly of lean buffalo meat or venison cut in thin slices, dried in the sun, pounded fine, mixed with melted fat, and packed in sacks. The name has also been given to various preparations of dried beef, sometimes mixed with suet or other forms of fat and either raisins, or sugar, carried by explorers by way of emergency rations.

PEPPER-POT

A West Indian hot-pot of flesh, fish or fowl and vegetables stewed with cassareep and red peppers and usually highly spiced.

To three quarts of water put a small cabbage, two large handfuls of spinach, a head of lettuce, two or three onions and a little thyme; cut them very small, and let them stew with 2 lb. of mutton, till they are quite tender; boil with them some little dumplings made of flour and water, and a piece of pork a little salted; half an hour before it is taken up, put in a lobster or crab, picked very small, and clean from the shell, with a little salt and chyan pepper.—c.m.a.

Philadelphia Pepper Pot
(American)
1 knuckle of veal (about 1 to 2 lb.)
1 lb. 'honeycomb' tripe
2 medium potatoes
6 peppercorns
Pinch dried marjoram
1 hot red pepper
1 cup flour
4½ pints cold water
1 large onion
Pinch allspice
1 dried bayleaf
1 tablespoon butter
Salt
Pinch dried thyme

Place the piece of knuckle of veal in a pan with the salt, onions, herbs, spices (tied in a small piece of muslin) and the hot pepper, cut into small pieces. Add the water and cook slowly until the meat falls from the bone, then remove both bone and meat. Clean the tripe well in several lots of water (adding a pinch of soda to the first of these and a little salt to the last) and cut it with scissors, into thin strips. Simmer these in the stock until they are soft; then add the pepper and the potatoes and cook until latter are done; then, strain the soup. It should be hot – in every sense of the word – as its name indicates. The strips of tripe may be left in the soup. Dumplings are served in this soup.

PESTELLE. PESTLE OF PORK
The name of a joint of pork, either the hock or the leg, which used to be popular in England. It is mentioned in the Star Chamber accounts in 1519, when it cost 8*d*., and in 1520 and 1534, when it cost 12*d*.

PETITE MARMITE
The name given in restaurants to a *consommé* (q.v.) served in the earthenware pot in which it was made. Pieces of toasted bread are usually added at the time of serving; some grated Gruyère cheese is also often served at the same time.

PETIT-SALÉ
French name of a joint of fresh pork after from three to six days' salting, boiled and served cold, as *hors-d'oeuvre*, or served hot, usually with cabbage and mashed potatoes.

PIES and PÂTÉS
(Meat and Game)
Terrine or Pâté en Terrine
½ lb. pork
1 small glass brandy
Thin slices pork fat

½ lb. veal
Salt
6 oz. beef
Pepper

Have an earthenware oven casserole, with a cover. Line the bottom and sides neatly with the slices of pork fat. Remove all skin, gristle and bone from meat before weighing. Cut it up, then chop finely together the beef and the veal. Cut the pork into ½ in. dice. Place a layer of the chopped meat, after seasoning with salt and pepper, on the bottom of the dish. Cover with the small pieces of pork and repeat until all meat is used up. Pour over all the brandy and cover closely. Cook in a moderate oven from one to one and a half hours. The terrine will be done when the point of a knife easily touches the bottom of the dish when plunged into the meat. Remove then from oven, take off lid and cover meat with a round of white paper and place a good weight on this, pressing meat evenly down. This should be eaten very cold and is nice cut into thin slices.

Terrines may be made with rabbit, hare liver and other kinds of meat. The method employed is invariably the same and some cooks paste the lid on firmly with a mixture of flour and water to seal in the aroma of the meats. A slice of the fat pork should be placed on top of the meat before the lid is put on, sealing the contents well in. Measure the dish before filling, as meat should come up to top of it when uncooked. When making rabbit or chicken terrine leave the nice white meat apart, cutting into long fillets and placing these on the layer of chopped dark meat. When the terrine is cut, these pieces of white meat add to the appearance of the dish.—p.w.

Beef Steak Pie
Cut 2 lb. of rump steak into strips; season them with pepper and salt; core and slice ½ lb. ox kidney, and season with pepper and salt. Pack the pie dish with a layer of meat and kidney mixed and sprinkle over it some finely-chopped shallot and parsley; then put on a layer of hard boiled egg in quarters or thick slices. Repeat the layers of meat and kidney and of hard-boiled egg until the dish be nearly full. Pour in some good stock level with the top layer, and cover with a layer of puff paste. Be careful first to brush the rim of the dish with a little cold water and to press the pastry well down to it. Make a small hole at the top of the pie with a skewer. Brush over with yolk of egg and bake for one and three-quarters hours or two hours in a moderate oven.

Puff paste: Mix 1 lb. of fine flour and half a coffeespoonful of salt; work it to a smooth paste with the yolk of an egg and a little cold water. Work the paste till it does not stick to the hands, the board or the basin. Flour the board and the rolling pin well, and roll the paste out, taking care to keep it very even, always rolling away from yourself, never towards you or sideways. Keep the paste about one third as wide as it is long. Now brush it all over with lemon juice and dot about it some 10 to 12 oz. of butter in small pieces; then flour the whole surface lightly and fold the paste over in three folds. Roll it out and set aside to cool. Roll it again one, two or three times more, allowing 10 to 15 minutes between each rolling. This paste requires a hot oven and the last rolling must be particularly even.

Little Raised Pork Pies

Ingredients: 2 lb. flour; ½ lb. butter; ½ lb. mutton suet, salt and white pepper to taste; 4 lb. neck of pork; one dessertspoonful powdered sage.

Mode: Well dry the flour, mince the suet, and put these with the butter into a saucepan, to be made hot, and add a little salt. When melted, mix it up into a thick paste, and put it before the fire with a cloth over it until ready to make up; chop the pork into small pieces, season it with white pepper, salt, and powdered sage; divide the paste into rather small pieces, raise it in a round or oval form, fill with meat, and bake in a brick oven. —B. (2).

Pâté de Porc en Terrine
(Mode de Cognac)

½ lb. fresh pork
4 oz. lean beef
Thin slices fresh pork fat (*bardes*)
½ lb. fresh veal
Good pinch mixed herbs
Salt and pepper
1 small glass brandy

Remove skin and sinews from all meat and chop *very* finely. Season with herbs and a rather large amount of salt and pepper. Mix well. Line an earthenware *terrine* (a sort of round or oval pot, having a lid) with thin slices of fresh pork fat (*couennes* or *bardes*). Place a layer of the mixed chopped meats on this, pressing down evenly. When the pot is half full, cover with strips of pork fat and fill up with remainder of chopped meats. Pour brandy over all. Cover and cook for an hour in a moderate oven. Remove lid and continue cooking *pâté* until the tip of a sharp knife easily penetrates to bottom of terrine and comes out quite clean. Place a round of buttered paper and a board on top of *pâté*, add a weight to press down evenly; slice when very cold.—P.W.

Pork and Veal Pie
(Canadian
(*Tourtière or Pâté de Noël*)

Filling: 1 lb. pork, ground; ½ lb. veal, ground; 3 oz. salt pork, ground; 2 cups (6) onions, minced; ¼ teaspoonful allspice, ground; 1 teaspoonful salt; ¼ teaspoonful black pepper; 2 teaspoonfuls granulated gelatine; 1¼ cups highly seasoned stock, or *bouillon*.

Pastry dough: 1 cup flour; ⅓ cup butter; 1½ tablespoonfuls lard; ¼ teaspoonful salt; ½ egg; 1 teaspoonful milk.

Mix ground meats together. Place in heated pan with onions and let meat brown in its own fat. Add allspice, salt and pepper. Prepare pastry dough by cutting butter, lard and salt into flour and working with fingertips. Add egg and milk and allow to chill for one hour. Roll out and line bottom and sides of buttered baking dish, leaving enough dough to cover pie. Put mixture in dish, cover with remaining dough and cut out a hole in centre of top crust. Bake in moderately hot oven (375° F.), lowering heat if crust browns too quickly. Bake for 1½ or 2 hours, and when done remove from oven. Mix gelatine with *bouillon* and pour through hole in crust. Let pie cool and chill so gelatine sets. Cut in thick slices and serve. Can also be eaten hot. Serves six.—P.V.M.

Cottage or Shepherd's Pie
For crust:

    2 cups flour
    2 teaspoons baking powder
    Cold milk or water
    1 cup cold mashed potatoes
    ½ teaspoon salt
    ½ cup mixed butter and dripping

Chop up cold beef finely and season well, adding a little mushroom catsup or Worcestershire sauce, a few drops of onion juice and some good stock or gravy. Be sure the meat is really nicely seasoned. To make the crust, sift the flour, salt and baking powder together twice. Rub in the butter and dripping (or good pure lard may take its place), work in the mashed potatoes and moisten with cold milk or water until ot rolling consistency. Roll out gently and use to cover pie. Bake in a hot oven until surface is nicely browned. Hand, separately, some rich mushroom sauce or serve with stewed tomatoes.—P.W.

Resurrection Pie

Ingredients: Equal portions of liver, steak and rabbit; two or three rashers of bacon, onions, potatoes, pepper and salt.

Method: Cut all meats into thin slices and put a layer into a casserole with a few pieces of bacon, then a layer of sliced onion and potato. Then, put another layer of meat and bacon, season to taste and cover with cold water; cover all with a good layer of sliced onion and potato. Put on the lid and cook for about 1½ hours in a moderate oven. —C.N.

Steak and Kidney Pie

Cut up 1½ lb. steak into small square pieces, and season them with pepper and salt; then dust them lightly with flour. Cut ¼ lb. kidney in thin slices, and fry them quickly and lightly in a little very hot dripping. Butter a pie dish and place a layer of the floured meat at the bottom, then some of the sliced kidney on top of it, and a sprinkling of thin bacon pieces, from a rasher of bacon which you will chop up. Place a second layer of meat, kidney and bacon on top of the first, and then nearly fill the dish with good stock. Cover and put in a moderate oven for two hours. Take the dish out then and let it cool before putting on a dripping paste brushed over with beaten yolk of egg. Bake in a brisk oven until the crust is brown and serve hot. Before putting the paste on a little more stock must be added to the dish if it looks dry.

Veal and Ham Pie

2 lb. veal, ¼ lb. ham, 2 hard-boiled eggs, a pinch of dried herbs, 6 oz. of flour, 2 oz. of lard, a small cupful of milk, a pinch of salt.

Wash and dry the veal, trim away any fat, then cut the veal into small slices and place the pieces in layers in a pie dish, alternating the veal with the ham. Sprinkle with herbs, cut up the eggs into sections, place here and there in the dish, fill up with gravy or meat extract. Melt the lard in milk, and stir into a basin containing flour and salt, mix to a paste and roll out, spread over dish and make edges and centre ornamental, also leave hole in centre of pie. Cook in a fairly hot oven for about an hour. Sufficient for eight people.

PIG

A young swine of either sex before it has reached the age of sexual maturity, when it becomes a *Hog*. The *Pig* is an omnivorous mammal and a wonderful converter. Pig used as food is known by its Norman name of *Pork* (q.v.), except the innards and odds and ends. Thus:

Pig's brains, *Cervelle de porc*
Pig's cheek or jowl, *Joue de porc*
Pig's ears, *Oreilles de porc*
Pig's face, *Groin de porc*
Pig's feet or trotters, *Pieds de porc* or *de cochon*
Pig's fry, *Menuises de porc*
Pig's harslet, *Frissure de cochon*
Pig's head, *Tête de porc*
Pig's kidneys, *Rognons de porc*
Pig's liver, *Foie de porc*

Pig's pettitoes
Pig's trotters, *Pieds de cochon*

'Useless during life, and only valuable when deprived of it, this animal has sometimes been compared to a miser, whose hoarded treasures are of little value till death has deprived them of their rapacious owner.' —E.B.

'Neither is all swines' flesh so commendable, but that which is young and best of a yeare or two old. Also better of a wilde swine than of a tame.'—Cogan. *The Haven of Helth*. 1589, p. 117.

PIG'S CHEEK

This is country fare and is sometimes known as *Pig's jowl* or *Pig's face*.

Ingredients: A pig's cheek, brown breadcrumbs.

Method: If the cheek has been cured and dried, soak it for five or six hours; if freshly pickled, simply wash it in two or three waters. Cover with warm water, bring to the boil, and simmer gently for about 2½ hours. Strip off the skin, cover rather thickly with lightly browned breadcrumbs and bake in the oven for about half an hour. Serve either hot or cold. *Time* to cook, about three hours. Sufficient for three or four persons.—B.E.C.

Pig's Cheek Collared

Lay two pig's cheeks, with the tongue, in a dish, and strew it well over with salt and saltpetre; let them stand for six days, and then boil them till the bones can be readily separated from the meat. Have ready a long strip of linen cloth, on which place the cheek, with the skin outwards, and on it the tongue, seasoning the whole highly with cayenne pepper, cloves, a very little mace, and salt; roll it up firmly and boil for two hours; when done, set it under a heavy weight till cold, when the cloth must be removed. A cow-heel can be boiled, boned, and rolled up with it.—M.B. (1).

PIG'S EARS

Unless they are quite plainly boiled (having first been well blanched) in seasoned water, and served with cabbage or some vegetable *purée* or, best of all, with *choucroûte*, they are first inevitably braised. They may then be sliced into fine strips dipped in batter or egg-and-breadcrumbed, fried in deep fat and served with fried parsley and a tomato sauce, or perhaps preferably they may be cut in half lengthwise, smeared with mustard, dipped in melted butter and then in breadcrumbs, and gently grilled, being accompanied by a *Sauce Robert*, or *Escoffier's*. They may also be prepared, after braising, in the same fashion as *Pieds de Cochon à la Sainte-Ménéhould*. (See *Pig's Trotters*.)—AMBROSE HEATH in *Wine and Food*, XXIII, p. 260.

Oreilles de Porc aux Légumes
Well-cleaned pig's ears
1 or 2 onions
Bouquet-garni
1 lb. brown lentils
2 or 3 carrots
Salt and peppercorns

Singe the ears, after thoroughly cleansing inside and out. Put them into a deep pot with the picked-over and pre-soaked lentils, the onions, *bouquet*, salt and peppercorns and carrots, sliced. Cook until all is tender, then keep ears hot. Scrape meat off cartilage and serve on the lentils, which must be pressed through a sieve and nicely seasoned. In France, the ears are served 'as is' and are sometimes boiled in a *court-bouillon* – like calf's head – then served with a hot tomato or *Piquante* sauce and mashed potatoes. Or they may be fried.—P.W.

PIG'S FACE
Pig's Face Collared
(A Breakfast or Luncheon Dish)
Singe the face carefully, bone it without breaking the skin, and rub it well with salt. Pour cold brine over the head and let it steep in for 10 days, turning and rubbing it often. Then wipe, drain, and dry it. Spread forcemeat equally over the head, roll it tightly in a cloth, and bind it securely with broad tape. Put it into a saucepan with a few meat trimmings, and cover it with stock; let it simmer gently for four hours, and be particular that it does not stop boiling the whole time. When quite tender, take it up, put it between two dishes with a heavy weight on the top, and, when cold, remove the cloth and tape. It should be sent to table on a napkin, or garnished with a piece of deep white paper with a ruche at the top. —B. (2).

PIG'S FRY
(A Savoury Dish)
Ingredients: 1½ lb. of pig's fry, 2 onions, a few sage leaves, 3 lb. of potatoes, pepper and salt to taste.

Mode: Put the lean fry at the bottom of a pie-dish, sprinkle over it some minced sage and onion, and a seasoning of pepper and salt; slice the potatoes; put a layer of these on the seasoning, then the fat fry, then more seasoning and a layer of potatoes at the top. Fill the dish with boiling water, and bake for two hours, or rather longer.—B. (2).

PIG'S HARSLET
Take some liver, sweetbreads and fat and lean pork, wash the whole and dry it; season with sage, minced onion, salt and pepper; lay the whole in a caul and sew it well up; roast it by a string, and when done enough, serve with port wine and some water boiled gently up with some mustard.—M.D.C.

PIG'S HEAD
(In imitation of Wild Boar's Head)
Procure the head with as much of the neck attached to it as possible; then singe it well over the flame of a fire, wipe it with a cloth; scrape it well with a knife, without scratching the skin, and place it on a cloth upon its skull; open it very carefully without piercing the skin, leaving no flesh whatever upon the bones; bone the neck part and cut it into small fillets 2 in. long; lay the head on a board and rub it with ½ lb. of brown sugar; let it remain for one hour; then place it in a salting tub, and throw over it 6 lb. of salt; pour in a separate pan two quarts of ale, add four bayleaves, ½ oz. of peppercorns, ¼ oz. of cloves, six blades of mace, eight sliced onions, 10 sprigs of thyme, 10 of winter savory, and two sliced carrots; stir it well up, and let it remain for two hours; then throw it over the head, which turn every day for eight or 10 days, rubbing it well; when sufficiently salted, take it out on a cloth; lay the head straight before you, skin side upwards; have ready 6 or 8 lb. of forcemeat, but using pork instead of veal, with which cover the head an inch in thickness at the thinnest part; put the fillets cut from the neck in a layer lengthwise in the head, with a long piece of fat bacon, ½ in. square, between each, sprinkle a little chopped eschalots, pepper, salt, and grated nutmeg over, and continue filling with forcemeat and the other ingredients until you have used the whole; join the two cheeks together with the above in the interior, sew it up with packthread, giving it the shape of the head as much as possible, and fold it in one or two large thin cloths leaving the ears out and upright.—A1.S.

PIG'S PETTITOES
Pig's Pettitoes consist of the feet and internal parts of a sucking pig. Set on with a quantity of water, or broth; a button onion or two may be added, if approved, also four or five leaves of sage chopped small. When the heart, liver, and lights are tender, take them out and chop fine; let the feet simmer the while; they will take from half to three-quarters of an hour to do. Season the mince with salt, nutmeg, and a little pepper, ½ oz. of butter, a tablespoonful or two of thick cream, and a teaspoonful of arrowroot, flour or potato starch; return it to the saucepan in which the feet are; let it boil up, shaking it one way. Split the feet, lay them round in the mince. Serve with toasted sippets. Garnish: mashed potatoes.—J.M.S.

PIG'S TROTTERS
Note.—Pig's trotters, tongues and even their tails may be boiled in a *court-bouillon* and

served with either a cold vinaigrette or piquante sauce or hot with any other sharp, well-flavoured sauce. They are nice grilled, after being boiled as indicated, and served hot. They may previously be dipped in beaten egg and breadcrumbs before grilling, hot butter being dripped over them during the process, as well as salt and pepper.

Pieds de Cochon à la Ste. Ménéhould
Thoroughly cleanse each foot and chop in two. Secure both halves together with a slice of fat fresh pork between the halves. Wrap up each foot thus prepared tightly in a band of linen or cloth, fastening ends tightly, like those of a roly-poly pudding. Prepare a *marinade* with half a bottle of white wine, salt, pepper, two or three cloves of garlic, a pinch or a sprig of dried thyme, a bayleaf, one or two cloves, a sliced carrot, a sliced onion and sufficient water to cover the feet. Cook gently for about five or six hours, the pan being covered. Allow the feet partially to cool; then unwrap them, dip each one first in beaten egg then in breadcrumbs, grill, turning frequently, and serve with French mustard and no sauce.—P.W.

Pieds de Cochon Truffés
Clean the feet and chop each longways, into halves. Cook gently for about six hours with salt, pepper, a *bouquet*, a carrot or two, an onion and a clove, as well as salt and a few peppercorns. When they are done sufficiently, carefully remove all bones and cut the fleshy part of the feet into fair-sized pieces. Now make a sort of stuffing with a little finely-minced veal or chicken and a little ham. Blend to a thick paste with two or three egg yolks, season rather highly with salt and pepper, adding a pinch of ground nutmeg and the peelings from a truffle. Cut a pig's caul into squares, lay in the centre of each one or two thin slices of truffle, on this spread a layer of the stuffing and on this, in turn, lay a few pieces of the cooked feet. Repeat until the preparation is sufficiently thick, shape like a cutlet, cover with the caul fastened securely, and either grill or fry light brown, serving hot with mashed potatoes and no sauce.—P.W.

POOKOO. PUKU
Lat. *Adenota vardoni*. A reddish African antelope allied to the *Waterbuck*. 'The only place where I ever met with this species was in a small tract of country extending along the southern bank of the Chobe for about 70 miles westward from its junction with the Zambesi ... The meat of the waterbuck is usually considered to be more unpalatable than that of any other South African antelope, but, if it will give any one satisfaction

to know it, I can conscientiously say that that of the pookoo is several shades worse'. —F.C.S.

PORK
Pork is the name given to the flesh of the hog, used for food from times immemorial, in China, and as far as records go back, in the West. One should always cook *Pork* well: beef and mutton may be underdone and even 'rare', if liked, but never pork. One should always bear in mind, when cooking *Pork*, that it must not be cooked *quickly*, as it is likely to be stringy, tough and indigestible if so cooked. For boiling and roasting, *Pork* should be the flesh of a young hog that is not older than six months, and the leg must not weigh more than from 6 to 7 lb.

'If fresh and young, the flesh and fat should be white and firm, smooth and dry, and the lean break if pinched between the fingers, or you can nip the skin with the nails; the contrary, if old and stale'.—Al.s.

Pork and Beans
(English style)
1 small shoulder pickled pork
2 carrots
1 strip celery
Pre-soaked dried white beans
1 onion
Slice turnip
8 or 10 peppercorns
Bouquet-garni
Parsley sauce

Put the pork into a deep saucepan, cover with warm water and bring slowly to boiling point, skimming as required. Now add the sliced vegetables and *bouquet*, as well as peppercorns. Cook gently for a couple of hours. At the end of one hour's cooking, add the pre-soaked beans and continue simmering until they are done. Slice the meat and serve in a border of the beans, over which a rich parsley sauce has been poured.—P.W.

Pork and Beans
(Boston baked beans)
1 pint small 'pea' beans (dried)
1 teaspoon mustard
1 teaspoon salt
1 teaspoon sugar
¾ lb. fat salt pork
¼ teaspoon pepper
2 tablespoons molasses

Very small white dried beans are used. They must be soaked overnight. Next morning, drain them well and parboil them for 20 minutes or so in slightly salted water. The salt pork must be in one square chunk, having the skin or rind on, which must be scored as for crackling. A special earthenware or sometimes iron pot, known as 'the bean pot' is used, but any deep earthenware or oven-glass casserole will do. Put half the parboiled beans in bottom of the pot. Wedge the piece of pork in them and cover this with remainder of beans. Mix together the mustard, pepper, salt, molasses (which is black treacle), sugar and sufficient hot water to blend and dissolve molasses and add to the beans with more hot water, in all just barely enough to cover the beans. Cover the pot closely and bake in a *slow* oven for about eight hours. About every hour or so take a look at the beans and if they seem dry, add more hot water. When the beans have been cooking for about six hours, bring the piece of pork to the surface and continue cooking with the pot uncovered, to crisp pork rind and top layer of beans. An hour before serving, cover again and continue slow cooking until ready to serve. The mixture should be thick, the beans soft but not broken up and the pork tender, with a crisp outer skin. A very satisfying but filling dish, best in winter.—P.W.

Pork Cheese
(An excellent breakfast dish)
Ingredients: 2 lb. of cold roast pork, pepper and salt to taste, 1 dessertspoonful of minced parsley, 4 leaves of sage, a very small bunch of savoury herbs, 2 blades of pounded mace, a little nutmeg, ½ a teaspoonful of minced lemon peel; good strong gravy, sufficient to fill the mould.
Mode: Cut, but do not chop, the pork into fine pieces, and allow ¼ lb. of fat to each pound of lean. Season with pepper and salt; pound well the spices, and chop finely the parsley, sage, herbs, and lemon peel, and mix the whole nicely together. Put it into a mould, fill up with good, strong well-flavoured gravy, and bake rather more than one hour. When cold, turn it out of the mould.—B. (2).

Chine of Pork
Score it well, stuff it thick with pork stuffing, roast it gently, and serve with apple sauce.—AL.S.

In the Star Chamber Accounts, a *Chine of Pork* cost either 7*d.* or 8*d.* each, in the earlier accounts (1519 to 1536); 12*d.*, in 1567; 3*s.*, in 1590 and 1605.

Fried Pork Chops
Unless the meat be very young and tender this is not a very satisfactory way of cooking pork chops. Cook them in plenty of fat – either butter or good lard. Turn them, while cooking, four or five times. They may, if desired, first be egg-and-breadcrumbed, then served with tomato sauce

Grilled Pork Chops
Select small chops with a fair amount of fat. Flatten them nicely, trim and grill, turning several times and sprinkling with salt and pepper. Serve with a *Sauce Robert*.

Ragoût of Pork Chops
Trim off a great deal of the fat before placing chops in an earthenware casserole with two cups of *bouillon*, a small *bouquet-garni*, salt, pepper, two or three sliced mushrooms and a good lump of butter. Cover closely and simmer until meat begins to get tender, adding more *bouillon* if and when required. When nearly done, sprinkle lightly with flour, add a glassful of white wine and a good tablespoonful of brown meat glaze or essence to colour. Continue cooking until meat is very tender, then remove chops, keep hot, reduce sauce by quick boiling, strain over chops. If wished, a teaspoonful of chopped chives, a clove of garlic and a whole ordinary clove may be added to other ingredients. Serve with *sauté* mushrooms, cooked separately.—P.W.

Pork Chops with Chestnut purée
Peel some fine large chestnuts and boil until tender enough to remove second skin, adding a little salt to water. When tender, press through a sieve, after draining well. Add to this *purée* the fat and gravy from the fried or grilled pork chops which are being served with it.

Pork Cutlets à la Bolognese
Small pork chops
Ground black pepper
1 egg
Butter
Shavings of Gruyère cheese
1 lemon
Salt
Brown breadcrumbs
1 truffle shaved thin
1 cup of good stock

Trim the cutlets neatly, removing a great deal of the fat and taking care they are not cut too thick. Strain the juice of the lemon in a dish, add a dash of freshly-ground black pepper and salt to taste. Put the cutlets in this and allow them to marinate for a couple of hours, turning once and again, in a cool place.

Drain each cutlet well, dip first in beaten egg then in breadcrumbs, which must be fine and sifted to make them of even size. Heat butter in a frying-pan, add the cutlets and brown evenly. Turn them over and, on browned side, heap the thin slivers of mixed truffle and cheese, cut as thinly as possible. Add the stock, which should be slightly heated, a spoonful at a time. Finish cooking and browning in a medium oven, serving with their gravy.—P.W.

Fillets of Pork

A fillet of pork may be cut into *filets mignons* or *médallions*. These may be either grilled, fried or braised, served with fried slices of apple, apple sauce or, alternatively, the usual pork stuffing. Braised, they are nice with young carrots and peas.

Fillet of Pork with Apples
(French)

Shape the fillet nicely; tying neatly with string. Surround with peeled and cored cooking apples ('reinettes' or pippins are best). Add butter, salt and pepper and roast in the usual way. Serve the apples around sliced meat, with gravy.—P.W.

Filet de Porc Lorraine

This requires a whole fillet. Shape and tie up neatly like a long sausage. Have a saucepan of suitable length and brown the meat on all surfaces in hot butter, turning without piercing the flesh, which would allow the gravy to run out. When browned, sprinkle with plenty of fine white breadcrumbs, mixed with salt and pepper, on all sides. Add a chopped onion and a shallot, a small minced clove of garlic and a little finely-chopped parsley. Place the joint in the oven, taking care to have a good heat. Baste frequently and, when the breadcrumbs are brown, add a cupful of good *bouillon*. Cover the pan and continue cooking until meat is done. Uncover 10 minutes before serving to crisp up breadcrumbs. When serving, add a small spoonful of good white wine-vinegar to gravy.—P.W.

Fried Pork, Country Style

Thin slices of salt (pickled) pork
Flour
1 tablespoon butter
Indian corn meal
Salt and pepper
1 cup milk
1½ cups boiled, cubed potatoes

Cut each slice of pork into about 2 or 3 in. pieces and snip through each rind four times to prevent curling up. Dip each in a mixture of yellow (Indian) corn meal and flour, using two-thirds meal to one-third flour. Have a very hot and lightly greased frying-pan and fry the prepared slices of pork quickly in this, turning frequently until well-browned. Remove meat from pan and strain the dripping through two thicknesses of muslin or a very fine sieve. Put 1½ tablespoons of this strained fat into a saucepan, add two tablespoons flour, stirring together until well blended. Add the milk gradually,

beating mixture to prevent lumps. Simmer for a few minutes, add salt and pepper and the butter, a small piece at a time, beating to mix well into sauce. Finally, add the boiled potatoes, cut into neat cubes, to this sauce. Pile them in centre of a hot dish, surround with slices of fried pork and garnish with parsley.—P.W.

Hand of Pork

This is the name of the *Shoulder of Pork*, which is usually boned and rolled, fresh or salted. When salted, it is usually boiled and eaten either hot, with green vegetables, or cold, with a green salad. When fresh, it is generally roasted.

Roast Leg of Pork

Select a small leg of a young pig. Remove bone up to knuckle. Have the skin scored into narrow strips, about ¼ in. wide. Rub in salt and pepper. Place on a rack in a baking tin, taking care to have the oven rather hot. When all surfaces are brown, reduce heat and continue cooking, basting with fat and gravy from leg very frequently. Allow a full 30 minutes cooking for every pound the leg weighs. If when done the skin is not very crisp, increase heat until it is; soggy crackling is horrible. Serve with sage and onion stuffing and green apple sauce.—P.W.

Roast Leg of Pork
(French Style)

The whole leg is not usually required for the preparation of this dish. Have a good thick slice, weighing about 2 or 3 lb., cut off the meaty end of the leg. Put it in an earthenware receptacle with half a bottle of white wine, one or two sliced carrots, a sprig or two of parsley, a bayleaf, a couple of cut-up shallots, a sliced onion and a minced clove of garlic. Add salt and pepper. Lay the slice of fresh pork in this, close receptacle hermetically and leave it to marinate 12 hours in a cool place, turning over once. Drain meat, brown on both sides in butter, sprinkle with flour and cook gently, adding from time to time a little of the *marinade*, strained. When almost done, remove skin, sprinkle fat surface with fine brown breadcrumbs and place in a hot oven to brown this crust of breadcrumbs. Put remainder of *marinade* in a small pan and cook gently until reduced greatly, when it may be poured over meat. —P.W.

Boiled Leg of Pork
(English Style

In order to seal in the meat juices, it is advisable to plunge a small young leg of fresh pork in sufficient boiling water to cover it completely. Boil up again, skim carefully then add carrots, an onion or two, a

476

few peppercorns, a strip of celery and half a turnip. Cover pan and cook gently allowing 30 minutes per pound of meat. Set aside stock for making pea soup. Cook, if wished, a cabbage and some parsnips and potatoes separately and serve around sliced meat, and hand a well-made old-fashioned pease-pudding at the same time. This is even better served cold with piccalilli pickles.

Roast Loin of Pork

Have the bones separated at the end, though not cut quite through, so that, when done, the joint may easily be carved into chops. Roast in the same way as indicated for beef or mutton and make good, rich gravy, also in the same manner as described for other kinds of roast meat. Sage and onion stuffing, cooked separately, is usual with this.

Pickled Pork

Wash and scrape it clean; put in a pan with warm water to cover; bring to the boil; then simmer gently until tender, removing scum as it rises. Serve hot with cabbage or any green vegetables; or else cold, with a green salad and some pickles.

Roast Pork

Small joints or young pigs are best for roasting. The lean meat should be almost as white as veal and the fat quite white. Have nothing to do with pork that is red and dried-up.

In England the outer skin is left on to provide crackling when the joint is roasted. The skin must be cut into thin strips, through to the fat, but not beyond, salt rubbed in and a little pepper. On the Continent, not only is the skin usually removed but the greater part of the fat is also removed in long thin slices, called *couennes* or *bardes*. These are used in many dishes when cooking meat which has little or no fat of its own.

Pork, like all white meats, *must* be well cooked. If crackling is part of the dish, set in a hot oven to start with, then reduce heat, allowing 25 to 30 minutes per pound for roasting a joint. When roasting pork, add halved or roughly-diced potatoes around meat when half done, shaking the pan gently now and then to colour potatoes on all sides. Small whole new potatoes are best. They may, if wished, be first parboiled, then continue cooking and colouring in the pork dripping with the meat.

A small clove of garlic gives an excellent flavour to pork which is being roasted.

Small button onions form a nice garnish to roast pork; also fried slices of apple.—P.W.

Rôti de Porc en Casserole

If the meat is rather old and not very fat this is an excellent way of cooking it. Pork, we must not forget, should *not* be cooked quickly or it will become tough, stringy and indigestible.

Have a heavy iron *cocotte*, or an earthenware casserole, having a well-fitting lid. Put in the pan a couple of tablespoons of butter and, when hot, brown the pieces of pork gently on all sides. A tiny clove of garlic may be added if flavour is liked as well as a pinch of dried sage, salt and pepper. When meat is coloured on all sides, turn heat very low, cover pan closely and continue cooking gently, turning the meat fairly frequently, until the butter is clear and there is a rich brown sediment in the bottom of the pan; add to this just a little hot water, rubbing the meat against sides of pan to remove sediment. Slice to serve, pouring rich gravy over it. Nice with boiled chestnuts or mashed potatoes.—P.W.

Epaule de Porc au Riz

Select a small shoulder of young pork and have it boned and rolled. Roast it in oven in the usual way, and when brown on all surfaces, remove and put into an iron or earthenware casserole. Add sufficient boiling water to come half way up side of joint. Add salt, pepper, a small *bouquet-garni*, an onion stuck with a clove, a clove of garlic, a bayleaf and one or two shallots. Cover and simmer gently allowing 25 minutes per pound of meat. One hour before the pork is to be served, add half a pound of picked-over and washed rice. Continue cooking gently, remove spices, etc., and serve rice around sliced meat.—P.W.

Roast Spareribs of Pork
(American)

This is a favourite dish in the U.S.A., whether roasted or boiled and served with sauerkraut.

To roast, ask for the meaty end of ribs and have them cracked to make carving easier. Two matching sets of spareribs, that is, of equal thickness and size, are mostly used to prepare this dish, and good sage and onion stuffing, or apple stuffing, is spread on one half of the ribs, the other half being used to cover; both being securely tied or sewn together. Sprinkle with salt and pepper and lightly dredge with flour. Put on a rack in a pan and brown in a hot oven until all surfaces are nicely coloured, then reduce temperature quickly and cook for about an hour or until tender, basting frequently. Remove string or thread before serving, but leave one half covering the other, enclosing the stuffing. Be careful to turn the meat to brown both sides.—P.W.

Boiled Spareribs with Sauerkraut

Select nice meaty ribs, wipe well, sprinkle lightly with salt and place in a saucepan, covering with cold water. Bring to boiling point, skim carefully, and simmer gently until meat is nearly done, then remove ribs, add about a pound of washed and drained sauerkraut, a few peppercorns and more salt if needed. Cover the pan closely and cook gently for about two hours. Replace the ribs, cook together for an hour longer, covered, then drain out sauerkraut, place ribs on top and serve with boiled potatoes. If wished, put the ribs, lying on the 'kraut, in a hot oven for 10 minutes, lightly to brown the meat; this also improves the flavour.—P.W.

Breaded Pork Tenderloin

Have tenderloin cut in crosswise sections and flattened with cleaver. Dip in fine dry breadcrumbs, then in beaten egg to which two tablespoons of water had been added, then again in breadcrumbs. *Sauté* in pork fat drippings until nicely browned on both sides. Serve with fried apple slices.—W.M.C.

PORPOISE

Lat. *Phocaena phocaena*. Old Eng. *Porpays, Porpeys* and *Porpus*. Any of the smaller cetaceans, such as the *Grampus* and *Dolphin*. It was served at Archbishop Nevill's enthronement feast and there are various recipes for *Porpoise*, rosted, salted, and in broths, in the *Forme of Cury*, written in 1381.

'The common or harbour Porpoise of the North Atlantic and Pacific was once considered a delicacy in this country, as are other Cetaceans in other lands at the present day. It formed a royal dish even so recently as the times of Henry VIII. The sauce recommended by Dr Caius for the "fish" was made of crumbs of fine bread, vinegar and sugar. Considered to be a fish it was allowed to be eaten on fast-days.'—F.E.B.

'There was formerly a considerable Porpoise fishery along the whole coast of Normandy, with laws on the subject as early as 1908. The flesh was sold in the markets and the oil used for lamps.'—F.C.F.

L.R.Brightwell says that the flesh is very dark red, somewhat oily, but not fishy, and that when properly 'casseroled' it might pass for jugged hare. He adds that it is very rich and sustaining.

Porpoise With Short Broth. Porpoise With Ragoust

Cut in pieces, and rost it on the spit, as it rosteth, baste it with butter, salt, vinegar and pepper; after it is well rosted, baste it with another sauce made with butter and minced onion, then mix all together, and bake it, mix a little flowre with it, and serve.—*La Va.*

POT-AU-FEU

A clear meat broth and the national soup of France. It is meant to be served in the *cocotte* or pot in which it was made.

    2 lb. soup beef
    2 tablespoons coarse (rock) salt
    2 whole cloves
    1 large onion
    3 or 4 carrots
    1 small parsnip
    1 small *bouquet-garni*
    Giblets from 1 fowl (if available)
    ¾ lb. bones
    12 whole peppercorns
    1 clove garlic
    3 leeks
    2 turnips
    1 stalk celery
    2 small stalks parsley
    Cold water

Top ribs, breast or leg of beef are suitable, but there must be some fat. The bones should include a good marrow-bone. Any French housewife will declare that a really excellent *pot-au-feu* must be made in one of those earthenware deep pots which are known by the very name of 'Pot-au-feu'. Failing this, a heavy iron saucepan will do, but earthenware is best.

Place the meat and bones, together with the giblets, if available, minus the liver, in the pot and add about a quart or a little more of *cold* water. Add salt. Place the pot on the fire – gas is very suitable as the heat can be regulated so easily – and allow contents to boil. As the scum rises, remove it very carefully. Then add a cupful of cold water when it comes again to the boil; skim again, most carefully. Now for the vegetables. Peel onion, carrots, turnips and parsnip. Cut leeks longways into halves after removing some of the upper green portion and, of course, the roots and first outer skin. Tie the leeks together with a little string. Stick cloves in the onion. Cut the carrots and other root vegetables into halves or quarters longwise.

Place the *bouquet-garni* in a small piece of muslin, with the parsley. When the soup has been skimmed for the second time, add all the foregoing, also the peppercorns, which may also be tied up in a small piece of muslin so that they may be removed easily when the soup is ready to serve. Cover closely and let the soup *simmer very gently* for four hours. Remember it is most important that this soup shall only just simmer, it must never boil fast, that is why a pin-point of gas is suitable as the heat is so regular.

When ready, remove the meat, bones and vegetables and keep warm. Place a piece of fine muslin in a strainer, having previously dipped the muslin in cold water. If you like the broth to look 'rich,' colour with a few drops of caramel or suitable brown colouring vegetable, after the meat has been removed. Have some very thin slices of French bread toasted a nice brown. Pour the soup over them, through the prepared strainer. This will remove any excess of fat from the soup.

In France, this soup is usually made in sufficient quality to serve two meals. The second time it is sometimes served heated up with fine vermicelli added, or it makes a perfect foundation for onion soup.

It is customary in France to serve the beef, which has then become *bouilli*, surrounded by the vegetables, as the second course in *bourgeois* homes. Coarse salt and pickled gherkins are served with the meat or thick tomato sauce in place of salt and pickles.

In some districts, half a cabbage is added to the *pot-au-feu*, but this destroys the delicacy of the flavour in the opinion of connoisseurs.—P.W.

Pot-au-Feu Varieties

There are countless variations of the *pot-au-feu*, of which the following are but a few:

A l'Albigeoise. Made with beef topside, calf's foot, ham, a little goose *confite* and small *saucisson*. The usual vegetables, plus some white haricots and a little garlic.

A l'Ancienne. Made of fore-ribs of beef, a fowl and some lean bacon.

A la Beauceronne. Made with beef skin, lean bacon and lard.

A la Berrichonne. Made with beef fore-rib, mutton and bacon.

A la Jambe de Bois. Made with leg of beef, lean bacon, a hen and a duck.

A la Languedocienne. Made with topside of beef, pork and goose.

PRONGHORN

Lat. *Antilocapra americana*. A small ruminant confined to the treeless parts of the Western United States and Mexico. It is usually referred to as *Pronghorn Antelope* or *Pronghorned Antelope*, but it is not a true *Antelope*.

'Its flesh, unlike that of any other plains animal, is equally good all through the year. In the fall it is hardly so juicy as deervenison, but in the spring, when no other kind of game is worth eating, it is perfectly good; and at that time of the year, if we have to get fresh meat, we would rather kill antelope than anything else; and as the bucks are always to be instantly distinguished from the does by their large horns, we confine

ourselves to them, and so work no harm to the species.'—TH.R., p. 181.

'We found antelope (i.e. pronghorn) liver the choicest delicacy to be had in the Rockies, and this fact perhaps led us to kill one or two more of these graceful and interesting creatures than we should otherwise have done.' *Dean Sage*, in the Book of the Boone and Crockett Club.

PUCHERO
(National Dish of Argentina)

The *puchero* is a dish for conventional occasions. It is, I think, the finest form of stew that has ever been evolved, but it must be made with *all* its ingredients.

Useless to suppose that this or that is not important, or that a substitute will serve.

If the proper things are not obtainable, *puchero* should not be attempted. It is made as follows: Take a large pot – iron, if possible – and half fill it with water. When this is boiling, drop into it large blocks of beef, with a normal proportion of fat, a calf's foot, and a boiling fowl cut in pieces. Salt this, let it boil, skim it, add a little more water, and skim again. When the meat is about half cooked, put in four carrots, four sweet potatoes, four potatoes, two onions, two whole tomatoes, four heads of sweet corn (corn on the cob), pieces of pumpkin, bacon cut into small pieces, and some thick slices of liver sausage. Let this boil, skim again, and leave it on a slow fire till the vegetables are cooked. Serve in three dishes, one for the meat, one for the vegetables, and one for the soup. Then, thank heaven for the good taste of the Argentines! (RUPERT CROFT-COOKE in *Wine and Food*, XXIII, p. 140.)

PUMA

Lat. *Felis concolor*. The American *Jaguar* or *Cougar*, also known as *American Lion, Mountain Lion, Catamount* and *Panther*. Although this dangerous beast is chiefly destroyed for safety's sake and not killed for food, we have the testimony of Charles Darwin, M.A. F.R.S., who ate *Puma* flesh in the Argentine, that 'the meat is very white and remarkably like veal in taste.'—H.M.S.

QUENELLES

    4 oz. lean beef
    1 oz. breadcrumbs
    1 egg
    Stock
    Salt and pepper
    Gravy

Mince the meat and pass it through a wire sieve. Add the crumbs, beaten egg, salt and pepper, and about a tablespoon stock. Fill some dariole moulds and steam slowly for 10 minutes. (*Lady Wilson* in R.R.E.)

RABBIT
Lat. *Lepus cuniculus*; Fr. *Lapin*. Hutch rabbit, *Lapin de chou* or *Lapin de clapier*; Wild rabbit, *Lapin de garenne*.

Selecting a Rabbit for Eating
Just as an egg is supposed always to be an egg, so a rabbit is always thought to be a rabbit; but both eggs and rabbit vary a good deal, and do not invariably afford the same food value. If you go to purchase a rabbit, one is lifted down from a hook and it is accepted and paid for without question; you would be diffident of accepting anything else in the way of meat without seeing it weighed. Rabbits, apparently of the same size, often differ much as regards weight, often to the extent of a lb. or more, and the loss to a purchaser may be that much. Very few understand how to select a rabbit for the table; if it has been killed some time, and is verging on becoming putrid, you have only to take a whiff of the interior to see if any sign of staleness is apparent. If the ear tears fairly easily the rabbit is not an old one, and if the kidneys are buried in fat a rabbit is certain to be in good condition. For eating, a doe is always preferable to a buck, especially as the season is nearing its end, when the male rabbit's flesh is often very strong in flavour. When the flesh is what is described as 'rabbity', it is far from appealing to the palate. As the rabbit season is approaching its end, selection should be even more careful, for all the old warriors are then being caught and consigned to market.

Trapped and snared rabbits are liable to be tasteless, devoid of flavour, particularly should they have suffered long in trap or snare. Those caught by both methods are not difficult to identify. A rabbit netted is always clean and free from injury except for a broken neck. Readers may not agree but my preference is for a rabbit shot, for its death has always been speedy. All shot rabbits have not been smashed, and if struck well forward there is no loss of value.

The tastiness of a wild rabbit greatly depends on what it has eaten, and it is never better than when its diet has largely consisted of bark and other dry material. When green food has become scanty in a warren, and bushes have been thrown in for rabbits to bark, they are always excellent eating. I once lived on an estate upon which one of the coverts was infested with wild garlic. Some of the rabbits developed a morbid craving for this, and became perfectly uneatable. The strong oniony smell was not apparent till cooking was in progress, and then it filled the kitchen. I have known a rabbit refused because its fat was golden-yellow, this being due to its having shared the maize scattered for feeding pheasants. Such a rabbit is most excellent eating. Quite the best rabbit of all is a nearly fully-grown one, killed about harvest-time, and cooked almost at once. Something depends upon the mode of cooking, for there are rabbits which should be roasted, and others fit only for stewing.—Salesman. From *The Gamekeeper*, August 1940.

Needless to say, rabbits have always been far more popular in Europe than in the U.S.A., where they are rather looked down upon.

A Few Points About the Breeds of Rabbit for the Table
by F. H. GOFFE
(Secretary of the Utility Poultry Society)

Practically all breeds of hutch rabbits produce flesh of about the same quality providing they are equally well fed.

Accordingly the main points to be considered are the size of rabbit required combined with economic points. In deciding on the breed some thought will have to be given whether a large or a small rabbit is generally wanted and whether baby flesh or more mature meat is appreciated. If a 3 to 4 lb. rabbit of about eight weeks still carrying its baby flesh is the objective then it is obvious that a Giganta breed must be employed, while if a small rabbit with full flavoured flesh is preferred a smaller breed will fill the bill.

No good purpose will be served by detailing the dozens of different breeds, and needs will be met with a few notes on the most popular varieties.

The Flemish Giant can be made to scale 4 lb. when about eight weeks old and will weigh up to 9 or 10 lb. at six to seven months. They are, however, very big eaters, and owing to exhibitors favouring heavy bone, a very big head, etc., the percentage of offal is heavy. Another point against them is that although the does have big litters they are poor mothers. The bucks however have a great influence on the size of the progeny if they are crossed with other breeds.

The Chinchilla Giganta, as the name indicates, is another big breed. It is an active small-boned rabbit and a moderate eater. The does are free breeders and good mothers. Youngsters will scale nearly 4 lb. at eight weeks, about 7 lb. when around five months, and will grow on to 9 or 10 lb.

The English and ordinary Chinchilla are both very good all round rabbits. The former makes up to about 6 or 8 lb., while the Chinchilla grows on to about 6 lb. or a little over.

The Dutch is an old favourite and good in all respects. It is, however, of small build, and adults are not expected to reach much more than about 5 lb. with the youngsters proportionally small. This is rather a drawback from a table point of view except for a curry. The breed does very well when crossed.

Anyone who has a fancy for any particular colour has a wide range of choice. The Chinchilla is a silver grey, the Havana a dark chocolate, the Beveren a light lavender blue, the Lilac a pink shade of dove, and, of course, there is a pure white, a pure black, etc.

There is probably no more accommodating animal in the world than the rabbit about food. They are vegetarians and will thrive on anything from the very best oats to waste cabbage leaves. They appreciate variety and this is probably what makes rabbit feeding a simple matter, nothing seems to come amiss. For example, the residue pips, etc., from blackberry jelly dried off with a little bran will be tackled with avidity. In the ordinary way a handful of wheat or oats or the hens' wet mash will form the main item of a rabbit's menu; this can be varied with dried crusts, porridge, or anything similar which happens to be handy. The second course should consist of a good helping of green food. Rabbits require a lot of bulk food and a supply of hay or oat straw should always be in the rack; likewise they should be always have fresh water before them in an unspillable trough. They thrive quite well if fed once a day, but if it is convenient to attend them twice a day then the green food can be given separately in the evening. Care should always be taken that all food offered to rabbits is fresh, as anything mouldy will upset them and their powers of recovery are poor. A note should be made against the return of more abundant days that milk, either cow's or goat's, given as a drink is the very finest food to get size into young rabbits.

If a well-fattened rabbit is starved, as it should be before it is killed, the dressed carcass will work out to 60 or 66 per cent of the live weight. The pelt will absorb about 12 per cent and the balance will be the weight of the paunch. A hare dresses out rather better with the carcass at about 75 per cent of the original weight.

A word or two must be given to the wild rabbit. The best that can be said about it is that when quite young the flesh is just passable but with age the flesh is hard and very dark. On the other hand the flesh of a hutch rabbit will come up quite white and even an old hutch rabbit will prove tender eating.

A hutch rabbit will always cut up white in colour but should extra whiteness be required soak the joints in salt and water for half an hour.

If there is any doubt about the age of a wild rabbit the best test is to take the head in one's hand and press the jaw bones together. If they appear to break the rabbit is young. Actually the point which gives way is between the two front teeth on the lower jaw where the two sides ordinarily join.

There is no relationship between a hare and a rabbit; they are different species and will not breed together.

No consideration is given in these notes to the merits of the pelts produced by the different varieties as pelt production is quite another story. A table rabbit is killed just when it is wanted but good pelts can only be obtained when the rabbit is full grown and in full coat. Of course the two may coincide and it follows that if the rabbit is in full coat it must be very fit and well and will be good eating. Generally speaking, however, table rabbits are killed long before they reach the full coat stage.

Augustus Muir, in *Heather Track and High Road* (Methuen, 1944), records that when Robert Ferguson, Edinburgh's own poet, was a bursar at St Salvator's, his turn came to say grace in the Hall, and he gave thanks as follows:

For rabbits young and for rabbits old,
For rabbits hot and for rabbits cold,
For rabbits tender and for rabbits tough,
Our thanks we render – but we've had
    enough !

Muir adds: 'Ferguson was duly haled before a professorial court, from which he received nothing more drastic than a reprimand; but for a long time after, rabbits appeared no more on the bill of fare.'

Lapin en Blanquette

1 young rabbit
Small 'button' onions
1 small piece lemon peel
2 tablespoons butter
1 or 2 egg yolks
Lemon juice
1 rather thick slice salt pork
1 small *bouquet-garni*
Salt and peppercorns
2 tablespoons flour
2 tablespoons cream (optional)
Small fresh mushrooms (optional)

This is first-cousin to the homely boiled rabbit, but it will be found to be a far more succulent dish. Cut the rabbit into neat pieces and soak them in cold salted water for a little while to remove excess of blood and so whiten the flesh. When ready, drain and put pieces of rabbit into a heavy stewing-pan, together with salt, a few peppercorns – tied in a piece of muslin – the *bouquet* and about 12 small onions. Add also a tiny piece of lemon peel, and the salt pork cut into neat pieces. Barely cover all with cold water and set the pan over a rather low heat, bringing contents slowly to the boil and skimming as required. Keep covered and cook until the rabbit is tender, then remove pieces of meat, keep them hot, strain the broth and also keep hot. Melt the butter in another saucepan, add the flour and stir until mixture is smooth then moisten gradually with the hot rabbit broth, of which there should be about two cupfuls. Add the cream, if used, beaten with the egg yolk (or yolks) after the stewing-pan has been removed from the fire. Season to taste with a little lemon juice. If mushrooms are used – and they improve the dish greatly – select small ones and slice French-fashion, that is, cut stems off to within ½ in. of caps, peel the mushrooms and the bit of stem, and slice each one from top of cap to bottom of stem, rather thinly. They should be added about 10 minutes before the rabbit is done. The pieces of pork, onions and mushrooms are, naturally, served in the creamy sauce, with the rabbit, and light hot mashed potatoes should accompany the dish.—P.W.

Brandy Rabbit

Marinade a rabbit, then lard him well or wrap in fat bacon. Put him in a casserole which will fit the oven and add large dice of raw ham, sliced carrots, an onion stuck with three cloves, herbs, salt, and a pinch of mixed spice. Add a cup of good stock and a port glass of cooking brandy. Cover and boil up for five minutes over a flame fire, which drives off the fierceness of the brandy, then place in a slow oven. Look at it from time to time and tilt so that the liquid bastes it. A rabbit takes an hour and a quarter, a young one fifty minutes, a baby not more than half an hour. When done strain and reduce the gravy to a demiglaze; pour over or serve in a sauce-boat.—M.H.P.

Lapin Chasseur

2 oz. butter
2 rabbits
6 oz. fresh pork
4 onions
2 sprigs thyme
2 bay leaves
3 glasses dry white wine
4 to 6 oz. mushrooms
2 dessertspoonfuls flour
Small cup cream or 2 yolks egg
1 spoonful chopped parsley

Sauté rabbit pieces in butter until brown, with diced fresh pork, small (or diced) onions, and allow to simmer in casserole with herbs, spices, and white wine until tender (about an hour).

Mushrooms cut up are fried in butter and added to rabbit in casserole.

The sauce is finished with addition of cream and yolks of eggs.

Sprinkle with chopped parsley before serving.—H.S.

Le Civet de Lapin

1 rabbit
2 slices bacon (streaky)
¼ lb. fresh mushrooms
Small pinch ground nutmeg
2 tablespoons flour
Blood of rabbit
1 thick slice salt pork
2 medium-sized onions
Bouquet-garni
Salt and pepper
1 bottle red burgundy
Fried *croûtons*

Cut the salt pork and bacon into dice and gently brown in a heavy iron pan (*cocotte*). Remove and set aside lean pieces of pork and bacon and brown cut-up rabbit in the fat in pan, adding the sliced onions. Stir frequently to colour pieces of meat on all sides. Now sprinkle the flour over all, stirring to coat pieces of meat. Allow this to brown a little, then moisten gradually with the wine. Add salt, pepper, *bouquet* and spice (also, if liked, a cut-up clove of garlic), the sliced mushrooms and the small pieces of browned pork and bacon. Cover pan and simmer contents very gently for about 1½ hours. 10 minutes before serving add the blood of the rabbit to thicken and flavour sauce. Remove *bouquet* and serve very hot with hot fried *croûtons*.—P.W.

Lapin à la Cosaque

1 young rabbit
3 or 4 shallots
1 tablespoon vinegar
1 pinch ground cinnamon
Salt and pepper
2 tablespoons olive oil
1 cup white wine
1 clove
2 tablespoons thick cream
1 tablespoon flour

Cut the rabbit into neat pieces and brown them in the hot oil, together with the minced shallots. When a nice colour on all sides moisten with the wine and the vinegar. Season with salt and pepper and add the clove and cinnamon. Cover closely and cook gently until rabbit is tender, then add to the gravy the thick cream into which the flour has been beaten or blended.—P.W.

Rabbit Cream

Cook a cut-up rabbit in 2 oz. of butter in a stewpan for about 20 minutes, and see that it does not get brown. Then cut off the meat, mince it and pound it in a mortar and pass it through a sieve, mix it with a quarter of a pint of cream, a little dissolved gelatine, pepper, salt and nutmeg. Steam it for an hour, let it get cold, turn it out, and mask it with a thick *Béchamel* sauce. (*Morning Post.*)

Curry of Rabbit with Rice
3 oz. butter
2 rabbits
4 large onions
2 soup spoons
Curry powder
2 large apples
4 spoonfuls raisins
Dash of lemon juice
¾ pint milk

Fry shredded onions in butter in stewpan until quite brown. Remove the onions and put them aside. Mix curry powder with milk and pour in stewpan, where it will simmer until it begins to look a rich yellow. Then add the rabbit (boned and diced) – the meat for a curry must be raw, but it can be lightly browned in butter – and allow to stew slowly for at least half an hour, adding a little milk from time to time. Then put back the onions, with diced apples and raisins, salt. Simmer slowly for another hour, and add lemon juice just before serving. Serve with boiled potatoes if rice is not available. —H.S.

Rabbit Cutlets
The fillets of a rabbit pounded (uncooked).
Soak about 2 oz. of bread in a little cold milk, squeeze it dry, and pass it through a sieve.
Mix with the bread 2 oz. of butter or margarine and add the pounded rabbit.
Pound the whole lot together again and pass through a sieve.
Add a mixture of one whole egg, previously beaten, and quarter pint of well-whipped cream or custard.
Season with pepper and salt.
Steam in a mould three-quarters of an hour.
Set in the cold or on ice.
When required, cut the mixture into the shape of cutlets, not too thick, or other appropriate shapes.
Egg and breadcrumb the cutlets.
Fry in lard.
Note.—The following sauce considerably improves the cutlets: Mix well together the yolks of two eggs, with two spoonfuls of cream or custard, 1 oz. of butter or margarine, pepper, salt, and a dessertspoonful of lemon juice. Stir all well together over a slow fire, until the sauce looks creamy. Serve hot in a sauceboat.—B.C.

Galantine of Rabbit (Glendelvine)
Ingredients
½ lb. minced cooked rabbit
½ lb. boiled ham
¼ lb. breadcrumbs
3 hard-boiled eggs, chopped coarsely
1 dozen pistachio nuts, if liked, for garnish
Season with salt, pepper and thyme.
Mix well and moisten with one raw egg and stock that rabbits were cooked in, until it forms a roll.
Boil for an hour.
When cold, glaze and decorate.—B.C.

Rabbit à la Marengo
2 tablespoons oil
Rabbit (sliced)
1 lb. mushrooms
Truffles (sliced)
Salt and pepper
Parsley (hashed)
2 tablespoons tomato sauce

Cut rabbit in medium slices. Put oil in saucepan and let heat. When oil starts smoking add rabbit, salt, pepper, and let cook on hot fire half an hour. Leave saucepan on side of the stove, take half the oil the rabbit has cooked in and put it in a small saucepan, let heat well and cook in it mushrooms, parsley and truffles; add tomato sauce. When mushrooms are cooked, serve rabbit and pour sauce over it.—(*From Mrs Francis Hallowell, N.Y.C.*, in S.D.L.M.)

Rabbit and Onion Sauce
Joint the rabbit and set it in a saucepan, covering completely with well-salted water to which you add a good squeeze of lemon juice.

Add two whole onions and a *bouquet-garni* of thyme, bayleaf, and parsley. Boil uncovered until all scum has come to the top. Remove this, and when the liquid is clear, cover the pot and let it simmer gently for three-quarters of an hour. Quarter three dozen very small white onions and toss them in butter, taking care that they do not take colour. When the rabbit has simmered for half an hour or so take it out and drain it, and remove the *bouquet-garni*. Strain off the gravy from the rabbit into a basin and put into the empty saucepan a dessertspoon of butter and an equal quantity of flour. Let the butter melt slowly and work in the flour, taking care that the heat is not enough to make it take colour. Slowly add the rabbit gravy, stirring continuously so that the sauce is smooth and free from lumps; let it come slowly to the boil and boil quietly for five minutes. Now, beat two yolks of eggs in half a teacupful of milk, pour it into the sauce, and stir in with the saucepan off the fire (it must not be allowed to boil). Add the rabbit and ónions and a little chopped parsley, stir well, warm up but do not boil, and serve.—M.H.P.

Lapereau au Porto

Cut the rabbit into neat joints and wash; leave it all night in a *marinade* consisting of three-quarter parts of port wine, a little water, ½ lb. prunes, a few raisins, a little sugar, pepper, salt, onion and diced carrots, a *bouquet* of bayleaf, peppercorns and celery seeds. The next day, put all into a saucepan and simmer two or three hours according to tenderness of rabbit. Just before serving, thicken the *jus* with a little *crème de riz* and add a teaspoon of red currant jelly or crab apple jelly.—EM.M.

Roman Pie (Rabbit)

Line a mould with good paste, not forgetting to make sufficient to make a lid and rose.

Boil a rabbit and cut the meat off the bone, as thin as possible.

Boil 2 oz. macaroni.

Grate 2 oz. parmesan.

Chop some shallot, and a mushroom (if possible).

Chop some ham and tongue.

Put all into the mould, adding a half pint of cream, or, if not available, some custard.

Bake for one hour; replace the rose, and serve cold.—B.C.

Rabbit Sauté à la Minute

Cut a very young and very fresh one in pieces, and *sautez* them in butter till they are nicely coloured; that is, for about 20 minutes. Season them and add a chopped shallot. Cook a few minutes longer, then pour a tablespoon of water into the pan to loosen the juices (having removed the pieces to keep warm), stir and scrape well till the water and juices are well mixed, and pour this simple sauce over the rabbit pieces, sprinkling them with freshly and finely chopped parsley.—AMBROSE HEATH in *Wine and Food*, II, p. 38.

Lapin Sauté au Vin Blanc

1 young rabbit
1 tablespoon butter
Bouquet-garni
4 tablespoons white wine
1 tablespoon olive oil
1 clove garlic
Salt and pepper
1 teaspoon tomato *purée*

Cut up rabbit, setting liver aside. Brown the pieces in mixed oil and butter, well but not over-heated. When brown, add to the stew the garlic *bouquet* – which should, if possible, include a sprig of wild thyme (*serpolet*) – salt and pepper. Reduce and cook slowly until meat is done, shaking the pan occasionally. A few minutes before serving, add cut-up liver and wine, continuing to *sauté* the contents of pan; finally add the tomato *purée*, increase heat to boil up contents of pan a second time and serve, sprinkling with a little chopped parsley. Mushrooms may be added, if liked. The sauce must be very 'short'.—P.W.

Rabbit Soup

Crème Cherville. A rabbit *velouté*, garnished with shredded morels and *escalopes* of fillets of rabbit. Add cream and a little Madeira wine at time of serving.

Rabbit Stew

To two jointed rabbits take 2 oz. of butter and ¼ lb. of fat bacon. Fry the bacon in the butter till crisp, then take it out and add three moderate-sized onions cut in rings, or a dozen button onions. When coloured remove, get the butter really hot, and drop in the rabbit and brown thoroughly, cooking well through and sprinkling with flour, pepper and salt. *Sauté* this for about twenty-five minutes. Stir in a dessertspoon of flour to thicken, and add three-quarters of a pint of stock and a glass of white wine. Season carefully with a *bouquet-garni* of herbs, bring to the boil, and put in the onions; cover the pan or casserole, and simmer very gently for an hour and a quarter. When done draw aside, strain off the sauce, remove the fat, and dish the rabbit on a round of toast in a hot dish with the bacon; pour over the whole the skimmed sauce after boiling up once more. Never boil the rabbit in the sauce. It should be cooked in butter, finishing slowly in sauce.—M.H.P.

Rabbit Stewed in Milk and Mushrooms

Colour in butter as usual, then add a glass of white wine and an equal amount of boiled milk (fresh milk will curdle), cover the pan, and stew.

Peel a pound of mushrooms and put the chopped stalks and peels into a little salt water to simmer for five minutes. Mince the heads of the mushrooms. Strain off the mushroom-peel water, add a hazel nut of butter, a moderate flake of garlic, and the chopped mushrooms; simmer it aside. The rabbit should cook for an hour in the original milk and wine stew, then add the mushroom stew, and cook for at least another half an hour. Long cooking is necessary if the rabbits are old. If young baby rabbits are chosen, the mushroom sauce will require longer cooking than the scant half-hour they need, so it should be started first.

When done, strain off the sauce from the whole and fold in the yolks of two eggs, broken up in two spoonfuls of water. Add a little chopped parsley, replace the rabbit, bring to the boil, and serve on very hot plates.—M.H.P.

Stuffed Roast Rabbit
1 young rabbit
Wine vinegar
1 sliced onion
1 small bayleaf
Freshly ground pepper
Butter
Slices of bacon
Larding bacon or pork
1 sliced carrot
Pinch dried thyme
Salt
Water
Forcemeat
Thick cream (optional)

The rabbit may be left whole, the head and ends of paws, however, being removed, and the liver should be set aside; or else the middle part only is used, the hind legs and breast being served in some other way. Lightly fry the liver in butter, chop and add to well-seasoned forcemeat, when ready to use. Marinate the rabbit overnight in a mixture of red wine vinegar and water, the sliced vegetables, the herbs, salt and pepper. Turn once or twice to marinate all sides evenly. Next day, drain rabbit and lard carefully. Fill interior with the forcemeat, sewing up carefully into shape. If the animal is whole, fasten both ends together securely with a skewer. Set in a baking-tin, spread with butter, lay a few thin slices of bacon on top, sprinkle lightly with salt and pepper and bake or roast, basting frequently with the butter and a few tablespoons of the strained *marinade*. When done and a nice brown, add, if wished, the thick cream, which should be gently stirred into the gravy and served in a sauceboat. Remove threads carefully from rabbit, unskewer gently, keeping the rounded shape, and serve very hot. If you have cause to suspect that the animal is a bit on the tough side, it is well to nick through the backbone at regular intervals to facilitate carving when done. White wine can advantageously replace the vinegar and water for the preparation of the *marinade*.—P.W.

Timbale of Rabbit
One or two rabbits; three yolks and one white of egg; 4 oz. breadcrumbs; a little milk or cream; salt, pepper and seasonings. Cut up the rabbit and allow it to stand in cold water for some time before putting the flesh through a mincing machine; then put it through a wire sieve, mixing in all the ingredients and beating it up very well all the time. Steam for two hours and turn out hot. (*Old family recipe.*)

RAT
Lat. *Rattus rattus*, the Black Rat, and *Rattus norvegicus*, the common, grey or Norway rat, a pest which has so far defied all the efforts of man to destroy it.

Captain L.C.Cameron wrote: 'Stuffed with a simple stuffing made of breadcrumbs, a sprinkling of sweet herbs, and a little pepper and salt, mixed with the liver and heart of the rat, and roasted for a few minutes in a hot oven, it proved to be a delicious dish not unlike a snipe in flavour. Young rats may also be made into pies, if meat stock, consommé or a piece of beef be added to provide the gravy.' 'I have eaten rats on more than one occasion. Once in England, and several times in Hungary and Roumania. Cameron is quite right, they are not at all bad. I know one gypsy family in this country that eats them quite frequently.' (Brian Vesey Fitz-Gerald, editor of *The Field*, in a letter to A.L.S.).

There are also those lines by an anonymous and *very* 'minor' poet, quoted in the *Australian Brewing and Wine Journal* (May 20, 1943):

'Rats are not a dainty dish to set before
    a king,
But for a really hungry man they're just
    the very thing;
Wrap each rat in bacon fat, roast slow
    before the fire,
Take him down and serve him brown
    you've all you can desire.'

RED DUIKER
Lat. *Cephalophus natalensis*. A pretty little antelope which the Boers call *Rooibosch-bokje* (*Little red bush-buck*); it is common in the densest kloofs of many parts of South Africa, wherever there is plenty of thick cover and a sufficiency of water.

'The flesh is tasty, and far superior to that of the grey duiker.'—F.V.K.

REEDBUCK. REITBOK
Lat. *Redunca arundinacea*. A small African antelope allied to the *Waterbuck*. It has a bushy tail and the buck has small, ringed horns which are curved forward. The doe is hornless.

'In the Matabele and Mashona countries on both slopes of the watershed it is very common along the banks of every river, except, of course, in the inhabited parts, where it has been exterminated.'—F.C.S.

'I do not agree with those who say that the flesh is unpalatable, for I consider a well "larded" leg of reedbuck a real delicacy, but *chacun à son goût.*'—F.V.K.

REINDEER
Lat. *Rangifer tarandus*; Fr. *Renne.* A most valuable deer, now confined to the sub-arctic regions, where it is kept in large herds for the sake of the milk, hides and, least important of all, its flesh. It is mostly used for drawing sledges, and is slaughtered for food when too old to work and to roast. It may be prepared for the table in any way suitable for *Venison* (q.v.). The most dependable part of the *Reindeer* from a gastronome's point of view is its tongue, when smoked.

RHEBUCK. VAAL-RHEBOK
Lat. *Pelea capreolus.* A South African Antelope nearly as large as the Fallow Deer, but more like the Chamois in shape and habits; its horns are short and upright.
'The flesh of this antelope is not in great favour as an article of diet owing to the fact that at certain seasons of the year the animal is subject to the attacks of the larvae of the bot-fly, which burrow under the skin and raise most unsightly-looking excrescences which, to say the least, do not tempt the appetite. The flesh, however, though dry, is as good as that of most of the smaller antelopes, which is not saying very much, that of the Klipspringer being decidedly the most tasty.'—F.V.K.

RHINOCEROS
Lat. *Rhinoceros simus.* This is the larger African species, or *White Rhinoceros*, so called to distinguish it from the common African species, or *Black Rhinoceros* (*Rhinoceros bicornis*); it is not white but slate coloured and now very rare. 'Selous states that between August and March this animal is in very good condition and that the meat is excellent.'—M.S.A., p. 303.

RILLETTES
Hors-d'oeuvre made up of a mash of pigmeat, usually highly seasoned. Also used for making sandwiches. The *Rillettes* enjoying the greatest popularity are the *Rillettes* and *Rillons de Tours*, but there are *Rillettes* made in many other parts of France.

RILLONS
Another name for the *Rillettes*, a pigmeat *hors-d'oeuvre*. The most popular *Rillons* are those of Blois.

Rillons de Tours
They may be used as a cold luncheon dish, with salad, or as a *hors-d'oeuvre*, in which case the meat should be cut up small. Cut fat

from breast of pork into 2 in. squares, after removing skin. Put them in a heavy saucepan with just sufficient water to prevent burning. Place on a rather hot fire, when the fat of the pork will speedily melt and the water evaporate. Shake or stir continuously during this process, pressing the pieces of meat down to extract fat – a wooden spoon is indicated for this job. Sprinkle with salt and pepper and the *rillons* will be done when they are a nice even brown. Drain them to serve cold, keeping the fat for cooking purposes.—P.W.

RISSOLES
Rissoles are a dish more than three hundred years old, of which the name is nowadays often misapplied to *Croquettes*, though strictly speaking they differ from them in that they are wrapped in a thin jacket of pastry. Here is a modern French recipe which differs from that given by la Varenne in 1654 only in paying greater attention to detail:
For eight or ten persons take 250 grammes (9 oz.) of short crust or puff paste. Roll it out to the thickness of a penny; cut it out in rounds with a bowl or jam pot; place on each a little heap of minced meat or of food prepared as for croquettes or godiveaux for quenelles; fold each round of pastry in two; stick them together by moistening the edges with a little water; fry in deep fat; take out when a nice colour; drain and serve garnished with fried parsley.—L.B.C.

ROCK RABBIT. KLIP-DAS
Lat. *Procavia capensis.* A small thick-set African ungulate, with short legs and ears and a rudimentary tail.
'Plentiful everywhere along the mountain ranges and in the kloofs. The flesh is eaten by the natives, but it is coarse and strong.' —F.V.K.

SABLE ANTELOPE. HARRISBUCK. ZWART WIT PENS
Lat. *Hippotragus niger.* A large and handsome African antelope, with large, horns, curved back, and annulated, a tufted tail and a slight mane.
'Its true home is the higher regions of the Mashona country to the north-east of the Matabele country. There it is the commonest antelope, and may still be met in herds of over fifty individuals, the usual number being from ten to twenty.'—F.C.S.
'The flesh is palatable, more so than that of the closely allied roan antelope.'—F.V.K.

SARMALAS
Rub a little garlic on some raw beef and mince the beef with a little ham, a scrap of onion, parsley and other seasonings. Dip

some spinach or young vine leaves in hot water and roll up the mince in them, tying with thread, which is removed before serving; braise very slowly and serve in the casserole in which it is cooked.

SASSABY. BASTARD. HARTEBEEST

Lat. *Damaliscus lunatus*. A large South African Antelope, dark purplish red in colour, with the back and face almost black; it resembles the *Hartebeest*, but its horns are regularly curved without angulation.

'When the young grass springs up, these animals become very fat, but the fat, like that of the waterbuck, is not pleasant eating, as it quickly becomes cold and clogs in the mouth.'—F.V.K.

SASSATIES

(South African)

Cut 3 lb. mutton in small thin round pieces, with pieces of fat in between.

Soak half a cup of dried apricots overnight, boil them and press through a sieve.

Slice three big onions with a piece of garlic and fry in two tablespoons of dripping. Mix together the apricots, onions, some cayenne pepper, six lemon or orange leaves, one tablespoon curry, one tablespoon sugar, half a teaspoon salt, three tablespoons vinegar, and boil it all together for a minute.

Let it cool off and then pour over the raw meat. Let the meat soak overnight in the sauce.

Now fry or grill the meat, boil the sauce again and pour over the grilled pieces of meat. Serve with rice.

SAUSAGE

A name that covers a multitude of tasty little 'bags of mystery', mostly finely-chopped and highly-seasoned meat encased in hog or sheep gut or some other non-edible but non-poisonous container. There are many different kinds of sausages, different as to size and shape, but chiefly according to the nature of the contents. The sausage is made up of pork, beef or any other meat or a mixture of different kinds of meat, bound by some starchy agent of neutral flavour, such as breadcrumbs, rusks, rice, cornflour, potato flour, soya bean flour, etc., and seasoned with pepper and salt as well as aromatic herbs, nutmeg or ginger, etc.

Here is a recipe for the commercial manufacture of a sausage of average quality and cost, immediately before the war, supplied by Frank Gerrard, and published in *Food Manufacture*, July 1939:

Recipe

    72 lb. meat (approx. ¼ fat)
    18 lb. dry rusk
    36 lb. water
    2 lb. seasoning

Stock Seasoning used

    18 lb. fine salt
    4 lb. ground white pepper
    7 oz. cayenne pepper
    6 oz. nutmeg
    6 oz. ginger

Method of manufacture: Meat prepared. Stored at 40° F. overnight. Broken down on ½ in. plate of mincer. Meat transferred to bowl chopper followed by seasonings and soaked rusk. Chopped fairly finely and filled to link six to the lb. Cooled at 40° F. prior to delivery. (Colour inclined to fade, seasoning and texture satisfactory, slight tendency to shrink on cooking.)

Final weight, 126 lb. (2 lb. loss); net cost per lb., 3.75*d*. approx.

Obviously, since the beginning of the war, the proportion of meat to binder and the quality of both have had to undergo many changes according to available supplies, and synthetic containers have also now replaced the hog and sheep casing to a large extent. There are also sausages without any casing. The *Oxford Sausage*, for example, is like a French *Crépinette*, a mere slab of sausage meat, not encased in a skin; whereas the *Cambridge Sausage* is also a pork sausage, but always encased in a skin.

There are four main kinds of American sausages: 1. *Fresh Pork Sausage*, 2. *Smoked Sausage*, 3. *Dry Sausage*, and 4. *Cooked Specialties*. Practically every variety of well-known European sausage is now made in the United States.

Home-made Sausage Meat

Select fat pork. Remove all skin, sinews, bones, etc., and chop or pass through a food chopper. Sometimes a little lean veal is also added as well as fresh breadcrumbs (very finely-grated), using one-third of these to two-thirds of meat and fat combined (or less fat and more lean meat may be used, if wished). Season rather highly with salt, pepper and mixed herbs. Shape into flat round or oval cakes, flour and fry in hot fat. This is easier than stuffing the preparation into special sausage-skins and the flavour is, of course, the same.

Pork Sausage

To be made entirely of pork.

Seven pounds lean to be cut from underneath the shoulder, 3 lb. fat to be cut from the backbone, three-quarters of a cup of ground and sifted sage, 1½ oz. of ground pepper, 3 oz. of salt.

If the sausage is cased, smoke it altogether three or four days by hanging up kitchen chimney or in a smoke-house until the skin looks dry and hard. Then hang it up in the garret or any dry place.—F.P.S.

SCRAPPLE

Scrapple contains delicate pork portions, corn meal, sage, and other spices, cooked and cooled in pans. To prepare it for the table you simply cut into flat squares and broil or fry it. It is made usually at butchering time and keeps well.—C.R.B.B. (1).

Maryland Scrapple

One jowl and one liver. Boil until it is well done, take out all the bones, run the meat through sausage cutter, then throw it in the water it was boiled in, season with salt, pepper, sage, thicken with cornmeal the consistency of thin mush; put in pans and slice off to fry. (*Mrs J.Morsell Roberts, Calvert County.*)—F.P.S.

SEAL

A name which applies to a large number of different marine carnivorous mammals, the flesh of which is not nearly so good as that of the marine herbivorous mammals such as the whale and dolphin.

D. F.C.Fraser told us that he had eaten the flesh of the *Crabeater Seal* (*Lobodon carcinophaga*), which was hung for some time on the ship's rigging before being used. The flesh, he said, was dark and not unpleasant, preferable, at any rate, to salt pork, which was the only alternative at the time. He added that the heart and liver of the *Leopard Seal* (*Hydrurga leptonyx*) were eaten.

Dr L.H.Matthews can vouch for the excellence of the tongue of the *Elephant Seal* (*Mirounga leonina*), when first of all boiled and then braised. He also calls the brain of the *Leopard Seal* a great delicacy, adding that it is excised, without breaking it up, soaked in salt water, carefully freed from all membranes, then cut in slices, grilled and served on hot buttered toast. Dr Matthews also recommends the tongue and the liver, when the seal is in good condition, but he does not recommend the kidneys: he has tried to eat some in a 'steak and kidney pudding' but they were like rubber tyres – very tough.

L.R.Brightwell told us that he found the seal flesh very palatable and not in the least fishy, and it was said to be nutritious. But the most informative account regarding seal's flesh as food for man is that given by Dr A.Horner, surgeon to the 'Pandora', who, in *Land and Water* (18th Dec. 1875, p. 475) has the following note:

'From the length of time these people have inhabited this cold country, one naturally expects them to have found some particular food well adapted by its nutritious and heat-giving properties to supply all the wants of such a rigorous climate, and such is found to be the case, for there is no food more delicious to the tastes of the Esquimaux than the flesh of the seal, and especially that of the common seal (*Phoca vitulina*). But it is not only the human inhabitants who find it has such excellent qualities, but all the larger carnivora that are able to prey on them. Seal's meat is so unlike the flesh to which we Europeans are accustomed, that it is not surprising we should have some difficulty at first in making up our minds to taste it; but when once that difficulty is overcome, every one praises its flavour, tenderness, digestibility, juiciness, and decidedly warming after-effects. Its colour is almost black, from the large amounts of venous blood it contains, except in very young seals, and is, therefore, very -singular looking, and not inviting, while its flavour is unlike anything else, and cannot be described except by saying delicious! To suit European palates, there are certain precautions to be taken before it is cooked. It has to be cut in thin slices, carefully removing any fat or blubber, and then soaked in salt water for from 12 to 24 hours, to remove the blood, which gives it a slightly fishy flavour. The blubber has such a strong taste that it requires an Arctic winter's appetite to find out how good it is. That of the bearded seal (*Phoca barbata*) is most relished by epicures. The daintiest morsel of a seal is the liver, which requires no soaking, but may be eaten as soon as the animal is killed. The heart is good eating, while the sweetbread and kidneys are not to be despised.

'The usual mode of cooking seal's meat is to stew it with a few pieces of fat bacon, when an excellent rich gravy is formed, or it may be fried with a few pieces of pork, or 'whiteman'', being cut up with the seal, or 'black-man''.'—J.A.A.

SHASHLICK CAUCASIAN

You take a very young lamb which would not weigh more than 5 lb. and cut off all the fat. The meat from the leg should be cut from the bone in little pieces, of about 28 pieces to a leg. Then take two lemons squeezed, one glass of olive oil, and a bit of salt and a few grains of pepper. All these are mixed together with the cut pieces of lamb and put in a cold place for three or four days. Then 15 minutes before you wish to serve, put the pieces of lamb on skewers and broil over charcoals. With this *Shashlick* you serve rice, lemon and a sauce called *Diable*. (*From Prince Serge Obolensky, New York City*, in S.D.L.M.)

SHEEP

(See also *Lamb* and *Mutton*).

The British breeds of sheep responsible for the best lamb and mutton may be divided in two main categories which bear a close relationship to environment, the Mountain and the Down breeds, the most important groups in each category being as follows:

Mountain or Hill Breeds. The *Scotch Blackface* and other varieties of Blackfaced sheep; the *Cheviot*, the old-established breed of the Cheviot Hills; the *Welsh Mountain* breed, small and hardy; the *Radnor*, which is not so hardy; the *Herdwick*, chiefly in Cumberland; the *Exmoor Horn*, a native of Exmoor; and the *Kerry Hill*, the old-established breed of Montgomeryshire.

Down Breeds. The *South Down*, the most highly-prized of all breeds in the South of England; *Shropshire, Suffolk, Hampshire Down, Oxford Down*, the largest of the Down breeds; and the *Dorset Down*. All Down breeds are hornless.

From these, the best breeds, a considerable number of cross-breeds have been raised, besides which there are also, mostly in low-land areas, some long-woolled breeds, the descendants of flocks formerly kept principally for the value of the fleece. They grow to considerable carcass weight and are readily fattened for the production of fat lambs. As late-fed hoggets, the carcasses usually carry too much fat, which is inclined to be tallowy and rather unpleasant; the meat is coarser than that of the Hill or Down breeds and it has not the same fine flavour. The best-known Longwoolled breeds are the following: *Leicester, Border Leicester, Lincoln, Wensleydale, Kent* or *Romney Marsh, South Devon, Devon Longwool, Dartmoor*, and, in Ireland, the *Rosscommon* and *Galway* breeds.

Sheep's Head

Clean the head well and soak it in warm water for two hours; then put it in a casserole with just enough cold water to cover it; when it boils add, for flavouring, one carrot and one onion peeled and sliced, a bunch of parsley, one teaspoon pepper and three of salt. Cover the casserole closely and let it simmer for 1½ or two hours. Skin the tongue and place it in the centre of the dish with the meat on either side. Throw over it a real good sauce, either caper, onion or tomato, the latter perhaps best.

Sheep's Heart

Proceed exactly as with calf's heart, only diminish the time of cooking in proportion to the size: about 30 minutes will be sufficient to serve with any kind of sharp sauce or any *ragoût* of vegetables.—Al.s.

Sheep's Tails à la Bourgeoise

Cook five or six sheep's tails in a thin, light sauce made of a little *bouillon*, a little salt, pepper, a bunch of parsley, shallot, two cloves, and half a garlic. Bleach for a quarter of an hour in boiling water the half of a large cabbage, rinse it in cold water and drain it by pressing. Cut off the stalk and chop up the rest. Cut into small dice a ¼ lb. to ½ lb. of bacon; put it with the cabbage in a small quantity of melted butter with a pinch of flour, mix together and moisten with some *bouillon* without salt, let this simmer on a slow fire for an hour until the cabbage and the bacon are cooked and the whole stew is of a good consistency. Put the tails to drain, arrange them in a dish at a little distance one from another; cover each tail with the stew and serve hot.—CLARISSE.

Sheep's Tongue Demi-Glaze

For one dish, take six, put them in water to disgorge, then dry them, put them in a stew-pan with two onions, half a large carrot, a *bouquet* of two bayleaves, a sprig of thyme, a quart of broth if handy, or water, half a spoonful of salt; put them on to boil, and simmer for two hours till done; try if tender with a pointed knife, if so take them out, skin them, trim out all the roots, cut the tongue in two, lengthwise, giving it a little of the shape of cutlets, skim the fat from the stock, reduce the whole or part to a demi-glaze, put your pieces on a dish; when ready to serve, make a thin roll of mashed potatoes, and dish them round it; add a little sugar to the demi-glaze, and a small piece of butter, stir round till melted, add the juice of half a lemon, pour boiling hot over the tongue. The sauce ought to adhere thickly to the back of the spoon.—Al.s.

Sheep's Feet or Trotters

Trotters can be cooked in a *blanc*, boned, egg-and-breadcrumbed, fried in deep fat and served with fried parsley and tomato sauce; or they can be rolled without boning in melted butter and breadcrumbs, carefully grilled and served with a *Sauce Diable*. A more savoury way is *à la Tyrolienne*, the trotters first being cooked as before. Then fry lightly some chopped onion and roughly chopped tomato with a seasoning of salt and pepper, a tiny bit of garlic and some chopped parsley. When this is ready, add some thin *Poivrade* sauce and the boned trotters, and simmer them gently for 10 minutes. (AMBROSE HEATH in *Wine and Food*, XXIII, p. 260.)

But the most popular way of all is to serve *Sheep's Trotters à la Poulette*:

Pieds de Mouton Poulette

Singe the feet carefully, scrape and blanch, then cook in a good vinegar *court-bouillon* until tender, when the meat will come off the bones. Drain and reheat without boiling in a rich *Sauce Poulette*.

Pieds de Mouton Frits

Cook some lamb's trotters as indicated in preceding recipe. Bone entirely when tender and cook gently for an hour in a *marinade* composed of salt, pepper, a touch of garlic, vinegar, *bouillon* to cover, a *bouquet*, a clove and a piece of butter, blended with a little flour. Cool, drain and dip each foot in beaten egg, shaping nicely, then in breadcrumbs. Allow surface to harden, then fry a golden brown in deep fat. Serve with a garnish of fried parsley.—P.W.

SPRINGBOK. SPRINGBUCK

Lat. *Antidorcas marsupialis*. An African Gazelle, dark buff-brown in colour, with darker markings, white underparts, and a conspicuous white dorsal stripe, expanding into a broad patch of white on the rump.

'Along the borders of the Kalahari desert it is common in many parts, and on the salt-pans between the Botletlie river and the wagon road leading from Bamangwate to the Zambesi it is also plentiful.'—F.C.S.

SQUIRREL

Lat. *Sciurus vulgaris*, the Red Squirrel; *S. carolinensis*, the American Grey Squirrel. Both are rodents and destructive by nature as well as necessity, but the *Grey Squirrel* is by far the more destructive of the two; it is also the fatter one and the best to eat, resembling very closely the warren rabbit in texture of flesh and flavour. It is eaten fairly commonly in some rural parts of the United States, but hardly ever available in England, although an offer to buy squirrels was advertised by some enterprising country butcher during the last war.

Squirrels en Casserole

3 squirrels
½ lb. chopped salt pork
1 cupful chopped onions
1½ cupfuls sliced parboiled potatoes
1 cupful green corn
1 cupful Lima beans
Black and red pepper to taste
1 quart (4 cups) peeled, cut tomatoes
1 tablespoonful sugar
1 tablespoonful salt
4 heaping tablespoons (4 oz.) butter
2 heaping tablespoons (2 oz.) flour
4 quarts (16 cups) boiling water

Clean, wash and joint the squirrels. Lay them in salted water for 30 minutes. Put the ingredients into a large casserole in the following order: First a layer of the pork, then one of the onions; next, of potatoes; then follow with successive layers of corn cut from the cob, the beans and the squirrels. Season each layer with black and red pepper. Pour in the water, put on the cover, and seal with a paste made of flour and water. Cook gently for three hours, then add the tomatoes, sugar and salt. Cook for one hour longer; stir in the flour and butter mixed together, boil for five minutes, and serve in the casserole.—M.H.N.

Squirrel Pie

'It may interest your readers to learn that grey squirrels, a pest from which it is admittedly desirable to rid this country, are not merely edible but provide an agreeable food. Young members of my family have been shooting them recently in a neighbourhood where they abound and are most harmful, and we are now finding them as useful as rabbits as a table dish. The meat is as tender as rabbit, can be similarly cooked, and resembles it in taste. If it were widely used to supplement the meat ration the double purpose might be served of addition to our food supply and the extermination of an animal destructive of that supply and of all bird life. Yours faithfully, Frances M.Rowe. Deancroft, Cookham Dean.' (*A letter to 'The Times'*, 19th February, 1941.)

Sautéed Squirrel

1 pair squirrels
2 tablespoons butter
1 onion, minced
1 garlic clove, finely minced
2 tablespoons minced ham
1 tablespoon flour
Bit of thyme, minced
½ bayleaf, minced fine
1 teaspoon grated rind of lemon
Salt and pepper
Cayenne
1½ cups claret

Wash and wipe the squirrels dry; cut in quarters; rub with salt and pepper. Slowly fry onion and garlic in butter until golden; add ham and squirrel, sprinkle with flour, and fry until brown. Heat claret and add with remaining ingredients. Simmer until tender.—C.R.B.B. (2).

STEINBUCK. STEINBOK

Lat. *Raphicerus tragulus*.

'This little antelope is found all over South Africa from the Cape to the Zambesi, except in the mountainous districts and tracks of very thick bush.'—F.C.S.

'They are dainty little things, and among the most graceful of all antelopes, their eyes being especially beautiful and lustrous. Their flesh forms a very desirable addition to a hunter's larder in the Low Country (Kahlamba-Libombo).'—F.V.K.

STEW, A
Fr. *Ragoût.*

STEW, TO
Fr. *Cuire à l'étuvée.* To cook with as little heat as possible as opposed to *roasting*, which is cooking with a fierce fire and in a minimum of time. Boiling point is 212° C. and stewing point about 170° C., which is sufficient for cooking food provided more time is allowed.

STOVIES
Ingredients: Potatoes, onion, fat, cooked meat, if liked, plenty of pepper and salt.

Method: This is a splendid way of using up the end of a roast. Cut off all the fat and melt it in a cast-iron pan. Put in as many potatoes as required, cut in thick slices. Add the onion and brown well. Lastly add any pieces of meat off the roast, cut in dice. Season well. Add a little water to prevent burning. Cook for about one hour.

(Usually served in the North-east with milk and oatcakes.)—C.N.

SUCKING PIG
Fr. *Porcelet.*

Roast Sucking Pig
I
Scarcely a recipe suitable for use in modern kitchenettes, but a goodly dish suitable for robust country appetites. The piglet must be thoroughly cleaned, particular care being given to the snout, ears and feet. Stuff with sage and onion stuffing, allowing plenty of salt and pepper. Truss and skewer. Make four parallel gashes, each about 3 in. long, through the skin on either side of the backbone. Put the piglet on a rack in a baking tin and brush over the whole surface with melted butter. Sprinkle well with salt and pepper, add two cupfuls of hot water to pan, and cover the roast with a well-buttered paper. Bake in a medium oven, basting frequently and allowing 25 to 30 minutes per pound in the usual way. When it has cooked for about 2 to 2½ hours, remove the paper and brush surface of sucking pig with thick cream. Dish up whole, placing a small red apple in mouth and cranberries in the eye sockets. Serve with sharp apple sauce and garnish dish with sprigs of watercress. Hand gravy separately.

Note.—If not already done by butcher be sure and scald then scrape entire surface of pig before stuffing and cooking. The liver may be added to stuffing, finely chopped and previously *sauté* in a little butter, and a tiny pinch of thyme or mixed herbs should

also perfume the stuffing. This is nice cold, though somewhat difficult to carve at table.—P.W.

II
(A South African recipe)
The sucking pig should not be more than about a month old, and to be eaten in perfection it should be cooked as soon as possible after being killed. Wipe the pig thoroughly, stuff it with green maize stuffing, then sew it up. Truss it like a hare, with the forelegs skewered back, and the hind legs drawn forward. Score it well with soft butter or Pastrine, sprinkle with salt and pepper, then wrap in greaseproof paper. Put into roasting pan in a hot oven of 450° F. and cook until crisp and brown, basting frequently. Remove paper, place on a hot dish, insert an apple or lemon in the mouth and garnish with parsley. Serve with apple or Cape gooseberry sauce, or fried pineapple slices.

Green Maize Stuffing. Cut green maize from the cobs, then put through a mincing machine. To two cups maize pulp add two cups stale breadcrumbs, one teaspoon salt, quarter teaspoon pepper, a few gratings nutmeg and two tablespoons finely chopped parsley. Add quarter cup melted butter, one well-beaten egg and enough cream or milk to moisten.

Apple Sauce. Peel and core four sour apples, then cut into quarters. Add just enough water to form steam, cook until tender together with two or three cloves and a squeeze of lemon juice. Rub through a sieve, add three tablespoons sugar, a pinch of salt and one tablespoon of butter. Reheat and serve.

SWEETBREADS
Although *Sweetbreads* (Fr. *Ris de veau* and *Ris d'agneau*) are always sold under that name alone, as if there were but one sort, there are two distinct white glands, taken from calves or lambs, covered by that name, the one placed immediately below the throat and the other, rounder in shape, lying nearer the heart, and very much the better from the gastronome's point of view. The first or 'throat' sweetbreads are elongated in form and neither so white nor so fat as the other sort, which should always be chosen by discriminating cooks.

Method of Preparation. Remove all hard tubes, blood, etc., and let them soak in cold salted water for three or four hours. Then simmer either in plain salted water or in a *court-bouillon*, according to whether they are to be served in a much-flavoured sauce or not. As soon as they are done – that is, in about two or three minutes only after the water reaches boiling point, they should be at once set in cold water, trimmed and set between two light boards having a small weight on top, to shape them nicely. When cold they may be sliced or used as wished. -—P.W.

Sweetbreads à l'ancienne

1 or 2 sets sweetbreads
Salt and pepper
Parsley
Butter
1 or 2 eggs
¼ cup cream
Bouillon
1 or 2 large spring onions
Flour
Dash of ground nutmeg
Lemon juice to taste

Blanch the sweetbreads in boiling water for a few minutes, then drain and put into cold water to harden a little. Drain, put in a casserole with about 1½ cups of good *bouillon*, salt, pepper, the onions and a branch or two of parsley. Add the butter, blended with a sufficiency of flour, and simmer for half an hour. Beat the eggs with the cream, add a pinch of chopped parsley and a dash of nutmeg. Remove pan from fire and blend the egg mixture carefully with hot sauce. Flavour with lemon juice and, if possible, add a sliced truffle. The sauce should be of the consistency of thick cream and must be poured over the sweetbreads after straining off all but the truffles.—P.W.

Croquettes of Sweetbread

Blanch, then cut into rather small dice. Cut some fresh mushrooms, after peeling, into pieces of equal size, as well as a slice of ham and, if possible, a truffle. Mix all the above with a cupful of very thick white sauce, well seasoned, adding two or three egg yolks. Cool the mixture, shape it and fry it as any other *Croquettes.*

Sweetbreads Jardinière

Blanch the sweetbreads, press them lightly, *sauté* them in butter after dividing into pieces or slicing. Add a tiny 'bouquet' and a few small onions. As brown sediment forms in pan, moisten with white wine mixed with *bouillon*, only about a tablespoon at a time. Mushrooms may be added as well as salt and pepper, of course. When done, toss a *jardinière* of vegetables in the gravy in pan, serving arranged around pieces of sweetbread.—P.W.

Calves' Sweetbreads larded, with stewed peas

Blanch, trim and place between two plates three 'heart' sweetbreads and press them slightly flat; they are then closely larded with strips of bacon in the usual manner. The sweetbreads must next be placed in a deep sautépan on a bed of thinly sliced carrot, celery and onions, with a garnished faggot of parsley and green onions placed in the centre, and covered with thin layers of fat bacon. Moisten with about a pint of good stock, place a round of buttered paper on the top, cover with the lid, and after having put the sweetbreads to boil on the stove-fire, remove them to the oven or on a moderate fire (in the latter case live embers of charcoal must be placed on the lid), and allow them to braise rather briskly for about 20 minutes – frequently basting them with their own liquor. When done, remove the lid and paper covering, and set them again in the oven, to dry the surface of the larding; glaze them nicely and dish them up on some stewed peas.—C.F.E.

Ris de Veau à la minute

Four slices of blanched sweetbread, brown in butter, season, add the juice of a lemon to butter in pan, a pinch of chopped parsley and pour this over slices when serving.

Breaded Sweetbread Slices

Cut into 1 in. thick slices. Dip in beaten egg, after seasoning on both sides, then in fine brown breadcrumbs mixed with a little flour. Press covering on with blade of a wide knife. *Sauté* in butter gently and serve, when browned on both sides, with a tomato sauce, a *Sauce Madère* or any other rich sauce, which is handed separately.

Sweetbreads Maryland

One medium-sized pair of sweetbreads. Sauce: one half cup mushrooms, two tablespoons butter, two tablespoons flour, one half teaspoon salt, a little white pepper and cayenne, one cup cream.

Soak sweetbreads in cold water 30 minutes. Drain and plunge into boiling water to which has been added a tablespoonful of lemon juice or vinegar, a bit of parsley and celery. Simmer 15 minutes and add salt before done. Drain and put in cold water, and remove tough parts and skin. Then put in sauce. (*Miss Louisa Ogle Thomas, Baltimore.*)—F.P.S.

Savoury Sweetbreads

Ingredients: 1½ lb. lambs' sweetbreads, 2 oz. butter, two level dessertspoons cornflour (or sufficient to thicken), a little milk, a small carrot and onion cut up roughly, a bayleaf, and a piece of mace, salt and pepper to flavour.

Method: Soak sweetbreads in cold water with teaspoonful of salt for one hour. Drain and put on to boil with fresh cold water and squeeze of lemon juice. Boil for half an hour, then lift out sweetbreads and clean thoroughly, breaking them up in small pieces. Melt butter in double saucepan and add sweetbreads. Place carrot and onion in small bag of muslin and put in pan with sweetbreads and cook slowly for one hour. Remove muslin bag and contents and add cornflour and milk to thicken, and salt and pepper to flavour. Cook for a further 10 minutes and then dish on a hot plate.—C.N.

Sweetbread Soufflé
Method: Line a mould with crisp pastry. Boil the sweetbread in milk, and with the milk in which they have been boiled make soufflé mixture. Cut the sweetbreads into small pieces and add some chopped mushrooms. Add these to *soufflé* mixture, put into the mould and bake in hot oven for 10 minutes. —C.N.

TAMALE
A Mexican dish, which may be prepared in a number of different ways, the foundation of which, however, always is some sort of minced meat mixed with crushed maize, and the outstanding seasoning of which is one of red peppers.

Tamale Pie
½ cup oil or other shortening
1 lb. ground steak
1 lb. lean pork (cut in small pieces)
2 large onions
1 can yellow cornmeal
1 garlic clove
2 eggs
2 cups milk
1 large can tomatoes
1 cup ripe olives (whole)

Fry in the shortening ground steak and pork with onions and garlic until slightly brown. Beat eggs; add milk, tomatoes, cornmeal and olives. Mix with meat mixture, place in greased baking dish and bake in slow oven for one hour. (*Mrs. Margaret Berr, Tucson, Arizona*, in SP.M.)

TOAD-IN-THE-HOLE
Although legend attributes considerable age to this rather dull partnership of meat and batter, we have not noticed any mention of it in cook-books prior to Mrs. Beeton, whose recipe runs:

Toad-in-the-Hole
1 lb. steak cut up small
4 oz. flour
½ pint milk
1 egg
Salt
Dripping

Mix the flour, milk, egg and a little salt into a smooth batter. Put into a Yorkshire pudding tin sufficient dripping to form a thin layer when melted, pour in about quarter of the batter and bake till set. Then add the meat, season it with salt and pepper, pour in the remainder of the batter, bake quickly until it has risen and set, and then cook more slowly until sufficiently cooked. Serve in squares arranged neatly overlapping each other on a hot dish.
Time to bake, about one hour.—B.

Many modern cooks improve on this by adding to the steak an equal quantity of cut up ox kidney, but unfortunately the generality of them save themselves trouble and coarsen the flavour by substituting sausages for other meat, achieving thereby a result barely fit to lay before hungry urchins at a grammar school. Another suggestion is to substitute for the steak crisp curls of fried bacon.

TOPI
Lat. *Damaliscus Korrigum*. An Antelope of Eastern Central Africa remarkable for the water-silk appearance of its glossy, purplish-brown coat. 'The Topi, when in good condition (and nearly every one I shot in this country – *Kéré* – was fat), furnishes splendid meat, and is one of the very best of the larger antelopes for the table; thus resembling, in this respect as well as in appearance, the "bastard hartebeeste" (though, for the matter of that, all the hartebeestes are good eating).'—A.H.N., p. 290.

TOURNEDOS
A French culinary name for small steaks cut from the fillet.

Tournedos Chasseur
Individual tournedos of beef
1 or 2 shallots
Salt and pepper
2 or 3 tablespoons good stock
1 scanty teaspoon potato flour
Butter
3 or 4 fresh mushrooms
1 small glass white wine
1 teaspoon tomato *purée*
Chopped parsley

Pan-fry the *tournedos* and keep hot. Fry chopped shallots and mushrooms in butter, without colouring. Moisten with wine, simmer to reduce a little, then add stock, previously blended with potato flour (*fécule*) and tomato *purée*. Season well, roll the *tournedos* in this sauce, without allowing to cook longer, and serve at once, sprinkling with finely-chopped parsley.—P.W.

Tournedos Dauphinoise

½ lb. fresh mushrooms
1 dessertspoon flour
Individual tornedos
Fried croûtons
2 tablespoons butter
½ cup thick cream
Salt and pepper

First prepare the mushrooms *à la crème*. Slice, after peeling and *sauté* in butter, until all liquid has evaporated and butter is clear; then reduce heat, add the cream previously blended with the flour, season well and keep hot while the *tournedos* are being grilled. Use their drippings as gravy to make the sauce. To serve, turn the mushroom *purée* into a hot dish, add as many fried *croûtons* as there are *tournedos*, placing one *tournedos* on each *croûton*; pour the gravy or sauce over them and serve hot.—P.W.

Tournedos Rossini

Thick, tender *tournedos*
Milk
Salt and pepper
Croûtons
Small pieces *foie gras*
Flour
A little port wine
Slices of truffle
Butter

This is a delicious way of serving *tournedos* for festive occasions. Season and grill in the usual way the required number of *tournedos*, then place upon each one a thin slice of *foie gras* previously dipped, first in milk, then in flour, and gently *sauté* in butter for a minute or two. Add to meat drippings and gravy as much port wine as you fancy, simmering for a while gently, with the slices of truffle. Serve each *tournedos* on a hot fried *croûton*, crowned with its slice of *foie gras*, and this, in turn, with a slice of truffle. Surround with gravy and serve at once.—P.W.

Some other favourite modes of serving *Tournedos*, according to the *Cuisine Classique*, etc.

Abrantès: Cooked in olive oil, garnished with aubergines, seasoned with paprika.

Archiduc: Cooked in butter, served on *galettes* of *pommes duchesse*, garnished with truffles, *croquettes* of calf's brains, sauced with sherry and cream.

A la béarnaise, grilled and served with a *sauce béarnaise*, and *pommes de terre château*.

A la bordelaise: Grilled, dressed on a slice of marrowfat (poached and drained) with a pinch of chopped parsley in the centre; *sauce bordelaise* served at the same time.

Henri IV: Cooked in butter and served on *croûtons* of fried bread, and on each *tournedos* a small artichoke bottom (boiled and drained), filled with a thick *sauce béarnaise* with a slice of black truffle on top; garnish with *pommes noisettes*.

Masséna: Grilled and then dressed on artichoke bottoms, with a slice of poached marrow fat on each *tournedos*, a sprinkling of finely-chopped parsley on the marrow fat.

A la portugaise: Cooked in butter and olive oil; garnished with very small stuffed tomatoes and *pommes de terre château*.

TRIPE

The first and second stomachs of a ruminant, more particularly of the ox, prepared as food for man. The first stomach is smooth and plain, the second is honeycombed.

Tripe à la Mode de Caen

4 lb. tripe and 2 cow heels or
    4 calves' feet
8 leeks
4 large carrots
6 large onions
6 cloves
4 bayleaves
4 sprigs thyme
2 pints cider or dry white wine
1 port glass of brandy

The tripe and cow heels or calves' feet are cut up in pieces, about 1 in. square, and put in a pan (earthenware, if possible) with the following seasoning: salt, pepper, thyme, bayleaves, parsley stalks, large quantity of onions stuck with cloves, large quantity of carrots and a few leeks, plus enough liquid (cider preferably, or dry white wine and a little water) and a small proportion of brandy, and the whole is allowed to simmer very slowly for at least 10 hours, with lid on.

Tripe must be served boiling hot, with chopped parsley.—H.S.

Braised Tripe

1 lb. cooked tripe; 2 oz. lard or oil; a few drops cooking sherry; 2 fresh mushrooms; 1 clove garlic; 1 tablespoon Soya bean sauce, Bovril or Marmite; 2 onions.

Cut tripe into strips; fry lightly for a minute in 2 oz. lard or oil with cut-up onions and garlic. Add a few drops of sherry, half pint water, half tablespoon Soya bean sauce or substitute; one or two fresh tomatoes and simmer for half an hour.—CH.C.

Tripe à la Lyonnaise

Cook your tripe well in water with salt, peppercorns, thyme, bayleaf, an onion stuck with cloves, two or three carrots and a piece of celery. When it is done, drain it and cut it into thickish strips. Fry some onions in butter, and when they are well cooked and golden-brown, add the strips of tripe. Cook together for a few minutes, and as they are served, sprinkle over a drop of vinegar and a good pinch of chopped parsley. It should be served very hot indeed.—AMBROSE HEATH in *Wine and Food*, IV, p. 23.

Tripe and Onions
1 lb. dressed tripe
1 or 2 onions
1 dessertspoonful flour

Cut the tripe into square pieces. Place in a pot and cover with cold water. Bring to the boil and throw away the water. Add to the tripe in the pot half pint milk and the same quantity of water, sliced onions, salt and pepper. Simmer for three hours and then thicken with flour mixed in a little milk and strained into the pot. Bring to the boil again, taste and add more pepper and salt if required and serve hot.

Broiled Tripe à la Parker
9 oz. portion honeycomb tripe
Flour
Oil
Breadcrumbs
Salt and pepper

Dry tripe well, season with salt and pepper, dredge in flour, dip in oil, then in breadcrumbs. Broil on both sides for about four to five minutes until golden brown. Butter well. Serve with lemon and fresh fried egg plant.—P.H.B.

Tripe Whitebait
Wash the tripe thoroughly in two or three waters till it is quite sweet, then wash in weak salt water. Cut the tripe in pieces the size of good whitebait. Lay each piece apart on a cloth to dry. Then shake them gently on to another cloth and dust them carefully with very fine flour.

Heat some fat till it smokes, then place the pieces of tripe separately in a frying basket and plunge them into the fat to cook for about one to two minutes. Turn them on to a sieve and continue till all the pieces are cooked.

Reheat the fat till smoke rises. All the pieces are now put together and reheated in the frying basket for a moment to crisp and brown them.

Drain well, first by shaking the basket over the fat and then tossing them gently on paper. Sprinkle with salt and cayenne or Nepal pepper and serve brown bread and butter and lemon.—D.T.

UDDER
'Mr. Creed and I to the "Leg" in King Street, to dinner, where he and I and my Wife had a good udder to dinner.'—*Pepys*, Oct. 11th, 1660.

Cow's Udder
Seeth it well, and when it is well sodden, cut it into slices, and garnish your entrées with it, or passe it in the panne with fine herbs, and chiboll whole; season all well, and soake it with the best of your broths, so that it be of a sharp tast, and the sauce well thickned, then serve.—*La Va.*

Udder of Roebuck
After you have blanced it well in water, cut it into slices, and fry it with juice of lemon, or seeth it with some ragoust. After it is fryed, or soft, mince it with lard, as that of the Beatills. Then serve it with the juice of lemon.—*La Va.*

UMBLES
The edible entrails of any animal, but more particularly of a deer, which used to be made into a pie: *Umbles Pie* was also called *Humble Pie* or *Lumber Pie*.

A Lumber Pye
Take the Umbles of deer, cut them in thin slices, season them with salt, pepper, nutmeg, and ginger; lay layings of them with inter-larden bacon, sliced dates, raisins and currants; and when it is going into the oven, pour into it, gravy, claret, and butter, beaten up together pretty warm.—W.D.W.

'I having some venison given me a day or two ago; and so I had a shoulder roasted, another baked, and the umbles baked in a pie, and all very well done.' (*Pepys*, 5th July, 1662).

'Mrs Turner came in, and did bring us an umble pie hot out of her oven, extraordinary good.' (*Pepys*, 8th July, 1663).

VEAL
Veal sold in England is not in any way comparable to Continental 'veau' or 'kalb', the reason being that it is not killed until too old and is already grass fed, whereas, to be perfect, it should be exclusively milk-fed.

The flesh should be *white*, not pink or even reddish, as is too often the case. It should look rather moist and the fat should be abundant and pure white. The outer skin must not be dry nor must the flesh be flabby or clammy to the touch.

'And as for excellent good Beef and Veale, there is no countrie in the world that can parallel, farre less exceed our beeves and veale here in England, whatsoever some talke of Hungary and Poland'.—(*Hart. The Diet of the Diseased*. 1633, p. 73).

In culinary French, *Veau* is used for both *Calf* and *Veal* and the chief cuts, with their English equivalents, are as follows:

Carré de veau: Best end of the loin, including kidneys.

Collet de veau: Neck of veal.

Côte de veau: Veal cutlet; chop end of the loin.

Côtelette de veau: Best end of the neck of veal.

Cuisse or *Cuissot de Veau*: Leg of veal.

Épaule de veau: Shoulder of veal.

Escalope de veau: Veal collop.

Filet de veau: Fillet of veal.

Jarret de veau: Knuckle of veal.

Longe de veau: Top part of the loin of veal.

Médaillon de veau. Veal Tournedos.

Noix de veau: Lengthwise cut of the chump end of the loin.

Pied de veau: Calf's foot.

Poitrine de veau: Breast of veal.

Quasi de veau: Part of the loin between the tail and the kidneys.

Ris de veau: Calf's sweetbreads.

Rognon de veau: Veal kidney.

Rouelle de veau: Fillet of veal cut across the chump end of the loin.

Tendrons de veau: Flat tails and ribs.

Tête de veau: Calf's head.

Breast of Veal Stewed

2 lb. breast of veal
2 carrots
2 onions
1 turnip

Put the veal into a saucepan with just enough cold water to cover it. Bring to the boil, removing all scum as it rises. Add vegetables cut in pieces; season with pepper and salt. Cover the pot closely and simmer gently for three hours. Serve the meat with a parsley sauce and save the broth for soups.

Veau en Casserole or Cocotte

Choose a piece of fillet or loin of veal and tie it up in a neat shape. Melt a couple of tablespoons of good butter in the pan, without allowing it to sizzle. Add the piece of veal, neatly tied into shape, and the bones, if any. Brown gently on all sides, add salt, cover closely and cook rather slowly on a low heat, turning now and then carefully and adding to the glazed gravy in the bottom of pan a few drops of water now and then. When done (and 25 to 30 minutes per lb. must be allowed for cooking large joints of veal) remove lid from pan to evaporate water and crisp up outer surface of joint. A few small onions and button mushrooms may be added about half an hour before veal is done. If liked, use white wine, or white wine and water in equal parts to remove glaze from bottom and sides of pan as meat cooks.—P.W.

Breaded Veal Chops

Egg and breadcrumb the veal chops, brown them in butter, reduce heat and cook slowly, turning to brown both surfaces. Season and serve when done with tomato sauce.

Côtes de veau en Papillotes

4 veal chops
Butter
4 or 5 ripe tomatoes
Salt and pepper
Flour
8 small slices York ham
4 or 5 mushrooms

Cut off ends of projecting bone on each chop and trim off excess fat. Roll each chop lightly in salted flour and brown it in melted butter, half-cooking it only. The slices of ham must be of the same shape and size as the chops. Peel the tomatoes, cut up and cook, with a little butter, salt and pepper, to a thick paste, which must be pressed through a sieve. Chop the mushrooms very finely, *sauté* them also in butter and add to tomato *purée*. Now prepare the dish thus: Take one slice of ham, on this spread a goodly layer of the tomato-mushroom *purée*, and on it, lay a chop; spread some more of the same *purée* on the chop and then, a second slice of ham. Press all together and roll each prepared chop up neatly and securely in sheets of strong white paper. Place these little parcels in a hot oven for 10 minutes and, to be correct, serve in the papers or papillotes. The only trouble about this is the fact that not only is it practically impossible to extricate the chops without using the fingers but, further, one never quite knows what to do with the papers, so it is best to remove them just before sending to table.—P.W.

Savoury Veal Cutlets

3 peeled onions
1 teaspoon salt
1 veal cutlet (about 1½ in. thick)
¾ cup sour cream
¼ cup flour
2 tablespoons fat
Paprika to taste

Slice onion and brown in skillet with fat. Flour cutlet and brown thoroughly in skillet. Flavour with salt, paprika and add sour cream. Cover and place over very low heat and allow to simmer gently for about an hour, or until tender, turning cutlet once.—(From *Mrs Charles E. Copeland, Jackson Heights*. L.I. in Sp.M.).

Escalopes de Veau au Beurre d'Anchois

Lightly flour some thinly cut steaks, or *escalopes* to give them proper culinary appellation, then fry gently in butter over a fairly quick heat to brown floured surface, instead of making a sticky mess of it. They should, when cut for individual servings, take no more than from six to eight minutes to cook through and brown on both sides. Season and add to brown glazed gravy and butter in pan a small quantity of either plain hot water or mixed white wine and hot water, stirring to convert sediment into brown gravy. Pour this over meat when serving. In this particular recipe, each steak, after being cooked as described, must be served on a fried *croûton* spread with anchovy butter, which is made by pounding together a fillet or two of anchovy, unsalted somewhat, and firm, fresh butter.—p.w.

Escalopes aux Olives Noires

Prepare and cook *escalopes* as indicated in preceding recipe. Remove stones from ripe black olives, roughly chopped and set on top of each serving before pouring gravy over them.

Escalopes à la Sauce Tomate

Prepare and cook *escalopes* as in the two preceding recipes. Mix with the gravy in pan a tablespoonful of either fresh or tinned tomato *purée*.

Escalopes Magyare

Cook as before, remove from pan, keep hot. Brown four or five chopped shallots in same pan with butter and gravy. Add a good strong pinch of paprika and two tablespoons of thick cream. Boil up once and pour over meat when serving.

Escalopes de veau à la Royale
(A recipe from Dijon)

Brown in a little hot olive oil very thin slices of veal *escalopes* together with sliced onions. Turn them frequently so that they will brown well on each side. Add salt, pepper and about four tablespoons of water to make the gravy. When the *escalopes* are cooked, remove and keep hot. In the meanwhile make the sauce with the gravy mentioned, and half a cup thick cream mixed with two beaten egg yolks, two tablespoons of brandy and two tablespoons of port. Mix this well, allow it to cook gently over a low flame to thicken slightly, pour back on the *escalopes* and heat until it bubbles again. Serve on large fried bread *croûtons* which have been prepared in advance.—cl.k.

Escalopes de Veau Panées
(Wiener Schnitzel)

Slices of veal from leg
Beaten egg
Salt and pepper
Fine brown breadcrumbs

Have the *escalopes* cut thin, trim and shape, after beating them evenly flat. Season with salt and pepper. Dip first in flour and then in beaten egg and then in breadcrumbs, coating

each piece of meat completely and evenly. Brown gently in plenty of good butter, turning once or twice with two spoons to avoid letting gravy run out. Serve when brown, with the strained butter from pan. Garnish with slices of lemon, or with a thin slice of lemon surmounted by a slice of hard-boiled egg, which has a coiled anchovy on it and a few capers.

Fillets of Veal Talleyrand

1½ lb. fillet of veal
1 shallot
1 gill rich white sauce
Salt and pepper
4 tablespoons butter
4 mushrooms
2 egg yolks
Lemon juice

Cut the meat into about eight fillets or steaks, flatten them out nicely, then brown them lightly in heated butter, seasoning to taste with salt and pepper. They must be very lightly coloured, if at all. Remove meat and keep hot. Chop the shallot and the mushrooms, first browning the former in the hot butter then, when nearly done, adding the mushrooms, cooking gently together until done. Strain off butter. Heat the white sauce, stir in the shallot and mushrooms, remove pan from fire and beat in the egg yolks. Season with salt, pepper and lemon juice as wished, adding also, if required, a small pinch of chopped parsley. Reheat carefully, taking care the sauce does not boil. Serve the fillets of veal on a bed of mashed potatoes and pour sauce over the meat. —p.w.

Fricandeau de Veau

2 or 3 lb. veal
Salt and pepper
Several carrots
A *bouquet-garni*
Large lardons of larding bacon
Thin slice fresh pork fat
Several onions
2 cups good meat stock

The best joint for this is what is known to French butchers as 'la noix', or the fillet. Season the *lardons* with salt and pepper and lard the joint. Wrap the joint up entirely in the thin slice of fresh pork fat (*barde de lard*) and place it in a heavy iron or earthenware braising-pan, with the vegetables and the *bouquet*, adding salt, pepper and the stock. Cook gently, keeping the pot covered, from three to four hours, then remove covering from meat and place it in another braising-pan, adding the fat and gravy from first pan. Increase heat, cook uncovered, and turn joint frequently to 'dry out'. This will leave in pan some clear fat, which may be skimmed off and kept for cooking other things. Serve with its own gravy and with a *purée* of fresh sorrel or spinach, slicing the meat crossways before sending to table.—P.W.

Jellied Veal à la Juivre

2 lb. shank leg of veal
1 small carrot
1 small onion
Salt and pepper
1 stalk celery
2 quarts water

Season meat with salt and pepper then place it in the water, with the vegetables. Boil very slowly until meat falls from bones. Strain the liquid, remove all bones, cut meat and vegetables into small, even-shaped pieces. Boil broth until reduced to half its bulk, pour it over the meat and vegetables. Turn into a mould, rinsed out with cold water, and set to harden, stirring while still liquid to prevent meat from sinking to bottom of mould. Cut into slices and serve with salad.—P.W.

Knuckle of Veal Stewed

3 lb. knuckle of veal
1 small turnip
1 stick celery
2 small carrots
1 onion
1½ oz. rice

Let the knuckle be cut in two or three pieces; put in a deep pan and add just enough boiling water to cover the meat. Boil, and remove the scum as it rises. Then add the vegetables, pepper and salt and a *bouquet-garni*. Simmer gently for two hours. Then add the rice and simmer for half or three-quarters of an hour longer. Take meat out of the pan and serve hot with parsley sauce and boiled gammon. Strain the liquid in which the veal was cooked and save it for soups.

Jarret de Veau Ménagère

The meaty part of a knuckle of veal
1 or 2 onions
1 shallot
1 glass white wine
Salt and pepper
Rashers of bacon
1 clove garlic
4 or 5 carrots
2 cups stock
Tomato purée
Butter

Have the meaty or upper part of knuckle cut into a thick slice. Brown on both sides in butter, remove from pan. Cut the bacon into dice and brown these in same fat, with the onions and sliced carrots, adding the minced shallot and garlic. When all ingredi-

ents are nicely browned, add meat, season well and moisten with wine, stock and tomato *purée*, the latter being blended previously with the other liquids. Cover closely and simmer gently for a couple of hours, turning once in a while. Remove lid, increase heat somewhat to dry out moisture until the fat in pan is clear. Remove meat and carrots, skim off excess fat and add more stock or water to gravy in pan, stirring well to remove all sediment. Pour over meat when serving. More carrots may be added, if wished, when meat is half-cooked, and they will serve as a substantial garnish.—P.W.

Veal Loaf

Take a cold fillet of veal, and (omitting the fat and skin) mince the meat as fine as possible. Mix with it ¼ lb. of the fattest part of a cold ham, also chopped small. Add a teacupful of grated breadcrumbs; a grated nutmeg; half a dozen blades of mace, powdered; the grated yellow rind of a lemon; and two beaten eggs; season with a saltspoon of salt, and half a saltspoon of cayenne. Mix the whole well together, and make it into the form of a loaf. Then glaze it over with beaten yolk of egg; and strew the surface evenly, all over, with bread raspings, or with pounded biscuit. Set the dish into a dutch-oven, and bake it half an hour, or till hot all through. Have ready a gravy made of the trimmings of the veal, stewed in some of the gravy that was left when the fillet was roasted the day before. When sufficiently cooked, take out the meat, and thicken the gravy with beaten yolk of egg, stirred in about three minutes before you take it from the fire.

Send the veal loaf to table in a deep dish, with the gravy poured round it.—L.N.R.C.

Jellied Veal Loaf

4 lb. knuckle of veal
1 small *bouquet-garni*
1 tablespoon chopped parsley
1 onion
Salt and pepper
4 hard-boiled eggs

Cook knuckle as directed in previous recipe, adding *bouquet* and onion to water. When meat falls from bones, remove it with care and chop it rather finely. Season rather highly. Add parsley. Garnish bottom of a flat round, square or oval mould with the slices of egg. Cover with meat. Reduce the broth, by fast boiling, to half its original bulk and pour it over the meat. Lay a plate or a small board on top, when liquid begins to harden, with a small weight to press contents of mould well down. Chill and serve sliced with salad.—P.W.

Loin of Veal, Braised

Sprinkle with pepper and salt and a little flour. Brown the whole of the joint in hot butter, turning it about continuously to avoid burning. Then add a little stock or water and two or three onions. Put a closely fitting lid on and cook slowly until the meat is quite tender, adding a little more stock or water whenever needed. When cooked, take the joint out of the pan and thicken the stock left in it with a little flour diluted with water.

Loin of Veal, Roast

Remove bone and fill cavity with veal forcemeat, tying the joint securely. Lay some thin strips of salt pork or some rashers of fat bacon on top of the joint. Season with pepper and salt. Add a little butter or dripping and a cupful of water in the pan. Bake in the oven as you would roast beef, basting frequently.

The fillet, shoulder or breast of veal may be roast in the same way.

Veau Marengo

2 lb. lean breast of veal
½ lb. onions
2 tablespoons flour
3 tablespoons olive oil
1 lb. ripe tomatoes
½ lb. mushrooms
2 cups *bouillon*
Salt and pepper
1 cup dry white wine

Heat the olive oil and brown in it the cut up meat, then add the chopped onion, browning a little also with meat. Sprinkle with flour, browning that too, then moisten with the mixed wine and *bouillon* or stock. Season well. Add the sliced mushrooms and the tomatoes, previously reduced to a pulp by slow cooking after peeling. Cover pan closely and allow contents to simmer gently for at least an hour and a half. Some gourmets add one grated clove of garlic.—P.W.

Veau Mimosa

1 or 2 lb. breast of veal
Flour
Port wine
Hard-boiled eggs
Butter
Hot water or *bouillon*
Chopped tarragon
Chopped parsley
Salt and pepper

Cut the meat into small, neat pieces, and brown well in the butter. Then sprinkle in a tablespoon or so of flour, brown this too and moisten with about two cups of stock, *bouillon* or hot water and a small wineglass of port. Season with salt and pepper, cover, and cook gently until meat is tender. Before serving add a scanty tablespoonful of chopped fresh tarragon leaves. Chop two hard-boiled eggs coarsely and use, with a little parsley, to sprinkle entire surface of the meat when sending to the table. Skim excess fat from gravy and serve around meat.—P.W.

Veal Olives
(Old English Recipe)

Thin veal steaks
Thin rashers of bacon
Grated lemon peel
Butter
1 teaspoon lemon pickle
½ teaspoon anchovy essence
Salt
1 egg yolk
Breadcrumbs
Chopped parsley
2 cups *consommé* or gravy
1 teaspoon walnut catsup
Dusting cayenne pepper
Flour

Prepare the meat as for *escalopes* and flatten each steak nicely, trimming to even shapes. Brush over with egg yolk. Lay a very thin rasher of bacon on top of each, strew over a few breadcrumbs, a little lemon peel and chopped parsley. Tie each olive up securely and put them into a baking tin, adding butter as for a joint, salt and pepper. Add to the tin the *consommé* (gravy, if rich, is better still), the lemon pickle, catsup, anchovy essence and as much cayenne as you wish. Dredge all over lightly with flour and cook until brown, basting with the seasoned gravy. Strain gravy over olives to serve. —P.W.

Olives of Veal

For to make them, take some veale, cut it into small slices, and beat them well with the knife halft, mince all kinds of herbs, beef, mutton suet and a little lard, and when they are well seasoned, and allayed with raw eggs, roull them among those slices of flesh, for to seeth them in an earthen or tourte pan; when they are sodden serve them with their sauce.—*La Va.*

Ragoût de Veau aux Petits Pois

2 lb. breast of veal
2 cups water or stock
2 or 3 onions
Flour
Salt and pepper
Green peas

Cut up the veal and brown in butter. Sprinkle lightly with flour when nicely coloured, and moisten with water or stock. Season well and add onions. Cover and simmer for at least one hour, then add freshly-shelled peas, cover and finish cooking until meat is tender.—P.W.

499

Veau à la Reboux

A square piece of nicely-larded veal
French mustard
Thick white sauce (*Béchamel*)
1 or 2 egg whites
Butter
Salt and pepper
Fresh mushrooms
Brown breadcrumbs

This is, when prepared with art and knowledge, a truly royal dish worthy of the gourmet whose name it bears. Select a piece of
lean, tender, white, milk-fed veal, as square
as possible and weighing not less than a
couple of pounds. Lard it either with ham or
the usual larding bacon fat. Blend to a paste
with firm butter some French mustard of
any of the following kinds 'Ravigote', or
'Estragon' or, again 'Aux Fines Herbes'.
Use a generous amount of this mustard without any fear that it may be too much. Spread
this mixture thickly on all surfaces of the
piece of veal, adding a good sprinkling of
salt and pepper. This mixture must be
spread on the joint both before placing in
the oven, and again when the meat is half
cooked. Roast as usual

Now take some good, rich and very thick
Béchamel sauce. Add to it the gravy from the
roast veal as well as the mushrooms, cut into
pieces no larger than green peas, then lightly
sauté in butter. Cut the joint into three or
four slices and spread each with the mush-
room-*Béchamel*. Place one slice on top of the
other giving the joint its original shape.
Beat the egg white or whites very stiffly and
incorporate them with about a cupful of the
Béchamel, set aside for this purpose. Season a
little if necessary with salt and pepper.
Spread this mixture thickly all over the re-
constituted joint, sprinkle entire surface with
nice fine brown breadcrumbs and replace in
the oven for a few minutes, until the surface
forms a brown crust. Serve at once ... com-
pliments should follow!—P.W.

Roast Veal
(English Style)

3 lb. fillet or loin veal
Salt and pepper
Rashers of bacon
Butter or dripping
Veal forcemeat

Remove bone and fill cavity with forcemeat, tying the joint into a neat round,
fastening it securely. Lay strips of salt pork,
cut thin, or rashers of fat bacon on top of
meat. Add butter or dripping, salt and
pepper and a little water to pan. Bake as beef
with the difference that the oven should not
be quite so hot. Baste very frequently when
cooking. Serve with quarters of emon,
crisp rolls of bacon or, if preferred, a piece

of boiled pickled pork and plenty of good
gravy.

Part of the shoulder, the breast or the loin
may be used instead of the fillet, if desired.
—P.W.

Roast Veal
(French Style)

If the selected joint be all lean, such as the
fillet, it is generally larded as is *Boeuf à la
Mode* (q.v.) and cooked in an iron cocotte or
a copper pan, slowly. In any event, two
rules must be borne in mind. Veal is a much
drier meat than beef, mutton or pork, so
that some form of fat should be added;
furthermore, it must cook gently or it will
be tough and stringy, and it must be very
frequently turned or basted while cooking.

Place in a pan, when roasting, after larding evenly through the entire thickness of
the joint. Spread generously with butter,
sprinkle with salt, add a very little water to
pan, and roast in a moderate oven, basting
every few minutes and turning often, but
without piercing meat with the fork.—P.W.

Rôti de Veau en Casserole

Take a small veal roast, or a good piece of
the lower part of the leg with the bone.
Brown it in butter, or other good fat, in an
iron or earthen covered pot. Add salt and
pepper, a little water, several onions, some
parsley and a bayleaf. From time to time if
necessary add a little more water and cook,
well covered, until tender. Serve in a not-
too-shallow dish with the natural juice or
gravy.—CL.K.

Rouelle de Veau Bourgeoise

1 thick slice leg of veal
2 thick rashers bacon
Small button onions
1 *bouquet-garni*
2 cups *bouillon*
Butter
Salt and pepper
Young whole carrots
Half a calf's foot
1 glass cognac

Trim the slice of meat neatly and brown
gently in butter to which the bacon, cut into
dice, has been added. Season well with salt
and pepper when brown. Add the vegetables, the *bouquet* and the calf's foot.
Moisten with the *bouillon* and the cognac
(white wine may be substituted) and cook
very gently for a couple of hours, frequently
basting the meat and turning it. When it is
done and golden-brown, serve, after skimming off excess fat, with its delicious gravy,
the calf's-foot, boned, and the vegetables. If
the vegetables are very young and tender,
use older ones, cut into pieces, to flavour
gravy while meat is cooking, and remove

them when half done, substituting the young carrots and onions which will thus retain their shape.—P.W.

VEAL LEFT-OVERS
Carnuffs
½ lb. cooked veal
Chopped parsley
½ cup stock or gravy
¼ lb. ham
1 cup white sauce
2 eggs
Salt and pepper

Mince the veal finely with the ham – or use tongue, if preferred. Add about a dessertspoon of chopped parsley and season well. Heat the stock or gravy, then add the meat. When hot, remove from fire and add beaten eggs. Blend mixture well and use to fill some small well-buttered moulds. Cover them with buttered paper and steam for an hour. Serve with sauce.—P.W.

Veau à l'Italienne
¼ lb. breadcrumbs
¼ lb. ham
2 eggs
Salt and pepper
1 lb. cooked veal
Grated peel of half a lemon
6 oz. macaroni
2 or 3 tablespoons stock

Mince ham with veal finely, season well, adding breadcrumbs and lemon peel. Bind to a thick paste with stock and beaten eggs. Boil the macaroni (or spaghetti) in salted water until tender. Drain well. Butter a mould well, line with the macaroni, fill centre with meat mixture and cover with more macaroni, enclosing meat. Cover with a buttered paper and steam from 30 to 45 minutes. Turn out to serve, covering with hot tomato sauce and hand-grated Parmesan, mixed or not with grated Gruyère.—P.W.

Timbales of Veal
1½ cups minced cooked veal
¼ cup thick cream
Salt, paprika or pepper
1 cup white sauce
3 egg yolks
⅔ cup white wine
3 egg whites
1 truffle

Mince veal very finely, then pound in a mortar, adding gradually the egg yolks, cream, wine and seasoning. Beat egg whites very stiffly and fold into mixture. Fill buttered moulds with the above, after filling them one-quarter full with the sauce, to which the chopped truffle has been added. Steam and serve as soon as the white sauce begins running down the sides of the moulds or timbales.—P.W.

A Dunelm of Cold Veal or Fowl
Stew a few small mushrooms in their own liquor and a bit of butter, a quarter of an hour; mince them very small and add them with their liquor to minced veal, with also a little pepper and salt, some cream, and a bit of butter rubbed in less than half a teaspoonful of flour. Simmer three or four minutes and serve on thin sippets of bread.—M.E.R.

VENISON
(See also *Deer*). The name used to apply to the flesh of any sort of game or wild beast hunted for food, but it is now restricted to the flesh of any kind of *Deer*. The flesh of the male, or buck, is of better flavour than that of the doe, but neither the one nor the other should be over three years old: they are at their best from eighteen months to two years. All venison is by nature dry and inclined to be tough, two faults which it is easy to correct, the first by larding the meat before cooking, and the other by hanging, first, and marinating after it has been hanging in a cool and airy place from 12 to 21 days, according to the temperature prevailing at the time, provided the animal has been well shot or killed and has not suffered in transit from kill to larder. The best parts of the deer are the haunch, the fillet, the loin and the chops.

Faune of a Hinde
Before it is mortified too much, dresse it very neatly, truss it up, take off some skirts which are on it and look like slime, then blanche it on the fire for to stick it, so that it be not too much blanched, because it would put you to too much trouble to lard it; take care also least you burn the head, or least the hare of it become black, spit it, and wrap the head with butterd paper. When it is rosted, serve it with a *Poivrade*.—*La Va*.

Legs of Roebuck, or Wild Goat
They may be done as the shoulder of Wildboare, as also the loyne and the shoulders; or else after you have larded them with great lard, you may passe them in the panne likewise with some lard and flowre, after which you shall seeth them with broth, and shall thicken the sauce alike.—*La Va*.

Fillet of Roebuck
After you have stuck it, rost it wrapped up in butter'd paper, after it is rosted, serve it with a poivrade.—*La Va*.

Loine of Stagge
Take off all the skinnes, stick it, and spit it, serve it with a poivrade.

The fillet is done up like the loyn, with poivrade.

The loins of Roebuck is also done the same way.—*La Va*.

Venison Chops with Purée of Chestnuts

Neatly trim and flatten six venison chops, season all over with a teaspoon salt and half ditto of pepper.

Thoroughly heat a tablespoon of melted butter in a *sautoire* and add chops one beside another, cook for five minutes on each side, dress a *purée* of chestnuts on a hot dish in a pyramid and arrange chops around. Remove fat from pan, add three tablespoons red currant jelly and mix until thoroughly melted; pour in a gill of tomato sauce, mix well, boil for two minutes, pour sauce over chops and serve.—A.F.

Filet de Chevreuil

Soak venison fillet for 48 hours in a *marinade* of wine, onions, spices and herbs to taste. Roast it or broil it 20 minutes to the pound, basting constantly with melted butter mixed with some of the *marinade*. Reduce the remaining *marinade* on very hot fire, and add it to the gravy. Bind with yolks of eggs and a few spoonfuls of good mustard. (From NOEL COWARD in *Spécialities de la Maison*).

Virginia or White-tailed Deer

'While a few persons cannot eat it, and other dislike it, to say the least, a majority of mankind admire it as a food, and others esteem it above all other flesh. It is dark colored, is fine grained, and has a flavor peculiarly its own. When cooked without accessories it is dryer than beef, but it is tenderer, *ceteris paribus*. This venison is tender and nourishing, and of good flavor, even in the summer time, when the animal is always poor, though of course far inferior to the luscious feast afforded by the fat buck just at the commencement of the rut, when he fairly swells out with new-made fat and flesh, which he has taken on in an incredibly short time. At this time I think the buck in the prime of life affords the best and most substantial venison, but at no time will the same quantity nourish the system as much as beef of the same quality, and so is vastly inferior in this respect to the venison of the elk.'

Venison Galantine

Ingredients: 3 lb. of the thick end of breast of venison, 3 eggs, 1 lb. pork sausage meat, ¼ lb. gammon of bacon, 8 peppercorns.

Method: Bone the venison and take away any gristle. Cut the gammon into small cubes and mix it with the sausage meat. Boil the eggs for 10 minutes and leave them till cold. Take the bones from the venison and put them in a saucepan with three quarts of water, a small teaspoonful of salt, a sprig each of parsley, thyme, marjoram, and the peppercorns. Bring to the boil. Put the boned meat on a board, the skin downwards, spread over it half the sausage meat, then the eggs cut in halves, then the remainder of the sausage meat. Roll it up and tie it in a cloth, just as you would a suet roll. Place it in the boiling stock, leaving the bones in the saucepan (they prevent the roll sticking to the bottom). Boil gently for four hours.

Take out, tighten the cloth by rolling it up again and place a dish with a weight on it to press it on the top. Leave till cold, then glaze. Strain the liquor from the bones and boil it rapidly until it is reduced to half pint. Turn it into a basin, and when cold chop it finely and put little moulds of it round the galantine alternately with sprigs of parsley.—C.N.

Grated Venison

(This is much the same as pemmican or biltong)

To dry Venison for grating.

Ingredients:

    ½ lb. bay salt
    ¼ lb. coarse salt
    ¼ lb. common salt
    Some black pepper

Rub these in well and leave the venison for about a fortnight or three weeks. Hang up first in a warm, dry place until hard. Then hang it up in the kitchen, or other dry place, but not near the fire.

When required, hack a piece off, and grate it. Eat plain with buttered biscuit or toast.

To use as a savoury, mix the grated venison with a grated hard-boiled egg, and pour a little melted butter or fat upon it in order to bind it. Make some buttered toast, spread the grated venison thickly upon it, and serve warm.

This also makes a good dish if mixed with mashed potatoes and a little butter or margarine, and rolled into small shapes like rissoles – a little fine-chopped yolk of egg improves it.

It saves trouble to grate a larger quantity than is required at a time and keep in a tin. —B.C.

Haunch of Venison

Put the haunch upon the spit (or make it ready for cooking in the oven).

Cover it with double kitchen paper, well buttered, greased, or dipped in sweet oil. (Greaseproof paper will do.)

Prepare a paste ¼ in. thick of flour and water, with as much butter (or margarine) as will make it stick together. Cover the paper with this paste, particularly where it covers the fat parts. Then put more paper over the whole and tie it well on with twine.

About five minutes before you take it from the fire, pull off all the paper and paste and froth it well.

A large haunch will take about three hours and a half to roast.—B.C.

A Venison Pasty

Bone your venison, beat it thin, season it with pepper, nutmeg and salt, lay it with layings of butter, or marrow, on your paste you design for the bottom, close up the lid, and bake it in a soaking oven four hours, then boil the bones in a pot, with claret, nutmeg, and a little pepper, and when it is hot strain it, and pour it into the pasty, and cut it up hot or cold, at discretion.—W.D.W.

Venison Pie or Pasty

Chop the meat, with one or two small onions, in pieces the size of an egg. (Neck or breast will do.)

Remove all bone and boil for three hours in broth, which should be preserved afterwards for soup.

Strain, then add half a pint of port wine and some good stock, also herbs, seasoning, etc.

Simmer till tender and withdraw from the fire.

When cold, put in a pie, again straining the gravy.

Bake in the usual way, with rose and hole at the top.—B.C.

Game Pie (Cold)

Ingredients: Take 2lb. of venison freed from all skin and sinew, 1 lb. of deer liver, pepper, salt, 1 teaspoonful finely chopped onion.

Method: Pass the venison and liver through a mincing machine and add the chopped onion, pepper and salt. Having a frying-pan ready with some hot bacon fat, fry altogether lightly, and put in a dish to cool a little. Add thin slices of deer's tongue, which has been cooked in a saucepan and a little vegetable. The tongue will want cooking for 1½ to 2 hours, so that the skin will come off fairly easily. Put some thin slices of bacon in the bottom of the pie-dish, then a layer of venison and liver. Sprinkle with chopped parsley and a little crushed peppercorn between each layer, then a layer of tongue, then venison and liver, and continue the layers until the pie-dish is full. Add a breakfast cup of stock, stand the pie-dish in a tin of water in a moderate oven, the pie-dish being covered with a closely-fitting cover. Cook for 2½ to 3 hours and when cooking fill up with good venison stock. The pie is improved by the addition of a hare, grouse or duck, and a glass of port wine.—C.N.

WAPITI

Lat. *Cervus canadensis*. The North American Stag or Elk, similar to the European *Red Deer* but much larger. The body is light reddish buff, becoming dark brown on the head

and limbs, and blackish on the belly. The short tail and large rump patch are buffy white.—(*Webster*.)

'Until comparatively recent years Wapiti were supposed to exist in a wild state only in America. In addition to being found in Central Asia they, or a very closely allied species, are also to be met with in certain districts of China.'—H.F.W.

WART HOG. VLAK-VARK

Lat. *Phacochaerus africanus*. Any African wild hog of the genus *Macrocephalus*, Syn. *Phacochaerus*, more particularly *M. aethiopicus*, of South Africa – and *M. africanus*, of North East Africa. They are distinguished by two pairs of rough warty excrescences on the face, and by large protruding tusks.

'Opinions vary considerably regarding the palatability of the wart hog, some considering its flesh to be dry and tasteless, others comparing it with very excellent pork.'—M.S.A.

'The flesh of the young wart-hog is very tasty.'—F.V.K.

WATERBUCK. KRING-GAAT

Lat. *Kobus ellipsiprymnus*. 'A large, coarsehaired, reddish-brown, African antelope.

'On the Zambesi and all its tributaries eastward of the Victoria Falls, it is very plentiful but it is never found in herds of more than about twenty together.'—F.C.S.

WHALE

The name applies to a large number of aquatic mammals of the order *Cetacae*, but more particularly to the larger members of the species, the whalebone whales, the flesh of which is very good eating. Speaking from personal experience, Dr F.C.Fraser said that 'provided the whale is young and freshly caught, the steaks are very good eating, in fact much better than much of the beef sold at present (1944). I have had the meat prepared in various ways, of which roasting was the least attractive. We most frequently had it fried with onions, but an alternative, and a very good dish, is to cut the meat in very thin pieces, wrap it up round portions of bacon or of ham, and serve it with a rather rich gravy like what is called "Beef Olives". Dr N.A.Macintosh says that he has had whale meat egg-and-breadcrumbed and pan-fried and that it was very good. Dr Fraser added that he felt certain that people would not be able to identify whale meat and would like it if they were not told what it was, and that existing prejudices against the smell, flavour, oiliness and fishiness of whale meat were quite unfounded: it never was in the least fishy nor was it ever excessively oily.

'The best of the (whale) meat is sent to Copenhagen, bought by Danish butchers at the stations for 18s. a barrel and sold at Copenhagen as a delicacy at £9 a barrel. It is very good to eat – between beef and veal, but rather better than either. The Japanese pay 25 cents a pound for it.'—W.G.B-M.

'Canned whale-meat is used for food in Japan. Cut into blocks of about 40 lb. it is transported in special refrigerators and sold at about half the price of beef. Only the best meat is used, and in a 50 ft. whale this may reach 2½ tons. There is (or was until recently) a small trade in canned whale meat with West Africa for consumption by the natives. The tougher it was the better they liked it.'—B.R.

The following 'protest' published in the *Licensed Victuallers' Gazette* (Johannesburg, 23rd September 1944) may be taken as evidence that whale meat was regularly used as food for man at the time.

'PROTEST AGAINST WHALE MEAT
BAN ON MEATLESS DAYS
The Durban committee of the South African Trades and Labour Council has passed the following resolution:
"This committee, representing 35,000 trade unionists in this area, lodges a most emphatic protest against the Food Controller's action in prohibiting the sale of whale meat on Wednesdays. We contend that the Controller's functions are to deal with such commodities as beef, mutton, and pork, not to prevent the sale of commodities which may alleviate the meat shortage to some extent." '

WILD BOAR

Lat. *Sus scrofa*. The wild hog of Continental Europe, southern Asia and North Africa which is believed to have provided the original stock from which all races of domestic swine have been raised. In England the gastronomic reputation of the wild boar stands on its head which was made into a fine *Brawn* (q.v.) and was also used as a table decoration and a tavern sign. In France, the Wild Boar (*Sanglier*) is still hunted in many parts of the country and the flesh of the young (*Marcassin*) is highly esteemed as a table delicacy.

Wild Boar's Head

Cut it off near the shoulder, to make it fairer, and of better shew, and to preserve the neck, which is the best of it, so that it be well seasoned; after you have cut it off, singe it, or scald it, if you will have it white; then cut the skin off round about the head four inches from the nose, least it may shrink and fall about other places; seeth and season it well, and when it is half sod, put to it white

or red wine, and make an end of seething of it, again well seasoned with pepper, onion, cloves, orange peel, and fine herbes. You may seeth and wrap it well up in hay, least it fall to pieces, after it is well sod, serve it cold, whole, and garnished with flowers. If you have wrapped it up, you may serve it in slices, which you may disguise with several sorts of ragousts.—*La Va.*

Slice of Wild Boar's Head

Cut it under the neck, or near it, or under the ear, and serve.—*La Va.*

Young Wildboar

Take off the skinne as farre as the head, dresse it, and whiten it on the fire, cut off the four feet, stick it with lardons, and put in the body of it a bayleaf, or some fine herbs; when it is roasted, serve.—*La Va.*

Shoulder of Wild Boare, with ragoust

Lard it with great lard, then put it into a kettle full of water, with salt, pepper, and a bundle of herbs; take heed you doe not season too much, because the broth must be reduced to a short sauce. When it is more than halfe sod, you shall put to it a pint of white wine, clove, and a bayleaf, or a sprigge of rosemary; then, when it is well sod, and the sauce short, you shall thicken it, which for to do, you must melt some lard, and fry a little flowre in it, then put to it an onion minced very small give a turne or two in the panne and poure it into your sauce, which you shall stove with capers and mushrooms; after all is well seasoned, serve.—*La Va.*

WILDEBEEST

Lat. *Connochaetus taurinus*. The *Blue Wildebeest*, so called to differentiate it from the *Black Wildebeest* (*C. gnu*), formerly abundant in South Africa but now practically extinct, whereas the *Blue Wildebeest* or *Brindled Gnu* is still found in many parts of the Union of South Africa. A third species (*C. albojubatus*) occurs in British East Africa.

ZEBRA

Lat. *Equus burchellii*. The name given to several varieties of *Zebra* inhabiting the plains of central and eastern Africa, with striped body and belly but the legs plain or nearly so, which differentiates it from the true or mountain Zebra (*E. zebra*), and the largest species of all, Grevy's Zebra (*E. grevyi*), with narrowed and more numerous stripes on body, belly and legs.

'The flesh is generally loaded with a yellow fat, and is very unpalatable to Europeans, but by the African natives it is regarded as a great delicacy.'—M.S.A., p. 294.

ZEBU

Lat. *Bos indicus*. A bovine mammal widely domesticated in India, China, the East Indies and East Africa. It usually has short horns, large pendulous ears, a large dewlap, and a large hump over the shoulders. In size, it ranges from that of the common ox to that of a large mastiff. Zebus are used as beasts of burden, for riding, for their milk and their flesh.

SECTION 7

BIRDS
AND
EGGS

SECTION VII

Birds and their Eggs: comprising an alphabetical list of

edible wild and domestic fowls, with a selection

of Recipes for their culinary preparation;

followed by an alphabetical list of

the best Egg Recipes,

savoury and sweet

BIRDS

A Coke they hadde with hem for the nones
To boille the chiknes with the mary-bones.

CHAUCER, *Canterbury Tales.*

INTRODUCTION

THIS Section of our *Concise Encyclopædia of Gastronomy* has been divided into two parts, the first of which deals with Game Birds and other birds that are called wild because they love to be free, and also with Poultry, or those birds that are sure of their daily corn and of an early death; the second deals with the best ways of cooking eggs.

With regard to the Game and other wild birds, invaluable help was most graciously given by and gratefully received from Mr N.B.Kinnear, of the British Museum (Natural History). Whilst there are both fish in the sea and plants in the fields that are distinctly poisonous, there does not appear to be any poisonous bird, so that a complete list of 'edible' birds would include every known species of bird. Such a list would not only have meant a book treble the size of the present one, but it would have been quite misleading, since the majority of the names included would have been of rare birds inhabiting inaccessible mountains or forests, and of others so rank and so tough that none but starving, shipwrecked sailors would ever think of eating them. Taking as an example one class of wild birds alone, the sea-birds, there are innumerable varieties of them, of all sorts and sizes, from tiny 'snippets', which visit our shores at different times, to the giant solitary albatross, which ranges the southern oceans, but very few of them have been included in the following pages – merely those whose flesh is deserving of the gastronome's attention, or those that lay their eggs where they can be easily collected: all sea-bird's eggs are good to eat, but most of them can only be collected at such expense and risk that they are left alone. Our thanks are also due to Mr W.B.Alexander, M.A., Director of the Edward Grey Institute of Field Ornithology, for his kindly advice and wise counsels.

In the second part, a selection of the best recipes for cooking eggs has been made, that is mostly hens' eggs and ducks' eggs. But all we know about penguins' eggs, ostriches' eggs and the eggs of other non-domesticated birds will be found in the first part, under the name of the bird responsible for the eggs.

NOTES ON AMERICAN GAME AND POULTRY

CHICKEN, turkey, duck, game birds – America abounds in all of them, yet only chicken and turkey, and to a certain extent duck, can be considered really popular favorites.

Raising chickens is a great American industry, and Europeans, passing by the poultry farms that dot our countryside, are simply staggered by the mass production of what to us is an everyday food and to them, an expensive luxury to be most judiciously used. They can't get over the scientific know-how which ordinary farmers who raise chickens possess, and the careful, systematic way the birds are fed. But what startles them most is that every reputable market here sells excellent chicken, turkey or duck, that there is no need to feel the bird, examine the bill and legs, pinch it – and all the other wiles of the European cook – to be sure that you're getting the best.

The excellence of American chicken, turkey and duck is due to experimental work by government research stations, government control, and to the efforts of the non-profit Poultry and Egg National Board which represents every branch of the poultry industry, and devotes itself to research and consumer education work on behalf of the industry and the housewife.

Since everybody in America loves chicken, and more importantly, can afford it, this *Encyclopædia's* noble array of recipes will be most welcome to all of us. About every possible way of cooking chicken seems to be here, with recipes for duck and turkey close runners-up. It is interesting, however, to see how much more inventive European cooks are when it comes to duck. You'll find many new delicious ways of cooking a bird that deserves to be at least as popular as turkey.

A thing you may find surprising in this section on birds is the gourmet's stress on game birds. Though our country is rich in wild game birds, as a nation we are not addicted to game as a delicacy the way the French and English are. But here are a few pointers on some of the best eating there is. Pheasant is unquestionably the most delicious of all the birds, and the most readily available. It ought to be hung from four days to a week. The bird called partridge in America is not a proper partridge at all (these are raised on game farms) but a ruffled grouse or one of the several varieties of quail, which can all be cooked in the same ways, allowing for the difference in hanging time. No hanging is needed for quail, which must be eaten right away. Grouse can be eaten within a day, or it can be hung for a short time. Partridge should be hung for at least four days to develop its fine flavor. Wild ducks are at their best with 48 hours' hanging. Since game birds are generally lean, they must be well larded to prevent drying out in cooking.

Most game birds eaten in America are raised commercially, and sold directly from the game farm or through superior markets. In either case, you will get with them the proper instructions for hanging and preparing them for cooking. Though it is a little more trouble procuring a game bird than a chicken, the effort is well worth it, with Mr. Simon's guide at hand. More than any other food, game spells true gourmandise; there is no more perfect luncheon or supper for any day of the year than a cold roast bird and a bottle of wine.

Nika Standen

Definitions and Recipes

AVOCET

Lat. *Recurvirostra avosetta*. A scarce passage migrant, in the British Isles, in spring and autumn, which formerly bred in various localities between the Humber and Sussex, but has not been known to nest in this country since 1842, though, in Ireland, two pairs nested in 1938. It still breeds in many parts of Europe, North Asia and as far south as Perisa; also in North Africa (Tunisia) and some parts of tropical Africa. In the New World, it is represented by the *American Avocet* (R. *americana*), which breeds in the U.S.A. and winters south to Guatemala. Two other varieties of *Avocet* are the R. *andina*, found in South America, from Peru southwards, and the *Red-headed Avocet* (R. *novae-hollandiae*) in Australia and New Zealand.

BALDPATE. AMERICAN WIDGEON

Lat. *Mareca americana*. One of the American ducks which is popular with both sportsmen and gastronomes, chiefly in Western Canada and some of the Western States of the U.S.A. It has occurred several times in the British Isles. It is given quite a number of other names, such as *Bald Crown*, *Bald-faced Widgeon*, *Poacher*, *Wheat Duck*, *Green-headed Widgeon*, *Baldhead*, *White-belly*, *Smoking Duck*, etc.

'My personal opinion is that the Baldpate of Currituck, and even those killed on our Massachusetts ponds, are second only to the Canvasback in its prime. Frank Forester extols its virtues, and yet it is surprising to find how little it is appreciated in comparison with the Canvasback or Redhead. Its great advantage for the table lies in its always being fat, averaging in this respect perhaps better than any other duck. Some have even classed it as better than the Canvasback. (Bird, Brewer and Ridgway, 1884.) On the Pacific coast, however, it is not always so "tasty," and does not enjoy so high a reputation.'
—J.C.P.

BARTRAM'S SANDPIPER. BATITU

Lat. *Bartramia longicauda*. Batitu is the name given to *Bartram's Sandpiper* or *Upland Plover* (q.v.), in the Argentine. It is a little larger than the *Snipe* and smaller than the *Woodcock*. During the winter months it is fairly common in many parts of the Argentine and it may be prepared for the table in any way suitable for the *Woodcock* (q.v.) to which it is in no way inferior.

BITTERN (COMMON BITTERN)

Lat. *Botaurus stellaris*. The *Bittern* is a nocturnal bird, haunting bogs, reedy swamps and marshes, where it hides during the day: it feeds during the night on fish, grubs and small animals of all kinds. Its curious call, during the mating season, is responsible for its different country names such as 'stakedriver' and 'Bull of the frog'. The *Bittern* was highly prized as an article of food in England during the sixteenth and seventeenth centuries, when it was also known as *Bittour*, *Byttor* and *Betowre*. It was served on numerous occasions to the Lords of the Star Chamber, and it was so highly prized that, in 1590, for instance, it cost 5*s*. when a capon cost but 2*s*. Its flesh is said to have much of the flavour of the hare's and none of the fishiness of the heron's.

'Hearon, Byttout, Shoveler, beying yonge and fatte, be lyghtyer digested than Crane, and the Byttour sooner than the Hearon ... All these fowles muste be eaten with muche ginger or pepper, and have good olde wyne drunk after them.' (*Elyot's Castle of helth*. London. 1539.)

The bittern was at one time common in the British Isles, but, in the nineteenth century, it became extinct as a breeding species. It has since returned to the Norfolk Broads.

'The flesh of the bittern was formerly in high esteem, nor is it despised in the present day: when well fed, its flavour resembles somewhat that of the hare, nor is it rank and fishy like some of its congeners. The long claw of the hind-toe is much prized as a toothpick, and formerly it was thought to have the property of preserving the teeth.' (*Hints for the table: or the economy of good living*. London. 1859.)

The common Bittern (B. *stellaris*) breeds in temperate parts of Europe and Asia, migrating south in winter to India and tropical Africa. In South Africa there is a resident race, and in Australia and New Zealand there is the *Australian Bittern* (B. *poiciloptilus*), while the *American Bittern* (B. *lentiginosus* is) found in the northern parts of the New World; in the south, it is replaced by another variety (B. *pinnatus*).

BLACKBIRD

Lat. *Turdus merula*; O.E. *Ousel*; Fr. *Merle* (*Marle*, in Mrs Glasse's *Art of Cookery*). A song bird related to the *Thrush* and ranging from the Outer Hebrides to the Volga, and from North Africa to Norway. In the British Isles and in Central Europe many *Blackbirds* do not migrate, whilst others do migrate in September or October and return in the following February or March. In England, *Blackbirds* are no longer killed for food, but there was a time when they were considered fit fare for a king. They were served to the Lords of the Star Chamber in 1590, when they cost 2*s.* per dozen; in 1605, when they cost 3*s.*, and in 1635, when the price had risen to 4*s.* 6*d.* per dozen.

'Black byrdes or ousyls, among wyld foule hath the chiefe praise for lyghtnes of digestion.' (*Elyot's Castle of helth*, London, 1539, *p.* 30.)

'Blacke-Birds, although esteemed by some a good nourishment, yet others are of opinion they are better to delight the eare with their musicke than to feed the belly, being bitter in taste, and hard of digestion.' (*Hart, The Diet of the Diseased*, London, 1633, *p.* 80.)

Be that as it may, gentle Mrs Beeton, in 1861, recommended *Blackbirds* in the following recipe:

Blackbird Pie

Have ready some blackbirds, rump steak, veal forcemeat, hard-boiled eggs, good stock, paste, salt and pepper.

Pick and draw the birds, and stuff them with veal forcemeat. Line the bottom and sides of a pie-dish with rather thin slices of steak; put in the birds, cut in halves; season them with salt and pepper and intersperse sections or slices of hard-boiled eggs; half fill the dish with good stock, cover with paste and bake in a moderately hot oven from one and a quarter to one and three-quarter hours, according to size. Add more stock before serving. Allow one blackbird to every two persons.

In Corsica the *Pâtés* and *Terrines de Merle* are among the most delicious local *spécialités*.

In the U.S.A. *Grackles* and other *birds* of dark plumage are called *Blackbirds*: they are not killed for food.

BLACK GAME. BLACKCOCK. BLACK GROUSE

Lat. *Lyrurus tetrix*. A game bird related to the *Capercaillie* and to the *Red Grouse*: it is smaller than the first and larger than the second: it is also better gastronomically than the *Capercaillie*, but not so fine a bird as the *Grouse*. The male bird is called *Blackcock* or *Heathcock* (*Heathpoult* in Devon); it weighs about 4 lb. when adult; its plumage is mostly of a rich, glossy black with white wing patches and outwardly curved tail feathers.

The female is called *Greyhen, Grayhen* or *Brown Hen*, and rarely weighs more than 2 lb. when adult: the plumage is mottled and barred. The French culinary name for both cock and hen is *Coq de Bruyère. Black Game* is widely distributed all over Northern Europe and Northern Asia.

There was a time when *Black Game* was known as *Grouse*, in England. Thus Henry VIII's 'Grows', at Eltham, early in the sixteenth century, were not Red Grouse but Black Game. Later they were called Black Grouse, as a distinction from the *Red Grouse*.

In England the season when *Black Game* is allowed to be shot is from August 20th (except in Somerset, Devon and the New Forest, where it is September 1st) up to December 10th, but the birds are not really fit to eat before the end of October.

The maximum retail price of *Black Game* was fixed in August 1942 at 7*s.* 6*d.* for black cocks and 6*s.* for grey hens, in feather, the sale of game birds otherwise than in the feather being prohibited.

To Truss a Blackcock

Pluck and draw the bird. Wipe it carefully with a clean cloth, both inside and out. Cut off the head and truss as you would a chicken. Scald the feet, peel off the skin and cut off the toes.

Roast Blackcock

Skewer some thin rashers of bacon over the breast of the trussed bird – and some fresh vine-leaves if available. Roast on a spit in front of a clear fire – coal, gas or electricity will do, but a wood fire is best; baste frequently and allow from 45 to 60 minutes according to size of the bird. If no spit be available, cook in a moderately hot oven, as you would a chicken, basting frequently. Dish up on thick slices of hot buttered toast, and serve with clear gravy in one sauce boat and bread sauce in another.

BLACK-THROATED DIVER. ARCTIC LOON

Lat. *Colymbus arcticus*. A fish-eating bird fairly common in the U.S.A., which also breeds in Scotland and occurs on English coasts in winter. It is considered the most acceptable, if not the only *Loon* worth eating. It is prepared for the table in any suitable way for *Wild Duck* (q.v.).

BOB-WHITE. VIRGINIAN COLIN. AMERICAN QUAIL

Lat. *Colinus virginianus*. This is the best-known as well as the most prolific of the game birds of the *Colin* found from Canada to Guatemala. It occurs chiefly east of the Rocky

Mountains, north to Minnesota and Ontario and south to the Gulf of Mexico. It has also been successfully introduced into Idaho and Oregon. In the north it is usually called a Quail, and in the south a Partridge. It resembles the Crested Quail, from which it differs solely by the absence of a crest. Its name of *Bob-white* is an approximation of the bird's ringing call when the covey is assembling for the night in the evening twilight. The *Bob-white* averages 10 inch in length of body; it is mottled reddish-brown above, with white on the breast: the male has the head striped with black and white and a white throat patch. The *Bob-white* lays from 12 to 18 eggs and is one of the most prolific of game birds. It has been introduced into different parts of Europe at different times but without success. The best ways to prepare *Bob-white* are those suitable for the Red or Scotch Grouse (q.v.).

In Florida there is a darker and smaller sub-species, and there is another in Texas which is greyer above. Related species occur southwards through southern Mexico to the borders of Guatemala, including *Grayson's Bobwhite* and the *Masked Bob-white*, with a blackish face and bright chestnut breast, which is also found in south-west Arizona.

BUSTARD

The name of various members of the family *Otididae*, but more particularly of:

The *Little Bustard* (*Tetrax tetrax*), the smaller European species, which is still found in most lands bordering the Mediterranean, in Southern Europe, North Africa and the Near East. It is the best, from the gastronome's point of view, and is known in culinary French as *Bastardau*.

The *Great Bustard* (*Otis tarda*), the largest of European land birds, ranges from Spain eastwards to China. It used to be found in the British Isles, and it was served to the Lords of the Star Chamber in 1519, when it cost 4*s*. on one occasion and 2*s* 10*d*. on two other days.

'Bustards, some twenty years since, were bred in the open parts of Norfolk and Suffolk, and were domesticated at Norwich. Their flesh was delicious, and it was thought that good feeding and domestication might stimulate them to lay more eggs; but this was not the case. There were formerly great flocks of bustards in England, upon the wastes and in woods where they were hunted with greyhounds, and were easily taken. The bustard is, however, now extremely rare in this country. Three female birds were shot in Cornwall in 1843; on Romney Marsh, in 1850; and in Devonshire, in 1851. In January 1856, a very fine male bustard was taken near Hungerford, in Berkshire, on the borders of Wiltshire, this being the only male taken for many years in England; it weighed 13¼ lb. and its wings measured from tip to tip 6 feet 3 inches.' (*Hints for the Table*. London. 1859).

Bastardau Double Beurre

Pluck your bustard and partly cook it in butter. Remove it and place it in a second lot of very hot butter. When cooked, cut it up, and pour over it a sauce made with red wine, before serving.—A.La.

CANNE-DE-ROCHE

The French-Canadian name of the female (*Cane*) of the *Rock-duck*, better known under the name of *Harlequin Duck* (q.v.).

CAPERCAILLIE. CAPERCAILZIE

Lat. *Tetrao urogallus*. This is the largest European member of the Grouse family: it is also known as *Cock o' the Wood*. It is found in the pine forests of the Jura, Alps, Carpathians and Siberia, and although it became extinct in the British Isles, it has since been re-introduced and is very plentiful in parts of Scotland.

Recipe for Capercailzie

Method: Truss and stuff first with breadcrumbs, chopped shallots and chopped parsley, two tablespoons of cranberry jam, pepper and salt. Boil slowly for at least 15 minutes in boiling water. Have a stewpan ready with onions and carrots fried in butter to a nice brown. Put in the bird and stew *very slowly* for two hours. For sauce put three tablespoons of cranberry jam into a small saucepan and strain the sauce that the bird was stewed in (with a tablespoon of flour added to thicken it) over the cranberry and bring it to the boil and put it round the bird when dished. (*Contributed by Mrs Lumsden, of Clova, Aberdeenshire*.)—C.N.

The cock capercaillie has an unfortunate habit of stuffing itself with pine needles, and Major Hugh Pollard recommends steeping the bird in new milk for an hour after it is plucked 'to abate too strong a turpentine flavour', but an old cock *Caper* is best dealt with in the manner recommended by Nazaroff in *Halcyon Days in the Urals*: 'Draw and clean it and rub the inside thoroughly all over with salt, pepper and mustard; stuff it with onions, sew it up and bury it in the ground for 24 hours. Then wash it well and let it soak in milk for 12 hours and for 10 in vinegar. After that, skin it, lard it well and roast over a slow fire for half an hour. Then steam it for three hours, butter it well all over and give it to the dog, if he will eat it, for nobody else could.'

The young birds are quite acceptable from September to November, although officially in season from August to December. The crop and ducts of the bird should be removed as soon as possible after it is shot, and it should be kept at least a week – two weeks would be better during the cold weather. Cover the breast with rashers of fat bacon and roast in a moderately hot oven, basting frequently. A rich chestnut and pig-meat stuffing is recommended.

In 1942, the Ministry of Food fixed the maximum retail prices of capercaillie at 10s. for the hen bird and 12s. for the cock, size and weight counting evidently more than palatability.

CAPON (and Chicken)

A Saxon word which has passed into culinary French as *Chapon* (Ger. *Kapaun* and It. *Cappone*). A *Capon* is a castrated cock, according to the dictionary, but, in the poultry trade, the name applies to a castrated cockerel which has been superfed, usually in solitary confinement, and killed when not less than six months nor more than ten months old. In England, where most chicks are reared in the spring, capons are usually available from November to March.

Capons figure on the Bill of Fare of all the great feasts given in England in olden times during the winter months, such as the marriage feast of Henry IV, in 1403, and the enthronement of George Nevile as Archbishop of York, in 1467. They also figure in most *Star Chamber Diet* Accounts, for Michaelmas or Hilary Terms, being referred to as either *Fat Capons, Roasting Capons* or *Boiling Capons*, the last being invariably cheaper. In 1519 and 1520, the price of a *Capon* was but 2s. In 1534, *Fat Capons* cost from 4s. to 7s. apiece, whilst two *Boiling Capons* cost 20d. only. In 1567 and 1568, *Capons* to roast cost 2s. 6d. and to boil 2s. each. In 1590, the prices were practically the same, but they rose later to 3s. in 1602 and 1605, 4s. in 1635, and 4s. 6d. in 1639.

'The capon is above al other foules praised, for as moch as it is easily digested.' (Elyot's *Castel of helth*, 1539. f. 30a.)

There are frequent mentions of capons in Shakespeare, such as: 'The justice in fair round belly with good capon lin'd' (*As You Like It*, II. 7). This is an allusion to corrupt magistrates who accepted fat capons as a bribe.

'Stand aside, good bearer. Boyet, you can carve;
Break up this capon.'
(*Love's Labour's Lost*, IV. 1).

This 'break up' for 'carve' is unusual, the correct term for carving being 'to sauce a capon'.

'Return'd too soon! Rather approach'd too late!

The capon burns, the pig falls from the spit.'   (*Comedy of Errors*, I. 2).

Sallet of cold Capon rosted

It is a good Sallet, to slice a cold Capon thin; mingle with it some Sibbolds, Lettice, Rocket and Tarragon sliced small. Season all with Pepper, Salt, Vinegar and Oyl, and sliced Limon. A little Origanum doth well with it. (*The Closet of the eminently learned Sir Kenelme Digby Knt. opened ... published by his son's consent.* London. 1669. p. 247.)

To know whether a Capon is a true one, young or old, new or stale

If he be young his spurs are short, and his legs smooth; if a true capon, a fat vein on the side of his breast, the comb pale, and a thick belly and rump; if new, he will have a close, hard vent; if stale, a loose open vent.—H.Gl.

CASSOWARY

Lat. *Casuarius casuarius*. A large, flightless bird living in some of the wooded parts of New Guinea and adjacent islands; also in Northern Queensland and Ceram, in the Moluccas. The eggs, of which there are usually six to eight to a clutch, are light green in colour when first laid, but they soon fade to a dirty white. They are highly valued for food and, like the *Plover*, the hen bird goes on laying more eggs to replace those taken from the nest. Then she loses interest in the nest and leaves the cock to attend to the incubation of the full clutch.

CHICKEN

A *Chicken* is just a barnyard fowl, and it may rightly be called the best of all birds covered by the name of *Poultry*. It is a more important article of food, all the world over, than any other domesticated fowl, and its claim to being the best of them all rests upon the fact that, like bread, potatoes and rice, *Chicken* may be eaten constantly without becoming nauseating.

There are a considerable number of recipes given in all cookery books for cooking a *Chicken*, but, just as you cannot possibly get good boiled or fried potatoes, whatever the recipes may be, unless you have mealy, floury potatoes for boiling, and firm, waxy ones for frying, it is not merely important but indispensable that you should make sure of the kind of *Chicken* given to you to cook, before deciding how you are going to cook it. Hence the recipes which follow have been grouped under three age groups, viz.:

1. The 'under age' or baby chicks and 'squabs' or broilers, known in culinary French as *Poussins*.

2. The 'of age', ranging from cockerels and spring chickens to fat fowls and 'capons', known in culinary French as *Poulets de grain, Poulets reine, Poulardes* and *Chapons*. This is, of

course, by far the most important of the three age groups.

3. The 'over age' or boiling hens, known in culinary French merely as *Poules*. Recipes for soups with a basis of chicken broth will be found in this group.

In the United States, birds under one year old are called 'chicken' and stewing hens of one year or more are known as 'fowl.' Chicken are classified as broilers, fryers, and roasters, depending on age and weight. They are sold 'packaged frozen eviscerated,' 'drawn' and 'market dressed' or 'New York dressed,' as well as by the piece. Frozen chicken is all ready to cook, 'drawn' chicken needs to have the lungs, kidneys, oil sac and pin feathers removed before being ready for the pan. 'Market dressed' or 'New York dressed' chicken comes to the market all plucked; it is then drawn and cut up by the retailer as requested when it is sold to the customer.

Broilers must not be over 8 to 12 weeks old and should not weigh more than $2\frac{1}{2}$ pounds market dressed. Fryers should weigh from $2\frac{1}{2}$ pounds to $3\frac{1}{2}$ pounds market dressed and be 14 to 20 weeks old. Roasters – though all young chickens are good roasted – weigh usually $3\frac{1}{2}$ pounds and more, market dressed. They should not be more than 5 to 9 months old.

How fresh should a chicken be?

The age of the chicken we are going to eat is important, and so is its freshness. If you buy a chicken from the poulterer, you cannot tell by looking at it whether it was killed overnight or a year ago: cold storage is so wonderful an invention. But you can use your sense of smell and if the bird offered to you has the faintest 'gamey' suggestion, you will be well advised to leave it alone and try your luck at the next shop. If you have your own barnyard or buy your chickens from a farmer whom you know, you may eat and enjoy a fowl cooked on the day it was killed; but a chicken which is not cooked 'warm', as soon as killed, should then be given three, four, five or even six days to hang in an airy and dry place, the shorter the time according to the warmer the weather.

To choose and to truss a chicken

The chief points to consider in selecting a tender bird for roasting are the following: (1) Good firm flesh; (2) The legs should be soft and free from scales; (3) Wings and end of breast-bone should be pliable. This denotes that the bird is less than one year old as the end of the breast-bone remains cartilage until the bird becomes adult; (4) There should be sufficient fat showing to make the chicken plump but not enough to increase its weight materially.

Poultry must be carefully singed over a gas jet or any clear flame, the wings being unfolded for this purpose. Wash well in cold water and wipe dry. Cut off the head, leaving a long neck, remove feet, bending the legs back until the top sinews are exposed. Use a wooden skewer to loosen these, one by one, and pull them out by grasping the upper part of the leg firmly and gently loosening the ligaments. Cut through the tough muscle at the joint, thus exposing the under-side ligaments, and, grasping the flesh of the leg again, draw them out, one at a time. Repeat this operation at the back of each leg. There are five sinews from the upper part of each leg and two from the under. In very young chickens this operation is unnecessary, as it is age – and much running about – which develops these sinews.

Now remove crop at neck, without breaking it. Remove intestines through an incision made at the end of the breast-bone, taking great care not to break the gall-bladder, which would make the flesh of the chicken bitter. Retain the heart, liver and gizzard. These with the wing-tips and the neck, are the 'giblets', from which many delicious dishes or soup can be made.

When a chicken is purchased in town, all this work has been done and the giblets are neatly replaced inside the fowl for use as required.

The chicken must now be trussed. To do this, fold the skin of the neck back, tuck the wings down neatly against the body as well as the legs, and, using a special 'trussing' needle, pass it right through the body, bringing the thread, or fine string, back over the leg joints and tying on one side. Carefully work the skin down over the ends of the leg bones and sew the legs close to the sides of the body, fastening them tightly together at the 'elbow'. This is the English method of trussing; in France, the breast-bone is often flattened and the fowl tied into a compact shape without the use of a trussing needle. The object of this operation is to keep the bird in shape while cooking.

Stuffing Poultry

After the intestines and giblets have been removed, the bird is washed out with tepid salted water. The stuffing, if stuffing is used, is put in, sometimes at one end, sometimes at both, and kept in place by sewing up the incisions previously made for emptying. Before serving, be sure to remove the thread by gently pulling. To clean the gizzard, or stomach, remove excess fat and pare off the fleshy part on both sides with a sharp knife. This is a better method than cutting the gizzard into halves as the undigested food contained in the interior frequently gives an unpleasant flavour to the dish. The feet may be used with the other giblets after they have been scalded and skinned.

All poultry is cleaned in the same way. Ducks and geese, however, having no crops, the intestines may be loosened at the neck and removed at the lower vent.

The liver of chickens is considered a culinary delicacy and can be used in several ways, as will be shown.

To Cut a Chicken into Pieces
Cut the legs off close to the body at the joints and separate each one into two portions – the drumstick and the second joint.

Cut off the wings in the same manner, removing the tips, which count as 'giblets' too. Separate each wing at the middle joint. Now remove the wish-bone, with whatever meat is on it, from the breast. This is situated at the rear end of the chicken. Using strong kitchen scissors, cut through the small ribs on either side of the breast, removing it in one piece, which must afterwards be cut into two halves lengthwise, if the chicken is large. Now cut the back or lower part of the bird into two pieces, lengthwise. This should give 12 pieces in all.

To Carve a Chicken at Table
The bird must be dished up lying on its back with the neck part towards the left of the dish. Insert a carving-fork firmly across the breast-bone. Cut through the skin between the leg and the body, bend leg over and cut it off at the joint, afterwards separating each into two portions. Cut off wing and divide also into two portions, unless the bird is small. Cut the white breast meat into thin slices along the breast-bone.

CHICKEN RECIPES
I. BABY CHICKS AND BROILERS
    (POUSSINS AND PETITS
    POULETS)
(a) Poussins and squab chickens
1. Alsacienne, Poussins à l'
2. Américaine, Poussins à l'
3. Belle-Meunière, Squab Chicken
4. Bohémienne, Poussins
5. Broiler, Planked
6. Châtelaine, Poussins
7. Souvaroff, Poussins
8. Véronique, Poussins
9. Viennoise, Poussins
10. Waynesborough, Squab Chicken à la

(b) Petits poulets
11. Amandines, poulets sautés aux
12. Bonne Femme, poulet cocotte
13. Créole, fried chicken
14. Devilled chicken, Mildred's
15. Diable, petit poulet à la

16. Grand'Mère, petits poulets
17. Grilled chicken
18. Mrs Mac's special fried chicken
19. Smothered chicken
20. Smothered in sour cream, chicken
21. Southern style, fried chicken
22. Tartare, fried chicken

II. COCKERELS,
     FARMHOUSE CHICKENS
     FAT FOWLS AND CAPONS
     (POULETS DE GRAIN,
     POULETS REINE,
     POULARDES ET CHAPONS)

(a) Roast or baked and served whole
1. Roast chicken
2. Poulet casserole
3. Bordelaise, poulet cocotte
4. Dixie, roast capon
5. Girenflot, chicken à la
6. Louviers, la poularde flambée comme à
7. Marengo, poulet sauté
8. Nantaise, capon à la
9. Nantaise, la poularde sautée à la
10. Pilaff, chicken
11. Sang, poulet au

(b) Poached or boiled and served whole
12. Albuféra, poularde
13. Anglaise, boiled fowl à l'
14. Aurore, poularde à l'
15. Béarnaise, poule farcie à la
16. Chimay, le chapon gratiné à la façon du Prince de
17. Demi-deuil, volaille
18. Estragon, poulet à l'
19. Gros sel, poularde au
20. Noodles, chicken with
21. Riz, poule au

(c) Chicken fricassées, stews, pies and puddings: chickens carved before they are cooked and served (en casserole, en cocotte, en pâte; suprêmes, filets et blancs de volaille)
1. Ancienne, fricassée de poulet à l'
2. Argentina, cazuela
3. Blanquette, poulet en
4. Chanteclair, chicken
5. Chasseur, poulet
6. Cider, chicken in
7. Coq au vin
8. Coq en pâte à la façon du pays de Foix
9. Coq en pâte à la Franc-Comtoise
10. Csirke paprika
11. Csirke pörkölt
12. Cuban style, Arroz con pollo
13. Curry, chicken
14. Demidoff, poulet
15. Dent du chat, poulet à la
16. Fricassée, chicken
17. Fricassée de poulet

18. Gumbo in casserole, chicken
19. Hotpot, chicken
19. Marengo, poulet
20. Maryland, chicken
21. Matelote, poulet en
22. Mulacolong
23–26. Pies, chicken:
     Chicken pies,
     Chicken corn pye,
     Country fair chicken pie,
     Pot-pie chicken,
     Welsh hermit's favourite chicken
         and leek pie
27. Pojarski, côtelettes à la
28. Portugaise, poulet sauté
29. Pudding, Williamsburg chicken
30. Reine, poulet à la
31. Romany chicken
32. Suprêmes et Blancs de Volaille
33. Suprêmes de Volaille Jeannette
34. Tortue, poule en
35. Trois Frères, poulet aux
36. Vin Blanc, poulet sauté au

III. Boiling Hens,
     Chicken Soups

IV. Left-overs and
     Sundry Made-up Dishes

1. Poulet en Capilotade
2. Chile con Carne
3. Coquilles de Volaille
4. 'Country Captain'
5. Creamed Chicken
6. Chicken Croquettes
7. Chicken Canneloni
8. Croustades de Volaille
9. Poulet en Daube Provençale
10. Devilled chicken bones
11. Devilled chicken croûtes
12. Left-over fricassée of chicken
13. Fritôt de poulet
14. Galantine de poulet
15. Gâteau de foie Lyonnais
16. Chicken au gratin
17. Chicken liver croustades
18. Gratin de Foies de Volaille aux nouilles
19. Chicken's liver balls (for soups)
20. Terrine de Foies de Volaille
21. Chicken loaf
22. Mayonnaise de Volaille
23. Minced chicken à la moderne
24. Mousse of chicken
25. Pain de Volaille
26. Potted chicken
27. Pressed chicken
28. Quenelles de Volaille
29. Chicken ramekins
30. Salade de poulet
31. Savoury canapés
32. Soufflé of chicken

I. Baby Chicks. Broilers.
     Poussins. Petits Poulets

The denizens of the barnyard have never yet staged a hunger strike nor lodged any other form of protest against the glaring inequality of the sexes and the unfair slaughter of baby chicks, all male birds, which are not allowed to live more than a short span of weeks, simply because they can never lay an egg. These little chicks are tender and tasteless: being tender, they are very suitable for grilling and frying; being tasteless they are often stuffed with all manner of savoury stuffings.

(a) Poussins and Squabs

Poussins à l'Alsacienne

Clean two fine *Poussins*, absolutely fresh; season them inside with pepper and salt; stuff them with a spoonful of cooked *foie gras* and their own livers cooked in butter.

Bind them and wrap round them some very thin bacon: cook them in butter and when done take them out of the pan and keep them warm.

Pour half a glass of white Alsatian wine into the pan in which they were cooked and leave it on the fire until reduced by half. Add two spoonfuls of *demi-glace* of veal gravy and two finely-sliced truffles. Dress the *poussins* in a *cocotte*, and keep warm.

In the meantime, poach ½ lb. fresh noodles in salted hot water; drain them well and bind them with 3 oz. fresh butter; season with salt and freshly-ground pepper. Dress the noodles in a *timbale*. Place on the noodles four or five slices of fresh *foie gras*, tossed in butter, and pour over them some of the gravy from the saucepan in which the *Poussins* were cooked; cover the *foie gras* with some more noodles and serve the *Poussins* with the Timbale of Noodles.—A.E.

Poussins à l'Américaine

The *Poussins* are cleaned and filled with a stuffing made of minced onions, breadcrumbs, butter and a little sage. They are then cooked in butter, in an open pan, and served, when done, with thin slices of grilled ham or bacon.

Squab Chicken Belle Meunière

Prepare three squab chickens for roasting purposes. Chop 12 oz. of fresh mushrooms. Fry 6 oz. of small-cut salt pork just a trifle. Chop chicken livers and giblets and three shallots very fine and cook in the salt pork dripping. Add the mushrooms, season with salt and pepper, a teaspoonful of chopped parsley and half a cupful of white wine or Sauce Bercy. Let simmer for a while, then stuff the chickens with this preparation. Truss and sew up chickens, place in a pan, pour melted butter over and colour in a very fast oven (400° F.). Then place them in a large earthenware casserole. Slice six mushrooms over them with four tablespoonfuls of butter. Cover the casserole and cook slowly for 40 minutes in a moderate oven. —E.E.A.

Poussins Bohémienne

The *Poussins* are cleaned and filled with a stuffing made of their own minced livers, to which have been added some breadcrumbs, mixed herbs and a little sweet paprika. They are cooked in butter in an open pan, with a chopped onion per bird. When about half cooked, dust them with sweet paprika and finish cooking on a slow fire. When cooked, take them out of the pan and keep them warm. Add to the butter in the pan a little white wine and some very fresh cream, stir well together over the fire and let it reduce for a few moments, to make a sauce which should be made richer still by adding to it some cooked and sieved *foie gras*. Serve the *Poussins* with this sauce and some potatoes cooked in their jackets.—A.E.

Planked Broiler

¼ cup butter
¼ tablespoon green pepper
¼ tablespoon red pepper
1 teaspoon minced onion
½ clove minced garlic
¼ tablespoon chopped parsley
1 teaspoon lemon juice
1 spring chicken, split
Hot, freshly-mashed potatoes
Salt
Sauté mushroom caps
Extra butter

A special seasoned 'plank' is required for this. Beat the butter to a cream, add to it the peppers, the onion, garlic, parsley and lemon juice. Put the chicken in a baking-tin, skin side down. Sprinkle with salt and pepper, dot over with small pieces of butter and bake in a hot oven for 15 to 20 minutes or until nearly done, basting twice with hot butter when cooking. Brush the plank over with melted butter, pipe a border of the mashed potatoes around the extreme edge of the plank, place chicken in centre, breast side upwards, and spread it with the butter mixture. Add the mushrooms, previously cooked in butter, and place the whole thing in a very hot oven to brown the potatoes evenly. Slip the plank on a platter to serve. If wished, the broiler may be jointed into serving portions before sending to the table, and sprigs of watercress may be used as a decoration.

Poussins Châtelaine

Clean two *Poussins*, season them inside with pepper and salt, and put their livers inside.

Chop up 2 oz. lean bacon; poach it for a few minutes in boiling water; drain it and put it in a pan with a spoonful of butter. Place the pan on a slow fire, and as soon as the bacon begins to cook, put in the pan two *Poussins*, six small new onions, six small new carrots, six new potatoes, one shredded lettuce, a cupful of freshly-picked green peas. Add enough boiling water to cover the *Poussins* and vegetables. Add salt and cover the pan: let the whole simmer for half an hour.

Take the *Poussins* out and dress them in a deep dish or a *terrine*. Bind the gravy in the pan with a spoonful of butter mixed with half a spoonful of flour. Let it boil for a few minutes and then pour over the *Poussins* and serve.—A.E.

Poussins Souvaroff

Stuff each *Poussin* with cooked *foie gras* and truffle cut up in dice. Half cook the birds in butter in an open pan. Unbind them and place them in a *terrine*, with a whole truffle per bird; the truffle to be of average size, not cooked but peeled and seasoned with pepper and salt.

Unglaze the pan in which the birds were half cooked, with chicken gravy and strong veal gravy, as well as a few spoonfuls of Madeira wine; let it all boil for a couple of minutes and then pour this sauce over the birds in the *terrine*.

Put the lid on the *terrine*, make it fast with paste all round, and finish cooking in the oven for 15 or 18 minutes. Serve in the *terrine*.—A.E.

Poussins Véronique

Cook the *Poussins* in butter in an open pan, dress them in a *cocotte* with 12 muscat grapes for each little bird, after having removed the skin and pips from each grape.

Unglaze the pan with some white wine, leaving it on the fire till reduced to two-thirds of the original quantity; add one spoonful of meat glaze per bird and three spoonfuls of very fresh cream. Let it boil for a few minutes and pour over the *Poussins* in the *cocotte*.—A.E.

Poussins Viennoise

Simply cut the little chicks in four, season them with salt and pepper, egg and bread-crumb them and fry them golden in deep fat. Nothing but fried parsley and quarters of lemon as a garnish, and a few new potatoes delicately rolled in butter and a fraction of finely-chopped mint.—*Wine and Food*, No. 14, p. 36.

Squab Chicken à la Waynesborough

6 squab chickens (1¼ lb. broilers)
4 tablespoons butter
1 onion, cut in half
1½ cups chicken broth
1 teaspoon meat extract
¼ glass white wine
Salt and pepper

Place the chickens, seasoned, in a casserole with the butter and the onion. Put into oven 375° F. and baste very often for half an hour. When both the chicken and onion are nicely browned, set on top of the stove and add the wine. Cover the pot and simmer for five minutes. Then place the chickens on a platter and put into a casserole the chicken broth and the meat extract. Boil for five minutes and pour over the chickens and serve in the casserole. Serve with Rice Créole or Spoon Bread.—A.W.R.

(b) Petits Poulets
Poulets sautés aux amandines

2 fresh-killed broilers cut in small pieces
¼ lb. shelled almonds (chopped very fine)
½ pint white wine
1 *bouquet-garni* (composed of several stalks of parsley, a sprig of thyme and a bayleaf, tied together in the form of a faggot)
1½ oz. of sweet butter
Salt and pepper
Roughly chopped parsley

Fry the chicken very slowly in butter with the almonds, salt and pepper and a *bouquet-garni*. When they are light brown add the white wine, the chopped shallots and two tablespoonfuls of Suprême sauce and cook for half an hour. Then add the chopped parsley and season to taste. Dish in a timbale. This dish can be served cold as well during hot summer days. (*One of Louis Diat's recipes, the Ritz-Carlton, New York.*)—M.A.

Poulet Cocotte Bonne Femme

Prepare a spring chicken as for roasting; season it inside with pepper and salt and stuff it with some sausage-meat to which you will have added some breadcrumbs and the chopped liver of the chicken; also some finely-chopped up parsley.

Cover the breast of the chicken with some thin rashers of bacon and cook it in butter in a *cocotte* (round earthenware or cast-iron pan). Put the *cocotte* on a low flame; add from 8 to 12 small onions and the same number of small pieces of lean bacon. Turn the chicken over and about now and again, and when about half cooked, add about ¼ lb. of diced potatoes, making sure that they all get their fair share of the butter in which the chicken is being cooked. Then put the lid on the *cocotte* and finish cooking in a slow oven.

Serve in a deep dish, after removing the rashers of bacon from the chicken, and with the vegetables that were cooked at the same time.

Fried Chicken Créole

1 spring chicken (2 to 2½ lb.)
2 eggs
¼ cup milk
1½ cups cracker meal
1 teaspoon white pepper
2 teaspoons salt
½ cup flour

Wash, split and cut the chicken in quarters. Season with salt and pepper. Make an egg-wash with eggs, milk and half teaspoon of salt. Pour the egg-wash over the chicken and let it stand about an hour or two. Roll chicken in flour and cracker meal which have been mixed together. Fry in medium hot fat from 12 to 15 minutes.—L.R.

Mildred's Devilled Chicken

2 large broilers
½ lb. butter
2 or 3 cloves of garlic
½ bottle of Worcestershire sauce

Remove skin from two large broilers, cut in six pieces each. Place them side by side in a shallow roasting pan. Melt ½ lb. of butter, add two or three cloves of garlic, and half a small bottle of Worcestershire sauce. Pour over the chickens, place in 375° F. oven and bake, basting every five minutes until well done, about 1½ hours in all; salt lightly when half-done. The chickens should have a deep brown, almost a black glaze when done, and there still should be sufficient juice left. If, however, it has boiled down too much, add about half cup of chicken broth to the roastin pan and simmer over a low flame for a minute or two, to make more juice.—J.P.

Petits Poulets à la Diable

Split the chickens down the back; clean the insides well and spread all over with freshly-made and fairly liquid mustard; then dip in breadcrumbs and melted butter and broil over a clear fire, or grill in the grilling pan of a gas oven. When done, serve with watercress in the dish and some sauce *Tartare*, in a sauce-boat.—P.W.

Petit Poulet Grand'Mère

This is another edition of the *Poulet cocotte Bonne Femme*, a small chicken cooked in butter in a covered pan on a gentle heat with small onions and diced potatoes cooked in the same butter and pan. The difference is in the stuffing with which the young but tasteless bird is filled before being cooked. To the sausage-meat, breadcrumbs, liver and parsley of the *Bonne Femme* stuffing, the *Grand'Mère* adds a fair amount of chopped onions and a dusting of allspice.

Grilled Chicken

Split down the back, without cutting through the skin of the breast, and break the joints. The breast-bone is usually removed. After cleaning interior well, sprinkle with salt and pepper and spread on both sides with softened butter. Place either on a grid over a clear fire or in the grilling-pan of a gas-stove. Grill carefully, turning on both sides to colour evenly. When done, place on a hot dish, spread with hot butter and serve at once, plain. If the bird be somewhat large, it is a good plan to bake it first in a very hot oven, skin side down, for a quarter of an hour, basting frequently with butter. At the end of this time, remove and finish browning on a grid.

Mrs Mac's Special Fried Chicken

Clean and disjoint young chicken. Sprinkle with salt and pepper. Pour over it the juice of half a lemon, one large wineglassful of wine, half a cup olive oil and the juice of one onion. Let stand for two hours. Then drain well but do not wipe. Dip each piece in flour that has been mixed with two table-spoonfuls chopped parsley. Fry in hot oil for about 20 minutes, slowly at first and then briskly. Arrange on hot, well-garnished platter and serve with French fried onions and apple rings. Serve very hot.—A.W.C.

Smothered Chicken

2 small broilers, split
Salt and pepper
½ cup butter
1 cup sour cream
4 rounds of hot buttered toast

A heavy iron pot, or *cocotte*, is the most suitable for this dish. Melt the butter, put in the broilers, sprinkled with salt and pepper, and brown them on all sides. Put on the heavy lid and place a weight on it; reduce heat and cook the chickens gently from 35 to 45 minutes, turning once and again. When tender and nicely coloured, remove them, add cream to fat and gravy in pan, heat well and pour over the rounds of hot toast. Place half a broiler on each round of toast to serve. The addition of a few drops of lemon juice improves the flavour of the sauce.—P.W.

Chicken Smothered in Sour Cream

Cut young chickens as for frying. Dip in flour, salt and pepper. Fry in deep fat until almost done. Drain off most of the fat, then pour some cream (one cup to each chicken) over the chickens, reduce the heat, cover well and simmer until done. This takes about 20 minutes. Arrange buttered toast on a platter and lay pieces of chicken on the toast. Pour remaining sauce over all. Serve with baked sweet potatoes.—A.W.C.

Fried Chicken, Southern Style

1 or 2 spring chickens
Salt and pepper
Flour
Fat salt pork

Plunge the bird or birds into cold water, drain well but do not wipe. Cut up and sprinkle with salt and pepper and coat on all sides with flour, as thickly as possible, pressing the flour into the meat with the flat of a knife. For two broilers, about 1 lb. of fat salt pork will be needed. Cut it into dice and fry these gently to get all the fat out, removing pieces of meat left in pan. When the fat is very hot and sizzling, fry the chicken in it. Brown well on all sides and serve crisp, with a rich white sauce.—P.W.

Fried Chicken Tartare

1 or 2 small spring chickens
Chopped parsley
Chopped fresh mushrooms
Salt and pepper
Frying fat
Butter
Chopped chives
1 clove minced garlic
Fine brown breadcrumbs
Ice-cold tartare sauce

Split the chickens down the back and clean interior well. Break the bones and soak in hot melted butter to which the chopped garlic and herbs have been added, as well as salt and pepper and the finely-chopped mushrooms. Cover and allow to marinate, turning occasionally for a couple of hours. Now drain halves of chicken, dip each in melted butter and coat evenly with the breadcrumbs, pressing them firmly on. Fry in an open pan or grill over a low heat, turning to cook evenly. Serve very hot with the sauce Tartare handed separately. In order to allow the pieces of chicken to marinate nicely, keep the mixture near the stove so that the butter remains liquid.—P.W.

II. Cockerels
    Farmhouse Chickens
    Fat Fowls and Capons
    Poulets de Grain
    Poulets Reine
    Poulardes et Chapons

This is by far the most important class both numerically and as regards culinary excellence. The bigger birds are cooked and served whole, mostly as *Roasts*, but also poached, braised or stewed; the smaller ones are cooked either whole, whether roasted, grilled, poached or braised; or else they are first of all cut up into pieces ready to serve and then cooked in many different manners, top-roasted, *sautés*, *poëlés*, *en casserole*, *en cocotte*, *en fricassées*, fried, baked or braised.

(a) Roast Chicken

Miss Lorna Bunyard, in *The Epicure's Diary*, paints a pretty picture of the Victorian culinary artist fixing meat or fowl to the spit with yarn or worsted that the meat be not pierced; basting the twisting joint with the sizzling, dropping dripping, and skilfully tending the fire with fresh coal at the back, glowing embers to the fore and a top-dressing of slack. And then she exclaims in sadness more than in anger: 'Roasting is no more!' But why? Large fires and cumbersome mechanically driven Victorian spits are no more, and let us not waste any tears over their loss. We have, in this our electrical age, compact and easily regulated electric fires fitted with electrically-driven spits, which can be fitted at any place in the kitchen that we find most convenient and at any desired height from the floor, so that we may watch and baste our chicken whilst it is slowly and surely revolving in front of the fire, without having to bend. The old spits are no more, but the new ones are much better than the old.

A fowl fit for the spit must not be old: the place of old birds is the pot, not the spit. If you have a spit and a young fowl, large or small, all you need do is to baste it occasionally and allow about 25 minutes per lb. weight of the bird for its cooking. If you have no spit, get one, and in the meantime use the oven since you must. Let the oven be brisk, but not *too hot*; smother the chicken with butter before putting it in; baste as often as possible and allow 20 minutes per lb. for the cooking. Serve with grilled, lean bacon and any vegetables in season or at hand.

A well-bred and well-fed spring chicken or fat fowl needs no stuffing nor any highly spiced sauces: they show their excellence best if served just plainly roasted with their own gravy, that is the blend of their own fat and the basting butter used in the cooking.

Other recipes for cooking a chicken whole either on the spit (rôti à la broche), in the oven (au four) or in a pan, covered or uncovered (en casserole or en cocotte).

Poulet Casserole

Next to 'spit roasting' (*à la broche*) this is the simplest and best way to cook a good chicken, one that requires no stuffing nor any other help.

Prepare the bird as for roasting, dust its inside with pepper and salt and settle it in a saucepan where it may have room to move about – or rather to be moved round. An earthenware pan is best. Smother the bird with butter first of all and let it cook without a lid on, on a fairly brisk fire, basting it with the hot butter and turning it about from time to time. When cooked, serve the chicken in the casserole, with its own butter as sole sauce, and no vegetables, but a crisp Cos lettuce barely dressed.

Poulet Cocotte Bordelaise

1 chicken
Salt and pepper
Artichoke bottoms
3 tablespoons butter
Small new potatoes
Small button onions

Prepare chicken as for roasting. Melt the butter in an earthenware or oven-glass *cocotte*, add the bird, salt and pepper. Brown on all sides evenly, reduce heat and cover *cocotte*. Meanwhile prepare the vegetables. If there are no small new potatoes available, turn some with a French 'baller'. Cut the artichoke bottoms – tinned ones will do – into diamonds of a decent size. Toss these, the potatoes and the onions lightly in a little butter in a separate saucepan. When done, add the vegetables and their liquor to the chicken and cook all together until the bird is tender. Serve in the *cocotte*, adding a few leaves of parsley just before dishing up. —P.W.

Roast Capon Dixie

Procure a plump 6 lb. capon. When cleaned, prepare a stuffing of 1 lb. stale bread soaked in milk or water. When well soaked, squeeze out all the fluid. Chop one onion fine, brown in skillet and add to bread; add one teaspoon of salt, quarter teaspoon of pepper, just a little grated nutmeg, one tablespoon of chopped parsley, one egg and a cup of pecans, walnuts or chestnuts. Mix well and stuff the bird with this preparation. Truss carefully and lay the bird in a roasting pan. Pour about half a cupful of hot lard over the bird. When this is done, sprinkle with salt. As soon as the bird gets a golden colour, pour over it six cupfuls of hot milk and keep on basting with this. Time of cooking should be about two hours in a fairly brisk oven. By browning a tablespoon of flour in four tablespoons of butter, a gravy should be made with the milk from the bottom of the roasting pan. Untruss and serve with watercress.—E.E.A

Chicken à la Girenflot

Prepare the bird for roasting; when on the spit, baste constantly with butter, into which you have mixed bacon and shallot, both chopped fine. When the chicken is of a fine golden colour, put one or two good slices of toast into the dripping-pan. Dish the bird on the toast, and serve with all the savoury contents of the dripping-pan.—G.A.S.

La Poularde flambée comme à Louviers

Choose a prize chicken, fat and tender. Put it in a pan with a little butter, cover it up, and toss it over a quick fire. When it has begun to perspire freely, take it out of the pan, pour some Calvados over it and set it alight for a few seconds. Carve it and place the pieces in a *cocotte*; let it stew gently, moistened with a little cider to begin with, adding plenty of rich cream towards the end. Add to the sauce some artichoke bottoms cut in quarters and some small mushroom caps which will have been cooked separately.

Dress the chicken in a dish, pour the sauce over it, and, at time of serving, sprinkle over it some ham and truffles finely-shredded *en julienne*.—A.E.F.

Poulet sauté Marengo

This old favourite way of cooking a chicken in an open pan is supposed to date from the Battle of Marengo, when, to save time, there was a *plat unique* served to Bonaparte, a chicken cooked in olive oil together with some eggs fried in the same oil and crayfish as well. The chicken and eggs cooked in oil are probably the only true part of the story, and we are inclined to believe that the tomato sauce and the *écrevisses* were additions to later editions of the dish. Here is Escoffier's recipe for it:

Sauter the chicken in butter and olive oil. Add a glassful of white wine, a dozen mushroom caps cooked in olive oil, just a little garlic, 1½ cupfuls of *demi-glace* (meat gravy) with a few spoonfuls of tomato sauce added to it.

When the chicken is cooked, dress it in a deep dish, pour over it the sauce and the mushrooms and place round it four *croûtons taillés en coeur* (pieces of bread cut the shape of a heart) and fried in butter, four fried eggs, four *écrevisses* (crayfish) cooked in a *court-bouillon*; dust the lot with a pinch of chopped parsley.—E.A.

Capon à la Nantaise

Make a farce with the liver, a dozen roasted chestnuts, a piece of butter, parsley, green onions, a very little garlic, two yolks of eggs, salt, pepper, and grated nutmeg. Roast the capon, after having filled it with the farce, and cover it with buttered paper; when it is done, brush it over with the yolk of an egg diluted in a little lukewarm water; sprinkle breadcrumbs all over it; let it brown well, and serve it with a sharp sauce.—G.A.S.

La Poularde Sautée à la Nantaise

Settle a plump fowl in the centre of a saucepan with pats of fresh butter upon its tender breast, a free dusting of pepper and salt, a carrot and an onion finely cut up on one side, and a bushy *bouquet garni* on the other side.

Place the pan on a moderate fire and let it be for a while. Then add a full glass of Muscadet wine and just a little white wine vinegar. Leave the fowl to cook gently for 30 to 40 minutes, according to size.

Remove the fowl and place it in a casserole. Then, attend to what is in the saucepan: add some chopped fresh shallots, plenty of them, and a little vinegar. Let it reduce itself, that· is steam itself away and then add a *Sauce Hollandaise*, and, by way of garnishings, some mushrooms cut up in quarters, some small onions, little carrots cut in the shape of olives and dice of artichoke bottoms, all of which will have been blanched beforehand.

Now taste the sauce and season as required with pepper and paprika, also a little tomato to make it look prettily pink. Pour this sauce and garnishings over the fowl, sprinkle some finely-chopped *fines herbes* before serving and serve very hot.—A.E.F.

Chicken Pilaff

I

1 chicken; 6 onions; ½ teacup rice; 18 raisins.

Braise chicken till brown. Fry onions. Take out chicken. Cook in oven for 20 minutes. Stew onions in stock for 1½ hours. Add rice and chicken and stew slowly for three-quarters of an hour. Add raisins. Serve chicken whole.—R.L.

II

1 lb. rice; ¾ lb. butter; 1 pint white stock; 3 oz. tomato *purée*; 1 head of garlic; 1 fowl, jointed.

Brown the rice and fowl in some of the butter in a casserole with the garlic, stirring over a slow fire for 20 minutes. Have ready the stock and the tomato and pour it on the rice, stirring well. Draw the casserole to the side of the fire and leave it well covered for an hour. When the rice has absorbed all the stock, add the rest of the butter and serve hot in the casserole. (E.S.P. Haynes's *Dragoman*. Greece 1913.—O.H.

III

To make a Poloe

Take a pint of rice, boil it in as much water as will cover it; when your rice is half boiled put in your fowl, with a small onion, a blade or two of mace, some whole pepper, and some salt; when 'tis enough, put the fowl in the dish, and pour the rice over it.—E.S.

(The only derivation that I can think of for *Poloe* is that it was an approximation of *Poule au riz*, contracted to *Poule au*.—ED.)

Poulet au sang

Keeping the blood of a plump chicken, you place the bird in a casserole with onions browned in butter and bacon, and when it is coloured, powder it lightly with flour. Moisten it with a very good red wine, preferably a Bordeaux, and let it stew for some time in the oven, well covered.

A few minutes before serving, add a large nut of butter and the blood of the chicken – the blood of two birds for every one will be all the better. Pour a small glassful of good brandy into the sauce and decorate the dish with *croûtons* and mushrooms. (*Recipe of the Hôtel Neuf, Pouilly-sur-Loire*.)—P.A.

(*b*) Poached and Boiled Fowls

A 'boiling hen' will make good chicken broth and it may be dished up in all sorts of ways, hot and cold, as we shall see later, but if one is to enjoy a poached or boiled fowl, it must be a young bird, large for preference, but large through intensive feeding and not mounting years. However, a fowl is bound to lose some of its flavour in hot water, so that boiled fowls are often stuffed before being cooked, and are served with savoury sauces as well.

Poularde Albuféra

Fill the fowl with cooked rice mixed with cooked *foie gras* and some fairly large-size dice of truffles. Truss the fowl and tie rashers of bacon over its breast; put it in a large pan and half cover it with veal stock. Let it simmer on a low heat for an hour or an hour and ten minutes, according to size.

Take the fowl out of the pan; unbind it and dress it in the centre of an oval, deep dish, and surround it with some fine mushroom caps and slices of truffles. Pour over it a rich white sauce made of meat stock and fresh cream.

Boiled fowl à l'anglaise

Put a young fowl into a panful of warm, salted water, just enough to cover it, and a *bouquet-garni* (parsley, thyme and bayleaf). Bring to the boil, then reduce heat, add a piece of bacon (1 lb. or thereabout) and simmer for an hour or a little more according to size. Serve with slices of boiled bacon, plain boiled potatoes and *Parsley Sauce*.

Poularde à l'aurore

Stuff and poach a fowl in the same way as *Poularde Albuféra* (q.v.), but cover either with a *Sauce Suprême* coloured with pink, sweet paprika, or with a *Tomato Sauce*.

Poule Farcie à la Béarnaise

1 large fat fowl
1 small clove garlic
1 slice stale bread
Salt and pepper
2 egg-whites
Pot-au-feu vegetables
1 rather thick slice lean ham
A few stalks parsley
A little milk
2 egg-yolks
1 lb. stewing beef
Uncooked rice
Hot tomato sauce

This is supposed to be the original recipe Henry IV had in mind when he suggested every French family should have a 'poule au pot'.

Remove crust from bread and soak it in sufficient rich milk to cover. When soft, squeeze milk out and beat lumps out of bread. Prepare fowl as for roasting after stuffing. Chop the liver, gizzard, ham, garlic, parsley and soaked bread together and bind with the well-beaten egg-yolks. Season to taste. Add to this stuffing the stiffly-whipped egg-whites to lighten mixture and use to stuff fowl, sewing up carefully and firmly at either end. Place fowl in an earthenware *pot-au-feu* pot, that is, a deep one, adding the beef and a small handful of rock salt. Add sufficient *cold* water to cover contents of pot, and a little over. Bring slowly to boiling point, skim well, then add the vegetables (carrots, an onion, a couple of leeks, a turnip and a small piece of celery) and a few peppercorns. Cover pot closely and cook gently for three or four hours, according to size and age of fowl. When nearly done, remove sufficient broth from the pot to cook the amount of rice required in a separate saucepan – allow one heaping tablespoonful for each guest. When all is done, serve the fowl in a deep dish on a bed of rice. Hand hot tomato sauce separately. *Note.*—The balance of the broth makes excellent soup and the beef may be used to stuff tomatoes or whatnot.

Le Chapon gratiné à la façon du Prince de Chimay

Choose a large capon or a fine *Poularde de Bresse*, and slip in some thin slices of truffle between skin and flesh. Poach the bird in a rich *fond blanc* for 35 or 40 minutes; take it out of the pan and keep warm in a slack oven. Simmer the liquor in which the bird was cooked until reduced by half and use it then as the basis of a *Sauce Suprême*. Bind it with the yolk of an egg and add a finishing touch of butter, away from the heat of the fire.

In the meantime, having cooked some fresh noodles, butter them up without stint and mix with them a *julienne* of ham and truffles. Fill a hollow dish with the noodles, making a nest in the centre. Carve the capon and dress the pieces in the centre of the dish, surrounded by the noodles. Add some minced mushrooms to the sauce and some *foie gras purée*, then pour it over the capon and the noodles. Put the dish under a hot grill for a few moments and serve hot and lightly gratinée.—A.E.F.

Volaille demi-deuil

This was for many years the great stand-by dish *Chez la Mère Fillioux*, Lyons. The recipe is simple enough: slip some thin slices of black truffle under the skin of a large fowl, without breaking the skin; sew up the bird in a thin cloth and poach it in salted simmering water, with a few leeks, an onion and a few slices of carrots; when cooked, serve the bird with just a pinch of *gros sel*, or rock salt. But you must not expect the fowl that you will cook in this way to come up to the *Volaille demi-deuil de la Mère Fillioux*. Hers were better because she could count upon a large demand and there were never fewer than a dozen *Volailles* being poached together in her great cauldron.

Poulet à l'Estragon

Fresh tarragon
Butter
1 large fowl
Hot water or *bouillon*
Salt and ground pepper
2 carrots
Small pinch thyme
1 or 2 onions
1 clove
Small stem tarragon

This is an old-fashioned and delicious method of cooking fowl. Chop some fresh tarragon leaves and mix with about three tablespoons of butter. Place this inside a tender fowl, sewing up neatly. Place the bird in a heavy iron pot, adding sufficient hot water or, which is far better, good *bouillon* half-way up its side. Add also all the other ingredients, removing all leaves from the branch of tarragon. Cook the fowl gently until tender. When done, remove skin from bird and keep hot without allowing it to dry up. Take a cupful of the chicken liquid and quickly reduce it until the residue in the bot-

tom of the saucepan is brown (*réduit à glace*). Add another cupful or two of the broth gradually to this and thicken with a little potato starch (*fécule*). Add some more chopped tarragon leaves. Pour brown sauce over the white chicken, decorating edges of dish with more tarragon leaves.

Poularde au Gros Sel

Truss a fowl and bind some rashers of bacon round it; put it in a pan with enough white stock to cover it; add about a dozen small onions and the same number of small carrots, or pieces of carrots and half a dozen leeks, without the green part. Cover the pan and let the fowl simmer from 50 to 60 minutes, according to size. When cooked, serve with the vegetables round it in a deep dish; also a sauceboat of the liquor in which it was cooked and a saucer of rock or sea-salt.

Chicken with Noodles

Boil a good tender chicken. Boil 1 lb. of noodles in one quart of boiling water for 15 minutes. Drain and season with salt, pepper, grated Swiss and grated Parmesan cheese. Butter a round baking dish and fill to three-quarters of its depth with the noodles. Place on top of the noodles the chicken, from which you have previously removed the skin, and cut into pieces about 2 to 3 in. long and 1 in. wide. Make a rich cream sauce with the *bouillon* of the chicken and thick fresh cream, and thicken well with the yolks of four or five eggs. Pour this sauce over the chicken and noodles. Sprinkle over the top a good covering of grated Swiss cheese and brown in a hot oven. (*Restaurant Philippe. Paris.*)—E.D.W.

Poule au Riz

1 large fowl
1 *bouquet-garni*
Salt and a few peppercorns
2 cups rice
3 onions
1 slice fat salt pork
1 clove

Place the fowl in a deep heavy iron saucepan and cover with hot water. Add all ingredients, except the rice. Cook gently until half done, then sprinkle the rice into the broth, laying the fowl on top. Reduce heat and gently simmer until the rice is done. Some French cooks brown the fowl in butter before boiling to give a nice colour to the rice. Remove *bouquet* before serving.

Fricassée de poulet à l'ancienne

For a *fricassée*, cut up a chicken as for a *sauté*, but divide the legs in two. Stiffen the meat in the stewpan without discolouring it and sprinkle it with about 2 oz. of flour per pound of chicken. Cook this flour with the chicken for a few minutes, then moisten the *fricassée* with white stock, season, and set to boil, stirring all the time. About 10 minutes before serving add 10 very small onions cooked in white *consommé* and the heads of 10 small mushrooms. Finish at the last moment with a pinch of chopped parsley, and thicken the sauce with the yolks of two eggs, four tablespoonfuls of cream, and 1 oz. of butter. Dish in a timbale, surround the *fricassée* with little flowerlets of puff pastry, baked without being coloured. (*Carlton Hotel Recipe, London.*)—R.L.

Cazuela Argentina

Cut up a chicken as for a *fricassée* and gild the pieces in sizzling butter over a slow fire; then cover them with stock and add sliced potatoes, carrots, pieces of pumpkin or vegetable marrow, sweet corn, turnips, a sprig of parsley, an onion, a pimento, a tomato, and a handful of rice. Cover this and allow it to simmer until the chicken is cooked to the point of tenderness.—*Wine and Food*, No. 22, p. 142.

Poulet en blanquette

Have a tender chicken not more than 2 lb. in weight. Remove the skin and carve it in five pieces (the four members and the breast). Put them in salted boiling water with a few pieces of carrots and onions and a *bouquet*; bring to the boil and simmer about 25 minutes.

Make a white *roux* in another saucepan with a piece of butter the size of a small egg and same quantity of flour. Add to it little by little and whipping well the chicken stock through a strainer, till you have enough to make a good quantity of sauce. It is then fairly liquid; bring to the boil and let it simmer five minutes; add the pieces of chicken and a few slices of mushrooms previously cooked three or four minutes only in butter. Stir occasionally; the sauce, reducing, will thicken a little.

Cook slowly a few minutes more and finish by a binding of one yolk of egg diluted in a little vinegar. The finished consistency should be that of thin cream.—X.M.B. (1)

Chicken Chanteclair

(Poulet Chanteclair as served at Antoine's in New Orleans)

Marinate a 3 lb. jointed chicken in good claret for 24 hours, with chopped carrot, minced small shallotts, minced celery, and two garlic cloves minced. Drain, season and *sauté* in butter. Then stew in wine with bacon *julienne*, and soaked dry mushrooms. Cook until tender, and serve with tarragon leaves sprinkled over.—C.R.B.B. (2)

Poulet Chasseur

1 chicken
1 tablespoon butter
1 or 2 shallots
2 cups good stock
1 glass dry sherry or white wine
Fines herbes, chopped
1 tablespoon olive oil
1 clove garlic
1 tablespoon flour (optional)
Salt and pepper
2 teaspoons tomato *purée*
Croûtons

Cut the chicken up into joints and brown these in the mixed oil and butter, previously heated, together with the minced garlic and shallots.

When all is nicely coloured on all surfaces, sprinkle with the flour, if wished, and moisten with the mixed *bouillon*, wine and tomato *purée*, adding salt and pepper to taste. A pinch of such *fines herbes* as chopped chives, chervil and parsley improves the flavour and just a little rosemary and thyme lends distinction but ... the faintest whiff only. Cover and cook rather quickly for about half an hour or until the chicken is tender. Strain gravy over chicken and garnish with hot *croûtons* and *sautés* mushrooms.—P.W.

Chicken in Cider

1 boiling fowl
¾ pint draught cider
¾ pint tinned tomatoes or 1 lb. fresh ones
1 onion, chopped
2 oz. margarine
1½ oz. flour
Seasoning and *bouquet-garni*

Joint and parboil the fowl. Dry the joints and peel off the skin, then dip in a little flour which has been seasoned. Heat half the margarine and fry meat and onion golden brown. Remove from pan, drain, and put in a casserole. Add remainder of margarine to that in pan and cook the flour in it a minute or two. Pour cider on slowly and when smooth, add the tomatoes and herbes. Bring to boil and season. Pour this sauce into the casserole and cook in slow oven till the meat is tender.

Le Coq au vin

Take a young chicken and divide into six pieces. Fry it lightly in butter in an earthenware saucepan over a quick fire, together with some lean bacon cut in dice, and the same quantity of fresh mushrooms or morels. When the whole has turned a good colour, add a bunch of mixed herbs and a chopped clove of garlic. Sprinkle with good brandy, set fire to it, and add a pint of good red wine. Cover the saucepan, and leave to cook for 20 minutes. Thicken the sauce with the blood of the chicken which has been carefully collected in a bowl, with a dash of vinegar to keep it from congealing.

Serve in a deep round dish, very hot, with little slices of bread which have been browned in the oven.—A.La.

Le Coq en Pâte à la Façon du Pays de Foix

Choose a good chicken; carve it; season the pieces with pepper, salt and allspice and let them lie overnight with odds and ends of left-over *foie gras* in a *marinade* made up of Madeira wine, livened up with a tot of Armagnac brandy and a sliced truffle. Also thyme, bayleaves, parsley, cloves and mushrooms cut in quarters.

Leaving the cut-up chicken in its fragrant and heady bath, blanch some calf's brains. Also prepare a chicken *velouté* with fresh butter and *foie gras* in equal parts, moistening with some of the *marinade* and leaving it to cook for an hour; reduce on a quick fire; add again fresh butter and *foie gras* in equal parts; also some more *marinade* and again 'reduce' this *fond*. Now is the time to add to it the chicken and, later on, the calf's brains cut up *quenelle*-wise, the cut-up mushrooms from the *marinade* and some small onions. In a *sauteuse*, or shallow saucepan, you will now toss some pieces of ham in butter and *foie gras* in equal parts, also some finely-chopped shallots; add what remains of the *marinade* and pour the lot over the chicken in the tourtière. Sprinkle over it the truffles from the *marinade*, which must be finely chopped, and place over it all a cover made of pie paste. Leave it to cook gently for at least an hour.—A.E.F.

Le Coq en Pâte à la Franc-Comtoise

Choose a good-sized cockerel with a fine comb. Save the head, to be breadcrumbed and fried later on.

Truss the fowl, season with salt, pepper, and four spices (see Section I, *SAUCES*), and cook gently with the giblets, carrots and onions and a good-sized piece of butter for about three-quarters of an hour in casserole.

Moisten your casserole with a glass of Armagnac, a glass of port, and a pint of thick cream.

At the same time prepare a garnish of small mushrooms, black Jura morels, a few large dice of ham, and braised sweetbreads.

Pour this sauce over the garnish, let it simmer a few seconds, and thicken the mixture with a savoury *purée of foie gras*.

Cut the fowl into quarters, put the pieces in a pie dish, pour over them the garnish and sprinkle thickly with truffles. Cover

with flaky pastry and finish cooking in a slow oven.

When serving, arrange the head of the cockerel in such a way that it protrudes from the pie, having previously dipped it in breadcrumbs and fried it.—A.E.F.

Csirke paprikás
(Hungarian)

Quarter and sprinkle with salt three spring chickens; wash, clean and leave them in water until needed. Warm thoroughly a thick stewpan (copper or iron), melt 2 oz. lard, mix in 3 to 4 oz. chopped red onions, do not allow to brown; stir in half teaspoon paprika and one teaspoon vinegar. Drain, but do not dry the pieces of chicken, add to the contents of the stewing pan, shaking it to prevent burning. As soon as the chickens are lightly fried, but not brown, add a little stock, cover and stew for 40 to 45 minutes. Then add three spoonfuls thick sour cream and small, boiled potatoes. Serve with Galuska or Tarhonya (q.v. in Section III, *CEREALS*).—L.D.

Csirke Pörkölt
(Hungarian)

Same method of cooking as 'paprikás', but instead of thickening the gravy with cream, use two to three spoonfuls tomato pulp. Same garnish.—L.D.

Arroz con pollo Cuban style

Cut two chickens in pieces for serving and brown them in quarter cup of olive oil. Add one large onion finely chopped and one or two cloves of garlic finely chopped and brown well with the chicken. Add two cups washed rice to the browned chicken and stir constantly until rice is well browned. Then add two cups raw, peeled and chopped tomatoes and let simmer for 15 minutes, stirring frequently. If more liquid is needed, add half cup of chicken stock and let cook slowly until chicken and rise are well done. Just before serving add a pinch of saffron dissolved in a very little cold water.—A.W.C.

Bengal Curry

Four oz. butter, 4 oz. onions, sliced thin, one clove of chopped garlic, to be fried on a brisk fire till brown.

Then add a tender parboiled chicken, or other tender meat, cut in small pieces. Add about ¾ pint of good stock, two tablespoonfuls of curry powder, medium hot, or one tablespoonful of hot curry powder, two tablespoonfuls of fresh tomato juice, or, if preferred, the juice of half a lemon, a small teaspoonful of salt, and a tablespoonful of milk. Keep stirring on the fire for about 30 minutes with a wooden spoon till all the stock is absorbed, and when the butter separates from the gravy the curry is ready for the table, and should be served with the rice in a separate dish. All dishes and plates must be hot. It takes about one hour to make a good curry, including 20 minutes for par-boiling the fowl, rabbit, veal, mutton cutlets or kidneys. All such meats should be fresh and tender.—B.H.

Cold Curry

An excellent breakfast or luncheon dish. Useful for camp or picnic hampers.

Take a large knuckle of veal, or one large fowl.

Cut the meat in slices and fry with some apples, onions also cut finely, and a tea-spoonful of chutney. No thickening is re-quired. Add a tablespoonful of curry powder and allow to simmer for four or five hours. Pour into a wet mould and turn out when cold.—B.H.

There are always a number of different pickles – called *Sambals* – served with all curries.

Poulet Demidoff

1 large fowl
2 or 3 young carrots
1 lb. or more fresh tomatoes
1 tablespoon olive oil
6 oz. best butter
1 quart good stock
¼ lb. ham
2 or 3 young turnips
1 lb. uncooked rice
Salt and pepper
1 cup dry white wine
Cayenne pepper (optional)

Cut up the chicken and brown well in two tablespoonfuls of the butter. Add the thinly-sliced vegetables, except the tomatoes, cover after adding the wine, salt and pepper, and cook gently. Meanwhile, brown the rice in the rest of the butter and, when lightly but evenly coloured, add the stock, cooking gently until the rice is done but not over-done. It should have gradually absorbed all the stock and be 'dry'. Cook the cut-up tomatoes in the heated oil, season and sieve. Cook *purée* gently until thick. Add a light dusting of cayenne, if liked. To serve, pile the rice in a hot dish in a ring, place the pieces of fowl in centre of this ring and pour the hot tomato *purée* over this. Dispose the sliced vegetables on the rice and strain the chicken gravy over all.

Poulet à la dent du Chat

Cut up a chicken and put it to soak in cold salt water. Slice an onion in rounds and brown it, either in an iron or an earthen-ware saucepan. Pour over it two spoonfuls of olive oil. Next make a thick sauce with five or six peeled tomatoes, and season it with a pinch of cayenne pepper, a pinch of curry powder, and a pinch of paprika. Add the pieces of chicken and let it stew for an hour, stirring it from time to time.

Mix the yolk of an egg in a pint of thick cream, and pour it over the chicken and the tomato *purée*. Set it on the fire for 10 min-utes or a quarter of an hour, and stir con-tinuously, so that the sauce thickens and mixes perfectly. Watch it carefully to see that it does not boil.—A.La.

Chicken Fricassée

1 young roasting chicken of 3 to 4 lb.
1 *bouquet*
2 peeled white onions
2 peeled carrots
2 tablespoons butter
2 tablespoons flour
3 cups chicken stock
½ cup cream
2 egg yolks
Salt and pepper to taste

Cut chicken in pieces, wash well, and put in a pot with cold water enough to cover. Add salt, *bouquet* and onions and cook until chicken is tender. Remove chicken and strain stock, beating until smooth between each addition. Beat egg yolks and add cream to them, then gradually stir into hot mix-ture. Cook about five minutes and pour over chicken on hot platter. Sprinkle with chopped parsley and paprika. Serve with baked tomatoes stuffed with rice and giblets. —A.W.R.

Fricassée de Poulet

1 chicken
2 tablespoons butter
1 tablespoon flour
1 cup water or stock
Salt and pepper
Small pinch grated nutmeg
1 or 2 stalks parsley
3 egg yolks
1 teaspoon lemon juice
¼ lb. fresh mushrooms
12 or 15 small onions
Fried *croûtons*

After having prepared the chicken for cooking, cut into neat pieces and allow them to stand for half an hour in tepid water, to whiten the flesh. Drain well and dry with a cloth. Heat the butter, add the flour, stirring until the mixture is smooth, moisten with the water or stock (some people prefer a mixture of water and white wine). Season with salt, pepper and nutmeg, add the pars-ley and, if available, some chives. Add the pieces of chicken, cover closely and simmer gently for 1½ hours or until the chicken is quite tender. Remove pan from fire and add beaten egg yolks and the lemon juice. The mushrooms and the small onions must be added when the chicken has been simmering for nearly an hour. Serve with *croûtons* as garnish, alternating with the small onions and the mushrooms caps. Sprinkle with a little minced parsley.

Chicken Gumbo in Casserole

1 roasting chicken, disjointed
1 chopped onion
1 chopped green pepper
¼ cup chopped celery
¼ cup olive oil
1 cup tomato essence
1 lb. okra cut in small pieces

Roll chicken in flour. Brown in butter and place in casserole. Brown onion, pepper, celery in olive oil, add tomato essence and okra and cook 10 minutes. Pour over chicken. Bake uncovered at 325° F. for 1½ hours. Rice should accompany this dish. Serves six or seven.—M.A.

Chicken Hotpot

1 chicken
2 oz. flour
2 teaspoonfuls grated lemon rind
Pepper and salt and nutmeg
6 slices bacon
½ pint of boiling water or stock

Cut up the chicken into neat pieces and roll in the mixed flour, nutmeg, salt, pepper and lemon rind.

At the bottom of the hotpot arrange the liver, gizzard and inferior pieces and then the best portions with bacon between them, and on the top add a few slices of onion and a squeeze of lemon juice.

Place in a saucepan of boiling water and cook for three hours. Remove onion before serving. Sufficient for six or seven people. —L.G.N.

Poulet Marengo

1 2-lb. chicken
5 or 6 tablespoons olive oil
1 clove garlic
Salt and pepper
1 small *bouquet-garni*
½ lb. sliced mushrooms
Flour
2 tablespoons tomato *purée*
3 tablespoons stock
Parsley
Fried *croûtons*
Fried eggs

Carve the chicken in seven pieces: wings, thighs, drumsticks, and breast.

The legs being toughest, lightly brown them first in the heated oil, together with the minced garlic, salt and pepper. When they have been cooking for five minutes or so, add remaining pieces of the chicken, together with the *bouquet-garni*, and continue cooking until all pieces are lightly browned. Add also the mushrooms and, if available, some sliced truffles. Moisten with the stock to which the tomato *purée* (or two raw cut-up and peeled tomatoes) has been added. Cover and cook gently until the chicken is done, then serve with the 'short' sauce, the fried *croûtons* and one fried egg per person. The garlic, unless entirely dissolved, and the *bouquet*, should be removed before serving. —P.W.

Chicken Maryland

First, select a 2 lb., or at most a 2½ lb., chicken. Draw and joint. Dredge each piece in flour and salt and pepper according to taste. Fry in *butter*, not lard, not bacon grease, not any of the numerous substitutes and subterfuges – just plain butter – and plenty of it. When fried to a rich deep golden brown, with bubbles of skin filled with gases of olfactory delight, turn down the heat, being careful not to cook it dry.

Here you have two alternatives, *fresh* corn fritters, or *water-ground* cornmeal mush cakes – also cooked till a brittle brown surface. Then, *thin* slices of well-candied sweet potatoes. Please don't have the slices so thick that they show a dry white in the centre. They should be candied through and through, and cut thin. These slices should garnish, with parsley around the edge of the platter.

Then – just before serving – cover the chicken and fritters or mush cakes with a piping hot, ever so rich cream gravy. The gravy must not remain on the chicken long enough to destroy the crispness of the chicken. The cook should stop the waiter *just before* he leaves the kitchen and gently poise *on top* of the gravy, brittle crisp strips of bacon, being most careful that the bacon lies *on* the gravy and *not* the gravy on the bacon.

There are those, and perfectly within their rights, who prefer to have the chicken served without the cream gravy, and the cream gravy brought to the table. This seems to be more or less of an academic choice as to whether you would risk the gravy being put on the chicken too early and the chicken losing its crispness or the gravy coming in a little late and the chicken not being quite so hot by the time the gravy bowl reaches your place.—Frederick Philip Stieff, in *Wine and Food*, No. 40.

Poulet en Matelote

1 cut-up chicken
2 medium-sized onions
2 carrots

1 tablespoon flour
1 cup red wine (claret)
1 cup stock or hot water
1 *boquet-garni*
Freshly-ground black pepper
Salt
1 clove of garlic
1 tablespoon butter
1 tablespoon olive oil
2 dozen small onions
Mushrooms (optional)
1 teaspoonful anchovy butter
A few French capers
Slices of fried bread

Slice the carrots and medium-sized onions and brown them in a little extra butter or in fat. Sprinkle with the flour, stirring for a couple of minutes, then moisten with the combined wine and stock or hot water. Add the *bouquet*, pepper, salt, garlic and the stems of the mushrooms, peeled and washed. Simmer this sauce gently by the side of the fire. Meanwhile, cut up the chicken and brown it in the mixed butter and oil. Strain the wine sauce over it. Set the pot over a brisk heat and reduce the sauce to half its original bulk, then add the small onions and the mushroom caps. Cover, reduce heat and continue cooking until chicken and onions are tender. Remove pan from heat, add the *Anchovy Butter* and the capers and serve chicken and sauce on slices of fried bread.—P.W.

Mulacolong

The marching rhythm of this name is entrancing. Its origin is as mysterious as the flavour of the dish itself.

A bird which has reached the age politely spoken of as 'uncertain' may serve as the *pièce de résistance* of any dinner and reflect glory on the hostess if it is prepared in this manner. Young chickens may also be cooked in the same way by using somewhat less veal stock and reducing the time of cooking.

1 fowl
3 pints veal stock
1 teaspoon turmeric
1 large onion
1 tablespoon lemon juice
Salt and pepper

Cut the fowl in pieces and fry it until it is well browned, then add the chopped onion to the fat and allow this to brown also. Add the veal stock, which should be very strong, and the turmeric mixed with the lemon juice. Season with salt and pepper and cook until the chicken is tender. The stock should cook down so that it forms a rich gravy, which should be served over the chicken. (*Carolina Housewife*.)—B.S.R.

Chicken Pie

I

Boil a young chicken, allow to cool and remove bones. To the chicken broth add a sliced onion, some celery and parsley. Boil for half an hour, strain, thicken and return to chicken. Add ½ lb. fresh mushrooms, which have been sautéed in butter. Prepare a very short pastry dough, roll thin and fit in to a casserole. Now place in the chicken and gravy, garnish with sliced hard-cooked egg. Cover with a pastry crust, crimp edges well and slash in vents. Bake until the crust is brown.—M.A.

II

Cover the bottom of a pie-dish with slices of raw ham or veal; season with salt and pepper; over this place two young raw chickens; cut each into four parts; season likewise with pepper and salt; add six yolks of eggs, boiled hard, and moisten with a gill of gravy; cover the pie with a flat of puff paste; adorn it, egg it, and bake it in a moderate oven for one hour and a half. If the pie is to be eaten cold, you can mix in the gravy two leaves of dissolved gelatine.—G.A.S.

Chicken Corn Pye

Boil up one cup of rice and butter it well while it is hot. Put a layer of rice in the bottom of a buttered baking-dish, add one chicken which has been cooked in a well-seasoned broth, and the corn scraped from three large ears. Pour over this one cup of broth, add three tablespoons of butter, salt and pepper. Cover with the rice, glaze it with a beaten egg and bake to a delicate brown. (*Old recipe: Henrico County, Virginia.* Prov'd 1937.)—H.B.

County Fair Chicken Pie

'In my mother's chicken pie were no alien or distracting elements such as carrots, onions, or peas. Hers was a *chicken* pie. And whether or not, circumstances and conditions permitting, I could emulate her artistry and set before you a dish of such outward beauty and inward relish. I can at least tell you how she used to make it.

In the first place she selected for such an occasion as the County Fair, two or more husky young roosters, corn-fed and ripe with oats from the field and grasshoppers from the meadow, the flesh moistened and seasoned with a spot of buttermilk from the churn.

These were killed but a day in advance of their honourable contribution to the feast, and drawn and hung up in the woodshed overnight to mellow. In the morning, they were rinsed, dried, and cut up. The leg yielded drumstick and upper joint; the back, for a pie, was deftly split down the centre, leaving an 'oyster' of meat on either side. The bones helped to support the crust. The wings were disjointed, and the wishbone separated from the breast, which was left whole, until after boiling, having been severed from the neck.

These parts, together with the giblets, were now put into the kettle and covered (but just covered) with boiling water. They cooked slowly until almost tender, when they were seasoned with salt and pepper. Now the cover was left off the kettle to let the water evaporate a little and so that the remaining liquid would absorb yet more flavour.

When the meat was finally done – *done*, but not dropping from the bones – it was transferred from the kettle into a pan, which was set on the back of the stove while the gravy was being made; with spring chickens there would be no grease to strain off, but when year-old hens were used, as was sometimes done for a Sunday dinner in the spring, the fat was skimmed off.

Now, to the amount of broth remaining – and there should not be three cups at the most – add a thickening made of three tablespoonfuls of flour mixed to a thin paste with milk. Cook until quite heavy, then add two cups of sweet cream previously warmed, and a tablespoonful of butter. Also further seasoning if needed. The giblets are reserved for another day. The gravy when done should itself have the consistency of thick cream. Season with pepper and salt.

Now lay the chicken, piece by piece (the white meat cut into suitable sizes for serving and the breastbone discarded) in the pan. Over the top is spread a rich crust of biscuit dough about a fourth of an inch thick. My mother made a sour-cream biscuit dough and there is none better, but do not give up making the pie if sour cream is out of the question.

The crust is laid on as for a fruit pie, with a slit in the centre to allow for the escape of steam. Biscuits on a chicken pie are all very well if that is the kind of pie desired, but it is not a 'County Fair Chicken Pie'.—D.L.

Chicken Pot-Pie

Take a fine chicken, from 3 to 4 lb., draw, wipe well and cut in twelve pieces. Put these in a pan, and cover them with cold water; leave them for 30 minutes, then wash well, drain, and return them to the saucepan. Cover again with fresh water, season with two pinches of salt, one pinch of pepper, and a third of a pinch of nutmeg; add a bunch of six small onions, and 4 oz. of salt pork, cut into square pieces. Cook for three-quarters of an hour, taking care to skim well; then add one pint of raw potatoes and three tablespoonfuls of flour diluted with a cupful of water. Stir till it boils, then let cook for 10 minutes. Remove the *bouquet*, and transfer the whole to a deep baking-dish; moisten the edges slightly with water, and cover the top with a good pie-crust. Egg the surface, making a few transverse lines on the paste with a fork, and cut a hole in the centre. Bake in a brisk oven for 20 minutes, and when cold, serve.—G.A.S.

The Welsh Hermit's Favourite Chicken and Leek Pie

Boil a chicken, cut it up into tidy pieces, not too large, flavour the chicken jelly which it will have produced with a little salt and celery, onion, and various herbs to taste; scald some leeks by pouring boiling water upon them, then split them, and cut them in pieces about an inch long; lay the pieces of chicken in the pie-dish with slices of cold boiled tongue, the pieces of scalded leeks, finely-chopped parsley, and the chicken jelly flavoured as above described. The paste for the pie is to be made with 6 oz. of flour, 3 oz. of the top fat taken off the mutton jelly, and put on the fire in a saucepan with a quarter of a pint of water; when the water boils make a hole in the middle of the flour and pour in the boiling water and mutton fat by degrees, mixing the fat in with a spoon; when well mixed, knead it till of the proper stiffness, and dredge the board with flour to make it smooth; cover your pie, make a hole in the top and form a little ornament with a small stem to fit into it. Fill your baking tin with water; when the paste is done, take off the top ornament, and with a jug pour in through the hole three tablespoonfuls of fresh cream previously heated by placing the jug containing it in a saucepan of boiling water, replace the ornament and serve.— Lady Hall. *Good Cookery*. 1867. Quoted by Ifan Kyrle Fletcher in 'Food and Drink in Wales', in *Wine and Food*, No. 5, 1935, p. 20.

Côtelettes à la Pojarski

1 large chicken
5 oz. fresh breadcrumbs
¼ cup thick fresh cream
1 or 2 eggs
Additional thick cream
A few carrots and turnips
Milk
Salt and pepper
Fine brown breadcrumbs
½ oz. flour

This is, in the words of a gourmet, 'the pearl of Russian cookery'. Scrape all the flesh from the bones of the fowl and set aside. Cook the carcass, with the giblets, the vegetables, salt and pepper, in just enough water to cover, for three hours, very slowly. When done, carefully strain this broth and set aside. Now finely-chop the raw chicken, after removing skin and sinews, and blend well with the fresh breadcrumbs, previously soaked in milk then squeezed dry. Add to this mixture the quarter cup of thick cream and the yolk of an egg as well as very little salt and pepper. This will give a thick smooth paste which may be shaped into 'cutlets'. Dip each one first into beaten egg, then in brown breadcrumbs and cook in hot butter – using either a sauteuse or a frying-pan – gently enough to cook chicken meat without browning exterior too much. Place a small piece of macaroni in the end of each 'cutlet' to simulate the bone. Serve up, in a crown, and keep hot. Pour the prepared broth into the pan where the chicken cooked, stirring to remove all sediment. Add about half a cup more thick cream, taste and season if necessary. Pour this thick sauce in centre of dish of bitoks. Serve very hot with fresh green peas.—P.W.

Poulet sauté Portugaise

1 chicken
½ oz. butter
Savoury rice
2 shallots
3 tomatoes
6 mushrooms
¼ gill white wine
1 gill tomato sauce
1 gill brown veal stock
1 teaspoonful chicken glaze
¼ gill oil
Salt and pepper and some chopped parsley

Cut the chicken into joints, chop the shallots, and slice the mushrooms. Put the butter and oil into a stewpan. As soon as it is hot, add the chicken, and fry it a light brown colour. Then add the shallots and cook a little longer. Now put in the mushrooms, the wine, stock, tomato sauce and the chicken glaze. Cover with the lid, and put it in the oven for half an hour to cook gently. Dish up the chicken on a hot dish, pour the sauce over, garnish round with the tomatoes cut in halves and filled with rice. Sprinkle over a little chopped parsley, and serve. Time required one hour. Seasonable at all times. Sufficient for four or five persons.—M.A.F.

Williamsburg Chicken Pudding

Cut up 4 or 5 lb. fowl as for *Fricassée*, put it in your kettle with water to cover, with one onion, a few celery tops, some sprigs of parsley, a teaspoonful of thyme, salt and pepper. Simmer gently until fowl is tender. Take from broth, remove skin and place in a

shallow baking-dish. Pour over it one cup of strained broth. Make a batter of one pint of milk, three well-beaten eggs, one-fourth cup of flour, one-fourth cup melted butter and one teaspoonful of salt. Pour this over your chicken and bake in a moderate oven about 35 minutes. Serve immediately with a gravy made of thickened broth in a separate dish. (Mrs Randolph's recipe, 1831. Adapted Market Square Tavern Kitchen, 1937.—H.B.

Poulet à la Reine

1 capon or fine and tender fowl
1½ lb. knuckle of veal
1 lb. carrots
Parsley
3 or 4 tablespoonfuls butter
Few stalks chervil
Flour
Butter
1 calf's foot
1 lb. onions
1 stalk celery
Tarragon
Salt and pepper
2 cups hot sauce Normande

This 'plat de haute cuisine' is said to have been the invention of Marie Leszcynska, who was an expert cook. The veal gravy, or 'jus', should be prepared the day before the chicken is to be served. To prepare it place the knuckle of veal and the calf's foot in a heavy iron pan with the cut up vegetables, salt, pepper, parsley, tarragon and chervil. Add just over a quart of cold water. Cover closely and simmer for five or six hours, over a very low heat. When done, remove bones and pass gravy through a sieve, pounding well both the meat and the vegetables. Place a couple of tablespoonfuls of butter in small saucepan, add the same amount of flour and lightly brown, making a 'roux'. Moisten this gradually with the strained veal broth and allow this sauce to simmer VERY gently on the side of the fire for three or four hours or until it looks like rather liquid jam in consistency. Season, adding a pinch of spice if desired. Set this aside until the morrow.

Cut up the fowl and brown the pieces in a sufficiency of butter. To serve, have a large deep dish, very hot. Pour into this a rich and creamy hot *Sauce Normande* and cover with the pieces of chicken. Re-heat the veal gravy and spoon it over the pieces of chicken. Each person takes his share of both top and bottom sauces.—P.W.

Romany Chicken

1 chicken
2 Spanish onions
Sweet raw Spanish pepper
4 tomatoes
1 large glass of sherry

Fry a chicken in a stewpan with bacon and a little butter, then stew it slowly with two Spanish onions, four tomatoes and a large glass of sherry in an earthenware pot. A little raw Spanish pepper is an improvement. Serve in the pot it was cooked in.—R.L.

Suprêmes

The *suprêmes* are constituted by the meat on each side of the breast, from the point where the wing originates to the extremity of the stomach. Under the *suprême* proper is the mignon fillet. If, in classic cookery, the *suprême* be taken from a large bird, the mignon fillets are separated, subjected to fanciful shaping, and after being cooked, used in the garnish of the *suprêmes* proper. There is no need for this in domestic cookery, provided the bird used be not too large, that is, of the chicken *à la Reine* class. The *suprêmes may* be rolled in seasoned flour and then very quickly cooked in intensely hot clarified butter (or a mixture of butter and pure olive oil), in which case the cooking should be stopped as soon as each side of the *suprême* is golden with a tinge of brown. It is better, however, to honour these exquisitely delicate things by a special mode of cookery instead of approximating them to chicken cutlets. That is, the slightly seasoned but unfloured *suprêmes*, first rolled over and over in some just melted butter to which a few drops of lemon-juice have been added, and then, in the same pan, made air-tight by putting a paste of flour and white of egg round the junction of lid and pan, are placed in a very hot oven for a few minutes.

In either case, *suprêmes* must be cooked at the latest possible moment and served-immediately, for even five minutes of delay very appreciably affects their quality.

The most luxurious garnishes suit these delicacies – truffles, *foie-gras*, asparagus tips, mushrooms, the Financière garnish, etc. —T.E.W.

Suprêmes are also called in culinary French *Filets de Volaille*, and when the *Suprême* or *Filet* is served with the joint bone of the wing attached it is called a *Côtelette de Volaille*. When the white meat or breast of a poached or boiled fowl is carved and served with a sauce or garnish specially prepared for it, it is not called *Suprême* nor *Filet* in culinary French but *Blanc de Volaille* or *Blanc de Poulet*.

Here are the *Suprêmes*, *Filets* and *Blancs de Volaille* for which Escoffier gives recipes. We merely indicate which is the informing flavour of each and refer the reader to Escoffier's *Ma Cuisine* for the recipes.

Suprême de Volaille Adelina Patti. Truffles.

Suprême de Volaille Chasseur. Mushrooms.

Suprême de Poulet la Villière. Mushrooms and truffles.

Suprême de Volaille Favorite. Foie Gras and truffles. A garnish of asparagus points.

Suprêmes de Poulet à la Bordelaise. Artichoke bottoms.

Suprêmes ou Filets de Poulet à la Hongroise. Paprika. Serve with rice.

Suprêmes ou Filets de Poulet à l'Indienne. Curry.

Suprêmes de Poulet Judic. Braised lettuce and truffles. Serve with green peas.

Suprêmes ou Côtelettes de Volaille a la Maréchal. Dipped in egg-and-breadcrumbs, grilled and served with truffles and lemon.

Suprêmes de Volaille Mascotte. Foie Gras, Crépinettes and truffles.

Suprêmes de Volaille Montpensier. Truffles and asparagus.

Suprême de Volaille Polignac. Sauce *Suprême, julienne* of truffles and mushrooms.

Suprêmes ou Côtelettes de Volaille Pojarski. The white meat of the chicken is chopped up, mixed with creamed breadcrumbs, seasoned, put together to look like a little cutlet, with a chicken bone at one end, dipped in flour and cooked in butter.

Suprêmes de Volaille Rosamonde. Served on a foundation of puff pastry covered with *Foie Gras*; also a *purée* of mushrooms.

Suprêmes de Volaille Rossini. Truffles. Serve well buttered and cheesed noodles at the same time.

Suprêmes de Poulet Verdi. Truffles. Served on a foundation of macaroni in which have been mixed some dice of *Foie Gras* and sliced truffles.

Blanc de Volaille Vicomtesse de Fontenay. Truffles, Parmesan cheese.

Blanc de Volaille Alsacienne. Foie Gras, truffles with a dish of *Nouilles a l'Alsacienne.*

Blanc de Volaille Angeline. Truffles, paprika, grated cheese.

Blanc de Volaille aux Concombres. Grated cheese and a dish of cucumber served at the same time, boiled with a Cream sauce.

Blanc de Poulet Bagration. Truffles, grated cheese and *Coquillettes.*

Blanc de Poulet Florentine. Grated cheese and browned; served on spinach.

Blanc de Poulet Mireille. Same as '*Florentine*', but with truffles added.

Suprêmes de Volaille Jeannette

Slices of cold breast of roast chicken
Slices of chilled *Foie Gras*
Aspic jelly
Tarragon

The chicken breast should be cut into thin slices of even size and thickness and should be laid on a serving dish, alternating with slices of *Foie Gras*, previously well-chilled also. The chicken aspic must be carefully spooned over all, after sprinkling the meat with chopped tarragon leaves, then set on ice until ready to serve.

Poule en Tortue

1 large fowl
1 large onion
2 cups hot *bouillon*
1 small *bouquet-garni*
Butter
2 scant tablespoons flour
1 or 2 carrots
Salt and pepper

This is a simple and useful recipe for using up a somewhat elderly and tough bird. Prepare as usual, cut into pieces and brown them in the heated butter – or a mixture of butter and olive oil. When nicely coloured on all sides, drain and set aside. Cut the onion up finely and brown gently in the fat used to brown chicken. When an even colour, sprinkle with the flour, stirring well, and moisten with the *bouillon* – or hot water. Add the pieces of fowl, the sliced carrots and the *bouquet*. There should be just enough liquid barely to cover the pieces of chicken; if necessary, add more *bouillon* or water as well as salt and pepper to taste. Cook over a moderate heat, stirring fairly often to prevent burning. Three hours cooking may be needed. Garnish with *croûtons* or *fleurons*. —P.W.

Poulet aux Trois Frères

Cut up a chicken into small pieces. Melt enough butter to cover the bottom of a casserole, *hot*. Add two full teaspoons of olive oil. Put in the chicken and cover with 24 *very* small onions, or shallots, carefully prepared, and 30 very small whole new potatoes. Flavour with salt and pepper and a pinch of mace. Add a few mushrooms cut in medium pieces. Put the whole in the oven. It should be well done in 40 minutes and the whole dish a good brown colour. Just before serving pour over three or four tablespoonfuls of dissolved meat glaze.—N.S.

Poulet Sauté au Vin Blanc

1 chicken
2 tablespoons butter
Salt and pepper
Chopped parsley
Small pinch mixed spice
1 cup white wine (dry)
1 cup stock or *bouillon*
2 shallots, minced
½ lb. mushrooms, sliced
2 tablespoons flour

Carve the chicken and brown the pieces in the butter, seasoning with salt, pepper, parsley and spice. When flesh is firm and brown, add shaliots, mushrooms and the flour, stirring well. Moisten with wine and stock and continue cooking until meat is tender. There should be very little of the excellent sauce. A small *bouquet* may be used in place of spice.—P.W.

III. BOILING HENS
CHICKEN SOUPS

Fowls, whether cocks or hens, of uncertain vintage and heritage, are not fit for the spit but for the pot. They can be used for puddings and pies, but younger birds are much better. Old birds, however, make good broth, chicken broth, *Consommé de Volaille* when the bird is boiled in water, with some vegetables and seasonings, but no milk; or *Crème de Volaille*, when simmered in milk and finished with fresh cream, but no binding of eggs is added. Here are recipes for the *Consommé de Volaille*, á *Purée of Chicken*, and a *Velouté de Volaille*, which are the basis of a large number of classical soup recipes, of which we give a list with a mention of their informing flavour.

Chicken Broth (Consommé de Volaille)

1 fowl
4 cups water
Salt and pepper
1 blade mace (or 1 pinch dried)
1 thick slice of onion
1 teaspoon pounded almonds

Place a cleaned fowl in a deep pot; add water and all other ingredients, except the almonds which, when pounded to a paste, must be added when the soup is strained and ready to serve. A carrot and a branch of celery, as well as a leek, may also be added. Simmering must be slow and the broth, when cold, must be freed of all fat before re-heating to serve.

Purée of Chicken

Prepare, the day before the party, a veal stock, and roast a chicken. Remove the flesh from the chicken as soon as it is cold, excluding all skin and brown parts. All the bones and trimmings, crushed with a chopper, should be cooked with the veal stock, of which there should be 2½ pints for eight basins. Strain this off in the evening. The next day, take the chicken-meat with half its weight of breadcrumbs soaked in milk, and pound together in a mortar, with a tablespoonful and half of ground sweet almonds, and the hard-boiled yolks of four eggs. Pass this through the sieve to get rid of lumps, gristle, etc., moistening it with a spoonful or so of stock to assist the operation. When this has been done, let cool, removing all the fat that may rise to the surface. Now take a pan and melt an ounce of butter at the bottom of it, stirring in a like quantity of flour; add a little stock, and work the *roux* so obtained without ceasing, gradually pouring in stock, and adding the paste. Let the *purée* now come to the boil; remove the pan from the fire, and as you pour it into the tureen, stir into it a coffee-cupful of the soup with which a tablespoonful of cream and the strained yolk of an egg have been mixed, and serve. Be careful to clear all white from the yolk, or it may set in flaky pieces, and spoil the look of the soup. Should this by any accident occur the whole should be passed through a strainer before serving.—A.K-H. (1).

Velvet Soup (Velouté de Volaille)

Make a good rich chicken *bouillon*. Thicken slightly with rice flour (one tablespoon flour to one pint of liquid). Remove the skin and bones of the boiled chicken and pound the meat in a mortar until absolutely smooth, then pass through a wire sieve. At the moment before serving, add the pounded chicken, and to one quart of *consommé* add the yolks of four eggs and one cup of cream. Stir well until absolutely velvety. —E.D.W.

Crème Agnès Sorel. Velouté de Volaille, with some mushrooms and a *julienne* of mushrooms, breast of fowl, ox tongue and cream.

Consommé aux ailerons. Consommé de Volaille, with some fowls' pinions boned, stuffed and braised; also some poached rice.

Consommé Alexandre. Consommé de Volaille, with a light tapioca binding, a *julienne* of chicken, some chicken *quenelles* and a *chiffonade* of lettuce.

Consommé des ambassadeurs. Consommé de Volaille, garnished with dice of *Royale* with chopped truffles, dice of mushrooms and of chicken.

Consommé ambassadrice. Consommé de Volaille, garnished with three sorts of *royale*, one with chopped truffles (black); the other with tomatoes (red); and the third with *purée* of green peas (green); also a *julienne* of mushrooms and chicken.

Consommé d'Arenberg. Consommé de Volaille, garnished with some very small balls – no bigger than green peas – of carrots, turnips, truffles, peas, *quenelles* of chicken stuffing and asparagus *royale*.

Consommé à la Bohémienne. Consommé de Volaille, with a light tapioca binding, garnished with dice of *foie gras royale* and served with *profiteroles*.

Crème Boïeldieu. Velouté de Volaille, garnished with *quenelles* of *foie gras*, truffles and chicken; also some fresh cream.

Consommé à la Bordelaise. Consommé de Volaille, with a tapioca binding, garnished with carrots cut up like marbles and green peas; marrowbone fat on *canapés* is served at the same time.

Consommé Bouquetière. Consommé de Volaille, with a light tapioca binding, and garnished with small, cut up vegetables, of as many different sorts as are available at the time.

Consommé Bretonne.' Consommé de Volaille, garnished with a *julienne* of fresh vegetables and sprigs of chervil.

Consommé Caroline. Consommé de Volaille, garnished with lozenges of *royale au lait d'amandes*, rice and sprigs of chervil.

Consommé Célestine. Consommé de Volaille, with a light tapioca binding and garnished with a fine *julienne* of pancake.

Consommé Chancelière. Consommé de Volaille, garnished with new peas, a *royale* of chicken, a *julienne* of chicken, some truffles and some mushrooms.

Crème Chantilly. Purée de Volaille, with some fresh cream and some *quenelles* of chicken.

Crème Charteuse. Chicken *velouté* garnished with pieces of tomatoes, small ravioli filled with *foie gras*, spinach and chopped herbs; also some fresh cream.

Consommé Châtelaine. Consommé de Volaille, with a light tapioca binding, garnished with dice of onion-cum-artichoke *royale*, and *quenelles* of chicken stuffed with chestnut *purée*.

Potage Cheveux d'Ange. Consommé de Volaille, garnished with some very fine vermicelli and served with grated cheese.

Consommé Chevreuse. Consommé de Volaille, garnished with large *quenelles* of chicken stuffed with an asparagus points *purée* and a *julienne* of truffles.

Crème Chevreuse. Velouté of chicken garnished with a *julienne* of truffles and chicken, a little semolina and a cream binding.

Crème Camelia. Purée of new green peas with a tapioca binding garnished with a *julienne* of chicken and white of leeks. Butter and fresh cream.

Consommé Carmencita. Consommé de Volaille, with tapioca and a little paprika; a glass of sherry added at time of serving.

Crème Chabrillan. Tomato *purée* garnished with *quenelles* of chicken and vermicelli.

Cock-a-Leekie

1 small fowl
1 large bunch leeks
2 tablespoons butter
Salt and pepper
1 or 2 tablespoons rice (optional)
2 to 2½ quarts good stock

Clean out fowl and cut into small joints. Wash the leeks thoroughly, taking off roots and outer skin as well as some of green top portion. Cut them up small and lightly fry in one tablespoonful of butter. Remove, leaving butter in pan. In this butter, to which the other tablespoonful has been added, fry the pieces of fowl brown on all sides, seasoning well with salt and pepper. Heat the stock, add leeks and pieces of fowl, simmer gently, after removing scum carefully as it rises, for about two hours or until fowl is tender. When ready to serve, put pieces of chicken in a hot tureen (they may be boned and cut up, if preferred) and pour soup over this. The rice should be added after the soup has been cooking for one hour, if rice is used. This soup is all the better for being made one day and reheated and eaten the next. A *bouquet-garni* is an improvement.

Consommé Colombine. Chicken broth garnished with vegetables cut up small, a *julienne* of pigeon and poached pigeon's eggs.

Consommé Comtesse. Chicken broth with a tapioca binding, garnished with lozenges of *royale* of white asparagus *purée*, stuffed lettuce, *quenelles* with minced truffles.

Consommé Crécy. Chicken broth, with a light tapioca binding and garnished with lozenges of *royale* of carrot *purée*, and a *brunoise* of carrots.

Consommé Dame Blanche. Chicken broth with a light tapioca binding, garnished with small pieces of *royale*, chicken meat cut up in the shape of little stars and *Perles du Japon*.

Crème Dame Blanche. Velouté of chicken garnished with dice of chicken breast, white *quenelles* and *Perles du Japon*.

Consommé a la Dartois. Chicken broth with a light binding of arrowroot and celery *fumet*, garnished with chicken *quenelles* and a *julienne* of truffles and mushrooms.

Crème Dartois. Purée of white haricot beans, garnished with a *brunoise* of vegetables, served with cream.

Consommé Demidoff. Chicken broth garnished with fresh vegetables cut up small; also truffles; and *fines herbes quenelles*.

Consommé Deslignac. Chicken broth with a light tapioca binding, garnished with dice of *royale* and lettuce leaves poached and stuffed.

Crème Derby. Ground rice *velouté* with onions and curry powder; garnished with rice, truffles and *quenelles* of chicken stuffed with *foie gras*.

Consommé aux Diablotins. Chicken broth garnished with little square cheese-coated *croûtons* dusted with cayenne pepper.

Consommé Diplomate. Chicken broth with a light tapioca binding, garnished with a *julienne* of truffles and rounds of chicken stuffing with crayfish *coulis*.

Consommé Divette. Chicken broth garnished with *royale* of crayfish, *quenelles* of smelts and truffles.

Consommé Doria. Chicken broth with cucumbers and short pieces of macaroni filled with chicken stuffing steeped in tomato sauce.

Crème Doria. A cucumber *velouté* garnished with cucumber cut up to be like small marbles and some rice. Served with cream.

Consommé Duchesse. Chicken broth garnished with *Perles du Japon*, some dice of *royale* and a *julienne* of lettuce.

Consommé Floréal. Chicken broth garnished with *Marguerites* of carrots and turnips, green peas, asparagus tips and small *quenelles* flavoured with pistachio.

Friar's Chicken. Chicken, veal, eggs, salt, pepper, parsley, water. Put 2 lb. of knuckle of veal into a pan with two or more quarts of water, boil for two hours, strain; cut a young fowl into joints, skin it, and add it to the boiling broth; season with white pepper and salt; let it boil for a little, then add a tablespoonful of chopped parsley. When the chicken is boiled tender, add three well-beaten eggs; stir them quickly into the broth one way, and remove immediately from the fire.—F.M.M. (1).

Consommé Garibaldi. Chicken broth garnished with *Perles du Japon* and spaghetti.

Consommé Gauloise. Chicken broth with a binding of yolks of eggs and garnished with small *crêtes* and *rognons de coq*, and rounds of ham stuffing.

Giblet Soup. The giblets of a couple of ducks or chickens; 2 oz. dripping; 2 oz. flour; three onions; one carrot; one turnip; tops of a stick of celery; a little thyme. Slice onion and cut carrot and turnip into dice; put dripping into a frying-pan and put the pan over the fire, stirring in the flour as the dripping melts, then add the vegetables. In about five minutes add the giblets (cleaned and chopped), and fry all for about ten minutes, stirring occasionally. Turn the contents of the frying-pan into a stew pan, add three pints of water, and simmer for about three hours. About an hour before the soup is ready, put in the celery, cut into fine shreds, and add the thyme, seasoning with pepper and salt to taste.—L.G.N.

Consommé Grande Duchesse. Chicken broth garnished with *quenelles* of chicken, a *julienne* of chicken breast and ox tongue, and some asparagus points.

Chicken Gumbo. Joint a young 4-lb. chicken. Roll in flour and fry till light brown in three tablespoons butter and three tablespoons lard. Put chicken and ham bone in large soup-kettle. Into the skillet in which the chicken was fried slice three medium-sized onions and fry golden brown. Put into the soup-pot with three cups stewed tomatoes, three pints of young okra sliced, three cups sliced celery and two quarts cold water. Simmer for four or five hours, adding one tablespoon salt and half teaspoon pepper towards the end. The chicken must drop from the bones. Take out the bones. Have boiled rice ready. Press portions into small buttered cups to mould and turn out on to soup plates. Pour the hot gumbo around it. (*Old recipe from Richmond, Virginia. Prov'd 1937.*)—H.B.

Consommé Impératrice. Chicken broth with *crêtes* and *rognons de coq*, asparagus points and *royale.*

Consommé Impérial. Chicken broth with tapioca and garnished with *quenelles, crêtes* and *rognons de coq*, green peas and parsley.

Consommé Infante. Chicken broth with a light tapioca binding garnished with *croûtons*, with a vegetable *purée* stuffing *gratinée.*

Consommé Jacobine. Chicken broth garnished with dice of potatoes, French beans, turnips, green peas and a *julienne* of truffles.

Consommé Jockey Club. Chicken broth garnished with dice of Crécy *royale*, mashed peas and chicken.

Consommé Joinville. Chicken broth garnished with *quenelles* of three colours: green, white and red.

Consommé Juanita. Chicken broth garnished with dice of tomato *royale* and the yolks of hard-boiled eggs passed through a sieve and made to look like vermicelli.

Consommé Judic. Chicken broth as meaty as possible: garnishings of braised lettuce with chicken stuffing and *julienne* of truffles served separately.

Consommé Lorette. Chicken broth with long pepper, garnished with *julienne* of truffles and asparagus points. *Pommes Lorette* served at the same time.

Consommé Marguerite. Chicken broth garnished with flowerlets of chicken stuffing, with hard-boiled yolks of eggs in the centre, and asparagus points.

Consommé Maria. Chicken broth with a light binding of tapioca, garnished with *royale* of haricot beans and fresh vegetables.

Crème Marie-Louise. Chicken *velouté* with barley cream, garnished with *printanière* of vegetables and dice of macaroni, egg binding or fresh cream.

Crème Marie-Stuart. Same as *Marie-Louise* but with dice of carrots in place of macaroni.

Consommé Marquise. Chicken broth garnished with *quenelles* of chicken and a tomato sauce; also *julienne* of lettuce and truffles.

Consommé Martinière. Chicken broth garnished with *rondelles* of stuffed cabbage, green peas and chervil. *Diablotins* are served separately with this soup.

Crème Martha. An oniony chicken *velouté*,

garnished with quenelles of chicken, with *fines herbes* and green peas. Egg binding or fresh cream.

Consommé Messaline. Chicken broth with tomatoes *fumet*, garnished with *julienne* of sweet peppers, *rognons de coq* and rice.

Consommé Mikado. Chicken broth with tomatoes *fumet*; garnished with dice of tomatoes and chicken.

Consommé Milanaise. Chicken broth with tomatoes *fumet*; garnished with *julienne* of mushrooms, ham, truffles and spaghetti. Grated cheese is serve separately.

Crème Milanaise. Chicken and tomatoes *velouté*; garnished with rice or macaroni and a *julienne* of grey truffles, ham and mushrooms. Egg binding or fresh cream.

Consommé Mimosa. Chicken broth garnished with three colours of *royale* dice: pink (carrots *purée*), yellow (yolks of hard-boiled eggs), green (green peas *purée*).

Consommé Mireille. Chicken broth thickened with semolina and garnished with rounds or stars of *royale* of chicken.

Crème Mogador. Chicken *velouté* with a *purée* of *foie gras*; garnished with a *julienne* of chicken, tongue and truffles.

Consommé Monaco. Chicken broth garnished with truffles, *Perles du Japon* and *profiteroles.*

Consommé Monte-Carlo. Chicken broth garnished with rounds of carrots, turnips and, stuffed pancakes and slices of truffles.

Consommé Montmorency. Chicken broth with a little tapioca, garnished with asparagus points, white *quenelles*, rice and chervil.

Crème Montorgueil. Chicken *velouté* garnished with a *chiffonade* of sorrel and fresh vegetables; also chervil; fresh cream added before serving.

Clear Mulligatawny

Half a raw fowl
2 tablespoons butter
1 small onion
1 oz. raw ham
1 scanty teaspoon curry powder
6 cups good veal stock
1 egg white, and shell
1 cup boiled rice
Salt and pepper
Lemon juice

This is an English recipe for this best-of-all Indian soups, but the ingredients required to make real Indian Mulligatawny being unobtainable in England, this must do, and is delicious, too.

Cut the fowl into pieces. Melt the butter in a pan; when hot add the sliced onion and ham, frying lightly. When a pale brown add the curry powder and stir into mixture, then add the pieces of fowl, browning nicely with other ingredients. Moisten with the stock (the broth from the other half of the fowl or from a knuckle of veal is suitable) and bring to boiling point. Skim, simmer for 25 minutes, then strain. Slightly beat the egg-white and add this, with the crushed shell, to the strained broth which has been reheated. Boil up once, then set pan aside and allow broth to settle for about 20 minutes; then again strain through a fine *tamis* or a cloth. Reheat, add the rice (more or less, as you wish) and the fowl meat, cut into dice. Season with lemon juice, salt and, if necessary, with pepper. Some people prefer to serve the rice – very hot and dry – separately. —P.W.

Thick Mulligatawny

1 small or half a large fowl
1 onion
2 tablespoons butter
1 dessertspoon curry
Flour
5 or 6 cups good meat stock
1 small apple
2 cloves
Salt and pepper
Lemon juice
½ gill cream

Cut the fowl into as small pieces as possible. Slice the onion and fry in hot butter. When they are a light brown, add the curry powder and flour, blending well; moisten mixture gradually with the heated stock; add the peeled and chopped apple, the cloves and the seasonings. Simmer soup for a good hour, then add the lemon juice and the cream after removing all bones from fowl and dicing the flesh. If at all possible, use fresh coconut milk in place of cream, alternately coconut water in place of half the quantity of stock mentioned above. To make this, soak 4 oz. grated coconut in a pint of water for an hour; then strain into soup when adding stock. Dry hot rice may be handed and, if you like it, a little good chutney.

Consommé Nemours. Chicken broth with a little tapioca, garnished with carrots, *Perles du Japon* and a *julienne* of truffles.

Consommé Ninon. Chicken broth, garnished with carrots and turnips cut in the shape of filberts and small beads of truffles; *tartelettes* filled with minced chicken and hard-boiled egg-yolk, with a star of truffle in the centre, are served with this soup.

Petits Pots de Volaille. To two jelly pots of strong chicken broth add the yolks of six eggs and a little salt. Steam in a stewpan for 25 minutes. When cold, turn out into moulds. Best served with *Salade Russe* or aspic. (*The Cookery Chronicle. Devon Nursing*

Association, Exeter, Xmas, 1932, *from the Countess of Antrim.*)

Poule au Pot. This was the national French dish from the time of good King Henri IV until the fall of the Bastille in 1789. It is made in the same way as *pot-au-feu* (q.v. in Section VI, *MEAT*) except that a fowl is substituted for the beef and a French country *saucisse* is added. This soup is not coloured and the boiled fowl is usually eaten as the second course.

Consommé Rachel. Chicken broth with tapioca; garnished with a *julienne* of artichoke bottoms. *Croûtons* with poached marrow from a marrowbone are served with this soup.

Crème Reine. Chicken *purée* with rice, garnished with dice of chicken. Fresh cream.

Consommé Reine. Chicken broth with a little tapioca, garnished with dice of *royale* of chicken *purée* and a *julienne* of chicken.

Consommé Rossini. Chicken broth with a little tapioca and some essence of truffles; garnished with *profiteroles* stuffed with *foie gras* and with dice of truffles.

Rossolnick. A Russian cucumber soup. Made like a *velouté de volaille* to which one adds some cucumber juice (*rossole*) and some pickled cucumbers (*agoursis*).

Consommé Sévigné. Chicken broth garnished with white *quenelles*, a *julienne* of lettuce and some asparagus points.

Crème Sévigné. Half *crème* of chicken and half *crème* of lettuce mixed; garnished with a *julienne* of lettuce and some *quenelles* of chicken.

IV. LEFT-OVERS AND SUNDRY MADE-UP CHICKEN DISHES

Poulet en Capilotade

Remains of cooked chicken
2 tablespoons butter
1 small glass white wine
2 tablespoons tomato *purée* or sauce
Salt and pepper
A few capers
1 or 2 onions
½ teaspoon vinegar
1 cup good *bouillon*
1 *bouquet-garni*
2 tablespoons flour

This is an excellent method for using up any left-over cooked chicken, whether roast or boiled; other kinds of poultry or even game may also be used up in this manner. Melt the butter, chop the onions, fry them a light brown in the hot butter, then add the wine and the vinegar and cook gently until liquid is almost entirely absorbed and forms a *glace* in bottom of pan. Moisten this with the tomato *purée* or sauce and the *bouillon*.

539

Add salt and pepper, the pieces of chicken, the *bouquet* and the capers, chopped. Simmer all this gently over a low fire for 10 or 15 minutes, then thicken the sauce by the addition of the flour, mixed with a little cold water or *bouillon*. This is an old recipe and fine breadcrumbs may be used to thicken the sauce in place of flour. Serve in a border of well-cooked rice or freshly-mashed, fluffy potatoes.—P.W.

Chile con Carne

Wash and split six large red chillies. Remove seeds, cover with boiling water and cook slowly till soft. Press through a sieve. Add half pint thick tomato *purée*, one large onion cut up, quarter teaspoon salt and a small piece of bayleaf. Cook slowly for 15 minutes. Cut up dark meat of a boiled or roast chicken into ½ in. cubes. Put this into the sauce and let it stand over boiling water for 30 minutes till the meat has absorbed part of the sauce. Serve with rice.

Coquilles de Volaille

If plenty of the white meat is left, use as indicated in recipe for 'Chicken Croquettes' and place a couple of tablespoons in real or silvered scallop shells, decorating all around the edge with small 'roses' of freshly-mashed potatoes, forced through a pastry bag having a rather large rose nozzle. Place small pieces of butter on top and a sparse sprinkling of brown breadcrumbs, and colour delicately in a moderately hot oven. A small round of truffle may be set in the centre of each coquille.—P.W.

'Country Captain'

A Sussex name for the following excellent dish of chicken: Cut neat slices off a partly boiled fowl. Dip the slices in flour and fry them to a delicate brown in 2 oz. of good margarine, with salt, pepper and a small spoonful of curry powder. When browned, add the sieved pulp of two or three tomatoes, half a pint of tomato sauce and a very little finely-minced parsley. Boil up again and serve in a pile with a garnish of fried *croûtons* and a dusting of minced parsley. —B.H.

Creamed Chicken

1½ cups cut-up cooked chicken
¼ lb. mushrooms
1½ tablespoons butter
2 tablespoons flour
Salt and pepper
1 cup chicken broth

Pick as much white meat as possible and cut it into small pieces or dice. Lightly fry the mushrooms in a little fat or butter, after slicing them. Mix with the pieces of chicken.

Melt the butter, add the flour, stirring until mixture is smooth, then add the broth and seasoning and beat until smooth and thick. Add chicken and mushrooms; let them simmer together for a few moments. A drop or two of lemon juice adds piquancy to the sauce. Serve on hot buttered toast or in a ring of hot boiled rice or spaghetti.

Chicken Croquettes

2 tablespoons flour
½ lb. cold cooked chicken
½ cup stock
Lemon juice to taste
¼ lb. small mushrooms
Salt and pepper
Fine brown breadcrumbs
2 oz. boiled ham
1 tablespoon thick cream
1 small truffle (optional)
Butter
1 egg
Frying oil or fat

The perfect chicken croquette is a delicious dish: the interior should not be too firm and the creamy substance must contrast with the crisp exterior.

Chop or mince the chicken finely with the ham. Toss the mushrooms, after chopping them, in a sufficiency of butter. Chop the truffle, if any. Blend all ingredients, add salt, pepper and a touch of cayenne, if liked. Melt a couple of tablespoons of butter without allowing it to brown, add flour and moisten with stock, beating to a smooth sauce which should be quite thick. Add the chicken mixture to this, with the cream. Cool mixture, then shape as desired into croquettes or 'corks', dip carefully first in the beaten egg, then in breadcrumbs; allow this to harden a little, then fry until a nice light brown in oil or fat at 475°F. if a thermometer is used, if not, in slightly smoking fat. Serve at once with any desired sauce handed separately. —P.W.

Chicken Canneloni

The chicken mixture indicated above may be enclosed in squares of thinly-rolled rough puff paste. Each square is then neatly rolled up, coated with egg and breadcrumbs, then fried, as suggested above. Crisply fried parsley is nice with either recipe.—P.W.

Croustades de Volaille

Slices of stale bread
Frying fat
Purée of cooked poultry or game

The slices of bread must be about 1½ in. thick and should be cut into points or 'sippets' about 4 to 5 in. long, one end being nicely rounded. With great care, remove the interior of each sippet, leaving a solid bottom and edge all around. This delicate operation should be done by first cutting with a sharp knife, then removing crumb deftly and evenly, leaving as much thickness at the bottom of each sippet as around the edges. There should be seven in all and also a round one, cut out in the same way. Fry a delicate brown in fresh frying-fat or oil, drain and fill each sippet and the round with hot *purée* of cooked game or poultry prepared as indicated in recipe for making chicken croquettes. Pile up round each one nicely, serve on a hot dish, in the shape of a circle with the seven points of fried bread touching one another in the centre and the round placed on top. Decorate with parsley and serve at once with or without a hot sauce handed separately. The pieces of meat may be finely minced, diced or, if a smooth *purée* is preferred, pounded, then pressed through a sieve after usual additions and seasonings.—P.W.

Poulet en Daube Provençale

1 large boned chicken
8 oz. raw veal
Carrots
Skins of fresh pork (couennes)
Giblets of chicken
8 oz. raw pork
A little cognac
Onions
1 calf's foot
Bouquet-garni
1 cup white wine

Chop or grind up in a mincing-machine the pork and part of the veal, leaving the best portions to be cut into long fillets. Allow these to marinate for an hour in a little good brandy. Add salt and pepper to the chopped meat and use to stuff the chicken together with the fillets of marinated veal which should be inserted longways in the fowl. Wrap the bird in a cloth and tie up at both ends securely. Cut the carrots and onions into slices and set them in the bottom of a heavy iron or copper stewpan. On them place a few pieces of skin of fresh pork, the cleaned and cut-up calf's foot, the *bouquet* and the cleaned giblets. Set on a moderate heat until bottom layer of vegetables begins to colour, then add the wine and sufficient *bouillon*, stock or hot water just to cover the chicken. Bring to boiling point, skim well, close with a weight on the lid and cook gently for a couple of hours. Press chicken under a board and weight after removing cloth. The gravy, strained, may be reduced by further boiling and used to coat the cold chicken.

This recipe resembles that given for 'Galantine of Chicken', but it is more savoury.—P.W.

Devilled Chicken Bones

Drumsticks and wings of chicken
1 tablespoon chili sauce
1 teaspoon mustard (made)
Flour
1 tablespoon walnut catsup
2 tablespoons butter
1 teaspoon Worcester sauce
Salt and pepper
1 cup chicken stock (optional)
Chopped parsley
Cayenne

This is an excellent way of using up drumsticks – which no one ever wants – wing tips or second joints of wings of chicken or turkey.

Melt butter, add sauces, mustard and a dash of cayenne. Cut several rather deep gashes in each piece of chicken, sprinkle with salt, paste all over with the butter, sauces, mustard, etc., and either grill or cook in a hot oven. A dredging of flour gives a crisp surface. The stock, if used, should be heated, the butter, sauces, etc., be added to it, and the plainly grilled bones added to this sauce, but most people prefer them crisp and dry, handing a separate sauce, if desired.
—P.W.

Devilled Chicken Croûtes

Cold chicken
Olive oil
Small rounds of bread
Butter
Meat glaze
Salt and cayenne
Pinch curry powder
Thick cream
Chopped parsley
Sprigs of parsley

Cut the bread about ½ in. thick, remove crusts and cut into rounds of desired size. Taking a smaller cutter, make a round cut in centre of each piece of bread, not, however, cutting right through to the bottom. Scoop out as much of this centre cut as possible, then fry these little cases brown in olive oil. Drain and keep hot. Mince chicken very finely, place in a small pan with butter, parsley, salt, cayenne and curry powder, and moisten to a thick paste with cream. Heat mixture through, then use to fill prepared bread cases. Glaze tops with the meat glaze and heat for a moment in a hot oven. Serve hot, garnishing with parsley.—P.W.

Left-over Fricassée of Chicken

With Rice. Cook the rice in chicken broth or any good stock or *bouillon* until tender but not too soft. Season well. Allow rice to cool, place a layer in a serving dish, cover with cold *fricassée* of chicken, freed from bones, cover this in turn with another layer of rice and so on, finishing up with a layer of rice. Smooth top surface with blade of a knife and serve cold, with salad.—P.W.

Fritôt de Poulet
(Left-over Boiled Fowl)

Cut any left-over boiled fowl into neat pieces and marinate in lemon juice, spices, a few drops of olive oil, salt, pepper and chopped herbs (parsley, chives, tarragon, etc.) for an hour, then drain well and dip each piece in frying batter. Fry in deep fat or oil until nicely browned. Serve at once, very hot, with a hot tomato or ravigote sauce. —P.W.

Galantine de Poulet

1 large tender chicken
8 oz. uncooked lean veal
Suspicion of powdered mace
Slices of fat boiled ham
Few stoned and chopped olives
12 oz. uncooked lean pork
Salt and pepper
Slices of cooked tongue
Few pistachio nuts
1 truffle or peelings

The worst part of this recipe is the boning of the chicken. If you are an old hand, you will probably – starting at the neck and gradually turning the bird inside out – be able to perform this delicate operation without breaking the skin, if not, it is best, frankly, to slit the skin down the entire back and gradually, using a very sharp, small knife, scrape the flesh from the bones. Set the latter in a saucepan, with some good beef and veal bones and soup vegetables, adding salt and a few peppercorns and simmering for an hour or so, then straining to use as will be directed.

The fowl being boned, chop together the raw pork, the veal and season well, adding the merest touch of mace. If the fowl has been split to bone, lay it, skin side down, on a wet slab. Cover inside part with the slices of tongue and these, in turn, with slices of fat ham. Flatten the chopped meat evenly on this and dot whole pistachios, the coarsely-chopped olives and either thin slices or peelings of truffles over entire surface. Roll up bird into its original shape. If it has been boned without splitting, wrap the chopped meats in the slices of tongue and ham and force through the neck, tying or sewing up firmly. Have a good, strong clean cloth. Tie the stuffed bird in this as you would a roly-poly pudding. Place it in hot stock made with bones or a knuckle of veal and simmer

gently for a couple of hours. When done, tighten up the cloth at both ends, lay a small board with a weight on top, and cool. When thoroughly cold, unwrap carefully, coat with chaudfroid sauce, and, when this is set, mask – i.e. cover completely – with cold but still semi-liquid clear aspic jelly. Serve with garnishing of mashed or diced aspic jelly and lettuce.—P.W.

Gâteau de Foie Lyonnais

1 or 2 fresh chicken's livers
Salt and pepper
2 egg whites
3 tablespoons flour
1 small clove garlic
2 egg yolks
2 tablespoons butter
½ cup milk

Lightly *sauté* the liver (one will do, if a good size) in a little butter, sprinkling with salt and pepper to taste. When cool, cut it up; then either press through a sieve or pound in a mortar until a smooth paste. Melt the butter, add the flour and stir until the mixture is smooth, over a low heat. Add the heated milk gradually, then the egg yolks, previously well-beaten. Season well; then add the chicken liver mixture, mixing it lightly in. Cool this mixture; then put in the stiffly-beaten egg whites *very* lightly, but be careful not to stir or beat the mixture in doing this, the most important operation. Butter a *soufflé* dish well after rubbing it over, bottom and sides, with the cut clove of garlic: this will lightly flavour the *gâteau*, no more. Pour the mixture carefully into the prepared dish and cook in a moderately hot oven, without once opening the oven door, from 20 to 25 minutes or until risen and nicely browned. This is, in reality, a *soufflé*, and may, when used as a savoury, be served in small individual ramekins.

Some Lyonnais cooks prefer the *gâteau* to have the consistency of a custard rather than that of a *soufflé*. If this is your choice – and this latter method is, of the two, the more orthodox – beat the eggs well without separating them and blend with the thick white sauce mixed with the chicken liver *purée* and seasoning. Pour into a deep, well-buttered dish rubbed with garlic (which can be sent to table – those oven-glass ones are very nice) and set in a panful of hot water before popping into a medium oven, there to cook until set through. When the fine blade of a small knife can be plunged into it and comes out quite clean, the *gâteau* is done and should be served at once.—P.W.

Chicken au Gratin

½ lb. cold roast or boiled chicken
½ cup grated cheese

Breadcrumbs
1 cup tomato sauce
2 oz. uncooked rice
Salt and pepper
Butter

Remove cold chicken from bones and cut into small pieces without chopping. Cook the rice in boiling salted water until tender but fluffy. Butter an oven dish well. Place a layer of the chicken on the bottom, cover this with a layer of cooked rice, pour some hot and, if possible, freshly-made, tomato sauce over this and sprinkle with grated cheese to which a few breadcrumbs have been added. The latter should be freshly-made, not brown. Repeat this until all ingredients are used up, finishing the operation with a top surface of cheese and crumbs. Dot with butter and bake in a hot oven to nicely brown surface. Hand more tomato sauce separately.—P.W.

Chicken Liver Croustades

½ cup chicken livers
½ tablespoon flour
2 tablespoons sherry or Madeira
Baker's loaf stale bread
1 cup small mushrooms
½ cup cream
Butter

Cut bread into 2-in. cubes. With a sharp knife remove centres, leaving neat box. Brush with melted butter and brown in oven. Fill with mixture: *Sauté* diced livers, sliced mushroom caps and chopped stems in butter. Sprinkle with flour, add cream and seasoning and simmer five minutes. Add wine, and when hot, fill the *croustades*. Garnish with a little minced parsley.—T.C.

Gratin de Foies de Volaille aux Nouilles

Cook some noodles (freshly made ones are best) in the usual way – that is, in hot, salted water; drain them well and after giving them a generous lump of fresh butter and a dusting of grated cheese, arrange them comfortably in a baking dish; they are the couch upon which the chickens' livers will rest. However, before they can enjoy this rest, the livers have to be prepared in the following manner: Cut them up in large dice and toss them in butter quickly with the same quantity of chopped fresh mushrooms; add a pinch of finely-chopped chives, chervil and parsley. A spoonful of good brandy is most acceptable at this stage, followed by twice as much fresh cream, both providing a suitable sauce for the livers and mushrooms while finishing cooking. Allow the sauce to reduce on a gentle heat, and the livers will then be ready to be dressed upon the

noodles; brown under a hot grill for a short while and serve hot.—A.E.F.

Chicken's Liver Balls (for Soups)

1 chicken's liver
1 teaspoon butter
1 tiny onion
1 egg
1 tablespoon flour
Salt and pepper

Chop the onion or grate finely. Melt the butter in a small pan, add the onion, then the finely-chopped or cut-up liver. Fry gently for a few minutes, then add the flour, mixing and seasoning well. Let the mixture cool; then add the well-beaten egg. This will give a dough which can be shaped into small balls which must be dropped into boiling soup 10 minutes before serving. A little finely-chopped parsley may also be added. —P.W.

Terrine de Foies de Volaille

Take a dozen good fowls' livers whole, or 1 lb. of calves' liver cut into 1 in. squares. Give them a few turns in a saucepan with a couple of tablespoonfuls of finely-minced shallot for five minutes, then drain them, wipe off any piece of onion that may adhere to them, let them get cold and wrap each in a jacket of cooked fat bacon. Line the *terrine* with slices of bacon, and then fill it in layers with forcemeat and the little rolls of liver; press all gently together and bake in a moderate oven for 1½ to 2 hours, adding a strong jellied broth made of giblets and remnants of chickens. A few truffles would, of course, greatly improve the *terrine*.— A.K.H. (2).

Chicken Loaf

1 large boiling fowl
1 onion
2 carrots
2 stalks celery
Parsley
Salt and pepper
2 tablespoons granulated gelatine (optional)

Cut the fowl up in serving pieces. Put in a pan with sufficient water to cover, adding the cut-up vegetables, salt and pepper. Simmer until tender. Remove fowl, strain broth and boil the latter down to two or three cupfuls. Remove all meat from chicken and cut it into smallish dice, keeping the white meat separate from the dark. Mix half the broth with the white meat and the other half with the dark. In warm weather, melt the gelatine in the broth while hot, stirring until dissolved. Allow mixture to cool thoroughly, then put the dark half in a loaf-shaped tin, placing the white meat on top. Set on ice to chill and solidify. Slice and serve with salad. —P.W.

Mayonnaise de Volaille

Cold roast or boiled fowl, freed from skin and bones, may be diced and marinated in a vinaigrette sauce for an hour or so. Drain, pile in centre of a dish, on a bed of cooked and diced potatoes or cooked mixed vegetables, the whole being then covered with mayonnaise sauce. Surround with lettuce leaves, asparagus tips, capers, fillets of anchovy and turned green olives.—P.W.

Minced Chicken à la Moderne

Finely-minced white meat of cooked chicken
Freshly-mashed potatoes
Butter
Thick cream
Asparagus tips
Hard-boiled eggs
Slices of ham
Mushrooms
Salt and pepper
Flour
Cream sauce
Lemon juice
Green peppers (optional)

This, too, is a tempting-looking and delicious dish. Mince cold roast or boiled chicken very finely. Chop, then pound, ham to a paste. *Sauté* the mushrooms in butter. Hard-boil the eggs and chop the yolks only. Mix together the ham paste, the chopped egg-yolks and some seasoned fluffy mashed potatoes, slightly cooled. Blend a little flour with some thick cream, heat gently, add chicken, season and flavour slightly with lemon juice and butter from *sauté* mushrooms. To serve, squeeze large 'roses' of the potato-ham-egg mixture around a hot dish. Pile creamed chicken in centre, garnish with hot, buttered asparagus tips, in *bouquets* around edge of dish at equal distances, surround with mushrooms and cover all with a hot, rich cream sauce. Set under a grill to brown lightly entire surface.—P.W.

Mousse of Chicken

Cold cooked chicken
2 tablespoons butter
2 chickens' livers
Dash grated nutmeg
1 onion
1 carrot
¼ cup aspic jelly
½ cup *Béchamel* sauce
Salt and pepper
1 tablespoon thick cream
2 rashers of bacon
1 turnip
1 *bouquet-garni*
Additional butter

Remove all skin, bones and gristle from cold game or poultry. Melt two tablespoons butter in a pan, add bacon cut into strips, the bones and carcass of fowl or duck, the *bouquet*, sliced carrot, onion and turnip. Cook gently together for about 20 minutes, then add sufficient water – or good chicken broth – to cover, salt and pepper, and continue cooking, over a low heat, for at least an hour, two if possible. When done, strain and skim off fat. *Sauté* the livers in a little additional butter and, when done, run them, together with the cold poultry, through the mincer then pound in a mortar, adding the nutmeg gradually. Moisten this mixture with a sufficiency of the gravy from the previous stewing and rub all through a sieve. Set in a cool place to become thoroughly chilled, then add the aspic, the *Béchamel* sauce and the cream, blending well. See mixture is adequately seasoned. Line bottom of a mould with cold but still liquid aspic jelly, decorate as wished, pour a little more aspic over the decorations and coat the sides of mould by gently turning it around, on ice, until the coating is smooth and even. When this is set, fill the mould with the prepared mixture and put on ice to stiffen. Turn out on a very cold dish, garnish with chopped aspic, salad, or any fancied trimmings.

Note.—Should the weather be warm, add about a heaped teaspoonful of powdered gelatine to warmed aspic to make it firmer. —P.W.

Pain de Volaille

2 chickens' livers
Butter
Salt and pepper
Cold poultry
Foie gras (optional)
2 eggs
2 tablespoons special sauce

Ingredients for Special Sauce
Carcass of bird, broken up
Bouquet-garni
2 tablespoons tomato *purée*
2 shallots
1 glass good red wine
Flour
Bouillon

This excellent recipe is suitable for using up left-overs of either poultry or game, such as pheasant, partridge, etc. First prepare the sauce. Break up the carcass of bird or birds as small as possible. Place this in a saucepan with the chopped shallots, the *bouquet*, the wine, the tomato *purée*, a sufficiency of good *bouillon*, salt and pepper. Cook gently until liquid is reduced to a third of its original quantity. Strain this extract and thicken by the addition of a little flour, previously mixed to a paste with cold water or *bouillon*.

Chop finely all meat taken from bones of poultry or game, pound in a mortar with the livers and as much *foie gras* as may be desired. Press this mixture through a sieve. Add to it the well-beaten eggs, salt, pepper, the butter required and the two tablespoonfuls of prepared thick sauce, keeping remainder hot for later use. Pour the prepared farce into a well-buttered mould and place it in a saucepan half full of hot water. Cover mould, allow surrounding water to boil gently – adding more to it as it evaporates – and cook thus, *very gently*, for about an hour; then turn out and cover with rest of hot special sauce. The quantity of butter to be added to farce depends, of course, on the quantity of meat used in its preparation, but there should be, roughly, one-fifth butter or less if *foie gras* is used.—P.W.

Potted Chicken

Butter
Salt and cayenne pepper
Pinch ground nutmeg
Cold cooked poultry or game
Touch of powdered mace
2 or 3 slices ham
Clarified butter

This is a useful recipe for large families where several birds are cooked at the same time and possibly a good deal is left over. Remove all meat from bones as well as all skin. To every pound of the meat, once chopped, allow a quarter of a pound of the finest fresh butter. The meat must be very finely chopped or minced, then pounded to a smooth paste with the butter, spices, salt and cayenne to taste. If time can be spared, it is advisable to press the whole mixture through a sieve. Press into glass or china pots and cover with a ¼ in. layer of clarified butter, turning the pot around while butter is still liquid to seal contents of pot in securely. Cover with paper or, in the modern way, with white cellophane.—P.W.

Pressed Chicken

This is a simple family recipe, a poor relation of the 'Galantine de Poulet', but delicious all the same.

Boil a nice plump fowl in as little water as possible until meat falls from the bones. Chop this finely, season with salt and pepper, adding if wished a little poultry seasoning. Have a rather large oblong mould. Cover the bottom with slices of hard-boiled egg, one slightly overlapping the other. Cover this with a layer of the chopped fowl. Press this down evenly and firmly. Pour over all a little jelly made by boiling down to one-half its original bulk the water the fowl was cooked in and adding to it 1½ tablespoonfuls of granulated gelatine. Add a second layer of meat when the jelly is set, press down, cover with a layer of jelly, allow this to set and repeat until both meat and jelly are used up and mould is full. Chill on ice, turn out when set and slice thinly, serving with mayonnaise and a green salad.
—P.W.

Quenelles de Volaille

½ lb. white meat from boiled fowl
2 tablespoons butter
2 tablespoons flour
Salt and pepper
½ cup chicken broth or stock
1 egg

Put the butter and the stock – chicken stock is best if available – in a small saucepan, bring to boiling point, then add the flour, all at once, stirring mixture fast the while and continuing to stir until mixture leaves the sides of pan quite clean. This constitutes a 'panada', which is the basis of *quenelles*. Cool mixture, add the finely-chopped and well-pounded chicken, blending and pounding the mixture well in a mortar or pressing through a fine sieve with a wooden spoon. Add the beaten egg, salt and pepper and, if liked, just a touch of nutmeg, grated. Shape the mixture into small sausages or into small 'eggs' and poach them in boiling stock or water for about 10 minutes or until they rise to surface of liquid and seem light. Drain and serve in a rich *Béchamel* sauce, or with cream, or use as a garnish to a rich entrée.—P.W.

Chicken Ramekins

1½ cups cooked diced chicken
½ cup chicken stock
¼ lb. fresh mushrooms
2 tablespoons flour
Salt and pepper
½ cup thick cream
Butter
Brown breadcrumbs

Melt a couple of tablespoonfuls of butter in a pan, add the same amount of flour, stirring until mixture bubbles gently, then moisten gradually with cream and stock. Simmer for a few minutes. Season well. Add the prepared cold chicken and the mushrooms, previously sliced and *sautés* in butter, adding the latter to mixture to flavour. Heat mixture well and pour into individual buttered ramekins. Sprinkle surface lightly with fine brown breadcrumbs and either bake or poach, turning out or not, as preferred, and handing with them mushroom, cream or tomato sauce.—P.W.

545

Salade de Poulet

Have some rice plainly boiled and well drained; season it, while still hot, with salt, pepper, oil and vinegar and let it get cold. Cut in small pieces the flesh of a roast chicken, and dispose it on the rice in a large bowl or deep dish, with slices of hard-boiled eggs all round.

Put a little mayonnaise (with a touch of mustard in it) all over, together with chopped parsley, tarragon and chervil. Stir at the last minute only, when the dish has appeared on the table.

There should be plenty of dressing in the rice and not too much mayonnaise.–x.m.b.(1)

Savoury Canapés

Uncooked chicken livers
Butter
1 small chopped onion
Finely-chopped lean ham
Chopped fresh mushrooms
Brown sauce
Salt and cayenne
Chopped white of hard-boiled egg
Yolk of 1 or 2 hard-boiled eggs
Rounds of bread
Parsley

Chop the raw chicken livers very finely, after removing nerves. Fry them in a little butter with a small quantity of onion and, when beginning to brown, add half as much finely-minced ham as there was chicken liver mixture, add also one or two chopped mushrooms. Cook all this gently together and bind to a paste with brown sauce, seasoning to taste with salt and cayenne. Spread this mixture thickly on rounds of toasted or sauté bread and sift hard-boiled egg-yolk over surface, placing in the centre of each round thus prepared a circle of chopped egg white and a tiny sprig of parsley. It is impossible to give definite quantities of ingredients as they depend on the number of canapés being made.—p.w.

Soufflé of Chicken

Finely-minced cold roast or boiled
    chicken
Salt and pepper
1 cup thick *Béchamel* sauce
2 tablespoons cream
Lemon juice
3 eggs

The chicken must be freed of all skin and gristle, then very finely chopped and pounded in a mortar and pressed through a sieve. Season, and add the thoroughly beaten egg-yolks, blending well. Beat the whites until very stiff and lightly fold them into the chicken mixture. Pour all into a buttered *soufflé* mould, and cook in a moderately hot

oven for about 25 to 30 minutes or until well risen and lightly browned on top. Serve at once.—p.w.

CHOCK

A local name of the *Wheatear* (q.v.). It is mentioned in the Letters of Sir Thomas Browne, M.D., published in *Notes and Letters on the Natural History of Norfolk*, in 1902: 'A small bird mixed black and white and breeding in cony borings whereof the warrens are full from April to September, at which time they leave the country. They are taken with an Hobby and a net and are a very good dish.'

COLIN. COLIN-LOUI

The American and Canadian names for the most prolific of all American game birds, the *Bob-white* (q.v.). It is known in culinary French as *Caille d'Amérique*.

COOT (COMMON COOT)

Lat. *Fulica atra*. A European water-bird which is more like a small wild duck, in shape and plumage, than other Rails. It is called in French *Foulque morelle, macroube* and *judelle*. It abounds in marshy lands and open inland waters. It is about 18 in. in length and weighs up to 2 lb. A slow and particularly stupid bird, the *Coot* owes its safety to the fact that it is hardly worth killing for food. But it is edible and it is eaten, under some other name, in some of the less reputable of London's Soho Restaurants, in salmis or pies. It should be skinned, not plucked, as soon as killed, like a *Rook*. There are regular *Coot* shoots on the Norfolk Broads and elsewhere in England, but there is only one part of Europe where the *Coot* is killed for food on a commercial scale: that is in Herzegovina, where *Coots* are smoked and kept as a highly valued winter food.

There are several species of *Coot* in the U.S.A. resembling the English or European bird of the same name, whilst in South America, there is a *Giant Coot*, larger than any which occurs anywhere else.

The *African* or *Crested Coot* (*Fulica cristata*) differs from its American and European cousins by the presence of a pair of red fleshy knobs above the white shield on the forehead.

The name *Coot* is often given in the U.S.A. erroneously to any small surf *Duck*.

According to the London market retail prices, the *Coot* is not nearly so much appreciated now as it was in the past. In 1807, coot cost 1s. 6d. each; in 1922, 8d.; and in 1941, in spite of the war and rationing, its price had dropped to 6d. apiece. In 1942, no records of official market sales have been found: but according to a letter to *The Times*, the shelves of one of the greatest London stores were 'lined with coots and moor-hens', one day in April, 1942.

CORMORANT

Lat. *Phalacrocorax carbo*. A large sea bird, abounding in practically all latitudes. If the Hebrews had not been forbidden to eat *Cormorant* (Deut., cap. xiv, v. 17), nobody would have imagined that anyone ever wished to eat the rank, dark flesh of this glutton among fish-eaters. Yet, it is on record that the 'squabs', or cormorant chicks, are highly valued by the northern islanders, and that 'sometimes young cormorants are used, instead of young pigeons, for squab pies, but in this case the birds have to be skinned before being used.'—C.R.

Cormorant squabs are said to taste rather like roast hare.

CORNCRAKE. LANDRAIL

Lat. *Crex crex*. A small migratory bird of real gastronomic merit. The plumage is of various shades of brown above and yellowish-white below, rendering it quite inconspicuous. It haunts the open country and agricultural land, and it has a way of running along the hedgerows or in the corn, instead of rising before the gun, which makes its life safer than that of other birds. 'Even when he (the Landrail) does rise, he often escapes, for his apparently slow, cumbersome flight is disconcertingly hard to judge.'—M.H.P. The *Corncrake* usually makes its nest in some long grass, on the ground, and lays from 9 to 11 eggs, cream coloured and blotched with red and grey.

The *Corncrake* arrives back in Europe, from its winter quarters in Africa, towards the second half of May, and its peculiar 'Crake-crake' pairing call is unmistakable. Full-fledged birds are but 10 in. in length, and they are not fit to eat until September, or after the harvest, when at their fattest and ready to embark upon their southward voyage to their African winter quarters.

In culinary French the *Corncrake* is known as *Roi des Cailles*, although it is not a *Quail*, but probably because it used to be said – maybe believed as well – that there was always a *Corncrake* acting as leader when the *Quail* returned to Europe in the spring. (It is also called *Re di quaglie, Rey de las codornices* and *Wachtelkönig*, in Italian, Spanish and German.) The *Corncrake* used to be considered a great delicacy but it is now too scarce to shoot.

In 1807, the market retail price of *Corncrake* in London fluctuated between 3*s*. 6*d*.

and 7*s*.; in 1922, between 2*s*. 6*d*. and 3*s*. There has not been any official quotation in recent years.

Landrail or Corncrake Roast

Pluck and draw three or four Landrail, wipe them inside and out with a damp cloth, and truss them in the following manner: Bring the head round under the wing, and the thighs close to the sides; pass a skewer through them and the body, and keep the legs straight. Roast the birds before a clear fire from 12 to 20 minutes, keep them well basted, and serve with fried breadcrumbs, with a sauce-boat of brown gravy. If preferred, bread sauce may also be sent to the table with them.

Note.—Landrail or Corncrake are seasonable from August 12th to the middle of September.—B. (1). *That was in Mrs Beeton's time; the birds are now protected by law.*

COURSER (CREAM-COLOURED)

Lat. *Cursorius cursor*. A fairly common plover-like bird found in North Africa, as far south as Lake Chad and as far East as Iraq. It has occurred in Europe and is a rare visitor to the British Isles. It is about 9 in. in length; the head bluish-grey behind, with a black and white band on each side. It owes its name to the fact that it runs with great speed and rarely takes wing. It is prepared for the table in any way suitable for *Quail* (q.v.). There are other related species in Africa and Asia, occasionally straying to Europe.

CRAKES

Little Crake (Lat. *Porzana parva*)
Spotted Crake (Lat. *P. porzana*)
Carolina Crake (Lat. *P. carolina*)
Besides the *Corncrake* (q.v.), there are other and less common species all of which may be prepared for the table like *Fieldfare* (q.v.).

The *Spotted Crake*, 9 in. long, olive-brown above with dark mottlings and white specks and grey below shading into white; yellow beak and green legs.

The *Little Crake*, 8 in. long, yellowish-brown above and the underparts mostly grey.

The *Carolina Crake* breeds in N. America and winters South, in Central America and Peru: it has occurred in the British Isles.

Hume and Marshall (1879) describe two other species of Asiatic *Crake*, the *Brown Crake* (*Amaurornis akool*); and the *Whitey-brown Crake* (*Poliolimnas cinereus*), as well as two other Rail-birds known as *Crakes*, the *Malayan Banded Crake* (*Rallina fasciata*) and the *Banded Crake* (*Rallina eurizonoïdes*).

CRANE

Lat. *Grus grus*. A wading bird, resembling the *Heron*, which is no longer considered fit for human consumption. But it had its admirers in the past among princes and kings and their courtiers. In 1519 and 1520, when *Crane* was served to the Lords of the Star Chamber, its cost was 4*s*.; in 1534 and 1535, when a capon cost 2*s*., a crane cost 6*s*. On 6 June 1543, the purchase of 'a yong pyper crane' from Hickling is mentioned in the accounts of the City Chamberlain of Norwich, which leads one to believe that cranes must have been bred near Norwich at the time. (*Trans. N. and N. Nat. Soc.*, VII, pp. 160 *et seq*.) In a MS. dated 1605 and published in Vol. XIII of *Archaeologia* (p. 315), entitled 'A Breviare touching the Order and Government of a Nobleman's House', there is a 'Dietarie' for each month of the year, and the crane appears from November to March only, when birds cost from 3*s*. 4*d*. to 5*s*. each. Further evidence that cranes were plentiful in Norfolk during the sixteenth century is supplied by the list of presents sent to William Moore, of Losely, on the occasion of the marriage of his daughter, on 3 November 1567, including nine cranes 'out of the marshland in Norfolk'. (*Archaeologia*, XXXV, p. 36.) 'Crane is hard of digestion, and maketh yll juice, but beyng hanged up longe in the ayre, he is the lesse unholsome'. (Elyot's *Castel of helth*, London, 1549, f. 31.)

The *Crane* is now found from Scandinavia to Spain and eastwards to China; it migrates to Africa and India in winter.

CURASSOW

Lat. *Crax nigra*. A short, heavy bird, with short wings, long, broad tail and a strong bill. It lives in small flocks in the forests of South America, east of the Andes, from Panama to Paraguay, nesting and roosting in tree-tops, feeding on fruit, seeds and insects. It has been domesticated and its flesh is white and delicate, not unlike that of the *Turkey* nor inferior to it. It can be prepared for the table like *Turkey*.

A related species, which is found in Mexico, is 3 feet in length and its plumage glossy black, except for the white abdomen and tail coverts. In common with the other species, its head bears a crest of feathers curled forward at the tips, which can be raised or depressed at will. The female is reddish-brown.

CURLEW

Lat. *Numenius arquata*. A migrant bird of the *Plover* kind, about 24 in. in length, drab coloured above, mottled with dark brown and white beneath. It has a remarkable sickle-shaped beak, 5 to 7 in. long, a slender and graceful body and long legs. Its chief breeding grounds are the northern lands of Asia and Europe. It is also called *Whaup* in Scotland. The eggs are usually four in number and brownish-green, with cinnamon markings. The *Curlew* feeds on berries, grubs and insects on the moors, where it breeds, and on small crustaceans and molluscs when it reaches the sea. This duality of diet is responsible for the apparently conflicting statements about the curlew's gastronomic merit. Young *Curlew*, 'stewed in milk and served with a plain rum butter and lemon sauce, are excellent', is the verdict of no mean judge, Major Hugh Pollard, who adds: 'Curlews are very good if they are inland birds fresh from their breeding-places on the moors, but after a short spell at the sea they get decidedly fishy.' M.C. writes: 'I have eaten curlew freshly shot from feeding on the black ooze of Belfast Lough and found them excellent, plainly grilled, while they have been good in salmi when purchased for 1*s*. 6*d*. from game-hawkers in Dublin.'

Curlews were served to the Lords of the Star Chamber in 1519 and 1520, when they cost 1*s*. each; in 1567, when they cost 1*s* 6*d*.; in 1590, when the incredible amount of 8*s*. was paid for one *Curlew*; and in 1605, when three cost 15*s*.

The *Curlew* is still shot and sold for food in England, but it does not enjoy the same measure of popularity, to judge from the London market retail prices. Thus, in 1807, the price was 3*s*. per bird; in 1922, from 8*d*. to 1*s*.; and in 1941, in spite of the war and rationing, curlew cost from 9*d*. to 1*s*. each. They were sold at one of the greatest London stores, in April 1942, at 3*s*. 6*d*. each.

There is an old Lincolnshire saying:
'Be she white or be she black,[*]
The Curlew has tenpence on her back';
and another, probably of later date to judge from the advance in price:
'A Curlew lean or a Curlew fat
Carries twelvepence on her back.'

Stuffed Curlew

After carefully removing the gall and the gizzard, chop up the giblets with chicken liver, bacon, and sausage-meat. Fry the mixture very lightly in a saucepan with thyme, bayleaf and juniper. When it is cooked, add a glassful of old madeira, and leave to cool in an earthenware pan.

Pass the whole through a wire sieve ,and add the yolks of a few eggs flavoured with spice, and some truffles.

It only remains to truss the curlews, and

[*] The *Black Curlew* is the *Glossy Ibis*, a rare vagrant in the British Isles.

fill them with this masterly stuffing, which is by no means easy to make. Then cover the birds with rashers of good bacon, and braise them gently, basting with a moderate amount of gravy.

Serve with game sauce, and garnish artistically with truffles, olives and mushrooms. —A.La.

DIKKOP. CAPE THICKNEE

Lat. *Burhinus capensis.* The commonest of the African members of the genus *Oedicnemus* or *Stone Curlew.* 'Its dark flesh is exceedingly good eating and is not so dry as that of most African game birds.'—B.HO.

DOTTEREL. DOTTREL

Lat. *Eudromias morinellus.* A bird of the *Plover* family, which occurs in many parts of Northern Europe and Western Asia. It is chiefly known in England as a summer visitor, appearing in small flocks of eight or ten towards the end of April and staying during May and part of June, when they are fat and much esteemed for their delicate flavour. Hence Drayton's reference to it in *Song xxv*:

'The Dotterel, which we think a very dainty dish,
Whose taking makes such sport, as no man more would wish.'

They were retailed in London, in 1807, at 3s. per bird, and it is on record that 17 couple were counted in one London poulterer's shop in 1845. It is now protected by law.

DOUGH BIRD. ESKIMO CURLEW

Lat. *Numenius borealis.* The name of an American *Curlew* which occasionaly straggled across the North Atlantic, but is now nearly if not quite extinct; this may be due to the fact that it was the best of all *Curlews.* In the summer and autumn months it fed on berries and seeds, and in the winter and spring upon rock snails and cockles.

DOVE

The name given to a large number of different species of small pigeons, all of them fit for the table and best prepared in any way suitable for *Pigeons.*

DOVE, ROCK

Lat. *Columba livia.* The ancestral form of our domestic pigeons. Many similar pigeons are found round the coasts of Great Britain, breeding in caves, but it is only in some of the more out-of-the-way places that the true *Rock Dove* exists.

DOVE, STOCK

Lat. *Columba oenas.* A small *Pigeon,* more compact than the *Wood Pigeon* and less abundant:

it is rarely found in large flocks. It is common in most parts of Europe, chiefly in the valleys of the Lower Danube; also in northwest Africa, western Asia, Palestine and Turkey. It is a resident in England. It is prepared for the table like a *Pigeon* (q.v.).

DOVE, TURTLE

Lat. *Streptopelia turtur.* One of the smaller species of wild pigeon abundant in the south of Europe and Western Asia, as a resident, and not uncommon in the southern and midland counties of England, as a visitor, from the spring to the end of September. Its Latin name *turtur*, pronounced tur-r-r ... tur-r-r, and its French name *Tourterelle*, are attempts at reproducing the bird's rather monotonous but not unmelodious 'moan'. It may be prepared for the table like a *Pigeon* (q.v.).

DOWITCHER

There are two game birds in the U.S.A. which are given this name; one is a visitor, wintering in Central and South America, and it is also called the *Red-breasted Snipe* (*Limnodromus griseus*). The other is a related species and a resident in some of the Western States only; it is also known as the *Long-billed Snipe.* Both may be prepared for the table in any way suitable for *Snipe* (q.v.).

DUCK

All *Ducks* can swim, but it makes all the difference to the gastronome whether they swim – and still more whether they feed – in fresh or salt waters. There is a considerable number of different species of wild duck all the world over: they provide sport for thousands and food for millions of appreciative people. In the British Isles, the commonest and best of wild duck is the *Mallard*, the ancestor of the majority of breeds of domesticated *Ducks* of Europe and the U.S.A. In the U.S.A., the prize for gustatory excellence is shared between the *Canvasback* and its cousin the *Redhead.*

In culinary parlance *Duck* is invariably used for both the male and female birds, the *Duck* and the *Drake.* In culinary French, the masculine forms, *Canard* and *Caneton*, are invariably used for *Duck* and *Duckling*, whether male or female, and the feminine forms, *Cane* and *Canette* are never used in menu language. The classical CUISINE recognises three different types of *Duck* for the table, i.e. (*a*) *Nantais*, a small duck ,from 3 to 4 lb., which is killed by having its head cut off and being left to bleed before being cooked; (*b*) *Rouennais*, a large *Duck*, from 5 to 6 lb., which is smothered so that it has lost none of its blood before being cooked; (*c*) *Sauvage*, which is generally a *Mallard*, but may be any sort of *Wild Duck*, usually shot but sometimes trapped.

To choose a Duck: The under-bill should be soft enough to be bent back easily, and the webbing of the feet should also be soft. If under-bill and webbing are hard, leave the duck alone. If they be soft, pinch its breast gently and make sure that it is meaty, as under-fed young birds have no flesh to speak of on their soft bones: they are not worth cooking.

To carve a Duck: Cut the crackling skin with the point of a sharp knife, and cut the meat from the breast in thin, long slivers along the bone. To find the wing joints is no easy task: use a carving secateur or scissors and save time and temper.

DUCK AND DUCKLING
CANARD ET CANETON
Aiguillettes de Canard Bigarade
Canard or Caneton à l'Alsacienne
Boiled Ducks
Braised Duck or Duckling
Marinated Duck
Ducks 'à la Mode'
Le Caneton farci et mijoté à l'ancienne mode de Provence
Le Caneton froid à la Montmorency
Duckling aux Navets
Duck with Olives
Pâté de Caneton
Duck and Green Peas:
   1. Canard à la purée verte
   2. Canard aux petits pois
Ragoût of Duck
Roast Duck or Duckling
Canard Rouennais
Duck Soups
Spoon Duck
Steamed Duck
Duck Villageoise

Aiguillettes de Canard Bigarade
Clean, singe and truss a large Rouen Duck, that is a duck that has been smothered. Put into a large *cocotte* or pan sufficient peeled and sliced onions and carrots to make a soft bed upon which to lay the duck. Add some veal bones and trimmings if possible; also a small *bouquet-garni*, pepper and salt and some *bardes de lard* (thin strips of fresh pork skin). Cook over a gentle heat until the duck is done, when you will remove it, drain it and keep it hot in the oven.

Strain the gravy from the *cocotte* through a fine sieve, make a light *roux* (see Section I, *SAUCES*) and moisten it with the strained gravy, from which you should skim all excess of fat. Cook gently for a few minutes and add the juice of a Seville orange.

Lift the *Aiguillettes* (thin slivers carved longways on both sides of the duck breast) and arrange them in the serving dish; pour the sauce over them and serve hot.

Canard or Caneton à l'Alsacienne
Choose a small tender *Nantais*, i.e. a duck with its head cut off; braise it (see *Braised Duck*) and serve with a dish of *Choucroûte* (see Section II, *VEGETABLES*).

Boiled Ducks
Put them, after drawing them, for a few minutes, into warm water; then put them into a pan containing a pint of boiling milk for two or three hours; dredge them with flour, put them into cold water, and cover them close. Boil them slowly for 20 minutes, and serve with onion sauce. Geese may be dressed the same way, and stuffed with onion and sage.—M.W.

Braised Duck or Duckling
Prepare the bird as for roasting, and then brown it on all sides in hot butter in a deep pan. Season with pepper and salt. Put in the pan a dozen or more very small onions and a bag of mixed herbs, then put the lid on and cook very gently on top of the stove or in the oven until the duck or duckling is quite tender. Turn it about from time to time, but take care not to prick the skin. When done, skim off the fat and serve with green peas and carrots or any other vegetables boiled first and then tossed in butter and well seasoned. Small braised turnips lose their turnipy flavour and acquire a taste of the duck when cooked in its company. Stoned green olives added to braised duck just before serving are always acceptable.

Marinated Duck
Disjoint a duck and place the pieces in an earthenware crock. Season with salt and pepper, 4 oz. (one-fifth of a pint) of brandy, two large glasses of claret, two large chopped onions, a little thyme, bayleaf, allspice, a sprig of parsley, and allow to stand four to five hours. Heat 4 oz. of fresh pork fat and one tablespoon of olive oil in an earthenware casserole. When hot, place in the pieces of duck and brown for 20 minutes. Add the wine in which the duck was soaked, with one clove of garlic, ½ lb. of fresh mushrooms, and simmer gently for one hour or a little longer. Serve on the table in the casserole. Serve with slices of brown toast and noodles.—M.A.

Ducks à la Mode
Take two fine ducks, cut them into quarters, fry them in butter a little brown, then pour out all the fat, and throw a little flour over them, add half pint of good gravy, a quarter pint of red wine, two shallots, an anchovy, and a bundle of sweet herbs; cover them close, and let them stew a quarter of an hour; take out the herbs, skim off the fat, and let your sauce be as thick as cream; send it to table garnished with lemon.—H.Gl.

Le Caneton farci et mijoté à l'ancienne mode de Provence

The duckling is simple: the stuffing is not.

To make the stuffing, take ½ lb. of streaky bacon, boil it and shred it finely. Add the duckling's liver. Add two or three onions, finely chopped and fried in butter; also a little shallot. Season with pepper and salt, and bind with the yolk of an egg.

Take a score of black olives; stone them; add to them the same quantity of mushrooms and a few long peppers; mince the lot and add to the stuffing. Add also some dice of black truffles; moisten with a fair allowance of Armagnac brandy, and coat the whole of the inside of the duckling with the stuffing 24 hours before it is going to be cooked. When the time has arrived, braise the stuffed duckling, allowing some 20 minutes per pound, and serve it with a *Sauce Périgueux*, creamy and winey, with garnishings of artichoke bottoms cut in quarters, mushroom caps, and a few stoned green olives.—A.E.F.

Le Caneton froid à la Montmorency

Stew gently in a white stock a young but fair-sized duckling and let it get quite cold in the pan in which it has been cooked. Then slit its back, raising three or four slivers (*aiguillettes*) from each side of the backbone. Cover these *aiguillettes* with a *chaufroid* (prepared from the carcass and giblets of the duck, to which add a spoonful of cherry brandy for flavour). The *aiguillettes*, with a good meat glaze over them and some tarragon leaves decorations in the glaze, are then dressed in a round dish and garnished with red, stoned cherries previously cooked in Madeira wine, and covered also with a clear meat glaze flavoured with some of the duck *fumet*.—A.E.F.

Duckling aux Navets

Make a concentrated stock of the giblets, and add a carrot, a leek, and a small bunch of mixed herbs. Having browned the duckling in butter, add onions, salt and pepper, and leave it to cook slowly for an hour.

Cook the turnips separately in 4 oz. of butter. Towards the end of the time of cooking (about half an hour), sprinkle with sugar, and brown.

Then make a *roux* of butter and flour, moistened with the giblet stock, and put into it the turnips and the duckling together with its liquor, previously strained, and leave to simmer for a quarter of an hour. Skim before serving.

Place the duckling on a hot dish and garnish with the turnips. The sauce should cover the whole. (Ali-Bab.)—A.La.

Duck with Olives

Truss the birds for boiling, and put them in a stewpan with a pint of good stock, a sliced onion, an onion stuck with two or more cloves, and a good *bouquet* (thyme, parsley, bayleaf, marjoram, green onions, and thinly pared lemon rind); cover with a buttered paper, bring it to the boil, then draw it aside and let it stew very gently for about 1½ hours, after which lift the birds out and glaze. Meanwhile, strain the liquor, free it from fat, mix it with about 1½ gills of good espagnole sauce, and about two or three dozen turned (or stoned) olives; let this boil up sharply for a minute or two to reduce it slightly, then pour it round the ducks and serve very hot.—Q. (2).

Pâté de Caneton

Four-fifths roast the duckling, that is to say, for an average duckling, roast it from 19 to 21 minutes. Cut the whole of the breast into the longest and almost the thinnest slices possible. Have ready the main part of the necessary forcemeat, prepared thus: Lightly and quickly fry some fat bacon and some calf's liver; remove these meats; swill the pan with some madeira; pound the liver and bacon, moistening with the madeira swilling; incorporate the pounded meat of the legs, etc., of the duckling; work in an appropriate quantity of yolk of egg; liven up with some thyme and a little powdered bayleaf. Now line a buttered pie-dish with 'short' pastry, and make a small slit at the bottom. Lay in alternately the forcemeat and the neatly arranged slices of the duckling. Finish with a layer of forcemeat. Put on the covering portion of pastry. Provide a small escape for steam by making a slit in the top. Bake for about one hour. Turn out the pie, upside down, on the hot dish on which it is to be served. Slice off the top, originally the bottom, horizontally. Cut this flavoured pastry into as many pieces as there are diners. Cover the exposed forcemeat with some very thick madeira sauce; place some cooked mushrooms on it, and see that each diner gets one of the mushrooms with his portion of the pie and some of the divided top, originally bottom, pastry. A dish for a king !
—T.E.W.

DUCK AND GREEN PEAS

I

Canard à la purée verte

Take rather more than a pint of green peas, boil them in a little broth, and rub them smooth through a sieve; stew a duck in broth, with salt, whole pepper, and a clove of garlic, some small onions, parsley, thyme, basil, and bayleaves. When done enough, pass the sauce through a sieve, and add it to the *purée* of peas; reduce the whole to a good consistency, about that of thick cream. Serve the duck with the *purée* over it.—L.H.

II
Canard aux petits pois

Clean, singe and truss a small and tender *Nantais* and brown it on all sides in some sizzling fat. Put into an earthenware pan a pint of freshly-picked and shelled garden peas, a small head of lettuce and two or three small onions; also a dozen little cubes of fat pork or bacon. Put the duck on top of all this, moisten with a large cupful of hot broth, or hot water if you have no broth; cover the pan tightly and simmer very gently until the duck is done.

Ragoût of Duck

1 cooked duck
2 heaping tablespoonfuls (2 oz.) butter
1 heaping tablespoonful (1 oz.) flour
1 pint (2 cups) stock
3 shallots
Few drops of kitchen *bouquet*
A few sprigs of parsley
1 teaspoonful lemon juice
Salt and pepper
1 teaspoonful red currant jelly
¼ teaspoonful meat extract

Cut the duck into neat joints. Melt the butter in an earthenware pan, toss the pieces of duck in it, then sprinkle in the flour, and fry it a light brown colour; then add the stock, stirring it in smoothly. Add the parsley, lemon juice, shallots, jelly, kitchen *bouquet* and meat extract.

Put on the lid and let it simmer for 30 minutes. Season it nicely. Pin a napkin round the casserole and serve it hot.—M.H.N.

Roast Duck or Duckling

Sprinkle with pepper and salt a cleaned, dressed and trussed duck or duckling. Spread a little softened butter over its back, but less than you would for a chicken. Roast in hot oven, allowing 15 minutes per pound of the trussed bird's weight. Baste every five minutes. All manner of different stuffings may be – and sometimes are – inserted in the duck before it is put into the oven; they are said to help a lame duck, but they are not wanted with ducklings. A dish of tender garden peas suits them best.

Canard Rouennais

1 good plump duck
1 shallot
Small pinch mixed spice
Milk
1 onion
Salt and ground pepper
1 thin slice stale bread
Butter

Rouen is noted for its ducks and the local method of killing them for the special preparation of this famous dish. The duck should be smothered so that all blood remains in it. Make the smallest possible incision to remove entrails and giblets. Chop the liver, heart and cleaned gizzard with an onion. Add the spices, salt and pepper and the crusted bread, soaked in milk, then squeezed dry, as well as a good tablespoonful of butter. Mix this stuffing well and use to stuff duck, sewing up firmly. Roast – if possible – in front of a brisk fire. Failing this, in a hot oven, for about 25 minutes, turning the bird once only from back to breast and once on one side then on the other. Baste during cooking. The breast should retain a little of the red colouring when cut, that is, it should not be too well done inside.

Note.—The duck thus killed should be cooked on the same day, as dangerous toxins develop if it is allowed to hang after suffocation.—P.W.

Duck Soup

Make a *Consommé* with bones, meat or fowl and some vegetables; flavour it with some duck *fumet* and garnish it with *quenelles* of duck. This soup is known in culinary French as *Consommé Cyrano*.

Another Duck Soup

Crème Danoise. Velouté of globe artichokes with an essence of duck; garnished with duck *quenelles* and a *julienne* of mushrooms. A small glass of Marsala wine added at time of serving.

Spoon Duck

Brown the duck in butter with sliced onions and carrots. Remove the duck from the casserole and strain off the butter. Stir into the pan some white wine to loosen the brown juices remaining in the pan. Add a good *bouillon*, sufficient to cover the duck, a *bouquet* of spices, and salt and pepper. Replace the duck and cook very slowly from three to four hours. After removing the duck from the pan, pass the juice remaining through a strainer and reduce until the quantity is about one cup. Thicken this gravy with arrowroot. Serve the duck whole and cover with gravy. (Recipe by Madame Jacques Lebel, Paris.)—E.D.W.

Steamed Duck

Rub the duck over with warmed butter, and tinge it a rich yellow colour, either before the fire, in the oven, or in the stew-pan in which you cook it. Put any bastings from this in the stew-pan, with a sliced carrot, a root of celery, an onion, a few cloves, a bay-leaf, two or three leaves of sage, and a little broth or water. Lay the duck on these, breast upwards, cover and let it steam till the vegetables are cooked well. Salt must be added, and more water, as it dries away. When thoroughly done, take up the duck. Pass the vegetables and sauce through a sieve, and thicken this with brown flour. Skim off the fat. Boil the sauce, and serve it with the duck.—G.N.C.

Duck Villageoise

5 lb. duck
1 bunch medium-sized carrots, scraped and quartered, and cut lengthwise in 2-in. pieces
14 small white onions, peeled
1 small leek, thinly sliced
1 bunch of celery stalks split and cut in 2-in. strips
¼ teaspoonful dried crushed rosemary
1 tablespoonful of sugar
1 tablespoonful of salt
¼ teaspoonful black pepper
1½ cupsfuls boiling water
4 tablespoonfuls of flour smoothed in 6 tablespoonfuls of water

Remove the pin feathers, if any, from the duck. Singe, dip quickly in hot water, and wipe dry. Cut off the legs, leaving the first and second joints together, as the drumstick alone is a little skimpy for a serving, and divide the breast into quarters. Save the back for soup. Brown the pieces all over in their own fat in a skillet, being careful not to overdo them. Remove the meat to a heavy kettle, cover with the vegetables, and sprinkle with sugar, rosemary and season-ing. Pour off all but two tablespoonfuls of the fat in the skillet, add the boiling water, and stir around the edges of the pan to mix in all the brown juices. Pour over the vegetables, cover, and simmer slowly for 1½ hours. The last 15 minutes, stir the smoothed flour into the gravy, a little here and a little there, guarding against crushing the vegetables. Before serving, sprinkle with chopped parsley. This way of cooking duck is a change from the all too usual roast. Serves five or six persons.—E.K.H.

DUCK, AFRICAN YELLOW-BILLED

Lat. *Anas undulata*. An African wild duck which occurs from the Sudan to the Cape.

'The flesh of this duck is described as ex-cellent in all parts of its range, even when the birds are moulting (Buckley, 1874; T.Ayres, 1880; Ogilvy-Grant and Reid, 1907; G.H.Gurney, 1909; *et al.*). In his book

on South Africa Bryden (1893) expatiates at length on the splendid condition and flavour of its meat when shot in the Botletle River country.'—J.C.P.

DUCK, AUSTRALIAN BLACK

Lat. *Anas superciliosa*. One of the commonest duck of Australia and New Zealand, abounding also in the Dutch Indies and the islands of the South Pacific. It is often re-ferred to as *Black Duck, Brown Duck, Grey Duck* or *Wild Duck*. It is a surface feeder and its diet is mostly vegetarian.

'The flesh is excellent especially at the beginning of the shooting season, when the birds are fat. Those from the interior lakes are quite naturally of a better flavour than those taken on the coasts. Buller (1888) re-gards it as perhaps the most valuable of the indigenous birds of New Zealand. The birds reach about 2.5 lb. (1.13 kilos) in weight, a little less than the *Mallard*, and invariably brought the highest market price in Mel-bourne (R.Hall, 1909). I can testify myself to the excellent eating qualities of hybrids between this species and the mallard, many of which I formerly raised on my ponds at Wenham, Mass.'—J.C.P.

'Regarded as an article of food the Grey Duck is in its prime during the autumn and commencement of the winter; but the qual-ity of the game differs according to the locality; those from the lakes and rivers of the interior having a richer flavour as a rule than birds living in the vicinity of the sea-shore, where the food is coarser.'—W.L.B.

DUCK, AUSTRALIAN SHOVELER

Lat. *Spatula rhynchotis*. One of the common duck of Australia and New Zealand: it is called indifferently 'Australian' or 'New Zealand' Shoveler; also *Blue-winged Shoveler* and *Spoon-billed Duck*.

'The flesh is not always first-class, and is generally rated as somewhat inferior to that of the *Australian Black Duck* or the *Teal* (Gould, 1865; White, in Mathews, 1914-15; North, 1913). Mr Charles Barrett writes that in Victoria it is favoured as a table bird and the poulterers' shops sometimes have good supplies.'—J.C.P.

DUCK, AUSTRALIAN WHITE-EYED

Lat. *Aythya australis*. This is a very common and widely distributed duck in Australia and New Zealand, also in New Guinea and New Caledonia. It feeds mostly on water beetles and broken shell-fish.

'Evidently this is considered a fairly good bird in Australia, for it brought from four to six shillings the pair in the Sydney market 35 years ago (Ramsay, 1876). In the market of Hobart, Tasmania, Legge (1905) found them even more plentiful than the Black Duck. Austin (in North, 1913) writing of New South Wales, says these ducks vary much in the quality of the flesh. I have known them shot at certain lagoons from which they are anything but a good eating bird, from other lagoons they are equal to the best of ducks, and yet we could not notice any difference in other species of ducks from the same waters.'—J.C.P.

DUCK, BAHAMA or PINTAIL

Lat. *Anas bahamensis*. A species of duck widely distributed throughout the West Indies and South to the Argentine. It is exclusively vegetarian.

'The flesh is excellent. During the dry season, when all ducks are forced to resort to the coast, in the Guianas, this species is said to be less oily in taste than the others.' F.P. and A.P. Penard, 1908-10.)—J.C.P.

DUCK, BLACK

Lat. *Anas rubripes*. The name given in the U.S.A. to a *Mallard* which is common along the north-eastern shores of Canada and New England, where it is considered as good eating as any *Wild Duck* (q.v.). The black *Cayuga* duck is believed to be a domesticated strain of the *Black Duck*.

'This species is so dear to the heart of our eastern shooters, that it is often put near the top of the list of ducks. I have eaten many which could not be improved upon. As a rule the young flight-ducks, which reach Massachusetts late in September and early October are tender but not fat, and the flesh is lacking in 'gamey' qualities. Most of them are still moulting. Later on they improve, and the large November "Red-legs" are excellent. In places where ducks are regularly baited, and given a chance to rest in a protected pond, they put on a layer of fat and become very fine for the table. Black Ducks which feed on minute shell-fish in winter are often in good condition but of stronger flavour, too strong for some palates, but just right for others. In the brackish sounds of North Carolina and in the abandoned rice-fields of South Carolina the flesh becomes even more delicious.'—J.C.P.

'In Abyssinia, East Africa and parts of South Africa, a duck which is dark of plumage is called *African Black Duck*, *Black River Duck*, *Speckled Duck*, *White-spotted Duck* and *White-barred Black Duck* (*Anas sparsa*). A note by Atmore (in Layard, 1875-1884), in which he describes the African Black Duck as "delicious eating" is the only direct information on the subject that I have found.' —J.C.P.

554

DUCK, BROWN

Lat. *Anas chlorotis*. A name which is often given to the *Grey Duck* or common *Australian Duck* (q.v.), although it belongs (according to Buller) to a distinct species distributed all over New Zealand, but not so often seen as the *Australian Duck* because it is a nocturnal feeder.

DUCK, BUFFEL-HEADED
BUFFLE-HEAD or BUTTERBACK

Lat. *Bucephala albeola*. One of the North American *Wild Ducks*, merely 15 in. long: it might be described as the small edition of the *Canvasback* (q.v.). In colour, it is black above, white below, with a white band extending around the back of the head from eye to eye, and with the rest of the head and the neck glossed with purple, green and blue. It is an excellent diver and feeds partly on small fish which it pursues and captures under water.

'Before they reach the coast, I should rank them among the harmless class of ducks. They are fairly good if one cannot get anything better, and they are often fat. As soon as they strike the coast, especially the old ones, I should place them among the worthless birds for the table. Opinions vary. Some have recorded them as "excellent eating", others as fishy and unpalatable.'—J.C.P.

This duck is also called *Robin Dipper*, *Dapper* or *Dopper*; also *Scotch Teal*, *Scotch Duck* or *Scotch Dipper*.

DUCK, CANVASBACK

Lat. *Aythya valisineria*. A North American diving duck related to the *Pochard* (q.v.). It owes its name to the light plumage of its back; the head is chestnut, the beak long and narrow. It occurs in most States of the U.S.A. as well as in Canada: it breeds in Colorado, Nevada, Minnesota and northwards to Fort Anderson. It used to abound in the Chesapeake Bay, where it fed on wild celery, a fact to which may be traced its high reputation among American gastronomes.

To roast a Canvasback

To roast a canvasback or a redhead or any good duck of similar size, rub a little butter on its breast, put it in the hot oven 'as is' – naked inside and out, roast 15 minutes, the door open the last two or three, and serve a breast to a portion. The carcass may then be put through the press and the gravy or juice (*not* thickened) served separately. Wild rice, either boiled and seasoned with butter and cayenne pepper, or fried *à la Corolla*, or hominy grits in fried cakes, or boiled pearl hominy (samp) in the chafing dish or with paprika and butter, should accompany the breasts of duck and then the juice from the carcass, and currant jelly optional – well, this and a bottle of Chambertin were 'paradise enow'.—C.B.

'The canvasback of the Mississippi Delta and Louisiana are as a rule good, but are not generally regarded as equal to those of the Chesapeake Bay. California birds are inferior as the *Vallisneria* (wild celery) does not grow there, but those from some of the north-central States and the Great Lakes region are very fine. ... To sum up, many discriminating palates have tried to damage the fame of the canvasback by lauding other species, and possibly they have in part succeeded. But his early reputation is too firmly established to be so easily shaken, and he will always remain, I think, at the top of the list. The large size places him above the ruddy and the widgeon, both of which ducks come very close to him in actual quality of flesh. The broad and deep chest gives him an ideal shape and he is far easier to pluck than the ruddy.'—J.C.P.

DUCK, CAROLINA or WOOD

Lat. *Aix sponsa*. A species of duck confined to the West Indies and to the U.S.A., where it used to be most abundant and so popular as a bird for the table that it was threatened with extinction and is now protected by Federal Laws at all times. It has been called in different parts of the States all sorts of names, such as *Acorn Duck*, *Bride Duck*, *Rainbow Duck*, *Regal Duck*, *Summer Duck*, *Tree Duck*, *Wood Duck*, *Widgeon* and *Wood Widgeon*.

'I can testify to the delicious quality of the Carolina Duck's flesh at all ages, and know of no writer in any part of the country who has found it other than excellent. The birds are almost always exceedingly fat, especially in the autumn.'—J.C.P.

DUCK, COMB or KNOB-BILLED or NUKTA

Lat. *Sarkidiornis melanota*. A peculiar-looking duck, also known as *African-humped Duck* and *Black-backed Duck*, which occurs in East Africa and India.

'Although this species cannot be considered as very popular for the table, all writers are in accord as to its flesh being fairly good eating; at least, it usually is better than the *Spur-wing* or the *Egyptian Goose*. The young birds are said to be excellent as food.

There is a related species in South America known as the *South American Comb-Duck*, *Black-backed Duck*, *Crested Duck* or *Wattled Duck*.'—J.C.P.

DUCK, CRESTED

Lat. *Anas speculariodes*. This *Duck*, which is also known as *Antarctic Duck* and *Gray Duck*,

is common in Western and South America and the Falkland Islands. It feeds mostly on fish and other aquatic forms of life. Its marine habits no doubt make this duck rather inferior eating, but in the Andes, Lane (1897) found it good. Mr J.L.Peters thus describes the meat of specimens taken in Western Patagonia: 'I cannot recommend this species very highly as a table duck. The flesh is dark and coarse and very ordinary in taste.'—J.C.P.

DUCK, FLORIDA DUSKY

Lat. *Anas fulvigula*. This American duck is common in Florida and the Southern States of the U.S.A., where it is known by a number of different names such as *Southern* or *Florida Black Duck*; *Striped* or *Summer Mallard*; *Texas Dusky Duck*; *Mottled Duck* and *Mexican Mallard*.

'Judging from the specimens which I ate in Louisiana, I should say that the flesh of this duck equals that of the mallard. I am told that the same is true of the birds killed in Eastern Florida, but Huxley remarks in his field notes that the flesh is likely to be muddy-flavoured. Kopman (1921) considers the flesh inferior to the mallard's.'—J.C.P.

DUCK, GREY

Lat. *Anas superciliosa*. One of the wild ducks of New Zealand and Australia, where 'it is considered an excellent table bird, and is much shot, under licence, and at certain seasons of the year'.—W.R.B.O.

DUCK, HARLEQUIN

Lat. *Histrionicus histrionicus*. One of the rarer Arctic ducks, also called *Painted*, *Mountain*, *Rock*, *Collar* and *Circus Duck*. The drake is one of the handsomest of ducks and the female is known in Canada as *Canne-de-roche*.

'Whilst feeding in fresh water, the Harlequin is, like the Golden-eye, a fairly good bird to eat. This applies particularly to young birds. After they have reached the ocean the flesh becomes strong, as in all other diving ducks that winter on the open sea. L.M.Turner (MS) remarks that the flesh was very nice and tender, but had a fishy flavour that could be removed by drawing the bird soon after it was shot. Hantzsch (1908), writing of the same region (Ungava), reported that the flesh was esteemed, but no doubt epicures are rare in that region. Slater (1901), speaking of the nesting grounds in Iceland, went so far as to say that Harlequins were better than any duck of his acquaintance.'—J.C.P.

DUCK, HAWAIIAN

Lat. *Anas wyvilliana*. 'The Hawaiian duck is a good table bird and was formerly shot in great numbers by sportsmen, chiefly about the ponds in the plains, but to some extent in the mountains also.'—J.C.P.

DUCK, MALLARD

Lat. *Anas platyrhynchos*. The commonest and most widely distributed species of *Wild Duck* (q.v.) in the Northern Hemisphere; it has a number of other names, such as *Stock-duck*, in the Orkneys, *Green-head*, *Moss Duck*, *Mire Duck*, *Muir Duck*, etc. In French it is called *Canard Sauvage*, but in culinary French it is always known as *Un Sauvage*.

Mallards figure in most of the ancient records of feasts and food in England, and, unlike swans, herons, bitterns and the rest, mallards still are highly prized for the table.

'In the spring and summer the birds are far less palatable than in autumn, when they begin to gain condition and lay on a reserve of fatty tissue. When feeding on wild rice or grain left on the stubble fields, they become exceedingly heavy; drakes weighing 3¼ lb. may be regarded as exceptionally fine, although 3¾ lb. has been recorded.* To many palates the mallard, when it has been driven to the sea-coast and forced to feed on marine molluscs, acquires a rank and all too gamey taste, but some people prefer the sea-flavour of these birds to the flesh of the inland grain-field duck.'—J.C.P.

DUCK, MANDARIN

Lat. *Dendronessa galericulata*. This is a strictly Eastern Asia species; it is also called *Chinese Teal* or *Duck*.

'The literature contains numerous references to the poor quality of mandarins as table birds, but I can see no good reason to believe this. Dörries (1888) speaks of them as "very tasty" as a rule, although some specimens in the springtime were unpalatable on account of having eaten the roe of dead fish. It would be very surprising if these ducks were really below par in food value.'—J.C.P.

DUCK, MARBLED

Lat. *Anas angustirostris*. A small duck confined to the warmer lands of southern Europe and North Africa, migrating to NW. India and SW. Asia.

'Irby (1875) considered these birds "excellent eating", but other, perhaps more discriminating, writers are of a different opinion. A.Chapman and Buck (1910) consider them very bad eating, and Hume (1879) is by no means enthusiastic about them. The species, he says, is not among the first-class ducks for the table. It ranks, I should say, little above the *Shoveller* and the

* *This was in Massachusetts; in Scotland, James Robertson Justice has shot 4lb. Mallard.*

White-eyed Pochard, and after obtaining a goodly array of specimens, we never shot it – first-class ducks, *Gadwall*, *Mallard* and *Pintail* as well as the *Pochard* (*Aythya ferina*) and *Common Teal* being always available. —J.C.P.

DUCK, MASKED or DOMINICAN

Lat. *Nomonyx dominicus*. A somewhat uncommon species found chiefly in the West Indies and south to the Argentine.

'Léotaud (1866) describes the flesh of the bird as excellent, and Barbour (1923) says that when sent to the market it is highly prized. Considering the nature of its food, this duck should be excellent eating, in spite of its diminutive proportions. I should guess that it can scarcely weigh more than one-half to two-thirds of a pound.'—J.C.P.

In South Africa the name *Masked Duck* refers to the *White-faced Tree-Duck* (*Dendrocygna viduata*), found in Africa and South America.

DUCK, MEXICAN

Lat. *Anas diazi*. A duck closely related to the *Mallard* (q.v.) confined to Mexico and some of the south-western States of the U.S.A. It is also called *Diaz's Duck*.

DUCK, MUSK or MUSCOVY

Lat. *Cairina moschata*. A native duck of Central America which is found in a domesticated form in many parts of the world.

In spite of the disagreeable association of its name this bird has no odour of musk about it, and the young birds are fairly good eating. The old birds are tough and have a strong odour. Heinroth (1911) tells us that they cease to be palatable after they have acquired their red wattles. Hill (1864) gives as an explanation of the name that they were originally procured from the Mosquito Coast, Nicaragua, the country of the Muysca Indians, whence was derived the name Musco Duck, corrupted later to Muscovy Duck. Nehrig says that they were imported to Europe in 1550 and spread rapidly to France.—J.C.P.

The Australian *Musk Duck* (*Biziura lobatus*) found in the southern half of Australia and in Tasmania is so coarse and has so unpleasant a taste as to be unfit for the table: the male birds smell strongly of musk during the breeding season.

DUCK, PARADISE

Lat. *Casarca variegata*. A colourful New Zealand *Duck*, related to the *Sheldrake*. 'Its flesh is considered good eating, especially when young, and formerly large numbers were killed in the Marlborough District for the Wellington Market.'—W.R.B.O.

DUCK, RING-NECKED or SCAUP

Lat. *Aythya collaris*. This is one of the less common ducks of North America.

'It is one of the best diving ducks for the table. I find only one writer who fails to give it a good name, and this one Elliot (1898), says it is about equal to the Little Black-head, which is hardly fair. In Louisiana, where it is much better known than any-where else, it is greatly prized by hunters, and is said to be always good. The older writers, Wilson, Ord and Audubon, ap-proved of it and found it was never "fishy". I see no reason why it should not rank as nearly equal to the Redhead. I have carefully compared the flesh with New England-killed Redheads, and although the texture is perhaps not quite so fine, the flavour is nearly the same, and there is no lack of "juiciness". It is perhaps as near the Ruddy Duck as anything.'—J.C.P.

DUCK, ROSY-BILLED

Lat. *Metopiana peposaca*. This is one of the commonest of wild ducks in Argentina at all times of the year, and it is also one of the best for the table, both as regards its size and its flavour.

DUCK, SCAUP

Lat. *Aythya marila*. A very widely distri-buted species of diving *Duck* of the North-ern Hemisphere and closely resembling the *Pochard* (q.v.) in size and habits. Its name of *Scaup* means 'broken shell-fish', which is its favourite food; it is also known as *Bluebill*, *Broadbill*, *Blackhead* and *Greater Scaup Duck*, to distinguish it from the *Lesser Scaup Duck*, a smaller American species, similar to the *Redhead* (q.v.). When in condition it can be very good eating. Another related species in New Zealand is known as *Scaup Duck* and *Black Teal*.

DUCK, LESSER SCAUP

Lat. *A. affinis*.

DUCK, NEW ZEALAND SCAUP

Lat. *A. novae seelandiae*. 'The specimens which I have shot on the pond at Wenham, Massachusetts, seemed to have come from the interior, for they had not fed on mol-luscs, and did not smell or taste rank. But these migrants are usually not fat and their flesh is always comparatively dry and taste-less, and far inferior to that of most ducks. Birds shot on the coast, both here and in Europe, especially old birds taken late in the season, may be fat, but they are strong, rank and by no means delicate in texture. Very few writers have a good word to say for them, though they are, no doubt, appreci-ated in localities where even Scoters are con-sidered fit to eat, as on Cape Cod, Mass. There are, however, certain waters on our coast where the Scaup is by no means to be despised. On the Chesapeake they enjoyed an excellent reputation in the old days, if they were feeding with Red heads and Can-vasbacks (E.J.Lewis, 1855), and on the freshwater sounds farther south their flesh is excellent. In Pamlico Sound, which is nearly salt water, they are considered about equal to the Redhead, but I did not find them so myself; shot on the same waters and eating of the same food, they were, I thought, coarse and strong.'—J.C.P.

SHELDUCK. SHELDRAKE

Lat. *Tadorna tadorna*. A common European wild duck, also known as *Burrow Duck*, *Stock-annet*, in Scotland, and *Tadorne*, in France. It is distinguished from the *Mallard* by its larger size, its upright stature and its striking black, white and bay plumage. The head and neck are a very dark, glossy green and the wing-spot (or speculum) bronze-green. The bill is pale red and bears a fleshy knob at its base. The *Shelduck* lays her eggs under cover, often in rabbit burrows, and in Friesia they make artificial burrows to entice the bird and to take the eggs.

'The flesh is very rank and the bird is unfit for the table, even when skinned. I find but one writer who considers the bird edible, and it is probable that his taste was not very discriminating. There are, indeed, people who prefer Mergansers to other ducks, but these "otherwise-minded" folks are best left out of account. The eggs of the Shelduck have a rank taste not suited to every palate, though apparently held in high esteem by the inhabitants of the Friesian Islands.'—J.C.P.

The *Radjah Sheldrake* (*Tadorna radjah*), which is known as *White Duck* in north-west Australia and as *Burdekin Duck* in Queens-land, occurs in the Moluccas, New Guinea and Australia. Hubbard (1907) says that its flesh is coarse and has an unpleasant flavour.

The *Ruddy Sheldrake* (*Casarca ferruginea*), also called *Brahminy* or *Ruddy Goose*, occurs in all parts of Asia, in south-eastern Europe and North Africa; also, occasionally, in Western and Central Europe. The flesh is generally regarded as worthless, although some of the natives in India are said to eat it. (Jesse, 1903).—J.C.P.

The *South African Sheld-Drake* or *White-fronted Sheldrake* (*Casarca cana*), known as *Berg-eend* in Africaans, occurs at the Cape, in the Orange Free State and in the Transvaal. 'Sheld-drake are most indifferent-eating, be-ing both rank and tough; but they are so wild and take such care of themselves, that they seldom get in position to appear on the table.'—B.HO. '... but the Boer farmers, who are not hypercritical in their tastes, consider them a delicacy.' (Sharpe, 1904.)—J.C.P.

There are other varieties of *Shelduck* in different parts of the world, but none of them deserving of the gastronome's attention.

DUCK, SHOVELER. SHOVELAR

Lat. *Spatula clypeata*. A widely distributed wild duck in most temperate parts of the Northern Hemisphere. It is also called *River Duck* and *Spoonbill*. Its French name is *Souchet*. It breeds in the British Isles and North America, wintering farther south, reaching India and Central America. *Shovelers* keep aloof from other ducks, but appear to be almost indifferent to the presence of man: this may be due to the fact that they are surface-feeding birds and scavengers delighting in decaying matter and filth, so that they are not considered as fit for human consumption. But their meat, like that of the least particular scavenger of the sea, the lobster, is of excellent flavour and very tender. In olden days, when the *Spoonbill* (q.v.) was called *Shoveler*, it was highly valued for food. In 1590, for instance, 5*s*. per bird was the price paid for some *Shovelers* served to the Lords of the Star Chamber, a much higher price than that paid for any other bird, wild or domesticated. In 1941, the price of *Shovelers* on the London Market varied from 1*s*. to 2*s*. per bird.

'Shovelars feed most commonly upon the sea-coast upon cockles and shell-fish; being taken home, and dieted with new garbage and good meat, they are nothing inferior to farred gulls.' (Muffet, p. 109.)

There are related species of *Shovelers* inhabiting the Southern Hemisphere and known respectively as *South African Shoveler*, *Australian Shoveler* (q.v.) and *South American Shoveler* or *Red Shoveler*.

'I know of no surface-feeding duck about the value of whose flesh there is more divergence of opinion. I once knew an old epicure from Baltimore, who considered himself an absolute authority on food and drink. At a certain shooting club, he used to pick out for himself as a breakfast dish, a young shoveler still with pin feathers in its plumage. Most American sportsmen consider this a fairly good bird for the table, although not equal to Mallard or Teal. Audubon almost goes into raptures in speaking of it, but he does the same for almost every other duck. Nevertheless, there is plenty of evidence to the contrary, and it certainly never fetched a high price in the markets. The truth is that the shoveler averages thinner than any of its relatives, and is seldom in really prime condition. The flesh, when poor, is not fishy in flavour but rather muddy.

'Among European sportsmen there is the same difference of opinion. Some consider it very good, others think it rather mediocre. But in India it seems to be universally despised, due no doubt to the very filthy nature of some of the village ponds on which it feeds. Both Hume and Marshall (1879) and Baker (1908) consider it one of the worst ducks. Undoubtedly it is strongly flavoured there, due to the abundance of animal food provided by the warm winter climate. On the other hand there may be a large element of prejudice involved in the stigma cast upon it.'—J.C.P.

DUCK, SPOTTED-BILL or SPOT-BILL

Indian Spot-bill. (Lat. *Anas poecilorhyncha*.) Eastern Spot-bill or Fray Duck. (Lat. *Anas zonorhyncha*).

The *Indian Spot-bill* occurs in most parts of the Indian Peninsula and in some parts of Indo-China. Hume and Marshall (1879) class it as second only to the Mallard and Pintail as a bird for the table, while Butler and Baker (1908) seem to consider it a close rival to the Mallard. It is said to be larger and more uniformly in good condition than that species, but at times it is thought to have a fishy flavour.'—J.C.P.

The *Eastern Spot-bill* occurs in the Far East (Manchuria, Japan, Formosa). They are fine large ducks and excellent for the table. The Chinese split them down the back, dry them and sell them in the Canton markets.

DUCK, TREE

Lat. *Dendrocygna*. A name which applies to a number of different species of arboreal ducks inhabiting tropical and sub-tropical fresh waters in America, Africa, Asia and Oceania. They have a long neck and are somewhat between the Shelduck and the Goose in size.

All writers agree to praise the excellence of the flesh of Tree Ducks, with the exception of Horsbrugh (1912) and Baker (1908), who found Tree Ducks of poor quality, the first in Africa and the second in India. J.C. Phillips says that 'the whole group is famed for the excellence of its flesh'.

DUCK, TUFTED, TUFTED POCHARD, or TUFTED WIDGEON

Lat. *Aythya fuligula*. One of the commonest palaearctic species of *Duck* in the Northern hemisphere. It is also called Magpie Diver, Old Hardweather, Lapmark Duck, etc. In France it is called *Pilet noir huppé* or *de marais*.

It is an omnivorous duck and poor eating, its one and only champion being Lord Lilford, who wrote, in 1895, that he considered its flesh far superior in flavour to that of the common Pochard, when living on fresh water.

DUCK, WHITE-BACKED
Lat. *Thalassornis leuconotus*. A widely distributed but uncommon *African Duck* which occurs chiefly in Abyssinia, East Africa, Rhodesia and Madagascar.

The flesh is oily and fat and generally regarded as unpalatable. (Nicolls and Eglington, 1892; Stark and Sclater, 1906). Still, Haagner and Ivy (1908) state that at times they are not bad, and Sibree (1892) quotes a certain Mackay who, in Madagascar, found them 'generally fat and plump and very good eating'. I tried several shot on Lake Chahafi where there was a great abundance of rich vegetable food and found them fat and fairly well flavoured, not very different from other ducks taken from the same waters. —J.C.P.

DUCK, WHITE-EYED
Lat. *Aythya nyroca*. Essentially a *Duck* of south-eastern Europe and south-western Asia. It is also called *White-eyed Pochard*.

'It is hard to estimate fairly the value of this duck's flesh as an article of food, for it varies greatly in different parts of its range. In the opinion of some it ranks along with the Pochard, whilst others consider it downright inedible. Most European sportsmen speak of it as moderately good, and in southern Spain, Colonel Irby considered it superior to either the Pochard or the Red-crested Pochard. This is the highest recommendation it has ever received. Indian sportsmen are particularly at variance on this point, although on the whole it is considered poor. (Hume and Marshall, 1879; Baker, 1921). Jesse (1903), however, found it "one of the best of Lucknow ducks", and Finn (1909) regarded it as "palatable enough". Taken altogether it must be relegated to a place distinctly lower than Pochards.'—J.C.P.

DUCK, WHITE-HEADED
Lat. *Oxyura leucocephala*. The real home of this duck is the Mediterranean basin, east to Turkestan, migrating south to Egypt, Iraq and India.

'Radde (1884) thought that their flesh was very poor. Henke (1880) found that the natives of the Kirgiz steppe region made a regular practice of taking their eggs and would eat them even though highly incubated. He adds that the Kalmucks would do the same were it not for their religious principles which prevent them from taking, not from eating, the eggs.'—J.C.P.

DUCK, WILD
Lat. *Anas platyrhynchos*. Most ducks are wild – and all would be if only they could be free – but, in England, *Wild Duck* means the *Mallard* (q.v.). It is in season from August to March, but at its best in the months of November and December only. In culinary French it is called *Sauvage* (short for *Canard sauvage*). In August 1942, the Ministry of Food fixed the maximum retail price of *Wild Duck* at 5s. 6d. each, 'in feather'.

'To eat Wild Duck, Widgeon or Easterling to perfection. Half roast them; when they come to table, slice the breast, strew on pepper and salt; pour on a little red wine, and squeeze the juice of an orange or lemon over; put some gravy to this; set the plate over a lamp, cut up the bird, let it remain over the lamp till enough, turning it.'—C.MA.

Canard Sauvage aux Bigarades
Take some wild ducks, allowing one for two or at most three people, as only the breast is really good and tender; it should be carved in thin slices.

Put a piece of butter in a shallow saucepan and roast the ducks in it; baste often, allowing about 20 minutes in a fairly quick oven.

Remove the ducks and keep them hot. Put very little flour in the saucepan and make a little *roux*; add a glass of port wine and one of veal stock; stir well and finish cooking the ducks in that for 10 minutes.

Meanwhile put in a small saucepan a little castor sugar and melt it. When it turns yellow, put in a liqueur glassful of curaçao. Add the sauce from the ducks, the skin of one orange (pith carefully removed) cut thin and small, like matches, and a little lemon juice. Bring to the boil and cook a minute or two.

Skin the birds and pour this sauce all over; serve with it quarters of Seville orange, carefully peeled with a very sharp knife, made hot in a small saucepan.

The only possible vegetable with this dish is potatoes in some form, *soufflées, sautées, Anna* or *Macaire*.—X.M.B. (1).

Braised Wild Duck
Season a duck with ground pepper from a pepper-mill and salt; place it in a braising pan lined with rashers of bacon, add a *bouquet-garni* and ½ oz. of butter, let it part cook in a hot oven till coloured. Remove, disjoint, etc., and place pieces in a stew-pan. Chop up the carcass, put it back in the braising pan, and fry it in the existing fat. Make half a pint of brown sauce, to which add the gravy but not the fat from the carcass and a quarter of a pint of good stock or giblet gravy. Cook for 10 minutes, then add the whole to the meat in the stew-pan and let

stew for 20 minutes. Five minutes before it is ready add a glass of white wine.—M.H.P.

Wild Duck (Roast)

Draw, truss and roast as indicated in previous recipes for domestic ducks, basting frequently and serving with orange jelly, or add a glassful of port wine or claret to gravy when nearly done, using to baste bird. An Espagnole sauce, enriched by the addition of the strained duck gravy, may be handed separately.

Marinated Wild Duck

Lay a wild duck for two or three days in a marinade of half a cup of vinegar, a bay-leaf, a few juniper berries, a little garlic or onion sliced, black pepper and three bruised cloves. Lard it for roasting. Baste frequently with butter. Put the marinade in the baking-dish, with a little water for sauce. Add salt, skim off the fat, and garnish with lemon slices. —C.N.C.

Canard à la presse

Clean, singe and truss a *Wild Duck* and roast it on a spit or, failing this, in a hot oven. The roast duck is then brought to the table and carved: first of all the *Aiguillettes*, or the breast cut up longways in thin slivers, are lifted and placed in a chafing dish; then the wings and legs. The *body* or carcass of the bird is then placed in a special *presse*, made for the purpose; it consists of a circular receptacle with a tightly fitting metal lid which may be raised and pressed down by a screw action. The bones and whatever meat is left on them when the *body* of the duck is put into the *presse* are so crushed that all their juices are forced out of them and collected in a lower rim of the *presse*, fitted with a spout. These juices are poured over the *Aiguillettes* in the chafing dish, a squeeze of orange juice is added and a glassful of good brandy, which is set alight. The *Aiguillettes* are turned over in the burning sauce and must be served as soon as the flames have died out. A *Salade d'Orange* (see Part IV, *FRUIT*) is usually served with the *Canard a la presse*.

Salmi of Wild Duck

I

Prepare a pair of ducks as for roasting; put a thin slice of bacon over the breast of each; place them in a pan with one half pint of water, and bake in a hot oven until nearly done, basting frequently with water; take from the oven and carve the ducks into as many pieces as convenient; stir two tablespoons butter and two of flour together until perfectly smooth; put it into a stew-pan and stir until a dark brown; add the broth; let it

come to the boil, stirring constantly; then add the bundle of sweet herbs, one tablespoonful onion juice, and one of lemon juice, one tablespoon mushroom catsup, salt and pepper; let all simmer together 20 minutes; take out the herbs; add the ducks and all the gravy from the dish on which you carve them; cover and simmer 20 minutes longer; add one half cup sherry, and serve on a hot dish. It is pretty served on a flat dish garnished with sliced bread cut into triangles before frying; arrange with the points up; scatter stoned olives over the top of the dish. (Old recipe, Richmond, Virginia).—H.B.

II

To one duck take 4 oz. of bacon and cut it in dice; fry these till crisp, then place half of them and the fat in a baking dish, keeping the remainder aside. To the baking dish add a sliced onion or a shallot, a *bouquet-garni* of fresh herbs and a pat of butter; put the duck on this layer, and bake for 20 minutes in a slowish oven. Remove before it is done and cut off joints and breast fillets.

Fry 1 oz. of flour in 1½ oz. of butter till brown; then add three-quarters of a pint of stock, preferably made with giblets, half a glass of claret, mixing the whole smoothly in, and bring it to the boil. Strain the fat off the duck gravy in the baking tin, and add the gravy to the sauce, boiling it up a second time. Arrange the meat in a clean fireproof dish, and add the dice of bacon and the flesh of six olives cut from the stone. Pour the sauce over this, and set the whole back in the oven to simmer for another 20 minutes before serving.

In this, as in all salmis, it is important to get the consistency of the sauce just right. If it has dried too much it must be liquefied with more stock or gravy; if too thin it should be poured off and reduced in a saucepan, taking care to stir all the time.—M.H.P.

DUCK, YELLOW-BILLED

Lat. *Anas undulata*. This is the commonest *Wild Duck* (q.v.) of East and South Africa. It is called *Geelbec* in Africaans and has practically the same habits as the European Mallard.

DUNLIN

Lat. *Erolia alpina*. A small wading bird, found in Europe, Asia and Western Africa; it resembles the *Snipe*, which it does not equal gastronomically. It is now protected by law in most parts of the British Isles.

EIDER

Lat. *Somateria mollissima*. This is the common *Eider Duck*. It is chiefly valued for the down from its breast, as its flesh and that of other related species is not fit to eat, but the fat of *Eiders* is of great value in northern latitudes and their eggs are also highly valued for food.

FIELDFARE

Lat. *Turdus pilaris*. A little bird which resembles the *Missel-thrush* and is a regular winter visitor to the British Isles, Southern Europe and North Africa, breeding in North Europe and West Siberia. It often takes the place of the *Lark* in the Steak-and-Kidney-and-Lark Pie. It is a poor singer, compared with the Lark, but just as good in a pie.

FIGPECKER. FIG-EATER. FIG-BIRD

The names of different little warblers, such as the *Lesser Whitethroat* (*Sylvia curruca*) and *Garden Warbler* (*Sylvia borin*), which feed, in the South of France and in Italy, on figs and grapes: hence their names of *Becfigue*, in French, and *Boccafico*, in Italian. They are now rare but nesting still in England and Scotland. They are eaten freshly shot, dressed without being drawn, sprinkled with a little salt, brushed over with melted butter, wrapped in vine-leaves and grilled. They may also be prepared in any way suitable for *Ortolan* (q.v.).

FRANCOLIN

Francolins form a large group of game birds varying in size from that of a Common Partridge to almost the size of a Guinea Fowl. They range from Cyprus to China, and the whole of Africa, which is the headquarters of the group. No less than 30 different kinds of the ordinary type (*Francolinus*) occur in Africa, and, in addition, four species of the bare-throated type (*Pternistes*). The more commonly met (and shot) *Francolins* of (*a*) the East and (*b*) Africa are the following:

Common Francolin (*Francolinus francolinus*), which ranges from Cyprus to Assam. It is the bird which Europeans in India call *Black Partridge*.

Grey Partridge (*F. pondicerianus*), Persia to India.

Painted Partridge (*F. pictus*), Peninsula of India.

Chinese Francolin (*F. pintadeanus*), Burma, Indo-China and Southern China.

And in Africa:

Grey-wing Francolin or *Cape Partridge* (*Francolinus africanus*), ranging from the Cape Province to Abyssinia. 'Plentiful in the grass-veld in the Sneeberg Mountains between Cradock and Graff Reinet. Thrive well and have been known to breed in captivity.'—B.HO.

Red-wing Francolin (*F. levaillantii*), Natal, and from Angola to Kenya.

Cape Francolin or *Cape Pheasant* (*F. capensis*).

Coqui Francolin or *Shwimpi* (*F. coqui*), 'excellent eating'.—B.HO.

Crested Francolin (*F. sephaena*), 'their flesh is excellent eating, not so dry as that of most Francolins'.—B.HO.

Kirk's Francolin (*F. kirki*), 'a woodland species fairly common in marshy parts of Portuguese East Africa'.—B.HO.

Natal Francolin (*F. natalensis*), 'it is called *Coast Partridge* in Natal and *Namaqua Pheasant* in the Transvaal'.—B.HO.

Orange Francolin (*F. gariepensis*), 'quite common on the kopjes which surround the Potchefstroom Commonage and round their bases; more plentiful still near Vryburg and right into the Kalahari Desert'. —B.HO.

Bare-throated Francolin (*Pternistes afer*), Angola and Natal to Kenya.

Swainson's Francolin (*Pternistes swainsoni*). Never far from cultivated fields and water; very partial to grain from ripening crops and sometimes a great nuisance to farmers. 'They are dry and indifferent eating, unless well hung and cooked with great care.'—B.HO.

According to the recorded sales of Game on the Kimberley Market during the 1904 season, there were 2,957 Francolins sold; they were entered as 'redwings', so that they must have been the *Cape Red-winged Francolin*. During the same period there were 3,565 Knorhaans sold, but merely 818 Guineafowls and 59 Paauw. There were also 22,626 'small birds' sold, and Major Horsbrugh thinks that these were probably the small *Coqui Francolin* or *Shwimpi*.

FULMAR. FULMAR PETREL

Lat. *Fulmarus glacialis*. An Arctic *Petrel*, smaller than the *Herring-Gull*, which it resembles in colour. Fulmars' eggs are greatly prized for food. At one time large numbers of *Fulmars* were snared annually, in the breeding season, by the people of St. Kilda, for winter use. In the last 50 years the *Fulmar* has increased enormously and its breeding range now extends to Southern Ireland, Wales and Yorkshire.

GADWALL

Lat. *Chaulelasmus streperus*. A wild duck of the same size as the *Mallard*, breeding in Europe, N. Asia and N. America, migrating south in winter. The *Gadwall* is highly esteemed as a bird for the table, and it may be prepared in any way suitable for *Wild Duck* (q.v.).

It is sometimes called *Gray Widgeon* or *Sand-Widgeon* in the U.S.A. It is more strictly vegetarian than the Mallard and other shoalwater ducks.

'Audubon classed the flesh of the Gadwall as equal to that of the *Redhead* (q.v.) and in only one place have I found it mentioned as inferior. Belding and Bendire (*vide* Grimmell, Bryant and Storer, 1918) speak of it as sometimes oily, fishy and inedible in California. Others have called attention to a "sedgy" taste. In India, its reputation is as high as in other parts of the world, and Baker (1908) regards it as not even second to the Mallard or Pintail. He says the birds always arrive in India in better condition than the Mallard, or else they fatten more rapidly after arriving. The fact that the Mallard comes a greater distance may perhaps explain this.'—J.C.P.

GALLINULE. MOOR-HEN. WATER-HEN

A name which applies to a number of different water fowls of the *Rail* genus, more particularly to two North American members of it, the *Purple Gallinule* (*Porphyrula martinicus*) and the *Florida Gallinule* (*Gallinula chloropus*). The first ranges over tropical and sub-tropical America, north to Illinois and south to the Carolinas; the second breeds further north, as far as Maine and Quebec, wintering in Southern California, the Gulf States and further South. Both are about 13 in. in length; they resemble the *Moorhen* (q.v.) and are neither better nor worse gastronomically.

GANNET. SOLAN GOOSE

Lat. *Sula bassana.* A large white sea bird with black-tipped wings which breeds on a number of rocky islands round our coast, on the Faroe Islands, and Gulf of St. Lawrence. From time immemorial the Solan Goose from the Bass Rock, near Edinburgh, has been esteemed as an article of food. Taylor, the Water Poet, writing in 1618, described 'the Soleand Goose' as 'most delicate fowle, which has very good flesh, but it is eaten standing at a sideboard, little before dinner, unsanctified without garlic; and after it is eaten it must be well liquered with two or three rowsers of sherrie or canarie sacke.' Up to about 1848 there was still a demand for young gannets from the Bass, and till at least 1885 they were sent to London, and many Midland towns, where they were eaten in the commoner eating-houses.

In London, gannets were sold as Scotch Grouse, plucked and cooked, at 10*d.* each, but gradually the demand ceased and the flesh was considered to be rank and fishy. Sir William Jardine, writing in about 1845, says: 'We have once or twice eaten them boiled like ham and considered them by no means either strong, fishy or unpalatable.'

The gannet is still eaten by the fishermen from Lewis in the Outer Hebrides, who annually raid Haskier for young birds, which they salt for winter use.

As late as 1856 eggs were sold in London at 6*d.* a dozen and, according to an old advertisement, were eaten at Buckingham Palace.

GARGANEY. SUMMER TEAL

Lat. *Anas querquedula.* One of the smallest duck and a summer visitor to England, breeding in the Norfolk Broads, where it is commonly known as the *Cricket-Teal*. It is a little larger than the common European *Teal* and much resembles its American cousin, the *Cinnamon Teal* (q.v.). The drake has a nutmeg-brown beard and a white line behind the eyes. It is called *Sarcelle d'été* in France. It is prepared for the table in any way suitable for *Teal* (q.v.).

'The flesh of the Garganey is everywhere graded lower than that of the Common Teal. It is more apt to have a rank and bitter taste, especially in the spring. Naumann considered it a very good bird for the table in the autumn, but Millais (1902), speaking of birds from the Rhone Delta and the brackish lakes of Algeria, classed them as very inferior. Hume and Marshall (1879) did not think them comparable to the Common Teal, and say that even the inland feeders are not always free from "a certain marshy twang".' —J.C.P.

GODWIT

Black-tailed Godwit (Lat. *Limosa limosa*)
Bar-tailed Godwit (Lat. *Limosa lapponica*)
Godwits are found in the Old World and in the New. They are large wading birds, with long legs, a long bill, and a body like that of a large pigeon, resembling the *Curlew*, to which they are greatly superior gastronomically. *Black-tailed Godwits* formerly bred in considerable numbers in the Eastern Counties, from Yorkshire south, but owing to their nests being robbed and the birds netted and shot in the spring, they ceased to breed in England from about the year 1829. In London, the price of *Godwit*, which was 3*s.* per bird in 1807, fluctuated from 1*s.* to 6*s.* in 1922. Godwits are cooked like *Woodcock* (q.v.).

The *Bar-tailed Godwit*, which is sometimes called the *Sea-Woodcock*, breeds from the north of Norway eastwards and is a common winter visitor in the British Isles.

In America there are the large *Marbled Godwit* (*L. fedoa*) and the small *Hudsonian Godwit* (*L. hudsonia*), which winter in Central and South America; while in Eastern Asia there is a form of the *Bar-tailed Godwit*, which winters in the Antipodes, as well as a slightly smaller race of the *Black-tailed God-wit*. All these Godwits have similar habits and haunt the seashore in winter.

The *Eastern* or *Southern Godwit* (*L. novae-hollandiae*) is one of the most wonderful of all the migrants; it breeds in Eastern Siberia and reaches the North Island of New Zealand in October, November and December: it then goes down the coast line to the very end of the South Island and as far as Chatham Island and the Stewart Group. Towards the end of April or at the beginning of May, this small bird returns by the same route to the North Polar lands from which it came, more than ten thousand miles away, with immense tracts of sea to cross. 'The Natives catch large numbers of them by spreading flax snares horizontally on manuka sticks 12 or 15 ft. high. ... They are esteemed good eating by both settlers and Maoris. The latter always cook the bird unopened and devour the contents of the stomach with relish. When very fat they are potted in the orthodox fashion and 'calabashed' for future use.'—W.L.B.

Sir Thomas Browne calls the Godwit 'the daintiest dish in England', and Ben Jonson refers to the bird in *The Devil is an Ass* (Act III, sc. 3):

'Your eating
Pheasant and Godwits here in
London, haunting
The Globes and Mermaids;
wedging in with lords
Still at the table.'

Dr Thomas Muffet, in *Health Improvement* (p. 99), writes that: 'A fat Godwit is so fine and light meat that the noblemen, yea, and merchants too, by your leave, stick not to buy them at four nobles a dozen.'

GOLDEN-EYE

Lat. *Bucephala clangula*. A diving duck which breeds in the far northern regions of Europe and Asia, migrating south during the winter. In spite of the fact that it is invariably fat, even in the depths of the hardest winter, it is too oily and not fit to eat, except in famine times. Its eggs, however, are excellent and greatly prized as food. In Iceland the *Golden-eye's* eggs fetch a higher price than other eggs, and in Scandinavia they fit artificial nesting boxes to attract the birds and rob them of some of their eggs. There are two American species of *Golden-eye* duck, but they are not killed for food.

GOOSE

The goose is one of the most valuable of our barnyard fowls. The male bird, when adult, is a gander, but in culinary parlance male and female birds are both called a goose, when adult, and either a gosling or green goose up to six months old. In culinary French, the adult bird, whether cock of hen, is always in the feminine: *Une Oie*, but up to six months old, always in the masculine: *Un Oison*.

'The spring is near when green geese are a breeding.'

(*Love's Labour's Lost*, Act I, Scene 1.)

'A young fat goose farsed with sweet herbs and spices, doth competently nourish.'

(Vaughan's *Directions for Health*, 1626, p. 36.)

In England, geese are at their best between Michaelmas and Candlemas, from September to February, and they are still mostly roasted and stuffed with sage and onion, as has been the practice for centuries past. Green geese or goslings, however, are roasted without any sage and onion stuffing.

The goose is much better eating than the swan, but not quite so good as the duck. Its gastronomic inferiority complex is due to the fact that it runs to fat very quickly, but advantage has been taken of this by the people of Alsace in the first place, and others since, who have used the goose's fat liver to make that delicious confection known as *Pâté de Foie Gras*.

A goose, when given the chance, lives to a great age, but a goose which is more than two years old, although it may be kept as a pet or a night watchman, is of no use for roasting. When buying a goose for the table, one should see that the bird still has some down on its legs, which are soft and yellow in young birds; also that the underbill is soft and pliable.

'The goose has long been domesticated, figures of two species appearing on many Egyptian monuments – the Egyptian Goose, *Anser egyptiacus*, and the Grey Goose, *Anser ferus*, the latter being the bird which, by its vigilance, saved the Roman capital from the Gauls. From the Grey Goose all our domestic breeds have descended. Pliny has given the following information on the subject of geese. "Our people," he says, "esteem the goose chiefly on account of the excellence of the liver, which attains a very large size when the bird is crammed. When the liver is thoroughly soaked in honey and milk, it be-comes specially large. It is a moot question who first made such an excellent discovery – whether it was Scipio Metellus, a man of consular rank, or Marcus Sesitus, a Roman knight. However, there is no doubt that it was Messalinus Cotia who first cooked the webbed feet of geese and served them up with cocks' combs, for I must award the palm of the kitchen to the man who is deserving of it. This bird, wonderful to relate, comes all the way from the Morini to

Rome on its own feet: the weary geese are placed in front, and those following by a natural pressure urge them on".'—E.G.B.

GOOSE. GOSLING.
OIE. OISON

Alicot of Goose
Goose boiled with mushrooms
Goose devilled en casserole
Le Cassoulet de Toulouse
Confit d'Oie
Oie farcie landaise
Minced Goose Breast (Vagdalt libamelle)
The famous white Goose Pie of Poitou
Ragoût of Goose with Apples
Ragoût d'Oie aux Choux
Goose Stew and Chestnuts
Roast Goose (English style)
Roast Goose (French style)
Roast Goose (German style)
Roast Watertown Goose
Pâté de Foie Gras
Pâté-Terrine de Foie Gras
Foie Gras au Porto

Alicot of Goose

First brown the pieces of left-over goose in goose fat; take them out, and in the same fat fry a couple of thinly-sliced onions and a slice of raw ham or bacon. Now skin four tomatoes, take out the pips and cut the flesh only and add this, with a *bouquet* of parsley, thyme, and bayleaf to the onion and ham. Add the pieces of goose and three cupfuls of beef stock well seasoned with salt and pepper; bring to the boil and simmer for a quarter of an hour. Then take out the *bouquet* and cook very gently for two hours.—AM-BROSE HEATH in *Wine and Food*, No. 4, p. 24.

Goose boiled with Mushrooms

Cut a goose in joints and boil till tender in salt water, with an onion, a carrot, celery or celeriac, a turnip, some parsley, a few mushrooms and mixed spice. Blend a spoonful of flour in 1 oz. of butter and cook it with three-quarters of a pint of goose-broth and half pint of cream. Add 1 lb. mushrooms stewed in butter. Cook the sauce for a few minutes, then dish up the goose and pour the sauce over it.—C.T.

Goose devilled en casserole

1 goose
Potato stuffing
4 tablespoons vinegar
1 tablespoon white pepper
2 tablespoons made mustard

After cleaning the goose and wiping it well with a damp cloth, plunge it into a saucepan of boiling water and boil gently for one hour. Take it from the saucepan, drain well and wipe it very dry.

Fill the body and neck with potato stuffing, truss and sew up, lay it in an earthenware pan, and roast in a very hot oven, allowing 20 minutes to every pound.

Mix the vinegar, pepper, and mustard together, pour them over the goose and baste it frequently. An old goose that can be cooked in no other way may be so dressed, two hours being allowed for the boiling instead of one hour.

To make the potato stuffing: Cook one chopped onion in a quarter of a cupful of salt pork cubes until brown, then add two cupfuls of hot mashed potatoes, salt and pepper to taste, half a teaspoon of poultry seasoning, one tablespoon of chopped parsley, and one cupful of cooked sausages cut in pieces. Mix thoroughly, then stuff the goose with the mixture.—M.H.N.

Le Cassoulet de Toulouse

2 lb. shoulder of mutton
1 lb. rinds of pork (couennes grasses)
¼ lb. onions
1 fresh Toulouse sausage
1 bayleaf
1 or 2 cloves garlic
10 pieces of confit d'oie
1 quart dried beans
¼ lb. fat salt pork
1 sprig thyme
Salt and pepper
1 pint white wine

This is a 'robust' dish such as French peasants, who do not possess modern squeamish stomachs, love. It should be enjoyed in good company, at leisure, and washed down with copious draughts of good white wine, followed by a cup of black coffee and a glass of Armagnac brandy.

Soak the beans overnight. Have a heavy iron saucepan – such as *de rigueur* for all these slow-cooked dishes – and line the bottom with the rinds of fat fresh pork. Cover these with the drained beans and the white wine, adding sufficient water to completely cover the beans. Salt with moderation. Add the herbs and a little pepper. Cover and cook gently 1½ hours when the beans will be half-cooked.

Brown the mutton, cut into pieces, in the fat rendered by the salt pork which has been gently fried to extract it. Add the sliced onions and the minced or grated garlic. Add all this to the beans, with the gravy from the mutton, cover and cook until mutton is done as well as the beans. Now add the pieces of *confit d'oie* and three tablespoons of its succulent fat. Turn all into a large earthenware pan and set in a fairly hot oven when, after a short while, a 'skin' will form on the surface. Mix this, very carefully, with the beans and replace in oven. Repeat this skinning and mixing operation six times, adding the browned sausage after the fifth mixing. Do not disturb the seventh 'skin'. Cut the sausage into rather thick slices, serve on top of the casserole and sprinkle all with finely-chopped parsley. Serve in baking dish, VERY hot.—P.W.

Confit d'Oie

This is a greatly-prized winter standby in the French countryside. The goose should – it is claimed – be killed on the name-day of St. Martin (11th November). Cut the cleaned bird – or birds if the family is a large one – into neat joints. Set aside the pieces of fat which should abound on the bird. Salt the former pieces well on all sides and set them in an earthenware pot, having a lid. Set a light board on the pieces of goose with a weight on top, and leave it in a cool dry place for 10 days. At the end of this time place the pieces of goose fat on the bottom of a large heavy saucepan. If there is not enough completely to cover, add a little pure lard. Wipe each piece of meat well to remove excess of salt and lay them on this bed of fat. Set pan over a rather low heat. The fat will soon begin to melt, and the pieces of goose will slowly cook. This operation should take about 1½ hours. When they are done, carefully remove them, place them in the deep earthenware jar and strain the hot fat over them, taking care the meat is well covered by it. To use, dip a long fork into the pot, fish out as much meat as you require – with its adhering fat – heat in a frying-pan and fry some thin rounds of raw potato with the goose, serving together. In some parts of France – notably Les Landes and Périgord – a mixture of finely-chopped parsley and a soupçon of garlic is sprinkled on top of all when serving. Kept in a cool, dry place, the *confit* will keep for months. It is, by the way, excellent cold, too.—P.W.

Oie farcie landaise

Take a young goose, prepare it for roasting and stuff it in the following manner: About ¼ lb. breadcrumbs, ¼ lb. sausage-meat, the liver chopped, and a handful of olives stoned and cut in half, a spoonful of anchovy butter, and a little chopped parsley.

All this should be well seasoned with salt, pepper, a little nutmeg, mixed together and bound with one egg. Before stuffing the goose, sprinkle the inside with a little lemon juice; stuff it, close the opening and wrap the bird with very thin slices of pork fat.

Roast, basting often, and half an hour before the end remove the slices of fat, so that the goose becomes nicely coloured.

Serve with potatoes baked in the goose fat. The gravy must remain as it is, and not be spoilt by the addition of anything else. Remove excess of fat if necessary. This fat is delicious and can be used in cooking.

The time of cooking for an average bird is 2½ hours, beginning with a hot oven and reducing to moderate.

The 'anchovy butter' is simply done by chopping and pounding fillets of anchovy in oil and working in well the same quantity (or a little more if the anchovies are very salt) of butter.—X.M.B. (1)

Minced Goosebreast
(Vagdalt libamelle)

Cut off the raw meat from the breast of a large goose, mince it very finely together with the goose liver, a spoonful finely-minced fried onion, two or three slices bread (previously soaked in milk); mix thoroughly, season with salt and pepper and add enough flour to hold together. Form into loaf, place on greased baking sheet or pan, baste with melted goose fat and roast for 45 minutes. Cut into slices and serve with the thickened gravy. This dish is sometimes eaten cold; in that case it is baked covered with pastry, similarly to an English pork-pie. It is a suitable dish for cold buffet or picnic.—L.D.

The famous White Goose Pie of Poitou

Make a crust of two parts flour to one part butter and yolk of egg, salt and water. Prepare a forcemeat of one-third lean fresh pork, one-third goose thigh flesh, one-third fat bacon, mixed herbs, fresh truffles, goose flesh cut in strips and some fat bacon cut in strips the same size, hard-boiled eggs cut in half, pie seasoning to taste. Soak the seasoned forcemeat in brandy for 2 hours. Line the pie-dish with the paste and place the forcemeat and the strips of goose and truffles and bacon in layers, and the eggs in the centre. The top layer must be of forcemeat. Cover the pie and take care to see that the two crusts are well closed. Make a small hole in the top and cook it gently in the oven for about 40 minutes. (Recipe of the Chapon Fin, Poitiers.)—P.A.

Ragoût of Goose with Apples

1 cut-up young goose
1 onion
Salt and pepper
Tiny pinch powdered cinnamon
Butter
2 lb. tart cooking apples
Small pinch nutmeg

If the family is a small one, either a small goose or part of one should be used. In towns – especially in French ones – it is possible to buy them cut into serving pieces, by the pound. Brown the pieces in very little butter as the skin contains much fat. Add the cut-up onion and the apples, peeled and cut into thick slices. Add a little salt and pepper and the spices. Cover pan closely and cook gently until pieces of goose are tender. Skim off excess fat before serving on a bed of the apples.—P.W.

Ragoût d'Oie aux Choux

Prepare this dish according to previous recipe, substituting blanched and shredded cabbage for the apples and adding a few caraway seeds – if liked – in place of cinnamon. Sauerkraut, cooked in white wine, may also be used instead of fresh cabbage.—P.W.

Goose Stew and Chestnuts

Cut up a small goose in 12 to 14 pieces and brown them in a hot pan. Run off the fat in a pot and keep in reserve. Dredge the pieces of goose with a tablespoonful of flour in a saucepan on a moderate fire, tossing them about until thoroughly brown. Then add a glassful of water and two tablespoonfuls of tomato *purée*; season with pepper and salt; add a *bouquet* of mixed herbs and cover the pan; let it stew on a moderate heat gently during an hour and a quarter or an hour and a half. In the meantime boil a pound of chestnuts, and whilst they are boiling, toss in the goose fat 15 to 20 very small onions and a carrot or two cut up in rounds or small squares, and then add them all to the pan in which the goose is stewing.

The chestnuts being fairly soft after boiling for 20 minutes, take them out of the water, one by one, peel them and add them also to the pan, when the goose will have already been stewing an hour. Remove all surface fat from the stew before serving and serve hot with the onions, carrots and chestnuts all mixed together. Taste before serving and add pepper and salt if wanted.—F.

Roast Goose
(English Style)

Prepare a goose, stuff the body of the bird well with sage and onion, then tie the ends of the legs together. Cover with fat and roast slowly, allowing 12 minutes to each pound. If not browning sufficiently well, dredge over with flour in the last half hour. When done, pour the fat from the tin, add to what is left one tablespoonful flour, half pint good stock made from the giblets, salt and pepper. Boil up, pour a little round the goose, and serve the remainder in a tureen. Serve with apple sauce.—E.W.K.

Roast Goose
(French Style)

Stuff a tender young goose with either boiled chestnuts or apples sliced rather finely. Bake in a hot oven, basting frequently with a little added fat, at first, and soon after with the plentiful supply of the bird's own fat. Allow 20 minutes per pound and the skin should be nicely browned and crackling.—P.W.

Roast Goose
(German Style)

When the goose is prepared for roasting, peel, wash and wipe dry a plateful of good potatoes; slice thin and cut them up into very little dice. Put 2 or 3 oz. of butter in a stewpan, and when this is hot put in the potatoes, with a middling-sized onion minced fine, or very little garlic; a saltspoonful of the latter when minced is enough. Cover the stewpan and set it over the fire, shaking it often that none of the potatoes may burn. Steam them for a few minutes till done but not softened. Take them from the fire and stir among them the finely-minced raw liver of the goose; season well with salt and pepper, and a saltspoonful of finely-minced or powdered sage; or, instead of the latter, a grating of nutmeg. Some prefer no flavour in this exceedingly good stuffing, but the potatoes, liver, a slight flavour of shallot or onion, as above, and salt and pepper.—G.N.C.

Roast Watertown Goose

Clean and prepare a Watertown goose, fill with a liver and mushroom stuffing. Truss together, place in a roasting pan with a *mirepoix*; pour hot drippings over breast; season with pepper and salt. Roast for about an hour before turning over, then add a few cupfuls of water. Baste for about two hours longer. Remove goose, add eight tablespoonfuls of flour to the roast pan and make a regular pan gravy. Strain. Serve with apple sauce.—E.E.A.

Pâté de Foie Gras

The liver of the goose is very good to eat and full of all goodness, vitamins and the rest. The liver of other birds is just as good, but the goose's liver is larger, and when the bird is crammed with food as well as deprived of all exercise, its liver attains a size five times larger than what it is meant to be. The Romans knew all about it two thousand years ago, and they were very fond of a goose-liver paste, the kind of confection which has been made in Alsace better than anywhere else in modern times and is known in all parts of the civilized world under the name of *Pâté de Foie Gras*.

Pâté-Terrine de Foie Gras

Ayez:

1 kilo de foie de veau
1 kilo foie gras
550 grammes de truffes
125 grammes de pain au levain doux
250 grammes de poitrine de porc frais
    sans couenne ni nerfs
750 grammes de panne de porc frais

Coupez le foie gras en morceaux de l'épaisseur de la moitié du doigt au plus.

Hachez et pilez au mortier une échalote et 2 branches de persil; ajoutez le foie de veau, la poitrine de porc frais et la panne; ajoutez à ce mélange le pain que vous avez fait mijoter 25-30 minutes avec un verre d'eau: assaisonnez de sel, poivre, épices. Hachez, pilez et mélangez bien le tout.

Etendez une couche de cette farce de l'épaisseur du doigt au fond de la terrine; mettez dessus des tranches de foie gras et des tranches de truffes; saupoudrez d'un peu de sel, de poivre et d'épices; mettez une nouvelle couche de farce, puis une nouvelle couche de foie gras et de truffes; et ainsi de suite jusqu'a ce que la terrine soit pleine; ayez soin de terminer par une couche de farce; couvrez d'une barde de lard très mince; mettez une feuille de laurier dessus; mettez le couvercle de la terrine et faites cuire au bain-marie trois heures environ.

Laissez refroidir complètement.

Si l'on veut la conserver longtemps, c'est une bonne précaution de la comprimer à la sortie du four avec une plaque ou une assiette que l'on charge d'un poids d'un ou deux kilogrammes, puis le lendemain on retire la plaque en la chauffant un peu; on recouvre le dessus du pâté d'une couche de saindoux; on remet le couvercle; on ferme hermétiquement en collant une bande de papier tout autour du couvercle et en mettant au trou du milieu. Conserve le pâté dans un endroit sec et frais. (*La Bonne Cuisine, par E.Dumont, A.Degorce, Paris.* n.d. circa 1895.)

Foie Gras au Porto

Although belonging to the Cuisine Riche, which is not that of every day, I think it useful to mention the method of cooking a *foie gras*. Without launching out daily into sumptuous expenditure on the table, one may have to treat one's friends or relations, and it is then that recipes like this are appreciated. Let me explain first how to tell a good *foie gras*. It must be rosy, firm to the touch and glossy. It is necessary first to remove with the point of a knife the greenish portion which was in contact with the gall; then season the liver with salt, pepper and four spices, put it in a *cocotte* with a quarter of a bottle of port wine (which can be replaced by madeira, champagne or good white wine).

Place round it two or three fresh scoured truffles and allow to marinate for 24 hours. Then wrap it in a 'cowl' (crépine) of pork and poach it without boiling in the well-closed *cocotte*, with the wine and truffles around. The best method of cooking is in the oven: 22 minutes for a liver of 500 grammes; 35 for a kilo.

This liver may be served hot with a sauce demi-glace with addition of the well-skimmed wine of the cuisson, or cold with jelly, to which is also added the wine during clarification. The truffles serve to decorate the liver. (*La Cuisine de Tous les Jours, par H.Pellaprat, Le Cordon Bleu, Paris.*)

GOOSE, BARNACLE

Lat. *Branta leucopsis.* A wild goose related to the *Brant* or *Brent Goose*, breeding in the Arctic regions and visiting the Hebrides, Solway and Ireland in the winter. There is a legend that it grew out of a fruit and had been plucked from the tree to which it was attached by its beak. There was another legend according to which the Barnacle Goose came out of an egg but of a sea-shell, the Acorn-shell, of the genus *Cirripides*, and shells of this genus have been named Barnacles, after the Goose. See *Goose.*

GOOSE, EGYPTIAN

Lat. *Alopochen aegyptiaca.* A non-migratory African Goose, the best-known of all the African members of the family *Anatidae.* It is also known as *Nile Goose* and *Zambesi Goose.* It is called *Berg Gans* in Africaans.

'The flesh of this species has been almost invariably described as unfit for the table, even the young being unpalatable, according to Horsbrugh (1912). Blandford (1870), however, speaks of it as good eating, and A.E.Brehm (1879) says the young are very tasty, whilst the mature birds make excellent soups.'—J.C.P.

GOOSE, SOLAN

See *Gannet.*

GOOSE, WILD

The *Wild Goose* is a fine bird from the sportsman's but not from the gastronome's point of view. There is a large number of different varieties, all of them difficult to shoot, and none of them comparable to the domesticated *Goose* (q.v.).

In 1942, the maximum retail price fixed by the Ministry of Food for the sale of *Wild Geese*, in England and Wales, was 10*s.* per bird for birds over 4 lb., and 8*s.* for birds weighing 4 lb. or less.

To cook a Wild Goose

I

Put a small onion, a slice of pork, pepper, salt, and a spoonful of red wine inside the goose. Lay it in a pan with water enough to make gravy. Dredge with flour and baste with butter frequently. Cook quickly and serve with gravy made from the thickened stock. (*Old recipe from Toano, Virginia.*)—H.B.

II

If quite young, it may be roasted like an ordinary goose, or it may be cooked like the swan, in paste, but stuffed with the following: Mince finely together 1 lb. of beef suet freed from string, etc., two shallots, a handful of parsley, a little thyme, sweet basil, and marjoram; to this add 1 lb. of breadcrumbs, ¼ lb. of butter, two whole eggs, and a good seasoning of pepper, salt and grated nutmeg; knead well together and use. A wild goose thus prepared takes about three hours, should be frothed up at the last with butter and flour, and be served with braised onions and Poivrade Sauce.—Q. (2)

GREENSHANK

Lat. *Tringa nebularia*. A European shore bird, allied to the *Snipe* (q.v.) but larger – about 14 in. Its legs are greenish and longer than those of the *Woodcock*; the plumage is brown and grey, the latter colour prevailing in winter, when the underparts are pure white; the beak is about 2 in. long; the tail is short. The *Greenshank* nests on the ground and does not sit on more than four eggs, like the *Plover*. It feeds on small animals of all sorts. In spring and autumn, small flocks occur on migration on the coasts of England and inland, on the Irish lakes and the Scotch lochs. It is prepared in any way suitable for *Woodcock* (q.v.).

'THE' GROUSE

Lat. *Lagopus scoticus*. In Great Britain and Ireland the name *Grouse*, when not otherwise qualified, applies exclusively to the *Red Grouse* or *Scotch Grouse*, the best, in our opinion, of all game birds in the world, during two months, from mid-August to mid-October of the year when it was born. It is generally regarded as an insular form of the *Willow Grouse* (q.v.), which has ceased to put on a white, protective plumage during the winter months. The *Grouse* is a very clean feeder, living upon the young and tender shoots of heaths which abound where it is bred, in Scotland, Yorkshire, and the Pennines; also in Wales and in the West of Ireland. All attempts to introduce the *Grouse* in France and elsewhere have failed, and there is no name for this bird in any other language. A young *Grouse*, that is a bird from 12th August to the end of December of the year when it was bred, has soft downy plumes on the breast and under the wings, pointed wings and rounded spurs.

The only other game bird which might dispute the claim of the *Grouse* to be the best of all would be the *Grey Partridge*, an excellent bird indeed. But if we give precedence to the *Grouse* over the *Partridge*, it is because of its greater individuality and the greater intensity of its flavour. A *Partridge* may be a little more or a little less plump, but it is otherwise exactly the same, whether shot in Norfolk or in Cornwall; and whether shot this year, last year or the year before. Not so the *Grouse*. It always has the distinctive grouse flavour, as any and every first growth of the Côte d'Or is obviously a wine of Burgundy, but there is between the birds shot in Derbyshire and those shot in Perthshire, as well as between the birds shot in one season and those of the previous year, the same degree of variation that exists between the different growths of the Côte d'Or of different vintages. Major Hugh Pollard, who acknowledges the influence of seasonal changes and locality upon what he calls 'that subtle alchemy of digestion which endows the bird with his special value', yet places the *Grouse* third in order of gastronomic merit, after the *Partridge* and the *Pheasant*. He considers the distinctive flavour of the *Grouse* a disadvantage, 'for it is not easily abated by other subtleties, so that, however you dress your bird, whether as soup or braise or pie, the dominant flavour is always grouse; and short of violence with a clove of garlic or a curry that would make coke palatable, it is impossible to cover it'. But why cover it? All the subtleties of delicious sauces and garnishings are devised to help chicken, veal, cod and all food without any flavour or one that is not attractive, but not the flavour of a young *Grouse*. What is true is that the flavour of grouse, good as it is, is somewhat too assertive to be enjoyed continuously, day after day, twice a day, like bread or potatoes. And there is yet another point in favour of the grouse: it is as good – some even say better – when eaten cold. Of course, an old grouse, that is a bird of the year before, is quite another thing, and a poor thing, and on no account should a young bird and an old one be cooked at the same time nor in the same way. Plainly and lightly roasted is the best way to deal with a young bird, whereas the most suitable funeral for an old bird is the soup pot or the game paste jar.

In 1757, the price of Grouse on the London Market was 3*s*. 6*d*. per bird; in 1922 it fluctuated from 5*s*. 6*d*. to 8*s*.; and in 1941 from 4*s*. 6*d*. to 7*s*. 6*d*. In 1942, the Ministry of Food fixed the maximum retail price at 6*s.* per bird, irrespective of age and condition.

The late Professor George Saintsbury, whose authority as a critic ranked very high in the realm of gastronomy as well as in the world of letters, wrote: 'While nearly all the game birds are good, and some eminently good, grouse seems to me to be the best, to possess the fullest and at the same time the least violent flavour – to have the best consistency of flesh, and to present the greatest variety of attractions in different parts.'

Grouse have *no* spurs.

Braised Grouse

Clean, truss and season the required number of old birds, and fry till brown in bacon fat. Put them into a casserole with a small quantity of stock, a piece of carrot, onion, celery, and braise for two hours, adding a small quantity of stock or water if required.

Thicken the sauce with cornflour and pour over them. Dish with vegetables in the centre.—M.F.

Broiled Grouse, with Bacon

Singe, draw, and wipe nicely two fine fat grouse. Split them in two through the back without separating the parts; lay them on a dish, and season with a pinch of salt, half a pinch of pepper, and a tablespoonful of sweet oil. Roll them in well; then put them to broil on a brisk fire for seven minutes on each side. Prepare a hot dish with six small toasts, arrange the grouse over, spread a gill of Maître d'Hôtel butter on top, and garnish with six thin slices of broiled bacon; then serve.—G.A.S.

Grouse Pie

Cut up a brace of grouse, each of them in five parts, and season with pepper and salt. Mask the bottom of a pie-dish with a layer of game forcemeat, on which place the pieces of grouse; sprinkle over a little cooked fine herbs; fill the cavities between the pieces with a few yolks of hard-boiled eggs, and place on the top of the grouse a few slices of raw ham; pour in good gravy, to half the height; cover the pie with paste, egg it, and put it in a moderate oven for 1½ hours; when done, set it on another dish.—G.A.S.

Pounded Game Pie

Ingredients: Two grouse or any other game; salt, pepper and 1 oz. butter.

Melt 1 oz. butter in a stewpan, split the birds in half, put them into the pan and brown well, but do not let them burn; then add a little water, pepper and salt, let it simmer gently at the side of the stove until tender, then take out the birds and free the meat

from the bones. Put all through a wire sieve, add a little of the gravy to moisten it, season to taste. Pack into a game pie-dish, decorate with vegetables cut in fancy patterns, and a thin layer of aspic jelly or a little melted butter; then it is ready for use as a breakfast or luncheon dish.—C.N.

Grouse Pudding

Take one old grouse, hack him in gobbets and cook him in an ordinary beefsteak suet pudding in place of the traditional kidney. It needs long cooking, and the addition at half-time of an extra cup of stock, but in the end all the steak takes the illusive grouse flavour. An ideal hot lunch for an outdoor party.—M.H.P.

Roast Grouse

Do not allow young birds to hang more than three or four days: they should not be 'high'. Pluck, singe, draw and truss as you would a chicken. Season inside and out with pepper and salt; insert a 'nut' of butter and a sprig of lovage or summer savoury inside, if any available, but no bayleaf, thyme nor any strongly-scented herbs. Slip on a waistcoat of thin rashers of fat bacon over the bird's breast and roast in a quick oven from 15 to 20 minutes, according to size of the bird. It must not be raw nor 'rare' but slightly underdone; not 'blue' but pink. Baste frequently during cooking with bacon fat or run butter; remove bacon, dredge lightly with flour and put back in the oven for a very little time to brown breast. The liver may be pounded and seasoned, then spread upon a square of toast, with the crusty ends cut off; this piece of toast is slipped under the bird to catch the gravy that drops from it during cooking, and the bird is dished on this piece of toast. It is served with some made gravy, a little cress or undressed salad, but *no vegetables* other than a few fried 'straw' potatoes.

Salmis of Grouse

Half roast or braise a brace of grouse, then joint them and place the pieces in a pan with sufficient good stock to cover them. See this is well seasoned and simmer gently for 15 to 30 minutes, according to age of birds. Serve with a 'short' sauce, garnishing with fried *croûtons*. A glassful of good port should be added to the sauce which is then reduced almost to a glaze, and it may, if desired, be slightly thickened with a little fécule or flour. —P.W.

Grouse Soufflé

Cold grouse; two handfuls boiled rice; 1 oz. butter; one tablespoonful meat glaze, dissolved in a little stock; seasoning; three eggs.

Remove the meat from the bones of the grouse, pound well with the butter, rice, and glaze; season well and rub all through a wire sieve, then mix in the yolks of the eggs, add the whites, beaten very stiff, steam gently for one hour, and serve with brown sauce. (Mrs Ellison, The Vicarage, Windsor.)—F.C.B.

Stewed Grouse

Take one or more young grouse, and after having cleaned them, cut up the back and front with a pair of kitchen scissors. Sprinkle with pepper, salt and flour and fry till brown in a flat pan so that the pieces do not overlap. When fried, draw the pan to the side, place a cover on it and simmer slowly for about 30 minutes, turning occasionally. Serve with the gravy in which they were stewed poured round. Button mushrooms may be added if desired.—M.F.

Cold Terrine of Grouse

Four old grouse: enough for eight people.
    Take some fillets off the breasts. Fry and pound and pass through a hair sieve the remainder of the flesh with the livers; a little parsley, thyme and bacon. Line a Pyrex dish with bacon and fill with alternate layers of fillets, forcemeat and rolls of bacon. Add garlic stock and season. Cook until quite tender, after which, if necessary, add a little gelatine stock. When set, turn it into another dish and cover with jelly.—R.L.

GROUSE, BLACK
See *Black Game*

GROUSE, BLUE or RICHARDSON'S
Lat. *Dendragapus richardsonii*. One of the North American game birds of the *Grouse* family. It is found in the Rocky Mountains from British Columbia and Alberta south to Wyoming. Further south it is replaced by the *Dusky Grouse* (*D. obscurus*), which extends to New Mexico.

GROUSE, CANADIAN
Lat. *Canachites canadiensis*. A game bird, also known as *Spruce Partridge*, of little gastronomic merit. It inhabits the wooded lands of south-eastern Canada and the forests of some of the eastern U.S.A., but is becoming rare. It is best prepared for the table in any way suitable for *Black Game* (q.v.).

GROUSE, RUFFED or PARTRIDGE
Lat. *Bonasa umbellus*. A North American game bird which occurs in the wooded parts of the Eastern U.S.A. and of Canada. It is also called *Partridge* in the north and *Pheasant* in the south. It is a handsome bird with a frilled ruffle of fanshaped feathers on each side of the neck. There is a related species

known as the *Oregon Ruffed Grouse*, which occurs along the Pacific coast of the U.S.A.

GROUSE, SAGE or SAGE-HEN
Lat. *Centrocercus urophasianus*. A game bird indigenous to the sage-brush plains of Western North America. The adult cock bird is from 26 to 30 in. long. In the winter months, when it has little if anything else to eat except the sage-brush of the plain, its flesh is not fit to eat, but in the summer, when its diet is more varied, it is acceptable and may be prepared in any way suitable for the *Capercaillie* (q.v.): it is no better. It used to be quite common, but it has now been almost exterminated in many of its old haunts.

GROUSE, SAND
Lat. *Pterocles arenarius*. A small game bird, of which there are many different species. *P. arenarius* is the largest sort and is known as the *Large* or the *Black-bellied Sand-Grouse* in Western Asia and Eastern Europe. The greater number of varieties of sand-grouse occur in East and South Africa, also in Arabia and India. Of one of these, the *Yellow-throated Sand-Grouse* (*P. gutturalis*) Major Horsbrugh writes: 'These sand-grouse are specially fond of the grain of Kaffir-corn and often feed in large numbers in fields ready for reaping. In consequence perhaps of this, they are generally very good eating, especially when split open and grilled with butter.' ... Then Horsbrugh quotes H.A.Bryden as follows: '*P. gutturalis* is much the biggest and heaviest of the four species, and in the deep chocolate or red-brown colouring of the underparts of the body, and in its cry, resembles most nearly the family of the Red Grouse of Scotland. ... The flesh of all sand-grouse is tough and compares poorly with that of many of the South African game birds.'—B.HO.

GROUSE, SHARP-TAILED
Lat. *Pedioecetes phasianellus*. A North American game bird, closely resembling the *Prairie Hen* (q.v.), but occurring further west, on the Pacific side of the Rockies as well as the wooded districts and tundras bordering the North American lakes. It has appeared at different times on the London Market, in a frozen condition.
    'In Middle West wheat fields prairie chicken (the sharp-tailed grouse) used to be so common that small parties would bag hundreds in a short sortie. These western grouse were even considered pests and vengefully shot down by irate farmers in and out of season. When game laws became more strict, it was the custom to invite the game warden to go along on all shooting parties out of season, to make everything perfectly

legal. To save plucking and cleaning, only the rick dark-meat breasts were jerked off and sent to the kitchen.'—C.R.B.B. (2)

GUILLEMOT

Lat. *Uria aalge*. Sea birds which abound on both the European and American coasts of the North Atlantic. The birds themselves are not fit to eat, but their eggs are collected on Flamborough Head and elsewhere in the British Isles, and eaten like *Plovers'* eggs (q.v.). They are twice as large but no better; and there is rather too much of it, more particularly too much of the white.

GUINEA-FOWL (COMMON GUINEA-FOWL)

Lat. *Numida meleagris*. The common *Helmeted Guinea-fowl* of West Africa was the bird originally called *Turkey*, in the sixteenth century, in England: it is the original stock from which the domesticated birds were bred. There are various forms of *Helmeted Guinea-fowls* (*Numida mitrata*) throughout Africa, as well as several species of *Crested Guinea-fowls* (*N. guttera*), differing from the others by their black, crested head, pale blue-spotted plumage and a white band along the wings. The wild *Guinea-fowl* is usually tough and very dry: it is best boiled or stewed with pork.

Major Boyd Horsbrugh describes the *Helmeted Damaraland Guinea-fowl* (*N. papillosa*) and also mentions a certain species of *Crested Guinea-fowl* (*Guttera edouardi*) which 'the Zambesi natives look upon with a certain amount of superstition. Nothing would induce them to eat it and they told us that its flesh was *poisonous*.'—B.HO.

GUINEA-FOWL

The *Guinea-fowl* is a native of West Africa which has been domesticated in England since the fifteenth century, when it was known as a Turkey, probably having been first introduced from Turkey. That was before the bird known to-day as a turkey had ever been seen in Europe. When Shakespeare speaks of a turkey, he means a *Guinea-fowl*. There are various species of *Guinea-fowl*, but they all have one characteristic in common, they never run to fat and their flesh is naturally dry. They are usually barded or larded and roasted on a spit or in a moderate oven or stewed in a *cocotte*, but may be prepared for the table in any way suitable for a chicken.

Guinea-fowls' eggs are excellent when boiled seven or eight minutes, that is hard-boiled; they may be described as a larger edition of the *Plover's Egg*, which they resemble in texture.

Guinea-fowl en Casserole

1 large guinea-fowl
1 onion
4 tablespoonfuls cream
Bunch of herbs
2 celery stalks
2 heaping tablespoonfuls (2 oz.) butter
Salt and pepper
2 heaping tablespoonfuls (2 oz.) flour
½ pint (1 cup) white stock
1 blade mace
6 whole peppers
2 slices carrot
½ pint (1 cup) milk

Draw and truss the guinea-fowl; then put it into a casserole with sufficient hot water to cover, then bring to the boil and simmer gently until the bird is cooked. Take it up and let it cool.

Measure half a pint of the water the guinea-fowl was boiled in. Put this into a pan with the milk, add the onion, mace, carrot, herbs, celery, whole peppers and the stock; bring slowly to boiling point; then simmer for 10 minutes.

Melt the butter, stir in the flour, then stir in the boiling stock. Cook slowly for 10 minutes, season with salt and pepper, add the cream.

Cut the guinea-fowl into neat joints. Put these into a casserole, strain the sauce over, put it on the fire, and heat up; make quite hot without boiling. Serve in the casserole. —M.H.N.

Guinea-fowl à la crème

Truss the bird with its liver inside it, and put it into a *cocotte* or oval stew-pan, with a small onion cut in four or five pieces and ½ oz. or so of butter. Cover and put into a moderate oven for 25 minutes, turning the guinea-fowl now and then so that it is nicely browned all over. Now boil a small cupful of sour cream in a separate saucepan, adding a pinch of salt and a little white pepper. When the guinea-fowl is ready, pour the boiling cream over it, put on the lid again and continue to cook in the oven for another quarter of an hour, basting with the cream at least three times. Serve as it is, in the *cocotte*, if it is of earthenware. If the cream is not sour, use fresh cream, and just on serving stir in a coffeespoonful of lemon juice.—AMBROSE HEATH in *Wine and Food*, No. 5, pp. 46–47.

Breast of Guinea Hen General Grant

Season six breasts of Guinea Hens and *sauté* in butter. Cook on both sides, which will take from 12 to 14 minutes. Place on a serving dish. Put two tablespoonfuls of sherry or Sauce Newburgh in the pan in which the breasts were cooked. Reduce a little, then add two cupfuls of rich cream, a little paprika and a dash of Worcestershire Sauce. If too thin, work in a little kneaded butter. Strain and pour over the guinea hen breasts. Serve with corn fritters and fried bananas. —E.E.A.

Guinea-fowl Calvados

Shred an onion and brown it in some sizzling butter; add a little raw ham cut up in dice, a handful of poached rice and three small sour apples (cider apples if available or green apples) finely-sliced. Moisten with a cupful of veal or chicken stock. Season with pepper and salt, and cook a little while but do not allow the rice to get stodgy.

Prepare as usual a young and tender *Guinea-fowl*; fill it with the rice-cum-apple stuffing prepared as indicated; sew it up securely; tie some bacon rashers over the breast and either braise the bird on top of the fire or roast it upon a spit in front of a brisk fire. When cooked, pour over it some *Calvados*, or Apple-jack, set it alight and serve with a rich cream sauce rather highly seasoned.

GULL

Black-headed Gull (Lat. *Larus ridibundus*)
Common Gull (Lat. *L. canus*)
Herring Gull (Lat. *L. argentatus*)
These handsome sea birds are no longer eaten, but there was a time when, in England, *Gulls* were netted and fattened during the winter months in the poultry yard, which may have been sufficient to make them lose their fishiness. They must have been highly valued since they cost the enormous price of 5*s*. each, in 1590, when bought for the Lords of the Star Chamber, at a time when beef cost but 20 *pence* per stone. In England to-day, since the sale of *Plovers'* eggs has been prohibited, *Gulls'* eggs have to a certain extent taken their place in the West End restaurants. The commonest species of Gull in the British Isles is the *Herring Gull*.

'During the seventeenth century young *Black-headed Gulls*, termed *Puets*, were netted and held in high esteem as a delicacy after being fed on bullock's liver or with corn or curds from the dairy, which may have imparted a more pleasant flavour.'—B.B.

HAZEL-HEN

Lat. *Tetrastes bonasia*. A game bird which inhabits chiefly the pine forests and birch woods of mountainous districts in many parts of Europe from the Alps to Russia and eastwards to Siberia and even Japan. It feeds mostly on berries and its flesh is white, tender and of fine flavour. It has never been appreciated to any great extent in England, although large quantities used to be sent to the London Market from Scandinavia and

Russia, but either frozen or chilled. Where the *Hazel-hen* is shot, it is best plainly roasted or prepared in any way suitable for grouse. It is very good when cooked with fresh cream, in the Russian way. Older birds and cold storage birds are best potted or in soups.

The French name of the *Hazel-hen* is *Gélinotte*.

Holodniy Teterka

(Cold potted grey hens or hazel-hens)
Ingredients: Three or four grey hens or hazel-hens, ½ lb. of fat bacon, two or three bay-leaves, six cloves, one small onion, one tea-spoonful of cinnamon, 1½ pints of light claret, salt and peppercorns.

Method: Cut the birds into neat joints and slice the breasts. Put a few slices of the fat bacon in a deep earthenware pot, over this put slices and pieces of the bird, with the spices, salt and peppercorns, cover with more bacon and continue putting in alternate layers till the pot is filled. Pour in the claret, cover with a cloth or with a lid of pastry, and cook in a very slow oven for five or six hours. This should be served cold. —C.M. (5).

Consommé Nesselrode

Boil a hazel-hen as you would a boiling hen to make chicken broth. Serve it with a garnish of rounds of *Royale* made of mashed chestnuts and game; also a *Julienne* of the hazel-hen white meat.

HEATH-COCK. GOR-COCK

Old English names for *Black Game* (q.v.).

'Heath-cocks are of much and laudable nourishment, and also of easy concoction.' (Venner's *Via recta ad vitam longam*, London, 1628, p. 61.).

HERON

Lat. *Ardea cinerea*. A long-legged and voracious bird which is never far from rivers and lakes in many parts of Europe; it destroys a considerable number of fish, frogs, water-fowl and even water-rats. The *Heron* is edible but it is practically never eaten now, although there are still a number of 'heronries', as the colonies of herons' nests are called, in different parts of the British Isles. There was a time when hunting herons with trained falcons was a fashionable sport and when herons were killed for food: they were served to the Lords of the Star Chamber in 1519, 1520, 1535, 1590 and 1605, their cost varying from 3*s*. 4*d*. to 5*s*. each. As late as 1807, their price on the London Market varied from 3*s*. to 4*s*. each. Elyot, Cogan and all who wrote about diet in England during the sixteenth century advise the drinking of plenty of good, strong, old wine with *Herons*,

Bitterns, Shovelers and all such 'weather-sore' birds.

Heron Pudding

'Before cooking it must be ascertained that no bone of the heron is broken. These bones are filled with a fishy fluid, which, if allowed to come in contact with the flesh, makes the whole bird taste of fish. This fluid, however, should be always extracted from the bones, and kept in the medicine cupboard for it is excellent for applying to all sorts of cuts and cracks. The heron is first picked and flayed. Then slices are cut from the breast and legs to make the pudding. The crust is made exactly like that of a meat pudding, and the slices of heron put in and seasoned exactly as meat would be. The pudding is boiled for several hours according to its size. (I have been told that, as a matter of fact, it tastes very much like a nice meat pudding).'—M.B. (1).

IBIS, HADADA

Lat. *Hagedashia hagedash.* One of the most widely distributed African *Ibises*; it is found throughout the whole of the Ethiopian region; from Senegal and Somaliland in the north down to the Cape of Good Hope.

'The Hadada is not really a game bird in the strict sense of the word, but it is most excellent eating and is always a welcome addition to the bag.'—B.HO.

JAY

Lat. *Garrulus glandarius.* A destructive, screeching but rather beautiful bird which is common in most European countries, including the British Isles. It is capable of doing great damage in the kitchen garden and has a passion for green peas. It must be shot in self-defence and it may be eaten, in austerity times: cats will not eat *Jays.* Its French name is *Geai.*

Here are two recipes, the one for dealing with old jays and the other for young birds.

Jay Pie

Cut off the jays' heads as soon as killed; slit with a sharp knife down the breast and skin each bird; do not pluck it. Cut off the whole of the meat on either side of the breast-bone; wash well and leave it all night in a *marinade* of olive oil, lemon juice, whole peppers and half a bayleaf. The next morning, take the jays' breasts from the *marinade* and half cook them in hot butter, in an open pan, for about half an hour. Then arrange them in a pie-dish in layers with some skirt of beef, cold boiled bacon, thick slices of potatoes and thin slices of onions. Moisten with half stock and half white wine. Season with pepper and salt. Cover the pie-dish with greased paper and cook in a moderate oven for a couple of hours. Let the pie get cold, then cover with

puff-paste and cook in a quick oven until paste is beginning to brown.

Suprêmes de Geai

Cut off the heads of six young jays, skin them and lift the breasts. Put them in an earthenware pan with a dozen button onions, a handful of freshly picked and washed sorrel, 6 oz. butter, a cupful of good meat stock and a wineglassful of white wine. Season with pepper and salt. Simmer very gently for an hour. Lift the breasts out of the pan and finish cooking them in cream. Serve with mushrooms tossed in butter and creamed.—F.

JUNGLE-FOWL

Lat. *Gallus gallus.* The parent of all domesticated fowls, but a poor bird to eat and a difficult one to find in the dense jungle of the Indian Peninsula, Indo-China and Malaya, where it hides.

'Except for its feathers or as a specimen, the Grey Jungle Cock is hardly worth shooting; the breast alone is really eatable, and even at the best the breast is very dry and hard.'—E.C.S.B. (2).

KALEEGE. KALIJ. SILVER PHEASANT

Lat. *Gennaeus melanonotus.* This is one of seven distinct varieties of eastern *Silver Pheasants* – not to mention intermediate racial forms – occurring in the lower and middle wooded ranges of the Himalayas; also in Burma, South China and Formosa.

'Gammie considers the flesh (of the *Black-backed Kalij*) poor eating, but most sportsmen in India are pleased enough to get it for the table, especially in out of the way spots where variety in food is not easily obtainable. Old cocks are, of course, tough, but young birds in the autumn are excellent eating. Like all Indian pheasants, they should be eaten as soon as possible after being killed, unless the weather is cold enough to allow of their being kept some days.'—E.C.S.B. (1).

'They are (*Black-breasted Kalij Pheasants*) very omnivorous in their diet and will eat practically anything from bamboo seeds to small snakes and lizards. Their favourite articles of food are the same as those of all other game birds with whose habits I am intimately acquainted, i.e. white ants, fruit of the various fici and bamboo seeds. To these must be added in the case of the Kalij, forest yams and the roots of small ginger-like plants very common over a great portion of their habitat. Birds which have been feeding on this extremely acrid, pungent root are almost uneatable, otherwise they are normally very good eating, though, naturally, old birds are tough unless cooked whilst still warm or hung for several days. Probably the best way of eating these birds is in the old gipsy manner, rolling them up in a mass of clay, feathers and all, chucking them into a heap of red-hot ashes until the clay may be broken, when the feathers come away with it and the dish is ready.'— E.C.S.B. (1).

KIWI

Lat. *Apteryx australis*. One of the strangest of all queer birds, brown or grey in colour, with a skin like a hide, curious primitive feathers and a long bill; with rudimentary wings only, but very fleet of foot. It is confined to New Zealand and it is becoming rarer every year. It is a burrower and a nocturnal feeder.

'We partook of the flesh of one of the Kiwis which the natives had boiled. It had the dark appearance of, and tasted very much like beef ... The Maoris, too, have a penchant for roast Kiwi, and travelling parties, when passing through the districts which these birds frequent, as soon as they have fixed up their camp for the night, start off with their dogs to hunt for them.' —W.L.B.

KNORHAAN

The general name for the *Bustards* (q.v.) of South Africa, of which there is a number of different species ranking among the largest and best African wild birds.

'Knorhaan are sometimes very good eating, but as a rule are rather tough and strong in flavour. They require to be well hung and very carefully cooked. The meat is dark and apt to be dry, but it makes a good addition to game-stew. They should always be skinned before cooking.'—B.HO.

During the 1904 season there were 3,565 knorhaan sold on Kimberley Market and only 818 guinea-fowls.

KNOT. KNOTT

Lat. *Calidris canutus*. A European *Sandpiper* (q.v.), breeding in arctic regions and migrating south, frequenting the shores of the British Isles in very large companies at certain times of the year. It is rather larger than the *Snipe*, having a shorter bill and shorter legs. They were taken in large numbers on the coasts of Lincolnshire in nets such as were used for catching *Ruffs*, and, when fattened, they were preferred to *Ruffs* by some people. They were provided for the Lords of the Star Chamber in 1605. They are also called *Robin Sandpiper* and *Robin-Snipe*. They may be served in any way suitable for *Snipe* (q.v.). Their loss of popularity is evidenced by the slump in their market value: in 1807 they fetched from 3*s*. to 4*s*. each, in London;

in 1922 they cost 3*d*. and in 1941 'from 2*d*. to 3*d*. each.

LAPWING. PEEWIT. GREEN PLOVER
(See also *Plover*)

Lat. *Vanellus vanellus*. Also called *Lappinch*, in Cheshire, and *Vanneau huppé* or *Dix-huit*, in France. It is the 'common' *Plover* in England, where it is a resident, its numbers being augmented by a great influx from the Continent in the autumn. It used to be shot and netted in large quantities and supplies were also imported from Holland. It is protected in most English counties. Its eggs, which may no longer be offered for sale in England, are excellent, whilst the bird itself is not generally considered as good as the *Golden Plover* (q.v.); yet its price on the London Market, rose from 9*d*. and 1*s*. in 1807, to 1*s*. 4*d*. and 1*s*. 6*d*. in 1922, and from 2*s*. 6*d*. to 2*s*. 9*d*. in one of the large London stores, in 1942.

'The Lapwing, by some called the Greene Plover, is by some likewise in high esteeme, and yet it is inferiour to the plover.' (Hart's *Diet of the diseased*, London, 1633, p. 81).

It is probable that the 'plover' which Dr Hart had then in mind was the *Golden Plover* (q.v.), the best of the Plover family from the gastronome's point of view. In French, whenever the name of *Pluvier* is used without any qualification, it means the *Golden Plover*, whilst the *Lapwing* is always referred to as *Vanneau*, a bird which appears to have enjoyed a greater measure of gastronomic reputation in the past than it does now. Thus according to an old French proverb:

'Qui n'a mangé grive ni vanneau
N'a jamais mangé bon morceau.'

And a Provençal proverb places the *Lapwing* on par with the *Woodcock* and the *Golden Plover*:

Se vuos mangea de buoi mousseu
Mangea bécassin, pluvié e vaneu.

There are two related forms of *Lapwing* in the East and Far East: the *Red-wattled Lapwing* (*Lobivanellus indicus*) and the *Grey-headed Lapwing* (*Microsarcops cinereus*).

LARK

Lat. *Alauda arvensis*. Larks, by which *Skylarks* are usually meant in England, are widely distributed in Europe and Asia. In France, the commonest species is the *Crested Lark* (*Galerida cristata*), known as *Alouette*, in the spring, when they are not killed for food, and *Mauviette*, after harvest and vintage, when they are fat and fit for the spit. Formerly *Skylarks* were caught in England on migration by bird-catchers, in nets and snares, and from 20,000 to 30,000 were often sent yearly to the London Market. (Yarrell.)

Larks are still occasionally eaten, in England, in the traditional steak, oyster, kidney and lark pie, but there was a time when considerable numbers of these little birds were also eaten roast. *Larks* were sent to the London Market, chiefly from Dunstable, during over 200 years; also, but not quite to the same extent, from Cambridgeshire. Yarrell states that 1,255,500 *Larks* were taken during the winter of 1867–68.

Larks were provided for the Lords of the Star Chamber on many occasions: they cost but 6*d*. per dozen in 1519 and 1520, rising to 8*d*., in 1534, 1*s*. in 1605 and 3*s*. 4*d*. in 1635. Their price, on the London Market, was 4*s*. per dozen in 1807; 3*s*. in 1922, and 4*s*. in 1941.

'What! Is the jay more precious than the lark
Because his feathers are more beautiful?'
> (*Taming of the Shrew*, Act IV. sc. 3)

'Let his grace go forward
And dare us with his cap like larks.'
> (*Henry VIII*, Act III, sc. 2).

This is an allusion to the method of catching *Larks* in Shakespeare's days, after attracting them and dazing them with small mirrors and a red cloth: in this case the 'cap' referred to is Cardinal Wolsey's red hat.

'Larks are of a delicate taste in eating, light of digestion, and of good nourishment.' (Venner's *Via recta ad vitam longam*, London, 1628, p. 61).

'Larks are not fit for the spit that do not weigh over 13 oz. to the doz.' (*Dr Lister, Queen Anne's physician*, 1703.)

Caisses of Larks

Bone the larks, and stuff them with fine farce. Have ready small paper cases dipped into warm oil. Give the larks a round shape, put into the cases some of the farce, and place over this the larks. Next, put them on a false bottom with some buttered paper over them, for fear they should dry while baking. When baked enough, dish them. If there is room enough, pour into the cases a little Sauce Espagnole and lemon juice. You must be very careful to drain out all the fat. —G.A.S.

Roast Larks

There is a difference between the French and the English way – but both agree in taking out only the gizzard. The French put the larks on a little larkspit, which, running from side to side, pins on them at the same time bards of bacon. The larks are then roasted briskly for eight to ten minutes, and served upon toast. The English season the larks with chopped parsley, pepper, salt and nutmeg, rub them with yolk of egg, roll them in breadcrumbs, sprinkle them with oiled butter, roll them in crumbs again, run them on a larkspit, roast them for 15 minutes

before a bright fire, basting them with butter, and serve them with plenty of fried breadcrumbs.—K.B.

Larks 'Crapaudine'

Pluck and singe the birds; cut off their feet, remove gizzards and bone with great care. Brush them over with melted butter, wrap up in thin rasher of fat bacon and roast in front of a fire or bake in a hot oven for 10 minutes. Then flatten the birds 'à la Crapaudine' and place them upon hot 'cases' of fried bread, i.e. *Croustades*, filled with a *purée* of mushrooms or any rich *Quenelle* mixture of your choice.—P.W.

MEGAPODE

Lat. *Megapodius nicobariensis*; *M. affinis*; *M. freycineti*. The name of a number of Australian and South Pacific birds, dull of plumage, and chiefly remarkable for their curious nesting habits. The eggs are laid in sand or in a mound of earth and covered with some decaying vegetable matter; the parents take no further interest in their young, which are hatched as if in an incubator by the heat of the cover; they leave the shell fully feathered, able to fly and look after themselves.

Davison, in Vol II of *Stray Feathers*, quoted by E.C. Stuart Baker, wrote of the *Nicobar Megapode*: 'As game they are unsurpassed. The flesh very white, very sweet and juicy, loaded with fat, is delicious, a sort of *juste milieu* between that of a fat Norfolk Turkey and a fat Norfolk Pheasant. The eggs, too, are quite equal if not superior to that of the Peafowl, and to my mind higher commendation cannot be given.'—E.C.S.B. (1).

Baker also quotes a letter which he received from a friend in the Andamans: 'To me they appear like large and very fat barndoor fowls, with abnormally small heads compared to their heavy, fat bodies, but even these latter were small in comparison of their powerful legs and huge feet.'—E.C.S.B. (1).

MOOR-COCK. MOOR-FOWL. MOOR-GAME. MUIR-FOWL

Lat. *Lagopus scoticus*. Local names which refer to the *Grouse*, in Scotland, but are also given to *Black Game*, in England.

Moor-fowl Pie

If the birds are small, keep them whole; if large, divide or quarter them. Season them highly, and put plenty into the dish above and below them; or put a beef-steak into the bottom of the dish. Cover the dish with good puff-paste and take care not to bake the pie too much. A hot sauce made of melted butter, the juice of a lemon, and a glass of claret, and poured into the pie when to be served hot, is an improvement and does not overpower the native flavour of the game.—C.I.

MOORHEN. MOAT-HEN. WATER-HEN. GALLINULE

Lat. *Gallinula chloropus*. The names of a small water bird very common in this country. It is about the size of a bantam hen, dark olive-brown above, iron-grey below, with white tail coverts, which are conspicuous as it swims, and a scarlet frontlet in both sexes. It lays from 7 to 11 eggs, dull buff in colour, with reddish spots. In country districts *Moorhens* haunt ponds, lakes and streams in safety as they are too poor fare to tempt poachers. Their price on the London Market was 1s. per dozen in 1807; from 4d. to 9d. each in 1922; and from 4d. to 6d. each in 1941. Major Hugh Pollard, no mean authority, has stated that 'waterhen skinned and then fried in hot fat makes an excellent salmi or braise'.

The *Moorhen* never appears to stop eating: it is a great devourer but a poor converter. Where it is plentiful the Mallard and other wild ducks do not come on account of the food shortage. To grow or scatter food to tempt wild duck is a waste of time, money and labour, unless *Moorhens* have been first of all destroyed or scared away.

MUTTON-BIRD. SOOTY SHEARWATER

Lat. *Puffinus griseus*. The name for a *Petrel* of the South Seas, which resorts to the islands south of New Zealand to breed. In New Zealand, it is so abundant that some 250,000 are said to be killed each year for food. In the Bass Strait there is another species (*P. tenuirostris*) which is also taken for food, but not in such quantities.

'Young Mutton-birds are taken at night-time, being enticed out of their burrows by lighted torches made of the bark of the mountain totatra ... They are usually killed by a blow of a stick on the head. The down and feathers are then removed by plucking and dipping into boiling water, and the birds hung for a night. Next day, the wings, legs and heads are cut off, and the birds split open, cleaned, and dry salt rubbed in. In this condition they are packed in casks for another day. Finally they are transferred to bags made from split thallus segments of the bull-kelp, which are packed in flax baskets protected with totara bark. Preserved in this manner, the birds will keep for a year or more ... At the present time over 300 persons are employed in the Mutton-bird industry from which they derive a substantial income.'—W.R.B.O.

The following announcement, which appeared in one of the London evening papers, prior to 1930, would lead one to believe that *Mutton-birds* were introduced to Londoners in recent years, but if the experiment was made it cannot have met with any large measure of success, since no further reference to the Mutton-bird appears in the London newspapers.

'TASMANIAN MUTTON BIRDS

'London is shortly to be introduced to an Australian delicacy. It is the Tasmanian mutton-bird (a species of Shearwater).

'Only the young birds, which are assiduously fattened by their parents, are caught to provide a table delicacy. They are taken before they are ready to leave the nest. A normal bird's weight is 2 lb. Its dressed weight ranges from ¾ lb. to 1 lb.; having been killed and plucked, they are split open, like kippered herrings and salted down in casks.

'The art of cooking mutton-birds consists in eliminating or neutralising the oil which still clings to them. Grilling and apple sauce are useful to this end. The flavour has something of duck, something of herring.'

ORTOLAN

Lat. *Emberiza hortulana*. The French name, which is used in English also, of a European Bunting about 6 in. long, enjoying a high degree of reputation among gastronomes. There was a time when they were plentiful but they have now become quite rare; they used to be netted, fattened and prepared for the table in any way suitable for *Quail* (q.v.). They migrate southwards in the autumn and return to breed in most countries of Continental Europe and Western Asia towards the end of April. They feed on insects and seeds, when free, but, unlike most other wild birds, they do not sulk when in captivity and very quickly get fat on oats and millet.

Roast Ortolans

Have ready some Ortolans, toast, bacon, bay-leaves or vine-leaves, butter for basting, brown gravy, fried breadcrumbs and water-cress.

Remove the head, neck and crop, but let the trail remain. Truss for roasting, brush over with warm butter, cover the breast of each bird with a vine-leaf or bay-leaf, and tie over them thin slices of bacon. Attach them to a long, thin skewer, running it through the body of each bird, and roast them in front of a quick fire for about 10 minutes. Baste the birds almost continuously with hot butter, and put the toast under them to catch the drippings from the trail. When cooked, remove the skewers and strings, but, if liked, the bacon may remain and be brushed over with warm glaze. Serve the birds on the toast, garnish with watercress, and send the gravy and breadcrumbs to table separately. Allow one bird to each person.—B. (1).

Consommé Rothschild

This is a meat broth which is flavoured with game *fumet* and garnished with rounds of *Royale* made of game *purée* and chestnut *purée* in equal parts; also some fillets of ortolans cut up *Julienne*-wise and some thinly sliced truffles.

OSTRICH

Lat. *Struthio camelus*. This, the largest of living birds, has a small and foolish head, but it lays an egg equal to about two dozen hen's eggs, and since the introduction and perfecting of the dehydrating methods, ostrich eggs have become a valuable source of supply of 'powdered eggs'.

Ostriches are African birds and their contribution to the gastronomic requirements of the people of other continents is restricted to their dehydrated eggs. In South Africa, however, the flesh of the *Ostrich* is eaten, dried in the sun, in the form of biltong.

'Biltong can be made from the flesh of birds as readily as it is prepared from the fles of animals. A considerable amount of ostrich biltong is sold in South Africa. This is probably biltong at its worst, for the flesh is black and wizened, and the taste unpleasantly oily.'—W.L.SPEIGHT in *Wine and Food*, No. 6, p. 34.

OWL PARROT. KAKAPO

Lat. *Strigops habroptilus*. A singular *Parrot*, peculiar to New Zealand, practically flightless and living in holes and burrows. 'It was a favourite article of food among the prospectors of the West Coast of the South Island. ... The Maoris used to snare them at night with the aid of lighted torches and dogs.'—W.R.B.O.

PARTRIDGE

Common or Grey Partridge (Lat. *Perdrix perdrix*)
Bearded Partridge (Lat. *P. barbata*)
Hodgson's or Tibetan Partridge (Lat. *P. hodgsoniae*)
Red-legged Partridge (Lat. *Alectoris rufa*)
Greek, Rock or Chukar Partridge (Lat. *A. graeca*)
Barbary Partridge (Lat. *A. barbara*)
The *Common Partridge*, sometimes called *Grey Partridge*, and known in France as *Perdrix grise*, occurs throughout Europe eastwards to Persia and the Altai Mountains. The live *Partridges* which used to be imported from Hungary, for a change of blood, are identical with the *Common Partridges* of England.

There are two other species of the genus *Perdrix*, the *Bearded Partridge*, which occurs in Northern China, from Mongolia to the Amur, and has been occasionally sent to England in cold storage; and the *Tibetan* or *Hodgson's Partridge*, which occurs from Kashmir to Western China.

In England, a *Partridge*, not otherwise qualified, means a *Common* or *Grey Partridge*, which, in Scotland, is also called *Paitrich*. Some rufous or chestnut-coloured *Partridges* are occasionally shot in England, chiefly in Northumberland, which have been described as a cross between the *Grouse* and the *Partridge*. They are nothing of the sort, but true members of the *Perdrix* family which happen to have exceptionally strongly marked plumage, which they lose after the moult. The *Grey Partridge* is the finest partridge of all from the gastronome's point of view, but there are others, such as:

The *Red-legged* or *French Partridge*, often referred to as a 'Frenchman', which is fairly common in most parts of Continental Western Europe, the Canary Islands and Northern Africa. It is not uncommon in England; it was introduced from France as far back as 1660, by Charles II, at the time of the Restoration, but not with any measure of success until 1770. In France it is called *Perdrix rouge* or *Bartravelle*, and in culinary French it is called *Perdreau*, always in the masculine, whether cock or hen, up to six months old; and *Perdrix*, always in the feminine, be it cock or hen, when over six months old.

'*A la St Rémi, les perdreaux sont perdrix.*'
(*The feast of St Rémi is on* 1st October.)

The *Greek* or *Rock Partridge* is a true Alpine bird ranging from North Italy and Switzerland eastwards to China. The *Chukar Partridge* is a racial form of the *Greek Partridge*, which varies a good deal as regards size and plumage: this is not surprising, since the species occurs on the shores of the Eastern Mediterranean, at sea level, and in the Himalayas, up to some 16,000 feet altitude.

The *Barbary Partridge*, which is very similar to the *Rock* or *Greek Partridge*, is fairly plentiful in North Africa.

In the Americas there are no indigenous *Partridges*, that is no species belonging to either the *Perdrix* or *Alectoris* genera, but the name is used for other birds. Thus the *Perdriz grande* of Argentina is a *Tinamou* (q.v.), and the *American Partridges* of the U.S.A. are also different birds.

In the British Isles the *Partridge* generally mates in March and its eggs are hatched out in a normal season during the first two weeks of June. Shooting is not allowed before 1st September and the young birds are at their plumpest and best in October. A young

Partridge – un Perdreau – should not hang more than three or four days, in a cool, airy place, after being shot. It possesses such a delicate and exquisite flavour of its own that it should not be 'high', nor should it be served with any strong sauce, such as onion sauce or sauce Madère. It is best served with just a little gravy, plainly roasted, baked or grilled, some straw potatoes and a little cress, if liked, but no brussels sprouts or any other bulky vegetable, least of all members of the cabbage tribe.

Young birds, that is birds of the year, are easily distinguished from their parents: their first flight feather is pointed at the tip instead of rounded until the autumn moult, and it is a sure birth certificate. The colour of the feet is not quite so sure a guide: in the earlier part of the season, the feet of the young *Partridge* are yellowish-brown, but as soon as the cold weather sets in they become pale bluish-grey, like those of the older generation.

Old birds, that is birds over fifteen months old, are an entirely different proposition and they are best stewed, braised and served with a variety of vegetables, not excepting cabbage.

Partridges have been highly prized in England for many centuries past, but it is somewhat disconcerting to our modern notions to find that game was eaten at all times of the year, quite irrespective of mating seasons, as we eat chicken all the year round. Partridges were served to the Lords of the Star Chamber at most of their sittings from 1519 to 1639, the cost of the birds rising from 6*d.*, 7*d.* and 8*d.* each in the earlier accounts to 2*s.*, 3*s.*, and as much as 3*s.* 8*d.* on one occasion, in the seventeenth century.

'The painted partrich lyes in every field
And for thy messe is willing to be killed.'
(BEN JONSON. *The Forrest. II.*)

'Killed' was the right word to use at a time when the poor little birds were set upon by trained hawks. Thus Dr Richard Layton, writing to the Lord Privy Seal, Thomas Cromwell, from Harrow-on-the-Hill, on 25 September 1537: 'I send by the bringer perisse (pears) of Harrow ... and partridges my own hawk kills'. The previous year (27 Hen. VIII) a Proclamation had been made 'to preserve the Partridges, Pheasants and Herons from the King's Palace at Westminster to St. Giles in the Fields, and from thence to Islington, Hampstead, Highgate and Hornsey Park.'—W.E.G.

'If the partridge had the woodcock's thigh
It would be the best bird that ever did fly.'
On the London Market the price of partridges has remained very much the same in recent years. In 1757, a partridge cost 2*s.* 6*d.*

in London; in 1807 the price varied from 4*s.* to 5*s.* per bird; in 1922 it was from 4*s.* 6*d.* to 5*s* 6*d.*; and in 1941 from 3*s.* 6*d.* to 6*s.* 6*d.* – the higher price being paid for young birds and the lower for old ones. In 1942 the Ministry of Food fixed the maximum retail price of partridges at 5*s.* per bird, young or old.

Partridge Biltong

'To provide a meal, at least one hundred birds must be killed and the breasts converted into biltong, which is softer and more tender than is usual with this type of food. The partridges are usually snared beside the water pans after the rainy season. Special nets are used for the purpose. When the necks of the hundreds of small partridges so caught had been wrung, the birds were plucked and cleaned and the flesh removed from the breastplates, when it was salted and dried. Large quantities of this biltong were taken home by the farmers. The Namaqua Partridge, which is smaller than the ordinary partridge, is held to have special dietetic qualities, for biltong made from the ordinary partridge cannot be compared with that produced from the Namaqua Partridge, which has a pale white flesh. Ordinary partridge biltong is black and sinewy and not appetizing.'—W.L. SPEIGHT in *Wine and Food*, No. 6, pp. 34–35.

Boiled Partridge

'Partridge roasted, and even *à la crème*, are superior to it, but if you have a young partridge just hung so and cook it in this way, you will capture a fleeting fragrance unflavoured by butter or cream. Salt the bird lightly inside and out. Wrap it first in vine-leaves and then completely in thin rashers of fat bacon. Boil it for 35 minutes in plain, unsalted water, and then at once plunge it into iced water, where it must remain only just long enough to get cold. Then unwrap, serve with a plain lettuce salad, and tell your friends about it.'—AMBROSE HEATH in *Wine and Food*, No. 3, p. 55.

Braised Partridge with Celery Sauce

Singe, draw, wipe and truss two partridges with their wings inside. Lay a piece of pork-rind in a saucepan, adding one carrot and one onion, both cut in slices, two bayleaves, one sprig of thyme, and the two partridges. Season with one pinch of salt and half a pinch of pepper. When they have assumed a good golden colour on the hot stove, moisten with half a pint of white broth, then put the saucepan in the oven, and let cook for 20 minutes. Dress them on a serving dish, untruss, pour a pint of hot celery sauce over, and serve.—G.A.S.

Chartreuse of Partridge

Take two old partridges; singe, draw and wipe them well; truss them with their wings turned inside, and lay them on a roasting pan, with half a pinch of salt, and a little butter well spread over the breast, and put them on to roast for six minutes. Take a Charlotte mould that will hold three pints; butter lightly and decorate with small pieces of cooked carrot and turnip, cut very evenly with a vegetable-tube. When ready, fill the bottom with a layer of cooked cabbage; cut the partridges into pieces, put a layer of them on the cabbage, covering the hollow spaces with more cabbage; lay on the top six slices of salted pork, add the rest of the partridges, and finish by covering the surface with cabbage, pressing it down carefully. Place the mould on a tin baking-dish, and put it in a moderate oven for 15 minutes, leaving the oven-door open during the whole time. Have a hot dish ready, turn the mould upside down on it, and carefully draw off. Serve with a little half-glaze sauce.— G.A.S.

Perdrix aux Choux

1 fine partridge
1 thick rasher fat bacon
Chipolata sausages
Tiny pinch powdered mace
2 or 3 carrots
Thin slices of fat salt pork
1 medium-sized white cabbage
Salt and pepper
Bouquet-garni
2 cups *bouillon*

This, too, is an excellent way of turning an old bird into a succulent dish. Prepare the bird as for roasting. Shred the cabbage finely. Cover the bird's breast with the thin slices of fat salt pork. Cut the bacon into dice and cook gently to extract all the fat, removing the lean portions when this has been done. Brown the bird on all sides in the bacon fat. Add salt and pepper, also mace and, if wished, another tiny pinch of mixed spices as well as the *bouquet*. Add the *bouillon*, cover the pan and cook the partridge gently until tender. The carrots, sliced, should be added with the other ingredients, or some chefs use them to line the pan, after browning the bird, placing it on the bed of carrots.

When the bird has been simmering for an hour, add the cabbage. As regards the latter, there are two ways of treating it before adding it to the partridge. Some 'blanch' it in salted boiling water which removes the 'strong' flavour, others lightly brown it in more bacon fat, then add to the simmering bird and other ingredients. In any case, the cabbage must cook at length and gently as it absorbs the juices of the partridge. When all is well done, serve the bird on the bed of savoury cabbage and surround with the chipolata, previously fried or baked separately. It is also possible to serve a piece of bacon, which has simmered with the other ingredients, cut into rashers and set around the dish. Should more liquid be required, add more *bouillon*. There must be enough to cook the cabbage in and a little over, which is poured over the partridge when serving. Boiled potatoes should accompany this dish. —P.W.

Perdrix à l'estoufade

Lardons of fat bacon or pork
Salt and pepper
1 or 2 carrots
Slices of fat salt pork (*bardes de lard*)
1 cup good *bouillon*
1 or 2 partridges
2 onions
Bouquet-garni
1 glass white wine

After the ordinary preparatory work, lard the birds with the lardons and rub over with salt and pepper. Slice the onions and carrots. Place the *bardes de lard* on the bottom of a heavy iron pan, cover with the sliced vegetables, add the birds, the wine and the *bouillon* and, keeping the pan very closely covered, cook contents gently until the birds are very tender. Strain the gravy over them when serving. Pease pudding is nice served with this dish.—P.W.

Perdreaux en Papillotes

2 young partridges
Brown mushroom sauce
Butter
Thin slices fat salt pork

Cut each bird in two and brown delicately in butter. When almost done, remove and wrap each half in the slices of fat pork, then in oiled paper. Grill gently for about 20 minutes, turning frequently and taking care the paper does not burn. Remove paper when birds are done and serve them very hot, pouring the sauce over them. The ordinary brown mushroom sauce should be enriched by the addition of the butter in which the partridges first cooked and a little good dry white wine. It should be gently reduced by slow cooking and really ought to be made well in advance of the cooking of the birds in order that it may mellow properly. —P.W.

Partridge Pie
I

Half roast some partridges – three, four or six, according to the size of your mould – joint them and cut them into neat pieces and cook them in a lb. of butter ($\frac{1}{4}$ lb. to each bird), sprinkle with a little salt and cayenne and a blade of mace. Cook till tender and put them into a mould or deep fire-proof dish, pressing the joints down and pouring the butter all over it. To be eaten when cold. (*My great-grandmother, Sarah Gillow*, 1801–66.)

II

> 2 partridges
> $\frac{1}{2}$ lb. of veal
> $\frac{1}{2}$ lb. of bacon
> Parsley
> Salt and pepper
> 2 hard-boiled eggs
> 1$\frac{1}{2}$ oz. butter
> 6 mushrooms
> Puffpaste
> 1 gill stock

Cut the partridges into four pieces each. Melt the butter in a *sauté*-pan, put in the birds, and fry them lightly. Cut the veal and bacon into thin slices, line a pie-dish with these slices, put on them the pieces of partridge, season with salt, pepper, chopped parsley, and mushrooms, then put over another layer of bacon and veal. Cover the pie with the pastry, and bake for about one hour in a hot oven. When done, fill up with stock, and serve either hot or cold. Time required 1$\frac{1}{2}$ hours. Seasonable September 1 to February 1. Sufficient for four persons.—M.A.F.

Roast Partridge

A plump, young partridge, not too fresh but by no means approaching the 'high' state, say four days after it was shot, is best just plainly roasted and with no other sauce but the butter which has been used to baste it and the fat and blood that have oozed from the bird and mixed with the butter during the cooking.

Pluck, draw and truss the partridge in the same way as you would a chicken. Season with pepper and salt. Cover the breast with a thin rasher of fat bacon and roast on a spit in front of a bright fire for 30 minutes, or in a moderate oven for 25 minutes, basting frequently with melted butter. Only straw potatoes and a little undressed cress may be served at the same time.

Salmis of Partridge

Truss the birds as for roasting and cut $\frac{1}{4}$ lb. of thick slices of streaky bacon into inch squares. Put these with an ounce of butter in a saucepan and fry till they begin to turn colour. Now dip in your birds and fry and turn them for 10 minutes; then take them out and allow them to cool. With a sharp knife carve off the wings, legs and breast and skin and trim them. Chop up the carcasses and return them and the trimmings to the stewpan, to which you add a couple of chopped shallots, sweet herbs, pepper, salt, a slice of ham, with as much stock flavoured with giblets as will cover the whole, and simmer for a couple of hours. Take this stew, strain and cool it, removing all fat, add a glass of claret, and place in the cleared stew the breasts, limbs, etc., of partridge, and again warm gradually to simmering point.

In a separate small saucepan melt a piece of butter and add flour to it, then pour in a little of the gravy and the juice of half a lemon. Stir this well and turn the whole into the salmis, which then thickens to the right consistency. Pile the portions of the bird in the centre of the dish and pour the sauce over them. Serve with sippets of dry toast. —M.H.P.

Cold Partridge Spliced

Roast or pot-roast the bird, being careful not to get it too dry if the former method be adopted, cut it up into the usual joints immediately, and put all these while still warm into a deep dish containing a couple of tablespoonfuls of very choice old rum. Cover the dish and let the pieces, which should be turned from time to time, remain in the rum until next day. Then drain them, but not too thoroughly, of whatever little rum the pieces have not absorbed, sprinkle a very few drops of lemon juice on them, and dish them surrounded by a salad of the hearts of lettuces.—T.E.W.

Partridge Soup

Consommé Cussy. A game *Consommé* with *partridge fumet*, garnished with *royale* of chestnut *purée* and partridge *purée*, *quenelles* of partridge, *julienne* of truffles; a small glass of madeira wine is added at the time of serving.

Perdreau au Verjus (old recipe)

> 2 young partridges
> Butter
> Some green grapes
> *Bardes de lard*
> 2 slices bread
> Salt and pepper

This recipe is suitable for very young and tender birds only. The grapes should be of the 'white' variety and unripe. Fasten the slices of fat salt pork (*bardes*) around the birds and place the grapes in their interiors. Heat a sufficiency of butter and *sauté* the young birds in this, colouring delicately on all sides and cooking for about 20 minutes. The slices of bread, from which the crust has been removed, should be half an inch thick. Once the birds are done – and, of course, they were seasoned during their cooking – remove the grapes and squeeze them dry, setting the juice aside carefully after straining. Keep the birds hot, and brown the slices of bread in the butter used for browning the partridges, adding more if necessary. Remove the bread when nicely coloured and add the grape juice to the brown sediment in the pan. Place the birds on their prepared *croûtons* and pour the gravy over them, serving at once.—P.W.

PARTRIDGE, BAMBOO

Lat. *Bambusicola.* Another name for the *Chinese Partridge* and other members of the genus *Bambusicola*, small Asiatic game birds which may be prepared for the table in any way suitable for *Pigeon* (q.v.).

PARTRIDGE, CHUKAR

Lat. *Alectoris graeca.* The name for the *Greek Partridge* found from Cyprus and Asia Minor, through Kashmir and Turkestan, to China. It is common in parts of the Himalayas and has been sent in cold storage to England from China.

PARTRIDGE, SPRUCE. GROUSE

Lat. *Canachites canadensis.* Names given in the U.S.A. to the same game bird, one that used to be common in the woodlands of the North Eastern States, but is now practically extinct.

TREE-PARTRIDGE. HILL-PARTRIDGE

Lat. *Arboricola torqueola.* This is the common *Hill-Partridge*, the most abundant of the many kinds found from the Himalayas to Formosa. They spend most of their time on the ground, running actively to and fro in search of insects and vegetable food, but at the approach of danger, as well as at night, they perch on trees.

PEACOCK

Lat. *Pavo cristatus*; Fr. *Paon.* This bird, a cousin of the Turkey, is never eaten now, but it used to have pride of place upon the tables of the noblest in the land in former times, in spite of the fact that its flesh was surely as tough and tasteless then as it is now. In 1470 the then Archbishop of York set before his guests one hundred peacocks, a wonderful sight if the birds were brought into the banqueting chamber, as they most likely were, in all the splendour of their stiffly displayed tails. It was customary at the time, and long after, for the peacock 'course' to be heralded and brought into the hall in a procession of dishes headed by a stuffed peacock in full feather, its tail sweeping over the bearer's shoulders and its head filled with soaked wool which was set ablaze, a practice which has survived in an altered

form, when the Christmas Pudding is set alight.

'Among the delicacies of this splendid table one sees the peacock, that noble bird, the food of lovers, and the meat of lords. Few dishes were in higher fashion in the thirteenth century, and there was scarce any noble or royal feast without it. They stuffed it with spices and sweet herbs, and covered the head with a cloth, which was constantly wetted to preserve the crown. They roasted it and served it up whole, covered after dressing with the skin and feathers on, the comb entire, and the tail spread. Some persons covered it with leaf gold, instead of its feathers, and put a piece of cotton, dipped in spirits, into its beak, to which they set fire as they put it on the table. The honour of serving it up was reserved for the ladies most distinguished for birth, rank, or beauty, one of whom, followed by the others, and attended by music, brought it up in the gold or silver dish, and set it before the master of the house, or the guest most distinguished for his courtesy and valour; or after a tournament, before the victorious knight, who was to display his skill in carving the favourite fowl, and take an oath of enterprise and valour on its head. The *Romance of Lancelot*, adopting the manner of the age in which it was written, represents King Arthur doing this office to the satisfaction of five hundred guests.' (*Antiquitates Culinariae; or curious tracts relating to the culinary affairs of the Old English, by The Rev. Richard Warner, of Sway, near Lymington, Hants. London. Privately printed. 1791.*)

PEACOCK-PHEASANTS

'Intermediate between the Pheasants and Peafowl is a beautiful group known as the Peacock-Pheasants (*Polyplectron*). The dense jungles and lower hill forests of the Indo-Malayan countries and the islands of Sumatra, Borneo and Palawan are their home.' —G.G.B.

'In some parts of Burma, the Grey Peacock-Pheasant is so common and so easy to trap that the villagers bring them instead of village fowls to the officers who are touring their districts, selling them at cheaper rates than they do the latter. In Siam also this Pheasant appears to be very common ... The flesh of the Bhutan Peacock-Pheasant is rather hard and dry, though white and of quite good flavour.'—E.C.S.B. (1).

PEAFOWL

Lat. *Pavo cristatus.* A magnificent game bird found throughout India, Assam and Ceylon, where it frequents broken and jungly ground affording good cover and plenty of water: where numerous, they can do a considerable amount of damage in a very little time among growing crops. It is the ancestral form of the domesticated *Peacock* (q.v.).

Besides the Common or Indian *Peafowl*, there is but one other species, the *Burmese Peafowl* (*P. muticus*), found in the Indo-Chinese countries, the Malay Peninsula and Java.

In many parts of India *Peacocks* are protected and considered sacred.

Pea Fowls

'These magnificent birds make a noble roast, and when young are very excellent. They are larded, plain roasted, and served with the tail stuck in them, which you have preserved, the head with its feathers being left folded up in paper and tucked under the wing. Roast about 1½ hours, take the paper from the head and neck, dress upon your dish with watercress, and a border of tulips or roses round, and serve the gravy separately in a boat.'—G.A.S.

PEE-WIT
See *Lapwing*.

PENGUIN
Lat. *Spheniscus demersus*. In *The Great White South*, by Herbert G.Ponting, there is a description of the last Christmas Day dinner enjoyed by Captain Scott in the South Pole ice pack, and it included 'an entrée of stewed penguin's breasts and red currant jelly – the dish fit for an epicure and not unlike jugged hare'.

Penguins' eggs are laid in holes in the ground on the little 'Guano Islands' off the rocky coast of South Africa; they are delicious when perfectly fresh, plain hard boiled and cold; they much resemble Plovers' eggs in taste and texture and are equal in bulk to about three of the latter.

PHEASANT (Common Pheasant)
Lat. *Phasianus colchicus*. The *Pheasant* is the most beautiful game bird in the British Isles. It is a native of the East, but it was introduced into Europe at an early date: it has never been domesticated, but it is largely hand-reared and almost hand-fed as well, or was in pre-war times. The cock-bird is much more beautiful than the hen, but the hen is more tender and as a rule fatter. Pheasants which manage to elude the sportsman's gun and the many snares and dangers threatening their existence from the day they are hatched – and even earlier – may live for fifteen years or more, but long before they reach such an honourable old age they cease to be of interest to the gastronome. Young birds are best. It is easy to tell a young cock pheasant by his spurs: they are rounded and

pointless for the first year, short but pointed up to the second year, very sharp and quite long in older birds. A young hen has soft feet and light plumage: an old one has hard and rough feet and a darker plumage. In the British Isles pheasants are in season from October to February and at their best from November to January. The flesh of the pheasant is dry and rather tasteless: that of the breast and wings is white, whilst the legs are dark and are more highly flavoured. To correct the natural dryness of the pheasant, it is supplied with a tightly-fitting waistcoat of bacon fat before cooking, and, if roasted, it must be basted abundantly. To correct its tastelessness, it must 'hang', not too long, of course, but long enough for the first signs of incipient mortification to be detected by sensitive nostrils. It is impossible to say how long a pheasant should 'hang' before it is cooked, as it depends upon the manner in which it was shot, the time that passes between the shooting and hanging, the weather conditions at the time and the place where it is kept. It should be a cool place, with lots of fresh air, and fresh cold air for choice. In warm weather, three days may be the limit of safety, whilst in the winter twelve days may not be excessive, provided the bird has not been badly 'shot' and has not suffered in the packing and transit from the shoot to the hook in the larder. Of all game birds the pheasant is the one that not only can be kept longest but must be kept. A pheasant cooked the day after it is shot, young and plump as it may be, will be tough and insipid: the same bird, a week later, will be tender and succulent.

We know from the Privy Purse Expenses of Henry VIII, that this monarch reared pheasants in large quantities at his palace at Eltham, and there is no lack of evidence of the high esteem in which the pheasant has been held by all gastronomes past and present, in spite of which the cost of pheasants in England has never been excessive. Thus, in the Star Chamber accounts, pheasants served in 1519 and 1520 cost 16*d.*, 18*d.* and 2*s.* each; in 1567, their cost had risen to 6*s.* 8*d.* per brace; in 1590, to 10*s.* per brace; in 1602 it was 8*s.* 4*d.* and, in 1605, 8*s.* 4*d.*, 13*s.* 4*d.* and 16*s.* 4*d.* per brace, on different occasions; in 1635, their cost was 8*s.* 6*d.* and 8*s.* 9*d.* per bird. By 1757, their cost had risen on the London Market to 6*s.*, and in 1807, to 7*s.* and 8*s.* 6*d.* per bird. In 1922 the cost of pheasants in London was 6*s.* 6*d.* for a hen and 8*s.* for the cock, and in 1941, these prices had risen to 12*s.* and 15*s.* 6*d.* In 1942, the Ministry of Food fixed the maximum retail prices for pheasants sold in England at 8*s.* for the hen and 9*s.* for the cock, irrespective of age and condition.

'Fesaunt exceedeth all foules in sweetnesse and wholesomenesse, and is equal to a capon in nourishing. ... It is meate for Princes and great estates, and for poore Schollers when they can get it.' (Cogan's *Haven of Health*, London, 1612. p. 132.)

'Fertile of wood, Ashore, and Sydney's copp's,
To crowne thy open table, doth provide
The purple phesant, with the speckled side.'

(BEN JONSON. *The Forrest.* II.)

Faisan à la Bohémienne

1 young pheasant
1 quail
1 or 2 truffles
Bardes de lard
Salt and pepper
1 small glass dry sherry
Slices of stale bread
Foie gras
1 shallot
Dash cayenne pepper
Butter

Pluck and draw the pheasant and the quail. Remove all the flesh from the quail and chop it with the truffles, setting aside the peelings of the latter for further use. Season with salt and pepper. Use this to stuff the pheasant, and either lard or cover breast of the latter with *bardes* (fat salt pork). Break up the carcass of the quail, brown it in butter, together with its liver and intestines, adding the chopped truffle peelings, the minced shallot, salt, pepper and the sherry. Cook this gently for half an hour, strain off the gravy and add as much cayenne as liked. Meanwhile, roast the pheasant, placing slices of bread on the bottom of the pan to catch the gravy as it falls from the stuffed bird. When ready, serve up on the slices of bread and pour the prepared sauce over the whole. As accompaniments this lordly recipe mentions slices of *foie gras*, cock's combs· and kidneys alternating with one another !

Roast Pheasant on Chestnut purée

After roasting as indicated, serve the bird on a *purée* of chestnuts to which cream and the gravy from the pheasant have been added.

Faisan à la Choucroûte

After braising a pheasant until nicely coloured, add to the pan a sufficiency of good sauerkraut, together with a thick slice of streaky salt pork and a glass of white wine. Cook gently until all is done and serve together, with boiled or steamed potatoes.

Cutlets of Pheasant

1 large pheasant
1 beaten egg
Salt and pepper
Fine brown breadcrumbs
Frying fat
Espagnole or other sauce

Cut up the bird and remove all bones from joints. Season each piece nicely and flatten, trimming into shape and folding the skin under, sewing up if necessary. Dip each piece thus prepared first into the beaten egg then in breadcrumbs. Fry in deep fat or, if preferred, *sauté* gently in hot butter, until well cooked. If frying fat is used, it should not be too hot or the inside of the fillets will be underdone. Serve with fried parsley and Espagnole or any preferred hot rich sauce, handed separately.

Lincolnshire method of cooking Pheasant

Cut up a tender pheasant, peel and shred an onion and a carrot. Melt 4 oz. of dripping in a pan, add a carrot and onion and fry for five minutes, stirring with a wooden spoon. Place the pieces of pheasant in this, with a little salt and pepper, and fry for another five minutes, stirring all the time; add two tablespoonfuls of flour and cook for three more minutes, gradually adding 1½ pints of stock and stir till it boils. Cut four tomatoes in quarters and ½ lb. of peeled mushrooms, one tablespoonful of chopped parsley; add these to contents of pan and simmer for half hour. Set the pheasant in the centre of a hot dish, pour over the sauce and garnish with mushrooms.—E.T.

Norwegian method of cooking Pheasant

Place the pheasant on the fire in a stewpan with 1½ oz. of butter and let it simmer for half hour. Roll a dessertspoonful of flour in 1 oz. of butter and a little salt. Add three tablespoonfuls of cream and shake the mixture well together. Put it in the pan and let it stand for five minutes.

Place the pheasant on a large round of toast spread with butter and the bird's liver (if possible, the liver of another pheasant as well). Strain the sauce through a fine wire sieve and pour over the bird.—E.T.

Pheasant à la Normande

Having hung your pheasant wisely and not too well, pluck, draw and truss her, and fry her in butter, in a *cocotte* till nicely browned. While this is being done, toss in butter separately half a dozen peeled, cored and finely-chopped apples. Put a layer of these apples in the bottom of the *cocotte*, the pheasant on top of them, the rest of the apples round her, and over all two or three tablespoonfuls of cream. Cover, cook in the oven for about half an hour and serve in the *cocotte*.—W.F. (3, p. 56).

Pheasant Pie

Cut up any left-over flesh of either roast or boiled pheasant into fairly small pieces and brown them in butter, with the addition of a little cayenne pepper and salt. Remove this and keep it hot. Chop one shallot and brown that in butter and mix with the pheasant. Add this to a sufficient quantity of spaghetti, according to the size of the pie-dish you are using. Mix well together, put into a pie-dish, covering with a flaky paste, and bake in a quick oven till the pastry is nicely browned. —E.T.

Pheasant and Sauerkraut Pie

Line a pie-dish with pastry and spread a layer of sauerkraut over the bottom. If the sauerkraut is tinned, it should first be cooked till nearly dry in a glassful of rather acid wine. If fresh, it should be stewed for 2 or 3 hours in gravy and a glass of wine. Then place pieces of pheasant on it. Sprinkle with the little sauce you can get out of the sauerkraut. Spread another layer of sauerkraut over this and dot pieces of butter here and there. Then cover with pastry and bake for an hour.—C.T.

Faisan poché au céleri

Prepare the following stock: put in a saucepan two onions and two carrots finely chopped, a *bouquet* of thyme, bayleaf and parsley, one or two cloves, half a head of celery cut in pieces, $\frac{1}{2}$ lb. of beef and veal and two pints of *consommé*. Season well, bring to the boil and let it simmer about one hour.

Meanwhile, prepare a pheasant as for roasting, put it in the stock when the stock is ready and cook it 35 minutes or a little more. Remove it, drain it and keep it hot. In another saucepan, melt about 1 oz. of butter and stir in the same quantity of flour. Cook it one minute without letting it get brown, and add, a little by little, some of the stock till the sauce reaches the consistency of a thin *Béchamel*.

Remove it to the corner of the fire and put in two tablespoonfuls of cream. Put in the pheasant, after having removed the skin, and cook a few minutes more. Put the pheasant in the serving dish. Garnish it with pieces of braised celery; add to the sauce, off the fire, a few small pieces of butter. Shake well till they have melted and bound the sauce, which you pour over the bird.—X.M.B. (1).

Roast Pheasant

Draw and truss a young hen pheasant as you would a chicken; season with pepper and salt in and out. Dredge the breast with flour and brown it in sizzling butter. Then tie some thin slices of fat bacon over the breast, push a piece of raw beefsteak inside the bird (it helps but it is not indispensable); roast upon a spit in front of a bright fire or in a quick oven for 35 or 45 minutes according to size of the bird: baste frequently with melted butter, and serve with mashed chestnuts or braised celery.

If you have put a piece of beefsteak inside the bird before roasting it, the meat must be taken out before the bird is sent to the table: it should be saved and minced to stuff tomatoes, egg-plants or vegetable marrows.

Roast Pheasant with Mushrooms

1 pheasant
2 oz. of butter
Some fat bacon for larding
1 dozen mushrooms
Salt and cayenne

Prepare the pheasant in the usual way, then lard it along each side of the breast with small lardons of bacon. Wash and skin the mushrooms; if large, cut them into halves or quarters. Stuff the pheasant with them; also add 1 oz. of butter, half teaspoonful of salt, a few grains of cayenne. Truss it neatly, and cover the whole breast with a thickly-buttered piece of paper. Let it roast for half an hour, basting several times. Remove the paper and roast 10 minutes longer. Serve with gravy and bread sauce.—S.C.

Salmi de Faisan

2 young pheasants
1 or 2 truffles
1 carrot
1 sprig dried thyme
Salt and pepper
1 tablespoon flour
Bardes de lard
2 or 3 shallots
1 bayleaf
1 cup red wine
2 cups good *bouillon*
Croûtons farcis

Prepare the birds as for roasting, wrapping each neatly in the *bardes* which are thin slices of fat bacon or salt pork. Roast in the usual way. When done, cut into five pieces: two legs, two wings and breast portion whole (if very large birds, cut this latter in two). Place these pieces of pheasant, with their gravy, in a small *cocotte* (or casserole) with the sliced truffles. Keep warm without further cooking. In another saucepan place the minced shallots, the thinly-sliced carrot, the thyme, bayleaf, salt, freshly-ground pepper, the carcasses of the birds and the wine and *bouillon*. Cook this gently until contents of pan are greatly reduced in volume, then add the flour, mixed with a small quantity of cold *bouillon* or water, and continue the gentle simmering for 10 minutes or so. Dish up the pheasant, surround with the *croûtons farcis* (see following recipe) and strain the sauce over the whole. This sauce should be smooth and 'short'.

Croûtons farcis

1 in. thick slices of stale bread
Forcemeat or sausage-meat
Frying fat or butter

Cut the bread into cubes and either fry in deep boiling fat until lightly coloured or *sauté* in butter but take care they do not become too crisp. Using the point of a sharp knife, scoop out the centres but do not cut through to the lower crust. Fill the hollow with forcemeat, fried sausage-meat or – *foie gras* ! Place for a minute or so in a hot oven before using as garnish to pheasants.—P.W.

Pheasant Soup
I

This can be made from your oldest and toughest bird.

Set the pheasant in a pan with enough water to cover it, a little salt, onion, and a head of celery. Simmer slowly for about 2½ to 3 hours, remove the bird and strain the stock. Allow to cool, carefully skimming all fat. This should now be beautiful clear stock, into which you put three leeks and a little white flesh of the pheasant, both cut in very thin slices. Boil together for about half hour quite slowly till the leeks are soft, and throw in a little finely-chopped parsley before serving.—E.T.

II

If a friend (?) sends you an old cock pheasant, make it into a good Potage St. Hubert and send your friend the recipe. First of all lift the meat from the breast and wings and put it aside. Then break up the bird's carcass, legs and wings and put them all in a pot with some good veal or beef bones and a variety of vegetables – onions, leeks, carrots and celery; also a *bouquet-garni* and let the lot simmer for four or five hours. Put the meat through a mincer, then pound it and rub it through a coarse sieve; mix it with breadcrumbs, moistening with some of the stock and the yolk of an egg to a paste; shape into small balls. Take out of the stock the *bouquet-garni*, and the bones and the vegetables: strain it and then add the balls of pheasant meat to it; bring again to the boil and serve with some fresh cream added at the last moment.

Pheasant en Daubière

Truss and lard a pheasant, and brown it with butter in a fire-proof dish. Pour over it from time to time as many as eight tablespoonfuls of port. Surround with freshly-peeled truffles, 12 small onions fried in butter, and 24 Chipolata sausages. Pour some veal stock over the bird, rich but not thick, and let it thoroughly soak in the liquor. Untie it and serve in the same dish.—H.G.

Stewed Pheasant with onions

Cut a young pheasant in pieces, cook in a small quantity of water with a dozen tiny young onions. Remove the pheasant to serving dish as soon as it is tender, and when the onions are soft drain from stock and reduce to about one cupful. Make the sauce of two tablespoonfuls of butter and the same of flour, add the stock and half a cup of cream, then add the yolks of two eggs, salt, pepper and lemon juice to taste. Pour the sauce over the pheasant and onions and serve very hot. —E.T.

Pheasant à la Guid Wife

Truss a pheasant as for boiling. Put it in a stewpan with a sliced Spanish onion and 1 oz. of butter, and fry together over a moderate fire. When the pheasant is brown all over, add two tablespoons of chutney and half a pint of stock, pepper and salt; cook for one hour.—C.N.

PHEASANT, ARGUS

Lat. *Argusianus argus*. A large and very handsome game bird, ranging from Tenasserim, in Burma, through the Malay Peninsula to Sumatra. It is quite distinct from the ordinary pheasant and, from the food point of view, it is little better than the *Jungle Fowl* (q.v.).

PHEASANT, BLOOD

Lat. *Ithaginis cruentus*. A small, grey, game bird with a black head and patches of blood-red on the breast. It is found in the mountains of Western China, Tibet and NE. India. There are other varieties, but they all feed on the tender shoots of pine and juniper, on the berries of the latter, on leaves, seeds and small fruits, so that the young birds should be very good to eat, but it is a case of 'first catch your hare'.—H.E.D.

(American ornithologists have renamed this bird *Blood Partridge*.)

PHEASANT, CHEER

Lat. *Catreus wallichii*. A crested form of Himalayan Pheasant, found from Southern Kashmir to Nepal.'It is said to be excellent for the table and one of my correspondents adds: "It is the only game bird I have shot in India which in any way reminds me of the English Pheasant, and the flesh, especially if kept for a short time during the cold weather, is much more like that of the true *Phasianus* than that of the Jungle Fowl or Kalij".'—E.S.C.B. (2).

PHEASANT, COPPER

Lat. *Syrmaticus soemmerringii*. A Japanese species of the Barred-backed Pheasants; also called *Ijima*, *Soemmering's* or *Scintillating Copper Pheasant*.

PHEASANT, ELLIOT'S

Lat. *Syrmaticus ellioti*. One of the *Barred-backed Pheasants* confined to the mountains of SE. China.

PHEASANT, FIREBACK or FIRE-BACKED

A name given to two groups of Asiatic game birds, one of them 'crested' and the other 'crestless', natives of the Indo-Malayan countries, Sumatra and Borneo. 'The Fireback appears to be a bird of the low-country, evergreen forest, not being found in the higher hills anywhere within its habitat. Over most of its range it is a comparatively common bird, many being trapped and kept in confinement by the natives. Easy to tame and easy to feed, it thrives even when kept in a comparatively small enclosure, though it has not yet been induced to breed. ... As might be expected, they are said to be good eating, though one of my correspondents refers to them as "very dry".'—E.C.S.B. (2).

Bornean Crested Fireback Pheasant (Lophura ignita).
Malayan Crested Fireback Pheasant (L. rufa).
Siamese or Diard's Crested Fireback Pheasant (Diardigallus diardi).
Bornean Crestless Fireback Pheasant (Houppifer pyronotus).
Malayan Crestless Fireback Pheasant (H. erythrophthalmus).

PHEASANT, (Mrs.) HUME'S

Lat. *Syrmaticus humiae*. One of the *Barred-backed Pheasants* found in Maniour, NE. Borneo and Yunnan.

PHEASANT, KOKLASS

Lat. *Pucrasia macrolopha*. This is the commonest of the various species of Koklass Pheasants occurring in the Himalayas, Tibet and China. 'It is common in the Western Himalaya, from Kumaon to Chamba, and generally found singly or in pairs. Its flesh is said to be superior to that of every other hill pheasant.'

PHEASANT, MIKADO

Lat. *Syrmaticus mikado*. One of the *Barred-backed Pheasants*: it is confined to the Island of Formosa.

PHEASANT, MOONAL

Lat. *Lophophorus impejanus*. This is the best-known as well as one of the handsomest of the *Moonals*, which are found from the Himalayas to Western China: the magnificent plumage of the males has been responsible for reducing the numbers of these birds.

PHEASANT, REEVE'S

Lat. *Syrmaticus reevesii*. One of the *Barred-backed Pheasants* found in North and Central China.

PIGEON

Lat. *Columba livia*; Fr. *Pigeon*; Germ. *Taub*; It. *Colombo*; Sp. *Columbis*. The *Columba livia*, or Rock Pigeon, is regarded as the original stock of the many different species of domesticated pigeons bred for food, ornament, sport or as messengers, such as pouters, carriers, homers, fantails, jacobins, nuns, turbits, tumblers, trumpeters, etc. The wild varieties of pigeons are mostly known under the name of *Dove*. The young pigeon, usually four weeks old, is known as a *Squab*.

Pigeons are mentioned in practically every one of the Star Chamber Accounts, a difference being made between 'house' pigeons, the tame birds, and the wild ones. In 1519, 1520, 1534 and 1535, the usual charge was a penny apiece or 10*d*. a dozen, but by 1590 the price had risen to 2½*d*. each for the wild birds and 6*d*. each for 'house' pigeons; in 1602 and in 1605 they cost 8*d*. each, and in 1635 and 1639, 13*s*. and 14*s*. a dozen.

'Pygeons be easily dygested and are very holsome to them whiche are fleumatike or pure melancholy.' (*Elyot's Castel of Helth. London.* 1539. *f.*31*r*.)

In France, young pigeons are killed, for roasting, before they have eaten hard grain. The legs are orange-pink, free from scales, and the breasts plump and tender.

Tame pigeons should be starved 24 hours before being killed and, if possible, all feathers should be removed while the bird is still warm. It is advisable to hang the pigeon head downwards as soon as it has been killed so that it may bleed freely, failing which the flesh will be very dark. It is most inadvisable to scald pigeons in order to remove feathers, as this toughens the skin and outer layer of flesh.

When trussing pigeons, turn the feet, which are left on, folded inwards across the rear of the birds.

Note on the Cooking of Pigeons

Whichever recipe is used, it is essential that the fat used in the cooking of pigeons be not too hot, as their flesh is delicate and overheated butter or oil would tend to destroy their flavour. If wished, when they are served plain roasted, a slice of toast, from which all crust has been removed, may be placed under the birds 10 to 15 minutes before they are ready to serve. This absorbs the gravy and interior fat and is delicious when eaten with the bird. In the British Isles the three principal species of *Pigeons* are the *Wood Pigeon* or *Ring Dove* (*Columba palumbus*), the *Stock Dove* (*C. oenas*), a smaller species wanting the white on wings and neck, and the *Rock Dove* (*C. livia*), breeding round the coasts, wherever there are cliffs, but now mixed with tame birds and only found in a pure state in parts of Scotland; the *Turtle Dove* (*Streptopelia turtur*) is a summer visitor, principally south of the border.

A large number of different kinds of pigeons are found throughout the world, some of large size, resembling the *Wood Pigeon*, others dressed in gorgeous colours, in which the green predominates. The green *Fruit Pigeons* found in the East and Africa, feed principally on wild fruits and nearly all are good to eat, but they should be skinned, not plucked, as the skins are very tough.

RECIPES

Angel's Pie
Pigeons en Casserole
Chaudfroid de Pigeons
Compote de Pigeons
Pigeons à la Crapaudine
Pigeons in Disguise
Pigeons en Fricandeau
Pigeons in a Hole
Pigeons aux Olives
Pigeons Cooked with Green Peas
Pigeons aux Petits Pois
Potted Wood Pigeon
Pigeons à la Provençale
Pigeon Pudding
To make a Pulpatoon of Pigeons
Pupton of Pigeons Cold
Roast Pigeons
Pigeon Soups
Stuffed Pigeons
Squabs en Casserole

Angel's Pie

'Many people would call this a pigeon-pie, for in good sooth, there be pigeons in it; but 'tis a pie worthy of a brighter sphere than this.

'Six plump young pigeons, trimmed of all superfluous matter, including pinions and below the thighs. Season with pepper and salt, and stuff these pigeons with *foie gras*, and quartered truffles, and fill up the pie with plovers' eggs and some good forcemeat. Make a good gravy from the superfluous parts of the birds, and some calf's head stock to which has been added about half a wineglass of old madeira, with some lemon juice and cayenne. See that your paste

be light and flaky, and bake in a moderate oven for three hours. Pour in more gravy just before taking out, and let the pie get cold.' *Cakes and Ale* by Edward Spencer. (*Grant Richards, London*, 1897.)

Pigeons en Casserole

Take three young pigeons trussed for boiling. Lard each with a strip of fat bacon, fry them in butter till nicely browned, drain them and put them into a casserole with just enough good gravy barely to cover them. Add three or four little green onions and a few button mushrooms, together with a good glass of claret and a seasoning of salt and coralline pepper. Let the birds cook very slowly for three-quarters of an hour at the side of fire, and then when cooked serve it up in same casserole.—N.S.

Chaudfroid de Pigeons

2 tender pigeons
1 onion
1 carrot
Salt and pepper
Chaudfroid sauce
1 *bouquet-garni*
Stuffing for pigeons
1 small turnip
1 cup good brown stock
Aspic jelly

Draw and clean the birds, singe and carefully remove the breast-bones and back-bones but not those of the legs. Cut off feet. Have some stuffing ready as indicated in recipe 'Stuffed Pigeons' and use to stuff birds, shaping them as nearly as possible in their original forms. Truss and bind securely and tie each one in a piece of muslin. Slice the vegetables, then place them, with the bones, herbs and stock, in a pan just large enough to cook the birds comfortably. A little dry sherry may also be added if wished. Place the pigeons on this 'bed', seasoning with salt and pepper and covering them with a greased paper, then the saucepan lid. Cook very gently on the stove or in a rather hot oven until the birds are tender, then allow them to cool as they are. When cold, carefully unwrap them and cut each bird into halves-or quarters, according to their size. Coat first with *chaudfroid* sauce, decorate surfaces as desired with fancy shapes cut from truffles or hard-boiled egg, and gently spoon cold but still liquid aspic jelly over them, very evenly. When this is set, serve the pieces of pigeon on a bed of lettuce or as wished.

Note.—It is a good plan to place the articles to be treated in this manner on a wire cake-cooler before adding *chaudfroid* sauce and aspic jelly.—P.W.

Compote de Pigeons

2 plump young pigeons
1 teaspoon flour
½ cup white wine
1 small *bouquet-garni*
Butter
¼ lb. fresh mushrooms
Fat bacon or salt pork
½ cup hot water
Salt and pepper
Small white onions
Pinch sugar
Tiny dusting nutmeg

Truss pigeons. Cut into small pieces a slice of either fat pork or bacon and cook gently to extract fat, removing pieces left over after the completion of that operation. Brown the pigeons in this fat on all sides and lightly dust with salt. When a nice even colour on all sides, add to the birds another rather thick slice of streaky bacon, cut into dice, and continue browning gently with the pigeons, taking care they do not colour unevenly. Dust with the flour, then add the hot water and the white wine. Boil up sharply for five or six minutes, then add *bouquet*, salt and pepper to taste, and greatly reduce heat or pull pan to edge of stove to finish cooking the pigeons. They must be closely covered during the cooking. Meanwhile, brown as many tiny onions as you may wish to use in a sufficiency of butter, adding a tiny pinch of powdered sugar. When the birds are half done, add these browned onions and, 2 minutes later, the mushrooms, slicing if large but use preferably the tiny 'button' mushrooms if available. Cook for 10 minutes longer. Drain the pigeons and keep hot after removing strings. Make the gravy in the usual way and serve the birds very hot, surrounded by the mushrooms and onions, straining the gravy over them and decorating with either watercress tips or parsley.
—P.W.

Grilled Pigeons (à la Crapaudine)

If very young and tender, pigeons are delicious cooked as 'broilers', that is, split open, flattened, spread with softened butter and then rolled in fine freshly-made white breadcrumbs, mixed with salt and pepper. Place under a grill and cook slowly, serving when done on both sides, with either a tartare sauce or, if preferred, simply with oiled butter to which a little lemon juice has been added.

Pigeons in Disguise

Draw and truss them, season them with pepper and salt; make a nice puff-paste and roll each pigeon in a piece of it; tie them in a cloth, and take care the paste does not break; boil them in a great deal of water; they will take an hour and a half boiling; take great care, when they are untied, they do not break; put them into a dish, and pour a little good gravy to them.—C.MA.

(In Mrs Glasse's *Art of Cookery* this recipe is given under the name of 'Pigeons Transmogrified'.)

Pigeons en Fricandeau

After having trussed your pigeons with their legs in their bodies, divide them in two, and lard them with bacon; then lay them in a stew-pan with the larded side downwards, and two whole leeks cut small, two ladlefuls of mutton broth, or veal gravy; cover them close over a very slow fire, and when they are enough (cooked), make your fire very brisk, to waste away what liquor remains: when they are of a fine brown, take them up, pour out all the fat that is left in the pan; then pour in some veal gravy to loosen what sticks to the pan, and a little pepper; stir it about for two or three minutes and pour it over the pigeons. This is a pretty little side-dish.—H.GL.

Pigeons in a Hole

Pick, draw and wash four young pigeons, stick their legs in their bellies as you do boiled pigeons, and season them with pepper, salt, and beaten mace. Put into the belly of each pigeon a lump of butter the size of a walnut. Lay out your pigeons in a pie-dish, pour over them a batter made of three eggs, two spoonfuls of flour, and half a pint of good milk. Bake them in a moderate oven, and serve them to table in the same dish.
—W.A.H.

Pigeons aux Olives

2 plump pigeons
1 slice streaky bacon
Salt and pepper
1 or 2 cups good *bouillon*
1 scanty cup stoned green olives
Thin slices fat bacon
2 tablespoons butter
1 cup white wine
1 teaspoon potato starch
1 medium-sized onion

Fasten the thin slices of fat bacon – or salt pork – securely on the breasts of the pigeons. Cut the slice of streaky bacon into dice and cut up the onion finely. Place these two latter ingredients into a heavy iron saucepan, with the butter, and brown them gently with the pigeons which have been added at the same time. When all ingredients are nicely coloured, add salt and pepper and the wine and simmer gently until the liquid in pan has almost entirely evaporated – taking care not to burn contents of pan. Now add the *bouillon*, using sufficient to come half-way up the sides of the birds. Mix the potato starch (*fécule*) with a little cold *bouillon* and strain this into the saucepan. Cover and allow contents to simmer gently over a low heat until the pigeons are done. Strain the gravy, replace it in the pan, with the birds, and add as many stoned green olives as you may desire, cook 10 minutes longer and serve them around the pigeons, with the gravy. It is well to 'blanch' the olives before adding to the sauce or they may make it too salt.—P.W.

Pigeons Cooked with Green Peas

Take a couple of young pigeons and roast them for about 25 minutes in a casserole with ½ lb. of fat bacon cut in dice and a dessertspoonful of butter. After 15 minutes cooking, season birds. While the pigeons are cooking, prepare the peas. Melt a tablespoonful of butter in a pot and then add a lb. of green peas, a large lump of sugar, a lettuce cut up, four or five small onions, cover the pot with a soup plate full of cold water, and this will prevent the evaporation of the juices of the vegetables while they cook. They will require to cook slowly for approximately 30 minutes; when done, add the sauce from the pigeons, thickened with a little flour. Serve the pigeons surrounded with the green peas.—B.G.

Pigeons aux Petits Pois

This method of cooking is suitable for older and tougher birds. Pluck, singe and truss birds, tie or skewer thin slices of fat bacon over their breasts and brown them, in a heavy iron cocotte. When nicely coloured, season with salt and pepper, add about a cupful of either *bouillon* or hot water and as many freshly-shelled green peas as may be required. When the birds are tender, serve surrounded by the peas and decorate dish with small fried *croûtons* or *fleurons*.—P.W.

Potted Wood Pigeon

Pluck and truss the pigeons and season them inside and out with a mixture of spices, cayenne and black, freshly ground pepper, ginger, cinnamon, mace, nutmeg and salt. Butter thickly the bottom of a fireproof dish, put the pigeons in it, breast downwards, packing them as closely as possible, put a good deal more butter round and over them, a piece of buttered paper over the jar and the lid tightly on that, and bake them until they are tender, about an hour for young birds. Take them out, and while they are still warm, scrape the flesh off them and put it into a terrine, pressing it down fairly tight. Let the liquid remaining in the casserole get quite cold, then remove the butter which has solidified on the top, being careful to scrape off any of the gravy adhering to it, melt it down again and pour it over the pigeon

flesh in the terrine. When this is cold, seal it with clarified butter.

These pots will keep for some weeks in a cold place. The stock under the butter is priceless for other dishes, as it is rich and spicy.

Pigeons à la Provençale

1 plump young pigeon
Olive oil
1 clove garlic
1 cup good *bouillon*
Lemon juice
Fillets of anchovy
Small button onions
Few sprigs chervil
1 cup dry white wine
Hot *croûtons*
Salt and pepper

A large Bordeaux pigeon is suitable for this excellent dish. Pluck, singe and truss neatly. Using a special larding needle, pass a few thin fillets of anchovy through the bird as when larding with bacon. Heat a couple of tablespoons of pure olive oil and lightly brown the bird on all sides in it when sufficiently hot. This should be done slowly. During this operation, brown a dozen or more tiny white onions in either a little butter or olive oil. When evenly coloured, add to pigeon together with the garlic and the chervil. Moisten gradually with the mixed *bouillon* and wine, add salt and pepper, cover closely and cook gently until the bird is done. Drain the pigeon of all fat. Skim excess fat from gravy and add to latter a little lemon juice – as liked – serving the bird whole surrounded by the onions and hot fried *croûtons*. If liked, a few fried chipolata sausages may be added also as a garnish.
—P.W.

Pigeon Pudding

Line a basin with rich paste half an inch thick; put in three pigeons, with about ½ lb. of beefsteak from well-hung meat, the yolks of three hard-boiled eggs, salt, pepper, and spices; and pour in gravy from the bones or trimmings, with brown stock as a foundation, to half the depth; cover with paste, and tie in a cloth. The pudding will require about three hours' boiling.—G.A.S.

To make a Pulpatoon of Pigeons

Take mushrooms, palats, oysters, sweetbreads, and fry them in butter; then put all these into a strong gravy; give them a heat over the fire, then thicken up with an egg and a bit of butter; then half roast six or eight pigeons, and lay them in a crust of forc'd meat, as follows: Scrape 1 lb. of veal and 2 lb. of marrow, and heat it together in a stone mortar, after it is shred very fine; then season it with salt, pepper, spice, and put in hard eggs, anchovies, and oysters; beat all together, and make the lid and sides of your pye of it; first, lay a thin crust into your pattipan, then put in your forc'd-meat, then lay an exceeding thin crust over them, then put in your pigeons and other ingredients, with a little butter on the top; bake it two hours.—E.S.

Pupton of Pigeon Cold

Take two wood pigeons. Cut off the meat, and cut up 3 oz. of fat bacon, a shallot, and a few mushrooms, and fry all quickly for five minutes. Then put on the lid and cook slowly for an hour with a *bouquet-garni*. Remove the *bouquet-garni*, pound the meat in a mortar very fine. Have ready a good meat jelly. Line a mould with it, then put in your pigeons, and when set enough pour in a little more jelly. You may if you wish decorate the top of the mould with a few olives or mushrooms. Enough for six.—O.H.

Roast Pigeons

Once plucked and singed, cover the breasts with thin slices of fat salt pork or bacon, truss up tidily, spread with fresh butter and roast in a rather sharp oven from 15 to 20 minutes, according to size of bird and degree of cooking required, removing the bacon slices half-way through the cooking to nicely brown the breasts. Baste well every few minutes and, after removing trussing strings, serve either whole or cut in halves, with watercress and the strained gravy. Season nicely before serving.—P.W.

Pigeon Soups

I

Simmer two pigeons in 1½ quarts of water and milk for two hours, adding a little more milk as and when necessary; season with pepper and salt and a dessertspoonful of aniseed seeds. Take the birds out, remove the flesh from the breast and cut up in *julienne* which return to the soup; pound all the other meat from the birds and make into *quenelles*, which are added to the soup at the time of serving. Add also some fresh cream and stir well in. This soup is known in culinary French by the name of *Crème Colombine*.

II

Crème Cambacérès. This is a very rich soup made up of a *velouté* of pigeons and a *bisque d'écrevisses* in equal parts and thoroughly well mixed; it is then garnished with *quenelles* of pigeons stuffed with a *salpicon* of crayfish tails.

Stuffed Pigeons

For Stuffing:

1 cup chopped fresh mushrooms
1 slice fat salt pork
2 tablespoons breadcrumbs
1 egg
Livers of birds
1 shallot
Parsley, chopped
Bouillon

Chop all ingredients, after previously lightly browning the livers in butter. Soak the fresh breadcrumbs in a sufficiency of *bouillon*, squeeze dry. Blend all ingredients with the beaten egg, season rather highly and use to stuff pigeons, sewing up carefully. Truss, and singe them before stuffing and roast as indicated, serving with hot tomato or Périgueux sauce.—P.W.

PIGEONS, AFRICAN

1. Speckled Pigeon (Lat. *Columba phaeonotus*)
2. Olive Pigeon (Lat. *C. arquatrix*)
3. Delalande's Green Pigeon (Lat. *Treron delalandii*)

There is a considerable number of *African Pigeons*, but these three are those which Major Horsbrugh praises as the best for food. The first is widely distributed throughout the greater part of Africa, and as it breeds at all seasons of the year, there are always some *Squabs* available. The second is the largest of the *African Pigeons* and it is found from Abyssinia to The Cape, principally in the mountains. It is very strong on the wing and carries a lot of shot. It is excellent to eat. The third is found in the Eastern Cape Province, and from Natal to the Tanganyika Territory. It is almost invariably fat, tender and well flavoured.

PIGEON, WOOD

Lat. *Columba palumbus*. The largest European *Dove* and the commonest form of wild pigeon in the British Isles. It is also called *Ring-Dove*, *Cushat, Queest* and *Woodie*, in England; *Cushie-doo*, in Scotland; *Pigeon ramier*, in France.

PINTAIL

Lat. *Anas acuta*. One of the most widely distributed of all the Old World migratory *Ducks*. It is one of the best from the gastronome's point of view. It is a handsome bird which used to be popular in France, where it is called *Pilet*, as one of the not-so-fishy vegetarian ducks which, in certain dioceses, were allowed on abstinence days, that is days when the eating of meat is not permitted. In August, 1942, the Ministry of Food fixed the maximum retail price of Pintail in England at 3*s*. 6*d*. per bird 'in feather'.

'Audubon seems to have held a rather low opinion of the pintail's flesh. Nevertheless it compares fairly well with that of several other species, when killed in regions well stocked with suitable food. I think it is apt to be thin, and it certainly seldom takes on the layer of fat which makes the widgeon so delicious. In the British Isles and in fact throughout Western Europe, it is at times quite "fishy" in flavour, sometimes simply uneatable. In India, it seems to rank high. Hume and Marshall (1879) class it next to the mallard, and say they have never come across one with a fishy taste.'—J.C.P.

Being so widely distributed, the pintail suffers from a number of different names in the vernacular, both in the British Isles and in the U.S.A. Here are the names given by Phillips: *Sprig-tail*; *Gray Duck*; *Pied Gray Duck*; *Gray Widgeon*; *Sea-Widgeon*; *Sea-Pheasant*; *Split-tail*; *Spike-tail*; *Pike-tail*; *Picket-tail*; *Water-Pheasant*; *Smee*; *Long-necked Duck*; *Winter Duck*; *Cracker*; *Pile-start*; *Spindle-tail*; *Lady-bird*, and *Harlan*.

In South America, there is a related species (*Anas spinicauda*), known as *Chilian Pintail*, *Brown Pintail* or *South American Pintail*, which is one of the commonest ducks of South America. In the Argentine it is one of the chief game birds of the country and its flesh is everywhere excellent.

PLOVER

All members of the family *Charadriidae* are entitled to the name of *Plover*, but there are three members of that large family which deserve more than any of the others the attention and gratitude of gastronomes: they are, in order of gastronomic merit, the *Golden Plover*, the *Grey Plover*, and the *Green Plover* or *Lapwing*. The *Golden Plover* (q.v.) and the *Grey Plover* (q.v.) are highly prized for food, in England, where they are still fairly common during the winter; the *Green Plover*, better known under the names of *Lapwing* (q.v.), *Peewit* or *Peweet*, is still abundant in many parts of the British Isles, and it is protected by law in some of the English counties. During the seventeenth and eighteenth centuries the name *Green Plover* was applied to the *Golden Plover*, but it was transferred to the *Lapwing* during the nineteenth century.

Another *Plover*, which is not protected and needs no protection, as it is unfit for human food, is the *Black-headed Plover* or *Crocodile Bird*: it is said to enter the gaping jaws of crocodiles basking in the sun, on mud banks, after they have enjoyed a square meal, and to feed upon the 'bits and pieces' which they find among the 'great reptiles' fangs or adhering to their jaws.

Plovers were served to the Lords of the Star Chamber on many occasions, sometimes under the name of *Green Plover* but usually merely under that of *Plover*. They cost but 2*d*. each, in 1519, 3*d*. in 1520, 3*d*. and 4*d*. in 1534. In 1567, ten *Plover* cost 4*s*. 4*d*.; in 1568, three *Green Plover* cost 15*d*. on one occasion, and 6*d*., 7*d*., and 8*d*. each on three other occasions. In 1590 and 1605, they cost either 6*d*., 8*d*. or 10*d*. each.

'Plover is of some reputed a dainty meat, and very wholesome; but they who so judge are much deceived; for it is of slow digestion, increaseth melancholy, and yeeldeth little good nourishment to the body.' (Venner's *Via recta ad vitam longam*. London, 1628. p. 63.)

To choose Plovers

'When fresh, they are limber-footed: when fat, they feel hard at the vent; when lean, they feel thin at the vent; when stale, they are dry-footed. These birds will keep sweet for a long time. There are three sorts of plovers, the grey, green, and bastard plover, or lapwing.'—C.MA.

The General Way of Dressing Plovers is as follows:

'Green plovers roast like a woodcock, without drawing; and the trail to run upon a toast; with good gravy for sauce.

'Grey plovers should be stewed. Make a forcemeat with the yolks of two hard eggs bruised, some marrow cut fine, artichoke bottoms cut small, and sweet herbs, seasoned with pepper, salt and nutmeg: stuff the birds then put them into a saucepan with some good gravy (just enough to cover them), a glass of white wine, and a blade of mace; cover them close, and let them stew very softly till they are tender; then take up the plovers, lay them into a dish; keep them hot; put a piece of butter rolled in flour to thicken the sauce; let it boil till smooth; squeeze into it a little lemon; scum it clean, and pour it over them.'—C.MA.

Ragout of Plovers

'Plovers are hardly fit for anything but roasting. Sometimes, however, they are prepared *à la bourguignonne*, which is indeed the only way of making a ragout of plovers. In this case, empty and truss them as neatly as possible; mask them in a stew-pan with layers of bacon; moisten them with a little stock or broth; when done enough, let them simmer a little in a *bourguignonne*, and serve up hot with a garnish.'—G.A.S.

Plovers' Eggs

Hard-boiled plovers' eggs are – or were once upon a time – a joy to which gastronomes looked forward in April. Well-meaning but ill-informed law-makers, in England,

591

made the sale of plovers' eggs an offence in order to protect the birds. As a matter of fact the plover invariably sits upon a four-egg clutch and no more; the eggs are pear-shaped and the pointed ends converge towards the centre of the saucer-shaped nest. Before Parliamentary interference with the plovers' eggs trade, expert collectors used to rob the plover's nest of two eggs out of the four and no more, which meant that the bird laid another two a little later on, and these were also taken away; the bird laid another two and was then left in peace, eventually hatching four birds, a couple of weeks later than she would have done had there been no tampering with her first clutch: this was all to the good, as the chicks had a much better chance to live after, rather than before the last bad frosts of the early spring. Plovers' eggs are olive-brown, thickly blotched with black and they harmonize perfectly with the dull meadow lands in which they are laid rather stupidly, since many thousands must be turned over every year by the plough.

If you live in the country, you may still 'find' plovers' eggs and enjoy them, although you may neither sell them nor buy them. They need barely five minutes simmering in all-but boiling water to be sufficiently hard-boiled. The yolk is of a rich orange colour, the white being of a translucid mauvy shade of mother-of-pearl appearance.

If you have no facility for gathering plovers' eggs yourself, you must needs be content with gulls' eggs, similar in shape but a little larger than the plover's, and also slightly greener or bluer in colour. See *Gulls*.

PLOVER, GOLDEN

Lat. *Pluvialis apricaria*. One of the European members of the large *Plover* family, and the best of them all, from the gastronome's point of view. It is called *Pluvier doré* in French, but in culinary French *Pluvier*. There is a related American species known as the *American Golden Plover*.

In London, the market price of Golden Plover has remained remarkably steady during the last century and a half. It fluctuated from 1*s*. 6*d*. to 2*s*. 6*d*. per bird in 1807; from 2*s*. to 3*s*. in 1922; and from 2*s*. to 2*s* 6*d*. in 1941. The golden plover escaped the attention of the Ministry of Food in 1942, when maximum retail prices were fixed for poultry and game.

Roast Golden Plover

A bird will be required for each person: they should be tenderly handled and, of course, not drawn. (*This is meant for the bird, but the courtesy may be extended to each person.*—Ed.) Roast them in the Dutch oven with their breast barded with fat bacon, baste with

butter, catching all the drips from the birds while cooking. Serve on crisp squares of toast, which have been spread with the melted butter and gravy thus saved, as hot as possible.—A.K.-H. (2).

PLOVER, GREY

Lat. *Squatarola squatarola*. A *Plover* which is very similar to the *Golden Plover* (q.v.), but a little larger. It is also the most cosmopolitan of its tribe, occurring on the coasts of all continents. Its average weight is 7 oz. and its flesh is very delicate. It is prepared for the table in any way suitable to the *Golden Plover* (q.v.). It is also called *Black-bellied Plover*.

In 1807, *Grey Plover* cost 3*s*. each in London, at a time when the smaller but gastronomically better *Golden Plover* sold for 1*s*. 6*d*. and 2*s*. 6*d*. But, in 1922, the *Grey Plover* was listed at its proper value on the London Market, at 1*s*. 3*d*. per bird; in 1941, however, the price rose to 1*s*. 6*d*. and 2*s*.

Muffet, in his *Health Improvement*, quotes a proverb: 'A Grey Plover cannot please him,' as applied to a discontented person, which shows that the bird was highly estimated as food.—C.S.

PLOVER, NORFOLK.
STONE CURLEW

Lat. *Burhinus oedicnemus*. The largest of the *Plovers*. It is widely distributed across Europe as far south as North Africa and as far east as India. It is a summer visitor in England and is found chiefly in Norfolk and Suffolk. It lays two stone-coloured eggs on the ground. The plumage is drab and the bird practically invisible when on the ground. It feeds on snails, insects, worms, frogs and any kind of small animal. It is now protected by law.

POCHARD (COMMON POCHARD)

Lat. *Aythya ferina*. One of the best diving *Ducks* for the table. It breeds in most parts of northern and central Europe, of western Asia as well as in Algeria. The name also applies to a closely related American species, and among the country names by which it is known in the British Isles are *Dun-bird, Dun-Curre, Red-headed Curre*; and in the U.S.A., *Red-head, Poker, Red-eyed Poker, Red-headed Widgeon*. The pochard is a vegetarian by choice, but, like most ducks, will eat anything when water grasses and seeds are not available.

'Considered one of the best European wild ducks, when shot on good feeding ground, it is quite equal to the American Canvasback and Red-head. Leonhard Baldner, of Strasbourg, wrote in 1653 that pochards were 'counted as good as mallard for meat'. —J.C.P.

Among the other species of Pochards, there are the Southern Pochard or Cape Pochard (*Aythya erythrophthalma*), also called *Nation's Pochard* and *Bruine-eend*, in Afrikaans; it is found chiefly in East Africa and western South America. It is a non-migratory duck, but it moves about according to the dryness of the seasons.

The flesh of this bird has been described as excellent, but not by Horsbrugh, who wrote: 'It is a poor fowl to eat, tasting strongly of mud; but as my office staff apparently thought them good, I usually shot these birds when possible.' Phillips wrote: 'I tasted a good few shot on Lake Chahafi and Lake Muanda, in south-western Uganda, and I think they were just about as good as the Yellow-billed Ducks from the same waters.'—J.C.P.

The following *Pochards* also deserve to be recorded:

Madagascar White-eyed Duck or Madagascar Pochard (*Aythya innotata*). This is a rare Pochard which is confined to the northern and eastern parts of the island of Madagascar.

Baer's Pochard (*Aythya baeri*) is also an uncommon Pochard breeding in Eastern Siberia, Japan and Northern China and occasionally visiting India.

Red-crested Pochard or India Pochard (*Netta rufina*) is an uncommon species, yet one that is widely distributed over Europe, Asia and northern Africa.

'Over most of its range, this bird is considered very good for the table, but in India, where at times they take a good deal of animal food, they are, like the Common Pochard under similar conditions, rank and coarse. (Baker, 1921.) When eating proper food, they are fully as good as the Pochard or the Widgeon.'—J.C.P.

PRAIRIE CHICKEN

Lat. *Tympanuchus pinnatus cupido*. One of the more important game birds of the U.S.A. It has been called the Grouse of the Mississippi Valley and is found from Manitoba to Texas. It is sometimes called the *Greater Prairie Chicken* in opposition to the *Lesser Prairie Chicken* (*T. pallidicinctus*), a smaller bird of the same type which occurs in Texas. It is best prepared for the table in any way suitable for the *Grouse* (q.v.).

PRAIRIE HEN

Lat. *Tympanuchus cupido*. A game bird of great gastronomic merit which used to be found in several of the Eastern States of the U.S.A. It has been extinct since about 1931.

PTARMIGAN (WILLOW-PTARMIGAN or WILLOW-GROUSE)

Lat. *Lagopus lagopus*.

PTARMIGAN (COMMON PTARMIGAN)

Lat. *Lagopus mutus*.

PTARMIGAN, ROCK

Lat. *Lagopus rupestris* and *L. leucurus*. Members of the *Grouse* family, of which there are two main sorts, the *Willow Ptarmigan* and the *Rock Ptarmigan*, also known as *White Partridge* and *Rock Partridge* (*Perdrix blanche* in French), although their feathered legs show they belong to the *Grouse* and not to the *Partridges*. It inhabits chiefly Northern Europe and Siberia, but it occurs on the mountains of Scotland, not below 2,000 ft. altitude, from Perthshire and Argyllshire northwards. It is the only bird in the British Isles to put on a white coat in winter. In the U.S.A. the *Ptarmigan* is represented by an almost identical species, known as the *White-tailed Ptarmigan*: it is found in the Rockies. The *Ptarmigan* may be prepared for the table in any way suitable for *Grouse* (q.v.) to which it is distinctly inferior gastronomically.

In 1922, ptarmigan sold on the London Market at from 2s. 6d. to 4s. 6d. per bird, according to quality, but in August 1942 the Ministry of Food fixed the maximum retail price of ptarmigan, 'in feather', at 3s. 6d. each irrespective of condition.

Ptarmigans roast

With some ptarmigans, take butter for basting, a slice of bacon for each bird, fried breadcrumbs, brown gravy, bread sauce.

Let the birds hang in a cool, dry place for three or four days. When ready for use, pluck, draw and truss them in the same manner as a roast grouse. Tie over each breast a slice of fat bacon, and roast in a moderate oven from 30 to 35 minutes, basting very frequently with butter. When about three parts cooked, remove the bacon, dredge lightly with flour, and baste well to give the birds a nice appearance. Dish on the toast, which should be previously put into the dripping-tin to catch the gravy that drops from the birds, and serve the bread sauce, gravy and breadcrumbs separately.

Allow one bird for every two persons, or if small birds one to each person.—B. (1).

PUFFIN

Lat. *Fratercula arctica*. Puffin is the name of several species of sea birds of the Auk family.

'Their flesh is excessively rank, as they feed on sea-weed and fish, especially sprats;

but when pickled and preserved with spices, they are admired by those who love high eating. Dr Caius tells us that in his day the Church allowed them in Lent, instead of fish; he also acquaints us that they were taken by means of ferrets, as we do rabbits.'

The *Puffin* is a rather ridiculous-looking bird, about one foot long, with a short neck and a deep-grooved, parti-coloured, laterally compressed bill: it has white cheeks, a blackish upper part and foreneck and white underparts. It lays but one egg a year. The *Puffin* provides the staple food of the Faroe Islanders and its flesh is dried and exported.

PURR

An Old English name, now obsolete, for the common *Dunlin*, a regular visitor to the British Isles, and a bird which nobody would think of killing, even if not protected by law, as it is in England. Yet they figure in the accounts of the dinners served to the Lords of the Star Chamber, in 1602, when *Purrs* cost 1*s*. 8*d*. each on one occasion, and 2*s*. on another.

QUAIL

Lat. *Coturnix coturnix*. The common *Quail* is a migratory game bird wintering in tropical Africa and India, and breeding throughout the greater part of Europe, and eastwards as far as NW. India. Considerable numbers formerly nested in the British Isles. The majority of birds exposed for sale in England were caught in Egypt on migration and imported alive in this country, where they were fattened and then killed. South of the Zambesi River, there is a resident African form, and in China and Japan another variety, the *Japanese Quail*. This bird has for long been kept in captivity by the Japanese for the sake of its eggs – one hen may lay as many as 200 eggs in a year. The *Black-breasted* or *Rain Quail* (*C. coromandelica*) is very similar to the common species but it is not such a fine table bird; it is confined to India. A handsome African species is the *Harlequin Quail* (*C. delegorguei*) (q.v.). In Australia, there is the *Stubble Quail* (*C. pectoralis*), which is considered the best game bird in the country. The *Swamp Quail* (*Synoicus ypsilophorus*), also known as the *Silver* or *Tasmanian Quail*, belongs to a different group: it is also found in Australia. Small *Quails* of the genus *Excalfactoria* inhabit SE. Asia, Australia and Africa. The *Blue-breasted Quail* (*Excalfactoria chinensis*) ranges from India and South China to Australia, where it is known as the *King Quail*. The African species (*E. adansonii*) occurs throughout the greater part of the Black Continent. In India, there are also two scrub-haunting forms, the *Rock Bush Quail* and the *Jungle Bush Quail* (*Perdicula asiatica*).

Quail should be eaten the day after they have been killed or as soon after as possible. They are plucked, singed and drawn from the neck; the head and neck should be removed, and the tips of the wings cut off: they can then be trussed like a small pigeon, or flattened out like *Squabs à la Crapaudine*. (See *Pigeon*.)

On the London Market, quail fetched 2*s*. 2*d*. each in 1757; from 3*s*. to 4*s*. in 1807; from 2*s*. to 4*s*. 6*d*. each in 1922; and from 3*d*. to 1*s*. 9*d*. each in 1941, at a time when prices had gone up generally. The explanation of this apparent anomaly is that the pre-war quails, in England, were fattened and imported birds, far better than the hungry and lean home-killed visitors of wartime days.

In the U.S.A. the names of *Quail* and *Partridge* appear to be interchangeable, one or the other being used for the same bird in different parts of the country. As a rule, however, *Quail* is qualified as in *Bob-white Quail* (q.v.), *California Quail* (q.v.), *Massena Quail* (q.v.), *Mountain Quail* (q.v.).

Quails en casserole

6 quails
2 heaping tablespoonfuls (2 oz.) butter
¼ pint (½ cup) red currant jelly
½ lemon
Salt and pepper to season
¼ lb. preserved cherries
1 wineglassful port wine
½ pint (1 cup) stock
¼ orange rind

Prepare and truss the quails. Melt the butter in an earthenware pan; when hot, put in the birds, and brown them all over. Cover with the lid, and put into a moderate oven till ready. Lift out the quails and keep hot. Drain the fat from the pan, add the stock, wine, and orange rind. Simmer for ten minutes, then stir in the jelly. Put in the quails for ten minutes; season with salt, pepper and the strained lemon juice.—M.H.N.

Quails à la Chasseur

Put the quails in a saucepan with a little butter, a bayleaf, sweet herbs, salt, and pepper; set them on a fierce fire and keep shaking them until they are tender, then add a dessertspoonful of flour, half a glass of white wine, and a little stock; when this is thick, and quite hot without boiling, take from the fire and serve.—G.A.S.

Chaufroid de Cailles

Draw and clean two quails; singe them and carefully remove the breastbones and backbones, but not the bones of the legs. Cut off

594

feet. Have some stuffing ready and stuff the birds, shaping as nearly as possible in their original form. Truss and bind securely and tie each one in a piece of muslin. Slice an onion, a carrot and a small turnip; then place them, with the bones and herbs, in some stock in a pan just large enough to hold the birds comfortably. A little sherry may also be added if wished. Place the quails on this bed, seasoning with salt and pepper and covering them with a greased paper, then the saucepan lid. Cook very gently on the stove, or in a rather hot oven, until the birds are tender, then allow them to cool as they are. When cold, carefully unwrap them and cut each bird into halves or quarters, according to its size. Coat first with *chaufroid* sauce, decorate surfaces as desired with fancy shapes cut from truffles or hard-boiled egg, and gently pour cold but still liquid aspic jelly over them, very evenly. When this is set, serve the quails on a bed of lettuce.

N.B.—It is a good plan to place the articles to be treated in this manner on a wire cake cooler before adding *chaufroid* sauce and aspic jelly.—P.W.

Caille à la Crapaudine

Split open as many quails as required, after having emptied and singed them. Flatten out nicely and set in a dish with salt, pepper, a pinch of mixed spice, a bayleaf (broken up), sprigs of parsley and thyme and a few rings of onion. Add the juice of a lemon and a couple of tablespoonfuls of olive oil. Allow the birds to marinate in this for several hours, then drain off all liquid and roll each bird in either fresh or brown breadcrumbs, to which salt and pepper have been added. Grill gently, turning frequently and moistening from time to time with a few drops of oiled butter.

Quail à la Mouqin

6 quails, dressed, cleaned and trussed
½ cup butter
2 shallots, finely chopped
2 cloves garlic, finely chopped
¼ bayleaf
1 teaspoon peppercorns
1 teaspoon finely-cut chives
2 cloves
1 pint white wine
1 pint heavy cream
½ teaspoon salt
⅛ teaspoon pepper
Few grains cayenne

Cook butter with shallots, garlic, bayleaf, peppercorns, and cloves for eight minutes, stirring constantly. *Sauté* quails in mixture until well browned. Add wine and simmer 30 minutes. Remove quails, strain sauce into

casserole, and add cream slowly. Add remaining seasonings and quails, cover, and heat to boiling point. Serve in casserole.— B.C.S.C.B.

Cailles en ragoût

Take some quails, cut them in two and toss them for a minute or two in a pan with a little pork fat and a sprinkle of flour. Add then a cup of *consommé* or of veal stock, salt, pepper, a *bouquet*, a few fresh mushrooms and pieces of globe artichokes. Cook very slowly and when it is nearly ready add the juice of an orange.—X.M.B. (1).

Cailles aux Raisins

Each quail should be wrapped in a vineleaf well soaked beforehand in cognac and a snow-white coverlet of bacon fat. Now, turning your attention to the little bird's inside, fill it up with a stuffing made up of the quail's liver, a little chopped bacon, some breadcrumbs soaked in cognac, the lot being made up into a paste. Cook in butter in a hot oven for about ten minutes; then add a dozen grapes per bird into the baking-dish or pan; they should be fresh grapes and both their skins and pips should be removed. Add a small glassful of brandy and cover the pan, leaving it in a moderately hot oven another five or six minutes. Take the birds out and remove their wrappings; set them in a serving dish with the grapes and the brandy gravy in which they were cooked and serve hot.—F.

Quails with Rice

3 or 4 tender quails
2 tablespoons butter
1 pint good stock or *bouillon*
1 *bouquet-garni*
Additional butter
1 large onion
6 oz. uncooked rice
Salt and pepper
1 glass dry white wine
Meat glaze (optional)

Having prepared the birds as for roasting, melt the butter and, when sufficiently hot, brown the birds on all sides in it. Add salt and pepper. Meanwhile, chop or slice finely the onion and colour it lightly in a little more butter, adding the rice at the same time and cooking gently together until slightly browned. Season moderately and moisten with the stock or *bouillon*, adding also the *bouquet-garni*. Cook the rice thus for about 15 minutes, then add the quails and their butter and gravy, placing them on top of the bed of rice. When this is done, cover pan and continue cooking from 6 to 10 minutes longer according to size, then add the wine and, if wished, a good tablespoonful of meat glaze, allowing the gravy to reduce gently until almost entirely absorbed by the rice. Serve the rice in a pyramid in a hot dish, surround with the birds and pour rest of gravy over all, after removing *bouquet-garni*, and straining.—P.W.

Roast Quails
The breasts of the birds should be covered with vine-leaves, then they should be wrapped in thin rashers of bacon. Roast for about 15 minutes in a good oven, basting constantly with butter and, of course, seasoning with salt and pepper. To serve, do not remove either vine-leaves or bacon and serve each bird on a fried *croûton* or on hot rounds of buttered toast.

QUAIL, AMERICAN
Lat. *Odontophorinae*. North American game birds, also called *American Partridges*, the best of which, from the gastronome's point of view, is the *Bob-white* (q.v.).

QUAIL, BLUE or BLUE-BREASTED
Lat. *Excalfactoria adansonii* and *E. chinensis*. The first is the African species of a small quail, and the second that of the Indian and Australian.
'The first is fairly common in Natal in some seasons and rare in others.'—B.HO.

QUAIL, BUSH
Lat. *Perdicula asiatica*. A small game bird found in different parts of India, where it is often called *Jungle Bush Quail* or *Rock Bush Quail*, and is prepared for the table in any way suitable to *Quail* (q.v.).

QUAIL, BUSTARD. HEMIPODE
Lat. *Turnix suscitator*; *T. sylvatica*; *T. plumbipes*; etc. The name given to a number of little quail-like birds found in Africa, Asia and Australia.
E.C.Stuart Baker, writing of the Ceylon species, says: 'Their food consists of seeds and insects and they are generally very fat and make delicious morsels on toast for those who can find in their hearts to shoot them.' —E.C.S.B.
The Anglo-Indian name of any variety of small *Bustard Quail* is *Button-Quail*. Its place for the gastronome is above the Lark and below the Ortolan. Hume and Marshall (1879) describe four eastern varieties: the *Indian Button-Quail* (*Turnix joudera*), the *Burmo-Malayan B-Q.* (*T. maculosa*), the *Nicobar B-Q.* (*T. albiventris*), and the *Little B-Q.* (*T. dussumieri*). Major Boyd Horsbrugh (1912) describes three African species, the *Kurrichane B-Q.* (*T. lepurana*), the *Natal B-Q.* (*T. nana*) and the *Hottentot B-Q.* (*T. hottentotta*). Sir Frederick J.Jackson says that the

Button-Quail is common in Kenya and Uganda, and he adds: 'It is almost invariably very fat and the skin being exceedingly tender, it is often badly torn, even by No. 10 shot, and requires very careful handling when skinning.'—F.J.J.
R.C.Stuart Baker, writing of the *Indian Button-Quail*, says: 'They feed both on grain, grass seeds, green shoots of crops, etc., and on insects, more especially ants. Their flesh is not bad to eat, though rather dry, unless very fat. Tickell, however, considers them "most delicious, and when in good plight as fat and delicate as an ortolan". Hume, on the other hand, always found them insignificant, dry, insipid little things.'—E.C.S.B. (2).

QUAIL, CALIFORNIA
Lat. *Lophortyx californica*. The most beautiful of all the game birds known under the name of *American Partridges* (q.v.). It inhabits the brush-covered hills and cañons of the Western U.S.A., ascending, in South California, to an elevation of above 9,000 feet above sea level. It is best prepared for the table in any way suitable for the *Partridge* (q.v.).

QUAIL, CAPE
Lat. *Coturnix africana*. This excellent little game bird is the representative of the *Common Quail* south of the Zambesi; it has a strange habit of appearing and disappearing in some districts.
'Quail when shot should not be hung as they decompose quickly. An excellent recipe for cooking them is to place a green chili inside the bird after drawing it, then wrap a piece of fat bacon round it and a green vineleaf round the whole, and roast fairly quickly. So cooked, they are appetizing to a degree.' —B.HO.

QUAIL, CRESTED
Lat. *Colinus leucopogon*. There is a number of different racial forms of the same species of *Colin* which are given this name. They are also called *American Partridges* (q.v.) and they may be described as the crowned brothers of the *Bob-white* (q.v.), from which they differ by wearing a crest and in no other respect. They occur chiefly in Central America and some of the north-western countries of South America. They are best prepared for the table in the same way as *Grouse* (q.v.).

QUAIL, HARLEQUIN
Lat. *Coturnix delegorguei*. An excellent little game bird, closely related to the *Cape Quail* (q.v.) caught in large numbers and greatly appreciated for food in Kenya and Uganda.
'In Kavirondo the natives catch, with the aid of decoys, great numbers of this bird for their own consumption and for sale.'—F.J.J.

In the U.S.A. the name is sometimes used and it applies to the *Massena Quail* (q.v.).

QUAIL, MASSENA. PARTRIDGE
Lat. *Cyrtonyx montezumae*. Two names which appear to be given indifferently to the same game bird, the handsomest of the *American Partridges* (q.v.). It is also called *Harlequin Quail* and *Fool Quail*, owing to its great tameness. It inhabits the rocky ravines among the higher ranges of Central America, Mexico and the south-western States of the U.S.A. In summer it is found at altitudes from 7,000 to 9,000 feet.

QUAIL, MEARN'S
A game bird which is closely related to the *Massena Quail* (q.v.) but its plumage is lighter in colour.

QUAIL, MOUNTAIN. PLUMED PARTRIDGE
Lat. *Oreortyx picta*. Two names which appear to be indifferently used for the same game bird, one of the *American Partridges* (q.v.), closely related to the *California Quail*, but a little bigger. It inhabits the mountains in some of the Western States of North America. Both cock and hen are alike in plumage, and both wear a very long crest composed of two feathers.

QUAIL, RAIN or BLACK-BREASTED
Lat. *Coturnix coromandelica*. A small game bird which is indigenous to India and the Malay Peninsula. It migrates during the monsoon to the drier parts of Upper and Western India. It is prepared for the table in any way suitable for *Quail* (q.v.).

QUAIL, SWAMP
Lat. *Synoicus ypsilophorus*. A small game bird found in Australia and New Guinea.

RAIL
There are a number of small, wading birds known by the name of *Rail* in the Old as well as in the New World. They all haunt bogs and marshlands, feeding upon the creeping, crawling life of swamps and they are very poor fare, not to be compared with their cousin, the *Landrail* (q.v.) which lives on the land and feeds on seeds and berries. In Europe, Western Asia and North Africa, the commonest *Rail* is the *Water-Rail* (*Rallus aquaticus*): it abounds in the British Isles. The plumage is darker than that of the *Landrail* and the bill is partly red. It glides with ease and speed through reeds and is a good swimmer. It is excellent eating, cooked and served like *Snipe* (q.v.). According to a letter of Sir Thomas Browne, M.D., written in the second half of the seventeenth century, and published in *Notes and Letters on the Natural History of Norfolk*, 1902, 'the Ralla or Rayle we have counted a dayntie dish' (p. 25).

In the U.S.A. there are a number of different species of *Rails*, the smallest being the *Sora Rail* or *Carolina Rail* (*Porzana carolina*), the largest the *King-Rail* (*Rallus elegans*) found on the Atlantic seaboard wherever there are salt marshes, whilst the only one fit to eat is the Virginian Rail (*Rallus limicola*), which prefers fresh water to salt.

All over the southern portion of the Australian Continent, as well as in Polynesia proper and the Philippine Islands, the commonest *Rail* is known as *Banded-* or *Land-Rail* (*Rallus philippensis*). It is a bird of semi-nocturnal habits, feeding on insects, seeds and the succulent parts of various native grasses.

Broiled Rail Birds
18 Rail Birds. Toast. Salt and Pepper. Clean and split the birds and season with salt and pepper. Spread on a very hot greased broiler, turning the inner side of birds towards the fire. Broil for two minutes in an oven of 400°. Turn and broil the other side for five minutes. They should be served underdone. Serve on canapé of soft buttered toast. Pour over them the essence caught in broiling pan, seasoned with salt and pepper. —A.W.R.

RAIL, BUSH
Lat. *Himantornis haematopus*. A plover-like game bird found in West Africa and the Congo; it may be prepared for the table in any way suitable for *Plover* (q.v.).

REDBILL. RED-BILLED PINTAIL
Lat. *Anas erythrorhyncha*. This bird, which is called *Rooibek-Eendje* in Africaans, is the African edition of the *Bahama Duck* (q.v.). It is common in the greater part of Africa.

'This is by no means difficult to kill; it falls to a fairly light blow, and is often very tame. It is excellent-eating.'—B.HO.

'This is an excellent bird for the table (E. A.Butler, Feilden and Reid, 1882; Sibree, 1892; Stark and Sclater, 1906). Davies called it "quite the best eating of all our ducks", referring in general to South Africa.'—J.C.P.

RED-HEAD. AMERICAN POCHARD
Lat. *Aythya americana*. One of the best known of American *Ducks*, although its range is more restricted than that of the Canvasback. It breeds in the north-western part of the U.S.A. and the south-western part of Canada, but is known as a bird of passage in many Eastern and Central States. It is mostly vegetarian in its diet and is very fond of the wild celery so dear to the Canvasback.

'To judge from market prices, the Red-Head, which is invariably cheaper than the canvasback, must be generally considered as inferior, but there have been many knowledgeable epicures to give it equal rank. It depends entirely upon their feeding ground. The Currituck Red-heads were never considered quite so good, and those from Pamlico, where the water grows salt, are distinctly inferior. I have eaten many New England Red-Heads which were hardly better than Scaup.'—J.C.P.

Among the country names given to the Red-Head in different parts of the U.S.A. the more usual are: Washington Canvasback, Red-headed Broadbill, Raft-Duck, Grayback, Fall Duck, Fool Duck.

REDSHANK

Lat. *Tringa totanus*. A common European shore bird, allied to the *Sandpiper* (q.v.). It is brownish above and white below, with bright orange-coloured legs and feet. When served to the Lords of the Star Chamber, in 1519, *Redshanks* cost 6*d*. for ten, and their price had not appreciably altered by 1922, when it fluctuated, on the London Market, between 4*d*. and 9*d*. apiece; in 1941, in spite of war conditions and rationing, they were offered in London at from 4*d*. to 6*d*. each.

REEDBIRD. BOBOLINK

Lat. *Dolichonyx oryzivorus*. A small, finch-like bird of the Southern U.S.A. It used to be greatly prized as a table delicacy and was served like *Ortolans* (q.v.).

ROOK

Lat. *Corvus frugilegus*. Opinions are divided as to whether the rook is the farmer's friend or his foe, but there is far greater evidence in favour of the rook than against it. The rook devours an immense quantity of grubs and wire-worms and other pests, of which there does not appear to be any shortage at any time, whereas there is very little evidence that rooks eat much if any grain. Rooks are both sociable and quarrelsome: they build their nests in large colonies, known as Rookeries, not for defence but for company. The Wild Birds Act of 1880 protects rooks in the nesting season, a protection which is a hollow mockery since a proviso of the said Act specifies that 'any person who owns or occupies land may kill rooks in the nesting season'. In 1940, an Order was issued that 'whenever a rookery becomes so populated that the birds are likely to damage crops, the occupier can be told by the local War Agricultural Executive Committee to reduce the numbers. Failure to do so will be a punishable offence.' Adult rooks being unfit to eat and difficult to kill, the 'reduction of numbers' of rooks usually takes the form of the most unsporting shooting of the fledglings still in the nests, and these are eaten in rook pies in many parts of rural England.

Rook Pies
I

'The birds should be young and be decapitated as soon as killed. For a good-sized pie take six young birds, slit with a sharp knife (through feathers and all) down the breast. Skin the bird, do not pluck it. Remove the slices each side of the breast-bone. Wash well in slightly salted cold water. Soak them all night in scalded but not boiled milk. In the morning, simmer the breasts for half an hour. When cold, place them in your pie-dish, add ¼ lb. skirt of beef, or a few slices of cold boiled bacon, and two or three hard-boiled eggs cut in quarters. Pepper and salt to taste, and add about 2 oz. of good margarine. Cover with good stock, adding a little gelatine. Cover the pie-dish with greased paper and cook for not less than one hour and a half. Allow to become cold. Then cover with puff-paste as for a pigeon-pie and cook in a quick oven. It is best eaten cold.' (*Mrs Jessop Hulton's* Recipe in *Wine and Food*, No. 28, December 1940.)

II

With six young rooks, take ¾ lb. of rump steak, ¼ lb. of butter, half a pint of stock, salt and pepper, paste.

Skin the birds without plucking them by cutting the skin near the thighs, and drawing it over the body and head. Draw the birds in the usual manner, remove the necks and backs, and split the birds down the breast. Arrange them in a deep pie-dish, cover each breast with thin strips of steaks, season well with salt and pepper, intersperse small pieces of butter, and add as much stock as will three parts fill the dish. Cover with paste and bake from 1½ to two hours, for the first half hour in a hot oven to make the paste rise, and afterwards more slowly to allow the birds to become thoroughly cooked. When the pie is about three parts baked, brush it over with yolk of egg to glaze the crust, and, before serving, pour in, through the hole in the top, the remainder of the stock.

This should be sufficient for five or six persons.—B. (1).

Rook Stew

Skin the birds (young rooks, of course) as soon as possible after they have been shot, and lift the meat from the breast; soak it in milk overnight and stew gently in a casserole with a number of available root vegetables, finely sliced; season with pepper and salt and serve hot.—B.H.

RUFF. REEVE

Lat. *Philomachus pugnax*. These birds used to appear in the Fens early in the spring and disappear about Michaelmas. The reeves laid four eggs in a tuft of grass the first week in May and sat about a month. Fowlers avoided shooting the *Reeves* (hens) not only because they were smaller than the *Ruffs* (cocks) but that they might be left to breed. They used to be caught by clap nets sometimes with decoy, in Lincolnshire, the Island of Ely, and the East Riding of Yorkshire, where they were fattened on bread and milk, hemp seeds and sometimes boiled wheat. When sugar was added to the diet, the birds became 'a lump of fat' in a fortnight and fetched 2*s*. and 2*s*. 6*d*. apiece.

In olden times, *Ruffs* and *Reeves* were highly prized as food for the rich, more particularly when game was out of season, and they were among the most expensive of the dainties served to the Lords of the Star Chamber, costing 6*s*. and 6*s*. 8*d*. each, in 1602 and 1605.

They should be cooked soon after being killed, being trussed and treated in any way suitable for *Woodcock* (q.v.).

'Ruffs and Reeves (which are particularly found in Lincolnshire and the Isle of Ely) are very delicate birds and must be trussed like the woodcock, but not dressed with the guts. When done, serve them up with gravy and bread sauce, and garnish the dish with crisp crumbs of bread.'—W.A.H.

At the beginning of the nineteenth century, ruffs and reeves were sold in London under two classes, 'fatted' or 'shot', the first costing on an average 5*s*. each, whilst the 'shot' birds rarely fetched 3*s*. and often sold for 1*s*. 3*d*. The last time when these birds appeared in the London Market quotations was in 1922, when they cost from 8*d*. to 1*s*. 3*d*. each, all, apparently 'shot' birds. (In Picardy the ruff is called *Paon* and the reeve *Sotte*.)

SANDERLING

Lat. *Crocethia alba*. One of the smaller sorts of *Sandpiper*.

SCOTER

Lat. *Melanitta nigra*. This is the common *Black Scoter*, a marine duck common both in the Old and the New World, breeding in the far north and migrating into temperate regions for the winter.

'The flesh, particularly in winter, is very strong, but I have often eaten young birds, before they reached the salt water, that were not really so fishy. The young birds, on our Atlantic coast and especially in New England, are still very much appreciated by those who have the patience and the courage to stew them in the proper way. The chief advantage of the scoter as a game dish lies in its abundance and the ease with which it can be secured. I confess I am not able to appreciate it.

'The art of cooking scoters seems to be dying out very fast in this part of the world. William Brewster tells of an ingenious way of baking them in a bean-hole in the North Woods, and subjecting them to one hour and a quarter treatment of such camp cookery. He says: "Before being consigned to this backwoods oven, the bird was stuffed with sage, onions and breadcrumbs, wrapped in several thicknesses of brown paper or birch bark, smeared with butter or lard. ... When taken out and unwrapped, it looked more like a boiled than a roasted duck, for the skin remained smooth and moist. Scoters cooked in this fashion were invariably tender, juicy and deliciously flavoured, even when old and excessively fat.'—J.C.P.

The *Velvet Scoter* or *White-winged Scoter* (*Melanitta fusca*), which breeds in Northern Europe, and the *Surf Scoter* (*M. perspicillata*), a related American species, which occasionally visits Europe, are no better gastronomically than the *Common* or *Black Scoter*.

SMEW. SMEE

Lat. *Mergus albellus*. A small saw-billed *Duck* breeding in Northern Europe and Asia; wintering further south.

'Feeding as it does almost entirely on fish, the smew is generally regarded as out of the question as an article of food. Pallas dismisses it with the brief characterization "pisculentissima". Finn (1915), however, asserts that one he shot was "quite good eating" and contrary to his expectations. Possibly the young birds in autumn, fresh from interior breeding grounds, may be edible, just as our young Hooded Mergansers are. Even young scoters, under similar conditions, are sometimes "inoffensive".'—J.C.P.

SNIPE (COMMON)

Lat. *Capella gallinago*.

GREAT SNIPE

Lat. *Capella media*.

WILSON'S or AMERICAN SNIPE

Lat. *Capella delicata*.

JACKSNIPE

Lat. *Lymnocryptes minimus*.

PIN-TAILED SNIPE

Lat. *Capella stenura*.

RED-BREASTED SNIPE

See *Dowitcher*.

Lat. *Limnodromus griseus*. The name, when not otherwise qualified, refers to the *Common Snipe*, a larger bird than the *Jacksnipe* or *Half-snipe*, but smaller than the *Great Snipe* or *Solitary Snipe*. The *Common Snipe* (Fr. *Bécass-ine*) is common in the sense that it is widely distributed from Ireland to Japan and from Siberia to the Cape of Good Hope. But it is one of the finest of all game birds, both for the sportsman and the gastronome. Its upper plumage is mottled with black and chestnut-brown, some of the feathers edged with straw-colour; the chin and throat are reddish-white; the lower parts white without spots; the flanks are barred transversely with white and dusky; its tail has 14 feathers. It is normally 11½ in. in length. It lays four eggs per clutch; they are olive in colour, spotted with brown and ash. It breeds in marshes and feeds upon worms and all sorts of creeping forms of life that it finds in mud, which it probes with its long bill, the tip of which is flexible and very sensitive. When disturbed, the *Snipe* rises suddenly, with a curious and most disconcerting twisting flight, and a sharp cry, and then settles down to very fast and quite straight-line flying. In September and October, large numbers of *Snipe* arrive in marshy districts of England, and after a short rest they distribute themselves among other and sometimes much farther suitable feeding grounds so that they are never long together. In the British Isles, *Snipe* are in season from October to February, but at their best in October and November.

In the U.S.A. the Snipe which is called *Wilson's Snipe* or *American Snipe* (*Capella delicata*) is the same as the *Common Snipe* except that it has 16 instead of 14 tail feathers.

In Africa, from Abyssinia to the Cape, the *Ethiopian Snipe* (*Capella nigripennis*) is very abundant and highly esteemed for food. It is just as good as the European Snipe. In India and some parts of Africa there is also the *Painted Snipe* (*Rostratula bengalensis*), which has the appearance of a *Snipe*, but a slow Rail-like flight and is of poor value for eating.

'The snite or snipe is worse than the Wood-cocke, being more unpleasant to the taste, harder of concoction and nourisheth lesse; and is very apt to engender melancholy.' (Hart's *Diet of the diseased*. London. 1633. p. 80.)

In spite of such uncomplimentary remarks, the *Snipe* has been – and still is – very highly prized as a table delicacy. During the period 1519–1639 covered by our accounts of the dinners provided for the Lords of the Star Chamber, *Snipe* were invariably served for their lordships' delectation during the winter months, the price of the birds rising from 2*d*. apiece in 1519, to 20*s*. for 18 in 1639. In 1757, *Snipe* cost a shilling each in London; and their price fluctuated from 2*s*. to 3*s*. 6*d*. in 1807, and from 1*s*. 6*d*. to 2*s*. 6*d*. each in 1922, and again in 1941. In 1942, the maximum retail price of *Snipe* was fixed by the Ministry of Food at 2*s*. per bird.

Snipe Roast

These birds, like the ortolan, plover and woodcock, are dressed without being drawn. They are trussed in the same way as other birds for roasting, but the head is skinned and left on, the long beak of the bird being passed through the legs and body instead of a skewer. Brush them over with warm butter, tie a thin slice of fat bacon over each breast, and place them in a moderately warm oven. Put some toast under them to catch the drip-pings from the trail, baste frequently with butter, and roast them for about 15 minutes, or less if preferred very much underdone. Dish on the toast, garnish with watercress, and serve with good gravy in a sauce-boat.

Allow one bird to every two persons, or if small birds, one to each person.—B. (1).

Snipe Pudding

Six fresh snipe; cayenne; lemon juice; one onion; one tablespoonful flour; chopped mushrooms; parsley; a suspicion of garlic; herbs; nutmeg; truffles; suet paste; half pint wine.

Halve the snipe, removing the gizzards and reserving the trail (*for entrail or intestines.* ED.). Season the snipe with cayenne and lemon juice and set aside till required. Slice up the onion, fry a light brown colour, add the mushrooms, parsley, garlic, nutmeg, and herbs, moisten with wine and boil all for 10 minutes, then add the trail and rub through a sieve. Line a basin with suet paste rolled thin, put in the snipe, the sauce and some truffles; cover the top with paste, steam 1½ hours, and serve hot. (Miss Walder, Horsham.)—F.C.B.

Snipe Soup

This is a *consommé* known in French classical cookery by the name of *Consommé Castellane*. It is made of good meat stock flavoured with a snipe *fumet* and garnished with a *julienne* of snipe fillets and a *royale* made as to one-third of snipe *purée* and two-thirds lentils mashed with the yolks of some hard-boiled eggs.

SNIPE, GREAT

Lat. *Capella media*. The largest form of *Snipe* found in England, mostly in the eastern counties, in the autumn. It is smaller than the *Woodcock* but a little larger than the *Com-*

mon Snipe, as well as very much less common in the British Isles. It breeds in Northern European countries and it is particularly abundant in Sweden. It is known also as *Solitary Snipe* and *Double Snipe*, in opposition to the *Half-Snipe* or *Jack Snipe* (q.v.). Like the *Woodcock*, the *Great Snipe* enjoys a more varied diet than the *Common Snipe*; grubs and larvae found in mud or soft ground are the main dishes of its daily menu, but it enjoys a vegetable *hors-d'oeuvre* of roots and a dessert of seeds. It may be prepared for the table like the *Woodcock* (q.v.).

SNIPE, JACK

Lat. *Lymnocryptes minima*. A smaller bird than the common *Snipe* (q.v.) but otherwise very similar to it in plumage and habits. It is but 8½ in. in length. It does not rise easily and is called in France *Bécassine la Sourde*, although it is probably merely wary and not at all deaf. In England it usually arrives in marshy country in September, but it does not reach France until November, hence its other French name of *Bécassine de la St. Martin*. In England it is sometimes called *Half-Snipe*, in opposition to the *Common Snipe*. It is prepared for the table in any way suitable for the *Snipe* (q.v.) and it is quite equal – some say superior to it from the gastronome's point of view.

SPARROW

Lat. *Passer domesticus*. No one would think to-day of killing any of these cheeky and friendly little birds for food, but they appear to have been eaten in the 'good old days'. In the English Edition of La Varenne's *French Cook* (London. 1654. p. 137), it is said that 'The Tourte of Sparrows is served like that of young pidgeons with a white sauce'. There is also John Webster, in *The White Devil*: 'You shall see in the country, in harvest time, pigeons, though they destroy never so much corn, the farmer dare not present his fowling-piece to them; why? because they belong to the lord of the manor; whilst your poor sparrows, that belong to The Lord of Heaven, they go to the pot for it.'

SPOONBILL

Lat. *Platalea leucorodia*. The name of a variety of *Heron*, sometimes and erroneously given to the *Shoveler*, *Shovelard* or *Popelar*. It nested with *Herons* in various parts of the British Isles, the young being taken from the nests with young *Herons*. The *Spoonbill*, under its former name of *Shoveler* (q.v.) was highly prized for food.

SQUAB

The name given to a *Pigeon* (q.v.) when about five weeks old and not weighing more than 12 or 14 oz.

Squabs en casserole

4 squabs
1 onion
¼ lb. raw, lean bacon
Bunch of herbs
1 tablespoonful chopped parsley
1 bayleaf
Salt and pepper
Small piece lemon rind
1 heaping tablespoonful (1 oz.) flour
1 heaping tablespoonful (1 oz.) butter
1 pint (2 cups) stock
1 wineglass marsala
1 blade mace

Cut each bird into four pieces. Cut the bacon in small pieces and the onion into large dice. Melt the butter in a casserole, put in the bacon, onion, herbs, mace, parsley, and bayleaf, and fry them for five minutes, or till a good brown colour.

Add the stock, and bring it to boiling point. Lay in the pieces of squabs and lemon rind, cover the casserole tightly, and allow its contents to simmer very gently for one hour. Next skim it well, remove the squabs, and strain the stock. Put the squabs back in the casserole. Mix the flour smoothly and thinly with a little cold water, add it to the stock, and strain both over the squabs.

Put in the wine and a good seasoning of salt and pepper. Allow the gravy to boil for five minutes to cook the flour, and serve it in the casserole. The wine may be omitted.
—M.H.N.

STARLING

Lat. *Sturnus vulgaris*. A small bird always met in large colonies, sometimes blessed as the farmer's friend and sometimes cursed as the gardener's foe. According to a letter to *The Times*, one could see, in 1942, on the shelves of one of the greatest London Stores, 'rows of starlings at 9*d*. each'.

One gastronome of our acquaintance has assured us that he had eaten some *Starlings* fresh shot, in Alderney, and had found them excellent.

STINT

A name given to many – almost any – of the small birds of the *Sandpiper* family or appearance, but more particularly to the *Dunlin* (q.v.). *Stints* were quoted on the London Market, in 1807, 3*d*. each, and in 1941, 2*d*. each, when it was not possible to obtain a more precise definition of the birds actually offered for sale than 'any small birds are called *Stints*'.

STORK

Lat. *Ciconia ciconia*. A European wading bird which nests about buildings and returns to its home-quarters every year, like the *Swallow*. Nobody would think of killing a stork for food to-day, and the birds are protected by law in most of the countries which they inhabit, chiefly Alsace, Belgium, Holland and Germany. But it was not always so, and a *Stork* figures in the food served to the Lords of the Star Chamber in 1534, when it cost 5s. 8d.

SWAMP-HEN

Lat. *Porphyrio melanotus*. One of the most widely distributed Rail-like birds of Australasia, abundant in the flax-swamps, lagoons and marshes of Tasmania, the greater part of Australia, New Zealand, the Chatham Islands and New Caledonia. It also frequents the banks of fresh-water streams. Its food is chiefly the inner succulent stems of the 'raupo' or swamp-reed.

'The swamp-hen may fairly be considered one of the best of our native birds. ... Along the sedgy margins of the lagoons and swamps it affords good shooting, although impossible to flush without a retriever; and if hung sufficiently long and properly dressed, it makes an excellent dish. When stewed, the flesh is hardly to be distinguished from that of the Capercailzie.'—W.L.B.

SWAN

Lat. *Cygnus olor*. A fine bird to watch on the water or in flight, but a poor one to eat. The male bird is called the *Cob*, the female the *Pen*, and the young, *Cygnets*. Cygnets used to be served on festive occasions in England.

At the banquet given by the Bishop of Durham for King Richard II, in 1387, fifty swans graced the board. On Christmas Day, 1512, five swans were provided for the Duke of Northumberland's table; on the following New Year's Day, four more, and on Twelfth Day of the same year, another four swans.

In London, cygnets are still eaten once a year, in the ceremonial and traditional manner, at the Vintners' Hall, in the City. The Thames swans are 'Royal' birds and are marked by the Swan Warden of the Vintners' Company, and his acolytes, with two 'nicks' in the shape of a V, on behalf of the sovereign. It is one of the privileges of the Vintners to enjoy a 'feast of cynets' once a year. The birds are brought into the Hall according to ancient usage, heralded by six musicians garbed in the old style of Swan Herds, playing an ancient lilt, 'All in a garden green', on wood-wind instruments: they are followed by six Swan Uppers, in their striped jerseys and white ducks; then by two

Swan Markers, in their blue and red old-time Watermen's coats, and each carrying his quaint Swan Crook. Next come the cooks, bearing on high the great pewter dishes of smoking hot cygnets. The procession advances to below the Salt, and opens outwards to admit of Mr. Swan Warden, in his flowing sable gown, his Stuart cap gaily embellished with a great white swan's feather: he is escorted by the Barge Master, resplendent in blue coat and silver lace and the silver badge of his office (of Barge Master) upon his right upper arm. Also in attendance the Bedel and Stavesman, in flowing gowns and armed with their silver-topped Quarter-Staffs; Mr Swan's silk standard is borne aloft behind him. The music stops; Mr Swan approaches the Salt, doffs his cap with flourish and reverence and proclaims in voice 'that all may hear': 'Master, I crave your acceptance of these roast cygnets for the delectation of your guests.' The Master replies: 'Let them be served, Mr Swan,' whereupon the procession withdraws with music as it came and soon after the cygnets are served according to the ritual which has not altered in any material point since the 'Presentation of Cygnets' was enacted on the same spot, if not actually under the same roof, for the first time, a great many years ago. (*From information supplied by Commander Harold B.Tuffill, Clerk of the Vintners' Company*.)

Roast Swan

Mince finely 3 lb. of rump steak with three shallots, and season liberally with salt, pepper and grated nutmeg. Truss the bird like a goose, stuffing it with the rump steak, etc., sewing it up to prevent the stuffing escaping. The old-fashioned way was to wrap the bird in well-greased or buttered paper, then in a flour and water paste (like venison), and lastly in another sheet of strong paper, and roast for about four hours, keeping it well basted all the time. Now it is only wrapped in one coating of paper, and very liberally basted, of course taking only about half the time to cook. When cooked, remove the coverings and froth it with a little flour and butter, and dish up with brown gravy round it, and port wine sauce. This is a Norwich recipe, which town was famous for swans. Swans are at their best from September to November.—Q. (2).

SWIFT

Lat. *Collocalia esculenta*. This small bird is neither shot nor snared for food, but it deserves the gratitude of gastronomes, particularly Chinese ones, for building the nest from which the *Swallow's Nest* soup is made. It builds its nest in caves in the south of China and in Malaya, and it manages to attach it to the face of the rock. The nests are collected, cleaned and dried for use, and, when wanted, they are soaked in water, when they resolve themselves into a gelatinous mass: this is no other than the glutinous secretion of the bird's salivary glands used to hold the nest together. When boiled, seasoned and properly spiced this soup can be both nourishing and stimulating, but it depends for its taste upon the seasonings used.

Consommé
aux Nids d'Hirondelles

Chicken broth, to which is added the nest built in China by the 'Salanganes' swallows. It must be soaked in cold water for a long time and thoroughly cleaned before use. The substances from which those nests are made contain some peculiar salts which are claimed by the Chinese to be most wholesome as well as of pleasant taste.

TEAL (EUROPEAN)

Lat. *Anas crecca*. One of the smaller wild ducks, which is excellent for the table. In the fen country it is also called *Half-duck*, a name which is given in other parts of England to wild ducks other than the *Mallard*. In France it is called *Sarcelle*, and is one of the waterfowls allowed to be eaten on abstinence days. It is also differentiated as *Sarcelle d'été* and *Sarcelle d'hiver*, the first being the resident bird and the other the visitor. The *Teal* is indigenous to the British Isles and breeds in many parts of Great Britain and Ireland, especially in the eastern counties and in Welsh bogs and Scottish moors with swampy tracts. There are 'summer teals', that is all-the-year-round birds, in England, but they are few compared to the considerable numbers arriving in September or October to spend the winter where food is not frozen or snowed up. They feed on water insects, worms, grubs as well as seeds and decaying vegetable matter. In England, they are in season from October to February, but at their best before Christmas.

On the London Market, the retail price of teal appears to have remained fairly constant: thus, in 1757, it was 1*s*. 6*d*. per bird; in 1807, from 2*s*. to 3*s*. 6*d*.; in 1922, from 1*s*. 9*d*. to 3*s*.; and, in 1941, from 2*s*. to 2*s*. 6*d*. The maximum retail price of teal was fixed at 2*s*. in 1942.

'Teal, for pleasantnesse and wholesomenesse of meat excelleth all other waterfowle.' (Venner's *Via recta ad vitam longam*. London. 1628. p. 62.) The price of teal provided for the Lords of the Star Chamber rose from 2½*d*. per bird in 1519 to 8*d*. in 1605.

'This bird for the delicate taste of its flesh and the wholesome nourishment it affords the body, doth deservedly challenge the first place among those of its kind.' (F. Willughby and J. Ray. *Ornithologiae Libri III*. Fol. London. 1676.)

TEAL (AMERICAN).
GREEN-WINGED TEAL

Lat. *Anas carolinensis*. In the U.S.A., the *Teal* is represented by several species, the most popular, because the most widely distributed, being the *Green-winged Teal* (*A. carolinensis*). The *Cinnamon Teal* (q.v.) is also fairly well known, whilst the *Blue-winged Teal* (*A. discors*) is comparatively little known, although it is by far the best from the gastronome's point of view. Its range is from the Gulf of St. Lawrence to northern South America, throughout the West Indies and Central America.

'In my opinion this species is equal to the Green-wing as a table bird. Perhaps it is a little better, just because it is a little larger. Audubon said that if it should ever be domesticated, so tender and savoury is its flesh ... it would quickly put the merits of the widely celebrated Canvasback Duck in the shade. Elliot (1898) and many others have eulogized the tenderness and good flavour of its flesh.—J.C.P.

In South America, there are a number of different species of Teal, of which four are fairly common and much appreciated as table birds; they are: Andean Teal (*Anas andium*); Puna Teal (*A. puna*), also known as Peruvian Teal, found in the high Andean regions of Peru, Northern Chile and Bolivia; the Ring-necked Teal (*A. leucophrys*), the range of which is the La Plata basin of the Argentine, Brazil, Uruguay and Paraguay; and Argentine Grey Teal (*A. versicolor*), one of the commonest ducks of South America; it is a resident in the southern parts of the Argentine, but some birds migrate as far north as Paraguay and Bolivia. It is also known as *Pampas Duck*.

In South America the Sharp-winged Teal (*A. oxyptera*) and its closely related cousin the Yellow-billed Teal (*A. flavirostris*) both enjoy a high reputation as birds for the table.

In the island of South Georgia, in the South Atlantic, one finds a distinct species of Teal, known as South Georgian Teal or Georgian Duck (*A. georgica*), of which Von der Steinen wrote in 1890: 'Their marine diet renders their flesh strong and oily, but the young birds are excellent eating, especially if skinned first.'

'In India, they (Teal) are so highly esteemed for the table that in the old days some of the epicures used to pen up several hundred teal in the spring in what Hume and Marshall (1879) called "Tealery". The birds were consumed in the hot summer months, when they made a delicious and appetizing meal, and apparently they were more easily kept in condition in these enclosures than other ducks.'—J.C.P.

In the Hawaiian Islands there is a distinct species of teal known as the *Laysan Teal* (*Anas laysanensis*).

See also *Whistling Teal* and *Cape Teal*.

Teal à la Bigarade

One of the most convenient ways of preparing teal is *à la bigarade*. Take four tender young teal, clean them thoroughly, singe lightly so as to burn only the down, and wash them with care.

Skin the four livers with the back of a knife and make from them a little stuffing, mingling with it a large piece of butter, salt, pepper, a little spice and some chopped lemon-peel. Stuff your teal with this mixture, so that their bodies are well-rounded. Truss them, and tie them neatly, so that they have an appetizing appearance.

Now is the time to impale them all on one skewer, and let them impersonate the brothers Aymon, fully armed. Their breasts will be covered with a slice of lemon, and on top of that is placed a rasher of bacon. Lastly comes a mantle of well-buttered paper to cover this succulent armour. Beside them lay their shields of golden toast. Be careful to tie the teal together at each end, so that the gravy may not escape.

After all these preparations, attach the skewer to the spit, and leave the birds in front of the fire for half an hour only: this is long enough for them to cook perfectly.—A.La.

Roast Teal

With some teal, take butter for basting, good brown gravy, bigarade sauce, watercress, lemons.

Pluck, draw and truss the teal for roasting. Brush them over with hot butter, and roast in a moderate oven from 25 to 30 minutes, basting frequently. Serve on a hot dish, garnish with watercress and quarters of lemon and send the sauce to table in a sauceboat.

Allow one small bird or half a large one to each person.—B. (1).

Teal in Wyvern's Way

Three teal will be enough for this dish. As soon as the birds are delivered plucked, but not trussed, in the morning, clean them, saving their giblets. Lay them on a board, and by passing a knife all round the ribs of each bird remove the whole of the breasts with the breast bones left in them. Put these three breasts on a dish, pour over them a marinade consisting of two tablespoonfuls

of salad oil, teaspoonful of good vinegar, ½ oz. of minced shallot, a teaspoonful of dried herbs, and the peel and juice of a Seville orange. Turn and baste them with this during the day. With the *débris* of the teal – back, legs, wing bones, and giblets well chopped up – proceed to make a strong broth by simmering them (covered with broth) very slowly, assisted by 3 oz. of each onion and carrot, a *bouquet*, a bunch of parsley and seasoning for about 1½ hours. Strain – there should be three-quarts of a pint of this – skim off any fat, add ½ oz. of glaze, a claret-glass of burgundy or claret, the juice of one lemon, and the juice of one orange; let this just reach boiling point, and then set it in the *bain-marie*.

When required, take the breasts from the marinade, wipe them carefully, then brush them over with butter and grill them. Divide each breast in half by a clean cut along the centre, lay the six pieces on six *croûtes* of fried bread, the sauce and Nepaul pepper with a salad of orange quarters accompanying.—A.K.-H. (1).

TEAL, AUSTRALIAN or CHESTNUT-BREASTED

Lat. *Anas castanea*. One of the small duck of Australia where it is commonly called *Chestnut Teal*. Savidge (in North 1913) says that the flesh of this bird is 'tender and excellent eating'.

TEAL, BRAZILIAN

Lat. *Anas brasiliensis*. A small duck which is found in some parts of Brazil in Bolivia and in Paraguay. Wied (1832) and R.G.Harris (in litt.) have described the flesh of this duck as 'very good'.

TEAL, CAPE or CAPE WIDGEON

Lat. *Anas capensis*. A small duck widely distributed from Ethiopia to Bechuanaland, but nowhere very common. Lieutenant H.A.P. Littledale (*Journal of the South African Ornithological Union*, April, 1908) says that the '*Cape-Teal* is good eating, but not to be compared with the *Redbill*'.

A closely allied species but a smaller bird is known as the *Hottentot Teal* (*Anas punctata*). It occurs from Uganda and Shoa to the Cape Province, and is uncommon, although not so rare as many believe, as it is often overlooked owing to its small size.

TEAL, CINNAMON

Lat. *Anas cyanoptera*. A small wild duck, closely related to the *Garganey* (q.v.): it is confined to the Western U.S.A., Mexico and also Peru. It is distinguished by the deep chestnut head and underparts of the male. It may be prepared for the table in any way suitable for *Teal* (q.v.) or *Wild Duck* (q.v.).

'In California the flesh of this Teal is considered as inferior to that of other Teal. Its 'keeping' qualities are said to be poor (Grinnell, Bryant and Storer, 1918). This is partly because it takes much animal matter, and because it is, or rather was, before the law prevented it, shot in warm September weather.'—J.C.P.

It is also known by other names, such as *Red Teal*, *Red-breasted Teal*, *Blue-winged Teal* and *Raffles Teal*.

TEAL, COTTON

Lat. *Cheniscus coromandelianus*. One of the smallest of the wild duck of India, and extending to South China Java, Borneo and Eastern Australia. It is also called *Indian* or *Green Pygmy Goose*, *Goose Teal*, *Quacky Duck*, *Rice Teal*, etc. No European eats it now.

'Very few travellers have waxed enthusiastic over the flesh of the Goose Teal as an article of food, though both Blasius (1884) and Legge (1880), speaking of Borneo and Ceylon respectively, note that it is very good eating. Finn (1915) considers it no better than a common house-pigeon. ... Robinson and Laverock (1908) considered these birds "a welcome addition to their larder" whilst travelling in Northern Queensland; and Rogers (Mathews 1914-15)says he shot many for food on Melville Island.'—J.C.P.

TEAL, FALCATED

Lat. *Anas falcata*. A small migratory Eastern Duck which is found from Japan to India and from Siberia to Persia. The bird has occasionally strayed to Hungary and Sweden. It is also called *Crested Teal* and *Bronze-capped Teal*. According to Walton (1903), the flesh of this bird is excellent for the table.

TEAL, FORMOSAN

Lat. *Anas formosa*. A Teal restricted to Northern Asia, Siberia, China and Japan. It is also known as *Japanese Teal*, *Baikal Teal*, *Clucking Teal* and *Spectacled Teal*: H.A.Walton (1903) says that this Teal is good eating.

TEAL, GREY

Lat. *Anas gibberifrons*. One of the best – even if rather small – wild duck of Australia, New Zealand and the Dutch Indies. It is highly prized by gastronomes and it fetches good prices in the markets of Melbourne and Sydney, either under its name of *Grey Teal* or other local names, such as *Mountain Teal*, *Slender Teal* or *Wood Teal*.

TEAL, WHISTLING or LESSER WHISTLING TEAL

Lat. *Dendrocygna javanica*. A small tree-duck found in India, Burma, Siam, Malaya, Indo-China, China and Africa.

'Some of the earlier travellers to the East spoke of this bird as a welcome addition to the larder, but the residents of India are almost unanimous in denouncing it. Baker (1908) states that young birds at the beginning of the cold weather are more likely to furnish an edible dish. The flesh has been described as having a "peculiar, faint, half-muddy and half-fishy" taste that makes it unpalatable.' (Hume and Marshall, 1879).—J.C.P.

TEREK

Lat. *Terekia cinerea*. A Sandpiper breeding in the far north of Eastern Europe and of Asia, migrating to South Africa and Australia.

TERN

Lat. *Sterna hirundo*. The common *Tern* of both coasts of the North Atlantic. It is not shot for food, but its eggs are valued as substitutes for *Plover's Eggs* (q.v.).

THRUSH

Song-Thrush (Lat. *Turdus ericetorum*)
Mistle-Thrush (Lat. *Turdus viscivorus*)
The name of a number of small song birds very widely distributed in all temperate parts of the world; in the British Isles, the *Song-Thrush* and the *Missel-Thrush* or *Mistle-Thrush*, a larger bird and not so good a singer, are the more common species. They feed on insects and grubs, seeds and chiefly berries, when there is no ripe fruit in season, but their love of all the fruits which man loves best has brought large numbers of them to an untimely and brutal death. The wise gardener, however, finds means of protecting his fruit without shooting or trapping *Thrushes*, as they are of the utmost usefulness in the lifelong war which all gardeners have to wage against insects and their grubs. No true gastronome would countenance the killing of a thrush for food, even if ready to admit that it was quite as good as a lark on occasions when a thrush found its way by accident into the classical steak-kidney-oyster-and-lark pie. On the Continent, thrushes are killed and eaten without any qualms of conscience, like many other small songsters, but it is rather unexpected to find a recipe given by gentle Mrs Beeton for roasting one.

Thrush roast

After trussing the bird, cover each breast with well-buttered paper, instead of bacon, which would impair the delicate flavour of the bird; place them side by side on a skewer, baste well with hot butter and roast before a clear fire for about 10 minutes, basting almost continuously with butter. Serve on *croûtes*, garnish with watercress, and send the gravy to table separately. Allow two birds to each person.—B. (1).

TINAMOU

Lat. *Rhynchotus rufescens*. The name of some South American partridge-like birds found in the open pampas from Mexico southwards. There are 50 different kinds, of which the commonest is the *Rufous Tinamou*, ranging from Brazil to the Argentine, where it is called *Perdriz grande*. It is not a partridge, but is quite as great a table delicacy.

'It (the *Rufous Tinamou*) has been introduced into England and stands our English climate well; but as a game bird it cannot be called a success, being of solitary habits and difficult to flush. Once on the wing its flight is very fast and extraordinarily noisy.—B.HO.

The *Tinamou* has been sent to England from South America in cold storage, but we have not found any record of its reception in this country.

TRAGOPAN

Lat. *Tragopan satyra*. The *Crimson* or *Sikkim Horned Pheasant*, the commonest of the *Horned Pheasants*. They are very handsome birds and are shot for their fine feathers more than for their food value, but they take good care of themselves and hide on the higher forest-clad ranges of the Himalayas and in China.

TRUMPETER

Lat. *Psophia crepitans*. This is the *Grey-winged Trumpeter*, which occurs from Eastern Venezuela to the Upper Amazon and adjoining countries. Other species of this bird are found in different parts of Brazil and northern South America. They owe their name to their peculiarly unpleasant and loud screeching. They are easily domesticated and highly valued for food, when young. In Brazil, it is not uncommon to find an old *Trumpeter* in the family barnyard, where it is kept to protect poultry; it is expected to raise the alarm by its screeching and to scare intruders.

There is a species of *Trumpeter* found in Surinam and Para which is called *Agami*, in French. There is a classical *Agami* dish: it is known as *Agami a la Chilienne*; the bird is braised like a *Duck* (see *Braised Duck*) and it is served with boiled rice and fried pimentoes.

TURKEY

Lat. *Meleagris gallopavo*. The usual 'short' or abbreviated form for *Turkey-cock* (Fr. *Dindon*), *Turkey-hen* (Fr. *Dinde*) or *Turkey-poult*

(Fr. *Dindonneau*), a large and excellent American game bird, domesticated for nearly four hundred years, and one of the most valuable domestic fowls.

The name was first of all given, in England, to the Guinea-fowl, which was originally introduced from West Africa before any of the birds now called *Turkeys* had been seen in Europe, and they were quite erroneously given the name already given to the Guinea-fowl, a name which has stuck to them ever since.

The first to be introduced into Europe was the Mexican Turkey; it had been domesticated in Mexico before the advent of the Spaniards, who brought specimens to Spain in 1530, some of which reached England round about the year 1540, before any specimens of the North American Turkey, and English colonists, soon after, introduced the *Mexican Turkey* to New England. In England, farmers breed chiefly the *Black Norfolks* and the *Cambridge Bronze*, the latter being the larger as well as nearer the original Mexican breed than the first, which was preferred by those who place flavour before size. In the U.S.A. the *Bronze Turkey* is the largest and most popular: the average standard weight of the adult cock is 36 lb. The *White Holland Turkey*, which is known in Europe as the *White Austrian*, comes next in popular favour: its average weight is 28 lb. for an adult cock. It is a pure white bird, whereas the plumage of the *Bronze* is distinguished by a rich, brilliant, bronze sheen, with white barring of the wings and edging of tail feathers. Another popular Turkey, in the U.S.A., is known as the *Bourbon Red*; the general colour of its plumage is a rich brownish red, with the primary and secondary feathers of the wing and the main tail feathers pure white. Its standard weight is 30 lb. for an adult cock. In England the tendency is to breed rather smaller birds. Turkeys have been domesticated so long that there are many sub-species, some better than others, but not even the best of them is likely to compare in flavour with the wild Turkey, which still inhabits the high tablelands of Northern Mexico and neighbouring States, up to an altitude of some 10,000 ft. above sea-level. During the eighteenth century several attempts were made to introduce some wild North American Turkeys into England, chiefly in Windsor Great Park and other royal forests. According to Jesse's *Country Life*, 'in the reigns of George I and George II, Richmond Park could boast a flock of two thousand wild turkeys. ... Turkeys are kept wild at Holkham Hall, Norfolk, by the Earl of Leicester, to whom they afford the same sport as any other bird in cover.'—H.W.B.

The *Turkey* provides the exception to the rule that it takes a long time to break down the prejudice of English people against anything new in the matter of food or drink. The *Turkey* was enthusiastically hailed and made welcome as soon as it appeared on the tables of the well-to-do people in England, and it displaced in a very short space of time the peacock, curlew, bittern, whimbrel and other fowls of the air and the sea, which figured on most bills of fare up to the beginning of the seventeenth century. One must bear in mind, however, that the name *Turkey* was first of all given to the Guinea-fowl, so that when we read in the First Part of *King Henry IV* (Act II, sc. 1, v. 19):

'Odsbody the turkeys in my pannier are quite starved'

one forgives Shakespeare for introducing a name that would have been quite unknown in the days of Henry IV, but one must not forget that he was referring to birds which we know as Guinea-fowls, two or more of which could be cooped in a pannier.

Even later, in the 1633 edition of Dr Hart's *Diet of the diseased* (p. 78), when we read:

'Turkies of a middle age and reasonably fat, are a good, wholesome, nourishing food, and little inferior to the best capon', it is obvious that the reference was to *Guinea-fowls*.

By the time of Queen Anne's reign, a turkey was a turkey as we know it, and people had probably already forgotten that the name had ever been that of the *Guinea-fowl*: it was already then the bird that was expected to grace every board on Christmas Day:

Sometimes with oysters we combine,
Sometimes assist the sav'ry chine,
From the low peasant to the lord
The turkey smokes on every board.

(*John Gay*).

Poultry breeders recognize two quite distinct breeds of domestic turkey in this country – the black-plumed Norfolk breed, and the more variegated Cambridge breed – and it is believed that the former is descended from the North American bird, and the latter from the more southern form ... The Turkey is ready for the table in about nine months, when a large cock may weigh as much as 20 lb. In the olden days, when big flocks were 'walked' into London – a journey often taking a week or more – the birds were protected from 'cold feet' by being shod, their feet being tied up in sacking and provided with leather boots. Geese do not allow themselves to be shod, and the feet of these birds, when similarly driven, were protected by a coat of tar covered with grit. As a result the phrase to 'shoe a goose'

was once a cant simile for attempting a hopeless task.—E.G.B.

The turkey cock is larger than the hen and less economical, as its bones are heavier; as a rule the hen is also more tender than the cock. A large turkey cock with sharp spurs is best stuffed by a taxidermist: it is an old bird to be avoided by all cooks. The best turkey is a hen from seven to nine months old which has been reared in semi-liberty, and given plenty of food, but made to scratch for at least some of it. Its legs should be black, the neck short, the breast broad and plump, and the flesh snow-white.

TURKEY.
DINDE. DINDONNEAU
Yorkshire boiled Turkey
Braised Turkey
Dinde en daube Provençale
Turkey Hash
Roast Turkey (English style)
Roast Turkey (American style)
Roast Turkey (French style)
Dindonneau roulé
Turkey Giblets Bourgeoise
Dinde Truffée

Turkey Left-overs
Creamed Turkey with Olives
Casserole of Turkey and Peas
Turkey Tetrazzini
Turkey Rissoles
Kromeskis of Turkey

Yorkshire boiled Turkey
After removing the legs, the bird is boned, but the wings are left on. It is then stuffed with veal forcemeat and a trimmed boiled tongue is thrust down the middle of the forcemeat. The bird is then sewn up, trussed as for boiling, with the feet thrust in their original position; the whole is wrapped in a buttered cloth and boiled very gently until done. It is served with a *Béchamel* sauce and a *jardinière* of vegetables, care being taken to carve it across, and not lengthwise, so that turkey, forcemeat, and tongue all appear in the same slice. This dish, served cold, makes an admirable luncheon or supper course.—AMBROSE HEATH in *Wine and Food*, No. 16, p. 59.

Braised Turkey
Take a plump turkey, cut off the claws, and tie the legs. When it has been thoroughly cleaned and singed, truss it and prick with thick pieces of bacon which have been seasoned with salt, pepper, *quatre épices* and herbs.

Next cover the bottom of your stewpan with rashers of bacon, lay the turkey on them, together with the claws, a knuckle of veal, a calf's foot, five onions – one pricked with three cloves – three or four carrots, two bayleaves, some thyme and a bunch of parsley and chives. Cover the turkey with rashers similar to the ones beneath it, baste with four spoonfuls of good stock, and cover the whole with buttered paper. Allow to simmer for 5½ hours, and then remove your stewpan from the fire, leaving the turkey in it for another half an hour. Strain the gravy through a fine cloth, put it back on the fire, and let it reduce to one-quarter the amount. Break an egg into a saucepan, beat it up well and add the gravy. Beat it up thoroughly together, taste the mixture, and put it on the fire. As soon as it starts to boil, stand it on the side of the stove, under a lid on which embers have been placed, and leave it for a good half an hour. Then strain it once more through a fine cloth, and pour it over the turkey.—A.LA.

Dinde en daube Provençale

Chop or grind in a mincing machine 8 oz. pork and 4 oz. veal, saving as much again of veal cut into long fillets. Allow these to marinate for an hour in a little good brandy. Add salt and pepper to the chopped meat and use it to stuff a boned turkey, together with the fillets of marinated veal, which should be inserted longways in the turkey. Wrap the bird in a cloth and tie up at both ends securely. Cut some carrots and onions into slices and set them in the bottom of heavy iron or copper stewpan. On them put a few pieces of rind of fresh pork, a cleaned and cut-up calf's foot, a *bouquet-garni* and the turkey's giblets. Set on a moderate heat until bottom layer of vegetables begins to colour, then add a cup of white wine, and sufficient *bouillon*, stock, or hot water just to cover the turkey. Bring to boiling point, skim well close with a weight on the lid and cook gently for a couple of hours. Serve hot if wished or if to be eaten cold press turkey under a board and weight after removing cloth. The gravy strained may be reduced by further boiling and used to coat the cold turkey.—P.W.

Roast Turkey
(English style)
1 medium-sized turkey
1 lb. veal forcemeat
Hot fat for basting (dripping)
1½ lb. sausage-meat
2 or 3 slices bacon
Salt and pepper

To make the veal forcemeat
8 oz. lean veal
2 oz. fat bacon
Chopped parsley
Pinch mace
2 eggs

¼ lb. beef suet
2 tablespoons breadcrumbs
Half a chopped onion
Pinch nutmeg
Salt and pepper

Mince veal very finely, pound in a mortar with the suet, previously finely chopped, and the bacon, also chopped finely. Pass through a sieve, add other ingredients. Season rather highly.

Prepare the bird, fill crop with sausage-meat and the veal forcemeat. Sew up neatly and firmly. Skewer the slices of bacon over the breast, cover with hot dripping, fat or butter, sprinkle with salt and pepper and bake from two to three hours in a moderately hot oven, basting frequently and removing slices of bacon about 20 minutes before serving, to brown breast. Remove trussing strings.

Serve with gravy, made in the usual way, and good bread sauce. Take care when turning bird to brown under-side not to prick the skin, and be sure to allow 20 to 25 minutes per pound for roasting, according to age of bird. Should the breast brown too quickly, cover with buttered paper to prevent burning if strips of bacon are not used.
—P.W.

Roast Turkey
(American style)

Dress, clean and stuff bird, then truss. Rub entire surface over with salt and spread breast, legs and wings with softened butter into which a little flour has been rubbed. Dredge bottom of baking tin lightly with flour. Place in a hot oven and, when flour begins to colour, reduce heat. Baste very frequently, using for this purpose more butter melted in a little boiling water at first, then use dripping in tin. Add a little more water during cooking if necessary and turn bird to brown all sides evenly. Garnish when serving with celery tips and allow eight cups of stuffing for a 10 lb. turkey. Use New England sausage and chestnut, giblet or plain chestnut stuffing. Cranberry sauce or jelly is always handed with turkey in the States.—P.W.

Roast Turkey
(French style)

For stuffing:
The turkey's liver
7 oz. chopped bacon
Truffles
Salt and pepper
8 oz. fat fresh pork
8 oz. boiled chestnuts
Foie gras (optional)
Butter

Prepare bird for roasting and use the above, chopped and well blended, to stuff interior. Some of the truffles, thinly sliced, may be inserted between skin and flesh the day before cooking and a few more may advantageously be simmered awhile in a little white port wine, the latter being set aside to blend with gravy when made. Serve with a garnish of fried apple rings or tart thick apple sauce. The quantity of *foie gras* used depends on your wishes – and means – and it may, of course, be omitted entirely. —P.W.

Dindonneau Roulé

1 small turkey
Salt and pepper
Thin slices fresh pork fat (bardes)
1 cup good *bouillon*
1 clove garlic
Pinch dried thyme
1 small bayleaf
Chopped veal and pork
Pinch poultry dressing
1 glass white wine
Few stalks parsley
2 whole cloves
Small pinch basil
2 large onions
1 small parsnip
2 tablespoons good meat glaze

Cut the turkey in halves, longways, after cleaning and singeing. Mince finely together about ½ lb. each of pork and veal. Season well. Remove all bones from each half of turkey. Spread the chopped meat over each piece, on the inside of course, and roll each one up neatly, tying with fine string. Tie or skewer a thin slice of fresh pork fat around each half. Place both in an iron *cocotte*, add the wine, *bouillon* and all other ingredients. Cover closely and cook gently until the turkey is tender. Remove and serve with strained gravy, to which meat glaze has been added.

Turkey Giblets Bourgeoise

1 set turkey giblets
1 *bouquet-garni*
2 cloves
Salt and pepper
2 tablespoons flour
2 tablespoons butter
1 clove garlic
1 pinch or small sprig basil
3 or 4 fresh mushrooms
2 cups good *bouillon*
Young white turnips

Clean thoroughly wing tips, feet, neck, liver and gizzard of a turkey. Brown all this in the heated butter and sprinkle with the flour. Moisten with the *bouillon*, season with salt and freshly-ground pepper and add the cut-up mushrooms and other ingredients.

Cover and cook until all is tender. Brown some small young turnips in butter and add to giblet stew when half-cooked. Remove any excess fat and serve with 'short' sauce. —P.W.

Dinde Truffée

Have a well-fattened young turkey ready for roasting. Take 8 or 10 truffles, peel them and cut them in quarters; boil the skins for two minutes in a glassful of sherry, chop them finely and mix them with about 1½ lb. of pork sausage-meat and two chopped chicken livers; season well and stuff the birds with the mixture, to which you add the pieces of truffles. Cut two of the truffles in thin slices which you insert between the skin and the flesh of the bird. Roast in the ordinary way, basting often. Remove the fat before serving the gravy.

The turkey should be well seasoned inside before inserting the stuffing, and the stuffing should be put in at least the day before you roast the bird, so that the flesh is well flavoured. Serve, if you like, chip potatoes and a plain salad of watercress.—X.M.B. (1).

LEFT-OVER TURKEY

Turkey Hash

Melt 1½ tablespoons of butter. Add one tablespoon flour, blend well and add three cups of cream which has been heated; add five cups cold turkey cut into pieces not too small. Add 1 lb. of peeled mushrooms cut in pieces and browned in butter.

Let cook until well heated through. Season with salt and pepper to taste and add four tablespoons of finely-chopped pimento 10 minutes before serving.

Serve in moulded rice ring and around edge of dish garnish with baked peaches. Or serve with a dropped egg on top of each serving.—A.W.C.

Creamed Turkey with Olives

2 tablespoons butter
Chopped parsley
Some large green olives
1 cup or more cold turkey
2 tablespoons flour
1 cup milk
Salt and pepper
Cooked rice or hot toast

Melt the butter, add the flour, blend well and moisten with the milk or, better still, thin cream. Season and allow to simmer gently until sauce is smooth and creamy, beating frequently. Add the cut-up or diced cold turkey, freed from skin, and cook gently until it is hot through, then add the parsley and the stoned olives, cut into strips. Cook a few minutes longer, then serve in a border of boiled rice or, for a light meal, on hot buttered toast. The sauce will be all the better for the addition of an egg yolk, beaten in off the fire, and, if wished, a few sliced and *sauté* mushrooms may be added.—P.W.

Casserole of Turkey and Peas
(Canadian)

Breadcrumbs
2 tablespoons butter
1 cup turkey broth
1 cup cold boiled green peas
2 tablespoons flour
Salt and pepper
Dash tomato sauce or catsup

Melt the butter, add the flour, stirring well, then moisten with the broth, which is made by stewing the carcass or bones well, with coarse vegetables, then straining and reducing by gentle cooking. Add the catsup, season to taste. Cut the cold turkey into slices or pieces and place them in a buttered baking dish, alternating with a layer of the green peas. Pour the hot sauce over all, sprinkle with breadcrumbs, dot with butter and bake until surface is brown.—P.W.

Turkey Tettrazzini
(American)

1 cup rich white sauce
½ cup boiled spaghetti
Butter
Salt and pepper
1 cup cold cut-up turkey
¼ cup *sauté* fresh mushrooms
¼ cup grated Parmesan cheese
¾ cup buttered breadcrumbs

The sauce should be very bland and smooth, thin cream being used if available and the yolk of an egg will still further improve it, though it is not essential. Boil the spaghetti, after breaking it into ½ in. pieces. *Sauté* the mushrooms in butter, after slicing. Cut turkey into thin strips, if possible; if not, into odd small pieces. Add the turkey, spaghetti and mushrooms, with their cooking butter, salt and pepper to sauce, blending well. Butter a ramekin dish, sprinkle interior with grated Parmesan cheese mixed with fine brown buttered breadcrumbs, fill with turkey mixture and place the ramekin in a dish or tin half full of hot water. Set in a moderately hot oven and bake until crumbs are brown. Turn out, if wished, and serve with hot tomato sauce.—P.W.

Turkey Rissoles

½ lb. minced cooked turkey
¼ lb. breadcrumbs
1 yolk of egg
Pepper, salt and white sauce to bind
¼ lb. mashed potatoes
Half a finely-chopped onion

Mix the dry ingredients together with seasoning and onion, then add the white sauce and stir well into the mixture. Make into round shapes, brush over with yolk of egg and dip in breadcrumbs. Drop the rissoles into hot boiling fat and fry both sides until golden brown. Drain on greaseproof paper before serving.

For the white sauce, melt 1 oz. margarine in a saucepan, add 1 oz. flour, a pinch of salt, and half cup of milk and water. Cook for wo minutes, stirring all the time.

Kromeskis of Turkey

Cut up meat of cold turkey into very small pieces and mix them with some equally small pieces of ham or tongue, a little minced onion and a few chopped mushrooms tossed in butter, and a little *Béchamel* sauce, so that they are well bound together. Mix in the yolk of an egg and let the mixture cool. When it is cold, shape it into little rolls and wrap each in a very thin rasher of streaky bacon. Dip them in fritter butter and fry them golden, serving them with whatever sauce you fancy.

TURKEY, BRUSH
Lat. *Alectura lathami*. Not a *Turkey*, but a mound-building bird of the *Megapode* family, found in the more thickly wooded parts of Eastern Australia. It may be prepared for the table in any way suitable for a *Turkey* (q.v.).

TURNSTONE
Lat. *Arenaria interpres*. A widely distributed, small shore-bird, no bigger than a thrush, about 9 in., which visits every year the shores of the British Isles, arriving at the beginning of August. It owes its name to its habit of turning over oyster shells or clumps of mud with its bill, and eating whatever it finds sheltering under the removed obstacle.

VELDT PAAUW
Lat. *Otis cafra*. One of the fairly common species of African *Bustards* (q.v.). It is also known as the Stanley Bustard.

'The birds I shot in South Africa were particularly good-eating, but the same species in British East Africa was coarse and tough, with a slight, but unpleasant flavour.' —B.HO.

WHEATEAR. FALLOWCHAT. WHITEEAR
Lat. *Oenanthe oenanthe*. A very widely distributed little migrant, breeding as far north as Greenland and wintering as far south as the Equator and southern India. They are among the earliest visitors to the British Isles, arriving on the Sussex Downs in

March, occasionally even as early as the latter part of February. They used to be trapped, chiefly on the Downs, in Kent and Sussex, and eaten like *Quails* (q.v.).

Potted Wheatears

They are a Tunbridge Bird; pick them very clean; season them with pepper and salt, put them in a pot, cover them with butter and bake them an hour; take them and put them in a cullender to drain the liquor away; then cover over with clarified butter and they will keep. (The *Compleat City and Country Cook*, 1732.)—M.K.S.

To roast Larks and Wheatears

When well cleaned, dip them in yolk of eggs, and roll them in breadcrumbs. Put a small bit of butter in these birds. Spit on a large spit, and fasten them to the spit. Baste with plenty of good butter, which is most essential in roasting all the small birds. Strew sufficient breadcrumbs on the birds as they roast. From 12 to 15 minutes will do them. Serve fried breadcrumbs, and garnish with fried crumbs or crisp parsley.

Obs.—Some good cooks put a thin small slice of bacon between the birds when they are spitted to nourish them. This is good practice.—C.I.

They feed on small flies, and are about the size of a lark, but far excel it in fatness and delicacy of flesh; we may rightly call them the English Ortolan, as they much resemble these birds in taste; and are so fat that they almost dissolve in the mouth like jelly, being so delicate. I shall not name the epicure who, being seriously asked his judgment concerning the abilities of a great lord, concluded him a man of very weak parts, because once he saw him at a great feast feed on chickens, when there were Wheatears at table. They are not in season till the middle of the summer, when, by reason of the heat and their fatness, they are so apt to corrupt that the London poulterers do not dare meddle with them, all the care that can be taken not being sufficient to keep them from putrefaction, which is a great disadvantage to the sale of them as well as a disappointment to dainty palates ...

It has been put on record that the victims (Wheatears) fetched from eighteenpence to three shillings a dozen, and that the shepherds, and their name was legion, reckoned to make any sums from four and five to thirty or forty and even fifty pounds apiece annually. These stalwarts, we are told, or at least part of them, were entertained once yearly by a firm of poulterers at Brighton, to which they had supplied the spoils, and after the jollification each man received his pay according to his prowess. After about 1880,

however, these dinners came to an end. Commerce in the bird had become dulled, not so much because the species had decreased, as because, it is said, the farmers objected to their underlings neglecting their daily routine for the less laborious pastime of waylaying wheatears. Still, even up to 1902, wheatears were sent in fairly large numbers to certain hotels at Brighton, and perhaps Eastbourne as well.—J.W.B.

WHIMBREL

Lat. *Numenius phaeopus*. A small *Curlew* which is also known as *May-Bird*, *Little Whaup* (Orkneys), and *Jack Curlew*. It breeds in the northern regions of Europe and Asia and migrates sometimes as far south as the Cape. It is no longer considered fit to eat, but there was a time when its cost was higher than that of a *Capon*: thus, in 1590, one *Brewe* served to the Lords of the Star Chamber cost the same as two capons.

WIDGEON. WIGEON

Lat. *Mareca penelope*. *Wigeon* was the name of the male bird, in Old English, and *Whewer* the name of the female, but *Widgeon* is now used for both duck and drake: Latham says that the young males used to be sold in London under the name of *Easterlings* and the females under that of *Lady fowl*; in Northumberland, they use the name *Whew* for both. In culinary French the bird is usually (and quite wrongly) called *Sarcelle*: its real French name is *Canard garrot* or *Canard siffleur*. It is a wild duck, a little larger than the teal but smaller than the mallard. It breeds in the British Isles, Sweden, Russia, Siberia and North America, migrating as far south as California and India. The widgeon is one of the clean-feeding wild duck and one of the most shy. It usually keeps away from the sea and salt waters, feeding for choice upon the short, sweet grass which geese also love. Hence its name *Grass Duck*, in Lapland. In the U.S.A., a closely related species (*Anas americana*) is also called *Baldpate* (q.v.). There is also a related South American species (*Anas sibilatrix*). In the British Isles, the widgeon is in season from August 1st to March 15th, but it is at its best in October and November only. Widgeons may be prepared for the table in any way suitable for *Teal* (q.v.) or *Wild Duck* (q.v.).

On the London Market, the price of *Widgeon* has never varied very much: it was 1s. 6d. per bird in 1757; it fluctuated from 2s. to 3s. in 1807; from 2s. 6d. to 3s. 6d. in 1922; from 3s. to 4s. 6d. in 1941, and it was fixed at 3s. 6d. (maximum retail price) in 1942, for birds 'in feather', no game bird being allowed to be sold otherwise than in the feather.

In India, they are considered as inferior to many other species (Hume and Marshall, 1879; Baker, 1908). On the Chinese coasts also there seems to be great variation in the quality of the flesh. According to La Touche, the Foochow Widgeon are very good, whilst those from Swatow are very bad. I see no reason why Widgeon feeding on *Zostera* alone are not just as good as our most delicious North American Brant from the East Coast.—J.C.P.

In the Argentine and Chile, the *Chiloe Widgeon* (*Anas sibilatrix*) is highly valued as an article of food.

Widgeon Roast

Procure some widgeon and take butter for basting, watercress and lemons.

Truss the birds for roasting. Baste well with hot butter, and roast for about 20 minutes in a moderately hot oven or longer, according to the size and age of the birds. Keep them well basted with hot butter, and shortly before serving sprinkle lightly with flour, to give the birds a nice appearance. Meanwhile, make a brown sauce, add to it port wine, orange and lemon juices, a pinch of sugar, salt and pepper to taste, simmer for 15 minutes, then strain, skim and serve with the birds on a hot dish, garnished with watercress and quarters of lemon, and hand the sauce separately.—B. (1).

WOODCOCK

Lat. *Scolopax rusticola*. A greatly-prized bird which is widely distributed from the British Isles to Japan and Java. In the U.S.A. there is a somewhat smaller bird, the *American Woodcock* (*Philohela minor*).

Woodcocks were provided on many 'meat' days to the Lords of the Star Chamber and at a cost which rose from 1*s.* per bird in 1534, 1535, 1567 and 1590, to 1*s.* 6*d.* and 2*s.* each in 1605. The price of *Woodcock* in the London Market was 2*s.* 6*d.* in 1757; from 3*s.* 6*d.* to 7*s.* 6*d.* in 1807; from 4*s.* 6*d.* to 6*s.* in 1922; from 3*s.* to 6*s.* in 1941; and its maximum retail price was fixed at 4*s.* in 1942.

'They (Woodcocks) come into England at the fall of the leafe, and depart again at the spring, but whence they come and whether they goe, it would trouble a good doctor to define. When the Woodcock goeth, the Swallow cometh.' (Cogan's *Haven of Health*, London. 1612. p. 133.)

'... four woodcocks in a dish'
    Love's Labour's Lost, (Act IV, Sc. 3).

The woodcock is not a marshland bird like its small cousin, the *Snipe*, and its diet is a mixed one of heather shoots, worms, insects and all forms of life hiding in mud, moss or foliage. As a result of its omnivorous habits, the woodcock carries much meat in proportion to its size, a 12 oz. bird being fully sufficient for one person of normal appetite.

In the British Isles woodcocks are in season from August 1st to March 15th, and at their best in October and November.

Both in France and in England the *Woodcock* has long enjoyed a high reputation for gastronomic excellence, whilst its name has been used when referring to brainless people. It is in that sense that Claudio uses it when he asks:

  'Shall I not find a woodcock too?'
    Much Ado About Nothing,
                    (Act V, Sc. 1).

Also, in Beaumont and Fletcher's *Loyal Subject* (Act IV, Sc. 4):

  'Go, like the woodcock,
  And thrust your head into the noose.'

But in Ben Jonson's *Every Man out of his Humour* (Act II, Sc. 3), when Savolina says: 'I love not the breath of a woodcock's head', she is not referring to any *fumet* but to the *fumée*, the tobacco smoke from a pipe which was known as a 'woodcock's head' owing to its supposed resemblance to the bird's head and beak.

In French, a *bécasse* is still commonly used in the vernacular for a 'simpleton', and the antiquity of its gastronomic reputation is evidenced by this very ancient quatrain:

  'Le bécasseau est de fort bon manger,
  Duquel la chair resueille l'appetet,
  Il est oyseau passager et petit,
  Et par son goust fait des vins bien juger.'

To choose Woodcocks

'They inhabit only with us in the winter, and are best a fortnight or three weeks after they first come in, when they are rested from their long flight over the sea; they are very high flavoured birds; if they are fat, they will feel thick and firm; that is a proof they are in fine condition; they will also feel thick and hard in the vent, and have a vein of fat by the side of the breast: a lean one will feel thin in the vent; if new-killed, it will be limberfooted, and the head and throat clean; when they are stale, the foot will be stiff and dry, the mouth and throat will be foul, and sometimes run at the nostrils.'—C.MA.

Bécasse Carême

Take a woodcock that is fairly high, and roast it for no more than nine minutes, so as to keep it markedly underdone, sprinkling at the outset and at least once again with olive oil, a few drops at a time. Cut it in two lengthways, and divide each half of the breast into two slices. Having ready almost a teaspoonful of well-flavoured French mustard diluted with a little fresh lemon juice, roll the slices in this quickly, cover and keep them very warm but not positively hot. With the chopped-up carcass of the bird and the invaluable trail, having added and somewhat reduced a tablespoonful of previously burnt brandy, and then a tablespoonful of game stock, prepare a sauce by about six minutes of cooking. Pass this through a strainer, under pressure with the back of a kitchen spoon, on to slices of the best part of the woodcock. Turn these slices in the sauce, so that they may be thoroughly covered with it; put the dish on the table or side-table over a spirit-lamp or electric heater for a minute or so, and serve.—T.E.W.

Woodcock Consommé
To soar to glory, for five or six persons, prepare one quart of *consommé* flavoured with woodcock, that is, with the carcass of a half-roasted woodcock added when the *consommé* is being clarified. Pound all the best of the meat of the half-roasted woodcock, and its trail, and, adding a good deal less than half as much lentil *purée* (or, in default of that, chestnut *purée*), make the basis of what is called a *royale* garnish by working in a little cold game or veal stock and some cream (nearly a quarter of a pint of the latter), little by little. Add a pinch of cayenne to this, after straining it, and thicken it with one whole egg and the yolks of two eggs. Pour the well-stirred mixture into small cases. Stand these in very hot water, coming well short of their brims, and let them cook, without allowing the water ever positively to boil, for about 14 to 18 minutes according to the size of the cases. Let these *royales* cool in their cases. When cold, slice them rather thinly. Add them to each plate of the Woodcock *consommé*.—T.E.W.

Woodcock flambée
(*Bécasse flambée à la fine Champagne*)
Roast your undrawn woodcock slightly underdone, then cut it into six pieces, the wings, the legs and the breast cut in half, and keep them warm. Take out the intestines and chop them finely, and press the rest of the carcass on to a pan to squeeze out as much blood as possible. Remove the carcass, mix the blood and the intestines together, pour over a glass of good brandy and set it alight. Let this mixture reduce a little, then add a tablespoonful of game *fumet*, or rich stock, a squeeze of lemon juice and a suspicion of cayenne pepper. Dish the pieces of woodcock and pour this sauce over them to serve very hot.—W.F. (3, p. 56).

Woodcock (Roast)
These birds should not be emptied. To truss, the usual method is adopted except that the head is skinned and left on, the long beak being used as a skewer to keep the bird in shape, it being passed through the legs and body. A thin slice of fat bacon should be secured over breast and a slice of toast should be placed under each bird to catch gravy and drippings as they cook. Fifteen minutes roasting in a moderate oven is considered sufficient by most amateurs, as woodcock is generally preferred slightly underdone. Serve on toast and garnish with watercress, serving gravy separately.

Stuffed Woodcock
The contents of body to which chopped bacon, parsley, onion and a little soaked bread are added, as well as salt and pepper, are used to stuff these birds which may then be roasted or cooked en casserole as indicated in recipe for 'poulet en casserole'. A small quantity of lemon juice may be added to gravy, after straining, and the yolk of an egg may be added to stuffing if wished. The stewing en casserole method is best for older birds.

Salmis of Woodcock
See recipe for *Salmi de Faisan*.

WOODCOCK, AMERICAN
Lat. *Philohela minor*. The name given in the U.S.A. to a bird which is smaller than the wading *Woodcock* (q.v.) but is greatly esteemed by gastronomes. It is shot chiefly during the winter months, in woodlands, and is best prepared for the table like a *Snipe* (q.v.).

EGGS

There is always a best way of doing everything,
if it be to boil an egg.

EMERSON, *Conduct of Life: Behavior*.

INTRODUCTION

IN China, it appears, there are connoisseurs of vintage eggs, but vintage eggs are a closed book to us, and we prefer new-laid ones.

The fresher the egg the fuller it is, and there are two ways of finding out how full an egg is, hence how fresh it is. One way is to place the egg between one's eye and a strong light, holding the egg vertically, when it is possible to see whether there is a void at the top end, and how great it is. The other way is the trial by water, laying the egg horizontally in sufficient cold water to cover it; if it lies flat, it is full and fresh; if it shows a slight tilt, it is probably good enough to fry or to scramble; if it sits up, it is not fit to eat.

The shell of an egg is porous, particularly so after it has been washed to look nice and clean, a process which removes the fine film covering all eggs when they leave the hen. If an egg is left on top of a piece of cheese or in too close quarters with smoked fish or anything else that is strong-smelling, the egg will acquire through its porous shell the next-door smell, and such a smell may be most acceptable 'next door', where it belongs, but most objectionable when it taints the egg.

If using eggs which are your own hens', they are best kept *unwashed* and in a cool, airy place, or in a refrigerator. If they are from a shop, they are best used immediately: there is every likelihood that their waiting has already lasted quite long enough.

If you are using eggs which have been stored in a refrigerator, it is advisable to run a little warm water over them before attempting to do anything else with them: if you put them straight into boiling water, they will crack, and if you try to whip them for an omelette they will sulk. When the whites are beaten for cakes or for adding to any sort of pastry, they will be lighter and make lighter work as well as lighter paste if beaten warm instead of cold. One must also bear in mind that whipped white of egg may be of fine or not so fine texture, looser or stiffer, according to the beater used. For meringues and soufflés, for instance, it is best to use a rotary beater or an egg-beater with small wires; it will produce a smaller volume of finer texture than a whisk with heavy wires; this sort of beater will produce a larger volume of looser texture, more suitable for angel cake, for instance; and the number of strokes will have to be double or more.

As a general rule all eggs ought to be cooked rather slowly, whether cooked in hot water, butter, olive oil or any other kind of fat. One should also bear in mind that eggs must never be boiled, except in their shell. Boiling curdles eggs, so that it is important not to let any preparation containing an egg or part of an egg to boil. To make sure, it is best to cook all dishes containing egg in a double-boiler, or in a saucepan which fits into another one filled with boiling water. Even then, if the smaller or inside saucepan be thin and the water in the larger pan boiling fast, the egg may curdle; to avoid which, it is best not to let the water in the larger pan boil fast, and it is even better not to stop stirring the egg preparation which is being cooked in the 'inside' or smaller saucepan.

There are a considerable number of different ways of serving eggs, but not more than half a dozen ways of *cooking* fresh eggs. Shell eggs are either *boiled, poached, fried, baked, scrambled* or *cooked* in *omelettes* or *soufflés*. We shall be content to give a few recipes showing how to serve eggs cooked in any of these ways, but it is obvious that poached eggs, for instance, may be served with any and every kind of vegetable purée, and not merely with sorrel or spinach; and that practically every kind of vegetable, fish, fungus, liver or meat may be served with fried or scrambled eggs or 'folded' in an omelette.

Definitions and Recipes

I. BAKED EGGS
Oeufs au four
Bourgeoise:

Slices of stale bread
Eggs
Thin slices of Gruyère
Salt and pepper
Dusting grated nutmeg

Melt a sufficiency of butter in a small frying-pan. Cut slices of stale bread and thin slices of Gruyère cheese into rounds of equal size and thickness, removing crusts from bread. Fry the rounds of bread slightly in butter, on one side only, remove and sprinkle with salt and pepper on fried side. Lay a slice of cheese on each round of bread, on the fried side. Set these, side by side, in a buttered baking dish in which they may be served. Gently break an egg on each round of bread and cheese, sprinkle with salt, pepper and a tiny dusting of nutmeg and bake until eggs are nicely done in a hot oven, or cook on top of stove.—P.W.

Eggs Columbus:

Small, firm tomatoes or green
   peppers
Salt and pepper
Butter
Fresh eggs
Squares of toast
Tomato sauce

Plunge the tomatoes or peppers into boiling water and slip off skins. Drain and dry well. Cut each one around stem and remove seeds and hard parts. Sprinkle interiors with salt and pepper. Place each tomato or pepper in a buttered small pan. Break a fresh egg into each, season and bake in a moderate oven for about 12 minutes or until eggs are set. Put one tomato or pepper carefully on squares of hot buttered toast and serve with tomato sauce, which may either be handed separately or poured over the prepared eggs. —P.W.

Oeufs sur le Plat Duxelle:

1 tablespoon butter
2 small onions
2 or 3 fresh mushrooms
1 small glass white wine
Butter
1 shallot
Salt and pepper
2 tablespoons minced ham
½ teaspoon chopped parsley
Fresh eggs
Tomato sauce

Heat the butter in a small pan until nut-brown with the minced shallot and the onions. Season well, reduce heat, add chopped mushrooms and chopped ham. Blend well, re-heating but not boiling, and moisten with wine to a thick paste. Cook very gently to reduce mixture to a smooth mass, then add parsley and place a layer of this mixture in small flat baking dishes, previously buttered. Break two eggs in each and bake in a hot oven for five minutes. Add a little tomato sauce when serving.—P.W.

Egg Fluffs:

Fresh eggs
Butter
Salt and pepper

Have small round individual baking dishes, well buttered. Break the eggs carefully, separate whites from yolks, whipping the former to a stiff meringue, beating in a sufficiency of salt and pepper. Now place the yolks in the small dishes, setting in the middle carefully. Pile the meringue around roughly, sprinkle with salt and pepper and place the dishes in a shallow pan containing hot water. Put in a moderately hot oven and bake until the eggs are set to your liking. —P.W.

Oeufs au Fromage:

Butter
Very thin slices Gruyère cheese
Grated cheese
Small rounds bread
Eggs
Salt and pepper

Have a large shallow baking dish. Butter it well and cover the bottom with rounds of thinly-cut bread previously dipped in oiled butter. Cover each round of bread with another of the same size of Gruyère cheese, cut thinly. Place the dish under the flame of a grill or in a very hot oven until the cheese has melted into the bread, without browning. Remove dish and quickly break an egg on each round of cheese and bread, taking great care not to break yolks. Add salt and pepper and a sprinkling of grated cheese, colour gently and serve in dish when ready. —P.W.

Green Eggs:

Cooked spinach
Butter
Minced parsley
1 or 2 finely-chopped mushrooms
Fried *croûtons*

White sauce
Salt and pepper
Onion juice
Eggs
Slices of ham

Having cooked and chopped or sieved the spinach, nicely seasoned with salt, pepper and butter or cream, add to it sufficient rich white sauce to make about two cupfuls in all. Take small ramekins, butter them well, place a little chopped parsley, a drop or two of onion juice and a teaspoonful of finely-chopped mushrooms, previously gently cooked in a little butter with salt in each ramekin and, on this, break an egg, seasoning with salt and pepper. Put the cases in a pan containing hot water, and cook gently in the oven until the eggs are set but not hard. Dish up the hot spinach in an *entrée* dish; on this set the *croûtes* of fried bread and carefully turn an egg on to each round. Serve with slices of mild ham as an *entrée* or supper dish.—P.W.

Oeufs au Plat Lorrains:
  Thin slices Gruyère cheese
  Thin rashers of mild bacon
  Eggs
  Pepper
  Butter
  Salt, if needed
  Very little cream

Butter an earthenware dish, cover bottom with the thin slices of Gruyère and these, in turn, with the bacon, previously fried crisply. Break fresh eggs over the bacon, using enough to cover surface nicely, and dribble a thin trickle of cream around edge of dish. Bake until eggs are set.—P.W.

Eggs Baked in a Nest:
  1 egg for each serving
  Buttered toast
  ½ teaspoon butter
  Salt
  Pepper
  Paprika

Separate eggs, keeping yolks intact; beat each white separately until it comes away from side of bowl; add salt and pepper. Place the beaten white in a buttered baking dish or ramekin; very carefully press a dent in the top of the mound and slip into it the egg yolk being careful not to break it. Repeat process until the desired number of eggs are prepared. Place in a moderate oven and bake until eggs are cooked and a bit golden on top. If desired, a sprinkling of cheese and paprika may be added on top of each egg just before placing in oven. Serve on a hot platter on slices of toast. If desired, a medium white sauce may be poured around toast after it is on the platter.—A.W.C.

618

Eggs à la Paderewski:
  Chicken forcemeat
  Salt and pepper
  Eggs
  Béchamel sauce

Butter some small ramekin cases, then spread with a thin layer of chicken forcemeat, using for the preparation of this the white meat only and seasoning to taste. Break an egg into the centre of each prepared case, cover with buttered paper and set in a pan of hot water. Cook for about 10 minutes in a moderate oven. Turn out and serve with a little good *Béchamel* sauce poured over each egg.—P.W.

Oeufs Parmentier:
  Large baking potatoes
  1 or 2 rashers bacon
  Butter
  Breadcrumbs
  Fresh eggs
  Grated cheese
  Salt and pepper

Bake the potatoes carefully and cut into halves, roundways, with a very sharp knife. Scoop out part of the centre of each half sufficiently to hold an egg. Fry the bacon until crisp, then chop coarsely. Pour a little melted butter into each prepared well, sprinkle with grated cheese and then with some of the chopped bacon. Poach carefully one egg for each half potato and when done and well drained place it carefully in the prepared well. Sprinkle top lightly with fine brown breadcrumbs, salt and pepper, dot with butter and put the prepared potatoes in a hot oven or under a grill to brown surface, serving at once. If a somewhat more elaborate dish is required, press the potato pulp removed from each half through a sieve with some boiling milk, salt and pepper and use to pipe around edge of the halves when ready to put in oven.—P.W.

Oeufs Presbytère:
  Poached eggs
  Grated cheese
  Salt and pepper
  Béchamel sauce
  Butter
  Few sprigs tarragon

Use for this dish small *soufflé* cases, either china or paper. Place a poached egg in each, sprinkling with salt and pepper. Cover with the sauce, nicely seasoned and flavoured to taste with grated cheese. Place a small piece of butter on this and bake in a hot oven for about five or six minutes. The tarragon, if obtainable, should be placed on the eggs before covering them with the sauce.—P.W.

Shirred Eggs: Butter a small dish, sprinkling bottom and sides with fine bread or biscuit crumbs, salt and pepper. Gently break an egg – or eggs – into this, cover with more crumbs and a little cream and bake in a gentle oven until crumbs are brown.—P.W.

Swiss Eggs:

> 6 eggs
> 3 tablespoonfuls butter
> 1 gill (half cup) cream
> Salt and pepper
> Swiss cheese

Melt the butter in a fireproof baking dish, break into it the eggs, cover them with very thin slices of Swiss cheese, and sprinkle over a little salt and pepper.

Bake in a moderate oven till the eggs are set and the cheese melted.—M.H.N.

La fondue: The following concise recipe for what the late lamented Marcel Boulestin calls 'this traditional Swiss dish' is given in his booklet on *Eggs*:

'The necessary ingredients for this dish are eggs, Gruyère and butter, though some people improve on it by adding slices of truffles *sautées* in butter, or gravy from roast fowl. The important thing is that the proportions are right: to the weight of the eggs, whatever it is, you must have a third of that weight of grated Gruyère and a sixth of good butter. First whip the whites, add one by one the yolks, then the butter in small pieces and last, the grated cheese. Put this in a saucepan, add salt and a good deal of freshly-ground pepper; cook, stirring well all the time, till the mixture is properly thickened. It should be smooth, thick like good cream, and served at once very hot.'

II. BOILED EGGS

(*Soft or Hard Boiled*)

Oeufs à la coque

There is nothing simpler than to boil an egg properly if you can attend to it and remember when it was put into boiling water. This cannot be so easy as it sounds, to judge from the uncertainty of the consistency of a boiled egg: it may be so 'runny' as to be very unpleasant as well as difficult to eat; or it may be quite hard. This should never happen. If an egg be slipped into sufficient boiling water to cover it completely and left to simmer gently for exactly 3, 3¼ or 3½ minutes, according to the size of the egg, from a pullet's egg to the largest egg laid by a well-bred and well-fed hen, the white will be just about 'set' and the yolk runny. If you are not good at mental arithmetic, buy one of the little sand-glasses which they sell for cooks who cannot trust their memory or their kitchen clock. It consists of two equal glass compartments, one above the other, and one with enough sand in it to take exactly three

minutes to run into the lower chamber when turned over.

There are people who put the eggs in cold water, in a pan on the fire, and take them out when the water boils: it is an unsatisfactory, because unreliable, manner to boil an egg, since the time during which the egg will be in warm, hot, and very hot water varies according to the fierceness or slackness of the fire.

There is yet another way, the lazy way. It consists in slipping the eggs in boiling water and moving the pan in which they are away from the fire; they will never get hard and may be left in the slowly cooling water 10 or 15 minutes. Cooked in this way, a boiled egg is called a *Coddled egg*; the white does not set but remains creamy and it is believed to be more easily digested by children and dyspeptics.

Soft-boiled or coddled eggs are called, in culinary French, *Oeufs à la coque*; they are eaten in the shell.

Oeufs Mollets

What is known in culinary language as an *Oeuf mollet* is an egg which has been boiled for a minute and a half longer than the *Oeuf à la coque*, and has been plunged in cold water when taken out of the boiling water. Its shell is then quite easily cracked and removed and the white is set and firm, whilst the yolk is still fairly runny. In that state the *Oeuf mollet* is served with spinach, a tomato sauce or a number of other sauces and garnishings, according to the various recipes for *Oeufs mollets*.

En Aspic: Place the required number of *Oeufs mollets* in the centre of the dish, surround them with well-drained canned cherries and cover the whole with some good aspic jelly.

Diplomate: Serve the *Oeufs mollets* in little china *cocottes*, each egg upon a thin slice of *foie gras*, and with a thin border of tomato sauce all round.

Grand'mère: Serve the *Oeufs mollets* on *croûtons*, garnished with asparagus tips and with a light covering of *Sauce Mornay*.

La Vallière: *Oeufs mollets* served in tartlets, upon a bed of creamed sorrel and asparagus tips, with a *Sauce Suprême* over them.

Milanaise: *Oeufs mollets* served in tartlets with some macaroni *à la Milanaise*, and a covering of *Sauce Mornay*.

Païva: *Oeufs mollets* served in *croustades* filled with a mushroom *purée*; a thin slice of truffle is placed on top of each egg and some *Sauce Mornay* poured over it all.

Renaissance: The required number of *Oeufs mollets* are placed on the same number of boiled and trimmed globe artichokes' *fonds* or bottoms, in the serving dish; the lot is then covered with a hot tomato sauce, and a little finely chopped parsley is sprinkled over it all just before serving.

Rosemary: *Oeufs mollets* served in tartlets filled with a white sauce into which some grated ham has been incorporated; also a sprinkling of finely chopped rosemary.

Rossini: *Oeufs mollets* served in tartlets with a slice of *foie gras* under and a sliced truffle over each egg; also a rich *Sauce Madère* over them.

Stanley: *Oeufs mollets* served in tartlets upon a bed of onion *purée*, seasoned with a little curry powder, and covered with a creamy white sauce, also seasoned with curry.

Swedish: *Oeufs mollets* served with a Swedish white sauce made of flour, milk and butter, and seasoned with pepper, salt, mustard and finely chopped parsley.

Oeufs durs

Hard-boiled eggs are rarely properly cooked because most people appear to think that it does not matter how long the eggs are left to boil and that it is safer to give them plenty of time to get really hard. But it does matter; Eight minutes from boiling point for a pullet's egg and ten for a hen's are fully sufficient for the egg to be hard boiled: longer cooking renders the white leathery.

There are all sorts of uses to be made of hard-boiled eggs, besides being safe for the picnic basket. They can be halved, quartered, sliced, mashed, scooped, stuffed, and used as a separate dish of their own or for garnishing, beautifying and improving all manner of other dishes.

Aspic: Sliced or quartered hard-boiled eggs, with a sprinkling of *Fines Herbes* and a thin covering of aspic jelly over them.

Egg Balls: Two hard-boiled eggs, chopped and mixed with a raw egg, and seasoned with pepper and salt, are rolled into balls on a floured board and poached in boiling water for five minutes.

Egg Charlotte: Alternate layers of well-seasoned mashed potatoes and sliced hard-boiled egg, in a pie-dish, with a layer of potatoes on top; breadcrumbs and pats of butter are then added and the *Charlotte* is browned in a hot oven.

Egg Cutlets: Make a rich white sauce with flour, butter and milk, and season to taste with pepper, salt and onion juice or lemon juice, grated nutmeg or paprika. Mix in this sauce the required number of hard-boiled eggs, chopped coarsely, and let the mixture cool; then shape it into cutlets. Dip each 'cutlet' into flour, a beaten raw egg and some fine breadcrumbs, and then fry in deep fat until browned: drain and serve hot with a *Sauce Béchamelle*. (A short stick of uncooked

macaroni may be used to pretend that the 'cutlet' has a bone.)

Devilled: Sliced hard-boiled egg covered with a sauce made with 1½ oz. butter, two tablespoons cream, Worcestershire sauce, cayenne pepper, chutney and mustard to taste.

Farced Eggs: Take sorrel, alone, if you will, or with other herbs, wash, and swing them, then mince them very small and put them between two dishes with fresh butter, or passe them in the pan; after they are passed, soak and season them; after your farce is sod, take some hard eggs, cut them into halfs a crosse or in length, and take out the yolkes, and mince them with your farce, and after all is well mixed stew them over the fire, and put to it a little nutmeg, and serve garnished with the whites of your eggs, which you may make brown in the pan with a little butter. (F.P.de la Varenne, *The French Cook*, Chas. Adams, London, 1654.)

Filleted Eggs: Rub a small saucepan with a cut clove of garlic; heat about a tablespoonful of butter and fry in it some fresh, sliced mushrooms; also a chopped onion. When this mixture begins to brown, add a pinch of flour and moisten with some meat stock or white wine or some of each; season with pepper and salt and let the sauce simmer for 15 minutes or so. Then slice the whites of some hard-boiled eggs into strips or 'fillets', and drop into the sauce; add the yolks also, keeping them whole if possible, and serve as soon as the egg is warm through.

Fried Sliced Eggs: Make them hard, take them out of the shell, and cut them into slices, then fry them with good butter, parsley, chibols minced, peper, gooseberries, or verjuyce of grapes; after they are well fryed and seasoned, put them into a dish with a drop of vinegar passed in the pan. If the sauce is too short, put in it a drop of broth; then serve with nutmeg; if you will, mix with it capers, mushrums, broken sparagus, fryed before you mixe them, as also mushrums, for it would not be good otherwise. (*The French Cook*, 1654.)

Egg Fritters: Sliced hard-boiled egg, dipped in batter, fried in smoking lard, and served with any strong sauce one may fancy.

Golden Eggs: Diced hard-boiled eggs, mixed with fried onion and dry mustard, and served on buttered *croûtons*.

Joinville: Slices of hard-boiled egg served with a 'pink' *Sauce Mayonnaise*, as hors-d'oeuvre; the 'pink' being due to the addition of some pounded shrimps to the sauce.

Khichuri (*Kedgeree*): Mix well-washed rice and lentils with salt, pepper and four cloves and simmer till it thickens but does not burn; fry one or two thinly-sliced onions in butter with shelled hard-boiled eggs cut lengthways (dipped in flour) till eggs are brown; then add some good curry powder to the rice mixture and 1 oz. butter and cook for another 10 minutes; serve hot with eggs on top of rice.

Egg-a-Leekie: Hard-boiled eggs cut in halves, longways, and served in a hot white sauce, together with small leeks, boiled till tender and cut in 1 in. lengths.

Lyonnaise: Brown some onions in butter and then add milk, stirring and adding pepper and salt to taste, so as to make a thin onion sauce. Arrange in a baking-dish the required number of hard-boiled eggs, sliced, and cover them with the onion sauce. Sprinkle the top with grated Gruyère or Parmesan cheese, also a few pats of butter, and bake in a moderate oven until nicely browned. Serve hot in the baking-dish.

Marie: Slices of hard-boiled eggs and of cooked beetroot, mixed, as a hors-d'oeuvre, with an oil and vinegar sauce, chopped *Fines Herbes* or capers; also, if liked, strips or dice of anchovies in oil.

Mexican: Slices of hard-boiled egg served on *croûtons* with finely chopped onion and sliced tomatoes.

Mousse of Eggs: Pass yolk of eggs through sieve; add Worcester and anchovy sauces (to taste), aspic jelly and seasoning; chop the whites finely and add to the mixture, whip the cream lightly and add at the last; put into a *soufflé* case, and when set, cover with a thin layer of aspic; decorate and cover with another layer of aspic.—*Cookery Chronicle* .

Roman: Sliced hard-boiled egg served in a thick onion sauce, made with milk or cream.

San Sebastian: Hard-boiled eggs chopped lengthways and placed on a dish, flat-side down, with a mixture of chopped cooked carrots and turnips between the half eggs, the whole is then covered with a meat-glaze and put in the oven to set. Serve when quite cold.

Santos: Hard-boiled eggs cut in halves and each half placed flat-side down upon a tomato, also cut in halves, in a hors-d'oeuvre dish, with some *Sauce Mayonnaise*, and a garnishing of diced beetroot and pimentoes.

Scotch Eggs: Make a forcemeat with finely chopped or minced cooked ham, two or three anchovies in oil, some fresh bread-crumbs; season with salt and pepper and mixed spices, if liked; coat the hard-boiled egg with this forcemeat, bind with raw egg, dip in egg-and-breadcrumbs, fry in hot fat and serve in halves on *croûtons*.

Spanish: Slices of hard-boiled eggs served in an onion sauce made with meat stock.

Stuffed Eggs: Hard-boiled eggs cut in halves, lengthways; the yolk is then pounded in a mortar and mixed with butter and a number of other tasty foods before being put back into the hollowed whites. The quantity of butter required to obtain a smooth, creamy 'stuffing' depends upon the nature of the materials used: the number of these and their combinations are considerable and the following are but a few of them given as examples:

1. Caviare.
2. Smoked Salmon, either alone, or with caviare.
3. Fresh Salmon, alone or with mayonnaise or other dressing.
4. Sardines, skinned and mashed, with or without capers.
5. Anchovies, in anyway mentioned for sardines.
6. Tinned Tunny Fish.
7. Finnon Haddock or Kippered Herring, well mashed.
8. Curried Prawns or Shrimps.
9. Lobster.
10. Cream Cheese.
11. Grated Cheddar or Parmesan Cheese, with mustard and-or other concomitants, *au choix*.
12. Chopped Olives with mayonnaise.
13. Chopped Tongue with or without anchovies.
14. Chopped Ham and capers.
15. *Purée* of artichoke bottoms and *Béchamel* Sauce.
16. Cream and scraped or shredded hung beef (boiled for 20 minutes and scraped with ordinary grater).
17. Grated Cheese, anchovy essence and Worcester sauce.
18. Egg and chutney.
19. Chopped Ham and horseradish cream.
20. Egg and pickled walnuts.
21. Cold buttered eggs, flavoured as liked.
22. Chopped ginger and cream cheese.
23. Chopped eggs with gherkins and pickled onions, anchovy essence and seasoning
24. Mock Caviare, Cod's Roe simmered in salted water for 40 minutes, crushed with a fork and mixed with anchovy essence, tomato sauce, lemon juice and cayenne.

Oeufs durs Tapénade: The *Tapénade* is made with black, ripe olives which are stoned and pounded with some fillets of anchovies, tunny fish, mustard and capers – *tapéno* being the Provençal name of capers. The mixture is then worked through a sieve and made of a creamy consistency by the addition of the required quantity of olive oil and brandy. It may be either piped into the hollowed whites of hard-boiled eggs, cut lengthwise, with a large rose nozzle, or spooned in and piled in to form a little dome. These eggs are usually served on lettuce leaves as a cold *entrée*.

Oeufs en tripe à la Lyonnaise: For half a dozen hard-boiled eggs you must stew in butter four medium-sized onions, chopped up finely. Take your time: do not let them brown, but simply become a rich, golden colour and quite soft. To these, when they are done, add a tablespoonful of flour, mix well and moisten with good stock (or, failing that, milk or even water), seasoning it with a *bouquet* of parsley, thyme, and bayleaf, salt, pepper, and grated nutmeg. Cook this sauce for 20 minutes or so; remove the *bouquet* and warm through in it the eggs cut in slices, halves or quarters, as you prefer. It is one of mankind's real inspirations.— AMBROSE HEATH in *Wine and Food*, No. 4, p. 21.

Soft Centre Braised Eggs
(Chinese)

4 eggs
1 tablespoon oil or lard
5 tablespoons soya bean sauce

Boil the eggs for five minutes and put them under running cold water for five minutes. Remove shells and put the eggs in a small saucepan with the soya bean sauce and lard and braise for five minutes, basting them with the sauce until they are dark brown. When fairly cold, cut into quarters with a sharp knife.—CH.C.

III. FRIED EGGS
(a) Oeufs à la poêle

Melt some butter, margarine or bacon fat in a frying-pan; break the eggs carefully into a wet saucer and when the butter or fat is sizzling or bubbly, slide one egg at a time into the pan. Cook on a slow fire until the white is no longer transparent and the yolk quite firm; dust with pepper and salt; baste the eggs with some of the hot butter or fat and serve hot with or without garnishings, according to selected recipe.

In the South of France, where olive oil is used for frying in place of butter, the technique is slightly different:

'The egg is usually broken into a saucer, salted and peppered. Then slide it very gently into a tiny frying-pan which holds two tablespoonfuls of hot oil, tilted down into one side so that it is deep. With a knife or wooden spoon you curl the white up around the yolk, keeping the pan tilted. This makes a handsome 'nest' for the yolk and also keeps it soft. You turn it or not as you please. But – you never cook more than one at a time – one egg, one frying-pan – no mass production! This is the secret of the pretty white ruffle.'—T.L.B.

In Spain, fried eggs are usually 'double-fried'. An egg is broken in a cup and slipped into a small pan of deep boiling olive oil, and as soon as it shows any signs of colouring, it is smartly turned over and given another minute or less to swell out like a fritter; it is then removed on a slotted spoon, drained and served.

Andalouse: Eggs 'double-fried' in olive oil and served with some slices of aubergines, also fried in oil: the eggs and the egg-plants are arranged in the dish in alternate lines and a hot tomato sauce is served at the same time in a separate sauce-boat.

Arroz a la Cubana: 12 oz. rice, one small onion, four bananas, five eggs, three large tablespoons olive oil, one bayleaf, salt.

Pour the oil into a casserole and when hot add onion, finely cut, and bayleaf; when they begin to take colour add rice and stir well for about half a minute. Add 1¾ pints boiling stock and let cook for about 14 minutes. Fry the eggs and bananas, skinned and cut lengthways, in olive oil, and serve with rice when ready.

Bill's Eggs:
    4 slices bread
    2 tablespoons butter
    8 strips bacon
    Small wineglass of sherry
    4 eggs
    4 tablespoons grated cheese
    1 cup cream
    Salt, pepper and cayenne

Broil bacon, melt butter in pan and when melted add cream. Drop eggs, without breaking, into this and sprinkle with salt, pepper and cayenne. When whites are nearly firm, sprinkle with cheese and finish cooking. Toast bread and cover with bacon. Lift out each egg and place on top of toast and bacon. To the remaining cream mixture add sherry and pour over eggs.—TH.C.

Créole: Eggs fried in oil and placed in the centre of a round dish, with a tomato sauce, within a border of rice: the rice is boiled and mixed with a good white sauce in which a little chopped ham and some grated cheese have been blended.

Lulli: Fried eggs served on fried slices of ham and garnished with some macaroni *à la Napolitaine*.

Rachel: Eggs fried in butter and served with a slice of poached beef-marrow and another of truffle on each egg; thickened beef gravy over all.

(b) Oeufs au Plat

This is one of the most usual ways of serving eggs, other than in an omelette, in France. Small china dishes, with two small 'lugs' are used, but anything which can stand heat may be substituted. Heat about a teaspoonful of butter in an individual 'plat'. When melted but not sizzling, break in one or two fresh eggs, sprinkle with salt and pepper and serve when the white is well cooked.

Oeufs au Plat à la Crème

Cook the eggs *au plat*, that is in small shallow dishes, in butter. When half-cooked, add as much thick cream as you wish, pouring it over the egg-whites. As soon as the cream begins to boil, serve, after seasoning with salt and pepper.

Américaine: Same as *oeufs sur le plat à l'anglaise*, with the addition of fried tomatoes, served with the bacon and eggs.

Anglaise: Eggs fried in the sizzling bacon fat of the bacon which is cooked and served at the same time.

Aurore: Fried eggs *au plat* with some tomato sauce.

Bercy: Same as *oeufs au plat à l'aurore*, but with small chipolata sausages added.

Béatrix: *Oeufs au plat* garnished with truffles and poached sweetbread, and seasoned with paprika.

Beauvilliers: Fried eggs served in small *sur le plat* dishes, on a slice of ham and with a *Sauce Madère*.

Beurre Noir, Oeufs au

Fry as many eggs as required, in ones or twos, in small china individual dishes, in which the eggs will be served. In a separate pan melt some butter and brown it slowly until nut-coloured, frying at the same time some chopped up pieces of curly parsley; pour the sizzling brown butter over the fried eggs; then put in the pan some vinegar and a caper or two per egg; let the vinegar come to the boil and reduce it by boiling for a moment, then pour it over the eggs and serve at once.

Beurre Noisette: Same as *Oeufs au beurre noir* but without the vinegar.

Carême: Fried eggs served with a *purée de volaille*, chopped truffles, a *Sauce Suprême* and a little sherry.

Catalane: Fried eggs served with an elaborate garnish of onions, red peppers, tomatoes and *cèpes*, all cooked in olive oil.

Chancelière: Fried eggs served with a garnishing of scalloped sweetbreads, truffles and carrots.

Chasseur: Fried eggs served with chopped mushrooms and shallots; also some chicken liver.

Choisy: Fried eggs served with diced potatoes and braised lettuce.

Colette: Fried eggs served with some shredded mushrooms, sheep's kidney and grated horseradish; also a fried half tomato with each egg.

Doria: Fried eggs served with grated grey piemontese truffles.

Duchesse: Fried eggs served with some *Pommes Duchesse* (See *Potatoes*).

Ermenonville: Fried eggs served upon a slice of ham and with a garnish of small mushrooms.

Esmeralda: Fried eggs served with aubergines, tomato sauce and paprika.

Espagnole: Fried eggs served with fried onions, tomatoes and sweet pimentoes.

Florentine: Fried eggs served on a bed of creamed spinach and with a *Sauce Mornay*.

Jeanneton: Fried eggs served with artichoke bottoms cut up in small pieces and a sprinkling of chopped chervil and tarragon.

Lyonnaise: Fried eggs served with fried onions and flat sausages (*Cervelas*).

Meyerbeer: Fried eggs served with sheep's kidneys and minced truffles.

Mirabeau: Fried eggs served with anchovies and olives; also a sprinkling of chopped tarragon.

Monégasque: Fillets of anchovies.

Monselet: Artichoke bottoms and truffles.

Nemrod: *Game Purée* and *Sauce Madère*.

Opéra: Chopped chicken livers and asparagus points.

Patti; Truffles.

Petit-Duc: Mushrooms and horseradish.

Piémontaise: Grey piedmontese truffles and grated Parmesan cheese.

Portugaise: Tomatoes.

Princesse: Asparagus points and truffles.

Reine: *Purée de blanc de volaille* and *Sauce Suprême*.

Richemont: Truffles and *Morilles*.

Romaine: Spinach, fillets of anchovies and grated cheese.

Rossini: *Foie gras* and truffles; *Sauce Madère*.

Sagan: Two small scallops of sheep's brains cooked in butter, Parmesan cheese and *Sauce Suprême* with curry.

Saint-Antoine: Chopped onions, bacon and *chipolatas* sausages.

Saint-Honoré: Lamb's sweetbread, truffles, mushrooms and fresh cream.

Sylvie: New carrots and small mushrooms with fresh cream.

Taillevent: Small scallops of calf's sweetbread and a *salpicon* of truffles and mushrooms; a little paprika.

à la Turque: Chicken liver and meat gravy.

Victoria: Salpicon of lobster and truffles.

Washington: Fresh cream and sweet corn.

IV. OMELETTES AND SOUFFLÉS

The perfect omelette is golden, plump and light. In France, its native home, the perfect omelette is served *baveuse*, that is, the interior is semi-liquid, or, rather, creamy.

Basic Ingredients:

They are four: (1) Eggs. (2) Butter. (3) Liquid. (4) Salt, or in the case of a sweet omelette, sugar. Pepper is usually added to savoury omelettes, and they may be filled with a large variety of foods, as will be seen.

Important Points:
The Frying Pan. A special pan should be kept for making omelettes only. It may be simply a cast-iron one, or a copper one or an enamelled iron one or even a nickel one, but aluminium, unless specially treated with a hard, bright, surface, should not be used for this kind of dish as eggs stick to rough surfaces. After use, never wash the omelette pan. Rub over first with some clean tissue paper, then with a piece of clean rag. If any particles of egg adhere to it – and none should – rub gently with a little salt, nothing else. When an omelette pan is new, season it before using by heating some fresh butter in it and rubbing this well on and in before attempting to make an omelette.

The Heat. Gas is most suitable for the making of a perfect omelette as the heat can be regulated at will very speedily. It should be rather high to begin with, then reduced almost as soon as the beaten eggs have been added.

Concentration. When you have decided to serve an omelette, everything but its care must be banished from your mind.

Immediate Serving. Once made, an omelette, like a *soufflé*, must not and cannot wait, not even a minute. If hors-d'oeuvre are to be served in a house where the hostess is at the same time the cook, let them be served in the Russian and American manner, that is BEFORE sitting down to table, with sherry or cocktails and, when the last few appetisers are on the point of disappearing, away to the omelette pan so that the guests may wait for it rather than it for them.

General Method of making Omelettes
For three guests:
       6 fresh eggs
       Salt and pepper
       2 tablespoons cold water
       2 tablespoons butter (1 oz.)

This is what is known as the omelette 'nature' which we shall call the 'basic' omelette.

Break the eggs into a basin, add water, salt and pepper to taste and beat energetically for a few minutes either with a chef's wire whip or with a rotary beater. This serves not only thoroughly to blend the yolks and whites of the eggs, but it also incorporates air into the mixture, making the omelette light. Add to this five or six small bits of butter each the size of a hazel nut; this also helps make the omelette light and prevents it from 'sticking' to the pan. Now take

your special pan and set it on a good heat. Add the butter; allow it to melt – almost (but not quite) to smoke; then pour in the egg mixture. The outer crust of your omelette will thus set and be crisp; it will serve as a sort of envelope to the interior part. Reduce the heat considerably, hold the handle of the pan in your left hand, tilting it slightly, and, using either a fork or, better, a broad smooth palette knife. lift the outer crust around the edges of the pan and let the liquid part of the egg mixture trickle in the hollow thus formed. Repeat this operation all around the pan and several times until only the centre portion retains any liquid. It is now ready to serve. Remove pan from the fire at once and gently shake it, when the omelette should slip out on to a hot dish without any trouble. If it should happen to stick a little at one point, however, detach gently by slipping the palette knife underneath.

To dish up, hold the dish in the left hand, gently slip half the omelette on it and, with a deft turn of the right wrist lower the second half on top of the first. There is, of course, a knack to this but, with practice, it can soon be acquired.

Fillings for Savoury Omelettes
Left-over vegetables, such as cooked green peas, asparagus tips, young carrots, etc., may be re-heated gently in butter and folded into a nice light omelette when serving.

Shrimps or Prawns, lightly *sautés* in butter.

Finely-chopped left-over chicken or veal, heated in butter.

Chicken Livers, *sautés* in butter, chopped finely and mixed with a little bread, soaked in milk then squeezed dry. Season well and, if wished, add a small chopped truffle. Tomato sauce may be poured around this type of omelette with good results.

Spinach, cooked and rubbed through a sieve, seasoned with butter or thick cream, salt and pepper.

Artichoke Bottoms. Boiled, or *sautés* in butter, drained and cut up.

Mushrooms, *sautés* in butter, etc., etc.

Here is a list of some of the Classical Omelettes with an indication of their informing flavour:

(a) Savoury Omelettes
Agnès Sorel: Minced mushrooms and *purée de volaille*.

Albina: Very small dice of truffles added to the egg mixture and beaten with it before cooking; cream and *purée de volaille* folded in the omelette.

Alsacienne: Goose fat used instead of butter to cook the omelette: *choucroûte* folded in and thin slices of ham placed on top of the omelette.

Anchovy Omelette:
 6 salted anchovies
 Olive oil
 Pepper and salt (if needed)
 Slices of fried bread
 6 eggs
 Butter
 Good meat gravy or tomato sauce

The salted, not the oily, anchovies are needed for this very Provençal dish. Put the anchovies in cold water for a quarter of an hour to remove excess of salt. Drain and split, longways, into fillets, removing backbone and trimming. Fry sufficient slices of bread in either olive oil or (if you must) in butter. Break three of the eggs into a basin, beat vigorously, and make a THIN omelette, using, if possible, good pure olive oil instead of butter. When done, turn on to a hot dish, cover with anchovy *croûtes* and cover these with a second thin omelette made with the three remaining eggs. It is advisable, if possible, when preparing this *spécialité*, to have two pans, frying the omelettes simultaneously so that there is no delay in serving as soon as ready. Ladle a little very good roast meat gravy over the slices of bread before covering them with the second omelette, in default of this, use fresh tomato sauce.—P.W.

André Theuriet: Morilles cooked in cream, and asparagus points folded in thin slices of truffles on the omelette.

Archiduc: Onion, paprika and truffles.

Argenteuil: Asparagus.

Omelette Arnold Bennett

Chop finely a fillet of cooked smoked haddock, beat up with the eggs and cream, add salt – not much, as the haddock is already salty – and pepper; put some butter in the pan and cook the omelette lightly. Do not roll the omelette when cooked, but turn out flat on to a plate. Spread over the top a little Sauce Mornay, sprinkle with grated cheese and pass under the gas grill to brown. (Savoy Grill recipe, London.)—R.L.

Bacon or Ham Omelette

Coarsely chop lean ham or mild bacon, cut rather thickly, and gently fry, or, according to the old American phrase, 'try out' in a pan. Add a little butter to the fat in pan and either mix pieces of ham or bacon with beaten eggs or pour mixture over them, cooking together with great care.

Omelette du Baron de Barante

(*Edward VII's favourite omelette*): Peel carefully 1½ lb. of firm, fresh mushrooms. Cut them into thin slices so that they can be cooked easily. Sprinkle with salt and cook in best butter. When they are a pale yellow,

pour over them a glass of good port. Cover the stewpan and reduce by half. Then add fresh thick cream and twelve slices of the tail of a lobster which has been cooked in a *court-bouillon*. Cover the stewpan and let the whole simmer. Place this mixture in an eighteen-egg omelette, fold omelette, sprinkle it liberally with Parmesan cheese, and brown a rich golden colour in a quick oven.–H.A.V.

Bercy: A *Fines Herbes* omelette (q.v.), served with small chipolata sausages and a tomato sauce.

Bouchère: Small cubes of poached marrowbone fat folded in.

Bruxelloise: Some very small brussels sprouts, cooked in butter, and folded in.

Champignons: Finely chopped mushrooms beaten in with the egg mixture to make the omelette; sliced, cooked mushrooms added on top of the omelette before serving.

Chasseur: Mixed chopped chicken livers and mushrooms, cooked in butter and folded in the omelette, and some added on top of it before serving, with a *Sauce Chasseur* poured over.

Châtelaine: Crumbled braised chestnuts folded in, cream sauce over.

Cheese Omelette: Allow two tablespoons of grated mixed Gruyère and Parmesan to eight eggs or *pro rata*. Mix with the latter and beat well, cooking omelette in the usual manner. If wished, a little more grated cheese may be sprinkled over surface of omelette when serving. Use a little less salt in egg mixture as cheese supplies some.

Choisy: A *Chiffonade* of braised lettuce folded in: cream sauce over.

Ciboulette: Chopped chives added to the egg mixture.

Clamart: Small green peas, cooked with onion and lettuce, folded in; small green peas on top of the omelette when serving.

Crécy: Finely shredded cooked carrots added to the egg mixture, or a layer of mashed and well-seasoned carrots folded in.

Diane: Shredded cooked mushrooms added to the egg mixture; minced, cooked meat of partridges or other game bird folded in, with chopped truffles added; garnish with slices of truffles.

Du Barry: Small flowerlets of cauliflower steamed and tossed in butter, then folded in.

Espagnole: Here there are two schools of thought. (1) Skin and cut up some nice red tomatoes, removing seeds. Cook gently in butter, seasoning with salt and pepper, until they are reduced to a thick *purée* or pulp. This should be folded when ready into the omelette. (2) Peel and cut firm red tomatoes into quarters. *Sauté* in butter, season but do not allow them to lose their shape. Make a plain omelette and fold the prepared tomatoes in the centre when serving.

Fines Herbes: Add to eggs, after a preliminary beating, finely chopped parsley, chives (or, failing this, a suspicion of minced onion) and, if possible, a blade or two of tarragon, as well as some chervil. Continue beating and cook omelette as indicated.

Flamande: Cooked chicory and cream folded in.

Florentine: Cooked spinach and cream folded in.

Forestière: Small dice of fried lean bacon added to the egg mixture; morels, tossed in butter, folded in.

Gasconne: Add to the egg mixture small pieces of cooked ham, finely shredded onion, browned in butter, and a little chopped garlic and parsley; then make the omelette in the usual way, using either butter or goose fat in the cooking.

Green Omelette: Break three eggs into one basin and three eggs into another basin. Pour nearly half pint of cream equally divided into each basin. Add to one ½ lb. spinach that has been boiled and passed through a hair sieve. Cook both mixtures separately in omelette pan and turn into dish side by side. Pour over a good sauce of gravy, slightly thickened with arrowroot, or better still a tomato sauce round the omelette, not over it. I find this omelette is rather too rich with only cream, so put some milk with the cream, it is really better.—N.S.

Japonaise: Japanese artichokes, steamed and tossed in butter, folded in.

Jurassienne: Small dice of bacon and *purée* of sorrel folded in.

Lorraine: Grilled lean bacon, wafers of Gruyère cheese and chopped chives folded in.

Kidney Omelette: Skin and cut up a small veal kidney or one or two sheep's kidneys, removing centre nerve. *Sauté* gently in butter, season lightly with salt and pepper, cool somewhat and add to beaten eggs or keep hot and fold in centre of plain omelette.

Lyonnaise: With cooked shredded onions.

Maintenon: Pounded cooked chicken meat, truffles and mushrooms folded in; cover the omelette with a *Béchamel* sauce, *soubisée* (with onions), dust it with grated Parmesan cheese, pour some melted butter over it and brown quickly under the grill or in very hot oven.

Ménagère: Shredded boiled beef and fried onions mixed together and folded in.

Omelette Moderne à l'Oignon:

    4 oz. stale breadcrumbs
    1½ tablespoons butter
    1 rather large onion
    ½ pint hot milk
    Salt and pepper
    3 eggs

Pour the hot milk over the breadcrumbs, stir until thoroughly blended, after covering.

Heat the butter and lightly fry the finely cut-up onion. When done, fold in the omelette.

Monselet: A *salpicon* of artichoke bottoms and creamed truffles folded in; garnish omelette with slices of truffles warmed in hot butter.

Mousseline: Beat the yolks of six eggs with two spoonfuls of cream; season with pepper and salt. Beat the six whites to a stiff froth and then add to the yolks. Mix very quickly and make the omelette in the usual way with this mixture.

Nantua: Crayfish tails and *Sauce Nantua*.

Niçoise: Tomatoes, garlic and chopped-up parsley folded in.

Normande: Shelled shrimps and shredded mushrooms folded in; garnish with poached oysters, truffles and *Sauce Normande*.

Parisienne: Add to the egg mixture some finely shredded onions and mushrooms, tossed in butter; serve with grilled chipolata sausages.

Parmentier: Potatoes cooked in butter and chopped parsley folded in.

Portugaise: A *fondue* of tomatoes folded in.

Princesse: Asparagus tips and truffles folded in; *Sauce Suprême* over the omelette.

Provençale: Quartered tomatoes, cooked in olive oil and with a little garlic, folded in.

Rossini: A *salpicon* of *foie gras* and truffles added to the eggs and beaten with them to make the omelette; serve with alternate scallops of truffles and *foie gras* on top of the omelette.

Rouennaise: Ducks' livers, cooked in butter and pounded to a *purée*, folded in; serve with a gravy made of stock and red wine simmered together.

Saint-Hubert: A *purée* of game meat folded in: serve with mushrooms cooked in butter on top of the omelette.

Savoyarde: Potatoes tossed in butter and thin wafers of Gruyère cheese folded in.

Verdurière: Add to the eggs before beating them a *chiffonade* of sorrel and lettuce, cooked in butter; also some chopped parsley, chervil and tarragon. Cook and serve the omelette as you would a pancake.

(b) Sweet Omelettes

Célestine: Small omelettes (one for each person) with apricot jam folded in. They are all dressed on a silver dish and liberally dusted with sugar before serving.

Omelette aux Fraises: Beat together six yolks and four whites of eggs, setting aside two whites. Mix some crushed strawberries with half the quantity of sugar, kirsch and lemon juice, setting, if possible, on ice an hour or so before being required for use. When ready, make the omelette, adding remainder of sugar and milk and beating well *before* folding in the two stiff egg whites, which must be lightly added at the last minute. Cook as an ordinary *soufflé* omelette. Drain juice from strawberries. Whip some cream very stiffly, adding a little sugar if wished, but it is better without. Fold the cream into the drained strawberries, having this mixture as cold as possible. When serving the omelette, fold the fruit and cream mixture quickly in centre and serve immediately, handing the juice separately or pouring it around the omelette, but it is best to serve it apart as it will otherwise cool the omelette too much. The omelette must be *very* hot and fluffy and the filling ice-cold. Serve very quickly to be a real success.–P.W.

Jam Omelette: Make a sweet *soufflé* omelette and fold in hot jam. Raspberry, apricot and strawberry are best. Sprinkle outside with sugar, pass quickly under the griller and serve immediately.

Normande: Sugar and cream are added to the eggs before beating them, and apple *purée*, sweetened and mixed with some thick cream, folded in.

Omelette au Rhum: The *soufflé* omelette is best for this, but use equal quantities of beaten egg yolks and stiffly-beaten egg whites only. Add to egg yolks the liquid (milk or thin cream) and about 4 oz. finely powdered sugar to six eggs, or less if not wished very sweet.

Make the omelette as directed, sprinkling as soon as done with powdered sugar and pouring over it a sufficiency of good, warmed rum. Set a match to this when taking to the dining-room. It is ready to serve as soon as the flames die down.

Rum Omelette 'de luxe': Fill the omelette with warmed apricot jam, pour warmed rum over, set alight, and serve with iced, unflavoured, whipped cream, which is handed in a separate sauce-boat.

Soufflé Omelette: This is quite easy and very effective, but this type of omelette will wait upon the guests even less graciously than its plain prototype: it will speedily become flat and tough.

To every yolk of egg used add two whites, beaten separately until very firm, then lightly folded into the beaten yolks to which the liquid and seasonings have been previously added. Instead of cooking *on* the stove, this type of omelette is best cooked in a *very hot* oven for about ten minutes, when it will puff up to huge dimensions and must be literally *run* to the table. Cheese, added in proportions already given, makes delicious *soufflé* omelettes. Some chefs begin the operation by frying on top of stove, as ordinary omelettes, putting it into the very hot oven as soon as outer surface is crisp and golden.

Omelette Surprise: Make a large omelette and a small omelette, and have the large one

ready a few seconds before the small one Coat the top surface of the large one with either apricot or greengage jam or freshly-made *purée* of those fruits; place the smaller omelette on this, and coat it with flavoured or unflavoured cream; roll up the preparation and serve.—T.E.W.

SOUFFLÉS

Soufflés are sweet or savoury confections which are made with a batter, similar to that used for pancakes (flour, butter and milk), and with eggs, of which the whites are beaten to a froth and added separately. They are best made in specially designed china dishes or cases, some of which are large and others small, the smaller ones being made of paper. All *soufflés*, large or small, must be light, and they owe their lightness to the fact that the air in the mixture expands when hot but is caught in the whisked white of egg: it stretches it but does not get through; hence the way the *soufflé* 'rises' and overflows the bounds of its case. Hence also the necessity to wait for the *soufflé* to be made and served immediately it comes out of the oven; if it has to wait, the air inside the meshes of the whites of egg cools and contracts and the *soufflé* just flops.

Soufflés are either baked or steamed and flavoured with either vanilla, chocolate orange, etc., for sweet *soufflés*, or cheese, steamed white fish, etc., for savoury *soufflés*.

Baked Soufflés: Make a batter with ¾ oz. flour, one gill milk and 1 oz. butter. Melt the butter in a white-lined pan, add the flour and cook for a few seconds; add the milk (or stock if making a savoury *soufflé*), beating well, over the fire, so as to get a smooth paste. Then add the yolks of three or four eggs per gill of liquid, one at a time, and beat them in thoroughly. Whisk the whites, one more than the number of yolks used, and as soon as they are quite stiff, fold them in carefully into the mixture. Then pour into a china, tin or paper dish, tin, or case, being careful not to fill it more than half, or less, to allow for the 'rise' of the *soufflé*. Bake in a moderate, steady oven, and serve as soon as it has risen and the centre is firm to the touch.

Steamed Soufflés: In the making of *soufflés* which are to be steamed, it is better to use a little more flour, say 1 oz. of flour to 1 oz. butter and one gill milk or stock, otherwise the procedure is the same.

Vanilla Soufflé: 1 oz. fine flour, 1 oz. butter, one gill milk, three yolks, four whites, one dessertspoon castor sugar, vanilla essence.

Method. Melt the butter, stir in the flour, add the milk and cook. Stir until mixture leaves sides of stewpan clean. Let the panana cool slightly; add sugar and vanilla essence and the yolks one at a time. Whisk the whites to a stiff froth, stir them lightly in and pour mixture into a well-buttered *soufflé* mould. Cover with buttered paper and steam very gently for 40 minutes or bake in a hot oven for 20 minutes, and serve with wine or jam sauce. Sufficient for three or four persons.

Chocolate Soufflé: 2 oz. finely-grated chocolate, 2 oz. sugar, 3 oz. flour, 1 oz. butter, half pint milk, three yolks, four whites, half teaspoon vanilla essence, custard or other suitable sauce.

Method. Place the milk and chocolate in a small stewpan and simmer gently until dissolved. Melt the butter, stir in the flour, add the chocolate mixture and boil well. Let it cool a little; add the vanilla essence, sugar and yolks one at a time; give the whole a good beating, then stir in as lightly as possible the stiffly-whisked whites. Turn into a well-buttered mould and steam gently for 45 to 50 minutes. Serve the sauce round the dish. Sufficient for five or six persons.

Oeufs à la Neige

This egg *entremets sucré* is more popular in France than any of the sweet omelettes. It is made with the whites of eggs beaten to a stiff froth with plenty of fine white castor sugar; with a tablespoon, take as much as the spoon will hold comfortably of this egg *meringue* and drop it into some boiling milk, sweetened with sugar and flavoured with vanilla; repeat until all the egg-whites have been used; they should have the size and shape of eggs. Cook these very light 'eggs' in the boiling milk, turning them over so that they cook on both sides equally; as soon as they are firm, take them out with a slicer and drain them. With the hot milk used for poaching the 'eggs', make a custard, pouring the milk on the yolks of eggs and stirring continuously, until the custard begins to thicken; let it be more liquid than for an ordinary custard and add the 'eggs' when the custard will be cold; they will float on top of the custard.

V. POACHED EGGS

Oeufs pochés, moulés, en cocotte, en cassolette

Poached eggs are eggs boiled without their shells. The tidiest way to cook them is to use the tin moulds sold for the purpose. Three or four together make a utensil. An egg is broken into each and the whole outfit put into boiling water slightly salted, and for choice with a dash of vinegar. When finished the sides of the mould are lifted from the bottom part, and the eggs slid off to their final destination.

628

But such a weapon is not necessary – the egg may be broken straight into boiling water and lifted out with a perforated spoon when finished. An average egg takes three minutes to poach, but it need not be timed, because it can plainly be seen when it is ready for removal from the water.—F.C.-W.

The French way of poaching eggs is somewhat different. Some water is put to boil in a deep saucepan, a tablespoonful of vinegar to about three pints of water is added; also half a tablespoonful of salt. When the water is boiling, a long-handled wooden spoon is used, practically in a vertical position, to create in the centre of the pan a sort of well, by rotating the water round and round in the same way as fast as one can without scalding oneself. The eggs are slipped, one by one, of course, in this miniature whirlpool, and the pan is moved away from the fire or the heat is reduced; soon the rotating egg will begin to set, and when the white is firmly set the egg can be taken out carefully, the pan put back on the fire, the water brought to the boil again, and the same operation repeated for the next egg. This method is more troublesome, of course, and the taste of the egg no better, but it retains its original 'egg' shape instead of being flattened.

Aline: Prepare a light batter as for *Fritters* (q.v.); poach the eggs, dip them in the batter and fry in very hot deep fat over a fierce fire for a very few minutes.

Ambassadrice: Poached eggs served in *croustades* upon a *salpicon* of chicken and mushrooms.

Archiduc: Poached eggs served in *cassolettes* with a garnishing of fried minced mushrooms and onions, and a dusting of paprika.

Argenteuil: Poached eggs served with asparagus points: these must be boiled till tender, then drained and made thoroughly hot again in a hot, rich, creamy sauce, seasoned with pepper and salt.

Aurore: Poached eggs served in *croustades*, covered with a rather thin tomato sauce.

Belle-Hélène: Poached eggs served with some *Croquettes de Volaille*; also asparagus points as a garnish.

Benedict: Poached eggs served on half a muffin, toasted and garnished with a piece of fried ham of the same size; a *Sauce Hollandaise* is poured over it all just before serving.

Bénédictine: Poached eggs served in a *Timbale* filled with *Brandade de morue* (q.v. in Section V, *FISH*).

Bohémienne: Poached eggs served in *croustades* upon two thin slices of equal size, the top one *foie gras* and the other ham; a *Sauce Madère* is poured over it all before serving.

Bretonne: Poached eggs served in *tartelettes*, upon a bed of haricot beans, cooked in good meat stock, with minced and browned onions, and then mashed to a *purée*. The eggs are covered with some rich veal stock and a sprinkling of finely-chopped parsley just before serving.

Bruxelloise: Poached eggs served on *croûtes* with a *purée* of brussels sprouts.

Cardinal: Poached eggs served in *croustades* with some shredded lobster and a tomato sauce.

Eggs in cases: These may be described as eggs set in china cases, or *coquilles*, that have been lined with some nicely made forcemeat the composition of which can be varied in numerous ways: fish, shell-fish, game, veal, chicken, ham, *foie gras*, etc., etc., being employed for the purpose. A simple example will suffice:

Oeufs en caisses aux crevettes: Work in a mortar to the consistency of pliant paste a quarter of a pint of picked shrimps, assisting the operation with 1 oz. of butter, and adding one yolk and a quarter of a pint of white breadcrumbs that have been soaked in milk; season with finely-chopped parsley, pepper and salt. With this line the bottom and sides of four small, previously buttered china cases, leaving a hollow in the centre of each to receive one egg. Slip the eggs into the cases carefully, sprinkle the surface with a little salt, and pour a small allowance of melted butter over them. Set the cases in a high-sided *sauté*-pan, with boiling water up to a third of their depth: cover and push this into a moderate oven, poaching gently for 8 or 10 minutes. On taking out the cases dish them in a *légumier*, giving each a cap of anchovy or capers butter, or of shrimp *purée*.

Taking this as a fair sample of the method, it is clear that by changing the lining ingredients you can produce a number of nice little dishes. This ought not to be difficult, for in many kitchens there are continually remnants of good things that can soon be turned into lining.—A.K.-H. 1.

Chantilly: Poached eggs served on *croûtes* with small, new, green peas and whipped cream.

Châtelaine: Poached eggs served on *croûtes* and upon a *purée* of chestnuts.

Chaufroid: The eggs are poached in the French way, drained, trimmed neatly and allowed to cool. Then a White Sauce (See Section I, *SAUCES*) is made, 1½ gills for four eggs; ¼ oz. of gelatine having been softened in water is strained into the White Sauce, and then 1½ tablespoons of aspic jelly; blend all together thoroughly and season with pepper and salt; stir frequently and allow to get cool. Put the poached eggs upon a wire tray and spoon over them the jellified sauce, with care and evenly. When one coating is set, add another and leave it to cool

and to set. Decorate the eggs with small pieces of black truffles cut in various fancy shapes, and cover them with a clear aspic jelly through which they will show.

Oeufs en cocotte: *Cocotte* means here a tiny casserole or ramekin, large enough for one egg. This is, perhaps, the simplest egg technique known to the French with the exception of the *à la coque*. A little butter is placed in the bottom of the *cocotte*, and the egg broken into it. It is placed then in a *bain-marie* – or, in ordinary kitchens, a pan of hot water – and cooked there. Simple in the beginning, it is served simply, too – with few garnishes, if any. If you want more calories, put a little cream in the bottom of the heated *cocotte* with a piece of butter. Break the eggs in, season, and cook in a pan of hot water, as above. Or mix the egg and cream gently, after a couple of minutes, and continue the cooking in the oven a few minutes covered. Sometimes minced mushrooms or ham or chicken livers are put in the bottom of the *cocotte*, and *Sauce Soubise* makes a tempting lining, but the simple method is really more popular.—T.L.B.

Daumont: Poached eggs served in *croustades* with some minced chicken, mixed with fresh cream, and duly seasoned with pepper and salt.

Devilled: Poached eggs upon which a little mustard is spread before dipping them in some beaten egg and rolling them in egg-and-breadcrumbs; they are then fried in boiling fat for one minute.

Diable: Cook some onions with a little curry powder, then chop them up and add a little sugar and a few drops of lemon juice; spread this mixture on top of *croûtons* which have been smeared with anchovy paste; serve with one poached egg on each dressed *croûton*.

Diane: Poached eggs served in a *timbale* upon a bed of game *purée* and minced mushrooms, with a *Sauce Madère* over it all.

Estragon: Poached eggs served in *tartelettes*, with a rich sauce made with half meat gravy and half tomato sauce, flavoured with chopped tarragon leaves; chopped tarragon leaves are also sprinkled over the eggs before serving.

Fédora: Poached eggs served on *croûtes* generously coated with *foie gras*.

Flamande: Poached eggs (or *Oeufs mollets*) served in *tartelettes* upon a bed of mashed potatoes and sprouts, with a cream sauce over it all and the smallest possible brussels sprout perched on top of each egg.

Flora: Poached eggs served in pairs, on *croustades*, one egg covered with a tomato sauce and a sprinkling of chopped parsley, the other with *Sauce Suprême* and chopped truffles.

Florentine: Poached eggs served in a *plat à gratin*, on a bed of creamed spinach and with a covering of *Sauce Mornay*.

Gilbert: Cold poached eggs served upon a couch of mixed salad of green peas, small French beans and asparagus points: grated nutmeg and a little cayenne pepper sprinkled on top of the eggs.

Gounod: Fry in butter some large mushroom caps and place them on the same number of round *croûtes* of the same size; then place a poached egg on each mushroom and sprinkle some finely-chopped parsley over the eggs before serving.

Grand-Duc: Poached eggs served on rounds of fried bread and arranged wreath-like in a round dish, with heaped up asparagus tips in the centre. Upon each egg there are two fairly equal pieces of lobster or crawfish (the latter for choice) and truffle, the fish below and the truffle on top. The whole is covered with a *Sauce Mornay* and quickly glazed under the grill.

Halévy: Poached eggs served on *croûtes*, richly spread with *foie gras*, and covered with a sauce made in equal parts with a tomato sauce and a *Velouté de Volaille*.

Jessica: Poached eggs served on *croûtes* with morels and asparagus points.

Massenet: Poached eggs served upon round *galettes* of *Pommes Anna* (See *Potatoes* in Section II, *VEGETABLES*), garnished with finely shredded boiled artichoke bottoms; a rich cream sauce is poured over it all.

Matelote: Poached eggs served with a *Roux brun*, made with flour, butter and meat stock, and flavoured with mushroom ketchup.

Metternich: Poached eggs served on artichoke bottoms, with a garnishing of strips of ox-tongue, a binding of *Velouté*, and a covering of *Sauce Mornay*.

Mirabeau: Poached eggs served upon *galettes* of *Pommes Anna* (see *Potatoes* in Section II, *VEGETABLES*), coated with a *Beurre d'Anchois* (see *Beurres composés*, in Section I, *SAUCES*), and with a sprinkling of chopped tarragon leaves on top.

Monselet: Poached eggs served on artichoke bottoms with a garnishing of truffles.

Mornay: Poached eggs masked with a *Sauce Mornay*, with grated cheese and breadcrumbs sprinkled over, and quickly glazed under the grill.

Normande: Poached eggs served in *croustades* with shrimps, mussels, oysters and a *Sauce Normande*.

Parisienne: Poached eggs served upon *galettes* of *Pommes Anna* (see *Potatoes* in Section II, *VEGETABLES*), and a garnish of braised lettuce.

Green Peas: Boil some large, elderly green peas until soft, rub them through a sieve, blend with pepper, salt, cream and butter to make a thick and unctuous *purée*. Cut some rounds of hot toast, butter them generously and coat them thickly with the *purée* of green peas; serve with a poached egg on each round of well-covered toast.

Petit-Duc: Poached eggs served upon the caps of grilled mushrooms, with a *Sauce Châteaubriand* and a little grated horseradish.

Poquelin: Poached eggs served on oval pieces of hot toast, with a garnish of salsify and a *Sauce Mornay*.

Princesse: Poached eggs served on *croûtes* which have been thickly coated with a *salpicon* of chicken; also asparagus points as a garnish and a *Sauce Suprême*.

Reine: Poached eggs served in *croustades* with pounded chicken meat mixed with a *Sauce Suprême*.

Rossini: Poached eggs served on *croûtes* with *foie gras* and truffles.

Royale: Large mushroom caps are grilled and then filled with a *purée* of truffles; one poached egg is then placed on each dressed mushroom cap and served.

Saint-Hubert: Poached eggs served upon a bed of minced venison.

Savoury Eggs: Put into one pint of hot milk a small sprig of marjoram, another of thyme, a small bayleaf, a blade of mace, a pinch of allspice, and four or five peppercorns: simmer gently for one hour and strain. Poach the eggs carefully in this savoury milk. Rub four or five anchovies through a fine sieve, after removing bones: mix with the anchovies a teaspoon of olive oil, a tablespoon of sherry wine, 1 oz. butter and a raw egg-yolk to bind the mixture. Heat throughout, but do not let the mixture boil, then coat with it some fried pieces of toast and serve with a poached egg on each piece of toast.

Soubise: Poached eggs served in *cocottes*, on a bed of thick onion sauce mixed with a little tomato *purée*; also some meat glaze round the eggs.

Surprise: Poach as many eggs as you need and when done slip into a basin of cold water. Allow two thin slices of ham to each egg. Put the drained egg on a slice of ham and cover it with another. Place on a long dish and cover with aspic jelly. When set, cut out with an oval cutter, put on a silver dish, garnish with green salad and serve with bread and butter.—O.H.

Tante Marie: Fill some *tartelettes* with cooked shrimps and a white sauce and serve with poached eggs on top.

Trianon: Fill some *cocottes* with a creamed *purée* of mushrooms, place a poached egg on top of the *purée*, cover with a *Sauce Mornay*, sprinkle some grated Parmesan cheese on top, brown in a quick oven and serve.

Villeroi: Poach the eggs in good meat stock, drain them, coat them with a thick

Sauce Hollandaise, dip them in egg-and-breadcrumbs, fry them in deep fat and serve with a tomato sauce.

Oeufs au Vin: Put some finely-chopped onions into an earthenware saucepan containing melted butter, and when browned, pour over them some good wine.

Next add salt, pepper, thyme, a bayleaf, a clove, and a sprig of fennel. After a quarter of an hour, the boiling wine, slightly reduced, will fill the kitchen with a fragrant steam. Break your eggs one by one on the edge of the saucepan, and let them fall into the steamy, bubbling wine. A white film will spread as you watch. When poached remove the eggs and set them all steaming with the sauce on a round dish. Then pour the wine quickly through a sieve, put it back in the saucepan, and thicken with a *roux* (flour and melted butter). After about five minutes you will feel a thick, firm sauce forming under your spoon, which you spread over the eggs like a brown eiderdown.—H.G.

Vosgienne: Poached eggs served with braised red cabbage, fried bacon and *cervelas* (flat sausages).

Xavier: Poached eggs served in *croustades* filled with a *salpicon* of crawfish, truffles and mushrooms.

VI. SCRAMBLED EGGS

Oeufs brouillés

To scramble eggs properly is quite easy, but it is even easier to scramble them into a nasty mess, with white streaks and a watery gravy, the result of allowing the mixture to come to boiling point. This *must* be avoided above all else, and the following directions carefully followed:

Break each egg (one per person is a minimum, two is a fairer allowance) into a cup and make sure that it is quite fresh; if it is not, throw it away; if it is, add it to the others in a basin, which must be large enough for the number of eggs proposed to be beaten to a froth comfortably. Add pepper and salt. Beat thoroughly with a rotary beater or a fork, but beat to a froth. Then choose the pan for scrambling. Never use an aluminium one for scrambling eggs: it is not suitable. Earthenware china and oven-glass dishes are really best for scrambling eggs and serving them in the dish itself; but a copper or iron pan will do, over a very low fire. A double boiler, or a smaller saucepan placed in a larger one full of boiling water is cumbersome but the safest for beginners. Whatever the pan used, put some butter in it and as it melts smear all the sides of the pan with it. As it is melting in the pan over the fire, add a little milk, cream or water to the beaten eggs, give one last 'rouse' (beating) and pour the mixture into the pan, before the butter begins to sizzle. Then stir the mixture evenly and constantly, scraping bottom and sides of the pan gently in order to prevent sticking and boiling, until the egg mixture is set to a soft creamy consistency. It is then ready to serve as it is, in small dishes, on pieces of buttered toast, by itself or with almost any kind of tasty food, asparagus tips, buttered shrimps, truffles, crabmeat, etc.

Scrambled Eggs with Bacon or Ham: Fry until crisp cut-up rashers of bacon or slices of ham, using as much as desired for quantity of egg used. The ham should be diced or, if preferred, shredded. When done, scramble eggs in with pieces of bacon or ham and in the fat in which they were fried; also if necessary, some more butter added.

Scrambled Eggs Bûcheronne:
> Rounds of toasted or fried bread
> Beaten eggs
> Round slices of ham
> Salt and pepper

A simple but excellent dish. Fry or toast rounds of bread and lay them side by side in a shallow oven dish which has been generously buttered. On each round of bread lay a slice of ham of the same size. Cover all with beaten and seasoned eggs and bake in a very hot oven for five or six minutes.—P.W.

Scrambled Eggs with Cheese: Allow about $1\frac{1}{2}$ oz. grated cheese for every two eggs used. Beat it with eggs and whatever liquid is used.

Scrambled Eggs with Chicken Livers: Lightly fry one or more chicken livers, adding, if liked, a drop or two of onion juice and, of course, butter as required. When done, chop livers coarsely and scramble with beaten eggs.

Scrambled Eggs and Corn:
> 1 small tin of corn or 3 cooked ears
> 4 eggs
> Salt and pepper
> 1 tablespoon butter

If fresh ears of corn are used, boil in salted water until it is tender enough to scrape off cob. If tinned corn is used, drain off all liquid and add none to eggs as the corn contains all the moisture required. Melt the butter in a frying-pan or on top of double-boiler; add the corn, season well and pour the well-beaten eggs on this, stirring and cooking as directed.

Scrambled Eggs Mirador: Butter copiously some small *cocottes* or ramekins. Half fill them with eggs beaten as directed for scrambling. Put in a moderately hot oven and, when set, turn out of moulds and serve with mushroom, Hollandaise or tomato sauce.—P.W.

Scrambled Eggs with Mushrooms: Cook sliced mushrooms in butter gently for a few minutes. Drain, cool and add to beaten eggs, using the butter the mushrooms cooked in for scrambling the eggs.

Eggs Rosebery: Scramble eggs and mix in any remains of cold salmon, adding salt and pepper. The dish, if properly made, should reproduce Lord Rosebery's racing colours: viz., primrose and rose. It looks pretty and tastes delicious (Lord Cobham).—N.S.

Rumbled Eggs:
> 5 eggs
> 1 tablespoon butter
> 1 teaspoon chopped parsley
> ½ teaspoonful salt
> ¼ teaspoonful pepper
> 1 dessertspoon water
> 1 or 2 tomatoes

The beauty of Rumbled Eggs is that they cook practically unattended – whereas the scrambled variety almost always overcook while you hastily make the coffee.

Put a baking dish or casserole on top of a saucepan full of boiling water. Beat the eggs, water, parsley, salt and pepper well together, while you leave the butter to heat and melt in the dish over the boiling water. When the butter has become liquid and really hot, pour in the beaten eggs and flavourings and stir twice. Then you can leave them over the gently bubbling water while you see to the rest of the preparations for the meal, giving them only an occasional stir as you pass the stove, just to prevent the egg nearest the water from sticking. Add the sliced peeled tomatoes after a few minutes.

As soon as the eggs are of the consistency of Devonshire cream, remove the saucepan from the flame, and the dish will keep hot over the water until the moment for serving arrives. (Ruth Morgan in *Woman*, circa 1938.)

Venetian Eggs:
> 3 eggs
> 1 heaping tablespoonful (1 oz.) butter
> ¼ pint (1 cup) strained tomato juice
> ½ pint (1 cup) grated cheese
> Salt and pepper

Melt the butter in a casserole, add the grated cheese, and stir until melted. Pour in the tomato juice, and when this begins to thicken, add the eggs, which have been lightly beaten.

Season with salt and pepper, and serve on hot toasted crackers.—M.H.N.

Scotch Woodcock:
> 3 or 4 slices toast
> 3 egg yolks
> 4 or 5 anchovies

½ pint thin cream
Pepper, very little salt

Cut the toast into fingers, buttering well. Keep hot. Wash, scrape and bone the anchovies, then pound or chop VERY finely. Spread them on the toast. Beat the egg yolks with the cream, season with pepper and a very little salt and scramble in a double boiler. When creamy, arrange prepared toast on a hot dish and cover with the egg mixture.

Another recipe: *Scotch Woodcock de luxe*: Take two slices of stale white bread, toast and butter it well on both sides, then spread over one side with a thin layer of anchovy paste. Place the other piece of toast on top and press together. Cut in strips 2 in. long and 1 in. wide, arrange in hot dish and pour over it a sauce made as follows:

Put two raw yolks of egg into the top part of a double boiler with four tablespoons thick cream, 1½ oz. butter, and pepper; mix with wooden spoon till the mixture is like a creamy sauce. Then strain through a strainer, add a little chopped parsley and pour over toast.

Scrambled Eggs with Tomatoes:
> 3 tomatoes
> 2 tablespoons butter
> 3 eggs
> Salt and pepper
> Toast or *croûtes*

Select firm tomatoes of equal size. Cut them in halves and remove seeds and centres without breaking skins. Put them on a buttered tin, add salt and pepper and a speck of butter on each and bake in a hot oven for four or five minutes or place under a griller. Scramble eggs, adding to them the softer portions of insides of tomatoes. Have round *croûtes* ready, or rounds of hot buttered toast, set half a tomato on each and fill with the egg mixture. Garnish with parsley and serve at once as eggs must not stand.

Another method. *Tomato and Scrambled Egg*: Peel some tomatoes, cut them up, remove seeds and drain liquid off; then put into a pan with a little butter, salt and pepper. Cook slowly, stirring frequently, until a thick tomato *purée* is obtained. Pour beaten egg mixture on this and cook as directed.

SUNDRY SAVOURY GARNISHINGS FOR SOUPS

Egg Balls
2 yolks of hard-boiled eggs
1 raw egg yolk
Pinch salt
Few grains cayenne pepper
½ teaspoon melted butter

Rub the hard-boiled yolks through a sieve, add the other ingredients, using the raw egg yolk to bind to a paste easy to handle. Shape into small balls, roll in flour and *sauté* in hot butter, shaking well. Nice with chicken broth or *consommé*. These, like the *croûtons*, should be handed with the soup; if put in it before serving, they soon lose their crispness.

Fritter 'Beans'

1 fresh egg
2 tablespoons milk
¾ teaspoon salt
½ cup flour

Beat the egg well, add to the flour and salt, mixing into a batter. Pour through a colander into deep boiling frying-fat, cooking until evenly brown and crisp. Drain on brown paper and serve hot with soup.

Soup Custard

2 egg yolks
Few grains salt
2 tablespoons milk

Beat the eggs lightly, add milk and salt. Pour the mixture into a buttered cup. Place this in a panful of hot water and cook in a moderate oven until firm. Cool, turn custard out of cup and cut it into cubes or fancy shapes with French vegetable cutters.

Marrow Balls

2 tablespoons of marrow fat
¼ cup soft breadcrumbs
2 eggs
½ teaspoon salt
Dusting of grated nutmeg

'Matzos' should really be used instead of breadcrumbs. These are large flat biscuits obtainable in certain foreign shops, but breadcrumbs will do. Soften the raw marrow by beating and pressing with a fork. Beat the eggs well, season and then add the breadcrumbs gradually, using only enough to bind the mixture to a soft dough. Let this stand in a cool spot or, better still, on ice until firm, then shape the mixture into small balls the size of a marble. Try one in boiling water and if it does not hold together, more breadcrumbs must be added. Drop the balls into boiling *consommé* or *bouillon* 15 minutes before serving. The crumbs must be fine and sifted before using.—P.W.

Cheese Drops

3 tablespoons milk or cream
1 teaspoon butter
2 tablespoons grated Parmesan cheese
2 tablespoons flour
1 egg
Pinch of salt

Mix the cream or milk with the butter and heat in a small pan. When the butter has melted, use mixture to moisten the flour and salt. Stir quickly and remove pan from fire. Add the egg and beat mixture until smooth; then add the cheese. Let the mixture stand in a cool place until it is stiff, then drop from the end of a spoon into boiling frying-fat and cook until brown and crisp. Drain. Delicious with onion soup.—P.W.

Chicken's Liver Balls

1 chicken's liver
1 teaspoon butter
1 tiny onion
1 egg
1 tablespoon flour
Salt and pepper

Chop the onion or grate finely. Melt the butter in a small pan, add the onion, then the finely chopped or cut-up liver. Fry gently for a few minutes, then add the flour, mixing and seasoning well. Let the mixture cool; then add the well-beaten egg. This will give a dough which can be shaped into small balls which must be dropped into boiling soup ten minutes before serving. A little finely chopped parsley may also be added. —P.W.

Royale

An egg custard cooked in a mould and allowed to set before it can be used. When it is firm and cold, it is cut in dice, lozenges, rounds, or any shape, and added to clear soups. It is usually white: when coloured, it is called:

Royale Crécy, with carrots and red in colour.
Royale à l'écarlate, with lobster or langouste *purée* and red in colour.
Royale Vert-Pré, with a *purée* of green vegetables and herbs (spinach, watercress, chervil and tarragon); green in colour.

SECTION 8
CHEESE

SECTION VIII

Cheese: comprising an explanation of the general quality of cheese, together with alphabetical lists of the most famous kinds made in England, on the Continent, and in the United States

CHEESE

Dans le Chester sec et rose
A longues dents, l'Anglais mord.

VICTOR MEUSY.

INTRODUCTION

BOTH Wine and Cheese represent man's effort to transmute the Perishable into the Durable. For a while – perhaps for thousands of years – our ancestors could refresh themselves with the juice of the grape only where the vine grew and its fruit ripened. Often must they have longed, in parched wastes and under brutal suns, for the grape's cool freshness; but at last somebody's carelessness or inquisitiveness left alone a bowl of pressed grapes long enough for Nature's miracle of fermentation to produce the first wine. Likewise with cheese. To draw from some tamed mammal – a cow, a goat, a sheep, a mare – the food-beverage which we call milk meant a great progress in civilization; but milk, like grape-juice, was as perishable as the daily manna of the wandering Israelites, until its controlled souring and curding made it durable and easily portable. In other words, both grape-juice and milk tend to 'go bad'; but human skill can make them 'go good' in the forms of wine and cheese.

A second resemblance between these two precious things is that they are made to 'go good' by processes which are fundamentally natural. The enemies of wine to-day love to misrepresent it as a non-natural and noxious potion, devised by perverse ingenuity for the undoing of mankind; yet the substitutes for wine, in contrast with it, are highly artificial. As for cheese, although its manufacture admits of manifold variations and refinements, it is, like wine, essentially a natural product.

This naturalness, however, does not mean that wine and cheese are simply grape-juice and milk largely purged of corruptibility. In each case the original material undergoes a

change
Into something rich and strange.

The first gourdful or skinful of cleanly fermented grape-juice was something new under the sun; and, although the first cheese may have been no more – perhaps much less – than Jael's 'butter in a lordly dish', or curds drained of their whey, this too was a thing different from mere bad and perished milk.

Beginning countless generations ago as more Nature's work than man's, wine has been elaborated within historical times to such an extent that, for more than two thousand years, its devotees have almost deified it, while poets have made it one of their fondest themes. Such men as the Deipnosophists, although they belonged to a pagan age, were not ancients but moderns in their talk-bouts on wine. Their œnological erudition was so definitely that of antiquaries and of *laudatores temporis acti* that we must smile at those contemporaries of ours who speak about *vins de luxe* and about precise territorial wine-names as recent innovations. But cheese, while resembling wine in its variety, has lagged heavily behind in respect of classification and description. Cheese is like wine in embodying local peculiarities of soil and climate; but, while the vintners have got so far as to give many a château or clos or schloss or garten or quinta full credit for its peculiar production of some noble or delicate wine, the curders have not advanced beyond broad regional categories.

Ernest Oldmeadow

Definitions

MILK

Milk is the secretion of the mammary glands of those vertebrate animals known as *mammalia* that suckle their young.

There is in milk, besides water, fat – the milk fat which is often called butter fat; proteins (lactalbumin, casein, globulin and others); carbohydrates (chiefly lactose); organic acids (chiefly lactic acid, also citric acid and very minute quantities of acetic acid). There are also in milk other organic substances such as urea, lecithin, creatinine, alcohol, hypoxanthin and lactochrome in minute quantities. And last, but by no means least, there are in milk small amounts of mineral salts of sodium, potassium, calcium, magnesium and iron; also some enzymes and vitamines.

Is there any water in milk?

There is far more water in milk than anything else; on an average 87 per cent of milk is water, before any milkman has even looked at it.

There are many different qualities of milk. First of all, according to the species and breed of the milk giver, whether cow, goat or ewe. Secondly, according to the condition of the animal, its state of health, the quantity and quality of its feed, whether grazed in the open in the summer months or fed indoors on patent 'cake' in the winter. Thirdly, milk varies from day to day, in fact from hour to hour, according to the temperature of the place where it is kept and the progress made by different bacteria which find in milk a most suitable breeding ground. Some of them are deadly; such are the tuberculosis bacteria present in the milk of cows suffering from tuberculosis. Others are most beneficial: such are the lactic bacteria which are responsible for lactic fermentation, or the conversion of most of the sugar present in milk into lactic acid.

Lactic acid is an organic acid with the chemical formula $CH_3 . CH(OH) . COOH$. It is formed during the lactic fermentation of sugars, starches and other substances in the presence of nitrogenous animal matter. It occurs in sour milk; it is the cause of the sourness of taste and flavour of sour milk.

Lactic acid in cheese is not only desirable, it is indispensable in cheese that is going to be kept and matured, that is to say practically every kind of fermented cheese.

CHEESE

Cheese is the curd of milk, separated by the action of rennet and suitably ripened. It is to milk what wine is to grape-juice. It is the most valuable and universally accepted milk food for adults.

There are ever so many different varieties of cheese, made in every civilized and some uncivilized lands, wherever grass grows and is grazed. The fundamental causes of differences in cheese are differences in the quality of the milk from which cheese is made and differences in methods of cheese-making.

Rennet, which is the chief fermenting agent used in cheese-making, is an unorganized ferment, a chemical substance found in the gastric juice of all mammals when still suckling. It is usually extracted from the fourth stomach – known as *vell* – of suckling calves. The amount of rennet used is governed, chiefly, by the variety of cheese which is being made; by the acidity, quantity and quality of the milk and by the time of the year. Thus when 3 oz. of rennet extract will be added to 100 gallons of milk in the spring, 5 oz. will have to be added to the same quantity of milk during the summer months.

Rennet contains two substances known as *rennin* and *pepsin*: they are proteolytic enzymes which make it possible for a number of changes to take place in the composition first of all of the milk – this is chiefly the part of the rennin – and, secondly, of the cheese – this is mostly due to the presence of the pepsin.

Rennin is responsible for the coagulation and precipitation, in the form of *curd*, of the casein which is present in the milk in partial solution and in combination with lime.

Curd is a combination of the paracasein with the lime and the calcium phosphate of the casein. It encases and holds most of the fat globules of the milk.

The temperature of the milk at the time is very important. Rennin acts best as a catalyst, that is to say a remover of hindrances, making molecular readjustments possible, at a temperature of about 105° F. However, this temperature is not practical in cheese-making, as the curd obtained would be too firm. For most kinds of cheese, the most suitable temperatures for renneting are between 80° and 90° F. The richer the milk and the colder the outside air at the time, the higher should be the temperature at the time of renneting. The danger of the temperature being too high is that the curd is sufficiently firm for milling long before it is acid enough. On the other hand, too low a temperature produces a weak curd which readily parts with its fat, and, if the milk is ripe, the curd will be much too acid before it is firm enough for milling.

Pepsin acts differently from rennin: it digests the curd, but it does this in a satisfactory manner only if there is the right amount of acidity in the curd. If there is not enough, the curd becomes cheese slowly and unsatisfactorily: it tends to develop a tough and leathery texture as well as producing evil-smelling gases. Should there be an excess of acidity in the curd, the cheese under the action of pepsin will age too rapidly; it will become dry and crumbly with too sharp a flavour.

The acidity of the curd is to some extent due to the natural salts which pass from the soil where cattle are being grazed into the milk; these minerals salts are the most important as regards the flavour which different cheeses acquire with age, although they are present in milk in very small quantities. The most important natural acid in milk, quantitatively, is lactic acid. It is the same in all milks. The acidity of the curd is primarily due to the acidity of the milk, which is due, chiefly, to lactic acid-producing bacteria; the acidity of the curd develops during ripening. The salt which is added at a later stage of cheese-making as a preservative or for the sake of greater palatability, must be of the purest sort and free from sulphates and salts of lime and magnesia. An inferior salt will spoil the flavour, texture and colour of the cheese.

The cheese with the greatest food value is the cheese made from cream, or from whole milk with added cream, whilst the cheese with the least food value is the cheese made from skimmed milk, the milk poorest in cream or butter fat.

The most digestible cheese is, in theory, that which is richest in pepsin; in practice it depends upon personal idiosyncrasies and upon what one drinks at the time, either vintage port in the winter months, tawny port in the spring, claret in the summer, or burgundy in the autumn; although it is really a matter of personal taste.

Note.   Cheese-mites are tasteless and inoffensive enough, but the terror of all strict vegetarians. Even they – the cheese-mites – have inspired one of the 'minor' English poets:

> The cheese-mites asked how the cheese got there,
> And warmly debated the matter;
> The orthodox said it came from the air,
> And the heretics said from the platter.

> > (*Notes and Queries.* 12th Series.)

CHEESE IN AMERICA

COMPARED to some European nations, Americans are not great cheese eaters, though during the last decade our cheese consumption has increased considerably.

Neither do we have a great cheese-making tradition, nor any original American cheeses. As a nation of settlers, we have hung onto the taste of our fathers for the cheeses of Europe, and preferred to reproduce them here – or import them – rather than develop new varieties.

Cheese-making on any kind of scale is only about a hundred years old in America. Until 1850 or so all the cheese was made on the farms, and most of it was cottage cheese, though some farmers made Cheddar in the way of their English forefathers. The first cheese factory was in Oneida, New York, where the surroundings were perfect – good pastures, ample water, fine cattle, a suitable climate.

New York State was the main cheese-producing area of the nation until, in the early nineteen hundreds, it became more profitable to send the milk to New York City, then rapidly expanding and wanting more and more milk for drinking. By and by the industry traveled westward, until today cheese is made in almost every state of the Union. Wisconsin, however, with ideal conditions, produces more than half of the cheese made in the United States.

About 80 per cent of American made and consumed cheese is Cheddar, which is what people mean when they call for store cheese, rat cheese, or plain cheese. Cheddar comes in various degrees of mildness or sharpness. It is also the basis of the 'process' cheeses, cheese 'foods' and 'spreads' on the market, which are rindless, long-keeping, easy to use and practically tasteless, which may be the reason why they have endeared themselves to the great American public with its preference for bland foods.

The nearest approach to a really American cheese is a Limburger-type cheese marketed under the trade-name of Liederkranz. But practically every kind of well-known foreign cheese is made here, provided there is enough demand for it. And the demand for more interesting cheeses is growing – there are cheese specialty stores in any sizeable city, and even the supermarkets carry a surprising variety of different cheeses.

Whether American cheese is as good as European cheese is a question that arouses passionate discussions among cheese fanciers. Our cheese is much more uniform in quality, because it is almost always made from Pasteurized milk (European cheese is not) which is much the same everywhere, though it does not give as tasty a cheese. Then, American cheese is mostly factory-made and systematized. We may have good cheese in

America that is always the same, but without the individual craftsman and his century-old tradition we will seldom have great cheese.

Neither can certain European climatic or geographical advantages be duplicated, like the sweet grass of the High Alps eaten by the noble cows whose milk makes Swiss cheese, or like the caves of Roquefort, where the cheese of the same name is ripened. Last of all, American cheese is very often not sufficiently aged. Aging is expensive, since it requires warehouse space, which is expensive, and besides it involves tying up large investments.

Certain European cheeses made in America are far more successful than others, and, with proper aging, quite as good. Cheddar and Swiss are the two outstanding examples. But to this day, we have not been able to make a really good Camembert or Brie.

When buying cheese, one should choose 'natural' cheeses – in most cases, they are so marked on the label. Whatever is claimed for process cheese, there is absolutely no substitute for the honest, true taste of natural cheeses.

Incidentally, what we in the United States refer to as Swiss cheese – either domestic or imported – is the same (or very nearly) as what in France is called Gruyère. What we call Gruyère is a process cheese, domestic or imported, made up into small wedges, foil-wrapped and packed in small round boxes. When a French recipe calls for Gruyère, you should use Swiss cheese, domestic or imported.

NIKA STANDEN

ENGLISH CHEESES

BLUE DORSET – BLUE VINNY

Blue Dorset is a hard cheese made from skimmed cow's milk, in Dorsetshire; it is more usually known as Blue Vinny, and sometimes as Blue Vinid.

It is as white as chalk with a 'royal blue' vein right through, a sort of *cordon bleu* which is the reason for its name.

Vinny is the corruption of the old West Country word 'Vinew' which means 'Mould', and used to be pronounced 'vinney' like 'sinew', which used to be pronounced 'sinney'; and vinid is the corruption of the old West Country word 'vinewed', meaning 'mouldy'.

The particular kind of mould responsible for the colour and the horizontal formation of the Blue Vinny 'blue' is different from other cheese moulds and behaves differently.

CAERPHILLY

Originally a Welsh cheese, but now made also in Somerset, Wiltshire, Devon and Dorset. It is a whole milk cheese, weighing usually from 8 lb. to 9 lb., lightly pressed and sold in its 'green' state, from 10 to 11 days old.

CHEDDAR

Cheddar is one of the oldest English cheeses on record. Here is what John Houghton said about it in a letter he wrote on 5th July, 1695: 'Cheddar being warmly seated on the south side of Mendip hills in Somersetshire, and at the foot of them near the town of Axbridge, is exposed only to the south and south-west winds, and has the moors adjacent to it on the south, being a warm and fertile soil for pasturage, whereby Cheddar is rendered famous for Cheese; and it has been long a custom there, as well as in some adjacent parishes, for several neighbours to join their milk together, as occasion requires, to make the said Cheese; which is of a bigger size than ordinary; and contends in goodness (if kept a due time, viz. from two years to five, according to magnitude), with any Cheese of England. The sizes of the same Cheeses are generally from thirty pounds weight to one hundred pounds.' (*Husbandry and Trade Improv'd*. Vol. I. Letter cliii.) Some fifty years earlier, in Samuel Hartlib's *His Legacy of Husbandry*, published in London in 1655 (p. 263), Cheddar is described as the best cheese in England, made in different weights from 20 lb. to 120lb.

The largest Cheddar cheese ever made was a monster Cheddar made from the milk of 750 cows by the people of East and West Pennard, in Somersetshire, in the Cheddar district, as a bridal offering to Queen Victoria, in 1840. Its weight was 11 cwt., its circumference 9 ft. 4 in., and its depth 20 in. The Queen graciously accepted the present, but the farmers asked that it might be exhibited. Their request was granted, but the Queen declined to have it back after the exhibition. The farmers then quarrelled among themselves, their cheese got into Chancery, and it never was heard of any more. In more recent times, at the Wembley Exhibition of 1924, there was a monster New Zealand Cheddar weighing 10 cwt.

Cheddar is a name covering a multitude of cheeses which have undergone the 'Cheddaring process'. It was made originally, and there is some Cheddar cheese still being made, in the Cheddar district of Somerset, but the same type of cheese is made also in other parts of England, in Scotland, in Canada, in Australia and New Zealand, and, more recently, in South Africa.

There are two main kinds of *Cheddar* cheese, the *Factory Cheddar* and *Farmhouse Cheddar*.

Factory Cheddar is made of cow's milk wherever and whenever cow's milk happens to be cheap: it is made in as large quantities as possible and as economically as possible. Its cost is usually half that of the genuine farmhouse Cheddar.

Farmhouse Cheddar is made from May to October, of milk from one and the same herd of cows when they are out at grass. It is made in ones or twos, from day to day, by a cheesemaker who is a specialist at his job. Its texture is close and buttery; its flavour is full and nutty but not strong, varying from fine to finest according to the skill of the cheesemaker and the age of the cheese; its colour is the same all through; above all, it will mature, that is to say improve, with time.

Cheddar cheese is made from the evening milk kept overnight and mixed with the morning milk. Rennet is then added and the *curd* – a bulky, soft, flocculent mass – is formed; it is stirred constantly whilst being heated slowly at the rate of 1° F. in every four or five minutes until a temperature of from 98° to 102° F. is reached and maintained during twenty to thirty minutes. The curd is then allowed to settle in a vat until it attains the proper degree of firmness, and it is also tested for acidity. The heating or cooking of the curd varies according to tradition followed by different farmers and according to weather conditions. As soon as the whey is drained off, the curd is removed from the vat and placed on a cooler over racks covered with a cloth through which more of the whey may readily ooze out. It is turned about and doubled up every half hour until it is ready for *milling, salting* and *pressing,* usually one and a half to two hours after being placed on the racks.

Milling consists in putting the curd through the curd-mill in order to extract what whey may still be in it. After it has been milled, the curd should have a smooth, velvety feel and its flavour should be that of ripe cream. It is then salted.

Salting consists in an addition of 2 lb. of salt to 100 lb. of curd, on an average, at the time when the curd comes out of the curd-mill and is broken up and stirred for about ten minutes so that the air may get at every part of it. It is then pressed.

Pressing consists in placing the milled and salted curd in a *chesset* or press where it is pressed lightly at first, the pressure being gradually increased to 30 cwt. by the end of three hours. The curd is usually pressed for three days, being turned over and covered with a fresh dry cloth each day. It is then given a bath.

Bathing is the plunging of the curd, now almost cheese, into water at 140° F. for one minute. Its object is to obtain a tough, thin rind which will not easily crack. After its bath, the cheese is well greased with pure lard and both its ends are protected with cotton cloth, whilst its sides are strongly bandaged to maintain its shape. It has now only to be cured.

Curing is maturing, or placing the new cheese in the curing-room, a dry, well-ventilated room with a temperature whenever possible of from 54° to 60° F.

A good farmhouse Cheddar must be given at the very least three months to 'set', and it should be given another three to six months to 'mature'. A good farmhouse Cheddar is usually 'ripe' when six months old; 'mellow' when nine months old. Provided, of course, that it is properly stored.

Cheddar should be stored whole and in a cool, dry and well-ventilated place. It should also be turned over regularly, to ensure an even distribution of the butter fat, and it should be well brushed to keep away cheese mites. A properly stored Cheddar has a clean, sound coat, free from mites and dampness, and without any trace of discoloration near the rind.

CHESHIRE
Cheshire cheese is a hard cheese, made from cow's milk, like *Cheddar.* It is the oldest English cheese. It was recommended by Sir Kenelme Digby, in the seventeenth century, in his *Closet Open'd,* as a 'quick, fat, rich, well tasted cheese' to serve melted upon a piece of toast.

Cheshire cheese is made in two colours: red and white, but the best *Cheshire* cheese is the Blue, because it is both the richest and ripest. Blue Cheshire is not made – it just happens; it begins by being red, the milk from which it is made being coloured at the time of the making. Some *Red Cheshire* cheeses mature early and remain mild, whilst others, a small proportion of the whole, first of all lose their carroty colour and then develop a blue system of veins which spread all over the cheese, as in the case of Stilton and other 'blue' cheese. The White Cheshire is made in the same way as the Red except that it is not coloured. It is not so mild as the Red, nor so rich as the Blue. It is a very fine 'medium' cheese, but there is not nearly enough made.

Cheshire cheese may be imitated like Cheddar and Stilton, but not with anything like the same success. This is due to the rich deposits of salt in Cheshire soil and the peculiarly saline composition of the milk of most Cheshire-grazed cattle.

COTHERSTONE
Cotherstone, a double-cream cheese made in Yorkshire; it is similar to Wensleydale cheese.

COTTAGE CHEESE. SMEARCASE CHEESE
One of the home-made English cheeses, the making of which came to an end with World War II. It used to be made from skimmed milk, heated and kept in a cool place for later use; it used to be eaten, generally moistened with fresh milk or cream. When this cheese had been kept some time and had grown rather soft, it used to be known as *Clabber Cheese.*

COTTENHAM or DOUBLE COTTENHAM CHEESE
A double-cream, semi-hard, blue-moulded cheese which used to be made in the Midlands, a little flatter and broader than *Stilton,* but otherwise quite similar to it, although, in flavour, somewhat richer and creamier than *Stilton.*

CREAM-CHEESE
Cream-Cheese is made in many parts of the country, but chiefly in Devonshire and Cornwall. In the making of cream-cheese all that is required, besides fresh milk, is a piece of muslin and a perforated box. The cream automatically drains away its own superfluous moisture and becomes about as firm as fresh butter in three or four days, when it is ready to eat.

Mrs Beeton did not value cream-cheese highly; she wrote: 'Cream-cheese, although so called, is not properly cheese, but is nothing more than cream dried sufficiently to be cut with a knife.'

'Cream-cheeses, when not only dried cream, are generally made from sweet, fresh milk, unripened by any acidity until after rennet has been added, are not pressed, are small, and as soft as good butter. The difference is that the whey is never allowed to drain entirely from them. This moisture permits the fermentation to grow quickly, and the absence of heating and pressing furthers, of course, the same end. The ripening proceeds from the circumference to the centre. Consequently, the temptation is to place them on the market too soon, and when this has happened, the purchaser finds a cheese oozy at its surface but sadly callous in the centre. Being short-lived, they are often salted and refrigerated for transport, so a genuinely creamy cream-cheese is found less by cunning than by grace.'—O.B.

In London and all large towns, cream-cheeses offered for sale in shops are practically always sold under the registered name or brand of the Dairy Company or other concern responsible for their processing. Such are the *St. Ivel* cheeses, made at Yeovil; the *Victoria*, made at Guildford; *Horner's* cream-cheese, made at Redditch, in Worcestershire; the little *Cottslowe*, a factory-made Cotswold cream-cheese with a Cheddar flavour; the *Farm Vale*, made at Wellington, in Somerset, and sold in little boxes of eight, wrapped in silver paper; and so on. In the country, it easier to come by freshly-made cream-cheeses, mostly sold under district names such as *New Forest* cream-cheese, *Guildford*, *Cambridge*, *York* and other cream-cheeses; but the best of all English cream-cheeses, or, at any rate, the one that has enjoyed the reputation of being the best for a very long time, is the *Slipcote* (q.v.).

DUNLOP

Dunlop, a Scottish cheese, similar to Cheddar, but more moist and of a closer texture. It originated in Dunlop, Ayrshire, and it is now made in all the best agricultural districts of Scotland. The best markets are at Wigtown, Kilmarnock and Kirkcudbright. The weight is approximately 60 lb.; the shape flattish, resembling that of Lancashire cheeses.

GLOUCESTER and DOUBLE GLOUCESTER

The County of Gloucester has given its name to two good cheeses, the *Gloucester* or *Single Gloucester*, and the *Double Gloucester*, which is both better and better known.

Double Gloucester

In shape it is the size of a large grindstone with convex edges – flat, round and large. Its texture is close and crumbly: a glorified Cheshire cheese. It has a pronounced, but mellow, delicacy of flavour, being pungent without being sharp. The tiniest morsel is pregnant with savour, nor does an ordinary greedier mouthful disappoint or cloy the palate. To measure its refinement, it can undergo the same comparison as that we apply to vintage wines. Begin with a small piece of Red Cheshire. If you then pass to a morsel of Double Gloucester, you will find that the praises accorded to the latter have been no whit exaggerated. Though popularly regarded as something of a rarity in places distant from Berkeley, where it was originally mâde, it is usually to be had in good West End shops. A slow-ripening cheese, it keeps reasonably well, but in its early days it suffers from draughts, and when cut, however ripe, has the tendency of crumbly cheese to become dry and friable. To mature properly it needs, say, six months.—O.B.

Single Gloucester

Single Gloucester, made during spring and summer, needs but a couple of months to mature. It is usually white, and is of a kindred shape, the same as Double, but smaller and flatter, and from this, though opinions differ, it presumably derives its name. Being a quick-ripening cheese, Single Gloucester has a texture not close but open, not firm but soft. Its mild flavour commends itself to its admirers, but it would be uncritical to compare its freshness with the mellow maturity of Double Gloucester. The quick-ripening and the slow-ripening cheeses are as different in quality of flavour as a young and crisp from an old vintage wine. Each offers distinct pleasures, which it would be a mistake to confuse. One suits one type of meal and weather, the other an opposite type of each.

Single Gloucester is good for toasting. –O.B.

LANCASHIRE

Lancashire Cheese, of which there is more than one sort, but the best is that from the Fylde, that part of the country north of the Ribble bordering the Irish sea coast. It is a hard cheese, more like Cheshire than Cheddar.

LEICESTER

Leicester Cheese, a hard cheese made from whole milk in the same manner as *Cheddar*, but in the shape of a millstone, and usually some 40 lb. in weight.

OXFORDSHIRE

The *Oxfordshire Cheese* which is mentioned by Swift in his *Polite Conversation* was evidently one of the loud-smelling sort, to judge from the dialogue when Lord Smart tells of 'an odd kind of fellow' who, 'when the cheese came upon the table, pretended to faint; so somebody said, Pray take away the cheese; No, said I; pray take away the fool: said I well?' To this Colonel Atwit rejoins: 'Faith, my lord, you served the coxcomb right enough; and therefore I wish we had a bit of your lordship's Oxfordshire cheese.'—O.B.

PACKET CHEESE

Packet Cheese is the trade name given to cheese which has been carefully treated by secret processes so as to arrest its development at the most favourable moment and thus prevent any further ripening. After it has been 'processed', the cheese is enclosed in airtight containers, usually wrapped in tin-foil, and is safe from the risks of deterioration. The 'processing' methods have now been so perfected that the standard brands of 'Packet Cheese' have secured a very large measure of public support.

SLIPCOTE

Slipcote, a soft cheese made at Wissenden, from fresh milk to which rennet is added in the usual way: the curd is made up into little cheeses (about 6 in. in diameter and 2 in. thick) which are placed in the concavity of plates to drain. As soon as it is firm enough, it is placed between cabbage leaves and it is ripe in a week or two. It owes its name to the fact that when it is ripe its skin or coat becomes loose and slips off.

'Pride of name and of position must be given to *Slipcote*, one of the oldest, which used to be considered the best of English cream-cheeses. Made in Rutland, and familiar until the War, it is apparently unobtainable in London. But, whilst it is no use asking for *Slipcote* or *Slipcoat* in London, where the Past is beginning to be despised as well as destroyed, if you ask for *York* you may be given something like it. This brick-shaped, thin-rinded cheese, lying on its straw mat, bears out the description of *Slipcoat*.'—O.B.

SMEARCASE CHEESE

See *Cottage Cheese*.

STILTON

Stilton is a seasonal, double-cream, blue-moulded, semi-hard cheese; seasonal because it can only be made from May to September in England; double-cream because Stilton is made from the richest milk, when it is not made from whole-milk, to which the cream of other milk is added; blue-moulded because it is inoculated with a mould, the *Penicillium glaucum*, which is responsible for the blue veining of Stilton; semi-hard, because it is not put through the curd-mill nor pressed like Cheddar.

Stilton is in Huntingdonshire, but very little Stilton cheese actually comes from Stilton. Most of the genuine Stilton cheese comes from Leicestershire and Rutland, as well as Huntingdonshire. William Augustus Henderson, in his *Housekeeper's Instructor*, published in London at the end of the eighteenth century, quotes one John Monk (p. 402) as stating, in a Report to the Board of Agriculture, that 'Stilton is made in most of the villages round Melton Mowbray.'

Mrs Paulet has been given credit for inventing Stilton, on the strength of a statement in Marshall's *Rural Economy*, published in 1790, that 'Mrs Paulet, of Wymondham, first made Stilton cheese', and later on, because of a description in *Memory's Harkback* (1889), by the Rev T.E.Gretton, of the great pile of Stilton which were to be seen in front of the Bell Inn, Stilton, where it was alleged, the cheese was sold for the first time in the last decade of the eighteenth century by one Cooper Thornhill, a kinsman of the 'inventor', Mrs Paulet.

There is, however, documentary evidence that Stilton cheese was known at a much earlier date. There is, for instance, the following passage in the *Sixth* Edition (p. 77), published in 1736, of R.Bradley's *Country Housewife and Lady's Director*:

'As for the famous Stilton Cheese, which I have already published the Receipt of, we are to make the Rennet strong of Mace, by boiling the Mace in the Salt and Water, for without that is done, the Cheese will not have the true Relish that the first famous Stilton Cheeses had; and without the people of Stilton keep up the antient way of making it, agreeable to the old Receipt, they must of necessity lose the Reputation they have gained by their Cheeses. I shall not pretend to affirm why the Cheeses now in that town are not generally so good as they were formerly; but perhaps it is because some of the Cheese-Sellers there depend upon the reputation of the first Cheeses, and now buy Cheeses from other parts, where nothing of the true Receipt is known but the Figure. However, it would be injustice in me if I did not take notice that the Master of the *Blue-*

Bell Inn in Stilton provided me with one that was excellent in its way, and yearly furnishes as many Customers with them as give him timely Notice. ...'

There are also the two following lines in Sat. VI of Pope's *Imitation of Horace*:
'Cheese such as men in Suffolk make,
'But wished it Stilton for his sake.'

The right colour of Stilton is white with veins of blue mould evenly distributed over the whole of its surface. The rind should be well crinkled and regular, free from cracks, and of a brown-drab colour.

Stilton is at its best when fully ripe, not less than six months and preferably nine months after it has been made.

It is quite wrong to add port or anything else to a good Stilton. It is only done to moisten it when it has been allowed to get too dry through exposure to the air.

Good Stilton has been made from rich milk and cream, in New Zealand, inoculated with the *Penicillium glaucum* mould from Rutland.

SUFFOLK

The hardness of *Suffolk Cheese* can be guessed from the saying: 'Hunger will break through stone walls and anything except a Suffolk Cheese'. A modern writer even exclaims: Suffolk, long infamous for its hard, horny, flet-milk cheeses, which Swift calls 'cart-

wheels' and farm-labourers designate 'bang'. JOHN CORDY JEAFFERSON: *A Book about the Table*, Vol. II, p. 261.

TRUCKLES

Truckles is a name given to two very different sorts of cheese. *Truckles* may be a blue veiny cheese made in Wiltshire, from skimmed milk, similar to *Blue Vinny*. There is also a full-cream loaf Cheddar, called *Truckle*, in the West of England.

WENSLEYDALE

Wensleydale is the name given to two distinct types of cheese made in the Vale of Wensleydale, which is part of the valley of the River Ure, in that part of Yorkshire which adjoins Cumberland; it also includes the smaller dales which open into the valley of the Ure with the delightful old-world village of Wensleydale as a sentinel at its opening.

The best-known variety of Wensleydale cheese, cylindrical in shape, like Stilton, but of smaller dimensions, which grows 'blue' when ripe, like Stilton, and is made only from June to September.

The other sort of Wensleydale cheese is a flat-shaped, white cheese which is eaten fresh and does not generally go blue. It is made mostly at the beginning of the year and late in the season, and even throughout the winter.

CONTINENTAL CHEESES

AETTEKEES
A Belgian winter cheese made from November to May.

ALENTEJO, Queijo do
A Portuguese soft cheese made from ewe's milk; average weight 6 lb.

ALISE SAINTE REINE
A French soft cheese made in the summer.

ALLGÄUER BERGKÄSE
A German hard cheese of the *Emmenthal* type, weighing from 50 to 100 lb. It is made of cow's milk from mountain pastures.

ALLGÄUER RAHMKÄSE
A German soft full-cream cheese, similar in flavour to the *Romadur*, but milder.

AMOU
A French winter cheese made from October to May in Béarn.

ARRIGNY
A French winter cheese made from November to May in Champagne.

ASCO
A French winter cheese made from October to May in Corsica.

ASIO
An Italian soft cheese made at Asio in the province of Vicenza.

AUGELOT
The name of the *Pont l'Évêque* cheese made in the Vallée d'Auge, in Normandy.

AURORE
An all-the-year-round French cheese made in Normandy.

AUTUN
An all-the-year-round French cheese made in the Nivernais.

AZEITAO, Queijo de
A Portuguese soft cheese made from ewe's milk.

BACKSTEIN
A Bavarian edition of the Limburger, which it resembles in flavour and fragrance, but it is smaller.

BAGNES
Otherwise known as *Fromage à la Raclette*. An all-the-year-round Swiss cheese. From 'Racler', French for scrape or rake. This is a very hard cheese and the proper manner to eat it is to cut a slice about ½ in. thick right across the cheese and then toast this in front of a wood fire (some of the up-to-date inns in this valley actually have electric grates for the purpose), until the cheese begins to run, then it is scraped off with a palette-knife and spread on bread and so eaten, hence the word 'Raclette'.

BANON
A French cheese made from May to November in Provence.

BATTELMATT
A Swiss cheese which is a speciality of one or two Alps in the St. Gothard district.

BEAUFORT
An all-the-year-round French cheese made in Savoie.

BEAUMONT
A French cheese made from October to June in Savoie.

BEAUPRÉ DE ROYBON
A French winter cheese made from November to April in Dauphiné.

BEL PAESE
An Italian rich, creamy cheese of mild flavour and weighing nearly 5 lb. each. It is made in different parts of Italy and mostly from October to June.

BELLELAY
A Swiss cheese which is not exported.

BITTO
An Italian soft cream cheese from the Valtellina.

BLEU D'AUVERGNE
French blue-mould cheese of the *Roquefort* type, made in Auvergne and mostly matured in the *Caves* of Pontgibaud. It is usually made of a mixture of goat's, ewe's and cow's milks.

BLEU DE BASSILLAC
A French blue-mould cheese of the *Roquefort* type made in the Limousin from November to May.

BLEU DE SALERS
A variety of the *Bleu d'Auvergne*, made in Auvergne from November to May.

BONDES and BONDON
A French, small, loaf-shaped, whole-milk, soft cheese, similar to *Gournay* in texture but with 2 per cent added sugar. It is made in Normandy, mostly round about Rouen. It is about 3 in. high and from 1½ to 2 in. in diameter.

BOSSONS MACÉRES
A French winter cheese made from December to March in Provence.

BOULE DE LILLE
The French name of a Dutch all-the-year-round cheese, known in Holland as *Oude Kaas*.

BOULETTE D'AVESNES.
BOULETTE DE CAMBRAI
Two names for the same cheese, a French all-the-year-round cheese made in Flanders from November to May.

BRA
An Italian soft, creamy, mild and small cheese made in the provinces of Turin and Cuneo.

BRIE
A French farm-made whole-milk, flat, round, mould-inoculated, soft cheese. It is usually 14 in. across, 1 to 1½ in. thick and 6 lb. in weight.

The best *Brie* is made in the autumn only and is usually obtainable from November to May. It is known as *Gras*. The spring and summer *Bries* are inferior and are known as *Migras* and *Maigre*.

Brie is named after the province where it was first made, La Brie, immediately east of Paris, and now part of the *Départements* of Seine-et-Marne and Marne. The best *Brie* comes from Seine-et-Marne, but there is a great deal of imitation or 'façon' Brie cheese made in other parts of France.

BRIE DE COULOMMIERS
Genuine *Brie* cheese made at Coulommiers from October to May.

BRIE DE MEAUX
Genuine *Brie* cheese made from November to May in the farms of the Meaux district. Usually very good.

BRIE DE MELUN
Genuine *Brie* cheese made practically all the year round in the Melun district. Not always the best.

BRILLAT-SAVARIN

A French soft cheese made all the year round in some parts of Normandy.

BROCCIO

A French soft cream cheese made all the year round in Corsica.

BRUXELLES, Fromage de

A Belgian, soft, fermented, washed cheese, made entirely almost of skimmed milk. It comes mostly from the *Hal* district and the environs of *Louvain*.

CACCIOCAVALLO.
CACCIO CAVALLO.
CACCIOBEURRE

An Italian hard cheese made from cow's milk, from *pasta filata*, i.e., drawn curd, as opposed to the *grana*, the rolled pellets of curd. The best Caccio – *Cacciocavallo* comes from the Province of Sorrento, but the same cheese is made also in the Abruzzi, Molise and Apulian province. It is a saltish, whole-cream cheese, weighing from 2 to 6 kilogs. and mild in flavour. It keeps for a long time and travels well.

CACHAT D'ENTRECHAUX

A French highly flavoured cheese made from May to November in Provence. Also known as *Fromage Fort du Ventoux.*

CAMEMBERT

A French soft cheese which has acquired a greater world-wide reputation than any other soft cheese. It is made of cow's milk, the curd being inoculated with a white fungus: *Penicillium album*. This is a colourless mould, which thrives upon and eventually disposes of every trace of lactic acid present in the curd. Once this first stage has been reached, a second fermentation sets in which results in the decomposition of the casein. When a certain proportion of the casein has been decomposed, the *Camembert* is ripe and beginning to get soft. It is at its best. When the state of decomposition is allowed to go too far, the cheese is too soft and a number of gases are generated which give to the advanced cheese a smell which most people find too violently assertive to be pleasant.

    Camembert was made originally at Camembert, a village of the Orne Département, but it is made equally well in the adjoining Département of Calvados and other parts of Normandy. The best *Camembert* is the cheese made of the richest cream, during the summer months; the poorest is that which is made from November to May when milk is poor in cream.

CANESTRATO

One of the most popular of Sicilian cheeses; it is made from the mixed milks of goat and ewe and requires at least a year to mature; yellow in colour and strong of flavour.

CANTAL

A French hard and strong cheese. It is made of whole milk, fermented, pressed and lightly coloured. It is pale yellow and cylindrical, with hardly any smell but possessing a peculiar sharp taste. It is made from the high plateaux pastures of Auvergne in different sizes, ranging from 40 lb. to 100 lb.

CARDIGA, Queijo da

A Portuguese hard cheese, somewhat oily and of mild taste.

CASTELO BRANCO

A well-known brand of Portuguese semi-soft, fermented cheese of the *Camembert* type, but made either from goat's milk alone or from goat's and ewe's milk.

CENDRÉ D'AIZY

A French all-the-year-round cheese made in Burgundy.

CENDRÉ DE LA BRIE

A French winter cheese made from September to May in the Seine-et-Marne Département.

CENDRÉ DES RICEYS.
CENDRÉ CHAMPENOIS

A French cheese made in the Aube Département from September to June.

CHABICHOU

A French cheese made from April to December in Poitou.

CHAINGY

A French cheese made from September to June in the Orléanais.

CHAMPENOIS.
FROMAGE DES RICEYS

A French cheese made in the Aube Département from September to June.

CHAOURCÉ

A French cheese made in Champagne from November to May.

CHAUMONT

A French cheese made in Champagne from November to May.

CHAVIGNOL

A French cheese made from April to December in Berry.

CHEVRET
A French cheese made from December to April in the Bresse, from goat's milk.

CHEVROTIN
A French goat's milk cheese made from March to December in Savoie.

CICLO
A small Italian cream-cheese.

CIERP DE LUCHON
A French cheese made from November to May in the Comté de Foix.

COULOMMIERS
A French whole-milk, mould-inoculated, round soft cheese *façon Brie*. It resembles *Brie* but is smaller: about 10 in. across. It is made in Seine-et-Marne, the 'Brie country', and surrounding districts, but it is not *Brie's* equal. It is sometimes called *Coulommiers Brie* to distinguish it from the *Coulommiers Frais*, a soft cream-cheese similar to the *Petit Suisse*. The *Coulommiers Brie* is mostly made from October to May, when there is no *Brie Gras* available.

CRÈME DES VOSGES
A French soft cheese made from October to April in Alsace.

CRÈMET NANTAIS
A French soft fresh cream-cheese made in the Nantes or Lower Loire country.

CREMINI
An Italian soft, small cream-cheese.

CROISSANT DEMI-SEL
A French double cream soft cheese slightly salted; it is made all the year round.

CROTTIN DE CHAVIGNOL
A French cheese made from May to December in Berry.

DANISH BLUE CHEESE
The name under which is known in England the Danish imitation of *Roquefort*.

DANSK SCHWEIZEROST
One of the popular makes of Danish cheese.

DAUPHIN
A French cheese made from November to May in Flanders.

DECIZE
A French all-the-year-round cheese made in the Nivernais.

DEMI-SEL
A French whole-milk soft cheese, about 4 oz. in weight, similar to *Gournay*, but with 2 per cent added salt. It is made in many parts of France but in Normandy more particularly.

DOMACI BELI SIR
A Yugoslavian cheese.

DOUBLE-CRÈME
French soft cream-cheese made in many parts of France during the summer when milk is richest in cream.

EDAM
A Dutch cheese, round like a ball in shape; about 5 lb. in weight, bright red outside and dark yellow or orange inside. It is made from cow's milk renneted at from 85° to 90° F., and coloured at the same time. It is not milled like Cheddar, but it is pressed in round moulds which give it its shape. *Edam* is often known as 'Dutch red balls', in England and 'Tête de Maure' in France. It is called *Edamer Käse*, in Germany, *Edammer Kaas* in Holland and Denmark where it is imitated on a large scale. The Yugoslavian imitation of *Edam* is called *Edamec*.

EMMENTHAL
A Swiss hard cheese which may be called an enlarged edition of *Gruyère*. It is made in different sizes weighing from 100 to 200 lb. It is slightly softer than *Gruyère*, and the holes are larger, sometimes very large, and placed irregularly. Cheeses similar to *Emmenthal* are made in France, in the Savoie, Haute-Savoie, Ain, Jura and Doubs Départements; also in Italy, in Germany, and other lands far more distant from Switzerland. The German spelling is *Emmentaler*.

ÉPOISSES
A French whole-milk, mould-inoculated, soft cheese made in the Côte d'Or Département (Burgundy), in the shape of a small cylinder with a flattened end, about 5 in. across. It is made in two thicknesses, the larger one, about 3 in. thick, being known as *Entier*, and the other which is only half the weight, as *Demi*. It is made from November to July. Some *Époisses*, pickled in white wine or local brandy, are known as *Époisses Confits au Vin Blanc* or *au Marc de Bourgogne*.

ERCÉ
A French cheese made from November to May in Languedoc.

ERVY
A French cheese made from November to May in Champagne.

ÉTUVÉ and DEMI-ÉTUVÉ
Full size and half size Dutch cheeses obtainable all the year round.

EVARGLICE
A Yugoslavian cheese.

EXCELSIOR
A French all-the-year-round cheese made in Normandy.

FEUILLE DE DREUX
A French cheese made from November to May in the Beauce country.

FIN DE SIÈCLE
A French all-the-year-round cheese made in Normandy.

FLEUR DE DECAUVILLE
A French cheese made from December to May in the Brie country.

FONTAINEBLEAU
A French soft, fresh cream-cheese made in the country round Fontainebleau, mostly in the summer.

FONTINA
An Italian soft, creamy cheese from the Val d'Aosta.

FONTINE
A French all-the-year-round cheese made in Franche-Comté.

FOURME D'AMBERT and FOURME DE MONTBRISON
French cheeses made from November to May in the Limagne country.

FOURME DE SALERS
A French cheese made in Auvergne, which resembles and is sometimes sold under the name of *Cantal*.

FRIESCHE KAAS
The name given in Holland to the soft cheese made from November to May.

FROMAGE À LA CRÈME
A popular Bourgeois dessert. It is merely milk left alone in a warm place until it has soured and become solid. It is then put in a piece of butter muslin and left hanging over a basin in a cool place to drain. When drained, it is mixed with a little milk and when dished it is served with a little cream. It is often put into a heart-shaped wicker basket which acts as a mould and is very widely known as *Coeur à la Crème*. It is nearly always eaten with sifted sugar.

FROMAGE BLANC
A French soft, white cheese, made from cow's milk which is left to sour and is then drained in a muslin bag and eaten without any cream being added – which differentiates it from the *Fromage à la Crème*. It is usually eaten with salt and pepper.

GAMMELÖST
A Norwegian cheese made all the year round.

GAPERON
A French cheese made from September to July in the Limagne.

GÉROMÉ
A French cylindrical, semi-hard, whole-milk, fermented cheese, made originally in and around Gérardmer, Saulxures, Remiremont and other places upon the western slopes of the Vosges; it is now made in many other places of Eastern France. Its flavour and aroma are very similar to the flavour and fragrance of the *Munster* cheese, but it is larger. A *Géromé* weighs anything up to 11 lb., and it can be up to 7 in. in diameter. The rind is brick red. It is made from November to April.

GETMESOST
A soft Swedish sweet whey cheese made from goat's milk.

GEX
A French blue-veined, skimmed milk, semi-hard cheese, made chiefly in the Ain Département, and also in the Jura, Isère and Hautes-Alpes, between November and May.

GIETOST. GJETOST
The national cheese of Norway. It is made all the year round, from goat's milk, in oblong blocks weighing about 4 kilogs. each.

GLUX
A French all-the-year-round cheese made in the Nivernais.

GORGONZOLA
is the name of a village near Milan and it is also that of a semi-hard blue-veined cheese which is made in the provinces of Pavia, Milan and Cremona in the following manner. The rennet is added to the evening milk when at a temperature of from 85° to 95° F. and the curd is obtained in about 15 minutes. The curd is broken up and ladled out into a cloth which is hung up in a cool place until the next morning so that the whey may run off during the night. When the morning milk is brought in, it is treated in the same manner but the curd in the cloth instead of being hung up and left for 10 to 12 hours is only left 10 to 15 minutes in a bucket to drain. Then the curd of the night before, which is cold, and the curd of the morning

milk, which is warm, are put together in a mould, the cold and the warm curds in alternate layers, in the centre, but only the warm curd all round. The mould is then left in a cool place for three or four days. Then the salting begins. The rennet being put in the fresh milk as and when brought in, evening and morning, there is a minimum of lactic acid in the curd and it renders the salting all the more indispensable. The curd is made by small grazers from the milk of their own cows, and sold to merchants who have the necessary facilities for dealing with it and the necessary capital to mature it. When duly salted, the curd is moved to cool and moist caves where it is left in a strong draught. At that stage, a red mould sets in and begins to grow over the surface of the curd which may then be said to have become cheese. From that time onwards, each cheese has to be frequently turned over and watched with great care whilst the mould penetrates and veins the cheese right through. This stage is not usually reached in less than four to five months, when the cheese may be sent to the market, but it should be kept another two or three months to be at its best.

Gorgonzola is made in round shapes weighing about 8 kilogs. each. Its fat content often exceeds 50 per cent of solid matter. Its excellence depends greatly upon the manner of its curing in the great curing houses of Milan, Crosico, Lodi, Codogno, Pavia, etc.

There is also a variety of Gorgonzola which is practically unknown outside Italy; it is the White Gorgonzola; it possesses a slightly bitter flavour greatly appreciated by Italian cheese connoisseurs.

GOUDA, GOUDSCHE KAAS

A Dutch cheese, similar in taste and texture to the *Edam*, but of different shape, being flat and very much larger. There are two grades of *Gouda*, the full-cream cheese with 45 per cent fats, and the inferior qualities which contain 40, 30 or 20 per cent fats and must be labelled accordingly. There is also a diminutive edition of *Gouda*, merely about 1 lb. in weight, which is known as *Little Dutch*. A similar cheese is made in Germany and sold under the name of *Goudakäse*. It is also made extensively in Sweden, where its different varieties are sold under the names of *Svensk Goudaost av Herrgardstyp*; *Svensk Goudaost av Vastgotatyp*; *Svensk Goudaost av Sveciatyp*.

GOURNAY

A French whole-milk, soft cheese made at Gournay, in Normandy, and surrounding district. It is a flat and round cheese, 3 in.

across, less than 1 in. thick and about 4 oz. in weight.

GRANA

The name of various Italian cheeses made from *pasta cotta* and more or less similar to *Parmesan*.

GRANA LOMBARDO

An Italian Parmesan-like cheese made in Lombardy.

GRANA REGGIANO

An Italian Parmesan-like cheese made in the province of Emilia, in the neighbourhood of Reggio. The *Grana Reggiano* brand is imitated on a large scale in the district of Mantua and in Lombardy.

GRAS

A Dutch whole-cream all-the-year-round cheese known in Holland as *Volvet Kaas* and in France as *Tête de Maure*.

GRUYÈRE

A cooked, hard cheese, pale yellow in colour, honeycombed with 'eyes' and weighing up to 100 lb. It is usually 2 ft. in diameter and 6 in. thick. Gruyère comes from the Canton of Fribourg in Switzerland. Later a similar cheese was made in the Emmenthal valleys and it has been imitated in the nearby Alps and Juras, as well as in Finland, Argentina, and the U.S.A. where it is called *Swiss*.

All Gruyère is made in the same way, but its goodness depends upon the goodness of the milk used and upon the length of time and the manner of its keeping. The milk is warmed to 93°F. and then the rennet is put in. The curd is formed in 25 to 35 minutes: it is broken up in little pieces the size of large green peas which are thrown into a large kettle placed over a wood fire. The curd is heated to 135° F., being stirred constantly until it has attained what is considered the proper degree of consistency. It is then lifted out of the kettle in a cloth which is passed under it and caught up by its four corners. It is dropped into a mould with one side opened and so designed that it can be tightened at will. The curd is gradually pressed in this way and then placed in the ripening room where it will be left to mature, being salted from time to time. The ripening room is fitted with three rows of shelves and the temperature varies from 52° F. on the lowest shelf to 60° F. upon the top shelf. The newly-made cheeses are placed upon the top shelves and brought down to the lower ones at a later stage, so that they may cool slowly. The rapid fermentation of the curd is responsible for the 'eyes' or holes in Gruyère, which are small and regularly spaced in the real *Gruyère*, but large and irregular in the *Emmenthal* cheeses. There is hardly any genuine *Gruyère* exported, but a great deal of *Emmenthal* which is called *Gruyère* and *Swiss* in the U.S.A.

GUÉRET. CREUSOIS
A French cheese made from October to June in the Limousin country.

HARZÉ
A Belgian semi-cooked cheese of the Port-Salut type made at Harzé.

HERRGARDSOST
Farmhouse, or Manor House, cheese, the most popular cheese of Sweden. It was first made in the western parts of the country and gradually spread to other parts, but the best is still that which is made in West Gothland and in Jamtland. It is a hard cheese of the *Emmenthal* type and weighs from 25 to 40 lb. It is made in two qualities, full-cream and half-cream.

HERVÉ
A Belgian soft, fermented and washed cheese made from November to May, in and around Hervé. It is turned out in cubes, in three qualities: extra cream, cream and partly skimmed milk.

HUSHALLSOST
The Swedish 'Household' cheese in common use throughout the country. It is made in three varieties known as *Herrgardstyp* or Farmhouse type; *Vastgotatyp*, or West Gothland type; and *Sveciatyp*, or Svecia type.

ILHA, Queijo da
Literally 'Cheese of the Isle', being a variety of cow's milk cheese made in various Portuguese islands. The name of the particular island where the cheese was made is sometimes mentioned, such as Queijo da Ilha Terceira, Queijo da Ilha do Pico (Azores), etc.

KACKAVALJ
A Yugoslavian cheese.

KAMEMBERT
A Yugoslavian imitation of *Camembert*.

KAUNAS
A Lithuanian all-the-year-round cheese.

KEFALOTIR
A Yugoslavian cheese.

KUMMEL. LEIDSCHE KAAS
A Dutch all-the-year-round cheese.

LA BOUILLÉ
A French cheese made from October to May in Normandy.

LAGUIOLE
Another name for *Cantal* cheese made from the Aubrac pastures of Auvergne from November to May.

LAMOTHE-BOUGON.
LA MOTHE ST. HÉRAYE
Two names for the same French cheese which is made from May to November in Poitou.

LANGRES
A French cheese very similar to *Maroilles* made in the neighbourhood of Langres. It is a square, semi-hard, full-flavoured and high-smelling, fermented, whole-milk farm cheese.

LEIDSCHE KAAS
See *Leyden.*

LES AYDES
A French cheese made from October to June in the Orléanais.

LES LAUMES
A French cheese made from November to July in Burgundy.

LEVROUX
A French cheese made from May to December in Berry.

LEYDEN. LEIDSCHE KAAS.
KUMMEL
A Dutch cheese made from partially skimmed milk with Cumin seeds added.

LIMBURGER
A semi-hard, fermented, full-flavoured, strong-smelling, whole-milk cheese made from December to May in Belgium, and also in Germany and Alsace. The best and mildest German *Limburger* is known as *Allgäuer-Limburger*.

LIPSKI
A Yugoslavian cheese.

LIPTAUER
A Yugoslavian cheese.

LIPTO
A Hungarian soft cheese made from ewe's milk; white of colour and mild of taste; it is sold in jars of different sizes.

LIVANSKI
A Yugoslavian cheese.

LIVAROT
A French semi-hard cheese made from skimmed milk. It is cylindrical in shape, about 6 in. across and 1¾ in. in height. It is

mostly made during the summer months when skimmed milk is plentiful and inexpensive, and chiefly in and around the village of Livarot in Normandy. There is a white – i.e. uncoloured – *Livarot*, but it is rarely offered for sale. *Livarot* is usually coloured dark red or brown, and it requires several months to mature in caves where the temperature varies but little. Hence *Livarot*, although a summer-made cheese, is not available until November, at its best from January to March and past its best in June.

MAINAUER
A German semi-hard, full-cream cheese, red outside, yellow inside, round in shape and weighing about 3 lb.

MANICAMP
A French cheese made from October to July in Flanders.

MANURI
A Yugoslavian cheese.

MARGHERITA
An Italian soft, small, cream-cheese.

MAROILLES. MAROLLES
A French semi-hard, full-flavoured, high-smelling, fermented, whole-milk cheese square in shape, the rind brown red, the cheese itself being yellow. It is a little more than 5 in. square and 2¼ in. thick and it should weigh 28 oz. It is made mostly from November to June and chiefly in and around Avesnes, in Flanders; also in Champagne and in many parts of Eastern France as far as Vervins.

MASCHERONE
A white, soft and delicate Italian cheese made from fresh cream; made mostly in Lombardy and chiefly in the autumn and winter. It is usually sold in muslin or gauze bags containing from ¼ to ½ lb. of cheese.

MESOST
A Swedish sweet whey cheese.

METTON
A French cheese made from October to June in Franche-Comté.

MIZITRA
A Yugoslavian cheese.

MONÇEAU
A French semi-hard cheese similar to *Maroilles* in shape and flavour, but of a smaller size. It is made chiefly in Champagne and Eastern France.

MONSIEUR FROMAGE
A French cheese made from November to June in Normandy.

MONTASIO
An Italian soft, creamy, small, mild cheese made in the Northern Friuli.

MONT-CENIS
A French semi-hard, blue-veined, whole-milk cheese made in the Maurienne country and on the Mont-Cenis plateau.

MONT DORE
Originally a cheese made from goat's milk in and around Lyons. Now it is made in all parts of the Rhône Valley and more usually from cow's than from goat's milk. It is whole-milk, soft cheese, yellow in colour, round like a *Camembert*, but thicker: about 3½ in. thick. It takes ten days to be ready for consumption in summer, and 15 in winter.

MORBIER
A French cheese made from November to July in Bresse.

MOZZARELLA
An Italian cheese made from buffalo's milk made chiefly at Cardito, Aversa, in the Mazzoni di Capua and at Salernitano. It is round in shape and weighs about ½ lb.

MUNSTER
A French semi-hard, whole-milk, fermented cheese, cylindrical in shape, made mostly from November to April in the valley of Munster, in Alsace, as well as in other parts of the Vosges country. It resembles the *Géromé*, but it is smaller, some weighing less that 10 oz. whilst others weigh up to 8 lb. The rind is brick red.

MUNSTER AU CUMIN
The same as *Munster* but flavoured with cumin seeds in the making.

MUROLS
A French cheese made from November to June in Limagne.

MYSÖST
The most popular all-the-year-round cheese in all Scandinavian countries.

NANTAIS. FROMAGE DU CURÉ
A French all-the-year-round cheese made in Brittany.

NEUFCHÂTEL
A French whole-milk, small, loaf-shaped, soft cheese, similar to *Bondon*, but rather softer. It is 2 in. across, 3 in. in height and

about 4 oz. in weight. It is made in and around Neufchatel, in Normandy.

NIOLO
A French cheese made from October to May in Corsica.

NOEKKELOST
A Norwegian all-the-year-round cheese.

OLIVET
A French whole-milk, mould-inoculated, farm-made, soft cheese, resembling in flavour and texture both *Camembert* and *Coulommiers*; it is a little larger than the first and smaller than the second. It is made in very limited quantities in the Loriet Département or Órléans country. The two best sorts are the *Olivet-Bleu*, which is made from October to June, and the *Olivet-Cendré*, which is made from November to July.

OLORON. FROMAGE DE LA VALLÉE D'OSSOUR
A French cheese made from October to May in Béarn.

OVÁR
A Hungarian cow's milk cheese weighing about 10 lb.; its crust is reddish brown; it is reddish yellow inside; its taste is mild, piquant but not too pungent.

PALADRU
A French cheese made from November to May in Savoie.

PÁLPUSZTA
A fairly strong-smelling Hungarian cheese of the Limburg type.

PARMESAN
The hardest cheese of all. It is made in Parma and Emilia from cow's milk which is first of all heated to 92° F. in a cauldron of solid brass resembling in shape an inverted bell. The rennet is not put in the milk as is the case with practically all other cheeses, but dipped into the heated milk, being enclosed in a little cloth bag, the size of a walnut, which is wrung in the milk and then thrown away. The curd is very quickly coagulated and it is then broken up to quite small pieces or grains, the size of big shot, hence, the name of *Grana* which is given in Italy to Parmesan cheese. The grana, or broken-up curd, is then heated to 104° to 110° F., and then it is pressed between two boards and packed into a mould, the shape of a millstone, in which it is left to mature in specially airy caves for not less than two and usually three years. When it is ripe, the crust is mostly black, but the cheese should be pale straw in colour and full

of small holes like pin pricks. When cut in halves it should exude a sticky sweet substance not unlike drops of honey, which is the reason why Parmesan cheese of the finest quality is called 'honeyed'.

Parmesan cheese is the best for grating. It is the proper and natural partner of macaroni.

The two best-known varieties of Parmesan cheese are known as *Parmigiano* and *Reggiano Lodigiano*, both similar in texture and taste, but made in different districts and of different weights: the *Parmigiano Reggiano* usually weighs from 25 to 30 kilogs.; the *Lodigiano* from 40 to 50 kilogs. each.

PASKI
A Yugoslavian cheese.

PAVÉ DE MOYAUX
A French cheese made from November to May in Normandy.

PECORINO
An Italian hard, all-the-year-round cheese made from ewe's milk. It is round in shape and weighs from 8 to 10 kilogs. It is a strong cheese with a piquant flavour and is mostly used as a flavouring agent, grated, with macaroni or in soups. It was originally made in the Latium and the more southern provinces, but it is now made on a considerable scale in Sardinia, being the principal article of export from that island.

PÉLARDON DE RIOMS
A French cheese made from May to November in Languedoc.

PERSILLÉ DE SAVOIE
A French cheese made from May to January in Savoie.

PETIT GRUYÈRE
A Danish form of imitation *Gruyère*, pasteurised and sold in cartons each containing six portions wrapped in tinfoil.

PETIT-MOULE
A local name for *Coulommiers*.

PETIT SUISSE
A French unsalted cream cheese, cylindrical in shape. It is made in two sizes, the larger being known as *Gros* and the smaller as *Demi*.

PICODON DE DIEULEFIT
A French cheese made from May to December in the Dauphiné.

PIE, Fromage à la, or FROMAGE BLANC
A French soft cream cheese.

PITHIVIERS AU FOIN
A French cheese made from October to May in the Orléans country.

PIVSKI
A Yugoslavian cheese.

POMMEL
A popular French brand of double cream cheese, unsalted, made all the year round.

PONT L'ÉVÊQUE
A French semi-hard, fermented cheese, about 4 in. square, 1½ in. thick, coloured yellow in the making and salted repeatedly during maturation. It is made practically all the year round in the farms of the Pont l'Evêque district, in Normandy, and varies in quality according to the milk from which it is made, either milk rich in cream or skimmed. Like Cheddar, *Pont l'Évêque* depends entirely upon the rennin and pepsin of rennet for its maturation; it is free from moulds and other fungoid maturing agents.

PORT-DU-SALUT or PORT-SALUT
A French semi-hard, whole-milk, fermented and pressed cheese. It is round in shape, from 1½ to 3 in. thick and from 7 to 10 in. across. It was originally made by the monks of the Trappist Monastery of Port-du-Salut, in the Mayenne Département, but it is made now in other parts of France at the Abbaye of Orval, for instance, as well as at Watou, Philippeville, Neerijsche and the Hervé district, in Belgium.

POULIGNY- ST. PIERRE
A French cheese made from May to December in Berry.

PROMESSI
A small Italian soft cream cheese.

PROVATURE
An Italian cheese made from buffalo's milk.

PROVELONE
An all-the-year-round Italian cheese.

PUANT MACÉRÉ
A French cheese made from November to June in Flanders.

PULTÖST
An all-the-year-round Norwegian cheese.

PUSZTADÖR
A Hungarian semi-hard, full-flavour cheese of the *Limburger-Romadur* type.

RABAÇAL
A soft paste, oily, Portuguese cheese made from ewe's milk.

RAHMATOUR
A German cream cheese made in Bavaria.

RAMADOUX
A Belgian cheese similar to *Hervé* made in the Arrondissement of Verviers.

REBLOCHON
A French cheese made from October to June in Savoie.

RÉCOLLET DE GÉRARDMER
A French cheese made from October to April in the Vosges.

REMOUDOU. FROMAGE PIQUANT
A Belgian cheese made from November to June.

RICEYS CENDRÉ. CHAMPENOIS
A French cheese made from September to June in the Aube and Marne Départements.

RICOTTA ROMANA
A rich, creamy and fragrant Italian cheese made from the butter-milk of ewes. It is sometimes served with sugar and cinnamon.

RIGOTTE DE CONDRIEU
A French cheese made from May to November in the Rhône Valley below Lyons.

ROBBIOLA
An Italian soft cream cheese.

ROCAMADOUR
A French cheese made from November to May in the Limousin.

ROKADUR
A Yugoslavian imitation of *Roquefort*.

ROLLOT
A French, soft, fermented, mould-inoculated cheese, similar to a *Camembert* in shape and flavour, but smaller and thicker. It is made in and about the parish of Rollot, Montdidier district, Picardy, from October to May.

ROMA
An Italian soft cream cheese.

ROMADUR
The Bavarian edition of the *Limburger* cheese. It is square and from 4 to 5 in. thick. It is made from November to April, and in three sizes weighing approximately 1lb., ½ lb. and ¼ lb.

ROMANA
A Yugoslavian cheese.

ROQUEFORT

This is the only ewe's milk cheese which has attained a world-wide reputation. It cannot be made except during the lambing season, that is at most during five months of the year. *Roquefort* comes from a Rouergue village of that name, in the Cevennes mountains, in the Aveyron Département, France. It cannot be made anywhere else not only because of the suitable sheep grazing land of the district but because of the limestone caverns of Roquefort itself which play a very important part in the maturing of *Roquefort* cheese. *Roquefort* is made from the evening and morning milk mixed and the rennet – which is taken from lambs' stomachs instead of calves' – is added when the temperature of the milk has been raised to 90° F. The curd is coagulated very quickly and it is piled up in layers with some mouldy breadcrumbs between each layer. It is then pressed and matured in natural caves or caverns where the temperature is about 46° F. and the humidity very great owing to the existence of an underground lake, under the caves. The mouldy breadcrumbs are a culture of the same mould used for the making of *Stilton* – the *Penicillium glaucum* which grows more rapidly being already in full activity when introduced into the curd.

ROUENNAIS

A French cheese made from October to May in Normandy.

SAINT-AGATHON

A French cheese made from October to July in Brittany.

SAINT-FLORENTIN

A French cheese made from November to July in Burgundy.

SAINT-MARCELLIN

A French cheese made from March to December in Dauphiné.

SAINT-MAURE

A French cheese made from May to November in Touraine.

SAINT-NECTAIRE

A French cheese made from October to July in Limousin.

SALAME

A small Italian soft cream-cheese.

SASSENAGE

A French semi-hard, skimmed-milk, blue-veined cheese made from November to May chiefly in the Isère Département. Similar in shape and flavour to *Gex* and *Septmoncel*.

SCHABZIEGER

A Swiss skimmed-milk, hard cheese, cooked with melilot green leaves and matured for several months. It is quite green at first but becomes brown with age. It is mostly used for grated cheese in cooking.

SEPTMONCEL

A French semi-hard, skimmed-milk, blue-veined cheese made from November to May chiefly in the Ste. Claude district of the Jura. Similar to *Gex* and *Sassenage*.

SERRA DA ESTRELLA, Queijo da

A Portuguese soft paste, oily cheese made from ewe's milk and weighing from 1 to 2 lb.

SJENICKI

A Yugoslavian cheese.

SMALTOST

A popular Swedish soft or 'melting' cheese.

SOMBORSKI

A Yugoslavian cheese.

SORBAIS

A French semi-hard, whole-milk, full-flavoured, high-smelling, fermented cheese. It is square, the paste is yellow and the rind reddish brown. It resembles the *Maroilles* in shape and flavour but it is a little smaller. It is made in Champagne and eastern parts of France.

SOUMAINTRIN

A French cheese made from November to July in Burgundy.

SPOSI

A small Italian soft cream-cheese.

STEINBUSCHER-KÄSE

A German full-cream, semi-hard cheese mildly sour and pungent.

STEPPE

A popular brand of Danish cheese.

STRACCHINO

A soft, fresh cream-cheese, somewhat pungent in flavour, made in various parts of Italy during the winter months.

SVECIAOST

The most largely consumed cheese in Sweden. It is of the same type as the West Gothland cheese; it looks the same but it is made differently and for much quicker consumption. It is ready from six weeks to six months old and it is no longer safe to keep after that time. It weighs usually from 25 to

30 lb. It is made in three qualities, full-cream, three-quarter-cream and half-cream.

SZÉKELY
A Hungarian soft cheese made in Transylvania from ewe's milk and sold in sausage skins or bladders. There is a variety of *Székely* that is smoked.

TAFFEL
A popular brand of Danish cheese.

TÊTE DE MAURE
A name sometimes given in France to the Dutch *Edam* cheese.

TÊTE DE MOINE
A cheese made in the Jura in small cylindrical loaves of 10 to 20 lb. each. It is made in the summer for sale in the winter.

TILSITER
A semi-hard German cheese made all the year round. There is an imitation *Tilsiter* made in Yugoslavia which is called *Tilziski*. It is also made on a large scale in Denmark and Switzerland. The Hungarian edition of this cheese is known as *Ôvàr*.

TOMME
A French cheese made nearly all the year round in Savoie. The best known *Tommes* of Savoy are those known as *Tomme des Beauges*, *Tomme au Fenouil* and *Tomme Boudane*.

TRAPPE. TRAPPISTES
A French cheese made by the Trappist monks, the best-known of which is the *Port-du-Salut*. The principal sources of supply of this cheese are the following monasteries:
    Banjaluka, in Bosnia
    Bricquebec, in Normandy
    Citeaux, in Burgundy
    Echourgnac, in Limousin
    Harzé, in Belgium
    Mont-des-Cats, in Flanders
    Port-du-Salut, in the Mayenne
    Ste Anne d'Auray, in Brittany
    Tamié, in Savoie
There is an imitation *Port-du-Salut* cheese made in Yugoslavia called *Trapist*, and a particularly good one made in Hungary.

TRAVNICKI
A Yugoslavian cheese.

TRIPLE AURORE
A French all-the-year-round cheese made in Normandy.

TROO
A French cheese made from May to January in Touraine.

TROYES
A French cheese made from November to May in Champagne.

VACHERIN
A French Savoy and Swiss cheese with a firm, leather crust and a very soft paste inside, similar to mature Brie or Camembert. It is made in the summer and sold in the winter.

VALENÇAY
A French cheese made from May to December in Berry.

VÄSTERBOTTENSOST
West Bothian cheese. A Swedish cheese made in the north of the country. It matures slowly and is not ready until 12 or 18 months old. It has a pungent and somewhat bitter taste. It weighs from 35 to 40 lb.

VÄSTGÖTAOST
West Gothland cheese. A Swedish semi-hard, pressed cheese from 20 to 30 lb. in weight, which requires about six months to be ripe. It has a pungent flavour.

VIC-EN-BIGORRE
A French cheese made from October to May in Béarn.

VIZE
A Yugoslavian cheese.

VOLVET
Dutch for 'Full Cream' cheese which must contain a minimum of 45 per cent fat in the dry substance, according to the law of the land.

WEISSLACKER-KÄSE
A German soft, full-cream cheese, cylindrical in shape, and with a somewhat sharp, pungent taste.

WILSTERMARSCH-KÄSE
A German full-cream, semi-hard cheese, a compromise between the Dutch *Gouda* and the Swiss *Tilsitt*.

Eugène Herbodeau's *Classement des Fromages de France*

FRESH CHEESES OF THE CREAM-CHEESE ORDER

Suisses	Demi-Sel
Gervais	Fourme d'Auvergne
Double-Creme	Cremets d'Anjou
Fontainebleau	Claqueret de Lyon

Can be eaten all the year round but preferably during summer.

FERMENTED AND REFINED CHEESES

Brie	Géromé
Coulommiers	Epoisse
Camembert	Goumantrain
Neufchâtel	Gex
Fort de Béthune	Blue d'Auvergne
Munster	Fourme d'Ambert
Soumantrain	Oust
Tardet	Castillon
Poustagnacq	Cendrée
Pelardon	Olivet
Septmoncel	

All these cheeses are excellent in winter. When July comes round again it is not so usual to serve them.

COOKED CHEESES

Comté	Gruyère
Cantal	Tommes de Savoie

Are served all the year round.

HALF-COOKED CHEESES

Livarot	Rollot
Maromme	Goyère
Pont-l'Evêque	Romatour
Maroilles	Géromé
Cancoillotte	Roblochon
Saint-Nectaire	Port-Salut

The Livarot, Maroilles, Rollot, Romatour, are not served during the hot months.

GOAT-MILK CHEESES

Bressans	Chabichou
Saint-Marcellin	Lerroux
Rigottes	La Mothe St.-Héray
Chevreton	Sainte-Maure
Saint-Loup	Selles-sur-Cher

Only good from February to September.

EWE'S MILK CHEESES

Roquefort	Brossons
Brousses	Cachat
Brocchio de Corse	

The Roquefort is served all the year round. The others are at their best only from February to September.

H. Androuët's *Calendrier régional des Fromages de France*

ALSACE

Crème des Vosges	*Oct.–Avril*
Récollet de Gérardmer	*Oct.–Avril*
Gérômé de Bruyères	*Nov.–Avril*
Gérômé au Cumin	*Nov.–Avril*
Gérardmer	*Nov.–Mai*
Munster	*Nov.–Avril*
Munster au Cumin	*Nov.–Avril*

AUVERGNE

Fourme de Salers (dit Cantal)	*Nov.–Mai*
Bleu de Salers (dit Bleu d'Auvergne)	*Nov.–Mai*

BÉARN

Amou	*Oct.–Mai*
Vic-en-Bigorre	*Oct.–Mai*
Oloron (dit fromage de la vallée d'Ossau)	*Oct.–Mai*

BERRY

Crottin de Chavignol	*Mai–Déc.*
Valençay	*Mai–Déc.*
Levroux	*Mai–Déc.*
Pouligny-Saint-Pierre	*Mai–Déc.*

BOURBONNAIS

Chevrotins de Moulins	*Mai–Déc.*

BOURGOGNE

Saint-Florentin	*Nov.–Juillet*
Cendré d'Aizy	*Janv.–Déc.*
Soumaintrin	*Nov.–Juillet*
Les Laumes	*Nov.–Juillet*
Epoisses	*Nov.–Juillet*
Trappiste de Cîteaux	*Janv.–Déc.*

BRESSE

Gex	*Nov.–Mai*
Morbier	*Nov.–Juillet*
Chevret	*Déc.–Avril*

BRETAGNE
Saint-Agathon	*Oct.–Juillet*
Trappiste de Port-du-Salut	*Janv.–Déc.*
Trappiste de Sainte-Anne-d'Auray	*Janv.–Déc.*
Nantais, dit fromage du Curé	*Janv.–Déc.*

CHAMPAGNE
Arrigny	*Nov.–Mai*
Troyes	*Nov.–Mai*
Chaumont	*Nov.–Mai*
Chaource	*Nov.–Mai*
Ervy	*Nov.–Mai*
Riceys-Cendré (dit Champenois)	*Sept.–Juin*
Langres	*Nov.–Mai*

CHAROLAIS
Chevrottons de Mâcon (dits mâconnais)	

COMTÉ DE FOIX
Cierp de Luchon	*Nov.–Mai*

CORSE
Asco	*Oct.–Mai*
Niolo	*Oct.–Mai*
Broccio	*Mars–Janv.*

DAUPHINÉ
Beaupré de Roybon	*Nov.–Avril*
Sassenage	*Nov.–Mai*
Saint-Marcellin	*Mars–Déc.*
Picodon de Dieulefit	*Mai–Déc.*

FLANDRES
Manicamp	*Oct.–Juillet*
Boulette de Cambrai	*Nov.–Mai*
Boulette d'Avesnes	*Nov.–Mai*
Dauphin	*Nov.–Mai*
Maroilles	*Nov.–Juin*
Puant Macéré	*Nov.–Juin*

FRANCHE-COMTÉ
Metton	*Oct.–Juin*
Fontine	*Janv.–Déc.*
Comté du Haut-Jura	*Janv.–Déc.*
Septmoncel	*Nov.–Mai*

ILE DE FRANCE
Brie de Meaux	*Nov.–Mai*
Brie de Coulommiers	*Oct.–Mai*
Coulommiers Brie	*Oct.–Mai*
Cendré de la Brie	*Sept.–Mai*
Fleur de Decauville	*Déc.–Mai*
Brie de Melun	*Janv.–Déc.*
Ville-Saint-Jacques	*Nov.–Mai*
Feuille de Dreux	*Nov.–Mai*

LANGUEDOC
Laguiole	*Nov.–Mai*
Pélardon de Ruoms	*Mai–Nov.*
Roquefort	*Janv.–Déc.*
Ercé	*Nov.–Mai*

LIMAGNE
Fourme de Montbrison	*Nov.–Mai*
Saint-Nectaire	*Oct.–Juillet*
Murols	*Nov.–Juin*
Gaperon	*Sept.–Juillet*
Fourme d'Ambert	*Nov.–Mai*

LIMOUSIN
Guéret (dit Creusois)	*Oct.–Juin*
Trappiste d'Echourgnac	*Janv.–Déc.*
Rocamadour	*Nov.–Mai*
Bleu de Bassillac	*Nov.–Mai*

LYONNAIS
Rigotte de Condrieu	*Mai–Nov.*
Mont-d'Or	*Déc.–Avril*

NIVERNAIS
Glux	*Janv.–Déc.*
Decize	*Janv.–Déc.*
Autun (dit fromage de vache)	*Janv.–Déc.*

NORMANDIE
Incheville	*Nov.–Mai*
Neufchâtel	*Oct.–Juin*
Rouennaise	*Oct.–Mai*
Villedieu	*Oct.–Mai*
Aurore	*Janv.–Déc.*
Triple Aurore	*Janv.–Déc.*
Excelsior	*Janv.–Déc.*
Fin de Siècle	*Janv.–Déc.*
Brillat-Savarin	*Janv.–Déc.*
Gournay	*Oct.–Juin*
Trappiste de Bricquebec	*Janv.–Déc.*
La Bouille	*Oct.–Mai*
Monsieur-Fromage	*Nov.–Juin*
Carré de Bonneville	*Sept.–Juin*
Pavé de Moyaux	*Nov.–Juin*
Pont-l'Evêque	*Sept.–Juillet*
Camembert	*Nov.–Mai*
Livarot	*Nov.–Juin*

ORLÉANAIS
Pithiviers au foin	*Oct.–Mai*
Chaingy	*Sept.–Juin*
Olivet-Bleu	*Oct.–Juin*
Olivet Cendré	*Nov.–Juillet*
Les Aydes	*Oct.–Juin*
Vendôme Bleu	*Oct.–Juin*
Vendôme Cendré	*Oct.–Juin*

PICARDIE
Rollot	*Oct.–Mai*
Guerbigny	*Oct.–Mai*
Trappiste du Mont-des-Cats	*Janv.–Déc.*

POITOU		Paladru	Nov.–Mai
Chabichou	Avril–Déc.	Persillé de Savoie	Mai–Janv.
La Mothe-Saint-Héraye	Mai–Nov.	Chevrotin	Mars–Déc.
La Mothe-Bougon	Mai–Nov.	Tomme des Beauges	Sept.–Juin
		Tomme au Fenouil	Sept.–Juin
PROVENCE		Tomme Boudane	Oct.–Juillet
Banon	Mai–Nov.	Trappiste de Tamié	Janv.–Déc.
Cachat d'Entrechaux (dit		Beaufort	Janv.–Déc.
fromage fort du Ventoux)	Mai–Nov.	Beaumont	Oct.–Juin
Bossons macérés	Déc.–Mars		
		TOURAINE	
SAVOIE		Troô	Mai–Janv.
Reblochon	Oct.–Juin	Sainte-Maure	Mai–Nov
Vacherin	Nov.–Mai		

CHEESE IN THE KITCHEN

Besides being a course in itself, and an important one since it is either the final or semi-final one, Cheese has a great place in cooking. In England and in the United States, the *Welsh Rarebit* is the supreme achievement of toasted cheese. In France, the *Sauce Mornay*, a *Béchamelle* with grated cheese incorporated in it, has brought the flavour of cheese to ever so many egg and vegetable dishes, as well as to fish dishes which have been rendered thereby much more acceptable than they would have been otherwise to the Wine Connoisseur. In Italy, the home of the *Parmigiano* or Parmesan cheese, the best cheese for grating, it has enhanced the flavour of most macaroni, spaghetti and other flour and eggs *Pâtes* which are somewhat insipid by themselves.

SOUPS

Soupe à l'oignon gratinée	II. 107
Macaroni Soup	III. 193
Potage Cheveux d'Ange	VII. 536
Consommé Milanaise	VII. 538
Consommé Catalane	VI. 422
Consommé a l'Italienne	VI. 422

SAUCES

Cheese Sauce	I. 18
Garniture Milanaise	I. 34
Sauce Mornay	I. 36

FISH

Chicken Halibut with Cheese sauce	V. 339
Coquilles St. Jacques Mornay	V. 371
Sole Mornay	V. 377

BISCUITS, CAKES, SAVOURIES

Cheese Biscuits	III. 163
Cheesecakes	III. 163
Chester Cakes	III. 163
Cheesed Rice	III. 219
Cheese Straw Biscuits	III. 163
Gnocchi Piémontese	III. 183
Gnocchi alla Romana	III. 183
Macaroni à l'Italienne	III. 192
Macaroni Milanaise	III. 193
Macaroni au gratin	III. 193
Paillettes au Parmesan	III. 203
Ravioli alla Romana	III. 218
Rice Cheesecakes	III. 222
Spaghetti Reggio	III. 232
Spaghetti Tuscan	III. 232
Tagliarini al fromaggio	III. 235
Tagliatelle	III. 236

VEGETABLES

Artichauts à la Milanaise	II. 57
Asperges Milanaise	II. 58
Asperges Mornay	II. 58
Asperges Polonaise	II. 58
Chou-fleur au gratin	II. 73
Cauliflower Soufflé	II. 73
Baked Celery with Cheese	II. 75
Leeks Mornay	II. 93
Mushrooms au gratin	II. 100
Potato Cheese	II. 113
Salsifis gratinés	II. 122
Epinards à la Mornay	II. 128
Tomato Fondue	II. 133
Small Marrows au gratin	II. 137

EGGS WITH CHEESE

Oeufs au Four Bourgeoise	VII. 617
Oeufs au fromage	VII. 617
Oeufs au plat Lorrains	VII. 618
Oeufs Parmentier	VII. 618
Oeufs Presbytere	VII. 618
Oeufs mollets Milanaise	VII. 619
Swiss Eggs	VII. 619
La Fondue	VII. 619
Oeufs dur Lyonnaise	VII. 621
Stuffed Eggs (11)	VII. 621
Stuffed Eggs (17)	VII. 621
Oeufs au plat Piémontaise	VII. 623
Cheese Omelette	VII. 625
Poached Eggs Mornay	VII. 630
Scrambled Eggs with Cheese	VII. 631
Venetian Eggs	VII. 632
Cheese Drops	VII. 633

SECTION 9
WINE

SECTION IX

Wine: including Beer, Cider, Spirits and other Beverages,
and many Recipes for making them

WINE

Wine whets the wit, improves its native force,
And gives a pleasant flavour to discourse.

JOHN POMFRET, *The Choice.*

INTRODUCTION

DRINK is the law of life. To live all must drink, man and beast, young and old, large and small. It was ever thus, and Anacreon said it, 2,500 years ago, in Greek verse, better than anybody else before him or since, in an *Ode to Wine,* which begins thus:

> 'The thirsty Earth drinks up the Rain,
> And drinks, and gapes for drink again . . .'

and ends with:

> 'Fill up the bowl, then, fill it high,
> Fill all the glasses there, and why
> Should every creature drink but I,
> Why, man of morals, tell me why?'

If, for an answer to so pathetic an appeal, we turn to Pascal – and who will challenge the right of Pascal to the title of 'man of morals'? – we learn that there are in man three natures: the physical, or animal; the intellectual, or human; and the moral, or divine.

Man's body is but matter, nought but moist clay: plain water is all that is needed to keep it moist.

Man's intellect, that is his power to think and to fend for himself, is so often dormant, or dulled by matter, benumbed by cares, paralysed by fear, that, in

665

all times and among all nations, the most highly civilized, as well as the least, man has managed to brew for himself some kind of drink more stimulating than plain water, something more helpful, and, of course, cheap enough for daily use. Hence the very *ordinaires* wines, in all wine-producing lands, and the mead, ale, beer and cider of more northern latitudes; also, in modern times, whisky and water and other forms of diluted spirits.

Man's soul is the greatest and most mysterious gift of all. It is the divine fount from which flows the milk of human kindness, the love of our neighbour, charity, that noble stock which brings forth none but noble fruits, and one of them is hospitality. The host worthy of the name has but one aim, that is to make his guests welcome and happy, to give them the best within his means and reach. In the matter of food his choice is great, but in the realm of drink it is even greater. There are fine wines and rare vintages, which are costly and the privilege of the wealthy, but there is also a considerable variety of other beverages within the thirst of all but the poorest in the land.

The best host is not he who spends most money to entertain his guests, but he who takes the most intelligent interest in their welfare and makes sure that they will have a good time, something good to drink, something that is both good and new, if possible. This Section of the *Concise Encyclopædia of Gastronomy* has been compiled to help such a host. He or she will find in its pages not merely a list of the chief wines of the world, but also all manner of recipes and suggestions for making cups and cocktails, fruit wines and punches, straight drinks and mixed drinks, hot and cold, long and short.

As regards the best way to serving different wines with different foods, there are a few general rules such as: dry wines should come before and never after sweeter wines; light wines before the heavier ones; white wines with fish and white meats; red wines with butcher's meat and venison; sweet wines with the sweets or dessert. But the best rule of all is to find out what your guests like best and give it to them, if you can.

Merely as a guide, which may prove helpful in the choice and service of different wines, we append a list of wines which, in our opinion, are best to serve before and with food.

BEFORE THE MEAL: *French Vermouth*, plain or with a little gin and served cold; or a dry Sherry, *Fino*, *Amontillado* or *Montilla*, and served slightly chilled; or a glass of *Dry Champagne*, iced;

WITH OYSTERS: *Chablis*, cool but not iced;

WITH HORS-D'OEUVRE: a dry white wine, chilled, either *Moselle*, *Alsace*, *Graves*, *Pouilly*; or a *Tavel rosé*;

WITH THE SOUP: A *Vino de pasto* Sherry or a dry *Madeira*;

WITH FISH: a fuller white wine than with the Hors-d'oeuvre, either a *White Burgundy* or a *Hock*, or else a dry *Champagne*, chilled but not iced;

WITH CHICKEN, TURKEY, VEAL OR LIGHT ENTRÉES: the same as with Fish;

WITH BEEF, LAMB AND MUTTON: *Médoc*, red *Graves*, *Beaujolais*, *Touraine* or any other rather light red wine, served at the temperature of the room;

WITH DUCK, GOOSE, PORK AND VENISON: *St Emilion*, red *Burgundy*, *Côtes du Rhône* or any other of the fuller red wines, served at the temperature of the room;

WITH THE SWEETS: *Sauternes*, *Anjou*, *Palatinate*, or any other sweet wine white, still or sparkling, and iced;

WITH THE DESSERT: *Port*, *Madeira* or one of the fuller types of *Sherry*;

WITH THE COFFEE: *Brandy*, never in a heated glass; or *Liqueurs*, chilled or served in iced glass.

Definitions and Recipes

ABBOCCATO
The local name given to the sweeter types of Italian white wines, particularly those of *Orvieto*.

ABRICOTA, ABRICOTINE
Two of the names under which a sweet Liqueur is sold which is made of spirit sweetened and flavoured with apricots.

ABSINTHE
A potent Elixir, wormwood (*absinthe*) being the chief of a number of aromatic plants used in the making of it. It was first invented by a Frenchman, a Dr Ordinaire, who lived at Couvet, in Switzerland, and who sold the recipe in 1797, to a Mr Pernod, whose name has been associated with *Absinthe* ever since. The right way to serve *Absinthe* is to dilute it with much iced water which is allowed to drip into it through a flat perforated silver spoon, when the glass is eventually filled with a cloudy, opalescent, aromatic liquid. The sale of *Absinthe* is prohibited in Switzerland, France and the United States.

ACETIC ACID. CH₃CO₂H.
The most prevalent of all undesirable acids in wine. Acetic acid is due chiefly to the oxidation of ethylic alcohol in the presence of a fungoid catalyst known as *Mycoderma aceti*. Acetic acid is responsible for the sour, sharp taste of vinegar and 'pricked' wines. The lower the alcoholic strength of a wine, the greater the risk of oxidation of its alcohol into acetic acid, and the freer the access of air to a wine, the more rapid will be the formation of acetic acid. Vinegar should never be kept in the wine-cellar: it adds to the ever-present danger of acetification of wine.

ACIDS
Acids are present in all wines, some being not only wholesome, but quite indispensable, whilst others are exactly the reverse. To the first group belong the aldehyde-acids, which are chiefly responsible for the *bouquet* of all wines; to the second belongs acetic acid, the principal cause of pricked' or 'vinegary' wines.

Free acids present in grape-juice before fermentation, and in wine after fermentation, in a more or less permanent or merely transitory state, are the following: carbonic, tartaric, tannic, malic and citric. Acids which are present in wine but not in grape-juice are:

succinic, acetic, matapectic, lactic and butyric acids. The variety of acids in wine is due to differences existing in the soil of different vineyards, the species of grapes and the nature of Saccharomycetes and other micro-organisms present in the must, or introduced adventitiously in the wine after fermentation. The majority of those acids are present only in minute quantities, too minute, in most cases, to be measured, but the importance of the part they play as regards the degree of excellence of different wines is out of all proportion to their volume.

ACQUAVITAE
An Italian form of *Aqua vitae* (q.v.) or *Brandy*.

ADEGA
The Portuguese equivalent of the Spanish *Bodega* (q.v.).

ADVOCAAT
One of the most famous Dutch Liqueurs and a valuable restorative. It is made chiefly of brandy and egg-yolks and might be called a bottled egg-nog. There are, unfortunately, some thick, yellow, semi-liquid compounds sold under the name of *Advocaat*, made with cornflour and raw spirit, which are an unwholesome travesty of the real thing.

AËRATED WATERS
There is a considerable number of aërated waters, some being naturally and the others artificially carbonated, or sparkling. The natural *Aërated waters*, also known as *Mineral Waters*, contain some carbonic acid gas in solution as they issue forth from the soil; they may be drunk at the spring, in their sparkling condition, or else in any part of the world, after they have been bottled, in which case their carbonic acid gas is usually collected at the spring and the right quantity of it is then reintroduced into the water under pressure at the time of bottling: this is the only way to ensure that their degree of effervescence shall be exactly the same from bottle to bottle and from year to year. *Aërated waters* which are artificially carbonated are also called *Minerals*: they are the more common and least expensive, but they contain none of the valuable mineral salts which many of the natural *Mineral waters* contain, besides carbonic acid gas. The commonest of all artificially carbonated *aërated waters* are soda, potash and lithia waters; they are

tasteless; other *Minerals* such as 'fizzy' lemonade and orangeade, are flavoured as well as carbonated. The principle upon which carbonated waters are produced is that water absorbs under the normal pressure of the atmosphere about its own bulk of carbonic acid gas, and twice as much if pressure equal to that of two atmospheres be applied; more as the pressure is increased. Carbonic acid gas is generated by chalk or whiting being treated with sulphuric acid; the gas thus obtained is stored in a gasometer, from which it passes into a condenser and eventually to the bottling machine. In the case of 'fizzy' lemonade or any other coloured and flavoured *Mineral*, the colouring and flavouring essences are run into the bottle, which is then filled with water charged with gas at the desired pressure. It is then immediately capped, corked, or otherwise securely locked into the bottle, so that the gas cannot escape before the cork or capsule is removed. The chief *Aërated Waters*, both natural and artificial, will be found under their own name in alphabetical order.

AESCULAP WATER

An aperient *Mineral Water* from the aesculap spring, in the Kelenföld, near Budapest. The salts of this water contain 90 per cent of purgatives, chiefly sulphates of sodium and magnesium.

AGAVE

The name of the American aloe (*Agave americana*) and also the name of a highly intoxicating drink which is distilled from its fermented sap. It is called *Maguey* in Mexico.

AGE OF WINES

The age at which wines are (*a*) fit to drink, and (*b*) at their best, varies according to their alcoholic strength and the poise or balance of their various acids. Age, in wine, is due to a series of molecular readjustments, chiefly at the expense of the carbon of alcohol and sugars and of the hydrogen of acids, and in the presence of oxygen. Many light beverage wines are at their best when a year old and even less, but all wines with any claim to real merit – wines made from wellbred stock, grown in suitable soil and in a favourable year – should be allowed to mature slowly under cork, that is to say in bottle, in the presence of a minimum of oxygen from the outside air.

AGLIANICO DEL VULTURE

A red table wine made from the Aglianico grape in the valley of the Vulture of the Basilicata (Italy).

AGUARDIENTE

The Spanish and Italian form of *Aqua vitae*, used in Spain, Mexico, Italy and South America for raw, potent spirit, mostly distilled from the grape in wine-producing countries, or from molasses in the West Indies and cane growing lands.

AHR

The Ahr is a tributary of the Rhine (left bank) and the vine has been cultivated in the Ahr Valley since the days of the Roman occupation. The vineyards of the Ahr Valley produce both red and white wines, the best and best known being the *Walporzheimer* and *Ahrweiler*, both red wines.

AIX-LES-BAINS WATER

There are two springs at this place, situated on the lower slopes of the hills which form the base of Mont Revard. The one spring is sulphurous; the other, called 'Eau des deux reines', is alkaline. The latter has a very decided diuretic action.—L.G.M.

AKVAVIT. AQUAVIT

The Scandinavian form of *Aqua vitae*, a highly rectified, practically neutral – and brutal – spirit, distilled mostly from grain or potatoes, and flavoured with caraway seeds. It is not sweetened and it is not aged. It is colourless and usually swallowed at one gulp, before meal, as a cocktail, or at the beginning of a meal with the *smörgasbrod* or Scandinavian hors-d'oeuvre. The *Aalborg Akvavit* is the best known brand of Akvavit exported from Denmark.

ALBA FLORA

The best white wine of the island of Majorca. It is made from Malvasia grapes.

ALBAN WINE

The wine of the *Colli Albani*, the Alban Hills, south of Rome, the quality of which must have greatly deteriorated since the heyday of the Roman Empire, when Horace sang its praises (*od.* IV, xi. 2, and *Sat.* II. viii, 16), and claimed that it was excellent when nine years old. Pliny, who was not a poet, places the Alban wine among the Third Growths of Italian wines; he adds that it was at its best when fifteen years old. The wines of the Alban Hills are now sold under the names of *Albano, Frascati, Genzano, Rocca di Papa* and *Ariccia*, all of them table wines of no great distinction.

ALBANA

A sweet golden wine made from the vineyards of Bertinoro, in the Province of Æmilia, in Italy.

ALBANIA

There are local wines, both red and white, practically everywhere in Albania and their quality is not too bad.

ALCOHOL

The name Alcohol covers a very large number of compounds of carbon, hydrogen and oxygen, but the member of the alcohol family which is such an important component part of all wines, beers and spirits is Ethyl Alcohol, or C_2H_6O, a colourless liquid with a faint and pleasant ethereal smell. There is absolutely nothing in the chemical composition of Ethyl Alcohol to warrant its description as a poison or a narcotic. Like other carbohydrates, it releases heat and supplies energy for muscular work; hence it is a food. But it is a food with a specific action upon the nervous system, an action which leads to perfectly normal functional changes, causing a gentle inner mental stimulation when taken in moderate quantities by normal subjects, but causing grave mental and physical deterioration when taken to excess or by subjects with undeveloped or impaired mental powers. The quantity of Ethyl Alcohol present in wine is reckoned in degrees of absolute alcohol, in France and in most wine-producing countries, but in England it is reckoned in degrees of Proof spirit, 100 of absolute alcohol being equal to 175 of Proof spirit.

The Ethyl Alcohol present in spirits is measured, in England, according to Sykes' method in degrees over or under 'Proof', which represent diluted alcohol equal to 57.05° of absolute alcohol by volume, and 49.85° by weight, at a temperature of 60° F.

ALCOHOLIC STRENGTH

The strength of wine refers to its alcoholic content, the greater the proportion of alcohol there is in a wine, the stronger it is.

Comparative Wine Strengths

In the United Kingdom the Duty is charged on the strength of wines described as 'not exceeding 25° or not exceeding 42° of Proof Spirit'. The following table shows the comparisons between degrees of alcohol and degrees of proof spirit.

Degrees of Alcohol	Degrees of Proof Spirit	Degrees of Alcohol	Degrees of Proof Spirit
1	1.8	13	23.1
2	3.7	14	24.7
3	5.6	15	26.4
4	7.2	16	28.1
5	8.9	17	29.9
6	10.7	18	31.6
7	12.4	19	33.4
8	14.2	20	35.2
9	15.9	21	37.0
10	17.7	22	38.9
11	19.4	23	40.7
12	21.2	24	42.6

ALE

The most popular beverage in all northern lands where there are no vineyards and where wine is accordingly too dear for daily consumption. *Ale* is made from barley, which is wetted, spread on a floor and allowed – or encouraged to germinate. It is then dried in a kiln and becomes malt. Malt is put in a tub with lots of warm water and some yeast, when fermentation soon starts and transforms the malt sugar into carbonic acid gas, which loses itself in the air, and alcohol, which remains in the liquid which may then be called *Ale*. It answers to Johnson's Dictionary's definition of *Ale*: *A liquor brewed from malt, to be drunk fresh.* This used to be known as *Common Ale*, in opposition to *Spiced Ale*, which used to be flavoured with a number of spices and herbs, other than hops. According to the Shorter Oxford English Dictionary, *Ale and Beer were originally synonymous; but now 'beer' is the generic name for all malt liquors, 'ale' being the name for the lighter coloured kinds.* This is not so, since there are *Ales* just as dark as the darkest *Beer*, other than *Stout*. Benskin's *Colne Valley Ale*, for instance, a very dark and full strength *Ale* and one of the best of 'bottled beers'.

Ale is from the Saxon *Eale*, and *Beer* from the Celtic *Bere*, barley, but whose thirst was greater, of Celts or Saxons, and who was the earlier or more skilled brewer, we may never know.

Stone Ale was not sold in stone bottles; it was *Ale* brewed originally at the monastery of Stone, in Staffordshire, which had the reputation of being the finest in the Midlands: the monks' skill in malting and brewing had probably something to do with it, but the excellence of the local water was mainly responsible then as it is to this day for the quality of the *Ale* brewed in Staffordshire.

March and October are the two best brewing months in England.

ALE FLIP or
ONE YARD OF FLANNEL

Put a quart of Bass & Co.'s barley wine, or strong ale, on the fire to warm, and beat up three or four eggs with 4 oz. of moist sugar, a teaspoonful of grated nutmeg or ginger and quarter good old rum or brandy. When the ale is near to a boil, put it into a pitcher, and the rum and eggs, etc., into another; turn it from one pitcher to the other till it is smooth as cream.—J. MAN.

ALEATICO

A sweet Italian red wine, made from the Aleatico grape, a species of black Muscat, grown in Apulia, Umbria, the Latium, and the island of Elba. There was a wine of Tuscany known in England by the name Aleatico as early as the time of Chaucer. Two of the best known Aleatico wines of to-day are made in the Latium, from the Castelli Romani vineyards, the *Aleatico di Terracina* and the *Aleatico di Gradoli*. There are also, among others, the *Aleatico di Puglia* and the *Aleatico Elba*.

ALEBERRY

Mix two large spoonfuls of fine oatmeal in sufficient sweet small beer, two hours before using it; strain well, boil, and sweeten according to taste. Pour into a warm jug, add wine, lemon juice, and nutmeg to taste, and serve hot with thin slips of toast or rusks.—F.F.

ALELLA

The name of a village of Catalonia (Spain) and also that of the wine – mostly white, made from the vineyards which surround Alella; it is sold in long, fluted bottles resembling Hock bottles, but the wine has neither the bouquet nor any other characteristic of Hock; it is just a plain, refreshing, homely wine.

ALGERIAN WINE

The progress made by the wine industry of Algeria has been very rapid. In 1864, Algeria produced 1,430,000 gallons of wine and imported 8,800,000 gallons from France. In 1878, Algeria produced 22,000,000 gallons and began exporting wine to France. In 1932, the vineyards of Algeria were responsible for the immense quantity of close upon 500 million gallons, mostly red wines, beverage wines of no great distinction but deep in colour and fairly high in alcoholic strength, the most useful type of wine for blending with poor, thin ones. There is also a very limited quantity of red and white still wines made in Algeria which are very pleasing table wines, but attempts at dessert, sweet wines and sparkling wines have not so far been very successful.

ALICANTE

One of the oldest centres of Spanish viticulture, and the name of the best known wine of the Province of Levante. The Alicante vineyards are responsible for the production of some 10 million gallons wine per annum; it is mostly red wine and rather sweet, and there was quite a fair demand for it, as a dessert wine, in England, during the nineteenth century, until the stronger and cheaper wines of Tarragona replaced it in public favour.

ALKERMÈS

A French Cordial, crimson red and rather sweet, which used to be very popular; it was coloured with what was called *Kermès* berries, which were not berries at all but small insects of the cochineal genus, full of red dye, gathered mostly upon some of the oaks of the Mediterranean uplands. There was also an Italian brand of *Alkermès*.

ALOQUE

One form of the name given in England to a white wine shipped from San Lucar, in Spain: it was also called *Xaloque, Hallocke* and *Hollock*. There is an *Aloque* silver Wine Label, dated 1834, in the Marshall Collection, and a *Xaloque* enamel Wine Label in the Ionides Collection.—N.M.P.

In the Dictionary of the Spanish Academy the present-day *Aloque* is described as a *Vin rosé*, made from black and white grapes mixed.

ALOXE-CORTON

One of the more important wine-producing Communes of the Côte d'Or Département of France. Its vineyards produce both red and white Burgundies of great distinction. The best red wines of the Commune are those of the following vineyards: *Le Clos du Roi, Les Bressandes, Les Chaumes, Les Combes, Les Fiètres, Les Grèves, Les Languettes, Les Maréchaudes, Les Meix, Les Pougets, Les Renardes* and *La Vigne au Saint*. Two of the most reliable red wines of Corton are the *Hospices de Beaune Cuvées* known as *Cuvée Charlotte Dumay* and *Cuvée Docteur Peste*. The average yield of red burgundy of the Corton vineyards is 100,000 gallons per annum. Their white wine yield is very much smaller: the two best white wines of the Commune are those of *Le Corton* and *Le Charlemagne* vineyards.

ALSACE

The easternmost province of France between the Vosges mountains and the Rhine. Alsace produces a very large quantity of quite ordinary wines from the Elbing and Burger grapes, as well as a fair quantity of very much better wines (white) from the Riesling, Pinot and Traminer grapes. The best growths of Alsace are the following:

Upper Alsace: Ammerschwihr, Beblenheim, Bergheim, Colmar, Eguisheim, Guebwiller, Hernawihr, Ingersheim, Katzenthal, Kayserberg, Jungholtz, Kientzheim, Mittlewihr, Ribeauvillé (or Rappoltsweiler) Riquewihr, Rouffach, Thann, Turkheim, Wintzenheim.

Lower Alsace: Andlau, Barr, Chatenois, Dambach, Epfig, Gertwiller, Goxwiller, Heligenstein, Kintzheim, Mittelbergheim, Molsheim, Obernai, Roosheim, Wolheim.

ALTAR WINE

Wine used for sacramental purposes. According to Canon Law, wine used for the Holy Sacrifice of the Mass must be unadulterated fermented juice of the grape. So-called 'unfermented' wines may not be used, but fortified wines have sometimes been considered suitable, as not being adulterated, merely 'assisted'.

AMARANTE

The name of one of the best white beverage wines of Portugal: it has little or no bouquet, but it has both body and freshness; it is very refreshing when young and served cold.

AMBROSIA

The mythical tipple of the gods in Olympus according to Greek mythology. It was said to be 'nine times as sweet as honey'.

AMERICAN WINES

The vine is indigenous to America, and the best European species have also been introduced both in North and South America. Vineyards flourish from Canada, in the North, to Chile, in the South, and wine is made, which is known by the name of the land of its growth, whether California, Mexico, Peru, Brazil, the Argentine or Chile. But the name *American Wines* is in practice reserved for the wines made in the United States, east of the Rocky Mountains, particularly in the States of New York, Ohio, New Jersey, Virginia, Missouri and Michigan. They are wines made from indigenous American vines, and they are known mostly by the names of the American vines from which they are made, such as Delaware, Catawba, Diana, Elvira, etc. Some are red and others white, some are still and others sparkling, and yet others are fortified like Port.

Viticulture and wine making, in the Eastern States, were in the hands of a comparatively large number of small farmers up to the last decade of the nineteenth century.

According to Frank Schoonmaker and Tom Marvel (*American Wines*, Duell, Sloan and Pearce Inc., New York, 1941) what made small-scale wine making unprofitable in the East and Middle West was a combination of two factors: (1) the increasing competition of cheap Californian wines, and (2) burdensome license fees, bonds, and various taxes.

During the last war the shortage of European wines, the greatly increased circulation of money and the exaltation of the national feeling all helped to bring about an unprecedented measure of prosperity to the wine industry of the East and Middle West, no longer in the hands of small farmers, but

in those of large and moneyed syndicates or powerful Co-operative Societies.

AMER PICON

A popular brand of French "Bitter' or *apéritif* cordial; it is usually served sweetened with a little *Grenadine* or *Cassis*, and diluted with two parts to one of iced water.

AMMERSCHWIHR

One of the most important wine-producing Communes of Alsace (France). Mostly white table wines. A little red wine made also in most years, and some *Vin de Paille*, in exceptionally hot years.

AMMINEAN WINE

One of the more lasting and most famous wines in the heyday of the Roman Empire, to which 'even the royal Phanaean paid homage' (*Virgil*):

'Sunt etiam Amminee vites, firmissima vina:

'Tmolius assurgit quibus, et rex ipse Phanaeus,

'Argitisque minor: cui non certaverit ulla,

'Aut tantum fluere, aut totidem durare per annos.'

(Georg. II, v. 97-100.)

AMONTILLADO

One of the most popular types of sherry, neither too dry nor too sweet. It may be a *Fino* or merely a *Vino de Pasto* wine, in quality, but it is meant to possess a fairly dry finish, somewhat similar to the finish of the wines of Montilla, near Cordoba. It is better served before the meal and slightly chilled.

AMOROSO

One of the fuller and somewhat richer types of sherry, darker in colour and sweeter than an Amontillado, but lighter in colour and body than a Brown Sherry. Best served with turtle soup at the beginning of the meal or with fruit, at the end.

AMPHORA

A jar or vase used in ancient Greece and Rome for storing wine and oil. It had an oval or egg-shape body, a narrow neck, two handles to lift it and a pointed end that used to be stuck in the earth or sand of the cellar or store. The Greek *Amphora* held 39 litres or 8½ gallons; the Roman *Amphora* 25 litres or 5½ gallons.

ANACREON

A lyric Greek poet (*c.* 532 B.C.) who had the reputation of being a great drinker, and who died of a grape-pip in his windpipe. He wrote the 'Ode to Wine' which Abraham Cowley translated, beginning:

"The thirsty Earth drinks up the Rain,"
and ending:
"Nothing in Nature's sober found,
But an eternal Health goes round.
Fill up the bowl, then, fill it high,
Fill all the glasses there, and why
Should every creature drink but I,
Why, man of morals, tell me why?"

ANDALUCIA

The province in the extreme south-west of
Spain, the eighth out of the twelve wine-
producing Provinces of Spain as regards its
wine production, but the first in the matter
of quality and reputation; it is the home
province of Jerez and of *Sherry*.

The *Almeria* vineyards of Andalucia produce grapes particularly rich in sugar: some
of them are used for making wine of the
Malaga type; others are dried into *Raisins*.

ANGELICA

(*a*) A Basque Liqueur of the *Chartreuse* type;
it is pale yellow in colour, very sweet and
highly aromatic. The best is made by Izarra.

(*b*) A very sweet white wine originally
made in the San Joaquin Valley of California
by the Mission Fathers. It is now mostly
made in various parts of Southern California
from grape-juice the fermentation of which
is checked by the addition of spirit. It is
more a *Mistelle* than a wine, that is a sweet
and alcoholic basis for the making of cordials
and *apéritifs*. The name also applies to highly
fortified dessert Californian wines, made in
the same way as white Port, that is fortified
after fermentation has started.

ANGOSTURA

The most widely renowned brand of 'Bitters'.
It is compounded in the island of Trinidad.
It may be used neat, as a medicine, in cases
of diarrhoea, but its chief use is as a flavouring agent, just a few drops being added to
cocktails and other drinks, both long and
short.

ANIS

The Spanish name of an aniseed-flavouring
cordial which is mostly drunk diluted with
iced water as a 'long' drink.

ANISETTE

The French name of an aniseed-flavoured
Liqueur which is very sweet and usually
served in very small glasses to the very
young and the very old, who like or need
sugar.

ANJOU

The Département of Maine-et-Loire produces a large quantity of very pleasing and
some really fine white wines; also a large
quantity of light white wines eminently

suitable for making sparkling wines. The
still wines of Maine-et-Loire and adjoining
vineyards are usually known as *Vins d'Anjou*,
the sparkling wines are known as *Vins de
Saumur*.

The finest white wines of Anjou, naturally
sweet wines, more suitable as dessert wines
than beverage wines, are those of the *Coteaux
du Layon*; the finest vineyards of the *Loire*
are *La Coulée de Serrant, La Roche aux Moines*
and *Château de Savennières*; the best of the
Layon are *Quart de Chaume, Faye, Beaulieu* and
Bonnezeaux. Two other celebrated white
wines of Anjou are those of *Château de
Parnay* and *Château de l'Aiglerie*.

The vineyards of Anjou, which produce
quality wines, cover some 40,000 acres.

APÉRITIFS

A French name for preprandial drinks which
differ from cocktails in being 'long' and
comparatively 'mild', instead of 'short' and
'brutal'. The oldest and most popular form
of *Apéritif*, in France, is the dry *Vermouth*,
Noilly Prat or *Chambéry*, with or without a
little *Cassis*, to sweeten it. Other very popular *Apéritifs*, sold under the name or brand
of the manufacturers, are *Amer Picon, Byrrh,
Dubonnet, Lillet* and *St. Raphaël. Pernod* and
all sorts of imitations of *Absinthe*, such as
Anis Mono, etc., are also drunk before meals,
as *Apéritifs*.

Strangely enough, a small glass of tawny
or white Port wine is also quite popular in
France before the meal, as an *Apéritif*.

APOLLINARIS WATER

An alkaline and strongly effervescent mineral
water from the Apollinaris Brunnen, a
spring in the valley of the Ahr (Rhineland).
It has no taste and is popular on that account
as a table water.

APPLEADE

Cut two large apples in slices, and pour a
quart of boiling water on them; strain well,
and sweeten. To be drunk when cold or
iced.—F.F.

APPLE JACK. APPLE BRANDY

Two names for the same colourless spirit
distilled from cider at usually very high
strength. That which is distilled in Normandy is sold under the name of *Calvados*,
from the Département of that name which is
famed for its cider and apple brandy.

APRICOT BRANDY

A highly flavoured and rather fascinating
Liqueur compounded in England and elsewhere; brandy is used in the making of the
better sorts; cheaper spirit for inferior
brands; in all cases the flavour is imparted by

dried apricots. The best *Apricot Brandy*, however, is distilled from fresh apricots and the crushed kernels of their stones, in lands where apricots bear abundant fruit, such as Hungary, where they make a very good *Apricot Brandy*; it is sold under the label *Barat Palinka*, in quite distinctive odd-shaped bottles.

APRICOT GIN
One of Messrs. Hawker's (Plymouth) liqueurs.

APRICOT LIQUEUR
A sweetened *Apricot Brandy* of rather low alcoholic strength. Many cordial and liqueur compounders produce *Apricot Liqueurs* which differ in strength, sweetness and attractiveness, as well as price: they are mostly sold under registered and advertised brands, such as *Abricotine*, *Apry*, *Capricot*, etc.

APRICOT WINE
Take 12 lb. of apricots, when nearly ripe; wipe them clean, and cut them in pieces; put them into two gallons of water, and let them boil till the water has strongly imbibed the flavour of the fruit; then strain the liquor through a hair sieve; and put to every quart of liquor 6 oz. of sugar; after which, boil it again, and skim it, and when the scum has ceased to rise, pour it into an earthen vessel. The next day bottle it, putting a lump of sugar into each bottle.—W.S.M.

APULIA
One of the most favoured of the wine-producing provinces of Italy. Its vineyards produce much dark and strong red wines of no great charm but very useful for blending with weaker wines. They also produce some excellent dessert wines known as *Moscata di Salento* and *Altramura*; also some good white beverage wines, more particularly those of *Bari*, *San Severo* and *Torre Giulia*.

AQUAVIT
See *Akvavit*.

AQUA VITAE
The early name of brandy, the elixir of life or *Eau de vie* (q.v.).

ARAGON
One of the most important wine-producing Provinces of Spain; its wines are mostly red and consumed locally. The only dessert wine of note produced in Aragon is a very sweet white wine known as *Cariñena*.

ARBANATS
One of the minor wine-producing Communes of the Graves district, 22 k. SSE. of Bordeaux, with the Garonne as its boundary

to the north. Its chief estate is *Le Basque*, with an average production of 100 tuns claret and 20 tuns white wine. The *Château Tourteau-Chollet-Lafitte* produces on an average 20 tuns claret and 100 tuns white wine, while the *Château d'Arbanats* produces merely 5 tuns claret but 30 tuns white wine.

ARBOIS
A picturesque little town of the Jura Département, on the lower foothills of the Monts Jura, and the birthplace of Pasteur. It is surrounded by vineyards which produce a fair quantity of red, white and *rosés* wines of no great distinction but very palatable when consumed locally. Some of the white wines of Arbois are also made into sparkling wines.

ARCINS
A Commune of the Médoc 33 k. N. of Bordeaux. The wines of Arcins have acquired by long usage the right to be sold under the name of the adjoining and better known Commune of Listrac. Its finest estate is that of *Château d'Arcins*, a Cru Bourgeois, which produces an average of 60 tuns claret.

ARF AN' ARF
A blend of half porter and half pale ale.

ARGENTINE WINES
The culture of wine-making grapes was introduced into the country by the early Spanish missionaries and it has been developed to such an extent that the Argentine now ranks fifth of the world's largest wine-producing countries with an annual average of some 160,000,000 gallons. The Province of Mendoza is responsible for nearly 75 per cent of the total wine output of the Republic; San Juan for 21 per cent; and Rio Negro for 4 per cent. The wines of the Argentine are produced by varieties of the European – or *vinifera* parent vine; most of them are red, beverage wines of no great distinction, but there are some wines of high quality made in small quantities, both red and white, as well as still and sparkling. Vermouths, dessert wines and brandies are also produced in the Argentine.

Some of the best Argentine wines are sold under the following labels:

Red: Trapiche viejo; Trapiche Derby; Puente viejo; Cabernet reservado; Pinot viejo; Carrodilla tinto.

White: Trapiche Sauvignon; Riesling; Château d'Anchon; Norton, San Félipe.

Sparkling Wines: Arizu, Alvear; Baron de Rio Negro; Monitor.

ARINTO
The name of the grape chiefly grown in the vineyards of Bucellas, near Lisbon: the golden wine which is made from it lacks

bouquet, but has body and is quite agreeable; it is mostly known in Portugal under the name of *Arinto*, but is sold overseas under that of *Bucellas*. One of the rarer English *Wine Labels* bears the name *Arinto*.

ARISTOPHANES (450–385 B.C.)

And dare you rail at wine's inventiveness?
I tell you nothing has such go as wine.
Why, look you now; 'tis when men drink
    they thrive,
Grow wealthy, speed their business, win
    their suits,
Make themselves happy, benefit their friends.
Go, fetch me out a stoup of wine, and let me
Moisten my wits, and utter something
    bright.
              Aristophanes, *The Knights*

ARISTOTLE (384–322 B.C.)

Founder of literary criticism, for twenty years Plato's disciple and a firm believer in wine. 'To know how to apply them (wine and honey) for the purposes of health, and to whom, and at what time, is as difficult as to be a physician.' *Nic. Ethics.* V, ix, 16 (Bohn).

ARMAGNAC

The brandy distilled from wine of the Gers Département of France. The centre of the Armagnac district is Condom. The best Armagnac Brandies are distilled from the Bas-Armagnac wines, and are divided into three classes: *Grands*, *Fins*, and *Petits* Armagnacs. The Armagnac district is divided into (1) *Bas-Armagnac*, from the Landes to the Gelize; (2) *Tanarèze*, from the Gelize to the Baize; (3) *Haut-Armagnac*, from the Baize to the Gers. Armagnac vineyards produce on an average a third of the brandy produced by those of Cognac. Good Armagnac can be very good and much better than ordinary Cognac, but the best Armagnac cannot hope to approach – let alone rival – the best Cognac.

ARRACK. ARACK

A fiery spirit distilled, chiefly in the Dutch Indies and British India, from rice. But the name, qualified or not, has also been used for 'native' spirits. Thus the *Pariah Arrack*, a spirit distilled from *Toddy*, the juice of the palm, drunk by the half-castes and lowest classes in India; *Batavia Arrack*, a spirit distilled from molasses with little cakes of dried Javanese rice added to the molasses. The worst *Arrack* of all is the *Tungusian Arrack*: it is distilled by the Tartars of Tungusia from fermented sour mare's milk. Although some *Arrack* is much worse than others, there is no *Arrack* pleasing to a cultivated palate.

676

ARROBA

Spanish wine measure: 16⅔ litres or 2⅜ gallons.

ARROPE

Not a wine, but unfermented grape juice (*must*) boiled to the consistency of a syrup; it is used for sweetening sherry and other Spanish wines.

ARSAC

A Commune of the Médoc 22 k. NW. of Bordeaux. Its best wine is that of *Château du Terre* (q.v.). Then comes those of *Cru Le Monteil* and *Château d'Arsac*, *Monbrison* and *Baury*, ranking as Bourgeois supérieurs and averaging 180 tuns of claret per annum. The red wines of Arsac have acquired by long usage the right to be sold under the better known name of the adjoining Commune of Margaux.

ASALI

An East African intoxicating native beverage, fermented somewhat like *Mead*, with honey as a basis.

ASCIUTTO

A name used in Italy, more particularly in Sicily, for a *dry* wine.

ASSMANNHAUSEN

An important wine-producing parish on the right bank of the Rhine, producing the best and best-known red wine of the Rhine; its bouquet is pleasing, but it is too thin to rank among the really great red wines. The best vineyards of *Assmannhausen* are *Hinterkirch*, *Höllenberg* and *Spitzerstein*.

ASTI SPUMANTE

The best-known sparkling wine of Italy, but not necessarily always the best. It is made from Moscato grapes grown in the vineyards of Asti and other Piemontese vineyards and is invariably sweet, sometimes very sweet. There is also a still *Asti* which was sufficiently well known in England for *Wine Labels* to bear this name in early Victorian times.

ASZTALI

The Hungarian equivalent of '*Vin ordinaire*'.

ATHOL BROSE

A Scotch 'night-cap' and sovereign cure for a cold: it is made up of boiling water poured over oatmeal, strained, sweetened with honey and braced with whisky.

A Victorian recipe for *Athol Brose*:

Add two wineglassfuls of Scotch whisky to a wineglassful of heather honey; mix well, and then stir in a well-beaten new-laid egg.
—F.F.

ATHOS
The home of some hospitable Greek monks who make quite a tolerable wine from the monastery vineyards (*Hagion Oros*).

ATTIC WINE
A name covering all the wines of Attica, the Athens Province, wines which cannot have been deserving of a very high place to judge from the fact that from classical times to the present they have been treated with resin. Martial (Ep. iii, 77) reproaches Baeticus with drinking nasty resinated wines in preference to Falernian, and Dr Miller, in *The Latins in the Levant*, endorses the verdict of the Metropolitan of Athens who, c. A.D. 1180, wrote that the Attic wine 'seems to be pressed from the juice of the pine rather than from that of the grape'.

AUBANCE
A small river of the Loire Valley: the vines gracing the slopes of the *Coteaux de l'Aubance* produce some light and pleasant white wines, the best of which are those of *Soulaines* and *Murs*.

AUBE
One of the French Départements adjoining that of the Marne. Its vineyards produce chiefly white wines, mostly rather thin and undistinguished wines, but, when the weather is favourable, they make a very pleasant sparkling wine of the champagne type from ripe Aube grapes.

AUDE
One of the three most important wine-producing Départements of France, quantitatively speaking. The other two are the Hérault and the Gard. The Aude vineyards produce very large quantities of undistinguished wines, mostly red; also a very limited quantity of fair white and red wines, more particularly those of *Limoux*, *Corbières* and *Minervois*.

AUROS, Château d'
A *Château*, parts of which date from the fourteenth century, at the extreme limit of the Graves de Bordeaux district, close to the Bazadais. The vineyards of *Château d'Auros* produce on an average 35 tuns of red wine and 125 tuns of white.

AURUM
A pale gold Italian liqueur highly aromatic and not too sweet.

AUSLESE
German for 'Specially Selected'; used for hocks and moselles made from the best and ripest bunches of grapes specially selected at the time of the vintage. When not only the bunches of grapes, but the best berries from each bunch, have been specially selected to make the wine, it is described as *Beerenauslese* or *Goldbeerenauslese*, with, sometimes, the qualificative *Feine* (Fine) or *Feinste* (Finest) before it.

AUSONE, Château
The first growth of St. Emilion. Average annual production, 15 tuns of claret. Always bottled at the *Château*. (There is also in the Graves district a *Château Ausone*, which produces about 5 tuns a year of red wine of moderate quality.)

Château Ausone is reputed to stand upon the site of the villa which the poet Ausonius built at Lucaniacum (St. Emilion) during the fourth century A.D.

AUSTRALIA
New South Wales is the cradle of the Australian viticulture, but it has been outpaced by Victoria, and above all by South Australia, which is responsible for nearly three-fourths of the Australian wine production. In both Queensland and Western Australia a little wine is also made, but not on a sufficiently important scale to provide wines for export. The principal types of Australian wines and the chief centres of production are as follows:

(*a*) The Hunter River district (New South Wales); the Great Western and the Lilydale districts (Victoria) produce chiefly light beverage wines, suitable for local consumption.

(*b*) The Irrigation Areas, all along the borders of New South Wales, Victoria and South Australia, where the greatest quantities of wines are produced, mostly distilled into brandy for fortifying 'sweet' wines.

(*c*) The Rutherglen and Corowa district, partly in New South Wales and partly in Victoria, which produce some of the best 'sweet' wines.

(*d*) The Watervale (Springvale) and other districts of South Australia, which produce the largest quantities of both sweet and dry wines suitable for export.

(*e*) The Queensland and Perth vineyards, which produce a limited quantity of both light and fortified wines.

AUSTRIA
Although Austria does not produce any wine in the class of the great wines of the world, there are many very pleasing red and white wines made from the vineyards of *Niederösterreich*, *Steiermark* and *Burgenland*, the three principal Austrian wine-producing districts. The best red wines of the country are those of the *Vösl'auer* and *Falkensteiner*; the best-known white wines those of *Grinz-*

ing, *Kremser*, *Sievering* and *Nussdorf*, the nearest vineyards to Vienna itself; and those of *Anninger Perle*, *Gumpoldskirchner*, and of the famous *Klösterneuberger*, an old monastery vineyard on the Danube.

AUXERRE
The chief city of the Yonne Département, the vinous glory of which are the white wines of Chablis. Among the best red wines of Auxerre vineyards are those of *Le Clos de la Chaînette* (12 acres), formerly owned by the Benedictins and now the property of the town of Auxerre; and those of the *Coteau de Migraine* (44 acres). The red wines of *Trancy* and *Coulange-la-Vineuse* enjoyed in the past a measure of reputation which their wines have ceased to deserve.

AUXEY-LE-GRAND
One of the lesser wine-producing Communes of the Côte d'Or (Côte de Beaune); its vineyards produce some very fair red wines which are usually sold under the better known name of the adjoining Commune of *Monthélie*.

AVA or ARVA
The most popular of the intoxicating beverages made by the natives of the Polynesian islands: it is fermented from a sweet mash which is obtained from the roots of the *Macropiper methysticum*, a plant which belongs to the Peppers genus. It is also called *Kava* or *Yava*.

AVALLON
An ancient market town which is the centre of some of the oldest vineyards of Lower Burgundy (now the Yonne Département), producing both red and white wines, the best of which are those of *Vézelay*, *Montcherin* and *La Côte Rouvre*.

AVELSBACHER
An attractive white wine from the Moselle vineyards in the Trier district. The best vineyards of Avelsbach – the name of a small river which joins the Moselle close to Trier – are known as *Herrenberg*, *Thielslei* and *Hammerstein*.

AVENSAN
A Commune of the Médoc, 29 k. N. of Bordeaux. Its best vineyards are those of *Châteaux Villegeorge, Citran, Meyre, Romefort* and *Vieux Clos*; they rank as Bourgeois supérieurs and average 225 tuns claret, *Château Citran* being responsible for 160 tuns. This Commune produces, besides the wines of these four growths, a good deal of fair quality claret, which has acquired by long usage the right to be sold under the better known name of the adjoining Commune of *Margaux*.

AVIZE
One of the more important wine-producing Communes of the Marne Département, on the left bank of the River Marne, between Cramant and Le Mesnil Oger, in the heart of the white grape vineyards of Champagne. The still white wines of Avize (of a good vintage) are among the most delicate and delightful of all light white wines.

AY
One of the more important wine-producing Communes of the Marne Département, on the right bank of the River Marne and merely a mile or so from Epernay. Its vineyards have produced some of the best wines of Champagne during the past five hundred years.

AYLER
One of the best white wines of the Saarburg district (Saar Valley). The best vineyards of Ayl are: *Kupp* and *Herrenberg*.

AZORES
Before they were destroyed by the Oïdium, in the fifties, and the Phylloxera, in the seventies, the vineyards of the Azores islands, chiefly Pico and Fayal, produced a fair amount of wines which were mostly exported to the United States, where they were known under the name of *Fayal* wines.

BABY
The name by which a quarter bottle, or *Nip* is sometimes known.

BACARDI
A popular brand of Cuban rum, particularly in demand for the mixing of a cocktail bearing this name.

BACCHUS WINE
The name of one of the wines of the Greek island of Santorin.

BACHARACH
An important wine-producing centre, on the left bank of the Rhine. Mostly white wines. Two of the best white wines of Bacharach are those of the Dell and Wolfshoehle vineyards.

BADACSONY
A hilly district of Hungary, chiefly famous for its white wines, which are usually known by the name of the grape from which they are made, such as *Auvergnas Gris, Kéknyelü, Rizling*. The best red wine of the district is made from Pinot grapes, known as *Burgunder*, and is sold as *Badacsonyer Burgunder*.

The best dessert wine, medium sweet and with a delicate and fascinating bouquet, is called *Badacsonyi Szurke-Barat*.

BADEN

An important wine-growing district of Germany. In pre-phylloxera days the vineyards of Baden covered some 22,000 hectares; they cover now about half. The wines of Baden are known as *Seeweine, Markgräflweine, Weine des Kaiserstuhls, Breisgauveine* and *Tauberweine*. One of the best red wines of Baden is the *Affenthaler*.

BADIANE

    3 pints brandy
    3 pints water
    1 lb. bitter almonds
    1lb. sugar
    1 lemon peel, rasped
    6 cloves
    1 oz. cinnamon

    Break up the whole, put it into a jar with the lemon peel; the sugar being melted in three pints of water, infuse for a month, strain it through a flannel bag, and then filter the liqueur and bottle it.—G.A.J.

BALM WINE

Take a bushel of balm leaves, put them into a tub, and pour eight gallons of scalding water upon them; let it stand a night; then strain it through a hair sieve, and put to every gallon of liquor 2 lb. of sugar, stirring it well until the sugar is dissolved; then put it on the fire, adding the whites of four eggs, well beaten up; when the scum begins to rise take it off; then let it boil half an hour, skimming it all the time; afterwards put it into the tub again, and when milk-warm add a gill of good ale yeast, stirring it every two hours; work it thus for two days; then put it into a cask, and bung it up. When fine, bottle it.—W.S.M.

BALTHASAR

A fancy name for a show bottle made to hold some 16 ordinary bottles, or 12.80 litres, equal to about 2.75 gallons.

BANANA LIQUEUR

One of the pre-war favourite liqueurs which was made in France, Holland, America, and elsewhere.

BANG

'Take a pint of cider, and add to a pint of warm ale; sweeten with treacle or sugar to taste, grate in some nutmeg and ginger, and add a wineglassful of gin or whisky'.—F.F.

BANYULS

The best and most popular French sweet or dessert wine during the eighteenth and nineteenth centuries. The vineyards of Banyuls are on the French side of the Eastern Pyrenees, in the former province of Roussillon, and they produce both black and white grapes. There are three grades of *Banyuls* wines: the red, which is made from black grapes, the must being partly fermented on the husks before it is fortified; the *rosé*, also made from black grapes, but the must being fermented away from the husks before being fortified; and the white, made from white grapes and fortified when partly fermented. Locally none but the wine of white grapes is given the name of *Banyuls*; the red and *rosé* wines are called *Grenache*, and when old in bottle and tawny in colour, *Rancio*.

BARBA-CARLO

One of the red table wines from the vineyards of the Broni district, in South Lombardy.

BARBARESCO

A red table wine from the easternmost vineyards of the Monferrato Hills, about 12 miles from Barolo. *Barbaresco* is rather lighter than *Barolo*, and not quite so fine a wine.

BARBERA

The name of a red grape grown extensively in Northern Italy. Also the name of the wine made from the Barbera grapes. The best Barbera wine is made in the Province of Alessandria, but Barbera wine is rarely of superlative quality, and some can be of the poorest quality.

A cheap and rather nasty sweet red wine which is supposed to be made from Barbera grapes is called *Barbera amabile*.

Red table wines of moderate quality, made from Barbera and other grapes blended are called *Barberati*.

BARBERONE

The name of a red Californian wine made from Barbera grapes and supposed to approximate the quality of *Barbera* wine.

BARDOLINO

One of the most acceptable of the red table wines of the Veneto Province of Italy; it is made from the vineyards on the eastern shore of Lake Garda.

BARLEY WATER

Take 2 oz. of pearl barley, wash it well, and boil for 10 minutes in a little water to clear it; when drained, put to it five pints of boiling water, and let it boil till reduced to one-half. Then strain for use.—L.G.M.

BARLEY WINE
A fancy name for *Beer* of high alcoholic strength and fine quality.

BAROLO
One of the best, if not the best, Italian red table wine. It is produced from a strictly delimited district of the Monferrato Hills, in Piedmont, known as *Le Langhe*, which includes, besides the vineyards of *Barolo* itself, those of *Castiglion Falletto, La Morra, Monforte, Verduno, Perno, Serralunga,* and *Grinzone*.

BARRACAS
An estate near Lisbon which used to be famous for its red wines.

BARREL
An English measure of capacity equal to 26¼ gallons, in London.

BARRIQUE
The French name for hogshead. Its official capacity varies with districts: Anjou, 56.108 gallons; Beaune and Sauternes, 50.246 gallons; Bordeaux, 49.786 gallons; Champagne, Cognac and Burgundy, 45.221 gallons.

In England, the name *Barrique* conveys the idea of a cask of 50 gallons.

BARSAC
The most important white wine Commune of the Gironde, after Sauternes, which it adjoins, producing somewhat luscious white wines, similar to those of Sauternes, but with a slightly drier finish and a bouquet quite distinctive. The two finest growths of Barsac are *Château Coutet* and *Château Climens*; then come the following *Châteaux*: *de Myrat, Doisy Daene, Védrines, Broustet-Nairac, Cantegril, Suau,* and *Caillou*. Among the less distinguished wines of Barsac are those of *Château Camperos* and *Mayne-Bert, de Carles, de Rolland, Guiteronde, de Lucquos, Cru de Montalivet, Châteaux Nairne, Piada* and *de Bastard*.

BAR SPOON
A 'mixing' spoon with a particularly long handle, the sort that Shakespeare never saw but anticipated when he wrote: 'He should have a long spoon that sups with the Devil'.

BASTARD
A sweet Peninsular wine, either white or tawny, probably blended and sweetened by the vintners, who sold it in England, in Elizabethan days and earlier.

Bastard was one of the wines familiar to Shakespeare:

Elbow. Nay, if there be no remedy for it, but that you will needs buy and sell men and women like beasts, we shall have all the world drink brown and white bastard. *Measure for Measure*, Act III, Scene ii.

Prince Henry. Why then, your brown bastard is your only drink ... First Part *Henry IV*, Act II, Scene iv.

Prince Henry. Score a pint of bastard in the Half-moon. First Part *Henry IV*, Act II, Scene iv.

BÂTARD MONTRACHET
One of the finest white wines of Burgundy, from vines in the Commune of Puligny-Montrachet (24 acres) and that of Chassagne-Montrachet (32½ acres).

BAVARIA
One of the wine-producing States of Germany, with an average annual production of 11 million gallons of wine, mostly white. Its best wines are those of the *Palatinate* and *Franconia*.

BAZAS
One of the (quantitatively) important Cantons of the Gironde; its vineyards produce much red wine and a little white, none of any great merit.

BÉARN
One of the most ancient wine-producing districts of the lower foothills of the Pyrenees, on the French side. Its best wine is that of *Jurançon*.

BEAUJOLAIS
The vineyard-clad hills facing the right bank of the River Saône, from Romanèche-Thorins, in Saône-et-Loire, to below Villefranche in the Rhône Département. The Beaujolais vineyards cover some 40,000 acres and produce an abundance of wine, mostly red, lighter than other red Burgundies from the Côte d'Or, and similar to those of the Mâconnais hills, immediately to the north. The best red wines of the Beaujolais-Mâconnais vineyards are those of *Thorins, Moulin-à-vent* (Commune of Romanèche), *Chénas, Fleurie, Morgon* (Commune of Villié), *Brouilly* (St. Lager) and *Juliénas*. The best white wines are those of *Pouilly* and *Fuissé*; the next best those of *Solutré, Vergisson* and *Chaintré*.

BEAUNE
An ancient Burgundian town which is, after Dijon, the most important hub of the wine trade of Burgundy. It is 38 k. S. of Dijon, surrounded by extensive vineyards, which adjoin those of Savigny and Corton, to the North, and those of Pommard, to the South. The vineyards of Beaune, which are responsible for the best red wines (1,340 acres) are: *Les Grèves (Enfant-Jésus)* and *Les Fèves*; also

Bressandes, Les Cent Vignes, Champs Mimonts, Le Clos de la Mousse, Le Clos des Mouches, Clos de Roi, Les Marconnets, etc. Among the more reliable red wines of Beaune, there are the *Cuvées Bétault Brunet, Clos des Avaux, Dames Hospitalières, Estienne* and *Guigone de Salins, Nicolas Rollin* and *Rousseau-Deslandes* of the *Hospices de Beaune* (q.v.). There is also a small quantity of white wine of no great distinction produced from Beaune vineyards.

BEAUSÉJOUR, Château
One of the First Growths Saint-Emilion. It was divided into two distinct properties at the death of a former owner, in the late sixties; the wines of one half of the vineyards have since been sold as *Château Beauséjour,* and those of the other half as *Château Beauséjour-Duffau*: each one averages 20 tuns claret. There are other *Châteaux Beauséjour* in the Gironde, two of them in the St. Emilionnais, two in the Médoc (St. Estéphe and Listrac), and one in the Graves (Villeneuve d'Ornon).

BECHTHEIMER
A white wine of Rhinehesse, from the vineyards of *Bechtheim,* in the Worms districts: the best vineyards are *Geyersberg, Katzenloch,* and *Rosengarten.*

BEER
The most popular thirst-quenching beverage in all lands where there are no vineyards and where wine is accordingly too dear for most people for daily use. Beer is fermented from malted and hopped barley, and filtered or fined before being drunk. The taste, flavour and gravity (or alcoholic strength) of *Beer* depend upon the quality of the malt and that of the water used, in the first instance; then upon the manner and method of brewing, bottling and keeping.

Malt is obtained by wetting and spreading barley on a floor, allowing it to germinate, when it is dried in a kiln. The method of drying the malt has much to do with the colour of the beer. The malt is then ground in a mill and becomes grist; the grist and plenty of hot water are mixed in a tub and become the mash – in the mash tub; hops are then put in, the wort is extracted from the mash and boiled with it, then cooled. The wort passes on into the fermenting tank. Yeast is then added and fermentation sets in; it produces carbonic acid gas, which loses itself in the air, and alcohol, which remains in what was the wort and now becomes *Beer.* Beer is then racked into casks or filled in bottles, and each brewer has his own method for fining, filtering, sweetening or not, dry-hopping or not, and otherwise giving the last 'finishing touch' to the beer he is going

to sell. The strength of the beer, of course, depends upon the proportion of water to malt; the more malt the greater the strength; the more water the milder the beer. The result of the late A.Chaston Chapman's analysis of a number of London and country brews of beer shows great differences in the strength of pre-war beers:

Alcoholic content by weight

Type of Beer		London	Country
Strong ale and old ale	..	8.43	5.36
Bitter and pale ale	..	3.92	3.62
Stout and porter ..	..	3.75	3.45
		English	*Foreign*
Lager	..	4.03	3.54
Mild ale and table beer	..	3.09	3.33

BEESWING
A very light sediment of bottled Ports; it is composed chiefly of mucilage, which does not settle upon the inside of the bottle, like the *Crust,* but does not spoil the wine when it happens to pass from the bottle into the decanter.

In the M.V.Brown Collection of Wine and Sauce Labels, given to the London Museum in 1915, there is an 1836 label bearing the inscription *Beeswing Port.*

BÉGADAN
A Commune of the Médoc 75 k. NNW. of Bordeaux, the vineyards of which produce a large quantity of fair quality claret, the best being the wine of *Châteaux Laujac, Laffitte, La Tour-de-By* and *du Barrail.*

BÉLAIR, Château
One of the First Growths of Saint-Emilion; the vineyards of *Château Bélair* adjoin those of *Château Ausone* and their owner is the same. This estate traces back its origin to Robert Knollys, one of Edward III's knights, whose descendants owned it until the French Revolution, the French form of their name having become Canolle. Average 30 tuns claret. There are no less than 24 different *Châteaux, Domaines* or *Crus Bel-Air* in the Gironde, according to Cocks and Féret's *Bordeaux et ses Vins.*

BELGRAVE, Château
A Fifth Growth of the Médoc (Saint-Laurent) so close to Saint-Julien that some of its vines are in the Commune of Saint-Julien. Its average production is 70 tuns claret. There are four different *Châteaux Bellegrave* in the Médoc, and one in the Graves district, but their wines are not of the same high quality as that of *Château Belgrave.*

BELLET
The Commune of the Alpes Maritimes Département (near Nice) which produces

the most and the best red and white wines of the Riviera.

BELLEVUE, Château
One of the First Growths of Saint-Emilion. Average 30 tuns. There are six other *Châteaux Bellevue* in the Gironde, but their wines are not of the same high quality as that of St. Emilion's *Château Bellevue*.

BÉNÉDICTINE
One of the oldest, if not actually the oldest, and one of the most widely renowned liqueurs in the world. It is distilled at Fécamp, in Normandy, and its origin has been traced to the Benedictine monks of Fécamp, as far back as 1510. It is highly aromatized and very sweet; many people prefer to drink it 'half and half', half *Bénédictine* and half *Brandy*, a blend which is known as B. and B. It is sold in bottles of distinctive shape, and the label bears the initials D.O.M. (*Deo optimo maximo*) of the Benedictine Order. *Bénédictine* is sometimes referred to as *D.O.M.* Liqueur.

BENICARLOS
A somewhat coarse, dark red, highly alcoholic and rich wine from Castellon de la Plana in the Province of Valencia, Eastern Spain. It had quite a vogue in England previous to the introduction of the wines of *Tarragona*.

BEREGSZÁSZ-NAGYSZÖLLÖS
A famous Hungarian wine district, close to Tokaj-Hegyalja, transferred to Czechoslovakia by the Treaty of Sèvres.

BERGERAC
One of the most important wine-producing centres of the Dordogne Département; (22,500 acres). The two most (locally) famous growths of Bergerac are *Châteaux Monplaisir* and *Peycharmant*.

BERNCASTEL-CUES
Twin villages, Berncastel on the right bank and Cues on the left bank of the Moselle. Berncastel produces the finer wines of the two. The most famous vineyard of Berncastel is known as the Doktor, from Doktor Thanish, its former proprietor. It consists of 13 acres owned by three firms: Thanish, Deinhard, and Lauerberg. Other good vineyards are: *Schlossberg, Graben, Badstube, Altenwald, Pfaffenberg, Rosenberg,* and *Lay,* in Berncastel; *Weisenstein, Herrenberg,* and *Königstuhl,* in Cues.

BERNE
The Canton of Berne is one of the minor wine-producing Cantons of Switzerland; its vineyards are practically the continuation of those of Neuchatel, on both sides of the lake of Bienne. The vineyards of the lake of Bienne produce both red and white wines from fair to middling in quality.

BESSARABIA
There are extensive vineyards in some of the valleys between the Danube and Dnieper, and much wine is made in Bessarabia, but none, as far as is known, of more than 'homely' quality. The largest wine-producing districts of Bessarabia are those of *Akermann* and *Kishineff*.

BEYCHEVELLE, Château
One of the Fourth Growths of the Médoc (Saint-Julien). The present Château was built in 1757 on the site of one of the oldest and most important outposts of Gascony. The Lords of Beychevelle were responsible for policing the water-borne traffic of the Gironde to and from Bordeaux. Average 160 tuns claret.

Beychevelle used to be a Commune of the Médoc with a port of its own on the Gironde, but, when the port became silted up, the Commune of Beychevelle was merged into the adjoining Commune of St. Julien, the official name of which became St. Julien-Beychevelle.

BÈZE, Clos de
The largest vineyard of the Commune of Gevrey-Chambertin (Côte de Nuits). Its 37 acres and the 32 acres of the Chambertin vines were formerly part of the same vineyard. The *Clos de Bèze* is not so universally known as *Chambertin,* although its wines are in no way inferior to those of *Chambertin.* There are half a dozen people who each own a share of the *Clos de Bèze* vines, a fact which accounts for differences in the quality of genuine *Clos de Bèze* wines of the same vintage.

BIBLE WINES
The different wines which are named in the Bible are the following:

Ahsis. A name used five times in Holy Writ for 'perfumed wine', or aromatic wine (Cant. viii, 2).

Khemer, Khamar. The poetical form of *Yayin,* Wine, used on eight different occasions in Holy Writ. (*See* Deut. xxxii, 14.)

Khometz. The name for 'small wine', 'poor wine' or 'vinegar'.

Mesech. The Hebrew name for a mixture of wine and water, or wine and anything else.

Mimsach. A name which appears twice only; it has been translated as wine in Prov. xxiii, 30, and liqueur in Isaiah lxv, 11.

Schechar. A name used 23 times in Holy Writ for Wine, more particularly in the sense of an intoxicating beverage. (*See* Prov. xxxi, 6 and 7.)

Soveh. A name used but three times for Wine, but what type of wine was intended is not clear. (*See* Isaiah i, 22.)

Tirosh. Wine in the sense of new wine or sweet wine. It appears 38 times. (*See* Joel ii, 24; Isaiah lxii, v. 8 and 9, etc.)

Yayin. The most commonly used name of wine in Holy Writ, in which it appears 140 times, from Gen. ix, 21, the wine from Noah's vineyard, to Prov. xxi, 17.

BIKAVÉR
Literally 'bull's blood', the name given to the darkest of red wines, almost black wine, which used to be made in the Eger district of Hungary; it was very strong as well as very dark.

BIN
The place in which bottled wine is stored and kept in a cellar. When wine is sold 'in bin' or 'ex bin', it means that the purchaser must supply or pay for straws and cases for packing and despatching. When 'a bin' of wine is sold, it refers to the contents of one and the same bin, wine that was bottled and laid down on the same day and should consequently be uniform in quality.

BINGEN-AM-RHEIN
An important wine-growing centre on the Rhine, at the mouth of the River Nahe, in Rhine-Hesse, opposite Rudesheim. The best-known growths are: *Schlossberg, Eisel, Rochusberg, Rosengarten, Scharlachberg, Schwatzerchen*.

BIRCH WINE
A fermented beverage which some people in northern countries contrive to make from the sap of birch trees.

Birch Wine as made in Sussex
Take the sap of birch fresh drawn, boil it as long as any scum rises; to every gallon of liquor put 2 lb. of good sugar; boil it half an hour and scum it very clean; when it is almost cold, set it with a little yeast spread on a toast; let it stand five or six days in an open vessel, stirring it often; then take such a cask as the liquor will be sure to fill; and fire a large match dipt in brimstone, and put it into the cask and stopt in the smoke, till the match is extinguished; always keep it shaking, then shake out the ashes, and as soon as possible; then pour in a pint of Sack or Rhenish, which taste you like best, for the liquor retains it. Rinse the cask well with this, and pour it out; pour in your Wine, and stop it close for six months, then if it is perfectly fine, you may bottle it.—c.c.c.c.

BIRKWEILER
A small wine-producing parish of the Oberhaardt (Palatinate), in the district of Landau. Its best vineyards are those of *Schwann, Gaisberg*, and *Herrenberg*. The wines of *Birkweiler* are white and rich.

BISHOP
The name given by Oxford and Cambridge undergraduates to a comforting winter-time brew of port, made hot, sweetened with sugar and flavoured with an orange stuck with cloves which is steeped in the hot port.

Here is Dean Swift's version of *Bishop*.

... 'Fine oranges,
Well roasted, with sugar and wine in a cup,
They'll make a sweet Bishop when gentlefolks sup.'

BISMARCK
A wonderful pick-me-up, one which Sir Gerald du Maurier enjoyed nightly for many years, whenever he was acting. It is made by pouring a pint of *Champagne* in a jug and adding a bottle of *Stout* to it. It is also called *Black Velvet*.

BITTERS
Fr. *Amers*. The name given to alcoholic tinctures of bitter roots and barks, flavoured in various ways and possessing a tonic action on the stomach. They are used mostly as *Apéritifs* and also in cooking, for flavouring. In the U.S.A., the law distinguishes between ordinary commercial *Bitters* and *medicinal Bitters*, which are not subject to the regular alcohol Internal Revenue Tax and may be sold by grocers, drug and departmental stores. During Prohibition, the fact that Dr Siegert's *Angostura Bitters* happened to be recognized as a 'medicinal bitter' was most fortunate, for the firm and for the American public. The most universally used *Bitters* are *Orange Bitters*, but there are many registered brands of bitters as well; such as, besides *Angostura*, Wolfschmidt's *Balsam of herbs* from Riga; *Bitter Sécrestat* and *Amer Picon*, in France; *Abbott's Aged Bitters*, prepared in Baltimore since 1865 by the Abbott family; *Fernet Branca* and *Campari*, in Italy, etc.

BLACKBERRY CORDIAL
A cordial compounded with spirit, crushed blackberries and sugar.

Mash and strain berries through sieve; to 1 gallon juice add 1 lb. sugar. Boil and add 1 tablespoon allspice and 1 tablespoon cloves; cook till thick; when nearly cold, add 1 quart whisky or brandy; bottle and seal.

BLACKBERRY WINE
Take blackberries when they are fully ripe, bruise them, and put to every quart of

berries a quart of water; mix them well, and let them stand one night; then strain them through a sieve, and to every gallon of liquor add 2½ lb. of sugar. When your sugar is dissolved, put it into your cask: to every 20 gallons of which add a gill of finings, and the next day bung it up. In two months bottle it.—W.S.M.

BLACKCURRANT LIQUEUR
A liqueur prepared from black currants, brandy and sugar: it is better known under its French name of *Cassis* (q.v.).

BLACK STRIPE
One wine glass of Santa Cruz rum; one tablespoonful of molasses. This drink can be made in either summer or winter. If in the former season, mix in one tablespoonful of water, and cool with chipped ice; if in the latter, fill up the tumbler with boiling water. Grate a little nutmeg on top in either case. —L.En.

BLANC FUME
The name of the best white wine of the vineyards of Pouilly-sur-Loire; it owes its name to its rather assertive bouquet, which is somewhat reminiscent of wood smoke, but quite pleasantly so.

BLANQUEFORT
A Commune of the Médoc nearly 10 k. NNW. of Bordeaux. Its best vineyard is that of *Château Dillon*, it is cultivated by the School of Agriculture of Blanquefort, and ranks as a *Cru Bourgeois*. Other Blanquefort vineyards: *Châteaux*: *Corbeil, Maurian, Haut-Duras, Breillan, Fongravey, Tujean*; *Domaines de Cimbats* and *Montgiraud* rank also as *Bourgeois* growths and average some 165 tuns of claret a year, as well as a little white wine.

BLANQUETTE DE LIMOUX
A peculiar, white, sparkling wine made from locally-grown grapes at Limoux, near Carcassonne.

BLAYAIS
One of the most important wine-producing districts of the Gironde Département. The name applies to all the wines, mostly red, of the Communes of the Canton of Blaye, on the right bank of the River Gironde, some 48 k. from Bordeaux, opposite the vineyards of Saint Julien, in the Médoc.

BOA VISTA
One of the finest and best-known *Quintas* of the Alto Douro (Portugal), for many years the property of the Forrester family.

BOCK
(France)
The name of a thick glass beer tankard hold-

ing quarter of a litre or nearly half a pint. The name is chiefly used for a half pint of draught beer.

BOCK BEER
(U.S.A.)
A special brew of beer, usually stronger and darker than most beers, as well as sweeter. It is brewed in the winter for use in the spring, *Bock Beer Day* being supposed to herald the arrival of spring.

BOCKSBEUTEL.
BOXBEUTEL
A flattish bottle of dark green glass, somewhat like the old saddle or pilgrim bottle, used chiefly for bottling the *Steinwein* of Franconia.

BOCKSTEIN
One of the finest white wines of the Saar Valley; it is made from the vineyards of *Ockfen* and is usually sold as a Moselle wine.

BODEGA
The Spanish name for a wine store or cellar: the name has been adopted in many lands for wine bars and cellars.

BODENHEIM
One of the more important parishes of Rhine-Hesse, the vineyards of which produce much white wine of very fair quality. The best vineyards of *Bodenheim* are: *Burweg, Bock, Kahlenberg, Neuberg*, and *Silberberg*.

BODY
Fr. *Corps*. The quality of a wine referred to as its body is due to a combination of its alcoholic strength, grape sweetness and flavour, which leaves on the palate a pleasurable and lingering, or lasting, impression. A wine which is lacking in alcoholic strength, sweetness or flavour, is thin, hard or dumb and lacking in *body*.

BOHEMIA
The vineyards of Bohemia have lost most of their former importance. The only wine of any note which Bohemia produced was that of the *Melnik* vineyards, some 12 miles north of Prague. Professor Bodkin describes it as a 'potent golden liquor which, when enjoyed with roast goose on the high terrace of the Château of Melnik overlooking the vineyards watered by the Moldau, is worthy almost to be compared with a Corton Charlemagne'.

BOLIVIA
Viticulture was introduced into Bolivia by the Spanish missionaries in the sixteenth century, and the vineyards of the Province of Chuquisaca, the highest probably in the

world, produce on an average 25,000 hecto-litres of wine every year, or about half a million gallons.

BOLZANO. BOZEN

The Italian and German names of a pictur-esque little town in the mountains of the Upper Adige Valley: its vineyards have pro-duced much white wines for many years past: the best is known in Austria under the name of *Leitacher*, and in Italy as *Santa Giustina* or *Giustina-Leitach*.

BOMMES

A Commune of the Sauternes district, ad-joining on the W. and N. the Commune of Sauternes. Its best vineyards are those of *Châteaux La Tour-Blanche, Lafaurie-Peyraguey, de Rayne-Vigneau, Rabaud-Promis, Sigalas-Rabaud* and *Clos Haut-Peyraguey*.

BOND

The store, vault or cellar in which wine and spirits are kept under Customs and Excise supervision before duty has been paid. The purchaser of wine or spirit 'in bond' is liable for the payment of the duty thereon before he can take 'delivery' of his purchase. To pay duty on and take delivery of wine and spirits in bond is 'to clear from bond'.

BONNES MARES, Les

One of the best red wines from vineyards partly in the Commune of Chambolle-Musigny and partly in the adjoining Com-mune of Morey (Burgundy).

BORDEAUX

The metropolis of the Gironde and the home of claret. The Gironde produces on an average some 84 million gallons of Bor-deaux wine every year, some 64 million being red or claret, and 20 million white. The finest red wines of Bordeaux are those of the Médoc, Graves, St. Emilion and Pomerol. The finest white wines of Bor-deaux are those of Sauternes; the better known and less expensive are the white Graves wines.

BOTA

Spanish for *Butt*, a cask of 108 gallons in which sherry is usually shipped from Port St. Mary.

BOTTLES

Bottles are containers in which to store and carry liquids. The earliest bottles were made of skins sewed together, but the Ancients also had bottles made of stone, alabaster, glass, ivory, horn, silver, and common earthenware. Modern wine-bottles are made of glass composed chiefly of silica, soda and lime in varying proportions. The shades of green of wine-bottles, other than plain white ones, are imparted by iron oxide. Quart and pint bottles must, by law, contain a fourth and an eighth of a gallon, but the actual liquid contents of bottles, half-bottles or quarter-bottles are not legally defined, a fact taken advantage of by some unscrupulous dealers in wine. According to current com-mercial usage, wine-bottles should never appreciably vary from the accepted standard of contents of 26⅔ fluid ounces per reputed quart, or 6 quarts to the gallon, equal to 4 imperial quarts of 40 fluid ounces each. The more usual names of bottles in Great Britain, besides half-bottles and quarter-bottles, are the magnum (two bottles), double-magnum (four bottles), tappit-hen (three imperial quarts), imperial pint (three-quarters of the reputed quart or ordinary bottle).

Outsize bottles, for show purposes more than for practical use:

Jeroboam or Double-Magnum	4 bottles or	3.20 litres or	0.70 gallons
Rehoboam	6 ,,	4.80 ,,	1.05 ,,
Methuselah	8 ,,	6.40 ,,	1.40 ,,
Salmanazar	12 ,,	9.60 ,,	2.10 ,,
Balthazar	16 ,,	12.80 ,,	2.80 ,,
Nebuchadnezzar	20 ,,	16.00 ,,	3.50 ,,

In France, the fluid contents of various bottles are fixed by law as follows:

Litre	= 100 centilitres or	0.220 gallon
Champagne	= 80 ,,	0.176 ,,
Burgundy	= 80 ,,	0.176 ,,
Bordeaux	= 75 ,,	0.165 ,,
Anjou	= 75 ,,	0.165 ,,
Alsace	= 72 ,,	0.158 ,,
St. Galmier	= 90 ,,	0.193 ,,
Vichy	= 80 ,,	0.176 ,,
Vittel	= 75 ,,	0.165 ,,

BOTTLESCREW
The eighteenth-century English name of the *Corkscrew*

BOTTLE SICKNESS
A passing distemper which affects some still wines when bottled, hence deprived of as much oxygen as reached them when in cask. Wine suffering from *bottle sickness* must not be condemned, but given time to get used to its rather airless home, which it does eventually, nearly every time.

BOTTOMS
The name given in the Wine Trade to Wine Lees.

BOUCHÉ
Fr. for *Corked*, in the sense of stoppered with a cork.

BOUCHONNÉ
Fr. for *Corked* in the sense of fouled by a defective cork, or *Corky*.

BOUQUET
The aroma and the greatest charm of a wine. Its name is due to the fact that there is a combination of various scents or smells in the bouquet of a wine. The bouquet of all wines should be 'sweet', that is 'clean'; the least trace of mouldiness, from a bad cork or dirt, or the smell of acetic acid, or any other trace of decay of the wine, puts the wine out of court at once; a wine condemned on the nose has no chance of appeal.

The bouquet of a wine is due to the oxidation of some of its acids in the presence of ethyl alcohol; hence the lack of bouquet in all wines lacking in acidity, such as the wines of Italy, Algeria, Australia, etc ; hence also the greater volume of bouquet in wines with a greater proportion of natural acidity, such as the wines of the Rhine and Moselle.

BOURBON WHISKY
A whisky distilled in the U.S.A. from a fermented mash of grain of which no less than 51 per cent is maize grain. The name is due to the fact that the first whisky distilled in Kentucky was obtained from ground maize at the mill of one Elijah Craig, in Georgetown, Bourbon County. It was called *Bourbon County Whisky* at first, and the name *Bourbon Whisky* has been used ever since for whisky distilled wholly or chiefly from maize.

BOURG. BOURGEAIS
An ancient stronghold on the River Dordogne, 28 k. N. of Bordeaux by river and 34 k. by land. It is the chief city of a Canton and has been a mart for the export of wine for many centuries. The vineyards of all the Communes of the Canton of Bourg produce mostly red wines, but some white wine also, all such wines being entitled to be sold under the names of *Bourg*, *Côtes de Bourg* or *Bourgeais*. Some of the more important Estates of Bourg are *Châteaux du Bousquet*, *Croûte-Charlus*, *Lalibarde*, *de la Grave*, *de Marsillac*, etc., which rank as Bourgeois Growths.

BOURGEOIS
Crus. A name given chiefly in the Médoc to growths responsible for quite respectable clarets, not the peers of the aristocratic *Grands Crus*, but better bred than the wines of the *Artisans* and *Paysans* growths.

BOURGUEIL
The name of a very pleasant red table wine from vineyards some 25 miles west of Tours, in the Valley of the Loire. The vineyards of Bourgueil and Saint Nicholas de Bourgueil, cover some 3,750 acres. *Bourgueil* is best served at cellar temperature, not chambré.

BOUZY
One of the more important wine-producing Communes of the Marne Département. Its vineyards are on the right bank of the River Marne, facing Châlons-sur-Marne: they produce none but black grapes which are used almost exclusively for the making of white sparkling champagne; some are also used to make a red still wine which has a delightful raspberry bouquet and, when made in a good year, is quite delicious: it should be served at cellar temperature.

BOXBEUTEL
The wrong but common spelling of *Bocksbeutel*, the flat-sided bottle used mostly for bottling the *Steinwein* of Franconia.

BOY
London 'Smart Set' slang for a bottle of champagne during the 'Gay Nineties' and for 20 years after.

BOYD-CANTENAC, Château
Third Growth of the Médoc, Margaux (q.v.). Average 25 tuns claret per annum. This vineyard is partly in the Commune of Margaux and partly in that of Cantenac. In 1855, *Château Boyd* comprised the vineyards of both *Boyd-Cantenac* and *Cantenac-Brown*; it was then purchased by the owner of the adjoining *Château Abel-Laurent*, who sold the *Cantenac-Brown* part of the estate, and retained the *Boyd-Cantenac* part, but sold its wines under the name of *Château Abel-Laurent*, from 1874 until 1920, during which time there was no *Château Boyd-Cantenac* sold under that name. The name has been revived

by the new owner of the property, Mr Ginestet.

BRACHETTO
One of the red wines of Piedmont which is made both still and sparkling: it has been described by the famous Italian oenologist Ottavo Ottavi, as a wine 'with a discreet bubble and a cherry-coloured foam.'

BRANAIRE-DUCRU, Château
One of the Fourth Growths of the Médoc (Saint-Julien). It was known for a long time as *Château Branaire-Duluc*, having been the property of various members of the Du Luc family during 140 consecutive years until 1879, when it was acquired by a Mr Ducru, and sold under the label: *Château Branaire-Ducru-Duluc*. Average 100 tuns claret.

BRANDY
Brandy is a spirit distilled from the fermented juice of fresh grapes, viz. Wine.

Brandy may be distilled anywhere in the world where there is wine to be distilled; it has no geographical significance. But if any and every wine may be distilled, it is only certain kinds of wine which are suitable for distillation, and there is none that yields a brandy comparable to Cognac brandy.

Cognac is the name of a small town on the River Charente, in the heart of a wine-growing district of France, famous all the world over for the excellence of its brandies.

After Cognac brandy, the brandies of the *Armagnac* district are the best brandies distilled in France. There are also brandies distilled in all wine-growing countries, from the wines of the country. The spirit distilled from the husks of grapes, that is the skins, stalks and pips, after the wine has been drawn, is not entitled to be called brandy: it is known as *Marc* in France, and *Grappa* in Italy.

Brandy and Ginger Ale. A lump or two of broken ice at the bottom of a tumbler; a tot or two of brandy poured on the ice and the glass is then filled with ginger ale. Mix with a spoon; give the ice time to cool the drink and away with it.

Brandy and Soda. A lump or two of broken ice at the bottom of a tumbler; a tot or two of brandy on the ice, and the glass may then be filled – more or less, according to taste and disposition, with soda water or seltzer.

Brandy Blazer. Use small thick glass. One lump sugar, one piece orange peel; one piece lemon peel; one glass brandy. Light with match, stir with long spoon for a few seconds and strain into cocktail glass.—H.C.

Brandy Broth. 'O, Brandy Broth is the King of Broths and royal in the rooms of the mouth. A good chicken and a noble piece of ham, with a little shoulder of mutton, small to have the least of grease; and then a paste of the roes of trout with cream; a bit of butter, and the yolks of eggs, whipped tight and poured in when the chicken, proud with stuffing of sage and thyme, has been elbowing the lamb and the ham in the earthenware pot until all three are as tender as a mother's heart. In with the carrots, and the turnips, and the goodness of marrow bones, and in with the mixture of milk and potatoes. Now watch the clock and every 15 minutes pour in a noggin of brandy, and with the first a pint of home-brewed ale. Two noggins in, and with the third thro' in the chopped bottoms of leeks, but save the green leaves until 10 minutes before serving, for then you shall find them still a lovely green.

Drink down the liquor and raise your eyes to give praise for a mouth and a belly, and then start upon the chicken.'

Brandy Cocktail. A glass of brandy poured on some cracked ice, flavoured with a dash or two of Angostura Bitters, stirred, strained and served in a cocktail glass.

Brandy Crusta. Twenty-five per cent Maraschino; 75 per cent brandy; the juice of one lemon. Fill the glass with ice; shake, strain in glass, and trim with fruit in season.—J.MAN.

Brandy Daisy. One teaspoonful sugar; juice of half a lemon; juice of half an orange; juice of half a lime; 25 per cent raspberry syrup; 75 per cent brandy. Fill glass with cracked ice. Shake and strain. Fill with fizz water and serve.—J.MAN.

Brandy Fix. One tablespoonful sugar; half a wine glass water; quarter of a lemon; one wine glass brandy. Fill the tumbler two-thirds full of ice, stir with a spoon, and ornament the top with fruit in season. —L.EN.

Brandy Flip. (1). One teaspoonful sugar; one fresh egg; 100 per cent brandy; half a glass cracked ice; shake well with shaker, strain and grate a little nutmeg on top and serve.—J.M.

Brandy Flip. (2). One teaspoonful sugar; one wine glass of brandy; fill the tumbler one-third full of hot water; mix, and place a toasted biscuit or pulled bread on top, and grate nutmeg on it.—L.EN.

Brandy Float. Fill pony glass with brandy, place whisky glass over pony of brandy, half a glass of water, then withdraw pony glass, allowing brandy to float on top of the water.—J.MAN.

Brandy Gump. One hooker of brandy; the juice of one lemon; two dashes grenadine. Shake well and strain into a cocktail glass. —H.C.

(A 'hooker' is a *copious measure* in American slang.)

Brandy High-Ball. One piece of ice in a glass; 100 per cent of brandy. Serve with fizz water and serve.—J.MAN.

Brandy Julep. Half teaspoonful sugar; add a little water to dissolve sugar; four sprigs of mint; 100 per cent brandy; one dash of Jamaica rum. Fill glass with ice. Trim with fruits in season and serve with straws. —J.MAN.

Brandy Punch. One tablespoonful of raspberry syrup; two teaspoonfuls of white, powdered sugar; one wine glass of water; 1½ wine glasses of brandy; 1½ small lemons; two slices of orange; one piece of pineapple. Fill the tumbler with chipped ice, shake well, and dress the top with berries in season. Sip through straws.—L.EN.

Brandy Rickey. One piece of ice in glass; juice of half a lime. Drop squeezed lime in glass. 100 per cent brandy. Fill glass with fizz water. Stir with spoon and serve. —J.MAN.

Brandy Sangaree. One teaspoonful of sugar; 75 per cent brandy; 25 per cent port wine. Fill glass with ice. Shake, strain and serve. —J.MAN.

Brandy Scaffa. One-half brandy; one-half Maraschino; two dashes Angostura on top. —O.W.B.D.

Brandy Shrub. To the thin rinds of two lemons and the juice of five, add two quarts of brandy; cover it for three days, then add a quart of sherry and two lb. of loaf sugar, run it through a jelly bag and bottle it.—H.C.

Brandy Sling. Dissolve a teaspoonful of sugar in water, add a glass of brandy, a lump of ice and fill with plain or soda water.

Brandy Smash. Half teaspoonful sugar; three sprigs fresh mint; 100 per cent brandy. Fill glass with shaved ice and stir well with spoon; ornament with fruit in season and serve.—J.MAN.

Brandy Sour. The *Brandy Sour* is made with the same ingredients as the *Brandy Fix,* omitting all fruits, except a small piece of lemon, the juice of which must be pressed into the glass. Use small tumbler.—L.EN.

Brandy Toddy. Put in a whisky glass: one teaspoonful of sugar dissolved in a little water; one small piece of ice; hand the bottle of brandy to the customer and let him help himself.—J.MAN.

Brandy Toddy may also be served *hot,* the same as above but without ice and a jug of very hot water being handed at the same time as the bottle of brandy.

BRANE-CANTENAC, Château
Second Growth of the Médoc (Cantenac). Average 150 tuns claret per annum. In some of the 'off' vintages, such as 1890 and 1896,

688

the wines of *Brane-Cantenac* have often been among the best of the Médoc.

BRASENOSE ALE
The name given to a bowl containing three quarts of ale, made hot, sweetened with sifted sugar, and with six roasted apples floating in it: it used to be brought in the refectory after dinner, and passed round, at Brasenose College, on Shrove Tuesday. In other Colleges, where the same custom prevailed, a similar brew was called *Lamb's Wool.*

BRAUNEBERG
One of the most renowned wine-producing districts of the Middle Moselle, near Berncastel. Best vineyards: *Juffer, Falkenberg, Burgerslay, Hasenlaufer, Nonnenlay.*

BRAZIL
Viticulture was introduced into Brazil by Italian emigrants during the latter part of the nineteenth century, and it has become one of the established branches of agriculture in the Southern States of Brazil.

BREED
The most seductive and rarest quality of wine; also the most difficult to describe. It is the privilege of the finest wine only, of wine that is endowed with an outstanding personality, a discreet yet fragrant bouquet, perfect poise of flavour and strength and a lingering, attractive 'farewell'.

BRESCIA
The chief city of one of the best wine-producing districts of Lombardy.

BRISTOL CREAM
The registered name of a *Sherry* rather rich and of fine quality, sold exclusively by Messrs John Harvey & Sons of Bristol.

BRISTOL MILK
The name used by several Bristol wine merchants for a fine quality *Sherry* of their own shipping and blending.

BRITISH WINES
The name covers all manner of alcoholic beverages produced in Great Britain, where they are known to the Excise authorities under the name of *Sweets,* and taxed as such. The oldest *British Wines* were the *Home-made Wines,* which, in olden days, were the pride of the still-room in all great, and even modest, households. *Home-made Wines,* when they were made on a commercial scale, were first offered for sale under the name of *English Wines.* Both were made from the same materials, mostly the fruits, leaves, flowers, seeds and roots of English grown plants, such as elderberry, apples and pears, cowslips and gooseberries; but also from

oversea produce, such as oranges and ginger, which were imported on a commercial scale into England from an early date. All such wines were mostly known under the names of the fruit or plant which formed their basis, but it was not at all uncommon to call some of them by the better-known or better-sounding name of some imported wine which they were intended to approximate. Thus was the *Gooseberry Wine* called *English Champagne*, and *Elderberry Wine*, *English Port*.

At present, however, the name *British Wines*, although it still covers *Home-made Wines* and *English Wines*, applies chiefly to a more modern type of alcoholic beverages made in England on more scientific lines, since the early part of the twentieth century. These, the latest form of *British Wines*, are made from either grapes, raisins, grape-juice or grape-sugar, imported in various forms – solid, liquid or semi-liquid – to which water is added, then some form of yeast to secure the fermentation of the sugar content of the brew: the resulting alcoholic liquid is then coloured and flavoured to taste, and with such skill that it has been calculated that during the years 1939–1945 not less than three out of every four bottles of wine sold in the British Isles were of this particular form of *British Wines*. Be that as it may, the figures published by the Treasury are there to show that the small Excise duty charged on *Sweets* brought in a greater revenue than the very high duties charged on imported wines.

BROCHON
One of the minor wine-producing Communes of the Côte d'Or (*Côte de Nuits*) immediately north of the Commune of Gevrey-Chambertin; its vineyards produce some red wines of fair quality but none of outstanding merit.

BRONTE
A wine-producing district of Sicily from which Lord Nelson took one of his titles, but the wine which Nelson sent from Sicily to England was *Marsala*: wine sold under the name of *Bronte* was *Marsala*. In the M.V.Brown Collection of Wine and Sauce Labels given to the London Museum, in 1915, there is a late eighteenth-century plated Label bearing the name *Bronti*. There are labels in other collections with *Bronte* and *Bronté*.

BROUSTET, Château
One of the second growths of Sauternes, in the Commune of Barsac (Average 30 tuns).

BROWN BETTY
Dissolve a ¼ lb. of brown sugar in one pint of water, slice a lemon into it, let it stand a

quarter of an hour, then add a small quantity of pulverized cloves and cinnamon, half a pint brandy and one quart of good strong ale; stir it well together, put a couple of slices of toasted bread into it, grate some nutmeg and ginger on the toast, and it is fit for use. Ice it well, and it will prove a good summer, warm it, and it will become a pleasant winter, beverage. It is drunk chiefly at dinner.—O.N.C.

BRUT
A French word used originally in connection with Sparkling Champagne to denote a wine which had not been sweetened, in the same way as *Nature*, which was adopted by other champagne shippers for their driest wines.

BRUTTIG
A small village of the Lower Moselle, near Cochem; its vineyards produce some very fair white wines, the best of them being from the *Rathausberg*, *Kuckucksberg*, and *Johannesberg* vineyards.

BUAL
The English spelling of the Portuguese *Boal*, the name of one of the best wine-making grapes grown in the island of Madeira, as well as of the wine made thereof. *Bual*, or *Boal* Madeira is a richer or sweeter wine than *Sercial*, but not nearly so rich as *Malmsey*.

BUCELLAS
The golden and pleasing wine named after Bucellas, a small town in the midst of vineyards, close to Lisbon. It is made from the Arinto grape, which is claimed to be the same as the Riesling. *Bucellas* wines were fashionable in England during the earlier part of Queen Victoria's reign.

BUDA
A red table wine from *Budafok*, now a suburb of Budapest, first mentioned in a Paper read by Douglas, Baron Glenbervie, before the Royal Society in 1774.—N.M.P.

BUDESHEIM
A small village of Rhinehesse at the foot of the 'Scarlet Mountain', or Scharlachberg, which overlooks the junction of the little river Nahe and the great Rhine, at Bingen. The vineyards which are cultivated on the foothills are partly in the parish of Büdesheim and partly in that of Bingen; they yield a very fair white wine which is sold under the name of *Scharlachberger*.

BULGARIA
There are many vineyards in Bulgaria and they produce some of the most acceptable wines made in the Balkans, although none of them claim to be fine wines. The best are

those of *Plevna, Rustschik, Sistowa, Sukindol* and *Varna*.

BULLAY
One of the smaller wine-producing parishes of the Lower Moselle, in the Zell district: its best vineyards are *Kronenberg, Herrenberg,* and *Bornlay.*

BURGSPONHEIM
One of the wine-producing parishes of the Nahe Valley, in the Kreuznach district. Its best vineyards are *Schlossberg* and *Sonnenberg.*

BURGUNDY
The name of a former Province of France, and also the name of the wine made from various vineyards within the boundaries of the said 'former Burgundy Province. There is both red burgundy and white burgundy. The best red burgundy comes from the vineyards of the Côte d'Or Département, and the largest output is that of the Saône-et-Loire Département. The best white burgundy also comes from the Côte d'Or, but the quantity made is very much smaller than the red. The best-known white burgundy is Chablis. There is also some red and white sparkling wine made in the Côte d'Or. There are quite a number of different types and styles of both red and white wines made in Burgundy, but the name Burgundy has a strictly geographical meaning, at any rate in France. Elsewhere, more particularly in England, the name of Burgundy is sometimes used in a generic sense to designate a dark red wine of rather more than average alcoholic strength whether imported from African, American or Australian vineyards or manufactured in England.

The finest red burgundies are usually accepted to be the following:

	Commune of
La Romanée Conti ..	Vosne-Romanée
Le Clos de Vougeot ..	Vougeot
La Tâche	Vosne-Romanée
Le Richebourg ..	,,
La Romanée	,,
La Romanée St Vivant ..	,,
Le Chambertin ..	Gevrey-Chambertin
Le Clos de Bèze ..	,,
Le Musigny	Chambolle-Musigny
Le Clos de Tart ..	Morey
Les Grands Echézeaux	Flagey
Le Corton	Aloxe-Corton
Les St Georges ..	Nuits-St. Georges

Then come all the best vineyards of the Communes of the Côte de Beaune, i.e. *Aloxe-Corton, Savigny, Beaune, Pommard, Volnay, Chassagne, Meursalt,* and *Santenay.*

The finest white burgundy, after *Le Montrachet,* sometimes ' called also *Le Grand Montrachet,* are *Le Bâtard Montrachet, Les*

Demoiselles Montrachet, Le Chevalier Montrachet,* and *Les Combettes,* all from the Communes of Puligny-Montrachet and Chassagne-Montrachet. Also *Les Perrières, Les Genevrières, Les Charmes* and *Les Gouttes d'Or,* in the Commune of Meursault. Also the *Corton Blanc* and the *Corton Charlemagne* from the Commune of Aloxe-Corton, and *Le Clos Blanc de Vougeot,* in the Commune of Vougeot.

BURIGNON
A noted Swiss white wine from Chardonnes, Canton de Vaud, the produce of a vineyard which is the property of the town of Lausanne.

BURRWEILER
One of the smaller wine-producing parishes of the Palatinate (Oberhaardt), in the Landau district. Its best vineyards are: *Schaber, Altenforst* and *Schlossberg.*

BURTON ALES
The deserved reputation which the *Burton Ales* enjoy all the world over is due in the first place to the fact that the water of the River Trent contains an unusually large proportion of sulphate of lime, together with carbonate of muriate of lime, or, in other words, it is an exceptionally hard water. The skill of the Burton brewers is, of course, an important factor also.

BUSHMILLS WHISKY
The distinctive whisky distilled in Northern Ireland with a particularly smoky flavour.

BUTT
An English wine and beer cask of 108 gallons.

BUTTAFUOCO
A brilliant-looking red wine from the *Canneto Parese* vineyards in South Lombardy, the colour of which is its chief asset: it is rather sweet and flat.

BUZAU
One of the best wine-producing districts of Wallachia (Rumania).

BYRRH
A French 'tonic' or *apéritif* wine: its basis is red wine from the south of France or Spain, fortified with brandy; its informing flavour is that of quinine. It is made at Thuir, Pyrénées Orientales, by Violet Frères.

CABERNET
One of the most extensively grown wine-making grapes for red table wines, the best of many different Cabernet grapes being the Cabernet Sauvignon. *Cabernet* is also the

name given in a number of vinelands to red beverage wines which are made – or supposed to be made – from *Cabernet* grapes.

CABINET WINES
A descriptive label used for fine hocks to convey the idea that the wine is worthy to be set aside for the private reserve (Cabinet or Kabinett) of the owners of the Estate.

CACAO, Crème de
A very sweet liqueur with a strong cocoa-cum-vanilla flavour. The name *Chouao* which usually figures on *Crème de Cacao* labels, is that of a district in Venezuela reputed to produce the best cocoa beans in the world.

CADAUJAC
One of the Communes of the Graves district, 11 k. SSE. of Bordeaux. Its one and only large vineyard is that of *Château Bouscaut*, average 120 tuns claret and 50 tuns white wine.

CADET
One of the three plateaux dominating the old city of St Emilion: the other two are *Pavie* and *La Madeleine*, and all three are covered with flourishing vineyards. The vineyards of Cadet are divided among several owners whose names have been hyphenated with that of Cadet: *Château Cadet-Piola* (average 15 tuns); *Le Cadet-Bon*, sometimes known as *Cadet-Pinaud-Bon* (average 30 tuns); *Château Haut-Cadet* (average 25 tuns); *Château Pavillon Cadet* (average 15 tuns); *Moulin-du-Cadet* (average 10 tuns).

CADILLAC
A Commune of the Gironde, 38 k. SSE. of Bordeaux, on the right bank of the River Garonne. Its vineyards produce both red and white wines of fair quality but of no particular merit: the white wines, which resemble those of *Sainte-Croix-du-Mont*, are in greater demand than the red.

CAECUBAN WINE
Horace's favourite wine and one of the most highly prized of the dessert wines in the heyday of the Roman Empire.
  'Absumet heres Caecuba dignior
  Servata centum clavibus, et mero
  Tinget pavimentum superbo
  Pontificium potiore coenis'
      (Od. xiv. Lib. ii. 11.25 *et seq.*)
  'Ante hac nefas depromere Caecubum
  Cellis avitis.'   (Carm. I. 37)

CAGLIARI
The centre of the best vineyards of southern Sardinia, the best wines of the district being those of the *Campidano*, both red and white, known as *Bianco* or *Rossi del Campidano*.

CAHORS
The chief city of the Lot Département (France), and the name given to the red wines of the district; they are the blackest of all French red wines.

CAILLOU, Château
One of the Second Growths of Sauternes, in the Commune of Barsac. (Average 40 tuns.)

CAJUADA
An alcoholic beverage fermented from the juice of the Cashew Nut, in some parts of West Africa.

CALABRIA
One of the southernmost wine-making Provinces of Italy; it produces much beverage wine quite undistinguished; also two red table wines of a little better quality known as *Savuto* and *Ciro di Calabria*. The best wine of Calabria is made from Greco grapes from the vineyards of the little village of Gerace, and it is sold as *Greco di Gerace*. They also make a dessert wine called *Moscato-Fior d'Arancio*, a sweetish Muscatel wine the bouquet of which has a faint orange blossom quality.

CALDARO, LAGO DI
A very agreeable red table wine from some of the Upper Adige vineyards which the Treaty of St Germain transferred from Austria to Italy, in 1919. Previous to the transfer the same wine was known as *Kaltererseewein*.

CALIFORNIA
The largest wine-producing State of the United States. Viticulture was introduced into California by the early Spanish missionaries, and the wine industry of California had reached considerable proportions, as well as a high standard of quality for its wines, before Prohibition ruined it. Since the Repeal, in October 1933, excellent progress has been made towards replanting the California vineyards for the production of raisins, table grapes and wine.

Professor Maynard Amerine, of the Viticulture Section, University of California, Davis, Cal. has suggested the following as a possible classification of the wine districts of California:

Dry Wine Districts
The Coast Range counties of Mendocino, Sonoma, Napa, Solano, Contra Costa, Alameda, San Mateo, Santa Clara, Santa Cruz, and San Benito.

Small amounts are produced in Santa Barbara, Monterey, San Luis Obispo, etc., counties.

Sweet Wine Districts

The southern California counties of Riverside, San Bernardino, Los Angeles, and San Diego.

The San Joaquin Valley counties of Kern, Tulare, Fresno, Madera, Merced, and Stanislaus.

The Sacramento Valley counties of San Joaquin, Sacramento, Placer, Yolo, and to a lesser extent Butte, Yuba, Colusa, Glenn and Sutter counties.

Note.—But in certain dry wine counties important quantities of sweet wines are produced, while in several so-called sweet wine counties there are notable amounts of dry wine produced. In the main the classification represents what may be the best separation.

CALISAYA

One of the bitterest of bitters. The *Calisaya* bark is supposed to be the bark of the *Chinchona calisaya*, but the name is also given to the bark of allied shrubs from which *Quinine* is extracted. It is used in the mixing of some *Cocktails*.

CALON-SÉGUR, Château

One of the Third Growths of the Médoc (Saint-Estèphe): originally known as *Château Calon*, later as *Calon de Ségur*. It is one of the oldest, largest and best of the Saint-Estèphe vineyards. Average 225 tuns claret.

CALORIC PUNSCH

The national liqueur of Scandinavian countries: there are a number of different varieties of it, but all have a foundation of rum and syrup.

CALUSO

A sweet dessert white wine, the best of its kind in Piedmont. It is made at Canavesano, near Ivrea, from grapes which are left in the sun on straw mats or else suspended from the ceiling in a warm room for a month or six weeks.

CALVADOS

Normandy *Apple Jack*, or cider distilled from the Calvados apple orchards. It is white in colour, of very high strength, and, unless kept in wood for many years, it is too brutal to appeal to any wine lover.

The best-known brand of *Calvados* in England, is *Un Trou Normand*.

CALVI

One of the wine-producing districts of Corsica responsible for some red, white and *rosés* table wines of fair quality.

CAMPANIA

One of the oldest and most beautiful of the vinelands of Italy, stretching at the foot of Vesuvius. Its vineyards produced the classic *Falernum*, which has greatly degenerated: modern *Falerno* is not the wine that poets would trouble about. The best wines of Campania are those known as *Lacrima Cristi*, some red, but most of them white, or golden and rather sweet.

CANADA

Viticulture in Canada is greatly handicapped by the severity of the winters, but some six million gallons of table wines, red and white, of no great distinction, are made on an average every year from Canadian vineyards.

CANARY ISLANDS

Viticulture was introduced into the Canary Islands by the Spaniards, and the wines of the Canaries, chiefly those from the largest island of the group, Palma, were famous in England during the seventeenth century under the name of Canary Sack. The vineyards of the Canaries were all but destroyed by the oïdium at the beginning of the second half of the nineteenth century, but they have now regained their former importance and they produce an average of four million gallons of wine. Teneriffe produces about a quarter of this total quantity.

CANARY WINE

One of the favourite wines of Shakespeare and Ben Jonson.

> *Host.* ... but, i'faith, you have drunk too much canaries; and that's a marvellous searching wine, and it perfumes the blood ere one can say, What's this?—
> Second Part *King Henry IV*, Act II, Scene iv.

> *Host.* Farewell, my hearts, I will to my honest knight Falstaff, and drink canary with him.
> *Merry Wives of Windsor*,
> Act III, Scene ii.

> *Sir Andrew Ague-cheek.* Never in your life, I think; unless you see canary put me down.
> —*Twelfth Night*, Act I, Scene iii.

CANNETO PAVESE

A small town in the south of Lombardy, the name of which has been given to a very undistinguished but sweet and locally popular red wine made from vineyards of the district.

CANON, Château

One of the First Growths of Saint-Emilion, usually sold under the label: *Château Canon-Saint-Emilion*. Average 75 tuns claret.

CANON-LA-GAFFELIÈRE, Château
One of the First Growths of Saint-Emilion.
It was formerly called *Canon-Boitard*. Average 45 tuns.

CANTEMERLE, Château
Fifth Growth of the Médoc (Macau). Average 100 tuns claret 'First' wine and 20 tuns
'Second' wine, which is sold under the label:
Château Royal-Médoc.

CANTENAC
One of the most important wine-producing
Communes of the Médoc; its best wines are
those of *Châteaux Brane-Cantenac, Kirwan,
d'Issan, Cantenac-Brown, Palmer, Le Prieuré*
and *Pouget*. Then come the wines of *Châteaux
Angludet, Martinens, Montbrun, Pontac-Lynch*
and *La Tour-Cantenac*, ranking as Bourgeois
or Bourgeois supérieurs and averaging 300
tuns of claret. There is, besides, much red
and some white wine made from the vineyards of Cantenac, and they have acquired
by long usage the right to be sold under the
better known name of the neighbouring
Commune of Margaux.

CANTENAC-BROWN, Château
Third Growth of the Médoc (Cantenac).
Average 90 tuns claret per annum. No
'Château bottling' between 1894 and 1910,
both included.

CANZEM. KANZEM
One of the best white wines of the Saar
Valley (Saarburg district). The best vineyards of *Canzem* are *Altenberg, Höreker,
Kelterhaus, Unterberg, Sonnenberg* and *Wolfsberg*.

CAPE SMOKE
One of the worst types of spirits distilled in
South Africa, solely for local consumption.

CAPILLAIRE
A syrup originally made by boiling maidenhair fern in sweetened water; it was used to
sweeten punches and other drinks, hot or
cold. Dr Johnson, according to Boswell,
'used to pour Capillaire in his port.'

To make Capillaire
To one gallon of water add 28 lb. of loaf
sugar, put over the fire to simmer, when
milk-warm add the whites of four or five
eggs, well-beaten; as these simmer with the
syrup, skim it well, then pour it off, and
flavour with orange-flower water, or bitter
almonds, whichever you prefer.—L.EN.

CAPRI
A beautiful island in the Bay of Naples; its
vineyards produce some very charming
white wines and a little red wine, which is not
nearly so pleasing. Most of the *Capri* wines
are consumed on the island and they are
rarely obtainable in the ordinary way of
commerce. The *Capri* wines of commerce
come chiefly from the Naples vineyards and
those of the island of Ischia.

CARBONNIEUX, Château
Villeneuve d'Ornon and Léognan. One of the
finest estates of the Graves district, producing on an average 150 tuns of red and 120
tuns of white wines.

CARCAVELOS
Red and white wines from the southern bank
of the Tagus estuary (Lisbon). This wine
must have been very popular in England
during the latter part of the eighteenth century, and at the beginning of the nineteenth,
to judge from the number of English wine
Labels in various collections bearing the
names *Calcavella, Calcavello, Carcavelle, Carco-
vello* and *Carcovellos*.

CARIGNANE
A dessert wine from the grape of that name
grown in Pyrénées Orientales (France).

CARIÑENA
A sweetish golden wine, somewhat reminiscent of a light Madeira; made in the neighbourhood of Saragossa (Spain).

CARLOWITZ
The only Serb wine which ever attained a
fair measure of popularity in England, during the 'sixties. It is grown on the right bank
of the Danube, thirty miles north of Belgrade, now within the borders of Yugoslavia.

CARYPTON
A 'green swizzle' from Trinidad, used chiefly
in the making of cocktails.

CASEL. KASEL
One of the important wine-producing
parishes of the Ruwer valley, Trier district.
Best vineyards: *Blindenberg, Dominikanerberg,
Herrenberg, Hitzlay, Kernagel, Nieschen, Stein-
kaul* and *Taubenberg*.

CASSIS

I

The French name for black currants and also
for a cordial made of black currants, brandy
and sugar. It is served either neat, as a
digestive liqueur, or with iced water, as a
long and refreshing drink; it is also used as a
sweetening agent with *Bitters*. The *Cassis de
Dijon* is reputed the best in France and
Bocksbeeren the best from Riga.

II

The name of red, white and *rosés* wines from
vineyards a few miles to the SE. of Marseilles. Jullien, in *Topographie de tous les
vignobles* (1848 edit.) says that the white

Cassis wine was the best, one cask costing as much as three of red *Cassis*. In the Ionides Collection of Wine Labels there is an English enamel label bearing the inscription *Cassis Blanc*.

CASTEL BRACCIANO
A dry white wine from vineyards upon the heights that rise above Lake Bracciano, north of Rome.

CASTELLI ROMANI
The generic name of the table wines, mostly white, from the Alban Hills vineyards, south of Rome, chiefly those of *Albano, Arriccia, Frascat* and *Genzano*.

CASTELNAU
One of the lesser wine-producing Communes of the Médoc. The wines of Castelnau have acquired by long usage the right to be sold under the name of its neighbour, the better-known Commune of Listrac.

CATALONIA
The second largest wine-producing Province of Spain. It produces on an average 200 million gallons of wine per annum, mostly red wines. There are many different types of Catalan wines, the best-known of them, although by no means the best, are the wines of *Tarragona*. Among the better-class wines of Catalonia are those of *Castel del Bosch* (both red and white) and *Castel del Remy* (white).

CATULLUS (87–54 B.C.)
A poet who was cursed with a great thirst and a great heart; his life was short and not edifying, for he loved wine and women too well. But his poetry still liveth: it possesses a directness and force which have never been excelled and but rarely equalled.

CAUDLE
Spiced hot wine given to women in child-bed, in Shakespeare's days; also, and chiefly, to anybody suffering from or threatened with a bad cold. There are numberless different manners of mixing *Caudles*, mostly with some kind of red wine as a basis, but some *Caudles* are made with hot ale instead of hot wine; others with tea and some without wine or ale or spirits of any kind:

Tea Caudle. Make a pint of strong green tea, pour it into a saucepan, and set over a slow fire. Beat the yolks of two eggs well, and mix with half a pint of white wine, some grated nutmeg and sugar to taste: then pour into the saucepan, stir well until hot, and serve.—F.F.

White Caudle. Mix two tablespoonfuls of fine oatmeal in a quart of water, two hours

before using it; strain through a sieve and boil it, then sweeten with sugar, and season with lemon-juice and nutmeg.—F.F.

CERASELLA
The best Italian *Cherry Brandy*.

CERDON
One of the most picturesque Communes of the Ain (France). Its vineyards produce some very fair red wines as well as a curious *rosé* sparkling wine, which looks like raspberry vinegar but is sweet and rather pleasing.

CÉRONS
A Commune of the Gironde, 35 k. SSE. of Bordeaux, the vineyards of which produce mostly white wines, rather sweeter than the average white wines of Graves, but not so rich as the wines of Sauternes. Jullien, in *Topographie de tous les vignobles connus*, placed the wines of Cérons among the Second Growths of Sauternes; they are no longer given so exalted a place but they have nevertheless many admirers. The white wines of the adjoining Communes of *Podensac* and *Illats* are sold under the better-known name of *Cérons*: the average production of the three Communes is 6,000 tuns white wine.

CERTAN, Château
One of the smallest of the First Growths of Pomerol. Average 10 tuns. The more important nearby Growth of *Vieux-Château-Certan* averages 40 tuns: it belongs to a Belgian firm of wine merchants and one never gets this wine outside Belgium.

CHABLIS
A small town of the Yonne Département (France), surrounded by vineyards from which a dry white wine is obtained which has made the name of Chablis famous all over the world. The best vineyards are the following: *Clos, Valmur, Vaudésir, Grenouilles, Blanchot*. Then: *Preuze, Bougros, Vaulorent, Fourchaume, Chapelot, Mont de Mileu, Montée de Tonnerre, Premiers Crus*; then *Vaillons, Montmain, Chatain, les Lys, Séchet, Epinotte, les Forêts*, and other *Deuxièmes Crus*. White wine sold under the labels (in England) *Chablis Village* or *Petit Village*, is rarely, if ever, genuine Chablis. *Chablis Moutonne* has been, since July 1932, a registered brand.

The true *Chablis* can still be tested by the standard set in the eighteenth century in a letter from Chanoine Gaudin to Madame d'Epinay:'...il enbaume, enchante le gosier, et laisse une suave odeur de mousseron'.

CHACOLI
A sharp white wine made in Vizcaya (Spain): it is refreshing although far from satisfying

as a wine, but, when distilled, it makes the best Spanish *Brandy*.

CHAGNY
The northernmost Commune of Saône-et-Loire (Burgundy); it produces some very pleasant white wines and also a small quantity of indifferent red wines.

CHAI
An above-ground storage place for wine in casks, as distinct from the *cellar* in which bottled wine is kept.

CHAINTRÉ
There are two wine-producing Communes of that name in France, hence two wines bearing the same name, and both are white wines; the better-known of the two is the white burgundy, from Saône-et-Loire, and the other a white Anjou wine from the district of Saumur.

CHALKIS
One of the more important wine-producing districts of Greece; it is chiefly renowned for its white wines.

CHALONNAIS, Le
CHALONNAISE, La Côte
The names of the wine-producing district of Burgundy which lies immediately south of the Côte d'Or and north of *Mâconnais*. Its vineyards are responsible for a large quantity of both red and white wines, mostly red. Its best-known red wines are those of *Mercurey* and *Givry*; the best white those of *Chagny* and *Rully*; also those of *Buxy*.

CHALYBON
The Greek name for the wine of the Lebanon vineyards (Syria).

CHAMBERTIN
One of the most famous red wines of Burgundy, from the vineyards of *Chambertin*, in the Commune of Gevrey-Chambertin (Côte de Nuits); they cover 32 acres and are divided among a dozen different owners, which accounts for differences in the quality of different wines entitled to the name of *Chambertin*.

CHAMBÉRY
One of the chief cities of French Savoy and the name by which is known one of the best and driest *Vermouths*.

CHAMBOLLE-MUSIGNY
One of the most famous of the wine-producing Communes of the Côte de Nuits). Its best vineyards are: *Les Musigny, les Petits Musigny, les Amoureuses, les Bonnes Mares, les Charmes, les Cras, les Fuées.*

CHAMBRER
A French word which means bringing a wine to the temperature of the room (chambre), that is the right temperature for the majority of red wines. Its English equivalent is 'to take the chill off', barbarous means to that end being to plunge a bottle or decanter of wine in hot water or to place it in front of a brisk fire: both methods are equally fatal to all wines except wines intended to be served as 'mulled' wine. A red wine which has not been brought up from a cold cellar long enough to acquire the room temperature is better nursed in the glass, when the warmth of the hands round the glass will soon improve matters; in any case it is better too cold than ruined by the ordeal of fire.

CHAMPAGNE
The name of a former Province of France, and also the name by which is known the most famous of the wines made within a strictly limited area of the said former Champagne Province. Both red and white still wines are made in Champagne, but, when not otherwise qualified, the name 'Champagne', in English, only refers to the white sparkling wines of Champagne. There are two outstanding differences between the making of champagne and the making of other high-class wines, be they bordeaux, burgundy, hocks or moselles. The first is that the wines of different vineyards – growths or crus – are blended together in order to make up *Cuvées* uniting the best qualities of individual vineyards, but at the expense of the individuality of the wine itself. The second, and more characteristic, difference between champagne and the great majority of other wines is that it is bottled early, and it finishes fermenting when in bottle, so that the carbonic acid gas generated by fermentation remains in solution in the wine, which it renders sparkling when it escapes, as soon as the cork is removed. When wines not only from different champagne vineyards, but also of different years, are blended together, in order to average quality and cost, they are known as Non-Vintage Champagne, as opposed to Vintage Champagne, which should be the wine of different vineyards but of one year only, and that year a particularly favourable one.

CHAMPAGNE, Fine
The name by which is known some of the best Cognac brandy; it is not allowed by French law to be used for any other but *Grande* and *Petite* champagne brandies.

CHAMPAGNE, Grande
The name given to a small part of the Charente Département, the vineyards of

which produce the wine from which the finest Cognac brandy of all is distilled. The name also applies to the brandy from the Grande Champagne vineyards, and to no other.

CHAMPAGNE, Petite

The name of the vineyards adjacent to those of Grande Champagne; they produce the next best Cognac brandy, which is also known by the name of Petite Champagne.

CHANTURGNE

The only red wine of merit made near Clermont-Ferrand, in Auvergne.

CHAPTALISÉS, Vins

Wines 'assisted' at the vintage time by the addition of sugar in order to secure a higher alcoholic degree than the wines would have obtained through the fermentation of merely their own grape-sugar. The practice was introduced by Jean Antoine Chaptal (b. 1756, d. 1832).

CHARNECO

A Peninsular sweet wine, probably from Charneca, near Lisbon, popular in London in Shakespeare's days.

> 'And here, neighbour, here's a cup of Charneco.'
> > Second Part *King Henry VI*,
> > Act II, Scene iv.

This wine is also mentioned in Dekker's comedy, *The Honest Whore* (Part II), in *Wit without Money* (Act II), in the *Black Dog of Newgate* (1612), in Heywood's *Fair Maid of the West* (Part I, Act III, Sc. iv).

CHARTREUSE

A world-famous liqueur which was manufactured at the Grande Chartreuse Monastery, near Grenoble (France), by Carthusian monks, from 1607 until 1901, when the monks left France for Tarragona, in Spain. There are two principal types of *Chartreuse* sold, the one being green in colour and of very high alcoholic strength, and the other yellow, not so potent and much sweeter. There is – or was at one time, a still stronger and dearer *Chartreuse*, pure white, and labelled *Elixir des Pères Chartreux*. All three kinds are highly aromatized, but the *Elixir* is the most remarkable restorative of the three.

After 1901, the French Government sold the Trade Marks of the Chartreux and an imitation *Chartreuse* was made and sold, in France, in bottles which were identical with those of the monks, except that in the left corner of the authentic *Chartreuse* in very small letters, one can read *Lith. Alier*, and on the post-1901 imitation *Lith.* without *Alier*,

the name of the printer of the original label. After World War II, the Chartreux returned to France, where *Chartreuse* is now being made again.

CHASSAGNE-MONTRACHET

One of the three Communes of the Côte d'Or producing the finest white burgundy. Its best vineyards are *Le Montrachet*, *Les Bâtard-Montrachet* (part of them), *La Boudriotte*, *Les Brussonnes*, *La Maltroie*, *Les Morgeots*, *Clos des Grandes Ruchottes*. Average production of white wines is 80,000 gallons per annum.

Some red wine of superlative excellence is also produced, in good vintages and in very limited quantity from the *Clos St Jean*.

CHASSELAS

The generic name of a number of table and wine-making grapes. The best wine-making chasselas is known as *Chasselas doré*, in France, *Gutedel*, in Germany, and *Fendant*, in Switzerland.

CHÂTEAU

French for 'Castle', in the sense of 'every Englishman's Home is his Castle'. The homestead of a wine-producing estate, large or small, ancient or modern. The most important feature of a 'Château' wine is that it is produced year after year from the same estate.

CHÂTEAU BOTTLED

A wine that has been *Mis en bouteilles au Château*, or bottled where it was made and by the people who made it. It is a guarantee of authenticity, and it used to be also a guarantee of quality when the owners of the Château refused to give the 'Château bottling' to any of their wines which they did not consider up to standard. But there are now Châteaux where every vintage is bottled at the Château, good or not so good: they claim never to make bad wine, sun or no sun.

CHÂTEAU BOTTLING

Sometimes *Mise en bouteilles du Château* and sometimes *Mis en bouteilles au Château*.

CHÂTEAU CHALON

Not the name of any 'Château' or estate, but that of the finest white wine made in the Jura Département, in the Communes of L'Etoile, Voiteur and Ménétrue. The grapes are gathered later than is usual elsewhere and the new wines are kept in cask much longer than is the case with other French white wines, the outside air being kept out by a thick film of *mycoderma vini*, similar to the *flor* on the surface of new sherry wines.

The result is that the white wines of Château Chalon have great vinosity and an admirable austerity, as well as great keeping powers. The *vin jaune* and *vin de paille* of *Château Chalon* are richer and even rarer than the other.

CHÂTEAU GRILLET
The name of a white wine of which there never was but a small quantity made, from the best vineyard of *Condrieu*, south of Lyons. It is one of the finest of the white wines of the Rhône valley, but there is so little of it that it is very rarely obtainable through the ordinary way of commerce.

CHÂTEAUMEILLANT
One of the best red wines of the *Berry* (France), but the quantity of it that is made barely suffices to meet the local demand.

CHÂTEAUNEUF-DU-PAPE
The best-known and one of the best of the wines of the Rhône valley. The vineyards of Châteauneuf-du-pape (4,500 acres) are on the left bank of the Rhône, near Avignon; they produce chiefly red wines. Among the best vineyards of *Châteauneuf-du-pape* are those of *Châteaux de la Nerthe, Nallys, St. Patrice, La Fortia, de Vaudieu, Clos des Papes, Domaine de Serres.*

CHAUCER
Chaucer, the son of the King's Butler, loved wine and knew all about the wines of his day; as a matter of fact, it is to Chaucer that we owe much of what we know of the wines which were popular in England during the latter part of the fourteenth century and early fifteenth century.

There were then, according to Chaucer, three distinct categories of wine, viz. beverage wines, dessert wines, and made or medicinal wines.

The beverage wines were known chiefly by their colour, as red, white, and claret. Red wines were mostly the very dark wines of Languedoc, whilst white wines came from La Rochelle or Nantes, being the produce of Angoumois, i.e. *Charente*, and *Anjou* vineyards. Claret, or Clairet, was the name given to the wines of Bordeaux, red wines which were not nearly so deep in colour as other red wines.

Must, or very new wine, is also considered by Chaucer as one of the beverage wines, wines for the thirsty, wines not to be sipped but swilled.

The dessert wines mentioned by Chaucer were, on the contrary, wines to be enjoyed when friend met friend, for pleasure's sake or hospitality. They were richer, stronger, and very much dearer than any of the red, white, or claret wines. They were brought chiefly by Venetians and Genoese to Southampton, Deal or London, where they were known under the following names:

Malvoisie or *Malmsey*, or *Candye*, from Cyprus.

Romany, Ribolle, Grenache, from Spain and Portugal.

Vernage from Florence.

Lepe, from Lepe, in Spain, between Moguer and Seville, now called Niebla.

In the third category we may include all the wines which were made up in England, being invariably sweetened with honey and flavoured with any and every kind of herb, seed or root; some of these had, and still have, marked medicinal properties, whilst others were supposed to possess, in Chaucer's time, the most uncanny virtues.

Chief among these queer wines was *Hippocras,* a name which covered a multitude of concoctions of which wine and honey were always at the base. Two other kinds of made or medicinal wines often named by Chaucer, *Piement* and *Clary* or *Clarree,* were also used chiefly for health's sake or for some dark ulterior motive.

CHAVIGNOL
One of the best red wines of *Sancerrois,* in the Cher Département of France.

CHERRY BOUNCE
The name appears for the first time in William Robertson's *Phraseologia generalis,* in 1693, and, according to R.G.Latham's *Dictionary* (1866), *Cherry Bounce* was really *Cherry Brandy* renamed in order to avoid the Excise duty on brandy. Thus, in *Poor Robin's Almanak* for 1740:

> 'Brandy ... if you chuse to drink it raw,
> Mix sugar which it down will draw,
> When men together these do flounce,
> They call the liquor Cherry Bounce.'
> —N.M.P.

Cherry Bounce has ceased to be made or sold under that name for many years past, in England, but the name survives in the U.S.A., where it is given to a cordial made as follows:

Strain the juice of the cherries through a coarse cloth, then boil it, and put in cinnamon, lemon peel, cloves, allspice, mace, and sugar (you are to be governed in the quantity of each by your taste). Then add one gallon of brandy to four of juice – at first it will be very strong, but in two months it will lose the strength and it will be necessary to add a quart of brandy to every four gallons of the bounce.—*Mrs William Courtland Hart, Somerset County.*—F.P.S.

CHERRY BRANDY
A liqueur distilled from the juice of ripe cherries fermented with some of the cherry

697

stones, crushed, as it is from these that a valuable oil is obtained which gives to *Cherry Brandy* its distinctive bitter almond finish. Cherry brandy is more or less sweetened with sugar or glucose, according to methods favoured by different distillers, and it is also made without brandy and cherries, with any kind of spirit and flavouring essences. The best cherry brandy is made where cherries are most plentiful and cheapest, in Kent, and in Alsace, Dalmatia and Germany, where it is called *Kirsch* or *Kirschwasser*. The best-known brand of Riga *Cherry Brandy* is called *Nalivka*.

CHERRY WHISKY
A liqueur made of whisky flavoured with cherries: it was known in Victorian days by the name of the black cherry used, the Gean (F. *Guigne*) and there are Wine Labels bearing the inscriptions *Gean Whisky*, *Guyne Whisky* and *Geen Whisky*. The modern version of *Cherry Whisky* is marketed under the name of *Chesky*.

CHERRY WINE
Take cherries, when the stalks are pulled off, and mash them without breaking the stones; then press them well through a hair sieve, and to every gallon of liquor, add 2 lb. of sugar; then turn it into a clean cask, until it is filled, and suffer the liquor to ferment so long as it makes any noise in the cask; afterwards bung it up close for a month, or more if not fine. When fine, bottle it off, putting a lump of loaf sugar into every bottle; but should the fermentation be too violent, you must draw the corks out for a while, then cork them again, and it will be fit to drink in a quarter of a year.—W.S.M.

CHEVAL BLANC, Château
The best Growth of the St. Emilion district known as *Graves de Saint-Emilion*: average 100 tuns claret per annum.

CHEVALIER, Domaine de
One of the best red *Graves* (*Léognan*): average 30 tuns claret per annum.

CHIAN WINE
The wine from the Greek island of Chios, the excellence of which has been recorded in prose and in verse, by poets and historians, for upwards of two thousand years, not merely by bibulous Horace (Od. iii. 19; Epod. ix. 34. Etc.) but even by sober Julius Caesar, who served it in 46 B.C., on the occasion of his third consulship.

CHIANTI
The best-known Italian red wine. It is made chiefly from the vineyards of the three parishes of Radda, Castellina, and Gaiole, a district known as Chianti Ferrese, in the Province of Siena. The wines made in the adjoining parishes of Castelnuovo, Bererdegna, the Terzo of Siena, parts of Greve, Barberino in Valdelsa and Poggobonsi are also entitled to the name of Chianti. One of the most reliable brands of Chianti is retailed under the name of *Chianti classico*, which bears the *Marca Gallo*, a black cock in a field of gold. There is also a small quantity of white *Chianti* made.

CHICHÉE
A small Commune of the Yonne Département (Auxerre) which produces a very pleasant white wine of *Chablis* character.

CHICLANA
A Cadiz white wine of the *Manzanilla* type (sherry).

CHILE
The largest wine-producing South American Republic after Argentina. It produces red and white wines of real merit, some of which are exported regularly to Europe and the U.S.A.

The vinelands of Chile stretch from Coquimbo in the north to Valdivia in the south, the best wines being those from the vineyards of the Maipo district. The average wine production of Chile approximates 75 million gallons per annum.

According to *La junta Reguladora de Vinos*, the official wine office of the Argentine, the average production of wine is 65.9 hectolitres per hectare in the Argentine and not more than 31.39 hectolitres per hectare in Chile, which accounts in no small measure for the much higher quality of the Chilean wines compared to those of the Argentine.

CHINON
The birthplace of Rabelais, some 30 miles west of Tours, Chinon is a picturesque old town surrounded by vineyards (2,700 acres); they produce a pleasing, light and fragrant red wine; it shows at its best when served at cellar temperature, not iced but cool.

CHOCOLATE
A beverage made from grated or ground chocolate allowing an ounce of chocolate to half a pint of milk. When the milk is very hot, put in the chocolate gradually, stirring all the time, and until the milk reaches boiling point, when it must be taken away from the fire. Add sugar then to taste and go on stirring a little longer. Serve immediately or keep until wanted and reheat to boiling point when required.

CHUSCLAN

A light or *rosé* wine of the *Côte de Tavel*, in the Gard Département, which must have enjoyed a fair measure of popularity in England in the early part of the nineteenth century to judge from the various Wine Labels which bear the names *Chusclan, Chuzelan, Schuzelan* and *Schuselan*, whereas no Wine Label of the period bears the name of *Tavel*.

CIDER

Cider is, with wine and beer, one of the oldest and most universally enjoyed forms of fermented beverage in the world. It is – or should be – obtained by the fermentation of the juice of ripe cider-making apples. These differ from eating or cooking apples, as eating grapes differ from wine-making grapes, chiefly because of their higher proportion of acidity. In cider, the principal acid is malic acid and the alcoholic content varies from 2 per cent to 8 per cent of alcohol. According to French law *Cider* must not contain less than 3.5 per cent of alcohol by volume. In England there is no limit to the alcoholization of *Cider*. In the U.S.A. normal *Cider*, i.e. slightly alcoholic *Cider*, is known as *Hard Cider*, in opposition to *Sweet Cider*, which is chemically treated, sweet and free from all alcohol. In Spain *Sidro* is practically always sparkling. There is some sparkling cider, which is naturally sparkling in the sense that it produces its own carbonic acid gas through finishing its fermentation after it has been bottled and securely corked. But the majority of sparkling ciders are carbonated, the desired quantity of carbonic acid gas being pumped into them.

CIDER CUP

Two quarts Cider (rather sweet Devonshire is best), two or three slices lemon, half glass Noyau, two small wine glasses of the Spice Mixture*, a piece of well toasted bread, 3 or 4 in. square and cut rather thick; sugar and ice; stir well together.

*Spice Mixture: ½ oz. cloves, ¼ oz. allspice; ½ oz. cinnamon. Simmer in one quart water for four or five hours, then strain off and bottle for use.—An Oriel College recipe, 1840.

CISSAC

A Commune of the Médoc, 7 k. NW. of Pauillac. Its more important vineyards are those of *Châteaux du Breuil, Larrivaux, Hanteillan, Cissac, Lamothe* and *Latour-Dumirail*; they average 680 tuns claret per annum. The majority of the wines of *Cissac* are sold under the better-known name of the adjoining Commune of St. Estèphe.

CIVRAC

A Commune of the Médoc, 72 k. NNW. of Bordeaux, the vineyards of which produce a good deal of fair red wines of no great distinction; the largest Estate of the Commune is that of *Château Panigon*.

CLAIRETTE DE DIE

A semi-sparkling light red wine from Dié, on the River Drôme (France).

CLAIRETTE DE GAILLAC

A semi-sparkling rose-red wine from Gaillac, near Albi, in the Tarn Département of France.

CLARET

The name by which the red wines of Bordeaux have been known in England ever since the twelfth century. The name is also used to designate natural, red beverage wines from other wine-producing districts, but in all such cases claret should be qualified as, Australian Claret, Spanish Claret, etc. Used without any such geographical qualification, the name claret only applies to the red wines of Bordeaux, the most natural and the most wholesome of all wines. There is no wine other than claret to possess so great a variety of styles and types, such perfection of poise and harmony between all that a wine should have: colour, bouquet, flavour and savour. (See *Bordeaux*.)

What was considered perfection in claret in Shakespeare's time has been described by Gervase Markham in the *English House-Wife*: 'See that in your choice of Gascoine wines, you observe, that your Claret wines be faire coloured, and bright as a Ruby, not deep as an Amethest; for though it may show strength, yet it wanteth neatness: also let it be sweet as a Rose or a Violet, and in any case let it be short, for if it be long then in no case meddle with it.'

Cade ... And here sitting upon London stone I charge and command that, of the city's cost, the pissing-conduit run nothing but claret wine this first year of our reign. ...
—Second Part *Henry VI*, Act IV, Scene vi.

CLARY WINE

Take 24 lb. of Malaga raisins; pick and chop them very small; then put them into a tub, and to each pound allow a quart of water; let them steep 12 days, stirring them twice a day, and taking care to keep it well covered; then strain it off, and put it into a clean cask, with about half a peck of the tops of clary, when in blossom; afterwards bung up for six weeks, and then bottle it. In two months it will be fit to drink. As there will be a good deal of sediment, it will be necessary to tap it pretty high.—w.s.m.

N.B.—*Clary* is a flowering sage (*Salvia sclarea*) common in most parts of the British Isles.

CLERC-MILON, Château

One of the Fifth Growths of the Médoc (Pauillac) which was divided, in 1881, among various people. Mr Mondon purchased the largest share of the vineyard, and none but the wines made from this part of the vineyard are now entitled to the 'Fifth Growth' privilege: they are sold under the label of *Château Clerc-Milon-Mondon*. Average 35 tuns claret.

CLIMENS, Château

One of the First Growths of Sauternes, in the Commune of Barsac. (45 tuns average).

COBBLERS

The American name of iced and sweetened summer drinks made up with various wines or spirits and usually decorated with fruit or foliage.

'There are cobblers to eat and cobblers to drink, both as all-American as pie and circus lemonade, and made with many different kinds of fruits and berries'.—A.C.

Here is a selection of 'Cobblers to drink':

Applejack Cobbler. One jigger applejack, half teaspoonful lemon juice, one tablespoon orange juice, one tablespoon maraschino cherry liquor. Mix and serve in old-fashioned cocktail glass partly filled with shaved ice. —A.C.

Champagne Cobbler. Put into a large tumbler one tablespoonful of icing sugar, then add a thin paring of lemon and orange peel; fill the tumbler one-third full of shaved or pounded ice, and the balance with champagne; stir with spoon, ornament with slices of lemon and berries in season, and place two straws in the glass.—F.D.S.D.

Claret Cobbler. Fill goblet with fine ice; add half jigger claret and half jigger syrup; stir and decorate with fruit.

Monongahela Cobbler. Put into a large tumbler one wineglass of bourbon whisky, one tablespoonful of icing or pounded sugar, one slice of lemon, and a slice of orange; fill up with shaved ice, shake well, and imbibe through two straws.—F.D.S.D.

Port Wine Cobbler. Fill goblet with fine ice; add half jigger syrup and 1½ jiggers port wine. Stir and decorate with fruit.

Sherry Cobbler. Two oranges, sliced thin, one lemon, sliced thin, pineapple wedges, one cup powdered sugar, shaved ice, one cup sherry, two cups cold water, berries to garnish. Lay oranges, lemon and pineapple in bottom of a bowl, alternating layers of fruit with sugar and shaved ice. Pour in sherry and water. Stir well. Serve in goblets with a bit of each fruit in each drink, and an extra garnish of berries.—A.C.

Whisky Cobbler. Fill goblet with fine ice; add one jigger bourbon and quarter jigger curaçao; also one slice lemon; stir and decorate with fruit.

COBLENCE

Also Coblenz and Koblenz. The chief centre, with Trier, of the Moselle wine trade. It stands on the Rhine and Moselle, where those two rivers meet.

COCHEM

Also Kochem. An important wine-producing parish of the Lower Moselle: its best vineyards are those of *Schlossberg*, *Rauschel* and *Rosenberg*.

COCHYLIS

One of the worst scourges of European vineyards. The cochylis moth lays its eggs in the wood of the vine and presently the grubs will attack one berry after another in each bunch of grapes.

COCK ALE

Take 10 gallons of ale and a large cock, the older the better, parboil the cock, flay him, and stamp him in a stone mortar till his bones are broken (you must craw and gut him when you flay him), then put the cock into two quarts of sack, and put to it 3 lb. of raisins of the sun, stoned, some blades of mace, and a few cloves; put all these into a canvas bag, and a little before you find the ale has done working, put the bag and ale together into a vessel; in a week or nine days' time bottle it up; fill the bottle but just above the neck, and give it the same time to ripen as other ale.—E.S.

COCKTAILS

The cocktail is intended to be like unto a bugle call to meals: it must not be sweet, nor warm, nor long, nor soft, but, on the contrary, in order to whet the appetite as well as to stimulate conversation, it should be flavoursome, cold, spirity, and served in small glasses, one sip or two, and no more. One cocktail helps, two do not, and three harm the flow of gastric juices which should be summoned at the beginning of a meal. The difference between *Cocktails* and *Apéritifs* is chiefly that *Cocktails* are always mixtures of a number of different ingredients, so well blended together that not any one of them overshadows the other. This is why most *Cocktails* are energetically shaken in a specially-constructed 'shaker' before serving. The most popular *Cocktail* is probably the *Martini*, one of the simplest, being half gin and half French vermouth mixed. There are variants, however, such as the *Dry Mar-*

tini, with two-thirds gin and one French vermouth, and a dash of orange bitters; the *Very Dry Martini*, with three-fourths gin and one-fourth French vermouth, and a dash of orange bitters; the *Sweet Martini*, half gin and half Italian vermouth. Another simple cocktail which is very popular in the U.S.A. is the *Manhattan*, two parts rye whisky to one of Italian vermouth, and a dash of bitters. But the number of *Cocktails* has positively no limits since everyone is free to use his imagination in the blending of various spirits, wines, flavourings and potable liquids of every description in the making of *Cocktails*.

Alabazam. One teaspoonful of angostura bitters; two teaspoonfuls of orange curaçao; one teaspoonful of white sugar; one teaspoonful of lemon juice; half a wine glass of brandy. Shake up well with fine ice and strain in a claret glass.—L.En.

Alaska. A dash of orange bitters; one-third yellow chartreuse; two-thirds Old Tom gin.—o.w.b.d.

Alexander. (1) One-third gin; one-third crème de cacao; one-third cream. Frappé. —o.w.b.d.

(2) Three-quarters jigger rye whisky; quarter jigger Bénédictine; twist orange peel on top. Stir.—L.T.C.R.

Anderson. Quarter jigger Italian vermouth; three-quarters jigger dry gin; orange peel. Stir well.—L.T.C.R.

Ardsley. Half sloe gin and half calisaya well shaken together.—L.T.C.R.

Astoria. One dash orange bitters; one jigger apple brandy; squeeze piece of lemon in mixing glass. Frappé.—L.T.C.R.

Atta Boy. Half French vermouth; two-thirds dry gin; four dashes grenadine. Shake well and strain into cocktail glass.—H.C.

Bacardi. Half teaspoon granulated sugar; half large or one small green lime (juice); one jigger Bacardi Gold Label rum; dash of grenadine. First shake up lime juice, sugar and grenadine until cold. Then put in the rum and shake until shaker frosts. Strain and serve.—H.J.G.

Barney Barnato. Dash angostura bitters; one dash curaçao; half Caperitif; half brandy. Stir well and strain into cocktail glass.—H.C.

Barracas. One-third Fernet-Branca and two-thirds Italian vermouth well shaken.

Bishop Potter Cocktail. Half dry gin; quarter French vermouth; quarter Italian vermouth. Two dashes orange bitters and two dashes calisaya. Shake well.

Biter. Four glasses of gin, two glasses of sweetened lemon juice and two of Chartreuse. Add a dash of Absinthe just before shaking.—N.T.A.

Black Hawk. 50 per cent rye whisky; 50 per cent sloe gin. Fill glass with ice. Stir,

strain and serve in cocktail glass.—J.Man.

Black Mammy. To the juice of one grapefruit and one lemon add a strip of thin orange peel and a strip of thin lemon peel, one heaping teaspoonful of sugar, two cloves, three glasses of Santa Cruz rum and one glass of brandy. Ice well and shake. —N.T.A.

Blackstone. Quarter jigger Italian vermouth; quarter jigger French vermouth; half jigger dry gin; one piece orange peel. Shake.—L.T.C.R.

Blackthorne. One dash orange bitters; one-third jigger Italian vermouth; two-thirds jigger sloe gin; lemon peel.—L.T.C.R.

Blanche. One-third cointreau; one-third anisette; one-third white curaçao. Shake well and strain into cocktail glass.—H.C.

Blue Blazer. Blue Blazes. One teaspoon powdered sugar; two jiggers Scotch whisky; two jiggers boiling water; twist of lemon peel. Put sugar and whisky in one metal mug and boiling water in another. Touch a match to the whisky, and when it's blazing well pour rapidly into the boiling water, then back and forth between the mugs in one running flame of fire, five or six times, until the blaze dies down. Serve in a small thick glass and twist a tail of lemon over for zest. —A.C.

Blue Train Special. Fill the shaker with cracked ice and pour into it one glass of brandy and one glass of pineapple syrup. Shake carefully, and then add three glasses of champagne. Give one or two more shakes and serve without further delay.—H.C.

Booby. One jigger gin; one-eighth jigger grenadine syrup; half jigger lime juice. Shake well.—L.T.C.R.

Brant. One dash angostura; quarter jigger white mint; three-quarter jigger brandy; lemon peel on top. Shake.—L.T.C.R.

Bronx. One of the most popular cocktails. It was first compounded by Johnnie Solon at the Old Waldorf Bar, New York, and named by him after the Bronx Zoo: The original *Bronx* was made up of one-third orange juice and two-thirds gin, and a dash of Italian and French vermouths, but it has since become a blend of one-fourth French vermouth, one-fourth Italian and one-half gin; a piece of orange peel and iced.–o.w.b.d.

Bronx Dry. Half dry gin; half French vermouth; one barspoonful orange juice. Shake.

Brooklyn. One dash amer picon bitters; one dash maraschino; 50 per cent rye whisky; 50 per cent Italian vermouth. Fill glass with ice. Stir, strain and serve.—J.Man.

Champagne. Place one lump of sugar saturated with dash of aromatic bitters in glass. Add cube of ice. Fill glass with chilled champagne. Twist small piece of lemon rind over glass and insert.—H.J.G.

Champs Elysées. Three glasses of brandy, one of Chartreuse and 1½ of sweetened lemon juice, put in the shaker with a dash of Angostura bitters.—N.T.A.

Chantecler. A Bronx cocktail with four dashes of grenadine syrup.—L.T.C.R.

Church Parade. Two-thirds Plymouth gin; one-third French vermouth; one dash orange curaçao; four dashes orange juice. Shake well and strain into cocktail glass.—H.C.

Clare. Half jigger sloe gin; half jigger Italian vermouth; dash of brandy. Stir well. —L.T.C.R.

Clove Leaf. Juice of half a lemon; white of one egg; one jigger dry gin; one barspoon raspberry syrup; shake well; serve with a spray of mint on top.—L.T.C.R.

Clover Club. Half jigger lemon juice; one jigger dry gin; white of one egg; one teaspoonful grenadine. Shake thoroughly with cracked ice and strain.—H.J.G.

Columbus. Two-thirds jigger French vermouth; one-third angostura bitters. Shake well.—J.T.C.R.

Coomassie. Break the yolk of a new-laid egg into a small tumbler, and mix with it a teaspoonful of icing sugar; add six drops of angostura bitters, two-thirds of a wineglass of sherry, and one-third of a wineglass of brandy; fill the tumbler with shaved ice; shake well and strain; dust with a little nutmeg and cinnamon.—F.D.S.D.

Covered Wagon. One jigger Tequila; one pony French vermouth; half lime; dash of Grenadine. This modern border cocktail, with its romantic name, depends on the Mexican cactus or century plant liquor 'Tequila' for its kick, and that, in turn, has the kick of a new Mexican burro. It's a nice tipple if you can take it.—A.C.

Cushman. Twenty-five per cent French vermouth; 75 per cent dry gin. Fill glass with ice, shake, strain and serve.—J.M.

Daiquiri. Juice of half green lime, freshly expressed; one barspoon granulated sugar. Put some cracked ice in the shaker and shake until it gets cold. Add 1½ oz. White Label Cuban or Puerto Rico rum. Shake until the shaker frosts. Strain and serve. *Important*: This cocktail should be drunk immediately because the rum, lime and sugar tend to separate if the drink is allowed to stand. —H.J.G.

Diana. Use port wine glass. Fill with shaved ice; fill glass three-quarters full with white crème de menthe and top with brandy.—H.C.

Down. Two-thirds dry gin; one-third Italian vermouth; one dash orange bitters. Stir and serve with an olive in the glass. —L.T.C.R.

Dry Martini. Half French vermouth and half dry gin.

Dubonnet. Half Dubonnet; half dry gin; one dash orange bitters.

Duchess. One-third French vermouth; one-third Italian vermouth, one-third absinthe. Shake well.—L.T.C.R.

Emerson. Half Italian vermouth; half Old Tom gin; three dashes of maraschino and the juice of half a lime. Shake well.—L.T.C.R.

Express. One dash orange bitters; half jigger Italian vermouth; half jigger Scotch whisky. Stir.—L.T.C.R.

Fairbank's. Ten dashes apricot brandy; one jigger rye whisky; one dash angostura bitters. Serve in old-fashioned glass.— L.T.C.R.

Feather. One-third French vermouth; three-quarters Italian vermouth; half absinthe. Shake well.—L.T.C.R.

Fifty-fifty. Half dry gin; half French vermouth. Shake well and strain into cocktail glass.—H.C.

Frank Hill. Half cherry brandy; half Cognac brandy; a twist of lemon peel. Shake well.—L.T.C.R.

Futurity. Half Italian vermouth; half sloe gin; two dashes angostura bitters. Stir well. —L.T.C.R.

Gin. Dry gin with a dash or two of angostura bitters.

Graham. Quarter French vermouth; three-quarters Italian vermouth. Stir well, strain and serve.—L.T.C.R.

Guggenheim. French vermouth with two dashes of Fernet Branca and one of orange bitters.—L.T.C.R.

Harvard. Two-thirds gin; one-third French vermouth; two dashes grenadine; one dash absinthe. Like Harvard beets and Harvard soup, the Harvard cocktail carries out the crimson colour note, here furnished by grenadine.—A.C.

Holstein. Half Cognac brandy; half blackberry brandy; one dash Amer Picon.— L.T.C.R.

Hunter. Two-thirds rye whisky; one-third cherry brandy.—L.T.C.R.

Iris. One-third lemon juice; two-thirds gin; one barspoon sugar; shake well and serve with a sprig or two of mint.—L.T.C.R.

Irving. Half dry gin; quarter French vermouth; quarter Calisaya; one slice orange. —L.T.C.R.

Jack Rose. Half large green lime (juice); one teaspoonful grenadine; one jigger applejack. Shake thoroughly with cracked ice and strain.—H.J.G.

Jack Zeller. Half Old Tom gin; half Dubonnet. Stir.—L.T.C.R.

Jenks. One dash Bénédictine; 50 per cent Italian vermouth; 50 per cent dry gin. Fill glass with ice. Stir, strain and serve.—J.MAN.

Jersey Lily. A *Martini* cocktail served with a sprig or two of mint.—L.T.C.R.

Jersey. Half cup cider; half teaspoon sugar; three or four dashes bitters; lemon peel. Mix and shake with ice. Twist lemon peel over top.—A.C.

Jockey Club. One dash orange bitters; one dash angostura bitters; two dashes crème de noyeau; four dashes lemon juice; three-quarter glass dry gin. Shake well and strain into cocktail glass.—H.C.

Knickerbocker. One dash Italian vermouth; one-third French vermouth; two-thirds dry gin. Shake well and strain into cocktail glass. Squeeze lemon peel on top.—H.C.

La Louisiane. Half jigger simple syrup; one dash Peychaud bitters; one dash angostura bitters; three or four drops absinthe; ½ oz. Bénédictine; ½ oz. Italian vermouth; 1 oz. whisky. This is one of the reasons that people still flock to La Louisiane Restaurant, founded in 1861.—A.C.

Lenora. Half dry gin; quarter orange juice; quarter raspberry syrup.—L.T.C.R.

Loevi. Quarter jigger French vermouth; quarter jigger orange gin; half jigger dry gin. Frappé.—L.T.C.R.

Lone Tree. Two dashes orange bitters; one-third Italian vermouth; one-third French vermouth; one-third dry gin. Shake well and strain into cocktail glass.—H.C.

Lusitania. Two-thirds French vermouth; one-third brandy; one dash absinthe; one dash orange bitters.—L.T.C.R.

McHenry. Half Italian vermouth; half dry gin; and one barspoonful Hungarian apricot brandy.—L.T.C.R.

Manhattan. One jigger rye whisky; half jigger Italian vermouth; dash of aromatic bitters. Stir well with cracked ice and strain into cocktail glasses. Decorate with maraschino cherry.—H.J.G.

Marquette. One-third Italian vermouth; two-thirds dry gin; one dash crème de noyau.—L.T.C.R.

Martini. Half Italian vermouth; half dry gin and a dash of orange bitters. Fill glass with cracked ice, stir, strain and serve.

Martini, Dry. Half French vermouth and half dry gin. Cracked ice; stir, strain and serve.

Merry Widow. Fifty per cent byrrh wine; 50 per cent dry gin. Fill glass with ice. Stir and strain in cocktail glass; twist of orange peel and serve.—J.MAN.

Montana Club. One part brandy; one part French vermouth; two dashes anisette. Half fill barglass with cracked ice, stir in ingredients, strain into cocktail glass and garnish with an olive.—A.C.

Nicholas. Fifty per cent orange gin; 50 per cent sloe gin. Fill glass with ice; stir, strain and serve.—J.MAN.

Nielka. Put three glasses of vodka into the shaker with two glasses of orange juice

and one of French vermouth. This is meant to be a very dry cocktail but sugar may be added if desired.—N.T.A.

North Pole. Half jigger dry gin; half jigger maraschino; the juice of half a lemon; the white of one egg well-beaten. Shake well, strain and serve with whipped cream on top.—L.T.C.R.

Old Fashioned. Put in an old-fashioned glass: one lump sugar muddled with half jigger water; three dashes aromatic bitters and one jigger rye whisky. Add cube of ice. Stir a little. Garnish with slice of orange and a maraschino cherry. Twist thin pieces of lemon rind over glass and insert. Serve with stirrer.—H.J.G.

Olympic. One-third orange juice; one-third curaçao; one-third brandy. Shake well and strain into cocktail glass.—H.C.

Opera. Half jigger Dubonnet; half jigger dry gin; two barspoons crème de mandarine; twist orange on top. Shake, strain and serve. —L.T.C.R.

Orgeat. Two oz. dry gin; 1 oz. orgeat; 1 oz. lemon juice; one teaspoon sugar. Shake with ice, strain and serve.—A.C.

Oyster Bay. Fifty per cent curaçao; 50 per cent dry gin; half glass ice. Shake, strain and serve.—J.Man.

Paradise. Two-thirds apricot brandy; one-third gin. Shake.—L.T.C.R.

Peter Pan. Quarter peach bitters; quarter orange juice; quarter French vermouth; quarter dry gin. Shake well and strain into cocktail glass.—H.C.

Ping Pong. Half jigger sloe gin; half jigger crème Yvette; three dashes lemon juice. Shake well.—L.T.C.R.

Pink Gin. A glass of dry gin with a dash of angostura bitters. (No shaking).

Pink Lady. Half jigger gin; half jigger applejack; half jigger lime juice; five dashes grenadine. Shake well.—L.T.C.R.

Planter's Cocktails. Rum, lime juice, orange juice or lemon juice mixed in varying proportion and sweetened or not according to the taste or fancy of the mixer. Such are the different cocktails known as *Planter's Cocktail* in the West Indies, where they are the most popular form of *Cocktail.*

Plaza. Three-quarter jigger dry gin; quarter jigger Italian vermouth; one slice pineapple. Shake.—L.T.C.R.

Presidente. One jigger White Label rum; two dashes orange curaçao; half jigger French vermouth; dash of grenadine. Add ice, shake well, and strain.—H.J.G.

Prince. One-third jigger white crème de menthe; one-third dry gin; one-third jigger Italian vermouth. Shake.—L.T.C.R.

Princeton. Two-thirds gin; one-third port; two dashes orange bitters; one lemon peel, twisted over. Shake with ice.—A.C.

Rob Roy. Half jigger Scotch whisky; half jigger Italian vermouth; two dashes aromatic bitters. Stir well with cracked ice and strain. —H.J.G.

Ruby. Half sloe gin; half French vermouth; two dashes raspberry syrup.—L.T.C.R.

Rue Royale. Two oz. dry gin; one teaspoon milk; three dashes anisette; one egg white. Shake with ice, strain and serve.—A.C.

Salome. Quarter French vermouth; quarter Italian vermouth; half dry gin; two dashes orange bitters. Well iced and served with two or three celery leaves.—L.T.C.R.

Sazerac. Muddle half cube of sugar with a little water in mixing glass. Add ice, one jigger of rye whisky, two dashes Peychaud bitters, and a twist of lemon peel. Stir until cold, then remove ice, add several drops of absinthe, and stir a little. Strain into a chilled glass and serve with iced water on the side. —A.C.

Side Car. A cocktail made up of one-third cointreau triple sec, one-third brandy and one-third lemon juice, all three well shaken with shaved ice, and strained into cocktail glasses.

Stinger. Half jigger brandy; half jigger crème de menthe (white). Twist a thin piece of lemon rind over the mixing glass and insert. Shake thoroughly with cracked ice and strain.—H.J.G.

Tango. Two dashes curaçao; the juice of quarter orange; quarter French vermouth; quarter Italian vermouth; half dry gin. Shake well and strain into cocktail glass. —H.C.

Thorp Cocktail. One teaspoon sugar syrup; one teaspoon orange bitters; five teaspoons Old Tom gin, five drops noyau or maraschino. Stir on ice with a spoon until thoroughly chilled and blended. The mixture must not be shaken, as that fills it with air. Lastly, take a piece of lemon just the size of a ten-cent piece, hold it over the cocktail and express a little of the oil, then drop it in the glass.—A.C.C.B.

Tom and Jerry. One dozen eggs; one tablespoon sugar; 1½ tablespoons ground cloves; one tablespoon allspice; 1½ tablespoons cinnamon; half cup Jamaica rum.

Beat yolks and whites separately. Mix sugar with beaten yolks, whip in the whites, add spices and lastly rum. This is only the foundation. Put one tablespoon of it in a small thick cup, and one jigger of bourbon whisky, and the same amount of boiling water. Stir until it froths, dust lightly with nutmeg, and toast the ghost of good old Professor Jerry.—A.C. ('Professor' Jerry Thomas is described as 'America's greatest bartender' by The Browns, Cora, Rose, Bob, in *America Cooks*, page 44.)

Van Wyck. Half jigger sloe gin; half jigger dry gin; two dashes orange bitters. Shake well.—L.T.C.R.

Van Zondt. Half jigger French vermouth; half jigger dry gin; one dash apricot brandy. Stir.—L.T.C.R.

White Lady. Quarter lemon juice; quarter cointreau; half dry gin. Shake well and strain into cocktail glass.—H.C.

Yale. Half gin; half Italian vermouth; a splash of seltzer; a squeeze of lemon peel on top.—A.C.

COCOA or CACAO

The pulverized form of Cacao or Cocoa Beans, the seeds of the Chocolate Tree (Lat. *Theobroma cacao*), a native of North America, now extensively cultivated in the West Indies, Mexico and elsewhere. The seeds are dried, partly fermented, freed from shell and germ and robbed of most of their fat, which is known as Cacao or Cocoa Butter, before they are ground to a powder.

The name cocoa also applies to the beverage made from cocoa powder as follows:

Put two teaspoonfuls of cocoa in a breakfast cup and pour over it sufficient cold milk to make it into a smooth paste, then fill the cup with boiling milk, boiling water or a blend of the two, stirring the cocoa paste all the while. Add sugar to taste. A cup of cocoa is a poor substitute for a cup of chocolate (q.v.) when made with water and unsweetened, but when it is made with rich milk in a saucepan, and boiled, instead of in the cup, it can be most acceptable.

COFFEE

1. A shrub or small tree with clusters of fragrant white flowers and bearing an abundance of small, round, or olive-shaped berries, the seeds of which, freed from the pulp, are roasted, ground and used to make the beverage of the same name.

The Coffee tree is a native of Arabia and it is now grown very extensively in Brazil – a country which is responsible for more than half the total production of coffee of the world; also in the Dutch East Indies, Java and Sumatra more particularly; the West Indies and Central America; Kenya, Mysore and elsewhere, in Africa and Asia.

2. The name of the infusion or decoction of roasted, ground coffee seeds.

The best coffee of commerce is the best blend of the best coffees. The best coffees are from the Blue Mountain (Jamaica), Bogota (Colombia), the Yemen, Costa Rica and Brazil; and the best blends are those made by the most skilful blenders.

Important as the choice of the variety of coffees may be, the excellence of a cup of coffee depends to an even greater extent upon the manner and the degree of the roasting, the freshness of the grinding, and finally the water used and the way in which it is used. Roasting makes all the difference to the taste of coffee, and grinding to its aroma. The somewhat bitter after-taste of most continental coffees is due partly to the admixture of ground chicory to the coffee, and partly to the fact that roasting is usually proceeded with nearer to the burning point than is usual in the British Isles or the U.S.A. On the other hand, the greater volume of aroma which coffee usually had in France was mostly due to the fact that the roasted berries were always freshly ground immediately before making the coffee instead of being ground in the shop and kept in the home cupboard in a tin or a paper bag until wanted. Whilst the degree of roasting is a matter of personal taste, there can never be any excuse for keeping ground coffee ready for use. Coffee must be ground when wanted and not before, and no more should be ground than the quantity to be used immediately.

As regards the making of coffee, there are two entirely different schools, the Eastern and the Western. In Arabia, the original home of coffee, the cup or pot is nearly filled with the freshly-ground coffee and sifted sugar; boiling water is poured over it and the cup or pot appears filled with a semi-liquid black and hot mass; presently the coffee sinks to the bottom of the cup or pot and the black liquid which comes to the surface is very strong, very aromatic and very good coffee, which must be sipped with care so as not to disturb the 'grounds' in the cup. This manner of making coffee is the most wasteful one and obtains chiefly in countries where coffee grows and is inexpensive. The Western way consists in getting boiling water to go through the coffee, carrying away colour and aroma and leaving the grounds in a separate section of the coffee-pot. A fair allowance is a tablespoonful of freshly-ground coffee per person, and it is better to press the coffee rather hard in the upper part of the coffee-pot, so that the boiling water will not pass through it too fast, but slowly filter through or 'percolate'. when it is poured over it. There are coffee-pots in which the coffee in the upper chamber is invaded from below by the water, which is made to boil by the flame of a spirit lamp placed under it. When all the water has ascended into the coffee chamber, the flame is removed and the water returns by gravity to its original home below, thus traversing the coffee twice, once up and once down. The process can be repeated, and each time the coffee will gain in strength and lose in flavour.

Black coffee must be strong and very hot; if strong coffee does not agree with you, do not drink black coffee. And if you do not drink black coffee, do not drink any coffee at all. Fresh cream added to black coffee makes the coffee less black but not less strong and it brings out the flavour admirably. *Café au lait* is an entirely different matter; it is a breakfast food and the milk is the most important partner: the coffee, which may be without offence doped with some chicory, merely helps to add a pleasing flavour to the tasteless milk. Coffee may be used similarly to flavour iced drinks, ice-creams, and many creamy cakes, such as *éclairs and Mokas*.

Moka, in culinary French, means *Coffee*, as in *Glacé Moka*. A cake with a coffee-butter coating is also called *Un Moka*. Originally a *Parfait* always meant a coffee ice-cream pudding, and it still does unless *Parfait* is qualified by *Chocolat, Vanille*, etc.

Iced Coffee

Make a pint of strong coffee and sweeten it to taste. Boil a pint of milk with a pod of vanilla in it; let it get cold; add a little cream to it; stir well; add the sweetened coffee; stir well in a jug, which can then be left in the ice-box for two hours or so, but not long enough for the mixture to become too thick or too stiff.

Coffee Royale

(The Californian edition of the New Orleans Café Brûlot.—Ed.)

(Proportions per cup)

½ part rum martinique
½ part cognac
1 clove
1 piece cinnamon stock about three times length of clove
½ strip orange peel
½ strip lemon peel
1 lump of sugar

Have coffee ready and piping hot. Put dry ingredients, cinnamon, clove, sugar, peels in hot pyrex bowl placed in boiling water (avoid all metal).

Pour in liquor. Take one lump of sugar, cover with liquor and start as wick for burning. (Richard Byrne, of Scarletts, Beverly Hills, Cal., is responsible for this recipe.)—M.A.

COGNAC

Cognac is the name of the brandy distilled from wine made in the Cognac district.

The vineyards of Cognac which produce the finest Cognac Brandies are those of the *Grande Champagne, Petite Champagne*, and *Borderies*.

The name Cognac has a strictly geographical meaning; it cannot be given to any other brandy than the brandy distilled from wine made from the vineyards of the district of Cognac.

Furthermore, the names of Grande Champagne, Fine Champagne, Petite Champagne are also geographical expressions corresponding to the peculiar chalky soil formation of a small and very distinct area, within the Cognac district, where the best Cognac brandies are made.

Cognac brandy is distilled up to 72° of alcohol: when distilled to a higher strength, up to 84°, it is called an *Esprit*, and over 84°, an *Alcool*.

Cognac brandy is sold under labels which are accepted in the brandy trade as guarantees of age, but not of quality; the more usually used are:

ONE STAR: not less than 3 years old.

TWO STARS: not less than 4 years old.

THREE STARS: not less than 5 years old.

Also V.O., V.S.O., V.S.O.P. and V.V.S.O.P.
V stands for *Very*; *S* for *Special*; *O* for *Old*; *P* for *Pale*.

COINTREAU

One of the best-known French orange curaçaos sold in a distinctive square-shaped bottle under the name of *Triple Sec Cointreau*; it is colourless and has a pleasing orange flavour. The shape of the bottle and the label are always the same, but the alcoholic strength of the liqueur itself varies appreciably according to the country in which it is sold.

COLLARES

The name of the table wines, mostly red, made from the vineyards of Cintra and other hillsides in the vicinity of Lisbon.

COLLINS

See *Tom Collins*.

COLOUR

The colour of wines and spirits is a matter of taste and, as such, a matter of importance; it is also a matter of fashion. Up to the first decade of the twentieth century, the demand, in England, was mostly for 'Old Gold' and 'Old Brown' sherries, vintage port as black as night, deep amber hocks and brown brandy. But public taste gradually changed, and now demands 'paper-white' hocks, pink or *rosé* red wines, tawny ports, and the palest of pale sherries and brandies.

All spirits being colourless as they leave the still, distillers, compounders and rectifiers have all the colours of the rainbow to play with, and give spirits, liqueurs and cordials any and every shade of colour likely

to prove attractive to the greater number of people, remembering that few use their senses of taste and smell, and that whatever pleases the eye is almost certain to be a winner.

COMÈTE, Vin de la

The wine of a vintage year remembered by the appearance of a comet, a natural phenomenon which was credited with some share in the excellence of the vintage. The first 'Comet' vintage on record is that of 1630; the most famous that of 1811.

COMMANDERIA

The best wine of the island of Cyprus; it is a rather sweet dessert wine.

COMO

A red fortified wine made in the island of Syra (Greece).

COMPLETER

The name of the strong and heady red wine made from Pinot Noir and Klevner black grapes grown in the Swiss Canton of Grisons.

CONDRIEU

The most famous wine-producing Commune on the right bank of the Rhône, south of Lyons. It produces much fair white wine, none, however, of exceptional quality except the one known as *Château Grillet*.

CONEGLIANO

A large village, north of Venice, with a number of vineyards producing both red and white table wines.

CONGIUS

Roman wine measure equal approximately to one gallon.

CONSTANTIA

The name of a dessert wine, made from the small muscadelle grape, which was very popular in England during the early part of the nineteenth century. It came from the vineyards of Constantia, at Wynberg, Cape Province. There are still three vineyards bearing the name of Constantia at the Cape: Groot Constantia, the oldest vineyard of the Cape Peninsula and the property of the Government; Klein Constantia and High Constantia, where both red and white wines are made from a number of different species of grapes, beverage wines and fortified wines of grapes, beverage wines and fortified wines, of a similar type to those made in other districts of South Africa.

CONSUMO

The Portuguese equivalent of the French *Vin Ordinaire*, a quite plain beverage wine.

COOLERS

An American name for a number of 'long' drinks, always served in a tall glass with a lump of ice in it. Some of the more popular forms of *Coolers* are:

Ardsley. One jigger of Tom gin to a pint of ginger ale, and decorated with a bunch of fresh mint.

Billy Taylor. One jigger of gin to a pint of soda water and the juice of half a lime.

Blackstone. One jigger of Jamaica rum to a pint of soda water; the rind of one lemon.

Bull Dog. One jigger dry gin to one pint ginger ale; the juice and rind of one orange.

Bull Pup. One jigger of dry gin to one pint of ginger ale; the juice of half a lemon.

Country Club. Half jigger grenadine syrup; half jigger French vermouth to a pint of soda water.

Floradora. Quarter jigger dry gin and quarter jigger raspberry syrup to one pint ginger ale; also the juice of half a lime.

Khatura. Quarter jigger French vermouth; quarter jigger Italian vermouth; half jigger gin; one pint of soda water and two dashes of angostura bitters.

Mint. One bunch of fresh mint leaves lightly bruised in a pint of iced ginger ale.

Narragansett. One jigger bourbon whisky to one pint of ginger ale; the juice and rind of one orange.

Orange Blossom. Two jiggers orange juice; one jigger gin; one small spoonful sugar; fill the glass with seltzer water.

Robert E.Lee: One jigger Scotch whisky; juice half a lime; two dashes absinthe; one pint dry ginger ale. Mix and stir with ice. —A.C.

Sabbath. Half jigger brandy; half jigger vermouth; the juice of half a lime, one pint of soda water; decorate with fresh sprigs of mint.

Sea Side. One jigger grenadine syrup to one pint soda; juice of one lime.

White. Half a jigger of Scotch whisky to a bottle of ginger ale; the juice of half an orange, and a dash of angostura bitters.

CORDIAL MÉDOC

A French brand of liqueur, made in Bordeaux, with a basis of brandy: it is highly aromatised as well as rather sweet.

CORDIALS

Sweetened and aromatised spirits intended to stimulate the circulation of the blood or invigorate the heart. Cordials are compounded; spirits are merely distilled.

Alkermès Cordial. A favourite cordial in early Victorian days; besides plain spirit and sugar, it contained some rose-water, mace, cinnamon and cloves.

Blackberry Cordial. Pound and strain one gallon of berries, and to every pint of juice add ¾ lb. of sugar, and to every two quarts of juice ¼ oz. each of mace, allspice, cinnamon, and cloves. Boil all to a rich syrup and fill bottles with equal parts of syrup and good spirits. Bottle and cork well.—*Miss Louisa Ogle Thomas, Baltimore.*—F.P.S.

Cloves Cordial. It is made from the essential oil of cloves, with a proportion of spirit and simple syrup. It usually has the colour of brandy. Sometimes it is of a pink colour, imparted by a preparation from the orchill weed, and is then sold as ambrosial nectar, or the drink of the gods.—CH.T.

Kola Cordial. Kola nuts, roasted and powdered, 7 oz.; cochineal powder, 30 grains; extract of vanilla, three drachms; arrac, 3 oz.; sugar, 7 lb.; alcohol, six pints; water, six pints. Macerate kola and cochineal with alcohol for 10 days, agitate daily, add arrac, vanilla, and sugar dissolved in water. Filter. —G.D.H.

Mint Cordial. Fill a large kitchen bowl three-quarters full of *young* mint leaves (no stems); cover with brandy. Let stay in broiling hot sun (July) all day. Strain, add sugar to taste. Bottle. *John Ridgely, Hampton, Baltimore County.*—F.P.S.

CORKED

Strictly speaking, a bottle which is not uncorked (Fr. *bouché*), but often wrongly used in the place of Corky.

CORKS

Stoppers made of cork bark; they vary in substance, some being softer and more spongy than others; in length; and in diameter. The cork must be larger than the neck of the bottle for which it is used, and the softer the substance of the cork the larger the cork must be. The cork must be pressed hard until it can be introduced into the neck of the bottle and forced into it, otherwise the wine may ooze out of the bottle, or the air from outside will reach the wine in excess of what the wine requires to 'breathe'. The longer the wine is intended to be left in bottle the longer should be the cork used, and the better should be the quality of the cork. The best corks come from Spain.

Corks were used as stoppers for wine in England from the earliest years of the seventeenth century, and were known to Shakespeare. Until the advent of the corkscrew, corks were cut conical in shape, the smaller end was driven as far as it could go into the neck of the bottle, leaving an inch or more of the thicker end out of it, so that the cork could be *pulled out*.

CORKSCREW

The gimlet-like 'screw' to draw corks out. The corkscrew was first introduced during the eighteenth century, but its inventor is not known. It was known at first by the name of Bottle Screw.

CORKY
(Fr. *Bouchonné*.) A wine tainted by a foul-smelling or diseased cork.

CORNAS
One of the best wine-producing parishes of the Ardèche Département in the Rhône Valley, near St. Péray: mostly red wines which are not unlike the red wines of the *Hermitage* hill, at Tain, opposite.

CORSICA
A large French island in the Mediterranean: it produces red and white wines, most of which satisfy the none too discriminating thirst of the island's population: also a limited quantity are wines of real merit; the best of them are the red wines of *Cauro, Cervione, Pino* (St. Florent); *Sciacarello (Sartène)*, and *Vescovato*; and the white wines of *Masaglio, Patrimonio, Tourinio, Fugari (Sartène)* and *Laetitia* (Ajaccio).

CORTAILLOD
The only red wine of any distinction made in the Canton of Neufchatel (Switzerland). The best vineyard of *Cortaillod* is the *Cru de la Vigne du Diable*.

CORTESE
The lightest – in colour – of the white table wines of Piedmont, named not after any particular district where it is made, but from the *Cortese* grape, from which it is made.

CORTON, Le
One of the best wines, mostly white, from the Commune of *Aloxe-Corton*. The vineyards responsible for *Le Corton* adjoin those which produce *Corton Clos du Roi* (red burgundy) and *Corton Charlemagne* (white burgundy).

CORVO DI CASTELDACCIA
A golden and rather heady Sicilian table wine, more of a dessert than a beverage wine, but not sweet, even rather austere. There is also a red *Corvo* wine but it is not nearly so attractive as the white.

COS D'ESTOURNEL
One of the Second Growths of the Médoc (St. Estèphe). Its annual production averages 150 tuns of claret. There was no 'Château bottling' granted from 1894 to 1904.

COS LABORY
One of the Fifth Growths of the Médoc (St. Estèphe). Its annual production averages 50 tuns of claret.

CÔTE DE BEAUNE
The vineyards of the Côte d'Or (Burgundy) from Aloxe-Corton, above Beaune, to the southern boundary of the Côte d'Or Département beyond Santenay.

CÔTE DE NUITS
The vineyards of the Côte d'Or from Fixin in the north to Prémeaux in the south.

CÔTE D'OR
The name of a French Département of which Dijon is the metropolis. Its vineyards produce the finest red and white burgundies. They are divided into the *Côte de Nuits*, which produces the finest red burgundy, and the *Côte de Beaune*, which produces the finest white burgundy. From north to south, the Communes which are responsible for the best wines are: Gevrey-Chambertin, Morey-St. Denis, Chambolle-Musigny, Vougeot, Flagey-Echézeaux, Vosne-Romanée, Nuits-St. Georges, and Prémeaux. They belong to what is known as the Côte de Nuits. Further south, the Côte de Beaune comprises the following Communes: Aloxe-Corton, Pernand-Vergelesses, Savigny, Beaune, Pommard, Volnay, Monthélie, Meursault, Chassagne-Montrachet, Puligny-Montrachet, and Santenay. Less important wine-producing Communes of the Côte d'Or are: Marsannay-la-Côte, Fixin, Brochon, Corgoloin, Comblanchien, Ladoix-Serrigny, Auxey-Duresses, and St. Aubin. The Côte d'Or produces an average of two million gallons of wines every year from the noble Pinot grape, not counting the production of commoner wines from the Gamay grape.

CÔTE DE PARNASSE
Some of the best red and white wines of Hatikoi (Greece).

CÔTE RÔTIE
The name of the vineyards and wines of the Commune of Ampuis, in the Valley of the Rhône, south of Lyons. The *Côte Rôtie* vineyards are on the right bank of the Rhône and they are divided in two parts, the northern-most or upper part, which is known as *Côte Brune*, and the lower part, known as *Côte Blonde*. Both produce none but red wines and those of the *Côte Brune* are of finer quality than all others.

COTEAUX DE LA LOIRE
The white wines of Anjou (France) from the hillside vineyards facing the River Loire. Some of the most renowned are the wines of *La Coulée de Serrant, La Roche aux Moines*, and *Château de Savennières*.

COTEAUX DU LAYON

The white wines of Anjou (France) from the hillside vineyards facing the small river Layon, a tributary of the Loire. The best-known Coteaux du Layon wines are the *Quart de Chaume*, and among the other good wines of the same district are the wines of *Faye, Beaulieu,* and *Bonnezeaux.*

CÔTES

Hillside vineyards. Vin de Côtes as opposed to Vin de Palus or Vin de Plaine, refers to wines grown upon the hills, hence presumably of better quality.

CÔTES DU RHÔNE

Both red and white wines, but chiefly red, from the vineyards of the Rhône Valley, below Lyons. The best Côtes-du-Rhône wines are *Côte Rôtie, Châteauneuf-du-Pape* and *Hermitage,* which are always sold under their own vineyards' names.

COULÉE DE SARRANT

One of the most fascinating of the naturally sweet white wines of the *Coteaux de la Loire* (Anjou).

COUTET, Château

One of the First Growths of Sauternes, in the Commune of Barsac. (Average 60 tuns.)

COWSLIP WINE

Take six gallons of water, and to each gallon add 2 lb. of loaf sugar; boil about an hour, and then let it cool. Toast a piece of bread, and spread both sides of it with yeast; but before you put it into the liquor, add to every gallon 1 oz. of the syrup of citrons. Beat it well in with the rest, and then put in the toast while it is warm. Let it work for two or three days; in the meantime, put in your cowslip flowers, bruised a little, about a peck together, with three lemons sliced, and one pint of white wine to every gallon. Let them stand three days, and afterwards put it into a clean cask; and, when fine, bottle it. —w.s.m.

In Wiltshire, cowslips used to be called 'peggles', and the 'Peggle Wine' mentioned in some old West Country manuscript books of home-made wines, is Cowslip Wine.

CRAMANT

A village of the Champagne district, immediately west of Avize, in the heart of the best white grape vineyards, on the left bank of the Marne. The still white wines of Cramant of a good vintage are delicious, and fully equal to those of Avize.

CRAMBAMBULL

Take two bottles of light porter or ale and boil them in a pan. Then put into the liquor half a pint of rum and from ½ lb. to 1 lb. of loaf sugar. After this has been boiling for a few minutes, take the whole from the fire and put into the mixture the whites and the yolks of from six to eight eggs, previously well whisked; stir the whole for a minute or two and pour it into a punch-bowl, to be drunk out of tumblers. It tastes well hot or cold.—f.f.

CRÈME

When applied to liqueurs, mostly French ones, *Crème* denotes a more than usual degree of sweetness: it is followed by the name o-the fruit or plant responsible for its informf ing flavour.

Crème d'Ananas. A sweet liqueur, the informing flavour of which is that of pineapples.

Crème de Bananes. A sweet liqueur, the informing flavour of which is that of bananas.

Crème de Cassis. A sweet liqueur, the informing flavour of which is that of black currants.

Crème de Fraises. A sweet liqueur, the informing flavour of which is that of strawberries.

Crème de Framboises. A sweet liqueur, the informing flavour of which is that of raspberries.

Crème de Menthe. A sweet liqueur, the informing flavour of which is that of fresh mint. It is one of the most popular of all liqueurs, and there are many different brands of it, many of them coloured green, but a few of them pure white.

Crème de Moka. A sweet liqueur flavoured with coffee.

Crème de Noyau. A sweet liqueur, the informing flavour of which is that of crushed kernels of stone fruit, mostly cherries.

Crème de Vanille. A sweet liqueur, the informing flavour of which is that of vanilla.

Crème de Violette. A sweet liqueur, the informing flavour of which is that of violets.

Crème Yvette. A sweet liqueur, violet in colour, which was distilled in Connecticut, U.S.A.

There are also *Crèmes de Cumin, de Prunelle, de Roses, de Thé,* etc.

CRIMEA

The Russian vineyards which produce the best wines, both still and sparkling, are those of the Crimea. The more popular white wines are the *Abran, Domski, Livadia, Massandra* and *Orianda.* The more popular red wines are the *Aï Danil, Aloupka, Bostandschi-Oglu-Kakour, Kobarn, Sapperavi* and *Soudak.*

CROIZET-BAGES, Château

One of the Fifth Growths of the Médoc (Pauillac), which is also known as Château

Calvé-Croizet-Bages; it has been the property of various members of the Calvé family since 1863. Average 50 tuns claret.

CROZES
One of the wine-producing parishes of the Drôme Département; its vineyards cover the lower slopes of the hills on the left bank of the Rhône, close to the vineyards of *Hermitage*; they produce both red and white wines. One of the best wines of *Crozes* is that of *Clostabry*.

CRU
French for Growth, i.e. a particular vineyard or range of vineyards producing wines of the same standard of quality and character.

CRUST
Lees, chiefly salts of tartaric acid, which are cast by some red wines, chiefly port, in the process of ageing, and adhere to the inside face of the bottle. The whitewash splash on bottled ports shows which way the bottle should be held so that the wine can be poured out without disturbing the 'crust' inside the bottle. When a crusted port is moved carelessly, the crust 'slips' and spoils the wine.

CRUSTED PORT
A wine old enough in bottle to have had time to throw a crust.

CRUSTING PORT
A full-bodied wine bottled early and intended to throw a crust.

CRUSTAS
An American name, the origin of which is obscure, for an elaborate cocktail.

Gin Crusta. Put into a small tumbler 30 drops of gum, 10 drops of angostura bitters, a wineglass of London gin and 10 drops of curaçao; fill one-third with ice; shake well, and strain into a coloured wineglass; pare half a lemon in one piece and place the paring round the rim, after damping with juice of lemon, and frosting by dipping the edge of the glass in sugar.—F.D.S.D.

CSOPAKI FURMINT
A somewhat heady, dry, white wine made from the Furmint grape grown in the vineyards of Csopak, in the Balaton district of Hungary.

CUPS
Summer drinks prepared in large jugs and made up of any kind of wine watered down by ice, soda, or seltzer, with the addition of some spirit – usually brandy or gin – one or two or even more sweet liqueurs, that bring strength and flavour to the *Cup*. Sprigs of mint or borage and some cucumber rind, as well as grapes, strawberries and pieces of other fruit, are added to make the *Cup* more attractive.

Badminton Cup. Peel half a middle-sized cucumber, and put it into a silver cup or bowl with 4 oz. icing sugar, juice of a lemon, a little nutmeg, half a glass of curaçao, and a bottle of claret; when the sugar is thoroughly dissolved, pour in a bottle of soda water, ice, and it is ready for use. A couple of sprigs of borage is an improvement when obtainable.—F.D.S.D.

Balaclava. Throw into a large bowl the thinly-pared rind of half a lemon, add two tablespoonfuls of icing sugar, the juice of two lemons, and the half of a small cucumber cut into thin slices with the peel on. Mix well; then add two bottles of soda water, two bottles of claret and one of champagne; stir well together; add a small piece of balm, put in a small block of ice, and serve.–F.D.S.D.

Bull's Eye. One pint sparkling cider; one pint ginger ale; one jigger brandy.—L.T.C.R.

Burgundy Cup. The same as *Claret Cup*, using red burgundy in place of claret. Good burgundy, however, is too dear and too good for a *Cup*, whilst cheap burgundy is usually not worth buying.

Champagne Cup. To a bottle of champagne add a glass of brandy and two slices of sweet orange, a piece of lemon peel, a sprig of verbena or borage, and a very thin peeling of a small cucumber. Let stand half an hour, add plenty of clear ice and serve.

Cider Cup. Put into a bowl one quart of sweet cider, one bottle of soda water, one wineglass of sherry, half a wineglass of brandy, the juice of half a lemon and the rind of a quarter; add sugar and nutmeg to taste, and a dash of extract of pineapple; a sprig of verbena and two sprigs of borage may be added. Strain and ice well.—F.D.S.D.

Claret Cup. To each bottle of ordinary claret add a bottle of soda water, a glass of sherry or curaçao, the peel of a lemon, cut very thin, with powdered sugar according to taste. Let the whole stand an hour or two before serving, and then add some clear ice. —C.T.C.

Dry champagne in place of soda water is an improvement.—ED.

Copus Cup. Heat two quarts of ale; add four wineglasses of brandy, three wineglasses of noyau, 1 lb. of lump sugar, and the juice of one lemon. Toast a slice of bread, stick a slice of lemon on it with a dozen cloves, over which grate some nutmeg, and serve hot.—C.T.C.

Hock Cup. To a bottle of hock add three wineglasses of sherry, one lemon sliced, and some balm or borage. Let it stand two hours; sweeten to taste and add a bottle of seltzer-water.—C.T.C.

Loving Cup. Rub the rind of two oranges on loaf-sugar, and put the sugar into a cup or bowl; add half a pint of brandy, the juice of one lemon, one-third of a pint of orange juice, and one pint of water; add more sugar if required and ice well.—F.D.S.D.

Velvet Cup. A pint of iced champagne and a pint of stout poured together in a large jug.

CURAÇAO

The most popular of all Dutch liqueurs. It was originally made in Holland from green curaçoa oranges and brandy or gin, but it is now made in many lands from all manner of oranges – and even without oranges by using fruit essences instead. So keen did the competition become that some distillers now sell their curaçao under quite other names, such as *Triple Sec, Cointreau, Grand Marnier Cordon Rouge* (or *Cordon Jaune*), etc.

CURRANT WINE

Take four gallons of currants, not too ripe, and strip them into an earthen steen, with a cover to it; then take 2½ gallons of water, and 5½ lb. of sugar; boil the sugar and water together, and skim it well; then pour it boiling on the currants, and let it stand 48 hours; afterwards strain it through a flannel bag into the vessel again, and let it stand a fortnight to settle; then bottle it off.—W.S.M.

CUSSAC

A Commune of the Médoc 33 k. NNW. of Bordeaux; its wines have acquired by long usage the right to be sold under the better-known name of the adjoining Commune of St. Julien. The best wines of Cussac are those of *Châteaux Beaumont, Lanessan, Lamothe-de-Bergeron, Bernones* and *Camino-Salva*; they rank as bourgeois supérieurs and average 400 tuns claret.

CUVE, CUVÉE

A *Cuve* is the French for *Vat* and *Cuvée* for a *Vatting*; also for a 'bottling', in the sense that a certain *Cuvée* is the wine bottled at a certain time under the same conditions. In the Champagne district, the *Cuvée* or *Vin de Cuvée* also refers to the first pressing, hence the best wine.

CYPRUS

A large island of the Eastern Mediterranean and the original home of the Malvasia grape and of the Malmsey Wine which was so popular in England during the sixteenth century. Both wine and brandy are still made from the vineyards of the island. The best Muscat grapes of Cyprus are reputed to be those of *Agros*.

CZECHOSLOVAKIA

The best contribution of this country to the thirst of man is its *Pilsener*, the light beer of Pilsen, the original and still the best of all lager beers. There are also wines made in different parts of the country, chiefly in *Bohemia* (q.v.), Ruthenia and Slovakia, but few, if any, of outstanding merit.

DAISIES

The name given to iced long drinks or *Coolers* of a somewhat superior kind.

Daisies are usually served in goblets, with shaved ice, and decorated with various fruits, flowers or leaves. The more popular *Daisies* are:

Brandy Daisy: One jigger brandy; half jigger raspberry syrup; the juice of half a lemon and half a lime.

Gin Daisy: One jigger gin; half jigger raspberry syrup; the juice of half a lemon.

Highland Daisy: Two-thirds jigger Scotch whisky; one jigger syrup; the juice of half a lemon, half a lime and half an orange.

Rum Daisy: One jigger rum; half jigger raspberry syrup; the juice of half a lemon.

Star Daisy: Half jigger gin; half jigger applejack; half jigger grenadine; the juice of half a lime.

DALMATIA

There are many vineyards in the mainland of Dalmatia, chiefly in the district of *Split* or *Spalato,* but their wine is not very distinguished, whereas the *Maraschino* of Zara is the best of all the liqueurs bearing this name. The only Dalmatian dessert wine of some distinction is the red *Almissa.*

DAME-JEANNE

The French name for a wicker-covered glass container, used mostly for storing spirits; the name has been anglicized into *Demijohn.*

DAMSON GIN

One of the more popular English liqueurs of pre-war days.

DAMSON WINE

Gather the fruit dry, weigh them, and bruise them with your hands; put them into an earthen pot with a faucet, having a wad of straw before the faucet; and to every 8 lb. of fruit add one gallon of water; then pour it over your fruit, scalding hot, and let it stand two days; afterwards draw it off, and put it into a clean cask, and to every gallon of liquor add 2½ lb. of sugar. Let the cask be full, and the longer it stands the better. It will keep very well a year in the cask; afterwards bottle it off. The small damson is the best. If you put a small lump of loaf sugar into every bottle, it will be much improved. —W.S.M.

DANZIGER GOLDWASSER

A curious liqueur made with grain spirit as a basis, flavoured with orange peel and various herbs, and decorated with small specks of gold leaf, which float about the colourless liqueur when the bottle is shaken: they are tasteless and harmless. It is also known as *Eau-de-vie de Danzig*.

D'ARCHE, Château

One of the Second Growths of Sauternes: it was known as *Cru de Braneyre*, previous to 1733, when M.d'Arche acquired it. Average 12 tuns white wine.

There are two other Second Growths of Sauternes: *Château d'Arche-Lafaurie* (35 tuns) and *Château d'Arche-Vimeney* (12 tuns).

DAUZAC, Château

Fifth Growth of the Médoc (Labarde): average 60 tuns claret a year. Some white wine is also made at Dauzac and is mostly used in the manufacture of a sparkling wine sold under the name of *Royal Médoc Mousseux*.

DEBRÖI HÁRSLEVELÜ

A very fair but rather sweet white wine made from the Hárslevelü grapes grown in the vineyards of Debrö, in the district of Eger, in Hungary.

DECANTER

'The half-way house between bottle and glass.'—GEORGE SAINTSBURY in *Notes on a Cellar Book*.

DECANTING

All wines are best decanted from their original bottles into perfectly pure white and well-polished decanters, simply because you can see them better, and the colour of all good wines is a joy for the eye. In the case of red wines which have been bottled for a number of years, decanting is not only a matter of looks but of leaving in the original bottle all the sediment thrown by the wine in the course of its slow maturing, and having in the decanter none but the brilliantly clear wine. To serve old red wines from a cradle is useless, unless seven or eight glasses are poured out at one and the same time from the bottle in the cradle, so that the cradle is only put down again when its work is over and nothing but sediment is left in the bottle.

DE HILDE, Château

One of the little-known Châteaux of the Graves de Bordeaux district, in the Commune of Bègles, between Martillac and Cadaujac. Its vineyards produce on an average 50 tuns of claret per annum and no white wine.

DEIDESHEIM

One of the most important growths of the Palatinate (Mittelhaardt). Its best vineyards are: *Grainhübel, Hahnenböhl, Hofstück, Hergottsacker, Kalkofen, Leinhölde, Maushöhle*.

DEKELEIA

Red and white table wines of moderate quality from vineyards near Marathon (Greece).

DEMI

The name given in France to a *Double Bock* or a pint of draught beer.

DEMIJOHN

A bulging, narrow-necked glass container holding from 3 to 10 gallons, used mostly for the storing of Madeira wine, and also for spirits. It is usually cased in wicker with wicker handles or lugs.

DEMI-SEC

A label used for champagne which is quite sweet.

DÉZALEY

The best white wine of the Canton de Vaud, and there are good judges who claim that *Dézaley* is the best white wine of Switzerland.

DHRONER

A very pleasing, light white wine from the vineyards of *Dhron*, in the Berncastel district (Middle Moselle Valley). The best vineyards of Dhron are *Sängerei, Hofberg, Kandel* and *Roterd*: the best-known wine of Dhron is the *Dhronhofberger*.

DIEDESFELD

One of the minor wine-producing parishes of the Palatinate, in the Oberhaardt district of Landau. Its best vineyards are *Wetterkreuzberg, Goldmorgen, Spielfeld* and *Hartkopf*.

DIENHEIM

One of the more important wine-producing parishes of Rhine-Hesse, in the Oppenheim district; its best vineyards are *Goldberg* and *Tafelstein*.

DIRMSTEIN

Palatinate. Frankenthal district. White wines. Best vineyards: *Himmelreich, Mandelpfad, Sandacker*.

DISTILLATION

The art of separating the alcohol contained in any alcoholic liquid by the application of heat. The art of distillation is based on the fact that alcohol is vaporized at a lower temperature than water, 78° instead of 100°. Wine, barley mash, molasses or any other liquid containing a certain proportion of alcohol will be vaporized at a temperature varying between 78° and 100°, according to the proportion of water to alcohol, as follows:

Percentage of Alcohol	Percentage of Water	Boiling Point
100	0	78.0°
90	10	78.8°
80	20	79.7°
70	30	80.9°
60	40	81.9°
50	50	83.1°
40	60	84.1°
30	70	88.3°
20	50	92.6°
10	90	99.6°
0	100	100.0°

The receptacle in which the liquid to be distilled is placed is called a still. Heat being applied, some alcohol-cum-water leaves the still in the form of vapour which is led away from the heated still through a tube or pipe until it reverts to the original liquid form, owing to lower temperature. By separating the tube or channel through which the vapour has to travel, before it is condensed, into a series of compartments, and by regulating the temperature of each compartment from 100°, the boiling point of water, down to 75°, the boiling point of alcohol, the whole of the alcohol in any alcoholic liquid could be separated from the rest. But the object of distillation, as applied to potable spirits, is not to extract the whole of the alcohol contained in wine, barley mash or the sugar cane, but to reduce the water contents of such alcoholic liquids, so that they shall contain a greater proportion of alcohol, a smaller proportion of water and the largest possible proportion of the most suitable 'by-products' or impurities present in the original liquid from which each kind of spirit is distilled. The distinctiveness of potable spirits is due to the nature and proportion of such impurities, in the first place; in the second, to methods of rectification and to later additions.

DOISY-VÉDRINES, Château
DOISY-DAËNE, Château
DOISY-DUBROCA, Château
Three of the Second Growths of Sauternes, in the Commune of Barsac; their average yield being 40 tuns, 12 tuns and 15 tuns of white wines respectively.

DOLE DE SION
One of the best red wines of Switzerland; it is made from Dôle grapes grown in the vineyards of Sion, in the Valais.

DOURO
The most famous river of the Iberian Peninsula from a wine point of view. It rises in the north of Spain and flows into the Atlantic shortly after passing between Oporto on the right and Vila Nova de Gaya on the left. During its run in a general east-to-west direction through Portugal, the River Douro may be divided into the Upper Douro, from the Spanish frontier to Regoa, and the Lower Douro, from Regoa to Oporto. The best wines of the Douro are those from the vineyards of the schistous hills of the Upper Douro; the Lower Douro hills are chiefly granite, and the wines which are obtained from their vineyards are more suitable for beverage wines than for the making of port.

DRAKENSTEIN
One of the best wine-producing districts of the Cape Province, S.A.; chiefly noted for its white wines.

DRAMBUIE
The only liqueur made in Scotland which has attained a world-wide reputation. It has for a basis Scotch whisky and heather honey. The name *Drambuie* is from the Gaelic *An dram buidheach*, meaning 'the drink that satisfies'.

DREIMÄNNER WEIN
A popular name given in Germany to the very tart red wines of the Neckar and other vineyards: a 'three-men wine' was supposed to be so sour that it took two men to make a third one drink it. The same type of wine was also called *Strumpf Wein*, or stocking-wine, the inference being that its acidity was such that it would draw together any holes in the stockings worn by the drinker.

DROMERSHEIM
One of the less-important wine-producing parishes of Rhine-Hesse (Bingen district). Its best vineyards are *Laberstall* and *Honigberg*.

DRY
An adjective with more than one meaning when applied to wine.
Champagne described as Dry is a wine not excessively sweet, but one which, as a rule, has been sweetened more or less according to age: the younger and more acid it is, the more sweetening has to be added to make the wine palatable.
White Graves and other white beverage wines described as Dry White Wines are not really dry; they are, however, dry compared with Sauternes and other naturally sweet wines.
Sauternes, Ports and other wines are intended by nature or designed to be sweet, that is to say, full of natural grape-sugar sweetness; if they are described as dry, it is that they have lost or have never had one of their chief assets.

Clarets and other red beverage wines are dry by comparison with fortified wines, but they should retain their 'fruit', and be free from tartness. When they lose their smoothness, they are described as 'going' or 'gone' dry, and they have lost much of their charm.

DUBONNET
One of the most extensively advertised and widely popular French *Apéritifs*. Its basis is red wine; its colour is dark red, its after-taste somewhat bitter and flat. It is drunk neat or with either brandy or gin to liven it up.

DUCRU-BEAUCAILLOU, Château
A Second Growth of the Médoc (Saint-Julien). Average 150 tuns claret.

DUHART-MILON, Château
A Fourth Growth of the Médoc (Pauillac), which was known during the eighteenth century under the name of *Mandavit Milon*. Its average is 140 tuns claret.

DURFORT-VIVENS, Château
A Second Growth of the Médoc (Margaux). Average 80 tuns claret per annum. The property of the Durfort de Duras family in the beginning, it was acquired by a Mr de Vivens in 1824.

DÜRKHEIMER
One of the best white wines of the Palatinate, from the vineyards of Bad-Dürkheim, in the Mittelhaardt. There is also a small quantity of red Dürkheimer made, the best of which is *Dürkheimer Feuerberg*. The best white grapes vineyards are: *Spielberg, Hochbenn, Steinberg, Schenkenböhl, Fuchsmantel, Frohnhof, Steinböhl, Klosterberg*.

EAST INDIA
A description often used in connection with madeira and sherry in the days of sailing ships and previous to the cutting of the Suez Canal. Casks of madeira, chiefly, and also of sherry, were then frequently used as ballast in ships going to the East Indies via the Cape of Good Hope and back, no freight or a nominal amount being charged. The long and slow rocking of the wine during the double journey aged and improved it. Now, however, owing to the vibration, the excessive heat in the hold, the more limited, hence more valuable, space available in steamers, the East India madeiras and sherries are merely a memory of more leisurely days.

EAU D'ARQUEBUSE
A very ancient French liqueur which long enjoyed the reputation of being a cure for all ills; it used to be made and was chiefly to be found in the Lyons region.

EAU DE LA BARBADE
A very popular liqueur of the *Chartreuse* type which used to be made in Bordeaux.

EAU DE MÉLISSE DES CARMES
A digestive liqueur flavoured with balm-mint (*Mélisse citronelle*), hyssop, cinnamon, sage and a number of herbs and spices. It used to be made in Paris, not by Carmelites, but Rue des Carmes.

EAU-DE-VIE
(Water of Life). The French name for brandy or potable spirit, not necessarily distilled from wine. When distilled from wine, it is called *Eau-de-Vie-de-Vin*; when distilled from cider, *Eau-de-Vie-de-Cidre*; when from grain, *Eau-de-Vie-de-Grain*; when from marcs, *Eau-de-Vie-de-Marc*; when from different kinds of fruit, *Eau-de-Vie-de-Fruits*. When blended with plain spirit, the word *Fantaisie* should be added after Eau-de-Vie; and when flavoured with essences (*Bonificateur*) the Eau-de-Vie must be described as *artificielle*.

EBULUM
To a hogshead of strong lusty ale add an over-flowing bushel of the berries of Elder and a $\frac{1}{2}$ lb. of the berries of juniper, both thoroughly crushed. Put the berries to the ale when you put in the hops and let the compound boil until the berries are burst apart by the scalding water, developing the liquor thenceforth as you would with simple ale. When the fermentation has ceas'd, add the following ingredients: $\frac{1}{2}$ lb. ginger, $\frac{1}{2}$ oz. cloves, $\frac{1}{2}$ oz. mace, 1 oz. nutmegs, 1 oz. cinnamon, all pounded and mixt together, $\frac{1}{4}$ lb. citron, $\frac{1}{4}$ lb. eringo root, $\frac{1}{4}$ lb. candied orange peel.

Cut the sweets very thin; put these & the spices together into a cloth bag which you will hang in the Cask before you stop it.

When the liquor is fine, serve it in glasses, into each one of which you have previously laid two lumps of refin'd sugar.—c.e.m.

EDENKOBEN
One of the smaller parishes of the Palatinate, in the Oberhaardt, Landau district, which produces some very fair and rather sweet white wines. Its best vineyards are *Mühlberg, Heilgkreuz, Klosteracker* and *Letten*.

EGGNOG
A kind of liquid custard and a wonderful pick-me-up. It is made up with egg, milk and sugar beaten together, braced with rum or brandy, and flavoured with grated nutmeg.

I

One dozen eggs; one gallon cream; three pints brandy; 1 lb. sugar; half gallon milk; one pint whisky; $\frac{1}{3}$oz. ground nutmeg.

Beat eggs and sugar together to a froth. Add all the other ingredients and pour from one vessel to another until thoroughly mixed and a deep froth stands on the mixture. *Mr Rudolph Kaiser. Anne Arundel County.*—F.P.S.

II

Two quarts of cream; 16 eggs; one pint brandy; one pint Jamaica spirits; 1 lb. loaf sugar. Beat the yolks light, and add the sugar and liquor slowly, then the cream. Beat the whites to a froth. *Mr and Mrs J. Spence Howard, St. Mary's Manor. St Mary's County.*—F.P.S.

Applejack Eggnog. Half jigger milk; half jigger applejack; one raw egg; two teaspoons powdered sugar; grated nutmeg. Mix milk, applejack, egg, and sugar together, and shake with ice until very frothy. Serve in tumbler with nutmeg grated on top.—A.C.

Tom and Jerry. The American name of a somewhat *de luxe* Eggnog. It is made by beating the yolk of an egg with a teaspoon of sifted sugar in a galss, then adding a liqueur glass of rum and another of brandy. Stir well. Then add the well-beaten white of an egg, and last hot milk, stirring all the time. A little grated nutmeg is usually sprinkled on top. The right way to serve *Tom and Jerry* is in coffee cups, or, better still, in specially-made 'Tom and Jerry' cups.

EGLISE, Domaine de l'

One of the First Growths of Pomerol, with an average annual production of 20 tuns of claret. There is another First Growth of Pomerol called *Cru l'Eglise*, and yet another called *Cru de l'Eglise*, the first producing an average of 25 tuns and the second merely 8 tuns of claret per annum. There is also a *Clos l'Eglise-Clinet*, still in Pomerol, with an average production of 30 tuns claret.

EGRI BIKAVER. EGRI KADARKA

Two of the best red wines of Hungary from the vineyards of Eger, a town about 120 miles NW. of Budapest. *Bikaver* is a very dark red and full-bodied wine.

EITELSBACH

A village near Trier surrounded by vineyards which produce one of the best wines (white) of the Ruwer Valley. The best vineyards are: *Karthäuserhofberg* and *Marienholz*.

ELDERBERRY WINE

A very old member of the English wines family. It is made from the juice of the little black berries of the elder shrub; they have diuretic and aperient properties but an unpleasant taste, a defect which is easily covered up by cloves and other spices. Drunk hot and sweetened, *Elderberry Wine* is comforting and helpful in winter time.

Elder Wine

Let the *elder-berries* be quite ripe. Put them in a stone Jug and set them in the oven, in a kettle of boiling water, till the Jug is hot thro'. Then take the berries out and strain them thro' a coarse sieve, pressing them well; then put the juice into a kettle. To every Quart of Juice put a Pound of fine Sugar and two ounces of Allspice; let it boil and skim it well. When it is clear and fine, pour it into a cask, and to every ten Gallons add an ounce of Isinglass dissolved in Cider, and six whites of eggs. Close it up; let it stand six months. Then it will be fit to be bottled and set aside for drinking.—C.E.M.

Elder Flower Wine

Pick from their stalks, while in full bloom, some blossoms of the Elder bush. To every Quart thereof allow one gallon of water and three pounds of sugar. Boil first the water and sugar together and pour it scalding hot on the flowers; when it has become cool mix it with a little juice of the lemon and of yeast a little, in the proportion of 6 lemons and 4 tablespoons of yeast to every 24 Quarts of liquor. Stir this mixture very hard. After you have let it ferment 3 days in a wood Tub cover'd with heavy cloths, strain thro' a sieve, add an ounce of melted isinglass to clarify it and rack it into a clean cask in the bottom of which you have previously laid 4 or 5 pounds of good ston'd raisins. When the fermentation has subsided, stop up the cask tightly, and at the end of six months it will be ready to be bottled.—C.E.M.

ELIXIRS

Liqueurs supposed to be the quintessence of various distillates. In the 'fifties, Picard et Cazot Fils, distillers of Lyons, offered the following *Elixirs* for sale: *China China*; *Elixir vital*; *Liqueur stomachique*; *Elixir des Braves*; *Elixir de Garus*; *Elixir de la Chartreuse*.

ELTVILLE AM RHEIN

One of the important centres of viticulture and of the wine trade of the Rhinegau. Its vineyards produce much white wine of high quality; the best of them are: *Steinmächer*, *Sandgrub, Ehr, Sonnenberg* and *Mönch-Hanach*.

EMILIA

An Italian Province which produces large quantities of very bad wines and a limited quantity of red and white wines which are just drinkable. The most acceptable white wine of Emilia is made near Bertinoro and sold under the name of *Albana*; the best red wine is made near Forli and is called *San Giovese*, the name of the grape from which it is made. The best-known red wine of Emilia is the *Lambrusco*, so named from the grape from which it is made.

ENGADDI

A small town in the valley of the Jordan, on the road to Bethlehem (Palestine). The vine still grows there as it did about a thousand years before Christ, when Solomon wrote the 'Song of Songs' and praised the vines of Engaddi:

'Botrus Cypri dilectus meus mihi, in vineis Engaddi.' (I, 14.)

(A cluster of Cyprus my love is to me, in the vineyards of Engaddi. *Vulgate*.)

The most remarkable feature of this line is that it shows that even in the days of King Solomon the vine of Cyprus, the Malvasia grape, was highly prized and had been introduced into Palestine as it was to be introduced into Italy by the Romans, into the island of Madeira by the Portuguese, in the fifteenth century, and by the Dutch, at the Cape, in the seventeenth century.

ENGLISH WINES

Although it is possible that the Romans, when they occupied Britain, and it is certain that, at a later date, the religious orders, when they civilized the same land, cultivated vineyards and made wine from home-grown grapes, there has not been any wine made from home-grown grapes in England for many centuries past, with the exception of insignificant quantities made more experimentally than commercially from time to time. English wines are alcoholic beverages made in England from roots, plants, flowers or fruit, mostly home-grown but also imported. Well over one hundred different sorts of alcoholic concoctions have been recorded which may claim the name of English wines, chief among them, in point of popularity and antiquity, are the following: *Blackberry, Cherry, Cowslip, Currant, Damson, Elderberry, Fig, Gilliflower, Ginger, Gooseberry, Mulberry, Parsnip, Peach, Plum, Quince, Raisin, Raspberry, Rose Sage.*

ENKIRCH

One of the more important parishes of the Middle Moselle (Zell district) renowned for the very delicate white wines of its vineyards: the best of these are: *Steffensberg, Löwenbaum, Kreuzpfad, Herrenberg, Nonnengarten, Ellergrub, Montaneubel* and *Klosterberg*.

ENTRE-DEUX-MERS

A wine-producing district of the Gironde Département rather loosely described as being situated between the Rivers Garonne and Dordogne: it includes hillside and riverside vineyards and produces red and white wines which vary greatly in quality and price, but none of them are of high merit.

ENTRE-MINHO-E-DOURO

The 'Entre-deux Mers' district of Northern Portugal. Its vineyards, north of the Douro and south of the Minho rivers, produce an abundance of *Vinhos Verdes* and other wines, suitable mostly for beverage wines.

EPPAN

South Tyrol. Red and white wines much in demand in Switzerland, South Germany and Austria.

ERBACH-AM-RHEIN

One of the more important of the Rhinegau wine-producing townships: its vineyards are responsible for some of the best hocks. Best vineyards: *Markobrunn, Brühl, Rheinhell, Hohenrain, Honigberg* and *Steinmorgen*. Close to Erbach is Prince Friedrich Henry of Prussia's famous *Schloss Reinhartshausen*.

ERDEN

One of the wine-producing villages of the Moselle Valley. Berncastel district. White wines. Best vineyards: *Treppchen, Herrenberg, Herzlay, Prälat, Bushlay, Pichter*.

ERLACH

The only red wine with a (local) reputation from the vineyards of the Lake of Bienne in the Canton of Berne (Switzerland).

ERLAU

One of the most important wine-producing districts of Hungary (Borsod County). The district of Erlau produces some white wines and some table grapes, but it is chiefly famous for its red wines; the red wines, which are sold under the name of *Erlauer*, are those made from grapes grown in the vineyards of *Erlau*, and also of the adjoining parishes of *Gyöngyös, Gyöngyöstarjan, Solijmos* and *Visonta*.

ESCHERNDORF

One of the wine-producing parishes of Franconis, in the district of Gerolshofen: its vineyards, which are responsible for the best white wines, are: *Kirchberg, Lump* and *Fürstenberg*.

ESCUBAC, Yellow

One of the early Victorian *Ratafias*.

1 oz. saffron
1 oz. Damascus raisins
1 oz. cinnamon
3 lb. sugar
1 oz. liquorice
1 oz. corianders
3 pints brandy
2 pints water

Pound these ingredients, and dissolve the sugar in two pints of water; put the whole in a jar to infuse for a month, taking care to stir it up every second day or the third at farthest.—G.A.J.

EST EST EST

The name of the golden Muscatel wine of Montefiascone, near Lake Bolsena, in the Latium, south of Rome. There are two types of *Est Est Est*, the one sweeter than the other, and the sweeter is considered the better of the two. The wine must have been known in England in the early part of the nineteenth century to judge from extant specimens of English wine labels of the period which bear the inscriptions *Est Est Est* and *Este-Este*.

ETTALER KLOSTERLIQUOR

A sweet liqueur of the *Bénédictine* style, made by the Benedictines of the Ettaler monastery, near Oberammergau, in Upper Bavaria.

EVIAN WATER

One of the most popular of French *Mineral Waters*. It is entirely free from carbonic acid gas and has no taste, but it is slightly alkaline and some people believe that it has some digestive properties. The best known spring of Evian-les-Bains, a Spa in Haute-Savoie, is the *Cachat* spring.

EXTRA SEC

The equivalent of *Extra Dry* for champagne, meaning that the wine has only had a little sweetening added to it before it was shipped.

EZERJO

The name of a grape and of a golden, full-bodied wine made from Ezerjo grapes at Mór, a small Commune near Budapest (Hungary).

FALERNIAN WINE

There is still much wine made in the Campanian vineyards round Falerno, under the shadow of Vesuvius; some is white but most of it is red and none of it is very good. Whether the wine has deteriorated, or whether Virgil, Horace, Pliny, Cato and all the Latin poets and historians who have praised *Falernian* in prose and in verse, were not so difficult to please and enthuse as we are, it is impossible to say.

FALSTAFF

Sir John Falstaff, probably the most sober, and certainly the most unfortunate of Henry V's generals, was both ridiculed and immortalized by Shakespeare, who makes him drink incredible quantities of *Sack*, a wine which Shakespeare loved above all, but the name of which had never been heard of in England in Sir John Falstaff's days.

FARGUES

A Commune of the Sauternes district, the vineyards of which produce some fair red beverage wines, for local consumption, and much more as well as much finer white wines, similar to those of the nearby vineyards of Sauternes and Barsac: the best are those of Châteaux *Rieussec* and *Romer*; then those of Château *Peyron*.

FEINTS

The 'heads and tails' or first and last as well as the worst parts of spirits from a pot-still.

FENDANT DE SION

One of the best of Swiss wines, made from *Fendant* grapes grown in the vineyards of Sion, Canton du Valais. It is a still white wine, but it often has a semi-pétillant or *spritzig* quality which is very attractive.

FERNET-BRANCA

The best-known Italian *Apéritif* wine or *Bitter*; it is made by Fratelli Branca.

FERRANDE, Château

The most important estate of the Commune of Castres, in the Graves de Bordeaux district, with an average annual production of 80 tuns of white wine.

FIASCO, pl. FIASCHI

A two-litre glass *flask*, round at the bottom, wrapped with matted straw, typical of Tuscany, where it has been used for many generations for wine, oil and water. A quart flask is a *mezzo fiasco*, or half a flask.

FIG WINE.
FARMINGDALE WINE

Take 6 pounds of dried figs, 6 pounds of fine sugar, and 2 cakes of yeast. Grind and chop the figs. Boil 3 gallons of clear, fresh water. To the water add the chopp'd figs and the sugar, and allow the mixture to cool. Now add the yeast. Let the mixture be well stirr'd every day for two weeks. Then it should be strain'd and put into bottles or a cask, where let it lie for three months.–C.E.M.

FILHOT, Château

A Second Growth of Sauternes. Average production 50 tuns.

FILZEN

A little village at the mouth of the Saar where it flows into the Moselle, near Trier. The vineyards of *Filzen*, the best of which is *Herrenberg*, produce some very delicate and charming white wines.

FINE

French for an indifferent brandy from some unknown source.

FINE CHAMPAGNE

A brandy which must be a Grande Champagne or Petite Champagne in France, but no real guarantee of quality outside France.

FINE MAISON
The staple brandy of the House (Hotel or Restaurant); as a rule the safest, but seldom fine.

FININGS
Finings act as a very small mesh net cast over new wine, a net which settles down slowly to the bottom of the cask, provided there is no draught nor trepidation, and carries with it every particle of mucilage or sediment in suspension in the wine. The chief finings are white of eggs for red wines, isinglass for white wines, and gelatine, also milk, fresh blood and a number of patent powders. But whatever the finings used, they must be thoroughly *whisked* (beaten up) before being poured into the wine, and the wine must be thoroughly *roused* (shaken) immediately after the finings have been added.

FINO
The most intensely clean on nose and palate of all sherries; the real *Fino* is dry without any bitterness, and delicate without being thin.

FIRKIN
The fourth part of a barrel of beer, i.e. nine gallons.

FIXES or TWISTS
These are iced summer drinks compounded in many different ways.

Gin Fix. Put into a small tumbler a table-spoonful of icing sugar, half a wineglass of water, the juice and peel of a quarter of a lemon, and one wineglassful of gin; fill the tumbler two-thirds with shaved ice, shake well, and decorate with berries in season; insert one straw, or use a straining spoon on top of glass.—F.D.S.D.

FIXIN
One of the smaller wine-producing Communes of the Côte d'Or, producing some red burgundy of very fair quality. Its best wine is that of *Le Clos de la Perrière*; its best-known that of *Le Clos du Chapître*. Average yearly production, 11,000 gallons.

FIZZ
A common name for any beverage which is effervescent, more particularly champagne.

FIZZES
American 'long' drinks made up of various kinds of spirits and some sugar or syrup, well shaken with plenty of ice, then strained and served in tall glasses which are then filled with a syphon: a pinch of carbonate of soda is sometimes used instead of a syphon to ensure effervescence

Bayard Fizz. The juice of 1½ lemons; one barspoon sugar; one jigger dry gin; one dash maraschino; one dash raspberry syrup. Shake, strain and fill glass with syphon. —L.T.C.R.

Brandy Fizz. The juice of one lemon; one barspoon sugar; one jigger French brandy; two dashes yellow chartreuse. Shake and strain, and fill glass with syphon.—L.T.C.R.

Daisy Fizz. The juice of half a lemon; juice of half a lime; half jigger orange juice; two-thirds jigger brandy. Shake, strain and fill glass with syphon.—L.T.C.R.

Galvez Fizz. The juice of one lemon; one barspoon sugar; four dashes raspberry syrup; one jigger dry gin; one white of egg; one dash orange flower water; one jigger cream. Shake well; strain into lemonade glass and fill with syphon.—L.T.C.R.

Gin Fizz. Put into a tumbler the juice of half a lemon and one wineglass of gin; fill with shaved ice, shake well, strain, add a teaspoonful of icing sugar, in which place a pinch of carbonate of soda, stir well, and drink while effervescing.—F.D.S.D.

Golden Fizz. Put into a tumbler the juice of half a lemon, one wineglass of gin; fill up to three parts with shaved ice, then break the yolk of an egg into the tumbler, shake well, strain, add a teaspoonful of icing sugar, in which place a pinch of carbonate of soda, stir well, and drink while effervescing. F.D.S.D.

Ramos Fizz. One heaping teaspoonful confectioner's sugar; two teaspoons lemon juice; quarter teaspoonful orange flower water; one egg white; 1 oz. dry gin; 2½ oz. milk; cracked ice. Shake 5–10 minutes and strain into 8 oz. glass.—A.C.

Sloe Gin Fizz. Half jigger of lemon juice; one teaspoonful of powdered sugar; one jigger slow gin. Shake thoroughly with cracked ice, strain and fill with charged water.–H.J.G.

FLAGEY-ECHÉZEAUX
One of the Communes of the Côte d'Or, producing some very fine red burgundy. Its best vineyards are: *Les Grands Echézeaux.* Other good vineyards are: *Les Beaux-Monts-Bas*; *Les Beaux-Monts-Hauts*; *Les Champs Traversins*, *Les Cruots ou Vignes Blanches*, *Les Echézeaux du Dessus*, *En Orveaux*, *Les Poulaillières*, *Les Quartiers de Nuits*, *Les Rouges du Bas*, *Les Treux*. Average 26,000 gallons.

FLAP
Put a little brandy in a tumbler and add a bottle of soda water.—F.F.

FLIPS
A spiced and sweetened drink with an egg beaten or 'flipped' in.

Cream Flip. Three jiggers cream; one egg; one dash curaçao; a grating of nutmeg on top.

Gin Flip. One jigger gin; one egg; one tablespoonful sugar.

Reviver Flip. One jigger sloe gin; one egg; one spoonful sugar; a grating of nutmeg on top.

Sherry Flip. One egg; one teaspoonful of powdered sugar; one jigger of sherry. Shake thoroughly with cracked ice and strain into glass. Sprinkle a little nutmeg on top.–H.J.G.

FLOR

Spanish for Flower. In wine parlance, it refers to a particular form of yeast, the *mycoderma vini*, which multiplies quickly on the surface of new white wines, in Andalucia, forming a filmy cover which shuts out the outside air from the slowly 'working' wine under it; it is responsible for some of the more distinctive characteristics of *Sherry*.

FORBIDDEN FRUIT

The only American liqueur which has achieved a fair measure of popularity in England. It is made of brandy and shaddock (originally) but nowadays presumably with the improved form of shaddock which is the grapefruit.

FORST

One of the finest growths of the Palatinate (Mittelhaardt) in the Neustadt district. Luscious white wines. Best vineyards: *Kirchenstück, Freundstück, Jesuitengarten, Ungeheuer, Ziegler, Langenböhl, Pechstein* and *Schnepfenflug.*

FOUDRE

The French name (*Fuder*, in German) of particularly large casks used either to mature or store wine in *Chais* and *Caves*, or for the transport of the cheaper sorts of wine.

FOXINESS

(Fr. *Queue de renard*.) The name given for the lack of a better one to the distinctive flavour of the wines made from the native American grapes of the Eastern States of the U.S.A. It does not resemble in the least the objectionable smell of the fox, but it is too assertive and too different from the discreet and flowery bouquet of the *vitis vinifera* or European vinegrape wines, to be welcome to a palate tuned to such wines.

FRANCONIA

An important wine-producing district of Germany, of which Würzburg is the chief city and market. The principal wine-producing parishes of Franconia are: *Würzburg, Randersacker, Eschendorf, Iphofen* and *Hörstein.* The wine of Franconia is known as *Frankenwein* or *Steinwein.*

FRASCATI

The name of an ancient and famous township of the Alban Hills, south of Rome; also the name of the white table wine from its vineyards.

FREEZOMINT

The most popular brand of French *Crèmes de Menthe* (Cusenier's).

FREISA

A pinkish or reddish and sweetish semi-sparkling wine made in Piedmont.

FRENCH HOEK

(South Africa). One of the oldest wine-producing settlements of the Cape Province, at the end of the Paarl Valley farthest away from Wellington.

FRONSAC, Côtes de

The registered name under which the best red wines are marketed which are produced by the vineyards of the different Communes of the Canton of Fronsac, on the right bank of the River Dordogne, in the Département of Gironde, a hilly and picturesque district known as Fronsadais.

FRONTIGNAN

The best dessert wine of Languedoc and one of the best of the naturally sweet wines made in France: it is tawny in colour and acquires with age a distinctive *rancio* flavour which is greatly prized by many people in France. This wine must have been popular at the end of the eighteenth century and during the early part of the nineteenth, to judge from the number of extant wine labels bearing its name, the spelling of which was rather uncertain. The following renderings occur in various collections: *Frontinac, Frontiniac, Frontignac, Frontignan* and *Frontigniac.*

FUISSÉ

A Commune of Saône-et-Loire adjoining the Commune of Pouilly. Both Communes produce a very agreeable white wine, similar in type, and it is often sold as *Pouilly-Fuissé.*

GAILLAC

The most important wine-producing centre of the Tarn Département (France) for quite ordinary red and white table wines: its best-known wine is the *Clairette de Gaillac.* It is a semi-sparkling rose-red wine of which the people of Albi are very proud. Their poet, Jasmin, wrote:

> Padure Champagno!
> Gaillaco t'espargno!
> Car, se boulio,
> Te toumbario!
> Poor Champagne!
> May Gaillac spare thee!
> For, if it wished
> 'Twould knock thee out.

GALAMUS
A tawny dessert wine made in some parts of Roussillon (France); it is rather sweet with a prematurely old or *rancio* flavour.

GALLON
Standard English and American wine measure which, up to 1826, was the same, i.e. 231 cubic inches for Wine, whilst the Ale gallon was equal to 282 cubic inches. In the United Kingdom these two gallons were replaced by Act 5 Geo. IV, c. 74 (1824), which came into operation on January 1st, 1826, when the present 'imperial' gallon was introduced. It is equivalent to 277.274 cubic inches; its weight is 10 lb. avoirdupois of distilled water: it is divided into 4 *Quarts* or 8 *Pints*. It is equivalent to 4.54 *Litres*.

The U.S.A. gallon is the old English gallon of 251 cubic inches or 128 oz.

GAMAY
One of the most extensively cultivated red-wine grapes. It produces much, but, as a rule, common wine. There are some vineyards, however, where the Gamay produces quite fair red wine; this is the case, for instance, in the Mâconnais, Chalonnais and Beaujolais.

GATTINARA
One of the better red table wines made in Piedmont north of the River Po.

GAU-ALGESHEIMER
The white wine of *Gau-Algesheim*, in Rhine-Hesse, Bingen district. Best vineyards: *Steinert, Stolzenberg, Rotberg.*

GAU-BICKELHEIMER
The white wine of *Gau-Bickelheim*, in Rhine-Hesse, Oppenheim district. Best vineyards: *Goldberg, Frohngewann* and *Steinweg.*

GAU-ODERNHEIMER
The white wine of *Gau-Odernheim*, in Rhine-Hesse, Alzey district. Best vineyards: *Fuchslock, Petersberg* and *Schallenberg.*

GAVI
One of the townships of the Monferrato Hills, in Piedmont; its vineyards produce some of the best white table wines of Italy, from the Cortese grape.

GEISENHEIMER
The white wines of *Geisenheim*, in the Rhine-gau. Best vineyards: *Katzenloch, Decker, Lickerstein, Rothenberg, Morschberg* and *Steinacker*. There is also some sparkling wine made at *Geisenheim.*

GENEVA
One of the names by which *Hollands*, or gin distilled in Holland, has been known for many years past. It has nothing whatever to do with the city or lake of that name; it is merely a corruption of the French name of gin, *Genièvre*, meaning Juniper, gin being a plain spirit flavoured with juniper berries. *Geneva* is either pure white or faintly straw coloured; colour is not due to the wood of the casks in which Geneva is kept, but to caramel. Geneva is sold as soon as distilled: it has nothing to gain by being kept.

GENTIANE
A digestive liqueur made in France and Switzerland; it is flavoured with the dried and ground roots of the *Gentiana lutea*, a herbaceous plant from three to four feet high, which is common in the Swiss Alps, the Burgundian Hills and the Pyrenees.

GERMANY, The wines of
Viticulture was introduced in the valley of the Rhine by the Romans, and it has occupied an important place in the economic life of many parts of the German Reich ever since, chiefly in the Prussian Rhineland, Bavaria, Hessen, Württemberg and Baden.

The best wines of Germany are the white wines of the *Rhinegau, Rhine-Hesse, Palatinate, Moselle, Saar* and *Ruwer*. The white wines of *Franconia* come next. There are no red wines made in Germany of the same excellence as the best white wines of the country, but there are a few Rhine red wines which enjoy a high degree of popularity in Germany.

GEROPIGA. JEROPIGA
Grape syrup used for sweetening wines, chiefly made in Portugal in the same way as Pedro Ximenez is made in Spain.

GEVREY-CHAMBERTIN
One of the most important Communes of the Côte d'Or, the two finest vineyards of which are *Chambertin* and *Clos de Bèze*. Other good vineyards of this Commune are: *Saint-Jacques, Charmes, Ruchottes, Latricières, Mazy* and *Clos de la Roche*. Average annual production, 226,000 gallons of red burgundy.

GEWÄCHS
German for 'The growth of', followed by the name of the estate or vineyard proprietor: on hock and moselle labels.

GEWURZTRAMINER
One of the best varieties (both red and white) of the Traminer grape, extensively grown in Germany, Austria and Alsace.

GILLIFLOWER WINE
To three gallons of water put 6 lb. of the best powder sugar, boil the water and sugar together for the space of half an hour, keep scumming as the scum rises; let it stand to

cool, beat up 3 oz. of syrup of betony, with a large spoonful of ale yeast, put it into the liquor and brew it well together; then having a peck of Gilliflowers, cut from the stalks, put them into the liquor, let them infuse and work together three days, covered with a cloth; strain it and put it into a cask, and let it settle for three or four weeks, then bottle it.—o.e.w.

GIMMELDINGEN

One of the wine-producing parishes of the Palatinate, in the Mittelhaardt, Dürkheim district. Its vineyards produce in good years some fine, rather sweet, white wines. Best vineyards: *Hofstück, Meerspinne* and *Nonnengarten*.

GIN

A spirit distilled from grain and flavoured with juniper berries. Its name is the abbreviation of its French name *Genièvre*, meaning juniper. *Gin* has been distilled in England to a far greater extent than any other spirit, ever since the eighteenth century. There are three main types of English gins:

1. *London Gins*, which differ according to the Distilleries responsible for them;

2. *Plymouth Gin*, a wholly unsweetened gin always uniform in quality and style, all Plymouth gin being distilled by the same Distillers (Coates & Co.);

3. *Old Tom Gin*, a sweetened gin of distinctive character.

English *Gins* are quite distinct from Dutch *Gins*, which are sold under the names of *Geneva, Hollands* or *Schiedam*.

Gin is the purest of all spirits, being distilled at a higher strength than other spirits. This is particularly so in the U.S.A., where the basis of *Gin* is practically neutral alcohol, that is a spirit out of which everything has been distilled; this means that it matters little from what material the *Gin* is originally distilled. It is entirely flavourless, as well as colourless, and is flavoured, coloured at will and brought down in strength by the addition of distilled water. *Gin* is not particularly welcome to the palate, but it is most helpful to the bladder. It is largely used in the mixing of *Cocktails, Collins, Slings* and other drinks, long and short.

Gin and Bitters. One of the simplest and one of the most popular forms of *Cocktails*. It is also known as *Pink Gin*.

Gin and Ginger Ale. A palate-paralysing and bladder-stimulating mixture, refreshing on a hot day, when well iced.

Gin and Tansy. This is an old-fashioned and excellent tonic. It is prepared by steeping a bunch of tansy in a bottle of Hollands Gin, which will extract the essence; when serving, set the glass, with the lump of ice, before the customer, allowing him to help himself. —j.man.

Gin Cocktail. Three dashes of plain syrup; two or three dashes of bitters; one wineglass of Hollands or gin; one or two dashes of orange curaçao. Squeeze lemon peel. Fill one-third full of ice, and shake well, and strain in a small tumbler.—l.en.

Gin Crusta. Peel of half a lemon in long string; place in glass; add half glass of fine ice; one dash bitters; juice of half a lemon; dash of maraschino; 100 per cent dry gin. And serve.—j.man.

Gin Daisy. The juice of half a lemon; quarter teaspoonful powdered sugar; six dashes grenadine; one glass gin. Use long tumbler. Half fill with cracked ice, stir until glass is frosted. Fill with syphon soda-water; put four sprigs of green mint on top and decorate with slices of fruit in season.—h.c.

Gin Fix. One tablespoonful of sugar; half a wine-glass of water; quarter of a lemon; one wine-glass of gin. Fill two-thirds full of ice, stir with a spoon, and ornament the top with fruits in season.—l.en.

Gin Fizz. One teaspoonful sugar; juice of one lemon; one dash cream; 100 per cent gin. Fill glass with fine ice. Shake, strain, fill glass with fizz water, stir and serve.—j.man.

Gin High-Ball. One piece of ice in glass; 100 per cent dry gin. Fill glass with fizz water, stir and serve.— j.man.

Gin Julep. One tablespoonful sugar; three sprigs mint; half a glass of fine ice; 100 per cent dry gin. Stir well, trim with fruits in season and serve.—j.man.

Gin Punch. Half pint of old gin; one gill of maraschino; the juice of three lemons; the rind of half a lemon; one quart bottle of German seltzer water. Ice well and sweeten to taste.—l.en.

Gin Rickey. One of the most refreshing of summer long drinks. *Recipe*: Put some ice (two cubes) in a tumbler, then the juice of half a ripe lime and some of the rind as well; add 2 oz. dry gin and fill with soda or seltzer water. Stir and drink slowly. This cooling drink was first served to Colonel Joe Rickey at 'Shoemaker's', a famous Washington drinking place, in the 'nineties.—o.w.b.d.

Gin Sangaree. It is prepared in the same way as the *Brandy Sangaree*, substituting gin for brandy.

Gin Sling. It is made in the same way as the *Gin Toddy* (q.v.), adding a little grated nutmeg on top before serving.—j.man.

Gin Sling (Hot). One lump of sugar dissolved in hot water; 100 per cent Hollands gin. Fill with hot water. Stir well, grate nutmeg on top and add slice of lemon.—j.man.

Gin Smash. Half a tablespoonful of white sugar; one tablespoonful water; one wineglass of gin. Fill two-thirds full of chipped ice. Use two sprigs of mint, the same as in the recipe for a *Mint Julep*. Lay two small pieces of orange on top, and ornament with berries in season.—L.En.

Gin Sour. Half a teaspoonful of sugar; 100 per cent dry gin; juice of one lemon; half a glass of cracked ice. Shake, strain, add a slice of orange and serve.—J.Man.

Gin Toddy. One teaspoonful of sugar; half a wine-glass of water; one wine-glass of gin; one small lump of ice. Stir with a spoon. —L.En.

GINGER ALE
One of the most popular forms of *Minerals*. It is made with a few drops of essence of ginger, or capsicum extract, and a few drops of colouring matter; also some sugar or glucose, put into a bottle which is then filled up with carbonated water. Occasionally a little mucilaginous matter variously known technically as *Froth*, *Heading*, etc., is added to give the *Ginger Ale* a 'better head' and the drinker thereof a greater thrill.

GINGER BEER
An effervescing beverage made by fermenting ginger, cream of tartar, and sugar with yeast and water, and bottling before the fermentation is completed. The carbonic acid generated within the fluid gives, after a few days or weeks, an aerated drink; but this variety of ginger beer is also an alcoholic drink, for the fermentation which is set up by the yeast in a part of the sugar gives rise to a little alcohol, as well as to carbonic acid. Two per cent of alcohol is the strict legal limit.—L.G.M.

GINGER WINE
A British Wine or liquor, generally made with water, sugar, lemon rinds, ginger, yeast, raisins, and frequently fortified with added spirit and a little capsicine.—L.G.M.

GIRO DI SARDEGNA
The most ambitious of the many ordinary wines made in the Island of Sardinia. It is a red dessert wine, quite sweet and fairly high in alcoholic strength.

GLASSES
Fine glasses materially add to the enjoyment of fine wines. Wine never tastes well in (*a*) coloured glasses, because one is unable to enjoy the beautiful ruby or gold of the wine; (*b*) thick glasses; (*c*) small glasses, because there must be a fair volume of wine for the bouquet to show off; (*d*) glasses filled to the brim. Glasses which have been dried with a dirty cloth, and glasses which have been left for any length of time bowl downwards, will spoil any and every wine by their foul or musty smell.

The size and shape of drinking glasses vary considerably, and the smaller the glass the farther the bottle will go. The 'reputed' quart, or ordinary wine bottle, should hold one-sixth of a gallon, or $26\frac{2}{3}$ liquid ounces.

It is generally advisable for the purpose of estimating how many glasses of a given size can be got out of a bottle to treat the quantity as 26 ounces only, as all bottles are not always one-sixth of a gallon. It also allows for any wastage, bottoms, etc. On this basis the following are the results:

Size of Glass (ounces)	No. of Glasses per bottle
$\frac{1}{2}$	52
$\frac{3}{4}$	$34\frac{2}{3}$
1	26
$1\frac{1}{4}$	$20\frac{4}{5}$
$1\frac{1}{2}$	$17\frac{1}{3}$
$1\frac{3}{4}$	$14\frac{6}{7}$
2	13
$2\frac{1}{4}$	$11\frac{5}{9}$
$2\frac{1}{2}$	$10\frac{2}{5}$
$2\frac{3}{4}$	$9\frac{5}{11}$
3	$8\frac{2}{3}$
$3\frac{1}{4}$	8
$3\frac{1}{2}$	$7\frac{3}{7}$
$3\frac{3}{4}$	$6\frac{14}{15}$
4	$6\frac{1}{2}$
$4\frac{1}{4}$	$6\frac{2}{17}$
$4\frac{1}{2}$	$5\frac{7}{9}$
$4\frac{3}{4}$	$5\frac{9}{19}$
5	$5\frac{1}{5}$

A *Pony* is a *small* glass and it often means a *very small* glass.

GOLDWASSER
A spirit which was originally made at Dantzig and continued to be made there exclusively for a long time. It is now distilled in other places as well. It is a highly rectified spirit, flavoured with aniseed, cinnamon, and a number of herbs and spices; it is colourless and as a rule of very high strength, but its outstanding feature is that it contains a large number of very small pieces of gold leaf or yellow and gold-like pieces which settle at the bottom of the bottle but float about like tiny golden snowflakes when the liqueur is being served.

GOOSEBERRY WINE
To every 4 lb. of gooseberries take $1\frac{1}{4}$ lb. of sugar, and a quart of spring water; bruise the berries and let them lie for 24 hours in the water stirring them frequently; then press out the liquor, and add your sugar to it. Afterwards put it into a clean cask and, when the fermentation has ceased, close it up, and let it stand a month; then rack it off into another cask, and let it stand five or six weeks longer: bottle it off, putting a lump of sugar into every bottle.—W.S.M.

GOÛT

French for *Taste*: as applied to wine, *Goût* is used in such expressions as the following:

Goût américain, denotes a fairly sweet wine, chiefly champagne.

Goût anglais, denotes a dry wine, chiefly champagne.

Goût de bois, meaning *woody*, tainted by too long a stay in cask.

Bon goût, pleasant to the taste.

Goût de bouchon, corky.

Goût d'évent, flat, stale, dumb, dead.

Goût de ferment, still fermenting, not ready to drink.

Goût français, denotes a very sweet champagne.

Franc de goût, perfectly clean on the nose and palate.

Mauvais goût, wrong, not fit to drink.

Goût de moisi, musty, foul.

Goût de paille, wet straw stink, foul.

Goût de pierre à fusil, a flinty and not unpleasant after-taste.

Goût de piqué, pricked, on the way to the vinegar tub.

Goût de rancio, bottle-stink; some people enjoy it, others dislike it.

Goût de taille, rasping (*taille* being the last pressing of the grapes).

Goût de terroir, a somewhat assertive quality, usually highly appreciated locally, where the wine is made, but not so much to the taste of the unbiased.

GRAACH

One of the more important wine-producing parishes of the Middle Moselle, in the Berncastel district. Fine white wines. Best vineyards: *Domprobst, Himmelreich, Abtsberg, Goldwingert, Münzlay, Rosenberg* and *Josefshöfer*.

GRADIGNAN

A Commune of the Graves district 9 k. SSW. of Bordeaux, the vineyards of which average some 300 tuns of claret and 25 tuns of white wine. The only large Estate is *Château Laurenzane* (average 100 tuns claret), and other well-known growths are *Châteaux Lafon, Moulerens* and *Lange*.

GRAND MARNIER

A brand of French curaçao marketed by Marnier Lapostolle under two distinct labels: *Cordon Rouge* and *Cordon Jaune*. The first is not so sweet as the second, and the second, which is very sweet, is not so strong in alcohol as the first.

GRAND-PUY-DUCASSE, Château
GRAND-PUY-LACOSTE, Château

Two of the Fifth Growths of the Médoc (Pauillac). Both belonged to the same owner, Bertrand de Jehan, until 1587, when the property was divided between his two daughters: the one, who had two-thirds of the vines, married a Mr de Saint-Guirons, and one of her daughters married a Mr Lacoste. This part of Grand-Puy was known as *Château Saint Guirons* up to the beginning of the nineteenth century, and as *Grand-Puy-Lacoste* since then. Jehan's other daughter sold her third of the vineyards to a Mr Ducasse, and the wine thereof was sold as *Château Ducasse*, up to the beginning of the nineteenth century, when the name was hyphenated with the original *Grand-Puy*. Its average is 40 tuns claret; that of *Grand-Puy-Lacoste* 120 tuns.

GRAND SAINT BERNARD,
Liqueur du

A Swiss liqueur, pale green, sweetened with honey, flavoured with leaves, flowers and seeds locally grown.

GRANDS ECHÉZEAUX

The finest wine of the Commune of *Flagey-Echézeaux (Côte d'Or)*. The *Grands Echézeaux* vineyards cover 22 acres and produce some excellent red burgundy.

GRANJO

A Portuguese white wine of the Sauternes type.

GRAPES

The fruit of the Vine.

(*a*) A bunch of grapes. Latin, *Botrus*. Italian, *Grappolo*. Spanish, *Racimo*. Portuguese, *Cacho*. French, *Grappe, Raisins*.

(*b*) The stalk of a bunch of grapes. Latin, *Scapus*. Italian, *Raspo*. Spanish, *Raspa*. Portuguese, *Engaco*. French, *Rafle*.

(*c*) The grape berries. Latin, *Uva*. Italian, *Uva*. Spanish, *Uva*. Portuguese, *Uva*. French, *Raisins*.

(*d*) What is left of the grapes after they have been pressed and their juice drawn, i.e. husks. Latin, *Vinacea*. Italian, *Vinaccio*. Spanish, *Orujo*. Portuguese, *Bagaco*. French, *Marc*.

(*e*) Grape-stones or pips. Latin, *Vinaceum*. Italian, *Vinacciuolo*. Spanish, *Granuja*. Portuguese, *Bagulho, Grainha*. French, *Pépins*.

GRAPPA

A crude Italian spirit distilled from the husks – the skins, pips and stalks of the grapes – after they have been pressed and the wine made.

GRAVES

The wines of Graves, when not otherwise qualified, are the wines from one of the most important wine-producing districts of the Gironde, a district which begins just outside

Bordeaux, extends about 5½ miles to the west and some 13 miles to the south. The Graves district produces both red and white wines, the red wines being of higher quality than the white, although the white are better known than the red under the name of Graves. There are 35 parishes or 'Communes' within the Graves district. Their average yield is half a million gallons of very fine red wine, a million and a half of fair wines and a quarter of a million gallons red wines of moderate quality. The Communes of Graves which produce the best wines are those of *Pessac, Léognan, Martillac, Villenave d'Ornon* and *Mérignac*.

After *Château Haut Brion*, the best-known Châteaux of the Graves district are: *La Mission Haut-Brion, Pape-Clément, Bellegrave, Phénix-Haut-Brion*, all in the Commune of Pessac. *Haut-Bailly, Malartic-Lagravière, Domaine de Chevalier, Haut-Brion-Larrivet, Carbonnieux, Haut-Gardère*, all in the Commune of Léognan. *Smith-Haut-Lafitte, de Lagarde, Ferrand* and *Latour* in the Commune of Martillac. *Carbonnieux* and *Pontac-Monplaisir* in the Commune of Villenave d'Ornon. *Bon-Air, La Tour-du-Pape* and *Pique-Caillou*, in the Commune of Mérignac. *La-Tour-Haut-Brion*, in the Commune of Talence.

GRAVES DE SAINT EMILION

The name given to a small district of the Saint-Emilion vinelands, the soil of which differs from that of other Saint-Emilion vineyards, being more gravelly. The finest wine of the *Graves de Saint-Emilion* is that of *Château Cheval Blanc*. Other famous Estates of this district are: *Château* and *Domaine Figeac, Châteaux La Tour-Figeac, La Tour-du-Pin Figeac, Lamarzelle, La Dominique, Grand-Barrail-Lamarzelle-Figeac* and *Ripeau*. Also *Château Chauvin*.

GRECO DI GERACE

An agreeably dry white wine made from Greco grapes grown in the vineyards of Gerace, in Calabria (Italy).

GREECE

Considerable quantities of wine have been made in Greece for a far longer time than in any other part of the world, China excepted. Much wine is still being produced in Greece, but none of outstanding merit. The largest wine-producing districts of Greece, in order of importance are: *Messinia, Attica, Achaia, Arcadia* and *Argolido-Korinthos*. The best Greek wines are the sweet wines of *Samos, Santorin, Patras* and *Cephalonia*. The best-known are the *Mavrodaphne* and the *Agios Georgios*, a sweet dessert wine, dark red like vintage port.

GREEK WINE

Wine from Greek vineyards. The Romans used to give the name of Greek or Greekish wine to an Italian wine which was sweet and potent.

Achilles. I'll heat his blood with Greekish wine to-night.—*Troilus and Cressida*, Act V, Scene i.

GRENACHE

A sweetish red or tawny dessert wine from the Pyrénées (Roussillon), made chiefly in the *Banyuls* district from Grenache grapes.

GRENADINE

A *sirop* of liquid form of sugar, bright red in colour, entirely free from any trace of alcohol. It is used as a sweetening agent in *Cocktails* or with *Bitters*.

GRIGNOLINO

A red wine of no great distinction but none the less greatly prized locally; it is made in various parts of Piedmont from Grignolino grapes.

GRUAUD-LAROSE, Château

A Second Growth of the Médoc (Saint-Julien). The vineyard was planted in 1757 by a Mr. Gruaud, whose heir, M. de Larose, added, in 1778, his name to that of Gruaud, as did le Baron Sarget when he bought the estate in 1812. In 1867 nearly half the vineyards were ceded to Messrs. de Bethmann and Faure whose heirs have acquired the Sarget part of the vineyard, so that now there is again but one *Château Gruaud-Larose* instead of two; *Gruaud-Larose-Sarget* and *Gruaud-Larose-Faure*.

GRUMELLO

One of the less distinguished of the Valtellina red table wines. (Lombardy.)

GRÜNHÄUSER

One of the finest white wines of the Ruwer Valley (Trier district). The best vineyard of *Mertesdorf-Grünhaus* is *Herrenberg*, and its wine is sold under the name of *Maximin Grünhäuser Herrenberg*. Another good vineyard is *Lorenzberg*.

GUINNESS

A name which several generations of the Guinness family have rendered synonymous with *Stout* (q.v.) all the world over.

GUIRAUD, Château

One of the First Growths of Sauternes; it was formerly known as *Château Bayle*. Average 80 tuns white wine.

GUMPOLDSKIRCHNER

One of the best-known Austrian wines chiefly red; the white is generally sold a

Gumpoldskirchner Steinwein, Himmelreich or
Goldtroepchen.

GUNDERSHEIM (Rhine-Hesse)
Worms district. White wine. Best vineyards:
Hunsrück, Höllenbrand, Bruchert, Hackgraben.

GUNTERSBLUM (Rhine-Hesse)
Oppenheim district. White wine. Best vineyards: *Steinberg, Vögelsgärten* and *Steig.*

GYÖNGYOS
Red and white table wines and also sparkling
wines (Hungary).

HAARDT
One of the wine-producing townships of
the Palatinate (Dürkheim district). Best
vineyards: *Letten, Schlossberg* and *Lehmgrube.*
White wines.

HALBROT
The Swiss equivalent of the German *Schiller-
wein*; it applies to beverage wines made of
both black and white grapes, the colour of
the wine being somewhat like that of raspberry vinegar.

HALLAUER
The best-known of the *Landweine*, the red
wines produced in the eastern Cantons of
Switzerland, from the village of Hallau, in
the Schaffhausen district.

HALLGARTEN
One of the more important wine-producing
townships of the Rhinegau. White wines of
fine quality. Best vineyards: *Schönhell, Deitels-
berg* and *Würzgarten.*

HAMBACH
(Palatinate.) Neustadt district. White wines.
Best vineyards: *Grain, Kirchberg* and *Schloss-
berg.*

HATTENHEIMER
One of the finest white wines of the Rhein-
gau. The most famous of the Hattenheim
vineyards are those of the *Kloster Eberbach*,
which produce the renowned *Steinberg*. Other
fine vineyards are those named *Engelmannsberg, Nussbrunnen, Wisselbrunnen. Rheinharts-
hausen*, where Prince Friedrich Henry of
Prussia had the most up-to-date wine-presses
and cellarage, is on the outskirts of *Hattenheim.*

HAUT-BAGES, Château
One of the Fifth Growths of the Médoc
(Pauillac); it belonged originally to a Mr
Libéral and was known for a long time
under the names of *Châteaux Libéral* and
Haut-Bages-Libéral. Average 40 tuns claret.

HAUT-BARSAC
That part of the Commune of Barsac which
lies furthest from the River Garonne, and
produces white wines of finer quality than
those of the vineyards nearer the Garonne
or *Bas-Barsac.*

HAUT-BENAUGE
A wine-producing district of the Gironde,
SSE. of Bordeaux, on the right bank of the
Garonne, adjoining *Langoiran*, comprising
nine Communes: *d'Arbis, Cantois, Escoussans,
Gornac, Ladaux, Mourens, Soulignac, Saint-
Pierre-de-Bat* and *Targon*. This district pro-
duces mostly white wines, similar to those of
Langoiran, as well as some red beverage
wines.

HAUT-BOMMES
A name which has been adopted for the
white wines of seven of the vineyards of
Bommes. There is also a *Château Haut-
Bommes* in the commune of Bommes: its
average yield is 10 tons of Sauternes wine.

HAUT BRION, Château
The most famous Growth of the Graves
district of the Gironde; it is situated in the
Commune of Pessac, at the very gates of
Bordeaux, and it ranks with Châteaux Lafite,
Latour and Margaux, the three First
Growths of the Médoc. The wines of Haut
Brion have been enjoyed in England ever
since the seventeenth century, but were
known under different phonetic spellings
such as Obrian, Hobrien, d'Aubrion, etc.
The average of Haut Brion is 100 tuns claret.
There is also a small quantity of white wine
made at this Château.

HAUT-PEYRAGUEY, Clos
One of the First Growths of Sauternes, in
the Commune of Bommes. (15 tuns average.)

HAUT-SAUTERNES
A commercial name for sweet white wines
of no particular merit but supposed to be a
little better – and dearer – than the similar
type of wine sold merely as *Sauternes*. It does
not correspond to any geographical or ad-
ministrative division of the Sauternes Commune.

HAWTHORN WINE
Pour one gallon of water on four double
handfuls of hawthorn flowers. Let it stand
for two days. Strain liquor off, boil and pour
again on same flowers. Let it stand two more
days. Again strain and add 3 lb. moist sugar
to the gallon and boil together 20 minutes.
Put back in pansion (? pancheon – it is a
large earthenware vessel with wide open
top: it was the local name in Notts) with
piece of toast with one tablespoon of yeast

on it to the gallon. Let stand one day, then put in barrel, and let it be till it has done working (about a fortnight or more); then lightly bung barrel and bottle in three or four months. (From *Lady Barker's grandmother's Mss. recipe book*.)

HEDDESHEIM
Nahe Valley. Kreuznach district. White wines. Best vineyards: *Kilb, Steingerüst, Honigberg, Goldloch, Höll* and *Scharlachberg*.

HERB TEAS
Hot drinks made with various herbs, flowers and seeds, most of them pleasant enough to taste, and usually highly-sweetened, but chiefly brewed for their real or supposed medicinal value. The principal *Herb Teas* were – and still are:

Sage Tea, aromatic and astringent properties.
Mint Tea, digestive and anti-spasmodic.
Pennyroyal Tea, a tonic.
Tansy Tea, good for colic and gout.
Fennel Leaves Tea, stimulates the kidneys.
Dillwater Tea, abates wind.
Marigold Flowers Tea good for the liver.
Rue Tea excites the circulation of the blood.
Hyssop Tea, good in chronic catarrhs and disorders of the chest.
Rosemary Tea, a cure for headaches.
Balm Tea, a favourite in cases of fever.
Camomile Tea, very aromatic and a fine tonic.

HERMITAGE
The red and white wines which are entitled to the name *Hermitage* are those from the vineyards which cover three sides of the hill rising sharply from the little town of Tain, on the left bank of the river Rhône, some distance south of Lyons and north of Avignon, opposite Tournon. Among the best vineyards of the Coteau de l'Hermitage are *La Sizer, La Chapelle Les Bessards* (red wines), and *Les Recoulles, Les Murets* and *Chante-Alouette* (white wines).

HIGHBALL
A 'long' drink of diluted spirits, usually whisky, served with cracked ice in a large, heavy tumbler, sometimes with a little glass stick for stirring.

When not otherwise qualified, a *Highball* is understood to be whisky, ice and syphon. There are *Bourbon, Brandy, Gin, Rye Highballs* made in a similar way with these different spirits. There are also less orthodox *Highballs* such as the:

Bermuda Highball: One-third brandy; one-third gin; one-third French vermouth.
Cascade Highball: Half Italian vermouth; half crème de cassis.

Pompier Highball: Half French vermouth; half crème de cassis.

HIPPOCRAS
One of the most popular forms of aromatized and spiced wines during the Middle Ages and even long after. There is every reason to believe that the basis of Hippocras was sour or pricked wine, of which there must have been an embarrassingly large quantity at a time when wine was kept on ullage, in casks, or in ill-stoppered bottles before the use of cork for stoppers. Such wine being heavily sweetened with honey and flavoured with herbs and spices was then filtered through a woollen bag, known as Hippocrates sleeve, hence the name *Hippocras*, often written *Ipocras* or *Ypocras*.

HOCHHEIM
At the extreme limit (south) of the Rhinegau, not far from Wiesbaden, on the River Main, close to where it joins the Rhine. The wines of Hochheim are believed to be responsible for the name 'Hock', which replaced, in England, the old appellation of 'Rhenish' for all Rhine wines. Best vineyards of Hochheim: *Domdechaney, Kirchenstück, Stein, Falkenberg, Daubhaus, Hölle*.

HOCK
Although no actual evidence has as yet come to light to place beyond all doubt the fact that the name Hock is derived from Hochheim, a village surrounded by vineyards, upon the right bank of the River Main, close to where it flows into the Rhine, such is the generally accepted origin of the name hock, a name which has completely replaced, in England, the older name 'Rhenish'. Under the designation 'Hock' are included the wines of the Rhinegau, Rhine-Hesse, Palatinate, Nahe Valley and Franconia. Hocks are bottled in red bottles, brown or brick red, whilst Moselles are bottled in green or blue-green bottles.

HOLLANDS
The name of a very distinctive type of *Gin*, made in Holland. Originally the Dutch used to crush the juniper berries and ferment their juice, which they distilled after. Now *Hollands* is distilled from a mash of barley malt mixed with ground juniper (or equivalent flavouring agent), and it is distilled at a much lower strength than *London Gin* or *American Gin*, so that it has a flavour of its own, greatly valued by those who are accustomed to it, but too pronounced for *Hollands* to be used in the mixing of cocktails and other drinks, where its assertiveness would not be welcome.

HOMER

The Father of Poetry was a true son of Bacchus, so much so that Horace dared call him 'vinosus Homerus' (Epist. xix. Lib. I, v. 6). Homer describes many wines in both the Iliad and Odyssey, as 'sweet', 'honey-sweet', 'sweet to the tongue', 'life-giving', 'mirth-provoking', 'worthy of the gods', 'beverage divine', etc.

HORACE (68–8 B.C.)

The bouquet of wine permeates practically the whole of Horace's poetry. The 19th Ode of the Second Book of Odes, *In Bacchum*, which begins with 'Bacchum in remotis', is assuredly one of his finest; and so is the 25th Ode of the Third Book, *Ad Bacchum*, which begins thus:

Quo me Bacche, rapis tui
Plenum?

Better-known, however, is the 37th Ode of the First Book, calling upon the Romans to rejoice at the news of Cleopatra's death:

Nunc est bibendum!
(Now is the time to drink!)

In many of his Odes, Horace sings the praises of the various Latin and Greek wines, chiefly the wines of Caecuba and Falernum, Chios and Lesbos.

The wine of Caecuba appears to have been the favourite wine of Horace:

Festo quid potius die
Neptuni faciam? Prome reconditum,
Lyde, strenua Caecubum.
　　　　　　Od. XXVIII, Lib. III, vv. 1–3.

(What is there for me to do on this Neptune's feast? Lydee, quickly let us have your best Caecuban wine.)

Horace admitted that the wines of Lesbos were the most fashionable of all Greek wines, but he preferred the wines of Chios:

Quo Chium pretio cadum
Mercemur ...
　　　　　　Od. XIX, Lib. III, v. 5.

But he liked the wines of Italy better than those of the Greek Archipelago: thus, addressing the serving boy, he asks that his glass be filled with wines of Chios or of Lesbos, then, thinking better of it, he adds: 'Give me rather some Caecuba wine which tones up the heart':

Capaciores affer huc, puer, scyphos,
Et Chia vina, aut Lesbia:
Vel, quod fluentem nauseam cöerceat,
Metire nobis Caecubum.
　　　　　　Epod. IX, vv. 33–36.

HORSE'S NECK

Peel a lemon in a long string. Leaving one end hanging over the rim of a large tumbler, anchor the other with a lump of ice. Add two dashes of lemon juice, a good measure of brandy and fill with ginger ale.

HÖRSTEIN

One of the townships of Franconia in the Alzenau district, noted for its white wines. Best vineyards: *Abtsberg, Käfernberg, Langenberg.*

HOSPICES DE BEAUJEU

Some of the best red wines of the Beaujolais Hills are sold under this name and for the benefit of the Beaujeu Hospital: the best of them is the *Cuvée de la Grange Charton.*

HOSPICES DE BEAUNE

A home for the aged and poor, founded in the fifteenth century at Beaune, in Burgundy. Its chief income has been for centuries past, and still is, the sale of the wines from the vineyards bequeathed from time to time to the Hospices. The wines of the Hospices are sold by auction every year. Genuine 'Hospices de Beaune' wines of a good vintage should always bear the name of the *Cuvée,* that is to say the name of the Donor of the vineyard from which the wine offered for sale was made; as well as the name of the Commune where such vineyards are situated. Thus:

RED WINES

Cuvées	Communes
Bétault	Beaune
Billardet	Pommard
Blondeau	Volnay
Boillot	Auxey-Duresses
Brunet	Beaune
Charlotte Dumay	Corton
Clos des Avaux	Beaune
Cyrot	Savigny
Dames de la Charité	Pommard
Dames Hospitalières	Beaune
Docteur Peste	Corton
Du Bay-Peste	Savigny-Vergelesses
Estienne	Beaune
Forneret	Savigny-Vergelesses
Fouquerand	Savigny-Vergelesses
Gauvain	Meursault-Santenots
Guigone de Salins	Beaune
Henri Gélicot	Meursault
Jacques Lebelin	Monthélie
Jehan de Massol	Meursault-Santenots
Nicola Rollin	Beaune
Rousseau-Deslandes	Beaune

WHITE WINES

Albert Grivault	Meursault-Charmes
Baudot	Meursault
De Bahezre de Lanlay	Meursault-Charmes
Goureau	Meursault
Jehean Humblot	Meursault
Loppin	Meursault

HRAD
The best wine of Bzenee, one of the more important wine-producing parishes of Czechoslovakia.

HUCKLE-MY-BUFF
Sussex slang for beer, eggs and brandy mixed. (*Cooper's Sussex Glossary.*) Farmer and Henley's *Dictionary of Slang* calls *Huckle-my-but*, 'beer, egg and brandy made hot.'

HUNGARY
Besides *Tokay*, the finest Hungarian wine, Hungary produces a great variety of red and white table wines, as well as many liqueurs and spirits. The more popular table wines are: *Red*: *Egri Bikaver*, *Egri Kadarka*. *White*: *Apczer*.

Among the dessert wines other than *Tokay*, the best known are the white *Debroë Hárslevelü*.

HUNYADI JANOS
A registered brand of Hungarian mineral water with valuable aperient properties.

HYDROMEL
Primarily honey diluted in water, with herbs and spices added according to taste and available supplies.

ILES DE LA GIRONDE
The principal vineyards of the islands in the course of the River Gironde are:

Ile Bouchard, opposite Blaye; average 400 tuns claret and 200 tuns white wine per annum.

Ile Fumadelle, Commune of Soussans, average 200 tuns claret.

Ile Margaux, average 200 tuns claret.

Ile du Nord, average 1,500 tuns claret.

Ile Nouvelle, also called *Ile sanspain*, average 450 tuns claret and 50 tuns white wine.

Ile Patiras, average 300 tuns claret and 200 tuns white wine.

Ile Verte, average 750 tuns claret and 175 tuns white wine.

ILLATS
A Commune of the Gironde 34 k. SSE. of Bordeaux, the vineyards of which produce a little red beverage wine for local consumption, and more as well as better white wines, similar to those of *Cérons* and usually sold under that name.

IMPÉRIALE
The name given to an outsize glass bottle, made in France, of green glass, for bottling fine clarets which are intended for long keeping. An *Impériale* should hold at least eight bottles of wine, allowing for the sediment; eight and a half bottles are commonly decanted from an *Impériale*, and occasionally up to nearly nine bottles.

IMPERIAL POP
Take 3 oz. of cream of tartar, 1 oz. of bruised ginger, 1½ lb. of white sugar, 1 oz. of lemon juice, and pour 1½ gallon of boiling water on them; add two tablespoonfuls of yeast. Mix, bottle, and tie down the corks as usual.—F.F.

INFERNO
One of the less distinguished of the Valtellina red table wines. (Lombardy.)

IPHOFEN
One of the wine-producing townships of Franconia (Scheinfeld district). White wines. Best vineyards: *Julius-Echter-Berg*, *Kronsberg*, *Pfaffensteig*.

IRISH WHISKEY
A grain spirit distilled from malted barley, and in pot stills. The chief difference between Irish and Scotch whiskies is one of flavour; it is due to the fact that, in Ireland, the malt is dried in a kiln which has a solid floor, so that the smoke from the fuel used does not come in contact with the grain, whereas, in Scotland, the malt is 'smoke-cured'.

Irish whiskey is sold at a much higher strength than any post-war Scotch whisky.

IROULÉGUY
One of the few red wines of the Basque country to possess real merit; it is a fairly heady wine, with a pleasing bouquet, rather light in colour but of higher alcoholic strength than one expects at first meeting. It is made some little distance from Bayonne, on the French side of the Pyrenees.

ISCHIA
A small island in the Bay of Naples; its vineyards produce a dry table wine (white) which is sold under the name of Capri, another island in the Bay of Naples.

ISSAN, Château d'
Third Growth of the Médoc (Cantenac). This Estate, one of the most ancient of the Médoc, was noted for the excellence of its red wine up to the 1929 vintage. After the three bad vintages 1930–32 its vines were done away with and the land given up to farming, but some of the vineyards have since been replanted.

ITALY
Italy produces more wine than any other country, France excepted: in good years, Italy's contribution to the relief of the thirst of man reaches a billion gallons. And wine

has been made by the people of Italy longer than by any other people, the Greeks excepted. But much of the wine of Italy is poor wine, made from their own grapes by poor people for their poor selves only. There are, however, many other wines made in all parts of Italy which are very fine wines indeed, and there are even more which, although merely from middling to fair in quality, are not only acceptable but enjoyable when drunk under favourable conditions, in sight of their native vineyards, for instance, and partnered with the food of the country.

The best table wines of Italy come from the north, from Piedmont (Turin), Lombardy (Milan) and the Tyrolese hinterland of the Venetian province; also from the 'Midlands' of the Peninsula, Tuscany (Florence), Umbria (Orvieto), and the Latium (Rome). Sweet wines are made almost everywhere, but the best come from the south, from Campania (Naples), Calabria (Reggio), as well as the islands of Sicily and Sardinia, Lipari, Capri, Ischia, Elba, and Pantellaria.

JAMAICA RUM
Rum distilled from molasses in the island of Jamaica. It is one of the best-known and one of the commercially most important of cane rums. It is distilled at a comparatively low strength so that it has a very pungent 'rummy' flavour. Its colour varies, with the proportion of caramel used, from a light gold to mahogany.

JEREZ DE LA FRONTERA
The hub of the sherry trade, in Andalucia, in the extreme south of Spain. It is called Xérès in French, a name which is used also for the wine of Jerez, *Sherry*.

JEROBOAM
In champagne the name is given to a double magnum, a large bottle holding the equivalent of four ordinary bottles, or 3.20 litres. In England the name is used for a very large bottle, one that may be larger than a double magnum. Professor George Saintsbury, in *Notes on a Cellar Book*, gives six bottles as the right contents of a *Jeroboam*.

JEROPIGA
See *Geropiga*.

JIGGER
An American barman's name for a small measure of spirits: 1½ liquid oz.

JINGLE
Roast three apples, grate some nutmeg over them, add sugar to taste, and place in a quart jug with some slices of toasted plum cake; make some ale hot and fill up the jug, then serve.—F.F.

JOHANNISBERG
One of the most famous growths of the Rhinegau, between Winkel and Geisenheim, but higher up the hill, with a beautiful view over the Rhine and Rhine-Hesse beyond.

The best wines of Johannisberg are the best of the *Schloss Johannisberg*, and these are sold under different labels according to a carefully graded scale of excellence, as follows:

1. Fürst v. Metternichscher *Cabinet* Spätlese.

2. Fürst v. Metternichscher *Cabinet* Auslese.

3. Fürst v. Metternichscher *Original Abfüllung* Auslese.

4. Fürst v. Metternichscher *Original Abfüllung* (not Auslese).

5. *Schloss Johannisberg*. Wachstum Fürst v. Metternich.

Next to the *Schloss* comes the *Klaus Johannisberg*, a growth always bearing the name of one of the proprietors among whom it is divided, such as the Royal Prussian Domains, Graf Schönborn, Kommerzierat Krayer Erden, etc.

The next best vineyards are known as Ernebringer, Kochsberg, Schlossberg and Hölle.

Plain *Johannisberg*, with the name of a grower and whether 'Auslese' or not, is never one of the best wines of Johannisberg, whilst the name *Dorf Johannisberg* usually is that of the worst wine of the district.

JOHANNISBERG (Vaud)
One of the best white wines of Switzerland, from vineyards of the Lavaux ridge: its best-known vineyard is the *Brule-Fer Johannisberg*.

JOIGNY
One of the oldest towns of the Yonne Department (Lower Burgundy), the vineyards of which produce much red and white wines of no outstanding merit. The best-known wine of Joigny is the *Vin gris* of the Côte St. Jacques, a wine which one occasionally sees listed in some Paris restaurants.

JONSON, Ben
Ben Jonson had a deep-rooted and oft-watered faith in the virtue of wine, more particularly Sack. Of Spenser's verses he liked most those in praise of wine, and he astonished a hard-drinking society by the depth and breadth of his potations. Aubrey says of him: 'He would many times exceed in drink: Canarie was his beloved liquor, then he would tumble home to bed; and when he had thoroughly perspired, then to studie'.

JORUM

A half-pint measure, named after Joram, 'who brought with him vessels of silver and vessels of gold, and vessels of brass' (2 Samuel, VIII, 10).

JULEP

The name, derived from the Persian *Julap* (a sweetened draught), of an old English favourite among *Cups*, which is now more popular in the United States than in the British Isles. *Julep* is said to come from the Southern States and to have been 'introduced' by Captain Marryatt in England, but that is not so, as Milton's lines clearly prove:

...'Behold this cordial Julep here,
  That foams and dances in his crystal
    bounds,
With spirits of balm and fragrant
    syrups mix'd.'

Applejack Julep. Three fresh mint sprigs, half teaspoon powdered sugar, one jigger *Applejack*. Crush leaves from one mint sprig in glass, cover with sugar, stir, and let sugar dissolve. Add applejack and fill glass with finely cracked ice. Stir until glass is frosted. Decorate with remaining mint sprigs.—A.C.

Brandy Julep. Fill the glasses or jug with finely cracked or shaved ice. For each person allow one port glass of cognac. Bruise several sprigs of mint with half a teaspoonful of sugar for each person, and strain into the glass or jug. Add a dash of rum for each glass, dress with fruit and a few sprigs of mint which have been moistened and dipped in sugar. Serve with straws.—N.T.A.

Mint Julep. Crush one lump of sugar at the bottom of a tall glass. Add half a dozen small sprigs of mint, which should first be lightly twisted between the fingers to break the skin of the leaves. Cover with whisky and allow to stand for 10 minutes. Then pour in balance of whisky (to make a long drink a full whisky glass should be used), fill the glass with finely-crushed ice and stir rapidly with a spoon until the outside of the glass is frosted. Served garnished with mint sprigs. The best Maryland Juleps are made with old rye. *Frederic Arnold Kummer, Baltimore.*—F.P.S.

Ben Clark Mint Julep. Crush in bottom of each glass five large crisp mint leaves, with a dash of sugar syrup. Let stand 15 minutes, if possible, to steep, after adding a generous shot of good bourbon whisky. Pack tight into each glass shaved ice, dried in towel. Stir gently until glass is frosted. Decorate with mint sprig and serve, wrapping bottom of glass in paper napkin to catch sweat.—A.C.

Rum Julep. Dissolve three tablespoonfuls of soft sugar in a little water and add a few sprigs of mint. Let this soak until the flavour of the mint is extracted, and then strain this juice into a tumbler. Add a brandy glass of rum, one or two cherries, a slice of tangerine and any other small fruits that are in season. Fill up the glass with finely-crushed ice and serve with straws.—N.T.A.

JULIÉNAS

One of the Beaujolais wine-producing Communes which is responsible for some of the best red wines of the Rhône Département. One of its best vineyards is that of *Château des Capitans*.

JURA

Many good wines are made from grapes grown upon the lower slopes of the Jura Mountains facing the Burgundian plains, but the two which have attained the greatest measure of fame are those of *Arbois* and *Poligny*, towards the east, and, further west, the wine made near Lons-le-Saulnier and known as *Château-Chalon*.

JURANÇON

A luscious, orange-coloured 'dessert' wine made from over-ripe grapes from vineyards (2,500 acres) near Pau. *Jurançon* is rarely obtainable commercially, as there is so little made.

JUVENAL, *c.* A.D. 60–130

Juvenal has left us a not too flattering picture of the Roman Society of his day: he watched his contemporaries with a critical eye and he showed himself far more indulgent of the wines they drank than of the life they led.

Juvenal was particularly partial to the wines of Albano, the *vinum Albanum* from the Roman hills, of which Pliny had but a poor opinion. But the chief interest of Juvenal's *Satyrae* lies in his descriptions of the table manners and drinking customs of his contemporaries; how, for instance, the host would provide his guests with hot or cold water to add to the wine he gave them, should they ask for either (*Satyrae* V).

One of the most amusing skits on the table manners of Imperial Rome is in the same *Satyrae* in which Juvenal describes the disgust of the guests, who had to be content with the most horrible wines, served to them in horrible glasses, common, thick glasses, cracked or chipped, whilst their host and his special friends at the top table were drinking rare vintages in the most exquisitely chiselled cups of gold or silver. (See *Satyrae* V, vv. 30–48).

KALAVRYTA

One of the red wines of Morea (Greece).

KALLSTADT (Palatinate)

Bad-Dürkheim district. Both red and white

wines. Best vineyards: *Nill, Saumagen, Kronenberg, Steinacker.*

KALMUTH
Formerly one of the finest ecclesiastical vineyards of the River Main valley, near Homburg.

KALTERERSEEWEIN
See *Caldaro, Lago di.*

KECSKEMÉT
One of the principal white-wine-producing districts of Hungary. The most renowned wines of this district are the Furmint Edes and Leanika.

KELLERABFÜLLUNG
German for 'Cellar Bottling', meaning bottled at the estate.

KELLERABZUG
German for 'Bottled at the Cellar of ... ', followed by the name of the grower, estate, or shipper.

KEPHESIA
The vine-growing district of Attica, which produces some of the best red and white wines of Greece.

KIEDRICH
One of the smaller wine-producing parts of the Rhinegau, near Eltville. White wine only. Best vineyards: *Gräfenberg* and *Sandgrub,* the estate of Graf Eltz.

KIRSCH. KIRSCHWASSER
A very popular spirit distilled chiefly in Germany, Alsace and Switzerland from the fermented juice of small, black and very juicy cherries which grow in a wild state in the Black Forest, the Vosges and other mountains. The *Schwartzwalder Kirschwasser (Black Forest Cherry Brandy)* has a world-wide reputation for excellence; so has the *Kirsch* of Alsace. *Kirsch* is always pure white: it is matured in demijohns, not in wooden casks from which it would extract some colouring matter.

KIRSEBOER LIQUEUR
The Danish name of the *Cherry Brandy* produced by the firm of Peter F. Heering, of Copenhagen.

KIRWAN, Château
Third Growth of the Médoc (Cantenac). Average 100 tuns claret per annum. The vineyards of Kirwan adjoin those of *Château Margaux* and *Brane-Cantenac.*

KISSINGEN WATER
A natural mineral water with marked medicinal properties. It is sparkling, saline and slightly astringent; its spring is in Bavaria.

KLEVNER
The name of a white grape grown in Alsace from which a white wine is made, which is sold under the same name, usually coupled with the name of the vineyard where it came from, or else that of the owner thereof.

KNIPPERLÉ
The name of a white grape grown in Alsace for the making of white wines, which are sold under the same name usually coupled with the name either of the vineyard where the wine came from, or that of the owner thereof.

KOBERNER
One of the good white wines of the Moselle Valley close to Coblence. The best vineyards of Kobern are *Uhlen, Nonnenberg* and *Weissenberg.*

KÖNIGSBACH (Palatinate)
Neustadt district. One of the finest growths of the Palatinate. Best vineyards: *Idig, Mühlweg, Hinterwiese* and *Haag.*

KREUZNACH, Bad
The most important wine-producing centre of the Nahe Valley. Mostly white wines. Best white wines vineyards: *Kronenberg, Narrenkappe, Mönchberg, Brückes, Krötenpfuhl* and *St. Martin.*

KUCHELBERGER
The best red table wine of Merano in the Italian Tyrol.

KUMMEL
One of the most popular of all liqueurs, with definite digestive properties. It has been made in Holland by Erven Lucas Bols and his successors since 1575, but Mentzendorff's *Kummel* from Riga, and *Gilka Kummel* from Berlin, used to be even more universally popular than the Dutch *Kummel. Kummel* has as its basis some highly distilled or almost neutral spirit, sometimes distilled from grain, sometimes from potatoes, rarely if ever from wine. It is flavoured with caraway seeds and cumin, to which it owes its digestive qualities. It is more or less sweetened, according to the formulae used for different brands, but is always pure white.

KVASS
A very refreshing Russian beverage which is made in many Russian households about once a week.
'With eight quarts water take 1½ lb. malt, 1 lb. rye flour, 1½ lb. sugar, ⅛ of a lb. mint leaves, half pepper pod, and half cake of yeast. Mix the malt and flour with boiling water and make a thick dough. Put into barely warm oven, and leave for the night.

Next day dilute dough with eight quarts boiling water and pour into a wooden tub. Let stand for 12 hours, then pass through a cloth. Pour one quart into an enamel saucepan, put on fire, add 1½ lb. sugar and an infusion made with the mint leaves (resembling weak tea). Boil once, then take off fire, cool until just warm, and add the yeast previously diluted with one cup of this same warm liquid. Let stand in warm place until it begins to ferment; then pour into the rest of the kvass in the wooden tub, and let stand until bubbles appear. Prepare clean bottles, putting one malaga raisin into each; pour in the kvass, cork the bottles, tie the corks with string to the necks of the bottles, and keep in warm place for a day or two. Then put in a cold cellar.'—R.C.B.

LABARDE
A Commune of the Médoc, 24 k. NW. of Bordeaux. Its best wines are those of *Château Giscours* and *Dauzac*. Then those of *Châteaux Rosemont, Labarde, Siran* and *Conseillant*; they average 177 tuns of claret per annum. The red wines of *Labarde* have acquired by long usage the right to be sold under the better-known name of the neighbouring Commune of *Margaux*.

LA BRÈDE
A Commune of the Graves district, 19 k. S. of Bordeaux; its vineyards produce a fair quantity of white wines and some red wines as well, none of them of particular merit. The most interesting Château of the Commune is *Château de la Brède*, Montesquieu's old home; its vineyards produce some 10 tuns of white wine. *Château Guillaumont* produces on an average 10 tuns of claret and 40 of white wines.

LAFITE, Château
One of the three First Growths of the Médoc (Pauillac). Since 1868, when it was purchased by Baron James de Rothschild, it has also been known as *Château Lafite-Rothschild*. Average 180 tuns claret, of which 150 'Premier Vin', 15 tuns 'Deuxième Vin' and 15 tuns sold as *Vin des Carruades*. Earliest 'Château bottling' was that of the 1846 vintage. The spelling of *Lafite* with two *f*'s and two *t*'s instead of one occurs in old records and even on old labels, but all forms are now obsolete other than *Lafite*. There are other Châteaux in the Gironde, however, bearing the same name with different spelling, such as *Châteaux Laffite* (Yvrac) and *Laffitte-Cantegric* (Listrac); *Laffitte* (Bégadan) and *Laffitte-Saint-Estèphe* (St.-Estèphe); *Cru Lafite* (Entre-deux-Mers), *Lafitte-Canteloup* (Ludon); *Clos Lafitte* (Bordeaux-Bacalan), *A Lafitte* (Entre-deux-Mers), *Château Lafitte-Bordeaux* and *Lafitte-Talence*, both red Graves.

LAGER BEER
A light type of beer which is brewed from malt, with hops and water, fermented, and then stored (*lagered*), during which time it is fined (freed from matters in suspension spoiling its looks), and carbonated (carbonic acid gas added to render it effervescent). *Lager Beer* is light in colour and body; it is slightly sparkling and brilliantly clear. It must be served cold.

In the U.S.A. most beers are *Lager Beers* and they are served cold. In the British Isles *Lager Beer* is not so good, nor so popular, nor is it always served cold.

LAGRANGE, Château
A Third Growth of the Médoc (Saint-Julien). Besides an average of 200 tuns claret sold as *Château Lagrange*, the vineyards of this estate produce other claret which is marketed under the registered labels of *Château Saint-Julien, Château La-Tour-Du-Roi* and *Clos des Chartrons*; they also produce some white wine which is sold under the registered label *Sirène Lagrange, Saint-Julien*.

LAGREINER KATZER.
LAGREIN ROSATO
The German and Italian names of an attractive Tyrol wine, light ruby in colour and 'lively', when still quite young.

LAGRIMA CRISTI.
LACRYMA CHRISTI
The names of a golden, rather sweet and very delicate wine made from grapes grown on the lower slopes of Vesuvius. There is also a little red *Lagrima Cristi* made, but it is not nearly so attractive as the white.

LA LOUVIÈRE, Château
One of the oldest wine-producing Estates of the Graves district, in the Commune of Léognan. Its vineyards produce on an average 85 tuns of claret and 10 tuns of white wine.

LAMARQUE
A Commune of the Médoc 36 k. NW. of Bordeaux; its wines have acquired by long usage the right to be sold under the better-known name of the adjoining Commune of Listrac. Its best wines are those of *Châteaux Lamarque, Cap-de-Haut, du Cartillon, Malescasse, de Carrasset* and *Reverdi*; they rank as bourgeois supérieurs and average 255 tuns claret.

LAMB'S WOOL
'To one quart of strong hot ale add the pulp of six roasted apples, together with a small

quantity of grated nutmeg and ginger, with
a sufficient quantity of raw sugar to sweeten
it; stir the mixture assiduously, and let it be
served hot'.—C.T.C.

'What would one have given to sit with
Pepys on a night, as he sat on November
9th, 1666, at "Cards till two in the morning
drinking Lamb's Wool".' That was two
months after the Great Fire of London.

LA MISSION HAUT-BRION, Château

One of the best wines of Graves (Pessac),
occasionally labelled *Haut-Brion La Mission*.
The vineyard was planted by the 'Prêtres de
la Mission', of Saint-Vincent-de-Paule, in
the seventeenth century, and they tended it
until dispossessed at the time of the French
Revolution. Average 35 tuns claret.

LAMOTHE-BERGEY, Château

One of the Second Growths of Sauternes.
Average yield 14 tuns white wine.

LAMOTTE, Château

One of the Second Growths of Sauternes,
its yield on an average is 10 tuns white wine.

LANDAU IN DER PFALZ

Palatinate. Oberhaardt. White wines. Best
vineyards: *Löhl, Steingebiss*.

LANGENLONSHEIM

One of the smaller wine-producing townships of the Nahe Valley (Kreuznach district). White wines. Best vineyards: *Steinchen,
Dautenborn* and *Rotenberg*.

LANGOA-BARTON, Château

A Third Growth of the Médoc (Saint-
Julien) which was purchased in 1821 by Mr.
Hugh Barton, who bought about a quarter
of the Léoville vineyards in 1826, and the
two properties have been run as one, from
Langoa, ever since by his successors. Average 125 tuns claret.

LANGOIRAN

One of the Communes of the Gironde, 26 k.
SSE. of Bordeaux, the name of which is
used, like that of Sauternes, for the wine-
producing district, including its own vineyards and those of seven nearby Communes:
*Langoiran, Baurech, Haux, Lestiac, Le Tourne,
Paillet* and *Tabanac*. This district is responsible for the production of a large quantity of
red wines, not of outstanding excellence, as
well as a larger quantity still of white wines,
of fair to middling quality, for which the
demand is keener. The vineyards of the Langoiran district are on the right bank of the
Garonne, opposite those of the Graves
district.

LAROSE, Châteaux

There are several wine-producing estates in
the Gironde bearing this name, mostly hyphenated with the name or names of present
or past owners. Much of the best wine is
that of the *Château Gruaud-Larose*, a Second
Growth in the Commune of St. Julien; then
that of the *Châteaux Larose-Perganson* and
Larose-Trintandon, two Bourgeois Growths
of the Commune of St.-Laurent (Médoc).
The least distinguished of all is the wine of
plain *Château Larose* in the Commune of
Baurech, Entre-deux-Mers, which averages
60 tuns of claret and 10 tuns of white wine

LASCOMBES, Château de

Second Growth of the Médoc (Margaux).
Average 35 tuns claret. This vineyard was
part of the *Château Durfort* originally; it was
sold to a Chevalier de Lascombes during the
eighteenth century.

LAS PALMAS

The chief wine-exporting centre of the
Canary Islands: it was responsible, in Shakespeare's time, for such names as Palm Sack
and Palm Wine, as alternative appellations
for the more usual Canary Sack. Average
production, 10,000 hectolitres (220,000 gallons) per annum.

LA TÂCHE

One of the famous vineyards of the Côte de
Nuits; produces some of the finest red burgundy; its wine is usually sold with the name
of its native Commune, *La Tâche Romanée*.

LATIUM

The Province of Italy in which Rome is situated; it produces a large quantity of both red
and white wines, the best-known of which
are those of the *Castelli Romani, Castel Bracciano, Frascati, Albano* and *Genzano*.

LATOUR, Château

One of the three First Growths of the Médoc
(Pauillac) and the most celebrated of all the
estates which bear the name of Latour. Its
average is 100 tuns 'Premier Vin' and 15 tuns
'Deuxième Vin'. There are numerous records
of purchases of *Château Latour* claret in England and Scotland during the eighteenth
century. *Château Latour* was then referred to
as standing in the Commune of Saint-Lambert, which was merged later in that of
Pauillac.

LA TOUR-BLANCHE, Château

One of the First Growths of Sauternes, in
the Communes of Bommes. (65 tuns.)

LA TOUR-CARNET, Château

A Fourth Growth of the Médoc (Saint-
Laurent). An ancient and picturesque Château, with a well-preserved keep and moat. It

used to be known as *Château Saint-Laurent*
and there are records of the sale of its wines
in 1354 and 1407, when a hogshead cost £36,
twice as much as the red wines of Graves. Its
yield was 100 tuns of claret at the beginning
of the present century, but it had declined to
merely half this quantity before the war.

LATOUR-POMEROL, Château
One of the First Growths of Pomerol; it be-
longs to the same owner as *Clos des Grandes
Vignes*, the adjoining vineyard, and the two
Growths are run as one; their combined
average is 40 tuns claret.

LAUBENHEIM (a.d Nahe)
Nahe Valley. Kreuznach district. Some fair
white wines.

LAUBENHEIM (b. Mainz)
Rhine-Hesse. Mayence district. Good white
wines. Best vineyards: *Berg, Edelmann, Kalkofen, Neuberg, Häuschen.*

LAUJAC, Château
The finest Estate of the Commune of Bégadan (Médoc), the first home in the Gironde
and still the property of the Cruse family. It
produces on an average 150 tuns of claret of
the most reliable even if not of superlative
quality.

LAVAUX
The name of a stretch of hills at the eastern
end of the Lake of Geneva, some 10 miles in
length from Lausanne to Montreux. Their
vineyards produce some of the best white
wines of Switzerland, none more renowned
than *Dezaley, Johannisberg,* and *Yvorne.*

LAYON, Coteaux du
Some of the best white wines of the Maine-
et-Loire Département (Anjou). The best
wines of the Coteaux du Layon are those
from the vineyards on the right bank of the
Layon, a small stream which loses itself in
the great Loire at Rochefort-sur-Loire:
*Thouarcé, Bonnezeaux, Faye, Rablay, Beaulieu,
St. Aubin-de-Luigné* and *Rochefort-sur-Loire.*
(See *Quart de Chaume.*)

LEANYKA
A light table wine from the Eger and other
wine-producing districts of Hungary. There
are two types of *Leanyka* wines, the *Leanyka
Szaraz,* which is an absolutely dry wine, and
the *Leanyka Edes,* which is fairly sweet.

LE COUVENT, Clos
One of the smallest of the First Growths of
Saint-Emilion, planted on the site of a
former Ursuline Convent, in the heart of St.
Emilion itself. Average 8 tuns claret.

LE GAY, Château
One of the First Growths of Pomerol. Aver-
age 25 tuns claret. It was known as *Manoir de
Gay* in former times.

LEITACHER
One of the more popular red table wines of
the Tyrol; it was renamed Santa Giustina
when the vineyards were transferred from
Austria to Italy, in 1919.

LEMONADE
A generic name for all manner of thirst-
quenching long drinks which taste of lemon
juice. The plainest form is made from the
juice of a lemon, cold water and a little
sugar, but sparkling water may be used and
different kinds of syrups in place of sugar.
The 'bottled' *Lemonade* is always sparkling;
it is usually made by filling with aerated
water a bottle in which there is a little syrup
of lemon – or merely a little citric acid
sweetened and coloured with saffron.

LEMON SQUASH
A bottled composition sold for the making
of *Lemonade* quickly and cheaply. One formula for its making is: Soluble essence of
lemon, 1¼ oz.; citric acid, 2 oz.; freshly boiled
water, 6 oz.; and syrup to make 40 fluid oz.
Colour, if desired, with a little saffron.
—L.G.M.

LÉOGNAN
One of the finest of the wine-producing
Communes of the Graves district, 13 k. S. of
Bordeaux. Its best wines are those of *Château
Haut-Bailly, Gazin, Rigailhou, Malartic-Lagra-
vière* and *Boismartin; Domaine de Chevalier* and
Cru Larrivet-Haut-Brion (claret only); and
*Châteaux Carbonnieux, Olivier, Le Désert, Le
Pape, Fieuzal, Haut-Gardère* and *La Louvière*
(both claret and white wines).

LÉOVILLE-BARTON, Château
One of the Second Growths of the Médoc
(Saint-Julien). It is the property of Mr R.
Barton, of the firm Barton and Guestier, of
Bordeaux, founded by the son of a Fer-
managh squire, born in 1694. His grandson
bought a fourth of the original Léoville vineyards and named it Léoville-Barton. There
is no Château attached to the property, the
vineyard being cultivated from and the
grapes pressed at *Château Langoa-Barton,*
which is under the same ownership. The
average yield of *Léoville-Barton* is 80 tuns
claret.

LÉOVILLE-LASCASES, Château
A Second Growth of the Médoc (Saint-
Julien) which consists of half the original
vineyards of Léoville: the other half is
divided between *Châteaux Léoville-Poyferré*

and *Léoville-Barton*. Its average yield is 200 tuns claret, of which 160 are sold as *Léoville-Lascases* and 40 under the name of *Clos du Marquis* (the *Marquis* being the Marquis de Las-Cases, the former proprietor). There was no 'Château bottling' at this Château between 1876 and 1906, both dates inclusive.

LÉOVILLE-POYFERRÉ, Château

A Second Growth of the Médoc (Saint-Julien). It is better-known because it is the best distributed of the three Léovilles abroad. There was no 'Château bottling' at this Château between 1894 and 1910, both dates inclusive. Average 120 tuns of claret.

LE-PIAN-MÉDOC

A Commune of the Médoc 17 k. N. of Bordeaux. Its best vineyards are those of *Châteaux Barthès-Pian-Médoc, Bellegrave-du-Poujeau, Duthil-Haut-Cressant, du Pian, de Malleret, Domaine de Lamourous, Moulin de Soubeyran* and *Château Sénéjac*; they rank as Bourgeois supérieurs and average 220 tuns of claret.

LESBIAN WINE

The wine of the Greek island of Lesbos. It was highly valued by the Greeks of old as a dessert wine, but it does not appear to have enjoyed the same measure of fame in ancient Rome as did the Chian wine. Horace calls Lesbian wine 'innocent':

'Hic innocentis pocula Lesbii
  Duces sub umbra'.
        (Carm. I. xvii. 21)

and he places Chian and Lesbian wines on par:

'Capaciores affer huc, puer, scyphos,
  Et Chia vina, aut Lesbia'.
        (Od. ix. Lib. v. 11.33-34)

Pliny places the wines of Chios and Thasos as superior to those of Lesbos.

LESPARRE

A Commune of the Médoc, 69 k. NNW. of Bordeaux, via Pauillac: it produces a large quantity of claret of no particular merit.

LE TAILLAN

A Commune of the Médoc, 11 k. NW. of Bordeaux. The largest estate of the Commune is *Château Fontanet*, and the best known *Château du Taillan*. Both rank as *Bourgeois* growths and average 150 tuns of claret per annum; *Fontanet* also produces a little white wine.

LIEBFRAUENSTIFT

(Rhine-Hesse)
The only reliable white wine of Worms. The best is sold as *Liebfrauenstift Klostergarten*.

LIEBFRAUMILCH

Formerly the white wine of Worms vineyards; now merely the name of a hock without any guarantee of origin or quality. The genuine wine of the Liebfrauenkirche vineyards, near Worms, is sold under the name of *Liebfrauenstift*.

LIESER (Moselle Valley)

Berncastel district. Very good white wines. Best vineyards: *Niederberg, Schlossberg, Pfaffenberg, Paulsberg* and *Helden*.

LIME JUICE CORDIALS

Preparations usually made from lime juice, sugar and water, and flavoured with lemon peel or orange flowers – say sugar 4 oz., syrup 16 oz., crude lime juice 16 oz., water 28 oz., and coloured with a little liquid saffron. It should be well filtered till fairly clear.—L.G.M.

LIMOUX

A small town, near Carcassonne, in the Aude Département, noted for a curious white wine known as *Blanquette de Limoux*, which is highly praised by some but not at all appreciated by others. There are also some red wines of Limoux: they are supposed to resemble *Beaujolais* wines.

LIQUEUR

A French name which has several meanings: (a) some form of it is chiefly used for flavoured and sweetened spirits. All *Liqueurs* have sugar and alcohol in common, although in varying proportions. They differ owing to the nature of the alcohol used in their manufacture, and to the number of aromatic substances used to flavour them, as well as to others used to colour them, unless, as is the case with a few *Liqueurs*, they are left colourless, as all spirits are when they leave the still. *Liqueurs* may be divided according to the spirit which is their basis, either brandy, gin, rum, whisky or a neutral spirit distilled from potatoes or sawdust. They may be further subdivided according to whether their chief flavour is derived from fruit, flowers, roots, leaves, or seeds, or a combination of a number of these. But there are many *Liqueurs*, among the oldest and more famous ones, such as *Chartreuse* and *Bénédictine*, which are sold under a name or brand giving no indication whatever as to the nature of the spirit used as a basis and the substances used as flavouring agents. All the principal *Liqueurs* will be found under their own name in alphabetical order.

Liqueur is also used for (b) a spirit of quality and age which is to be enjoyed 'neat', i.e. not watered down; such are *Liqueur Brandy* and *Liqueur Whisky*, and (c) a very

735

sweet syrup used for sweetening wine. Such are *Liqueur de tirage* and *Liqueur d'expédition*, the confection of candy added to champagne at the time of bottling (*tirage*) and when ready for sale (*expédition*).

LIQUEUR D'OR
A white *Liqueur* with specks of gold leaf floating in it, when the bottle is shaken. It is an imitation of the *Danziger Goldwasser*, but it is flavoured with lemon rind and zest instead of orange.

LIQUEUR JAUNE
The name given to a number of more or less colourable imitations of Yellow *Chartreuse* (q.v.).

LIQUEUR VERTE
The name given to some more or less colourable imitations of Green *Chartreuse* (q.v.).

LIQUOR
A term which in usual parlance includes all forms of alcoholic beverages, but in the 'Liquor Trade' itself, more particularly in the distilling industry, *Liquor* means distilled water used for breaking down spirits.

LISBON WINES
The red and white wines of the valley of the Tagus, down to the Atlantic from Lisbon, were fortified and shipped to England in large quantities during the eighteenth century and the early part of the nineteenth. There was a time when they cost more than similar wines from Oporto, but they deteriorated and became a cheaper type of port, until they ceased to be in demand, when Tarragona first, and Australia and South Africa next, supplied low-priced fortified wines. The wines of the Lisbon vineyards are now sold unfortified as *Collares* and *Bucellas*.

LISTRAC
A Commune of the Médoc, 34 k. NW. of Bordeaux. It produces an average of 2,000 tuns of very fair claret per annum, a further quantity of more ordinary red wines and a little white wine. Some of the claret from the adjoining Communes of Moulis, Lamarque, Arcins and Castelnau have acquired by long usage the right to be sold under the better-known name of Listrac. The best wines of Listrac are those of *Châteaux Fourcas-Dupré* and *Cru Fourcas-Hostein*; *Châteaux Fonréaud, Clarke, Lestage, Saransot-Dupré*, which rank as Bourgeois supérieurs, and *Châteaux Semeillan, Listrac, Lalande, Veyrin, Veyrin-Domecq, Lafon, Laffitte-Cantegric* and *Clos de Fourcas*, ranking as Crus Bourgeois.

LITRE
French standard liquid measure; the one-hundredth part of an hectolitre; 61.027 cubic inches; 1.7608 pints (Britain); 1.0567 quart (U.S.A.).

LIVENER
Fill tumbler with chipped ice: put in two or three drops of angostura bitters, two or three drops of lemon juice; add a teaspoonful of raspberry syrup, a liqueur-glassful of brandy, half a glassful of champagne; then stir well with large spoon and strain off into a pony tumbler; put a piece of lemon on top. —ch.p.

LIVERMORE VALLEY
A wine-growing district in the Alameda County of California: it is chiefly noted for its unfortified sweet wines.

LJUTOMER
The Slovene name of the chief wine-mart of central Slovenia and also the name of some of the best white wines of Yugoslavia, famous for many years throughout Austria under their German name of *Luttenberger*.

LOMBARDY
An important Italian wine-producing Province. Its principal wines are *Broni, Canneto Pavese, San Gimignano* and *Valtellina*.

LONGUICH (Moselle)
Trier district. White wines. Best vineyard: *Probstberg*.

LORCH
One of the most ancient vineyards of the Rhinegau, but not one of great importance as regards the quality of its white wines.

LORRAINE
One of the wine-producing provinces of eastern France, the wines of which are mostly light and somewhat sharp. They are highly appreciated locally but nowhere else. The best are those of the Moselle Valley. There are red and white Lorraine wines; also *Vins Gris*, a dirty pink in colour, not attractive to look at but quite refreshing on a hot summer's day. The best white wines are those of *Gueutrange* and *Dornot*; the best red those of *Thiaucourt, Pagny* and *Gueutrange*; one of the best *Vins Gris* is that of *Bruley*.

LOUPIAC
One of the Communes of the Gironde, 40 k. SSE. of Bordeaux, on the right bank of the River Garonne. Its vineyards produce some fair beverage red wines, but more and better white wines, similar to those of the adjoining Commune of *Sainte-Croix-du-Mont* (q.v.).

LUCIAN

Juno. And, soon, too, thou wilt dare to praise that fine novelty, the Vine and Wine! What matters to thee all the misdeeds of drunken unsteady fools, their blasphemies and the mad fury they find at the bottom of the cups they drain ...

Jupiter. What thou sayest is foolish argument. It is neither wine nor Bacchus who is responsible for such accidents, but the stupidity of those fools who gorge themselves with wine. Wine sensibly used, used in moderation, makes men amiable and joyous.

Lucian's XVIIIth *Dialogue.*

LUDON

A Commune of the Médoc 16 k. N. of Bordeaux. Its best wine is that of *Château La Lagune.* Next comes the wines of *Domaine de Fonbonne-Agassac, Château d'Arche, Cru de Bizeaudun, Châteaux d'Egmont, Lafitte-Canteloup, Ludon-Pomiés-Agassac, Nexon-Lemoyne, Paloumey, Pomiés-Agassac,* all Bourgeois or Bourgois supérieurs, averaging 350 tuns of claret per annum.

LUNEL

One of the most attractive of the French unfortified, sweet dessert wines; it comes from the vineyards of Lunel, in the Languedoc, on the French side of the Pyrenees. It is tawny in colour and has a delicate bouquet.

LUTTENBERGER

See *Ljutomer.*

LUXEMBOURG

The Moselle flows unhurriedly through the rich meadows and gentle hills of Luxembourg, on its way from France into Germany, and wherever there are hills there are vineyards; these produce quite a large quantity of white wines, light, dry and refreshing wines, not unlike some of the better white wines of Switzerland.

The chief city of the Luxembourg vinelands is Grevenmacher-sur-Moselle, where they hold a festival of wine every year, on Maundy Thursday.

LYNCH-BAGES, Château
LYNCH-MOUSSAS, Château

Two of the Fifth Growths of the Médoc (Pauillac) the recorded history of which goes back to the sixteenth century; they both belonged then and for long after to various members of the Lynch family and were known as *Château Lynch.* When the vineyards were divided, the larger part became *Château Lynch-Bages* (average 130 tuns claret), and the smaller *Château Lynch-Moussas* (average 20 tuns).

MACAU

A Commune of the Médoc, 21 k. N. of Bordeaux. Its best wine is that of *Château Cantemerle.* Next comes those of *Châteaux des Trois Moulins, Constant-Trois-Moulins, La Houringue, Maucamps, Cambon-La Pelouse, Rose-La Riche, Larrieu-Terrefort, Cusseau, Gironville, Priban, Maucamps, Bellevue*; all rank as Bourgeois supérieurs and average 400 tuns of claret per annum.

MÂCON

The metropolis of the Mâconnais and an important mart of the wines of Lower Burgundy.

MÂCONNAIS

An important wine-producing district of Lower Burgundy, south of the Côte Chalonnaise and north of Lyons. It includes the Cantons of St. Gengoux, Lugny, Mâcon, Tournus and Cluny.

MADEIRA

Madeira is a wine made not from any kind of grape grown in the island of Madeira but only from certain suitable grapes. Madeira is a fortified wine which owes its excellence to the grapes from which it is made, to the way in which it is made, and to the climate of the island of Madeira where it is made. Time is an all-important factor in the making of madeira, a fact which means that it is impossible for true madeira – the only kind of madeira worth drinking – to be very cheap. Madeira is not necessarily a sweet wine: *Sercial* madeira has a distinctly dry finish; *Bual* madeira is rich, and *Malmsey* madeira is the sweetest of all.

Standard gauge of a madeira pipe 92 gallons. Average yield, 44 dozens.

The wines of Madeira were not known in England in the time of Henry IV but they were known to Shakespeare:

Poins. ... Jack how agrees the devil and thee about thy soul that thou soldest him on Good Friday last for a cup of Madeira and a cold capon's leg?

First Part *Henry IV,*
Act I, Scene ii.

MADÈRE

The French name for both the wines of the island of Madeira and imitations made mostly at Cette now written Sète.

MADÈRE, Château de

One of the Estates of the Podensac Commune of the Graves district: its average production is 4 tuns of claret and 25 tuns of white wine.

MADÉRISÉ

The polite French word to use to describe the bottle stink of a wine which has been kept too long.

MADIRAN
The best red wine of Bigorre (Basque country). The best Madiran wine is that from the vineyards of *Anguis* and *Tichanères*.

MAGDELAINE, Château
One of the First Growths of Saint-Emilion which has remained for the past two hundred years the property of various members of the same family. Average 20 tuns claret.

MAGNUM
A bottle holding two reputed quarts or one-third of a gallon.

MAIKAMMER-ALSTERWEILER
Palatinate. Landau district. White wines. Best vineyards: *Mandelacker*, *Petersbrunnen*, *Weinsger*, and *Spielfeld*.

MAJORCA
A Spanish island off the coast of Catalonia. Palma, the only city on the island, is surrounded by vineyards which produce a quantity of beverage wines of moderate quality.

MALAGA
Malaga is one of the best sweet wines made in Spain. It comes from the Province of Eastern Andalucia and is shipped from the port of Malaga. It is a blend of new wine and old wine, known as *Vino Tierno* or *Vino Maestro*, and a dark sweet wine known as *Vino de Color*. The best wine of Malaga is made from the Muscatelle grapes and known as *Lagrima*: it is made in very much the same manner as Tokay. Average production, 100,000 hectolitres (2,200,000 gallons) per annum.

MALESCOT-SAINT-EXUPÉRY, Château
Third Growth of the Médoc (Margaux). Average 50 tuns 'Grand Vin' and 10 tuns 'Deuxième Vin', which is sold under the name of *Cru de la Colonie*. This estate was purchased by the London firm of W.H. Chaplin & Co. Ltd. at the beginning of the present century.

MALMSEY. MALVASIA
A sweet fortified wine made in Madeira, Cyprus, the Canary Islands and other southern vineyards from the Malvasia grape, when available.
The popularity of this wine must have been great, in England, during the latter part of the eighteenth century and the first half of the nineteenth, to judge from the large number of English Wine Labels of the period, in various collections, which bear its name, the spelling of which appears to have been rather uncertain. The following renderings occur: *Malmsey*, *Malmslay*, *Malvoisie*, *Malvasia*, *Malmsly*, *Malmsey*, *Madeira*, *Malvasia di Madera*.

MANDARINE
A sweet liqueur the informing flavour of which is that of Tangerines.

MANZANILLA
A very pale and dry type of *Sherry* from the vineyards of San Lucar, to the west of Jerez. It has a peculiar and attractive flavour of its own, which is easy to recognize but impossible to define.

MARASCHINO
A liqueur distilled from marasca cherries, in Dalmatia. It used to be shipped to all parts of the world from Zara in very distinctive straw-covered bottles. The popularity of this excellent liqueur is responsible for the many imitations of it offered for sale by distillers of different countries where the Dalmatian cherry is not obtainable.

MARC
A spirit distilled from the husks of grapes or the pulp of apples after the wine or cider has been made. Usually distilled at a very high strength, it requires many years to become tolerably palatable.

MARCHE
One of the least important of the wine-producing Provinces of Italy: its only wine above the *très ordinaire* class is a dry white wine called *Castelli di Gesi*.

MARGAUX
One of the most famous Communes of the Médoc, 28 k. NW. of Bordeaux. It produces a very large quantity of good claret which is sold the world over under the name of *Margaux*, a name which covers the claret made from the vineyards of the adjoining Communes of Cantenac, Arsac, Soussans, Labarde and Avensan. The finest wines of Margaux, however, are sold under the names of their respective vineyards, no less than eleven of the classed Growths of the Médoc being in the Commune of Margaux. They are: *Châteaux Margaux*; *Rausan-Ségla*; *Rauzan-Gassies*; *Durfort-Vivens*; *de Lascombes*; *Malescot St. Exupéry*; *Ferrière*; *Desmirail*; *Marquis d'Alesme Becker*; *Cru Boyd-Cantenac*; and *Château Marquis-de-Terme*. Besides these, *Châteaux de Labégorce*, de l'*Abbé-Gorsse*, de-*Gorsse*, *Abel-Laurent* which used to be known as *Séguineau*; *La Gurgue*; *de L'Estonnat*; *Doumens* and *de Lamouroux* rank as Bourgeois supérieurs and average 200 tuns of claret.

MARGAUX Château

One of the three First Growths and one of the oldest vineyards of the Médoc. In the fifteenth century it was called *Château de Lamothe*; it was known as *Margoo*, in England, in the seventeenth and eighteenth centuries: in 1703, the first Earl of Bristol paid £27 10s. for a hogshead of *Margoose Clarett*, and, in 1706, £43 for a hogshead of *Margous claret-wine*. Prior to the French Revolution, Château Margaux stood first of the three First Growths of the Médoc and produced 440 hogsheads of claret. Prior to 1914, it averaged 600 hogsheads of *Grand Vin* and 40 tuns of the next best, which used to be sold under the name of *Pavillon Rouge-Margaux*. Since 1924, a white wine has been made at *Château Margaux* which is sold under the label *Le Pavillon Blanc*.

MARKOBRUNNEN. MARCOBRUNNER

One of the most famous growths of the Rhinegau, in the parish of Erbach, adjoining Hattenheim. The name means 'Springs of St. Marcus', St. Marcus being the Patron Saint of Erbach.

MARQUIS-D'ALESME-BECKER, Château

Third Growth of the Médoc (Margaux). Average 25 tuns claret. The vineyard was planted originally in 1661 and was purchased early during the present century by the London firm of W.H.Chaplin & Co. Ltd.

MARQUIS-DE-TERME, Château

Fourth Growth of the Médoc (Margaux). Average 75 tuns claret. A 'Deuxième Vin' is sold under the name of *La Mariotte Margaux*. Its name dates from 1762, when the Marquis de Terme married its owner, a niece of M. de Rauzan.

MARSALA

The best and best-known dessert wine of Italy; it is made from grapes grown in Sicily, between Palermo and Messina, north and south of Marsala. Standard gauge of a Marsala pipe, 93 gallons. Average yield, 45 dozens.

This wine which was popular in England during the greater part of the nineteenth century, figures on some English Wine Labels as *Massaly*, *Marcella* and *Marsalla*. Two labels, one dated 1812 and the other 1832, in the M.V.Brown collection of Wine and Sauce Labels given to the London Museum in 1915, bear the name *Marsella*.

MARTIAL

c. A.D. 40–104. Bacchus never had a more devoted disciple than Martial, to whom we owe much of our knowledge of the table manners and drinking customs of the Romans.

Martial not only gives the names of a number of wines of Italy, Greece, Gaul and Spain, and the dates of the best vintages, but also a number of details about casks and glass bottles, the cooling of wine in summer, the frauds of certain unscrupulous Roman vintners, the order of toasts and the manner of drinking healths.

MARTILLAC

One of the Communes of the Graves district, 17 k. S. of Bordeaux, the vineyards of which produce some 400 tuns of claret and 100 tuns of white wine. The largest estate of the Commune is *Château La Garde* and the best wine that of *Château Smith-Haut-Lafitte*. Other reputed growths are *Châteaux Ferran, Rochemorin. Saint-Augustin-La-Grave, Latour, de Nouchet, L'Hermitage* and *La Solitude*.

MARTINI COCKTAILS

The straight *Martini*, oldest and simplest form of this very popular cocktail, is just half *Gin* and half *French Vermouth* well mixed together. Then there is the *Dry Martini*, with two-thirds of dry *Gin* to one of *French Vermouth*, and a dash of orange bitters. If a *Very Dry Martini* should be called for, the proportion of the *Gin* is increased to three-quarters or four-fifths and that of the *French Vermouth* is correspondingly reduced to one quarter or one fifth. When *Italian Vermouth* is used to sweeten the *Martini*, it is no longer a *Martini* but is called a *Bronx*.

MASDEU

Red, fortified wines of Roussillon, very popular in England in early Victorian days. Also written *Masdu* and *Masdieu*.

There is no mention of *Masdeu* in the 1833 edition of Cyrus Redding's *History of Modern Wines*, but the following remarks appeared in the 1851 edition: 'This wine is not a factitious (sic) French port from the harbour of Cette, or it would not have merited notice. It is a genuine production called Masdeu, from the vineyard which produces it, between Perpignan and Collioure. The vineyard once belonged to the Knights Templars, and afterwards to the Hospitallers … It is shipped from Port Vendres. Yet this wine, five hundred years old, was new to England till 1838. The house of Robert Selby imported in one year into England, between 1836 and 1837, no less than 1,648 pipes of this wine, and it may be said to be fixed in the English market.'

In the M.V.Brown Collection of Wine and Sauce Labels given to the London Museum in 1915, there is a *Masdeu* plated label of the latter part of the eighteenth century.

MAVRODAPHNE
One of the best known of the modern Greek wines: it is a red wine, fortified, rather sweet and satisfying, usually served in quite small glasses. It is made from the grape of the same name.

MEAD
A mildly alcoholic beverage of great antiquity which was fermented from honeyed water, and flavoured with various strongly scented herbs.

'*Mead.* There are different kinds of this wine; but those generally made are two, namely, sack-mead, and cowslip-mead. Sack-mead is made thus: to each gallon of water put 4 lb. of honey, and boil it three-quarters of an hour, taking care to skim it well. To each gallon add ½ oz. of hops, boil it half an hour longer, and let it stand till the next day. Then put it into the cask, and to thirteen gallons of liquor add a quart of brandy or sack. Close it tight till the fermentation is over, and then stop it up very close. It must stand a year before you bottle it.'—E.

MEDICINAL and
MEDICATED WINES
'Wine took an important place in ancient dietietics, and the custom of adding spices and drugs to wine is very old. Some of these medicated wines, particularly the *condita*, which usually contained pepper, were drunk as appetizers ... Other ancient medicated wines were straight remedies prescribed by physicians to their patients. Dioscorides, Galen, Oribasius, Aëtius, Paulus of Ægina and other medical writers have numerous recipes for the preparation of such wines, and they also discuss the diseases for which they were supposed to be good. The mediaeval physicians followed the ancient tradition. The medical use of wine is mentioned in all *regimina sanitatis* and recipes for the preparation of medicinal wines occur incidentally in the works of many mediaeval medical writers.' (From Dr Henry E.Sigerist's Introduction to *The Earliest Printed Book on Wine*. New York, Schuman's. 1943.)

In modern times, in the British Isles, medicinal or medicated wines are mostly mixtures of the cheaper sorts of red fortified wines with extract of meat or extract of malt, quinine, coca, and other substances; they are made and advertised on a commercial scale. Such wines may not be sold to the public except by holders of wine licences. Pepsin wine and ipecacuanha wine are simply medicines; they, and other such wines rendered so medicinally nasty as to be incapable of being used as beverages, may be sold by chemists who do not hold a wine licence.

740

MEDINA
A Spanish red wine which Jullien (*Topographie*) mentions as being the best in the then kingdom of Leon. It must have found its way to England since there is an Enamel Wine Label bearing its name in the Ionides Collection.

MÉDOC
A strip of land barely 50 miles long and six miles wide, along the left bank of the Gironde, responsible for the output of about half the quantity of really fine red wines produced in the world. There are 70 parishes, or 'Communes', in the Médoc where vineyards are cultivated. The 60 best estates, or 'Châteaux', of the Médoc were classed by order of merit, as regards the excellence of the wines they produce, as far back as 1855, and this classification still holds good. They are all situated in what is called the *Haut Médoc*, that part of the Médoc which stretches from Blanquefort to Saint-Seurin-de-Cadourne. The part of the Médoc nearest the Bay of Biscay, from Saint-Germain-d'Esteuil to Soulac used to be known as *Bas-Médoc*, but is now called *Médoc*.

OFFICIAL CLASSIFICATION OF THE GROWTHS OF THE MEDOC

First Growths
Lafite		Pauillac
Margaux		Margaux
Latour		Pauillac
Haut Brion		Pessac

Second Growths
Mouton-Rothschild		Pauillac
Rausan-Ségla		Margaux
Rauzan-Gassies		”
Léoville-Lascases		St. Julien
Léoville-Poyferré		”
Léoville-Barton		”
Durfort		Margaux
Lascombes		”
Gruaud-Larose		St. Julien
Brane-Cantenac		Cantenac
Pichon-Longueville		Pauillac
Pichon-Lalande		”
Ducru-Beaucaillou		St. Julien
Cos d'Estournel		St. Estèphe
Montrose		”

Third Growths
Kirwan		Cantenac
D'Issan		”
Lagrange		St. Julien
Langoa		”
Giscours		Labarde
Malescot St. Exupéry		Margaux
Brown-Cantenac		Cantenac
Palmer		Margaux
La Lagune		Ludon

Desmirail	..	..	Margaux
Calon-Ségur	..	..	St. Estèphe
Ferrière			Margaux
Marquis-d'Alesme-Becker	..		,,

Fourth Growths

St. Pierre-Bontemps and			
St. Pierre-Sevaistre	..		St. Julien
Branaire-Ducru	..	..	,,
Talbot	..	..	,,
Duhart-Milon	..	..	Pauillac
Pouget	..	..	Cantenac
Rochet	..	..	St. Estèphe
Beychevelle	..	..	St. Julien
Le Prieuré	..	..	Cantenac
Marquis de Terme	..	..	Margaux

Fifth Growths

Pontet-Canet	..	..	Pauillac
Batailley			,,
Grand Puy-Lacoste	..	..	,,
Grand-Puy-Ducasse	..	..	,,
Lynch-Bages	..	..	,,
Lynch-Moussas	..	..	,,
Dauzac	..	..	Labarde
Mouton-d'Armailhacq	..	..	Pauillac
Du Tertre	..	..	Arsac
Haut-Bages	..	..	Pauillac
Pédesclaux	..	..	,,
Belgrave	..	..	St. Laurent
Camensac	..	..	,,
Cos-Labory	..	..	St. Estèphe
Clerc-Milon	..	..	Pauillac
Croizet-Bages	..	..	,,
Cantemerle	..	..	Macau

The classed growths of the Médoc, on an average, produce about three-quarters of a million gallons of fine red wines every year. Besides those sixty classed growths, there are, in the Médoc, a large number of other wine-producing estates graded as 'Bourgeois Supérieurs', 'Bourgeois', 'Artisans' and 'Paysans'; these produce an average of some seven million gallons of very fair red wines every year. In low lands, close to the Gironde, and in islands in the Gironde, vines are also grown, and they are responsible for the production of about a million gallons of red wines every year, bringing up the total average output of the Médoc to nearly nine million gallons of wine, mostly red.

The name 'Médoc' does not correspond to any administratively defined area, but it is given, according to local usage, to all red wines or claret made from grapes grown between La Jalle de Blanquefort, as the point nearest to Bordeaux, and Le Verdon, as the farthest point, close to the Bay of Biscay; also from the vineyards planted in the islands of the River Gironde.

MENDOZA
The oldest and most extensive wine-producing centre of the Argentine Republic, at the foot of the Andes.

MERANO
The principal wine mart of the Upper Adige vineyards which were transferred from Austria to Italy in 1919.

MERCUREY
One of the best and most extensive vineyards of the Côte Chalonnaise, in Burgundy. Most of the *Mercurey* wines are red, and they are also of better quality than the few white wines of that district.

MERCUROL
A village of the Rhône Valley, a little to the south-west of the *Hermitage* Coteau; its vineyards produce both red and white wines, the whites being of finer quality than the reds.

MÉRIGNAC
A Commune of the Graves district 6 k. west of Bordeaux; vineyards, mostly very small ones, tended by about fifty different owners, produce about 200 tuns of claret per annum, none of them of outstanding merit. The best or best-known are those of *Châteaux Bon-Air, La Tour-de-Pape, Le Burck* and *Pique-Caillou*.

MESCAL
A potent spirit distilled in Mexico and South America from the *Maguey*, or American aloe.

MESSINIA
The largest wine-producing district of Greece.

METHEGLIN
The anglicized form of the Welsh name for *Hydromel, Medey-glin*, a honey drink.

'To 9 gallons of boiling water put 28 lb. of honey, add the peel of three lemons, with a small quantity of ginger, mace, cloves: and rosemary; when this is quite cold, add two tablespoonfuls of yeast. Put this into a cask and allow it to ferment; at the expiration of six months, bottle it off for use.'—C.T.C.

METHUSELAH
A giant bottle, used for show more than for maturing wine: it holds eight reputed quarts or 6.40 litres, equal to 225,350 fluid ounces. The name is also used in connection with wine to convey the idea of great age.

MEUNG
One of the Orléanais red wines which enjoyed, once upon a time, a far greater reputation than it does at present.

MEURSAULT
One of the chief Communes of the Côte d'Or for white and red burgundy. Its best vineyards are: *Les Perrières*; then *Les Genevrières, Les Charmes, Les Bouchères, Les Tessons, La Goutte d'Or* (white wines). *Les Santenots du*

Milieu; then *Les Cras, Les Santenots-Blancs, Le Clos des Mouches, Les Pelures* (red wines). Average yearly production, 100,000 gallons.

MEXICO
The cultivation of vines and the production of grapes for wine-making purposes are not on a very large scale.

MIDI WINES
The *Vins du Midi* are generally understood to be the wines of the Hérault, Gard and Aude, the three largest wine-producing Départements of France. They are mostly characterless red and white wines, chiefly red. They are used blended with Algerian wines or not; the whites are also used as a basis for *Vermouths* and the reds for *Bitters*.

MIGRAINE
One of the best red wines of the Auxerre district in Lower Burgundy. (There is not a headache in it.)

MILLÉSIMÉ
French for 'date of the vintage'.

MILLÉSIMÉ, Vin
French for a wine bearing the date of its vintage, i.e. a Vintage wine.

MILTON, 1608–1674
When writing to his friend Diodati, who had complained to him that the Christmas festivities interfered with his writing poetry, Milton could not agree with him:
> Why dost thou say that poetry hath been put to flight by meat and wine?
> Poetry loves Bacchus, Bacchus loves Poetry;
> Phoebus was not ashamed to wear green corymbs
> And to prefer the ivy to his own laurel.

He reminds his friend of the intimacy between Bacchus and the Muses; also of Ovid, Anacreon and Pindar, in whose poems, he says:
> Every page is redolent with the wine they have absorbed ...

It was after having drunk a four-year-old wine that Horace
> Sweetly sang Glycera and fair-haired Chloe.

It will be the same with Diodati if he drinks deep enough, so sang Milton in Latin verse.

MINERAL WATERS
Spring waters which are impregnated with mineral salts to which they owe their medicinal value, if any, and their individual flavour. Some are naturally and others artificially sparkling, having some carbonic acid gas forced into them at the time of bottling.

Some mineral waters contain a minimum of mineral salts and have no taste and no specific action upon any of the human organs: they are called *Table Waters*: such are *Perrier* and *Apollinaris*. Others are slightly alkaline and may also be used as *Table Waters*: such are *Malvern, Evian Cachat*, and *Vichy Célestins*. Others contain sufficient sulphate of magnesia to be bitter to the taste and aperient, such are *Apenta, Hunyadi-Janos* and *Rubinat*. Others are known as ferruginous or Chalybeate Waters; they are supposed to have stimulating properties on the digestion and blood circulation: such are *Homburg, Marienbad* and *Vittel*; others are impregnated with sulphuretted hydrogen and smell of bad eggs; such are *Bath, Harrogate* and *Barèges*: they are never drunk except under doctors' orders. Others are even worse, being distinctly arsenical, such as *La Bourboule* and *Royat*; they are medicinal and not merely mineral waters.

MINT
The highly scented leaves of *Mint* are used in the making of liqueurs usually sold under the name of *Crème de Menthe* or *Peppermint*. Mint is also used in wine cups, cordials and juleps.

MINT JULEP
Dissolve one teaspoonful of granulated sugar in just enough water to cover it. Fill the glass with cracked ice. Then pour in some *Bourbon Whisky* to within ½ in. of the top. Stir until the glass is frosted. Decorate freely with fresh mint. (If desired a sprig of mint may also be crushed with the sugar and water and left in the glass.)

MIRABELLE
An Alsatian spirit distilled from the small golden plums of that name, which grow in many parts of France, but nowhere better than in Alsace. *Mirabelle* is pure white and sometimes slightly sweetened. Like *Kirsch* and all *Eaux-de-vie Blanches, Mirabelle* is matured in glass.

MISTELLE
A white wine of no particular quality made chiefly from the vineyards on both the French and Spanish sides of the Pyrenees, by the addition of a comparatively small quantity of brandy to partially fermented grapejuice, soon after the vintage. It is sometimes sold as a cheap dessert wine, but it is mostly used for making *Vermouth*, or as a basis for *Apéritifs* wines.

MIXED DRINKS
The following *Mixed Drinks* are described

under their own name in the alphabetical order:

Apéritifs	Lemonades
Cobblers	Orangeade
Cocktails	Puff
Collins	Punches
Coolers	Rickeys
Cordials	Sangarees
Crustas	Shrubs
Cups	Slings
Daisies	Smashes
Eggnogs	Sours
Fixes	Swizzles
Fizzes	Toddies
Flips	Tom and Jerry
Highballs	Twists
Juleps	Zoom

MONBAZILLAC
A rich, golden wine from three Communes of the Dordogne Département: Monbazillac, Colombier, and Pomport.

MONCHHOF
One of the white wines of the Burgenland (Austria).

MONFERRATO
The name of a chain of hills, in Piedmont south of the River Po, where stand the townships of Asti, Canelli, Barolo, Gavi, Barbaresco, surrounded by extensive vineyards which are responsible for considerable quantities of red and white wines, still and sparkling.

MONTEFIASCONE
A sweet white wine made from Muscat grapes grown in the vineyards of Montefiascone, just over the border of Latium, a few miles south-west of Orvieto.

MONTEPULCIANO
One of the best red wines of Tuscany. Jullien, in his *Topographie*, places it first of red muscat dessert wines; Redi, in *Bacco in Toscana*, calls it the king of wines, and there is a Wine Label bearing this name in the Ionides Collections of Enamel Wine Labels.

MONTHELIE
One of the Communes of the Côte d'Or (Côte de Beaune), which produce some red wines of very fair quality: its best vineyards are: *Le Cas Rougeot, Les Champs Fulliot* and *Le Château-Gaillard*.

MONTIBEUX, Clos de
One of the best white wines of the Valais (Switzerland).

MONTILLA
One of the driest types of sherry wine, which is not really entitled to the name of sherry, as it is made from grapes grown in the Mon-

tilla Mountains, in the region of Cordoba, about 100 miles from Jerez. Yet it is from this 'outsider' that the true Jerez wine called *Amontillado* owes its name: it is a wine in the Montilla style, that is dry, light, with a clean and nutty finish.

MONTLOUIS
One of the best red wines of the Loire Valley (Touraine).

MONTMÉLIAN
One of the few really good red wines of French Savoy.

MONTMURAT
The only good red wine of the Cantal Département.

MONTRACHET, Le
The finest white burgundy, First Growth Puligny-Montrachet (Côte d'Or). Sometimes sold as *Grand Montrachet*.

MONTRACHETS, Les
Le Chevalier-Montrachet; Le Bâtard-Montrachet; Les Demoiselles-Montrachet; First and Second Growths Chassagne-Montrachet, and Puligny-Montrachet (white burgundy).

These are, with *Le Montrachet*, the best of all French white wines other than the sweet wines of Sauternes, which are in a different class altogether.

MONTROSE, Château
One of the Second Growths of the Médoc (Saint-Estèphe). During the sixties and seventies, the name of the then owner, Dollfus, figured on the labels of *Château Montrose Dollfus*. Average 100 tons claret.

MOREY-SAINT-DENIS
One of the important Communes of the Côte d'Or, producing much fine red burgundy. Its most famous vineyard: the *Clos de Tart*. Other good vineyards are: *Les Lambrays, Clos de la Roche*, and *Clos Saint-Denis*. Average annual production, 33,000 gallons.

MOROCCO WINES
Although viticulture in Morocco dates from the twentieth century only, it has progressed at such a rate that the country now produces considerable quantities of both red and white wines as well as much grape-juice exported as such for the making of British wines and similar beverages.

MOSCATEL
A generic name for wines made in Spain from muscat grapes; none of them are dry wines, but some are sweet to a fulsome degree. The best *Moscatel* of Spain is that which is made from the vineyards of *Sitges*,

a small seaport south of Barcelona: it is fully sweet enough, has an alcoholic strength of from 16 to 18 per cent by weight, and a very distinct muscat flavour.

They make a wine of the same style in the Argentine, and it bears the same name.

MOSCATELLO. MOSCATO

The name of a variety of sweet Italian dessert wines made from muscat grapes. The less sweet of such wines are called *Moscato secco* and the sweeter sorts *Moscato passito*. Some of the better-known *Moscato* wines are the *Moscatello di Montefiascone*, a Latium wine; the *Moscato di Salento*, of Apulia; the *Moscato Fior d'Arancio*, of Calabria; the *Moscato di Noto*, from Syracuse; the *Moscato Zucco*, from Palermo; and the *Moscato di Pantelleria*, from the small island of that name.

MOSELLE

The Moselle is a long twist of a river which rises and has its longest run in France: it then forms the boundary between Luxembourg and Germany and enters Germany at Wasserbillig, only 7 miles from the old Roman city of Trier. It then buckles its way in a northerly direction with an easterly inclination for more than 120 miles, as far as Coblenz, where it meets the Rhine. Strangely enough, none of the many vineyards which the Moselle passes by, both in France and Luxembourg, produce any wine of distinction, certainly none comparable to the wines made from the vineyards which grace both banks of the 'Mittelmosel', in the Berncastel district, or from the vineyards of the Saar and Ruwer, close to the junction of those two small rivers with the Moselle, the first above and the second below Trier.

The best wines of the Moselle are those of the middle course of the river between Trier and Coblenz (*Mittel Mosel*) they are, in alphabetical, not geographical, order: *Avelsbach, Berncastel, Brauneberg, Cues, Dhron, Enkirch, Erden, Graach, Lieser, Piesport, Traben, Trarbach, Trittenheim, Uerzig, Wehlen, Zell* and *Zeltingen*.

The following wines, from the Saar and Ruwer Valleys, are of the same high standard of excellence as the wines of the Middle Moselle, and they are usually sold, in England, as Moselle wines: *Ayl, Canzem, Eitelsbach, Filzen, Grünhaus, Ockfen, Oberemmel, Saarburg, Scharzhof, Serrig, Waldrach, Wawern* and *Wiltingen*.

Next, as regards the quality of their wines, come the vineyards of the Lower Moselle: *Bruttig, Cochem, Pünderich, Senheim, Valwig* and *Winningen*. Last of all are the wines of the Upper Moselle from *Nittel* to *Wincheringen*.

MOTHER-IN-LAW

A Cockney name for 'Half-andHalf' – stout and bitter.

MOULIN-À-VENT

The best and best-known red wine of Beaujolais (Burgundy), from vineyards partly in the Commune of Chénas and partly in that of Romanèche-Thorins. There are thirty-two named vineyards, the wines of which are entitled to the name of *Moulin-à-Vent Grand Cru*.

MOULIS

A Commune of the Médoc 33 k. NNW. of Bordeaux. The red wines of Moulis are sold under the name of their own Commune or under that of the adjoining and better-known Commune of *Listrac*. The best wine of Moulis is that of *Château Chasse-Spleen* (average 90 tuns claret); then come the wines of *Châteaux Gastebois, Brillette, Poujeaux-Marly, Mauvesin, Pomeys, Duplessis, Anthonic, Dutruch-Grand-Poujeaux, Biston-Brillette, Gressier-Grand-Poujeaux; Cru Biston-Brillette; Châteaux du Testeron, Moulis, Bouqueyran, Ruat-Lamorère; Cru Bergeron; Châteaux Guitignan, Maucaillou, Lestage-Darquier, Moulin-à-Vent, Bel-Air-Lagrave, Haut Bourdieu, Granins; Au Grand Poujeaux*, etc., all rank as bourgeois supérieurs and average 1,000 tuns claret.

MOUTON D'ARMAILHACQ, Château

One of the Fifth Growths of the Médoc (Pauillac). Average 250 tuns claret, of which 175 'Premier Vin' and 75 tuns are sold under the name of *Cru des Carruades d'Armailhacq*.

MOUTON-ROTHSCHILD, Château

The first of the Second Growths of the Médoc (Pauillac). The wines of this Château of recent vintages have been fully equal to those of the First Growths. Before 1853, when it was purchased by Baron Nathaniel de Rothschild, it was known as *Château Brane-Mouton*, and it was known by that name during the greater part of the eighteenth century; before that it was called *Cru de Mouton*. Its average is 150 tuns claret.

MULBERRY GIN

I

Fill a large jar with ripe mulberries, then pour highest strength gin obtainable over them; stopper the jar tightly and leave the fruit to macerate in the gin for not less than six weeks, when it will be ready to serve, unfined and undecanted.

II

Mash some ripe mulberries and strain the juice through a coarse cloth; flavour with lemon peel and a stick of cinnamon; sugar may be added, according to taste; bring to the boil and remove scum carefully, then let the juice cool and then add one gallon of gin to every two gallons of fruit juice. Mix well and serve in coloured glasses.

MULBERRY WINE

Gather your mulberries when they are ripe, beat them in a mortar, and to every quart of berries, put a quart of spring water. When you put them in the tub, mix them well, and let them stand all night: then strain them through a sieve, and to every gallon of liquor put 3 lb. of sugar: when your sugar is dissolved, put it into your cask, into which (if an 8-gallon one) you must put a gill of finings. Care must be taken that the cask be not too full, nor bunged too close at first. Set it in a cold place, and, when fine, bottle it.—W.S.M.

MULLED WINE

One of the most acceptable – and most ancient – forms of prevention or cure for a cold. Any wine may be used, not necessarily the finest, of course, and red for preference. Plenty of sugar is first of all dissolved in a little hot water, in a pan over a slow fire; then the wine is put in and brought to the boil; it must be moved away from the fire as soon as it reaches boiling point, and served to the patient with a little grated nutmeg on top. This is the 'straight' form of *mulled wine*, the form which Falstaff, and Shakespeare himself without a doubt, approved of. But there were in Shakespeare's days and there are now people who believe in adding a well-beaten egg to *mulled wine*, stirring it well in the hot wine *off* the fire.

MUM

A brew which once upon a time had its admirers in England; it is now practically unknown in the British Isles, but it is still popular in Brunswick. It is brewed from a blend of malted wheat, oatmeal and ground beans, in the proportion of seven bushels of wheat to one each of the other two. The mash is then boiled with fir-rind, tops of fir and beech, and a variety of herbs, till one-third is evaporated.

MUNSTER-BEI-BINGENBRUCK

One of the wine-producing parishes of the Nahe Valley, in the Kreuznach district. White wines. Best vineyards: *Pittersberg* and *Kappellenberg*.

MUSCADEL

A sweet dessert wine made from muscat grapes. It was popular in England from early

times and it was well known to Shakespeare.

> *Gremio*. ... *A health*, quoth he; as if
> He had been aboard, carousing to his mates
> After a storm: quaff'd off the muscadel,
> And threw the sops all in the sexton's face; ...
>
> *The Taming of the Shrew*,
> Act III, Scene ii.

MUSCADELLE

A small but delicious grape which used to be extensively cultivated at the Cape in the early part of the nineteenth century and made the reputation of the famous Constantia wine.

MUSCADINE WINE

Another name for *Muscatel wine* or any wine made from muscat grapes.

MUSCAT

The generic name of the most highly scented varieties of *Vitis vinifera*, the European parent grape. The Muscat d'Alexandrie is grown on a very large scale in California for wine-making, but in Europe it is mostly grown for table grapes. Wines made from other muscat grapes are known as plain *Muscat*, or *Muscat de Frontignan*, *Muscat de Samos*, etc.; they are sweet, muscat-scented, dessert wines.

MUSCATEL

The name of a sweet fortified wine made in California. Also, in England, that of a cheap sweet white sparkling wine, usually flavoured with elderberry flower essence.

MUSIGNY, Les

The most famous vineyards of Chambolle-Musigny, Côte d'Or. They produce chiefly red wines of very fine quality; also a little very good white wine (about 14 acres). The Musigny vineyards are cut in two by a small road, the larger half being sometimes called *Grand Musigny* and the smaller half *Petits Musigny*.

MUSKOTÁLY

One of the best white muscat wines, chiefly from Villány (Hungary).

MUSSBACH (Palatinate)

Neustadt district. Some fine white wine and some quite ordinary. Best vineyards: *Stecken, Pabst, Lauterbach, Spiegel*.

MYRAT, Château

One of the Second Growths of Sauternes, in the Commune of Barsac. (Average 40 tuns.)

NACKENHEIMER

One of the best white wines of Rhine-Hesse, in the Oppenheim district. Best vineyards: *Roteberg, Feuchelberg, Engelsberg, Fritzenhöll*.

NAHE

A tributary of the Rhine. The vineyards of the Nahe Valley produce both red and white wines, the white being the better of the two. The best vineyards of the Nahe are those of: *Bad Kreuznach, Burgsponheim, Heddesheim, Langenlonsheim, Münster, Niederhausen, Norheim, Schloss Böckelheim, Winzenheim.*

NAIRAC, Château

One of the Second Growths of Sauternes, in the Commune of Barsac. (Average 30 tuns.)

NANTZ

An eighteenth-century name for French brandy, large quantities of which used to be shipped from Nantes, on the River Loire.

NAPA VALLEY

(Northern California). Some of the best Californian table wines come from the Napa Valley.

NAPAREULI

White Caucasian wine (U.S.S.R.).

NASCO

One of the best dessert wines of Sardinia.

NATURE. NATUR

The French and German words used to convey the idea of a wine which has not been 'sweetened'.

NEBBIOLO

One of the best black grapes grown in the North of Italy for the making of red table wines. Many of the wines made from nebbiolo grapes are sold as *Nebbiolo* wines, sometimes with the name of their vineyards coupled with it.

NEBUCHADNEZZAR

A giant bottle, made for show purposes, and too unwieldy for use.

NECTAR

'The drink of the gods', in Greek mythology. Milton describes *Nectar* as follows:
  '... one sip of this
  Will bathe the drooping spirits in delight
  Beyond the bliss of dreams.'
                    (*Comus*. 813)
  A number of French liqueurs used to be given the name of *Nectar*, such as *Nectar de Bonaparte, Nectar de Mazagran*, etc.

NEGUS

To every pint of port allow one quart of boiling water: ¼ lb. loaf sugar, one lemon, grated nutmeg to taste. Put the wine in a jug; rub some lumps of sugar (¼ lb.) on the lemon rind until all the yellow part of the skin is absorbed; then squeeze the juice and strain it; add the sugar and lemon juice to the port wine, with the grated nutmeg; pour on the boiling water, cover the jug, and when the beverage has cooled a little, it will be ready for use.—L.EN.

NEMES KADARKA

One of the best red Hungarian wines, from the *Kadar* district.

NEPENTHE

The family name of some sixty varieties of 'pitcher-plants' from which a drug is extracted. Homer mentions it in the *Odyssey* (*IV*, 221) as an Egyptian drug, and it has often been used in ancient times as a draught of 'doctored' wine given by the gods above to men below to help them forget their cares.

NEUCHÂTEL

A Swiss Canton which produces both red and white wines. Most vineyards of Neuchâtel have been cut at great cost ledge-wise along the steep foothills of the Juras, a narrow band of terraced 'Clos', mostly facing south-east and the lake of Neuchâtel. The best red wine of Neuchâtel is the *Cortaillod* and the best white that of *Champreveyres*.

NEUDORF (Rhinegau)

Between Nieder-Walluf and Frauenstein. White wine. Best vineyards: *Mückenberg* and *Pfaffenberg*.

NEUMAGEN (Moselle Valley)

Berncastel district. White wines. Best vineyards: *Lasenberg, Hambach, Engelgrube, Rosengärtchen* and *Laudamusberg*.

NEUTSTADT

One of the wine-growing districts of the Palatinate (Mittelhaardt). White wines. Best vineyards: *Grain, Erkenbrecht, Vogelsang*.

NIEDERHAUSEN

One of the smaller wine-producing parishes of the Nahe Valley, in the Kreuznach district. White wines. Best vineyards: *Rosenbeck, Hermannshöhle* and *Steinwingert*.

NIEDER-INGELHEIM

One of the wine-producing townships of Rhine-Hesse, in the Bingen district. White wines. Best vineyards: *Horn, Nonnenberg* and *Steinacker*.

NIERSTEIN

The most important wine-producing parish of Rhine-Hesse. It produces much white wine, some of which is of very fine quality. Best vineyards: *Glöck, Auflangen, Hipping, Rehbach, Orbel, Heiligenbaum, Domtal, Spiegelberg* and *Fuchsloch*.

NIP

A quarter bottle.

NOAH

A name sometimes given to a very old wine, Noah having planted the first vineyard on record.

> And Noah began to be an husbandman, and he planted a vineyard: and he drank of the wine, and was drunken; and he was uncovered within his tent.
>
> *Genesis* IX, 20–21

NOGGIN

An English measure equal to a quarter of a pint.

NITTEL

Upper Moselle: Saar district. White wines. Best vineyards: *Vogelsberg, Leiterchen* and *Gipfel*.

NONNOS

A Greek epic poet, who lived probably at the end of the fourth century A.D., and whose chief work is an epic in forty-eight books entitled *Dionysiaca*.

> Give way, ye warrior, to the wine-grower:
> To Mars ye offer a bloody offering,
> But to Bacchus the other offers
> The sparkling blood of the inebriating grape.
> Ye, Ceres, and ye also, Pallas,
> Both, indeed, own yourselves beaten.
> Olive trees make not men merry,
> Nor does golden wheat charm their soul.
> Greater am I than either of you;
> Without wine where would they be
> The pleasures of the table
> And the joys of the dance.
>
> *Nonnos*, Canto XII, vv. 218–225

NORHEIM

One of the smaller wine-producing parishes of the Nahe Valley, in the Kreuznach district. White wines. Best vineyards: *Delchen, Schmalberg, Hinterfels* and *Hufels*.

NUITS-SAINT-GEORGES

One of the most important Communes of the Côte d'Or. It produces much red wine of very fine quality, chiefly from the following vineyards: *Aux Boudots, Les Chaboeufs, Les Chagnots, Aux Cras, Aux Murgers, La Perrière, Les Porrets, Les Poulettes, Les Procès, Les Pruliers, La Richemonne,* and *Les Vaucrains*. But its best wines are those from *Les Saint-Georges* and *Les Cailles* vineyards. Average annual production, 121,000 gallons of red burgundy.

OBER-INGELHEIM

One of the wine-producing parishes of Rhine-Hesse, in the Bingen district. White wines. Best vineyards: *Paares, Horn* and *Burgweg*.

OBEREMMELER

One of the finest white wines of the Saar Valley (Trier district). The best vineyards of Oberemmel are: *Rosenberg, Rauler, Falkenstein,* and *Junkerberg*.

OCKFENER

One of the best white wines of the Saar Valley (Saarberg district). The best vineyards of Ockfen are: *Bockstein, Herrenberg, Geisberg, Neuwies* and *Heppenstein*.

OFEN-ADELSBERG

One of the best red wines of Hungary, from Ofen-Pest, it is also sold under the name of *Aldesberg*.

OKOLEHAO. OKE

A spirit distilled in the Hawaii Islands from a fermented mash of the right proportion of sugar-cane molasses, Koji rice lees and the juice of the baked root of the Taro or Kalo plant (*Colocasia antiquorum*) to which water is added. The spirit is bottled at from 80° to 90° proof and is dark in colour; it has a smoky flavour and a fierce action.

OLD FASHIONED

One of the most popular and one of the most palate-paralysing forms of cocktails, fashionable in the U.S.A. It is served in specially designed glasses together with pretty little glass sticks or 'stirrers'; it is made as follows: Melt a lump of sugar in a little water in an *Old Fashioned* glass; add a dash or two of some aromatic bitters and a 'jigger' (1½ liquid oz.) rye whisky. Add some cube ice. Stir with stirrer. Some people garnish with a slice of orange, a maraschino cherry and/or a thin twist of lemon rind.

OLD TOM GIN

Another name for Plymouth gin, a sweetened *Gin*, always pure white.

OLIVIER, Château

One of the oldest and best-known of the Châteaux of the Graves district of Bordeaux. Its vineyards produce both red and white wines.

OLOROSO

One of the most popular types of sherry wine: it is golden in colour, full-bodied and rather sweet.

OMAR KHAYYÁM

Persian poet and astronomer, born probably at Nîshâpûr, between A.D. 1025 and 1050, whose fame rests upon the collection of quatrains (rubá'is) known as *The Rubá'iyát*.

And lately by the tavern door agape,
Came stealing through the dusk an Angel
  shape
Bearing a vessel on his shoulder; and
He bid me taste of it: and 'twas the Grape!
The Grape that can, with logic absolute,
The two-and-seventy jarring sects con-
  fute;
The subtle Alchemist that in a trice
Life's leaden metal into gold transmute.
                    The Rubá'iyát, vv. 42–43,
              Edward FitzGerald's translation.

OPIMIAN WINE
The wine that was vintaged when L.Opimius
was Consul, the year 633 of Rome (121 B.C.).
Pliny says that the heat of the summer was
so great that the grapes were literally cooked
and the wine which was made from them
lasted as no other wine ever did. But not all
Opimian wine was actually wine of that
extraordinary vintage, the name being sometimes used merely to mean a very ancient
vintage.

OPORTO
The Port of Portugal, on the right bank of
the River Douro, immediately facing *Vila
Nova de Gaia*, originally named *Cale*. It is to
the conjunction of the names of both towns,
Porto and *Cale*, that *Portugal* owes its name.
They are together the hub of the port wine
trade, most port shippers having their
residences and offices at Oporto and their
cellars at *Vila Nova*.

OPPENHEIM (Rhine-Hesse)
Between Mayence and Worms. White wines.
Best vineyards: *Sackträger, Herrenberg, Kreuz,
Goldberg, Krötenbrunnen, Reisekahr, Daubhaus*
and *Vielweg*.

ORANGEADE
A refreshing long drink which is made in
the same way as *Lemonade* (q.v.) using
oranges in place of lemons, and, if liked, a
little sugar, but when sweet oranges are used
there is no need to add any sugar. The commercial article sold as *Orangeade* in a bottle is
a different proposition; it is usually made
with essences and acids.

ORANGE BITTERS
The most popular form of bitters used for
flavouring cocktails and other mixed drinks.
It is made from the peel of the bitter Seville
orange.

ORANGE BRANDY
One gallon best brandy; rind of eight Seville
oranges and two lemons cut very thin, and
2 lb. loaf sugar; put into a stone jar, cork
down and shake daily for a few minutes for
three weeks; then strain off, bottle and cork.

ORDONNAC-ET-POTENSAC
A Commune of the Médoc, 62 k. NNW. of
Bordeaux, the vineyards of which produce
some undistinguished claret, the best of
which being the wine of *Châteaux Gallais*
and *Potensac*, two of the Crus Bourgeois.

ORGEAT
Blanch and pound ¾ lb. of sweet almonds
and 30 bitter ones, with a tablespoonful of
water. Stir in by degrees two pints of water
and three pints of milk, and strain the whole
through a cloth. Dissolve ½ lb. of loaf sugar
in a pint of water, boil, skim well, and mix
with the almond water, adding two tablespoonfuls of orange-flower water, and a teacupful of good brandy.—F.F.

ORLEANS
The wines of Orleans have enjoyed in the
past a great reputation which none of the
wines of the Loiret Département deserve to-
day. The red wine of Beaugency, from vineyards between Orleans and Blois, was a great
favourite at Court, during the eighteenth
century, and still enjoys a certain measure of
popularity locally. The white wines of
Tavers and Meung-sur-Loire, more particularly the Vin des Mauves, of Meung, are
pleasant summer wines in great demand in
Orleans restaurants and estaminets.

ORVIETO
One of the most picturesque cities of Umbria
perched on a hilltop and surrounded by
vineyards, the best wines of which are the
white *Orvieto*: there are two varieties of it,
the dry or *secco* and the sweet or *abboccato*,
which is the finer of the two. Both are straw-
coloured and bottled in straw-covered flasks
similar to the *Chianti* fiasco.

OSOYE. OSEY. AUSSAY
Various forms of the name of a wine which
was popular in England in the time of
Chaucer: its nature and origin have never
been ascertained satisfactorily.

OESTRICHER
One of the finest white wines of the Rhinegau. Among the best vineyards of Oestrich
are: *Lenchen, Eiserberg, Doosberg, Klostergarten,
Deez, Mühlberg* and *Neuberg*.

OUZO
The most popular apéritif of Greece: it is a
spirit flavoured with aniseed and is usually
served in a tall glass, like *Absinthe*, and mixed
with iced water, when it turns milky and
opalescent. It is most refreshing served thus.

PAARL VALLEY
One of the most beautiful as well as the most
important wine-producing valleys of the
Cape Peninsula.

PAJARETE. PAXARETE

A small town of the Jerez district, near Arcos, where there was a famous monastery, now no more; also vineyards still flourishing and noted for their Pedro Ximenez grapes. These grapes are gathered when fully ripe and exposed to the sun for a week or two before being pressed, when they yield a very sweet juice. This is treated with brandy so that it does not ferment, and the *Pajarete* or *Paxarete* liqueur wine thus obtained, although it may be drunk as a sweet liqueur, is mostly used for sweetening high-class sweet sherries. That this wine was popular in England during the latter part of the eighteenth century and the first half of the nineteenth is shown by the number of Wine Labels bearing its name, under various spellings. In the M.V.Brown Collection of Wine and Sauce Labels given to the London Museum in 1915, two labels bear the name *Paxarette*, the one dated 1794, the other 1802; two others in the Ionides Collection of Enamel Wine Labels bear the names *Pacaret* and *Pagares*. The spellings *Paxarete* and *Pajarete* also occur.

PALATINATE

A plateau on the left bank of the Rhine, South Germany, the vineyards of which produce some of the most luscious and delicious hocks, as well as a quantity of white wines of fair to moderate quality. The Palatinate is divided into three parts, the Upper, Middle and Lower Haardt, all the best wines being those from the Middle Haardt vineyards.

    MITTELHAARDT: *Bad Dürkheim, Deidesheim, Forst, Gimmeldingen, Haardt, Kallstadt, Königsbach, Neustadt, Ruppertsberg* and *Wachenheim*.

    OBERHAARDT: *Birkweiler, Burrweiler, Diedesfeld, Edenkoben, Hambach, Landau in der Pfalz, Maikammer-Alsterweiler, St Martin* and *Siebeldingen*.

    UNTERHAARDT: *Dirmstein* and *Zell*.

PALESTINE WINES

The grape-vine is indigenous to Palestine, where wine was made for centuries before the advent of the Turkish rule. Vineyards were replanted at the end of the nineteenth century, and still more during the years immediately after 1918, when Jewish settlers were encouraged to return to Palestine. The most important centre of viticulture is at *Richon-le-Zion*, about eight miles south of Jaffa.

PALM WINE

A generic name for any of the many alcoholic beverages obtained through the fermentation of the sap of tropical trees, chiefly the date palm (*Phoenix dactylifera*) and the coconut palm (*Cocos nucifera*).

PALMA

A name which is used for three distinct types of wine: (1) the wine of Majorca, one of the Balearic islands; (2) that of Palma, the chief city of Teneriffe, one of the Canary Islands; (3) the driest, palest and most delicate types of sherry in the making, marked with a chalk *Y*, which is supposed to represent a palm (*Palma*).

PALMER, Château

Third Growth of the Médoc (Cantenac). Average 100 tuns claret. The vineyards of *Palmer* are partly in the Commune of Cantenac and partly in that of Margaux, and their wine is usually sold under the name of *Palmer-Margaux*. Previous to 1830 the Château and its wines were known as *Château de Gasq*. There is also some white wine made at *Château Palmer*, but it is not nearly so fine as the red.

PALOMINO

A species of white grape which is extensively grown in the Jerez district for the making of the best sherry wine.

PALUS, Vins de

The red wines made from grapes grown in the low-lying vineyards along the banks of the Rivers Garonne and Gironde and in the islands of the Gironde. They are mostly cheap wines of no great distinction but none the less wholesome and most acceptable.

PAPE-CLÉMENT, Château

One of the best Growths of the Graves district of Bordeaux, in the Commune of Pessac. It was once the property of the Archbishop of Bordeaux, Bertrand de Goth, who, on becoming Pope, in 1305, when he took the name of Clement V, donated the property to his successors on the See of Bordeaux. Its annual average production is 50 tuns claret.

PAREMPUYRE

A Commune of the Médoc, 16 k. N. of Bordeaux. Its two best estates are *Châteaux Parempuyre* and *Ségur*, both *Bourgeois supérieurs* averaging 145 tuns of claret.

PARFAIT AMOUR

A sweet liqueur of violet hue, the informing flavours of which are violets and vanilla. (Probably owes its name to some elderly spinster who knew no better.)

PARSNIP WINE

Cut the roots into thin slices, and boil them in water, pressing out the liquor, and fermenting it. This wine, when made strong, is highly approved of by many *bons vivants.* —W.S.M.

PASOLATO DI TRAPANI
One of the more popular sweet dessert wines of Sicily.

PASSE-TOUS-GRAINS
A red burgundy made of mixed grapes, Pinot and Gamay, or grapes not specially selected. It never is a very fine wine, but, in good vintages, some Passe-tous-Grains wines are quite good and inexpensive.

PASSITI
The name of a number of sweet dessert wines made in many parts of Italy.

PASSOVER WINE
A dark red and very sweet wine made in the U.S.A. from the concord grape, chiefly by the Monarch Wine Company. It is a fully fermented wine, not fortified but sweetened with cane sugar.

PASTEURIZATION
The raising of the temperature of newly made wine to a degree sufficient to kill or render definitely inactive the ferments and germs it may contain. The *pasteurized* must is thus freed from the cause of most diseases likely to affect wine made from grapes that are not quite sound. Safe, i.e. pure, yeast is then added, and fermentation takes place under conditions which are natural, although not nature's. Pasteurization has saved untold quantities of unsatisfactorily made wines from the still or from the vinegar butt, but no wine that has been pasteurized will ever reach the same perfection as wine made from sound grapes and allowed to ferment unchecked with its own self-supplied ferments.

PASTOSO
A sweetish, because imperfectly fermented, white wine from the Alban Hills vineyards.

PATRAS
One of the best wine-producing districts of Greece. Mostly white.

PAUILLAC
One of the most important wine-producing Communes of the Médoc, 48 k. NNW. of Bordeaux, between Saint-Julien to the south, Saint-Estèphe to the north, and the broad Gironde to the east. Two of the three First Growths of the Médoc, *Châteaux Lafite* and *Latour*, are in the Commune of Pauillac, as well as three Second Growths, *Châteaux Mouton-Rothschild, Pichon-Longueville* and *Pichon-Longueville-Lalande*; one Fourth Growth, *Château Duhart-Milon*; and eleven Fifth Growths, *Châteaux Pontet-Canet, Batailley, Grand-Puy-Ducasse, Grand-Puy-Lacoste, Lynch-Bages, Lynch-Moussas, Haut-Bages, Croizet-Bages, Mouton-d'Armailhacq, Pédesclaux* and *Clerc-Milon.* Besides these there are a large number of *Bourgeois supérieurs* growths responsible for a very large quantity of very fair claret: the more important are: *Châteaux Balognes-Haut-Bages, Colombier-Monpelou, Malécot, Constant-Bages-Monpelou, Bellegrave, Haut-Bages-Avérous, Fonbadet, Bichon-Bages, La Tour-Milon, d'Anseillan, La Tour-Pibran, Haut-Milon, Grand Saint-Lambert, Grand-Milon, Bellevue-Saint-Lambert, La Couronne, Bellevue-Cordeillan-Bages, Belle-Rose,* etc.

PAVIE, Château
One of the largest of the First Growths of Saint-Emilion now divided among a number of different owners. By far the largest share of the vineyard is that which belongs to a Mr Porte; it is usually sold as *Château Pavie,* with the name *Albert Porte* added on the label; it averages 200 tuns. The next largest share of Pavie vineyards belongs to the heirs of a Mr Macquin, and is sold under the name of *Domaine de Pavie-Macquin*; it averages 70 tuns. A smaller share, which belonged originally to a Mr Decesse, is sold under the label *Château Pavie Decesse*; it averages 25 tuns. The wines of yet another vineyard close by are sold under the label *Château Saint-Georges-Côte-Pavie*; it averages 20 tuns.

PEACH BRANDY
A cordial made with brandy which is flavoured with peaches.

PEACH LIQUEUR
A liqueur with a brandy, or any other spirit as a basis, flavoured with fresh or dried peaches and sweetened with sugar or glucose. The best *Peach Liqueurs* are, of course, those made with brandy, cane sugar and fresh fruit.

PEACH WINE
Press thro' a cloth with wide meshes the juice of 50 pounds of fresh, ripe Peaches, treating the fruit the same as in making Marmalade; then put it to ferment in a large half-cask. After covering the liquor with a cloth, place it in a moderately warm place, until it has fermented well, which should be in 2 or 3 weeks. When there are no longer any signs of fermentation and you are well satisfied with the clearness of the liquor which you will find below the surface or a scum formed on top, and which you must skim off carefully from time to time, you may pass it all thro' four thicknesses of cheese-cloth. Then you shall add a pint of

spirits of wine, well rectified, and 2 pounds of sugar. Rack the Liquor into a cask, bung it tightly, and let it stand for a year. And then you can bottle it.—C.E.M.

PÉCS
The centre of the *Villany-Fünfkirchen* vineyards, in the Baranga Komitat of Hungary, noted for their wines and table grapes.

PEDRO XIMENEZ. P.X.
The name of a grape which is particularly sweet, because it is lacking in acidity, and also the name of a sweet wine which is made from it, chiefly in the south of Spain. The grapes are gathered when fully ripe, left to dry in the sun on straw mats for a week or two, and then pressed. Their very sweet juice is then run into casks in which there is some brandy, so that it cannot ferment. It is more a liqueur than a wine and may be drunk as a very sweet liqueur, but it is chiefly used for sweetening high-class sherries. In the Ionides Collection of Enamel Wine Labels, there is one bearing the inscription *Peixi Meles*, which is probably an attempt at some phonetic spelling of *Pedro Ximenez*.

PERALTA
Jullien, in his *Topographie*, mentions this wine as a dessert 'rancio' wine, made from muscat grapes, at Peralta, in Navarre. As evidence that the wine must have enjoyed a certain measure of popularity there are two labels in the Ionides Collection of Enamel Wine Labels bearing the names of *Peralta* and *Peralte* respectively.

PÉRIGNON, Dom
The Cellarer of the Abbey of Hautvillers who helped to make champagne more popular in France, at the close of the seventeenth century, by suitably blending wines of different vineyards and introducing cork stoppers, which made 'Sparkling Champagne' possible. But Dom Pérignon never claimed to have 'discovered' Sparkling Champagne, which was known at an earlier date, in England, where cork stoppers were in common use long before they were obtainable in France.

PERNAND-VERGELESSES
One of the smaller Communes of the Côte d'Or, which produces some fine red burgundy. Its best vineyards are *L'Ile des Vergelesses*, *Les Basses Vergelesses*, and *Les Fichots*. Average yearly production, 31,000 gallons.

PERNOD
A name that was for many years synonymous with *Absinthe*, in France and Switzerland. The firm of *Pernod*, of Pontarlier, in the Jura

Département of France, close to the Swiss frontier, was the oldest and largest to distil *Absinthe*. Since the sale of *Absinthe* has been prohibited in France, they sell an apéritif under the name of *Pernod*, which has no *Absinthe* but *Aniseed* as its basis.

PERRIER WATER
One of the best-known mineral waters from the south of France. It is highly effervescent, colourless and tasteless, hence suitable as a *Table Water*.

PERRY
The fermented juice of fresh pears, and usually sweetened as well as filtered before it is bottled. There is both still and sparkling *Perry*, the sparkling kind is the more popular of the two and it is sold as *Medium Dry*, which is sweet enough for most grown-up people, and *Sweet*, which is very sweet.

PERSIA
Once upon a time the country was famous for its wines; to-day the making and sale of wine is not allowed to Persians, but there are a few Armenians who make and Jews who sell wine.

PERSICO
A peach liqueur or cordial which was well known under that name, and also as *Persicot* and *Persicoa*, in England, during the eighteenth century. Mrs Manley mentioned *Persicoa* in her *New Atlantis*, in 1709, and Addison speaks of 'Cordials, Ratafias, Persico, Orange-flowers and Cherry-Brandy', in the *Spectator* (No. 328, 17 March 1712). —N.M.P.

PERUVIAN WINE
The vineyards of Peru are chiefly in the regions of Ica, Locumba, Lima, Pisco and the Sicamba River; their wines are made from European species of grapes, but their limited quantity and their homely quality have restricted their consumption to Peru itself.

PESSAC
The nearest Commune WSW. of Bordeaux and the most famous of the Graves district, being the home of *Château Haut Brion*, the finest wine of Graves and one of the greatest of all clarets. *Châteaux La Mission-Haut Brion*, *Pape-Clément*, *Bellegrave*, *Laburthe-Brivazac*, *Camponac*, *des Chambrettes*, *des Carmes-Haut-Brion*, *Phénix* and some thirty-six other smaller wine-producing estates are situated in the Commune of Pessac.

PHYLLOXERA
The American vine louse. It was first recorded in England, at Kew, in 1863, and it

751

has since spread to every continental and island vineyard of the world with but few exceptions. The indigenous North American vines, having become partly immune to this pest, are now largely used in European and other vineyards as the briars upon which the various species of *Vitis vinifera*, the European vine, are grafted.

PICARDAN

One of the golden sweet dessert wines from vineyards on the French side of the Eastern Pyrenees, it enjoyed a certain measure of popularity in England during the eighteenth century.

In *Notes on a Cellar Book*, Professor George Saintsbury refers to *Picardan* as 'the northernmost wine of France and the worst.' We are unable to account for this curious verdict. Maybe the Professor was misled by the analogy between *Picardan* and *Picardie*, where there are no vineyards. The only wine of the name that we have ever heard of is a wine very similar to the wine of *Banuyls* and made in the same district of the Pyrenees.

PICCOLIT. PICCOLITO

Piccolit is the name of a white grape which used to be grown in *Friuli*, a Venetian province, and *Piccolito*, the name of the wine made from it. Cyrus Redding, in his *History of Modern Wines*, says that 'the luscious wine made at Piccoli is equal to the *Vino Santo* of southern Italy'. There is a Wine Label with the name *Picolito* and another, in the Ionides Collection of Enamel Wine Labels, with *Piccolit de l'année*.

PICHON-LONGUEVILLE,
Château
PICHON-LONGUEVILLE-
LALANDE, Château

Two of the Second Growths of the Médoc (Pauillac), originally one and the same property which was owned during over two hundred and fifty years by various members of the Pichon-Longueville family. During the first quarter of the nineteenth century, some three-fifths of the vineyards were acquired by Comtesse de Lalande and their wine has been sold ever since under the label '*Pichon-Longueville. Comtesse de Lalande*'. The average of *Château Pichon-Longueville* is 75 tuns claret; that of *Château Pichon-Longueville-Lalande* is 100 tuns.

> *Pichon-de-Longueville, en face de La-Tour,*
> *Est élégant, musqué comme un homme de cour.*
> *Dans son parfum, son ton, enfin dans tout son être,*
> *Il a l'étincelant éclat d'un petit-maître:*
> *Et, quoiqu'il soit léger, coquet et sémillant,*
> *Son esprit est solide autant qu'il est brillant.*

PICPOUL

The name given to a number of light, rather thin and characterless white wines made in the Midi, chiefly in the Aude Département; they are chiefly used as a basis wine in the making of vermouth. There is, however, a better and sweet dessert wine of that name made in the Pyrénées Orientales Département.

Piedmont produces some of the best red table wines of Italy as well as most Italian sparkling wines and vermouths. The best wines of Piedmont are those of the Monferrato Hills, south of the River Po, chiefly the red wines of Barolo and Barbaresco, and the white wines of Gavi and Canelli; also the sparkling wines of Asti, but many of the wines of Piedmont are sold under the names of the grapes from which they are made, such as Nebbiolo, Barbera and Grignolino, for the red wines, Cortese for the white ones, and Moscato for the sweet wines.

PIESPORT

Moselle Valley. Wittlich district; fine white wines. Best vineyards: *Goldtröpchen, Falkenberg, Lay, Günterslay, Schubertslay, Pichter, Taubengarten.*

PILSNER BEER

The most renowned of all *Lager Beers*, from Pilsen, in Bohemia. The name has been freely borrowed by brewers in other parts of the world, who sell the best *Lager Beer* they know how to brew under the name of *Pilsner*.

PIMM'S No. 1

The original and best-known of the four 'Cups' marketed as *Pimm's Cups*. Its basis is gin and bitters. It is used neat, iced, and for *Gin slings*, etc. Pimm's No. 2 has whisky, No. 3, brandy, and No. 4 rum as a basis.

PINARD

French Army slang for the ration wine issued to the troops.

PINOT. PINEAU

The variety of grapes, both black and white, from which the best champagne and the best burgundies are made. There are a number of different members of the noble *Pinot* family: *Pinot Noir, Pinot Blanc, Pinot Chardonnay*, etc.

PINT

English standard wine measure, the one-eighth of the gallon, or half the quart. Contents: 34.659 cubic inches, equal to 5.68 décilitres. The old English pint (pre-1826) was only 0.8331 of the present or 'Imperial Pint'; it is still the legal pint in use in the U.S.A. (28.875 cubic inches). There used to be also a Stirling Pint in Scotland, which was equal to nearly three Imperial Pints (2.9834).

PIQUETTE
The French name of an imitation wine which is usually made out of the husks of grapes, after the juice has been pressed for making wine; they are flooded with water, sweetened with the cheapest available sugar and fermented with brewer's yeast.

PISCO
A very potent spirit popular in Peru, where it is distilled from wine made in the Valley of the Ica, near Pisco. A milder form is also shipped, from Pisco, to the U.S.A. in porous clay jars.

PIPE
The standard cask for port in the British Isles; its gauge is 115 gallons, averaging 56 dozens when bottled.

PLATO
'When a man drinks wine, he begins to be better pleased with himself, and the more he drinks, the more he is filled full of brave hopes and conceit of his power ... What is better adapted than the festive use of wine, in the first place to test, and in the second place to train the character of a man, if care be taken in the use of it? What is there cheaper or more innocent?'

Plato, *Law* I, 648–650

PLUM WINE
Take 20 lb. of Malaga raisins, pick, rub, and shred them, and put them into a tub; then take four gallons of fair water and boil it an hour, and let it stand till it is blood-warm; then put it to your raisins; let it stand nine or ten days, stirring it once or twice a day; strain out your liquor, and mix with it two quarts of damsin (*sic*) juice; put it in a vessel, and when it has done working stop it close; at four or five months bottle it.—E.S.

PLYMOUTH GIN
Completely dry and pure white gin distilled at the Black Friars Distillery, Plymouth by Messrs Coates & Co.

PODENSAC
One of the Communes of the Gironde, 32 k. SSE. of Bordeaux, the vineyards of which produce some red wines of no particular merit but more and better white wines, similar to those of the adjoining Commune of *Cérons*; they are mostly sold under the name of *Cérons* wines. The best wines of Podensac are those of *Châteaux de Madère* and *de Mauves*.

POLIGNY
An important wine-producing Commune of the Jura Département, it is chiefly noted for its white wines, more particularly some of the *Vins jaunes* and *Vins de paille* which are similar to those of *Château Chalon*.

POMEROL
One of the more important wine-producing Communes of the Gironde. Its vineyards occupy a small plateau between Libourne and St Emilion: they produce no white wine but a large quantity of claret of high quality, as well as a greater quantity still of whole-some and pleasant but commoner red wines. Some of the best-known growths of Pomerol are the following: *Beauregard, Château; Bourgueneuf, Château; Certan, Château; A Certan; Clinet, Château; Gazin, Château; Grand Champ, Cru; Grandes Vignes, Clos des; Gravette, Clos de la; Guillot, Château; La Conseillante, Château; La Croix, Château; Lagrange, Cru; La Pointe, Château; La Tour Pomerol, Château; L'Eglise, Clos; L'Eglise, Cru de; L'Eglise, Domaine de; L'Eglise Clinet, Château; L'Evangile, Château; La Fleur, Château; La Fleur du Gazin, Château; La Fleur Pétrus, Château; Le Gay, Château; Nénin, Château; Petit-Village, Château; Pétrus, Château; Presbytère, Enclos du; Rouget, Château; Trotanoy, Château; Vieux-Château-Certan.* All these call themselves First Growths. *Château La Commancerie* and many others, which produce some very fair claret, are content to be known as *Second Growths*.

POMMARD
One of the best-known Communes of the Côte d'Or (Côte de Beaune) which produces a large quantity of red burgundy, much of it being of very fine quality and much more of little distinction. There is also sold, under a name which is more easily remembered and pronounced than many other Burgundian names, much wine which never came from Pommard. The best vineyards of Pommard cover some 845 acres; they are: *Les Argillières, les Arvelets, les Bertins, les Boucherottes, les Chaponnières, les Charmots, le Clos Blanc, le Clos de Citeaux, Clos de la Commaraine, les Croix Noires, les Epenots, les Fremiers, le Clos Micot, les Pezerolles, les Rugiens*. Some of the most reliable wines of Pommard are the *Cuvées Billardet* and *Dames de la Charité*, which belong to the *Hospices de Beaune*.

POMMARÈDE, Château de
One of the oldest Châteaux of the Graves de Bordeaux district, in the Commune of Castres. Its average production is 20 tuns of claret of fine quality and 8 tuns of white wine of fair quality.

PONTAC
The name of several red wines of the Gironde (Claret), none of them of any outstanding merit. But in the seventeenth century *Pontac* was considered one of the finest clarets in

England. John Locke wrote in 1677: 'The Vin de Pontac, so much esteemed in England, grows on a rising opening to the west ...', and John Evelyn wrote, on 13th July, 1683, that he had met Monsieur Pontac, 'the son of the famous Bordeaux President, who owns the excellent vineyards of Pontac and Haut-Brion, whence the best Bordeaux wines come from.' *Pontac* is also the name given to a sweet and highly fortified red wine made at the Cape, where it is highly popular locally, chiefly among 'gentlemen of colour' on Saturday nights.

PONTET-CANET, Château

The first of the Fifth Growths of the Médoc (Pauillac). It was purchased in 1865 from the heirs of Mr de Pontet by Mr Herman Cruse and has belonged to the Cruse family ever since. Its average is 200 tuns claret and its name is more widely known than that of most other clarets.

POOR MAN'S DRINK

Take two quarts of water, and place in a saucepan with 4 oz. of pearl barley, 2 oz. of figs split, 2 oz. of stoned raisins, and an oz. of root liquorice sliced; boil all together till only one quart remains; then strain and use as a drink.—F.F.

PORT

Port is a wine made from grapes grown in the valley of the Upper Douro, fortified at the vintage time and shipped from Oporto. When the grapes are pressed, their sweet juice begins to ferment; but before fermentation has transformed the whole of the grape-juice sugar into alcohol, brandy is added to it and all further vinous fermentation is immediately checked. At that stage, port is a blend of wine (fermented grape-juice), brandy, and unfermented grape-juice. But of such materials Time, that great artist, fashions two different and equally seductive wines: Vintage Port and Tawny Port. *Vintage Port* is a wine made in one year, shipped usually two years after it is made, and bottled in England soon after it is received. *Tawny Port* is not a wine made from any one year's grapes, but a blend of wines of a number of years. Tawny Port is kept at Oporto in the Shipper's Lodges for many years and matured in wood. It ages more rapidly than early-bottled Vintage Port, and is shipped when ready for drinking. *Ruby Port* is a compromise between the early-bottled Vintage Port and the matured in wood Tawny Port. Ruby Port may be the wine of one vintage kept in cask long enough to lose some of its 'fire', but not long enough to lose much of its colour. Ruby Port may be a blend of wines of different years and

style – a blend which may be made at Oporto by the Shipper, or in England by wine merchants. Although the first duty of Port is to be red, there is such a thing as *White Port,* and it has many admirers, more particularly among the ladies.

The standard gauge of a Pipe of Port is 115 gallons; its average yield 56 dozens.

PORTETS

A Commune of the Graves district, 25 k. SSE. of Bordeaux, the vineyards of which produce much red and white wine of fair quality, but none of outstanding excellence. The best wines of the Commune are those of *Châteaux Millet, Lognac, de Portets, Cabannieux, Pessan* and *La Tour-Bicheau.*

PORTUGAL

One of the more important of the European wine-producing countries and the only one of all wine-producing countries in the world to export, on an average, 1,000 gallons of her own wines for every gallon of wine imported from other vinelands. The average wine-production of Portugal is, approximately, 170 million gallons.

The principal centres of production of the Vinhos Verdes, that is 'green wines', which are not green but 'new', are the districts of Viana de Castelo, Braga, Porto, and Aveiro. Other table wines, mostly red, are those chiefly of the districts of Castelo Branco, Coïmbra, Leiria, Santarém, Lisbon, and Setubal. Port wine is made exclusively in the Douro Valley, chiefly in the districts of Vila Real, Bragança, Guarda, and Vizeu; whilst other fortified wines are made in the districts of Evora, Portalegre, Béja, and Faro.

PORT-VENDRE

(Pyrénées Orientales). A Commune which produces wines similar to those of Banyuls.

POSSET

One of the most popular forms of hot drinks to prevent or cure a cold. Its basis is hot milk, curdled with hot ale, sweetened with sugar, and flavoured with grated nutmeg. In the *de luxe edition* of the *Posset*, sherry is used in place of ale.

POTASH WATER

The real article should be a solution of bicarbonate of potash, say 15 grains in half a pint of distilled water, and aërated with washed carbonic acid gas. It is an antacid, and more of a medicine than a beverage, but its continued use is said to lead to depression of spirits.—L.G.M.

POTEEN. POTHEEN

A home-brewed Irish Whiskey, the produce of an illicit still.

POTTLE

English wine measure equal to one half of a gallon or four Imperial Pints. The pre-1826 English Pottle was, and the present American Pottle is, equal to 3.3324 Imperial Pints.

POUGET, Château

Fourth Growth of the Médoc (Cantenac). Average 30 tuns claret. One of the old Bénédictine vineyards of the Médoc, enlarged, in 1929, by the acquisition of a part of the adjoining vineyards of *Rauzan-Gassies*.

POUILLY

There are two quite different French white wines of this name, the better known of which is a white burgundy from the vineyards of two adjoining Communes of the Saône - et - Loire Département, the one called *Pouilly* and the other *Fuissé*; hence the hyphenated name of *Pouilly-Fuissé* by which the wine is sometimes known. The other wine is from the Loire Valley, from the vineyards of the Commune of *Pouilly-sur-Loire*, in the Nièvre Département; it has a very pronounced bouquet – it may almost be called aggressive – and this *Pouilly* wine is generally called *Pouilly-Fumé*.

POUSSE-CAFÉ

Original New Orleans Pousse-café

This *pousse-café* is made by pouring equal parts of brandy, maraschino, curaçao, and rum in a glass, in that order, so each remains separate, forming a different-coloured ring. More elaborate ones call for as many as seven different tinted liqueurs.—A.C.

PRAMNIAN WINE

One of the most famous of ancient Greek wines, the wine that was Nestor's – and presumably Homer's – favourite (*Iliad* X. 780). There is every reason to believe, from the descriptions of Pramnian wines which have reached us, that it was not the wine of any particular vineyard, but a wine made from overripe grapes, which were not actually pressed, their very sweet juice being collected as it oozed out under the weight of the gathered grapes: if so, it may have been somewhat like some of the *Tokay Essenz*.

PREIGNAC

One of the Communes of the Sauternes district, 42 k. SSE. of Bordeaux. Its vineyards stretch from those of the Communes of Sauternes, Barsac, Bommes and Fargues to the banks of the Garonne. The best wines which they produce are those of *Château Suduiraut* and *de Malle*: next come those of *Châteaux Bastor-Lamontagne, du Pick, Saint-Amand*, and a number of others.

PRÉMEAUX

One of the wine-producing Communes of the Côte d'Or, immediately south of Nuits-Saint-Georges; it produces a fairly large quantity of good red burgundy. Its best vineyards are *Aux Corvées, Aux Didiers, Aux Forêts, Les Argillières, Clos Arlots, Clos Maréchal, Clos Saint-Marc, Les Perdrix*.

PRIEURÉ, Château de Cantenac

Fourth Growth of the Médoc (Cantenac). Average 30 tuns claret. One of the oldest ecclesiastical vineyards of the Médoc; its wine was praised by Brillat-Savarin and Grimod de la Reynière. *Château Prieuré* is the name used on the Château-bottled labels, but Château *Le Prieuré* and *Château de Cantenac Prieuré* also occur; *Château Pagès* was the name which replaced that of *Prieuré* when the owner of the Château was Mr Pagès, in the sixties. An average of 15 tuns red wine of less distinguished quality is made at this Château and is sold under the label *Château Latour-Cantenac*; also some 10 tuns of white wine sold under the label *Château Cantenac-Blanc*.

PROOF SPIRIT

In the U.K. Proof Spirit is 'that which at the temperature of 51° F. weighs exactly '12/13 of an equal measure of distilled water.' This means that at a temperature of 60° F. Proof Spirit contains 49.28 per cent by weight or 57.10 per cent by volume of alcohol. Any degree or degrees of alcohol over or under 57.10 by volume is stated with the mention 'o.p.' or 'u.p.', meaning 'over proof' or 'under proof'. Thus a spirit containing 60.6 of alcohol, by volume, and another 53.8, would be described as: the first 6.13 o.p.; and the second 5.78 u.p.

In the U.S.A., what is known as 'Proof Spirit' is a spirit containing 50 per cent by volume of alcohol at 15.6° C. (60° F.) (Trailles alcoholometer). Thus 1 per cent of Proof Spirits equals 0.46 per cent of absolute alcohol by weight and 0.57 per cent of absolute alcohol by volume.

PROVENCE

A former Province of France divided into the Alpes-Maritimes, Bouches-du-Rhône, Var, and Vaucluse Départements. It produces a great deal of wine, both red and white, those of *Châteauneuf-du-Pape, Cassis*, and *La Gaude* being among the best.

PRUNELLE

A French liqueur, the informing flavour of which is that of fresh sloes. It was first marketed by the firm Naltet-Menand & Fils, of Chalon-sur-Saône, under the name of Prunelle Naltet.

PRUSSIAN STATE DOMAINS

The vineyards were those owned by the Prussian State, the largest vineyard owners in the Rhinegau, and they spared no expense nor trouble to secure the best wine possible. Their stamp, on a hock bottle: *Original-Abfüllung Preuss. Staatsdomane*, is a guarantee of quality as well as of authenticity. The Prussian State vineyards were the following:

Hochheim. Part of the Domdechaney and Kirchenstuck vineyards.

Rüdesheim. Parts of Schlossberg, Burgweg, Roseneck, Bronnen, Zollhaus, Bischofsberg, Hinterhaus.

Steinberg. The whole of Steinberg.

Hattenheim. Most of the Engelmannsberg vineyards.

Markobrunn, Rauenthal, and *Kiedrich.* Parts of quite a number of vineyards in each.

PULIGNY-MONTRACHET

One of the three Communes of the Côte d'Or (Burgundy) responsible for the finest white wines of Burgundy. Like the adjoining Commune of Chassagne, Puligny has hyphenated the name of its most famous vineyard, *Montrachet*, with its own, *Puligny*. Its best wines are those of *Montrachet, Chevalier-Montrachet, Blagny Blanc, Caillerets, Bâtard-Montrachet, Bienvenue-Bâtard-Montrachet,* and *Les Pucelles*.

PULQUE

An intoxicating beverage fermented, chiefly in Mexico, from the sap of the Maguey and other kinds of aloes.

PUNCH

Punch in its oldest and simplest form is rum and water, hot or iced, with sugar to taste and orange or lemon (for hot *Punch*), or fresh lime (for cold *Punch*). It was in 1655, when they took Jamaica from Spain, that the English were first introduced to Rum and to Punch. During the eighteenth century *Punch* became much more elaborate, in England, as well as the recognized Whig drink: it was 'brewed' or mixed at table in a Punchbowl, by the host, with rum as one of the ingredients but other spirits as well, brandy nearly always, and either hot water or hot tea, oranges and lemons in thin slices, grated nutmeg and sundry decorations or flavourings to the taste or discretion of the holder of the Punch Ladle.

'Punch cures the Gout, the Cholic, and the Phtisic,
And it is to all men the very best Physic.'

Ale Punch. Put into a bowl one quart of mild ale, one wineglassful of sherry, the like quantity of brandy, a tablespoonful of icing sugar, the peel and juice of one lemon, a little grated nutmeg, and a small piece of ice; serve in small tumblers.—F.D.S.D.

Army Punch. Two dozen lemons and two dozen oranges. One quart of light rum; 3 lb. of sugar; bottle and cork it and serve with crushed ice. *Mrs Wm. H.Thomas, Carroll County.*—F.P.S.

Chilean 3-day Punch. First day: Pare yellow rind from nine lemons with sharp knife, so thinly that none of the bitter white adheres. Put in a quart jug and pour on one pint fine Jamaica rum. Screw cover right down and set aside for use on third day.

Second day: Put 2 lb. sugar loaf in another jar and squeeze over them the juice of those nine skinned lemons. Screw cover down and set snugly by the side of the rum-and-rind jar.

Third day: Mix contents of both jars in a big punch-bowl, pour in three pints rum and five quarts distilled water, or water that has been boiled and cooled, with two pints boiling hot milk. Let it drain slowly through a flannel bag, without squeezing.—A.C.

Duke of Norfolk's Punch. To a gallon of rum or brandy take six lemons and six oranges. Pare them as thin as you can and put the parings into the spirits and let them steep 24 hours. Afterwards take six quarts of spring water and 3 lb. of loaf sugar and boil the water and sugar for quarter of an hour and clear it with whites of eggs. When the sugar and water is cold, strain the parings from the brandy or rum and squeeze in your juice of oranges, etc., through a strainer to keep out the seeds. Then mix all together and turn it in a vessel where it must remain six weeks at least unbottled. (Anne Wynne of Bodewryd, 1675.)—D.A.

Fish House Punch. One pint lemon juice, three pints mixture, viz.: one pint Jamaica spirits, one pint brandy and one pint peach brandy, 4 lb. sugar, nine pints water. Make lemonade first, then add other liquors. *Mrs Charles H.Tilghman, Talbot County.*—F.P.S.

'Fish House Punch has been the main speciality of the "State in Schuylkill" since this association was founded, in 1732. This drink has made countless thousands happy, including George Washington, Lafayette, and, later, General Pershing.'—C.B.D.

Milk Punch. One tablespoonful of fine white sugar, one tablespoonful of water, one wineglass of cognac brandy, half a wineglass of Santa Cruz or Jamaica rum, a little chipped ice. Fill with milk, shake the ingredients well together, and grate a little nutmeg on top.—L.EN.

Old Medford Punch. One quart Medford rum, half pint brandy, half pint claret, one cup strong tea. Sweeten to taste and add three sliced oranges, one sliced pineapple. Stand 24 hours. Chill, and to serve add two quarts champagne.—A.C.

Planters' Punch. The planters' punch, according to one writer, gets its name because it has been drunk by the sugar planters in Jamaica for over a hundred years. Unfortunately, like a mint julep, it is made in a hundred different ways and seems to reflect the idiosyncrasies of the various bartenders. Generally speaking, a planters' punch is made with a good drink of rum (1¼ to 2 oz.) in a long glass with cracked ice and water, shaken up with lime juice and sugar and served unstrained with a straw. In some places orange juice is used instead of water. —C.B.D.

Peabody Punch. (Named after the maternal great-grandfather of August Peabody Loring, Jr., Hon. Secretary of the Wine and Food Society of Boston, Mass.).

    1 bottle best Jamaica rum
    6 glasses cognac
    3 glasses madeira
    1 doz large limes or 2 doz. small
    1 jar guava jelly
    1 pint green tea
    Sugar to taste

Rub sugar on limes to get the essential oil diffused into the sugar. Dissolve two-thirds of sugar in tea. Then cut the limes, squeeze and add their juice to the remainder of the impregnated sugar. Dissolve the guava jelly in a pint of boiling water. Mix all these until you get the right sweetness; then add the rum, madeira and cognac. It should stand for at least 12 hours, or better, 24. Let large lump of ice float in the punch for an hour before serving, which serves two purposes – making the concoction cool and pleasant to the taste, and diluting it to a pleasant consistency. Bottle any punch left over for a future occasion, as it improves with age.—C.B.D.

Roman Punch. Six oranges, four lemons, one quart whisky or one bottle champagne, eight egg whites, 2 lb. sugar, one gallon water. Grate the rinds and add to the juice one gallon water, one quart whisky and eight whites of eggs beaten to a froth. Freeze. *Mrs Robert Goldsborough Henry, Myrtle Grove, Talbot County.*—F.P.S.

Royal Punch. One pint of hot green tea, half a pint of brandy, half a pint of Jamaica rum, one wineglass of white curaçao, one wineglass of arrack, the juice of two limes, a thin slice of lemon, white sugar to taste, a gill of warm calf's foot jelly. To be drunk as hot as possible.—L.En.

Rum Punch. Put into a large tumbler a tablespoonful of icing sugar, a wineglass of brandy, the like quantity of rum, two teaspoonfuls of arrack, the juice of one lemon, quarter of a wineglass of green tea, a teaspoonful of essence of spice. Half fill the glass with shaved ice, shake well, strain, and add sufficient milk to fill the glass. Dust with nutmeg and cinnamon, and serve with a straw.—F.D.S.D.

Tea Punch. One pint rum, 1½ cups sugar, six lemons, one tablespoonful brandy, two cups strong tea. Peel the lemons thin and pour the tea boiling hot over them. Squeeze the lemon juice on the sugar and let remain an hour or more. Mix altogether and mix over a bowl of crushed ice. This would serve about six people before prohibition. *Mrs Anne Merryman Carroll, Hayfields, Baltimore County.*—F.P.S.

Webster's Punch. Two dozen lemons, strained; 2 lb. sugar; half pint green tea, strained; one quart best brandy; three quarts claret. Bottle and stand overnight. Then add champagne to taste, strawberries, bananas, oranges, cherries, pineapples, and any fruits desired. Serve in punch-bowl with ice.

PÜNDERICH

Lower Moselle. Zell district. White wines. Best vineyards: *Rosenberg, Marienberg, Falkenlay, Golday,* and *Petersberg.*

PUPILLIN

A village of the Jura Department, near *Arbois,* hemmed in by vineyards which produce wines, mostly white, similar to those of *Arbois* and usually sold under the name of *Arbois.* In particularly good years, however, they also produce a white wine of the style of the *Vin Jaune* of *Château Chalon;* such a wine, according to the *Loi des Appellations* may not be sold as *Vin Jaune* until it is at least six years old.

PURL

An old-fashioned English winter drink, of which there are many variants. One kind used to be made up of a mixture of ale and beer with gin and bitters. The gin and bitters are first put into a pint pewter pot, the ale is warmed over a brisk fire and poured into the pot when warm enough for the drinker to be able to toss the whole down at a single draught.

Here is another Victorian version:

Put a quart of mild ale into a saucepan, add a tablespoonful of grated nutmeg, and place over a slow fire until it nearly boils. Mix a little cold ale with sugar to taste, and, gradually, two eggs well-beaten; then add the hot ale, stirring one way to prevent curdling – and a quarter of a pint of whisky. Warm the whole again, and then pour from one vessel into another till it becomes smooth.—F.F.

QUART

A standard English wine measure equal to one-quarter of a gallon, 1.136 litres or 69.318 cubic inch. This standard or legal quart is also known as 'Imperial Quart', as distinct from the 'reputed quart,' which is only one-sixth of the Imperial Gallon. The *Winchester Quart* was a noble bottle holding five pints.

QUART DE CHAUME
The best white wines of Rochefort-sur-Loire, in Anjou, where the little river Layon joins the great Loire.

The vineyards now bearing this name formed originally the Clos du Seigneur de la Guerche who demanded a fourth of the yield every year from the vignerons who farmed them. They now belong to various owners and the *Quart de Chaume* which was considered the best, up to 1940, was that of a Mr Mignot, at *Château de Belle-Rive*.

QUETSCH
A spirit distilled from plums, chiefly in Alsace: it is always pure white, as it is not coloured nor matured in wood.

QUINCE WINE
Take your quinces when they are fully ripe, and wipe off the fur very clean; then take out the cores, bruise the fruit as you do apples for cider, and press out the juice; to every gallon of which add 2½ lb. of loaf sugar, stirring it together till the sugar is dissolved; afterwards put it into your cask, and, when the fermentation is over, bung it up well. Let it stand till March before you bottle it. This wine will improve by being kept two or three years.—W.S.M.

QUINQUINA
The French name of *Quinine Wines*, mostly served as *Apéritifs* (q.v.).

QUINTAS
The Portuguese equivalent of the *Château* of the Médoc, 'Estates', of which the best-known are: *Boa Vista, Noval, Roriz, Malvedos*, etc.

RABAUD, Château
One of the First Growths of Sauternes, in the Commune of Bommes (60 tuns average).

RAIN WATER MADEIRA
The name originated in Savannah, where a madeira enthusiast, a Mr Habersham, evolved a special mode of fining and maturing his wines which acquired a distinctive colour and bouquet. But his secret died with him and since then the name has been registered as a brand which is the property of Welch Brothers, of Madeira.

RAISIN WINE
Take two gallons of spring water, and let it boil half an hour; then put into a steam pot 2 lb. of raisins stoned, 2 lb. of sugar, and the rinds of two lemons. Pour the boiling water on the above ingredients, and let it stand covered four or five days; then strain it out, and bottle it off. In about 15 or 16 days it will be fit for use. It is a very cool, pleasant drink in hot weather.—W.S.M.

RANCIO
Spanish for rancid or rank: where used in connection with wine, it refers to a certain concentration of ethers chiefly noticeable in the sweet dessert wines kept a long time in bottle.

RANDERSACKER
One of the best wine-producing parishes of Franconia in the Würzburg district. White wines (Steinwein).

RASPAIL
A French digestive liqueur.

RASPBERRY WINE
Pound your fruit, and strain it through a cloth; then boil as much water as there is juice, and, when cold, pour it on the dry strained fruit, letting it stand five hours: after which strain it again, and mix it with the juice. To every gallon of this liquor add 2½ lb. of sugar: let it stand in an earthen vessel closely covered for a week; then turn it into a clean cask, and let it stand well bunged up for a month, till it is fine. Afterwards bottle it off.—W.S.M.

RATAFIA
A generic name for a number of cordials, usually home-made, always sweet and often of very highly alcoholic strength. Ratafia may be made with new wine or grape juice and sufficient spirit to stop its fermentation; being further flavoured with various fruits, herbs and spices; or else by the infusion of the same ingredients in brandy.

'Every liqueur made by infusion is called *Ratafia*; that is when the spirit is made to imbibe thoroughly the aromatic flavour and colour of the fruit steeped in it: when this has taken place, the liqueur is drawn off and sugar added to it; it is then filtered and bottled.'—G.A.J.

In early Victorian days the more popular Ratafias were the orange, raspberry, currants, mulberries, green walnut.

RAUENTHAL
Rhinegau. White wines of very fine quality. Best vineyards: *Hühnerberg, Siebenmorgen, Burggraben, Berg Edellse, Steinnacher*.

RAUSAN-SÉGLA, Château
Second Growth of the Médoc (Margaux). Average 60 tuns claret. No Châteaux bottling. The estate belonged to members of the

de Rausan family from 1661 until 1866, since when it belonged to the Cruse family.

RAUZAN-GASSIES, Château
Second Growth of the Médoc (Margaux). Average 50 tuns claret. One of the oldest vineyards of the Médoc; it has been owned by a Gassies since 1530 to 1789; a Mr de Rauzan added his name when he became the owner during the early part of the nineteenth century.

RAYNE-VIGNEAU, Château
One of the First Growths of Sauternes, in the Commune of Bommes. (75 tuns average.)

REFOSCO
A semi-sparkling, sweetish, red wine, which used to be sold in Trieste. It was made from the grapes of Carso and Triestino vineyards and was highly esteemed by the natives.

REHOBOAM
The name of a 'mighty King of Israel'; also that of a large bottle holding eight reputed quarts. It is or was used for champagne served at weddings or some such festive occasions.

RETSINA WINES
The name under which resinated Greek wines are known.

RHENISH
The name by which the wines of the Rhine were known in England from a very early date down to the eighteenth century, when they began to be called *Hocks* (q.v.). Rhenish is mentioned by Shakespeare:

Portia. Therefore, for fear of the worst, I pray thee set a deep glass of Rhenish wine on the contrary casket: for, if the devil be within and that temptation without, I know he will choose it. ...

     The Merchant of Venice, Act I, Scene ii.

Salarino. There is more difference between thy flesh and hers than between jet and ivory; more between your bloods than there is between red wine and Rhenish.

     The Merchant of Venice, Act III, Scene i.

Hamlet. The king doth wake to-night, and takes his rouse,
Keeps wassail, and the swaggering up-spring reels;
And, as he drains his draughts of Rhenish down,
The kettle-drum and trumpet thus bray out
The triumph of his pledge.

     Hamlet, Act I, Scene iv.

1st Clown. A pestilence on him for a mad rogue! 'a poured a flagon of Rhenish on my head once. ...

     Hamlet, Act V, Scene i.

RHINEGAU
The district on the right bank of the Rhine which produces the finest German wines, both red and white, but chiefly white. The principal wine-producing parishes of the Rhinegau, as one goes up the Rhine, will be found in the following order: *Assmann-hausen, Rüdesheim, Geisenheim, Johannisberg, Winkel, Oestrich, Hallgarten, Hattenheim, Kiedrich, Erbach Eltville, Rauenthal,* and, further on, *Wiesbaden* and *Hochheim.*

RHINE-HESSE
The district on the left bank of the Rhine, practically opposite the Rhinegau, which produces the largest quantity of German red and white wines of fine quality; chiefly white. The principal wine-producing districts of Rhine-Hesse are: *Alzey, Bingen, Mayence, Oppenheim,* and *Worms.* The most important wine-producing parishes of those districts are: *Alsheim, Bechtheim, Bingen am Rhein, Bodenheim, Dienheim, Dromersheim, Gau-Algesheim, Gau-Bickelheim, Gau-Odernheim, Guntersblum, Laubenheim, Nackenheim, Nieder-Ingelheim, Nierstein, Ober-Ingelheim, Oppenheim am Rhein, Sprendlingen, Wallertheim, Worms am Rhein.*

RHODES
One of the isles of the Greek Archipelago, which has been famed for the excellence of its wines for the past two thousand years. Thus Virgil:

    'Non ego te mensis et dis accepta secundis,
    Transierim, Rhodia, et tumidis, bumaste, racemis.'

     (Georg. II. v. 101–102)

RHÔNE
A fine river with vineyards more or less the whole of its course. The Rhône vineyards produce some fair wines, in Savoy (Seyssel), but the best are those from vineyards below Lyons and before Avignon. The most celebrated are the wines of Hermitage, Châteauneuf-du-Pape, and Côte Rôtie. Many others are sold under the name of Côtes-du-Rhône.

RHUBARB WINE
One of the old English 'wines' made of rhubarb stalks washed and crushed heavily, sugared and fermented with the help of some yeast. It needs a little lemon and a great deal of much else to have any flavour and to be acceptable.

RIBEAUVILLÉ
One of the best white wines of Alsace comes from the vineyards of this picturesque little town, the German name of which is *Rappoltsweiler.*

RICHEBOURG

A red burgundy wine of superlative excellence from a small vineyard (12 acres) of the Commune of Vosne-Romanée (Côte de Nuits). The *Richebourg* and *Romanée Conti* vineyards are near neighbours and their wines are considered by many good judges as the finest of all red burgundies, but whilst the smaller *Romanée Conti* vineyard belongs to one owner, the larger *Richebourg* vineyards are divided among three owners, a fact which accounts for possible differences in the *Richebourgs* of the same vintage.

RIESLING

The finest white grapes grown for the making of high-class white wines in Alsace, Austria, Germany and Hungary. It is very similar but not identical with the *Pinot Blanc*. The white table wines made from the Riesling grape in Alsace, in the Italian Tyrol and elsewhere are often offered for sale under no other name but *Riesling*.

RIEUSSEC, Château

One of the First Growths of Sauternes (Fargues). Although most of the vines of Rieussec are in the Commune of Fargues, part of the vineyard is in the adjoining Commune of Sauternes. Average 70 tuns white wine.

RIOJA

A district of Aragon, in Spain, which has been famous for centuries past for the excellence of its fruits and vegetables. It was, however, rather less than a hundred years ago that its vineyards were developed, and they have since gained the reputation of producing the best Spanish table wines, mostly red. They have more body than charm and greater alcoholic strength than 'finesse'.

RIONS

A Commune of the Gironde, 33 k. SSE. of Bordeaux, on the right bank of the River Garonne, the site of *Ryuncium*, an important Gallo-Roman city. Its vineyards produce both red and white wines of fair quality but of no outstanding merit.

RIQUEWIHR

One of the best white wines of Alsace comes from the vineyards of this picturesque little Alsatian town.

RIVESALTES

A picturesque little town on the lower slopes of the Pyrenees, at their Mediterranean end: it is surrounded by vineyards, the best wine of which is a white, sweet dessert wine, not unlike *Lunel*.

ROCHET, Château

One of the Fourth Growths of the Médoc (Saint-Estèphe). In the 1840's the owner was a Madame Veuve Lafon de Camersac, and it was known as *Château Lafon de Camersac* or *Château Lafon-Rochet* until the end of the last century. Average 100 tuns claret.

ROMANÈCHE-THORINS

A well-known Growth of the Beaujolais (Lower Burgundy). One of the best wines of the district is that of the *Hospices de Romanèche-Thorins*, which, since 1926, are always bottled at the Hospices.

ROMANÉE, La

The smallest of the 'Romanées' vineyards (2 acres) in the Commune of Vosne-Romanée (Côte de Nuits), but their two acres are responsible for some of the finest red burgundies.

ROMANÉE CONTI

A small vineyard (4½ acres) of the Commune of Vosne-Romanée (Côte de Nuits) responsible for the finest of all red burgundies.

ROMANÉE SAINT-VIVANT

The largest of the 'Romanées' vineyards (24 acres), in the Commune of Vosne-Romanée (Côte de Nuits); they are responsible for very fine, even if not the finest, red burgundy.

ROMANÉE LA TÂCHE

A very small vineyard (3½ acres) of the Commune of Vosne-Romanée (Côte de Nuits); responsible for some of the finest red burgundies.

ROMER, Château

One of the Second Growths of Sauternes (Fargues). The Estate was divided in 1881 among three purchasers; the most important part of the vineyards was bought by a Mr Lafon and its wine is sold with the name Lafon on labels and corks. Average 20 tuns.

ROSBACH WATER

A mineral water, naturally effervescent, from a spring near Homburg. It contains the carbonates of calcium and magnesium and the chlorides of magnesium and sodium which are supposed to be helpful in cases of gout and acid dyspepsia.

ROSE WINE

Put into a well glazed earthen vessel three quarts of rose-water, drawn with a cold still; put into it a sufficient quantity of rose-leaves, cover it close, and set it for an hour in a kettle or copper of hot water, to extract the whole strength and flavour of the roses. When it is cold, squeeze the rose-leaves into the liquor, and steep fresh ones in it, repeating it until the liquor has got the full strength of the roses. To every gallon of liquor put 3 lb. of loaf-sugar, and stir it well, that it may dissolve; then put it into a brandy cask, or other convenient vessel, to ferment, and throw into it a piece of bread toasted hard and covered with yeast; let it stand a month, when it will be ripe and have the flavour and scent of roses; by adding some wine and spices, it will be considerably improved.—w.s.m.

ROSÉ, Vin

Pink wine. The best natural *Vin Rosé* is that of Tavel (Rhône Valley), but *Vins Rosés* are made elsewhere, both still and sparkling, either with red grapes which are not left long to ferment on their husks, or white wines coloured with cochineal or blended with red wine. The cochineal colouring is harmless enough and the colour is more stable, but its use is not to be encouraged, since it introduces into the wine an animal dye quite foreign to it.

ROSSOLIO. ROSSOLIS

Rossolis is one of the oldest of all French liqueurs, now all but forgotten. It used to be home-made always, brandy and sugar being the basis of the liqueur, which was flavoured with any and every kind of fresh fruit available at different times and places. *Rossolio*, or *Rossoglio* or *Crème de Rose* is a bright red liqueur, coloured with cochineal, and flavoured with oil of roses, made chiefly in Zara. In Turin they distil an *Orange Rosoglio*, also red in colour, and flavoured with tangerine rind and orange juice as well as orange blossom.

ROUMANIA

One of the largest wine-producing countries of Europe. The average wine production of Roumania was about 150 million gallons annually, 80 million being the average production of old Roumania, 50 million that of Bessarabia, and 20 million that of Transylvania. The best wines of Roumania are those of *Akkerman*, in Bessarabia; *Cotnari*, in the Province of Moldau; *Dealul Mare*, in the Province of Muntenia; *Dragashani*, in the Province of Oltenia; *Sarica*, *Constanza*, *Silistria*, and *Turtucaia*, in Dobrudscha; *Alba Julia*, *Tarnavale*, *Arad*, *Biho-teleagd*, *Satul Mare*, and *Halmei*, in the Siebenbürgen district.

ROUSSETTE

The most popular white wine of Seyssel, Savoie; the best come from the Ain, or right bank of the Rhône.

ROUSSILLON

One of the southernmost former Provinces of France which produces a great deal of strong, dark, red wine. Its vinous reputation, however, rests on the vineyards of three of its main valleys: (1) Vallée du Tech, the vineyards of which are responsible for the wines of *Banyuls*, *Picardan* and *Collioures*; (2) Vallée du Têt, from which come mostly red and white beverage wines; and (3) Vallée de l'Agly, the vineyards of which produce the wines of *Corbières* and the muscat of *Rivesaltes*.

ROZET, Château de

One of the best-known white wines of *Pouilly-sur-Loire*, in the Nièvre Département.

RÜDESHEIMER

One of the best-known hocks, from the northernmost vineyards of the Rhinegau. The best vineyards of Rüdesheim are grouped under the name of *Rüdesheimer Berg*. Other well-known vineyards of Rüdesheim are: *Schlossberg*, *Burgweg*, *Roseneck*, *Häuserweg*, *Bischofsberg*, *Engerweg*.

RUM

A spirit distilled from molasses; it can be, has been and still is, distilled from the fermented juice of the sugar cane, but it is not a commercial proposition. There are many types and styles of *Rum*, most of which may be classed in one or the other of the following three main categories: (1) the very dry, light-bodied *Rum*, of which the Cuban *Rum* is the prototype; (2) the rich, full-bodied *Rums*, of which the *Jamaica Rum* is the acknowledged standard; (3) the more aromatic *Rums* such as are made in the Dutch East Indies; Martinique, Puerto Rico, Trinidad, Barbados, Demerara and many other islands and mainland sugar cane districts all produce *Rums* which possess some characteristics of their own.

Rum Collins. The juice of half a lemon, half a tablespoonful powdered sugar, one glass Jamaica rum. Shake well and strain into long tumbler. Add one lump ice and soda water.

Rum Daisy. One teaspoonful sugar, a teaspoonful raspberry syrup, juice of half an orange, juice of half a lime, juice of half a lemon. 75 per cent Medford rum. Fill glass with cracked ice. Shake, strain, and fill glass with fizz water and serve.—j.m.

Rum Flip. Prepare grated ginger and nutmeg with a little fine dried lemon peel rubbed together in a mortar; to make a quart of *Flip*, heat rather more than 1½ pints of ale; beat up three or four eggs with 4 oz. of moist sugar; a teaspoonful of grated nutmeg or ginger; and a gill of good old rum or brandy; and when it is nearly boiling, put it into a pitcher and the rum and eggs, etc., into another. Mix and pour it from one pitcher to the other till it is as smooth as cream.—L.En.

Rum Shrub. Put three pints of orange juice and 1 lb. of loaf-sugar to a gallon of rum. Put all into a cask, and leave it for six weeks, when it will be ready for use.—H.C.

Spiced Rum (Hot). One lump sugar, half teaspoonful mixed allspice; dissolve with a little water; 100 per cent Jamaica rum. Fill glass with hot water. Stir, grate a little nutmeg and serve.—J.M.

Rum Toddy. One lump of sugar and one jigger of Jamaica rum. Fill glass with boiling water. Insert one small piece of cinnamon, one slice of lemon garnished with four cloves and a thin slice of lemon rind twisted over glass and inserted. Stir mixture a little and serve with a spoon. Also serve a small pitcher of hot water on the side.—H.J.G.

RUPPERTSBERGER

One of the finest of the white wines of the Palatinate (Mittelhaardt). Among the best vineyards of Ruppertsberg are: *Hoheburg, Reiterpfad, Spiess, Mandelacker, Hofstück, Kieselberg, Linsenbusch, Gaisböhl* and *Mühlweg.*

RUWER

A small river which joins the Moselle a short distance north of Trier. The vineyards of the Ruwer produce some very delicate white wines, usually sold in England as 'Moselles'. The best are the following:

Parishes	Vineyards
Casel	*Nieschen, Taubenberg, Hitzlay, Blindenberg, Herrenberg, Dominikanerberg, Steinkaul, Pauliusberg, Kernagel.*
Eitelsbach ..	*Karthäuserhofberg, Marienholz.*
Grünhaus ..	*Maximin Grünhäuser, Herrenberg, Bruderberg.*
Waldrach ..	*Ehrenberg, Laurentiusberg, Krone.*

RYE WHISKY

A straight whisky distilled from a fermented mash of grain of which not less than 51 per cent is rye grain.

SAAR

A tributary of the River Moselle. Many vineyards grace both banks of the Saar; the best, in geographical order, from Saarburg to Filzen, where the Saar joins the Moselle, below Trier, are those of *Saarburg, Ockfen, Ayl, Wiltingen, Scharzhof, Oberemmel, Canzem, Wawern, Serrig,* and *Filzen.*

SAARBURG

The chief wine centre of the Saar. White wines. Best vineyards: *Mühlenberg, Leyenkaul, Rausch, Antoniusbrunnen, Niederleukener Kupp.*

SACK

A dry, amber wine, occasionally sweetened with honey or sugar, mentioned for the first time in a Proclamation fixing the retail prices of wine in England, in 1532. It came mostly from Cadiz or Jerez, in Spain, and was sometimes referred to as *Sherris-Sack* (or *Jerez-Sack*) in opposition to *Canary Sack* and *Malligo Sack,* wines of the same nature shipped to England during the sixteenth and seventeenth centuries from Teneriffe and Malaga. But the Jerez or Sherris wines were the best and have alone survived under the name of Sherry. Shakespeare was very partial to Sack, and it is the wine which occurs in his plays more than all the other names of wine put together.

Falstaff. ... A good Sherris-sack hath a two-fold operation in it. It ascends me into the brain; dries me there all the foolish and dull and crudy vapours which environ it; makes me apprehensive, quick, forgetive, full of nimble, fiery, and delectable shapes; which delivered o'er to the voice, – the tongue, – which is the birth, becomes excellent wit. ...
Second Part *Henry IV*, Act Iv, Scene iii.

SAGE WINE

Take spring water, Malaga raisins and green sage, the same proportions; pick the raisins and rub them, cut them and the sage small, and put them in a tub; boil the water for 18 minutes, and let it cool down to milk-warm; then pour it upon the sage and raisins, and let it stand six days, stirring it once every eight hours during that time; then strain off the liquor from the pulp, and put it into a clean cask: when it has stood for half a year, draw it clear off into another cask, and, in a short time, when it is fine, bottle it off for use, which may be in two months. This wine will improve much in keeping.—W.S.M.

SAINT-AUBIN

A Commune of the Médoc, 15 k. NW. of Bordeaux. Its best vineyard is *Château de Cujac,* a *Bourgeois* Growth, averaging 20 tuns of claret and 10 tuns of white wine per annum.

SAINTE-CROIX-DU-MONT

A Commune of the Gironde, 43 k. SSE. of Bordeaux, on the right bank of the Garonne, opposite Langon and the Sauternes district. Its vineyards produce some ordinary beverage red wines, but more and better white wines, as sweet as most Sauternes but not so refined, nor so costly. The best-known white wines of this Commune are those of

Châteaux Lamarque, Loubens, de Tastes, Lafue, La Rame, du Pavillon, Domaine de Morange.

SAINT-EMILION

The quaint old City of St. Emilion stands in the centre of a cluster of hills, about two miles from the right bank of the River Dordogne, above Libourne. It is surrounded by extensive vineyards which run into some fifteen different parishes, but all the wine they produce is known as St Emilion wine. It is deeper in colour than most Médoc wine, and has more body than Graves wines; but it does not last long and seldom possesses so refined a 'bouquet'.

The finest wine of St Emilion is that of *Château Ausone* (q.v.). Among the best estates of the district are the following Châteaux: *Beauséjour, Belair-Marignan, Bellevue, Berliquet, Bragard, Cadet-Bon, Canon, Canon-La Gaffelière, Capdemourlin-Magdelaine, Chantegrive, Corbin, Corbin-Michotte, Coudert, Couperie, Coutet, Croque-Michotte, Curé-Bon-La-Madeleine, Fonpéglade, Fourtet, Fonroque, Franc-Mayne, Gaubert, Grandes Murailles, Grand-Mayne, Grand-Pontet, La Gaffelière-Naudes, de Laroque, Laroze, Magdelaine, Malineua, Mazerat, Palat, Pelletan, Pavie-Porte, Pavie-Macquin, Petit-Faurie-de-Soutard, Peyreau, Saint-Emilion, Saint-Georges-Côte-Pavie, Sansonnet, Soutard, Terte-Daugay, Troplong-Mondot, Trottevieille, Villemaurine.*

Some of the St Emilion vineyards, the soil of which is a mixture of sand and gravel, are known as 'Graves de St Emilion'. They produce a slightly different style of wines, the best and most typical being the wines of *Château Cheval Blanc.* The other best-known estates of the Graves de St Emilion are the following Châteaux: *Figeac, La Tour-Figeac, La Tour-du-Pin-Figeac, Yon-Figeac, La Dominique, Lamarzelle,* and *Ripeau.*

Besides the wines of the Commune of St Emilion, those from the following Communes have acquired by long use the right to be described as St Emilion wines: *Saint-Christophe-des-Bardes, Saint-Hippolyte, Saint-Laurent-des-Combes, Saint Étienne-de-Lisse, Vignonet, Saint-Pey-D'Armens, Saint-Sulpice-de-Faleyrens, Montagne, Saint-Georges, Parsac, Lusac, Puységuin.*

SAINT-ESTÈPHE

A Commune of the Médoc, 9 k. N. of Pauillac, in which there are two of the Second Growths of the Médoc, *Cos d'Estournel* and *Château Montrose;* one-third, *Château Calon-Ségur;* one-fourth, *Château Rochet* and one-fifth, *Cos Labory.* Besides these, there are many other vineyards responsible for a large quantity of very fair claret, chief among them being the following, which rank as bourgeois supérieurs: *Châteaux Le Roc, Tron-*

quoy-Lalande, Meyney, Le Crock de Marbuset, Le Boscq, Beau-Site, Fatin, Fonpetite, Phélan-Ségur, de Pez, Houissant, Canteloup, Capbern, Pomys, Micard, Beauséjour, La Haye, Clauzet, Morin, La Commanderie, MacCarthy, Cru Roche, etc.

SAINT-GERMAIN-D'ESTEUIL

A Commune of the Médoc 61 k. NNE. of Bordeaux, which is responsible for a large quantity of red wines of no great distinction, and some white wines as well. The best vineyards of the Commune are those of *Châteaux Livran* and *Briès-Caillou,* both of them the property of Messrs James L. Denman & Co., of London; also *Châteaux Beaulieu, du Castera* and *Hauterive;* they all rank as Crus Bourgeois.

SAINT-JULIEN

A Commune of the Médoc, 44 k. NNW. of Bordeaux, which is responsible for some of the finest clarets, chiefly those from six of the Second Growths of the Médoc, i.e. *Châteaux Léoville-Lascases, Léoville-Poyferré; Léoville-Barton; Gruaud-Larose-Sarget; Gruaud-Larose-Faure;* and *Ducru-Beaucaillou;* also two of the Third Growths, *Châteaux Lagrange* and *Langoa;* and five of the Fourth Growths, *Châteaux Saint-Pierre-Bontemps; Saint-Pierre-Sevaistre; Branaire-Ducru; Talbot;* and *Beychevelle.* Of the many bourgeois supérieurs and other lesser Growths of Saint-Julien, the most important is *Château Médoc,* averaging 80 tuns claret per annum.

SAINT-LAURENT

A Commune of the Médoc 43 k. NW. of Bordeaux. Its best wines are those of three of the Classed Growths of the Médoc, i.e. *Châteaux La-Tour-Carnet* (Fourth Growth); *Belgrave,* and *Camensac* (Fifth Growths). Then come the wines of the following bourgeois supérieurs: *Châteaux Larose-Trintaudon; Larose-Perganson; Barateau; du Galan; Caronne-Sainte-Gemme; de Cach; Mascard; La Tour Sieujan; La Tour Marcillanet; Marcillan-Bellevue; Balac; du Peyrat; Cruscaut;* and *Cru de La Chatolle.* The red wines of Saint-Laurent have acquired by long usage the right to be sold under the better-known name of the adjoining Commune of Saint Julien.

SAINT-MÉDARD-EN-JALLES

A Commune of the Médoc 13 k. NW. of Bordeaux. Its best vineyard is *Château Le Bourdieu,* a *Bourgeois* Growth averaging 20 tuns claret.

SAINT MORILLON

One of the minor wine-producing Communes of the Graves de Bordeaux. Some of its best wines are the red and white wines of *Château Camarset*.

SAINT-PÉRAY

One of the wine-producing Communes of the Ardèche (Rhône Valley); it has been famous for centuries past for its white wines, both still and sparkling.

SAINT-PIERRE-BONTEMPS, SAINT-PIERRE-SEVAISTRE,
Châteaux

Two Fourth Growths of the Médoc (Saint-Julien) which were reunited, in 1920, under the same ownership. Their combined yield is 100 tuns claret.

SAINT-PIERRE-DE-MONS

One of the wine-producing Communes of the Gironde, south of the River Garonne and east of Langon. It produces some very fair white wines, similar to the unclassed wines of Sauternes; they are entitled by long usage and by law to be sold as Sauternes wines. This Commune is also called *Saint-Pey-de-Langon*. Its best-known wine is that of *Château de Respide*.

SAINT-POURÇAIN

A Commune of the Allier (Loire Valley), famous for its still, white wines; the white wines of the adjoining villages of Louchy, Saulcet, and Montord are also sold under the better-known name of *St. Pourçain*.

SAINT-SATUR

One of the best white wines of the Sancerre district (Berry).

SAINT RAPHAËL

One of the well advertised and popular French *Apéritifs*; its basis is white wine and its after-taste is that of quinine. It is usually served chilled and undiluted.

SAINT-SAUVEUR

A Commune of the Médoc, 6 k. W. of Pauillac. Its most important vineyard is that of *Château Liversan*: average 150 tuns claret; it ranks as bourgeois supérieur. *Château Peyrabon* produces but 15 tuns of claret, on an average, but it has the reputation of being much the finest wine of the Commune.

SAINT-SEURIN-DE-CADOURNE

A Commune of the Médoc, 13 k. N. of Pauillac. It produces a great quantity of fair red wines, but none of great distinction; also a little white wine. Its largest vineyards are those of *Châteaux Coufran, Verdignan, Sénilhac* and *Bel-Orme-Tronquoy-de-Lalande*.

SAINT-YZANS

A Commune of the Médoc 68 k. NNW. of Bordeaux, the vineyards of which produce a good deal of sound red wine and a small quantity of white wine as well. The most important Estate of the Commune is that of *Château Loudenne*, the property of Messrs W.&A.Gilbey, of London, averaging 400 tuns of claret per annum.

SAKÉ

A Japanese rice beer obtained by two consecutive processes of fermentation of a brew mostly of rice, but occasionally of other grain. Its alcoholic content is usually from 14 to 16 per cent of alcohol by volume; it is colourless, quite still, and is served warm in tiny porcelain bowls holding little more than an ounce. The first taste of *Saké* is rather sweet but its after-taste is bitter. Its name is supposed to come from Osaka, which has long been famous for its *Saké*. *Saké* is sometimes served in specially made little bowls with an air tube so devised that one draws air when sipping the *Saké* in the bowl, thus producing a whistling sound: these little bowls are called singing *Saké* cups.

SALMANAZAR

A large glass bottle for show more than for use: it is supposed to hold 12 reputed quarts (9.60 litres) or 338.012 fluid ounces.

SAMOS

One of the Greek islands producing some of the most popular tawny dessert wines sold in the Netherlands and Scandinavian countries.

SAMSHU

The Chinese *Saké*, a kind of beer brewed from rice that is treated with a special yeast, *Aspergillus oryzae*, which converts the starch of the rice into sugar.

SANCERRE

A picturesque old City of the Cher Département of France; its vineyards produce chiefly red wines, which are consumed locally. They also produce a white wine under the name of *Château de Sancerre*.

SANGAREE

The name given to long, mixed, iced drinks in some parts of the tropics: whether wine or spirits be used as a basis, and if so which sorts and in what proportion, is left to the ingenuity or imagination of the barman or whoever offers to mix the *Sangaree*.

Port Wine Sangaree. One and a half jiggers of port wine, ½ oz. of simple syrup. Stir well with cracked ice and strain into highball glass with two cubes of ice. Grate nutmeg on top.—H.J.G.

SANGIOVESE

A ruby red wine, rather coarse by itself, but refreshing when diluted with water, which is the only vinous glory of the minuscule Republic of San Marino. It is also made in the adjoining Italian Province of Emilia.

SANGUE DI GIUDA

One of the 'blood' red table wines of Lombardy, from Broni vineyards.

SANKT GEORGEN

There is a white wine from the vineyards of Freiburg im Breisgau sold under this name; also both red and white wines from the vineyards of Pressburg.

SANKT MAGDALENER
SANTA MADDALENA

The German and Italian names of the same wine, the red table wine of Bozen or Bolzano, in the South Tyrol.

SANKT MARTIN

Palatinate. Landau district. White wines. Best vineyards: *Goldmorgen, Schlossberg, Kirchberg, Spielfeld.*

SAN SEVERO

The best table white wine of Apulia. It comes from vineyards in the vicinity of Foggia and is one of the few Italian white wines to be quite dry.

SANTA CLARA VALLEY

One of the more important wine-producing districts of California, its vineyards are responsible for some very fair wines.

SANTENAY

The southernmost Commune of the Côte d'Or (Burgundy); its vineyards produce a good deal of red wine of fair quality as well as a little of real merit: *Les Gravières* and *Le Clos Tavannes* are its two best vineyards.

SANTORIN

One of the minor and the most volcanic of the Cyclades, formerly called *Thera* and, even earlier, *Calliste.* It produces a number of different types of wine, known as *Thera,* a wine not unlike a dry madeira; *St. Elie,* described as 'dry, delicate, spirituous, fresh-tasting and ambrosial'; *Vino Santo,* a sweet muscat wine, and a sweet, red *Santorin,* similar to the *Lachryma Christi.*

SARDINIA

The best wines of Sardinia are the sweet, dessert wines, of which the best-known are the *Giro, Monica, Moscato di Cagliari, Moscato del Tempio* and *Malvasia.* Among the table wines of the island, the best white wine is the *Vernaccia del Campidano,* amber in colour, dry, with an almost bitter finish, and a very

pleasing almond-blossom bouquet. One of the best red table wines is the *Sassari.*

SASSELLA

The best of the red wines of the Valtellina (Lombardy). It is bright ruby and it has more bouquet than most Italian red table wines.

SAULCET

One of the best wines of the Allier Département of France: it is usually sold under the better-known name of the adjoining Commune of *Saint Pourçain* (q.v.).

SAUMUR

The chief city of the chief wine-producing part of the old Province of Anjou; it is the centre of vineyards which produce an abundance of white wines and a little red wine. Some of the white wines are quite suitable for the making of sparkling wines, but the best white wines of the district are still wines.

SAUTERNES

The Sauternes district comprises not only the vineyards of the Commune of Sauternes, but those of the adjoining Communes of Bommes, Barsac, Preignac, and Fargues.

The Sauternes district adjoins that of Graves, but its soil is entirely different and the species of grapes cultivated in the vineyards of Sauternes are also entirely different.

They are white grapes which are picked over-ripe, and from which is made the most marvellous of all naturally sweet wines.

The finest Sauternes wines were the following when 'classified' in 1855.

Château *Yquem* or *d'Yquem* – in a class by itself.

First Growths

Château La Tour-Blanche	..		Bommes
,,	Peyraguey	.. ..	,,
,,	Vigneau	.. ..	,,
,,	De Suduiraut	.. ..	Preignac
,,	Coutet	.. ..	Barsac
,,	Climens	.. ..	,,
,,	Bayle (Guiraud)	..	Sauternes
,,	Rieussec	.. ..	Fargues
,,	Rabaud	.. ..	Bommes

Second Growths

Château De Myrat	..	..	Barsac
,,	Doisy ..	.. ..	,,
,,	Peixotto	.. ..	Bommes
,,	D'Arche	.. ..	Sauternes
,,	Filhot ..	.. ..	,,
,,	Broustet	.. ..	Barsac
,,	Nairac	.. ..	,,
,,	Caillou	.. ..	,,
,,	Suau ..	.. ..	,,
,,	De Malle	.. ..	Preignac
,,	Romer	.. ..	Fargues
,,	Lamothe	.. ..	Sauternes

The white wines of St. Pierre-de-Mons, a little to the east of Langon, may now be sold as Sauternes.

SAUVIGNON
One of the finest species of white grapes. *Sauvignon* and *Sémillos* grapes, in the proportion approximately of one-third and two-thirds, are responsible for the excellence of the sauternes wines. Other fine white wines, such as the white wines of *Pouilly-Fuissé*, are made entirely from the *Sauvignon* grape.

SAVIGNY-LES-BEAUNE
One of the Communes of the Côte d'Or, immediately north of Beaune, which produces much red burgundy of fair quality and some of outstanding merit, similar to the wines of the adjoining Communes of Aloxe-Corton and Pernand-Vergelesses. Its best vineyards are *Les Vergelesses*, *les Marconnets* and *Les Jarrons*. Average annual production, 110,000 gallons. The Hospices de Beaune (q.v.) own four *Savigny* vineyards.

SAVOIE
The French part of the mountainous country between the Rhône valley, Switzerland and Italy known as Savoy. There are many vineyards in Savoie which produce wines, both red and white, still and sparkling, of local fame, but none of superlative quality, nor any made in sufficiently large quantities to be sold in other parts of France or overseas. The *Rousette* is the name both of the grapes mostly used in the *Seyssel* district and of the white wine best known in Savoie. A fair white wine is made near Evian, at *Féternes*; at *Jongieux*, the *Marétel*. Near *Thonon*, the *Ripaille Blanc* has many admirers, as has the *Crépy Blanc*, at *Douvaine*. The *Marignan*, at Sciez, and the wine of the *Coteau d'Altesse*, to the left of the *Lac du Bourget*. Among red wines, the *Montmélian*, from vineyards in the vicinity of *Chambéry*, is one of the best; whilst the red *Chignin* is the most popular.

SCHAFFHAUSEN
One of the less important wine-producing Cantons of Switzerland. Its best white wine is the *Siblinger* and the best red the *Osterfinger*, from the vineyards of Hallau.

SCHARZBERGER
One of the best wines of the Saar and Moselle valleys, from the vineyards of Scharzhof, in the valley of the Saar.

SCHARZHOF
A small township of the Saar valley, also known as Scharzhof-Wiltingen. Its vineyards produce some of the most delicate white wines of Germany; the finest are those sold under the names of *Scharzhofberger* and *Scharzberger*.

SCHIEDAM
The *Gin* distilled at Schiedam, one of the oldest centres of *Gin* distillation in Holland. It is pure white and the best-known brand of *Schiedam Gin* is sold in black bottles with flat sides, known in the vernacular as *Square-face*.

SCHILLERWEIN
The more ordinary beverage wines, chiefly of Württemberg and Baden, light red in colour, usually made of both black and white grapes mixed in the pressing.

SCHIRAZ
The cradle of viticulture and wine, in Persia, if not, as has been claimed, of the world. There is wine still made in the Schiraz district, but its quality cannot be said to deserve Omar's and other poets' praises.

SCHLOSS BÖCKLEHEIM
Nahe Valley, Kreuznach district. White wines. Best vineyards: *Kupfergrube*, *Felsenberg*, *Mühlberg*.

SCOPELO
One of the minor Greek Islands of the Eastern Mediterranean, north of Euboca, where they make a rich *Malmsley* type of wine of some repute: it must have been known in England formerly, since there is, in the Ionides Collection, a Wine Label bearing the name *Scopoli*.

SCOTCH WHISKY
The most popular of grain spirits all the world over, but since the latter part of the nineteenth century only. Up to 1814 every laird in the Highlands had his own still and never bought *Whisky*, nor did he sell any. In 1814, no still was permitted under 500 gallons and the distillation of whisky became a commercial proposition which has been exploited ever since with such vigour and intelligence that *Scotch Whisky* has earned fortunes and peerages for distillers.

The four main regions of Scotland chiefly concerned in the production of *Malt Whisky* are the Highlands, the Lowlands, Campbeltown and Islay. *Scotch Whisky* is made from barley (Scotch grown or any other barley), which is (1) malted; (2) mashed; (3) fermented; (4) distilled in pot stills. The spirit thus obtained was the only one to answer to the name of *Scotch Whisky* until 1853, when the firm of Andrew Usher is credited with having been the first to introduce an all-important innovation: the blending of 'straight' malt *Whisky* with plain grain spirit, distilled from barley or other grain, un-malted, and from a patent still, which is not only a much cheaper method of distillation, but one which produces a lighter type of spirit which appeals to Lowlanders in general and Englishmen in particular. The differences in the flavour of different brands of whisky is chiefly due to the differences in the types and proportions of any of the four above-mentioned *Malt Whiskies* which have been blended with plain grain spirit. Their alcoholic strength is a matter of added water; their colour is naturally white but it can be and is made golden, light or dark, accord-ing to taste.

The finest *Malt Whiskies* are those of the Highlands, chiefly Banffshire; and within Banffshire, the Glenlivet and Speyside dis-tricts are reputed the best. Next in import-ance comes Moray. Campbeltown malts are heavy and smoky; Islay malts heavier still and more pungent; Lowland malts the least smoky of all. All whiskies must be matured for at least three years before the law allows them to be sold. They are matured in well-seasoned oak casks and often kept longer than three years. The blending of Malt Whisky and Plain Grain Spirit is done after whisky and spirit have been matured; it is the last as well as the most difficult and the most important step taken by the distiller to transform barley into a spirit of exactly the same strength, colour, flavour and taste as has been bottled by him for years and years in any particular shape of bottles and under any particular label.

SEC
French for *Dry*, in the vernacular, but for *Sweet* on the label of a champagne bottle. *Sec* is not so sweet as a wine labelled *Demi-Sec*, which is very sweet, but it is sweeter than another labelled *Extra-Sec*, which is but slightly sugared.

SEDIMENT
Organic matter discarded chiefly by red wines kept in bottle for any length of time. The sediment varies as to both volume and nature: it may take the form of a crust which adheres to the glass of the bottle; or it may be mud-like or dust-like. In any case it must remain in the bottle and not be allowed to spoil both the look and taste of the wine poured out to drink: hence the necessity of *Decanting* old wines with great care.

SEKT
The German name of a typically German wine, a cheap imitation of champagne; a sparkling wine not necessarily made from German wine but from any cheap wine avail-able, or even from apple juice.

SÉMILLON
The species of white grapes which, together with the *Sauvignon*, is responsible for all the best white wines of Bordeaux and many other vinelands.

SENHEIM
One of the less important wine-producing parishes of the Lower Moselle, in the Zell district. White wines. Best vineyards: *Lay*, *Eulenkopf* and *Kuckucksbusch*.

SERCIAL
One of the finest and most distinctive types of madeira wine; it has a dry finish and great breed as well as power, when made, as it should be, from Sercial grapes, which have become very rare in Madeira since the Phylloxera disaster of the late seventies.

SERRIG
One of the wine-producing parishes of the Saar Valley, in the Saarburg district. White wines. Best vineyards: *Vogelsang*, *Heiligen-born*, *Hindenburgslay*, *Herrenberg*, *Marienberg* and *Wurtzberger*.

SERRIGNY
One of the lesser Communes of the Côte d'Or, the vineyards of which produce some fair red burgundy.

SETUBAL
A white, or rather amber, Portuguese dessert wine made from muscatel grapes grown in Estremadura.

SEXTARIUS
The standard *Sextarius* was the 12th part of the *Modusi*, or hogshead, but there was also a *Sextarius minor*, one-sixth of the *Congius*, about half a litre.

SEYSSEL
Two villages bear the same name, the one in Haute-Savoie, on the left bank of the Rhône, and the other in the Ain Département, exactly opposite, on the other bank of the same river. There are vineyards on both sides of the Rhône from which both still and sparkling *Seyssel* wines are made, the best being the still white wine called *Roussette*.

SHANDY GAFF
A long drink made up of a bottle of ginger beer and a pint of good ale.

SHEBEEN, SIBIN
A shop or bar, chiefly in Ireland or the Irish-occupied parts of Scotland, where excisable liquor is sold without a licence.

SHERBET
A refreshing semi-liquid concoction usually having some form of water ice as its found-

ation, and flavoured with any and every variety of fruit. The finest sherbet is said to be that flavoured with the *Soursop* (*Granabana*).

SHERRY

Sherry is a wine made from white grapes grown in the Jerez district, in the south of Spain.

The grapes from which sherry is made are pressed, when ripe, at the vintage time, and their sweet juice is allowed to ferment in its own sweet way. After a time this grape juice becomes wine, but it is not yet *Sherry*.

Sherry is made from the best wine of each vintage, to which some brandy is added, after which it is kept for many years with the best wine of other vintages.

Sherry is a blended wine – the blend of many wines of different years kept together long enough for each to lose its individuality and for all to become an harmonious whole.

Sherry is pale amber in colour, and dry, but it can be made dark and sweet by adding to it a particular dark and very sweet liqueur wine made specially for the purpose.

The best pale, dry, delicate sherries are usually those sold under the names of *Amontillado, Fino, Vino de Pasto*, and *Manzanilla*. The best dark, rich and full sherries are usually those sold under the names of *Oloroso* and *Amoroso* and *Brown Sherry*. But there are a great number of other names of sherry, mostly brands registered by shippers and merchants.

The standard gauge of a butt of sherry is 108 gallons, its average yield, 52 dozens.

Sherry Cobbler. Fill a tumbler nearly full with shaved ice. Pour in a spoonful of sugar syrup, then a wineglassful of sherry. Decorate with squares or slices of fresh fruit in season and a maraschino cherry; stir well with a spoon and serve with straws.

Sherry Flip. Beat a raw fresh egg into a glass of sherry, add cracked or shaved ice and a teaspoonful of granulated sugar; shake thoroughly, strain into a glass, and grate a little nutmeg on top.

SHIVOWITZA

A plum liqueur made in southern Hungary from the *Shiva* plum.

SHRUB

A bottled home-made cordial kept in the store cupboards for emergencies.

Brandy Shrub. Put the juice of five lemons and the rind of two into two quarts of brandy, cover it over for three days; then add a quart of sherry and 2 lb. of loaf sugar, run it through a jelly bag, and bottle.
—F.D.S.D.

768

Raspberry Shrub. Two quarts raspberries; one pint cider vinegar. Sugar. Combine berries and vinegar and let stand 48 hours. Mash and strain through a jelly bag. Add 1 lb. sugar to each pint of juice. Boil 20 minutes, bottle, and seal. In serving put one or two tablespoons shrub in a tumbler and fill with iced water.—A.C.

SICILY

The southernmost Province of Italy and one of the more important for the extent of its vineyards and the variety of the wines which they produce. The best-known wine of Sicily is that of *Marsala*, whilst the *Moscato* of Syracuse is one of the sweetest and best muscatel wines, and the *Zucco*, of Palermo is also an attractive dessert wine. Of Sicilian table wines, the best are the white *Corvo di Casteldaccia* and of *Ætna*; also the rather heady *Albanello*, some of which is dry and some sweet.

SIEBELDINGEN

One of the wine-producing parishes of the Palatinate (Oberhaardt). White wines. Best vineyards: *Hohenberg, Zelter* and *Sommerseite*.

SILLERY

One of the Communes of the Marne (Champagne), which was made famous by its wines, still and sparkling, a very long time ago. The still white wines of *Sillery* continued to be made and to be shipped long after sparkling champagne had become first favourite in the world's markets.

SITGES

A small port of Catalonia (Spain), the vineyards of which produce the best sweet muscatel wine of Spain. 'The Malvasia made at Sitges, about fifteen miles west of Barcelona, is considered very good. It is pale and clear, but acquires colour with age.' (Cyrus Redding: *History of Modern Wines*.) There are Wine Labels bearing the names of *Sietges, Setges* and *Sieges*, probably referring to this wine; it is even possible that wine labels with the names *Sayes, Scyes* and *Seyes*, are misspellings for the same wine.

SLINGS

The name of a number of cold mixed beverages, more particularly popular in the tropics.

Singapore Sling. One oz. lime juice; 1 oz. cherry brandy; 2 oz. dry gin. Shake well and ice. Top with seltzer and decorate with slice of orange and fresh mint. Then add through middle with a medicine dropper: four drops of Bénédictine and four drops of brandy.
—H.J.G.

SLIVOVITZ. SLJIVOVICA

The names of the spirit which is distilled

from plums, in Hungary and Serbia; it is similar to the Alsatian *Plum Brandy* called *Quetsch*.

SLOE GIN

A cordial, the basis of which is *Gin* and the informing flavour that of *Sloes*, the berries of the black thorn.

Four quarts sloes; one gallon gin; 2½ lb. sugar candy; ½ oz. bitter almonds. Put into a two gallon jar, shake twice a week for three months, then strain.

Sloe Gin, like Van der Hum and many other liqueurs, is cloyingly sweet and sticky to the palate if drunk too soon after being made. It becomes deliciously clean and mellow if kept for about nine or ten years after bottling.

The most popular English brand of *Sloe Gin* is Hawker's *Pedlar Brand Sloe Gin*.

Sloe Gin Fizz. To one glass of sloe gin, add half a glass of lemon juice and a teaspoonful of powdered sugar; shake well and pour over cracked ice in a tumbler; then add as much soda water or seltzer as may be desired.

Sloe Gin Rickey. Put in a tumbler two cubes of ice, the juice and rind of half a fresh lime and a glassful of *Sloe Gin*. Fill the glass (more or less according to taste) with soda water or seltzer, stir and sip through straws.

SMASHES

Mixed iced drinks always with a spirit foundation and some mint flavouring:

Brandy Smash. Crush half lump of sugar with three sprigs of mint, one jigger brandy, one lump ice; stir in old-fashioned glass and serve.—L.T.C.R.

Gin Smash. Same as *Brandy Smash*, using gin instead of brandy.

Whisky Smash. Muddle one lump of sugar with a half jigger of water and a few sprigs of mint in glass. Add two cubes of ice. Pour in one jigger of whisky. Decorate with four or five sprigs of mint. Serve with small barspoons, and a glass of charged water on the side.—H.J.G.

SMITH-HAUT-LAFITTE, Château

One of the important Châteaux of the Graves district, near Bordeaux (Commune of Martillac). Its annual average production is 200 tuns of Premier Vin (Red); 50 tuns Deuxième Vin (Red); and 10 tuns white wine.

SOAVE

One of the best of Italian table wines (white). It is made from grapes grown in Veneto; it is dry but not harsh and has a pleasing and delicate bouquet.

SODA WATER

The true aerated alkaline water known by this name is, strictly speaking, a medicament of the antacid type. It is not a beverage, if by this word we mean a pleasant thirst-quenching drink. Each 10 oz. egg-shaped bottle should consist of from 5 to 15 grains of bicarbonate of soda, dissolved in half a pint of water, and highly charged with carbonic acid gas. Indeed the British Pharmacopoeia orders 30 grains per pint, but that is not at all palatable and only intended as a medicine. It is a valuable remedy for sourness on the stomach, etc., but should not be taken as a regular beverage. To meet the public taste, or for other reasons, manufacturers of soda water and potash water vary the quantities of alkaline bicarbonate, according to their individual judgement or fancy.—L.G.M.

SOLERA

Solera is not a type of sherry; it is really equivalent to 'Blend' or 'Vatting'. A sherry described as 'Solera 1860', for instance, is, or should be, a wine from a vat first laid down in 1860; it is a blend of wines of which the oldest dates back to 1860.

SOLUTRÉ

One of the best of the cheaper descriptions of white burgundies. From the Saône-et-Loire Département. The parish of Solutré adjoins Pouilly and Fuissé, and its wines are usually sold as Pouilly-Fuissé.

SOMERSET WEST

One of the noted wine-producing districts of the Cape Province (South Africa).

SOMLOI FURMINT

One of the best white wines of Hungary, from the vineyards of *Somlyó*, on Lake Balaton. It is also marketed under the name of *Somlauer Auslese*.

SONOMA VALLEY

One of the best wine-producing districts of California.

SOURS

Alcoholic long drinks for thirsty days; they are really *Sweet-sour*.

Apple Jack Sour. Put into a large tumbler, with half a tablespoonful of icing sugar, the juice of half a lemon, and dissolve the same with a squirt of seltzer water from a syphon; add one wineglass of old cider brandy. Nearly fill the glass with shaved ice, stir well, strain, ornament with a little fruit, and serve. —F.D.S.D.

Brandy Sour. Juice of half a lemon; one barspoon sugar; one jigger cognac; shake, strain, dress with fruit and serve.—L.T.C.R.

Brunswick Sour. Juice of one small lemon; one barspoon sugar; one jigger rye whisky; shake, strain and float claret on top. Decorate with a slice of orange, a slice of pineapple and one cherry.—L.T.C.R.

Champagne Sour. Juice of half a fresh lemon; one lump of sugar, dissolved; fill with champagne, stir well and dress with fruit.—L.T.C.R.

Egg Sour. Juice of half a lemon; one barspoon sugar; yolk of one egg; one dash anisette; one jigger brandy; shake well and serve.—L.T.C.R.

Gin Sour. Juice of one small lemon; one barspoon sugar; one jigger dry gin, Old Tom gin or sloe gin; shake, strain and dress with fruit.—L.T.C.R.

Hancock Sour. One jigger bourbon whisky; four dashes rock candy syrup; two dashes rum; juice of lime. Stir, strain, splash with seltzer, and dress with fruit slices.—A.C.

Jersey Sour (or *Teddy Roosevelt Sour*). One jigger applejack; one teaspoon sugar; juice of half a lemon; one slice lemon. Shake, strain, and garnish with lemon juice.—A.C.

Whisky Sour. Half a glass of lemon or lime juice; one glass of rye or bourbon whisky; one teaspoonful of sifted sugar; shake well with some cracked ice, then strain and pour into glass decorated with a maraschino cherry and a slice of orange.

SOUSSANS
A Commune of the Médoc, 30 k. NNW. of Bordeaux. Its best wine is that of Château *Bel-Air-Marquis d'Aligre* (average 40 tuns claret); then come the wines of *Châteaux La Tour-de-Mons*, *Paveil*, *Haut-Breton-Larig-audière*, *Domaine de La Bégorce-Zédé*, *Châteaux Marsac-Séguineau*, and *Grand-Soussans*: they rank as Bourgeois supérieurs and average 380 tuns claret. The more ordinary red wines of Soussans have acquired by long usage the right to be sold under the name of the adjoining and better known Commune of Margaux.

SOUTH AFRICA
Vines grow, and wine is made, in the Transvaal and elsewhere, within the borders of the Union of South Africa, on a very limited scale. It is only in the Cape Province that viticulture attains to real importance and that wine is made on a sufficiently large scale to supply a growing export demand.

The oldest and most famous South African vineyards are those nearest to Cape Town, at and near Wynberg, which produced the renowned wines of Constantia so much in demand during the early half of the

nineteenth century. Wine is still made on an important scale at Wynberg, at 'Groot' Constantia itself, which is a South African Government property, and adjoining vineyards.

The finest stretch of vineyards is further inland, from French Hoek to Wellington, along the Paarl Valley, and in the Stellenbosch district close by. Further inland still, at Worcester, Robertson, Montagu, Ladysmith, and Oudtshoorn, larger quantities of wine are obtained from grapes grown on richer soil, but wine of inferior quality.

South Africa can, and does, produce a very large quantity of different wines, some very fair, dry beverage wines, both red and white, and some palatable sweet fortified wines, as well as some sparkling wine and a good deal of brandy.

SOUTH AMERICA
The two more important wine-producing lands of South America are the Argentine, for quantity, and Chile, for quality. There are vineyards also in Brazil, Uruguary, Peru and Bolivia, but they do not produce wines in sufficient quantities nor of sufficient merit to compete in the world's markets.

SPAIN
The third largest European wine-producing country. Its best-known wines, in England, are *Sherry*, *Malaga*, *Tarragona* and *Rioja*, but *Sherry* a long way first. The red and white wines of *Valdepeñas* did enjoy a fair share of popularity in early Victorian days but are rarely heard of now, and the same may be said of the *Alicante* wines, once a popular dessert wine of moderate price.

SPALATO
The Italian name for two different types of wines, one 'sour' and another sweet, i.e. table and dessert wines, from the vineyards of Splt, on the Dalmatian coast of Yugoslavia. Both are red wines, but the dessert *Spalato* is a fortified wine, the fermentation of which has been checked.

SPARKLING WINES
Sparkling wines belong to two quite distinct categories: the best are wines, the fermentation of which is completed after they have been bottled and securely corked, so that the carbonic acid gas, a by-product of fermentation, cannot escape and remains in solution in the wine; the prototype of these sparkling wines is sparkling champagne. The others are still wines which are rendered effervescent by having some carbonic acid gas forced into them at the time of the bottling; the said carbonic acid gas may have been generated by their own fermentation in a close tank, saved and used again, or

it may be any carbonic acid gas: it makes no difference. Most sparkling wines are white wines; they are better than red sparkling wines, which, however, have their admirers.

SPÄTLESE WINES

The German name for 'late vintaged' wines, that is wines made from the last and ripest berries to be gathered at the time of the vintage.

SPIAGGA DE LESINA

The Italian name of one of the best white dessert wines of Dalmatia, in Yugoslavia.

SPIRITS (Potable)

Alcoholic liquids obtained by distillation from some wholesome materials such as wine in the case of brandy, sugar in the case of rum, grain in the case of gin and whisky, rice in the case of arrack and saké, etc. In all spirits the nature, but not the proportion, of ethyl alcohol is the same. The great differences between them all are due to the by-products or impurities, which vary according to the nature of the 'mash', or fermented liquid from which they were distilled.

Some of those impurities can be, and often are, poisonous, but present in quantities too small to be injurious. Thus spirits distilled from potatoes (vodka) and cider (applejack) can be quite injurious if consumed in more than very small doses. But spirits distilled from sawdust and all kinds of other materials are usually *rectified* in such a way that they consist in the end of merely ethyl alcohol and water.

SPRENDLINGEN

One of the wine-producing Communes of Rhine-Hesse, in the Alzey district. White wines. Best vineyards: *Geyersberg*, *Wiesberg* and *Horn*.

SPRITZIG

German for 'lively wine', denoting the presence in a still white wine of just a little carbonic acid gas, the result of a very limited secondary fermentation of the wine in the bottle, which gives a pleasant impression of liveliness on the palate.

SPRUCE BEER. BLACK BEER

A brew which is concocted without any barley, but with black spruce branches, cones and bark which are boiled for several hours, then put into a cask with molasses, hops and yeast. It is left to ferment and is considered fit to drink in 24 hours by the fishermen of Newfoundland, Labrador and the Gulf of St. Lawrence.

STARBOARD LIGHT

An after-dinner, 'Digestive', cordial made up of about 90 per cent green crème de menthe and 10 per cent brandy, and no ice.

STARS

One, two or three stars have been used upon cognac labels for a great many years to denote the age of the brandy in the bottle. One star denotes that the brandy is not less than three years old, two stars four years old, and three stars five years old. Beyond that number, stars, like crowns, are merely ornaments.

STEINBERGER

The finest wine of Hattenheim, and one of the finest of the white wines of the Rhinegau. The vineyard of *Steinberg* covers nearly sixty acres; it belonged for many years to the Dukes of Nassau, and then to the Royal Prussian Domains. *Steinberger* was always sold by public auction in an ascending scale of excellence, first of all the plain '*Steinberger*', and then the *Auslese*, *Spätlese*, *Feine Auslese*, *Hochfeine Auslese*, *Beeren Auslese* and *Trockenbeeren Auslese*. During the Nassau régime, the finest *Steinberger* of all was the *Kabinet* wine or ducal reserve.

STEINWEIN

A dry white wine, somewhat hard when young, which well repays keeping as it develops with age a very attractive and distinctive bouquet and softness. The genuine *Steinwein* is the wine of the *Steinmantel* vineyards, 350 acres, north of Würzburg, in Bavaria. *Steinwein* is usually sold in *bocksbeutel*.

STELLENBOSCH

One of the districts of the Cape Province (South Africa), important for the production of red and white wines as well as brandy.

STILLS

The apparatus used in the distillation of spirits, that is the separating of the alcohol present in any alcoholic liquid from most of the water in it. This may be done in two quite different ways, by Pot Stills or Patent Stills. In Pot Stills, the alcohol in the 'mash' is vaporized by the application of heat and collected by condensation. Patent Stills, which also bear the name of Coffey Stills, from one Æneas Coffey who perfected Robert Stein's apparatus, are continuous stills, in which the alcohol in the 'mash' is gradually, step by step, freed from not only water but all else, so that in the end one gets a spirit which is called pure or plain, because there is nothing left in it, other than ethyl alcohol, of what there was originally in the 'mash': it is free from all impurities, and free also from all taste and distinctive merit.

STONE FENCE
(A highball with cider)
Pour one jigger of whisky into highball glass, with ice. Fill glass with cider.

STONEWALL JACKSON
1½ jiggers applejack; two cups hard cider. This is the genuine New Jersey recipe, although outside of the State is has degenerated into a sort of highball made with only one jigger of applejack and with sweet cider substituted for hard.—A.C.

STOUT
Stout is the darkest ale or beer brewed: it is also the sweetest, both colour and sweetness being due to the amount of kilning and degree of roasting of the malt used. The quality of the water also has a great deal to do with the quality of *Stout*, as it has with the quality of all ales and beers, hence the best *Stouts* are brewed in Dublin and London. In Ireland *Stout* is commonly known as Porter.

STRAIGHTS
An American name for brandy, gin, rum and whisky if, when called for, the bottle is placed before the customer with two small tumblers, a lump of ice in one and the other three-parts filled with iced water.

STRAW WINES
Fr. *Vins de paille*. Sweet wines made from very ripe grapes which are left in the sun, after being picked, and laid on straw mats to become almost like raisins before they are pressed.

STREGA
One of the more popular liqueurs made in Italy.

SUAU, Château
One of the Second Growths of Sauternes, in the Commune of Barsac. (15 tuns average.)

SUDUIRAUT, Château de
One of the First Growths of Sauternes. The vineyards of *Suduiraut* are in the Commune of Preignac and produce an average of 100 tuns of white wines per annum. There was a time when *Suduiraut* was known as *Cru du Roi*.

SUISESSE
One teaspoon sugar; one egg white; 2 oz. charged water; cracked ice; one pony French vermouth; half pony green crème de menthe; two ponies absinthe; cherry. Mix

sugar with water, vermouth and absinthe. Add egg white, fill glass with cracked ice, and shake well. Drop one maraschino cherry into a champagne glass, pour crème de menthe over, and strain the drink over all. No drink is more typically New Orleans than this exotic Suisesse.—A.C.

SWEDISH PUNSCH
A cordial with rum as its basis; it is highly spiced and may be drunk neat as a liqueur, or with hot water, by way of a chest protector in cold weather.

SWEETS
According to English law, the name of 'any liquor made from fruit and sugar, mixed with any other material, and which has undergone fermentation in the manufacture'.

SWEET WINES
These are mostly dessert wines; their sweetness is due to the original grape-sugar of the must which was prevented from fermenting by added spirit, but much less than is customary or necessary for 'fortified' wines. Some 'sweet wines' are made from such sweet grapes that some of the grape-sugar in the must is unable to ferment, even if there is no spirit added. The best sweet wines are made from muscat grapes in the south of France, Italy, Spain, Portugal and some of the Greek islands.

SWITZERLAND
There are vineyards in 20 out of the 22 Cantons of Switzerland, many vineyards in some of them, and a few only in others. The vineyards of Switzerland may be divided in three main groups: (1) The Rhône Valley or Western region, nearest France; (2) The Rhine watershed or Eastern region, nearest Germany; (3) The Ticino and Grisons country or Southern region, nearest Italy. The best wines of Switzerland are those of the Cantons of Vaud, Valais, Neuchatel and Berne.

SWIZZLES
Cocktails which, instead of being shaken in a 'shaker' are mixed with a swizzle-stick, acting as a whisk. The ice is omitted from the *Swizzle*, but the other ingredients may be the same as for any *Cocktail* (q.v.).

SYLLABUB
Season rich milk with sugar and wine, but not enough to curdle it. Fill the glasses nearly full and crown them with whipped cream, seasoned.—F.P.S.

SYNTHETIC WINE
Synthetic wine is artificial wine. A 'wine' made up of water, spirit, glucose, glycerine,

and colouring matter is a synthetic wine, artificially made from materials, some of which are artificial insomuch as they are never present in any real wine.

A 'wine' made from concentrated must to which water and yeast are added in order to provoke fermentation, as is the case with the majority of 'British wines', is artificially made but not from any artificial materials. It may, on analysis, be found to contain no substance that might not be found in real wine.

It may be argued, therefore, that 'British wine' made from must from which the original water has been evaporated and the original yeast killed, but only to be replaced at a later stage by water and yeast of a different kind, but of the same nature, has produced its alcohol through fermentation and is not a 'synthetic wine', a term the use of which should be restricted to 'wines' made artificially without the fermentation factor.

SYRACUSE
A red dessert wine from the vineyards of Syracuse, in Sicily; it is made mostly from muscat grapes and is always sweet.

SZEKSÁRD
A red table wine from the vineyards of the Tolna district of Hungary.

SZOMERODNY
One of the best-known Hungarian white table wines.

TABLE WATERS
Bottled waters, whether natural mineral waters or artificially aërated waters, which are colourless and flavourless, hence suitable for drinking at mealtime either by themselves or with wine or spirits.

TAIN L'HERMITAGE
A small town on the left bank of the Rhône opposite Tournon, at the foot of the vine-clad hill of *L'Hermitage*.

TALBOT, Château
One of the Fourth Growths of the Médoc (Saint-Julien) dating back to the fifteenth century and named after General Talbot, who lost the battle of Castillon, in 1453. It belonged for some time to the Marquis d'Aux and it is sometimes called *Ch. Talbot d'Aux* or *Ch. d'Aux Talbot*. Average 150 tuns claret.

TALENCE
The Commune immediately south of Bordeaux, in the Graves district. Its vineyards yield some very fair claret but none of out-standing merit. The best growths are those of *Châteaux La Tour-Haut-Brion*; *Rostan-Haut-Carré*; *Raba*; *Lafitte-Bordeaux* and *Clos Lafitte-Talence*.

TAPPIT-HEN
A Scotch bottle, always made of black or very dark green glass, and holding approximately three imperial quarts or 4½ reputed quarts.

TARRAGONA
The fortified red wines of Tarragona were shipped to a very considerable extent, and enjoyed a great measure of popularity in England, for many years as 'the poor man's port': they were very dark, very sweet, very strong and quite cheap. Their sale was checked by the Anglo-Portuguese Treaty of 1916 and further by the Imperial Preference Conference, and their place has been taken to a great extent by the port-style wines from South Africa and Australia at first, but more recently by port-type British wines.

TART, Clos de
The best vineyard of the Commune of Morey (Côte de Nuits); it is but 17 acres in extent but produces some very good red burgundy.

TAVEL
A village on the right bank of the Rhône, the vineyards of which, together with those of the adjoining Commune of Lirac, produce the best *Vin Rosé* of France.

TAWNY
The peculiar brownish-red colour of ports matured in wood. Also the name of port matured in wood until it has acquired a tawny complexion.

TEA
Tea is made from the dried and prepared leaves of a small evergreen tree or shrub of the Camellia family. The first reference to tea is found in Chinese writings of the year 2737 B.C.; it was introduced to India in 1837–8 and to Ceylon in 1870. The varieties in general use in the U.K. are *China Tea*, which has an aromatic fragrance, *Indian Tea* – Darjeeling, Assam, Cachar, Sylhet, Dooars, Terai, Nilgiri, etc.; and *Ceylon Tea*.

Teas are also classed according to their method of preparation as *Green*, *Black* or *Oolong*, and graded in order of quality as *Flowery Orange Pekoe*; *Broken Orange Pekoe*; *Orange Pekoe*; *Pekoe*; *Pekoe Souchong* and *Souchong*. *Pekoes* are made from the smaller leaves and *Souchong* from the larger and coarser ones.

Use a really good quality of tea, for flavour and economy. Water for making tea must be freshly drawn and boiling fiercely: tea made with water which has been reheated, or has simmered for some time, will be stale and flat. Warm the teapot, or rinse with boiling water, before putting in the dry leaf. Use one teaspoonful of leaf for each person. Pour the boiling water on to the leaf, and allow to stand for not more than six minutes.

Milk Tea. Make tea in the ordinary way, but boil only half the usual amount of water. Infuse for five minute. Pour out, half filling each cup; fill up with warm (not boiled) milk. Sugar to taste.

American Iced Tea. Make a brew of strong tea. Fill a tall glass with cracked ice to the brim; pour the tea over the ice, straining carefully; add sugar to taste. Serve with a slice of lemon hung on the side of the glass. Excellent served after lunch or dinner.

Russian Iced Tea. Pour two pints of freshly boiling water over four teaspoonfuls of tea leaves; infuse for five minutes. Strain carefully through a piece of muslin or a fine strainer, into a jug containing the juice of one lemon and one orange, one teaspoonful of sugar, and ice.

Iced Mint Tea. Pour a pint of boiling water over four teaspoonfuls of tea leaves. Fill each tumbler a third full with crushed ice, and three bruised mint leaves to each, fill up with the hot strained tea after this has infused for four or five minutes. Serve with sugar and lemon slices.

(*Information and recipes supplied by M.C.G. Gardiner, Assistant Commissioner, Empire Tea Bureau.*)

TEMPERATURE

All white wines are better served cool or cold, that is to say, at the temperature of the ideal white wines cellar, i.e. 48° F., and all red wines at the temperature of the ideal red wines cellar, i.e. 55° F. There is no great harm in cooling white wines rather quickly in a frigidaire or ice bucket, if they come from too warm a cellar, but there is a very grave danger of ruining red wines past all hope of redress by bringing them up to a higher temperature than that of the cold cellar out of which they come. To put a red wine in front of the fire, or to plunge it into hot water, 'to take the chill off', is a sin that cannot be forgiven because there is no atonement for it. If your red wine comes from too cold a cellar, leave it in the dining-room long enough, and it will soon acquire the temperature of the room, which is all that is desirable. If you cannot leave it long enough in the room, warm the glass in the hollow of your hands, and you will soon have the wine at the right temperature.

TENERIFFE

The most important of the seven Cape Verde Islands. The vineyards of Teneriffe occupy a district called 'Monte', some seven miles from Las Palmas; they produce on an average a million gallons a year of red and white table wines, as well as some sweet muscatel white wines, practically the whole of them being consumed locally.

TENT. ROTA TENT.
TINTILLA DE ROTA

The name of the darkest of all Spanish red wines. Mostly used for blending with lighter red wines.

TEQUILA

A fiery spirit which is distilled in Mexico from *Pulque* (q.v.).

TERLANER. TERLANO

The German and Italian names of the same wine, a white wine of the Tyrol.

TERMO

The name of a plain, white Portuguese table wine made from the vineyards of the Lisbon region.

THERA

The chief wine-producing district of the Greek island of *Santorin* (q.v.). Also the name of one of the best white wines of Santorin.

THORINS

One of the best red wines of the Beaujolais. The name of Thorins may be given to all the wines made from the vineyards of Romanèche-Thorins and some of those in the Commune of Chénas. But only the wine made from 46 named vineyards in the Commune of Romanèche-Thorins may be sold as *Thorins Grand Cru*.

THURGAU

One of the minor wine-producing Cantons of Switzerland. Its only wine of note is a red wine known as *Karthauser* from the vineyards which flourish between Worth and Ittingen.

TICINO

One of the more important wine-producing Cantons of Switzerland, producing much red and white wine of moderate quality.

TODDY

The name of two distinct types of drinks. In tropical and sub-tropical countries, *Toddy* is the name of the sap of various palms, and also of the beverages which are fermented from such sap. The name is also sometimes given to some iced long drinks of fairly high alcoholic strength.

In northern latitudes, a *Toddy* is a hot drink usually made with sugar, spirits and hot water, with a squeeze or a slice of lemon. Here are two examples of Hot Toddies, one simple and one not so simple. Also a hot weather American iced *Toddy*.

Hot Apple Toddy. This is a toddy that has been brewed at the State in Schuylkill in Philadelphia for a couple of hundred years, and for the last fifty or sixty at the 'Rabbit' in the same city. It is used and useful on a cold winter's night, and is made as follows:

Bake in an earthenware dish 13 Newton Pippin apples. Do not core, but remove eyes and stems. Put baked apples in a 2½ or 3-gallon jug and add two quarts of Jamaica rum, one quart of brandy, 12 to 15 lumps of sugar, and two quarts of boiling water. Cover jug with plate and place near an open fire to steam for at least two hours before serving. Stir gently with a wooden spoon occasionally, while brewing.—C.B.D.

Pendennis Toddy. Crush half lump of sugar with a little water in an old-fashioned glass; one jigger bourbon whisky; one lump of ice.—L.T.C.R.

Rum Toddy. One lump of sugar; one jigger of Jamaica rum.

Fill glass with boiling water. Insert one small piece of cinnamon, one slice of lemon garnished with four cloves and a thin slice of lemon rind twisted over glass and inserted. Stir mixture a little and serve with a spoon. Also serve a small pitcher of hot water on the side.—H.J.G.

TOKAY

The wines of Tokay take their name from the small village of Tokaj, in the Hegyalja district of north-eastern Hungary, at the foot of the Carpathians. The best *Tokay* wine is known as *Tokaij Essencia*, the next best as *Tokaij aszu*, which is not quite so rich but very sweet and of greatly concentrated flavour. Both will keep longer than any other wine, but they both deserve Professor Saintsbury's verdict: 'No more a wine but a prince of liqueurs'.

The next grade is called *Tokaij Szamorodner* and is more of a table wine, being fairly dry, unless made in a great vintage, when it is also quite rich: it is then labelled *Tokaij édes szamorodner*. Wines sold under labels such as *Tokay Forditás* or *Tokay Maslas* are commercial wines not in the same class as the others. They are made from the lees of the pressings of the real *Tokay* wines. These are always made from the *Furmint* grape and from overripe grapes, called *trockenbeeren*. They are gathered in wooden vessels known as *puttonyos*, holding about 25 quarts, and it is the number of these *puttonyos* full of over-ripe Furmint grapes per cask which deter-

mines the quality of the wine. When the label on the bottle records '1 puttony', it means that about 10 per cent of the grapes used were *trockenbeeren* when that particular cask of wine was made; if '3 pottonyos', the proportion was 30 per cent, and if '5 puttonyos', as much as 50 per cent, which is the richest and finest *Tokay Aszu* made, except in exceptional years, such as 1920, when a '6 puttonyos' wine was made. When the *Tokay Aszu* is offered under the German name of *Tokay Ausbruch*, the German for puttonyos is büttig.

TOM COLLINS

A wonderful thirst quencher in hot weather. It is made of a glass of dry gin and half a glass of lime juice or lemon juice and a teaspoonful of powdered sugar well shaken with some cracked ice and then strained in a long glass: a cube or two of ice are then added and the glass is filled with soda or seltzer water.

There are also a number of bastard Tom Collins known as:

Bourbon Collins, made with bourbon whisky.
Brandy Collins, made with brandy.
Irish Collins, made with Irish whiskey.
John Collins, made with Hollands gin.

TONIC WATER

A bottled water with a slightly 'quinined' or bitter after-taste.

TONNERRE

One of the three most important towns of Lower Burgundy (Yonne Département). The vineyards of Tonnerre produce distinctive and pleasing wines, some of the best being the·red and white wines of *Les Olivottes,* in the Commune of Dannemoine; the white wines of *Vaumorillon,* in the Commune of Junay, and *Les Grisées,* in the Commune of Epineuil.

TORRE GIULIA

One of the best table white wines of Italy; it is made from the vineyards of Foggia, in Apulia; it is quite a dry wine, it has a good bouquet and is full-bodied.

TORRES VEDRAS

Plain beverage Portuguese wines from the parishes of *Lourinha* and *Mafra,* near Lisbon.

TOURAINE

One of the fairest of the old Provinces of France, chiefly noted for its Châteaux and its wines. The best white wines of Touraine are those of *Vouvray,* and its best red wines those of *St Nicholas de Bourgueil.*

TOURNON

An ancient little city on the right bank of the Rhône, immediately facing Tain-l'Hermitage; its vineyards produce both red and white table wines, the red wines being the better as well as the more plentiful of the two.

TOURNUS

One of the most important wine-producing centres of the Saône-et-Loire Département (red burgundies mostly).

TRABEN-TRARBACH

Twin villages on opposite banks of the Moselle; Zell district. Good white wines. Best vineyards of Traben (left bank of the Moselle): *Königsberg, Würzgarten* and *Kräuterhaus.* Best vineyards of Trarbach (right bank of the Moselle): *Schlossberg, Hühneberg* and *Burgberg.*

TRAMINER

A species of white grape extensively grown in Alsace and in Germany for the making of high-class wines.

TRIER. TRÈVES

One of the chief markets of the Moselle wines trade and a very quaint old city, on the Moselle, close to where the Ruwer and Saar join the Moselle, the first above and the second below Trier. The white wines from the vineyards of Trier itself are of very moderate quality.

TRIPLE-SEC

A curaçao liqueur which was first sold under that name by the firm of Cointreau, of Angers, and *Triple-Sec Cointreau* has always been acknowledged as the best. *Triple-Sec* is always sold white (uncoloured) and usually in square-sided flagons copied from the original Cointreau flagons.

TRITTENHEIM

A wine-producing parish of the Middle Moselle, in the Trier district. The best vineyards of Trittenheim are *Laurentiusberg, Falkenberg, Olk* and *Apotheke.*

TROCKENBEEREN AUSLESE

The German name for a wine made from a special selection of overripe grapes, the grapes from which the richest, sweetest and finest German white wines are made.

TULARE COUNTY

A Californian county, south of Fresno County, both of them very important fortified wine-producing counties.

TUN

An English wine measure for a large cask containing 210 Imperial gallons or 252 U.S. gallons or 954 litres.

TUNISIA

That part of French Northern Africa immediately east of Algeria; its vineyards produce an average of 30 million gallons of wine per annum, mostly red wines.

TUQUET, Château du

The only important Estate of the Commune of Beautiran, in the Graves de Bordeaux district. It produces on an average 20 tuns of claret and 65 tuns of white wine per annum.

TUSCANY

The most important wine-producing Province of Italy: the home of *Chianti.*

TWANN

A deep golden and full-bodied wine from the vineyards of Twann near the Lake of *Sienne* in the Swiss Canton of Berne.

ULLAGE

An *ullage* means a bottle with a faulty cork which has allowed some of the wine to escape. An ullaged bottle of champagne, provided the loss of wine has not been excessive, may be excellent, whereas an ullaged bottle of claret or burgundy is always flat and poor. *On ullage*, refers to a cask of wine which is no longer full to the bung, a dangerous condition for any wine if so left for any length of time.

UNGSTEIN

Palatinate. Dürkheim district. White wines. Best vineyards: *Herrenberg, Spielberg, Roterd.*

UNICUM BITTERS

A well-known brand of *Bitters* made by Zwack, a Hungarian firm of liqueur distillers.

URUGUAY

There are some 6,455 hectares of vineyards in Uruguay and practically every one of the chief types of European wines are imitated: beverage wines of the chianti and hock types; fortified wines made to resemble sherry, port, marsala and malaga; sparkling wines and vermouths. Five-sixths of the vineyards of Uruguay are in the districts of Canelones and Montevideo.

ÜRZIG

One of the best wine-producing parishes of the Middle Moselle (Wittlich district). Best vineyards: *Kranklay, Würzgarten, Schwarzlay.*

USQUEBAUGH

The original Celtic name of the modern *Whisky* (q.v.).

VALAIS

A Swiss Canton renowned for the white and red wines of the upper Rhône Valley, from Martigny to the Visp Valley, chiefly those of Sion, made from Fendant grapes, which are white, but also those made from Dole grapes, which are red.

VALDEPEÑAS

A small town in the Province of La Mancha, in Spain, surrounded by vineyards which produce both red and white wines of somewhat higher alcoholic strength than that of most table wines.

VALENCIA

Dark, red, rich wines from the Province of Levante, Spain; chiefly used, in England, for blending purposes. Average production 850,000 hectolitres, or nearly 19 million gallons per annum.

VALPOLICELLA

A truly dry, almost bitter, red wine of Veneto, in Northern Italy. It is made from the grapes which grow on the foothills rising from the shores of Lake Garda.

VALTELLINA

The name of both the red and white wines of some of the table wines made in the region of Sondrio, in the north of Lombardy, which was formerly Swiss. The same wines were then known as *Veltliner*. The better class of *Valtellina* wines are sold under individual names of their own, such as *Sassella* or *Inferno*.

VALWIG

Lower Moselle. Cochem district. White wines. Best vineyards: *Herrenberg, Schwarzenberg*.

VAN DER HUM

The best and best-known of South African liqueurs. It is made with Cape brandy, and flavoured with naartjes, the South African tangerine, as well as various other fruits and herbs, and, like all liqueurs, it is sweet.

Van der Hum. 12 bottles brandy; 2½ nutmegs; 50 cloves; 12 dessertspoons cinnamon; a few seeds cardamon; 12 wineglasses ship's rum (six tablespoons Seville orange peel greatly improves the flavour); 12 wineglasses orange flower water; 24 tablespoons naartje peel finely cut.

All spices to be bruised and put into thin muslin bags. The brandy should *not* be weaker than 22 degrees, or the liquor will not be clear.

Method: Mix all well together and let the ingredients remain in the brandy for 1½ months, shaking occasionally till all virtue

is extracted from them. Then take 6 lb. clear light brown crystallized sugar, one cup sugar to two of water, and boil to a thick rich syrup. When quite cold, mix one cup syrup to two of the spiced brandy; stir well till quite mixed. Add one wineglass *best* rum to every bottle of Van der Hum; this mellows the mixture.

Put all back into a cask and clarify with the whites of two eggs, well whisked, and lightly put on the top of the Van der Hum; then, with a cane split up like a whisk, swirl it round until the whites are quite admixed, and let it stand without disturbing it for three weeks, when it will be beautifully clear and ready for bottling.

It is advisable to bottle through filtering paper.

VAT

In English, a *Vat* is a tub, the size of which varies, but in Dutch *Vat* means 100 litres (hectolitre) or 22 gallons.

VAUD

This Canton produces the finest white wines of Switzerland. Its vineyards may be divided in three groups: (1) *La Côte*, facing the northern shore of Lake Geneva, west of Lausanne; (2) *Lavaux*, a stretch of hills facing the eastern end of the Lake of Geneva, with the great Bernese Alps towering behind them, some 10 miles in length from Lausanne to Vevey and Montreux, two of their more renowned wines being those of Dezaley and Johannisberg; (3) Upper Rhône Valley, from Villeneuve to Bex, their finest wine the Yvorne, from the vineyards of Aigle.

VÉDRINES, Château

One of the Sauternes Second Growths (Commune of Barsac). Average production 40 tuns white wine. The vineyards of *Védrines* were originally part of the *Château Doisy* Estate.

VERDELHO

One of the driest types of Madeira wines, and one of the best; it used to be made from the Verdelho grape, now all but extinct.

VERJUICE

The acid juice of unripe grapes: it used to be in demand chiefly for cooking. Latin, *Omphacium*; French, *Verjus*; Italian, *Agresto*; Spanish, *Agrazo*; Portuguese, *Agraço*.

VERMOUTH

A white wine prepared chiefly on the French and Italian sides of the Alps, with aromatic Alpine herbs and various ingredients, which are cooked in the wine before it becomes vermouth. The Italian vermouth is usually darker in colour and sweeter than the French.

The well-known brands of Italian and French vermouths are not only the best but the safest. There is also a number of imitation vermouths manufactured in wine-producing countries and elsewhere; they look like *Vermouth* and are in great demand.

Vermouth Achampanado. A thirst-removing long drink much in demand in Cuba. *Recipe*: Twist a small piece of lime rind into a tall glass, pack in some cracked ice, add a teaspoonful of sifted sugar, a wineglassful of French vermouth, then fill the glass with seltzer water, stir a little, drink the lot and be grateful.

Vermouth Cassis. One of the most popular *Apéritifs* in many parts of France. *Recipe*: Pack some cracked ice at the bottom of a tall glass, pour a liqueur glass of crème de cassis on the ice, then a wineglassful of French vermouth and fill with seltzer water.

VERNACCIA
The name of one of the species of grapes largely cultivated in Italy for the making of wines which are sold under the name of *Vernaccia*, with the name of the vineyard or region of their birth added: thus *Vernaccia di Campidano*, a dry, amber-coloured wine from Sardinia; *Vernaccia di San Gemignano*, from Sienna, in Tuscany, etc.

VERTHEUIL
A Commune of the Médoc, 8 k. NW. of Pauillac, which produces a large quantity of fair claret, but none of great distinction; some of its best vineyards are those of *Château Victoria* and *Domaine de l'Abbaye-Skinner*; they rank as Bourgeois Growths.

VERZENAY. VERZY
Two of the more important wine-producing Communes of the Marne Département, upon the Reims side of the *Montagne de Reims*.

VESPETRO. VESPITRO

2 pints brandy
1 oz. aniseed
1 lb. sugar
2 oz. corianders
1 oz. fennel
2 drachms angelica
2 lemons

Break up these ingredients, and put them in a jug with two pints of brandy; peel the two lemons, which you must add to the mixture, and squeeze in the juice, break the sugar; dissolve it in water, and put it into the jar; let it stand for a fortnight, then

strain it through a flannel bag, filter and bottle it.—G.A.J.

VICHY WATER
Mineral waters from a number of natural springs in the valley of the Allier, near Vichy. They vary greatly according to the spring from which they originate, thus *Vichy Célestins* is practically flavourless and may be used as a table water, whilst *Vichy Grande Grille* and *Vichy Hôpital* should not be drunk at meals, nor at any time except on doctor's advice.

VIDONIA
One of the sweet dessert wines which had a fair measure of popularity in England during the eighteenth century and early part of the nineteenth. It came chiefly from Teneriffe, the vineyards of which never recovered from the phylloxera disaster.

VIEILLE CURE
A popular French liqueur, distilled at Bordeaux; its basis is brandy and it is highly aromatic, somewhat on the same lines as *Bénédictine*, although not so sweet.

VIENNE
The chief city of the Isère Département of France, in Dauphiny: its wines were famous in Rome in the days of Pliny and Plutarch, and they are referred to by Martial in one of his Epigrams:

Haec de vitifera venisse picata vienna:
Ne dubites misit Romulus ipse mihi.

The vineyards of *Vienne* still produce some fair beverage wines, both red and white. Some of the best white wines of the Isère Département are those of *Tullins, la Tronche, Château-Bayard, Lapierre* and *Marquises*. The best reds are those of *St. Ismier, St. Jean de Moirans* and *Fares*. The best white wine of Vienne is the white wine of the *Côte St. André*: the reds, which are more ordinary than the whites, are those of the valley of *Grésivaudan* (vineyards of *St. Savin, Jailleu* and *St. Rambert*).

VIESCH
One of the white wines of Switzerland from vineyards of the upper Valley of the Rhône close to where the river enters France.

VILA NOVA DE GAYA
Oporto's twin city, one the left bank of the Douro, where most port shippers have their wine stores.

VILLAFRANCA DEL PANADES
One of the most important wine-producing districts of Northern Spain (Barcelona Province). It consists of 33 parishes with an

average yearly production of 44 million gallons of wine, both red and white, the best mostly white.

VILLANY-PÉCS
One of the most important wine-producing districts of Hungary. The best white wine is known as *Villányer Riesling* and the best red as *Villányer Auslese*.

VILLENAVE-D'ORNON
A Commune of the Graves district 9 k. S. of Bordeaux, which produces a large quantity of claret as well as a fairly large quantity of white wine. The best and best-known Châteaux of the Commune are *Châteaux Carbonnieux, Haut-Madère, Lahontan, Baret* and *La Ferrade*, which produce both red and white wines; *Châteaux Duc d'Epernon, Pontac-Monplaisir* and *Lalanne-Monplaisir*, which produce none but white wines; whilst *Château Couchins* produces none but red wines.

VIN
Fr. for *Wine*.

Vin blanc, white wine.

Vin bourru, new wine, before it has fallen bright.

Vin chaud, mulled wine.

Vin cuit, grape-juice boiled to the consistency of a syrup.

Vin de côtes, wine from hillside vineyards.

Vin de coule, wine of the first pressing of grapes.

Vin de cuvée, wine of the first pressing (champagne).

Vin de garde, a well-balanced wine suitable for laying down.

Vin de goutte, wine from the last squeezings of the grapes.

Vin de liqueur, grape-juice, the fermentation of which has been checked by the addition of brandy.

Vin de messe, altar wine.

Vin de paille, a sweet, golden wine made in the Jura from grapes which are left on straw mats when picked, to dry in the sun, before they are pressed.

Vin de palus, claret from the vineyards nearest the banks of the rivers Garonne, Dordogne and Gironde.

Vin de pays, local wine; wine with a local reputation but not made in sufficiently large quantities to be exported.

Vin de paysan, homely wine; the poorer quality *Vin de pays*.

Vin de plaine, wine from plain vineyards, never so good as that from the hillsides.

Vin de presse, an inferior wine made from the pressed husks of grapes.

Vin doux, grape-juice before it ferments and becomes wine.

Vin gris, light red wine of Lorraine usually made of mixed black and white grapes.

Vin jaune, the best wine of Château Chalon, Jura.

Vin mousseux, sparkling wine.

Vin nature, unsweetened wine.

Vin non-mousseux, still wine.

Vin ordinaire, the more homely type of table wine.

Vin rosé, 1. A pink wine made from very ripe black grapes, the skins of which are not allowed to ferment with the wine, so that they only impart to it a pink tinge instead of a dark red colour.

2. A pink wine made from black and white grapes mixed in the pressing.

3. A white wine coloured with cochineal to the degree of pink required.

Vin rouge, red wine.

VINEGAR
An acid liquid prepared from various substances by acetous fermentation of the alcohol present in all alcoholic beverages, which becomes in the presence of oxygen, acetic acid. In all wine-producing countries winevinegar is the rule; in the others, it is maltvinegar. Vinegar is also made from cider, and to a much less extent from perry, honey, rice, maize and all manner of other vegetable substances which are susceptible to produce alcohol by fermentation.

VINHO
Portuguese for *Wine*.

Vinho claro, unfortified wine.

Vinho generoso, fortified wine.

Vinho spumoso, sparkling wine.

Vinho verde, the more homely sort of table wine; new wine.

Vinho estufado, Madeira wine matured in an *estufa*.

Vinho trasfugado, the *Vinho estufado* after it has been racked.

VINO. VINOS
Sp. for *Wine* and *Wines*.

Vino blanco, white wine.

Vino corriente, ordinary table wine.

Vino de anada, young Jerez wine before it is blended.

Vino de color, grape-juice boiled to the consistency of a sweet syrup.

Vino de cuarte, a *Rosé* wine from the Province of Valencia.

Vino de la tierra, local wine.

Vino de pasto, dinner wine, a 'utility' type of sherry wine.

Vino maestro, a very sweet and strong wine used for blending with harsh or weak wines.

Vino spumoso, sparkling wine.

Vino tierno, another name for *Vino maestro.*

Vino tinto, red wine.

VINO, VINI

It. for *Wine* and *Wines.*

Vini bianchi, white wines.

Vini di lusso, expensive dessert wines.

Vini rossi, red wines.

Vini rosati, Rosés wines.

Vini tipici, standard wines.

Vino cotto, grape-juice boiled to the consistency of a sweet syrup.

Vino della riviera, wines from the Lombardy side of the Lake Garda.

Vino de arrosto, wine of breed.

Vino frizzante, cheap, fizzy wine.

Vino spumante, sparkling wine.

VINTAGE

The gathering of the grapes. Also the particular year when the grapes were gathered and the wine made. There is a *Vintage* every year, but the quality of the grapes vintaged varies from year to year. There are wines shipped under the date of their vintage and others shipped without any such date; all were made alike from grapes gathered in one or more years. The chief difference between dated (Vintage) and undated (non-Vintage) wines is that the first show greater promise of improving with age and should be kept, whilst the others are ready for immediate consumption and may – but need not – be kept.

I

Some of the greatest Classical Vintages of the nineteenth century:

Port. 1834, 1847, 1851, 1853, 1863, 1868, 1875, 1884, 1887, 1896.

Claret. 1848, 1864, 1869, 1870, 1871, 1875, 1878, 1899, 1900.

Burgundy. 1858, 1877, 1881, 1885, 1889, 1895, 1898.

Champagne. 1874, 1880, 1884, 1889, 1892, 1893, 1899, 1900.

Hocks. 1868, 1889, 1893, 1900.

II

Some of the best Vintage Years of the first half of the twentieth century:

Port. 1904, 1908, 1912, 1920, 1922, 1924, 1927, 1931, 1934, 1935, 1941, 1947, 1948.

Claret. 1909, 1914, 1920, 1923, 1924, 1928, 1929, 1934, 1937, 1943, 1945, 1947, 1949.

Burgundy. 1904, 1906, 1911, 1915, 1919, 1923, 1926, 1929, 1933, 1934, 1937, 1945, 1947, 1949.

Champagne. 1904, 1906, 1911, 1920, 1921, 1926, 1928, 1929, 1934, 1937, 1942, 1943, 1945, 1949.

Hocks. 1904, 1906, 1911, 1915, 1920, 1921, 1929, 1933, 1934, 1937, 1945, 1947, 1949.

There is some poor wine made even in the best of vintages, and there is also some good wine made even when the vintage is, generally speaking, a failure. Hence one should pay more attention to the quality of the wine in one's glass than to the label on the bottle.

VODKA

The national Russian spirit. It is as nearly 'plain' as a spirit can be, being distilled from the cheapest material at hand, which used to be wheat in Russia, and neither flavoured, nor coloured, nor matured. It is served very cold and swallowed at one gulp: there is no need for nose or palate to waste any time over *Vodka.*

VOLNAY

One of the best-known Communes of the Côte d'Or, producing much red burgundy of very fair quality. Its best vineyards are: *Les Angles, La Barre, Bousse d'Or, En Caillerets, Caillerets Dessus, En Chevret, Fremiet, Les Mitans, Pointe d'Angles* and *En Verseuil.* Average annual production, 100,000 gallons.

VOLLRADS, Schloss

One of the finest growths of the Rhinegau. The castle dates back to the fourteenth century. It stands in a little valley at the back of the twin villages of Winkel and Mitteheim, and has been for generations the property of the Matuschka-Greiffenklau family.

VOSNE-ROMANÉE

One of the most famous of the wine-producing Communes of the Côte d'Or (Côte de Nuits); its vineyards stretch from those of Vougeot, in the North, to those of Nuits-Saint-Georges, in the South. The most renowned of all is *La Romanée Conti*: it is closely challenged, as regards the excellence of their wines, by *Les Richebourg* vineyards, and then come the wines of other fine vineyards, *La Romanée, La Tâche,* usually called *La Tâche Romanée*: *Romanée Saint-Vivant, Les Grands Suchots, Les Gaudichots, Les Malconsorts,* and other vineyards produce very fine red burgundy although not quite of the same superlative excellence.

VOUGEOT

One of the most famous of the wine-producing Communes of the Côte d'Or (Côte de Nuits), the vineyards of which produce an average of 100,000 gallons of fine red burgundy per annum.

VOUGEOT, Clos de

The most celebrated of the vineyards of the Commune of Vougeot, as well as the largest and best-known of the vineyards of the Côte de Nuits (125 acres). A former property of the Abbey of Citeaux, the *Clos*, which is still partly enclosed, is now divided among more than forty different owners, who have not all the same standards, means and methods of vine-growing and wine-making: hence marked differences in the quality of the wines entitled to the name of *Clos de Vougeot*. Up to 1789, when the *Clos de Vougeot* was owned by the Cistercians, its vinous production was divided into three Cuvées, the *Cuvée des Moines*, the wine made from the grapes grown nearer the main road; the *Cuvée des Rois*, from those grapes that grew about half-way between the road and the foothills; and *Cuvée des Papes*, from the grapes grown on the higher ground, furthest from the road.

On the other side of the road which skirts the top corner of the *Clos de Vougeot*, to the south-west, there is a vineyard known as *La Vigne Blanche*, which produces the finest white wine of the Côte de Nuits. It belongs to a firm called *Etablissements l'Héritier-Guyot* and its wines are sold as *Clos de Vougeot Blanc*.

VOUVRAY

The most important wine-producing district of Touraine (Loire Valley). It is chiefly noted for its white wines, both still and sparkling.

V.S.O.

'Very Special Old' brandy from 12 to 17 years old.

V.S.O.P.

'Very Special Old Pale' brandy, from 18 to 25 years old.

V.V.S.O.P.

'Very, Very Special Old Pale' brandy, up to 40 years old, which is as old as any brandy need be and older than it is in the ordinary course of commerce.

WAAD

See *Vaud*.

WACHEMHEIM

One of the wine-producing parishes of the Palatinate, in the district of Neustadt. White wines. Best vineyards: *Goldbächel, Böhlig, Gerümpel, Wolfsdarm, Mandelgarten, Luginsland, Dreispitz, Fuchsmantel, Königswingert, Büchelein.*

WALDBÖCKELHEIM

(Nahe Valley.) Kreuznech district. White wine. See *Schloss Böckelheim*.

WALDRACH

(Ruwer Valley.) Trier district. White wine. Best vineyards: *Ehrenberg, Laurentiusberg, Krone.*

WALLERTHEIM

Rhine-Hesse. Oppenheim district. White wines. Best vineyards: *Wiesberg* and *Homberg*.

WALLIS

See *Valais*.

WALPORZHEIM

(Ahr Valley.) Red wines. Best vineyards: *Berg, Pffaffenberg, Domlay* and *Kräuterberg*.

WASSAIL BOWL

A kind of Loving Cup which is referred to in *A Midsummer Night's Dream*. In many parts of England it was – and it may still be – partaken of on Christmas Eve.

'Put into one quart of warm beer 1 lb. of raw sugar, on which grate a nutmeg and some ginger; then add four glasses of sherry and two quarts more of beer, with three slices of lemon; add more sugar, if required, and serve it with three slices of toasted bread floating in it.'—C.T.C.

WATER

The liquid form of a compound of two parts of hydrogen to one of oxygen. Its solid form is called ice and as a vapour it becomes steam. Water is as necessary as air to the fishes that swim in the sea, the birds of the air, the beasts of the field and jungle, as it is for the grass to grow and every tree and plant on earth to bear fruit. Man also needs water and he gets a great deal of it from the food he eats, whether meat, fish or fruit, and the drinks he drinks, wine or beer, tea or coffee, and all other kinds of foods and drinks. There are people, however, who drink water from necessity or choice, and there are different waters for them to choose from, good, or not so good water, safe or not. The best water to drink is spring water, the running water of Highland 'burns' or other mountain streams; also deep-well water. Water from shallow wells, lowland rivers and storage tanks is neither so good to taste nor so safe to drink. Water should never have any colour or smell, but it has a taste which varies according to whatever may be in it besides hydrogen and oxygen, organic and inorganic matter collected in the passage through sub-soil strata in the case of spring water, through the sulphurous and sooty air hanging over towns, in the case of rain water collected in built-up areas, to say nothing of all the refuse that finds its way into surface water. Bacteria of all sorts thrive in all such waters and render them dangerous for human consumption. Distilled water, or boiled water, is safe enough but has a 'flat' taste which is unpleasant. This is sometimes assisted by carbonic acid gas forced into the distilled water at the time of its bottling, the result being a water like *Salutaris* which is effervescent, tasteless and safe. Most natural (other than sea) waters are roughly divided into hard and soft waters. Hard waters are those which have been impregnated with minerals of different kinds. When such waters contain no more than from 8 to 10 grains of solids per gallon, or at most 14 grains for water that is impregnated with lime, they are considered as acceptable; when they contain more they should be artificially 'softened' before use. Hard waters make the best ale, soft waters the best stout.

WATERVALE
South Australia. The wine-producing district in which are situated the Spring Vale vineyards.

WAWERN
(Saar Valley.) Saarburg district. White wines. Best vineyards: *Herrenberg, Ritterpfad, Jesuitenberg, Goldberg.*

WEEPER
A bottle showing the first signs of a defective cork; one that should be recorked, or, preferably, drunk, before it becomes an *Ullage.*

WEHLEN
(Moselle Valley.) Berncastel district. White wines. Best vineyards: *Sonnenuhr, Nonnenberg, Lay, Feinter, Klosterberg.*

WELLINGTON
(South Africa)
One of the most prolific wine-growing districts of the Cape Province, at the end of the Paarl Valley, furthest away from French Hoek.

WERTHEIM
(Baden)
White wines; Steinwein type. Best vineyards: *Schlossberg* and *Altenberg.*

WHISKEY. WHISKY
A grain spirit distilled from barley, rye and other cereals which are first of all malted and then fermented. The strength, colour, flavour and 'quality' of different whiskies depend upon the grain used in the first instance, the manner and degree of the malting, fermentation and distillation, the length of time of maturing and the skill of the blender. Some indication of the main differences resulting from all such factors is given under the headings of the principal whiskies of commerce, which are, in alphabetical order: *Bourbon, Canadian, Irish, Rye* and *Scotch.*

Whisky Cobbler. One teaspoonful sugar; 100 per cent whisky; one teaspoonful fine apple syrup. Fill glass with cracked ice. Stir with spoon, dress with fruits in season, serve with straws.—J.M.

Whisky Cocktail. Three dashes of plain syrup; two or three dashes of bitters; one wineglass of rye or bourbon whisky, and a piece of lemon peel. Fill one-third full of fine ice, shake, and strain in a fancy white wineglass.—L.EN.

Whisky Daisy. Use small bar glass. Three dashes Gomme syrup; the juice of half small lemon; one wineglass bourbon or rye whisky. Fill glass one-third full of shaved ice. Shake thoroughly, strain into a large cocktail glass, and fill up with Apollinaris or seltzer water.—H.C.

Whisky Fix. One teaspoonful sugar; juice of half a lemon; 100 per cent of rye whisky. Fill glass with cracked ice. Stir well with fruits in season. Serve with straws.—J.M.

Whisky Fizz. One teaspoonful sugar; 100 per cent whisky; juice of one lemon. Fill glass with ice. Shake and strain, fill glass with fizz water and serve.—J.M.

Whisky Flip. One teaspoonful sugar; one egg. Fill glass with cracked ice. Add 100 per cent of rye whisky. Shake, strain and grate a little nutmeg on top and serve.—J.M.

Whisky Punch. (Use large bar glass half full of ice.) One teaspoonful sugar; three or four dashes lemon juice; 100 per cent whisky and rum mixed; one dash angostura bitters. Shake well, strain into punch glass, with slice of orange, three or four dashes of curaçao on top, with seltzer, and serve.—J.M.
In Ireland *Whisky Punch* is served at almost boiling point, with the aid, if possible, of a Waterford glass 'muddler'.

Whisky Rickey. One piece of ice in glass; juice of half lime; drop squeezed lime in glass; 100 per cent of Scotch whisky. Fill glass with fizz water. Stir with spoon and serve.—J.M.

Whisky Sling (Hot). One wineglass of whisky. Fill tumbler one-third full of boiling water, and grate nutmeg on the top. —L.EN.

Whisky Smash. Muddle one lump of sugar with a half jigger of water and a few sprigs of mint in glass. Add two cubes of ice. Pour in one jigger of whisky. Decorate with four or five sprigs of mint. Serve with small barspoon, and a glass of charged water on the side.—H.J.G.

Whisky Sour. Half jigger lemon and lime juice; one jigger bourbon or rye whisky; one teaspoonful powdered sugar. Shake thoroughly with cracked ice. Put in serving glass a cherry and a slice of orange. Strain mixture and pour into glass —H.J.G.

Whisky Toddy. One teaspoonful of sugar; half wineglass of water; one wineglass of whisky; one small lump of ice. Stir with a spoon and serve.—H.C.

WILTINGEN
Saar Valley. Saarburg district. White wines. Best vineyards: *Rosenberg, Klosterberg, Dohr, Schlossberg, Kupp, Gottesfuss, Braunfels, Braune Kupp.*

WINCHERINGEN
Upper Moselle. Saarburg district. White wines. Best vineyards: *Fuchsloch* and *Mühlenberg.*

WINE
Wine is the suitably fermented juice of freshly-gathered ripe grapes. The colour, bouquet, flavour, strength and 'quality' of any wine depend upon a number of factors, chief among them being (1) the species of grapes from which the wine is made; (2) the nature of the soil and aspect of the vineyard in which the grapes were grown; (3) the incidence of rain and sunshine responsible for the quality and ripeness of the grapes when gathered at the time of the vintage; (4) the care given to the cultivation of the vines and to the gathering of the grapes; (5) the manner and degree of the pressing of the grapes, the fermentation of their sweet juice, and the treatment accorded to the newly-made wine; (6) to the methods adopted for blending and maturing; the time and manner of bottling, packing, despatching, binning, uncorking, decanting and serving.

Fermentation may be slow or rapid, complete or partial, satisfactory or not, but it is as inevitable as it is natural, and it transforms part or the whole of the sugar present in fresh grape juice into alcohol: the sweeter the grape, the stronger the wine. Fermentation may be checked by the addition of spirit or of chemicals, but there cannot be any such thing as a 'non-alcoholic wine': it is a contradiction in terms.

Light beverage wines, which are 'natural' wines, contain from 8 to 12 per cent of alcohol; fortified wines twice as much; water always is the bulk of the wine (from 66 to 90 per cent), but there are also minute quantities of quite a large number of other substances which are responsible for the colour, bouquet, flavour and keeping quality of every wine. There are as many types of wine as there are types of men and women in the world, a few are very good, some are very bad but the great majority are neither good nor bad, just 'ordinaires'. Some are long lived, they are the exception; some are short lived; some are sound and others are sick, but all must die. A wine need not be rare nor costly to be enjoyable: it must be suited to the food that is served with it, to the occasion and mood of the moment, and, whatever its price, name or pedigree, it is quite indispensable that it should be *sound*. A sound wine is a wine that is pleasant to look at, sweet smelling and intensely clean on the palate; it is a wine that has got over the distemper of youth, but shows as yet no signs of decay, of approaching its end.

WINKEL
One of the best-known villages of the Rhinegau. Fine white wines. Best vineyards of Winkel are: *Hasensprung, Jesuitengarten, Dachsberg, Honigberg, Bienengarten* and *Schloss Vollrads.*

WINNINGEN
Lower Moselle Valley. Coblence district. White wines. Best vineyards: *Uhlen, Hamm, Rosenberg.*

WINTRICH
Moselle Valley. Berncastel district. White wines. Best vineyards: *Ohligsberg, Geyersberg, Simonsberg, Geyerskopf, Geierslay, Sonnseite.* Occasional spelling: *Winterich.*

WINZENHEIM
Nahe Valley. Kreuznach district. White wines. Best vineyards: *Honigberg, Rosenbeck* and *Kranzgraben.*

WOODY
A wine or spirit having acquired the smell of the cask in which it has been lodged too long. If one of the staves of a cask is mouldy, the wine or spirit in it soon acquires a musty taste which renders it undrinkable. But *Woodiness* is the smell of *sound* oak; it is unwelcome but not unwholesome, and it can, as a rule, be remedied.

WORCESTER
One of the important wine-producing districts of Cape Province (South Africa).

WORMS
An important centre of the Rhine-Hesse wine trade. The best wines of Worms are: *Liebfrauenstift, Katterloch, Luginsland, Kirchenstück* and *Klostergarten.*

WÜRZBURG
The chief centre of the Franconia wine trade (Stein wines). Best vineyards: *Steinmantel*, formerly known as *Jesuiten-Stein*, *Stein*, *Herrenberg*, *Schalksberg*.

WYNBERG
The oldest wine-producing district of the Cape Peninsula (South Africa).

YALUMBA
The name of Messrs S.Smith & Son Ltd.'s vineyards, at Angaston, South Australia, and the name under which they market their wines.

YERBA MATÉ
The dried leaves of a South American shrub of the holly family, also known as *Paraguay Tea*, chiefly used in Argentina, Uruguay and Paraguay to make a refreshing kind of tea. It is often called *Yerba* for short and sometimes Yerba de maté. The native way of drinking maté is to plâce the leaves in a hollowed, dried calabash gourd, which is then filled with boiling water. A *Bombilla*, which is a specially made tube, usually of silver, with a strainer at the lower end, is then put into the gourd and the hot maté is sipped through the *Bombilla*.

YONNE
A wine-producing Département of France which, at one time, was part of Burgundy. Its best-known wines are the white wines of *Chablis*.

YQUEM, Château d'
The finest wine of Sauternes and the finest of all French sweet white wines. The gathering of the grapes at Yquem may last a whole month, none but the ripest berries of each bunch being picked at a time. The average yield is 125 tuns, and the wines from the earliest and following pressings are so blended together that the whole product of the one vintage is of the same quality. There are vintages, however, when some of the last pressings are kept apart and sold as *Tête de Vuvée* or *Crème de la Tête*.

YUGOSLAVIA
One of the more important wine-producing countries of the world. The more extensive vineyards of Yugoslavia are those of Slovenia and Dalmatia, whilst some of the best of the country's wines are from the vineyards of Gorizia, in the extreme south-west of Slovenia, and from those of the Adriatic islands off the coast of Dalmatia.

YVORNE
One of the best Swiss white wines, from Aigle, in the upper valley of the Rhône.

ZACO
The best white wine of the Rioja district of Spain.

ZELL
Palatinate (Unterhaardt). White wines. Best vineyards: *Schwarzer Herrgott*, *Schnepfenflug*, *Osterberg*, *Philippsbrunnen*.

There is also a village of the same name in the valley of the Middle Moselle. White wines. Best vineyard: *Schwarze Katz*.

ZELTINGEN
Middle Moselle. Berncastel district. White wines. Best vineyards: *Kirchenpfad*, *Stefanslay*, *Steinmauer*, *Schlossberg*, *Himmelbreick*, *Sonnuhr* and *Rotlay*.

ZOMBIE
  ¾ oz. lime juice
  ½ oz. pineapple juice
  1 teaspoonful Falernum or simple
     syrup
  1 oz. White Label rum
  2 oz. Gold Label rum
  1 oz. Jamaica rum
  ½ oz. 151° proof Demerara rum
  ½ oz. apricot liqueur

Shake well and strain into 14 oz. Zombie glass, quarter filled with ice. Garnish with slice of orange and several sprigs of mint. Serve with straws.—H.J.G.

ZUBROWKA
A Russian spirit which is just as 'raw' as *Vodka*, but not quite so plain. It is *Vodka* (q.v.) in which some Zubrowka grass is steeped, so that it has a little colour, aromatic bouquet and bitterish taste, whereas *Vodka* is colourless and free from all bouquet or taste.

ZUCCO
A dessert wine from Sicilian vineyards, chiefly those of Palermo.

List of Sources Quoted

A.A. *The Family Director or Housekeeper's Assistant*, by Addison Ashburn. Coventry. 1807.

A.A.B. *All About Biscuits*, by H.G.Harris and S. P. Borella. Maclaren & Sons. London.

A.B. *The Receipt Book of Mrs Ann Blencowe*. A.D.1694. London. Guy Chapman. 1925.

A.C.B. *The Ayrshire Home Cookery Book*, compiled by the Misses J. and C. Kerr. Cunninghamhead, Kilmarnock. John Ritchie.

A.C.C.B. *The Anglo-Chinese Cook Book*, compiled and edited by Mrs R. Calder-Marshall and Mrs P. J. Bryant. Vol. I. English 2nd Edition. Shanghai. Kelly & Walsh Ltd. 1926.

A.E. Auguste Escoffier. *Ma Cuisine*. Paris. Flammarion. 1934.

A.E.F. *Quelques Recettes Culinaires Classiques et Régionales*, par Eugène Herbodeau. London. 'A L'Ecu de France'. 1943.

A.F. *The International Cook Book*, by A. Filippini. New York. Doubleday, Page & Co. 1907.

A.G. Anne Gurney. *Vegetable Variety*. London. The Medici Society Ltd.

A.H. (1). Ambrose Heath. *Good Sweets*. Faber & Faber Ltd. London.

A.H. (2). Ambrose Heath. *Good Soups*. Faber & Faber Ltd. London.

A.H. (3). Ambrose Heath. *Vegetable Dishes and Salads for every Day of the Year*. Faber & Faber Ltd. London. 1938.

A.H.N. *Elephant Hunting in East Equatorial Africa*, by Arthur H.Neumann. London. Rowland Ward. 1898.

A.K.-H. (1). *Common-sense Cookery*, by Colonel A. R. Kenney-Herbert. London. Edward Arnold. 1913.

A.K.-H. (2). *Picnics and Suppers*, by Colonel A. R.Kenney-Herbert. London.

A.La. Alin Laubreaux. *The Happy Glutton*. Ivor Nicholson & Watson. London.

A.L. (2). *New American Cookery or Female's Companion*, by an American Lady. New York. D.D.Smith. 1805.

A.L.S. André L.Simon's *French Cook Book*. Boston. Little, Brown and Company. 1938.

Al.S. *The Modern Housewife or Ménagère*, by Alexis Soyer. London. Simpkin, Marshall. 1850.

A.L.W. Andrew L.Winton and Kate Barber Winton. *The Structure and Composition of Foods*. New York. John Willy & Sons Inc. 1935.

A.Ma. Recipes by Magarian.

A.S. (1). Arnold Shircliffe. *The Edgwater Salad Book*. The Hotel Monthly Press. Chicago. 1934.

A.S. (2). Arnold Shircliffe. *The Edgwater Sandwich Book*. The Hotel Monthly Press. Chicago. 1930.

A.W.C. *Pan-American Cook Book*, compiled by the American Women's Club, Buenos Aires. The B.A. Herald.

A.W.M. *The Galley Guide*, by Alex.W. Moffat. New York. Kennedy Bros. 1936.

A.W.R. *The Philadelphia Cook Book*, by Anna Wetherill Reed. New York. M.Barrows & Co. Inc. 1940.

B. (1). Mrs Beeton's *Poultry and Game*. London. Ward, Lock & Co. 1926.

B. (2). Mrs Isabella Beeton's *Book of Household Management*. 1st Edition. London. S.O. Beeton. 1861.

B.B. *British Birds*, by H.F.&.G.Witherby Ltd. London.

B.C. Recipes from Blair Castle.

B.C.B. *The New Butterick Cook Book*, revised and enlarged by Flora Rose. New York. Butterick Publishing Co. 1924.

B.C.S.C.B. *The Boston Cooking School Cook Book*, by Fannie Merritt Farmer. 6th Edition. Boston. Little, Brown & Co. 1938.

B.E.C. Mrs Beeton's *Everyday Cookery*. New Edition. London.Ward, Lock & Co. 1923.

B.G. *Bouquet Garni*, by David de Bethel. London. Medici Society. 1939.

B.H. Blanche Hulton. Recipes supplied by Mrs Jessop Hulton.

B.Ho. *The Game-birds and Waterfowl of South Africa*, by Major Boyd Horsbrugh. London. Witherby. 1912.

B.J.C. *Book of Jewish Cookery*, by Mrs J. Atrutel. London. 1880. P.Valentine.

B.L.L. Blanche L.Leigh. *A Household Book*. Published by N. G. Morrison, Leeds, Yorkshire.

B.R. *Whale Oil and the Products of the Whaling Industry*, by Brian Roberts, in *Polar Record.* The Cambridge University Press. 1939.

B.S.R. 200 *years of Charleston Cooking*. Recipes gathered by Blanche S. Rhett. New York. Random House. 1934.

C.B. Charles Browne. *The Gun Club Cook Book*. Charles Scribner's Sons. London and New York. 1934.

C.B.D. *The Gun Club Drink Book*, by Charles Browne. New York. Charles Scribner's Sons. 1937.

C.B.J. Mrs C. B. Jennings' Recipes.

C.C.C.C. *The Compleat City and Country Cook*, by Charles Carter. London. Bettersworth. 1732.

C.Cum. *The Guinea Pig or Domestic Cavy*, by C. Cumberland, F.Z.S. London. Upcott Gill. 1905.

C.E.F. *The Modern Cook*, by Charles Elmé Francatelli. London. Bentley. 1873.

C.E.M. *The Squire's Home-made Wines*, by Charles Edmund Merrill. New York. T. B. Holliday. 1924.

C.F.L. (1). *The Gentle Art of Cookery; with 750 recipes*, by Mrs C.F.Leyel and Miss Olga Hartley. Phoenix Library. London. Routledge. 1928.

C.F.L. (2). Mrs C.F.Leyel. *Herbal Delights*. Faber & Faber Ltd. London. 1937.

C.F.M. *Culina Famulatrix Medicinæ*, written by Ignotus and revised by A. Hunter, M.D., F.R.S. York. Wilson S. Spence. 1806.

C.G. Crosby Gaige. *New York's World's Fair Cook Book*. New York. Doubleday Doran and Company Inc. 1939.

Ch.C. *Chinese Cookery*, by M. P. Lee, with decorations by Chiang Yee. London. Faber & Faber. 1943.

Ch.J. *Chez James*, by Rose Henniker Heaton and Duncan Swann. London. Elkin Mathews and Marrot. 1932.

Ch.P. *American and other Iced Drinks*. Recipes mainly chosen by Charles Paul. London. Farrow & Jackson.

Ch.T. *British and Foreign Spirits*, by Charles Tovey. London. 1864.

C.H.S. *Hunting the Elephant in Africa*, by Captain C. H. Stigand. London. Macmillan. 1913.

C.I. *The Cook's and Housekeeper's Manual*, by Margaret Dodds. The Cleikhum Inn. 4th Edition. St. Ronan's. 1829.

CLARISSE. *Clarisse or the Old Cook*, translated from the French by Elise Vallée. London. Methuen. 1926.

Cl.K. *Clémentine in the Kitchen*, by Phineas Beck (Samuel Chamberlain). New York. Hastings House and Gourmet. 1943.

C.M. (1). Countess Morphy. *Vegetable Dishes*. Vol. 5 of the Kitchen Library. Herbert Joseph Ltd. London.

C.M. (2). Countess Morphy. *Soups*. Vol. 1 of the Kitchen Library. Herbert Joseph Ltd. London.

C.M. (3). Countess Morphy. *Sweets and Puddings*. Vol. 6 of the Kitchen Library. Herbert Joseph Ltd. London.

C.M. (4). Countess Morphy. *Good Food from Italy*. Chatto & Windus. 1937.

C.M. (5). Countess Morphy. *Recipes of all Nations*. Published for Selfridge & Co. Ltd., by Herbert Joseph Ltd. London.

C.M. (6). Countess Morphy. *The Memorandum Cookery Book*. Herbert Joseph Ltd. London.

C.Ma. *The Lady's Assistant*, by Mrs Charlotte Mason. Robert Burton. Dublin. 1778.

C.M.D.R. *Savour: A New Cookery Book*, by Claire McInerny and Dorothy Roche. 3rd Edition. Oxford University Press. 1939.

C.N. *Cook o' the North*, edited by the Lady Forbes and Miss Mitchell-Thomson. Aberdeen. 1936.

C.R. *Cornish Recipes*, by Edith Mason. Truro. 1929.

C.R.B.B. (1). *America Cooks: Practical Recipes from 48 States*, by Cora, Rose and Bob Brown. New York. W.W. Norton Co. 1940.

C.R.B.B. (2). *The Wine Cook Book*, by Cora, Rose and Bob Brown. Boston. Little, Brown & Co. 1934.

C.S. *Provincial Names and Folk-lore of British Birds*, by Rev Charles Swainson. London. English Dialect Society. 1885.

C.T. *Cook's Tour of European Kitchens*, by C. and M. de Schumacher. London. Chatto & Windus. 1936.

C.T.C. *Cups and their Customs*. London. John van Voorst. 1869.

C.W.C. *My Indian Journal*, by Colonel Walter Campbell. Edinburgh. Edmondstone and Douglas. 1864.

D.A. *A Book of Scents and Dishes*, collected by Dorothy Allhusen. London. Williams & Norgate. 1927.

D.B. David de Bethel. *Bouquet Garni*. London. The Medici Society. 1939.

D.D. 88 *Danish Dishes, or Dining in Denmark*, by Hetna Dedichen. Copenhagen. A. F. Host & Son. 1937.

D.F. David Fairchild. *The World was my Garden*. New York. Scribners. 1938.

D.H. Recipes from the late Sir Daniel Hall.

D.L. Della Lutes. *The Country Kitchen*. London. G. Bell & Sons Ltd. 1938.

D.L.S. Recipes from the Dowager Lady Swaythling.

D.L.T. Recipes from Mrs Doris Lytton Toye.

D.M. *The New London Family Cook*, by Duncan Macdonald. London. Albion Press. 1812.

D.T. Recipes from the (London) *Daily Telegraph*.

E. *The Economist or New Family Cooker*, by Anthony Haselmore. London. McGowen. 1823.

E.A. *Modern Cookery in all its Branches*, by Elizabeth Acton. London. Longmans. 1854.

E.B. *Recipes from Hungary*, by Evelyn Bach. London. The Shenval Press. 1938.

E.C. (1). Elizabeth Craig. *Family Cookery*. Collins. London and Glasgow.

E.C. (2). Elizabeth Craig. *The Stage Favourites' Cook Book*. London. Hutchinson. 1924.

E.C.S.B. (1). *The Game-birds of India, Burma and Ceylon*, by E. C. Stuart Baker. The Bombay Natural History Society. 1930.

E.C.S.B. (2). *Indian Pigeons and Doves*, by E. C. Stuart Baker. London. Witherby. 1913.

E.D.W. *Recipes for Successful Dining*, by Elsie de Wolfe (Lady Mendl). London. William Heinemann Ltd. 1934.

E.E.A. Ernest E. Amiet. *Palmer House Cook Book*. Chicago. John Willy Inc. 1940.

E.G.B. *A Naturalist at the Dinner-table*, by E. G. Boulenger. London. Duckworth. 1927.

E.K.H. *Edith Key Haine's Cook Book*. Farrar and Rhinehart Inc. New York and Toronto. 1937.

E.L.B. *The Epicure's Companion*, by Edward and Lorna Bunyard. London. Dent. 1937.

E.M. *Cornish Recipes, Ancient and Modern*, compiled by Edith Martin. Issued by the Cornwall Federation of Women's Institutes. Truro. 1931.

E.M.L.D. Recipes supplied by Mrs E.M.L. Douglas, of Innerleithen.

Em.M. Recipes given by the late Mrs Emile Mond.

E.O. Ernest Oldmeadow. *Home Cookery in War Time*. London. Grant Richards. 1915.

E.P.V. E. P. Veeraswamy. *Indian Cookery for Use in all Countries*. London. Herbert Joseph. 1936.

E.S. *The Compleat Housewife*, by E. Smith. 11th Edition. London. 1742.

E.Sp. *Cakes and Ales*, by Edward Spencer. London. Grant Richards. 1897.

E.S.R. (1). Eleanour Sinclair Rohde. *Vegetable Cultivation and Cookery*. London. The Medici Society. 1938.

E.S.R. (2). Eleanour Sinclair Rohde. *A Garden of Herbs*. Philip Lee Warner, publisher to the Medici Society Ltd. London and Boston (U.S.A.).

E.T. *Fifty ways of Cooking a Pheasant*, by Elsie Turner. London. Spottiswoode, Ballantyne & Co. Ltd. 1932.

E.W. Emelie Waller's *Cookery and Kitchen Book for Slender Purses*. London. Faber & Faber Ltd. 1935.

E.W.K. *Tried Favourites Cookery Book*, by Mrs E.W. Kirk. 15th Edition. Edinburgh. J. B. Fairgrieve. 1917.

Ex.B. *The Experienced Butcher*. London. Darton, Harvey & Daryon. 1816.

F. Recipes by André L. Simon, published in *The Field*, in 1939 and 1940.

F.B. *The Book of Menus*, by Fin Bec. London. Grant. 1876.

F.C.B. *The Feill Cookery Book*. Glasgow. M'Naughtan and Sinclair. 1907.

F.C.F. *Giant Fishes, Whales and Dolphins*, by J. R. Norman and F. C. Fraser. London. Putnam. 1937.

F.C.S. *A Hunter's Wanderings in Africa*, by Frederick Courteney Selous. London. Richard Bentley & Son. 1890.

F.C.-W. Sir Francis Colchester-Wemyss, K.B.E. *The Pleasures of the Table*. London. Nisbet. 1931.

F.D.S.D. *Drinks of all Kinds*, by Frederick Davies and Seymour Davies. London. Pitman.

F.E.B. *A Book of Whales*, by Frank E. Beddard. London. Jo'n Murray. 1900.

F.F. *The Family Friend*, Vol. III. London. 1850.

F.G.F. F. George Frederick. *Cooking as Men like it*. Business Bourse. New York. 1930.

F.J.J. *Notes on the game-birds of Kenya and Uganda*, by Sir Frederick J. Jackson. London. Williams & Norgate. 1926.

F.K. *French Household Cooking*, by Mrs Frances Keyzer. 3rd Edition. London. Country Life. 1915.

F.L. Recipes received from Francis Latry when in charge of the Savoy Kitchens.

Fl.B. *The Flowing Bowl*, by Edward Spencer. London. Grant Richards. 1899.

Fl.W. *Good Things in England*, by Florence White. London. Jonathan Cape. 1932.

F.M.M. (1). *The Scottish National Cookery Book*, by F. Marian McNeill. Edinburgh and Glasgow. John Menzies & Co. Ltd.

F.M.M. (2). *The Scots Kitchen*, by F. Marian McNeill. London and Glasgow. Blackie. 1940.

F.N. *Farthest North*, by Dr Fridtjof Nansen. Westminster. Archibald Constable. 1897.

F.P.S. Frederick Philip Stieff. *Eat, Drink and be Merry in Maryland*. New York. G.P. Putnam. 1932.

Fr.B. *Log-book of a Fisherman and Zoologist*, by Frank Buckland, M.A. London. Chapman & Hall. 1875.

F.V.K. *In the Haunts of Wild Game*, by Frederick Vaughan Kirby, F.Z.S. Edinburgh. William Blackwood & Sons. 1896.

F.W. *Farmhouse Fare*, collected by *The Farmer's Weekly*.

G.A.J. *The Italian Confectioner*, by G. A. Jarrin. 3rd Edition. London. Ainsworth. 1827.

G.A.S. George Augustus Sala. *The Thorough Good Cook*. London. Cassell. 1895.

G.D.H. *Henley's Twentieth Century Formulas, Recipes and Processes*. Edited by Gardner D. Hiscox, M.E. New York. Henley Publishing Co. 1921.

G.H. (1). *The Good Housekeeping Cookery Book*. New York. Farrar & Rinehart. 1942.

G.H. (2). *Invalid Cookery Book*, by Florence B. Jack. *Good Housekeeping*. 1938.

G.H. (3). *Good Housekeeping. Sweets and Candies*, by D. D. Cottington Taylor. London.

G.H. (4). *Good Housekeeping. Cakemaking*, by D. D. Cottington Taylor. London.

G.L.B.R. *Godey's Lady's Book*. Receipts by Annie Frost. Philadelphia. 1870.

G.L.H. *Perfect Cooking*, by Miss Gwen L. Hughes. The Parkinson Stove Co. Ltd. Birmingham 9.

G.M.B. Geoffrey Boumphrey. *Cunning Cookery*. Thomas Nelson & Sons Ltd. London. 1938.

G.N.C. *German National Cookery for English Kitchens*. London. Chapman & Hall. 1873.

G.T.L. Gladys T. Lang. *The Complete Menu Book*. Houghton Mifflin Company. Boston. 1939.

H.A.V. Recipes supplied by Horace Annesley Vachell.

H.B. *The Williamsburg Art of Cookery*, by Mrs Helen Bullock. 2nd Edition. Williamsburg, Va. 1939.

H.C. Harry Craddock of the Savoy Hotel, London. *The Savoy Cocktail Book*. London. Constable. 1930.

H.E. *Country Recipes of Old England*, by Helen Edden. London. Country Life. 1929.

H.E.D. *A Manuel of Palaerctic Birds*, by H. E. Dresser. London. The author. 1902.

H.F.W. *The Big Game of Central and Western Asia*, by Harold Frank Wallace, F.R.G.S., F.Z.S. London. John Murray. 1913.

H. & G. *Cooking without a Cook*. Selected Recipes from *Homes and Gardens*. London. Country Life. 1926.

H.G.B. *Hendy's Gourmet's Book of Food and Drink*. London. John Lane, The Bodley Head Ltd. 1933.

H.Gl. *The Art of Cookery made Plain and Easy*, by Hannah Glasse.

H.J.G. *Grossman's Guide to Wines, Spirits and Beers*, by Harold J. Grossman. New York. Sherman & Spoerer, Inc. 1940.

H.L.D. Henrietta Latham Dwight. *The Golden Age Cook Book*. New York. Alliance Publishing Company. 1898.

H.M. *The Game-birds of India, Burma and Ceylon*, by Hume and Marshall. 1879.

H.M.S. *Journal of Researches* into the Natural History and Geology of the countries visited during the voyage of *H.M.S. Beagle* round the world. London. John Murray. 1860.

H.P. Hilda Powell. *Vogue's Cookery Book*. Condé Nast. London. 1939.

H.S. '*Hermitage' Recipes*, as published in the Quarterly Circular of the Wine and Food Society of New South Wales, Sydney, N.S.W.

H.W. Hannah Widdifield's *New Cook Book*. Philadelphia. T. B. Peterson & Brothers. 1856.

H.W.B. *Hints for the Table*, by H. W. Brand. 1859.

I.B. *The Meatless Menu Book*, by Ivan Baker. Herbert Joseph Ltd. London. 1936.

I.N. Inga Norberg. *Good Food from Sweden*. Chatto & Windus. London. 1935.

I.O.E. *Illustrations of Eating*, by a Beef-eater. John Russell Smith. London. 1847.

J.A.A. *A History of North American Pinnipeds*, by J. A. Allen. Washington. Government Printing Office. 1880.

J.B. *Cook It Outdoors*, by James Beard. M. Barrows & Co. New York. 1941.

J.C.P. *A Natural History of the Ducks*, by John C. Phillips. Boston. Mass. Houghton, Mifflin Co. 1922-26.

J.H. Jason Hill. *Wild Foods of Britain*. Adam and Charles Black. London. 1939.

J.M. *The Art of Cookery Made Easy and Refined*, by John Mollard. London. J. Nunn. 1801.

J.Man. *Jack's Manual on Wines, Liquors, etc.*, by J. A. Grohusko. New York. Copyrighted 1910.

J.M.S. *The Complete Cook*, by J. M. Sanderson of the Franklin House, Philadelphia. Lea & Blanchard. 1843.

J.N.L. J. Neil Leitch. *Dietetics in Warm Climates*. London. Harrison & Sons. 1930.

J.P. June Platt's *Plain and Fancy Cookbook*. Boston. Houghton Mifflin Company. 1941.

J.R. Janet Ross. *Leaves from our Tuscan Kitchen*. London. Dent.

J.W. Recipes and Definitions received from John Wright (London) Ltd.

J.W.B. *A History of Sussex Birds*, by John Walpole-Bond. Witherby. London. 1938.

K.B. Kettner's *Book of the Table*. London. Kettner's Ltd. 1877 (Reprint 1912).

K.C.B. *Kookaburra Cookery Book*. G.W. Cole. Melbourne.

La Va. *The French Cook*, written in French by Monsieur F. P. de la Varenne and in English by J. D. G. London. 1654.

L.B.C. *La bonne Cuisine*, par E. Dumont. Paris. Degorce. 1900.

L.C. Recipes received from Lady Carew.

L.D. *Hungarian Cookery*, by Lilla Deeley. London. Medici Society. 1938.

L.E. *The New England Cookery*, by Lucy Emerson. Montpelier. Joseph Parks. 1808.

L.En. *American and other Drinks*, by Leo Engel. London. Tinsley Bros. 1878.

L.G.A. Lucie G. Allen. *Choice Recipes for Clever Cooks*.

L.G.M. *Law's Grocer's Manual*, 3rd Edition. Edited and revised by C. I. T. Beeching, O.B.E. London. Wm. Clowes & Sons Ltd.

L.G.N. Lucie G. Nicholl. *The English Cookery Book*. London. Faber & Faber Ltd. 1936.

L.H. *Dainty Dishes*, receipts collected by Lady Harriet St Clair. 13th Edition. John Hogg. (First published in 1866.)

L.M. (1). *More Caviare and more Candy*, by Alice Martineau (Lady Martineau). London. Cobden-Sanderson. 1938.

L.M. (2). *From Caviare to Candy*, by Lady Martineau. Cobden-Sanderson.

L.N.R.C. Miss Leslie's *New Receipts for Cooking*. Philadelphia. T. B. Peterson. n.d. 1854.

L.R. *New Orleans Cook Book*, by Lena Richard. Boston. Houghton Mifflin Company. 1940.

L.T.C.R. *A Life-time of Collecting of 688 Recipes for Drinks*. London. Herbert Jenkins. 1934.

M.A. Merle Armitage. *Fit for a King*. New York. Longmans, Green & Company. 1939.

M.A.F. *The Ideal Cookery Book*, by M. A. Fairclough. London. Routledge & Sons. 1912.

M.B. (1). *Pot Luck*, the 8th Edition of Mary Byron's *Home Cookery Book*. London. Hodder & Stoughton Ltd. 1932.

M.B. (2). Mary Byron's *Cake Book*. London. Hodder & Stoughton Ltd. 1932.

M.C. *Round the World with an Appetite*, by Molly Castle. London. Hodder & Stoughton Ltd. 1936.

M.C.B. *Mothers' Cookery Book*. Published by the National Association of Maternity and Child Welfare. London.

M.Co. *The Lady's Complete Guide*, by Mrs Mary Cole. London. G. Kearsley. 1788.

M.D. *The Scots Book*, by Macdonald Douglas. London. Alex. Maclehose & Co. 1935.

M.D.C. *Modern Domestic Cookery*, by Elizabeth Hammond. London. Dean & Munday. 1816.

M.D.Cr. Mrs M. D. Crittall's Recipes.

M.E.A. Mary Ellis Ames. *Balanced Recipes*. Pillsbury Flour Mills Co., Minneapolis.

M.E.R. *A New System of Domestic Cookery*, by a Lady (Mrs M.E. Rundell). London. John Murray. 1814.

M.F. *A Highland Cookery Book*, by Margaret Fraser. London. John Lane, The Bodley Head. 1930.

M.F.C.S.C. *Easy Chinese Dishes for Today*, by Moira Field and Chung San Chao. London. John Lane, The Bodley Head. 1943.

M.G. *Wild Vegetables and Salads*, by Mrs M. Grieve, F.R.H.S., Whin's Cottage, Chalfont St. Peter, Bucks.

M.H.N. *How to Cook in Casserole Dishes*, by Marion Harris Neil. London and Edinburgh. W. & R. Chambers. 1912.

M.ʌ.f.P. *The Sportsman's Cookery Book*, by Major Hugh Pollard. London. Country Life. 1926.

M.K. *A Collection of over 300 Receipts in Cookery ... by several hands.* Printed for Mary Kettilby. 1728.

M.K.S. (1). *Sussex Recipe Book*, by M. K. Samuelson. London. Country Life Ltd. 1937.

M.K.S. (2). Recipes supplied by Mrs Margaret Samuelson.

M.S.A. *Mammals of South Africa*, by W. L. Sclater.

M.W. *Cookery Made Easy*, by Michael Willis. London. John Bumpus. 1829.

N. Nieves. *Ramillete del ama de casa.* Luis Gil. Barcelona. 1925.

N.A.B. *Check List of the North American Birds*, prepared by a committee of the American Ornithologist's Union. 4th Edition. Lancaster. Pa. 1931.

N.M. Recipes supplied by Mrs Norah Mather.

N.M.P. *The Book of the Wine Label*, by Dr N. M. Penzer, Litt. D., F.S.A.

N.S. *Food for the Greedy*, by Nancy Shaw. London. Cobden-Sanderson. 1936.

N.T.A. *Drinks, Long and Short*, by Nina Toye and A. H. Adair. London. Heinemann. 1925.

O.E.W. *Old English Wines and Cordials*, compiled by J. E. M. Bristol. High House Press. 1938.

O.H. *Cooking and Curing*, by Oriana Haynes. London. Duckworth. 1937.

O.N.C. *Oxford Night Caps.* Oxford. H. Slatter. 1827.

Or.C.B. *The Oriental Cook Book.* Shanghai. American Presbyterian Mission Press. 1889.

O.W.B.D. *Old Waldorf Bar Days*, by Albert Stevens Crockett. New York. Aventine Press. 1931.

P.A. Pearl Adam. *Kitchen Ranging.* London and Toronto. Jonathan Cape. 1935.

P.Ar. Pellegino Artusi. *L'arte di Mangiare bene.* Firenze. Adriano Salani. 1907.

P.B. A. Paillieux and D. Bois. *Le Potager d'un Curieux.* 3rd Edition. Paris. Librairie Agricole de la Maison Rustique. 1899.

P.D.P. Pearl Droste Plogsted. *The American Women's Club Cookery Book.* London and New York. G. P. Putnam's Sons Ltd. 1928.

P.G. (1). Peter Grieg's *New York Wine and Food Newsletters.*

P.G. (2). Petrona C. De Gandulfo. *El libro de Doña Petrona.* Buenos Aires. 1940.

P.H. *North Country Cooking Secrets*, by Peggy Hutchinson. London. Werner Laurie. 1935.

P.H.B. Recipes received from The Parker House, Boston, Mass.

P.R.M. Mrs P. R. Midgley. *Food for today in the Land of tomorrow.* Maseru. Basutoland. 1941.

P.S. *Travel and Big Game*, by Percy Selous and H. A. Bryden. London. Bellairs. 1897.

P.T.L. Mrs Percival T. Leigh. *Souvenir Cookery Book.* J. D. Hunter & Sons. Union Press, Armley, Leeds. 1905.

P.V.M. *The World-Wide Cook Book*, by Pearl V. Metzelthin. New York. Julian Messner. 1939.

P.W. Mrs Pauline Willsher's Recipes.

Q. (1). *The Queen Cookery Books.* No. 11. *Bread, cakes and biscuits*, collected and described by S. Beaty-Pownall. London. Horace Cox. 1902.

Q. (2). *The Queen Cookery Books.* No. 5. *Meat and Game*, collected and described by S. Beaty-Pownall. London. Horace Cox. 1902.

R.H.G. *Mrs Gardiner's Recipes from 1763.* Hallowell, Maine. White & Horne Co. 1938.

R.L. *Lovely Food*, by Ruth Lowinsky. London. The Nonesuch Press. 1931.

R.R.E. *Recipes Rare from Everywhere*, edited by Mrs Geoffrey Peto. Butler & Tanner. Frome and London. 1932.

S.B.P. S. Beatty-Pownall. *The Queen Cookery Books.* No. 10. *Vegetables.* London. Horace Cox. 1902.

S.C. *Superior Cookery*, by Mrs Black. London and Glasgow. Collins.

S.D.L.M. *Spécialités de la Maison*: compiled and published in New York by the American Friends of France. New York. 3 Sutton Place. 1940.

S.H. *A Kitchen Manual*, by Sheila Hibben. New York. Duell, Sloan & Pearce. 1941.

St.J.C.B. *The St. James Cookery Book*, by Louisa Rochfort. London. Chapman & Hall. 1894.

S.W.R. Scottish Women's Rural Institutes. *Farmhouse Recipes.* 1938.

T.B. *British Quadrupeds*, by T. Bell. 1837

T.C. The Thimble Club. *Choice Collection of Cherished Recipes.* Manchester (New Hampshire). 1937.

T.E.W. *Away Dull Cookery!* by T. Earle Welby. London. Lovat, Dickson Ltd. 1932.

Th.R. (1). *Big Game hunting in the Rockies and on the Great Plains*, by Theodore Roosevelt. London. Putnam. 1899.

Th.R. (2). *Through the Brazilian Wilderness*, by Theodore Roosevelt. London. John Murray. 1914.

T.L.B. *French Cooking for English Kitchens*, by Therese and Louise Bonney. London. George Allen & Unwin Ltd. 1930.

T.S. Townley Searle's *Strange News from China*. London. Alex. Ouseley Ltd. 1932.

U.P.H. U. P. Hedrick *Cyclopedia of Hardy Fruits*. New York. Macmillan. 1922.

V.S. *My Life with the Eskimos*, by Vilhjálmur Stefánsson. London. Macmillan. 1913.

W.A.C. *Williamsburg Art of Cookery*, by Mrs Helen Bullick. Williamsburg. 1939.

W.A.H. William Augustus Henderson. *The Housekeeper's Instructor*. London. J. Stratford. (*c*.1790).

W.B. *A Monograph of the Pheasants*, by William Beebe. London. H. F. & G. Witherby. 4 vols. 1918-22.

W.D.W. *The Whole Duty of a Woman.* London. J. Gwillim. 1695.

W.E.G. *A History of the Birds of Middlesex*, by William E. Glegg. London. H. F. & G. Witherby. 1935.

W.F. *Wine and Food*, a Quarterly Magazine published by the Wine and Food Society.

W.F. (4). *Winter in the Kitchen*, by Ambrose Heath, in *Wine and Food*, No. 4. December, 1934.

W.F. (28). *Regency Recipes*, by Mrs M. K. Samuelson, in *Wine and Food*, No. 28. December, 1940.

W.G. *Gunter's Confectioner's Oracle*, by W. Gunter. London. Alfred Miller. 1830.

W.G.B-M. *Modern Whaling and Bear Hunting*, by W. G. Burn-Murdoch. London. Seeley, Service & Co. 1917.

W.H.T. *Someone to Dinner*, by Winifred Hope Thomson. London. Cobden-Sanderson. 1935.

W.H.W.F. Recipes from Mrs W. H. Wynne Finch.

W.K. *The Cook's Oracle*, by William Kitchiner, M.D. Edinburgh. Robert Cadell. 1843.

W.L.B. *A History of the Birds of New Zealand*, by Sir Walter Lawry Buller. London. 1888.

Wm.B. *The Book of* 100 *Beverages*, by William Bernhard. London. 1850.

W.M.C. *Wilson's Meat Cookery*, revised by George Rector. Chicago. Wilson & Co. Inc.

Wn. Wyvern. *Sweet Dishes.* 3rd Edition. Madras. Higginbotham & Co.

W.R. *Of Cabbages and Kings.* A Cook Book by William Rhode, New York, Stackpoole & Sons. 1938.

W.R.B.O. *New Zealand Birds*, by W. R. B. Oliver. Wellington, N.Z. 1930.

W.R.O.G. *The Gun at Home and Abroad*, by W. R. Ogilvie-Grant and others. London. The London and Counties Press Assn. Ltd. 1912.

W.S.M. *The Wine and Spirit Merchant's Companion*, by Joseph Hartley. London. Simpkin, Marshall.

X.M.B. (1). X. Marcel Boulestin. *The Finer Cooking: or Dishes for Parties.* Cassell & Co. Ltd. London, Toronto, Melbourne and Sydney. 1937.

X.M.B. (2). X. Marcel Boulestin. *What shall we have today?* 365 *Recipes for all the Days of the Year.* London. Heinemann. 1931.

X.M.B. (3). X. Marcel Boulestin. *The Evening Standard Book of Menus.* Heinemann. London and Toronto. 1935.

Index

Many items have been grouped in sub-sections and entered, alphabetically, under the following heads: Ales and Beers; Apéritifs and Bitters; Biscuits; Brandy; Breads; Buns and Cookies; Cakes (Large); Cakes (Small); Cheese (American); Cheese (Continental); Cheese (English); Cheese Recipes; Desserts; Drinks (Soft); Eggs; Flours, Cereals, etc.; Fritters; Garnishes; Gins; Grapes; Herbs; Ices and Iced Sweets; Jams and Jellies; Liqueurs and Cordials; Nuts; Pastry; Rolls; Sauces; Scones, Pancakes, etc.; Soups; Sweets (Puddings); Waters; Whisky; Wine (Chateaux); Wine (Districts); Wine (Terms); Wines.